I0788593

SERIES 1 THE DARKSLAYER BOOKS 1-6

OMNIBUS

Wrath of the Royals
Blades in the Night
Underling Revenge
Danger and the Druid
Outrage in the Ourlands
Chaos at the Castle

CRAIG HALLORAN

THE DARKSLAYER
Series 1 Books 1-6
By Craig Halloran

Copyright © 2015 by Craig Halloran
Print Edition

TWO-TEN BOOK PRESS
P.O. Box 4215, Charleston, WV 25364

ISBN Hardback: 978-1-946218-42-1

THE DARKSLAYER is a registered trademark, #77670850
http://www.thedarkslayer.net

Artwork by Ernie Chan, Randy Linbourn and David Chen.
Map by Gillis Bjork

THE DARKSLAYER: Wrath of the Royals Copyright © 2010 by Craig Halloran
THE DARKSLAYER: Blades in the Night Copyright © 2010 by Craig Halloran
THE DARKSLAYER: Underling Revenge Copyright © 2012 by Craig Halloran
THE DARKSLAYER: Danger and the Druid Copyright © 2013 by Craig Halloran
THE DARKSLAYER: Outrage in the Outlands Copyright © 2013 by Craig Halloran
THE DARKSLAYER: Chaos at the Castle Copyright © 2013 by Craig Halloran

Publisher's Note

This book is a work of fiction. Names, characters, places, and incidents either are the product of the author's imagination or are used fictitiously, and any resemblance to actual persons, living or dead, events, or locales is entirely coincidental.

THE WORLD OF BISH
KEY LOCATION GUIDE
Hohm City
City of Three
The Mist
Hohm Marsh
Dwarven Hole
City of Bone
Red Clay Forest
The Warfield
Great Forest of Bish
Two-Ten City
Nameless Mountains
Outpost Thirty-One
Outlaw's Hide
Caves of the Underland
Lush Lakes
Outer Outlands
The Mist
N
W
E
S

TABLE OF CONTENTS

Series 1 THE BOOK 1

THE DARKSLAYER

Wrath of the Royals

CRAIG HALLORAN

1

TWO SCARLET MOONS CAST SHADOWS on the city structures, adding a strange hue to the colorful flowers and curtains in the apartment windows above. It was one of those rare, almost pleasant, nights.. The alleys seemed less putrid and the puddles of urine far fewer than usual. Tonight, the screams of pleasure and laughter outweighed the cries of terror that filled every night in the City of Bone. It was a hot and dry evening, and many strolled along the sidewalks as the brilliant banners of the Royal housing districts billowed.

A brawny warrior strutted through the streets with a broad grin on his face. Brushing back the locks of his blond hair, revealing his hard blue eyes, he belted out an alarming tune, startling the passersby. His name was Venir, a hunter of the Outlands returned to the city to unwind. The foul city had raised him, albeit in a callous manner, and its harsh elements were little more than entertainment to him.

At his side, a slender man called Melegal matched him stride for stride, not making a sound. The two had been together a long time in the city they recognized as home. The skinny man jostled by a basking couple, tipped his cap, and hurried alongside the bigger man, eyeing a small brooch of gold in his palm.

"Heh heh," the rogue laughed, pinning the jewelry to his vest. Venir looked up at the pair, who had stepped beneath a sign. A foul beast was colored on the placard that read: The Chimera.

"What do you think?" Venir asked, nodding to Melegal.

"Not the kind of place for our ilk. Remember the last time we dawdled with those Royals?"

Venir slapped the man on the back and smiled, "Ah, as you always say, 'The bigger the risk, the bigger the reward. Come on. I'm sure the ale's just fine."

Melegal scowled. "Royals don't like being cheated."

"Does anybody?" Venir lead them inside and took a seat at a table.

The Chimera was more than just another tavern of the middle districts. It was well-known for the low-key discretion of the young Royals that tended to do whatever they wanted.

"Do as they say or die in the dungeons," the poor storekeepers would say. "Do as they say or disappear," the commoners would warn. When the Royals were around, one could never be too careful.

Blending in the best they could, Venir ordered the first round of drinks. "To the skim," he said, hoisting his tankard.

Melegal nodded and said, "Certainly, but don't overdo it tonight. You know how vengeful the Royals can be."

His eyes met with Melegal's, whose chin dipped a tad as he savored a goblet of wine. "I'll try."

The atmosphere was accommodating as Venir gambled with nubile girls in scant clothing of the finest cloth. He told tales of his exploits while rolling the rocks.

"It's true! It's true!" Melegal said, confirming every outlandish tale.

The minutes turned into an hour, and one hour to two as tale after tale came from Venir's mouth. As Venir finished one swig of grog and ordered another, a tall young man clonked his tankard on their table and silence fell over the tavern. Venir's eyes flitted towards Melegal's. He could read the thieves lips.

"Here we go."

The young warrior bore the mark of a higher Royal house, wore clothes of the finest craft, and had the chin of a nobleman. A sword of high quality gleamed on his hip.

"My, what have we here? A warrior from the City of Three?"

"Your big ears have served you well," Venir said, forcing a smile. "Are you here to welcome me? In Three, we have the courtesy to offer a bottle of wine or a pitcher of ale."

"The only thing big in this tavern is your mouth, and it would do you well to close it."

Melegal eyed Venir and gave a slight shake of his head.

Something about the young man irritated Venir, and he could not let it go. "A challenge, perhaps?"

"Hah!" The Royal dropped his fists onto his hips, head craning around. "I'll tell you what, warrior, for the honor of the City of Bone, I accept your challenge!"

Cheers erupted from the cajolers mouths, jostling the entire tavern.

Melegal gave Venir a disappointed side nod.

The gathering crowd dragged tables and chairs from the center floor and surrounded the two challengers.

Melegal scooted along Venir's side and said, "You are an idiot. This is not the skim I envisioned, but a contest between a young and old bull."

"I'm not an old bull." Venir took a drink as he rose to his feet.

"Just make it quick," Melegal muttered.

The crowd roared as Venir squared off against the leering Royal. The clinks of coins shuffled among their hands. The bar maids were pushed and pulled, back and forth, as the crowd demanded their thirsty gullets filled.

Venir's voice rose above the mutterings of the room. "So what will it be, boy?"

The challenger stared hard in his eyes, replying in a demanding tone. "I challenge you to the Quick Fence!"

"I accept!"

The Quick Fence was one of many common tavern challenges of skill and bravado. They were a long-standing tradition in the City of Bone and beyond.

A heavy-set man in a bartender's apron, smoking a cigar, with tattooed forearms and a pitted face, strode between the two men. He carried a chest-high, heavy, wrought-iron candle stand and set it between them on the planks.

A tiny woman with silver hair squeezed through the crowd and stuck a long, thick white candle on the stand's spike, then disappeared. The barkeep took the big cigar hanging from his mouth and ignited the wick. He placed the cigar back in his mouth and wiped his meaty hands on the sides of his apron.

Venir placed himself a sword's length from the candle.

The barkeep raised his arms, bringing a hush into the room as he flipped up his hands. He blew a thick ring of yellow smoke into the air. "Best of three!"

Venir squared off on the man before him. He wanted to knock the scowl off the Royal's face. Something about the young man didn't sit well with him. "What's your name, boy?"

The young warrior's cheeks reddened. "Don't call me boy, Three-born! You'll never forget who *I* am when this is over! Not after I carve my name, Tonio, into that ruddy hide of yours."

Venir rubbed his calloused hands over the grip of his broadsword. The women whispered in excited voices, stating their preferences, either the rugged man from Three or the captivating Royal. Their colorful words brought a thin smile to his face.

"I hope you have plenty of coin, Three-Born. By the looks of you, I'd say you don't."

A handful a snickers spread across the room.

Venir retained his poise as things began to simmer in his gut. The face of the spoiled man before him reminded him of so many of his transgressors from before. He focused on the candle's burning light.

"I'll have plenty after this," Venir said, fingering his pommel.

"We'll see." Tonio readied himself.

The barkeeper hushed the crowd and raised his arms high.

"Go!"

Venir yanked his sword from the scabbard, swinging hard, but the candle was already falling to the floor.

Tonio pumped his arms, raising his blade high in the air and spinning on his heel.

In unison, part of the crowd chanted, "Tonio! Tonio! Tonio!"

Venir handed his sword over to the barkeep, who eyed it, wiped the blade down, and returned it back to him. He slammed his weapon back in the sheath with a grunt.

Melegal was almost smiling as he pressed the betting odds with the excited crowd. The skim was on.

The barkeep wiped the waxy residue off Tonio's blade and handed it back.

"One for the Royal—Tonio!"

It drew another raucous cheer from the crowd.

Tonio pounded his chest and sucked in several quick breaths as he waited for the next signal.

Venir eyed the Royal as the candle was replaced.

He's good.

He rubbed his hilt again and closed his stance in a bit farther.

The crowd quieted as the barkeep raised his hand.

Quick. Quick. Quick.

"Go!"

Blades licked out faster than the ale-glazed eyes could gather.

The top of the burning candlestick fell to the floor. The crowd looked at the barkeeper, muttering about who had won. Many voices spoke up for the Royal.

"Tonio!"

"He won!"

"I saw it!"

"Me, too!"

Even Venir wasn't certain.

"Hold! Hold!" the barkeep shouted at the top of his lungs, forcing back the eager crowd. "I must check the blades!"

The barkeep first inspected Tonio's sword with a keen, smoke-reddened eye, wiped it down, and returned it to the somber-faced young warrior.

Venir watched as the barkeep's fingernail revealed the residue of white candle wax at the tip of his blade. *Yes!*

"The warrior from the City of Three is the victor!" declared the barkeep.

More shouts of encouragement came to the aid of Tonio.

"You can do it, Tonio!"

And the insults flew at Venir.

"Son of a trollop!"

"Inbred cattle molester!

While the barkeep replaced the candle, Melegal placed more bets and glared at Venir. The rogue's hands and lips worked the gamblers like a master magician. Slender fingers flashed up and down, beckoning for more coins. He could see that icy glimmer in Melegal's eyes saying to him, *Don't foul this up.*

He prepared for the final round. *Focus, Venir. Focus.*

Tonio spit at his feet.

"Luck! I haven't been beaten in two years, and I'm not about to end my streak to some cretin like you. I'm the best, and you won't ever beat me again."

Venir glowered back. Something about the Royal went under his skin, into the bone. Win or not, he wanted to chop the young man's head off. *One slice.* "For Bone!" the Royal shouted to his mouthy cadre decorated in pompous clothes.

"Bone — Bone — Bone …" they chanted.

Venir eyed the flame. Tonio gripped his blade as the sweat began to bead on the man's creaseless forehead. Smoke and sweat smothered the tavern air. The barkeep stepped back and raised his arms high as the chants subsided.

"GO!"

Shing!

The thick white candle-top hit the floor, still burning.

Tonio looked at the candle with his jaw on the floor. The crowd gasped, many rubbing their eyes. The Royal's sword was half drawn from its sheath.

Venir stood there with his thick arms crossed over his broad chest, smirking as Tonio's eyes met his.

"Looks like you lost your streak — boy!" He wanted to laugh, but held it back.

"Keep practicing! You can only get better!"

Tonio shook with rage as his brethren dragged him away, kicking and screaming.

"Cheater!"

Venir paid him no mind as he headed back to his table.

Melegal was collecting money from several scowling faces as the wary barkeep gave him an odd look, gathered the candle stand, and sauntered away. A minute later, the crowd went back to their drinking and swindling, while Tonio and his ilk slunk farther away.

Venir sat down, grinning from ear to ear.

"Pretty fast, huh Melegal," he said with a wink.

"Did you have to draw that fast?"

"I couldn't take any chances. Besides, he's good. But … he's a cocky one, even for a Royal. He needed a lesson. Who knows, maybe it'll do him some good." He gulped from his mug and wiped the froth on his sleeve.

Melegal shook his head.

"I doubt it. Not those Royal types; they're all rotten to the core!"

It was true. The Royals were a vindictive bunch. But so was he.

"Yes, so why pass up an opportunity like that? Nothing like a little pleasure at their expense for a change. They've had plenty at ours."

The thief's face only darkened.

"Uh … anyway, how'd we do?" Venir said.

"Better than usual. These guys have deeper pockets than the crowds we're used to skimming. Let's get a couple of drinks and then get out of here. I'm leery of these Royals and the City Watch."

The tavern was full of drunkenness, raunchy jokes, and coarse laughter. Arguments, broken pottery, and the occasional whiff of vomit wafted in the air. Melegal watched the beefy bouncers escort debilitated men outside by the scruffs of their necks, adding a solid kick in the pants that sent them reeling into the dirt. Only the Royals were exempt from such treatment.

Still, Melegal worried. As Venir relished the company of the comely women, he became loud and rowdy. Venir bought escorted women drinks, recited piss-poor poetry, offered flirtatious words, and even bought a drink for a thirsty-looking dog. Most didn't mind his bold behavior, but others began to grumble. *He's going to find a knife in his throat.* Still, free drinks made many friends—as long as the gold lasted.

Venir had the remaining dwellers' attention as Melegal slunk farther from the table and fingered his recently acquired coins. The muscles in his back became taut as he noticed the younger Royals had further isolated themselves from the crowd. Their heads were down and they stared Venir's way. There was venom in their whispers. The Royals of Bone never took losing well, even worse to an outsider. He motioned Venir's way, *Time to go.*

As a beauty twirled her finger in Venir's ear, the big man frowned and shook his head.

He'll never learn. So be it; I'm going. As Melegal got up, two voluptuous ladies in short silk dresses pressed their full bodies into his face. Their wily whispers in his ears raised goose bumps on his arms. One moment Melegal's skinny legs couldn't find the exit fast enough, the next his instincts beckoned for him to stay. He eased back in his chair. *Why can't all of Bone's women smell and look so amazing?* Overwhelmed by the women's arousing splendor, he soaked it in. The Royals were the furthest thing from his mind when those thoughts were interrupted as the women suddenly slid away.

2

"**B**ISH! WHERE ARE YOU WOMEN going?" Venir said it as if he'd been woken from a dream. All of the women scurried away from his table as Tonio and his brethren arrived. Venir eyed them. "What now, ladies?"

One Royal with shifty eyes and a goatee spoke up. "Tonio, challenge him to a real man's game! The Strength Test!"

Word of a new challenge energized the deadened crowd. Unintelligible shouts of encouragement rang out from all corners, shaking the crystals that dangled from the chandeliers.

"What do you say?" Tonio demanded of Venir. "Care to put your coin on a true challenge, Three-born?"

Venir looked at Melegal, who shook his head, his slender smile turned upside down. Venir felt good, loose, up for anything—and his pride wouldn't let him back down from a man like Tonio. He swung his arm over the back of his chair and teetered back on two legs.

"I don't know, boy," he slurred, "I'd be afraid I might end another one of your streaks!"

"Ooh!" The growing throng laughed along.

Tonio pulled off his shirt and tossed it to the ground. Underneath he wore a sleeveless leather jerkin that revealed his long, muscular arms. "Let's see what you say after you eat the floor, mongrel!"

Venir staggered up, pointing and winking at one of Tonio's friends. "Let's go then, you double-cur-eating son of a mid-wife!" he said with a smile.

But no one laughed. Instead, the charged up crowd began exchanging coins.

Melegal struggled to keep up with the bets, salivating as his gray eyes gleamed with silver.

The roars rose to a deafening crescendo as Venir and Tonio squared off. The Royal was a towering athlete, with broad shoulders and powerful arms. The younger man's chestnut eyes glared into Venir's.

Renewed agitation stirred inside Venir. How many Royal faces like this one had tormented him? His humorous side was replaced by something else. His inner anger stirred.

Tonio was almost spitting as he thumped his chest.

"I'm taking you down, Three-Born! No one's ever beaten me at this!"

The barkeep stepped between the two large bodies and spoke loudly.

"No kicking, biting, head butting, or tripping! Your hands must be locked on the other's upper arms at all times. Whoever forces his opponent on his back first, wins!"

The onlookers sized up the pair of giants, and many coins shuffled in Tonio's favor. Venir removed his heavy hooded smock with white wolf-fur shoulders, typical of a man from the City of Three. Underneath, he wore a leather tunic that exposed his iron-thewed arms.

"Great Bish!" someone said.

The bets began to shift again. Tonio's friends looked at one another.

"Take up your positions!"

Tonio's eyes widened when he clamped his large hands onto Venir's biceps. Tonio's nails dug into his scarred arms. A look of uncertainty filled Tonio's face. He locked onto Tonio's smooth and sinewy arms, gripping right below the biceps, and held them tight. He could hear metal coins shuffling as Melegal continued taking more bets. His blue eyes blazed into the man.

"Are you ready?" the barkeep shouted.

He nodded as Tonio stared at him in anticipation.

"Last chance to save your gold, boy."

"Never!"

"We'll see, then!"

"GO!" the barkeep shouted.

Venir pulled his arms in a terrific upward tug, drawing Tonio in close. He was shoved back, boots digging for footing on the planks below. The young man was every bit as strong as he appeared.

"Blast!" Venir murmured as he fought for his balance.

The crowd whooped and hollered at the thrilling sight of the two men going head to head.

Venir twisted and jerked, back and forth, like a stubborn child. Tonio moved with speed, balance, and power. He was proving to be a difficult match. Venir's mind became slow and groggy, but he held on.

He's good. Bone!

He shuffled back and forth as the two danced like bears, knocking over tables and chairs. The crowd filled his ears like thundering horses. Venir was in a lull, his body trying to awaken as he battled to shove the aggressive man back. One slip and he would be on his back.

Venir slammed into the bar.

The crowd let out a triumphant roar.

The young warrior's comrades, full of fire and liquor, chanted obscenities at his back. The Royal of Bone was good, very good, and the crowd knew it.

Venir looked up just in time to see his opponent spit snot in his face. His blood bristled. *Enough!* The time for the charade was up. He took the offensive, his large hands squeezing hard, choking the blood flow in Tonio's arms. Tonio gasped as Venir half-jerked the young warrior's arms out of their sockets. Tonio bit his lip. Venir squeezed deeper.

The younger warrior tried to pull away.

"No!"

"Yes—boy!"

The Royal fought back with skill and natural athleticism. Hatred grew between the two as they tossed back and forth. Venir was awake now, the droll of ale and grog flushed out in battle. He strained against the Royal's powerful limbs. The crowd was going wild.

The match was taking longer than he had anticipated. What started out as a simple skim for extra gold was now a full-fledged battle. He could feel the man's labored breaths on his neck, while his own lungs began to burn. He short-stepped the man back and forth, but Tonio fought on, bumping his head under Venir's chest and trying to wrench his arms from his shoulders.

"Had enough," Venir snorted.

The Royal's forehead walloped him in the nose, watering his eyes. Blood trickled down Venir's face, covering his chin and dripping to the floor. The sight of blood drove the men and women into such a frenzy that the head barkeep stood atop the bar waving a large oaken club.

Venir growled and snarled; half-man, half-bull, and all warrior. Enough was enough. With arms locked on Tonio like a vice, he drew the young man in close.

"Down you go!"

"Never!" Tonio cried out.

Venir crossed Tonio's arms and pulled him in tight, turned his hip under the man, and lifted Tonio's entire body over his own head. He slammed the Royal into the hard oaken floor with all his might.

CRACK!

The air exploded from Tonio's mouth.

Silence filled the room.

Most of the crowd gawped at Venir, but some cheered. It was a contest that would be remembered. Venir wiped his hair from his face, sucking in breath as he looked down at his opponent.

Tonio was limp, yet breathing. As they lifted him from the floor, Venir noticed it was the planks on the floor that had cracked, not the warrior's back.

Too bad.

Venir watched them go, holding a rag to his nose that a patron handed him. With a sigh her rubbed his head. Taking a seat, he watched Melegal retrieve their winnings from many hapless faces. The crumpled heap of his opponent disappeared with his companions out the back of the Chimera. For some reason, he wished he had killed the man.

Melegal sat down beside him, pointed at his nose and said, "Want me to fix that?"

"Huh? Oh, no, I wouldn't want you to get dirty." Venir pinched his hands over his nose, and, with a nasty crunch, shoved it back into place. Tears streaked down his cheeks. "Is it straight?"

"Straight enough … like it matters."

3

IT WAS WELL INTO THE morning as Melegal and Venir sat in the tavern, which had begun to clear out. A couple of ladies had made their way back to the table, and Venir was beginning to act like his old self.

Quick to act, but slow to learn, Melegal thought, patting the tiny purse of coins concealed along his thigh.

"By Bone, Venir," Melegal said, "it almost looked like you weren't in control of that whole bout. It could have cost me."

"You mean, us, don't you?"

Melegal shrugged. "You've already spent your share."

Blue eyes glowered at him as Melegal motioned to the women in the nooks of Venir's arms.

Venir smiled, squeezing the ladies as he tossed his head back. "Ha! That Royal surprised me is all I can say. I have a broken nose to show for it. But don't worry, I won't be so careless next time."

Now it was Melegal's turn to laugh.

"You said that last time."

"No I didn't."

"I'm certain you did. But memories often escape that thick skull of yours."

"Don't worry, warrior," said one of the buxom honey-blonde women who hung on Venir's bruised arms. "We'll take care of you."

"That's a great idea." Venir rose from the table. "Let's get out of here."

Melegal grabbed his woman by the hand and followed.

Into the empty streets they went as Venir belted out a rousing tune.

"Shush, fool, you've made enough noise down here tonight. I don't want the City Watch all over us," Melegal said, looking over his shoulders.

If Venir heard, he didn't show it as on and on he went.

Somewhere hidden in the nearby shadows, eyes watched them go, following every staggered step. The Royal games had just begun.

4

DAYS LATER, THE HEAVY RAINS washed the stagnant filth back into the sewers of the city. People filled the streets with buckets and soap, storing fresh water and washing off weeks of the sandy grime that caked them. Rain was a rare blessing in the city centered in the Outlands, and baths were not a commodity of the impoverished.

Sheets of the warm drops drenched Venir. Dark, wet, and drunk, he sloshed through the flooding streets, a jug of wine nuzzled in the nook of his arm, singing a warrior's song. People shuffled away. He belched and bustled past them, saying, "Get out of the way!"

Venir was on his own, doing what he wanted—escaping the pursuits of the Outland world. He wanted to live another wild night. Women, song, drink, and dance—the best his remaining coins could buy. He smiled as rain dripped over the chiseled features of his face. There was more amusement to be found.

Hours earlier, Melegal had opted out of a return to the Chimera. The rogue tried to talk Venir out of it, but his mind was set. He would go back and win the crowd once more with his tales of glory.

"Have at it," the thief had said as he stormed away.

Pah! Venir didn't need a babysitter if he was only going among the city bred children.

He whistled a tune he had heard somewhere earlier in the dreary day. He hoped to bump into some of the people he'd impressed a few nights earlier. Venir no longer wore the special hooded smock from the City of Three. The significance of that never entered his inebriated mind.

Now, he looked like nothing more than an oversized commoner in the garb of a layman. His mind was on more of that premium dark grog, and maybe a bottle for the road. His dry mouth began to water despite the soaking rain.

Maybe someone would want to buy him a bottle, he thought, laughing out loud. He wouldn't stay too long. He would bump elbows and soon be out of there, without any trouble. *It's the least I can do.*

Dripping wet and wearing a tattered brown cloak and muddied boots, he stomped inside, oblivious to the glares. He couldn't have been more out of place if he had a dead cat strapped to his head. It was early, the tavern was quiet, and only a handful of commendable types and others filled the room. Frowning faces looked up from their food, then down again, muttering amongst themselves. He went up to the bar, sat down on a stool, and barked out a greeting.

"A fine evening! A bottle of grog, if you will." He dropped his coins on the bar.

The same pock-marked barkeep from nights earlier nodded, pouring the grog in a polished rock-cut tumbler that he placed on the bar. Venir took it in his hand, sipped it, nodded at the cigar-smoking barkeep, and drained it.

"Ah!" he said, clonking the empty tumbler back on the surface. Behind him, another patron scurried into the back, looking back and forth. The barkeep nodded as the patron slipped away. Venir paid the gesture little mind, only watching the man's meaty forearms pour more dark amber fluid into his cup.

"Thanks," he muttered, tossing the man another coin.

"No problem," the barkeep replied, sweat beading his brow.

Venir stared at the man's smoky eyes and sniffed the intoxicating liquor, pausing before he drained it. He licked his teeth and smacked his lips. Something didn't seem quite right, but the grog tasted fine.

"That was good," he said, grinning. "How about another? Make it two!"

It wasn't long before he was feeling at home. More rain-soaked patrons sauntered in, leaving burning looks on his broad back as he welcomed them. Satisfied, Venir sat at the bar, hunched like a yeti. He caught a fine red head eyeing him. Smiling, she came over as he gestured for her. She was voluptuous, smelling like a dozen different flowers, with the mouth of an ornery troubadour. He captivated her with his story from a few nights before. Her painted eyes were inviting as she twirled a lock of his hair and straddled one long leg over his.

She whispered in his ear, jostling his manhood.

"I wish I could have been there to see it."

They shared a few more rounds, and the barkeep offered him another drink. She tried to pull his arm away.

"Perhaps you should slow down. I want your company all night. Another round might put you down."

Venir laughed.

"There's no chance of that," he said, ogling her.

He turned to the other patrons and toasted her, roaring his drunken thanks and describing her comely body in a booming voice that all could hear. Then he shot back the grog and slammed the tumbler down. There was a low, wicked chuckle from somewhere in the room.

The grog had tasted different this time—more bitter and intoxicating. The face of the captivating woman before him began to twist and contort.

"What is happening?" His arms stretched out towards the woman's contorted face.

Venir's body shivered and the floor wobbled. He heard her voice, but couldn't understand her words. Distorted laughter came from her perfect red lips. His brows buckled as he growled, clutching at the bar, hanging on for his life. Then the floor smashed him full in the face. He didn't feel a thing.

5

H E AWOKE DISORIENTED, CHAINED, AND hanging by his arms in the middle of a small, smelly cell. An angry grunt aggravated the throbbing in his head. His hands were numb, and they bled within the tight shackles on his thick wrists. His sudden snort jostled an unkempt, heavyset guard who was leaning against the wall, asleep in his chair. The young guard rubbed his eyes and tilted all four legs back to the stony floor, then scratched his unshaven chin and looked through the bars at him.

"Finally got yer hide, didn't they, thug?" The jailer spit tobacco through the cell bars, but it fell short of Venir's swelling feet.

Venir uttered a faint laugh, drawing a perturbed look from the man's pimply face. The guard unlocked the cell, swung back its barred door, strode up to him, and spat thick, dark tobacco juice full in his face.

"What d'ya think of that?"

"I think," he replied in a threatening voice, "you'll be the first to die."

The guard slammed his fat fist straight into his stomach. "Ow! Blast it!" The guard winced, shaking his wrist and gave him an uncertain look, then stepped out of the cell, locking it shut. Holding his wrist, the man skittered out of sight, and a heavy door opened and closed in the distance.

Venir checked out his dreary surroundings. *Bone!* Dungeon floors were like a second home to him. They were all the same, no matter where you were—foul, and slick with centuries old muck and grime. It was not something he ever got used to, but he had been in worse. The chubby city guard was the same as the rest, fresh meat, trained to punish or kill.

As black spittle ran down his chin onto his chest, he tugged at his chains. They were rusted, and made for a lesser man. The cell door looked like its better days passed decades ago. A solid kick would take it from the hinges. He had barreled through thicker steel when he had to.

Why was he here? He traced the last steps he recalled. *The Chimera.* A cherry headed woman with an unrivaled plunging neckline and soft milky thighs was there. A faint smile crossed his cracked lips. The grog—syrupy, biting, and divine—had turned his belly sour. *Drugged? Poisoned?* He wanted to figure it out. He thought of wrenching the chains from the walls and walking out, but he was drained and sluggish. His eyes ached when they opened. It wasn't in him.

Patience was the better plan, but one could never trust the City Watch, controlled by the Royal brethren. They would slit a woman's throat with little more than a word; he had seen it before. If someone had drugged him, he wanted to know who and why. He was perturbed and embarrassed to have been duped at the tavern. To make matters worse, his nose was aching, and the rest of his body throbbed under his skin. But it could have been worse. Nothing felt broken, not even a rib. He was lucky all he had was a headache and not a cracked skull. He had tasted steel-toed boots before. But who would have gone to all this trouble over him? It must have been the Royals; he had crossed their turf once too often. *I hate it when Melegal's right.*

He drifted into sleep only to awaken to biting pain and discomfort as he shifted in his shackles. The next few hours were agonizing. He dozed off and was heavy in dreams when the sound of footsteps disturbed his sleep. His mind seemed to trudge through the mud, eyes cracking open to see what was about to befall him.

Four figures strode into full view at the cell door: the chubby guard who had spat on him, a rugged-faced man marked as a warden, a tall, familiar brown-haired man, and an older, elegant and powerful-looking man. *Royals.* His blood began to stir.

The pair of Royal men both towered over the guards and looked to be father and son. He knew one of them well enough, and his nose ached at the sight. Their rich clothing bore the insignias of upper-class Royals, and their appearance in the dungeon seemed misplaced. He shifted in his shackles, head down and eyes up.

The ugly warden with the rough voice spoke first.

"It hasn't taken you long to wind up here again, I see."

Venir didn't reply, but was all ears.

"You've been brought in for assault on a Royal and theft," the warden continued, "and threatening a city watchman. What do you say to that, scum?"

"It's crap," Venir responded, his voice dry and cracked. "I'm here because I beat that loudmouthed little braggart in a fair challenge. I embarrassed him and all of his little brood."

Tonio's face reddened with fury as he gripped the hilt of his longsword.

"That's not true!"

A strong hand held his grip in place.

"Father, he tried to cheat me. I broke his nose for it. Look!"

Venir winced at the lies.

"Did you tell your father how many coins you lost, *boy*? It was quite a bit, I recall!"

Tonio shook with rage.

"Lying crook! You attacked me from behind and stole my money!"

It was preposterous now. One lie would come after the next. It was their kind's way. *I should have killed him.* He knew it was best to remain silent, but silence was not his forte.

"You mean your father's money? And how would you have seen me attacking you from behind?" He was almost laughing now.

"He's a liar, Father! He didn't beat me! He's a thief! Open the door! Open it so I can slit his throat!" Tonio was losing control. "I'll tear this vermin to pieces! You scum! You'll rot in this cell or die by my sword!"

A sharp backhand slapped into Tonio's frothing face. Venir laughed out loud. Silenced and dejected, Tonio looked away, holding his lip.

"I bet that stung," Venir said. "Ooof!"

The warden slammed his stick into Venir's gut. It could have been worse; he could've lost his tongue for it, but he couldn't resist. *You gotta keep a sense of humor, even on the worst days.*

Tonio stormed from the room, wailing obscenities. When the young Royal was out of shouting distance, the father prepared to speak. The city guards kept their eyes downcast like fearful children about to be stricken. Whoever the man was, he had great command of his subjects. An uneasy feeling crept over Venir. He crossed the wrong people. His vacation in the City of Bone was over.

The older Royal's words seemed to control the air with the power of a strong breeze.

"No food and ten lashes a day until I return." Before the man left, he turned, casting a sharp glance his way. "What a waste of a man. I could have used a brute like you. If you were one of us, you might not be left in the rot. See to it he doesn't regain his strength. I like seeing them die at their worst, not their best."

The Royal father turned and walked away, leaving Venir with a sinking feeling.

"Unless you're lucky enough to die within a week," the warden told him, "you'll be calling this dungeon home for most of your life. You'll probably just have your decrepit body hanged or quartered. I'd like to see a big fellow like you pulled apart. Now that'd be something I'd pay for. Heh heh. You messed with the wrong people. They've got the power to make you pay every moment of your last days. You should know that."

"I can leave when I choose," Venir said, shifting in his shackles, but his words were not convincing. "Nobody can do anything about it."

The warden laughed.

"Sure. Go ahead! Run all you want, they'll catch you. The Royals always get their man. War games, and you're less than a pawn."

6

THE GUARDS LEFT HIM HANGING alone in his cell, crushed by his thoughts. *War games.* Those were things he had avoided over the years, now he was caught in the middle. He was but a commoner to them, no more or less, to die at their whim.

He had taken his own games too far. The Outlands were dangerous face-to-face with the elements, but the belly of Bone was just as bad. Now he was in the same place he had crawled out of years ago. He had been charged with lesser charges before, but not by a Royal. His prior shenanigans roused little fervor and cost no more than a few days in a dingy hole. This time, Royals had it in for him, and his future in City of Bone, and perhaps in all of Bish, was uncertain.

If a Royal accused you, you were guilty. You were either indebted with impossible fines, killed, or spent years—decades even—in the dungeons to rot. Many opted for suicide, which sometimes passed the burden onto a family member to finish suffering their fate. The easiest way to thrive in Bone was by steering clear of the Royals or doing as they said. It was slavery without saying so.

As bad as that seemed, it was easy to avoid such troubles because the Royals were a fragment of the wretched population. One could lay low after a frivolous encounter; the twisting city offered many places to hide, and the common faces were easy to forget.

In addition, the City Watch was incapable of enforcing all the ludicrous accusations of the Royals. There was too much crime and not enough manpower. The City Watch and Royals had enemies that didn't like them, either, and did not fear to strike back. Several areas were not even patrolled, and these were the areas Venir frequented. He was safe in the dark, local areas, and the guards there only pursued criminals who had just committed a major offense. And anyway, major crimes were more lucrative for the city guards. The petty ones were given little regard.

So why was he captured, shackled, and left to perish in the rot? After some hard thinking and remembering his encounter with Tonio several days ago, it dawned on him. The Royal warrior's ego was bigger than his own. *All of this over a fair bet.* There was no honor in it, but Royals only had honor among their own.

As he hung in the gloom, his own faults became clear. He had ignored his friend's warnings, failed to play by their own rules, even. Booze and ego intertwined into a bad mixer of poor judgment and lust. *Ah, but that fire-topped wench was worth the shot.* Still, his actions were a no-no in their business. A rich, smart, and vengeful man could just pay a spotter to alert him when a foe was around. It wouldn't take more than an urchin or a decrepit geezer seeking a goblet of wine to track a man for miles around.

He winced as he struggled within his confines, noting the trickle of blood oozing down his wrists.

He should have known this bratty Royal would have it in for him, but Venir was cocky and stupid sometimes. Unlike most people in the City of Bone, he never felt in danger there. He hadn't since he was a boy. He was too weathered by his ventures in the Outlands, a hardened soldier, and he had seen horrors the common people had never heard of. Besides, dark grog could make a red-blooded man feel invincible, and in his case, it worked most of the time. Only one thing made him feel mightier: *Brool,* his war-axe.

So here he was in a dank gray cell, hanging in chains, feeling hungry, foolish, and hung-over. A slow hour had passed before he heard a scratchy voice from a pile of rags adjacent to his cell.

"Ahem … are you enjoying yourself?"

It was Melegal, huddled in a heap of cloth that began to take shape. He was glad to see the man. He had long gotten over his amazement at the rogue's way of appearing out of nowhere.

"No … just hanging," he replied in a sour voice.

"Better hanging in here than outside from a noose," Melegal said, dusting off his clothes. Melegal explained that as soon as he'd found out Venir was in the dungeon, he had himself arrested for calling a City Watchman a "big, ugly, cow-loving orc-face." Then the rogue had escaped his first cell and managed to sneak into Venir's. Melegal wanted to make sure he got out of jail; he needed him around for protection and profits. This was the surviving nature of their relationship, and it worked well. The thief had been raised from birth in the City of Bone and knew its history well. Venir had met with him in one of many orphanages he wound up in not long after the underlings slaughtered his family. Venir hit it off with Melegal, though most did not. The orphanage offered the adventuresome boys few comforts or choices. Their days were filled with hard labor, which they performed beneath the castles of the great city. Months would sometimes pass before he ever caught a glimpse of sunlight.

Many hopeless and pain-filled years passed for him, but Melegal always hung by his side. Days went by without food, and he watched many die without hope. Others disappeared. Out of all the children he had come to know, Melegal would have been the last he guessed would survive. He did what he could, and the scrawny crumb-snatcher did the same for him. He and the thief grew bold enough to escape and live on their own in the cCity of Bone. Once they found freedom, they never looked back. Their past was best forgotten, but it always lingered.

The pair managed just fine despite their young age. But over time, Melegal branched out to test his own skills, while he, who had been born in the Outlands, was drawn to the barren landscapes and forests where he felt most at home. It wasn't long after the underlings overtook outpost thirty-one that Melegal had come back to settle again in Bone. Venir spent his time in many lands and cities, but much of the time he came back to Bone. This had been going on for the past five years.

He looked across at Melegal, thinking how funny it was that this gaunt man always looked the same. The thief's face was neither welcoming nor threatening and his steel-gray eyes drew a savory woman now and then. The man had a smile, but saved that for the fairer sex. His half-shaven face, salt and pepper hair, and dimpled chin gave the man an older appearance. As far as he knew, they were about the same age, but neither could tell for sure.

The rogue was still wearing loose-fitting drab clothes and had on an odd black cloth hat. It hung like a wet leaf down the right side of his head. Why it was so special to his friend, he did not know.

Their friendship had been sparked in the orphanage, the day some bullies snatched a similar hat from Melegal. Venir had whipped the bullies that same day and taken back the hat. He did not know why he did it, but he was beaten for it, as good deeds were often punished along with the bad. The raw-boned boy had been at his side ever since.

Men always hated Melegal's hat, but women of late, for some reason, loved to play with it and comment on it. He never understood the importance of the hat, but found it funny when his friend explained that it made him look "distinguished."

"So, do you want me to get you out of this one?" Melegal unlocked his cell and walked in. "Shall I sneak you out again? Maybe I'll unchain you, stupid."

"Just get me some food and drink, Melegal."

"Oh no." The thief wagged his finger. "They clearly stated you're not to eat for two days. Sorry, but rules are rules."

Not this again. He knew Melegal was mad at him for his blunder, because it would cost them business while he wasn't on the streets.

Melegal leaned against the wall, cleaning his nails with a thin blade. Venir knew his friend wanted him to admit his mistake. Melegal always played these games, but had never gotten him to acknowledge any failure. And Melegal was always too impatient to pass up the next business transaction. The man wanted to regain his lost profits.

Venir closed his eyes for a moment. When he opened them, the man had disappeared. He grunted and closed his eyes again. He heard nothing. *Where is he?*

The minutes seemed like hours. The sound of footfalls caught his slumbering ears. He cracked his eyes open, expecting to see his friend. Instead, two familiar guards entered, one carrying a whip in a coarse hand.

The dungeon warden looked at him with big, cruel fish-eyes. The chubby recruit fidgeted with his neck collar, eyes wide, like a child on the first day of school.

"On yer feet, dirt!" The warden snarled. "Time for yer beating."

"I'm sorry, trout face, but I can't," he said, twitching his feet.

"Ew … that will cost ya an extra ten, deadman. I'm gonna enjoy this," said the warden with a sinister gap-toothed smile.

The recruit gave a nod, sticking his chest out a bit farther, while looking over the warden's shoulder. It was a bonding moment between student and teacher. Venir almost laughed, but his head hurt too much. His limbs were stiff and aching, his head still full of bad medicine.

"Spread yer legs!" said the torturer in his ear.

The man's foul breath reeked of tobacco juice and decaying teeth. The warden kicked his legs into a wide straddle. His predicament was getting worse, and the cavalry didn't seem to be coming his way. *Where is that thief?*

He hoped the thief was hidden somewhere in the dungeon, but there was no sign as he strained his head around. The warden punched him in the jaw, rocking back his head as he closed his eyes and grimaced. He heard the rattle of chains as the warden went over the steps.

"One, two, three," the warden flipped his wrist, "wupash!"

Venir heard a sharp crack. There was no pain, but sweat began to glisten on his head.

"That's how you do it, boy. What you learned in training has no meaning here. Go ahead, give my lash a go." The warden passed it over to the eager recruit's hands. *Crack!* The warden rubbed his chin. "Not bad. Not bad at all."

Venir chest tightened. His breath became short. *Where are you Melegal? They're about to get cracking!*

"Tell you what, I'll do the first fifteen," said the ugly torturer, holding out his hand, "and you finish the last five. Well … maybe seven. It'll be good training for you. Now, pay attention. You don't have to hit hard to make it hurt. Just watch the ol' expert. I've done it a thousand times."

The warden snapped the whip with another crack that cut through the stale air. The recruit nodded as the warden reached to rip off Venir's shirt.

Suddenly, the door burst open.

Finally!

Tonio strode in, shoving his way in front of the two guards. The Royal was consumed with rage and began spitting obscenities in Venir's face.

Not Melegal. Not good!

He mustered enough strength to roll his eyes at the belligerent man.

"Hand over the whip!" Tonio screamed at the warden.

"Don't you give me orders!" the warden said in a growl. "That's my job!"

Tonio rolled up on his toes and sneered down on the man.

"Oh, so you don't mind losing favor with a high-ranking Royal, do you?"

The warden started to stammer, but a hard slap across the cheek stopped him.

"I could have you killed, and you know it!"

The grizzled warden stood his ground, looking for a moment like he might turn the whip on the Royal brat.

Tonio hissed in his ear, "If you even think of using that whip on me, I'll flay the skin off your back and the backs of everyone in your family, while the fat farm boy over there digs your grave to dump you in."

The warden held Tonio's gaze while fire burned in both men's eyes. At last, the warden handed over the whip. Venir braced himself. Impending pain was on its way.

"Remove his shirt!" Tonio ordered the recruit, who looked at the warden.

"Do as he says," the warden said with a quick, begrudging nod.

"I'm gonna scar every inch of his filthy back," Tonio said, strutting around the room cracking the whip, "and make him scream for mercy! I may even bust his nose again!"

The chubby recruit ripped Venir's cotton jerkin down to the waist in a few tugs. The recruit stumbled back, staring at Venir in confusion. Imprinted between his knotted shoulders over the bullish muscles of his scarred back was a large black **V**.

Tonio cracked the whip.

"Let me flay that stupid tattoo off your back, dog!"

Venir was subdued, and his head drooped. Yet, his breathing was growing heavier, and the room seemed to darken as something bustled in the torch light. Unnoticed, he appraised the rusty shackles around his ankles. *Gotta do this before he tears the skin off my back.* He had been whipped before and never gotten used to it. If he could avoid it, he would, but his body wasn't responding to his commands fast enough. No woman was worth a whipping. *Redheads.*

Tonio drew back the whip. The rookie guard took a long step back while the warden grinned. The musty hot air filled with anticipation.

The whip came down in the middle of the tattoo spanning his expansive back.

Crack!

Venir had no control over the snarl that ripped from his parched lips. His corded arms were as taut as steel as he wrenched the metal loop out of the stone ceiling. He twisted his legs from the rusting shackles on the floor. A loud ringing followed as he ripped the chain clean from the weathered wrist cuff. A full two feet of heavy chain now hung in his clutched palm like a snake of steel. He glowered at Tonio with blazing fury. .

Tonio shuffled back alongside the stunned warden. On a foolish instinct, the grim warden charged him.

Crunch!

Venir shattered the man's jaw with his fist, dropping him to the cobbled floor. The warden was out cold. He turned on Tonio. The Royal dropped the whip and went for his sword, which was half out of its sheath when the thick chain smote his hand, breaking bone. Tonio screamed, cursing and clutching his wrist.

Tonio grabbed for the whip with his other hand, but Venir whipped the chain across Tonio's shoulders. The painful expression on Tonio's face would last the young warrior his lifetime.

With a face full of agony, the tough Royal stood straight up, one fist raised as the other dropped to his side. "You're nothing but a street dog!" Tonio cried, too arrogant to acknowledge the danger. "That's all you'll ever be!"

Venir twisted the chain off his right cuff and tossed it to the floor. He closed in on the defiant Royal, who punched him in the jaw with a hard smack that drew blood. He spat it out, blocked the next punch, and countered with a right uppercut to the belly, lifting the man off his feet.

"Ooomph!" Tonio fell to his knees, winded but groaning as he rose again. Venir unleashed his anger, shattering his ribs with hammer-like blows, dropping the Royal to the floor like a bag of sand.

Somehow, Tonio struggled back to his feet. He tried to spit out a curse, but only produced bloodied spittle that ran down his scabbed chin. Venir blackened the man's eye, broke his nose, and shattered that loudmouth's jaw with a mallet of a punch. Tonio was out cold, his face bleeding on the cobblestone floor.

Venir breathed heavily as he eyed his surroundings. He noticed the trembling recruit holding out a ring of keys with his eyes shut. He knocked him out with a single blow, and scooped up the keys.

Despite all of the violence, only a minute had passed since the whip had crossed his bleeding back. The constant rumblings from the streets above had muffled the chaos from those who might have been close enough to hear. Guards would be coming soon. He scanned for Melegal, but the thief was gone, leaving behind only a small red apple in his cell. With the keys and the apple, Venir slipped out of the old dungeon.

It was dusk outside the small compound as he made his way deep into the worst part of the city. He snatched a cloak from a merchant stand and pulled it over his shoulders before heading back to his stomping ground, the Drunken Octopus. Melegal sat back in the corner, by a stone fireplace, with food, grog, and ale ready.

Venir wasn't feeling happy. "What happened to you? I got whipped—blast you!" He grabbed a loaf of bread and stuffed it in his mouth, washing it down with pitcher of ale.

The thief tilted his head and matter-of-factly said, "You had it coming, buffoon."

He would have split another man for saying that, but Melegal was his friend. He nodded as he wiped his mouth and sat down. "So I did."

Not much was said while he stuffed bites of cheese and meat in his face, his hunger surpassing his anger.

"Coffee!" he yelled, hitting the table.

Melegal sipped at his wine.

"So, the new guard seemed to recognize you."

He shrugged. "He didn't look familiar. I may have met him sometime, somewhere on the outskirts of the city. There are still normal people out there, you know. Where do you think all this food comes from?" He waggled a chicken bone in his friend's face.

"Smarter than he looked, taking a shot on the jaw to save his job. It might even get him a promotion."

Venir gave the thief a funny look. How had Melegal gotten back here so fast? He let it go.

"It was either that or die."

"Oh, I know how you farm boys stick together. You wouldn't do that."

"Sure." His once snarling lips now began to form a relaxed smile. "You could at least have stolen the whip!"

"Oh, I thought you pig herders enjoyed that sort of thing. Why end your fun? Besides, I thought you were looking a little homesick."

"You're sick in the head, Melegal," he said, losing his smile.

"Well, who'd notice better than you?" The thief retorted with a deadpan face.

Venir grunted and chewed as his friend poured more wine. A scrawny waitress with short-clipped hair brought over a pot of coffee and poured him a cup, spilling it on the table. He scowled at her, and she scowled back before walking away.

"I hate her. She always spills something."

"Well, you'll live. She looks better than the orcs of Two-Ten."

"Not much prettier, though."

"Hah. She's not that bad. Just a dirty little waif. She'll come around."

Venir didn't say a word, he just sipped his coffee.

Melegal continued, "I'm getting curious. You've changed since I last crossed the Outlands with you, and you spend so much time out there these days. One day, I might even follow you there again." The thief began cleaning his nails. "People around here talk about you, you know."

Venir half smiled.

"You wouldn't want to go back. There are no easy pickings in the Outlands. Still, it would be good to have you along again."

"I hear stories, you know. Most of the good ones mention the Darkslayer. Do you ever come across him?"

"Don't start."

The thief leaned back in his chair. It had been almost five years since Melegal had left Bone. The Outlands and the thief didn't mix well. No comfort or companionship. It was the city life for the rogue, and Melegal wanted no part of the underlings, either.

Venir hated to leave, but the Outlands drew him back. The underlings beckoned him. He was the Darkslayer, and he relished that role. He even liked the rumors he heard about himself, even the most ridiculous ones. Still, his identity was safe because his alter-ego didn't play inside the City of Bone. Venir broke the awkward silence.

"Quit patronizing me and drink some grog, girlie boy!"

The morning came, and the small suns burned bright again. The pair talked little, and ate and drank much. The blazing surfaces of the Outlands were calling for Venir, and he could think of nothing else. The underlings awaited him. Crawling inside dank caves, buried in foul marshes, they dug in, and he was beginning to lose sleep over it.

7

S OUTHWEST OF THE CITY OF Bone was the Underland, home of the underlings. It was a catacomb of caves that began in a vast mountain range and went down as far as the mountains were high. Aside from the underlings, only a few people of Bish knew much about the Underland. Not many would dare to venture into the belly below those breathtaking mountains whose icecaps were miles high.

Those captives who went in didn't escape, but were sometimes released. Their ghoulish tales had helped fuel the fabled fear of the underlings. The horrors they spoke of swept through the lands of Bish like the wind itself. Hence, no one ventured near the mouths of the Underland. By underlings, the Underland could be reached through a network of cave entrances, large and small. The entrances sat like open mouths at the base of the Nameless Mountains. There were stories of monsters, treasure, and lost cities in those mountains, but only the icy winds knew for sure. The underlings kept the daring adventurers at bay. Whatever lived in the mountains stayed there, and everyone preferred it that way.

The caves that led down into the Underland were steeply graded, dropping away from the light that disappeared with every step. No guards could be found at any of them, for there was no need. Anyone other than an underling fool enough to enter would be lost, if not ensnared.

The black walls were slick and shiny when illuminated, and the dripping water sometimes echoed and created endless streams through the dark caverns. The black tunnels contained no light or life, but if one ventured deep enough, a faint blue glow began to outline the subterranean walls. This was called the underlight, and its source was said to be magic from deep below Bish itself.

The true source came from the powerful underling magi that ruled the Underland. The underlight had arisen from ancient spells cast millennia ago, and even the underlings did not have record of who was responsible. This day, deep beneath the mountains, the underlight illuminated a disturbing scene.

Side by side, two robed figures hovered over a puddle of blood. One rubbed his hands together as the other nodded his head. Unlike common underling soldiers, each radiated great mystic power. The pair wore dark robes laced and inlaid with intricate patterns that gave off a faint silver glow.

Only their hands and heads protruded as they floated above the damp cave floor. Their thick black hair was short and wiry above the ears. Like all underlings, their physical frames were humanoid, but lither than their hated human rivals. Their ashen skin was covered with a fine, silky fur like that of rats. Their hands ended in long, thick black nails filed into points. Only their eyes and faces distinguished one underling from another. Their eyes could be any color on Bish, and their heads could be round or thin, large or small. But they all had an evil countenance and gray teeth.

"What a work of art!" one elated. His silver eyes were narrow as he surveyed dozens of deep lacerations and scalpel-like wounds on three humans shackled to the wet cavern wall. "Master Sinway will like this one."

"It's one of our best yet, Verbard," the taller of the two agreed, his golden eyes sparkling while gazing at the humans.

Lord Verbard held out his index finger, and with a quick hiss his finger ignited in a red hot glow. The underling ran its nail over the fresh blood on the leg of the middle human. The man's hairs began to curl away and stink. The underling jabbed his burning fingernail into the man's flesh, ripping a deep laceration on the thigh.

"Wonderful sounds they make, don't they, Catten?"

Catten studied the man's tormented face and clapped. "Like music. Did that hurt, human? Was that a sound of pleasure or pain? Are you trying to say something?" He floated closer to the man. A sound was coming from the corner of the man's torn mouth.

"The Darks... slaaaa... kilz... filth...unders-s-s..."

Catten's gold eyes became molten with anger. All five of his nails glowed red hot as he tore out the flesh of the man's thigh in a single stroke. "Are you falling asleep on me? Verbard, we cannot allow him to sleep again. It's the ninth time today. I will not be treated like this by my guests."

"And we can't have them sleeping when Master Sinway arrives," Verbard replied.

Catten shared his brother's look of concern and snapped his fingers.

"Let's remove their eyelids."

8

I NFINITY WAS NOT ALWAYS THE best place to be. Although it was considered heavenly, it was sometimes quite hellish. Anything imaginable was at your disposal, yet it was boring. Trinos was complaining to herself again, and seemed to enjoy it. At least it kept her entertained.

Trinos was a being from a created race that had achieved its greatest potential. Her race had been created by some other infinite being, like her, millennia ago. How long that was exactly didn't matter, because time was infinite. What mattered was that Trinos belonged to a race of overachievers. As wonderful as that sounded, her life had become a mundane grind, leaving her to contemplate the sanity of her cosmic thoughts.

There had once been a time, so very long ago, when Trinos's life was filled with joy, sorrow, adventure, and love. But all of her dreams had come true once her race learned the greatest secret of the cosmic expanse itself. And this discovery had allowed her race to become immortal.

It was thrilling at first, having the time and the power to do whatever she wished. But now, she sometimes thought it might have been better to have died. Those Trinos loved had drifted away to explore their own newly found capabilities and responsibilities. Like them, she could do or create anything at will, anywhere in the vastness of space. So could the rest. Everything was simple ... all too easy.

To keep beings like Trinos from overrunning the universe like power-mad children, there were rules. The infinite ones had all agreed to a set of endless tasks that kept them occupied. Some had to make new worlds, and others had to destroy them. The majority tried to discover what had created their own universe. Despite their ability to do and create anything at all in their universe, they still could not find the end of it. It just kept going.

Trinos had the task of evaluating the worlds created by the many other infinite beings. She would watch the worlds begin and end. Different races would be born to these new worlds, all created by the hands of various supreme beings. But try as they may, the infinite beings just kept making the same types of worlds over and over and over again.

It was always the same scenario. A new world was made and then new races gained knowledge, made fire, made weapons, went to war, struggled for survival, fought alien invaders, and ultimately destroyed themselves or were exterminated by others.

On occasion, maybe one race in thousands would evolve into the omnipotent status her kind enjoyed. Trinos had seen this happen a few times, and it gave her a tingle to welcome the newcomers to the expanse. This joy was always short-lived because she had to go back to watch the other worlds destroy themselves. War, famine, and disease finished them all off. In some cases, the infinite creators didn't even build worlds that could last. It was always much the same. Trinos had become aware that, in the grand scheme of things, her monitoring was pointless.

She always reported her findings to the world creator, who would ignore them and simply make another world. Yet, it remained her job to watch after them. Sometimes, just to pass the time and try to get a taste of life, she would show up on one of the created worlds. But it made no difference what she did; she had become redundant.

One time, Trinos was busy evaluating a new world in a small corner of her universe. It was blue and beautiful. She had visited and could feel that this race had the potential to become infinite. It was a rare treat, indeed, and Trinos felt something almost like excitement, if such a thing were ever again possible.

The beings of this world were by far the most promising and colorful Trinos had seen in eons. They made great strides in technology, medicine, and science in short spans of time. One of the cultures of that world had become a melting pot of all of its greatest minds and races. They showed so much promise.

She began to enjoy the enthusiastic characteristics of the world's people. It seemed to her that when they worked together they were unstoppable. Maybe they would make it. Maybe she would not always be so bored in infinity. But, her moment of hope was brief. They were not going to make it after all. The prominent young race had too much success too early. They lost their creativity as technology and convenience led them to self-indulgence and internal strife. They who had overcome so much now began fighting among themselves. Their pride and greed were to be their world's undoing.

It became clear to Trinos that it would not be long before they were all gone, but they still had some time. Unfortunately, as much as Trinos liked this world, she could not interfere. It just wasn't allowed. *Such a shame.* It made her restlessness grow. None of these worlds ever lasted long.

Of course, not every world could achieve infinite status, but why did they always have to become extinct? Couldn't some of these worlds remain in an interesting state forever? Why did all of the infinite and knowledgeable beings keep creating such short-lived worlds?

Trinos pondered these annoying thoughts. She had endured enough. There had to be something, somewhere, to look forward to. Yet, every time she went back to check on a promising race, they were gone.

At last, inspiration struck. Trinos would build her own world. She would build a world that would remain locked in strife and survival every minute. She would build a world that could keep her eternally entertained. It would be one that would always be there for her to come back to. A child that never grew old.

Trinos took great care to plan her new creation. She selected the unique characteristics of that shiny blue world she was so fond of, and then added in some of the otherworldly races as well. Survival was of the utmost importance when developing their genetic codes. There were millions of details to attend to. The basic laws of their universe would apply. The laws of alignment, good and evil, were to be in place. Races would only achieve an archaic form of technology. That would prevent them from ever leaving the world. The study of science would be replaced by the study of magic. Life spans would be abnormal. Humanoids would rule. A powerful mystic equalizer would be in place to prevent either good or evil from achieving full supremacy. No evolution.

It would be a brutal world, one that ran the gauntlet of emotions every second. Man would rule beast. Monsters would cause mayhem. Heroes would be born with great willpower, and villains with unparalleled greed.

These people would like it there, thought Trinos. And she would like it there.

She tucked her little world away, deep in the expanse within their universe, in the hopes that no would find it. Then, after many moments in infinity, Trinos gave birth to her new world. She called it Bish.

9

V ENIR AWOKE TO THE SOUND of pounding rain. He was in the little apartment he shared with Melegal during his stays in the City of Bone. On the top floor of a dingy four-story apartment building, it was adequate for the two full-grown men to live in comfort within the miserable city.

The candles mounted on the walls were unlit, but a lantern glowed, and there was a hint of light at the small window where the rain splattered the glass pane. Another empty cot was by his side, its satin pillow fluffed and the blankets folded in perfect squares. A wood stove burned, filling his nostrils with the smell of fresh coffee. A metal carafe of Melegal's best percolated on the stove.

He yawned as he watched his roommate's rigorous routine of calisthenics taking place on the floor. The thief was in a hand stand, doing push-ups.

"Ninety-nine … one hundred." Melegal rolled down, silent as a cat, and hoisted his feet behind his head.

"Morning," he yawned again.

"Morning, crap!" the thief replied. "It's almost noon."

"What!" He turned to the single window by his bed and peered through the water-coated glass.

"Slat! It's just gone dawn."

"No fooling you." Melegal switched positions and began one-armed pushups.

Venir got up and went to the water basin beside the wood stove and rinsed his face. He sucked in some water from a pitcher, washing out his cottonmouth, and spit into a large metal pipe between the wood stove and the basin. The indoor waste shoot was the reason they had chosen the top apartment. That way they would not have to listen to any other occupants spit, wash, and urinate down into the nasty sewers below from the spouts above.

Indoor plumbing was one of the marvels of the City of Bone, rumored to be the only city with such advancements. In truth, this ancient city was almost the only one with buildings several stories high. The humans that claimed they built City of Bone often bragged of being the most advanced race on Bish. They enjoyed their comforts. But, over the centuries, even they had forgotten most of what they had or hadn't done, or who had done it and why. For the City of Bone had been torn down more than once in its long life, only to be rebuilt on the bones of its dead. That was how it had acquired its current name. And, chances were, as with all things on Bish, it would fall again.

He sat down alongside his roommate and tried duplicating the routine calisthenics. It was agonizing. *If he can do it, I can.* Ten minutes later, he was sweating like a pig. Melegal's forehead was still dry as a bone as the man crouched with his legs behind his head. Venir strained to attempt the same.

Melegal snorted a laugh as he hopped up and poured some coffee.

Venir stayed on the floor, struggling to put his legs behind his head. He grunted and pulled. He used to do it all the time, years ago. "Hah!"

Melegal's face said it all. "How'd you get your legs over those monstrous shoulders?"

"Don't know," he replied, flopping back to the floor. "But I can."

Melegal stirred his coffee, shaking his head.

He took a deep breath and exhaled.

"Ahh!" His head was clearing, and he was beginning to feel better. "How 'bout some coffee?"

Melegal poured it into a handle-free mug and passed it over to him.

"So, what's the plan for the day? Are you going to be around any longer, or head back to the wilderness already?"

Venir sniffed in the intoxicating aroma, feeling the warmth from his ceramic mug. He took a slurp.

"Mmmm … it's that time again, it seems. Besides, after that last run-in, I'd better be going. Are you gonna come this time, or hide under your cot again?" He managed a smile, but the truth was he felt cooped up. He couldn't tear his mind from the underlings. The things they did to people, the shredded faces were always haunting his thoughts and dreams. The longer he stayed inside, the more people died.

Melegal frowned.

"With all that gold we just made … would I rush off and risk dying again? You get me into one life-threatening mess after another. It's insane. You're insane! I like the easy life inside the walls."

"Ah, bullslat. You get bored outta your mind when I'm gone. You just sit in here and whittle away. You like it on the edge with me. And I always keep you safe; you know that."

Melegal sipped his coffee, shaking his head. "No … I don't miss you. I like the quiet. I like the coin, but the quiet is better. You cause such a racket."

There was an odd silence while he gave the thief a look.

"Venir, every time you leave, you come back less … civilized. Sometimes you're out of control. Maybe if you stayed in the walls longer you could unwind. You are tighter than a bowstring these days."

The words stung a little, but he knew his friend was right. He had to drink himself into a slumber when he was home. His warrior sense fired up at every odd noise, and his mind was in a constant race for battle. The women, sex, and alcohol, as enjoyable as they might be, were just distractions. *Fleeting and foolish.* He had a problem that he couldn't control, unless he was out there.

He got up and pulled a large, worn leather sack from underneath his cot. He tossed it on the bed with a clank that brought him a flickering memory of Jarla, an old foe, her beautiful face scowling from years ago. He hunted for her, but never found her because the underlings got in the way.

"Pulling out the artillery," the thief said in a dour tone. "Seems your mind's made up."

Melegal was all eyes as Venir reached inside the leather sack and pulled out the shield. It was a strange design, a grid of worn iron bands welded over a body of dark gray metal unknown anywhere in Bish. He had no idea what metal it was. The shield appeared grim and heavy, but he flipped it around with ease. It fit his powerful frame like a glove. He had stopped countless life-threatening blades and arrows with it, but it didn't have a single notch or dent. He rubbed its framework and smiled. "You're a strange man." Next, he pulled out a colossal battle axe and whispered in a loving tone, "*Brool.*"

Melegal grimaced. "You would have a name for that nasty thing."

"All good friends have names!" Venir swung the axe like a toy. The weathered shaft felt like an extension of his arm. Its warmth filled him with vitality. He couldn't help but grin. Brool was a four-foot long, double-bladed battle axe, with an iron-shod dark oak handle. A serrated spike at the top made the weapon almost five feet in length. It was long enough to impale a man. The metal of its double blades shimmered like that of the shield as he began whirling it around his body like black lightning. The tip and edges were just a hair from destroying the interior of the room.

Melegal followed the fluid movements with a silent shudder.

Brool had an odd design for a weapon—bigger than a battle axe, yet smaller than a great war axe. It looked unwieldy, awkward, and heavy. He liked to call it a "hand-and-a-half axe." There was no other like it in all the world. He fought one-handed with it, a feat in itself, but he could deal out even more damage two-handed. It was a terrible thing to face Brool in his hands.

"So, why have you decided to head out this time? Is there another brood of orcen princesses you're trying to rescue?"

"Hah," he said, chopping the air. "There's word of some trouble in the southern provinces that's moving north. They're getting aggressive out there. The Royal soldiers have their hands full keeping tabs on Outpost Thirty-One. I can make good coin on underling heads, assuming they pay before they perish this time. The caravan officials say the carnage along the trails is increasing." Venir ran his thick forearm across his sweaty head as he put down his weapon and fetched the final object out of the bag.

He placed the burnished gray helmet over his great skull, buckling the leather chinstrap. The sound of the rain on the window became louder, his senses crisp and clear. The helmet was banded with iron like the shield, with another sinister spike on top like Brool's, only smaller. It covered everything above the nose, including his eyes, which peered out through eyelets.

He was a menacing sight, and eeriness settled over the small apartment. Here was the figure that the outlanders, farmers, and villagers all hailed as the Darkslayer.

Melegal shifted in his chair, sucking hot coffee though his teeth. The man nodded his head. "That is one disturbing get-up, but it goes great with your trousers."

He was in a semi-trance, only half noticing the words. "Huh? Oh," he replied, "guess I do look a bit foolish, don't I?"

"Yep, you do."

"The underlings won't think so when Brool and I get a fix on them. I'm itching for it."

It had been weeks since he slaughtered any of the heinous creatures.

His broad smile had Melegal shaking his head.

"Think they're the ones causing trouble on the caravan trails?"

"They're always causing trouble, little monsters," he retorted. "I hate 'em. The smaller farms seem to be suffering, and the villagers don't stand a chance. There's lots of people showing up dead or disappearing. It's a shame. The Royals couldn't care less about the people who feed them."

"Well, they say the Darkslayer has their number. At least, that's what I've heard," Melegal added with a straight face.

"That's right!"

He gave the air a two-handed chop with the axe as Melegal jumped over the table.

"Watch it with that thing, will you? You could put a dragon's eye out."

"Sorry." He grinned, kissed Brool on the blade, and began shoving the armaments back into the sack. The thought of leaving the city put a spring in his step. He needed something he could sink his blade into. He used to enjoy it here, but he had changed so that now he felt like a caged animal inside of Bone's mighty walls. His purpose was out there now. He began pulling on his clothes, giving his friend a hard look as he buckled his belt. "Why not tag along on this one? It's been a while, and you're getting rusty. These city walls make you soft, Melegal. Even though you've got it all under control here, there's bound to be a day when the walls come down. You might not be ready."

Melegal stood in front of the mirror, arranging his beloved hat. "I've got it better now than ever. Why give it up to risk my neck with you?" The thief showed himself a satisfied and handsome smile of perfect teeth. "There's no comfort outside these walls. It's brutal out there! The ants are bigger than my hands. The ground is as hard as stone. What's to gain? Here, I have coin, privacy, and a roof over my head." He poured another cup of coffee. "I'm going to enjoy it while it lasts. And the women are a lot prettier here, too. Out there they usually have three eyes, hairy backs, and a row of rotten canines. I'll pass!"

"No need to be nasty. Besides, I recall you liking those little hairy lycan gals from time to time," Venir said with a laugh. "No more of those."

The thief's eyes closed, and then he opened them with a sigh.

"That last lycan about did me in. Cripes, she killed a handful of women just for looking at me one night. I don't want to take the chance of running into her again. My guess is she's still around."

Venir pulled on his boots and said, "Fair point. She was fetching in the light, though, if you ignored her tail. Look, I'd like to stay, but … I gotta go before I wind up killing somebody, myself." Venir attached a large belt pouch around his waist.

Melegal gave him a rueful look and said, "I'll walk you to the stables so I can check on Quickster. If Georgio isn't doing his job, I'm gonna kick his fat butt. Maybe he can go with you. Then you won't need me along."

"If you say so. How about heading down to the market with me? I need to load up with supplies before I get outta this stinking city."

Venir tossed the remainder of his belongings into a backpack while Melegal started setting some homemade intruder traps. As the two adventurers went out, the door quietly shut behind them. Venir locked it with his own key. Next, Melegal produced a razor-thin key, self-made, and stuck it in a well-concealed key hole. The lock tumbled into place with a quiet *click,* double locking the door.

"Is that necessary? Nobody's gonna break in before you get back." Venir scratched his head. "Not our spot anyway."

"I'm trying to not go *soft,* being prepared, like you were lecturing. Now, let's get you outta here, before you hurt someone."

The two companions headed down four flights of creaking steps onto the empty floor of the Drunken Octopus. They took to the malodorous city streets as the stinging rain hit their faces. The showers from above disguised the sound of footsteps following from behind.

10

As the suns rose, Melegal finished haggling with the local grocers as their arguments over prices with him didn't hold salt. Nothing was worth what he didn't want to pay. He was doing them a favor by not stealing it. *Stupid merchants. Just thieves in fancy clothes.* His lumbering friend's backpack was now stocked up with plenty of dried meat, fruit, and water to last the journey south. It was a stupid place to go, but at least his grinning friend could have a full belly. Anything was better than nights of eating bark and fried toad. Melegal had enough of those retched days in the wilderness. This city might smell worse, but it tasted so much better. He pinched a pair of plums from a wart-faced woman's cart and padded back alongside Venir, handing him one.

The walk was much longer than he was used to, and his narrow legs began to ache. "I hate long walks like this. It feels like ten miles to the stables. You need to find a stable closer to the Drunken Octopus." He bit into the plum and spit a tiny seed at a cat's nose, causing it to hiss and bound away.

"Quit crying, we're almost there," Venir said with a mouth full of fruit. "Mmmm … besides, you'll be happy to see me go."

"Sure will!"

The back alleys of the massive city remained gloomy even in the daylight. Most of the city wasn't safe, even on the brightest days on Bish. Only the main streets offered any safety. The two companions took shortcuts, leaving a confusing trail in case of unwanted pursuit. Melegal always led Venir on a different route, but he never got used to the big warrior moving like a ghost behind his shadows.

He looked back at stern-faced Venir, who paid his glance no mind. Melegal knew his friend's mind was elsewhere, tracking and killing something. As adolescents, the pair had managed to survive some of the worst punishment the Royals had to offer. It was Venir who was the beacon that pulled them through. Even back then, Venir reminded him that Bish had better things to offer.

Venir had told him about his family, pets, fish fries and more about his home village, Throhm. Melegal could almost taste and smell the words as they had rolled off Venir's enthusiastic lips. Venir had given him something he never had before—hope.

The Royals tried to beat it from Venir, but never could. How anyone could find humor in that was beyond Melegal, but somehow Venir always had. The man's face was dark and distant, these days. His strapping friend had been full of mirth many years ago, yet hard as iron inside and out. That festive smile was now replaced with something grimmer. Ever since the man came back from the clutches of the Brigand Queen many years ago, the crafty ranger was not the same.

As each year passed, the hardy warrior returned thickened by battle and time, rangy muscles turned to bullish brawn. Now, the youthful face was scuffed and hard as stone. His friend was on a lone mission that even his forthcoming words could not explain. Every time Venir left, Melegal felt it would be the last time he saw the man. He assumed the armament protected the man, but it did harm as well. Another piece of his jovial friend had disappeared whenever he returned.

"Do you think that Royal brat learned his lesson?" Melegal wondered aloud. "Or do you think he'd have the gall to come after you again?"

He stopped as Venir caught up.

"I mean, the beating you gave him, it should have scared the life out of him."

Venir gave him a strange look.

"Are you really worried about that, Melegal? Don't, because if he comes after me again he'll die."

Melegal picked up the pace.

"Well, I discovered he's from a very high Royal house," he said with a sheepish look. "They don't like scum like us screwing with their own. They can be vengeful."

Venir's face curled up, half-sneer, half-smile.

"Pah, I'm sure I put an end to it. Besides, he shouldn't be able to walk or talk for days."

"If you say so."

After several more minutes of walking, his fleet feet fell onto a wide cobblestone street that crossed between the alleys. People plowed through one another, bargaining in the buzzing market places. Shouting and bartering could be heard everywhere, passing from slick lips and hefty hips. The streets were alive with trading, soliciting, and stealing, amid shouts of joy, shock, and surprise.

Not far from the cobbled road loomed the great southern gate, standing five stories high. The mighty portcullis was a woven steel maw locked shut. People, wagons, carts, and mounts were directed in and out, through a smaller gate on the east side, by an assertive squad of the City Watch. It was the main gate that controlled the passage of all vehicles and pedestrians in and out of the southern part of the city. Desperate people tried to press inside, only to be beaten back by whips and thick clubs called watch sticks.

The wall surrounding the City of Bone stood over four stories high, made of massive stones no group of men could have ever moved. No one knew for sure where they came from, nor did they care. The story of the old seers was that giants had built and occupied the City of Bone. There was no evidence to support such a tale. Only the boulders knew, and they had no interest in talking. On top of the huge stone walls stood many battlements lined with smaller walls of brick and mortar. Dozens of guards in studded leather armor and gleaming helmets were posted in pairs, spaced along the wall, as far as the eye could see.

"Exciting job," Melegal said, gazing at those guards. He would almost prefer the Outlands to standing hours on end along that wall. He turned his eyes away. "Let's get you to the stables and out of my hair."

Along the foreboding wall, a few hundred yards east of the main gate, a dozen large wood-framed barns were laid out in two rows, each over twenty feet high and a hundred yards long. Melegal headed toward the barn in the rear, farthest from the gate. His feet were beginning to burn, and the thought of a blister ate at his brain.

Gonna have to buy new shoes, too.

Melegal tugged open a small, nondescript door.

Finally here. Ew. The smell of hay and manure magnified ten times as he stepped inside. He tucked his nose inside his cloak. *Filthy.*

Hundreds of stalls lined the walls, and the sounds of stabled beasts rose to the rafters. Banners of the militia and Royal houses were displayed at the utmost northern end. An open roof cast light on several well-bred horses that stood in the distance, being tended by stable hands hard at work with chores. He remembered those long days, frail arms shaking, face filled with sweat and grime. Urchins — the bottom of the barrel — worked here.

Pitiful, but at least I was smart enough to make it back to the castles and out of the stink.

Venir followed him into the southern end, away from the rustles and neighs that fell behind. The open roof was shadowed by the city's wall, leaving the area quiet, undisturbed, and run down. Another wooden fence, several feet in height, barricaded the south from the north. He climbed between the rotting planks as Venir pushed his gear through and climbed over the top, landing by his side.

In the distance, a curly-headed boy seated on a stool buffed his shoe with a horse brush. Seeing the two coming his way, the young fellow squinted, jumped up, and ran toward them while trying to put his shoe back on.

"Venir!" the boy yelled, running up and wrapping two arms around his waist.

"Georgio!" He patted him on the head, trying to pry his arms off. "Easy, big fella. You're getting stronger every day, I see." Seeing the boy brought a smile to his face.

Georgio released him, beaming with pride. "I want to be strong like you. The strongest man in the world! I moved five hundred hay bales this week!" The big boy flexed his arms and stuck out his chest. "Taking care of Chongo is a lot of work. I didn't think you were ever gonna come back by." Georgio began to skip away while motioning for him to follow, but Melegal grabbed his arm.

"What about my mount?" Melegal began with a hiss. "I hope you haven't been neglecting him!"

"Aw, let me go!" Georgio tried to jerk his arm away, but was held fast. "Your stinking donkey's just fine! All he ever does is sleep and poop everywhere."

"Don't smart mouth me," Melegal said, poking him in the chest.

Venir stepped between them.

"Can't you two ever get along? Melegal, you know Georgio always takes care of Quickster."

Venir grabbed the boy by the shoulder and turned him away as Melegal retorted, "Not last time he didn't. Quickster was sick 'cause of him."

"That wasn't my fault. That dumb donkey started eating from the slat bins."

"He's not a donkey! He's a pony!" the thief said.

"It's a pony that looks like a donkey and eats crap!" Georgio jumped away as Melegal swatted at his curly head.

The hefty boy moved with speed that belied his formidable girth as Melegal started after, but Venir obstructed him again.

"Let it go. I'm sure he's fine this time."

"He'd better be, or I'll bust Georgio's butt." Melegal straightened his cap as he walked away, saying, "Take the boy with you, eh. If you run low on food you can always cook him."

Venir watched Georgio finish his trot to a stable many yards away. The boy was nodding and mumbling between the planks of the gate. The stable was quiet, more so than normal. Something was missing. He craned his neck, expecting to hear the eager baritone yelps of Chongo. The barking did not come. As he watched Melegal walking towards the boy, the skin on his neck began to itch. Something was amiss. Venir started to turn.

"Don't move!" a raspy voice said from behind.

He froze.

Ahead of him, Melegal whirled back his way, daggers drawn. The thief's chin dipped, eyes flaring wide. Melegal's lips were mouthing the word, "*Tonio.*"

Another chill slivered to his toes as he made a slow turn to face his assailant. Indeed, it was his latest adversary. The man he'd busted to bits stood there without a noticeable scratch around his curled sneer. The pupils of the man's eyes were big dots of coal, glaring back at him. The quivering hands were now wrapped about the trigger of a double crossbow that pointed dead at his chest. Venir fought the urge to lunge underneath it. He began lowering his two sacks slowly to the ground.

"Keep those sacks up! You in the back, toss the blades."

Venir heard the daggers clatter behind him.

"Who's that man?" the boy asked.

Tonio's voice was tense, slurred, and wavering. "Can't believe I'm better, can you?" Tonio said in a throaty voice. "You should have killed me. We Royals have the best healing at our disposal. And now I've got you, dog! Nobody beats me and lives to tell about it!" Tonio motioned him backward with the crossbow, and he backed up, stopping as he came alongside Melegal. The Royal spat, made a tight face, then spat again. "Let's take this a little farther back. A stable full of manure should make a nice grave." Tonio's chuckle was low and wicked. "Fat urchin back there, stop fidgeting! Get those hands back up, all of you!"

"Do as he says, Georgio." Venir stepped back until they all stood side by side.

He watched the tip of the bolt swing from belly to belly. The boy's labored breathing caught his ears. He couldn't have been in a worse situation if his pants were down. No weapon or armor. How did they miss the man? Tonio was sweating, hands clammy and eyes dilating, fingertip fidgeting on the trigger. Sweat dripped into Venir's eye and off his nose. *Slat!*

"Don't stop, you two! Boy, go open that empty stable back there, or I'll shoot your friends." Tonio said.

Georgio tripped over his feet, scrambled up, clutched at another stable door and pulled it open. He managed to conceal himself behind the planks on the other side.

Venir and Melegal moved backward, step by step along the opening of the stable, and stopped again.

"I said don't stop!" Tonio yelled. "Are you deaf? Keep moving! Get in there! "

Venir's chest tightened as Tonio's finger twitched on the crossbow's trigger. Ten paces away, he side-stepped, blocking Tonio's view of the boy.

"Fine!" the Royal shouted, aiming the crossbow at his throat. "You can die right there!" Venir prepared to spring away.

A low growl erupted from the stable by Tonio's side. The Royal took a peek over the closed stable gate. "Eh …?" A pair of lion-like paws reached over the gate and tore into Tonio's face. A burst of snarls and barks followed as the claws pinned the man to the gate. "Aagh!"

Tonio wailed and thrashed as a massive dog snapped at his head. He raised his crossbow, eyes bearing down on Venir like charging lances.

Clatch! Zip! Zip!

Venir dove to the ground as a bolt shot his way and clipped the back of his calf. He scrambled back to his feet. The crossbow fell from Tonio's limp hands as he screamed and fought for his life. The beast kept pulling at him, tearing his clothes to bloodied shreds.

"No! No! NOOOOO!"

A massive maw bit down on Tonio's horrified face, gripping it tight, while another set of teeth sank into his neck. A resounding crunch sent a flock of doves from the rafters in a plume of white and gray. Outside the stables, few noticed their flight, for it was nothing extraordinary to a commoner's eye.

Venir saw Tonio's body go limp. Two giant dog heads came into full view, shaking the body a couple of times and dropping it to the stable floor like a discarded toy. Venir pulled the man's still breathing body out of the way and swung the door open.

The two faces of Chongo bounded out, his two tails wagging with enthusiasm. The pair of monstrous, bloodied heads licked Venir like a happy puppy. He tried to fight the giant dog off in vain. Chongo came out of the gate, standing as tall as a small horse, but broader. The shaggy red-brown coat shone in the morning light as Venir tried to calm his excited pooch. He rubbed the massive dog's chest and belly as it rolled onto its back.

"Good boy, Chongo. Good boy."

He scratched all four of the dog's ears and looked about for the thief and boy. Georgio stood shaking at the gate, staring at the crossbow bolt embedded in it. Venir signaled the boy over. Melegal, with a foul look on his face, led a shaggy, dark gray pony out of another stable.

"See what you've done!" the thief yelled at Venir. "The City Watch is gonna be all over us. The Royals will have a price on our heads so high we'll never be able to come back. They'll be hunting us nonstop. Blast you, brute!"

Melegal paused as he inspected the teeth and ears of his pony.

"Now, I'm gonna have to go with you. I knew this would happen. I bloody knew it! I told you we shoulda been worried!" Melegal began cursing under his breath, glaring at him. "Now what?"

"Be silent," Venir growled under his breath, looking about. Tonio couldn't have been alone.

Venir held two fingers to his chest, paused, and held up one. Melegal repeated the signs back to him, and handed Georgio the saddle of his pony. With a parting glare, Melegal shook his head and disappeared.

"Where's—"

Venir tugged at the boy's ear.

"Oh."

Georgio scrambled to saddle the pony. They moved like soldiers breaking down a camp. Venir slung Chongo's leather saddle over his back and was ready to move out.

Georgio stepped into Chongo's stable and pulled an old rake off the wall. The boy stretched it upward, caught it high above the rafters, and yanked at something. An angled wooden walkway dropped down at the back of the stable. It opened into a deep passage facing south and slanting down.

The mysterious passage had been revealed to Venir by an old stable hand. The old man said he had seen it used only once when he was a boy. It was just another forgotten secret among a thousand in the great City of Bone.

Venir grabbed the big dog by the scruff of its chest and led both animals into the tunnel. Back inside the stable, the boy raked at the hay, manure, and dirt, and waved. The secret door closed and Georgio's broad smile left his sight.

It was pitch black. Venir traveled at a sluggish pace for over a mile. He crossed over a large metal grate with the sound of water running far below. Venir always assumed it was a large storm drain, but wondered if that was its only purpose. From there, the passage began sloping upward, and he came to a dead end. There, he waited....

At last, the dead end opened up, and scattered daylight poured in. They were inside a small cave. Georgio's flushed pie-face appeared, whispering, "Coast is clear."

"Good job, Georgio. Now, help me adjust Chongo's saddle. I'll keep him calm while you tighten the buckles."

The husky boy closed off the secret passage and took the large saddle from Venir's shoulder. Venir sat Chongo down, talking to him and scratching his head while the dog-beast growled as Georgio saddled him. Venir kept Chongo calm long enough for the boy to finish the last buckle, and tossed each head a red apple. Chongo chomped them down, whirled, and began barking at the boy, who backed up gingerly.

"Heel!" Venir said.

The dog lowered his heads and lay down at his feet. He loaded his two sacks onto the giant dog. One head licked at his boots, while the other kept a wary eye on the boy.

"Why's he doing that? He never does me like that in the stables," Georgio said as he clambered onto Quickster's saddle.

"Ah … he's just testing you. Besides, he doesn't like me saddling him, either."

Venir slung himself up on Chongo's back and led the way. It was late morning, and the two suns were hot over the dry, open land. The City of Bone's southern wall stood like a blackened monolith more than two miles away. In the south, the barren Outlands looked dry and dreadful. Venir smiled.

The air was fresh and pure, the sunlight hot on his face. The clouds had broken apart as the rain traveled into the distant north. He could still see several groups of nomadic people and farmers clustered near the distant walls. Most were not welcome in the City of Bone. It was either sell or be sold if you weren't careful. The main caravan trail was busy with the comings and goings of all types of trade. Heavy clouds of dust from beasts of burden obscured the figures traveling along with their carts and wagons. *Fools.* But what better choice did they have?

Georgio rode at his side as he set off. "Where to?" The boy looked eager.

"I'm taking you home. Melegal will meet us in a couple of hours. You'll be safe; the City Watch won't come out more than a day's ride."

Georgio frowned as they rode on in silence. The dog led the way with a fluid gait, tongues hanging out in the heat, ears and eyes all alert.

"Why didn't Chongo bark when you showed up?"

"He sensed danger and wanted to sneak up on it, I guess. He's smart. He doesn't like bad people. I think he can sense evil."

"How come Melegal has this dumb pony? Why can't he have a real horse or something?"

"I told you before," he said as irritation rose in his voice, "quick ponies move just as fast, but they carry like a pack mule. Melegal thinks he's going to find a hoard of treasure one day. Besides, it didn't cost him anything; he won Quickster in a bet."

"Well, Quickster's a stupid name. He should be called Poopster."

"Enough, Georgio!"

The land south of the city was mostly clay, dirt, and rocks, vegetated with cacti and thick thatches of thistles. It was flat, and the footing hard. The suns burned front and back on a day like this. The Outlands offered little comfort to those who were ill prepared.

Not much was to be encountered between cities or villages, except in the cool of the evening. Bandits knew the pickings on the trails were riskier at night, but that was when they came. During the day, the dreaded blistering heat of the suns helped to protect travelers. Still, day or night, you could never get comfortable. The bandits watched, and laid their traps as soon as you did. Many wearied travelers perished under their desperate steel. It was only one of many terrors to be encountered in the Outlands.

The two hadn't traveled far when they came upon a dry well with sparse vegetation. The cacti were abundant; it was good fortune. Venir found a nice round cactus, lopped off the top, and started pulling out the watery pulp and feeding it to Chongo. Georgio did the same for Quickster. In the distance, the City of Bone hovered like a mirage, wavering in the sunlight like a ghostly castle. He squinted towards it. Georgio, soaked in sweat, grabbed a waterskin and gulped it down.

Venir went to one of his large sacks and pulled out two beige cotton cowls. "Put this on your head. It'll keep you from frying." It had been over an hour, and Melegal was nowhere in sight. "Bloody thief's gonna be late," he muttered to himself. "I told him he was getting rusty."

"Rusty? I've been following you for an hour," a voice shot from behind. "I just couldn't decide who I would kill first."

Venir turned around, grinning. The thief was dressed in tones as drab as the landscape, hands on polished steel at his hips.

"Well, maybe I was wrong. Any news?"

"I moved the body, covered the tracks. There was a stir as I left the stables. The City Watch filed in with some Royals. I thought I saw a familiar face from the Chimera, but I recognized no one else. But, you can bet your ears they'll be looking for us for a long time coming. He wasn't alone, I'm sure."

Melegal turned back towards the city and waved.

"Good-bye my dear tavern dwelling. Good-bye soft and simple life."

As the wind whipped across their faces, Venir began thinking out loud. "Who could've seen us? I know Tonio's father knows what I look like and a few guards, too, but I seriously doubt—"

"You know as well as I, not a man in all of Bone can hide forever when he's on the List. All you can hope is to not make the List. But now that Chongo's turned one of their own into a chew toy, I'm pretty sure *we are* on that List! Something I'd taken pride in avoiding all these years."

Venir kept his own discomforting thoughts to himself. All this trouble over him was excessive, even for a Royal.

Melegal snatched the waterskin from Georgio's hand. "I don't understand why that Royal bastard even conceived of coming after you. Usually, they get their dirty work done for them. It was insane!"

"Maybe we became pawns in something bigger. The Royals like doing one another in."

"My gut's telling me the same, but there is no evidence."

The thief rinsed the grit from his mouth, spit, and continued, "Not that they need it. That's why I gotta get my happy arse out of Bone!"

Venir tried to sound reassuring.

"One way or the other, they were coming after us. At least we didn't get cornered in the city. We'll head down to Two-Ten first. We'll hail well there; they hate Bone."

The thief shook his head and swung his leg up unto Georgio's saddle.

"Oh great! Orcs and bad wine. I can't wait!"

"Well, I guess you're coming after all!" Venir said.

"Why not? I've nothing to live for anymore, might as well die trying to live." They loaded up as Georgio hopped onto Chongo's back behind Venir. Despite their quick pace, it was a long, hot ride south, where he hoped to leave Georgio at his home village. But they'd have to pass through Red Clay Forest first, and Venir had reservations about going in there. *It can't be as bad as last time.*

It was just dusk when the small party finally stopped, just inside the shadowy edge of the forest.

11

LORDS CATTEN AND VERBARD FLOATED at attention as another underling hovered before the hanging humans. Catten's icy heart worked overtime. Master Sinway had arrived. The master of all underlings was dark-robed, hawk-nosed, and not so different from his brethren. Still, Master Sinway's greater height and breadth distinguished him from all others. He made Catten feel small.

Iron-colored irises outlined Master Sinway's black pupils that glinted like cut coal. The underling master's countenance radiated an endless river of wisdom. His heavy robes were traced in exquisite patterns flecked with traces of silver and rust. Oh, how Catten craved the magic he could feel permeating those clothes. Master Sinway turned, catching his eye, causing him to look away. His brother Verbard, fidgeted at his side.

Master Sinway's face was broad and hairless, more like a human. His hair was black and short, hanging just below his ears. His thin lips hid small, flat gray teeth, and his hands were large, black-knuckled, and hairless. His iron-colored eyes were deep, ageless and omnipotent. Black robed, he stood taller than the brothers.

Master Sinway was not alone. Catten's golden gaze fell on two of the most impressive beasts in the Underland, known as the Vicious. The Vicious stood flat on the ground only a few feet from the underling master. The imposing pair were black and genderless.

The Vicious were unlike underlings. They had round, cat-like faces with long, pointed ears, and small noses with flared nostrils. The creatures were known to track prey for leagues on scent alone. Thick, claw-like black fingernails came to points, like five small daggers on each hand. Wide platinum eyes without lashes shone bright under their protruding brows. Their countenances revealed the cool intelligence of predators, and their lips turned up in matching sinister sneers. Pain and destruction.

That was what Catten thought of them. He watched as the pair moved, silent and fluid, over the cave water that mixed with dripping human blood. They were difficult to see against the cavernous background. These great assassins were heralded throughout the Underland as legends of death.

Catten had seen them only a handful of times over the centuries. He dug his nails into his palms. The Vicious were as tall on the ground as he was floating. *Why are they here?* Their heavy muscles rippled underneath their hairless, leather-like skin. Catten recalled a time when one Vicious had twisted an imprisoned gnoll's head from its neck. An unwelcome tingle raced down his spine.

Sinway was believed to have been an apprentice to Master Sidebor. Master Sidebor was the greatest of all underlings back then, and he had created the Vicious from a blend of man, underling, and magic. Sidebor was believed to have perished in long-past centuries in a great battle some said was against Sinway. No underling knew for sure what had caused the demise of Sidebor, though Catten was certain Sinway knew the truth. The evidence casting suspicion on Sinway was the powerful magic robe he wore. It too had been Sidebor's. Of course, as far as he was concerned, Sidebor could still be alive, for his body had never been found.

If Catten's brother Verbard was as uncomfortable as he was, he didn't show it. Verbard looked up and down, fingers twitching like a bored child. Catten hoped his brother could keep his mouth shut, just this once. Tension continued its slow ascent up his neck.

After several uncomfortable minutes, the master spoke.

"What a unique piece of humanity you have displayed."

Catten was surprised. His master's voice was almost reassuring.

Master Sinway floated toward the bleeding humans as his black index fingers ignited in sharp blue flames. "Perhaps a few finishing touches." Master Sinway drew agonizing symbols into the men's burning flesh. "Much better," Sinway said, adding a mild chuckle as he blew out his fingers.

Catten clapped in unison with his brother, sharp teeth bared wide. Sinway cut their efforts off with a short hand gesture, his iron eyes sliding back and forth between the two.

"So, what have you to report about the world above? I gather our troops have been—oh, how shall I put it?—diminished!"

Catten felt like he was hit in the stomach. He doubled over as heavy drops of water and debris fell from the stalactites above. He wanted to slither away. Instead, he pulled his tongue down from the roof of his mouth and began to speak, but Verbard beat him to it.

"All is fine, Master Sinway. The troublemakers have been vanquished, and our troops are in good order."

Catten couldn't believe his ears. *Idiot!*

"Really, Verbard?" Master Sinway stood inches from Verbard's face, and Catten could feel his master's cool breath. "The last I heard, a few score raiding parties perished a few weeks ago—and two score just before that!"

The drops began to fall again as Catten covered his queasy stomach with his arms.

"So, how do you consider the problem to be resolved?" Master Sinway's face was taut.

Don't say a word, Verbard. Catten knew the numbers were even greater, but he had no desire to admit to that. In all of his centuries alongside Master Sinway, Catten had never seen him more angered. The time to grovel had come.

Verbard dropped to his knees, robes dangling in the stream below.

"My lord, we did not know—"

Verbard was lying, but Catten kneeled alongside his brother anyway.

"We have been so busy with other projects. We were assured the problem was taken care of," Verbard pleaded in a stammering voice.

Catten had seen the soft ploy before. He didn't care for it, but it worked.

"Be silent! I am no fool. You two have never failed me—up until now, that is."

Catten pulled himself into a tighter ball. His master's fingers twitched at his sides. He tucked his chin deeper into his chest, and caught Verbard's silver eyes for a split second. The fool was smiling. *Quiet, fool!*

Sinway's tone softened a hair as he said, "This situation is unusual, but it is not the first time this has happened." There was a pause, and Catten swore he heard Sinway sigh.

"It seems our troops and run-of-the-mill soldiers are no match for this Darkslayer. He kills with less mercy than we ... and he hunts us down!"

A stalactite fell to the cave floor. Sinway's ancient voice was almost a yell.

"No one dares to hunt the underlings!"

Catten expected the cave to collapse as more debris fell around them.

"So, I am dispatching the Vicious to finish the task you have clearly mismanaged." *What?* Catten's golden eyes were as wide as saucers, as well as his brother's. He tilted his head upward, eyes still down. Sinway resumed. "Assuming this Darkslayer works alone, he will be unable to handle the Vicious. None has ever lived to fight the Vicious another day."

Catten watched as Sinway's robes billowed and floated away. When he looked up, the Vicious and Sinway were gone. Sinway's words lingered in his mind. *I am dispatching the Vicious.* Catten stood up at his brother's side, and the two faced one another with evil grins. With the Vicious gone, Sinway would be at his most vulnerable. But it was only a whim; even together they were still no match for him. Yet the thought was pleasurable.

"Do you think this solves our problem?" Catten asked.

"I don't know, but it's one less burden. That Darkslayer is a pain in my bollards. The Vicious are going after him ... incredible." Verbard bobbed his head. "Now we will learn what we are really dealing with."

"I imagine so. It should be a great battle. What do you think Master Sinway meant by 'It is not the first time this has happened'?" Catten searched his brother's eyes.

"I don't know, but I'm not sure he intended to let that out."

Catten agreed. Sinway knew something he didn't want to share. Catten shuddered as he looked at the fallen rocks on the floor. The fact they both were unharmed was astounding. Sinway hadn't become the master of all underlings by showing mercy. Whatever the Darkslayer was, it had Sinway concerned. It had Catten concerned as well. *Stay or go.*

The two magi lords dusted off their robes and floated away, abandoning their dead human masterpiece. Cave rats scurried forth, nipping into the succulent human nutrition, rather than the crisp cave bugs that always fought back.

12

VENIR AWOKE JUST AS THE light of the two suns cracked over the horizon and warmed his face. He sat up and stepped onto the grassy edge of the Red Clay Forest. He could hear the chittering of small creatures bouncing among the tree tops and rustling in the branches above. Shade and food were in abundance just inside the forest, but danger lurked in there as well. Venir thought about going around. *Too long. Too hot.* The suns would dry his companions out like twigs if they ran out of water. All of a sudden, he was uneasy, hot, and thirsty.

He pulled Georgio off the ground and gave him a firm shake. The boy rubbed his groggy eyes with his meaty fists and said, "I'm hungry."

Unlike the dry plains they had crossed the previous day, the Red Clay Forest appeared alive, eerie, and magnificent. But travelers would risk the heat over the forest most of the time. The rough and uncertain terrain wasn't made for wagons or slow-footed folk. Still, with his experienced eye Venir recognized the faint pathways. They always seemed to move. He paced back and forth along the edge then knelt down to feel the ground and peered ahead. A pair of large brown squirrels scurried in the distance. This would be it. He dusted his hands off.

The Red Clay Forest was known for its inviting beauty, lush vegetation, and delicious wildlife. Travelers didn't pass through it for the view though, no, most passed when there was little choice left. The inviting beauty was uncomfortable amid the odd serenity. Despite Venir's misgivings, it was the fastest way to Georgio's village.

"I don't wanna go into that filthy forest!" Melegal was packing Quickster's saddle bags. "It's easier in the Outlands. Now, bugs and vermin are gonna crawl all over me. I remember last time. I barely made it out alive, and I lost my gold! Let's go around!" Melegal swatted at a mosquito bigger than his hand. "Bone! How'd I get into this?"

"It wasn't so bad last time. You just overreacted. And we aren't going around; it'd take days. We don't have that much water. Do you want to die of thirst?"

"I don't drink so much as you. I have plenty," Melegal said, patting one of his two flasks.

"Don't worry, the bugs will leave you alone once they realize you're made of stone," Georgio said, smiling and turning away.

Melegal flung a stone, hitting the boy in the back of his head.

"Ow!" Georgio rubbed his head. "You didn't need to do that."

Melegal and Georgio had been at each other without ceasing, and Venir had reached his limit. "Get your gear ready! This forest isn't gonna make the trip any less miserable, so stop it, both of you!" He slung his pack over his shoulder and pulled Chongo along.

It didn't take but a few dozen steps before Venir felt like he was in another world. The forest trees rose out of sight in many places, and even the lowest branches were too high to reach. The leaves were an assortment of reds, greens, and blues that never fell from the trees inside Red Clay Forest, unlike in other parts of Bish. It could not be explained; no one on Bish cared anyway. *Why*, never came to mind.

They walked over the red clay and stepped through areas covered in various mosses, shrubbery, and flowers of great beauty. Venir pulled Georgio away when he began picking at blackish berries on a thorny bush.

"Poison," Venir muttered.

Georgio stuck his tongue out, flicking the berries away. "Yuck."

Step after step, Venir led them down a narrow path. Without the rustle of leaves beneath their feet, it was as if the forest had been recently swept.

Much of Venir's time in the Outlands was spent in Red Clay Forest. He used it both as a safe haven and for shortcuts during his travels. Most people knew better than to be too curious about the forest; too often the curious never came back out. The forest was risky, filled with violence of all sorts. At times, the forest left Venir alone, and at other times it did not. It had been a while since Venir traveled with company in the forest. It was more risky. Still, his knowledge of the shortcuts through the forest often threw the more experienced pursuers off his trail.

The minutes felt like hours, and despite the wonderful shade of the mammoth leaves, it was still hot and humid. There was no breeze. Chongo's two heads made loud panting sounds, tongues hanging out like red carpets. Quickster panted too, and Georgio's curly hair was bushed out and soaked with sweat. It was almost as miserable as being under the suns. There was little cool comfort anywhere in the Outlands, except in the caves or high in the nameless mountains.

"This forest makes me itch all over," Melegal said, scratching his neck.

Venir looked back towards the thief, who'd changed some of his clothes. "Eh … changing attire again?" he said.

Melegal shrugged.

"I don't think that will scare the bugs away."

"No, but it will make me a less obvious target than you."

"Have it your way, then."

He led Chongo up a steep slope of rocks and slippery moss. Georgio clutched at the saddle as the big dog lurched upward. Onward they went; one hour became two. When they leveled out on a plateau, a stiff wind cut through their damp clothes. "Ah … that feels great," Georgio said, widening his arms.

Even Melegal seemed to think so, closing his tireless eyes. Venir's nostrils widened as his hand fell to the hilt of his knife. The wind picked up, bending the saplings and tall grass, raising goose bumps on his sweat-slickened skin.

The smell in the wind was foul, like molded bread. Georgio and Melegal held their noses. Venir knew what it was the foul breeze spoke in his ears. *Bone – the magi come!*

13

R OYAL LORD ALMEN WAS SEATED in his elaborate throne room. His primped brow was drawn down, and his chest heaving. His fist was clenched in the face of another man, all clad in black.

"Why? Who? How?" he yelled in the cowering man's face.

His bellows echoed off the high ceilings, down the corridors, and throughout the rooms of his castle. There was a crash of glass coming from somewhere, a gasp and the sound of footfalls scurrying away. It was not good to be around the wrath of Lord Almen of the Fourth House of Bone.

Lord Almen seethed inside, far worse than his shaking voice. His finest son was lost. His enemies, any hundred of them, would see this as a weakness in his powerful house. He had to take precautions so that news of his son's demise would not travel.

"Why haven't the culprits already been brought to me? I want the culprits. Now!"

"It seems that the criminal has fled the City of Bone." The man's voice was silky, but mindful. The swarthy figure spread out his hands and began to fan himself with a wide brimmed hat.

"Go on, Detective McKnight!" Lord Almen bellowed.

McKnight drew himself up, but left his head dipped down. "There is no specific evidence, except that Tonio was mauled to death." He spoke fast, but fluidly as he went on. "By what, I haven't discovered yet. It's taking time to gather up all of the locals. But we'll make them talk. The stable master and his help were found dead. Others seem to have vanished. It seems to be the work of an assassin from another family, although the mauling is inexplicable at the moment." The detective shrugged. "I don't understand it yet, but I will."

Lord Almen grabbed the detective by the collar of his cloak, and pulled him up on his toes. "You better!" He searched for the man's eyes, but could not find them. He wanted any reason to kill—any man would do—but McKnight he needed. He sat down in thoughtful repose, dipping his jeweled goblet into his wine bowl. "It is assassination then?" *Evil vermin, those assassins.*

"I believe so, lord, but who and why is curious."

"That much I know, fool." Lord Almen folded his arms and leaned back into his cushions. "I believe I shall deal with this without your help, Detective McKnight. In the meantime, make sure this recent debacle of my son's demise does not get out, especially to my wife." He waved his hand. "You are dismissed."

Detective McKnight could not have been more relieved. *Let him find his deviant son's killers. That way, my back will be covered, not buried.*

Detective McKnight was one of the finest in the business, having done the dirty work for many Royal families for more than twenty years. He had seen the worst. This mess, however, was unique. Whatever had mangled the foolish Tonio was no assassin of a Royal house. It was perhaps a clever setup, though. It seemed more likely that Tonio had gotten caught up with the wrong locals. *It happens.*

McKnight knew all too well that the City of Bone contained people and creatures that even the mighty Royal houses should not mess with. He had given up warning them, as they would never believe a commoner. *They'll have plenty of time to think it over in the grave.*

Dozens of scenarios ran through his mind. He strode through the castle like a ghost in black garb, stroking his thin sideburns and pointed chin. A thin film of sweat built up on his pallid face. Lord Almen was one of the few who made him nervous. He looked straight ahead as he passed the hard stares of the sentries in the exit corridor. *Morons.*

McKnight, unlike most in his profession, enjoyed the limelight. He suspected that this was why Almen had hired him long ago. He also knew how to handle delicate matters—in the dark. He stepped out from under a small portcullis and into the streets of the city.

"Whew," he said, scratching a small bald spot on the crown of his head. He had to find out who killed Tonio. That information would be worth something. It might even get him a room in the castle. *But first … a drink.* He put on his wide black hat and disappeared into the city, singing a cheerful melody. "Ding dong, the brat is gone …"

14

CHONGO'S FOUR EARS PERKED UP like horns, and his tails moved in rigid unison. The big dog made low howling sounds. Melegal reigned in Quickster along Chongo's side, tucking his nose inside his cowl. The foul air cut through the scented leaves. Venir stood on the grassy plateau, holding his hand out in warning. This was no normal breeze.

The wind picked up around the group as Chongo began to howl louder at the whine of the whipping wind. Georgio clutched Chongo's saddle, shaking on the dog's back. The howling wind tore at their clothes; louder and louder it came. Venir squinted, but he couldn't see a thing. The wind knocked him around so that he grabbed Georgio and held him tight.

He yelled for Melegal, "Hang on to something!"

The howling continued for more than a minute before the wind died. Venir looked about. Melegal was adjusting his hat, and that's when he saw them coming.

He heard a *whoosh*, like broken branches flying in the wind. Several floating figures in earthen robes hovered above the ground and began circling the party. Venir squinted as he searched the hooded faces. He had no idea what race they were, as the races of the magi were known to be many.

"Don't anyone make any sudden moves," Venir said. "Just be still."

He wanted to drop his hand over the hilt of his knife; instead he tugged at the reigns. Chongo pressed his ears down and growled while Quickster chewed on a piece of grass.

"Where are their feet?" Georgio whispered, drawing a sharp elbow from Venir.

The magi came to a stop, and two of the misshapen figures floated toward Venir, Chongo, and Georgio. Another set bore down on Melegal and Quickster. Melegal reached for something.

"Don't move; it's all right," Venir warned.

Melegal sat like a stone, a scowl crossing his slender face.

Like greedy thieves, the four forest magi pawed and rummaged through all of their belongings. Their groping was uncomfortable, but the smell was worse. Rancid breath filled Venir's nostrils, and Georgio gagged behind his back.

"Venir!" said Melegal, pleading as the magi turned his sack upside down, spilling the contents to the ground.

"Hold off … I don't think they'll take anything."

"Easy for you to say, you don't—"

"Ssh! For all I know, they speak our tongue. We won't have what they want. Be still!"

One of the forest magi shook Venir's large leather sack up and down.

Oh no. If anything fell out of that sack, a fight was on. He waited for Brool to drop out, but nothing fell. He saw one of the magi toss the sack away, and he swore he heard a *clank*, but all the clatter elsewhere covered the sound. Venir let out a soft sigh.

They watched as all of their meager belongings were picked through and dropped. The magi gathered, circled around them once more, broke off into a uniform column, and disappeared back into the forest. The stink dispersed.

The normal forest sounds resumed, and Chongo's twin tails wagged again. Quickster still chewed at the ground, their supplies strewn about the forest floor around them.

"Whew!" Georgio said. "What were those nasty things?"

"Forest magi!" Venir picked up his knife and jammed it back in his sheath.

"Oh … then what were they looking for?" Georgio asked, retrieving some items.

"Magic, no doubt. They're whores for magic, those smelly fiends. That's why they live here." Venir picked up his large leather sack and shook it.

"Why?" the boy asked.

"It's isolated, and the forest is supposedly magical. I don't know if it is, but then again, it doesn't change like the rest. So I'm told."

Venir was picking up more provisions when he noticed Melegal making no effort to help.

"What's the matter, Melegal? Did they rob you of your magic hands?"

Melegal sat motionless, his face dark with emotion.

"Your hat!" Venir exclaimed. Georgio gasped.

Melegal unleashed a fury of profanities never before heard in the Red Clay Forest. He ranted in an unbroken stream for a full minute, until at last his outburst began to subside. "I told you! I told you! I told you! Just like the last time, you idiot!" He stopped, took a breath, and turned on Venir.

Venir was not there. In his place was the form of a brutish man wearing a spiked helmet, a round shield, and a massive battle axe. It was a chilling sight.

The words from the man's lips were more scary than reassuring.

"I'll get it back."

Melegal and Georgio stepped out of his way.

15

Trinos was pleased with Bish. Whenever she checked in, it seemed to be stuck deep in a mud puddle of chaos. Yet, it was not as entertaining as she had hoped, because she knew what was going to happen most of the time. She remembered something called repeats from other worlds; so still she watched, even when she had seen it all before. But sometimes a ripple here and there would catch her off guard, for good and evil were always somewhat unpredictable. It was those precious thrills that gave her world meaning. The infinite ones had escaped from good and evil over time, as their eternal life transcended it, or so it seemed.

Whenever Trinos saw that things had become too mundane, she would place a ripple in the world—a new creature, race, or ecosystem—and come back later to see what effect it caused. This proved the most effective way to keep things interesting, or to create the feeling she had once referred to as *fun*. Life on the world of Bish always reacted to her interventions. The balance would tip in favor of good or evil. Currently, things were much in favor of evil. So, Trinos had her tool in place to protect the good for the time being. And it was a bloody creative tool at that.

16

Venir took off at a flat run, angling to cut off the forest magi somewhere down the winding paths. His bulk achieved amazing speed as his ragged hair waved like a banner under his helm. His unusual breadth was deceptive, for he could shoot off in a blink.

"I'm going after him," said Georgio, dashing after Venir as fast as his chubby legs would carry him.

"Crap." Melegal placed Quickster's reins in one of Chongo's mouths and caught up to Georgio in several quick bounds.

It wasn't long before the pair were caught up in the thatches and had to slow. Melegal's ears were keen though, and what he might not see, the seasoned thief could hear. He grabbed Georgio and pulled him along.

Ahead in the distance, Venir stopped. He had almost overrun the pinched path where he intended to cut off the forest magi. He knew the forest well enough to track them down. There he stood, his stout legs shoulder-width apart, with a slight bend in his knees. His helmet was keen to his needs, but it didn't feel like a boiling pot on his head, not like when the underlings were near. No, he was in control, but his anger was far from in check.

He laid his banded shield behind him while Brool twirled in his left arm, cutting the air in short strokes. His head rolled, making his neck crackle as he grumbled beneath his black-spiked helm. The forest grew quiet, and a score of birds burst away as the magi rounded the bend.

The tallest of the forest magi floated forward, twirling around while making odd gestures with its hands.

Venir flexed his grip on his axe, thick blue veins rising in his arm like small roots. He had played their games before, but he hadn't always won. *What's it gonna be this time?* The rest of the magi began forming two columns on opposite sides of the path, centered on their leader.

"One of you took something that was not yours," Venir said in growl. "I will be taking it back!"

The forest magi weren't known to take material things, such as a commoner's cap. This was considered dishonorable among them. They loved magic, though. They were greedy little pests, and not often challenged about what they took. Gripped in fear, most would leave the forest magi alone. Travelers were often happy for the inconvenience when they felt their lives had been spared.

Venir watched as a lone mage floated from the back of one of the columns. Much shorter than the others, the mage came alongside his leader and removed his hood. Venir could make out a human face covered in bright red blemishes. A nasty grin crossed the little man's face, revealing missing teeth and a swollen tongue that licked dirty lips. Atop the mage's mangy tufts of red hair sat Melegal's floppy hat.

The little man spread his arms wide, pointing outward, and brought his fingertips to the hat. He then tapped his chest and twirled while waving the hat in the air.

Venir's temper unshackled. He strode towards the mage, axe brandished before him. He drew back to swing, but the cackling forest pest floated out of his reach. The gruesome little man weaved in and out of his kindred, taking the hat off and waving it high in the air.

Despite his efforts, Venir could not square up on the floating man for a single swipe. He was being set up for something—these were magi after all. Time ticked on as he felt their mutterings inside his head. If something didn't happen soon, they would be gone, or he would be dead.

Nearby, Melegal and Georgio crept up and peeked out from the brush. To Melegal's surprise, Georgio wasn't making a sound. The thief watched a mage who was doing a strange dance of sorts. *It's wearing my hat!* Fury swelled in his belly. The remaining forest magi kept their distance as if captivated by the spectacle, but Melegal's keen ears picked up on something else.

They were muttering underneath their hoods.

He nudged the boy, dangling a sling in front of him, and Georgio followed suit. Melegal's eyes darted back to the magi as he withdrew some stones, but they seemed preoccupied and unaware of their presence.

"I'll take the one with the hat. You take the tall one," Melegal whispered.

Georgio gave several quick nods, brushing his hair from his eyes. It was a rare thing when Melegal felt his heart thump in his chest. *Ten of those things, Bone!* He low crawled over to a clearing as the boy squirmed behind him. He looked back and watched the thick beads of sweat drop from the boy's brow. His breathing became shallow and rapid. *Calm.* He closed his eyes and thought of a burning candle. He blew it out, and his body began to cool. *Better to die doing something than nothing.*

Melegal continued to watch the unpleasant song and dance between the ugly forest mage and Venir. Venir's blue eyes burned under his helmet, and his feet shuffled back and forth as he made clumsy swings at the mage. The other magi voices became louder. Suddenly a tree root rose from beneath the dirt, tripping Venir and forcing him to one knee. As the big warrior faltered, his tormentor took advantage of the moment by muttering a spell. Melegal signaled to Georgio. *Now!*

The tiny mage's lips shimmered as more roots burst from the ground.

Whoosh-thunk!

The mage's next word was stifled with a stone, broken teeth, and blood. The forest mage sputtered toward the ground with an anguished groan, trying to spit out the stone. In a flash, Venir slung Brool as if shot from a heavy crossbow, its spike tip penetrating the mage's sternum. The weightless man was flung backward and pinned to a red forest tree.

Whoosh-thunk!

Georgio's stone crushed the temple of the leading mage, who collapsed onto the hard forest floor with a thud. It all happened so fast that the other magi watched in disbelief, and the roots they summoned began to seep back into the clay ground.

Venir leapt over to the tree, plucked the hat from the dangling mage's head, and tossed it away. Somehow, the strange mage lived, still struggling to spit out the stone. Venir clutched the handle of his weapon, braced his leg on the mage's chest, and jerked it free. The thief couldn't control his wince. Venir whipped the blade in a full circle and severed the ugly mage's head from his body.

The lifeless head floated away from its body, leaving a trail of red blood bubbles in the air.

The others! When Melegal looked for the rest of the forest magi, they were fleeing. Venir took the flat of his great axe and batted the floating head at the rest of the pack. The head smacked into a tree and dropped to the ground.

This time, the forest magi had lost.

"That was incredible!" yelled Georgio.

"Here," Venir said, tossing Melegal his hat. "You should wash it."

Melegal sniffed the hat, scowled, and jammed it into his pocket. "Thanks."

Venir slung the blood from his dripping axe. "I don't think the forest magi will mess with you two again."

"Yeah, because next time they won't just get a few sling bullets," Melegal said, pulling out a small knife, "but the whole battle package."

Georgio and Venir huffed a laugh.

Melegal allowed himself a grin. "Now, let's find a creek so I can wash my hat."

"Sure, sure, Melegal."

Venir stopped and looked around. "So, where's Chongo?"

Georgio offered the answer." Melegal left them."

The warrior turned on Melegal with a deep frown. "You what?"

17

A SMALL ARMY OF SLAUGHTERERS TRAVELED at a rapid pace from the great caves of the Underland. Five squads, with twelve heavily armed underlings each, cut through the brush. They were the Badoon underlings, each well known for their stealth, skill, and tactics.

The Badoon were the most sinister warriors in the underling world. This Badoon brigade, in particular, had been battle tested time after time over the decades, and many of them bore scars from the wrath of the Darkslayer. The stories of the surviving Badoon inspired the other cold-hearted soldiers as they marched through the landscape like a giant black caterpillar.

The Badoon were armored in dark leathers, woven with stud and mail. Weapons jangled at their hips as the glimmer of blackened steel revealed curved blades, knives, swords, daggers, and crossbows. Some of the dark faces chittered from underneath cloaks, while others were brazen with shaved heads, bare bodies, and long clawed hands hanging at their sides.

It was night, and the fields of cacti and thatches that lay between the dark, hairy little race and the nameless mountains of Bish did little to slow their pace. The towering Vicious led the Badoons with great vigor as the underlings followed mile after mile, day and night on blistering feet.

A couple of the soldiers stumbled along the way, drew off their boots of hide, and wrapped their bloodied feet. When they returned to the column, the Vicious barred their way, snapped their necks, and mounted their heads on spears at the fore and aft of the column. It was a gruesome sight, unless you were an underling. For an underling, it was a great honor to die at the hands of a Vicious, and that sacrifice left the Badoon brigade feeling as invincible as ever. They picked up the pace.

They had lost more than enough men to the Darkslayer, and they all shared in the hatred for this enemy of their kind. In the past, their numbers had never seemed to be enough. The human had foiled them time and again, but this time the odds would be in greater favor of the underlings. Their time for vengeance had come. The Vicious had never lost.

18

V ENIR HOOFED IT THROUGH THE forest as Melegal and Georgio struggled to keep up from behind.

Venir yelled over his shoulder, "You'd better hope Chongo hasn't eaten yer little pony!"

"You'd better hope he hasn't, either," Melegal said under his breath.

Georgio bounced in and out of the trees, mimicking the now perished forest mage.

"Nya, nya … you can't catch me." The boy waved a handkerchief over his head. "I'm the ugly-faced moron, and I'm too fast for you!"

Leaping upward, Georgio attempted to float by clutching at branches, only to fall on his butt. The boy broke out in giggles as he pretended to impale himself to a tree with a stick. Melegal and Venir continued to storm ahead while Georgio looked around, scratching his head.

"Wait up!" the boy said, tripping and falling before getting on track again.

Venir was several yards from the clearing when he squatted down. He smelled something. Closing his eyes, he focused on the sound of the mounts. Melegal was at his side, swatting the winded Georgio on the back of the head.

Venir motioned for them to follow. Melegal nodded, towing Georgio behind him by the shirt cuff. Venir crept toward the clearing with Brool clutched in his hand. He came to a stop and coiled like a big ape ready to spring. His eyes grazed back and forth where Quickster and Chongo seemed undisturbed. Each lay in a thick patch of tall grass.

What is that smell? It was driving him crazy.

Chongo's head and ears perked up over the grass, and his fat paws began stamping. The dog howled as Venir emerged into the clearing, and licked his face like it was covered in beef gravy.

"Why all the excitement, Chongo?" Venir said. "I haven't been gone long." He scratched Chongo's ears while trying to avoid the soaking saliva. "The last time you acted like this—"

Venir whirled, his axe ready.

"Ahh! Humans! More scrawny little humans in Mood's forest?" A booming voice erupted from the foliage.

A figure, broader than Venir and almost as tall, hoisted Georgio and Melegal off the ground like rodents. They kicked and flailed like children as the red-bearded fellow pinched the life out of them between the nooks of his elbows.

"Put them down, Mood; you're gonna kill them," Venir said, laughing and dropping his helm and Brool, spike first, into the dirt. Chongo howled and stamped his paws at the sight of the husky figure.

"Oh, why not let me kill them?" Mood said with a snort, dropping them unceremoniously to the ground. "Humans are about as useful as underlings nowadays."

He came and stood toe to toe with Venir, his mighty hands grasping and almost engulfing Venir's forearms. Melegal and Georgio just shook their heads and looked over at each other with uncertain glances.

Mood's head was almost as wide as one of Chongo's, his features indistinguishable behind his bushy red hair, eyebrows, and beard. Only a pair of glinting green eyes gave evidence of the dwarf within. Beneath a heavy chain-mail shirt, Mood wore a long-sleeved leather jerkin with matching pants and high, floppy-cuffed brown boots. Two giant hand axes crisscrossed over his broad back, and a large belt pouch wrapped around his waist.

Melegal dusted himself off and pulled Georgio back to his feet.

"Good to see you, Mood! Chongo's even more pleased, I see," Venir said.

"Oh Chongo, it's been too long!"

Mood hugged both of the dog's thick necks as Chongo licked the giant-sized dwarf's broad face. "You just keep getting bigger and bigger." Mood reached into his pouch and produced two purple fruits, which he tossed to Georgio. Chongo leapt after them, and knocked Georgio back down, fruits falling from his hands. The dog licked them up and belched.

Noticing Melegal's perched eyebrows, Venir began the introductions.

"Ahem … Melegal, Georgio, this is my friend, Mood. He's the giant dwarf who used to look after Chongo."

Mood patted Melegal on the shoulder.

"Hello to you. And to you, too, little fella."

Georgio stared back at the wide, fuzzy face, squinting toward the bright green eyes beneath the bushy brows.

"Yer almost bigger than Venir!" Georgio blurted out. The boy's gawking face caused Mood to turn away.

"Er … so I saw you and those little forest magi having a tussle, eh?" Mood chuckled. "You sure scared the slat out of them, I'll tell you! Never seen 'em scatter like that."

"That's the first time they've done something so blatantly ignorant," Venir replied.

"Times are tough. The underlings have been creeping around the borders, making trouble. The forest magi aren't used to anyone messing with their territory, never mind invading it. It makes them edgy, thinking the fiends want their magic. But you'd think by now they'd know you're on their side."

"Whose side? Yours?" Melegal said, glaring at Venir. "Maybe they need to spend more time with just you and not me or my sling. Forest magi, underlings, and giant dwarves? Another fine mess you've gotten me into. One right after the other!"

Venir shrugged and Mood let out a chuckle.

"I told you, Melegal; you've been in the city too long."

Venir almost started laughing, but he held it in by taking a deep breath, and smiled.

"You don't need to worry about the forest magi; they're lightweights. You and Georgio could have handled them. You just didn't know it."

Venir winked at the boy, but his statement wasn't exactly true. The forest magi were well known to trap and eat a traveler from time to time, but only the ones that used magic. Still, he saw no need to raise a panic in his companions. He needed to defuse their worries.

"Just save it, Venir," Melegal said, checking his cap. "You always try to downplay the dangers, but I know better than that. And I'd remember any story about your red-bearded friend here, too."

"I've told you about him," Venir disagreed.

"No you haven't," Melegal retorted.

"I don't remember," Georgio confirmed.

"Uh … well anyway, he's an old friend and so are his people. Sometimes we track underlings together. As a matter of fact, he's the one who taught me most of what I know about such things."

Melegal's expression wasn't satisfied.

Shrugging, Venir added, "I try to tell you about these things, but you don't like to listen."

"As for the underlings," Mood piped up, lounging against Chongo who was lying down, "I don't think you need to worry about them, either. Your buddy with the big axe over there goes through them like slat through a … well, I forget how it goes, but you get the idea. It's like nothin' I ever saw. Almost enjoyable to watch."

Venir sighed and sat down. "Anyway, we're gonna be just fine." *As long as we don't run into any underlings.* He was thirsty and tired, and his friends looked the same. He broke out a canteen and tossed it to Georgio, then opened another for himself.

Melegal strolled forward, arms crossed.

"And what about the Royals that we assume to be chasing us? Is that no longer a concern?"

"No. They won't follow us here."

"Royals?" Mood sat up. "Uh, that would be something I'd definitely worry about. Why are you running from Royals, Venir?"

"You're leaning against the reason."

"Oh."

The big dwarf leaned back, deep in thought. A silence fell over them, and the forest quieted as a gentle breeze wheezed through the glossy blue, green, and red leaves of Red Clay Forest. Mood lit a massive cigar, and its aroma began to calm their nerves. Exhaustion filtered through Venir's body. His eyes grew heavy, and in moments he was fast asleep. Melegal and Georgio followed suit while Mood chewed on his cigar.

"Royals … sheesh!" Mood said in a whisper.

There was a faint roar somewhere nearby. Chongo's tails began a fast twitch. Mood pulled his massive hand axes off his back and rose from the ground. A second roar came, closer now, but the men didn't stir from their slumber. Mood watched the trees shaking in the distance as another growl came.

19

TWO DAYS HAD PASSED SINCE Tonio's demise in the stables near the south gate of the city. During that time, Lord Almen's detective had figured out that Tonio had not been assassinated.

An old stable hand, haggard and leathery, stood shaking in his sandals. The man's hair was salted with white flakes and lice, forcing McKnight to avert his eyes from the man's wispy crown. The old man continued to tremble as McKnight spoke in a threatening tone.

"So, you don't know what on Bish it was, do you?"

The old man trembled as he spoke.

"Yes, a two-headed beast. Like a d-dog … m-m-master. It's nothing like I-I've ever seen."

"Anything else?" McKnight asked, pulling the man's chin upward, and studying his eyes.

The old man's teeth chattered. "No … I've worked all my life in this stable, and I only saw this creature once, a few months ago. Me thinks it was what you're asking for."

McKnight shoved the old man to the ground. "I'm not asking what you think!" He twirled a blade between his fingers.

The stable hand watched him with eyes full of terror.

Why is this stuttering fool scared? Killing him would be a kindness. Wait, that can't be right. Killing someone would be kind? Doing them a favor? I have been going about this the wrong way all of these years. "Well …" he said, shaking his blade at the old man, "I don't like your story, but I've gathered little more than the same from others. You say this is the stable the dog-beast was in?"

He looked around the stable.

"So, how did it leave without being seen?"

The old man held his shaking skull as he muttered, "I don't know."

McKnight jerked out another knife from his scabbard, and the old man flinched. He nodded his head and began poking all over the stable. *I hate these foul smelling places.* After several minutes, he stormed from the stable, looking up and down the rows, stepping back and forth. *Something's not right here.*

"Close that stable gate, you useless sack of bones."

The old hand crawled up from the ground and began to dust himself off.

"Quickly, fool!"

The man jumped and pushed the gate closed with a loud clank, then backed away. McKnight opened and closed some other gates. They latched without the same sound. *Interesting.* He looked back at the first gate, noticing it was set a little lower than the others. He chuckled. Brushing the old man aside, he opened the stable gate and closed himself on the inside. From there, his long fingers searched for a handhold or latch. Two big grooves hid under the main support beam of the stable gate. McKnight lifted it, felt some give, and stopped. He tried again. *Bone!* He squatted down, braced his arms on the bar, and pushed up with his legs. The heavy piece of wood popped, but nothing happened. He looked around and noticed a small wooden lever protruding from one of the rafters. *Clever.* He jumped up and pulled it down. The floor at the back of the stable dropped open as he turned around, a gaping hole leading down into the ground.

"This could come in handy," he whispered to himself. "Well, there we have it. Fascinating."

He looked back over the stable gate and saw that the old man was no longer there. Instead, he was hobbling away down the middle of the barn.

He's horribly slow. He pondered whether to kill him or let him go. *Living is a much worse fate. Perhaps he will be of some use to me later.* His curiosity had the better of him today.

McKnight studied how the latching mechanism worked. After a minute's time, he had it figured out. He gathered a small bull's-eye lantern, stepped into the secret corridor, and closed the passage behind him.

20

IT WAS EARLY IN THE day when Lord Almen strolled from his chamber. His handsome face was heavy in thought as he passed by the nervous bows and downcast eyes of servants. Castle Almen was decorated with the finest materials available in Bish, a marvel in comparison to the other houses ranked below it, as well as some above. The marble pillars sparkled with intricate inlaid copper designs that reflected the candlelight from the golden wrought chandeliers. Every chamber oozed with wealth as his footsteps echoed down the hall.

None in Bish ever needed so much, but each Royal house competed with the others to obtain more material, slaves, and bragging rights, and Lord Almen would not be outdone. It was his passion—the acquisition of beautiful things—but how he acquired them was dark, dark indeed. Fear and killing were the formula for success in ruling this cruel world, and Lord Almen excelled at it.

He descended down a spiraling set of stone-cut stairs. At the bottom, a lone door and sentry appeared. The sentry saluted, opened the door, and closed it behind him. He stood in a makeshift bedroom with a large, plush bed. The room was dry and dusty, unlike the chambers of the rest of the castle. Two figures stood beside the bed, and one turned to greet him with a bow. It was the house cleric, Sefron. The other figure was scrawny and black-robed, with a sharp fuzzy face and a sparkle of violet in his eyes—an underling.

Sefron was flabby and naked, except for a small cloth around his waist. His body was shaven from head to toe, and his crystal blue eyes bulged and were watery. The look on Sefron's face drew questions about his sanity, and Lord Almen never got used to it. The strange man had his uses, though. Many clerics in the City of Bone had disturbing ways, but Lord Almen made the most of it. Sefron shuffled forward, wheezing, and went down on his knees in front of him. The underling stood silent, without a single glance his way.

Lord Almen walked past Sefron and stood alongside the bed. The figure of his son lay prone on exquisite blue silk sheets and spreads. Tonio's face was bandaged with wet salves of damp medicated cloth. Only his nostrils and eyes remained uncovered as his chest rose and fell. The rest of the young man's mangled body was wrapped like a mummy with strange symbols drawn on the blood stained wraps.

"He lives?"

Sefron shuffled at his side, speaking in an excited lisp. "Oh yes, he lives, dear Lord Almen. He lives, indeed. I did not think it could be done when we found him after many hours of bleeding. He is strong like you, lord." Sefron cast a wary glance at the black-haired underling. "Of course, I merely stopped the bleeding and applied the bandages. Your lordship's … er … underling acquaintance brought him back to life … it seems."

Lord Almen gave Sefron a stern look.

"Of-of course, you know that, my lord." Sefron edged back and checked Tonio's bandages.

"I appreciate your service to my son, Oran," Almen said as he turned and gave the small underling a slight smile. "My most promising son would have been a great loss to the family."

The underling was almost the size of a child by comparison, but Oran's dark eyes showed power and wisdom unlike that of any human child—or man, for that matter.

"I care not, Royal Almen," Oran said in an insulting retort. "My race will never understand this human attachment to family. We underlings do not mourn the dead." It was a lie, as underlings cherished their lives more so than men. "It is pathetic. There are always more to take a dead one's place."

Oran, black to the bone, was also a cleric among his kind. The underlings were Bish's most prominent race in the mastery of magic. Underlings could heal, but they focused more on the aggressive forms of magic. Still, in order to dominate, even underlings sometimes needed their lives saved, though none would care to admit it.

Oran was advanced among underling clerics, for rather than merely healing, he had also mastered ways of causing great harm—especially to other races. But, as much as he hated humans and other races, he could not help but be fascinated by them. Oran's meddling with the other races had made him a renegade among his kind.

He was a studious underling whose eyes revealed a deep knowledge of the black arts. His coal black hair was thick, long, and matted. Simple robes and shoes adorned his body. His face was narrow, with high cheeks, a strong chin, and the sharp gray teeth of his kind. His eyes were round and hypnotic, causing Lord Almen to struggle to keep his stare. Yet, Almen feared no underling, or he would not have been where he was today.

"Do you have my payment?" Oran asked. "I, unlike humans, have no time to waste. I have studies to complete and travel to make." The underling began to fidget. "I would like to inspect the specimen now, if I could."

Lord Almen's voice took a harsher tone as he studied his son.

"I was wondering if you have discovered the cause of my son's death, Underling Oran. Your work is not complete until I know this. Surely, you know what brought my son to such a brutal end?"

Oran huffed and gritted his teeth before he answered. "I don't know what stabled beast could have done this. It's not the bite of a horse, a mule, or a giant bug, for that matter. It seems to be an Outlands creature, but I cannot say what. It had four legs with paws and canine teeth, possibly a Fenris Wolf." The underling shook his head. "It is odd because they reside in the far north. Big though, big enough to ride, I would say." Oran rolled his eyes with indifference. "He has spoken a bit. He has said 'heads' over and over. Odd … he may mean a symbol, or something else, but I found no evidence on his — "

"How about a giant two-headed dog?" a bold voice offered from inside the doorway.

Sefron and Lord Almen looked up to find McKnight standing in the entrance of Tonio's chamber.

"A what?" Lord Almen said with a look of surprise and agitation.

McKnight removed his hat and bowed. "I am sorry to interrupt, Royal Lord Almen, but I could not pass up the moment."

"I have never heard of such a creature. Did you see it?" Oran's eyes were enlarged, almost fearful.

"No, but I've questioned enough people to know there is such a creature, and I've tracked it outside the city heading toward Red Clay Forest."

Lord Almen caught the moment of shock showing on Oran's furry face.

The underling composed himself and asked in a soft hiss, "How many were there?"

"The dog thing, a pony, and three people; two men and a boy, based on the tracks I found."

Lord Almen was thrilled, but his expression remained grim. "It seems you have earned your keep this day, McKnight. Your interruption is forgiven. Ready a score of my finest — "

"Wait, Lord Almen," interjected Oran. "I can help you here. I think I know who and what attacked your son."

"Do tell?"

"We call him the Darkslayer."

"And why is that?" questioned McKnight.

"Well … he has been a scourge of my people for quite some time now," Oran said, dejected.

"A scourge of the underlings?" Lord Almen was incredulous. "Can this be? Hah!" He smiled at the thought of a man that troubled underlings.

"Is it the beast or his rider that you call the Darkslayer?" McKnight asked.

"Ah," Oran grew flustered as he spoke, "… he is a man, a thickset man at that! He is like no other, and he wields a war-axe like a stick. He appears a split second before he kills, made of magic and changing shapes. He is the only one known to ride a two-headed beast."

The candles seemed to flicker as the room became silent.

Oran continued, "But maybe I can help track him down and kill him."

Almen, McKnight, and Sefron looked at one another, and all eyes fell back on the underling. It was common knowledge that underlings feared neither human nor any other race. The fear and respect with which Oran had spoken of the human was unheard of — not that any man ever dared — or survived long enough — to repeat what an underling had said. It was an amazing turn of events.

"What now, Oran?" Almen asked as his mind was beset with more questions. *Has a rival house hired out this man's services? Is this man a member of another house? The Klings? The Caapes? The Crones? Slergs? Who could it be? How did Tonio fall into their midst?*

"Let us finish today's business with my payment. I shall contact you soon. Your servant has provided helpful information to me," Oran said.

McKnight cocked a brow at Oran's words.

"Tomorrow then, Oran," Almen said, pointing towards the doorway. "I think you know the way to your payments. I bid you farewell."

Without any further courtesy, Oran turned and walked through another doorway in the back.

"My lord," McKnight said, "may I ask what his payment is for the resurrection of your son?"

Sefron looked up from checking a bandage, his watery eyes feverish with interest.

"More humans," Almen said. "He wanted twenty of them: men, women, boys, girls and some elderly."

"What does he do with them?" McKnight stroked his goatee.

The room seemed to darken before Lord Almen replied.

"Various experiments. While they are alive, he studies their reactions to torture. Once they have breathed their last, he tries to find other practical uses for their bodies."

McKnight's skin turned as pasty as Sefron's.

"Yes, McKnight, we are cruel. But the underlings are so much crueler."

21

VENIR JERKED UP FROM HIS slumber, eyes darting back and forth. A monstrous howl cut through the branches. He snatched Brool and charged through the foliage. He burst into a clearing just as Mood cut the neck out of a silver-backed grizzly bear. The massive animal fell to the ground. Mood wiped the blood from his axes before looking toward him. "Enjoy yer nap?"

Mood and Venir skinned the beast as Mood devoured lumps of the raw flesh, its blood deepening the color of his beard. Georgio still napped while Melegal sat grim-faced, holding his stomach, and retching. Venir shivered a tad himself. *Some things you never get used to.*

Chongo devoured his portion of the treat with vigor. Venir then bundled up the remainder of the meat and gathered the hide and head for Georgio's poor family, knowing they would be thankful for such a fine gift.

Moments later, Mood led them into a stream that was as cool as cave water. Georgio jumped in with a splash while Melegal rinsed out his dingy hat. Chongo barked away the fowl on the water as Mood flushed the blood out of his beard. The familiar scene of content faces splashing in the water tugged at his heart. He was thinking about home, his family, so long ago. Venir's eyes began water. His heart swelled a bit. He dunked his face in the stream.

"Let's go!" Venir said.

"Aw …" Georgio frowned, kicking at the water.

Venir let Mood take the lead over the rough, slick, steep, and narrow terrain . Ahead, Mood chopped brush like wheat with his axes, and Venir towed Chongo behind him. Georgio bounced as he rode on Chongo, sweating with a funny smile.

Melegal brought up the rear on Quickster, scowling as he shifted in his saddle.

"When will we see the suns again? We've been half a day in this tangled mess, and then some. My butt hurts, the bugs are eating me alive, and the humidity's sweating me dry."

"Oh, shut up. It won't be much longer," Venir said, shaking his head. *Too much time in the city.*

Venir didn't care how hot it was; anything was better than sweltering inside city walls. Here the air was fresh, and he didn't miss the odor of muck that filled his nose in the city. Of course, the climate could be perfect and Melegal would still complain. Venir knew what to expect from the thief, but it was still annoying.

"Almost out," added Mood. "A few more miles and we'll be back in that blazing desert." Mood's broad body trudged forward, unfazed by the briars and thorns that tore at his clothes. The giant dwarven people preferred cool, dark, and damp places most of the time. They were the hardiest of races on Bish and not ones to complain. Venir had seen dwarfs lose ears, even limbs, and never shed a tear. They were tougher than chewed leather, and Mood was no exception—rather the exceptional.

22

TONIO'S FATAL EXPERIENCE STILL DIDN'T add up in the mind of Detective McKnight. Why was the young lord alone at the stables on the day of his debacle? Did he encounter the Darkslayer? And why was he armed with a crossbow—a weapon rarely carried unless one was guarding the wall or marching off to war?

Maybe Tonio would be able to recall why he was there, if the brat wasn't too ashamed to tell. Even with his pride on the line, a man like Tonio would not venture into danger alone. Had a friend or an ally accompanied him? Had someone set him up?

The young Royals kept tight circles. They competed with one another, jumping at openings to grab more power. After all, Lord Almen's house had been moving up over the years. Had Tonio been set up by another house, or had the brat messed with the wrong man this time? McKnight was out to get the whole story, even if Tonio was not willing to talk.

McKnight had just finished choking some fresh information from a disheveled chap he found wandering around the barns. He slit a piece off the man's ear, whispered a warning, and headed for the Chimera. He knew it to be a seedier place where Tonio and many others among Bone's finest jackanapes hung around.

It was evening as he stepped inside the heavy doors. It was just as he thought, *Pompous snobs and overbearing arses pretending to be scoundrels,'like me.* McKnight felt flattered as small groups of eyes darted his way from every corner. He would find out what he needed to know, with or without their cooperation, and their evil little minds need never know. He set his wide brimmed hat on the bar and ordered. "A goblet of your finest, please."

23

O RAN DID NOT WASTE ANY time before traveling home with new information about the Darkslayer. The lords and masters of the Underland might find his musing useful. Oran the cleric, also known as Oran the outcast, might regain some lost favor. They had not been very approving of his dealings with the other races. In fact, they had forced him from the Underland, his home.

The underlings feared he might reveal too much about his own kind, despite his proven reliance. He had not betrayed his kind, but still he was mistrusted and shunned. The pit in his stomach deepened at the thought. He was an odd underling— that much he would admit. He was more concerned with the pursuit of knowledge than the pursuit of world domination. *You cannot have one without the other.* But they did not listen.

Oran was one of the few underlings to have stepped inside a human city of his own free will. An underling in the City of Bone was unheard of and so far as he knew, he may have been the only one inside of Bone in centuries. He had crossed paths with Lord Almen after the siege of Outpost Thirty-One. Lord Almen became a person of interest to him, and he allied himself with the man.

Oran wasn't a fool though. He knew Lord Almen was a dangerous man who liked to take risks. He saw it as an opportunity to learn more about his enemies. Oran was one of the main reasons the Almen house had moved up so fast over the recent years. So far, their relationship had paid off, for Oran also liked risk—and its rewards. One day, Oran would make Almen pay much more for his services, but so far Almen had served his needs well.

He left Almen's castle via the dungeons, and traveled by torch with his twenty new captives through secret tunnels winding through massive caves until they reached an underground river. There, an ample barge waited, and he loaded the slack-jawed humans aboard. They offered no resistance as he shackled them with chains and gagged them with dirty rags. *Pathetic.* Their glassy blank stares showed no alarm. He tossed the torch into the murky black river, where it extinguished with a hiss and sank.

The cavern that hosted the stagnant river was pitch black, and the sound of dripping water echoed inside the tunnel. Oran sat, soaking up the darkness, and muttered an incantation. The barge slid over the water, deeper and faster into the darkness. A mild breeze ruffled his robes, raising goose bumps under the hairs of the naked prisoners.

The prisoners sat, silent and helpless in the darkness, in the last moments of peace they would ever know.

24

B ISH'S ORANGE-RED SUNS CAST LONG shadows over the burnt plains as they set on the skyline.

"Stop staring at the suns, Georgio," Venir said with a snap. "It'll burn your eyes into the back of your head."

It was a fair warning, for many on Bish had lost their eyesight trying to stare down the suns. Georgio, however, loved the suns and seemed unfazed by his staring. Even Mood held a perplexed look over the paunchy boy's obsession. Venir gave it no serious thought. They had arrived at Red Clay Village, and he was keen to dispatch the boy, even though Georgio resisted being left behind.

"I'm going with you!" he said, hands locked on Chongo's saddle.

The boy's pleas grew until Venir decided to bargain with the boy.

"Now Georgio, you keep your mouth shut. No talk about Mood or Chongo. Your people here won't understand," he lectured. "Your folks don't trust outsiders, and you're lucky they finally came to trust me."

He hoped they did. It was not long ago that he had saved their village from a nasty brood of brigands, but trust was still hard to come by.

"So, keep your silence, boy, and we'll come get you in a few weeks. If you don't, you won't see me or Chongo for a very long time."

"But..." The boy's large brown eyes filled with tears.

"I said not a word."

"How am I s'posed to last that long? You know I can't shut up forever."

He shook the boy. "You don't have to—just a few weeks!"

Georgio slid from the saddle, and kicked up some dirt. "All right."

Venir spoke a few moments with Georgio's parents. Their wary looks turned to tear-filled eyes as they hugged their boy. The grizzly meat and pelt would take care of the family for weeks.

"What a good influence you've been on Georgio," they said. It was true, Venir knew, although not quite the way they thought; yet he took pride in the matter, and their comments warmed his battle-hardened heart.

Venir said his goodbyes and headed out of the village with Melegal at his side. A few miles away they would catch up with Mood and the mounts.

"So, what's this about bloodthirsty brigands you saved the village from?"

"Oh my, I wouldn't want to take any time away from your complaining."

Melegal smiled. "Don't worry, I'll get my complaining in, all in due course."

"I think you already know that story anyway."

Venir felt heavy now, and Melegal let it go. Venir and Georgio's relationship was not born of sunshine and rainbows, but from tragedy and loss. That was why the big man cared for the boy and protected him from things he wasn't yet ready to know. Venir carried this burden so that Georgio could remain happy and carefree.

Venir was thinking back to the time he'd been hired to track some bandits and had caught up with them pillaging Georgio's village. Venir and his small force of mercenaries managed to run off those they had not slain. The skirmish was one against superior numbers, and Venir's leadership, battle tactics, and instincts had blossomed that day. His valiant efforts were never forgotten by the folks in the small village. Yet, the victory was not without its tragedies. Many of the brigands had escaped with captives before he arrived. Georgio's teenage sister, Silvia, had been among them. Georgio was just a toddler then. For his own good, his heartbroken parents never mentioned her to the boy. As far a Venir knew, Georgio no longer remembered her.

Georgio's parents had described her to Venir, and several years later he found her by chance, working in a tavern in the City of Bone. She had grown to be a comely woman with long locks of curly brown hair, and round chestnut eyes like her mother and Georgio. Venir spoke with her, but it did not go well. Shame and humiliation had hardened her, and she would not acknowledge any pleasant memories of family and home. Venir wound up walking away. He had kept tabs on her for a while, but soon lost track of her. It was a memory he wished he could leave behind.

It was nightfall when Venir and Melegal came to a massive crevasse in the ground where signs of light wavered from deep inside. Below, Mood had made a campfire inside the steep, rocky gorge. From the dry plains at the upper rim of the gorge, the moon's illumination was dimmed in the crevasse, concealing the smoke that drifted into the hazy night.

The pair of men navigated into the crevasse and found Mood and Chongo on a large, jutting crag. Venir knew this spot as he and Mood had spent many nights here before. A few snakes and vermin ventured here from time to time, but most dangerous humanoids or predators were not likely to travel this terrain. It had been this way always, as far as he knew. Something in this chasm seemed to preserve this spot as a safe haven for select travelers.

"Ah, in time for some chow," said Mood as Chongo slobbered over Venir.

"Whatcha got for us, Mood?" Venir asked.

"We're lucky. Snake, big green snake. The best. Chongo and I have had our share. You and yer little buddy help yerselves to the rest."

"Ooh, Melegal, you're gonna like this!" Venir nudged his friend in the back.

"Not if it isn't cooked."

"It's cooked. And better than anything you've ever had in Bone."

Venir took a big bite of snake meat that Mood had skewered on a stick. The meat was tender, juicy, and delicious.

"Mmmm … now that's good. I haven't had this in years."

Melegal picked off a piece, his skinny face drawn tight, and nibbled at it. A look of curiosity crossed his brow as he took a bigger bite.

"Incredible!"

"I told you it was good." Venir shook his skewer.

"Good? It's great! Is it really snake?"

"Yes."

"Bone!" Melegal exclaimed above a whisper, sinking his teeth into the succulent dinner from the wild.

"So," Mood said, "you never told me about this mess you're in back at Bone. What exactly did Chongo do?"

Venir made himself comfortable. "Well, Melegal and I skimmed a Royal who tracked me down and got me thrown in the dungeons."

Mood chuckled.

"Then, at the dungeon, the fool boy decided to take a whip to me." Venir's lip turned up as his voice dropped down. "I didn't really care for that, so I gave him the beating of his life."

Mood perched his brows and said, "Shouldn't mess with ta' Royals. Most er' pretty bad company. Looks like you got a beating yerself — if that's what happened to yer nose?"

Venir rubbed his nose, frowning at Mood's *ho-ho* chuckles.

"Uh … I didn't really think. I was too ticked off. I guess I shouldn't have skimmed the fool, but we can never pass up a sucker—can we?"

Melegal gave him the thumbs up, still stuffing his face.

Venir singed more of his meat on the fire. "So, I left the dungeon and decided it was time to get out of the city for a while. But this Royal shows up at the stable—with a loaded crossbow, mind you—and tries to kill me. That's when ol' Chongo got hold of him." He scratched Chongo's heads affectionately. "Chewed him up good, but the stubborn boy was still breathing when we bolted. Bleedin' pretty bad, though."

The giant dwarf lounged on his side, shaking his head. Venir knew what Mood was thinking. His friend had warned him, but he already knew. Mood had fought Royals before. Crafty, selfish, and sly they were. They ran Bish despite the attempts of the underlings to subdue the surface.

Good Royals were uncommon, and somehow the bad Royals ruled in unison with them. Whenever there was a threat to the humans on Bish, all Royals, good and bad, stuck together. They had the numbers and the resources, and they had always ruled, as far back as anyone could remember.

It was fine during the wars, when the Royals left everyone else alone. But when Bish wasn't at war, the Royals didn't have much to do. Then they were a pain in the neck. If you weren't a Royal, the last thing you wanted was to be a part of their daily affairs. If you crossed one, you crossed the whole family and sometimes other families, too. They wouldn't let up until you were humiliated, punished, or in your grave. It was what the commoners called the Royal War Games.

Mood grunted as his bushy eyebrows buckled. Venir unrolled his blanket between Chongo and the warm fire and lay down. The ravine was quiet. No crickets, no howls, just a whistling between the small crags and other outcroppings at the upper rim. It was neither a soothing nor a threatening sound, just eerie. The blackness crept in as the party slept, and the coals began winking out. Venir's eyes drifted open and closed.

Mood and Chongo snorted on occasion, sometimes in unison. Melegal slumbered, belly now filled with the wonderful green snake meat. Quickster slept at Melegal's side, seemingly dead, but for the bursts of green snake gas that stirred from beneath the mount's tail from time to time. All were at rest, except Venir. The mammoth man lay quiet and still, but tormented. Above him, the two full moons, one white and one red, cast shadows that outlined the warrior's form like a statue. The stress lines etched in his face seemed to deepen. His head was filled with anguish as nightmares seared his mind with images of death.

Venir's eyes snapped open. The moonlight shone a bluish hue in his burning gaze. He crested the lip of the ravine, adorning his helm, shield, and Brool without disturbing a thing.

There he stood, an onyx statue of a man, a mighty two-bladed axe in one hand, and a fattened black shield in the other. The black spike atop his helm sparkled in the moonlight. He murmured in fury. His eyes were like burning coals behind the iron eyelets. He could feel them—the underlings were near. He sprang into a quick stride, running along the plains of dirt and sand like an armored panther. This big cat would find his prey tonight. The underlings were his favorite gifts to death, and he was coming for them. A new hunt had begun ….

Melegal's fantastical, moonlit dream of a bosomy dwarven woman came to an abrupt halt as Chongo let loose the barking of a dozen bloodhounds. He bolted upright, his once blissful face a fuzzy knot of concern.

"What in all of Bish?" he said, jumping up and fumbling to reach his short sword. Quickster remained sound asleep at his back, bent legs up in the air.

"Come on, human." Mood strapped on his axes. "Venir's gone."

Melegal rubbed his blurry eyes as he started snatching up whatever he thought would help.

"What?"

"Just grab yer gear and get on that shaggy thing. Yer friend has his weapons, which means he's huntin' underlings. If we can catch up, things'll be … well … you can just see for yerself."

Melegal was ready and on Quickster's saddle in moments. Mood was on Chongo, leading them out of the ravine. The great two-headed dog charged southwards, following the scent of Venir.

Melegal watched ahead as he followed behind the two tails of the ridiculous dog and the odd-looking giant dwarf. He rubbed his eyes some more and shook his head. He was accustomed to many things, but not this. The warm night air confirmed to Melegal that he was indeed awake, and so did Mood's bellowing voice.

"Huzzah! Ride, Chongo, ride!"

And ride they did, through the night, over the barren plain, beneath the bright white and red glow of the moons. Melegal was so caught up in the rush that he had almost forgotten where they were going. Venir was hunting underlings, and they were headed that way as well. He wanted no part of that. *Underlings! Not me!* He almost pulled back on the reigns, but where would he go?

"Son of Bish!" he yelled, whipping the reigns, catching up to Chongo in no time. *He's gonna owe me big.*

25

THE STRANGE MOONLIGHT ON BISH hindered the movement of most inhabitants at night. The moons were at times white, red, orange, or blue. Their colors changed; so it was, so it had always been. The light could come and go, sometimes hidden by clouds and other times disappearing altogether. Tonight, a red moon sat on the edge of the world of Bish, offering little light and darker shadows. Only a few races could see at night, and humans were not among them. But at this particular moment, one human inhabitant on Bish was not hindered at all. Venir could see every bit as well as an underling at night. The mystic helm allowed for that. It was something he'd grown fond of over the years.

The underlings used their infravision to take advantage of unsuspecting people. They could see the warmth of living bodies, sneak up on them, and kill. It was one more tactic they used to instill terror on the surface world. Over the years, Venir had learned how to turn the underlings' own guerilla tactics against them. He thrived on it.

Venir was far south of the ravine where he left Melegal and Mood. A thick coat of sweat covered his armored body. A dream had woken him, a sixth sense of sorts he couldn't explain. Such dreams had become more frequent over the years and had saved him a time or two.

He stood inside the edge of a stagnant and foul-smelling marsh. Many dark groves such as this were scattered about, providing on Bish's outlands a source of water, which, by a cruel twist of nature, was undrinkable for humans. It was refreshing for underlings, however, and they often sought refuge in such places. Venir felt their presence inside as his heart began thumping in his brain.

The nervousness in his belly was choked down by his burning desire to kill. Venir was compelled to venture into this nasty grove to put an end to the filthy inhabitants that sought its sanctuary. He pushed through the brush, boots sinking into the muddy waters, and merged deep into the shadows. It wasn't long before he picked out several warm shapes huddled together, muttering their ratty chit-chat.

Silent as a cat, he crept forward and counted as many as twenty underling hunters. The small humanoids wore cloaks and leather. They were armed with steel and shields. He could smell their rancid breath, and their chittering voices aggravated him. He scanned around, but did not feel the presence of any guards. *Good.* No guards meant something else, a magic ward perhaps, if he ventured close enough. Magic—all underlings had magic. Underling hunters, though not powerful in magic, still had spells that would aid them. But, Venir thought, he was privy to most of it. Fighting the urgings within the helm, he crouched down and waited. His sweaty hands squeezed the shaft of his axe. *Patience!*

26

AFTER SEVERAL MINUTES OF HARD riding, Mood and Melegal pulled their mounts to a stop. Ahead lay several groves scattered throughout the barren landscape. Chongo's heads snorted the air, paws stomping. Mood hopped to the ground, pulling the dog's wet noses to the dirt.

"Sometimes, smells get mixed up in these areas. The acidic trees and marshes give off strong odors that kill a scent. It makes underlings hard to find."

The man-sized dwarf stuck his nose in the air and sniffed long and hard. "Chongo's the ultimate tracker … noses ten times better than mine. But sometimes the two pooch heads clash. One wants one thing, one wants another. It happens." He ran his sausage-like fingers through the dirt and pointed to a marsh ahead. "Dog heads seem right, usually are."

"Why didn't Venir take Chongo?" Melegal asked.

"Have you ever gone hunting underlings with him at night?"

"No."

"Underlings can see at night, and Chongo's so big he'd be spotted. It's harder for them to see Venir. The underlings, like me, see the warmth we give off, but I don't think they see Venir when he has that get-up on."

"I'd like to see him fight underlings at night," mused Melegal. "I've been out with him here and there, but never encountered much. I have seen him in his scary outfit, though. It's hard to believe they can't see him!"

Mood chuckled as he swung himself back up on Chongo's saddle and pointed.

"I think he's in that grove ahead, if you can make it out. Go, Chongo!"

Melegal could make out the foggy grove's outline in the distance. Tall, ugly trees seemed to spike the sky, and the ever-changing glow of the moons cast an eerie haze over the strange marsh. Melegal hoped they wouldn't have to enter it; the Red Clay Forest seemed far preferable to a swamp. But, for some silly reason, Melegal knew Quickster would enjoy it. *What a strange pony*, he thought.

An abhorrent stench assaulted Melegal's nose.

"Oh slat, don't tell me that's the grove!" The thief pinched his nose. *What's with all these smells?*

But Mood and Chongo were galloping out of sight. He had no desire to be left alone, so he dug his heels into Quickster. The thought of fighting underlings terrified him, but so did being left in the Outlands alone.

27

V ENIR WATCHED AS AN UNDERLING hunter broke from the main group and came his way. He choked the neck of his axe, knuckles white, head aching with fury. The underling's eyes sparkled, peering around as it began to piss into the murk, releasing a sound of relief. Finished, the underling shook his waist and headed back to his group, this time followed by a silent, axe-wielding shadow.

Venir closed within five paces, mimicking the smaller underling's movements step for step. He listened as the returning underling stood before the group and rambled something amusing. The group chittered in the odd way of the underlings. Venir had heard those twisted laughs before. He could no longer contain the savage cry within.

As the underling before him giggled on, the laughter of the others came to a stop. Their colorful eyes were transfixed, and their mouths dropped open when his great shadow rose up before them. The underling turned just in time to see Venir thrust down the double-bladed axe, splitting it from head to belly. Venir rushed between falling body parts before the first drop of blood hit the ground.

The nearest underling stood stupefied as Brool exploded through its chest, spraying blood like a rainbow across the grove. Another underling's neck was punctured from his backswing. Venir ripped out its throat and prepared his next swing. *Three!* The next underling turned to run as he swung Brool around his head and down onto the creature's shoulder. The heavy blade crunched through the clavicle, severing the shoulder and arm from its body.

Stepping onto the dying underling's bloodied corpse, Venir moved forward for more kills. He could sense them if not see them, spreading out and preparing for action. The surprise was over, now the work was about to begin.

The remaining underlings readied curved short swords and hand axes as they chittered orders. Five of them, armed and ready, formed a semicircle before Venir, but it didn't slow his coming.

His voice was loud like an enraged animal as the words burst from his lips.

"Prepare to die, vermin! I'm coming for you!"

The underlings didn't quiver or turn; they dug in, spitting threats of their own.

Venir dove into them, sweeping Brool left to right, keeping the five underlings at bay. His axe blade whistled, making an eerie sound that many underlings had come to know as the "last call."

Two flanking underlings charged Venir. He leapt forward, chopping through the head of the astonished center figure. The two beside the fallen underling swiped at his legs, striking a pain-filled gash and drawing blood. Venir slammed his shield edge into the head of one, cracking its skull. He howled in bloodlust as he swept Brool into another underling's side. It fell in a gurgling heap. *Seven!*

The last two underlings cut into his shifting thighs. The hot blood oozing down his leg did little to slow him, but it burned. He fought back, Brool hacking from the right and the shield defending on the left. The underlings ducked and dodged under his swings. Blood seeped from his wounds. There was no time for these games. They only wanted to wear him down, and it wouldn't be long before help arrived.

In a blink between underling attacks, he whirled a hundred and eighty degrees, cutting deep into the leg of one underling and shattering the other's knee with his shield. Their howls of pain cut off as Venir put them to death. *Nine!*

The long run to the grove, the fury of his attack, and the loss of blood were taking a toll. This was the part he hated, the torture of being pushed on despite his agony. He couldn't tell if it was in him or from the helm, but he would not quit until the underlings were all dead. He was like one possessed, all reason banished by his hatred and rage.

His chest heaved, and his lungs burned like fire as he slunk through the murk. *Control it!* His heart pounded as he pressed himself into the thatches, fighting the drive that urged him forward. A voice deep in the back of his battle-raged mind reminded him that there were still many more.

The red haze of battle began to subside. The marsh was filled with sounds of crickets, toads and squawking birds. *Maybe they all fled.* He sucked in a deep breath, closed his eyes, and focused.

No, they were still out there. Venir had almost cleared himself from the thatch when something caught his feet. Roots, vines, and grasses of the marsh wound around his legs, pulling him down. He bit his tongue. *Bone!*

The dark magic coiled around his thighs like tightened rope. Plants cut into his torn skin. He chopped and tore at his tangled assailants, Brool's honed edge slicing the cords away. The vines crawled up his back and around his face and mouth. If he didn't escape he would be overcome and suffocated. Brool cut through the twisted foliage, his arm and elbow working like a saw. He was on his knees now, coughing and fighting to stay alive. He gave another gasp and wrenched at his binds, tearing himself free.

He pulled himself upright, spitting vegetation from his mouth, his legs held fast from below. Venir's eyes shot up just as three more underlings encircled him. Heavy darts assailed his body, stinging like a nest of wasps, causing him to wriggle with pain.

"Arghh! Curse you little maggots!" he cried out from behind his shield as the poison burned like fire in his straining biceps.

Venir wiggled and sliced. The vines finally gave way, sinking back into the marsh. He was free now, free to destroy. A small, robed underling turned on him, a foot long pipe protruding from its lips. Venir bashed its brain in with the edge of the shield. Another flurry of darts came from behind with several landing in the backs of his legs. His knees buckled as pain raced into his chest. *Poison!* He whirled to attack, anger blinding his mind from the pain. The underlings fired from the left and right, turning him into a human pin cushion.

Venir hurled his spiked axe like a spear, impaling the chest of one. The other underling yanked out its sword, a hiss of triumph parting from its lips. Venir charged as the underling thrust at his thigh, but the blade bounced off his shield with a clang that brought sparks. As the underling drew back for another attack, Venir's steel-toed boot crushed its chin, dropping the stunned creature. He stomped his heel into its chest a few more times, collapsing its ribcage and pulverizing its lungs. The underling convulsed on the ground as the edge of his shield dealt the death blow to its skull. *Twelve is good!*

Venir bounded after Brool, and plunged into the darkness of the marsh. Time was running short. His body burned like fire, and his strength was ebbing. He had to rest, but rest did not kill underlings, and he drove himself on in pursuit. The underlings were in hiding, planning another attack on him. It was time to flush them out.

He was moving southward, quiet as a deer, when he spotted them. Three bulges of heat hunkered down in the murk. Their colorful eyes shifted back and forth, axes and swords gripped in their clawed hands. He could assault them all, chop them down one by one, but more were bound to come with poison-filled darts. *No need for more of that.*

Like a shade, Venir moved behind their line and crept back up on the one in the middle. Setting his axe and his shield down, he slipped behind the hunkered-down underling. He struck like a cobra, clutching its neck in his mighty hands, lifted the creature from the ground, and choked the life out of it. Its feet dangled and twitched in the air. Venir fought the urge to snap its neck before setting the limp creature down. *Good.* The dead underling's legs gave one last violent twitch, kicking the thicket.

Two enraged fiends charged at his sides. There Venir stood, weaponless, with their brother dangling in his grip. Venir flipped the corpse feet up into his hands and swung it like a sack of melons into the body of the closest attacker. Bowled over by the impact, it underling collapsed in a heap. Venir dropped it in his hands just in time to dodge the two-handed axe attack of the other.

The underling moved in, chopping in a fury. Venir lashed out, catching it by one of its wrists, restraining it like a toddler swinging a stick. It countered, swinging its free arm at his neck. Venir caught it in the same manner, now squeezing both wrists like a vice, causing the underling to drop its weapons. It released a high pitched wail. Venir silenced it with a crotch-crunching kick. It dropped to its knees. Venir snatched one of the fiends hand axes from the ground and slammed it deep into its brain. Now, the other enemy was back on its feet, charging full force, just in time to receive a flying hand axe between its eyes.

Grimacing, Venir grabbed Brool and his shield and ran toward where he sensed more of them lurking in the grove. His battle-raged mind became sluggish, and each step was filled with pain. Although his body was burning and weakening with every stride, he forced himself to find the last few before he collapsed. The helm assisted in beckoning him on. He saw them nearby, bodies warm and red in the blackness. He cut between two trees, closing the distance between him and them.

Venir was held fast by a giant spider web. "Bone!" he cried out. He struggled to free himself. "Slat!" he shouted again.

The cords stuck fast as he struggled, peeling off loose pieces of skin. His mind was in a frenzy to escape. He needed to remain calm, but those thoughts were gone. Two underlings appeared, strapped in leather, with long blow pipes.

Venir's neck hairs rose. He tried pushing through the web, but iron would have been easier to cross. His axe and arm were held fast, but he groaned while pulling Brool back and forth to cut through. The trees bent from his efforts. The blades cut through the tiny fibers, little by little, giving him more leeway by the second.

Toowah! Toowha! Toowah!

The barrage of bigger darts bit into him and his blood coursed like fire once more. He cut into the web as fast as he could, but the poison slowed him. Second by second, he felt his strength fade as the fire inside him was smothered by the life-draining poison. He was numb from head to toe. *Not now! Not now ….*

Relief entered a splinter of his mind. His pursuit was coming to an end. The cold dirt of a grave to lie in was welcoming to Venir. His lazy eyes looked up as the garbled sounds of the underlings chittered away. He still wanted to kill just a few more, but he would have to rest first. Venir's eyes rolled up into his head, and he no longer moved at all.

28

T HREE HAUNTING FIGURES EMERGED FROM the grove.

"Underlings! He musta missed some!" Mood roared, spurring Chongo to attack.

Chongo growled and charged, all four eyes bearing down on the underlings that burst from the marsh. Two underlings broke to the right, dashing away from the fearsome sight. Chongo closed in on the fleet-footed pair, great jaws snapping at the heels of the one half a step behind the other.

"Bite that vermin, Chongo!" Mood bellowed, axe shining in the light.

The underling ducked, swerving away, but Chongo snatched up the underling in his massive jaws. The underling swung its sword, and Mood knocked it away with his axe. One head of Chongo crushed down on the underling, killing it. The other dog head led the pursuit of the underling still running away.

The underling managed further separation as Chongo slowed to drop his prey. The open plain and its moons assisted Mood with keeping the underling in his line of sight. The dwarf spurred the beast onward.

"Yo ho!" Mood yelled as they closed the gap.

The underling turned and kneeled with a crossbow pointing their way.

"Whoa!" Mood pulled at Chongo's reigns, but the dog charged on.

The underling's wicked smile danced in the moonlight as it squeezed the trigger.

29

T HE UNDERLINGS STARED AT THE mass of flesh in the web that was as prone as a possum. One launched another dart into his leg, but Venir did not react. They gave a loud whistle, a strange, inhuman sound that only underlings could make. Two underlings drew their swords as they approached their fallen foe.

Avoiding the webs, one went behind Venir's back. The other underling stepped in closer to get a better look at Venir's face. The underling's lips curled up in a merciless grin. If this were truly the Darkslayer, they would be honored and praised indeed.

Venir saw and heard everything as if he were in a distant land. The figures, the sounds and smells were still there, vivid in his mind. Something ignited inside his head and raced down to his toes. The sluggishness was wearing off. His thickened blood began to thin and flow again as a fresh spring of life beat between his temples. He felt the nearby danger racing down his spine. *Die doing something or die for nothing!*

As the underling's rancid breath reached Venir's nose, his bloodshot eyes popped open. The underling lurched back with a hiss as Venir punched Brool through the web, puncturing its neck. It dropped, gurgling, to the marshy ground. The underling behind Venir drove its blade at his back, but it clanged off his shield as he pulled free. The webs were dissipating now that their caster was dead. The underling swung its blade in a high arcing swing.

Venir stepped out of the blade's way and chopped off the underling's head. "I hate webs," he muttered, trying to pull the tacky substance away. He spun slowly around. "Where are they?"

He didn't feel them close by, but the helmet wasn't always right. He cracked his neck side to side and spat blood and saliva from his mouth. His arms and legs ached, and he coughed up blood. He gritted his teeth and then started running towards the north end of the marsh.

"Slat," he muttered, running through the murk, not wanting to believe that the last few underlings had gotten away.

30

A SUDDEN *WHOOSH-THUNK* ERASED THE UNDERLING hunter's grin as a sling bullet glanced off the back of its head. The underling shook off the blow and jerked up the tip of its crossbow, with Chongo's heart still in its sight. *Whoosh-thunk!*

The underling's head pitched forward and dropped it like a stone as the crossbow bolt sailed over Mood's ducking head. Chongo tore into the helpless creature, both heads chomping and devouring the bloody underling treat. The bone-crunching sounds turned Melegal's stomach as he pulled along Mood's side, sling dangling from his hand.

"Sorry about that first shot," Melegal said with a sheepish look.

"No harm done. Where's da other underling?" Mood wiped the sweat from his brow.

"Hard to say. He ran like he had a hive of angry bees up his arse. I never saw anything like it. He just ran faster and faster, then he was gone."

"Hmm … those underlings have some sneaky magic," Mood commented. "That musta been their leader blinking out like that. No matter, just hunters by the looks of 'em. I don't think there'll be any more left in this party. Our friend musta taken care of the rest, seeing how they was run outta dat grove 'n all."

Mood's brow furrowed.

"Let's head over to where they came out; Venir should be coming our way, anytime."

Mood waited a bit as Chongo gulped down the remains of the underlings, and then they made their way toward the grove's edge. While they waited, mosquitoes hummed in their ears and attempted in vain to drink their blood. It wasn't long before a rustle stirred not far from where they stood.

Venir stepped into the clear. Muscle, sweat, blood, and metal all combined into a horrifying sight: a great gory man that the world of Bish called the Darkslayer. He was splashed with mud and guts from head to toe. His muscled legs and arms bled from a dozen wounds. Darts were still embedded and jutting from his skin, leaving black and purple marks. His chain mail shirt glimmered in the moonlight. His eyes blazed like a blue inferno, and his voice was as dry as a bone.

"Any left?" he rasped.

"No, one got away," Mood answered.

Venir approached with a bitter face, his tanned skin now ashen.

"So, how many?" Mood asked of the warrior.

"Fourteen."

His voice was almost inaudible as he removed his helm, revealing long sweaty locks of blond hair on a damp brow. Under his helmet, his head had remained as clean as the rest of his face was filthy with grit. Venir spat more blood.

"Fourteen?" Melegal was incredulous. "You killed fourteen underlings?"

"Would'a been more if I hadn't hit a spider web. Bone! Would've had them all."

He stretched his arms, grimacing, but then managed a small grin.

"That was good. Close, but I live." Venir began scratching Chongo, who started to lick the dirt off him.

"Your legs are purple!" Melegal said, looking on in concern.

"Yep," Mood said. "He's been poisoned."

"Poisoned?" Melegal cried, appalled at Mood's indifference. "We have to do something!"

"We already did," Venir replied.

"We did? What?"

"Ate green snake meat."

Melegal folded his arms over his chest. "Oh, and I suppose you told me that before as well." *He's got the memory of an ox.*

"Probably," Venir said as he coughed and hacked, spitting more bile. "You see, green snake meat does more than just taste good. It remedies poisons and such. It's saved my hide more than once. It's already taking the pain from my legs."

"Really, because you look like you're in pain," Melegal added. "Perhaps it hasn't reached that grog imbibed brain of yours?"

"No, I couldn't be better." Venir winked.

One second the warrior looked fine and in the next his eyes fluttered and rolled up in his head as his body sagged towards the ground. Melegal leapt forward just in time to break his friend's fall.

"Never seen 'em do that before," the big dwarf said, rushing along their side.

"He'll be all right with your snake meat, I trust?" Melegal asked with some sarcasm.

Mood shrugged. "Maybe so, but we better get some water in 'em. If he ran all that way and then jumped all those underlings, he should 'a been dead by now anyway. Them wounds are pretty bad, and I can't say for sure green snake meat cures everything. No telling what those underlings shot him with."

Melegal returned with some water, made Venir drink some, and then slipped Venir's helmet back on his head. "Maybe this will help."

Mood began stitching up the passed-out warrior whose breathing was very shallow for so robust a man. They plucked the poisoned darts from his body, revealing more ugly purple wounds. Blood and pus ran freely as Mood squeezed and drained them. It looked painful to Melegal, but his friend lay still as a corpse. *Slat, just what I need, to drag his husk around.*

Mood had done all that he could, and now all they could do was wait. Melegal couldn't sleep as he sat huddled at Venir's side, rocking with his hands wrapped around his knees. Chongo lay alongside his master, eyes drooping and ears flicking up from time to time. Melegal couldn't help but wonder what he would do if Venir didn't make it. His best friend's mortality had never occurred to him. He drew a blanket over his shoulders as the aroma of Mood's cigar lulled him back into a relaxing sleep, dreaming of more green snake meat.

31

TRINOS FELT SOMETHING LIKE ENJOYMENT from the affects her ripples were having on Bish. Actually, it was not so much the ripples themselves as the ripples upon ripples that filled her with mild amusement. Was this how some worlds were able to reach infinite status? Worlds that were not supposed to make it made it anyway, while those that should have made it did not. Had other beings like herself tinkered too much for their own good, perhaps sending in ripples of good that turned bad?

Trinos felt she should know the answer to this, but then again, many of the laws of their universe had not been revealed. The edge of their universe was yet to be found, and certainly that was where the answers would lie. And without an objective outside view of the universe, how could the universe ever be fully explained? This, of course, was not the problem Trinos had been assigned by her kind. But it did spark a thought now and again. She would see parallels between her life within the universe and the life on Bish. *Interesting.*

Trinos had also found certain points in her captivating world that required additional study. In particular, there was the matter of conflict. She had created a world that contained both boundaries and conflict. The main boundary was a lack of interest in understanding any complicated formulas of science. The creatures of Bish lacked either the intelligence or the drive to study why they existed or why there were two suns and moons, all changing as she so desired. The people of Bish did not care about her stars or why they were there. It all just was.

The only driving force was for power and control over the other beings in their world. Some races wanted peace, while others wanted war. One race could not ignore or survive without the other. In general, the races of Bish exhibited very little compassion, friendship, or joy. The people were hard, and their need to survive and conquer always outweighed their need for affection. Greed and betrayal kept breaking down alliances and friendships, leaving all in Bish forever watching their own backs.

The creation of Bish had also led Trinos to contemplate the nature of good and evil. She had instilled both good and evil—although she herself was unable to engage in either—in order to confer strife. There had to be acts that resembled one or the other. Or, had she merely created persons with good and evil traits for the sake of her own entertainment?

Trinos began to wonder if Bish was perhaps not such a good idea after all. She pondered destroying it, but could not. Would a mother destroy her own children? So, she continued her study.

Most worlds she had studied were created on a basis of neutrality and shaped by the natural will of the creator. How these worlds turned out depended on those rules. The specific needs of the world would then either enlighten or extinguish it. Trinos, however, had created a world differently. And she had instilled characteristics of other worlds, but not allowed room for change. She had, in a sense, created good and evil from her own free will. Did that mean she was not the neutral being she had always thought she was? Had she bent the rules of her kind for her own entertainment? *So be it.*

All this contemplation took place in mere seconds before she arrived at her conclusion. Whatever she may have done, the world she had created could not possibly affect anything else in their universe other than itself. With that last thought, Trinos abandoned her observation of Bish, and returned to her study of the comings and goings of the other worlds. Perhaps she would discover some similarities to her world while the world of Bish kept on churning.

32

" **A** AAUGH!"
A man screamed from the dusky chamber below Castle Almen.
"My skull hurts!"

Tonio was on his feet, screaming and clutching his head. The young man tore at his bandages, jostling over tables and chairs. The cleric Sefron offered soothing chants, only to see the rampaging man square off on him. The flabby cleric was all alone when Tonio's hands wrapped around his neck.

Sefron's bald head purpled like a turnip, wet eyes almost bulging from the sockets, tongue curling like a salted slug. Tonio shook the man, squeezing harder as he spat through his busted lips.

"Vee-Man!"

Sefron's hypnotic eyes locked onto Tonio's torn and twisted face. The young man's pupils were black dots, lips curled in pain, brows buckled with hatred. Sefron couldn't breathe, but he could think. *Let go. Let go.* The cleric's eyes made the suggestion as he was forced downward on the pillow-filled bed. Sefron fought to hold the man's gaze, refusing to look away as his air began to fade. *Let go. Stop. Let go. Stop.* Sefron's eyes and mind pleaded for escape.

Tonio's screams began to soften, and his grip slackened. Sefron felt himself regain control, slowly, very slowly. *Let go. Stop.* Tonio became still. Sefron rolled off the bed and sank to the floor, gasping for air. The cleric's pasty skin turned from purple to red to pink and finally white. The cleric struggled back to his feet, knees wobbling as Lord Almen burst through the door.

"What has happened, Sefron?" he demanded, looking at his son, who was standing on the bed. "I heard screams from the kitchen." Almen's voice betrayed a hint of worry.

Sefron rubbed his throat, trying to find his voice. A few croaks came out as he turned toward Lord Almen.

"Good news … eh … good news … uh … my Royal Lord Almen," he answered grimacing. "Er … He woke up!"
Lord Almen's heated scowl almost sent him running. *Slat! Think fast!*

"When they do awaken … it is usually with a great deal of delirium and pain. But I … I mean he … is fortunate."

The shifty cleric had a fit of coughing as he recovered his wind and tried to smile. "He is surprisingly powerful, and had I not kept my composure, I would surely be dead now, with Tonio on a rampage. Your son is powerful indeed."

"Hmmm … I know how this goes. But I thought you would have it under better control, Sefron." Lord Almen walked around the bed's edge and studied the mangled skin of his son.

Sefron could see Lord Almen's face tighten, dry eyes becoming moist. "I thought so, too, my lord," Sefron's tone was upbeat, "but he came out of his healing slumber sooner than expected. He is a fine specimen and a true warrior. I've not seen one recover so fast."

Despite Sefron's ingratiating manner, his words were true.

"I have something else I discovered as well, my lord." Sefron bowed, awaiting notice from his master.

"What?" Lord Almen's voice came like a crack of thunder.

"He was drugged," a new voice said from the doorway.

Lord Almen's broad shoulders twisted around as Sefron whipped his neck around. It was McKnight, hat off and head bowed. Sefron glared at McKnight with all his hatred. *Arsehole!*

"How do you know this, McKnight?" asked Almen.

"Well …"

Sefron stepped between them, blocking McKnight from Lord Almen's view.

"I found traces of various inducers in his body, my lord. This detective is only guessing. I have proof. He couldn't possibly know this. I'll show you."

Sefron hurried to the tall body of Tonio that stood like a statue, staring blank at the wall. The cleric took the battered man by the hand and led Tonio from the bed like a pliant child. Lord Almen nodded and Sefron continued.

Sefron caught McKnight's grinning face, but hid his heartless scowl. Sefron hated McKnight, his charm, his privileges, and the trust Almen gave him. The detective was a pain in the neck, always keeping a wary eye on his spiny back.

"My lord, when a person is drugged — in this case it was consumed — the inducers that are used do not dissolve in the system. They are thick juices of specific types; in this case it is the Purple Leaf from Red Clay Forest. It is one of the rarest plants on Bish. The juice does dissolve out of the body, but slowly, sometimes over weeks. However, the effects of Purple Leaf only last a few hours, but this is quite long enough for a person to implant one, or maybe two, solid suggestions."

"I know what purple leaf is, fool!" Lord Almen shouted. "Do you think I need a refresher course in manipulation? Poison?"

Sefron dropped to his knees, cringing at the edge of the Royal lord's robes.

"Forgive me, master!"

McKnight backed toward the door.

"Get up!" Lord Almen said.

Sefron feebly rose to his feet, head down.

"Very well then, Sefron," Lord Almen said in a softer tone. "How did you know?"

The cleric bounded toward Tonio, flabby arms jiggling.

"I cast a minor spell designed to extract poison. It bled out from Tonio's bowels. And it showed up purple in his urine and stool, my lord. I have it over here, my lord," Sefron said, grabbing a bowl from the bed.

"I'm glad that you checked him out thoroughly this time, Sefron. The last time you were not so careful."

Sefron couldn't hide the look of surprise and fear growing on his face as McKnight watched him, needling his chin.

"Now, when can I expect Tonio to be back to normal?" Lord Almen asked.

Sefron set the bowl back down. "My lord, I am sure Oran's resurrection will have the same consequences as the others. Tonio will operate as a better warrior with greater strength and pain tolerance, but his constitution will not be quite what it was. Resurrection takes a lot out of a person—as you know. But as he wasn't dead long, I think his mind will be almost eighty percent. Such resurrections don't restore a person's full humanity. And the scars he shall wear may make him rather irritable."

There was a long pause. The cleric's eyes twitched, darting back and forth between the three superior men.

Lord Almen let out a sigh. "Indeed. My son was a fine-looking warrior. He will be, how shall I put it, maniacal and sick from time to time—and his mother is not to know of this. Understand!"

Both the detective and cleric nodded.

Lord Almen walked around his son, continuing his inspection, running his fingers over the wounds of the hypnotized young man.

"Dear Tonio," he muttered in a low, callous voice, "what a life you have set up for yourself from now on."

The Royal turned back to Sefron.

"Make sure he is calm when I next come to see him. When you get him under control, I need him dressed—and induced if need be—so I can make sure he is prepared for his new role."

"Yes, my lord," Sefron said, bowing.

Lord Almen turned to a guard's corpse that lay alongside the wall.

"What happened here, Sefron?"

"When Tonio awoke, screaming, the sentry charged in and tried to restrain him. Tonio slammed the man into the wall like a rag doll."

Lord Almen lifted his chin and nodded.

"McKnight, come with me. I'd like you to explain what you've discovered. Sefron, I'll send another sentry."

The two men left Tonio and Sefron alone in the healing chambers. Sefron saw McKnight shoot him a wink, and he responded with an obscene gesture of his own. *Arsehole!*

33

ORAN ARRIVED HOME WITH HIS barge full of slaves. He led them off the barge and into the underground river called the Current. Their feet and legs sank into the sandy bank, forcing him to pull them along by the ropes that held them. They followed him, silent and hopeless, in a labyrinth filled with stalagmites, stalactites, streams, ponds, and bats. It was pitch black, the setting into which all underlings were born and raised. These human men, women, and children were some of the few creatures that ever ventured beneath the surface of Bish.

When he could see a faint blue light in the distance ahead he let out a sigh. It wasn't the Underland, but it wasn't far from there either. He took his prisoners inside a cave cell and closed an ancient iron door behind him. He took a key off a metal peg in the rock and locked the door. Blue light danced off his prisoners shivering faces. He had plans for them.

He shuffled his robed feet over the dry cave floor until he found himself back in a large cavern. Over his head, jagged stalactites jutted from the ceiling, casting shadows in the eerie light. Candles burned, large and small, not with yellow and orange flames as on the surface of Bish, but in flickering hues of pink, green, and blue. He walked along a wall of shelves, filled with a myriad of glass jars containing heads, arms, legs, hearts, and every other appendage imaginable. What most beings would regard as a show of timeless horror was stylish décor to Oran. This was what he called home.

The thick glass tanks and jars on all of the shelves and tabletops were filled with human contents. The tormented faces of men and women, and sometimes an entire child, could be seen in their liquid graves. Oran chuckled as he tapped on the glass with a twisted sneer. This was his research for the greater advancement of his race, and for his quest for knowledge.

The acquisition of humanoids had its price, of course. Oran was neither a hunter nor a slayer. He had to provide payment or service for the creatures he sought. Magic, metal, or precious stones—the humans were suckers for it all. The human remains were plentiful in his labs, but the more difficult races appeared in jars as well. There were dwarves, dog-faced gnolls, orcs, and even some long-legged striders to be discovered, among others. But most of the less-common races were of little threat compared to the insurmountable numbers of humans. Only the underlings came close to matching them in number, but their numbers still weren't enough.

Oran felt tired as he trekked into the most welcoming part of his lair. He slumped into a massive couch layered with red and purple velvet pillows. He stared into a jar with the pickled head of a black-bearded dwarf, a victim from centuries ago. He blew dust from the corked opening on the top and stretched. He wanted to take a nap for only a week or so, but more pressing matters were at hand. News of the Darkslayer could not wait. He pulled one of his black toes to his lips and bit off one of his nails. He spat the black bits into a small bronze bowl filled with driftwood shavings. As he twitched his fingers over the bowl, the bits crackled, and black smoke rose from a yellowish flame. The scent of acid filled his flaring nostrils as he closed his eyes and began murmuring a spell.

For many minutes, Oran murmured and chittered in various high and low crescendos. Sometimes fast-paced and sometimes slow, he kept the rhythm steady. His body stiffened as his face drew tight. Every syllable he uttered tingled in his bones. Power filled him. Magic coursed through his unwavering lips while his mind harnessed the magic of another realm. The energy he summoned felt like a river rushing over him, and then it passed, leaving him as dry as a desert. Oran collapsed back on his couch with a gasp.

Several hours went by before he awoke. He sat up on his couch, rubbing his blurry eyes with his hands and wiping the drool off his sleeve. Staring at him was a big, unblinking eye. It was Eep the imp. Eep was just over three feet tall, with two legs, two arms, two leathery wings, and a head with just one large eye. His muscular arms ended in three clawed fingers and a thumb, and his thick, bumpy skin was a mixture of gray, brown, and black. The imp had a hawk nose, and his wide nostrils seemed to point to his grin. Eep opened his mouth full of white, razor-sharp teeth and a long tail-like tongue. Eep was a small horror with a very big smile.

"It's been long, Eep," Oran said, stretching.

"You could say so!" Eep spoke in a scratchy rasp. "Years! We used to spend so much time together, killing humans and the like. Those were the days. So, master," Eep asked clutching its claws, "what wicked bidding awaits me now?"

Oran got off the couch and poured himself a glass of underling port.

"I need you to run a message to lords Verbard and Catten for me."

"What?" The imp's wings fluttered, raising him in the air. "Deliver a message? To them? Can't we go and kill like we used to? Please?"

Oran took a long draw of his drink. His throat was dry, and there was nothing like the fermented juices from underneath Bish to soothe it.

"No, Eep. That can wait. I need haste! You are the only one who can give me that."

Eep's wings slowed as his clawed toes landed on the ground. Imps fed well on compliments.

"Please, master! I haven't been summoned in a very long time. You gotta let me kill someone."

Eep gnashed his teeth and clawed the air.

"I gotta kill something, Master Oran. I just gotta! It's been too long!"

"Oh, quit begging, Eep! When you get back, I have some fresh meat ready for you to play with. My word. Now, properly deliver the message to Lord Verbard and Lord Catten. I can't have you killed like last time, either, so watch your tongue."

The imp bunched up, its tongue rolling back in its mouth. "Ooh, I hate those two. They had no business doing that. It was just for their pleasure—and it hurt. Nothing can hurt me usually, but they did." Eep paced back and forth, his orbish eye blinking.

"They'd better not kill me this time … no-no … Master Oran. Each time it happens, it's harder to come back. I think so, anyway; I can't remember because it's been so long."

"Quiet Eep!" said Oran with his palm out. "The news you shall deliver is positive news about the tracking of the Darkslayer. They will be pleased, and we shall gain favor. I assure you, not even lords Verbard and Catten will want to tease you with their twisted musings."

Eep's head was down. "If you say so, master. What message am I to deliver?"

34

ONE MOMENT, EEP WAS RUNNING across the open plains of Bish faster than the fleetest deer, and in the next the little imp vanished in a blink. The mystic powers of the world came from a different dimension of Bish that few could tap. Creatures of magic that existed in those unseen dimensions could be summoned, and Eep was one of those. He could view Bish from his own dimension and re-enter it in a different place. It made Eep faster than any other known creature and very powerful.

Eep knew his orders, no special stops on his way to the Underland. He soared through the air and buzzed over the plains, snorting in his freedom. His bat-like wings flapped as the air whistled through his ear holes. He spied a golden eagle miles in the distance. The bird was beautiful, and he hated such things.

He pictured the spot he wanted to go and blinked. He reappeared, smashing mid-air into the unsuspecting eagle. It shrieked as Eep tore at it in a lustful frenzy. Its feathers and blood scattered in the sky, sprinkling on the aghast faces of the farmer's below. The noble bird struggled for its life as Eep pulled them toward the ground in a gray streak. He bit off the eagle's leg when he saw the surface rushing up from below.

"Eh!" Eep said as he crashed into the plains.

"Oooph!"

The great bird was dead, but Eep felt fine. He stood up; dusted off his elbows, and saw the terror-stricken faces watching him. He wanted more. Eep showed them a mouthful of blood and feathers as he licked his lips. The farmers scattered like children running from a crack of thunder. Eep hovered off the ground, his leathery wings beating like a giant hummingbird, and then attacked. It was a bad day to be a farmer.

"Look who we have here, Catten," said Verbard as he lounged on his pewter throne, "a visitor. It is Oran's little imp."

Eep stood inside the magi lords' audience hall, eye averted and wings still. The chamber was dark and ornate with sparse decorations other than two man-made thrones of pewter encrusted with jewels. The two brothers lounged atop puffy velvet cushions, wrapped up in their heavy robes. Eep felt their gold and silver eyes boring into him, picking at his mind. The underling brothers had no respect for his kind, or for his master Oran, for that matter.

"Is he not dead, Verbard?" Catten inquired, shifting in his throne. "Did we not kill him?"

Eep tried not to cringe as they stepped from their seats and approached him.

"Ah, you know how these imps are," Verbard sighed. "Kill them, and they just come on back. I wonder how we can erase this weird little one for good. After all, we don't really like Oran, nor his little pets."

Eep's urge to attack burned in his tiny mind, but he was shackled by magic he could not break. Instead, he stood like a soldier, head bent down. He must do as commanded.

"Agreed," Catten said, "but perhaps the imp brings good news, or something we can use. A gift? What say you, imp? Have you some news to deliver?"

Eep almost didn't hear the question. All he could think about was the last time he met with them. Eep, who hated all life on Bish, did not fear death from the lords, for they could only kill him temporarily. However, they could bring him a lot of pain and suffering during his stay. Eep sucked back his biting tongue. Too often, his big, grinning mouth had got the better of him. The underlings liked to trick him, and then make him pay. Eep's squat little figure dropped to one knee.

"Yes, Lord Catten, Lord Verbard, I do have a message of importance from the cleric, Oran. I have been sent to tell you about a human called the Darkslayer. It seems this man was in the City of Bone recently, with his two-headed dog. He is now sought by a Royal house called Almen. This human is believed to be heading through Red Clay Forest at this time. Oran believes the man and beast will continue their flight further south, and that they could be cut off."

Verbard and Catten looked at each other before they turned their eyes back on the imp.

"Impling, this news from Oran is of some regard, but it would be better if we knew *exactly* where he was. Tell your master that his message shall be remembered by us. In the meantime, give him this message."

Eep felt a moment of relief.

"If he can deliver the precise location of this man in the next two days, the chances are that our underling community could find a new place for him. If he cannot, I would suggest he never bother trying to be a part of this community again. Am I clear, wretched imp?"

"Yes! Yes, Lord Catten … very clear," Eep said in a hiss that revealed his excitement.

Eep's fantasies of killing them both faded for a moment. He often thought about it, but was certain it wasn't something he could accomplish. No creatures in all of his existence were as dangerous as Catten and Verbard. That there was an underling more powerful was hard to believe. Eep was mindful of the power of Oran, but he felt that the power of either one of these two was like Oran's multiplied. It made him resent them even more.

The imp stayed on one knee, listening for the next command. His head was still bowed, and his eye grew tired of counting the pieces of grit on the cavern ground. As the underling lords loomed over him, he listened to Verbard's recount of the previous time he spent with them. Eep remembered the pain as the dogs tore him, muscle from bone. Their words bored into him, and he was certain they would do it again. Verbard's voice rose with more exciting ways to torment him.

Oran was wrong, Eep thought. They would show him no mercy again. Eep heard a sharp whistle and the padding of cave dogs coming his way. His small body yearned to bolt away, but Oran's command held him fast. Eep wanted to look up at the dogs, but a glance at anything could provoke them. If he left on his own, Oran would banish him again, somewhere else, until summoned again. Eep would rather be tortured than bored. He closed his eye and readied himself for the worst.

Several long and horrible minutes passed before Verbard broke off and said, "You may go, imp."

Eep's wings buzzed as he floated up, turned his back to the underling lords, and flew through the winding caves as fast as he could. The imp felt a rush of joy and relief. In a blink he would be back in Oran's lair.

Verbard and Catten sat back on their thrones as the gruesome and mangy cave dogs lay at their feet.

"This is good timing, Verbard. We haven't heard from Oran in years, and now this. Right when we have sent a Badoon brigade after this human. Now we just need to get word to the Vicious and send them that way. We may finally catch the element we have always lacked—surprise!" Catten said, clutching his fist.

"Yes, brother, but I don't wish to take chances. We should send the Vicious and the Badoon farther southeast, *and* I think we should go as well. We can head him off in case he returns north."

Lord Catten's golden eyes darted towards his brother. Verbard's head was cocked, and his eyebrows raised. The brothers preferred to operate from behind the scenes, pulling the strings.

Catten added, "Brother, if you think that is best, I have to agree, but if we are to go out, let us make the most of this trip. Let's fill it with screams of human terror."

"Well, let us not limit it to humans."

35

MELEGAL WOKE AT DAWN TO a stench as foul as anything he had known in the City of Bone. Shaking his head as he held his nose, he peered toward a mysterious rustling. Venir was on his feet, packing his gear on Chongo.
"Venir?"
Melegal could not tell the man was a dream or a ghost in the strange morning mist rising from the marsh.
"How are you?"
"Doing better." Venir forced a smile as he stretched the straps on Chongo's saddle. "How 'bout you?"
"You are?" Melegal looked around, rubbing his eyes. "Well, you were pretty nearly dead last night."
Venir cocked his pale face.
"Really? I don't recall seeing you last night."
"You don't?" Melegal stood and walked over to his friend. "You're telling me you don't remember coming out of that grimy, stinking marsh and telling me about green snake meat and all?"
"No."
"Well—and there I was worried about you. Bone!" The thief kicked up some dirt. "You are invincible, aren't you? Well, fine, I guess if you can't be killed, then I don't have to bother myself worrying about you," he said, snatching his blanket from the ground. "So, why don't we just go kill all the underlings right now?" He strutted over to Quickster and slapped the pony on its rear, startling it from its slumber.
"Hah!" Venir managed. "Would you rather I was dead then, Melegal? Then you'd have another reason to be miserable on this trip. Would that make you feel better?"
Melegal folded his arms. "Maybe it would. I mean, look at you! Your legs were purple last night. Now they're just plain ugly and white."
Melegal felt bad for saying it as he came closer and noticed that Venir's battered appearance had been hidden by the mist. The man had a haggard expression, and his torn body was bandaged and scuffed as if he'd been dragged

by horses for several miles. Melegal didn't understand how Venir endured all of the scrapes. *Well, he should know better by now.*

"It's the snake meat. But, does it make you feel better to know I ache from head to toe? My stomach is nauseous and my head is dizzy!"

Melegal fought to contain a smile. "A little bit." He didn't know why, but it actually did make him feel better. He didn't like feeling vulnerable in the wake of Venir and Mood.

"Besides, it's not like you haven't seen me pass out a dozen times before. Why are you so bothered this time?" Venir took a draw from a waterskin.

"Oh, well forgive me for still being riled up from last night's skirmish. My underling killing skills are a little rusty." Melegal glanced at Venir's gory helmet that lay beside the extinguished camp fire. "It's disturbing."

"You'll get over it," replied Venir.

"Sure ... sure." *I always do.*

"Have you ladies finished squabbling over not being dead yet?" said Mood's grizzly voice from close by. "I'm ready ta go."

It took a full day's travel before the company arrived a few miles north of Two-Ten City. Dusk was setting in, and the two blazing suns were melting down over the southern treetops and onto the burnt plains of Bish.

Unlike the City of Bone, Two-Ten City could not be seen as well from a distance. It had no giant wall enclosing it, only the open plains. Venir's keen eyes could see the few scattered lookout towers ahead, some with militia and others without. Two-Ten City was a community without civil care. All comers were welcome. Venir led the way along an older caravan trail leading into the rundown city.

Venir admired how the people of Two-Ten City lived without the fear of being overrun by hordes of underlings, or any other race for that matter. It had a motley army at best, that was made up of various races. Nobody cared if you were human, orc, half-orc, or dwarf, just as long as you weren't an underling. This odd mixture of people made for the most unique culture on Bish. It was where all the misfits, adventurers, profiteers, and thieves came when their status as an outcast or criminal had all but banished them from elsewhere. For the most part, the races tended to stick with their own kind, but in this city, everyone was welcome.

"Well, this is close enough for me, Venir," Mood said under his bushy beard, green eyes following along the disused trail. "The smell of city, ooh, it's as bad as the marsh. I'll take care of Chongo and the pony if you like, while you two dogs go into that hole and do what you gotta do."

"I figure we won't be long," Venir said as he hopped off Chongo and started gathering his necessities. "But, if we decide to lay low here, you may have to keep Chongo with you longer."

Venir rubbed the big dog's floppy ears.

"I don't know how persistent those Royals will be. They may look here, but they won't get much help. The Royals here aren't like the ones in Bone. But they'll get other help, I'm sure."

"They won't find us in this city," said Melegal, straightening his hat. "And as long as we're here, I plan on enjoying myself. Oh, and I'm keeping Quickster with me. I'm not gonna walk any more than I have to." Melegal scratched the black mane of the shaggy mount.

"That's one thing I like about Two-Ten. Nobody messes with Quickster."

"Fine, keep your stinkin' pony, stick-man," Mood said with a gruff laugh. "I'm sure as slat nobody will want to eat or steal that smelly beast, not even an orc. Ho-ho!"

Mood slapped Venir on the shoulder, and hoisted himself on Chongo. Venir watched them go, then turned and followed Melegal into the city.

Venir's body throbbed with every step. The green snake meat did its part countering the poison, but his body was far from one hundred percent. When he awoke earlier that morning, he wished he was dead, but the survivalist inside him kept him going. It always did. He could see Melegal's sharp and shaven face was now wooly and haggard. Guilt settled in his thoughts, so he tried to lighten the mood.

"Ah, Melegal, it'll be good to be back in Two-Ten City. I can smell the ale, grog, and cheap perfume already. And some of Bish's best-kept secrets are in Two-Ten. There's always something new every time I come."

"Well, you got that right," Melegal said, stretching out his arms, "It's been years, and I can't believe I've been in Bone so long. I used to like it here."

The thief's gray eyes began to dance.

"I wonder if our old tavern's still standing. Wasn't it almost destroyed the last time we were here together?"

Venir smiled and said, "I'm pretty sure." The truth was he couldn't remember a thing about the last time. It seemed strange.

It wasn't long before the neglected trail led them toward the bustling activity on the outskirts of the city. Every type of commerce could be found scattered around the borders of the city as well as within. Merchants and farmers fought for space to sell their baubles or food. The worst of the harlots aggressively foisted their wares in the faces of the two adventurers. Their lurid tongues promised unforgettable favors. Their expressive seduction added a bounce to Venir's step, and he watched a thin smile cross Melegal's lips as he brushed the women away.

There was something about Two-Ten City that represented the high life he enjoyed most in Bish. Maybe it was the oddity of it all. The strumpets were not just human, but orc, dwarf, and halfling. They all jostled to find seekers of their tricks, each race offering its own specialties. The open fondness of the different races was not represented in the City of Bone. The Royals there considered it something of a crime to intermingle with other races within city walls. But the Royals of Two-Ten cared not, for they, too, were of different races.

It wasn't long after the first wave of jobbers that the ragtag urchins, faces wrought with filth, swarmed around the men. Venir shoved them away with a growl, sending them in a scurry, except for one who clung to Melegal's heels.

"Lord, shall I find you a stable for your jackass?" asked an ugly orc boy with a tuft of blond hair, snaggled teeth, and a slimy pig nose.

"No," Melegal answered in a gruff tone, tugging Quickster along.

The orc boy grabbed Quickster's reigns.

"It will only cost a few coppers, skinny man, and I shall groom and feed him," the orc boy insisted.

"What?" Melegal snatched the reigns away. "Go away, you ignorant boy, and don't call me skinny man again!"

The persistent boy blocked Melegal's path. "Sorry, I didn't realize you were just an ugly woman."

Venir coughed a laugh. He had almost forgotten how smart-alecky orcs were by nature.

Melegal came to a stop. The thief waved his finger across the orc boy's watching eyes.

"Leave me and my pony be, orcling, or I shall be forced to use this."

"Whatcha gonna do with that finger, miss?"

Venir covered his mouth.

Melegal's frown turned upward. Striking like a snake, he poked his finger in the boy's throat. The orcen child dropped to his knees, clutching his neck, and kicking at the air. He bent over the unfortunate boy, whispering in his ear, "That's what I'm gonna a do. And if I ever see you again, I'll be the last thing you ever see. Got it?"

The orc boy turned purple as he began to pee himself. The boy's growing eyes blinked over and over. A small crowd gathered. Melegal looked around and then poked the orc's throat again. The orc gasped, looked back at Melegal, screamed, and ran clumsily away and out of sight. The laughing crowd began to disperse.

"Tsk, tsk. Pickin' on children already, are you?" Venir said.

"That wasn't a child; it was an orc. And he reminded me too much of Georgio."

"That's low," Venir said, shaking his aching head. "Just plain low."

"You know, I'm starting to remember why we left this wretched place. Those orcs are stupid, a real nuisance, and I can see they haven't changed. I'm starting to recall another reason why we had to leave last time."

"Me too, and I wouldn't be surprised if they were still around," Venir said as something he hadn't considered entered his mind.

"I'd be surprised if they weren't."

Venir forced a chuckle, giving the thief a big slap on the back. "I guess we'll know soon enough."

He led the way toward a rundown tavern that stood near three stories high. The oak building was covered in dirt and grime. It was as ugly as it was unnatural. On the wall hung a cock-eyed sign that read: THE BEATEN BOAR'S BUM. The plank walls creaked as the building swayed in the breeze. The Bum stood in defiance of its odd and decaying appearance. Some said it was magic that somehow held the giant tavern together, while others said it was how soundly the dwarves had built it centuries ago. The stories had grown in extravagance over the decades. The Beaten Boar's Bum was one of the lowest and dirtiest places to be found on Bish, without being underground.

"Shall I stable your pony?" enquired a small, black human lad sporting a heavy afro, blue eyes, and a small nose.

Melegal gave the boy a thoughtful look. "Keep him close to the Boar's Bum." Melegal handed over the reins and a few coppers, "and be sure to feed him well." The thief flashed a few more coins and the young boy smiled as he led Quickster away.

Venir stood before the decrepit building and gave a sigh. The refreshing thought of ale, grog, and women began to surge over his aches and pains. A bosomy older woman in a revealing short dress rocked in a chair on the porch. Her leathery lips and crooked fingers beckoned for him to enter. Venir's thoughts shivered in mid-fantasy as he turned his boot away from the porch's front step. "We'd better go in the back. Let's fetch that boy and have him get us a room."

The thief gave an excited clap. "I'm with you," Melegal said, winking at the woman, "but let's make haste. My tongue's dry, and my belly's groaning, and I'll be having enough wine to pickle me purple. I want to forget all about that rough trip down."

"Go on after the boy, then," Venir urged. As Melegal hurried away, he looked back at the older gal and gave her a quick nod. Her seedy smile gave him pause. Maybe coming back to Two-Ten City wasn't such a good idea after all.

36

ORAN'S FACE FILLED WITH GLEE as Eep took his pinned-up frustrations out on many of the imprisoned humans. He made swift notes of the reactions the people had defending themselves from the blood-thirsty imp.

"Pace yourself," Oran said, but the imp tore through them like a milling stone.

Oran jotted down quick sketches with his deft hand, black lips mimicking their shrieks as he recorded their final words at the threshold of death. They all pleaded, begged for mercy, and promised everything a human could imagine. Every word of it would have made him laugh, but he didn't know how.

He watched all of them cringe in horror, but for one. A lone woman fought for her very life, a short mop of strawberry hair hanging down in her eyes. Oran noted how she bit, clawed, and kicked, one time clipping the imp's eye with a long fingernail. Eep silenced the screaming woman after that brief moment of triumph with a quick-clawed blow to the neck. It was one of the better sessions Oran had ever recorded, all five seconds of it.

In a separate cell, the remaining humans emerged from their drugged calm. Four stout men stood at the bars, while the rest wailed with tear-filled faces as he let Eep out from the cage. The imp walked by, snapping at them. The men shuffled back as the blood-drenched imp hissed and walked on.

"Eep, come over here so we can get moving," Oran said, strolling back to his lab. "It's time for part two of your journey."

"Ah, thank you, Master Oran, thank you," said the imp. "That was just what I needed. I just had to rip something apart. They were perfect."

The imp wiped the blood from the lid of his large eye. "I'm sorry it went so fast. Catten and Verbard made me so angry I couldn't contain myself." Eep's wings buzzed as he shook off the blood like a rain-soaked dog, splattering Oran with droplets.

"Foolish imp!" shrieked Oran. "Look what you've done!" Oran tore off his modest robes and hurled them at the distracted imp. "Nah-rollah!"

The robes caught Eep full in the face, coming alive and smothering the imp like a living thing. Eep struggled as the robes constricted around his small body, restraining his wings, dropping him to the ground with a plop. Oran watched his robes confine the entirety of the imp like a waxy mold as he focused on the robes squeezing every crevice air tight, suffocating the imp. Eep's body lurched and kicked from within, then lay still. Oran gathered his composure, considering all he had to do.

"Stupid imp." His hand passed through the air. "Rollahkem."

The robes slackened, and Oran walked over, pulled his heavy robe off the limp imp, and kicked Eep in the head.

"Ooch," the imp whimpered as it struggled to draw breath.

"No more games, Eep. Let's track this Darkslayer and be done with it. Come."

Eep dragged himself up and followed Oran into a study that was filled with less experiments and more paperwork. Oran sat down on a stool and rolled out a long weathered parchment—a map—and pointed at it.

"This is the plan. I have to return to the City of Bone. You need to head southeast to this area. The Darkslayer has to be somewhere between Red Clay Forest and Two-Ten City. Our human troublemaker will most likely be in the city, so look there first." Oran's black nail circled the spot.

Eep's head tilted, nodded, and he said, "Yes."

Oran continued, "We have to resolve this quickly in order to help Verbard and Catten. Even if we don't actually catch him, at least we'll have aided them. That will go a long way with the underling lords. Then hopefully," he paused and hissed through his teeth, "I can finally go home."

Oran thought back to the last time he had met with Lords Catten and Verbard. Oran was outspoken, and they didn't like it. He had dared to speak against them in the presence of brethren on the issue of mingling more with humanity and the rest. The mistake had almost cost him his life. Instead, he had been banished. Oran once had power and status in the Underland, but Verbard and Catten had it removed. Since then, he had hardly spoken with another underling, but he had his ways of staying informed.

With a wave of his hand, Eep sped out of the cave, and over the Current as fast as his wings could take him. Oran headed that way as well, stepping onto his barge while muttering a spell. The barge glided over the black river toward the City of Bone. He could still hear the screams of the humans calling for him as he went—begging for food and pleading for freedom. He wondered if any would die of starvation while he was gone. *Will they eat one another?* He hoped he wouldn't miss it. Oran's stomach rumbled. It had been days since he himself had last eaten.

37

I T WAS LATE EVENING BEFORE Venir and Melegal sauntered down the wooden steps leading to a balcony that surveyed all below. He inhaled the smells of exotic smoke and long-brewed ale. It gave him a welcoming burst of vitality. Melegal stood at his side, rubbing his eager hands together, his eyes glinting at the roughshod faces below.

Venir bustled past scornful faces as he made his way to the main floor below. The smell of mead and grog was so strong he could taste it on his watering tongue. Bravado blinded his manners as he created a path through the crowded bar. He thought of Mood, thankful of that last sliver of snake meat that had melted in his mouth. His aches and pains were beginning to wash away.

Melegal cruised, flanking his side. The thief toyed with a nubile waitress and dispensed winks, kisses, and nods to others as he went by. A curious kind of music filled the main tavern, mingling with the sounds of laughter, anger, and triumph. Venir rocked his shoulders with the rhythm as he shoved into a spot along a waxy, blackened bar.

Unlike the taverns in the City of Bone, the Beaten Boar's Bum had few fully human occupants. There were plenty of part-humans, but the full-blooded ones stood out like flowers among the thorns. Also absent were the expensive perfumes and beautiful ladies in elaborate silks and colorful make-up. There was nothing to hide in Two-Ten City, and the miscellaneous folks were proud of that. Appearances weren't as important as coin.

The room was weathered, yet maintained. The tables, chairs, and wooden mugs seemed as well-worn and hardy as the heavy planked floors. Torches lit the room on all sides, their orange flames casting shadows onto the mishmash of faces as they laughed, drank, smiled, cursed, and even wept. Despite the plethora of torches, it was not hard to find enough privacy to commit an unscrupulous act or two. The room was live and engaging. No judgment was to be found here among Bish's unwanted. It provided a respite for its occupants from the harsh realities they all faced, whether due to shame, ugliness, or their crimes. It was a tavern that didn't know a stranger even though it was full of them, coming and going just like the light. And tonight, Venir had returned to a scene where he had once thrived.

Memories swelled up inside him that he hadn't anticipated. The room and its ambience made him feel as if he had stepped back in time. He felt like the younger man he had been before he became something else. He thought back to other nights like this and about what had happened before he acquired Brool and the armament. In those times he had lived so free, as a soldier, a mercenary, a scout, and even a brigand.

Best of all were the days when he had lived for the hunt, his reputation as a tracker and killer of underlings and beasts preceding him. He had been vibrant, whispering words in jeweled ears that drove the ladies in the taverns wild. Things had never been the same since. Venir had buried the flickers that longed for those days, but tonight it hit him like a great slap in the face. So much had happened since he last left this place. Two-Ten City may have been the last place he remembered truly having any fun.

He watched Melegal talking up two formidable part-orcen soldiers at the bar, their grim faces turning upward at the words of the thief's uncanny jokes. A soothing expression crossed his face as he recalled some of his daring, foolish, and even childish adventures with the thief. It seemed as if they had come from nothing, only to have the whole world of Bish at their very feet. But she had changed it all. A woman, an inhuman woman some would say, whose exploits he had heard about in Two-Ten City one sweltering night. It was with more than a mere glance that Jarla had caught his eye. Friendships like his and Melegal's were put to the test, and changed forever. A familiar voice jostled him away from the unwanted thoughts.

"Venir, it's the same band!" Melegal said, nudging him with a knobby elbow.

Twin orc men with large noses strummed tall basses, one with three strings and one with four; a halfling man banged a tambourine and danced while a bald and beardless dwarf played a lengthy cone-shaped flute. It seemed as if the band had never changed, never left the stage since the day they were last here, many years ago. Venir snapped out of his daze. It was time to unwind.

Venir's booming voice cut through the room like a cymbal, causing heads to turn. "The Bone if it isn't!"

Venir tapped his hands on the bar, trying to catch the eye of the barkeep. It felt like it had been days since he had a drink of anything, and his throat felt as dry as sand. The barkeep was at the far end of the bar that ran the full length of the tavern's floor, his back turned on Venir. The barkeep hadn't so much as glanced his way.

Venir slammed his fist down on the bar. "Pardon me, you big black son of a boar!" He bellowed, drawing dozens of eyes on him. "How about some tankards down here!"

Parts of the tavern fell silent, but the band still played, while the bartender stayed leaning over the bar, continuing his conversation.

"Are you deaf? If you don't send me my mead, I'm gonna come back there and get it myself." Venir hopped onto the bar counter.

Bewildered folks snatched their drinks and vacated their bar stools. The barkeep stood straight up, head towering above the rest, muscles thick and supple under his apron.

As Venir opened his mouth again he saw a small cask of ale hurling across the counter like a missile. Off-balance and unable to dodge it, Venir caught it fully in his chest and was sent tumbling off the end of the bar with a resounding crash.

The tavern jumped and fell silent as the music lingered in the background. Melegal stood alone at the bar, eyes down on his friend on the floor. People murmured and craned their necks, peeking back and forth between the floor and the bartender.

"If I catch it, it's free!" Venir said with a roar as he bounced up, hoisting the keg over his head, flashing a smile. The crowd stared and shouted out in astonishment.

"You better not have spilled any, you big oaf, or I'll bust yer tail!" the big black man said with a broad, white-toothed smile.

The man reached Venir's end of the bar in a few strides, leapt the bar in a single bound, and snagged the keg of ale. "What on Bish brings you back to this rat hole, Venir?" The big man lowered the keg on the bar as another man, frail as a fiddle, tapped it. "I didn't think you could leave the pretty women of Bone behind!"

The ragged and motley crowd of humanoids shifted around as whispers of Venir's name spread from lip to lip.

"You know me, Mikkel, I can't stay in one place too long. Besides, I missed the finest mead ever brewed, by a man, that is!" Venir and Mikkel faced one another, both standing tall and proud, like men among babes. Venir slapped and clasped the bartender's shoulder.

Mikkel's broad smile turned downward.

"Yer not saying I don't make the best mead in Bish, are you?"

"Come now, there is one better, made by a beautiful gal in Bone—"

"You shut your mouth!" Mikkel's light eyes were hot with anger. "You know that heifer stole my recipe!"

Venir poked the man in his chest.

"She said it was hers."

"By Bish! It's from my grandfather's grandfather, and it's older than his tavern, you know that!" Mikkel clutched his head and squeezed his eyes shut. "Why do you torture me with her memory?"

"Ah, I just like toying with you."

"As long as it ain't with her," Mikkel said, giving him the eye.

"You know me better than that. The last time I saw her, she was as big as a six-legged cow."

Mikkel let out a thunderous laugh.

"Now you're talking; she was that big when I kicked her out. Now let's drink the best brew ever made." Mikkel snatched the barrel off the bar. "Nikkel! Get us some mugs and tumblers and a bottle of grog. Today, I drink with old friends!"

The three men took a separate table near the bar, and each pulled up a chair. The young black boy with blue eyes brought over the bottle and mugs. It was clear to Venir who the boy's father was, although Mikkel wasn't sporting an afro anymore.

"So, why did you start shaving your head, Mikkel?" Venir said.

"Don't ask," the big bartender frowned as he filled the glasses.

Puzzled, Venir started slurping some drinks before it hit him.

"You went bald!"

Mikkel stiffened. "Well, you aren't so far off, yourself. But I am older than you, so show some respect." He turned to Melegal. "How are you, Melegal? What kinda trouble has he got you into this time?"

"Oh?" Melegal straightened from his slump. "Are you going to start acting as if I'm here, now?"

"Ah, come on, you know better than that. I'd never snub you," Mikkel said in a sincere apology.

"I know that, Mikkel, I'm just deviling you." The thief finished off his first mug. "Ah! Anyway, to answer your question, let's just say some simple skimming turned ugly, and we're trying to avoid any further Royal trouble."

The slender thief took a solid slug of his second mug of delicious mead. Mikkel nodded, his blue eyes looking upward as he rubbed his silvery chin.

"So, we thought we'd lay low awhile until this situation clears," Venir piped up, scarfing down one mug after the other. The gratifying taste of Mikkel's mead seemed to shave the past ten years off his life.

The Broken Boar's Bum was alive and kicking, and he felt his body begin to unwind. He ate and drank like a Royal as they talked far into the morning. Each had a story that marveled the other. But none could tell a story like

Venir, as one tale after another rolled off his drunken lips. The middling women, swooning at his words, became more tempting by the hour.

It took some time before Venir ran out of words and fell asleep at the table, alongside the rest. The day had passed from dawn and back and into the dusk before he stirred. After a belly full of steak, eggs, red potatoes, and biscuits, Venir's tongue was back up to speed. Stoking more stories with mead and grog, Venir continued to have one of the best times he had had in years. It was good to be alive for a change. However, peaceful moments on Bish never lasted long.

There were many kinds of silence. There were silent nights, silent shadows, silent terrors, silent murders, and silent suffering. But this silence, the silence that fell now, was perhaps the most unnerving and unpleasant of them all. The band of the Broken Boar's Bum had fallen silent. The rest of the occupants gawped as if a spreading doom had crept upon the tavern. All were quiet, wide-eyed, and unmoving, as a menacing bulk overshadowed the room with heavy steps that caused the plank floors to groan. All living creatures in the tavern were transfixed, hairs standing on end, except for one. Venir carried on as ever, finishing off another pitcher of mead.

He was sharing a compelling misadventure with Nikkel, whose head had turned away. He continued his rambling as loud and offensively as ever. Seldom was such talk even noticed in a place such as this. But when all went quiet, his audience became as stiff as wrought iron. Something about this voice seemed out of line, inappropriate. He hardly noticed his friend's words.

"Oh no," Mikkel breathed, "not again."

The entire room darkened as a giant shadow fell over the massive shoulders of the ever-rowdy Venir.

"Who turned the lights off and the stink on?" Venir turned toward the source of the disturbance.

He looked up and saw one of the biggest humanoids he had even seen. Much broader and far taller than himself, a rare half-ogre man loomed over him, arms crossed over a hairy, muscled chest. He peered down at Venir through what appeared to be only one good eye. The ogre had thick black-brown hair with streaks of grey, brown eyes and canine teeth. There was little facial hair, and his arms and legs were covered with coarse black hair. This one in particular stood nearly seven feet tall, and must have weighed well over four hundred pounds.

"Ah … it's Farc," Venir slurred, peering up through one eye, trying to keep things from looking twice as bad. "I gather you haven't taken a bath since I last saw you. You smell like orc slat!"

Farc sounded like ten voices in one.

"Venir—close mouth! Listen while Farc talk," the glowering half-ogre said. "Farc not forget you smashing eye! Farc pay you back! Farc pay you now!"

Gasps filled the room, and those who had actually been around at the time the two had clashed scattered to spread the news.

Venir slouched back in his chair. "And how do you plan to do that?" He said in a rising voice, "I crippled you. And even you wouldn't be stupid enough to fight me again, 'cause then your other eye would be useless, too!"

Farc leaned in and Venir could feel his fetid breath on his face.

"You promise Farc another fight. Remember, human?"

Venir nodded.

"But, I not said you fight Farc, did I? I just said you fight. Right?"

"Yes," Venir said, nodding again as he slurped the last of a mug of ale and wiped his mouth on the inside of his arm. Venir began waving his mug in the air.

"Say, Farc, why don't you buy me another drink? I'm all empty."

Farc slapped Venir's mug across the room.

"You say anytime, anyplace, last time," Farc growled. "Time now! Place the same! Me and my boy will be waiting!"

The half-ogre stormed through the dispersing crowd like a behemoth and disappeared.

Venir looked around and smiled.

"I bet he's got one ugly boy, and I bet that boy has an ugly mother to boot. Poor lad!"

Melegal chuckled, but Mikkel's face was grim as he cleared his throat and said, "Uh, Venir, I think it's his boy he wants you to fight. He's been the champ for the last two years."

Venir didn't pay any notice to the tension in his friend's voice.

"You might wanna stop drinking. This is gonna go down soon," Mikkel said.

"I thought you were the champ, Mikkel." Venir looked around for his mug.

"Not since Farc beat me. Then you beat him, and after you left it was wide open for a while. His boy, Vee, is better, much better and younger. Farc wasn't the youngest, or even in his prime when you defeated him. But his son! Well, he's an abomination! He makes his ugly old man look like a halfling."

Nikkel was just putting two refilled mugs of mead in front of Venir when Mikkel grabbed them away.

"Gimme my drinks now, Mikkel!" Venir said in a slur, as his face began to redden.

"You better stop drinking and start thinking! You're on in about an hour!"

Venir scowled. He wanted to just walk away, grab a wench and go to bed. He glanced at the concern expressions around him. He rapped his fist on the table.

"Coffee then!"

38

THE VICIOUS AND THE BADOON brigade moved fast, cutting through the southwestern part of Bish and leaving a trail of blood over hill and dale. Many unfortunate inhabitants that weren't quick enough to flee died, their final moments filled with pain and anguish. The possibility of surviving a Vicious-led Badoon attachment was slim. Dozens of Bish's more peaceful inhabitants had already perished, and dozens more would meet the same fate before the brigade caught up with their enemy.

The two hulking Vicious led the trek through high and low landscapes, unhindered by rugged terrain, inclement weather, or natural hazards. Even the most senior and weathered elite underling hunters were pushed to keep pace with them. The best of the Badoons, as nasty as they were, felt some discomfort in the presence of the Vicious, for the Vicious did such things to torture and mutilate their victims that even the hardened Badoon had never imagined them. The word "cruel" was inadequate in describing their deeds. The worst the soldiers could imagine was little more than a bad dream compared to what the Vicious would, could, and did do. Still, the Badoon soldiers found it inspiring.

Little of Bish had heard about the legendary Vicious, for none had lived to witness such events unfolding. Their appearances on the surface were rare at best. But now, from high in a tree perch, a rare, yellow-haired halfling boy named Lefty Lightfoot had seen the Vicious in action.

Lefty had watched in numb dismay as the bodies of his family and friends were torn, shredded, bludgeoned, and strewn from one end of his village to the other. The muscle-laden Vicious were responsible for almost all of it. He saw many of the frightened halflings escape the clawed clutches of the Vicious only to be cut down by the crossbow bolts of the surrounding warriors. It had all happened so fast, and then the underlings were gone.

Lefty's mind was seared with the nightmarish screams of his brothers and sisters, bigger and smaller, being bitten, broken, and eaten. He only wished he had not survived to see such horrors befall his people. He wept until he could weep no more and then ran as fast and far as his speedy little legs would carry him.

39

ORAN MADE HASTE RETURNING TO the belly of the City of Bone. The Current ran just below Castle Almen, as well as many other castles. The cavernous stone-cut chambers far below the castle, ancient beyond recorded history, could not possibly have been the handiwork of humans. Dwarves possibly, but even dwarves were not known for engineering feats as spectacular as this. In an eerie cave room, Lord Almen stood in the torch-lit semi-darkness with the resurrected Tonio, Sefron, and Detective McKnight.

"What information do you have for me, Oran?" Almen's loud voice echoed through the large chamber.

"South, most positively. He will be found no matter where he goes. An underling Badoon is en route to dispose of him now."

Lord Almen folded his arms across his golden-etched clothes.

"What is your point, Oran?" asked Lord Almen. "I thought the underlings could not handle this Darkslayer, so what makes you think he'll be dispatched now?"

Oran kept his groan to himself as Lord Almen's flickering shadow enveloped him. Oran felt no fear of this powerful Royal. He respected the man, but it was beneath an underling to fear a human.

"Lord Almen, my reliable sources leave me in no doubt that these are the final days of the human pest. He has never been taken seriously by our people. But, over time, word got back to some of the upper echelons, so to speak, and they were not happy with these losses."

"Ha, Oran!" Lord Almen said, letting loose a chuckle. "Yet you tell me that this man, this one man, has required the effort of a whole underling badoon? My, what I wouldn't do to have a fellow such as that on my side. This has to be the most astonishing news I've heard in over a decade!"

Lord Almen's continued chuckles drew a sneer from Oran. He wanted to rip the man's tongue out. He was an underling after all, and human mockery wasn't something he had ever experienced. Sefron laughed along, his naked belly jiggling, while McKnight stood fanning himself with his hat, grinning.

Oran let things sink in, it became an awkward moment for him. He had been too busy to give the situation much thought. Struck now by the preposterousness of it, he felt somewhat embarrassed for his kind.

Even Tonio managed to choke a laugh: "Huh ... huh."

Once a loudmouthed braggart, Tonio was much quieter now. Oran stared at the young man. Since Tonio's resurrection, he was clearly not all there, but he was still a soldier to contend with. Just not one of Oran's better jobs, something he kept to himself.

Oran shook it off.

"Lord Almen, you need no longer trouble yourself with this matter. I could try to recover the body of the man for you, or a piece of it, at least. It is unlikely even a shred will remain, but I will do my beh—*urk!*"

Tonio's strong gray hands squeezed his neck.

"Lead me to Vee-man," the young warrior forced from his throat, "or die now!"

"Drop him, Tonio!" Sefron shouted.

The Royal son obeyed, dropping him to the ground, where he gasped for air.

Lord Almen continued, "This is prophetic. Oran, you will see to it this Darkslayer is dead. You can take my son with you on your journey."

What! But Oran could not muster the words. He was only happy to breathe again as he watched Sefron calm his zombie-like attacker.

Lord Almen stepped over him and said, "Give me your word, underling; you will take my son to find the Darkslayer."

Oran searched the eyes of the men that surrounded him. Hatred began to swell inside him. He didn't feel as if he had much of a choice—at least, not at this moment.

"My word," Oran agreed.

Sefron stepped farther into view and added, "Perhaps McKnight can be of some assistance, Lord Almen. He's an excellent tracker."

McKnight's enlarged eyes shot arrows at Sefron's insidious suggestion.

Lord Almen perched his brows and said, "Good idea, Sefron."

McKnight's jaw dropped.

A few words were exchanged as Almen clasped his son's hands and gave him a final blessing.

"Kill him without mercy, son. Avenge yourself. Good hunting."

McKnight could not believe how quickly his life had worsened. Sefron had gotten him, and gotten him good. It had all been fun and games to him over the years, tormenting the perverted cleric. Now it seemed to have caught up with him. McKnight had exposed the cleric's twisted behavior time and again at Castle Almen. He had caught the cleric peeping on the ladies, young and old. He had returned the cleric's small hoard of "misplaced" castle jewels and other rare baubles, some of which he still kept for himself. McKnight had always been two steps ahead of him, until today.

Now, he found himself smack in the center of a mess he would have done anything to avoid. He was now stuck with the Royal brat, Tonio. *At least he doesn't talk as much anymore.* McKnight knew nothing about underlings, either. It was pitch black other than the lantern he carried. He was at the mercy of the foul-looking underling, and of Tonio as well. It was an unlikely cadre of adventurers.

Oran chittered something in underling, which he didn't comprehend. "What's that, underling?" enquired McKnight, brandishing two long, silver-hilted daggers of a unique design.

"Oh, be silent!"

It was the last thing he heard Oran say for a while. McKnight wasn't used to traveling in total silence and darkness. He had always felt darkness was his friend, but now it was like a drape that covered him so that he couldn't escape. He kept Oran and Tonio in sight before him, fingers toying with his daggers. The craft glided over the water—how, he did not know. The cool wind wafted in his hair. It did little to ease his thoughts. For all he knew, they were headed for the Underland.

40

A FTER AN ENTIRE POT OF Nikkel's strongest coffee, Venir's head was only a little more clear. Things were beginning to annoy him as he contemplated how such a promising night had turned bad in a moment's notice. And as if things couldn't have been worse, he was now being harassed by things that should have been settled years ago.

"Ooh, honey, now don't get beat up too bad," a half-orcen woman cooed. She stood before him, hands on hips, wearing a purple satin dress that was slit to reveal one of the most curvaceous bodies he had ever seen.

"I just love the rough and rowdy type, and I was counting on you the moment I saw you walk through that door."

She winked at him and flashed a promising smile.

"Don't worry, dear, you won't be waitin' long," Venir said as he brushed into her body.

As the sexy part-orcen woman's swelling chest smashed into his, more bravado pumped through his body. The woman's muscular thighs and pumpkin-round behind caught his attention as well. His lust-addled mind was blind to her blonde pigtails, sweaty lips, crooked teeth, and piggish nose. After countless drinks, compounded by hard travel and no companionship, Venir's particulars no longer registered.

"See you later, mighty warrior."

She blew him a kiss and waved as Melegal and Mikkel pulled him away.

"Venir, if you survive this, you might not survive that!" Melegal said with a wide open smile.

"You two guys are both sick!" Mikkel said, shaking his head. "She is trouble. Trust me, I know. Win, lose, or don't fight at all tonight, she's still gonna try and tear your legs off!"

Venir responded with a foolish grin and a shameless comment. Nikkel gagged as his father covered his ears.

41

T RINOS FOUND HERSELF STYMIED FROM time to time. A degree of frustration had even set in, which was odd to one who had the ability to do anything.

More often than one would expect, created things would turn into things that were not supposed to happen. Still, her endless universe offered some surprises for the omnipotent ones who seemed to roam and do whatever they pleased. Trinos would run across unique changes to worlds that had come and gone. She would be fascinated and begin to study them, looking for answers. It did not happen as often as she would have liked, but by her eternal frame of reference, that was still quite often.

Her world of Bish was safe, tucked away from the meddling eyes of others. The rules were in place to avoid a catastrophic change. And so, while she roamed, she had left the tiny world hidden deep in their universe, in a place impossible to find. But within the infinite, there still remained infinite possibilities.

Another being like herself had been lurking near her precious world. Scorch made his discovery of her odd world quite accidentally. He began to study it with divine interest. Its unique set-up gave him enjoyment. *But*, he thought to himself, *it could be even better.*

42

A STAIRWELL OPENED UP IN THE back of the tavern and sloped down. It was wide and steep, flattening out deeper under the ground. Venir looked ahead at a large tunnel that was cut from rock and gleaming iron ore. A muffled roar rose in the distance. Warmth filled the air with every step, and the salt of sweating bodies made him flare his nostrils.

All races sweated, but half-ogre sweat distinguished itself above and beyond the rest. You could not smell it from a mile away, but you always wished you had. Once you got too close, it stuck to you. It was best described as a mix of salt, manure, and urine. Venir fought the urge to hold his nose as the foul odor assaulted his senses.

The tunnel opened into an enormous cavern hosting a circular arena. Hundreds of shouting faces crowded on wooden benches. This was the home of the greatest game on Bish: Pit Battles. Every race on Bish had fought here—except the underlings. Fights inside the Pit were ongoing, twenty-four seven. Many of the spectators were known to stay a week at a time. Others couldn't leave, they either owed the Royals too much, or they were addicted to the madness. That madness crept into Venir's bones.

The Pit itself was a simple setup. It was a six-foot deep and fifty-foot wide circle cut into a stone floor. Heavy iron bars were bolted into the lip of the stone circle and rose in a crisscross pattern over ten feet high. Two large grates on opposite ends of the ceiling allowed the contestants to drop inside. Venir had seen dwarves and halflings hang from the ceiling bars, legs dangling as they got their fingers smashed before falling to the pit floor. Broken legs and ankles were never a good thing. A man or woman needed every advantage they could find. A cripple stood little chance, but some had prevailed.

As he scanned the room, it appeared nothing had changed. Venir didn't have to struggle to remember the rules. They were simple: no weapons other than a single blunt weapon that hung from a chain in the middle of the cage.

The weapon varied; it could be a staff, a mace, a flail, or a big wooden club. Whoever got it first would often have the advantage, and once again, dwarves and halflings had a hard time jumping up to reach the weapon, especially with a busted ankle.

On the other side of the cage, Venir eyed a handful of the Royals from Two-Ten City. They were unlike any Royals in Bone. Most of the Royals on Bish were pure human, while the Royals in Two-Ten City were humanoid, but little human showed. Long ago, Two-Ten City had been pure human, until it was invaded by a multi-racial horde who usurped the city. They bred with the Royal humans by force and claimed to be Royals themselves. The other Royal families of Bish no longer recognized a Royal from Two-Ten City. They considered them a disgrace and a mockery of humankind, so Two-Ten City was left to fend for itself.

Venir stood along the rim of the cage with his comrades. Mikkel's light-hearted expression was as grim as he had ever remembered. Even Melegal seemed to shift uncomfortably by his side. The battle with Farc from so long ago was never as glorious as it had been portrayed. It had become a classic that had spread throughout the land, taking the shape of legend over the years. Farc was past his prime, and battered from an earlier fight. Venir just never allowed himself to admit that a desperate punch saved him from a crushed neck when he busted Farc's eye.

Mikkel nudged him with an elbow. Several more Royals now perched in their seats high above the pit. Their unpleasant faces were part-orc, gnoll, or ogre. There was some portion of humanity in all of them, maybe an eighth, or a quarter. They all were adorned in fashionable attire and gaudy jewels. Most had large eyes, flaring nostrils, rough skin, course hair, and iron jaws. They were bigger and more muscular, on average, but many mixed orcs sometimes looked very much like their pure human counterparts. It was the orcs that called the shots.

If there was uncertainty about whether one was more orc than human, the brash orcen personality would usually reveal the more prominent lineage. The more human, the more bearable in all cases, as the orcs were one of the strongest and ugliest races on Bish. Their stupidity was a marvel of its own accord. They all despised humans, and of course denied being any part other than orcen. Still, they tried to imitate humans as best they could. Humans were still tolerated in Two-Ten City. Someone had to keep the books and encourage order.

Venir turned his gaze inside the pit as a tall, heavy human dispatched a family of six halflings. The robed pony-tailed man seemed intent on breaking every bone he could in their tiny bodies. His strikes were hard and fast, and his movements as fluid as water. The crowd roared at the sounds of the man splintering bones. The crippled halfling family begged for mercy before they were finally dragged out of the cage. Orcen men tossed their broken bodies into a cart, and they were wheeled down another tunnel. Nikkel shuddered at his father's side. Mikkel whispered in his son's ear. He saw Nikkel mouth the words, *"I'll be all right."*

Bad memories swam inside Venir's head.

Melegal's hand slipped on his shoulder as he said in his ear, "Should I bet on this?"

"Why not?" Venir nodded. "One of us should enjoy himself." Melegal was already moving away as Venir added, "It's just my life."

Farc approached with a patch drawn over his eye, chin jutting in what could have been mistaken for a smile. The ogre leaned down and pointed into Venir's somber face. He spit with rotten breath as he spoke. "Tonight, Farc finally pay you back! Tonight, your eyes get smashed good!"

Farc flipped up his patch, revealing his crushed eye socket.

"Then you know what it like for Farc. Son of Farc bust you good. Every bit of you!"

Mikkel turned away, covering his nose, but Venir held Farc's gaze as his blood pumped harder behind his temples. "Whatever makes you happy, Farc."

Venir stood with his hands behind his back, glaring into Farc's milky eye.

"Time to get in … and die!" Farc said, breaking off his stare and seating himself with the Royals.

Now that the cage was being prepared, the room filled beyond capacity. The betting began. People craned their necks to get a look at the legend who had walloped Farc long ago. On top of the cage, two full-blooded orcs in studded leather armor opened the drop-down gates and beckoned for Venir. He strode to the cage and climbed the bars like an ape until he stood on top.

The crowd fell silent. The two armored orcs looked at one another and then at him. They were the same two that had badmouthed him the last time. Now they nodded and stepped aside. The crowd was full of puzzled looks. He could feel the inhuman Royals' burning gazes, and he shot them all a fiery glance. He spit, punched his fist into his hand, and hopped inside. The orcs slammed the cage door shut.

BANG!

The crowd erupted with jeers. Venir could feel the power in their blood-thirsty voices, but it wasn't for him. Then the chanting began.

"Son of Farc! Son of Farc! Son of Farc!"

The rafters shook with every lung-bursting syllable. Venir didn't remember hearing such cheers last time. He gritted his teeth and stared down the tunnel. A large head appeared, coming his way through the dim light. The crowd's roaring became deafening as the son of Farc stepped into full view. The ogre pumped his fists high in the air, stirring the frenzied crowd into another high. Being in the cage seemed like the safest place as scuffles broke out all around.

The son of Farc was much more ogre than his father. By the looks of things, the son of Farc was all ogre, but for his blue eyes. The part-ogre was the biggest Venir had ever seen, standing over seven feet tall and every bit of four hundred pounds. Venir swallowed hard and waited. Farc's son was more than a chip off the old block, rather the block itself.

The son of Farc had coarse black hair all over his half-naked body. His muscles were thick, his heavy brow protruded, and his legs were like solid oak trees. His nostrils flared wide under a fattened nose, and his shoulders had the girth of a bull's. All Farc's son wore were faded blue pants, tattered at the bottom, and a belt made out of hair. Farc had worn a similar belt, a variety of hair pulled from the heads of the ogre's vanquished opponents. Venir tied his long locks back. He had no desire to become a part of the ogre's strange trophy.

Son of Farc reached up, grabbed the upper rim of the cage, and bounded to the top. The ogre shoved the two armored orcs off the top, opened the drop-down gate, and jumped inside. Looking down at Venir, Farc's son displayed a smile full of rotting yellow teeth above his jutting jaw. Above, the orcs slammed the gate down and prepared to lower the weapon. But, as a morning star was about to be lowered, Farc, from the audience, made them stop, signaling "no weapon" with his fists in the air. The crowd booed and hissed, but then Farc's roar settled them down. This fight was to be bare knuckles, teeth, knees, elbows, you-got-it you-use-it; just the way it had been the last time.

It was all on Venir now. No help, no Brool, no choice. He cast a glance at his friends, who all looked worried. *Better me than them.*

He was dripping like a waterfall as he removed his sweat-soaked jerkin. He tried to shake the flow of blood into his fingers. He felt numb, lethargic and unprepared, but a twinge of anger was burning somewhere.

Voices in the crowd shouted about the big V-shaped tattoo on his over muscled back. *Vermin, Vulgar, Vile, Villain,* the mixed races screamed. *Victorious* said another, much to the laughter of the others. A few coins exchanged in favor of the man that had beaten Farc before. The son of Farc snorted, staring at his sneering father who stood on the balcony above.

Venir wasn't the less-experienced man Farc had fought years earlier. He was different—weathered, and frightening. Venir looked at his comrades, all pressed near the cage. Mikkel gave him a puzzled look, while Melegal gave him a meager thumbs up.

The crowds' voices became a manageable rumble as a gray-bearded dwarf sauntered over to a bronze gong as tall as an ogre. The ancient dwarf stared up at the Royals in the bleachers, hoisting the mallet high above his head. A tall orcen man, leaner than the rest, stood and raised his palms outward in the air. The crowd hushed. A handful of coins clinked onto the bleachers and rattled down. Venir's eyes locked on Farc's son. There was ice in the ogre's stare, and fire behind the ice. The rush of blood flowed behind Venir's ears. *Die doing something!*

The tall orc's palms knotted into big fists. Two long, hairy thumbs flicked upwards.

BONG!

In an instant, Venir sprang like a panther and punched Farc's son straight in the nose. The ogre's head rocked back with a notable crack, and first blood had been drawn. The roar of the crowd was a dull hum in Venir's pulsating ears.

The son of Farc held his broken nose, furious, swatting his long arms back and forth, and forcing Venir to dodge away. The ogre grinned, smearing the dripping blood with his forearm along his chin. Now, the ogre beckoned to the man with his finger. The crowd went wild. Venir's hand ached, and he realized it was going to be a hard and dirty fight.

The two circled each other, and the son of Farc made his move. He lunged in low with a powerful right upper cut. Venir ducked in and pounded a flurry of hard shots into the ogre's ribs. A man would have dropped like a sack of broken glass, but the ogre shoved him away.

The son of Farc circled, agile on his massive feet, then lunged once more. Venir dropped to a crouch, punching into the ogre's belly.

"Ooph!"

A rush of air burst out above him, and then a massive fist slammed down, glancing off his head and onto his neck and shoulder. Blinded by the shocking blow, Venir dropped to one knee. Two huge fists slammed into his shoulders like hammers, driving Venir to the ground. Pain exploded into his upper body as the crowd leapt to their feet. Venir sat on both knees, waiting as the son of Farc brought his mallet-like fists down again. Venir bolted up, catching both wrists, and rose up, staring the ogre in the face.

"You got nothin', human," the ogre said with a growl. "You gonna die."

Venir pushed the ogre back, its feet sliding in the dirt. Venir's bull neck was red, blue veins rising along his arms and back. Farc's son snarled, using his superior weight as leverage, bending Venir back. Venir squeezed the ogre's wrists and screamed. With a yank, he pulled the ogre down and inward, rolled onto his back, planted his feet in the ogre's belly, and launched him over his head. The son of Farc slammed into the rocky arena wall.

Mikkel and Nikkel jumped into the air as the ogre lay stunned on the floor.

Venir pounced on the ogre's back, raining down punches as hard as he could into his ribs and kidneys. Howling in pain and anger, the son of Farc tore himself away from the vicious onslaught. Venir lost his grip on the ogre's head of hair, dropped down, and crouched on the stony floor. He gasped. His legs felt wobbly, and his lungs were bursting.

The son of Farc stood before him, tall as a tree, clutching his side and spitting a mouthful of blood. One thing was for sure, the son of Farc was a lot tougher than his father. If Farc had not become overconfident, Venir might not have won that battle. It seemed Farc had certainly prepared his son well for this day.

Do something or die trying. Venir rushed back in, throwing powerful haymakers and uppercuts into every vulnerable spot on the ogre's body. The ogre returned in kind, and the apparent mismatch became a clash of titans. In a furious assault, the son of Farc struck, dodged, and countered. Venir was quicker and more precise, but the ogre took the pain and kept up the pressure. Frustration settled on the son of Farc's bewildered face as Venir's hammering blows raised knots on his body. Venir punched harder and harder, his hands feeling like they were about to break as the ogre's big arms absorbed most of his powerful blows. The son of Farc's massive fists swung all around as Venir dodged and ducked his head. His quickness and instincts saved him from punches that might have killed a lesser man. Stunned at what they were witnessing, the crowd squealed in delight.

Battered, bruised, and bloodied, the seconds began to feel like minutes. Venir was on the verge of collapse, his arms as heavy as lead. *Not going to make it.* The son of Farc had worn him down with sheer weight and endless strength. Suddenly, the ogre broke it off and backed away.

Venir gasped for air, clutching at his aching sides. The ogre's chest heaved while it clutched at its sides. Blood dripped in Venir's eyes from where the ogre's clawed fingers had ripped open the skin on his skull.

The son of Farc charged with a thunderous roar. Venir tried to dodge, but was barreled over and crushed into the ground. Something inside of him cracked, and he let out a yell of pain.

From beneath, he tried to break free of the big ogre's grapple and squirm away. The ogre's powerful grip held him fast. Venir was determined to wrestle his way out. He didn't hear Mikkel screaming at him, "NO!"

It was a mistake. There was an old saying in Bish, "Don't wrestle the ogre, wrestle the bear instead."

Outmatched under the ogre's weight, Venir's wrestling was fruitless, and something stabbed inside his chest. He was as good a wrestler as any man on Bish, but humans weren't the natural-born wrestlers that ogres were. Venir tried in vain to grab ahold of something, or pull away to escape.

The Son of Farc was relentless, countering every move as if he was one step ahead. Venir's strength sapped as his blood dripped to the ground in a steady stream. The half-ogre slammed him, belly first to the ground. *Bone!* The ogre grabbed his long hair in his hand and jerked his head back with a painful snap. He cried out. The crowd went wild, screaming for his blood. He caught a glimpse of his friends' shocked faces, now filled with internal anguish. Nikkel turned his head away.

The Son of Farc wrapped his arms under Venir's and locked his hands behind Venir's head. Venir was in a full headlock by the strongest creature he had ever known. *Slat! What have I done?* He forced his head backward against the growing pressure. The pressure in his corded neck kept building, and his nerves were on fire. He struggled as his chin bent down into his chest. He turned red with rage, his veins bulging like purple snakes. Every ounce of his strength was exhausted. He waited for the sound of his cracking neck. He wondered if that would be the final sound, or would it be the son of Farc laughing in his ear. Blood streamed out of his nose as his eyes rolled up in his head. *Better dying ....*

43

McKnight couldn't have been happier when the barge stopped and the dreadful journey that seemed to take an eon came to an end. The sound of rippling water and Tonio's raspy breath had worn on McKnight like a festering earache. Just when he was contemplating stabbing his own dagger into his ears, they arrived.

McKnight had never been more thankful for the ground below his feet as they climbed out of the barge and into a cave. The cool, gritty dirt clutched in his fingers might as well have been gold. The dark cave winded and twisted and there was light ahead, moonlight. Its orange light burned like sunshine to him. He enhanced his efforts, scraping over the shale and slime, welcoming the illumination.

The cave opened somewhere in the Outlands, but where exactly Detective McKnight could not be sure. It wasn't the Underland, and that was all that mattered. He studied the moon high above, calculating his position. It offered little comfort, but the terrain told him much more. Vegetation was not so sparse, trees and grass appeared near and more so in the distance. He surmised that they were far from the City of Bone. The detective basked in the light until a shadow blocked it out.

"Let's eat," Tonio said in a ragged voice.

It was the first words the man had spoken since they departed. McKnight wanted nothing more than to feed the man his sword. The blank expression on Tonio's torn face was almost as bad as the twisted grimace of the underling. Both men seemed unnatural to McKnight, but he kept his shudders to himself. He rubbed the pommel of his blade with his hand and watched their every move.

He shared a brief and tasteless meal of baked cornmeal and soured wine with Tonio, while Oran stared unmoving at the sky. McKnight watched as Oran began moving away from them.

"And where are you heading off to, underling?" asked McKnight as his daggers glinted in the moonlight.

Oran hissed and said, "At ease, human. I am not venturing out of sight. I have to call for some help to find the whereabouts of our … I mean, your prey. It would be wise to let me be so we can get this over with."

McKnight brushed the crumbs from his chest, sucked in a swish of wine, and ventured over by Oran's side. His tone was threatening as he said, "I don't trust you. What you have to do, you can do right here."

"Pah! Surely even you must know that I have nothing to gain at this point. You clearly have the advantage." Oran looked toward Tonio who was facing him as well, brandishing his longsword.

McKnight shook his head. *Ah yes, a mute swordsman that moves like a slug. How dangerous!* McKnight looked away from the Royal, pointing his dagger at the underling's neck.

"What kind of help are you calling on, Oran?" he asked. "I at least need to know what to expect."

"Since you insist, it is my familiar, an imp. You do know what an imp is?"

McKnight had not heard the word *imp* in decades. But he knew that imps were creatures mentioned in stories to scare children. It had never occurred to him that they might be real, but he was not going to let Oran know that.

"If an imp shows up here, underling, it had better not make any suspect moves, got it?" He flashed his daggers before Oran's eyes before stuffing them back into their sheaths.

Oran sighed.

"I only want this over. The imp won't bother you; just don't bother it."

"Do your summoning then, and tell us how long until the imp arrives," McKnight said, stepping away.

He was nervous and curious now. The stories he remembered described imps as wretched creatures, dangerous and wild. He drew his daggers and leaned against a tree. *Maybe it will kill Tonio.*

Oran sauntered off, but remained within sight. McKnight could hear the chaotic chirping that made his stomach sour. After a minute, Oran came back, head down, black eyes slack.

"Eep should be here any second, flying or just appearing, I cannot tell."

Tonio's ugly face scoured the sky, clutching his sword, while McKnight's eye stayed on the dark and frustrated underling.

Eep, bored with killing forest vermin, was relieved to receive a tingling summons from Oran. His master wasn't too far away for flying. Eep's wings buzzed to a shriek as he spit out a squirrel head and flew like lightning toward his master. *Finally*, the imp thought, *I can get this done and receive my due.*

Eep flew low over the plains, grazing the cactus tops, in a straight bead of flight toward the underling. His leathery wings buzzed like a thousand bees, cutting the air with a zipping sound that could be heard from a hundred yards.

Eep saw a man in his path, a large one holding out a sword. Why would a human—no, two humans—be with his master? Imps, for all their magic and power, were not known for complex thinking; they were impulsive creatures, creatures of action. They followed simple orders to attack and kill. *Master's in danger! Destroy!*

44

L ORD ALMEN HAD BEEN BUSY pursuing an additional investigation of his son's recent demise. He had already set things in motion to try and catch the person responsible for filling Tonio with inducers. He toyed with a garrote in his fists as he sat on the bed where Tonio had lain in recovery. How many men had died in his clutches on his rise to power? He remembered every face, castle, and name. He was subtle and swift, an assassin of high pedigree. Killing had gotten him everything he wanted … almost.

Now others did his dirty work, but the urge to mangle and torture another person still stirred inside him. He needed someone to take out his frustrations on. He needed it soon. He tossed the garrote on the bed, folded his hands behind his back, and headed up the stairs. His emboldened enemies would have to pay.

He simmered at the thought of the attempt to eliminate his son. Indeed, nothing intimidated one who had raised his house from the lowliest of Royal rankings to almost the very top. More than anything, he was insulted that the attempt appeared to have been made by an inferior house. The use of inducers was amateurish. Though rare and costly, they were child's play for any upper ranking Royal family or assassin. Whoever had used it was desperate.

Such evidence eliminated the houses ranked just ahead and behind his. But with almost unlimited resources at his disposal, Almen was confident of finding his answer soon. In the meantime, he played within his wondrous castle, entertaining people from near and far. The garden variety of guests came and went all hours of the day, some using different doors than others. Everyone was a suspect. Even in his own castle he had to be careful.

45

OBLIVIOUS TO ORAN'S LOUD PROTESTS, Eep dove into an attack on the lower legs of the large human brandishing the gleaming longsword. Tonio's downward thrust cut into the imp's flight path, nearly cleaving it in two. Eep barrel-rolled away, wings buzzing as the imp prepared another run. As Eep turned back toward Tonio, two daggers, hurled like streaks of lightning, caught him in mid-air. One dagger lodged in a wing, while the other found the imp's large eye. Eep fell to the ground, screaming in anger.

Tonio leapt to finish off the imp.

"*Charlonock!*" Oran bellowed.

The grass and foliage burst from the ground, coiling around Tonio's lower legs. The man let out a raging howl.

"Oran!" McKnight warned. "You had better not be double crossing me." The detective's sword tip dug into the underlings back.

Oran waved his hands about his head. "I'm not!" he yelled back over Tonio's clamor. "Just don't kill the stupid imp. He must have thought you were attacking me!"

A moment of silence fell as the two men watched the imp dislodge the dagger from its oozing eye. McKnight shivered and gaped as the imp slid the other from its wing. Nearby, Tonio struggled with the vines that grew back as quickly as he snapped them. The imp took a confident step their way, mouth wide, red tongue flickering in the air. McKnight pressed his sword tip deeper into Oran's back.

"Eep," Oran commanded. "Stay still!"

The imp froze; not a muscle moved. Tonio was on the verge of cutting off his own legs, hacking at the roots and dirt. The man's sword came up and sliced down. Oran looked over his shoulder at McKnight, who shrugged. Oran chittered another word and the foliage slunk back under the dirt.

Tonio lunged with his blade at the imp, who simply slipped through the air and away. It was perfect. McKnight wanted nothing more than to see the imp tear the man asunder.

"Call off your friend, human," Oran said with a snap. "The imp will not tolerate this aggression forever. They aren't the smartest creatures. My control of his rage has limits."

Whatever happens, happens, McKnight thought. Tonio chopped into the air like a blind man as the imp cackled and flew away. It went on for several agitating minutes, and then Tonio sheathed his sword and walked away. *Not the outcome I was hoping for.* However, with the immediate drama resolved, the natural tension among underling, imp, and humans resurfaced.

McKnight got them back to the subject of their journey.

"So, exactly how is this awful imp going to help us?"

Oran paused, twisting the black hairs on his head.

"I'll be brief, and maybe you will grasp it. Eep can travel from our dimension to his own, the magical dimension. But imps are not ordinary magical creatures. From their dimension they can see into ours, as if looking into a crystal ball."

McKnight fanned himself with his hat. *Preposterous.* "So, are you planning for the imp to find the people we're tracking?"

"Unless he has already."

McKnight was surprised. "Continue."

"Eep, catch us up on what you've found out so far."

Eep lead the small, miserable party south, playing question-and-answer with Oran and McKnight, while Tonio strode slack-jawed at the rear. McKnight found the conversation with the imp as intimidating as it was fascinating.

"Two humans and a donkey, you say, entered Two-Ten City?" repeated McKnight. "Did this donkey seem capable of killing Tonio? Was it a rare, killer donkey, perhaps, distinguishable from a normal donkey?" He couldn't help himself, as his indifference for the spoiled Royal seemed to grow with every step.

Eep eked out a few more details. It left McKnight with little to go on, except that the people they sought *might* be in Two-Ten City. Hundreds of other humanoids traveled in and out of that city each day. He was not confident that they could find the right people, and time was pressing. He wanted this over with.

"All of that imp blather and that is all you have. Eep thinks he saw them enter Two-Ten City. Certainly the powerful underlings rely on better resources than this."

Of course, a visit to Two-Ten City wouldn't be bad about now. After all, they made the best mead in all of Bish.

Oran's glassy black eyes twinkled in the moonlight. He said, "I shall send Eep ahead to find who he is talking about. I have a spell that allows us all to see what he sees. This will have to do. It would have helped if Tonio could have given a better description than just, *Vee-man.* Go, Eep!"

In a violent buzz, the imp blinked out of sight. McKnight's spine tingled. *I should have been a mage.*

"Now, McKnight, I need your word that you will not interfere with my spell casting."

"My word, underling. Anything to get this over with."

Oran stepped away and closed his eyes. McKnight felt the air thicken as the underling muttered an incantation under his breath. Several minutes passed, and then his spell began to take form. Colors exploded before his eyes, sparkling, fading, swirling, and popping in and out like the crackling of hot embers in a fireplace. McKnight was enthralled; he would be much more mindful of Oran's abilities from now on.

The collage of colors began to take on a shape in the air before him, forming an oval boundary enclosing a black space. A blurry picture formed from what seemed to be inside of the imp's single eye. Then the barrier of the eye vanished, and in its place, everything the imp could see, they could see.

Tonio mumbled, "Wuh."

McKnight was high above trees and hills, then streaking towards the ground below. He hovered above a city where he could see the people coming and going. Then, through the city he zipped, viewing sight after sight in an instant.

Flashing before his eyes were humanoids of all kinds doing all sorts of things—much of which seemed indecent or inhumane—and in just a few moments he had toured most of the city. A lump formed in his throat as his gaze passed straight through beasts and buildings, and after many moments the images began to slow and settle. McKnight felt a wave of nausea. The image settled inside an old tavern that appeared deserted, except for a band of misfits playing music.

McKnight looked down a stairwell and into a corridor that opened into a wide arena. He knew this place. *The Pit.* All types of humanoids were gathered and whooping it up. It was odd to watch such a thriving sight and not hear a sound. *Is this how the deaf feel? Pity.* McKnight tried to read the lips of those he saw. *Farc.* The people chanted. His blood turned cold. He recognized Melegal. *What's that little rat doing there? It looks like he's having a bad time. Must be losing money. Good.*

"Well done, Oran," McKnight said in a disgruntled voice as the spell faded and the image paled.

The fading picture went toward the inside of an iron cage. A large, hairy ogre had an overgrown man locked up and was forcing his neck down. A big V-shaped tattoo was visible on the man's back.

"Vee-man!" screamed Tonio, diving straight through the image and into a tree with a tremendous thud.

The spell fizzled out with a flash as Oran let out a heavy sigh.

"Like I was saying, Oran, well done!" McKnight said as he began to chuckle. "Bone of a good job! I think we've found who we're looking for. And it would appear that this Vee-man is practically dead already."

With relief, McKnight could see his mission nearing its end. But there was another thing. *Melegal! Why isn't that worm dead?*

46

I T WAS NOT THE CHOKING hold of the son of Farc that was to be Venir's final memory. It was the blackness, the sinking into unconsciousness in his last gasping moments of desperation. Venir's colleagues, Mikkel, Nikkel, and Melegal, all cried out in horror as his rigid body started to slacken. An odd silence settled on the battle arena as the excitement in the air changed from a blasphemous hostility to a collective shiver. All awaited the sound of the son of Farc snapping Venir's neck. All the faces faded to black, and the roaring sounds muted.

Farc's son yelled something in his ear. The ogre strained, bending the iron muscles in his thick neck. If Venir was still fighting, he didn't know what with. He was oblivious to the breathless crowd. Something stirred deep inside him. A black, suffocating hole opened up in his mind. Sounds of chittering underlings filled his ears. Evil. Mocking. Laughing.

His life rushed past his eyes, the moments of promise destroyed by the masses of underlings. They killed family, friends, innocent men, and beasts. He recoiled. Images of Chongo, fish, Georgio, and silver flashed in his mind, and a volcano erupted inside him.

The ogre wrapped his mighty arms around his head, ready to apply his final spine-shattering twist to Venir's neck. The crowd was wild-eyed. The Royals of Two-Ten were on their feet. At any second that resounding *crack* would come, or had they just not heard it? They peered deeper into the caged arena, lips pursed, knees bent and arms half raised. And then the crowd saw Venir's body flex and stiffen. He growled in rage. His white eyes snapped open. The crowd went into an uncontrollable frenzy.

Venir's work on Bish wasn't finished.

NO! He remembered the most hated and despised moment in his violent life; the day that he, an innocent boy, was supposed to die in a ditch. The rage had come upon him then for the first time. And now that rage, an unforeseen creation of the underlings, was triggered along with something else. A spark ignited inside him. His blood coursed through his veins like liquid lightning. From the inside out, he grew.

Venir lurched up, his bloodshot eyes rolling up in his head, his face turning purple. As the crowd looked on, fear and excitement surged through every one of them. Venir fought himself into a sitting position. The son of Farc continued to crank up his hairy forearm around his neck.

"NO!" Venir spat.

He shook in unfettered fury, his rage and blood lust blocking all rational action. Only his instinct to survive was thinking, and that kind of thought meant destroying whatever he saw. His elbows hammered into the half-ogre's ribs, causing the son of Farc's grip to slip. Bellowing in objection, the ogre kept trying to squeeze the life out of him. The pressure was unrelenting, but Venir wouldn't give way. The ogre's wind waned. The Darkslayer sensed it.

"Get him, Venir!" shouted Nikkel, his excited young voice shattering the moment of spellbound silence.

"Go Vee!" Melegal and Mikkel yelled in unison.

"VEE! VEE! VEE!"

The name rang out as the crowd throughout the arena rejected their own champion. The human haters' faces turned to outrage at the impossible sequence of events.

He was on his knees now, struggling back to his feet. The son of Farc draped over his back, dead weight trying to force him back to the ground. Venir continued his rise, legs shaking from the effort. Every muscle on the son of Farc strained as Venir's corded muscles knotted all over his body. The son of Farc shouted in defiance, but Venir surged on. Venir's legs sprung upward. He charged toward the stone wall of the arena, dragging the clinging half-ogre with him. Ducking, he slammed the man-beast's head into the hard rock.

The thrust jarred the ogre. Chips of stone hit the floor. A nasty gash opened on the ogre's head, and blood gushed over his face and hairy arms.

Venir dragged the stunned ogre toward the other side of the arena, repeating the same tactic with another tremendous effort. The son of Farc's grip slipped away. Venir backed away from his opponent, fists clenched, feeling ten feet tall.

The crowd was split. Fights broke out all around the arena. None was more shocked than Farc. In disbelief, he waded unnoticed through the fracas toward the arena. Inside the cage, an enraged man was about to give the Farc family their just due. Farc looked determined to not see that happen.

The son of Farc rose back to his feet as the two warriors charged each other. The son of Farc tried to pound Venir's body back down, but he didn't feel a thing. He would have none of it. He was far too quick for the sluggish ogre to land a solid hit. Venir's energized punches were like mallets driving spikes through the ogre's body. Son of Farc groaned under every blow.

Venir could not hear the rising crescendo of the crowd, but he smelled the blood of the ogre as it began spitting it up. The ogre's rock-hard ribs snapped and cracked like twigs, and its energy was all but dissipated. Then the son of Farc's legs wobbled; his head rolled on his slumped shoulders as he fell. Venir sensed the kill and went for it.

Smash!

Venir's head was rocked from behind by the big fist of the once mighty Farc. Venir reeled from the blow and fell, rolling backward before he leapt back onto his feet. The ogre father now stood between him and the ogre son.

Farc shouted, blocking him with his hands.

"Stop!"

Venir came at him.

"Stop!" Farc pleaded louder, once more.

It would have been easier to make such demands of the wind.

The son of Farc, in a heap behind his father, struggled to regain his feet. The movement seized the heightened instincts of Venir. His prey was alive still, not dead. He charged and leapt into the massive body of Farc, crushing his last good eye socket with a devastating haymaker and shattering his jaw with a knockout. Farc fell face first onto the bloodstained stone floor.

The son of Farc's face turned into a pit of fire as he gazed upon his fallen father. He charged Venir, attempting to bowl him over once more, but Venir didn't care. He braced himself, latched onto the enemy's large head and neck, and squeezed so hard that the son of Farc made a noticeable choking sound.

Venir heaved with all his remaining strength, turning the ogre's head purple. He wasn't letting go. The son of Farc's legs kicked, and his body twisted, but to no avail. Venir had full control of his opponent this time, forcing it to drop to his knees. The crowd watched as the remorseless man cranked it up, squeezing with all of his might. His muscles popped out all over his sweaty and blood-soaked body.

No one imagined that he could possibly choke the ogre out, for it had never been known to happen, nor did it. Instead, something else that had never happened … happened. As the son of Farc roared, his voice was cut off by a sound never heard before in the Pit.

CRACK!

His neck broke in the arms of the berserk human warrior. So far as anyone remembered, an ogre's neck had never been broken.

It was over. A huge silence overcame the stunned crowd. Before their eyes, the man who had pulled off the improbable five years earlier had, this day, pulled off the impossible. When the cage was opened again and Venir climbed out, a frenzied chant erupted.

"VEE! VEE! VEE!"

47

HALFLINGS WERE FAST. TO HAVE survived on Bish with such feeble bodies, there had to be magic in the feet of the halfling race. So the people would say. No matter how dire their situation, somehow halflings managed to move fast enough to survive.

But other than being quick and hardy, halflings were considered little more than an occasional inconvenience. They were amusing little people who traveled with caravans or in small nomadic packs, fetching supplies as needed. Often, they would not leave a person alone until they had traded whatever it was they had for whatever it was they wanted. People would take what they neither wanted nor needed just to see them gone. It was as if halflings could talk people into letting themselves be robbed. Yet, there was much more to these little people.

Georgio was bored. He missed the city—the sights, the sounds, and the mouth-watering food. His parents wouldn't pay him for his chores like Venir did. Then again, there weren't any biscuits or fruity pie for him to buy with his tiny coins, either. He huffed as he walked along a creek bank after abandoning his usual chores. The tall reeds of grass and patches of woods gave him the privacy he needed. The small village was a hive of nosy old women and smelly old men.

Heedless of his parents' warnings, he found time to play. He was deep in his own fantasy in the forest, imitating his hero, Venir. Equipped with his own hand axe, Georgio tossed it with surprising accuracy into a tree. Suddenly, he heard a rustle. He turned just as a little blond head slammed into his chest and knocked him to the ground.

Georgio studied the halfling in puzzlement. He had never seen one up close before. The sight of this little blond halfling fidgeting in a panic made him giggle.

"Human, what you are laughing at?" the halfling said, eyes darting all around.

The sound of the halfling's tiny voice turned Georgio's giggles into an eruption of laughter. The halfling turned and walked away, head down, little hands stuffed inside the tiny pockets of his pants. Georgio scrambled up, still laughing, and followed, but slipped on the slick embankment and fell into the creek. He climbed back out, chuckling with a mouthful of water as the halfling kept going.

"Stop!" called Georgio. "Stop—please!"

The halfling boy stopped and turned. Georgio got a closer look at the dark rings around the halfling's sagging blue eyes, and his heart sank. "I'm sorry for laughing," he said as he lumbered over to the tiny person and took a knee. "I've just never met a halfling before. He held out his hand. "I'm Georgio!"

The halfling extended his little hand that fit just inside Georgio's meaty palm. "I'm Lefty Lightfoot, sir. I need help. We all do! There's great danger!"

Lefty slumped to the ground and started crying. It made Georgio want to cry as well, but he sat down and patted the back of the tiny, weeping boy.

48

FEW LIVING THINGS SURVIVED IN the wake of the Vicious-led Badoon brigade. The evil that radiated from the Vicious stifled the life force of lesser living things. But despite the path of devastation—where most vegetation and small vermin lay dead—the Badoons did not kill every living thing along their route.

This unusual migration of strong life forces on Bish sent creatures fleeing and sparked alarm across the Outlands. The disturbance reached Dwarven Hole, a little known place that was as ancient as Bish itself. It was home of the dwarves and the giant dwarves, known as the Blood Rangers.

The Blood Rangers were great hunters that thrived in seclusion. They lived within Dwarven Hole, protecting their kind. Few other races, if any, had ever seen a Blood Ranger, for there were only one hundred. Their hold was buried deep in the plains of Bish, north of the Underland. Dwarven Hole was practically a secret, and the dwarves liked to keep it that way.

At this moment, no more than ten miles separated the Badoon brigade and the Blood Rangers. The giant dwarf rangers had been privy to the activity and movements of the Badoon within hours of their departure, and though the dwarves most often stayed in isolation, the Blood Rangers had often been involved in defending Bish and its peoples. It seemed that another such time was on the horizon.

49

DESPITE BEING BEATEN WITHIN AN inch of his life, Venir somehow mustered more than enough energy to entertain himself. The bodacious part-orc woman he had flirted with minutes before stepping into the cage with the son of Farc had scurried him away. His animal instincts had been awakened, and Dolly, the entertainer, was eager to oblige.

He lay inside the stone walls of her candlelit chambers, sprawled out on her big, round bed. Dolly stood before him in a tight black dress with a deep slit that showed off her muscular thighs. Another deep slit plunged down the front to show her full and swelling chest. Lust shielded him from any decent thought he ever had.

As Venir lay down amid comforting pillows, Dolly pursed her puffy lips and blew out some of the candles. She brushed her long straw locks away from her batting eyes. A giggle burst from behind her snaggled teeth. It wasn't the worst face he'd seen, and far from the prettiest, but Dolly's body could make an old dwarf cry. Standing before him, she let her dress slide slowly to the floor. He pulled her onto the bed, crushed her into his arms, and ravished her all night long.

Early the next morning he was having breakfast with Melegal, Mikkel, and Nikkel inside the tavern. The aroma of baked dough, eggs, and sausage filled the air, and Venir ate enough for ten men. All were quiet, including the usual patrons of the tavern. The buzz of the battle had dissipated, yet the lingering silence seemed unnatural. Venir washed down another biscuit, then clonked his wooden cup on the table.

"All right, out with it! Why is everyone acting like they're eating with a ghost?"

Mikkel met Venir's eyes and glanced away.

"I thought you were dead," Melegal answered. "The fact that you aren't isn't easy to understand. Don't get me wrong, Venir, but I don't quite follow how you survived last night."

Venir took a deep breath and winced. His ribs were sore. He had felt them crack in the iron cage, he was certain. He shouldn't be up and about, and he knew it, but here he was, just like any other day. He sipped his coffee and helped himself to some more bread and scrambled eggs. Melegal's question was fair, but it wasn't something he could explain. He remembered the feeling of dying, something inside slipping away as the cold grip of death was on him. Then somewhere deep, a spring of energy rushed through him like a crashing wave and his body crackled like fire. It was something he didn't understand.

Mikkel forced a broad smile and added, "You must have wanted Dolly pretty bad, huh, Vee?"

They all gave a half- hearted chuckle.

"Venir?" Nikkel asked, his curious eyes staring, head cocked. "How come you're bigger now?"

"What do you mean, Nikkel?" his father asked.

"Why, he's bigger, he's taller. How come?"

"You know," said Melegal, looking perplexed, "when you came down here, I thought something was off. I figured it was all the swelling, but … stand up, Vee. I think Nikkel's onto something."

Venir shrugged, pushed himself back from the table and stood up.

"Mikkel, stand back to back with Vee."

Mikkel obliged.

"Don't tell me he's taller than me now, Melegal."

"Well, no … but he's the same height!"

"What!? Turn around, Vee," Mikkel ordered.

Venir turned and met Mikkel eye to eye.

"You have grown. I think I saw it happen!" said Melegal. "I mean, when you were in the ring making your escape from the son of Farc … I thought you grew that moment. Your entire body lurched like it was hatching from a shell. The whole room shuddered. I felt it. You are bigger, no doubt about it!"

Mikkel's voice was distant.

"I never heard of anything like that before."

Venir had. This wasn't the first time, either. He sometimes thought the armament had something to do with it, but it had happened long before that. Bish offered plenty of strange things no one cared to investigate, so why should he?

Venir grinned and said, "It's happened to me before actually, when I was a child."

Everyone sat back at the table and pulled their chairs in.

He continued: "When I was a boy, I caught a fish … a silver fish. Nothing like I'd ever fished before. I was hungry, so instead of taking it home with the rest, I ate it. It was the most wonderful thing I ever tasted. Sometimes when I burp, I swear I can still taste it. The next day, my grandfather said I was bigger. I grew overnight."

"That's amazing! I want some silver fish, too!" said Nikkel

Melegal then asked, "So did Chongo eat some, too?"

"Yes, but he didn't grow and get his second head until a long time after that."

"Are you pulling our legs, Vee?" asked Mikkel.

Still grinning, he replied, "Maybe."

"Aw!" Mikkel got up and walked away. Melegal rolled his eyes. They finished their meal without another word about it.

The next day, early in the morning, the small group of friends began to part ways. Nikkel fetched Quickster, and the two adventurers headed north out of Two-Ten City. To Venir's embarrassment, Dolly came running out, begging him to take her with him and causing a scene that caught the fancy of everyone within a hundred yards.

Somehow, Venir managed to break away, whispering, "I'll be back for you one day."

Dolly fell for it long enough for him to speed off out of sight. Mikkel's laughter was audible all the way out of the city, while Nikkel waved goodbye to his father with a sad look in his eyes.

Melegal was still chuckling when he came upon the same smart-aleck orc boy he had encountered on the way in. Melegal locked eyes on the boy and scowled, causing the boy to tremble and run off.

"Is there any chance," Melegal said, breaking the odd silence, "that could be Dolly's boy?"

Venir didn't reply. His shameful closed-door encounter with Dolly was still sinking in. The thief had a fair point that he hadn't ever considered. In the past, he had never given such things a moment's thought. But today, for some reason, he began to ask himself some searching questions. Venir's head was downcast as he vowed never to return to Two-Ten City again.

From high above, Eep's magic eye stared down on the warrior and the thief. Oran and McKnight were keeping a close watch, having convinced Tonio to gather firewood.

"I can't believe that big, tiresome human is still alive," hissed Oran as the swirling, scintillating colors at the edge of the vision began to fade.

"He must have had help," said McKnight.

The two paused, trying to imagine what they might be up against.

"Did you see that ugly orc woman? I find it hard to imagine that he ..." McKnight couldn't bear the thought. He knew Two-Ten City had much better to offer.

"Clearly, you do not get around Bish much, human. You are rather sheltered in your City of Bone. Two-Ten is the most normal city. You should visit it," said Oran as he examined his long black nails. "You will be a changed man."

"No thanks! I've been there before, and I have a pretty good idea why I left." McKnight flicked a stick into the campfire. "Unlike your kind, I see no need to maintain sub-human standards."

"The human heart is as wicked as the rest ... even yours," commented Oran.

"Maybe so, but at least it's human. Now let's cut the chat. We have about a day to wait until they show up. In the meantime, let's go over our plans again, because getting that over-sized menace back to Bone alive won't be easy. Are you sure you and Tonio can handle it? I'm quite sure I can dispatch his friend," McKnight said as he slung one of his daggers, impaling a squirrel to a tree.

Oran said, "I have Eep, remember? He will tip the scales in our overwhelming favor."

"Good," said McKnight. He gathered his blade and prepared to skin the squirrel. He held the vermin in his face and looked it in the eye. "Ah, Melegal, what a nice little fur coat you have," he said as he crushed it in his hand.

50

THE OMNIPOTENT SCORCH HAD EXISTED longer than most all eternal beings. But to Scorch it did not matter how long he had been there; it mattered only that he existed. Unlike many of his counterparts in the universe, he had no assigned realm of responsibility, for he pre-existed even that.

He had dealt with his eternal frustration long before most infinite beings arrived. He told them—*There is no end*—but they did not listen. So he made the most of his situation by doing whatever he wished. Time and time again, his meddling led to the demise or the enlightenment of other worlds and their civilizations. And now Bish was to become his latest exploit as he tossed one additional ingredient into Trinos's secret stew. Bish would never be the same.

51

THE WINDS ON BISH WERE brisker than normal, but not as refreshing as one might expect. The change was strange. The typical warm and dry season was replaced with something else. Venir's thoughts had been elsewhere for most of the journey since leaving Two-Ten City. For whatever reason, he wasn't himself. Instead, he tried to somehow distance himself from his past.

Lost in his memories, Venir had all but forgotten that Melegal was behind him when Quickster sneezed, jolting Venir back to the present.

"Ah ... did Quickster startle the deep-thinking lout?" Melegal said with snicker. "You're not even humming a tune. What's going on in that thick skull of yours, Venir?"

"Uh, just thinking back to when things were different, is all."

"You mean, before Brool?"

"Yeah, but not just that."

Melegal remembered those days, too. But that had all come and gone, and Venir was able to move on, as most people did in Bish. Few dwelled upon the past, although long journeys could cause a man to reflect from time to time.

"Two-Ten City stirred you up, didn't it? But I think we've had as much good luck as bad there. I mean, you wrestled an ogre and lived—you should be happy. I'm glad for you," Melegal said.

"Bet you are, thief," Venir said, managing a smile. "And where's my share of the winnings?"

"In due course, Vee. You gotta get me back to Bone first. Now, quit thinking so much. You're gonna hurt yourself."

Venir nodded as he remembered the exact moment it had happened, that he had become the Darkslayer. He could remember the sweltering weather and the sight of the setting moons glowing in the dawn. On that day, life on Bish had opened up like a black cave and swallowed him like a drop of water. He didn't regret it, for somehow it had helped him survive, again and again. It took him a moment before he realized Melegal was still talking to him.

"Why are we heading this way, Venir?" Melegal sat sideways on his saddle. "Not that I mind heading back this way. I think the stench of the marsh has finally cleared my nose."

There was a pause. He didn't really have an answer. Venir replied in a somber voice, "I don't think it makes much difference which way we go."

Melegal cocked his head as he fanned himself with his hat.

"Really? It's barely a week since we left home, but if we're going back, shouldn't we go straight? Why northwest instead of north?" The thief turned forward in his saddle, spurring Quickster along his side. "Surely there are other northward paths we can take that aren't the same as the one we took southward?"

"This way we'll catch Mood and Chongo quicker. I have a feeling he's gonna be this way. He won't be expecting us so soon, so he's unlikely to be at our original rendezvous. Besides, I need to try and track what I can. It's not as easy to do without Chongo, though. It'll be harder to find them on our own."

"Well, that was a mouthful, considering you're not drunk," Melegal said. "That's more words than you've said all day."

Venir realized his friend was attempting to lighten the dour mood, but it did little. He was dead inside. Things hadn't felt right since he left Two-Ten City. He felt different. The weather had changed. Grimness had settled over him like a damp quilt. It was not an overwhelming feeling, but bad enough. Something was wrong. He kept scanning the sky, the small suns burning like ghostly beacons behind a patch of rolling clouds ahead. The heat seemed to sizzle his neck, but there was something else.

Venir jogged with determined footfalls, crunching down a path in the tall grass.

"Eh …" Melegal said, watching him go and shaking his head, then trotting along behind.

In the distance, a wall of thickened forest lay. Tall treetops bunched together for miles across from east to west. Dark clouds seemed to sit on the gray treetops with rays of sunlight breaking through and displaying bright splotches of green leaves here and there. Flocks of birds swooped by the hundreds, disappearing in and out of the clouds. Venir slowed his brisk pace and eyed the thundering sky.

"Something's ahead. I can't quite say what, but I feel it might be waiting for us." Venir pulled a canteen from Quickster's saddle, bringing a soft neigh from the beast.

"Well, should we venture in, or find another way?" Melegal took the canteen Venir offered him and had a sip. "Do you think it's Royals?"

Shaking his head, Venir twisted the cap back on the canteen and said, "I think whatever it is will find us anyway. Maybe it already has, so let's take the fight to it. Or sneak past it."

Shaking his head, Melegal sighed and forged on ahead. They had traveled a few miles farther when Melegal asked, "Which forest is ahead of us, anyway?"

"That, my friend, is the Great Forest of Bish. Its trees are triple the girth and height of any other trees on Bish. It's spectacular. It's actually twice as far away as it appears. And those birds you see are pretty large, too. Don't get spooked, though. Travelers make it through, on the whole. Well, in most cases." Venir allowed himself a slight smile.

"Man, one day nothing, then the next it's talk, talk, talk."

The sound of Melegal's complaining voice made him feel better.

"Maybe you should write it down. Of course, there isn't enough paper in Bish once you get going, story teller," Melegal said, snapping the reigns.

"Hmm, I like that idea."

"Uh … maybe you should start acting like the brute you are and stop blathering. That ogre must've squeezed something loose in you. Did he finally get the blood flowing in your thick skull?"

Maybe he did, thought Venir.

Melegal checked his equipment. Encounters were something the thief fought hard to avoid. It would have bode him well over the years if he had more reservations like the thief, but that just wasn't in him. He was always go, go, go.

Venir started his jog again, straight ahead toward the Great Forest of Bish. Action was better medicine than talking. But the Great Forest left him uneasy, more so than Red Clay Forest. At least there was shade in the trees, but the suns kept your enemies from creeping up on you.

52

L ORD ALMEN'S STOOD, ARMS CROSSED, with two henchmen on either side. With satisfaction, he watched the torture of a member of another Royal family from a discreet location far away from his palace walls. Two others also witnessed the torment of one man who had assisted in Tonio's fall.

The tormentor was none other than Sefron. The flabby, half-naked cleric had just finished dripping drops of acid on the wailing man's toes. The other witness, a mysterious man named Teku who was no newcomer to dispensing pain, stood alongside Lord Almen. He was taller than the Royal lord, olive skinned, and dressed from head to toe in loose, nondescript white robes that draped over his fingers. His brush-green eyes were intelligent and deep.

Lord Almen smiled at the man from time to time as they exchanged elegant words back and forth. Sefron sneered when they weren't looking his way. Teku's voice was deep and soft, and his body as still as calm water. He smiled along with Lord Almen, and his sharpened white teeth shone like pearls in the torchlight.

The leather-bound prisoner was from the Slerg house, a once prominent house that had fallen from the ranks of the city's hierarchy. Lord Almen knew their story quite well, for it was he who had led them to their fall. Now, the Royal Slerg's vengeful tactics had caught up with him, and he was to be another sacrifice of the Slerg family.

The tortured man laughed at the sight of Sefron opening another vial. He had already told them everything, almost.

"Curse you, Lord Almen!" the man said as spit dribbled down his chin. "Payback's coming!"

Sefron's sweaty face looked back, but Lord Almen remained stone-faced as he gave his final nod.

53

MOOD RESTED UNDERNEATH THE LEAFY branches of the Great Forest of Bish. A steady breeze swept through his blood-red beard as he wondered how his friends were doing. Chongo was sleeping, small snorting noises coming from his nostrils, while Mood leaned back against a tree wider than twenty bunched men. He stretched his arms and propped up his stout legs on Chongo.

All the while, he was smoking a rolled-leaf cigar of the dwarven kind. The rare leaves burned slowly around the tobacco that was harvested unseen in the caves of the dwarves back home. The smoke from his bearded lips was light blue. It hung in the air like a ghost before the breeze took it away. Mood's mouth opened wide as he yawned. The cigar was the only thing that caused that. A dwarf like him wasn't accustomed to fatigue, no, not the king of the Blood Rangers.

The forest was his escape from the massive holes that confined his pressing people. His kin always seemed to do well without him, so he roamed. Why not, he was the king? But today, neither the powerful narcotic of his dwarven cigar, nor the rich green mossy forest with its gentle plant life and blooms were able to take the edge from his mind. At length, the ears of the double-headed mastiff perked up—one pair anyway, while the other remained asleep. Mood's blurry eyes showed a sliver of green beneath his brows, for he, too sensed that something—maybe dangerous—was amiss.

He nudged the dog with his boot.

"Let's go, Chongo."

Chongo rolled up on all fours, one head still sagging down as the pair slipped through the forest like an apparition. Mood felt small as he negotiated the enormous forest. The plant life was gargantuan. A single leaf could shield you from the heavy rains. He almost liked it as much as Red Clay Forest, where he was the most at home.

The Great Forest of Bish was open to all comers. It wasn't as particular as the others, it seemed too big for the smaller matters of life that surrounded it, but sometimes the wrong creature would bother the forest, intentionally or not, and the ramifications were often fatal.

Mood took a long sniff of the air. He had a feeling something was about to happen. He hoisted himself on Chongo's back. There he sat in thick canvas-like clothes of brown and green, two giant-hand axes forming an X across his back, wearing high, soft leather boots, and a large belt pouch containing various requirements. He blew half a dozen smoke rings in the air as Chongo's thick muscles shifted under his seat. Both necks rose on the dog, all four ears alert. Mood rubbed each thick neck and said, "Let's go get 'em, boy."

54

GEORGIO HAD STOPPED TO PEE. His feet ached and he was leagues away from his village, east of the Great Forest of Bish.

"Run! Run! Run!" Lefty Lightfoot said, running Georgio's way at full speed.

"Wait! What's going on?" Georgio hollered, struggling to stop in midstream and getting splashed as he turned. "See what you've made me do … again!" He pulled up his britches and started to run. "What are we running from, Lefty? We need to keep westward."

Lefty's hands were in a frantic wave. "No! Come, or we'll be eaten!"

Georgio had already seen the little halfling panic several times over nothing in their brief travels to find Venir. The poor little boy couldn't sleep a wink. Georgio pitied him, but it was becoming annoying.

"Will you stop a second and tell me what you're talking about?"

Any creature seemed to spook the halfling, but the curly-headed Georgio was beginning to gain Lefty's trust.

Lefty stopped and tugged at his wrist. "It's a gigantic two-headed beast with a huge red man-thing! Run!"

The poor halfling's ashen face almost broke Georgio's heart, and he had to bite his tongue to keep back the giggles that had offended Lefty earlier. He stuck out his chest. "I'll handle the beast. Don't fear, Lefty. I'll protect you!" Georgio patted his shoulder, turned, and pulled out his hand axe, leaving Lefty frozen in his tracks. The past few days had left the poor halfling not knowing what to expect.

Lefty let Georgio talk him into heading back the way they had come. Lefty thought the human was a fool, but the boy had been convincing. Now the prolonged wait began to cause further doubts. Lefty's feet became clammy as his eyes darted all around. Was he wrong about what he had seen? Then he heard something, and his hairs stood on end.

Lefty froze with fear in his hiding place among the great trees. The forest seemed so still and quiet that his heartbeat was all he heard. Nearby, Georgio stood in a clearing with his broad shoulders beginning to slouch. Georgio turned and walked back toward him, his hand axe swinging back and forth at his side. The big boy had a look of disappointment on his face. It did little to comfort Lefty.

The closer Georgio came toward him, the more Lefty knew something was about to happen. He imagined a pair of massive jaws jumping out to devour the boy at any moment. The bright day had dimmed, leaving the forest cast in an eerie darkness. *What is he doing?* Lefty thought. *We must run!*

Salty sweat dripped into his eyes, and he dabbed them with a handkerchief. Lefty bit his nails as he looked at the boy with horror. *Here it comes!* He wanted to scream for Georgio to run, but the boy kept walking, in circles now, his eyes to the ground. *Oh, look up, stupid man!*

He's going to die, and so am I. Georgio looked up and around and their eyes locked. Georgio smiled. Lefty felt a moment of relief, but then Georgio froze in his tracks. Lefty felt hot breath on the nape of his weensy neck, and he couldn't move as a warm gob splashed down his spine. *Oh my!* Somehow, he turned.

Facing him were four huge eyes, two heads, two massive sets of teeth, and above those a giant hairy red man-thing. Lefty's limbs froze. He would soon be dead.

Squeezing his eyes shut, he managed to stammer, "Eat me. Please get it over with."

His fate came in the form of two soaking licks and an uproarious laugh and Georgio shaking his shoulders saying, "It's all right. It's all right."

"I'm dead, aren't I?" he said, shivering with a squeak.

"No!" Georgio answered. "We're saved!"

Lefty cracked open his eyes and saw the blood-red beard in his face, then fainted before his new friends.

"Now ain't that somethin'," Mood said, scratching his head. "He sure is tiny, even for a halfling."

"He is?" Georgio exclaimed.

Mood just shrugged and grabbed Georgio under his armpits, dropping him onto Chongo's saddle.

"What's going on? Where's Venir?"

A big hand clamped over Georgio's mouth.

"Hush boy."

He hated it when people did that, but thought the better of taking a bite from Mood's hand.

Mood looked upward and Georgio did, too. Thunder rolled overhead, but he hadn't noticed it before. The forest began to darken as Mood picked up the limp halfling and put him in Georgio's arms. Something made Georgio shiver as he felt the halfling boy's ice-cold skin.

"Mood, I want to go home now. My friend needs help."

"It's too late for that, boy."

The Blood Ranger grabbed the reigns and led them deeper into the Great Forest of Bish. Georgio's head kept twisting around, noticing many other odd sounds and movements coming from above them. "I hope Venir's in there," he whispered.

55

V ENIR MOVED AHEAD AT A slow run. One setting sun had dipped below the horizon while the other began to sink behind the treetops of the Great Forest. The man was only focused on what lay ahead. Melegal wasn't so determined.

The incongruity in the distance made for a strange sight. The treetops were thrice as high as normal, casting an early shadow over the grassy plain. Venir ran ahead, picking up his pace. He had emptied his arsenal from his sack, except the helm. The large iron-banded shield was slung across his back, and his menacing battle axe, Brool, whistled sharply as it cut the wind. Melegal followed on Quickster, staying close behind, careful of the distance he kept between him and the axe. Something about that blade always left him uncomfortable. Whenever it was out, death soon followed.

A nagging crept between Melegal's narrow shoulders. His back was stiff from the long ride, and he wanted to stop and stretch. A moment of relief came as Venir came to a halt and dropped to a knee, peering through the waist-high grass.

Melegal pulled on Quickster's reigns, saying, "Whoa."

Quickster's legs continued on, whisking him onward and well past his friend.

"What the …?" Gritting his teeth, Melegal yanked at the reins, but Quickster kept right on going. As the forest began to close in, dread overcame him. He tugged once more, snapping up Quickster's bullish neck. Quickster didn't slow.

"Bish!"

With a quick hop, he abandoned the saddle. He watched Quickster go, faster and faster, now a speck against the tree line, and out of sight. He smoothed his floppy hat down along the side of his head and stood dumbfounded and silent. Then he cursed at the top of his lungs.

With a sigh and a grimace, Melegal marched back to where he had passed Venir. *I'm sure the big lout will have another new humorous story to tell. Stupid mule!* He didn't hear the laughter he expected, though. In the dimming light, he caught Venir running toward the forest in full battle gear. He saw the spiked helm strapped to Venir's chin, his large shield on his back, and Brool swinging in cadence from his right hand. The helm's iron eyelets glowed with menace. He felt something cold inside him, and he crouched down. Venir was not there. No, this was the Darkslayer, running as fleet and quiet as a forest stag. *Not you, too!*

Melegal stood alone in the dusk. He turned back and stared at the looming forest. Should he follow Venir, or try to find Quickster? There was no time to waste. *I've got to get my gear.* Deciding that Venir was capable of taking care of himself, he set off along Quickster's path. He ran as fast as he could, but the Great Forest was farther than he had anticipated. How fast had his pony gone? He was out of breath before he was half way there. All of his judgment was based on what he had learned in the City of Bone, and that seemed wholly inadequate now. With great caution and misgiving, the thief jogged as he entered the forest. *Dimwitted animals.*

56

O RAN'S SPELL WAS WORKING. THEIR surprise attack was underway, and soon his mission would be over. It would not be long before they could all go back home. Through the eye of Eep, Oran and McKnight viewed the swirling image of the Darkslayer and the pony rushing towards the Great Forest of Bish.

"I must say," said McKnight, fighting the urge to slap the underling on the back, "I'm rather glad you and Tonio have chosen to tackle the big fellow. I can't say I have any desire to be in your boots. He looks rather menacing. Good hunting to you."

"It should be you, in fact, human," said Oran, without looking up from his mirage. "But I shall do what I must. Be thankful I have set you up with easy prey. In a few moments that animal will deliver into your lap the other resident of your tiresome city."

"Rather a shame, really, to lose another fine citizen of Bone. I suspect we will need every sneaky human we have in order to keep you underlings under control." McKnight pointed his finger at Oran.

McKnight didn't want to let on about his past with Melegal and how this was his opportunity to see his former apprentice undone. He dabbed some poison on his bolts and blades, then tucked them back under his cloak.

"Tsk, tsk—such decisions—which lives to take and which to let be!" McKnight's eyes perked up at his comments. "I ought to make note of that; it sounds rather profound." He turned as he left, saying, "I shall try to be quick and return to help you, underling. I rather think you may need it."

Staring at the fading mystic image, Oran stroked his jaw with his long-nailed fingers. The time had come to forever be rid of this impudent human. As the image died, Oran caught a faint glimpse of what was coming his way: a large man, armed like a war machine, eyes glowing black fire, and moving like the wind. Oran couldn't contain his audible gasp.

"Tonio! Take your position ... he comes!" He closed his eyes with the imp hovering by his side. "Eep, you know what to do!"

Eep turned on a nasty smile and buzzed away.

57

L ORD CATTEN AND LORD VERBARD arrived in the southwest corner of Red Clay Forest.

"It's as good of a place to wait out the Darkslayer as any," Verbard commented as they landed near the colorful forest's edge.

"What have we here?" Catten remarked.

Ten gangly robed figures floated around them, making odd sounds, but not getting too close. Catten could feel the magic within the strange figures of the forest magi, and he knew they were drawn to his as well.

Arms folded across their chests, he and his brother didn't bother to introduce themselves. A tall, brown-robed figure ventured before Catten, hands motioning in arcane patterns. Then the forest mage froze.

Verbard let out a hissing chuckle.

The forest mage bent in a slight bow and backed off. The rest did the same, slowly floating away as their robes brushed over the ground. Catten felt their earlier confidence turn into fear.

The air shimmered as Catten called the magic within him. Tendrils of lightning burst from Verbard's clawed hand. The first bolt of chained lightning blasted into the nearest forest mage's retreating form. Catten let loose his own bolt of energy, slamming into the one opposite the leader. The silver-blue bolts shot counter-clockwise, gaining speed, spinning like grinding stones and growing brighter and brighter as they passed through each of the forest magi. Catten and Verbard stood in the middle of the mayhem, sadistic faces filled with glee. As they closed their eyes, one final brilliant flash followed, and when they opened them just ten piles of ash remained. As the brothers inhaled, they found the smell of smoldering skin and charred bones refreshing

"That felt good, but they didn't have time to scream. I like it when they scream," Catten said with disappointment.

Verbard continued his chuckle. "Me, too."

58

V ENIR CHARGED INTO THE GREAT Forest of Bish like a human juggernaut shot from a catapult. He grew angrier with every stride as the scent of an underling consumed him. He was wary of a trap, but he couldn't fight the urge to take things head on. His battle instincts always served him best when he took the fight to them. But who was he trying to face?

His blue eyes flashed beneath his spiked helm as Brool slashed through any foliage that barricaded his path. The Great Forest had darkened a great deal since he had entered from the more open plains. It was of little concern. He knew this forest as well as the rest, and his quick feet carried him through the woodland as if it were daylight in the desert.

He was about two hundred yards inside when trouble appeared. Spider webs, giant spider webs, engulfed the trees from the ground to as high as the eye could see. *Underling magic.* His helm shimmered around his head. Great power awaited him somewhere ahead.

Venir slowed his pace and picked his way past the webs through the gaps between trees that were not covered. Meanwhile, the recesses of his raging mind asked a question whose answer he already knew, for this maze reminded him of the fish traps he had set as a boy in the silver streams of Throhm. But this was a crueler version, designed by underling hunters to trap their prey.

The labyrinth of webs let you think you were finding your way through, but at the end, if you succeeded without getting stuck, you were boxed in and killed. He had dealt with the webs before, and his spine tingled as he recalled the last time, but he trudged on.

The underling labyrinth opened into a cove laced with webs around all of its vast trees. There was no other way out but back. Venir turned and watched as new webs grew along the trees, sealing off his path. Whoever it was, they were not far ahead. He could sense it, strong and evil.

He spat from his dry mouth.

"Bone with this!"

Running straight, he charged the webs ahead at full speed. Brool sliced a gap in the entanglement, and the thick webs began to curl away and dissipate.

The forest opened wide again, but was darker. Venir pressed his back along a massive tree and listened. He heard nothing. His helm ebbed around his skull, and he started moving again. A high buzzing sounded right on top of him. Pain raced up his arms as a hunk of skin was sheared away.

"Argh!" He slashed Brool high in the air.

He was on the defensive now, searching for the source of the buzzing sound that seemed to come from all over the forest. Venir circled where he stood, scanning the high branches. A rush of wind came his way as he swung Brool up. Two talons skinned his neck, and a nail nicked his throat. The wound burned as hot blood flowed down his chest. Whatever it was, it had Venir's attention.

The creature zipped in and out, and his mocking bird-like sounds seemed to echo from all sides. More webs coated the trees, and Venir became ever mindful of where he turned, lest he be stuck. The imp cut past the webs, but Venir chopped Brool in the imp's path at every turn. Brool's spike jabbed and poked at the imp as Venir tried to work his shield free from his back.

Brool cut through the spider webs, creating room to work, but the axe could only do so much. The imp came from every direction. Venir couldn't tell how many of the creatures were out there. He did all he could to contain the imp attacks. *Blasted things are ripping me to ribbons!* The imp rushed in and out, just beyond Brool's metal, darting away in the nick of time. Venir readied his shield, as the chronic buzzing faded away.

Silence fell. Venir labored for his breath. Somewhere, an underling was waiting, that and something else he had never encountered before, what seemed like a horde of imps. *Go!* His mind urged him onward, even as his shield arm drooped and blood dripped down his injured hand. He cut away the thick webs and headed for the beacon of evil deeper in the forest. Suddenly, the buzzing was back from somewhere high above. It agitated him. His wounds seemed to fester from the annoying sound. The smacks of flapping wings split through the air as the imp flew in and out of range.

Venir stayed low. More silence came. Sweat rolled off Venir's chiseled face in large drops. He waited. A distant hum rattled in the high branches. He groaned. Aggravation, pain, and throbbing licked at his limbs. He was thirsty. He wanted a good look at his assailants, but only cold and black surrounded him. He scanned the trees. Beating wings and mocking bird-like sounds were hidden in the blackness above.

The brawny warrior pressed deeper through the forest at a trot. The webs continued to peel away as he cut through them. The underling presence ahead refueled his anger. He was getting closer. In an instant, a beating of bat-like wings shrilled from behind, and thick claws ripped into the chain mail on his back. He twisted away, striking back with his axe. Nothing was there. A gaping slash was torn in the chain along his gouged back. Venir fought the urge to scream. *What was that?*

He moved on, his mystic eyelets not sensing the cold shadow squatted like a stump as he passed by. Then Venir heard something scuff the dirt behind him. He whirled, shield raised, as there was a bone-jarring sound.

CLANG!

A shower of sparks lit up a familiar face that his mind could not comprehend. *It cannot be!*

59

I HAVE HAD ENOUGH OF THIS *misadventure*! Venir and Quickster had frustrated Melegal to his limit. He stomped through the Great Forest, peering about for Quickster's tracks. Doing his best imitation of a ranger, he ran his hands through the dirt and leaves. He followed a straight line as best he could, trying to guess where a pony might go, but to no avail.

The darkness had settled, and that left him uneasy, especially without Quickster and most of his gear. The odd rustles, hoots, and chirps of the forest only added to his growing discomfort. Muttering and cursing under his breath, he finally heard a familiar scuffle of hooves not far ahead: the soft neighs and munching sounds of his ever-hungry quick pony.

Thank Bish! He thought as he strolled to the side of his shaggy mount, wrapped his arms around its neck and squeezed. Resisting the urge to choke the stupid beast, he stroked its mane instead.

He sighed, but the tickle between his shoulders was still there, telling him something abnormal hung in the air. Now he had to find Venir, in a forest bigger than Bone. Finding a man in the city was one thing, but in the forest was another. He checked all of his belongings. *All there.* It left him with little relief. Pony or no, he still felt awkward and alone. He stuck his boot in the stirrup.

"Whatever made you drag me into this cursed forest better have been worth it," he huffed, glancing around. "Now let this be the end of it, Quickster."

"I should say it was *worth it*," said a familiar voice.

The tickle in Melegal's spine turned to a sheet of ice.

"... and this *will* be the end of it, for you at any rate," the voice added.

It can't be! Here? Melegal let his foot back out of the stirrup and began to turn.

"No sudden moves now," the sinister voice continued. "Just stay put. I'm pretty good with a crossbow at such close range … Rat."

The ice in his veins simmered. *Rat!* Melegal hated being called that. The character's chuckle was most disturbing, indeed. It was a sound he wished he never would have heard again. Now he stood on flat feet, no idea where to run, and a long way from home. Melegal shook off his fears. "I was figuring you'd swallowed your tongue, McKnight. In that wretched hat, I thought you'd be too embarrassed to open your mouth."

"Hah! Fine guess, Melegal, but compared to that filthy sock on your head, my hat is simply glorious." The man's feet shifted in the dirt. "My, my, you've certainly grown since I last saw you living like a rat in Bone. You must be rather uncomfortable outside the city."

"No more than you. It's not the first time I've been here, and far from the last."

Melegal stood with his arms wide, palms outward. McKnight came around in front of him. The two men from the City of Bone—the thief and the former thief turned detective—stood eye to eye, while between them Quickster continued to munch at a tuft of green grass. A few quiet seconds passed as Melegal's mind raced with a hundred thoughts.

McKnight stood there, beady eyes shifting in the darkness. The man had been his friend and mentor once. McKnight had taught him just about everything he knew at one time: climbing, stealing, skimming, picking, throwing, and fencing. The detective had been like a bad father, big brother, or uncle that he trusted despite the abuse. Melegal had betrayed him and turned his back on his brethren just when McKnight needed him most.

Melegal had his reasons. He couldn't stomach snatching children and stuffing them into the dungeons beneath the castles. Instead, he had freed them. It had been costly, and McKnight had longed for his head ever since.

"Why exactly are you looking for me, McKnight?"

"Well, now," McKnight mused, "it's a funny thing. I could offer you an explanation, but I'd rather shoot this bolt through your eye socket and get paid. Hard feelings, of course."

The detective took aim through his sight at Melegal's eye socket. *Move or die!*

McKnight then eased off and continued, "You knew you were being pursued by the Royals, which is why you and your large companion, the Darkslayer or whatever, fled Bone."

McKnight kept his steady aim on him as Melegal allowed a gentle bend in his knees. *Keep talking, please.*

"Myself … I'm merely the hired help of the Royal Almen House. This situation is rather unusual, in that it's taken me out of the city. Somehow, you fellows managed to tangle with that Royal Almen brat, Tonio, who—you may wish to know before you die—is alive and at present with me."

Melegal's brows peaked. *How can that be?* He watched McKnight's finger tighten on the trigger.

"As a matter of fact, he's just preparing to dispatch your brutish friend once and for all, with some additional assistance from an underling and a foul magical creature called an imp."

Very little of what McKnight said made sense at all. Why would humans be tangled with an underling? It was considered forbidden without anyone ever having to say so. Of course, it had happened before. Melegal didn't have time to sort it all out. *Time to move.*

"McKnight, all of this trouble over little ol' us? It seems a bit much. So, how much is this charge supposed to pay you? I'd hate to think you went to all of this effort for nothing. I mean … what if you don't achieve your objective?"

Melegal caught McKnight staring at him eye to eye. *Freeze. Freeze. Freeze,* Melegal's mind suggested to the detective. His floppy hat was warm, his mind glowing. *Please work!*

McKnight thought he noticed a twinkling wink in Melegal's eye. He felt dizzy, and the image before him began to blur. Somewhat perplexed, he regained his composure and refocused his crossbow on Melegal's eye.

"It's the end of the road for you, rat."

He squeezed the trigger.

Click. No bolt fired. Alarmed, he pulled the second trigger.

Click.

The unexpected misfire of the crossbow sounded like breaking glass in the silence. McKnight's narrow chin dropped. Before him, Melegal chuckled, twirling the crossbow bolts in and out of his fingers in a blur.

"How?" McKnight dropped his crossbow and reached for his swords. They too were missing. He tried to jump aside, but his paralyzed legs didn't budge. A small dart was stuck in each of them. *Bone, those are mine!*

Two silvery flashes caught a dash of red moonlight as they sliced through the air and buried themselves in his chest. McKnight clutched at them, trying to remove his cherished daggers. The poison set fire to his veins. He tried to scream, but his tongue was thick and garbled. He tasted blood as he coughed. His body teetered and fell. He had killed all of those people, and now he knew what it felt like.

His former protégé had turned the tables on him, again. Melegal strolled over with one of McKnight's shortswords in each hand.

"How did you do that?" McKnight somehow managed through blood-splattered lips.

"I could tell you, but somehow I don't think that would make you feel any better."

Melegal stood straight up and examined the fine craftsmanship of the shortswords. The blades shimmered in the night, edges sharp as razors. Melegal's eyes and hands caressed the fine craftsmanship.

"Thanks, McKnight. Nice to have them back after all these years."

Melegal gathered Quickster by the reins and departed.

McKnight lay on his back on the hard ground, staring at the sky between the treetops, and for a moment wondered what would happen when he died. His chest burned like fire, but his hatred for Melegal was hotter than an inferno.

60

THUNDEROUS BLOWS RESOUNDED IN VENIR'S ears. The fury of Tonio's assault had his full attention. Every jolt sent a wave of pain down his gashed arm. Venir felt as if his arm was about to shatter as the deranged half-dead Royal swung heavy two-handed blows down on his shield. It didn't help that the man trying to carve a chunk out of him should have been dead.

Tonio's scarred faced was a twisted sneer, ashen with hatred. His flashing sword came down with the power of an ogre, almost driving Venir to his knees.

His demented foe was one issue, but the buzzing of what turned out to be just one imp was another.

The creature kept buzzing in, high and low, jabbing at Venir's exposed limbs with thick, sharp talons. Venir shrugged off what he could as Brool's spike did well to parry the swift imp. Fresh cuts littered his body now, and his helmet still ebbed in warning of the underling. An angry hiss rushed between his teeth as he strained to push back and deflect Tonio's blows with his shield.

A short distance from the melee, Oran stood alone, a mask of concern. He was fascinated that the human was somehow withstanding Tonio and Eep's unrelenting attacks, blow after ringing blow. It was the first time Oran had witnessed either man or underling withstand such heightened ferocity. He was beginning to understand that the Darkslayer was no mere man and why he had become the scourge of his kind.

As fast as Eep was, the imp had managed only a few good cuts to the sinewy arms and legs of the man. Oran watched for the final blow to be struck by the imp, but the axe's tip would lick out like a snake's tongue, almost impaling the imp. The man was dripped in blood, but the fatal wounds had not landed. The whirling figure did not slow, and it worried him.

Oran wrung his rat-furred hands together. The longer his pawns went on struggling to dispose of the big warrior, the more likely they would miss their chance. It was time to put an end to this. From his thin purplish lips, Oran began to mutter an incantation in a low, barely audible tone.

Venir was taking a pounding. The relentless attack wore down his inner fury. His chest labored, while his opponents didn't seem to have the same need for air. Wave after wave, they came on, hard and fast. A split second of missed timing and he'd be dead. He had to counter somehow before all his energy ebbed. *Blink and die!*

The whispers of an underling spell caster hummed in Venir's ears. It was a beacon of fire in his mind. Tonio's tireless blows still hammered into his shield in a chronic rhythm. The one-eyed creature zipped in and out. It was time to let it all out.

As the imp flew in, Venir parried and countered with Brool, nicking a leathery wing. The mystic creature hissed and retreated. Venir whirled as Tonio's sword clanged one more time off his shield. Tonio's corded arms rose high, face mired with hatred and scars, lips letting out a wrath-filled groan. The man's arms thrust down, dead eyes unblinking. Venir bellowed as he swung Brool in return with all of his might.

Slice!

Tonio's face remained unchanged as his arms were cut off at the elbows. The Royal lord's fresh stumps went on chopping the air with vigor, up and down. Astonishment and anguish set in as the remaining shred of humanity crossed the young man's face. Armless and trying to cover his face, he looked up, watching the axe coming. Venir wrenched Brool down with such force it cleaved the man's head and body in two. One half of Tonio fell to the left and the other to the right.

That better do it!

More buzzing combined with a screech of fury and came from behind. In a flash, Venir spun, jabbing his spike as he turned, impaling the screaming imp through the chest.

Crunch!

It squealed as its ribs cracked. It was the first good look Venir got of the thing. Powerful claws clutched at his neck, and a large red eye bore into him with hatred. It was the essence of evil. The thing dangled on the spike, trying to push itself off. Venir's laugh was gruesome as he charged deeper into the forest.

Oran felt a renewed sense of confidence and power. Time seemed to be at his command, and everything seemed to take place in slow motion; he had never felt such magic within him. It was as if the gates that held the magic of Bish had burst open for him. It was unexplainable and delicious. He waited for the man to enter his path so he could wipe the brutish human from the face of Bish forever.

The Darkslayer charged into his clearing with Eep skewered on the spike of his axe like a chicken for a roast.

Eep screamed, "Now you will die, human! Drop your axe and surrender, fool!"

The Darkslayer's eyelets were like black fire.

"No, you all die today!" the man said in an inhuman bellow.

The imp laughed scornfully as the man hoisted the war-axe high above his head and charged into Oran's path. Oran felt the hatred grow in his belly and fuel his power. He was screaming aloud now, his spell fully prepared, and his triumph imminent. Power filled him like a blast of hot air. Tree limbs bowed and leaves blustered all around.

"Die now, Darkslayer, at the hand of the great underling, Oran!"

A bolt of red-blue fire shot straight at the man as he swung down his axe.

"No!" Eep shrieked as the spike caught the bolt, frying the thrashing imp into blackened char.

"Impossible!" Oran howled.

The bolt should have destroyed the axe and the man. Instead, its blast had knocked the warrior flat onto his back, intact. The smell of fried flesh and hair was heavy in the air. Oran stared wide-eyed at the brute still gripping the axe, body smoking on the ground at the end of the scorched path. One more spell should finish off the prone man once and for all.

Oran was on his own now. His imp was blasted to smithereens, the man chopped asunder. The scourge of the underlings was knocked flat, chest laboring up and down, feet shaking. *He's mine*, Oran thought. *All mine!* He summoned more of the world's energy into his fingertips. It came slow, easy and willing, filling him from head to toe. Oran wanted the power to wipe out everything that lived and breathed within a mile. One final shot was all he needed. He eyed the twitching figure on the forest floor, hungry to turn the human into a crater of flesh and steel. It was Oran's time for glory. His eyes turned to violet-black saucers as the Darkslayer rolled onto one knee.

Venir felt like a piece of shattered glass. Pain coursed through his hardened body. His finger tips were numb. His mouth tasted like metal, and his ears rang. He saw the axe in his grip as he lay on his shield. His sluggish mind urged a warning. The underling was near. It felt like an army of them. *Move or die.* There were no other options. His body longed to rest, but his survival instincts would not let him give in, not until he was dead. He rolled onto one knee.

A radiant swirl of energy surrounded a robed underling whose small hands were rolling before his chest. Venir took a deep, painful breath. The black eyes of the hairy fiend bore into him, boiling with rage. His pain was replaced with the urge to destroy his enemy. It chittered like a hundred voices, waving its robed arms high in the air.

Venir's legs felt as heavy as iron as he sprang to his feet, lifted Brool high above his head, and charged. The underling wavered back a step as Venir ran onward like an angry bull. Oran slapped his hands together above his head. A crackle came, and a burst of brilliant light shot forth. Venir jerked up his shield and dived to the ground. The shield ripped away from his arm, his breath knocked from his lungs. Everything was black, and the world rang all around him.

He gasped for air, saw fire, and patted the flames from his clothes. The blond hairs on his arms were tiny black curls, and his teeth hurt. He could see the underling screaming at him now, like a muted nightmare.

Then he heard it, something unnatural. The hideous shriek would have torn out his eardrums, if not for the helm he wore. His stomach twisted into sour knots at the horrifying mystic siren. Somehow, he rose from the ground, Brool still in hand, and stormed against the sound and down the seared path. The underling's filed teeth hung in its shouting maw like daggers as Venir delivered the final swing. Brool struck the side of Oran's screaming head, slicing it off between his eyes and nose. Black blood gurgled from the top as the silenced body collapsed on the forest floor.

Venir stood shaking. Only his boots and his shorts remained. His chain mail was scattered in chunks and links along the burnt path. Scorch marks and red welts rose on the rippling muscles of his torso. His V tattoo remained unscathed between his shoulder blades. His purple veins pulsated, and the blood and gore was baked red and black all over him He was the picture of every raw, wild, and powerful element on Bish. Brool hung in his right hand, and his blue eyes still blazed through the eyelets. His chinstrap was still tight under his grizzled chin.

A hundred sets of eyes watched from high above as he banged Brool's spike onto the heel of his boot, knocking the charred remains of the imp off. He inhaled, and then groaned and tried to spit the taste of metal from his mouth. He inhaled painfully again, filling his chest with the hot night air. He let out a bellowing battle cry so loud and deep that time seemed to stop. The throbbing in his head subsided as he tried to remember where he was. Another concern came his way. Where was Melegal?

61

CHONGO'S FOUR EARS PERKED UP as an inhuman shriek cut through the forest. Lefty covered his ears, stomach in twisted knots. The halfling looked around, dizzy, his blue eyes rolling up in his head. The sound stabbed at the back of his mind, and he began to sag. A meaty hand gripped him. Then the horrible sound was gone. Lefty's stomach curled. Georgio puked on the ground. Everything seemed to stop for a long moment as they tried to regain their senses.

"What was that?" Georgio gasped and then gagged again.

"Turn back!" Lefty wailed with one hand over his eyes and a finger in his ear. "I can't take it, make this beast turn around!"

But Georgio held him tight.

"Don't worry, Mood and Chongo won't let anything happen to us!"

The grizzle-faced Mood just grunted through his red beard. Chongo lay down—ears flat as he gave a low whine. The giant dwarf urged the dog back on all fours, forcing Lefty to hang on to the saddle, Georgio still holding him from behind. They moved on, between the massive tree trunks, at a brisker pace.

A faint human-like roar reached his ears. Chongo's feet began to stamp, his tails wagging back and forth in excited bursts. Mood turned back with a smile as Chongo howled. Georgio gave a reassuring squeeze on Lefty's shoulders, causing him to lurch. Georgio yelled in his ear, "Lefty, you're gonna meet Venir!"

"Oh …" he said, wishing when he met Georgio he'd kept on running.

Lefty rolled his neck back, peering upward to the ceiling of blackened leaves. Something moved high above. He hoped it was just a roost of birds. But it was not.

62

A BONE CHILLING SOUND RIPPED THROUGH the air. Quickster bucked and Melegal was sent reeling to the ground. He covered his ears and choked back bile. He lay there, sucking in breath after the foul noise was gone. His legs felt like jelly as he got up. He heard another cry, more human this time. It took several more minutes before Quickster would budge.

Melegal trotted through the forest towards the thunderous cracks, screams, and howls he had heard. He choked down his fears; there was nowhere else to go. The forest was black as night, but his eyes were as good as a man could have. He moved on towards the last sound he heard.

The battle cry had to have come from Venir. *I miss Bone.* It was the simple things about the City of Bone that Melegal enjoyed so much. He pilfered his wants and needs. He tickled the toes of wanton women. He sipped from goblets filled with the finest wines. He was always one step ahead of the authorities. Now, with McKnight out of the picture, there could only be more to come. A satisfying smile crossed his thin lips. He rubbed the pommels of the twin swords on his hips. It was good to have his *sisters* back. Now, all he had to do was get his arse out of the forest.

Quickster slowed, interrupting his daydreams and making him notice the massive cobwebs all around. His homesickness intensified, and he took a deep swallow. He glanced upward. Soft movements scuffled in the monstrous branches high above. Quickster nickered as he slowly weaved in and out among the web-covered trees. The cobwebs were disintegrating, but Melegal was as stiff as a board.

A clearing opened up ahead. His gray eyes made out a hulking silhouette coming his way — a familiar figure with a spiked helm and axe. Melegal could see a wide smile reflecting in the faint moonlight.

"Hah!" roared the Venir. "Another great night in the forest!"

Melegal gave him an unforgiving look. Venir looked like he was just spit out of a furnace. Dried blood and long scabs were scattered all over the man's half-naked frame. He didn't care.

He couldn't hold back his outrage; his fists shook when he let it out.

"You go berserk and run off! My pony does the same! I get stuck in this jungle, trapped against all odds! McKnight! Do you remember him, you idiot?"

Venir's faced pinched in thought as Melegal continued.

"Well … I had to kill him and then come and try to save your butt — great night! Bah!" Melegal felt better. He waited for Venir to lay back into him like an overbearing ogre, maybe split him in two.

Venir just stood there, emotionless. "You killed someone from Bone? McKnight?" The big man paused, scratching his chin. "Good!" Venir added with a slap on his shoulder. "Then I guess that's the last of them. I don't figure anyone else is still looking for us. But it's not time to run back home just yet, Me."

Melegal rolled his eyes. "Great." How much longer would he have to wait things out? It seemed like this had been the longest week of his life.

"Come, take a look at who I killed here. It's that Tonio guy from the Chimera and the stables."

Tonio's body lay in two equal parts, his innards seeping toward the ground. Melegal's face was aghast. He didn't think he'd ever seen a man cut in twain like that before.

Venir picked up one of the man's dismembered arms and waved it at him.

"Shouldn't he have been dead already? You almost beat him to death, and then Chongo chewed him to death. How does that work?" Melegal said.

"Magic. Evil, powerful, magic. Take a look."

Melegal looked at the corpse. As horrible as it appeared, Tonio had bled very little. A chill ran up Melegal's spine.

"Vee, that is some serious magic. He was already dead when you killed him — or killed him again, that is. Who has that kind of power?"

"Well, did you hear that battle earlier?"

Melegal nodded. "I heard something awful. Don't know if I'd call it a battle."

"That's who, is my guess."

He pointed at the robed corpse of an underling.

"That was an underling, very powerful. Certainly the most powerful I've ever crossed. He's dead as a rock now, though. I'm more concerned that an underling and a human were both coming after us."

"Or after you." What had Venir gotten him into? Melegal felt the pressing need to head back to Bone. There were no underlings there. Or were there? Melegal didn't know what to think, but he'd rather be home.

"It's strange. This alliance makes no sense. And you didn't even see the other thing?' Venir said.

"What other thing?"

"An imp, I believe."

Melegal shook his head in disbelief. "So, now what?"

"We make a fire and find something to eat. I'm starving."

"Good."

The surrounding sounds of the Great Forest of Bish had returned to normal. Owls hooted and crickets chirped while the orange fire glowed. It was only a small camp fire, but its warmth and light softened Melegal's always stern expression. The skinny man City of Bonelay back against the furry black belly of Quickster. All was well in the forest, leaving Venir alone in his thoughts.

Venir squatted down, stoking the fire with a stick. He was concerned that he had dragged his friend bone deep into all of his affairs. He was aching, his faculties stretched to the limit, but he couldn't let that on. It was his fault. *Just smile, and people will think all is well.* Someone had told him that once. It seemed to work. He would do anything to be back in Bone, soaking in some cool water, getting soaped down by a savory wench. Venir figured that was how Melegal felt most of the time. He did his best to enjoy the finer things in Bone, but the underlings seemed to call. He heard something faint over the whistling nose of Quickster. He stood up, peered around, and grabbed his axe. Something was out there. He didn't stop, just slipped by his friend and plunged deeper into the forest.

All too quickly, the morning crept up on Melegal. The scuffles of the awakening forest became louder with every moment. Unlike the sounds of the city, these noises couldn't be quashed by closing a window or a thick oaken door. Melegal rubbed his groggy face. He heard loud snoring on the other side of Quickster. Somewhere close by he noticed Venir's low voice talking. Sunlight warmed his face as he rose and stretched. His hand brushed against something humanoid.

"Agh!" Melegal jumped clear over the smoldering fire in one bound. With McKnight's blades drawn, Melegal peered at a small humanoid disappearing behind Quickster.

Georgio yelped from behind his pony.

"Get off me, Lefty. I'm trying to sleep."

Venir and Mood let out two thunderous laughs from behind him, both bright-eyed and bushy-tailed. Melegal sheathed his swords with a scowl. It seemed several people had snuck up on him last night. It was an embarrassing feeling.

"What's the matter, scrawny man? Got a bed bug?" Mood said in his gruff voice.

Out of place as Melegal felt around the dwarf, he was glad to see him back. He waved the bushy face off with his hand.

"What was that creature, Venir?"

"That's Georgio's new halfling friend, Lefty," Venir said, still chuckling.

"Me, it's me!" Georgio popped up from the other side of Quickster, face beaming. "Meet my friend, Lefty Lightfoot. He's a halfling! See? Look!"

Georgio pulled Lefty by the arm, but the halfling escaped his grasp and almost ran onto Melegal's toes, stopping short when Melegal's sword almost pierced his tiny neck. The halfling froze.

"Easy Melegal, he's just greeting you. Haven't you met a halfling before?" asked Venir.

Melegal stuck his sword back in his sheath and walked away.

Georgio put his hand on Lefty's shoulder.

"It's not you. He's not a morning person … or any other time of the day, for that matter."

Georgio and Lefty sniffed the air, and Lefty stamped his little feet and clapped in excitement.

"What's for breakfast?" the boys asked in unison.

"Mood's been cooking up a young elk, big as a deer, but tastier than a stag. That'll hold your hunger for most of the day," said Venir, as Mood presented the boy's breakfast.

"Delicious, don't you think, Lefty?" said Georgio, chewing the steaming meat.

Lefty put a piece in his mouth and spat it out. He fanned his tongue.

"It's too hot!"

Georgio gave him a funny look, saying, "No it's not." He bit into another mouthful.

Lefty set his food aside. As he waited for it to cool, his hand strayed to his pocket, and he smiled. He had tucked something away in there after hearing Venir's tale late in the night. The curious halfling had gone to explore the battle site, and among the robes of the dead underling cleric he had found two red, bullet-sized gemstones that had a sparkle of light inside.

Georgio had just finished his stag meat when Venir walked over and stuck Tonio's sword in the ground at his feet.

"This is yours, Georgio," Venir said.

The boy's jaw dropped as he stared at the sword. It was magnificent and gleaming with tiny jewels around the hilt. His hand latched on the hilt, yanking it from the ground.

"Venir! This is the best gift ever!" The boy made several awkward cuts in the air and Lefty dashed away.

"Are you going to teach me to use it?"

Venir kneeled alongside the boy and said, "Certainly. It's one of the finest swords I've come by. I couldn't believe it didn't break against my shield. It came down with great force on every blow, but there isn't a nick on it."

Georgio ran his pudgy fingers along the shiny blade, slicing his skin. "Ow!" he said, but no blood surfaced.

Venir gave the boy a funny look and continued on. "It's big, but it's light. Those Royals must have one mighty good weaponsmith. It's a keeper, Georgio. You take good care of it, and I'm sure it'll take care of you." Venir squeezed the boy's shoulder, and Georgio could do nothing but smile up into the eyes of his hero.

"All right, already! Can we go home now?" asked Melegal.

"We're gonna try," said Venir. "But I still think it's too soon."

"I don't care!" Melegal snapped back.

"I know. We aren't out of the thicket yet, Me. Mood says that many more underlings are about. Farther north than us, which is odd. No one knows what they're up to, but we can only hope they don't get too close before I get you home," Venir replied.

Melegal wanted to throttle something. Underlings and who knew what else might pop up on this misadventure. No chest of treasure to be found and no new coins to spend. He had lost their money betting on the son of Farc in the Pit. His friend cost him. He would never tell Venir that, though. He knew better than to ever bet against his comrade again. He slung his saddle back on his pony.

"Well, if anyone's still looking for us, I'd rather take my chances back in Bone. I'll die in the comforts of my home. I just hope that there are no witnesses left to bother me … er … us there." Melegal swung his leg over Quickster's saddle. "So get me back. I need a hot bath, and so do you. Look at you, letting your dog lick the muck off you. It's disgusting!"

63

THE TWO SUNS BLAZED OVER the Outlands like distant orange beacons, making the ground hazy to the naked eye. The sparse brown vegetation yielded little for the humanoid appetite. Enormous green cacti, bone trees, fire bushes, red toads, leather lizards, palm trees, and occasional sunflowers somehow survived without an oasis. Water in any form was hard to come by here.

This particular section of the Outlands was southwest of the Great Forest of Bish and northeast of Dwarven Hole. It was the most dangerous place in the whole of this barren land, maybe all of Bish. It had been home to more battles, wars, and acts of terror than any other place in the world. This dry and dusty area had come to be known as the Warfield. The Warfield was a flat piece of rock and desert that lay like a torched graveyard in the center of Bish's Outlands.

There were small villages near the Warfield, but they maintained a respectable distance. It was inhospitable for occupancy or commerce, and no place for children or adults to play. It blanketed its trespassers with chronic sweat and pain. Only the toughest creatures occupied it. It was also the place where the chest beating of the races began and ended, for no skirmish, battle, or war was worth recalling that did not take place at the Warfield. As with so many other things in Bish, no one knew or cared why they battled in that place; they simply did. It was where true warriors came to earn their badges of honor and horror.

For centuries, the Warfield had been devouring the remains, weapons and armor of the greatest warriors and wizards that ever lived. All surviving traces of these events dissipated in the hard and bitter land and were forgotten. No one ever cared to visit the final resting place of the Warfield's fallen heroes and villains. There was no graveyard, only rust turned to dust. It was as loathsome a place as there could be, where tempers would flare, and best friends could become bitter enemies. The survivors of the battles that broke out never returned for the fallen; they took whatever they could and left the rest to the impossible climate.

There were survivors, though. Many had survived battles, and some became renowned throughout the land. The toughest of each and every race were Warfield veterans, and their names were revered among their kin.

Some had survived more than once, and were the toughest men and women on Bish. One would know it at a glance, for the Warfield always left its mark. Some boasted of their excursions, while others kept silent about their personal triumphs and tragedies. It was the quiet ones that always seemed to revisit their restless war demons in the hope of putting them to rest forever.

One man and woman who returned had never been able to erase their demons, and so they remained. Unfit for society, they were the Nameless Two—clothed in sandy white robes from head to toe, sandaled, and insane.

They lived in a cave behind a rocky crag on a gargantuan hill on the Warfield. With little left to live for, these tormented veterans practiced nothing but fighting for survival. They both tempered their skills and remained perfect Warfield warriors. They were known as nothing more than ghosts, and they showed up whenever they chose and fought whoever they wished. Often, they killed without mercy those too disabled to make it home after a battle.

Today, the Nameless Two stood outside on their craggy stoop high above their cave. A strange event was unfolding in the distance. The underling Badoon brigade had ventured onto the Warfield and blocked the passage northwards. A squadron of Blood Rangers appeared from the western horizon.

The Nameless Two saw this distant event from a powerful mystic source they had harnessed deep within their cave. The strange magic left them all-knowing of the occurrences on the Warfield. It gave them vision for miles around. It was this secret that had allowed them to survive for so long, and a secret they would never risk losing to another. It came at a price, but they were willing to pay.

64

V ENIR LED THE WAY NORTH toward the lower rim of the Outlands. He could feel Melegal glowering at his back. Georgio and Lefty sat atop the pony scrunched behind the thief, with uncomfortable looks on their faces.

"Why are we heading north again, and not back through Red Clay Forest? I have absolutely no desire to try to pass through the Warfield," Melegal said.

Venir's reply was grim.

"We're just going to the rim, Melegal. Take it easy. Besides, it's Mood's understanding that underlings are near Red Clay Forest."

Melegal's voice was defiant and quick as he shook his head. "How could he know that? And if you're going anywhere near the Warfield, count me out." He hunched over and scooted up on his saddle, shaking his head. "I know you'll go on, but I want nothing to do with that dreadful place. I've heard enough of your stupid bar room squalor to know that you'll never pass up the chance of another story to brag about, and if even half the slat you say is true, it's more than enough reason to know that the Warfield's clearly no place I want to be. So, *I* am heading west to Red Clay Forest, with or without you. I'll take my chances."

Georgio and Lefty nodded. Everyone knew about the Warfield, the place of *fight or die*. Venir got a good look at the boys' faces as they scooted closer on the thief's saddle. Melegal gave Georgio a sharp nudge with his elbow.

"What do you think, Mood?" Venir asked.

"I smell a trap," Mood replied cautiously. "If it ain't, I'm a halfling's uncle. The creatures say someone is there, waitin' on someone. I can sense it, too. Chances are that someone's you. I feel a northeastern way is not safe."

Venir was ready to go it alone, but if he left his friends, they might perish. "North then, maybe we can slip by."

"Maybe, but I don't think it matters." Mood pulled out a cigar from his pouch and lit it as he said, "They'll be waiting."

"Who's waiting, and who's setting traps?" Georgio asked.

"Underlings," answered Mood.

"More underlings?" Lefty's shrill voice shouted from behind. "Not the ones that killed my family?"

"I'm afraid so, Lefty," Venir answered. "To get home, we're gonna have to try and go around them."

It was one thing for Venir to get by—the armament provided for that—but not his friends. Underlings had their ways of finding a needle in a haystack.

The hot winds ebbed and flowed. Venir sensed it wasn't natural. The party traveled on in silence while he contemplated what might be their next—and possibly final—move. He could handle underlings, but this time it was different. This time it was not him hunting for them, but rather them hunting him.

"Well, I don't care." Melegal said, breaking the silence. "I'm going back through Red Clay Forest, with or without the rest of you. Whatever's looking for *you* probably isn't looking for *us*."

Venir faced Melegal. "We're not splitting up now! They know enough about where we are. If you want to get home alive, stick with us. And that means *all* of you!"

With a gruff command, Venir nudged Chongo forward, and Mood followed. Melegal hesitated in his saddle. Then he sighed and spurred Quickster ahead. The ever-growing dread befell them all.

Mood trotted up to Venir and said, "Let's head northwest towards my dwarven kin. We can possibly avoid these underlings that way. Or at worst, perhaps, I can slip our friends around the underlings and back home. Whatcha say?"

Venir didn't like the idea. Underlings were thick in the Outlands below Dwarven Hole. Still, anything was better than trying to pass through the Warfield. It was a place that oft times drew him in like a bear to honey. He tried to sound positive.

"That's as good a plan as we've got, I guess. I hate to drag 'em into all this. You'll have to look out for them in case I can't."

Venir looked into the sky, where white clouds streaked with gray rushed overhead,. He had never seen that before. He fingered the chin straps on his helmet. Mood looked at him warily, and Venir donned his helmet. No sense in getting caught off guard. He saw Mood's bushy face cocked at him, and nodded back. He felt fine, and took it off. He'd give it another go later.

"Just don't go any farther north, and let's see what happens when it happens," the dwarf said with a wink, puffing on his cigar. Its mellow smoke filtered back, bringing dizzy smiles to the faces of the boys. Melegal was busy fanning it away.

65

Verbard and Catten were in the midst of a long meditation when Verbard said, "I sense the Darkslayer might be on to us, brother. Shall we wait, or shall we depart for the Warfield?"

"Oh, I say we have waited enough. If the man were headed this way, we'd have been alerted to it by now." Catten didn't sound disappointed, however. "It has been such a long time since I witnessed a lengthy battle. And the Vicious-led Badoon does promise a salivating new amusement."

Verbard licked his lips, gold eyes flashing in anticipation.

Catten clenched his fists, eyes flickering with power.

"I would think the risk worth taking, brother. I don't know about you, but I feel the day has come to finish off this man."

Verbard's silver eyes shone with elation.

"Quite so, I feel ready for anything." He glanced at the piles of smoking ash at their feet. Their spells had been more effective than he anticipated. *Excellent. We read the same page.* It was quite the natural high. "I wonder, is it just us, or do all of our kind feel this way, Verbard?"

"Well, if it is all of us—underlings, that is—then the Darkslayer is doomed, and Master Sinway will be very pleased."

"Ah, I had almost forgotten that Master Sinway had set us on this charge. Perhaps he does not feel as we do," he hissed.

"Yes," Verbard answered as the corner of his mouth rose.

Both of the underling lords had longed to remove Master Sinway at some time during their lengthy existence, but neither could hope to achieve it without the other. Although they never spoke of it, each brother plotted to wrest the rule of the underlings from Master Sinway. But for now, first things first. Verbard gave his brother a nod, they uttered an underling syllable, and sailed high in the air towards the Warfield.

One lone forest mage had tucked himself deep in the brush. He had avoided the devastation Catten and Verbard had wrought on his brethren. It was a good day to be late, and live. Still, he had witnessed the whole thing, cringing like a babe. He had never realized such raw power existed in Bish. He dared a glance as they departed like ghosts into the sky. His heart pounded in his chest, but he felt relief.

Morty was his name. His grungy robes billowed as he floated over and slumped beside the ashes of his fallen family. Sobbing, he created a makeshift wooden urn and put what he could of their remains in the shabby container. He could still feel the magic within those ashes. It was faint, but still there nonetheless.

As he scooped up another pile, a glint of silver caught his eye. A peculiar-looking silver coin lay on the ground. It seemed not everything had been destroyed. Picking it up to study, Morty saw the wicked face of an underling looking back at him. It was one of those who had just departed. Terrified, the forest mage tried to throw the coin away, but it would not leave his hand.

"No! Get away!"

Morty screamed at the object, squirming and wriggling as he tried to brush the token from his hand against the ground and branches. But it was futile. He stared in horror as he looked at the underling's face on the gleaming token and pleaded, "Please, be gone!"

But the evil image looked back, winked his silver eye, and hissed, "Goodbye!"

Thunder crackled from above. Morty lifted his hooded head. Filled with terror, he looked into the darkening sky. He saw a blinding white flash as he was blown to smithereens. The talent dropped to the ground and crumbled away. Somewhere far away, Lord Verbard chuckled.

66

The Warfield was living up to its name this day. From the west, one squadron of giant dwarven rangers had flanked and fully surprised the Badoon Brigade. A dozen underling hunters lay dead and baking in the sun. The expert aim of the crossbow bolts fired by the Blood Rangers was responsible for the surprising onslaught. The stunned Badoon warriors recovered, howling in fury, gathering themselves as one of the most violent skirmishes to ever take place on the Warfield began.

Twelve Blood Rangers, dressed in leather and metal armor, squared up against the remaining Badoon brigade.

Six powerful dwarven warriors, wielding their renowned giant hand axes, chopped into the raging black masses. Six more rangers fired bolts at the underlings with bull's-eye precision. The waves of underlings screamed, fell, and recoiled. The Blood Rangers chopped down the wounded underlings and continued to press them back.

Heavily armored dwarven women with braided hair and stern faces reloaded the crossbows. Smaller dwarven women mumbled as they prepared healing and protection spells.

The underlings were repelled back; many lay in pieces on the ground, reddish-black blood sinking into the sand. The Blood Rangers, faces mired with blood and sweat, ignored their painful wounds. The underlings gathered back from the volley of the crossbows, deflecting missiles with an unseen shield. The dwarves stopped and waited. Six of the Blood Rangers stood facing the underlings, axes dripping wet, bushy beards caked in blood. Behind them, on the higher ground, their brethren kneeled as loaded crossbows were set by their sides. The underlings' razor sharp weapons glistened in the suns. Their mouths snapped back and forth as they tightened the buckles on their armor and loaded small crossbows. The fine rat-like hair on their dark gray skin was as wet as rain. The Vicious barked commands in their ears, faces twisted with rage. The underlings raised canteens to their lips and drank. Their multi-colored eyes shone with renewed vigor, and with a single command they charged.

The Blood Rangers stood their ground. Small bolts glanced off their hide-thick leather armor. Four underlings to one dwarf surged ahead on fleet legs.

Twenty steps away — ten — five.

A giant wall of flame leapt eight feet into the air. The underlings screamed to a halt, crouching away. The barrier ran a hundred yards, north–south, bright orange and yellow fire licking the air. The underling hunters came as close as they could, firing volley after volley through the flames.

The infuriated Vicious ordered a small group to run through the burning wall. A single Blood Ranger stood within the fire, unharmed, protected by the dwarven magic. With their swords drawn again, a dozen underlings charged into the flames, attacking the lone Blood Ranger. They drove him beyond the fires, singed and scorched, overwhelming him.

He chopped hard with his axes, each hitting its mark and dropping underlings dead and knocking them back into the inferno. The underlings' discipline and hatred drove them on in the scorching inferno. Still, his axes felled them one by one. The Blood Ranger was more than a match for burning Badoons. The underlings' own magic countered some of the fire's effects, but the next wave of dark bodies slowed down the ranger's efforts.

The powerful dwarf was cut and stabbed as the underlings pinned themselves to his arms. He could swing no more. He struggled to his feet, a yell bursting from his throat as he dragged himself and the underlings into the fires, where he fell and died. Screaming in glee at their triumph, the Badoon underlings turned to find more prey. They burst through the blaze to the other side. The relentless rear rank of Blood Rangers cut them down with the repeating fire of crossbow bolts.

Scrambling to escape, the underlings turned to retreat through the flames. The silhouettes of the Vicious on the other side of the fires suggested something else. They swung back, ready to fight, but their hesitation cost them. Heavy bolts pierced their temples, throats, eye-sockets, and black hearts. Falling, bleeding, and burning, another dozen underlings died quickly at the hands of the Blood Rangers.

Over two dozen Badoons were now defeated, and less than four dozen more remained. The Warfield was quiet but for the roaring wall of flame. The Vicious stood boldly in front of the ranks, their hardened black bodies glistening under the two red-hot suns. Long, clawed hands opened and closed in unison with the gnashing of their teeth. The savvy dwarven Blood Rangers ignored the provocation.

The Blood Rangers stood confidently on one side of the blaze, ready, with the underlings uncertain and defeated on the other. Two robed underlings floated down from the sky. Dwarven bolts zipped toward them, but bounced harmlessly away. The Vicious and the underlings began to scream and cheer as the two magi lords landed alongside the Vicious. With little more than a whisper, Lord Catten extinguished the fires.

67

VENIR LED THE WAY, NOW on foot, shoulder to shoulder with Mood, towing Chongo behind him. Melegal found renewed strength for complaining with every passing minute. Georgio giggled at his profanities, many of which the boy claimed he had never heard before. Lefty took mental note of all this, but his knowledge of the common language was not enough to follow most of the gutter-mouthed squalor that passed Melegal's lips.

Lefty tried asking Georgio the meanings, but the boy just shrugged and giggled. Lefty took a keen interest, however, assuming that these strange words were some sort of thieves' cant. Lefty focused. *I can learn this.* He tried to filter out the garbage, but Melegal's caustic mutterings were only making his efforts to understand worsen. Finally, Lefty could take no more.

"Please, human," he said, raising his little voice, "Be silent!"

"You can walk if you like, halfling," Melegal retorted.

"Fine, I can keep up." Lefty hopped off.

Lefty chose to catch up to Venir and Mood, leaving Georgio with his bad-tempered friend. He came up beside Chongo, whose left head stared at him like a tiny morsel while the right head tried to lick him. "All right, dog-thing, don't eat me, and I'll pet you," he said, putting a tiny hand on one of the dog's wet noses. Chongo's other head began licking his hand. "Whew! Can I ride you?"

Chongo flopped down so Lefty could climb on, and then reared up and was on the move again. He shot a glance at the boy and thief behind him. Melegal's scowl made him turn away. Lefty found the big dog's company much more pleasant than Melegal's, and he enjoyed scratching his four big floppy ears.

Venir halted.

Mood pulled his axes from his back.

The sky above was a swirl of gray clouds. Suddenly, the big warrior jammed his helmet on and turned toward them, his eyelets black as the night. His knuckles were white around the handle of his axe. Venir howled like a hundred warriors gone mad, and sprinted away.

Chongo howled as well, but Mood held the dog tight by the reigns. Mood hopped up behind Lefty.

"Who was that?" Lefty exclaimed.

"That was Venir," answered Mood, puzzled by the question.

"It was? It didn't look like him."

"I suppose not, but he's on our side, you know."

"I'd hate not to be on his side."

"Me, too, Melegal," the giant dwarf shouted back, "what do you want to do, follow Vee, or keep going west?"

"Follow Vee!" screamed Georgio like a battle cry, hoisting his new longsword high into the air and howling like his hero.

Melegal averted his eyes, and with a huff yelled back, "If I have to fight a hundred underlings to get home, so be it!"

"Well, I hope you can keep up then! Yah!" Mood shouted as Chongo took off.

"Now you're ticking me off," Melegal said, kicking his heels into Quickster.

The shaggy mount darted forward like a race horse. Georgio clutched the thief's sides and howled with glee. Quickster's legs thundered alongside Chongo and edged past. Lefty hung on to Mood and closed his eyes while Mood whipped at Chongo's reigns. "Ye've made yer point, man," Mood bellowed to Melegal. "Now let me lead so we don't get lost."

As Melegal slowed, Mood came up beside him. The city thief had a clever smile on his face. "Pretty fast, eh?" he said, lifting his brows.

"Guess so," Mood answered gruffly. "Now let's get after him."

The party galloped over the plains, mile after mile. Lefty expected to see Venir at any moment now, but the big man was gone like a ghost.

"Did we lose him?" the halfling cried as he leaned back into the dwarf's chest.

"No, Chongo's got the scent. But somehow the man's moving much faster than we are."

"How's that possible?"

Mood said nothing as they continued galloping. Lefty's feet seemed to tingle. He wished he could run that fast.

68

SOMETHING IN THEIR UNIVERSE WAS raging, but then again, there were always things raging. Time and time again, chance or manipulation would cause such an event to occur. Scorch had manipulated Bish, as he had done elsewhere many times before. And now Bish was like a candle burning at both ends—until Trinos arrived.

She was just in time to subdue the havoc Scorch had wrought. The damage had been done, however, to her tiny world. The ripple effects could not be reversed, for a door had been opened and innocence lost. Trinos implemented some hasty protection to her world to mend this catastrophe. It would have to hold. Scorch had not stayed long enough to see his meddling through. Her pet project seemed done for. She seethed inside, and it felt good.

Why? Such things should not bother her, yet this did.

She turned her eye away from Bish and began to track down Scorch while the trail was hot. She would not stop until she had found him and held him accountable for his actions.

69

WHEN THE WALL OF FIRE went out, the Blood Rangers repositioned themselves as if they had been in this same situation a dozen times before. The closest Badoon squadron was almost upon them by the time they retreated to higher ground. Cries of alarm and shock went up. The underlings found themselves falling into a massive hidden pit. Thick bolts pierced the underlings who were trapped in the pit, while others fired back over the chasm.

The Vicious stormed around in hulking fury, but Catten and Verbard cackled. Invigorated, the two underling lords pushed back the Blood Rangers with their own brand of firepower. Bolts of energy shot like missiles from their hands, blasting their targets with devastating accuracy. They relished roasting dwarven flesh, driving many to their knees, only to rise again in retreat. The underling brothers laughed at all the crossbow bolts bouncing off their invisible shield. There was little harm Blood Rangers could bring to them.

Doom was upon all of the fighting giants of Dwarven Hole; they were cornered and overpowered with the arrival of the underling lords. The remaining eleven Blood Rangers circled their women and fought valiantly. The underlings attacked them at all points with spells, bolts, arrows, and swords. The intensity was indescribable.

In complete defiance of the siege, the Blood Rangers sang in thunderous voices. Axes carved deep into underling bone as more heavy bolts impaled them left and right. The sheer numbers of the enemy fighters and the superior magic of their lords overwhelmed the brave fighters. Magic rocked the ground beneath their boots. Tiny poisoned bolts stuck in their arms and faces. Again and again the Blood Rangers rose.

Their wonderful working women shouted encouragement and stayed within their men's protective circle, casting spells of healing, strength, and vitality to help get them through each and every critical second. The Blood Rangers held their own as their blood and sweat formed pools on the rugged ground of the Warfield.

From their crag not far from the fight, the Nameless Two saw it all. The battle they were witnessing was a beautiful thing to them; so beautiful that it spurred them to thoughts of action. But the two troublesome underling lords caused them to hesitate.

Verbard looked at Catten and said, "Are we being watched?"

"I believe so." Catten agreed.

"How can that be?" Verbard said, looking at the hill in the distance. "Up there," He pointed.

"I see," Catten said. "Perhaps it's worth our investigation."

"I agree. The Vicious will finish things off. These dwarves won't hold out much longer."

Verbard looked downward. The dwarves were surrounded by the underling hoard. Mangled bodies littered the ground, but the Vicious pressed the Badoon forward. The rest of the Warfield was barren, plain, and abandoned. Something was missing.

"I would have expected that impudent human to be here by now. I can't bear the thought that he might have avoided us." Verbard shrugged. "Let us go and see what lies inside that crag."

Catten nodded, and like two wraiths they sailed through the air towards the rocky hill in the distance. Verbard felt drawn towards the powerful source of magic inside the out-of-the-way landmark. It looked like a mountain, but was merely a rocky hill with a large cave mouth yawning wide open.

Inside, Verbard noted very little, but his glance showed the primitive comforts of occupancy. Catten strolled around the room, hands out, golden eyes alert.

Verbard paced about, trying to find the source of power, but it stayed hidden. When he stepped out of the cave mouth, he looked on in wonder. Verbard sucked in his breath. He could see every detail of the fight. Bodies hewed down. Dwarven forces scattered. He saw everything above, the sky, below, the sand and plains, and even the forests behind the mountain where he stood. From over a mile away, he could clearly see the angered face of a dwarf, chopping a Badoon down.

"Brother, come quick! Do you see this?"

By his side, Catten let out an excited hiss. "I see it all, my brother. This is new, completely fascinating. I can see the whole area for miles just as plain as the nose on your face. Stunning!"

"Those stubborn dwarves are still fighting, and the Vicious have still not acted," Verbard admonished.

Catten's golden eyes flashed. "This whole thing should be over by now. I hate to think that we might have to go back to clean up when we could be enjoying the victory from here."

"Perhaps we can do what we must from here," Verbard said, the corners of his mouth turning up. "It's certainly worth a try."

"Ooh … a good idea, indeed, but let's wait and see what happens first. The suns will be setting soon, and I like doing such things at night rather than in the blazing sunlight."

"Certainly, assuming we can afford to wait … eh."

Verbard noticed an object charging in the distance.

"Do you see something coming from the south? It's rather faint, but coming this way."

Catten leaned over the edge. "Hmm, I don't see it." He squinted. "Ah, now I do. Is this who I think it is? Finally—our nemesis comes!"

Verbard watched in silence. Just as he and his brother planned, the Darkslayer approached the trap. He had never relished the thought of battling the scourge of the underlings himself, but he'd never felt so robust before. His brother stiffened at his side. Their hatred ran deep for this human who had managed to slay hundreds—possibly thousands—of underlings over the years, to their great embarrassment.

The toll had grown high. The stories they had heard and the variety of descriptions of the man had never seemed believable, until now. The closer the man got, the more eager they felt to bury him once and for all.

Catten spoke up and said, "Let us see if we can take him out from here, Verbard."

"What shall it be, then? I say as soon as he hits the clearing—we turn him into dust!"

"No, we slow him down, smother him, and burn him alive with all means at our disposal. I am sure the Vicious can handle what is left. After which, we walk down there, skin him, remove his head from his shoulders and march it to the Underland on a pike!"

The pike won Verbard over. He nodded, stepping back to summon forth his energy. It grew inside him, something powerful and delicious, begging to be set free. He wanted to hold the intoxicating feeling a bit longer, the magic felt so good. Catten stood before him, his face a mask of concentration and limitless power. There was nothing to fear, nothing left but the urge to destroy one lone man. Verbard felt supreme, capable of leveling a city with the wave of his hand.

His silver eyes became saucers, staring at their target closing the distance, barreling toward where the Vicious still battled the giant dwarves. Powerful energy surged between both underling magi, unifying them in their thoughts. It felt like it would take little more than a single word to wipe out the whole lot of them.

"Don't try to kill them all." Catten urged Verbard.

Verbard cackled.

"Why not?"

70

T HE BLOOD RANGERS, ON THE edge of obliteration, fought on with fury.
The underlings unrelenting forces closed in.

There would be no meaningful tally. Only victory. Only death. Trinos had made it so.

However, Scorch had caused an imbalance, which Trinos had to correct. There had always been an equalizer for good and evil on Bish. As the battle between these two forces swung back and forth over decades, centuries, and millennia, the score had remained the same—until Scorch decided to tilt the odds. Although Trinos had changed it back, Bish would never be the same. And to get things back on course, the equalizer of Bish had work to do, whether he knew it or not.

Venir ran over the terrain with the speed of a galloping horse. He could not comprehend how he had moved so far so fast, but it was beyond him to slow his pace. His body no longer seemed his own. He felt like he had the strength and stamina of ten men. He was not the wind, but a gale. Not a river, but a waterfall. Not the rain, but a storm. His mind was a maelstrom of anger and violence.

The spiked helm was strapped to his clenched jaw, the eyelets burning like black fire. A streak of darkness filtered through the air behind him. His tattered clothing, grimy pants, and bloodied boots whistled through the wind. With white knuckles, he gripped Brool in his right hand while his iron-banded shield was tucked against his side. He could see the underlings now, tiny little specks in the distant Warfield. He smelled them; he heard them; he loathed them … he wanted to annihilate them.

He paid no notice to the two brutish heads with pointed ears and long claws barking orders at the mass of battle ahead. The creatures, underlings called the Vicious, were of the likes he had never seen before. Their backs were turned, and they screeched an awful sound as he ran past. The hulking creatures ran like lions on all fours, fanged mouths gnashing at his heels, but he was only concerned with the embattled throng of underlings ahead.

The two underling predators were fast enough to catch any human in seconds, yet they could not close in on the Darkslayer. They were close enough to see the wide V-shaped tattoo that stretched across his expansive back. Their cries were impassioned from behind, but now Venir was a human juggernaut that would not slow.

He raised his axe high.

Before him, the dark underling bodies were a synchronized mass of skill, armor, and steel. A singing Blood Ranger hurled two underlings over his head as their stabbing weapons pierced his belly, doubling him over.

Venir's battle rage blossomed. He ran roughshod into the backs of the Badoons that pressed in on the small circle of Blood Rangers. Brool carved out a path of mangled little figures. Sinking the axe into the shocked bodies of the underling soldiers intoxicated him. With every stride, he became quicker and his body stronger. Dark bodies fell in piles at his feet. Limbs were severed, bones shattered, and throats punctured.

Venir leapt high in the air, roaring his battle cry. He crashed like a great boulder, crushing two or three beneath him, while slamming into others with his shield. The front ranks of the underlings faltered as the Blood Rangers let out a cheer. Venir rolled across the hard, dusty ground and sprang to his feet. Instantly, Brool became a whirling razor's edge of death. The Darkslayer had arrived. The underlings howled with their weapons raised in alarm.

All pairs of colored underling eyes set on Venir. They looked like children with sharp toys pointed at him. They chittered back and forth. More cries rose up from the other side of their circle. In an instant, the mass swarmed him. Venir swept Brool into the first onslaught; the Blood Rangers anchored his sides. Within moments, the red-black blood of the underlings began spreading like spilled oil.

Limbs fell. Heads rolled under the fury of the man's corded arm. The underlings trampled over one another, alive or dead. Heavy dwarven blades cleaved into their bodies, but they continued to surge toward the man they hated beyond reason. Venir felt a few stinging blows, but more and more underlings fell mutilated at his feet. Brool's sweeping twin blades were as fast as a pair of short swords, weaving back and forth, striking like snakes. Venir and his axe were one. An underling leaped out of the fray, latching itself onto his shield. A dwarven hand axe chopped into its back. The Vicious were far from the melee, screaming orders to their single-minded minions. Not a single head turned. Not a single order was obeyed. The fine-tuned Badoon brigade was little more than a frenzied horde. The ensuing chaos resembled rats in a whirlpool; the more they struggled and thrashed, the more useless their attacks became. On they came, and down they went.

Venir's body seemed to move with a mind of its own. His own consciousness hovered in his mind, but it was as if he watched another's work unfold. Elation tingled up his spine. Wrath rushed through his blood. He was a mass of muscle and mayhem, steel and stone.

He split the face of an emerald-eyed underling. He was strong. He disemboweled another. He was invincible. He was outnumbered a hundred to one. Hah!

The surrounding Blood Rangers, exhausted and bleeding, did not hesitate to take hold of the new advantage. Crossbow bolts rocked out again, penetrating the heads of underling warriors with unfailing accuracy. The Blood Rangers, long beards dripping blood, chopped from all angles, slowing the underling pressure toward Venir.

Still, the Badoon Brigade's numbers were overwhelming. The Blood Rangers' heavy wounds took a toll on their valiant efforts. The underlings were only falling one by one now, rather than in heaps.

Venir swamped the fiends with a renewed surge that came upon him. He swung in large arcing circles at such speed that the underlings hesitated. One ventured inside the arcing perimeter, and Brool chopped its leg out from under it. Venir swiped his axe forward and backward. The underlings darted back and forth, stabbing away.

Venir's thigh burned from a nasty slash. He cried out as he crushed the underling's head with the edge of his shield. Another nipped in and out, only to have the tip of Brool's spike tear out its knee. Poisoned bolts from underling crossbows zinged over his head. His arms felt like anchors. His raging mind began to become his own.

One moment, Venir seemed to be slaughtering at will, and the next there were none within striking distance. Gasping for air, he watched his remaining foes rush away.

Two black hulking creatures, as tall as men, circled him. They had fluid gates, flawless physiques, and fingers clutching open and closed like daggers. The onyx-skinned humanoids were like nothing he had ever seen before. The invincible sensation was vanquished from his spine. Only courage remained.

He stood covered from helm to toe in baking gore. His eyes shone like boiling blue water. The blackened steel of Brool glinted as he swung it like a sickle back and forth. His body and mind were pushed past their limits. Every wound festered and ached. *Keep moving.* His helm, axe, and shield would not relent.

In unison, the armaments he had donned seemed to consume his whole body, driving him onward without mercy. His mind screamed, wanting it all to end, once and for all, but there was only one way it could ever end. *Fight or die.* It was time to dish out more revenge.

Venir leapt into action, charging after one Vicious only to be pursued by the other. The first Vicious whirled, readied hungry claws and teeth, and braced for the attack. Venir brought Brool full circle, swinging hard over the creature's ducking head. It slid away with astonishing speed. It popped up, claws clutching, beckoning for more.

"Blast your slick hides!" Venir roared.

The pursuing Vicious pounced at his back. Brool's blade chopped down, clipping it's shoulder. It sprang away. Venir held his shield close, looking back and forth. Whatever they were, they weren't underlings. The helm offered him no help anticipating their moves.

They rushed him. Brool cut and whirled in offense and defense, in short and long arcs, keeping the Vicious at bay. He shuffled over the dusty ground, grit blowing in his teeth as he gasped for breath. He strained with every swing, his boundless energy sapped. The claws of the Vicious managed a nick here and there, and more severe cuts followed. Venir groaned again.

He saw their eyes, calm and evil, knowing they were wearing him down, like jackals and a wounded lion. Their claw marks burned. He bled freely, soaking the legs of his tattered pants. He chased, chopped, and swung, but they danced away. Angry, his swings became wild. His limbs like lead. Brool burned in his clutches.

He knew he was losing, but hung on. He chopped. He battled. Death meant nothing but rest to him. He could bleed to death at their mercy, or try to kill at least one of them before he went. *Fight or die!* Reaching deep within himself, he summoned all his anger and hatred for one more valiant onslaught.

He slung his shield into the fang-like teeth of the nearest Vicious, drawing a howl of pain and surprise. High over his head, Venir gripped Brool in two hands and wrenched it down with such speed and accuracy that the air winced at the blow. The Vicious dodged, losing its entire left leg in the effort. It cried out like a banshee.

Defiant, the one-legged Vicious regained its balance and crouched to attack. Its stump showed not a drop of blood. As the Vicious leapt, Brool chopped through the air and slammed to the ground. Venir raised the axe and dropped it with furious strikes, hacking off flesh like chunks of wood. With a shudder, the creature's magical life force subsided forever.

The remaining Vicious grappled Venir from behind. His shredded, battle-weary arms could swing no more. Venir let Brool slip from his shaking hand. The dead weight of the monster hung on his back. The vile beast choked him and ripped his helmet from his head.

The Vicious hung onto him like an enormous blood leach. Its sharp claws cut and bored under his skin like lances. The opened holes gushed. It was man versus Vicious now, skin on skin.

Venir could feel icy breath on his neck and cold skin sliding on his back. Strong as tempered steel, the muscles of the creature squeezed him like a vice. His blood-soaked hair was ripped from his head. Painful claws dug into his skin. His exhausted body could no longer respond to the demands of his angry mind. Venir had little fight left inside him, but it would have to be enough.

Fight or die!

The two thrashed about the barren, rocky ground, entwined like pythons. Venir's hard head, powerful elbows, and honed instincts kept the Vicious from taking complete control. Venir's head butted under the creature's rock hard chin, drawing spots in his eyes. The Vicious twisted away, howling back at him in fury. *I live!* He gasped and wiped the blood from his eyes. *I fight!*

Little more than the span of a man separated the two warriors. The Vicious clicked his talon-like fingers together. Venir sucked his breath in with deep, pain-filled draws, noticing the creature didn't appear to have a scratch. He scanned the ground, but Brool was nowhere to be seen. He shook his mangled head, not knowing why the Vicious hadn't finished him; maybe it was just punishing him first.

This was it for him. The Warfield was his last stand. Letting out a final scream, Venir charged like an ox. The Vicious struck like a snake. Two clawed hands punctured him deep in his chest. He looked it in the eyes, choking down the urge to cry out. He clutched the evil thing's throat in his powerful hands and squeezed with all his might. The eyes of the Vicious bulged from their sockets, and its black tongue gagged soundlessly. Blood and saliva spit from Venir's lips as he wrenched the thing's iron neck with all his effort.

Venir sneered at the hatred and mockery in its face as its eyes receded back into their sockets. The gaping maw of the Vicious turned into a smile. Venir's grip went slack as his body began to pale. Every ounce of strength had been sapped from Bish's ultimate survivor. He didn't feel a thing when the creature hoisted him listless into the air, claws still buried to the knuckle in his chest. All he saw was the white hot light above. There was a rush of blue and brown as he was driven into the ground. He twitched like a fish out of water.

His body stopped.

Somewhere, somebody screamed.

Chongo's keen ears picked up on the battle from over a mile away. The big dog burst forward, heads howling in the wind. Mood was the first to see the carnage as they crested the ridge above the Warfield. Melegal rode Quickster right on his heels. They charged into the scene. Someone screamed. They all saw Venir's battered body pushed high in the air and slammed into the ground.

Mood leapt from Chongo's back and began bludgeoning the clinging Vicious with the backs of his big hand axes. The creature was balled up over Venir, claws still sunk deep in his sides. The Vicious scowled at Mood as it hung onto Venir like a giant black tick. Mood tried the blades of his axes, but his dwarven steel had no effect. The thick skin of the Vicious showed no sign of blood.

"What in the seven cities of Bish is this *thing*?" Mood bellowed. The giant dwarf pounded the evil thing on the head with his fists, avoiding the mess of Venir's gaunt face. Chongo barked and bit, but the Vicious just tightened its grip.

"Vee!" Georgio screamed, rushing to his hero's side. The boy jammed his sword into the creature's back. The Vicious let out a terrific scream of pain, but still it held on.

"Gimme that, boy!"

Mood snatched the sword away from Georgio and jabbed at the monster. It shrieked in pain, each poke going deeper. Finally, letting go in a howl of rage, it jumped away.

Chongo and Mood had the Vicious surrounded, their feet shuffling, cutting off any avenue of escape. Chongo managed to bite deep into its leg and hold it, while Mood carved a nasty groove in its chest. The Vicious drove its claws into Chongo. The big dog yelped and let go, but the furious Vicious remained at bay, with the dog and dwarf in relentless attack.

Melegal slipped past the melee and knelt at Venir's side. The man was caked with blood and dirt, his face almost unrecognizable. The thief tore off a sleeve from his shirt, then struggled to figure out which place to bandage first.

"Vee, what do you need?" Melegal's voice was dry and pleading. Venir was pale, his eyelids fluttering, his breath shallow and raspy. Venir's lips moved, so Melegal leaned his ear over his mouth.

"Helm." This single, almost inaudible word was all his busted lips could muster. "Helm."

Melegal's head snapped up.

"Georgio! Lefty! Find his helmet *now!*"

The boys scoured the area in a frenzy of action. Georgio appeared, dragging Brool along Venir's side.

"I said *helmet*, Georgio!"

Not appearing to notice the words, the boy just kneeled alongside Venir. Lefty appeared with the helmet.

Blinking, Melegal struggled to slip the helmet on his friend's sticky and matted head. There was no response from Venir, whose eyes remained closed. His breathing appeared to have stopped. Melegal slipped the helmet's buckle under Venir's chin.

"Is he going to die?" Georgio asked, tears running from his eyes.

A current of emotion stirred inside the thief, who ran his hand along his friend's arm. He was empty. Lefty curled up on the ground, weeping, body turned away from the sight.

Georgio pleaded,

"No! No! No!"

71

L ORD VERBARD'S MOMENT OF TRIUMPH had come. He didn't care about anything other than the destruction of the Darkslayer. The Vicious had his enemy surrounded, but he didn't care about them. His brother would have to understand. Every battle had casualties. He summoned bolts of bright energy that coiled along his robed arms. Catten turned toward him, gold eyes knowing his intent, lips mouthing the word, "Yes!" Feeling their unity was complete, Verbard turned his focus back to the Warfield.

Verbard took another glance at his brother, who whirled at him, face full of surprise. Two swords burst through the front of Verbard's chest with a bolt of pain. The appearance of the Nameless Two could not have come at a worse time. Verbard looked down at the dark red steel jutting from the front of his robes. It disappeared as they wrenched it out of him. Falling to his knees, Verbard murmured under his lips, and a shimmering magic coat formed around his body.

The robed warriors darted toward Catten, blades high and low. Catten raised his hands, igniting the Nameless Two's heads. In shock, Verbard watched the sandaled pair press silently forward, blades still poised in the air.

"Catten, help me!" Verbard cried out the best he could while trying to wipe the blood from his chest. His wounds were critical. He couldn't focus enough to summon the words that would stop him from bleeding to death.

Catten waved his hands, raising the Nameless Two off the ground. With another wave, Catten sent both figures sprawling out of the mouth of the cave, over the hillside, and hurtling down to the hard ground below.

When Verbard looked up, Catten was by his side, whispering in his ear. He could feel his gaping skin closing up, the pain subsiding from his body. His internal bleeding had slowed, but the wounds were still grave. The underlings were not known for their healing. Verbard would need more help. He had to get back home.

Verbard saw the grave look in his brother's eye. His situation was more serious than he was ever accustomed to. Something else flickered in the gold rim of his brother's eyes, too. Now would be an excellent opportunity for Catten to kill him. In Catten's place, would he not be tempted to do the same? Verbard watched with caution as Catten walked back over to the ledge of the cave mouth and let out a shriek.

Somehow, Verbard dragged himself to his feet and took several agonizing steps back to the ledge. "What now? Have they not yet killed him?" He saw one Blood Ranger and the two-headed dog fighting the lone Vicious. The man was lying still on the ground, surrounded by crying faces. *Please be dead!* His evil face soured when he saw that the Blood Rangers were routing the Badoon underlings.

At his side, Catten trembled with rage. "We have to finish him now, Verbard. Not a shred shall remain," Catten said. "We may not get another chance!"

Verbard was grim. He needed all of his energy to keep his own heart beating. "I have nothing for you, brother. I need all my strength to get home. Do what you can, and do it now."

The air began to shimmer with energy as Catten began a new incantation.

72

V ENIR FELT NOTHING. HE HEARD nothing. He saw nothing. Everything he was seemed to seep somewhere else. There were memories—faces and moments drifting in his mind. It all appeared in a distant haze, only to break up like smoke in the wind. He was ready to go to the abyss of the unknown ....

Thump. He heard a faint heartbeat and felt the burning of his skin mending together. *Thump-thump!* His heartbeat grew louder and faster, his blood igniting everything from his head to his toes. The sounds of battle awoke him from the darkness. Cries and sobs were nearby. Something powerful felt white hot on his head, but it didn't burn. His eyes snapped open to the blood-smeared and bewildered face of Melegal.

Venir gasped in a huge gulp of air. He lurched upright into a sitting position and rose to his feet. He searched for the creature that almost put him in the grave. It was there, trapped between two of his oldest friends. His helmet was no longer white hot. His mind was his own again, and his body was whole. The Darkslayer was back.

Venir extended his hand to Georgio and said, "*Give me my axe.*"

The boy dropped the handle in his awaiting hand.

The Vicious chomped its jaws up and down, baring its teeth. Venir rushed out to greet it. Unfettered, he was determined to kill it. It hissed and surged his way. Venir braced himself, arms springs of steel, axe ready to split the monster like a log. A loud chime of warning rang inside his head.

Thunder cracked from a distant rocky hilltop, and lightning exploded beneath his feet in a blinding flash. Everyone tumbled to the ground, and chunks of rock and debris fell through the air. Venir was down and stunned. The thunder continued to roll. Winds swirled above the battlefield. Chongo howled as he struggled back onto his feet. Whatever sent the magic must have missed.

The others lay still on the ground, struggling to regain their feet. Venir could see Mood, Melegal, and Lefty, but where was Georgio? A clicking sound came from nearby. The Vicious had seized its opportunity and snatched up the curly-locked Georgio by the neck. It dangled the screaming and kicking boy in front of his eyes. Georgio's face went purple as he stood there dumbfounded.

The Vicious hissed out an evil laugh and ran a clawed finger across the boy's throat, cutting it wide open. "NOOO!" Venir felt like he had been stabbed in the heart.

It dropped Georgio to the ground, where he lay in a growing pool of his own blood. Delighted, the Vicious snickered in its own evil way. Melegal and Lefty screamed. Mood howled in outrage.

Venir went on a rampage.

The cackling monster ducked and dodged Venir's blade. Brool's keen edge got closer and closer with each swing. He wasn't going to let it get away. He would have vengeance. The Vicious could not run, for Mood and Chongo kept it corralled. It had no choice but to face Venir.

Then, quick as a cobra, the powerful creature leapt at Venir, hands clutching for his throat.

SLICE!

One Vicious hand was gone, but another came.

SLICE!

Off came the other. The Vicious wailed in rage.

RIP!

The mocking maw of the evil creature fell to the ground.

CHOP!

CHOP!

Brool cut into bone and marrow.

CHOP!

CHOP!

CHOP!

That was for Georgio.

It was over in a few seconds. Nothing remained of the Vicious but a blackened heap and two severed hands.

Melegal held Georgio's limp body in his arms, his head in his lap, with Lefty giving what aid and comfort he could. Tears streamed down Lefty's face. His makeshift bandages were soaked red around Georgio's neck. Melegal's face filled with anguish.

Venir rushed to the boy's side. Georgio's face was sunken and listless.

Lefty cried, "You have to save him! He can't die!"

Venir took off his helmet and lowered it toward his young friend's head. Tears and sweat streaked down his grimy cheeks. He was torn with his own personal agony.

Yet, before the helmet touched him, the boy coughed up blood, and then some more. Melegal pulled the boy up and patted him on the back. Georgio screamed.

"Save me, Vee! Save me!"

Venir dropped the helmet and grabbed the boy in his arms. "You're alive!" Venir's eyes were as wide as the boy's. "Let me see your neck!" He gently removed the bandages. The boy's neck was caked with drying blood, but the nasty slash was closed and healed, almost as if nothing had happened. Venir fell back onto his seat. "By the giants of Bish! You're a Regener, Georgio! You're gonna be fine!"

Georgio hugged him tightly, crying and refusing to let go. Venir let the boy get it all out.

"He's a what?" asked Melegal, busy trying to rub the filth off his clothes.

"He's a self-healer; he regenerates. I'll be." He rubbed his chin. "Anyway, he's gonna be your friend for a long, long time, Melegal. I don't think we could get rid of Georgio if we tried! And I wouldn't want to, either!" he said, still hugging the boy and rubbing his head.

"Oh great." Melegal kept his head down, trying to hide his watery eyes. Mood showed a glint of yellow teeth behind his bearded face. Lefty jumped onto Georgio's back, shouting with glee, while Chongo devoured the remains of the Vicious. That's when Venir noticed that they all were gathered around the edge of a smoldering crater. He grabbed his helmet and axe.

73

"**I** CANNOT BELIEVE THIS, VERBARD. I cannot believe this," Catten said, shouting and trembling in outrage. "We had him. And now we have lost a brigade of our finest underling fighters, as well as two of Master Sinway's precious pets. My spell did not make a direct hit! It faltered!" Catten spluttered, dumbfounded. "And that human boy appears to have revived!"

"Something has changed this day." Verbard's voice was weak and raspy. "Something does not add up. Does this impossible turn of events make sense to you?"

"Yes, I think it does. You have no time to spare, however. We must go now."

Verbard was relieved at his brother's words. He had no desire to die at the Warfield. Nodding, he offered what magic power he could. The two brothers concentrated and blinked out of the cave. It was the first step of a strenuous journey back to the Underland.

74

NO MORE LIGHTNING CAME FROM the distance, and Venir sensed no more danger nearby. Only a smoking pit of busted rock and shining globs of glass remained. Instead of more fighting, he put his newfound energy to use in aiding those who were left alive.

Only four Blood Rangers remained at the Warfield, plus their king, Mood. In no other battle had more than two

Blood Rangers ever died. But not a single underling hunter from the Badoon brigade remained. Venir's arrival had enabled the Blood Rangers to rally and carve up the underlings.

Still, the loss of eight Blood Rangers did not seem possible, and Mood was left wondering about it. The past few days had seen strange events that many people of all races on Bish had begun to take note of, including the halfling Lefty Lightfoot.

Georgio was shaken, but the curvy dwarven ladies cleaned him up and calmed him with their soothing touches. Melegal, Lefty, Mood, and Venir were all amazed that he lived and had not the slightest scar as evidence that he had almost died.

Venir himself had scars all over, but the ones inflicted by the Vicious proved the worst of them all. Venir's thoughts went back to the lightning.

"Did anyone notice where that lightning came from?" he asked.

"I saw it come from that mountain hill," Georgio said, pointing.

"I wonder if that's something we need to check out. Any ideas?" Venir asked.

"Let's get back to Bone. That's been my idea all along." The thief had a cheerful sound in his voice, perhaps because he was sipping on a flask of dwarven ale. "Besides, our other pursuers are vanquished as well. Thanks to me."

"Ha. Well, as I recall, it was your idea to leave Bone in the first place. And look at you, not a scratch on you!" Venir took the buckskin flask from his friend and sucked it dry.

"It was your fault we had to leave. And I do my best to avoid wounds, unlike you, the human pincushion."

"Come to think of it, I don't even remember why we left!" Venir said, tossing the thief the empty flask.

"I'll refresh your memory on the way back then."

A dwarven woman with big hips, standing almost four feet tall, brought him another flask and began rubbing his shoulders. The thief was putty in her strong little hands.

"Thanks, Melegal," Venir said. "I'm looking forward to it already."

"Can I come?" Lefty Lightfoot had been so quiet he was all but forgotten; he had been busy writing something all along. "Please?"

Venir and Melegal looked at each other.

"Shall we let Georgio decide?" suggested Venir.

"Oh ... he's definitely coming!" The boy rubbed his neck and looked all about. "But what about the mountain that shoots lightning?"

"It doesn't appear to be shooting lightning right now, and I don't feel like fighting any mountains tonight." Venir just wanted to put this entire saga behind him. He'd had enough sun and sand to last a lifetime. But such was life on Bish.

"Me either," Georgio said. "And I really hate underlings now, Vee. I'm glad I'm not dead. I'd have missed you guys. What would've happened if I was dead?"

Venir shrugged. He had no answer for that. "Let's have no more close calls, Georgio. Let's get you back home, safe and sound. But we'll take a trip back to the big city first. Sound good?"

"Yes!" Georgio, Lefty, and Melegal all agreed.

<h1 style="text-align:center">75</h1>

R OYAL LORD ALMEN HAD BEEN so busy that he had not given much thought to the absence of McKnight, Oran, and Tonio. But now he began to wonder if he would ever see them again. His son had been the pride of Castle Almen, and although his new condition did not bode well for him, Tonio could still be useful.

Detective McKnight had always been a resourceful ally and henchman. His loss would be difficult to replace. It was something Almen did not need while he was under pressure from rival houses. He needed all of the loyal bodies he could find, and his son and McKnight were two of them.

The underling he could do without, however, for he could not be trusted. It had occurred to Almen when they left that it might be the last time he saw any of them. He hoped that he had not been right. In the meantime, he got back to his normal daily activities. He would find out about them soon enough.

McKnight's body lay motionless and still. Paralyzed and in pain, he wheezed softly through his nose. The poison hadn't killed him, but he wished it had. Night had fallen, and a foreign sound crawled inside his brain. Several spider-like beings the size of large dogs scurried down the massive trees and surrounded him. These strange creatures had never before been seen on Bish. They had the bodies of tarantulas, but the torsos, heads, and arms of humans. The vile faces of these creatures were like those of other men on Bish, except that they had eyes like those of insects. Two small antennas protruded from their heads, which were covered in jet-black hair. They carried small spears and had no need for clothing.

McKnight tried to recoil, but they dragged him along the ground. He thought he caught a glimpse of a man's face staring back at him. Two of the arachna-men lifted each body off the ground, while two others stood before the men and began blowing at them.

McKnight felt himself spinning around. The creatures opened their mouths wide, and threads of spider silk emerged to wind around him. *No! No! Noooo!* Enclosed in a cocoon, he was gathered up and carried high into the giant tree tops of the Great Forest.

76

A FRESH POT OF COFFEE BREWED in the apartment room above the Drunken Octopus inside the City of Bone. The room had little of worth: a small cupboard alongside an iron stove, a round table and four hapless chairs, a couple of cots and some blankets and pillows. It was very warm, but compared to the Outlands it was paradise. Lefty Lightfoot took up the least amount of room. He sat cross-legged in a corner, deftly writing on a sheet of parchment. He felt compelled to chronicle all that they had done. He asked question after question of Venir in particular, and Venir was more than happy to answer. The big man enjoyed having his own personal scribe, and Lefty found him very entertaining after his reveling. It took some getting used to, but Lefty was beginning to feel safe inside of City of Bone. He had friends there he knew he could count on.

Melegal lay stretched out on his cot, a jug of wine by his side, the smell of sweet perfume on his clothes. The women of Bone had something to offer that he swore he'd never part with again. If someone came for him again, he'd crawl into the sewers first. But maybe, just maybe he'd adventure to the City of Three.

Melegal had run out of complaints about the last adventure, and decided to give Venir a break. He couldn't help but notice that his friend had suffered more than he let on. The wounds from the last battle ran deep, and the near loss of Georgio had frightened them all. But it was clear that Venir was affected the most. Every day, Venir swore he'd take Georgio home, but he couldn't do it, much to Melegal's chagrin. The boy wasn't half bad, though. At least he made a good pot of coffee, not that Melegal ever said so.

Georgio was not much worse for wear. He sat at the round table and sliced his finger open with a knife. It hurt, more like a sting, but then he watched the wound close in seconds. It amazed him every time. He stuffed his third piece of pie in his face and washed it down with a glass of warm milk in one big gulp. Then he patted his belly. The Warfield was no more than a memory now. From time to time, he woke up at night coated in sweat and screaming, but a friend was always there, and getting back to sleep was never a problem.

Venir sat at the small table as well with Georgio. The boy talked but he paid Georgie's words little mind. Instead, he wondered how many underlings he had killed and how many more he still had to kill. He reached over to the stove and grabbed the pot of coffee, refilling his cup.

Venir was protective of the people in this room. Guilt had crept inside him and responsibility ate at him. He wasn't comfortable with such thoughts. A man of the Outlands couldn't survive with such soft feelings. Bish took who it pleased, and there was nothing he could do about that. *Just smile and laugh*, an old friend had told him, *it makes people think everything is all right.*

Recreation and relaxation wasn't such a bad thing, either. The women and ale had never tasted sweeter. Georgio lay down on the blankets beside his cot. The boy would be fine. Venir got up, heading for the door, and Melegal's soft footsteps fell in behind. Lefty waved his feathered quill, and out the door they went.

77

I T TOOK EVERYTHING UNDERLING LORD Catten had not to shake. He had been on a single knee, beaten and stripped, for what seemed days. All he heard was his brother's ragged breath, kneeling by his side, trembling, and sick. Verbard had been healed soon after they made their return to the Underland, but Verbard's body had paid a price, and Catten could only see a dull reflection in his brother's once bright silver eyes.

It was little more than two days after they returned home that the eruption of rumors crawled back to greet them. Catten knew full well that their colossal failure had spread throughout the under realm. He and his brother avoided their kin as best they could, but they couldn't hide forever. Master Sinway called them to his throne. He had been kneeling in silence ever since, every joint in his body aching. Only the use of his magic allowed him to maintain the uncomfortable position. A drop of sweat fell from his brow, the first one in days. Catten tried to imagine what the underling master had in store for them next. Would he have to fight his brother to the death, be devoured by cave dogs, dropped in the caves of infernos, or have his skin flayed from his face and back for all to see? The punishment for failure was always extreme. A beating was little punishment if any at all, still his pulped face ached. If only his fool of a brother hadn't been so careless and gotten stabbed, this all would have been over.

Ahead of him, Catten felt the mighty presence of Master Sinway, bearing down on his bowed head. The master of all underlings sat in robes blacker than night, on a large throne carved from rock and filled with scintillating metals and stones. The three of them were all alone. Catten wanted to grovel, but not doing so was his best hope. All he could do was wait.

Master Sinway's voice was soft and powerful, sending shivers into his core. "Do you have another plan?"

"Yes," Catten managed to reply.

Catten felt his body lifted up and hurled through the room in a rush of wind. He landed hard on the ground. When he looked up, he caught a glimpse of his master on the throne as two towering metal doors slammed closed.

I'm alive! Catten couldn't believe it. He looked at his brother's busted figure, struggling to rise from the floor.

His brother chittered as he floated away.

"He must be getting soft."

Catten couldn't disagree more.

ORIGINS OF
THE DARKSLAYER

1

VENIR WADED IN THE COOL silver stream, checking the trout snares he had set at the end of the previous day. His long, straw hair was pulled back into a ponytail that hung to shoulder length. A fisherman since birth, the twelve-year-old fished like a man of thirty. He wore only a pair of brown cotton trousers rolled up above his ankles as he sloshed into the water.

His gritty fingers gathered fishing line from a large pouch on his belt. He cut the line with a very long hunting knife and sheathed it back at his side. It had been his grandfather's, and he wore it with pride. His young muscles were fluid and supple as he moved the trout out of the traps, into nets, and into sacks for transport. It was hard work, but it had its rewards, for some of the fish he brought home were grilled or baked into delicious meals. He swore he could smell it cooking now. He had never missed such a feast.

With a smile, he hefted two large half-filled sacks over his back and whistled an ancient song of cheer.

A dog barked. *What now?*

From somewhere upstream, his agitated dog raced toward him. Unworried, he wandered up to find out what was upsetting his pet. The ordinary reddish-brown dog appeared along the stream bank, barking at something floating down the rippling waters. Venir set down his sacks with a grunt and waded into the water to try to catch it.

"It's just a stick, Chongo! Quit barking," he said in an irritated voice.

He had to check it out or his pooch would follow it to the mouth of the river, miles away. The last time they took a long trip down stream together he had almost drowned. His family had thought he would never fish again after that, but the incident only enhanced his resolve.

Peering upstream, he noticed some darkening of the water. Slowly, it started flowing past him, becoming thicker, darker, and reddish. He focused on the object floating toward him, Chongo splashing and barking in the water nearby. He grabbed it when it came within reach, and gasped in horror. It was a leg—a human leg—pale and clammy like a fish belly. He slung it as far away as he could. The dog howled, but recoiled from crossing the reddening water.

He tried to gather his thoughts, but only numbness and confusion set in. Something unnatural crawled inside him. Standing in water that was becoming something else shook the very innocence of his being. The once refreshing stream that had fed him all of his life had filled with blood, and he ran out of it, screaming. The young fisherman tingled from head to toe. Something was amiss … something awful.

"Chongo, come! We have to get home!" he yelled as they sprinted back toward the village.

It was not long before he heard the sounds; shrieks and wails gripped him with fear, but his legs pumped faster and faster. His imagination was paralyzed in terror. Billows of thick smoke burned his nostrils and water filled his eyes as he approached his home. The paths became more distinct, and his pace made the wind whistle in his ears. Screams of agony and terror filled his ears. His stomach turned. Tears streaked down his face. He wiped them from his eyes and forged ahead.

Chongo burst toward the center of the village, barking. Venir's burning eyes lit upon furry, black and gray hawk-nosed humanoids who ran wild through his village with bloodied weapons and dismembered body parts. They were smaller in size and frame than men, but he knew what they were. He didn't know how he knew, but these were underlings. Venir had heard enough terrible stories about Bish's Underland to know what to expect at the sight of an underling. Hearing about the foul menace at campfires was nothing compared to seeing them in action. It was overwhelming.

He froze, trying to comprehend the black and bloody madness surrounding him. Women, children, men, friends, and family were dead, dying, bleeding, and crying. They ran all about in desperation, trying to evade their pursuers, only to be cut down. The villagers had been taken by surprise, and their weapons were little match for underling magic and steel. Many lay in bloodied heaps on the ground.

Venir froze amid the chaos. A dark figure was coming his way. He gripped the hilt of his ancient knife. An underling hunter rushed directly into his path and screamed in his face. The underling's face was covered with thin fur and blood. It bared its sharpened gray teeth and raised an odd shaped dagger before him. Venir struck. His hunting knife tore out the throat of the surprised underling, who gurgled and fell into its own pool of dark blood.

Venir was in motion—running, screaming, and slashing at the wild horde. His long blade sank deep into flesh and bone. Howls of pain and fury assaulted him. The heat that had surged through him from fear now fueled his limbs as he punched holes into the dark bodies of his enemies. In the confusion, many underlings backed away, staring back and forth at one another with uncertainty. Amid the smoke, fire, and chaos the hunters faced the wild slashing boy. A couple of them were felled by his anger.

The seasoned attackers barked out commands, surrounding him. Venir squared up to three underlings in his path, swinging and stabbing with all of his heart. They parried his attacks, toying with him, chittering in mockery, as they awaited their moment. Wearing black armor and cloaks, they brandished weapons of all sorts, and stared at him with scintillating eyes of everlasting evil.

Venir fought on, determined to spill their blood. Several poisoned darts hit his exposed body. He burned inside for a moment, and then his limbs went numb. He fell backward onto the ground, cold and stiff.

Before his frozen gaze, the sneering faces of underlings passed by. He felt himself being dragged across the bloodied grass. He could hear their mocking, smell their sweat and dark blood. They did painful things to him, but he felt no fear of them. His smoldering will protected him from utter despair. The moments became like hours, tortuous and dragging as the sounds of shovels dug into the ground. One shovelful at a time punched into the dirt nearby, a sound that ground into his brain like a chisel. What had happened to his family and Chongo? It was time to cry, but no tears came. *Mother? Father? Where are you?*

Venir was grabbed by his feet and turned around. He saw piles dead bodies. His people. The underling with the shovel walked back into his line of sight and sneered. Raising the spade over its head, it began bashing his people one by one. They all died before his eyes in a heartless and cruel moment of twisted triumph. His heart cried out, bursting inside his chest, burning with fire, and as it all came to an end, a single tear ran down his grimy cheek. The underling chittered with laughter, laid the bloody shovel down before Venir's eyes, and dragged him away. He passed more corpses. Many of them were buried head first in the ground with only their legs sticking out. *Buried alive? No! No! No!*

His limp body was pitched face first into a man-sized ditch. In a final, tortuous twist of fate, the dirt hole became his personal grave. He heard the metal spade digging into the ground. Dirt gathered around his head, shovelful by shovelful. Each heap of dirt brought him closer and closer to his last moments on Bish. Soon, the light was no more. He was finally covered and laid to rest, not hopeless but angry. The blackness suffocated him, but his rage burned bright until the end. Yet, without oxygen, all fires extinguish, and the young hunter from the village of Throhm blacked out.

He heard something. A popping and cracking sounded. He felt grit in his eyes and struggled to wipe it out. He lay on rugged ground. A blurry image of a man with bushy hair squatted by the fire with a slab of meat roasting on a spit. Venir tried to move toward the fire, but he only managed to let out a feeble groan. The stocky figure turned his way as something else stepped into his view and licked his face.

A deep voice rumbled in his ears.

"Yer gawn bee fine, boy.

Venir shivered.

2

D ESPITE THE TRAGEDY DURING HIS boyhood, more than ten seasons later Venir's spirit remained unbroken. His freedom among the cities, forests and dry lands kept a grim smile on his face most of the time. A good meal and a comfortable place to sleep was more than enough to satisfy him. And so, with trial, he lived on.

Where the thick forests ended and the harsh grit of the Outlands met, the young outlander had settled in Two-Ten City. Inside the falling city—an unimpressive tavern called the Orc's Elbow—he carried on with his colleagues. It was an unusual oaken tavern with a grimy gray-brown exterior, in a two-story building with few support walls. It appeared that the second story would tumble down at any moment.

Despite its name, no full orcs were to be found inside. The tavern's previous owner, a full orc, had wagered the Orc's Elbow on a fight between Venir and another. The orcen man had lost. Since then, not a single full orc had re-entered it. Venir had been comrades with the new owner, Billip, ever since.

"So Billip, what's the wager tonight?" he said as he sat his big body on a groaning stool. The man behind the bar sent a fresh mug of mead sliding his way.

"Ah, wouldn't you like in on the action! Well, I'll tell you. I've got ten good gold against Melegal. That dirty donkey of his will be mine if he can't throw a bulls-eye, blindfolded, from ten paces." Billip cracked his knuckles, grinning with greed.

A lean figure in loose fitting clothes looked up from farther down the bar and rolled his eyes. Billip glared at the skinny man and fidgeted. His dark eyes always seemed to be calculating odds under his mop of short black hair. Nothing appeared extraordinary about his stout, wiry frame or his weathered skin as he moved with fluid purpose about the bar. The tavern owner was a tireless tracker and an unrivaled archer, and as loyal a man as could be found on Bish. Older than Venir, Billip had much more experience as a soldier, a trader, and a gambler, which was what might have led to him living in Two-Ten City in the first place.

The scout kept his private thoughts to himself and never confirmed it, but Venir suspected that Billip had got in over his head somewhere along the line. The security of this undesirable multi-humanoid city was as good a place to hide as any.

The other man at the bar pulled his sleeves up along his bony wrists, adjusted his floppy hat, and savored his purple wine. Billip dug around under the bar and produced a black cloth. Venir, comfortable in his spot, slurped his mead and watched.

Melegal pushed himself away from the bar, walked over to Billip, and stood as still as a crane. Billip strapped the thick black cloth around the man's narrow head and walked over to the adjacent wall. He outlined a large gold talent with a white piece of chalk. The blinded man's ear bent as the raunchy tavern dwellers closed in. Melegal stiffened, but Venir cleared his throat a few times, and the thief's rigid posture loosened. Being blindfolded wasn't something one normally did in treacherous taverns, but the gold made it worth the risk. Venir bristled in his chair, and the audience retreated. They all had enemies, and no one was ever safe, especially in Two-Ten City.

"Listen now, Melegal. Let me remind you of the rules. Your hit has to be inside the mark," Billip rapped his knuckle on the spot, "… not touching it. Not even close to touching it!"

Melegal smirked and drew a short, flat throwing dagger from inside his shirt. The betting crowd quieted to a hush. With a flick of his wrist, Melegal's dagger sliced the air and landed with a loud *thunk*, dead center as Billip jerked away his calloused fingers.

"I didn't say go yet!"

Venir laughed out loud. He couldn't remember the last time he had done so. When the others got over their amazement they began laughing, too. Billip snatched the dagger out of the wall and threw it into the floor.

"You wait until I say go—and you don't get to use your *own* dagger! That's cheating, and you didn't let me finish the rules. Don't move!" Billip said as he scurried away with a furrowed brow.

Melegal waited, hands on hips, sighing while his challenger hunted, crashed, and cursed from inside the kitchen. The barkeep returned, showing a thin row of white teeth, and placed an object in Melegal's waiting hand.

This should be good, Venir thought, leaning back on the bar.

The blindfolded man ran his delicate fingers over the object and twirled it around with a scowl. Melegal said, "Are you expecting me to throw a wood-handled steak knife into that wall?"

"Sure," Billip answered with cheer.

"Surely you jest?"

"I don't jest when it comes to my wages. House rules. My house, my rules."

"It doesn't even have a point. Its round on the end," Melegal said, fingering the edge. "I'm surprised you didn't give me a spoon. This is ridiculous."

"Too bad. Double or nothing. No—triple! Make your throw or give me your mule—plus ten gold!"

Venir covered his mouth as Melegal bristled at the remark. The two challengers burst into a flurry of unpleasant words. Billip was trying to get inside Melegal's head. There had been a hot issue between the two for some time over the pack animal, Quickster. The two argued another five minutes over the issue of true ownership. He watched the agitated men, wondering who would swing first. Someone else from the crowd told them to shut up and get it over with or they would all leave. As quick as it started, it was over. The two men got back to business, but both men's lips were tight. Billip looked over at him and shrugged. *Nice try,* Venir thought. "Wait until I say go," Billip added.

"I'm waiting," the thief replied.

Billip paced about, checking the blindfold until he was satisfied. The room tingled with anticipation. Coins shuffled between eager hands. The barkeep raised his arms and voice.

"Well enough—Go!"

The knife flicked out of the man's hand like a snake's tongue and lodged itself inside the circle. The knife handle hung down at an angle, but held firm to the wall. The crowd cheered.

"Nooo!" Billip fell to his knees, holding his head, teeth clenched. "How did he do that? He does it every time. He's gotta miss one of these days!"

Billip tugged at his black hair, screamed, and stormed into the kitchen. A loud crash came from behind the wall. His staff rushed out with ashen faces.

The tavern erupted with praise and laughter as Melegal joined Venir at the bar.

"Good show, Melegal," he said, refilling the rogue's wine glass.

"Indeed." The man saluted before slinging the blindfold away.

Billip resurfaced and dropped his coins on the bar. The man's cheeks had cooled, and he didn't watch as the coins disappeared faster than they appeared. The two men gave a quick nod to one another

"Come on," Billip said, motioning with his head. Venir and Melegal followed him to a more discrete booth near the back end of the bar.

"All right, so what's the big news?" Venir asked in an eager voice, while Melegal fingered a piece of his winnings, drawing a hard look from the barkeep.

Billip turned to Venir, scratching his head.

"You know, I love the Outlands and the forests and all, but I don't see how you live out there as long as you do and survive. Don't you miss the comforts of the city? The food and companionship? The girls keep asking me where my tawny-headed friend is. I ain't got time to answer to your whereabouts all the time. I'm not your keeper, you know."

"Yeah, me neither," Melegal added.

Venir shrugged. They never understood before, so why bring it up now?

"Someone's got to keep tabs on the underlings."

Billip just shook his head and said, "I don't understand you."

Venir beckoned for the man to continue.

Billip popped his knuckles.

"Anyway, things are stirring up around here. I'm not used to it. A detestable bunch of mercenaries—not at all like us—are doing a lot of recruiting here in Two-Ten. Some of our fellows say they're paying well—extremely well—and some have even joined up."

A steaming meal of steak and potatoes arrived with a strong-smelling pot of coffee. The powerful aroma roused his senses; Venir hadn't had any in weeks. He took a few welcome gulps of the fresh brew straight from the pot. "Ah" he moaned. *Too long.* Venir topped off his mug and shrugged again. "That's it? More mercenaries for hire? It is just Royals up to their dirty tricks. I don't see the big deal—"

"I'm not finished," Billip stammered, almost spilling his glass. "Mind your elder, Venir. I've been chatting them up when they ask for people, and Melegal has been listening in, too. They keep pretty hush-hush about their purposes, but we're pretty sure we've figured it out."

Venir leaned back in his chair and took a long, hot sip.

"Well, what?" he asked.

"You sure you wanna know?'

"Yes. What is it?"

Billip's voice was excited as he continued.

"They're raising a brigand army of the likes never before seen on Bish. I'm talking at least three hundred brigands. And they ain't all human, either. They send humans to recruit, but it's the orcs that are leaving in masses."

"Great! The fewer full orcs in Two-Ten the better. What's the problem?"

"They're being led by a woman—a human woman."

There was a moment of pause.

Venir tugged on the locks of his braided hair that hung over his shoulder. "A woman? That can't be. And it's hardly an army. Maybe a small one. I'll believe it when I see it."

Melegal interjected,

"It's true, Vee. They call her Jarla, the Brigand Queen. They revere her. They say she started with a small band near the White Blaze Pass beyond the Underland, and she's been slowly carving her way through Bish for years. According to her men, they've been devastating merchant trains, human settlements, and even Royal outposts."

Melegal kept his voice at a harsh whisper as a group of merchants glanced their way.

"Now, that's not normal protocol for brigands. They might rob men, but now they've been slaughtering them, too … and their families as well."

Venir's flaxen brows creased over his eyes as he rubbed his square cut chin. He and his own mercenary troupe had seen and done much that very few would understand. They always drew the line at what had to be done. As for common brigands, they tended to scare rather than harm their own kind, and there were usually no more than a dozen or so to the gang. The thought of a brigand army that plundered, killed, and battled organized soldiers didn't make sense. He hadn't been far south lately, but maybe it was time he went and checked on some old friends.

"What are you thinking, Venir? You wanna go check if the rumors are true? I'm ready when you are," Billip offered, "and Mikkel's keen, too."

"Count me in," Melegal said, to Venir's surprise. "Even I need to get out of this stinking hole sometimes."

"All right, but I want to enjoy myself some first," Venir remarked. "We'll figure something out tomorrow. I need to unwind. Say, where are they keeping the pretty women these days? Clearly they still aren't coming in here."

"Melegal runs them off every time he offers them a ride on his donkey," Billip said.

Venir laughed. It was time to revel into the hot night. As he got up, he felt an uncomfortable presence looming nearby. Scanning the room, he noticed nothing odd. He gulped down the remaining pot of coffee and tried to let the feeling go, but it hung in the air. Hopefully, a few stiff drinks and wayward songs would wash the feeling away.

3

T WO DAYS LATER, A SMALL band of men began the journey south toward the camp of Jarla, the Brigand Queen. The terrain they traveled was far more hospitable than the barren north, as the thick forests offered refuge from the two blazing suns. The southern lands of Bish contained less marsh, less desert dust, and more blue-green foliage. Cooling oases with large streams cropped up in their midst. But, unlike the north, the terrain was anything but flat. Unforgiving hills and valleys slowed travel, forcing a narrow traverse through winding passes, rather than straight over the hilltops. It kept the small party on edge, as it was a perfect place for an ambush.

The high ground was good ground, as small Royal outposts could be seen in the distance, flying the flags of their people. The Royal soldiers kept watch over this lush land. Farms and villages thrived in the rich soil, where food, water and timber were valuable commodities among the world rulers. The Royals protected their investments well, yet the southlands of Bish were just as treacherous as those of the north.

Brigands, orcs, dog-faced gnolls, and kobolds thrived and raised their kind in this land as well. Most of the time, they fought one another, but they also raided and pillaged the more peaceful inhabitants. It had been the natural order of things for as long as anyone remembered. Not a day passed in the world without violence of the most treacherous nature. It made for hardened people everywhere.

As the men passed through the villages they happened upon, the tales of Jarla's brigand army became more intriguing. Venir could not tell if what they heard was truth or rumor, but the people seemed convincing enough. The repeated claims of a large army of orcs, kobolds, humans and gnolls, all functioning as a single unit under a woman's command, toyed with his imagination.

Still, it was a hard story for Venir to swallow. In his experience, two races almost never fought in a cohesive unit, let alone four. The leader must be the biggest, ugliest woman a woman could be, he thought. He was compelled to see for himself, and his thoughts of hunting underlings uncharacteristically drifted away.

Female leaders were uncommon in Bish. Most races were not led by fighting women. Venir was astonished that the rough races were following a female, let alone one of another race. As for female soldiers, he had known plenty among the human ranks, but they never ventured together too long. The men tended to want the women as more than just fellow soldiers, and those men often suffered dire injuries as a result. So how had this one woman created an army that threatened the southern lands of Bish? He had to find out.

The long hours of silence were broken when Mikkel spoke with the voice of a rushing river.

"Man, I can't believe there are kobolds in that army. That's stupid!" the powerful black man said, spitting.

"Aye, I'm not so sure we need to get too curious about all this," Billip added, wiping the sweat from his brow with a handkerchief.

"We've come this far. Let's just get a quick look. It's hard to imagine the stories are true, but who knows." Venir sipped from his canteen.

The small band pushed through the slippery terrain on foot, pressing deeper into the forests. He and the company had traveled like this dozens of times over the years, and they all knew how to handle things if they ever got into a pinch. They were all dressed in tunics of leather or woodsman garb, except for Melegal, who wore drab clothes of his own design. Backpacks, canteens, belt pouches, and weapons of choice made up the rest of their personal gear. The humidity in the south was as thick as water. Sweat rolled off the men's heads and soaked their attire. Venir and Mikkel's bare biceps were thick with oily sweat. Billip's cloth-covered arms were soaked, while Melegal appeared as dry as a bone, drawing a frustrated grunt from Billip.

The men did not brandish arms as they navigated the difficult territory. Instead, they left their grubby fingers free to fight for miniscule grips as they crossed over jutting hillsides and down into plunging gorges. Billip led the way with a short composite bow across his back, and Mikkel had a heavy crossbow strapped across his. Venir carried a short bow, and each had a quiver, while the wiry scout ahead carried a spare. Swords, daggers and knives could be seen at their hips. Whatever the thief carried was not apparent.

"So what's the plan, Vee?" Mikkel asked from behind. "I know you have one. Do we take a look? Spy, attack, join?"

"I thought we'd just rob them. I'm sure we can take them all on since you're with us, Mikkel."

"Well, I'm the only true fighter in this pack, besides you. I've no idea why you brought these other two sandbags along." Mikkel jutted his thumb back over his shoulder. "They never fight closer than thirty feet."

"Don't talk like that," Billip said, glaring back. "I do my fair share, unlike Melegal. Just look at him, he even avoids his own sweat."

"Hah, you can say all you like, but someone's gonna have to dig your graves one of these days," Melegal chimed in from the rear, "… so be grateful. And just to be clear, I won't do the digging. I'll use Billip's money to pay his urchins to do that."

"Melegal, you are cruel. But I like it!" Mikkel shot him a grin, white teeth gleaming in the sun. Billip scowled and huffed forward over a mossy ledge.

Chongo appeared at Venir's side after he stood atop the ledge. The shaggy brown mastiff licked his face as he poured water into his meaty palm. The dog was lapping it up when he suddenly stopped, ears perking up, and began scurrying back and forth, barking in low puffs.

"All right, Chongo's found something. Let's step it up. I've got a feeling we're about to happen upon the brigand army."

"Great, so when you gonna share your plan, Vee?" said Mikkel. "Or do I have to come up with one myself?"

"Bad idea, we know how your plans turn out," the scout said.

Mikkel folded his arms over his powerful chest.

"What you talking about, Billip?"

"Oh, well, how 'bout the time you wanted to—"

"Silence!" Mikkel retorted. "Venir, what's the plan?"

"If we get caught, I say we just act like we're interested … play dumb is all. Hopefully we won't arouse any problems. I figure we can get a closer look first."

"Well, don't expect me to act too friendly with the kobolds," Mikkel said, clutching his studded club. "If they get too close, I'll crack their stupid little skulls."

"We know!" they all replied, causing the man's light blue eyes to widen.

As quiet as cats, they followed after Chongo, deeper into the belly of the southern forest.

<h1 style="text-align:center">4</h1>

I T HAD TAKEN ALMOST THIRTY minutes of diligent pursuit for the weathered group to catch up with Chongo. The dog's growl was low and excited as its stiff tail whipped back and forth. The men crouched down. The sound of clashing steel and raised voices traveled from not far in the distance. The trees and broad foliage muted the battle sounds, and the men glanced at one another, their faces drawn taut as Billip and Mikkel readied their missile weapons.

Using hand signals, Venir directed Billip and Chongo to scout ahead, followed by him and Melegal, with Mikkel in the rear. They moved like big gray foxes through the flourishing green, ignoring the briars and bugs. They stopped and waited in a small clearing while the archer and dog disappeared. He could now distinguish the voices of men crying out in battle. He gestured to Melegal, *How many?*

The rogue's eyes were closed, hand cupping his ear. With a slight shrug he flashed ten fingers.

We can take them, Mikkel mouthed back.

He wanted to laugh as Melegal's scowl deepened. Venir had no intention of engaging anyone, even if his companions liked to attack first and think later. In nervous anticipation, they waited in the agonizing heat. He took out his short bow and rubbed a dab of oil along its taut string. Ten men were a lot to take on, and they would need to be ready to fight at a second's notice—or flee if necessary.

As a trained ranger with seasons of hard soldiering, he knew better than to take things head on; sometimes it paid better to just watch and report. The seconds dragged as the sounds of pain and agony droned on. Concern showed in all of their faces when the dog appeared with the scout running behind. "It's safe to talk low," Billip said, slightly out of breath. "Ten Royal foot soldiers are already dead, and about six are left, heavily armed and battling four gnolls and an armored woman." Billip pulled out his canteen, shaking his head. "The soldiers have their hands full. They're below this ridge; looks like they got trapped."

"Any others?" Venir asked.

"I took a good look. No signs. But that woman fights better than two gnolls together. Never seen anything like it. What do we do? You want to go around?"

Everyone looked at Venir.

He didn't want to risk anyone, but he couldn't stand the thought of men falling to the gnolls. The tall, wolf-faced humanoids with canine teeth were dreaded warriors. They killed for pleasure and were known for their lengthy torture of prisoners. Despite their hairy, wolf-like appearance, gnolls spoke the common tongue well and could track like dogs. They were not vast in number, but were well-trained, armed, and formidable warriors. The fact that a woman fought with them suggested that he was about to encounter the brigand army. A wave of excitement overcame him, turning his guts. "Let's all take a look. I have a feeling this is what we came to see."

Billip led, drawing from his quiver as they fell behind in a small column. They crept to the edge of a ridge, flat on their bellies with weapons drawn, bolts locked and arrows nocked. Below, the battle was furious and bloody. The seasoned Royal soldiers fought with gleaming longswords and crested shields. Their breastplates and battle helmets were battered and smeared red.

Corpses of hacked down men littered the scene, gashed and punctured, still as logs on the ground. More soldiers were cut down with swords and hacking axes, overwhelmed by greater speed and power. Venir fought the urge to charge down into the fray. He kept his bow ready, rising to a knee. At times like this, the inhabitants of Bish had to weigh their own odds of survival before getting involved. *What's this?*

A striking female warrior carved up the soldiers as if they were just boys. She wore only a sleeveless chain mail dress of bronze, ending high above her knees. Her sinewy arms and legs were blood-splattered, and long jet-black hair flowed from beneath a spiked helmet of an ornate design. The only other protection she wore were iron-banded bracers around her forearms, but most impressive were the pair of battle axes she used with intense ferocity. One in each hand, she commanded the matching weapons as easily as a jester tossing apples. Her viper-like strikes were powerful and devastating. He had never seen the likes of her before.

He watched from above in awe, uncertain how to react. Seeing men die under the banner of a good Royal house was not easy to watch. It was even harder as the evil gnolls were taking part. Anticipation and the passion to act built up inside him. Melegal gripped his broad shoulder and pulled him back. Venir eyed the man and nodded. *Not our fight.* He maintained his position and continued to watch the battle unfold.

The woman warrior's haymaker axe blades felled her opponents one by one. Her axes, spiked on the back, penetrated their shields and ripped them from the soldiers' grasps, leaving the men to defend with only their longswords. The gnolls were engaged as well, heavy bastard swords swinging hard and deadly, keeping the valiant men from escaping her wrath. She fought each man, one by one, as if there was a personal score to settle. The blood curdling screams she let out after each victory made it clear that she relished what she was doing.

One soldier snatched a second longsword from the ground and fought her two-handed. He held his ground in feverish parries and she pounded away at him. The exhausted man stabbed at her only to catch a spike in his skull, finishing his valiant efforts. She slung the gore from her axe and was on to her next victim. Despite the demoralizing situation, the Royal foot soldiers did not cower; they faced her, one by one, with the bravado of the best from Bish.

Now the soldiers were down to just two, fighting back to back, pinned in by the woman and the remaining three gnoll warriors. Surrounded, they began to defend more than they attacked. The woman cursed and barked at her men; these soldiers were proving more formidable than expected. She demanded her opponents surrender, but the exhausted men did not lower their blades. They cursed back and spit on the ground. *Fight and die … no shame in that.*

One soldier was bleeding heavily, his leg useless, and head sagging under a heavy iron helm. Two gnolls pounced on him, batted away his sword, stabbed his wavering figure deep in the back of the neck, and the man crumpled lifeless to the ground. Now there was just one Royal left— the commander.

Two big gnolls loomed to the man's left and right, barring his path, leaving him squared up against the approaching woman. The soldier readied his sword that gleamed bright red in the sunlight. The man showed no fear, his face as hard as stone, ready to take his fate head on. *Klatch!* A heavy bolt struck a bull's eye into one gnoll's forehead. The Royal commander flinched, but the woman didn't. Two more arrows zipped through the air, burrowing into the armored chest of the other gnoll, dropping it wailing to the ground with a thud.

Bish! Venir charged down the ridge.

Uncertainty didn't slow the helmed woman. She responded, moving in like a panther. Swinging low, she tore out the armored commander's left knee with her axe-blade. The soldier cut back with a powerful two-handed blow, which she deflected with her bracer, skinning her arm. She screamed in fury. She countered with a crunching blow, punching through his breastplate and deep into his clavicle. The sword dropped from the man's lifeless grip as he fell to one knee.

Venir charged in behind her, yelling for her to stop, but her finishing blow was too fast. She crowned the man between the eyelets of his helm. The soldier was dead. She turned just in time to see him coming for her, and began laughing.

"It seems you are too late to save this man," she said, ripping her axe from the man's head. "Now, can you save yourself, yellow hair?"

Venir paused ten steps away from her, heart thundering in his temples, and brandished his longsword and hunting knife. Beside him, Chongo barked and growled.

"Mmm … dog meat, my favorite," she said, licking her maroon lips.

He measured his next move. He had more support than she. She did not seem worried about him, though, or the rest of them. She stood before him, tall and proud. Now, Venir was so close that her features captured his imagination. Her dark blue eyes burned from behind the eyelets of her helmet, intelligent and cunning. He yearned to know more about the woman who dripped blood from the axes that hung loose in her hands.

"Hey, yellow hair," she said in a taunting voice, "if you see something you like, why not just come and get it?"

He didn't know what to say as she added,

"Seems I have a mute boy here. It's a shame, all muscle and no tongue."

A bright white smile grew under Venir's nose as she stepped forward, then back. He sheathed his sword and knife and folded his arms over his chest.

"I can't help but wonder why a woman such as you would run around with filthy gnolls? Surely you can keep better company?"

"Ah, the boy has a tongue. I might have use for you yet."

She stared back and took better measure of the man she faced. Her battle-hardened body loosened. Her eyes bored into his chest as if she liked what she saw. He was ready for her to spring at any moment, fighting to maintain his composure. He felt something churn inside of him as she continued to look him up and down.

Rivulets of blood slid off her coated helmet as she removed it. Her face was beautiful, slender and strong. Her dark eyes searched his. Her blood-smeared skin was browned by the suns, her cheekbones, high and noble, were scarred and somewhat disfigured, but he kept his gaze on her eyes alone. She seemed to like that; a smile kept coming and going from her lips. She walked down the bank, and the closer she came the more he seemed to fall under her shadow. She seemed taller than him. *If this woman isn't the Brigand Queen, she must be the queen of something.* She stopped just out of striking range as he hushed his barking dog and it dropped to its haunches. Danger still prickled the air, but it could wait.

"So, tell me, yellow hair," she said in a voice as polished as silver, "why did you kill my men? They had no quarrel with you … or yours." She looked around, but there were no signs of his companions.

"My name is, Venir," he said, "and gnolls are not men. They are beasts that we like to kill. Luckily for you, you are not a gnoll, and we don't like to kill women, or you would be dead, too."

"Hah!" she said. "Even if I were a gnoll woman, you wouldn't be able to kill me." She waved her battle axes in front of his face. Their craftsmanship was of the likes he had never seen. He found them almost as fascinating as her.

A few silent moments went by. The tension in the forest seemed to ease.

"I'll tell you what, *Vee-neer*. I'll spare you and your men if you tell me what business you have in my forest."

"Spare us? Now it's my turn to laugh. Hah!" he said, not hiding his chuckle. "Anyway, we are looking for some people."

"What kind of people?" she said, wiping blood from her lips.

"Ones who follow a brigand queen named Jarla. If she lives in your forests you may have heard of her," he said, not withholding an ounce of sarcasm. "I hear she mates with gnolls and has a butt like an ogre. Ever hear of her, princess?"

"You are a witty one, Venir, I will give you that. It's been a long time since a man made me laugh." She gave him another once over as she looked around. "It seems I'm in need of a new escort. I need to report back to this *queen* you spoke of." She rolled her eyes. "Perhaps I can help. She is very fond of me."

"Eh … that would be nice."

"I suggest you watch your tongue in the meantime, yellow hair. I think you have seen what I can do to people I don't like."

He nodded, not certain what to say.

"So … why did you take them down? Royal houses are not often trifled with."

Her face darkened into another identity. "It was payback," she responded.

Seeing her glare, he backed off the topic.

"So, now what?"

"Tell your two men to come on in. I'll take you back to *my* camp and feed you. But, don't kill any more of my gnolls. Got it?"

"I'm not promising anything."

Billip, Mikkel, and Chongo were all quiet as they accompanied Venir back to the woman's camp. It was unsettling. Marching a more-than-capable warrior back to her own camp that contained natural enemies among its ranks was not the best idea for survival. Venir, however, was oblivious to those concerns. He didn't understand that his passion was overcoming his reason as he followed her. He just knew he had to follow her. He paid no mind to the dour looks behind his back.

Melegal, however, had managed to evade the situation. She had given no indication that she knew of his presence.

From the trees on the higher ground, the rogue watched them go, shaking his head. Melegal wondered if he'd ever see his comrades again.

"Stupid …"

<h1 style="text-align:center">5</h1>

S HE LED THEM MILES DEEP into a wide, ravine-like pass. The farther they went, the more sluggish the hikers became. Few words were said among them. Venir would have followed her athletic figure anywhere across Bish. Watching her long, glistening legs pass through the brush and climb over mossy edges made him thirst more than usual. He looked back at his friends, whose faces were grim and downcast. *They'll be all right.*

The ravine was narrow and wet. He felt the aim of notched bows bearing down on his chest as he looked up into the thick tree branches. The singing birds became silent as the pass bottomed out before a massive hill, made up of jagged rocks and vine-like trees, rising toward a flat top. *Good place to hide.* She crested the hill, disappearing from his sight. A foul smell began to choke the humid air. Doubt grew inside his chest before he scrambled after her, sending shards of rock sliding down the hill, bringing sharp complaints from below. When he made it over the top and crouched by the rim, he stared on in wonder at the brigand camp.

Billip, Mikkel, and Chongo gathered at his side. The brigand camp was laid out similar to the army camps they had served in over the years. Most noticeable was the variety of races that grouped together and the slaves they had acquired to serve them—a cruel and despairing life.

"This is disgusting," Mikkel muttered as he climbed down the hill.

Billip grabbed him and said, "If you leave, they'll feather you like a chicken." The big man frowned, but stayed his ground in silence.

Humans, full orcs and half-orcs gathered by fires, armored and as filthy as pigs in the mud. The stench of sewage and rotting flesh filled their nostrils, and large flies buzzed in their ears. Venir knew at that moment that they had seen all they needed to see—but they weren't going anywhere.

Venir and the rest stood stupefied as the woman spoke.

"Make yourselves at home."

She strode away, her head held high as the men of the camp stood at attention and saluted her. *Jarla the Brigand Queen.*

A few humans were a welcome sight in the midst of the other brash races. It was clear to Venir, however, that their time in the brigand army had worn down their humanity. Many of the men chewed food and grunted like beasts as they tormented the hapless slaves, women and children among them. He wanted to run the beastlike men through.

Billip whispered in his ear.

"Just act like we're new recruits?"

He nodded.

"Vee, what have you gotten us into?" Mikkel asked.

Venir shook his head. He wasn't so sure he knew. The suns were setting, so they made a small camp near the edge of the plateau. No one approached them as he watched humans abusing humans. The brigand men didn't seem to care what happened to their own kind at the hands of the gnolls, orcs, or kobold bandits. They made sport of a pair of human boys wrestling in the slime of sewage. A gnoll, tall and powerful, barked fearsome commands as one child beat the other senseless in the muck. They wanted to avert their eyes, but could not. Instead, they looked right in the yellow eyes of the dog-faced gnoll. It snarled and turned away.

Two days passed while the men did all they could do to blend in while staying removed. It was evident that Venir and his men were not welcome, but their arrival with Jarla'd had an impact. No one dared approach them, but it was awkward. Jarla busied herself, controlling her camp like a field general. The decrepit army was an organized shuffle at her beck and call. She said little to him, but ignored his companions like the plague.

"Vee, we got to go!" Mikkel pleaded for the hundredth time.

Venir sat, toying with a log and his ancient hunting knife. If he could only get used to the smell it wouldn't be so bad, that and the chronic griping. He convinced them that he was still figuring things out, so they had to trust him and wait.

Venir listened to the hundred different ways Mikkel would kill the kobolds. Those small humanoids looked a bit like halflings, with ruddy, snake-like skin, dog-like faces and two tiny horns on their heads.

Mikkel rambled on through his sneered lips, "I'll shoot them in the back of the head. I'll bust their little heads. I'll cut them in the belly. I'll—"

"Why do you hate them so much, man?" the somber scout blurted out.

The big man paused, crooked his neck, and looked up into the starry sky.

"I don't know … I just do. You don't have to have a reason to hate anything, you know. Now where was I?"

Billip rolled away from the campfire as Venir let out a chuckle.

Venir knew his friends were concerned, but he assured himself he had things under control. He told himself he really wanted to find out what this brigand army was all about, but in truth he was infatuated with Jarla. The powerful warrior woman had captivated him in ways he did not understand. He was uncomfortable with it, but wanted to discover what she was about and why he was drawn to her. Indeed, she might be his enemy. It seemed only prudent to keep a close eye on her—a task he hoped to enjoy.

Venir was sleeping by the burning coals of the campfire when a ferocious growl from Chongo stirred him. They all sat up, hands gripping hilts. Two heavyset half-orcs with beady eyes, sweaty snouts, and flails approached.

"Jarla wants to see the one called Venir," one said.

The other spat, "Come with us."

Venir shrugged and couldn't help but grin at his men as he followed the pair away. Mikkel and Billip looked at each other and rolled their eyes, then lay back in their grassy beds.

"Venir's a dog!" groaned Mikkel. "He has all the luck. I was just dreaming about being in the sack with my woman right now."

"Aye, your woman is something," said Billip.

"What!" he said, sitting back up.

"Go back to sleep; I'm just messing with you. Don't get me thinking about it, too. Things are bad enough. Even that orc woman with the missing eye is starting to look attractive to me."

"Well, just you dream about her then, not about my woman—got it?" Mikkel said, giving his friend a shove in the back.

"Got it, now go to sleep," Billip said, hiding his grin.

Mikkel rolled over and fell fast asleep, but Billip kept churning the whole night. He was ready to leave and determined to convince Venir to do the same. The hills didn't have walls, but he could feel them closing in. He rolled up, stoked the coals, petted Chongo, and cracked his knuckles. *This place is evil*, he thought, as he waited for dawn to break. He swore he heard voices laughing at them somewhere in the distance.

6

THE ESCORTS LEFT HIM AT the entrance to Jarla's extravagant tent. It stood in the center of the camp, ten feet high, with the makings of a Royal field general. *How did she get this?* His nerves were on edge. Dozens of favorable scenarios inside her quarters raced through his mind. He pulled his flaxen hair back from his eyes, took a deep breath, and entered with a smile.

Her tent was plush, filled with purple and red pillows, hand stitched carpets and curtains. Sparkling silverware and china lay out on the tables. The shining candlelight was absorbed in the dark tapestries, and there was a fragrance, overwhelming at first, but soothing. It was so much better than the foul air that had surrounded him earlier. He saw no sign of her as he walked toward the center, spinning around on his heel. He wanted to dive into the sofa and guzzle the crystal carafe of wine on a table nearby. He rubbed his filthy hands on his dirty trousers.

From behind one of the curtained sections he heard a playful and sultry voice.

"I'll be with you in a moment, Venir."

He was all too eager to find out what awaited him behind the purple and gold curtain. He swallowed the lump in his throat. His temples began to pound, as if he were entering the battlefield to face an enemy he had never seen before.

After a few more agonizing seconds, she emerged from behind the curtain, wearing thick gold hoop earrings and a sleeveless black silk gown that stopped mid-thigh. Her dark blue eyes were magnetic, drawing into his as she approached him. Her jet-black hair lay over her shoulders, and her wine-colored lips revealed a small welcoming smile.

She brushed her chest against his and looked up into his eyes.

"Come," she whispered, lips brushing his ear. Taking his eager hand in hers, she led him farther back into her tent ….

7

HIS GROWING RELATIONSHIP WITH THE queen began to bear fruit on his men. They were given a decent tent within the camp and were supplied with better rations. Venir and Jarla were not often together, but it was clear that she favored him over all others. As time passed, he felt her bringing him in deeper, but she hinted little about her plans for the brigand army.

His friends still urged him to leave, but he would have none of it, despite the numerous arguments. The brigand camp was rotten; no amenities could make it any better, and they wanted to go, regardless of his assurances. Every day, he told them they would soon depart, but the weeks still passed. Mikkel had trouble looking him in the eye, and Billip had little to say.

The woman was calling the shots, whether he admitted it or not. She made both his friends uncomfortable, and they stayed busy when she was around. Venir had never met a woman like her. He considered himself a good judge of character, and it was against his normal cunning to take up so tight with a woman of any kind. He wanted her.

Somehow, the band of men managed to work through it all, despite the intrusive and unpleasant woman. Before long, they were in it thicker than thieves, moving along trails and raiding merchant caravans that ran commerce south to north. The brigand army and its queen's reputation had spread, and the merchants brought along more men-at-arms on their travels. It was not enough. The misfit army continued to grow. Still, the brigands were forced to plan better, and the merchant trains became more difficult to sniff out.

Jarla was a brilliant bandit. She planned her raids using resources and preparations unrivaled by the best war generals on Bish. Venir learned much from her, and was impressed by her knowledge of the field. He had spent many years soldiering in Bish, but few soldiers were her equal. She would locate the caravans and exploit their weaknesses with uncanny precision. He could not work out how she did it. He asked questions, but often was cut short.

She charged into every melee that came their way on her large, dapple-gray steed, Nightmare. Nightmare was a lightly armored warhorse and a force unto herself. He had seen the horse trample bodies under powerful hooves that crushed bones to dust. As if on her own two feet, Jarla fought on horseback, with both spiked battle axes. The carnage she wrought was a spectacle to any observer, but to Venir it was an inspiration. Even he could not match Jarla's body count in battle, but he was the only one to come close.

She complemented his fighting skills, and so his acceptance among her ranks grew. He was not comfortable with the bloodlust of the brigands—it seemed unwarranted. Billip and Mikkel kept their distance from the fray, relying on their wits and their range weapons. No one complained, as they were the best shots among the band. He knew they pulled back when they could, as did he. It was a risk.

Over the passing months, the army had great success and had grown to more than five hundred strong. Jarla's leadership and battle skills allowed her to control the various races of her army well. When she was challenged by one of her commanders, a powerful gnoll of noted repute, she cut him down in a fight to the death. Her victory was quick, her leadership unquestioned.

Venir had the pleasure of watching her dress for battle. She had her own sequence for putting everything on and taking it off. He watched, eyes intent, as she put on her iron-toed boots, and a sleeveless white cotton shirt, followed by her bronze chainmail dress. The sight of the magnificent warrior woman never failed to capture him.

She would grab a large, stitched-up leather sack, kneel down, and pull out an iron-banded bracer for her left arm, followed by another for her right arm. She reached in with her left hand, pulling out the first spiked battle axe, and followed with the right. The axes drew his attention because they were as compelling as she was. They did not stand out as extraordinary, but they were special in design. Each was about three feet in length. Their dark steel blades and serrated spikes seemed forged from an unfamiliar metal, and their thick oaken handles were shod with hammered iron. Setting them at her sides, she pulled out the helmet, a similar design and material as the axe and bracers, with a small iron spike on top. She was a sight to behold, like two separate women in one.

When she returned from battle, the blood was gone from her armament. It retained its dim shine and didn't have a nick. Neither was there a notch on the blades. She rubbed them down, never sharpening, then would kneel down and put them back in the leather sack, right first and left last, and toss it beside her bed with a *clank*. The sack never clanked except when she did that, and it never appeared big enough to hold all its contents. *Is it magic?* He wanted to ask, but never did. He was just enjoying being there, and he knew she would tell him if there was anything she wanted him to know. Those comments never came. The pit in his gut still festered, but he ignored it.

8

VENIR'S REASSURANCE LEFT BILLIP NO comfort. Billip pushed for departure every time his comrade came around. His young friend didn't know the ways of the world as he did … or women. The brigand queen had a smile that could crack a rock, but he swore she had a tail she somehow concealed. He jammed an arrow in the ground as he strung and unstrung his bow. *Stupid boy.*

Stupid, but brave and loyal as well, and Billip knew he had no fiercer friend than the tall-shouldered ranger. The pay of a few silver coins a week, plus some of the additional booty from their raids, appealed to his greedy nature, but the company he kept failed to grow on him. *A bunch of animals.* Every day, he felt his own humanity slipping away—and he might be starting to like it. *Why am I here?* He missed the Orc's Elbow and Mikkel's mead.

He eyed the swinging figures near the fringe of camp. They were the remains of deserters of the brigand army that had been chased down and hung. Those humanoids rotted in the wind, tongues swollen and dry, carrying the stench of decay. *No thanks.* He had to talk Venir into leaving.

Mikkel's overbearing hatred of the kobolds had expanded to include gnolls and orcs as well. The big man clutched his studded club and squeezed. His arms were thick with cords, like black pythons, as he banged his glimmering skullcap, muttering obscenities. Even Billip, who didn't really hate anything but losing, found fires burning inside him against other races and men as well. The two men passed their time finding ways to wound or kill the kobolds, during the raids, without being noticed. He and the big man used quivers other than their own. This had become a contest between them. Mikkel would argue that his was the superior marksmanship, which was not true, impressive though it was. The sight of a screaming kobold impaled to a tree by one of those heavy crossbow bolts made it great target practice for him as he shot from horseback. *This isn't so bad.* Mikkel took his own sort of pride in it, while the rest did not care enough about the kobolds to suspect foul play.

Mikkel squatted by the fire, roasting a kobold's toe.

"You've got to get us out of here, Billip," Mikkel said in disgust. "Venir's lost his mind over that woman. She scares the slat out of me!"

Billip wasn't listening, but contemplating. Their exploits had garnered them respect among many of their fellow human brigands, but Jarla's longest-standing fighters still held too much close to the chest. He had heard the snickers of gnolls and orcen commanders when their backs were turned, and it was more prevalent when Venir was around. His gut told him something was not right, and it was in his nosy nature to find out what it was.

He looked at his friend as he said, "I hope you aren't going to eat that."

The basher just shrugged, let out a hollow chuckle, and tossed the burnt toe away. Chongo sniffed it, walked over and lay down with a yawn.

Mikkel said, "Chongo, get your master out of here." The dog's ears perked up and flattened back down with a human-like sigh.

It was early in the morning when Billip began to snoop around. The cloudless sky left the campground pitch black, except for the flicker from dozens of burning campfire embers. Any mercenaries who were not sleeping were drinking and not paying much attention to anything else. Boredom was the most dangerous element in the brigand camp, but the commanders kept it under control with swift and painful punishment. Billip scuffed himself up and sauntered through the camp, offering slurred tidings as he shuffled along.

His goal was to reach the center of camp where Jarla's tent was surrounded by the four smaller tents of her commanders. As far as he knew, only she and Venir occupied her tent most nights, but Venir did not always get the comfort of her quarters. He chuckled at the thought of his pouting friend being kicked out from one of Jarla's searing moods.

Billip spent several nights within range of these tents, watching the commanders—gnoll, human and orc—come and go. They would meet late evening or early morning at one of the four tents, and Jarla would attend from time to time, but always without Venir. *If he'd gained her trust, he'd be in by now.* Like a night owl, he watched the armored guards with spears standing at both the entrance and the rear of each commander's tent. During the meetings, one was stationed at each side of the tent.

Late one evening, Venir strolled into her tent, and not long afterward the army commanders gathered, one at a time, in the tent behind Jarla's. It seemed sudden and uncharacteristic, and in their haste they had not doubled the guards, leaving the right and left sides unguarded. Nervousness set in, turning his hands clammy.

What are they doing? It was his only opening after days of recon, and he had to take it. The red moon cast a shadow over the right side of the tent, leaving it pitch black even to his keen eyes. He crept into its shadow and lay flat on his back. His heart pounded in his temples so that he could hear almost nothing else. He took slow breaths until he could focus and listen in. Small groups of dark clouds passed over as tiny insects crawled over his warm body and sweat dripped over his brow, burning his eyes. *Get on with it, fools.* He fought the urge to pee.

The orc guarding the front of the tent stepped into view and mumbled something in orcen. *Slat!*

The other orc guarding the rear stepped around. He closed his eyes, lest the whites give him away, and listened. They whispered in orcen, but did not move any closer. If they saw him, he would have to run and try to blend in elsewhere.

They'll interrogate the whole camp. We'll be first!

Dry grass crunched under the foot of the guard in front. Another step came his way, followed by another. The one in the rear continued his chat, stepping farther from the tent corner. Regret flooded through Billip's mind.

I should have gotten out of this camp long ago!

His heart thumped so hard he was certain the guards would hear it.

Get ready!

He thought about where he would run first, and waited for the alarm to sound.

Another loud orcen voice sounded from within the tent; someone was on his way out. The guards trotted back to their posts, and he overheard the front guard being reprimanded. In defense, the guard pointed out to his commander that the tent was not properly secured with the additional guards at the sides. That only complicated Billip's problem, for now the commander took it upon himself to check both sides, peering with intent around the corners. After many long seconds, Billip squinted, raising his head just a few inches. He thought he saw the commander shrug and walk back into the tent. No one seemed to be dispatched to find more guards.

Yes!

Despite his better judgment, he chose to wait it out, chancing that there was little likelihood of anyone coming in his direction again. Inside the tent, the meeting was heating up. It was being conducted in human tongue, but he did not hear Jarla's voice. The doggish voice of a gnoll was in control. Billip flicked a mosquito from his nose and pulled his hair behind his ear. The tones were low, but he could still hear through the thick canvas of the tent. Excitement rose in the voices of the commanders, followed by cruel laughter. He heard something he could never have anticipated — the ambition and evil plans of Jarla and her commanders … and it did not bode well for humans. He learned something else was behind the army's exploits that he found incomprehensible.

Oh no!

The meeting began to unwind; the savvy scout had no time to waste. He rolled out of the tent's shadow and made his way back to the campsite.

It can't be!

9

"M IKKEL," HE WHISPERED, POKING THE snoring man in the ribs, "wake up!"
Mikkel sat up as if he'd been shot, his black bearded face groggy and perturbed. Chongo stirred at his side, greeting him with a few licks.

"You'd better have a good reason, Billip. I was dreaming of my woman, and those dreams don't come often in this stinkin' camp. What's going on?"

"Listen to me, we're in danger."

"Me? Why's Melegal in danger?"

"Not *Mee-legal*. Blast your sluggish brain! You, me, and especially Venir." Billip pointed to Mikkel and then himself. "Now get your gear ready, and don't make it obvious."

The big man shook his head as he rolled out of his army blanket. Mikkel fumbled around the tent and pulled on his boots. He cracked his thick knuckles in a chronic cadence. Mikkel's large hands clamped down on his and then continued rounding up his gear.

"Billip," Mikkel said, staring down into his eyes, "tell me what you heard. You're worrying me."

"I will, but keep calm; I know how you get. Hear me out."

Mikkel gave a faint nod.

"I just listened in on one of the commanders' tent meetings. They're planning to attack Outpost Thirty-One in the next few days, and —"

"There ain't no way!" the warrior almost shouted. "Outpost Thirty-One has a thousand well-armed soldiers of the Royal house legions."

"Keep your voice down." Billip motioned. "Let me finish. They already have help; over two thousand strong are waiting to help sack the outpost—"

"Even with that many, it'll be hard to take. They'll have to starve them out, and by then help will have arrived. Besides, no one just attacks a Royal army outpost. It would be suicide—an act of war. Even gnolls and orcs don't have the numbers to face the humans when you come down to it." Mikkel sighed, stuffing everything in a sack and looking uncertain what to do.

Billip nodded.

"Let me finish, *again*; it's not orcs or gnolls or humans or dwarves or even halflings, for that matter."

Billip paused, raising an arched brow. Mikkel gave him a funny look. Billip waited as his friend scratched his cheek.

Mikkel's eyes brightened, something flicked on in his mind, and smacking his hands together he said, "Ogres!"

"No, Mikkel, not ogres, worse. Worse than all of them combined," he said through clenched teeth.

"Will you just tell me?" Mikkel said, loading his crossbow.

"If you'd just let me finish you'd know by now."

"Well, if you'd quit arguing, maybe I'd let you finish."

"We got more important things to do now than have another stupid argument."

Mikkel chuckled as he plucked a straggling hair from his head and blew it in the air.

"Since when?" An odd silence fell as Mikkel looked at Billip with a blank stare.

He's as dumb as Venir. The archer caved in.

"Underlings, you idiot! Jarla's brigand army is in league with the underlings! And has been for quite some time! It's no wonder she's been so successful. And we've been helping her!"

Billip crossed his hands behind his back and paced inside the small tent.

Mikkel sat back down, leaning against the tent post. "Bone … we gotta tell Venir. He's gonna go berserk. Bish, he hates underlings more than I hate kobolds."

"Uh … that's the other thing. I'm glad you're sitting down for this next bit of news."

Mikkel looked up at him, his chestnut face fresh with loss.

Billip squatted down beside his friend.

"It seems Jarla has no more need of Venir's services. I assume that includes us, too. And I think the last guy that slept with her is dead. And the guy before him is dead. And so on. You catch my drift?"

Mikkel clutched his skull.

"My, she is one evil lady! No wonder those guys always chuckle when he walks by. Glad it wasn't me, after all. Dreamin's better than dyin'. "

"Except you're the one that gets to save him," Billip said, slapping Mikkel on the shoulder.

"What? Me?" Mikkel pointed to himself as he stood up. "I'm not gonna run in there and pull him out of her bed! He might as well go happy, I say!"

"That's not the plan. And shame on you!" he said, wagging his finger.

"Sorry, just teasing. I knew she was evil, though. It's like she hates everything. I have never seen that woman smile," Mikkel paused. "Still, she's tempting as a fox. Tough break for Vee, though. So, what's the plan?"

"First off, I gotta warn Outpost Thirty-One. I'm gonna need to clear a hole through the wretched ravine watch. There are five guards on each side of the ravine, spaced out over a mile."

Billip drew with his finger in the dirt.

"They use bird pipes to signal. I'm gonna cut off the west side of the ravine . . . here!"

Using a stick, he made an X in the dirt.

"That's the side you and Venir will have to take to get out of the camp and past the brigand squadron at the end of the ravine. They're only orcs, and they usually sleep between the whistles, especially right before dawn. I shouldn't have much trouble taking them out. If I have time, I'll take out the other side as well, and you guys will hopefully be able to disappear from camp altogether. Got it?"

"I'm with you," Mikkel said with a nod, rubbing his club.

Billip scratched his scruffy chin.

"It should be dawn before long. I hope Venir will make his way back here as usual, to tell us his exploits. Break the news to him and get the Bone out of here! Meet me at Outpost Thirty-One. Got it?"

Mikkel nodded again.

"I'm going on foot, so have my horse ready for Venir. His horse is stabled, so don't fool with it, it might draw suspicion. And you," he grabbed Chongo's face, "make sure he doesn't screw this up."

"Good fortune, Billip. You're gonna need it," Mikkel said.

"I like my chances better than yours, so hang on to that fortune," Billip said, grim-faced as he slipped out of the tent.

Billip drifted like a shadow over the plateau edge and into the ravine. The forest was black and slick as he passed through thickets and hours-old cobwebs.

Got to do this.

He had to be at his best and not miss a single shot in the blackness. If he had to, he would sneak up and cut their throats. This do-or-die mission was as frightening and exciting as any he had ever faced, but he was determined not to let down his friends — or the rest of his race, for that matter.

Men and underlings — why me? He had friends in that outpost; they all did. It was a key stronghold that had helped keep the underlings from gaining control in the north for as long as anyone knew. Without it, the tide between man and underling would shift. The foul creatures had been gaining ground for quite some time. This might be the strike the fiends were waiting for. He had to get there in time.

I hope Venir and Mikkel make it.

10

MIKKEL'S FOREHEAD BEADED WITH SWEAT as he prowled their campsite. *Where is he?* Dawn was breaking, and Billip had been gone for hours. Waiting was agonizing; he felt like a dead duck among the now awakening army. Chongo's ears kept perking up and flattening back down.

"Bad deal," he muttered.

At least he had killed some kobolds. If things didn't go his way, he might have a chance to kill more. The brown dog sniffed and snuffled at his side, enhancing his frustration. He was ready, though. He didn't know what for, but if a fight was coming, he was ready. He had packed their gear and loaded the mounts. The horses gave soft neighs. The beasts were well-trained and ready to be ridden out of camp at a second's notice. That second couldn't come soon enough.

He paced around the tent countless times, chanting an old war song.

Come, come ye dire dogs,
It's time to taste my wrath.
The bow is strong,
The battle long,
As we embrace the throng.
Come, come ye dire dogs, come!

"Where is he, Chongo? He should be back by now!"

He clenched his teeth as he tightened the leather cords around his burgeoning biceps. Smears of dark gray paint coated his cheeks and lips. It burned with a strong scent, arousing his senses and warming his blood. He couldn't contain himself.

Wait or flee? Fight? Bone! Billip's probably in a fort full of women by now. Dog!

Chongo looked up at him, giving only a low yelp. If Venir took much longer, he would have to leave without him. The thought was disturbing, but no more so than the thought of what might be happening to Venir in Jarla's tent.

Come on, Venir!

11

VENIR AWAKENED, REFRESHED FROM HIS slumber, inside the brigand queen's tent as he had many times before. *It's good to be me.* She wasn't there though, so maybe it wasn't going to be such a good start after all. Most mornings, she was already up, busy with all the tasks of maintaining command of her army, or her "hapless horde" as he liked to call them. Venir never understood how she kept company with such an assortment rather than the company of her own, but if she could live with it, so could he — for now anyway.

She was capable enough to command any army, so why she chose this one he could not figure. In the meantime, he made the most of it. He was confident that he had a good handle on his situation and that it would not be long before he gained her total trust. *Today is the day.*

He sat up, shaking from an unusual chill as he rubbed the thick cords of his forearms. Combing his fingers through his thick hair, he spied himself in a tall mirror on the other side of the bed. Venir ran his fingers over his pale stubble. *Time to shave.*

Venir flexed his sinewy arms over his head as he yawned, noting the scabs and bandages from the recent slaughters won. He stretched out his great arms and then ran his fingers over the heavy scratches that littered his tan skin. *Those might go away.* He didn't like the scars and healed patches of torn skin that had cropped up over his athletic physique over the years, but there was little choice in it. Each one meant he had survived, and he enjoyed the questions women asked about them. It was the scars they couldn't see that he never talked about. He rinsed his face off in a porcelain basin. *Where is she?*

There was no sound of the usual activity in the tent. He was used to Jarla muttering to herself like a hermit, but not this morning. He searched for his trousers and knife then decided to look beyond the curtained quarters to see if she was there. The heavy tent brightened from the rising suns. The candles were expired, and the odd quiet was his only companion. *Strange.*

Jarla was very thorough with the details of her business. The tent was the same as always, yet something seemed amiss. There was a nagging in his gut.

His head began to ache like when he drank too much the night before. How late had he slept? Why were there no plans on the tables? *Where's my food?* The familiar smell of coffee was not there. *Hmmm.* But he wasn't one to be paranoid. He was sure that whatever might be going on had nothing to do with him. After all, she was rather fond of his prowess — both on and off the battlefield — and he had the marks on his back to prove it. If anything important was up, he'd be the first to know.

He wandered back toward the bed and snatched his shirt and trousers. Footsteps approached the tent's entrance, so he went back. In she came, and he greeted her with a welcoming smile. Clothed in her typical attire, she shot back a rueful smile, nodding as she looked his unclothed body up and down. He responded, ready to crush her in his arms, when two gnoll commanders, Throk and Keel, entered behind her, fully armed for battle. Brazen though he was, he was embarrassed.

Venir shouted at the gnolls,

"Don't you two ever enter Jarla's tent uninvited! Now get out of here!"

Throk and Keel chuckled like jackals, their yellow eyes full of mockery. Venir looked at Jarla, but she did nothing but smile. There was an awkward moment before he turned back toward the two gnolls, regaining his composure.

"So, I guess you two want a closer look at the best looking man, and I emphasize *man*, in the camp?" He stood, head high with arms wide. "Well, here I am."

Again, there were surly chuckles, and he started to feel uneasy.

"Jarla, what in Bish are these two doing in here? What's going on?"

"They're here to help me take care of some business," she said, in a soft unpleasant voice.

Another chill ran the course of his spine.

"I'm sure I can help. Let me get some clothes on," he said, turning back towards the bed.

"No!" she almost shouted, "Stay right there, my pet. I like you as you are."

Venir's dander started to rise. He looked her square in the eyes.

"Pet? I am not your pet, Jarla."

"Pah! You've been my pet all along, buffoon!" Her voice was as sharp as a dagger. "You're no different from all the other fools I've had before. You aren't the first, and you won't be the last. But I'll give you credit, you were one of the best."

What? He stepped back, not expecting such words. The sugar and spice had turned to salt and mud. He felt himself sinking into the ground. The uneasiness that had crept in earlier turned into something he had never dealt with before — uncertainty. Her beautiful eyes burned with hate now. Her features twisted into a persona he had never encountered. This was not the woman he thought he knew. She looked at him like he was just another man, among a hundred, who had wronged or spurned her in some horrible way. The tent shrank around him, and he felt as helpless as a babe.

He swallowed hard and said, "What are your plans for me, then? Am I to be expelled from your army? I wouldn't miss it. I'd be happy to leave."

"It's not that simple, yellow hair. No man who shares my bed lives long enough to tell about it," she said, stepping back between the sneering gnolls.

His body went cold, and his mind numb at the heartlessness of her statement. He knew she meant it and was prepared to end his life with a single command. He felt like a fool as he stood flat-footed with no means to defend himself. He was about to be slaughtered. Sweat broke out on his brow. The gnolls' hairy hands dropped onto their sword hilts. He wanted to scream, but who would come? *Think!*

"Are you going to at least give me a fighting chance?" he blurted out, unable to mask the defeat in his voice.

She laughed.

"No. I've seen you fight. Giving you a chance is too dangerous."

Venir's voice trembled.

"So what then?" He shrugged, fighting the urge to vomit.

"Throk and Keel normally eliminate my pets while they're sleeping, or sometimes as they try to escape. They've been begging to kill you and your men as payback for the loss of their comrades and one of my best commanders, Durn. But that's in the past."

Venir was agape. *Billip and Mikkel!* Were they dead? A wave of guilt swept over his fear now. He had ignored their warnings. He was a fool whose folly might have led to the death of two good friends. Yet, despite the news she had shared with him, he still found her magnificent. To her surprise, he even managed a grin. *Smile, no matter how bad it seems.* Who told him that?

"Well, that's a first, a fool grinning in the face of death. You are something, I'll give you that," she said, almost smiling herself.

"Oh, I know you think at least that much of me, and more," he answered, managing a wink.

Throk and Keel chuckled. Jarla slapped Keel on the back, and continued with the bad news.

"But in your case, my pet, there's a pretty steep bounty on your head."

"What bounty?" *A bounty from who?*

"The one my outside supporters have put on you, fool."

"You have me at a loss, again, it seems. Who is this outside interest, witch?" he asked.

Jarla sneered.

"I was careful not to disclose anything to you before, because I know how you feel about them, but there's been a war going on for a long time—a secret war." Deep creases crossed her forehead as she stroked her silky hair.

"I'm part of it, a distraction for the most part, but I'm very well paid, as we all are. And I don't mind carving into the supporters and forces of the Royals who led the humans. They put me through great pain long ago, so it satisfies my thirst for revenge. The truth is, I don't feel much for any race; I just enjoy what I do."

She licked her upper lip.

"I could do it for either side in this war, but right now, I'm on the side that's gaining on the humans."

Venir's neck hairs rose. Was she about to say something he never would have believed? She mustn't. He simply could not believe it to be true, and that he too, may have become a part of it.

"The bottom line is, it doesn't matter to me who wins or loses, but when it comes to tendering for my services, the *underlings* pay far better."

Rage exploded inside Venir's chest, flushing his cheeks with fire. He had been sharing a bed with this traitor for months. She had been in league with his most despised enemies, had even known how he felt, and had used him anyway.

Still helpless and almost shaking, he gathered his thoughts.

"I'll make you pay, Jarla! You'd better kill me now if you ever want to sleep again! I will hunt you down!"

Her scoffing laugh doused his fire.

"I've survived bigger threats. Don't worry, yellow hair, the underlings have agreed to let me be present when they run you through. Apparently, some of the underlings you've allowed to escape would like to apply your own methods to you. We're going to watch them put your head on a pike. They're even going to let you lead their army as we take Outpost Thirty-One. Won't that be an honor, you leading the march on the Royals?"

He stared at her with growing hatred. His mouth was dry as he choked out his next words. "They won't take me alive! You'll have to kill me! I won't give you a choice!"

"I assure you, that won't happen. Give yourself up. You're unarmed, and the whole tent is surrounded. It won't be hard to wrestle you down. Be good, and I'll try to make your suffering quick."

His lust and pride had made him a fool. He didn't know who he hated more, her, the underlings, or himself. Perhaps he deserved to die, but not his friends.

Not Chongo!

With the desperation of a cornered tiger, he eyed his surroundings for a weapon of some sort. The only object close to him was the large, worn leather sack lying on the map table. He had looked in the sack several times before, unbeknownst to Jarla, and never found a thing. He knew it was futile to try it again, but he felt compelled to—he had nothing to lose.

"Well?" she said. "What's it going to be? Do you give yourself up, or do my men wrestle you down like a child?"

He sprang like a deer, grabbing the leather sack off the table and reaching down deep inside it.

Throk, Keel, and Jarla laughed with vigor.

"They do that every time," Jarla sneered, patting Throk on the back. "These poor brutes just can't come up with anything better."

Venir turned to face them, straw hair hanging over his face, shoulders slumped.

"Put my sack down, Venir. It's time to end this game."

There was a pause, all eyes intent on him, seeing him for a fool. Throk and Keel took a half step forward and then stopped.

A smile cracked under Venir's nose.

"Why would I do that ... when I have this?"

The gnolls looked at one another and Jarla's face froze. He pulled out an object and watched their eyes widen, none more than Jarla's, for she was not gazing upon either of her twin battle axes, but a much larger one that looked like both of hers put together. Venir felt something incredible and powerful in his grip.

"Bone!" Venir elated.

Jarla's dark eyes locked on his for a moment and returned to the great axe he now wielded.

"Put that back, Venir! Put that back in the sack now! Do it, Venir!" She screamed in rage. "Do it! Do it! Do it now!"

He had never seen a woman so angry in his life, and he had seen plenty. Her frenzy almost persuaded him, but he caught himself, realizing that he no longer cared for her anymore than a marsh witch.

He flashed them all a hardy grimace.

"I think, I'll cut you all down instead!"

Jarla dashed from the tent, screaming at the top of her lungs.

"Kill him! Kill him!"

Throk and Keel drew their bastard swords in time to parry his attack, but Venir was on them like lightning in a rainstorm. Blades shattered and bones broke under his fury as the two gnolls fell dead on the ground in pools of blood. His new weapon felt alive in his hands, and power seemed to course through his body. It felt good—very good. More soldiers pressed in, but the sight of the convulsing gnolls' bulky bodies blocking the entry caused them to hesitate.

Venir yanked a helmet out of the sack and put it on. A wave of awareness overwhelmed him. He could sense everything. Then he pulled out a round shield. *Great Bish!* He prepared himself for a stand. He felt like he could fight the entire army. It suddenly struck him that the back of Jarla's tent faced the entrance to the ravine and the path back to his tent.

He grabbed his gear. He at least had time to warn Billip and Mikkel. As the guards charged in, he slit open the tent and slipped through the canvas as fast as he could.

12

MIKKEL HAD BEEN ON TENTERHOOKS for what felt like an eternity. Through a small spyglass, he surveyed the rear of Jarla's tent. He had watched her leave it, seen brigand soldiers surround it, and watched her re-enter with the two heavily armed gnoll commanders.

Son of a Bish! He was about to witness the assassination of his friend. No one seemed to have noticed Billip's departure, and no one seemed concerned with him, either, so he waited, keeping watch for a few more minutes.

He was about to pack it in and go when Jarla bolted around from the front of her tent and started barking commands. The guards converged on her tent's entrance. The camp was still in a slumber, but many were now alert and sounding the alarm. A figure emerged through a slit in the back of the tent: a naked man with a great axe, a shield, and what looked like the brigand queen's helmet ran out of the opening, straight in Mikkel's direction. When two orc brigands intercepted his path, the naked warrior cut one in the neck and punched another down. Mikkel saw a V-shaped tattoo on the big man's broad back. He snapped his spyglass shut.

"It's him!"

Chongo bolted to his master's aid while Mikkel jumped on his horse and led the other mount into his friend's path. Two more brigand soldiers tried to cut Venir off, but Mikkel shot one clean through his skull and Venir severed the other in two with a wide swipe through the belly.

"Come, Vee! Let's go!"

Jarla's men came, shouting in alarm. The whole army seemed to be awake and on the move. Venir leapt onto Billip's readied horse, and they raced down the hillside and into the ravine. Chongo took the lead. Hard and fast they rode, and to their surprise nothing seemed to stand in their way.

Mikkel cried out, "Billip did it!"

They even passed the ravine watch at the end of the pass. Mikkel shouted back to Venir, "Billip must have led them on a fox hunt!"

As they galloped clear of the ravine, he shouted to Venir, "Good thing Billip left his horse for you!"

"Why?"

"There's no way I'd let you ride with me looking like that!"

Venir had forgotten all about his nakedness.

"We'd better get you into some clothes. If Billip or anyone else sees us now, we'll never live it down! "

"I'm just happy to be alive, either way!" Venir yelled.

"I heard that!" he said.

They rode hard toward Outpost Thirty-One with a large portion of the brigand army in heated pursuit.

Series 1 THE Book 2

DARKSLAYER

Blades in the Night

CRAIG HALLORAN

1

BENEATH TWO BLAZING SUNS, THE restless man known as Venir trudged along. His hair was pulled back in a thick braid that ended just below his brawny shoulders. Venir's bright blue eyes contrasted with his tanned skin. He wore nothing more than a light set of tanned leather armor over outdoor garb, with a white cowl around his neck. A long hunting knife hung from his belt, the sheath's tip tied against his lower thigh. His dark leather pack seemed small hanging from his expansive back.

Venir pulled a grimy hand across his forehead to wipe away the sweat. He swore his already reddened skin was cooking. Looking up toward the two fiery orbs in the sky, he longed for the night, but felt compelled to press on. The Outlands could send an unprepared person into a delirium—especially in this kind of heat—but Venir still had his bearings.

Stopping and kneeling, he took off his backpack and extracted two canteens. He chugged a few thick sips from one, then set it down beside the empty one. Venir waited, watching the breeze create tiny whirlwinds over the sun-baked surface. Mirages shimmered in all directions as far as he could see. Greenish brown cacti of all shapes and sizes stood scattered over the landscape. None of these would aid him. He needed to travel farther east for water, but he would not. Venir's mission was to cut down the underlings, and they were close. He had to find them, and he had to do it on his own.

The underlings were not accustomed to the broad daylight. They stayed just below the surface until the time was right. They used magic to burrow into the ground, where they would wait, spying, before killing at will. This was one of the reasons they were such formidable enemies.

If he could just find a burrow, he would have the jump on them. Just like any other beast, underlings left signs of their movement. Few knew their signs or cared to know; who would want to follow an underling, anyway? But Venir did—he always did. He and a handful of others knew that the underling burrows formed a network throughout the hard surface of Bish. More caves and tunnels went far below the burrows for safety.

The dwarves kept tabs on many of these tunnels. Underlings tended to travel on the surface in small groups and only at night. Their tunnels were small, more like giant snake holes, and on occasion one might find an abandoned one on the surface. Over the past few days, Venir had found several, hoping they were traps he could spring, but there had been no shred of life in any of them.

Wiping the sweat from his brow again, Venir reached into his backpack. He pulled out a large, worn leather sack and dropped it down with a clank. He began to unroll it, then held it in both hands and stared at it. A sour expression crossed his grizzled face. *I don't need you.*

Yes, the contents of the leather sack would give him what he needed to find the underlings, but the sack would not be in his possession forever. What would he do then? Before he'd gained the items, Venir had survived fine without them while hunting underlings—better than any other man alive. Yet the sack gave him what he needed to make it much easier and even more … delightful.

He shook his head. *I can do this on my own.* He rolled up the sack and stuffed it back into his pack along with the canteens, then slung it onto his shoulders once more. Venir walked southeast into the empty landscape. Red Clay forest wasn't far away, but he would wait until night to stop and camp there.

The ground tremored beneath his feet, and a large hole opened before his eyes. He backpedaled, but another hole opened behind him. As two gigantic sand spiders emerged, his gut told him to run, but four underlings scurried out of the holes and surrounded Venir. The small humanoids wore black leather armor and were armed with short swords and crossbows. Their fingers were clawed, their teeth sharp, and they had coarse black hair and colorful, wicked eyes.

"Bone!" Venir cried, whipping out his hunting knife and charging toward the two closest underlings on his left.

His incredulity at their sudden appearance was only surpassed by his hatred of them—a hatred that had blinded him into waging this fight without his prized items. Venir bounded forward. How had he ever imagined that he could take them on alone, without the help of the armament that remained tucked away in his leather sack?

Pride had overcome instinct. Venir should have known better. But it was too late now.

Caught off guard by the rushing warrior, the two underlings dropped their hand crossbows to draw their short swords. His long knife sliced through the neck of the first like the underling was a chicken in a slaughterhouse. The other lunged at Venir's armored chest. He side-stepped the attack and drove his knife straight through the underling's heart, pulling it out again and again with a bellow of triumph. Black blood splattered onto him and spilled over the dusty ground.

He whirled toward his other attackers. The remaining two underlings mounted the pony-sized sand spiders.

They attacked. He ran.

The sand spiders were far worse than underling hunters, and it would take more than a hunting knife and courage to handle a single one. The enormous, tarantula-like arachnids bore down on him, chittering at his heels. They were fast.

He was faster.

Got to make it to the forest.

Pushing himself beyond his known limits, Venir increased the distance between himself and his pursuers. *Blast my Pride.* He needed time to get out his mystical armament. Slowing down would be his end, so he sprinted onward.

Venir cocked his head. A shrieking sound ripped through the air. There had to be more underlings in the area. His legs pumped faster and faster toward the edge of Red Clay Forest far off in the east. His best chance was to lose them in the trees — if he survived that long. His legs and lungs felt ready to burst.

The forest's edge shimmered in the distance. *Might make it.* Sand whipped into a small storm all around him. He ran on, sure of his direction. The wind picked up and confusion beset his course. He could not see to move. *Underling magic!* Hot sand tore at his skin. His frustration and frenzy mounted. He couldn't breathe amidst the swirling, thick sand. He pulled his cowl over his face and stumbled on until he could walk no more.

As he crawled forward, four more lightly armored underlings — wielding odd swords and small crossbows — surrounded him. They chittered back and forth in cruel mockery, knowing that their sandstorm would suffocate him and render him unconscious — if not kill him. They banged their short swords together in triumph, loud screams erupting from their twisted faces.

Venir heard it all through the whipping wind as he struggled to breathe. Blood pounded through his thick blue veins. They had him; he knew it and so did they. He fought through the storm, sand and dirt stinging his skin like a thousand bees. He only had one chance. He yanked off his backpack, pulled out the leather sack, and reached deep inside.

It was time to make them pay.

As their sandstorm subsided, the underlings waited with grins of anticipation on their faces as they continued to bang their swords together.

In the center of the dying storm, the large silhouette of the rising man took shape before their eyes. The swirling ceased and they froze.

The man stood in place — ominous — like a statue, coated head to toe in the harsh grit of the Outlands and the storm they'd conjured for him. A black helmet sat strapped to the man's head, the helm topped with a single serrated spike that glinted faintly in the blistering sunlight. Dirt and sand encrusted the rectangular eyelets of the helm. Strapped to the man's left arm was an ornate round shield. In his right hand, he held a massive twin-bladed battle-axe with a smooth spike protruding from the top.

The underlings hovered before the unexpected sight, eyes wide with curiosity — and surprise.

They had the Darkslayer within their grasp.

Venir remained motionless, as if petrified by the storm that was no more. He could not see the enemy through the dirt-sand film that covered him from helmet to boots ... but he could hear them.

Come closer, fiends.

His head pulsed underneath his helmet. Venir wanted to destroy them, and he would wait no more. He let out a deep growl and shook off his sandy cocoon.

Venir lifted up his great axe, Brool, and banged it flat against his helmet. The grit fell from his eyelets. He grinned. He felt like he had stepped out of an iron furnace, his muscle and steel now joined as one.

The underlings stepped back, their bright eyes darting back and forth as they chittered. He knew what their hisses meant. They thought they had trapped the infamous Darkslayer — the scourge of their kind. Within their reach, they no doubt thought, was revenge for the countless brethren that had fallen at the hand of the Darkslayer.

And he would let them take their chance at him — just like all those that had fallen before them. "You have me, rodents! So come and get me!" Venir lunged toward them like some starving bobcat chasing rabbits, all the while brandishing Brool.

The underlings rushed in, screeching as Venir whirled his battle-axe around his body in a blistering tornado of steel. He swept the heavy blade into the nearest underling. Sinking Brool deep into its chest, Venir dropped the creature with a sickening crunch. Another underling took advantage of Venir's focus and cut him in the midsection.

With a roar, Venir slammed his head toward the underling, jabbing his helm's serrated spike into its eye socket. He twisted it out, leaving a ghoulish hole in the fiend's head.

He spun around, sensing something.

Zip! Zip! Zip!

Venir ducked and raised his shield. A volley of crossbow bolts ricocheted off his helmet and shield. Another embedded itself in his shoulder, drawing a grunt of pain from him. His head throbbing, he felt bloodlust begin to overcome him.

Four more. Stay with them — and the spiders.

The two underlings hopped off the spiders that scampered in to flank him. Both spiders scurried forward, and Venir's gaze darted back and forth between them, eyeing their hairy legs, black eyes, and gaping maws. He smashed one in the face with his shield. Green acid erupted from the spider's mangled face and sizzled when it struck his shield. Raising his axe high, Venir prepared to brain the creature.

Something from behind entangled his feet and jerked him down. As he hit the dirt, Venir saw that the other spider had caught him with a cord of its webbing and now reeled him in like a fish. He kicked at the sand as he was dragged toward the creature. Every second brought him closer to the beast's open jaws, which dripped with venom. He only had seconds left. He kicked harder at the slippery sand, trying to slow himself down, even as the underlings cackled at his impending doom.

From the other direction, the wounded spider lunged at his head. He lifted his shield and fought it off. Its hairy arms tried to tear the shield away from him. He heard the snapping jaws at his feet.

"Bone!" Venir felt something tug at his toe. Battle heat raced through him. He let go of his shield. "Enjoy it, beast!" he yelled.

He jerked up into a sitting position as his boot entered the mouth of the spider. With one arm, Venir brought down Brool with all his might.

Crunch!

An ear-shattering screech came from the foul creature's mouth. Its head burst open and its eight legs flailed. Venir let out a howl as venomous acid splashed onto his leg, burning more than fire itself. He turned and crawled in the opposite direction, fighting the webbing on his lower legs.

His eyes fell upon the other spider, which seemed intent on destroying his shield. He took Brool's edge and cut away the corded web from his legs. Grimacing, Venir stumbled back onto his feet in time to see two more underlings charge at him in a rage. His arms felt heavy as he swung his axe back and forth. The clangs against their swords resounded loud and sharp. Venir felt his leg going numb. And two other underlings — the ones who had ridden the spiders — hung back, no doubt waiting until he'd been further weakened, or killed, by the two now facing him.

He had to end this.

One underling hacked at his legs while the other pressed him backward. Venir slashed his axe at arm's length. The underlings leaped back in time to avoid decapitation then prowled around him. He could feel their hesitation.

One barreled toward him, sword arcing high. Venir parried, his axe spike sinking through the underling's breastplate and into the flesh of its chest.

Even as he drove the spike deeper into the enemy's chest, the other underling hacked at his back, slicing deep into his mail.

"Enough!" Venir yelled. Whirling around, he let go of his axe and grabbed the underling by the wrists, squeezing. It screamed and dropped its weapons. Venir jerked its arms wide as it kicked at him. Leaning into the creature, Venir slammed his metal helmet into its skull.

Bang! Bang! Bang!

Feeling the underling's blood all over his face, Venir slammed the helmet into its skull one last time.

Bang!

Crunch! Its face bones cracked. It hung there, limp in his arms. He flung the dead underling through the air. It landed in the gaping maw of the spider that had been chomping his shield.

Venir's blood-smeared helmet glistened like black oil in the sunlight as the two remaining underlings flanked him. Their hand crossbows bore down on his chest.

"Come on!" Venir cried.

For all his bravado, he knew he was about to faint. He couldn't feel his legs. His chest heaved in dry gulps of air. But the underlings didn't seem to realize that. They looked back and forth at one another and backed away. He took a painful step forward, snarling as loudly as he could. Chittering sounds burst from their lips, and they turned and buzzed across the landscape like fireflies. Venir dropped to his knees and croaked out a laugh. He became aware of the burning in his shoulder and legs. He was not yet out of jeopardy.

"Ah!" he shouted, wrenching out the small bolt that had lodged in his shoulder.

He had survived, but he needed a remedy—fast. Time was running out. He could see the sand spider's poison eating the skin off his leg. Red, swelling boils rose up as large strips of skin peeled off. He had to act.

A sudden sucking sound rose behind him. He looked over and caught the grotesque sight of the remaining spider. It was drawing the last drops of blood and juice out of the underling. The black creature was almost a husk.

With a groan, Venir limped in agony to where his axe protruded from an underling's chest. Nauseated and gagging, Venir grabbed the underling's short sword. He could feel the acid on his leg spreading. Black and purple spots hung before his eyes. The only cure lay in the belly of the beast itself.

Venir made it over to the spider he had brained earlier. He dropped beside the twitching beast. Grimacing, he rolled the foul thing onto its back, hoping it was a female. It was. There between the head and the abdomen lay a small, hairy, black egg sack. He sliced it open. A thick, milky pus with a horrible stench seeped out.

"Ooh … Smells like an orcen shower," he said, spitting the foul taste from his mouth.

He plunged his hand in and pulled out a glob of the thick milky goo, and smeared it over his leg. The relief in his burning ankle was instantaneous, and he fell flat on his back in elation. He was now so woozy that he was on the brink of passing out, but he willed himself to stay awake. If he fell asleep, he'd be baked alive—or maybe eaten by the other spider once it finished its underling meal.

Water …

Extracting his canteen from his backpack, Venir gulped down all that was left and chucked it. Then he gathered up his gory axe and shield, ignoring the preoccupied sand spider. He set off, running with a limp toward Red Clay Forest.

The trek seemed to take forever under the diminishing suns, but after an hour's trot, he made it to the edge. He staggered as deep inside the forest as he could, then collapsed on a thick patch of amber moss beneath leaves of emerald, sage, violet, and red, and passed out.

The crackling of a campfire stirred Venir from his slumber. He sat up in a lurch to check his surroundings. Night had fallen in Red Clay Forest. He was pretty sure he had not made the fire; he could barely recollect reaching the forest's edge. Brool, his helmet, and his shield laid out beside him with the rest of his gear resting by his side. It had to be Mood. He was safe. His stomach growled and his head began to hurt.

Venir leaned back and took a deep breath of the cool night air. Red Clay Forest was not a place for everyone—it seemed to choose who it liked and who it did not. He had always found safety within its thick trees and shrubs, though. As its name suggested, the forest was set on red clay soil, and its pathways wound for miles among colorful leaves that were not only green, but also gold, red, blue, purple, and even white. Unlike all other plant life on Bish, the leaves in the forest never withered with the seasons. Here, one could travel quick and quiet.

Some referred to this forest as a magic garden, others a haven of treachery. None really knew if it had a mystic secret or not. What Venir cared about was that underlings in particular steered clear of it.

He grimaced as he stretched for his backpack. Inside, he found a filled canteen. He drank it down gulp after gulp. "Ah!"

He stood up with a groan and peered about. The fire glowed and crackled a few feet away, and its warmth relaxed him. Smoke from somewhere else wafted into his nostrils. It was Mood, all right—along with his usual cigar—but where was he? Venir walked beyond the firelight and scanned the black shadows of the forest. He picked up a stone and cocked his arm to throw it.

"You don't want to chuck that at me, human," a familiar voice rumbled ahead.

"And if I do?" Venir said.

"You'll miss."

The voice was behind him. Venir whirled and discovered Mood on the other side of the fire. "Getting sneaky in your old age, Mood?"

"Absolutely," he said, grinning underneath his thick beard. The giant red-haired dwarf stepped around the fire and clasped hands with Venir. They stood almost eye to eye, but Mood was a bit shorter and much broader. Like the rest of his kind, Mood boasted blood-red hair and ruddy skin. He wore leather woodsman's garb in green, brown, and red, and had two giant hand axes strapped in an X across his back. Typical dwarves on Bish stood much shorter than humans, but Mood was one of the Blood Rangers—a rare breed of giant dwarves that protected their kind and others. Unlike the rest of the Blood Rangers, Mood did as he wished, and being their king he was allowed that privilege.

"So, Venir, what's bringing you to me forest this time?" Mood took a puff of his cigar and aimed a smoke ring over Venir's head. Mood liked to call Red Clay Forest his own, although it wasn't, but it was where Venir had met him long years ago.

"You've bailed me out again, Mood. I was tracking underlings and almost bit the dust. I didn't think I'd make it here, and if I did, I didn't think I'd still be alive," he said, checking his wounds by the fire.

"Ah, I've seen you much worse 'n that. Not so long ago when you came out o' that marsh, now, that was a sight. You'd have made it on your own if the bugs hadn't got after you. The creatures told me you were here. I didn't know it was you, though … just a man, they said. So I thought, what the Bish, I'll check it out, and there you lay, snoring like a baby! Ho-ho!"

"I don't snore!" Venir said.

Mood laughed even harder. "Eh, so what's goin' on? How many underlings did you kill? Twelve? Twenty? Fifty?"

"No," Venir said, disappointed.

"Well?" Mood tossed another log on the fire.

"Just six. Two more got away. There were two sand spiders—caught me by surprise."

"I thought that never happened when you had that get-up on. You usually surprise them." Mood nodded toward the armaments that turned Venir into a one-man army—the heavy three-foot round shield of dark gray metal overlapped with large woven iron bands, the glistening helmet with similar iron banding wrought over the back and neck, and, of course, Brool, which was now stuck spike-first into the ground, with its thick, dark oak handle shod with the same iron banding. Venir called it his hand-and-a-half axe. It was a weapon unlike any other—Bish's great equalizer between good and evil.

Venir grabbed his helmet and axe. "I didn't have the gear on—not at first, at least. Didn't want to. I always used to do just fine carving up the creepy little rodents with my wits and usual weapons."

Mood stepped back, a concerned look on his dark face. No man hated the underlings more than Mood. He had warned Venir more than once about taking greater risks with the underlings.

Sighing, Venir set the axe back down.

"Do you really think the underlings would hold back if they were tracking you? They sure didn't last time." Mood slammed one of his axes into a nearby stump.

"No," Venir finally answered.

Then they were both quiet. The crickets and the owls seemed to fall silent too. The breeze, the fire, and Mood's cigar smoke began to soothe Venir's nerves, making him reflective. He had survived much in the harsh world of Bish and was the better for it, but of late, things seemed out of place. It had never been normal for him to even ponder such things. Now it seemed common in his thoughts.

Mood cracked some branches and tossed them on the fire. "The underlings are thick as roaches, nowadays. My brethren and I are hard pressed to keep tabs on 'em. They're bolder, using daylight more. Of course, you've figured that out the hard way. They're getting ready for a surface war, I think, but not doing it like they used to."

"My problem, Mood, is that I used to be able to pick them apart and hunt them on my own terms. But once I put on that armor …" Venir looked over at his armaments. "I can't stop till I kill them. It just keeps … pushing me. I have to be careful there aren't a hundred too close to me or else I'll go after all of them. That's why I do what I can in the Outlands. There aren't too many large groups."

Venir sat down by the fire.

"Ah, now, it can't be that bad, can it?" Mood said.

Venir shook his head. "Besides, I don't think I'm going to be wielding the armaments forever."

Mood raised an eyebrow, but went on chewing and puffing on his cigar. "Looks like you're stuck with 'em now. Stop thinking and keep fighting. I've seen a lot o' things on the battlefield in this world, but never anything that could go through underlings like you do. You're a strong man and born that way. You can handle it." Mood pulled Venir to his feet. "So make the most of it and kill all the underlings you can. You'll be happier for it. I know you."

"I guess you do." Venir rubbed his hands together over the fire. "I can't believe I'm putting all this thought into it. I need to … Eh, I'll just stick with carving them into little chunks of troll food. Just don't let me get too close to the Underland."

The husky dwarf began carving a chair out of a massive log he'd downed. "I'd be glad to help. Now, how's Chongo? I assume he's safe since you didn't bring him along. He would have smelled 'em out long before you did."

"That's true. And he's fine. I let him sit this one out. Georgio's been keeping an eye on him."

"Really? And how is the boy? Silly little fella, but he makes me laugh," Mood said, still carving away.

"He seems to be doing well, given the circumstances. He's none the worse for wear." Even as he said it, though, Venir felt guilty for having not done a better job protecting Georgio in the Outlands. If only the boy had learned to stay put, things would have turned out better for him.

"Glad to hear it," Mood said. "Now, let's fetch us something to eat. I bet I can catch dinner before you can!"

"You're on!"

The two hulking figures separated and slipped into the deep shadows of the forest.

2

T HE WORLD OF BISH WAS a secret place, resting deep within the vast, wondrous folds of a cold, dark universe. Trinos, its creator, was once a mortal on a similar world. Her kind had discovered the means to travel the stars and gain limitless power. With this power, they created their own worlds.

As her kind had spread out across the vastness of space, they found that they were not the only ones. Other races, too, had discovered the endless expanse of time and space. They all thrived within the universe, united in their quest to find its purpose, its end. Yet, they could not. Once great and powerful, these beings now seemed to themselves as minuscule as molecules, scattered like stardust among the galaxies and stars—free to do as they pleased, yet feeling trapped within the enormity of space, where the limitlessness of their power often left them bored and restless.

Still, each had an agreed undertaking to fulfill. Trinos took the charge of monitoring new and old worlds that had been created by beings such as herself. These worlds came and went, rarely reaching the limitlessness that Trinos and other infinite beings had acquired. Most worlds extinguished over time.

Many had shown hope and promise, but sooner or later, all manner of creatures seemed to display self-destructive patterns of behavior. Selfishness, greed, and ambition outweighed more cohesive, constructive behaviors like love, peace, and joy. At one time, Trinos had also experienced such things as joy, pain, and love, but that was long, long ago—now just a fragment of her consciousness.

The creators of these worlds were often careless in their projects, and they lacked the vision to give their worlds a purpose. Often, they would merely abandon them, as they were not permitted to interfere. None, it seemed, could duplicate what their own race had achieved, and the source of their own power remained a mystery to them.

Trinos had grown rather disenchanted with her charges as she watched these worlds collapse again and again. Those to whom she reported these outcomes seemed not to mind how they fared, one way or the other. It frustrated her. In a moment of inspiration, she decided to create her very own world. It would be one that could survive under the harshest of conditions and bear humanoids, whom she had come to favor.

It would be a place where magic would supplant technology. Its people would have no desire to understand or care why they were there. Good and evil would be locked in eternal conflict, but a delicate balance would be maintained by a powerful source of magic that would change sides before one conquered the other, and so avoid ultimate destruction. The world would be full of colorful survivors—desperate, greedy, passionate, and fierce. Chronic mayhem and conflict would leave little room for peace among the races, with villainy pitted against heroism, each striving to eliminate the other at all costs.

Unknown to its inhabitants, the power to keep this world in check would be wielded by only one individual at a time. And at this particular moment in time, the magical power lay in the hands of a warrior—a furious juggernaut relentlessly opposed to evil.

At present, Trinos had little interest in the matter. Over the course of the world's existence, she had been pleased with its results. It had survived. Teetering on the edge of its own self-destruction, it had managed to recover time and again. Bish was a marvel, and had remained her secret for quite some time, which pleased her. But nothing lasted forever, for even those with limitless power were not beyond the reach of chance, fate, or chaos.

And so, upon her most recent return to enjoy the delights of her world, Trinos had discovered that another infinite being—Scorch—had come upon her jewel and tampered with it. Now, Bish was in decline, destined for destruction. She felt the stirring of anger in her once emotionless belly, and embraced it. It gave her a sense of purpose to pursue this meddler. But before she gave chase to Scorch, Trinos managed a quick fix to try to staunch the damage by bestowing additional power to the magical equalizer, hoping that this would be enough to check the decline. Then she set off, abandoning the world of Bish to deal with its predicament on its own.

3

B ELOW THE BLAZING SURFACE OF Bish, Lord Catten sat deep in thought, tapping his index finger into the pewter armrest, now riddled with tiny dents from his black, pointed nail. He was a black robed underling with a covering of light gray rat-like fur over his body. His head hair, eyebrows, lips, and sharp nails were all black, and his teeth gray and pointed.

The underling populace terrorized the surface world, although the massive, convoluted caves of the Underland remained their home. His race was matched against the humans in the battle for dominance on Bish. The underlings were more powerful in magic and had superior longevity to all other races, except for the dwarves. The humans, however, had superior numbers and other formidable talents that made them difficult to extinguish. There was nothing he hated more.

The humans, meanwhile, remained divided among themselves, torn between good and evil in their daily struggle with the harsh elements on Bish. By contrast, the underlings' fierce hatred for surface dwellers united them. Catten and his kind had one quest—seeking the utter destruction of their enemies. They were cruel, calculating, and merciless, hunting and torturing their victims more for power and pleasure than necessity or survival. Catten himself so delighted in these efforts that it was often a game for him and his kin.

Underling soldiers came and went across the surface of Bish at all hours of day and night, as orderly as worker ants. They were small in stature, more the size of small human women, and their movements were fluid and lithe, and purposeful. They would watch, observe, and report—then maim and execute helpless inhabitants throughout the land.

Though daylight did not bother them, they usually struck at night—it was their way. Leaving a bloodied trail of corpses, they left horror in their wake, and often took prisoners deep into their caves, never to be seen again. Sometimes they would leave a mutilated survivor or two with stumps for hands to recount the nightmare to others on the surface, and those demoralizing horror stories had no equal in instilling deeper fear.

Of late, however, successful underling invasions had been less numerous. It had been years since the underlings had engaged in a full-scale battle on the surface, yet they kept busy plotting and scheming while practicing guerrilla-like games. They were still the most dangerous race, but they had become more cautious of their losses and casualties, simply because they did not reproduce as easily as other races. They had to be careful when they struck, for a single miscalculation could wipe out a score of soldiers.

Lord Catten was not enjoying the pressure of tracking the formidable Darkslayer any more than a mouse would enjoy trying to catch a cat. He simply could not understand why this one man was so hard to kill. He sighed, though his narrow gold eyes remained unblinking over his hawkish nose. The eyes were the feature that most clearly distinguished one underling from another. Their heads could be a variety of shapes, but it was the uniqueness of their eyes in which they took most pride. Eyes came in all possible shapes, sizes, and any color of the spectrum, and anyone who survived a face-to-face encounter with an underling would never forget the sight.

Underlings so valued their eyes, in fact, that they would preserve those of their fallen brethren, though what they did with the bodies was uncertain. Their enemies would burn their bodies rather than bury them, lest underling magic revive them, as had sometimes been rumored.

Catten frowned. The battle casualties had been growing for the underlings. Yes, the Royal forces of Bish had gone on the offensive, preparing the villages and small farming towns under their watch, but there was another force that had steadily racked up a body count of underlings over the years, a force whose deeds alone had rallied the most inept of farmers to fight for their survival.

The Darkslayer had become the greatest thorn in the side of the powerful underlings, and because of him, their fearsome grip on Bish was weakening. At first, the Darkslayer had been only a pest, but now he had spread the poison of inspiration among their enemies. Catten and his brother, Lord Verbard, had been charged with his elimination, but these two powerful underling magi had been unsuccessful so far.

The two underling brothers were centuries old and stood a full five and a half feet tall, towering over their brethren. But now they sat on their pewter thrones in a cavern filled with objects of their desire, the dark walls glowing with the faint blue hue of the underlight, which derived from magic more ancient than even their knowledge.

Lord Verbard seemed less concerned than his brother; at the moment, his silver eyes were absorbed with the spectacle of the two urchlings before them, who were beating a captured human to a pulp. Urchlings were half-sized underlings with limited intelligence. They wore no clothing, had hunched backs, coarse body hair, knotted muscles, and white eyes, yet they were every bit as malicious as other underlings. Right now, their shrieks and chittering made Catten long to jam a spike into their heads to stop their wails of twisted triumph.

Bored at last, Verbard dismissed the two from his chamber with a sharp *chit*, and the urchlings dragged the disfigured and bloodied corpse of the man out of sight, much to Catten's relief.

"Did you not enjoy the show I arranged for you, brother?" Verbard inquired, leaning back in his throne.

Catten remained silent and brooding.

"Come now, Catten. You used to *adore* that! You have been quiet for weeks. If you will not talk, you may force me to return to my mate, and you know how it is when women are pregnant." Verbard scratched his chin and ground his teeth.

A slight smile came and went from Catten. "I sometimes think your mind is gone, Verbard, you are so unfocused on our task. I fear Master Sinway has lost patience. We need to see this deed done, yet you sit watching urchlings and mocking your mate."

"Patience." Verbard got up from his chair. "I will not let this task consume me. Besides, if Master Sinway wished, he would have castrated or eaten us already. No." He wagged his finger. "He needs us. We know our enemy best."

"Perhaps. Still, I think you are being a bit of a fool these days. People realize that you have changed, and this may be taken for weakness," Catten said.

"Ah … but am I not giddy about my heirs to be? Besides, the woman has been in an unbearable state of pregnancy for almost a decade. I cannot be in the same room with her." Verbard's round and wicked face seemed to recoil at the thought.

Catten could not avoid another smirk. His brother did have a way of cheering his own dark heart. Underlings were not without personality and emotion, though no one on Bish knew much about their lives in the Underland, for none cared to risk finding out. Of all the races on Bish, only the underlings were entirely bent on causing destruction and mayhem. Catten did not like waiting for Master Sinway to call, but he had no choice but to wait until he did. Then he could plan for vengeance again. In the meantime, he was determined to survive alongside his agitating brother. He needed him, and he'd have to make the best of it, for now.

"Come, brother," Catten said, getting up and floating down the dank corridor. "Come and stay with me. Let's go."

Verbard clapped his hands together and followed.

4

The lust for revenge was all Detective McKnight had to keep himself alive. He had been captive for an unknown time in a place entirely foreign to him and Tonio, his fellow prisoner. McKnight had been without food, but was somehow sustained. Lying on his back and immobilized from head to toe, he could see and hear little, but just enough to turn his stomach foul. The smell of rot filled his nostrils. He wanted to puke, but could not. Darkness was his constant companion, but he was not without company.

McKnight had no idea how he and Tonio had come to be where they were, yet he remembered what he had been doing before they became captives—dying. Were they not dead already? At times, he wondered if indeed this was death. Thoughts of revenge somehow reassured him that they both were still alive.

Revenge burned inside him like black fire. If they ever managed to escape their horrifying predicament, he would track down and destroy Venir and Melegal. Their blood would flow no more. McKnight figured—at least, hoped—that this thought was shared by Tonio, the son of Royal Lord Almen.

Now, though, McKnight was more concerned about escaping from the wiry silken cocoons covering them. Up to their necks they were sealed—and they had been captive for an unknown length of time.

It seemed like forever since McKnight's services had been requested by Lord Almen, after Tonio had unknowingly crossed paths with Venir and paid a dire price for his arrogance. The young warrior had everything in life, but his pride had cost him it all. What the detective did not know at the time was that Tonio had been set up. Other enemies of the Almens had actually struck down the young man.

McKnight eventually discovered that Tonio had been drugged with inducers. It led to the arrogant young man being mauled by Venir's giant two-headed dog and left for dead. The powerful magic of an underling cleric named Oran kept Tonio's heart beating. But he suffered, a large shred of his humanity was lost, and now Tonio lived with only a single thought—to kill Venir. McKnight never pitied the man—had always hoped to be rid of him on their quest—but now he was his only friend, and maybe the last he would ever see.

The swarthy detective, long-tenured in Royal Lord Almen's service, had been sent out to track Venir down. Accompanied by Tonio and the cleric, Oran, they'd set a trap. McKnight tried to remember himself then. He'd walked tall in his cloak, black boots, and a wide-brimmed hat. He'd been dangerous, cunning … and overconfident. Venir's friend Melegal had somehow undone McKnight. It ate at his insides.

McKnight and his allies had tracked Venir and Melegal far south into Two-Ten City. In the Great Forest of Bish, they'd sprung their trap. *It was perfect,* he mused. Yet it had failed, and he and Tonio had been left for dead.

In fact, McKnight had been sure he was dead until he awoke into his current nightmarish situation. The tingling in his body confirmed that it was real, which was horrific and healing at the same time. He could move his head a little and wiggle, but that was all. The little he witnessed in the gloom turned his stomach. He squinted in the dimness.

In the eerie light that illuminated the dark cavern around them, he could discern no ceilings, walls, or floors. He made out vast cobwebs stretching in all directions. Piles of web-like cocoons of every shape and size lay scattered around. Inside were carcasses, some as big as horses, others as small as rabbits.

Scurrying around and over him by the thousands were spiders of varying sizes. This place, he thus deduced, was their pantry and he was trapped inside. McKnight felt and saw the spiders crawling over his prone body and head. He could not get used to their hairy legs probing and crossing over his mouth.

Even worse, he could sometimes hear powerful sucking sounds nearby. The sound was sickening and unforgettable, as if the marrow were being wrenched from inside their bones.

A cacophony of moans and screams from tormented men and beasts continued for long hours through day … or night. He knew not which. McKnight found little relief that it was not him. He had sobbed his last teardrop long ago and now only vengeance filled his head and heart.

It appeared that he was getting what he deserved—a fate worse than death. But he and Tonio needed only one chance, and soon he would have it.

McKnight looked again at a glint of steel nearby. If he could only get a fighting chance, he would take it. He noticed Tonio's head facing that glint as well, as they were entwined side by side. Tight as his tacky web-strung bonds had him sealed, McKnight finally managed to move just a little. He found it odd that he felt fine. The poison that had taken him in the forest seemed to have disappeared from his system. He felt rejuvenated. But then, maybe it was only a hopeful delusion from his imagination.

McKnight began discussing another impossible plan with Tonio. The man never responded with any more than a grunt. *Idiot.* There was little else to talk about and he said nothing he hadn't said a hundred times already, but just saying it gave McKnight a reason to survive. He waited, hoping his captors would soon come for them as dinner. His vengeance could not be kept in check forever.

Soon something came his way. The spiders crawled off. McKnight bounced up and down as something approached. His blood turned cold as they came.

5

L ORD CATTEN WAS IN HIS cavern castle, looming over his desk and engrossed with his studies. While his brother Verbard was being entertained by Catten's family, Catten chose to spend long hours planning.

The underling's home ran deep beneath the rock that made up the mountain ranges of Bish. Scintillating and colorful minerals formed magnificent swirling patterns in the walls that stretched from cave to cave. Though the entrance to his home was small with no discernible door, the inside was as vast as any great castle in the city of Bone. Some of the caverns were natural formations, but most had been carved out by enslaved hands or powerful magic long ago. Unlike the outer caves of the Underland, here there were no dripping stalactites overhead or troublesome stalagmites on the cavern floors. Stairways and catwalks of metal, wood, or stone traversed the spaces, leading in and out of dark holes, crisscrossing from high to low. To one who lived topside, it would have been either an engineering or magical marvel that appeared to wind from everywhere to nowhere.

Catten's home was dry and comfortable, every bit as luxurious as any in the world above. None would have guessed that such a malevolent race could have such an appreciation for finer things. On the wall hung paintings of exquisite beauty, among others so horrifying that no human eye would be able to look upon them. Indeed, the underlings were much like humans, but their hearts had been twisted inside out.

Catten's intense gold eyes darted over an ancient scroll spread across his massive onyx desk. His study held his most treasured possessions, most of which were records of dark magic, for he knew the more magic one controlled, the more power one wielded, and he and Verbard were already in a league of their own.

The blue glow from his fingertips illuminated and moved the parchment he was studying. He sought assistance to capture or destroy the Darkslayer, for Master Sinway, ruler of the Underland, was on his way to visit Catten's home, an unprecedented event. Catten needed answers and a convincing plan.

Thus far he had nothing.

Sitting atop a scarlet pillow on his black oak chair, Catten closed his eyes. Magic failed to track the Darkslayer. He was like a ghost. But he was a man, a warrior—yet his armaments had to originate from a mystic source. Catten scowled—his lack of understanding infuriated him.

Time and again, he'd scoured the few records he had. The underlings were irresponsible in their documentation of history, just as the rest of Bish. This bothered the underling wizard, who now spent more time recording magic on scrolls and studying them than anything else. Nowhere could he find mention of the weapons and armor of the Darkslayer—nor of the man himself, other than what had passed from others' lips in the past few years. It was all a great mystery.

More than brute force would be needed to destroy the Darkslayer. Once again, he and Verbard would be required to venture out into the dreadful landscape of Bish, which he dreaded. He slumped in his chair, face in his hands.

His festering hatred—along with his brother's—helped drive Catten's determination to pursue this detestable human. He wanted the Darkslayer destroyed—but at the peril of his own life? That he did not know. This time he would see to it they were better prepared and more careful.

But first they had to track him down.

Catten rubbed his eyes as Verbard strolled into the study. His brother was accompanied by Catten's own mate and twin daughters. He watched in agitation as they chatted and smiled at his brother's comments.

The women wore dresses of sheer white silk, displaying their nubile bodies. Their long fingernails were painted to match the colors of their radiant eyes, which were framed by long, seductive lashes. He frowned as the three women smiled more than he had seen in quite some time.

"I see they've been taking good care of you, brother," Catten said, hiding his disgust. He rose from his chair, walked over, and pulled his mate away from Verbard, his eyes averted from hers. "Now, let us gather our thoughts before Master Sinway gets here!"

"Your family has treated me quite well, thank you," Verbard said. "I do feel able to focus on our task now that my head is cleared of ominous thoughts of my overbearing and pregnant mate."

As Verbard scowled, the females snickered. Underling women underwent a startling transformation during their ten-year pregnancies. By the end they bore no resemblance to normal female underlings. Their faces became monstrous and their mouths fanged, and they experienced supernatural growth that left them bedridden.

Urchlings were called upon to be the unfortunate caregivers, a dangerous task, as pregnant underlings became violent, moody, and unpredictable. They would eat anything, including urchlings. Some underlings, Catten included, enjoyed their women like this, but Verbard loathed it.

"You're faint of heart, brother," Catten said, squeezing his mate.

"Sorry, but I prefer our women beautiful," Verbard said, hugging his nieces, who stroked his cheek in return.

Underling women were the most beautiful creatures on Bish, yet none had ever been above the surface. Their dusky skin and gray fur gave them a deceptively soft, gentle appearance. Yet, despite their exotic beauty, they were demanding and calculating—intense and vicious when competing for the men at the top positions in society. Such was their nature.

As skilled as their men were in weapons and magic, the women were skilled in more subtle means of survival and conquest. They used their magic to create potions and toxins, and to make themselves charming, hypnotic, and irresistible. And just like Catten and Verbard, these three women were proficient and powerful. At Catten's gesture, they departed without a word. Verbard snickered, watching them go, then flopped into a chair at the black table.

"Your mate and daughters are as delightful and devious as ever," Verbard said, checking his pointed nails.

Catten fought the urge to slap his face. "I am glad you enjoyed their company. Now, let us get on with the task at hand."

"Ah, but first you must tell me their names," Verbard said.

"No, brother, never! We will not go down this road again." Catten turned away, face down toward the table.

Part of the underling courtship culture was for the male to discover the female's name. It was a puzzle. Once a male had figured it out, she fell under his full authority and became his mate.

It was rare for underlings to have mates, as these brothers did. A name might be discovered through a variety of means, sometimes to the detriment of the female. Hence, Underland society allowed open relationships between males and females, and many underling houses had several women and children under their guard, yet no husband-and-mate relationship.

Underling women received names from their father. Not even a mother knew her daughters' names.

An underling who wished to court and mate with an underling daughter needed to learn her name from the daughter herself. A father could bestow the name as a gift, but this was rare. A daughter would never give up her name to another underling. Instead, she gave clues, often decades apart. Underling courtships could last a hundred years or more, but great power was gained through such unions. Catten, in fact, had received his mate's name from her father.

"Just teasing, Catten. Loosen up some. Now, let's go over whatever it is you want," Verbard said, sitting up and pulling his chair to the table.

Catten sat on the table, looking down at his brother. "When Master Sinway arrives, we need to be very forthcoming. Make no bones about our plans …" He wagged his finger. "I will propose that we venture above once more. First, we will take the Current below Bish, but we need to decide who should join us. Last time we failed to take the Darkslayer by force. So this time we will have to show more patience."

"We will take him by force this time!" Verbard almost shouted. "We'll blow him into bloody chunks and pieces. We had him last time!" he said, clutching his chest.

Catten could see the anguish in Verbard's face as he remembered the fatal wound from the Warfield not so long ago.

"He should be dead!" Verbard finished with a rap on the table.

"I agree, but there are forces in the world we don't understand. He is one of them. If we can separate him from his armaments, I think we can put an end to him, but it's going to take patience and cunning."

A quiet moment passed as he watched his brother consider the plan.

"Agreed. Besides, I think this is how Master Sinway prefers us to go about it. We will do this, brother. The Darkslayer will die," Verbard said.

Catten looked deep into his sibling's eyes and felt they were united by a single burning desire—to see the Darkslayer dead. Verbard froze as his silver eyes widened. Catten's shoulders felt cold, as if an icy stare lingered on his back.

No ... Not yet!

Catten turned and saw Master Sinway's foreboding presence fill the doorway.

6

L ORD CATTEN DROPPED TO ONE knee, head bowed, alongside his brother. Master Sinway and a dozen Badoon warriors crowded his study. Master Sinway wore thick black robes with an inlay of dark patterns and mystic signs. He towered over the others, a full six feet in height.

Catten peered up, spellbound as always. Sinway's chiseled face was aimed at him—the ominous eyes beneath a thick head of receding black hair. His master's furry hands waved long fingers with marvelous rings and razor-sharp nails. The underling overlord's feet skimmed over the marble surface with each step, never touching the ground. It made Catten feel even smaller. The shadow-walk came naturally to some, but not all. Catten looked down again as he felt his master's robes pass.

"Get up, you two," Master Sinway said with clarity. "Your insincere groveling does not impress me."

Catten stood at attention, pulling up his smirking brother by the arm.

Idiot.

"Welcome to my home, Master Sinway," Catten said, head bowed. "This is a great honor you have bestowed on my family. Is there anything I can get you?"

"As a matter of fact, yes. The Darkslayer. Do you have him here by any chance?" Sinway's iron-red irises locked onto his. Catten held his stare for a moment then dropped his eyes. *He's furious.* His brother took a half step back.

"No, Master," Catten said, keeping his head down. "My brother and I are working on it."

Sinway walked around them both, stopping to regard his brother. His brother looked up and returned Master Sinway's stare. *Don't do it!*

Sinway stopped. From the corner of his eye, Catten watched Verbard's eyes stream with tears. Catten's twin cried out, grasping his eyes as he fell to his knees.

Sinway's voice shook the room, jolting objects from the shelves. "You fool, Verbard! I do not understand your behavior of late, but do not do that again. Ever!"

Catten helped his brother back to his feet, but Verbard pushed him away. Sinway moved to the black table, preoccupied in thought. Catten envied Sinway's power over them and all others. Verbard felt the same. It was what they desired for themselves one day. Sinway had more secrets than all the days of their lives, but over time Catten would acquire the same through his service.

Catten heard his lord behind him. "I have given you two the benefit of the doubt long enough. You had been fine servants until this last failure, but the loss of my precious Vicious and a whole Badoon brigade was colossal. And embarrassing!"

Invisible fingers poked Catten's back, nudging him forward. It hurt.

"I cannot fathom how you managed to fail," Sinway said. "I armed you well. You had great power at your disposal. Yet the Darkslayer still lives, while underlings die in multitudes."

There was a long silence. Catten turned to see his master gripping the edges of the table.

"Last time, Master Sinway," Catten said, stepping forward, "we allowed ourselves to be distracted. It was a costly error and we did not foresee it. It was the first time we had taken the matter directly into our own hands. We have learned much about our enemy now. We will not fail again."

"No, you will not," Sinway said, "because if you do, you will never set foot in the Underland again. Do not return if you fail this time!" he yelled as the edges of the onyx table crumbled in his glowing grip.

Catten fell to his knees. *No!* He felt like a child caught one too many times, shrinking under his master's hot glare. He searched his brother's face and saw his shock as well. He should not have been surprised, for the Darkslayer had been a constant thorn in their sides. What would he have done in his master's shoes?

"Kill this human," Sinway said. "Bring me his body and his weapons. I want everything he has. I don't know what it will take and I don't care. Stop him!"

Two clawed fingers pointed at their chests. Catten's heart stopped. He pitched forward, clutching his chest as Sinway released his spell. He was sweating now, gasping for air, trying not to writhe like a worm all over the floor. *Point taken.* With a groan, Catten gathered himself, still shaking as Sinway shadow-walked through the doorway and disappeared. As the door closed, silence enveloped the room.

He couldn't have been more relieved. Then he noticed Verbard lying on the floor.

"I told you he was mad," Catten tried to shout, but couldn't find his breath. "And you had to try to stare him down! You are fortunate to still have your mind left."

Verbard still clutched his chest, his face a drooling grimace. *That old wound is quite bad. Interesting.* He pulled his brother up and watched as his ashen face returned to gray.

Verbard dusted himself off. "He still has it, I will say that. I have not tried that with him for over a century, but I lasted longer than ever. Either he's getting weaker or I am stronger!"

"You are a fool! He almost killed you," Catten said.

Verbard's silver eyes sparkled. "No, he respects it. He doesn't like it, but he respects it."

Catten took a deep breath, walked over to his table, and began rolling up the scrolls.

"What are you doing?" Verbard asked.

"Gearing up. I suggest you do the same."

"Why bother with that?"

"We will be gone awhile. It is not wise to leave anything on the table."

"Well, if that is the case, then we will not go alone. I will bring some help and protection," Verbard said with strange cheer.

Catten knew what his devious brother had in mind, but he didn't resist. His brother was right, it was time to pull out all the stops. Never in their lives had they been faced with a kill-or-be-killed mission, but the time had come. It was their charge.

"Hurry back," Catten said, shaking his head at the ruined table. "I cannot wait to see what you return with."

Catten looked up and saw Verbard's wicked smile as his brother walked out through the open door.

7

V ENIR HAD REACHED THE OUTSKIRTS of Bone after leaving Mood and Red Clay Forest behind. A mile away from the main south gate, he stood and gazed at the massive stone walls surrounding the city. They were unlike any others on Bish, enclosing well over a hundred thousand occupants as if in a giant castle.

There was little evidence of how the great city had come into existence, but the dungeons and catacombs below were filled with tombs and bones from a long-forgotten time.

The wall's enormous portcullis opened like a gaping maw ready to devour its next meal. The southern outskirts of the city walls always bustled with activity as merchants and farmers plied their trades day and night like worker ants.

The City Watch was thick in the area. They were strict in enforcing who could enter and who could not. The Royals did not welcome other races, but allowed inhabitants to barter with them on the outside. The City Watch also recruited citizens. Anyone with skill or charm would be welcomed and escorted inside, never to be seen again by their families. It was considered a great honor by outsiders to be taken into the city's sanctuary, but often those persons met a most unpleasant fate. This, in fact, was how Venir had arrived in Bone as a boy.

He had been a strapping young twelve-year-old with bright blue eyes and shiny, thick blond hair. But he was alone; his family had long been slaughtered by underlings at his village of Throhm. Bandits had taken him in and traded him to devious merchants, who then took him to the city of Bone to exploit his skills. There he worked as a slave below several Royal castles.

His only friend then was a fellow slave boy named Melegal. Their days were filled with cleaning the muck and grime of the excesses of those above. The nights were filled with lashings and fitful sleep on a cold, damp dungeon floor with only grimy cleaning cloths for blankets.

The only good thing was that the slavers educated them so that they could understand their duties and how Royal systems worked—reading and writing were needed to meet the demands of their superiors. As they grew more skilled, they rose up to the less subservient positions. It was still slavery, but a better life than many had on Bish. Those without skills did not survive long.

But the slavers took the older ones as they approached adulthood, and they were never seen again. The younger ones were left wondering where they had gone. Unbelievable rumors had struck terror in their hearts. Even today, Venir still did not know where the older slaves had gone, but he knew of many who had survived.

He and Melegal had been lucky—they had picked up the reading and writing. Melegal had the precious gift of being able to take dictation with a fluent hand. Venir, conversely, relied on his strength, and was made a sparring dummy for Royal sons to develop their battle skills. He never fought back as they dished it out to him over and over. It was a time in his life he preferred to forget, and he pretty much managed to do that—until times like these that brought him back to Bone.

Returning his thoughts to the present, he headed far off the beaten trail up a barren hillside. He started to feel good about returning back to civilization and his friends—good food, strong drink, and feisty women.

Venir entered a cave opening hidden by thick bushes. It was just big enough to get a small horse through. Inside, it fanned out in a variety of directions, and he walked ahead a hundred feet or so. The caves were neither deep nor dangerous, but those who came across them were invariably too scared to enter for fear that underlings were nearby. Venir liked them to think this. He would even litter the cave paths with old bones of various animals—and sometimes even underling skulls.

He took several turns in total darkness before finding a door, felt around in the rock for the keyhole, inserted a key, and gave it a turn. The door swung open.

Inside was a stone tunnel, taller than a man, sloping down toward the distant sound of rushing water. He approached the source of the noise—a large storm drain with an old steel grate, beneath which water rushed some fifty feet below. As soon as he had passed over it, the corridor sloped upward again. By the time he reached the end of the tunnel, Venir had risen again to ground level. There, a large ancient wall loomed before him. He tripped a simple latch and the low ceiling dropped downward, revealing a large opening. He walked up a massive plank, tripped another hidden mechanism, and the floor raised back up, sealing the secret opening.

He was now in a hay-filled stall inside the great stables of the city of Bone. Only he and a few others knew of this long-neglected secret passageway. He stepped out of the stall into a barn of massive proportions. Hundreds of stalls and stables lined two rows north to south, illuminated by a massive hole in the roof, its rim streaked with gray-and-white pigeon litter. Venir welcomed the strong smells of hay and manure after the barren Outlands he had jogged across in the sweltering heat.

In the distance, he could see some activity in the northern stalls, but the southern stalls seemed mostly vacant. This barn had always been the least active of the six giant buildings that housed mounts for Bone's City Watch and the Royal families. He peered over the stable gate to see if anyone was in the immediate area then treaded out. He hadn't taken two steps before he heard a yell.

"Vee!" Georgio ran toward him from a mere twenty paces away, causing an unwanted commotion. "Vee, you're back!"

"Hush!" Venir said with a wave of his arm.

Georgio covered his mouth and ran on tiptoes, stumbled to the ground, then scrambled back up again, sending pigeons fluttering. No one seemed to be around. Venir hugged the husky farm boy, who smiled and nodded in return.

"Man, I'm so glad you're back, Vee!" Georgio whispered.

"It's been little more than a week, Georgio. You act like I've been gone a year." He rubbed the large boy's head. "So, how's it been going?" He regretted the question as it left his lips.

"Melegal's grouchy all the time. Lefty keeps writing. I get bored. It's no fun when you aren't around. They won't play with me. Melegal and Lefty play games, but they say I'm not smart enough. I tell them I am, but they still don't let me play. And after I take care of Chongo and Quickster, Melegal asks fifty questions about Quickster and I tell him to go check himself. Then he starts cursing and lecturing. He gives me a headache with all his yakking. It's better when you're here."

Georgio sighed, shaking his brown curls. Then his eyes grew round with excitement. "So, how many underlings did you kill? Tell me! Ten? Twenty? Tell me, tell me!"

"Six," Venir responded.

"Six?" Georgio shook his head again. "That's it?" His eyes lit up again and he snapped his fingers. "Wait! You killed them all! Only six were left on Bish?"

"No," Venir said.

Georgio frowned.

"I didn't have much luck tracking them down," Venir said. "It happens. Besides, there were enormous sand spiders, too."

Georgio perked up again. "I've heard about them. How many did you kill?"

Just one wasn't going to impress the boy. Lefty would want all the details, plus Venir was eager to hit the town, so he opted for the truth—at least this once. "I fought two, but I only had to kill one. See what the spider spit did to my legs."

The boy's eyes grew at the sight of the thick red burns healing on his hero's leg. "Wow! That's nasty."

"I'll tell you all about it later. Let's see how Chongo's doing. Where is he?" he asked.

"I moved him over this way," the boy said.

Venir followed the boy deeper into the southern end of the barn. Chongo occupied a variety of different stables in case anyone became too curious about the unique animal. Georgio did a fine job of relocating him regularly and making sure no one messed with Venir's favorite pet, mount, and friend.

Georgio stopped before an old, worn stable gate. Unlike the others, it was over six feet high, so one could not see over it. Set into it was a smaller door that latched from the inside.

The boy climbed over followed by Venir. He was set upon by two large, wet tongues of black and pink. Two lion-sized paws pinned him to the wall as the two-headed Chongo licked him up and down. Venir laughed and scratched one of Chongo's heads and then the other. Chongo's two stiff tails snapped back and forth like cattails.

"Ow!" Georgio shrieked as a tail whipped across his cheek, leaving a red welt.

Venir gave a little frown, then smiled at Chongo again. The bull mastiff—known also as a dwarven setter—was the size of a small horse. Chongo's heavy coat, unusual for a mastiff, was deep brown and red, and as soft a retriever's. And his two snouts made him an excellent bloodhound, able to pick up a scent for miles, maybe even leagues. Chongo had been with Venir on and off since his boyhood. They had always managed to find one another again, despite the odds against survival on Bish.

As soon as both of Chongo's heads had calmed down, Georgio passed Venir a rag to wipe off his coating of saliva. After drying himself, Venir looked around the oversized stall, noting that it was layered with clean hay and that the food and water troughs were freshly filled.

Another beast lay snoring in the corner. It was Melegal's gray pony, Quickster, who looked more like a mule than a pony—except for his furry black underbelly. Venir laughed again, thinking about how it always annoyed Melegal that everyone called Quickster a mule or donkey, though the beast didn't seem to mind. As usual, he just lay there on his back in his own world, hooves dangling below bent knees, oblivious to the presence of Venir and Georgio.

"Why does Melegal keep that silly donkey, Vee?" Georgio asked, rolling his eyes.

"Don't start, Georgio, or I'll tell Melegal he looks hungry."

Georgio grunted. "But that's the dumbest animal I've ever seen! All he ever does is eat, sleep, and fart. He even tried to eat a live chicken. Ever seen a donkey chase a chicken, Vee?"

"Shut up, Georgio. I just got back. Save your words for Melegal."

Georgio pouted and muttered and finished up his chores in the stall. Venir watched the boy as he scratched Chongo's ears and belly. Despite the boy's endless questions and pointless comments, Venir was glad to see Georgio.

He had taken care of Georgio over the years like a kid brother—ever since rescuing him from an underling attack on Red Clay Village, south of the forest, when Georgio was just a toddler. Now about twelve years old, Georgio reminded Venir of himself at that age—full of energy and a thirst for adventure. Georgio had remained cheerful despite his circumstances, and had grown on the hardened warrior. Truly, the boy gave Venir another purpose besides slaughtering underlings.

"Things look to be in good order, Georgio," Venir finally said. "Let's head back so I can wash. On the way, I'll take you by the market and get you some of the fruits you like, for your fine work. How's that sound?"

"About time! I'm starving. Quickster eats better than me. Oops … sorry. I didn't say that. Uh, so, can I get some jerky, too?"

Venir squeezed the boy's thick shoulder. "Sure, all you can eat."

"Man, all the jerky I can eat?" Brimming with joy, Georgio skipped out through the small door in the gate.

As the two of them stepped out into the seductive grasp of Bone, an old stable hand emerged from an adjoining stall. He hobbled across the barn and out of the main entrance. Wide-eyed, he kept muttering over and over to himself, "I *must* tell him. I *must* tell him."

8

Catten's thoughts were heavy as he made haste from the Underland. He had been banished from the seclusion, power, and comfort of the cave lands. It was unsettling. His mind played countless scenarios of the task ahead. The destruction of the Darkslayer was a challenging assignment and his only way back home.

He blamed himself for their failure less so than his brother. Verbard had been careless and cocky the last time.

Catten didn't doubt that his twin blamed him for the failure. His brother never found fault with himself. Neither did Catten, for that matter. The truth was, failure was something he hadn't experienced in a long time. It disturbed him.

A fifteen-foot-long barge made of black wood glided over an underworld river called the Current. The Current was a black stream of ice-cold water that didn't flow. Few creatures lived in the waters that ran through a catacomb of cave tunnels. The tunnels were narrow and low to enormous and high, but one could little tell the difference in the sheer blackness if you were not an underling. The water of the Current had a foul sulfur-like smell. Even the underlings could not drink it, but they found its waters cleansing, and some life thrived within the murky deep.

A steady breeze billowed Catten's robes as he stood at the fore. He and his brother were not unaccompanied. They traveled with new companions, just as the clever and silver-eyed Verbard had promised. Catten preferred to rely on his scrolls as well as some other unique oddities to accompany him. Still, he'd brought some added security for himself.

As Catten stood at the bow of the rudderless barge, two other underlings stood behind him. They were not hunter warriors such as the elite Badoon that had failed them before. Instead, they were armed with flexible black-plated armor, bracers, closed-face helms, and twin scimitar-like swords on their hips. They were Catten's personal bodyguards that had protected him for over a hundred years. Their skills in battle were rivaled by few in the Underland. They were called the Juegen, and as long as he had them with him, he was confident he would stay alive.

Farther behind him, he could hear the heavy breathing of his brother's escorts. They were the opposite of his perfect guards—armorless, filthy, stupid, and savage. All six of the disturbing creatures huddled in the back, smacking their twisted lips and growling at one another. Catten kept his distance, glaring at his brother who stood in the middle of the barge, cleaning his nails. Catten didn't know which disgusted him more, Verbard's nonchalant attitude or their other escorts.

The others who accompanied them were urchlings, but much different from the rest of their kind. Whereas typical urchlings were smaller, hunchbacked, and hairy, these were a taller, stocky, corded, albino version of their kind. They had four nostrils on their bat-like faces and could track like a bloodhound. Their clawed hands were that of a ferocious wolverine and their tiny brains followed simple orders to perfection—hunt and destroy. His brother had spent generations breeding their kind for occasions such as these, but this group had never hunted with the underling lords before. *He'd better have control of them.*

After countless hours of whisking over the black water, Verbard asked, "So, I can't help but let my curiosity overcome me. Where exactly are you taking us?"

Catten turned and faced his brother. "Oran's lair."

Verbard nodded. "That was my suspicion. Of course, you never are one for surprises, now are you?"

"Would you have made a different choice, Verbard?"

"No, I am just saying if I made the choice, it wouldn't have been so obvious," Verbard said.

"Then why did you ask me?"

Verbard tossed a scrap of human flesh to his pet urchlings, who tore into it—and each other—with vigor. Catten didn't like the sound of his brother's voice. It irritated him. He hoped Verbard would say nothing else.

Catten turned forward again, straddling the bow. His brother's behavior was an increasing agitation. It never bothered him this much before, though. As a matter of fact, Catten often looked forward to his brother's clever ideas and daring. Now, though, it had become tiresome. He huffed.

And then Catten heard his brother again at his back. "I couldn't think of anything else worth asking … brother. So, how much longer will this trek to Oran's be? The scenery on the Current is becoming dreadful."

Catten remained silent.

9

M CKNIGHT SUCKED IN A BREATH as he saw ahead of him several spider-like creatures the size of large dogs with man-like torsos and faces, and the legs of a tarantula. He felt horror as the strange creatures advanced on him and while they carried him away.

As they hauled him along, McKnight studied them, for they were like nothing he had ever seen before. The creatures had strange, bearded faces, large insect eyes, small bent antennas, and neutral, insect-like expressions. A chill raced through McKnight's spine, and he writhed inside his cocoon, obsessed with the thought of driving his dagger into their ugly bodies over and over again.

Calm down, man, McKnight chided himself.

He looked around, glimpsing more of his surroundings.

This might be your chance.

Two of the strange creatures carried McKnight in and out of webs within an enormous room. The odd light illuminated more than just corpses and cocoons, and the edges of the room began to form. It seemed to be designed for some other, larger humanoid race. McKnight noticed tables, chairs, and other furnishings much larger than those for ordinary men. There was even a massive fireplace, and a variety of weapons lay scattered about as if a battle had taken place.

Where am I? The detective strained his eyes. *And where are the people who used this furniture?*

Perhaps the losers had been cocooned. He had no idea what race might claim the belongings in this enormous and apparently endless room. *Giants?* Maybe the legends were true. He was so disoriented he could not even tell if he was above or below ground. Nausea overcame him as he bounced along upside-down under the ceiling and sideways along the walls. He spit bile and groaned.

McKnight was dropped to the floor and dragged through a winding, twisting corridor that seemed to have been bored through wood. The creatures stopped in darkness. A door opened and hot air blew on his face. He filled his nostrils with exhilaration. *Sweet Bish!*

He was plucked up again and dragged out into a burst of blinding sunlight. Purple and blue spots danced before his eyes. His vision slowly returned as he felt the warmth of sunlight on his cheeks. *Be ready.*

He craned his neck and noticed he was on the limb of a monstrous tree. It felt as if he was free again, despite the inescapable bondage. A tremble of hope entered his mind. He'd had little need for simple joys in the past, other than those supplied through various pleasures in Bone. But now he felt what it meant to be free—or at least close to freedom. A spark consumed him that only a fighting man would understand. He just needed one chance. He looked into the stoic insect eyes of his strange captors.

"Have mercy on me!" he said with a croak.

I sure as Bone won't return it, though.

As he lay flat on his back, he could see more enormous branches above, covered with bright leaves of emerald and gold. Then he was hoisted up and, without warning, tossed off the massive branch.

"Nooooooo!"

Tonio plummeted alongside him.

Anger overtook his fear, and McKnight yelled out, "You idiot, Tonio! That I should die like an urchin because of your arrogance—ulp!" McKnight's stomach lurched as he jerked to a halt upside-down in midair and bounced in suspension on a web-like cable.

The cocooned Tonio swayed before him.

McKnight looked below, expecting to see the ground, but only another massive branch stared back at him, along with some of the arachnamen. Still overwhelmed with helplessness and fury, McKnight used his momentum to swing toward Tonio and butt the warrior hard in the chin with his head. The jolt was painful, but he continued his assault. Tonio soon responded in kind, and the two butted each other like legless rams.

The arachnamen on the branch below pushed McKnight and Tonio into each other. The subsequent laughter sounded to McKnight like night owls hooting. His tether snapped, and he plunged onto a hard branch with a painful thump. The buys hands of the arachnamen clutched at him, rolling him over and over again, until he plunged into a hole. He screamed as he slid downward through the blackness. It was a long, fast ride, which ended as he vaulted into the air. McKnight plopped onto a hard wooden floor. He rolled over just in time to see Tonio plummeting his way.

"Oomph!" McKnight groaned as he reluctantly softened the big man's landing.

Lying on his back, his body aching, McKnight glanced around at their new surroundings the best he could. Hundreds of pairs of insect eyes gazed down on him and Tonio from row upon row of tiered seats—all filled with arachnamen.

An arena carved right into the heart of the tree?

McKnight struggled against his bonds and managed to sit up on the wooden floor. Nearby, Tonio rolled around like a burning earthworm.

A second later, several arachnamen surrounded them both, poking their chests with spear tips. Two of the ugly beings cut their cocoons with slender blue-bladed daggers. The cords of webbing became brittle as soon as the blades cut across them. A powerful tingling coursed through the detective from head to toe at the feel of the air.

McKnight held his nose as a stench filled his nostrils. Thick pools of liquid drained from his cocoon onto the ground around him. He wondered if it contained some of his own excrement, but the muck that covered him seemed to dry fast and he found his clothing still intact, though soaked and misshapen. He might as well have stepped out of a sewage monster's belly. He let it go.

His moment had come.

Ignoring the stiffness in his cramping muscles, McKnight exploded into action. Tonio, too, wasted no time, catching the closest arachnaman by the neck and snapping its spine like a twig. The young warrior snatched a dagger from its lifeless grip and leapt at the others.

McKnight disarmed another arachnaman and used its blade to poke a hole clean through its throat. The kill felt good. And even though McKnight knew the odds were not in their favor, he sensed no serious fight in the creatures that now surrounded them with their spears lowered. No doubt they'd all been shocked by the onslaught he and Tonio had wrought already.

As he focused on his foes, hoots of excitement came from the creatures watching from the tiered seats. McKnight snarled, and he and Tonio waded into the arachnamen, stabbing and carving them into puddles of milky blood.

McKnight pulled his blade from one of the creatures and glanced to his right. Tonio tore into them like a rabid animal. He pinned one to the ground with its own spear and stomped its spider body into goo. *We're gonna get out of here,* McKnight thought, liking their chances more by the second.

Seeing the flash of a spear to his left, McKnight hurled a dagger into the open mouth of his attacker. A bubble of webbing erupted toward McKnight's face as the creature tried to spit the blade out. Another arachnaman rushed straight at him with a spear, bent low. Feeling his legs limbering up, McKnight leaped forward, vaulting over the creature and landing on its back. Twisting quickly, McKnight threw an arm around its neck and strangled it from behind. It crumbled, lifeless, to the floor.

Another rushed in, spear tip bearing down on McKnight's belly. He snorted a laugh, leaping and kicking it square in the face. Its nose crunched under his heel. At the same time, Tonio rammed a spear through its body and it spit globs of bloodied webbing in all directions. Falling to the ground, it writhed in agony.

All but one lone arachnaman scurried over the walls and disappeared. Glancing around, McKnight counted eight dead. He picked up a spear, and together he and Tonio flanked the last arachnaman, who fell to its knees, trembling. McKnight kicked it onto its back and pinned it there with his right foot on its chest.

"Let us go!" McKnight yelled to those in the audience. "If you do, we won't kill him! We have no quarrel with any of you!" He heaved for his next breath, his burst of energy dwindling.

McKnight heard only silence, as if his words were being considered—if they even understood him at all. It was an odd moment. The strange creatures did not blink, but only looked at one another with their insect eyes. McKnight looked around, but could see no discernible way out. Iron spikes and barbs seemed to prevent any escape from within the arena—which had been carved out right in the heart of the giant tree.

How many more must I kill? McKnight lacked Tonio's strength. He hadn't fought so much in years. He didn't figure his skill with a sword and his excellent marksmanship would serve him now. He was too exhausted. But ... *Fight or die.*

At his side, Tonio stood still, gray as a granite statue splattered with red, black, and white blood. The roughhewn man seemed to barely even be breathing while McKnight himself gasped for air.

A deep chant rose in the seats around them, like a thousand hooting owls. Were they singing a horrendous song or were they summoning something? Something moved under McKnight's feet. Looking down, he saw hundreds of hand-sized spiders squeezing up out of small holes all over the arena floor. His stomach dropped to the floor.

The spiders were white with tiny fangs. Red stripes and spots covered their hairy backs. McKnight froze as they swarmed onto the creature he had pinned to the ground. McKnight jerked his foot off the arachnaman's chest as the spiders completely covered its body. The spiders' tiny mouths began to devour the arachnaman alive. McKnight's stomach turned to mush and he gagged. *Please no!*

Fifteen seconds later, all the spiders scurried back into their holes. Only the arachnaman's spear remained.

McKnight felt an overwhelming sigh of relief run through his shivering body. *I hate spiders, I hate everything.* McKnight thought of jamming his spears into the little holes. Tonio stood nearby, ready to drive his spear into the tiny holes as well.

"If we ever escape this cursed tree, Tonio," McKnight said, "I swear I'll burn it to the ground!" McKnight stopped. A creaking sound caught his ear. He turned to see a tall door opening on the far side of the arena. The arachnamen in the arena seats stared at the door like dogs waiting for a treat. From deep within the tunnel came an eerie growl, the likes of which McKnight had never heard before. Then a clacking sound echoed from within the corridor behind the doorway. It grew louder. Tonio gripped a spear in each hand while McKnight studied the blue-bladed daggers in his own grasp. The mysterious blue metal matched the spear tips, and he wondered what it might be—but right now, he wondered even more what on Bish was coming down that corridor.

The crowd cheered, balls of web floating from their mouths like smoke in the air. Something fearful was emerging from the tunnel. McKnight really wanted to run. *Son of a Bish!*

And then it appeared.

A great hairy humanoid creature filled the entryway. It stood over six feet tall with brutish muscles covered in red and black fur like a tarantula. It also had a tarantula's head, with eight tiny insect eyes glowing green. Its mouth was a wicked maw, opening and closing like a snapping turtle's, all the while showing four curved fangs. McKnight noted the man-like hands and arms, and that, even stranger, it wore insignia pants like a Royal soldier, but no shirt.

It appeared as if a formidable human had been transformed into a spidery predator. Whatever it was had been a man at some time. McKnight felt something stir beside him. He glanced that way and saw Tonio's white knuckles squeeze the shaft of his spear. Did he recognize the spidery humanoid? Had a Royal son like Tonio been turned into this perverse abomination?

The creature squatted, brandishing its blade—a broadsword of excellent craftsmanship. Tonio stepped forward, obviously trying to flank the creature, and McKnight followed suit on the other side.

Tonio charged, flinging one of his tiny spears at the beast's chest. In a flash, the spider-human leaped into the air and the spear sailed beneath it. McKnight froze in place, watching in awe as the monster landed behind Tonio, who whirled around in confusion. The spider creature swung its broadsword blade toward Tonio's head, but Tonio intercepted the blow with the shaft of his other spear. The sword tore through the shaft, splitting it in two, but at least the spear had deflected the blow off Tonio's neck and into his muscled shoulder. The big man groaned.

McKnight shook off the numbness of the moment and leapt onto the creature's back. His daggers sank deep into its spine and shoulder blades. It howled, and spit burst from its mouth. The creature grabbed at him and flung him headlong to the ground. He rolled up to take a knee. *That should have killed it!* Bluish blood oozed from the creature's wounds.

It came at him, sword raised to smite him down.

"Bone!" McKnight cried, trying to crawl away.

Tonio stepped in and delivered a crushing blow to the creature's jaw. The spider monster responded with a slice from its broadsword. Tonio ducked. Rolling with his momentum, Tonio grappled at the thing's legs, trying to drive the beast to the ground. McKnight stood on shaky legs as the creature dropped its sword, grabbed Tonio around his belly, and flung the warrior over its ugly head into the closest wall with a sickening smack. Even as he thought to defend himself, the detective was amazed to see Tonio rise back to his feet.

It was clear that Tonio was no longer an ordinary man.

With the creature advancing on him again, McKnight dashed for the broadsword. As he grasped it, a stream of web was spat onto his feet, holding him fast. He considered trying to cut the webbing away, but feared to, lest his blade also stick. The creature stepped toward him. *I'm doomed.*

The creature turned to Tonio, who strode toward them, shaking his fists in challenge.

The creature peered back at McKnight. Then the spider beast shook its own red-haired fists at Tonio with a shrill screech—in obvious understanding. The audience erupted with elation. Tugging against the bonds that held him fast, McKnight could only watch as the two warriors squared off like traditional Royal soldiers. Some shred of humanity certainly still lurked deep inside the hulking spider creature.

The two combatants had something in common—both were once full-blooded men of Bish. Now, though, both had been twisted by fate into something perverse and unnatural. Tonio had more humanity on his side, plus an iron will blackened with desire for vengeance, while his freakish counterpart sought only its survival, it seemed. The detective could only watch and look for an opportunity to escape. If Tonio didn't pull this off, they were both dead.

The spider creature bounded toward Tonio in quick bursts, like a deer. Tonio shifted his feet, eyes focused. The creature leaped high above the warrior and dove toward him. Tonio dodged, avoiding its full weight and possibly a broken back. Tonio still went down on one knee with the blow. The creature punched him in the face, knocking him onto his back.

McKnight grimaced. In an explosion of rage, Tonio surged back to his feet.

Wham! Wham! Wham!

As fast as Tonio had risen, he fell back to the ground even quicker. Two blows to his belly and another to his head knocked him to the dirt again.

Oh no! McKnight looked around, seeing no chance of escape, even if he could get free of his bonds.

The arachnamen in the audience were on their many legs, making a strange clamor with their arms and legs.

As McKnight shifted his gaze back to the fight, the lightning-fast spider creature jabbed Tonio again and again, finally roaring in triumph. Now on his hands and knees, Tonio seemed no match for the beast's power.

But Tonio rose yet again, his body busted and bruised with welts raised on his head. And then McKnight saw something he couldn't believe—a small smile cracked across Tonio's bloody lips. McKnight's heart pounded faster with inspiration. Maybe, just maybe, they still had a chance. He jerked at the cords holding him. He needed just one more chance.

As the battle intensified, the audience of arachnamen screeched with such fervor that the great tree seemed to shudder. Fire burned in Tonio's brown eyes as he faced his assailant once more. Taking advantage of the distraction, McKnight stretched to his limit, trying to grasp the blue steel dagger that lay just out of reach. His fingers strained just inches from its hilt, but he could reach no more. Twenty feet away, the spider-creature caught sight of McKnight's efforts and turned toward him. Tonio seized the moment to rush it from behind, but the creature's leap was too great. It landed by the blade.

And kicked it away.

"Bone!" McKnight yelled. "Tonio! Get me a dagger! It'll cut the webs!"

Tonio focused on the creature facing him again.

"Get the blade stuck in its back, Tonio!" McKnight shouted.

Tonio snarled, beckoning the next blows. They came in a flurry of jarring snake-like strikes. Tonio matched them blow for blow with his own ferocity. They hammered one another all over the arena with fists, knees, and elbows, each blow enough to break a lesser man's bones.

The hulking creature shuddered under several of Tonio's powerful blows. Its midsection cracked, and jabs into its face shut some of its eyes. Still, it landed two blows to each one of Tonio's. Tonio's body was taking a beating from head to toe, and pale, red blood dripped slowly from his nose and lips.

Tonio punched on until at last he sank with a gasp to both knees. He dropped his chin as the deafening crowd jumped around with excitement. Apparently, no one in the arena had witnessed a battle such as this before.

Caught up in the intensity of the battle, McKnight almost failed to notice the dagger he'd tried to reach earlier had been kicked almost within reach. Using the broadsword in his hand, he nudged the dagger his way.

The creature turned at the scraping of the sword against the dagger. It rushed at him in a red blur. Sweating and quivering, McKnight hurled the sword at the creature's chest. It dodged it with ease and the blade stuck in the ground. McKnight reached the dagger and slashed at the webs. The monstrosity grabbed his wrist and snapped it.

The blade fell free.

"Argh!" McKnight screamed, dropping to his knees.

It roared in his face as he spat at it. Stars exploded in his head as the spider creature punched him in the chest, snapping ribs and dislodging his breath. It drew back its hairy red hand for a final lethal strike.

At least I'll die fighting.

The tip of a broadsword exploded through the front of the creature's chest. The blade disappeared, only to emerge again through its belly and disappear again.

The creature released McKnight's wrist in a howl of pain. It whirled on Tonio as the man brought the heavy blade down. The sword bit deep, almost severing the creature's arm from the shoulder. Red and black blood flowed like pus from its gaping wounds.

It spewed webbing onto Tonio's sword arm, trapping it to his chest. As Tonio grasped the blade with his free hand, it stuck, leaving him helpless.

"No, you idiot!" McKnight screamed.

The creature stumbled toward a small spear on the floor. Its dangling arm dragged wet across the wooden surface. The detective recovered the blue-bladed dagger and cut himself free. He ignored the burning pain in his chest and charged as the spider creature bent toward the spear. McKnight jumped onto its back and stabbed the blade deep into its brain.

It fell to the arena floor.

McKnight gasped in relief, then grasped his broken wrist and felt a surge of pain in his shattered chest. He fell to the floor next to the dead spider monster.

Summoning his last strength, McKnight crawled over and pulled a dagger from the creature's back. *Please … no more fighting today.* He stumbled to his feet and hobbled over to Tonio, then sliced through his bonds. The webbing tore away as the blade ran through it.

They both stood still, smeared with blood and gore, in the midst of the totally silent arena. Thousands of arachnid eyes stared down on this pair who had just defeated their champion. McKnight expected the little red and white spiders to swarm from their tiny holes at any moment and devour them. *So be it.*

Instead, a dozen armed arachnamen descended from above and surrounded them. Two wielded webbed whips that they snapped around the men's ankles. Two more blew webs around their arms to secure them to their chests. McKnight didn't struggle.

The dead spider creature was cocooned and hauled down the tunnel it had come from. He was glad to see it go, but he hoped that the abomination of a man within was dead for good, never to be brought back.

McKnight was jerked off his feet again. He and Tonio were hauled upward above the arena, into one of many large holes in the ceiling. *Now what?* He was dragged, winding upward through spirals inside the tree's core. Bright light finally washed over his face.

Once again, he found himself outside on a giant branch. Lying there, he wondered what was next. He was heaved off the branch. *What!* He'd never get used to freefalling. Green grass below rushed up to greet him. Panic overcame him as he sensed the end of his life. *Anything to get this day over with.* Something jerked at his feet and he juddered like bowstrings. He bounced and dangled in midair a dozen feet above the ground.

He couldn't believe it. *I'm alive!* Then, as quick as he stopped, he plummeted to the hard ground again.

Thud!

To his surprise, the webs began to dissipate. Gingerly, he sat up, rubbing his chest and wheezing.

He still held the blue dagger in his hand. Tonio still had the broadsword. McKnight laughed and rolled along the ground in joy. "Ow!" He rubbed his crushed wrist, but he didn't care.

Tonio stood up, the shadow of a smirk on his battered countenance. McKnight could barely recognize the man's swollen face. He slapped him on the shoulder as they surveyed the familiar surroundings together. They were back in the Great Forest of Bish, not far from the city of Bone, their home.

"Tonio, we're going home!" McKnight said. "Let's go while we still have daylight left. To Bish with these rotten woods and foul spiders. I need women and wine!"

"Kill Vee," was all Tonio said.

"Hah, Tonio, be glad you live. If Venir still lives, we'll find him, I swear it. But right now, let's get home. His death can wait a little longer. Then we'll make him pay, if someone else hasn't already."

McKnight had little idea how much time had passed since their abduction, but he no longer cared. More on his mind now was that he'd bonded with Tonio—and how odd that seemed. From the beginning, he had disliked the proud young man whose arrogance had almost cost him his life. But now, he'd gained a new respect for the warrior. The spoiled young man had become a survivor. Tonio had been boastful all his life, but now he had earned the right to his pride. Perhaps his father had been right about him after all. McKnight had to admit that he was rather glad to have the fearless warrior on his side.

McKnight trudged north, Tonio lumbering behind, wheezing. McKnight didn't know if he could completely trust the Royal. The detective wanted revenge on Venir as much as Tonio, but then what? Would the Royals take them back into their fold? The former Royal brat wasn't exactly the handsome warrior he used to be. Personally, McKnight didn't even think a mother would want him. McKnight looked back at Tonio. The silent, gray-skinned man with heavy scars tottered like a child in the forest. Every so often, Tonio took time to marvel at the birds and bugs.

What is going on in that head? McKnight wondered.

His thoughts ceased at the sound of something large disturbing the bushes behind them. A low growl burst forth. He bolted for the bushes.

10

UNDERLING LORD CATTEN AND COMPANY entered a strange lair alongside the Current. The cavern sanctum below Bish's hot surface was one of a kind

The bleak establishment was illuminated by green-flamed smokeless candles and decorated with dripping stalactites. Common furnishings sat about—sofas, garments, tables, and chairs from many races in the world above. *Too much time among the humans I see.* A strange scent hit his nostrils. He and Verbard covered their noses; whatever it was would take some getting used to. His brother tapped his finger on the odd plethora of glass jars.

Why must you be a child? Catten thought.

Some of the jars were tiny, and others as large as a man. Many jars were empty, but most were full of a clear, thick liquid that preserved a creature within, some in part and some not. *I would like to stuff you in one of those,* Catten mused as he watched Verbard.

Within the jars, Catten saw ogre and orc heads and hair, women and children of all races, some strange insects, parts from one race sewn together with another, and more. The scene was dark, insidious, twisted, and disturbing, even for Catten. He picked up a large jar that contained a dog's head on a halfling girl's body. He shook it, nodded, and set it down.

Oh, Oran, what have you done?

Even the more vile land races would cringe at the sight of the collection. Catten took his time, trying to piece the atrocities together, trying to understand. There were too many things he could neither imagine nor explain. Finally, he let it be. They were here for another reason.

He led Verbard to a barred dungeon room. Catten eyed the source of the stench—torn and shredded human bodies that had been decaying for weeks, if not months. Verbard laughed as he swung the door open and studied the corpses. Catten wondered what had killed them—and why his brother found the whole scene amusing. Whatever killed these individuals was neither underling nor human. Catten walked around, eyes flashing. Whatever had killed them might still be around. Oran's lair was littered with caverns and tiny dungeons like this one. Whatever it was could be anywhere.

"Oran really was a strange one," Verbard said. "His obsession with all the other races was out of control. I think it would have been best to have killed him, rather than banish him. I just don't see the point in all of this and do not care to, either."

His brother's words echoed but Catten remained silent. Verbard dropped down on a velvety red couch and uncovered his nose. He chittered an order, and the albino urchlings dragged the foul carcasses into the Current one by one.

Moving down the corridor, Lord Catten's gold eyes widened when he discovered a study-like room. A table of papers, scrolls, and notes sat in the room. Just what he was looking for. Using magic, he sorted through the objects and notes, suspended them before his eyes, then moved them with a wave of his hand. There must be a clue here, but Oran would have taken due care in leaving his objectives behind so they were hidden from others. Catten took his time, and eventually Verbard came in and sat down on a small couch opposite the table.

The hours passed in long silence. As he worked, the thought of facing the Darkslayer didn't exactly thrill Catten, but he felt himself relaxing in the odd ambience of Oran's lair with some newly found admiration.

Maybe Oran was smarter than all of us.

While Verbard slept, Catten went on trying to familiarize himself with Oran's dealings. It revealed a lot of details about the races and creatures on Bish that he did not know, but none of it mentioned any dealings with the Darkslayer. It was very clear that Oran took great care in not revealing his intentions about anything he was going to do, but only recorded what he'd already done.

Feeling frustrated and weary of his search, Catten wriggled his pointed nails into the table while his brother snored. He overturned the table.

Verbard snapped up. The Juegen guards surrounded Catten, as the urchlings did with Verbard.

Verbard stood and walked toward Catten. "I don't think Oran would appreciate that," he said with a hiss.

Catten turned away and raised his hands to chest level, palms out. He muttered as magic swelled into him. Power surged into his hands, and his fingernails glowed a faint blue. Verbard stepped back.

Shutting his eyes and trusting his magic to guide him, Catten turned and moved around the cavern. Catten had always been a natural with magic, some for protection, but also for detection, which he relied on now. His hands brightened. Step after step, he was drawn to powerful magic. His hands burned like fire when he let the spell go. Before him stood several big jars on the floor. He moved them and discovered a small chest hidden beneath them in the ground.

"It seems you have found something, brother," Verbard said, smiling.

"Indeed." Catten nodded. "Now, let's see what Oran has really been hoarding over the years."

Catten reached down, but Verbard pulled him back. Verbard's hand glowed before him as he levitated the painted chest from the cave floor. A pair of white-fanged serpents slithered out and struck the chest at the handles, embedding themselves into the wood. Catten grabbed each serpent, snapped their necks, and tossed them away. Verbard guided the chest to another table and set it down.

Standing over the table, Catten inspected the dark chest. Images of fiends were painted on it, and the chest seemed almost alive in the green candlelight. Catten looked at his brother, who shrugged. With a wave of Verbard's palm, the chest lid opened. Inside, on top, were trinkets and treasure. Catten tossed all of it out. Digging deeper, he found scrolls, potions, and vials. He set them on the table as he pulled them from the chest.

Verbard bent over, sniffing the vials. "Hmm … good stuff."

Oran, you dirty underling, Catten thought. *You have a nice hoard here. No wonder you kept to yourself.*

Catten smiled at his brother, who returned his own in kind. He felt connected to him again. An odd feeling crept into Catten's mind — they weren't alone.

Catten turned in time to see a long, barbed tentacle snag one of the urchlings. It screamed, helpless, as the tentacle tore into its body, dragging it into the river. Something ancient and foul crawled out of the Current only a dozen yards from where they stood inside the study room. The remaining urchlings gathered in front of Verbard, while the armored Juegen defended Catten.

Seeing the creature rise from the Current, Catten shook his head. He had never seen anything like it before. It was a black mass of flesh with a snapping maw the size of a watermelon. Dozens of long tentacles protruded from its muddy, jellyfish-like body. It hissed with a twisted, long tongue that looked to have an eye at its tip. Then it moved toward them.

The Juegen burst into action, cutting the whipping tentacles away. Their curved twin blades sliced with precision and ease through the tentacles, but they were being overwhelmed by the thrashing monster. The urchlings threw any object they could find at the creature — including items from the table.

"No!" Catten screamed. "Brother, take care of this!"

Catten scrambled to save the potions before they were all gone. The screams of the Juegen distracted him. They were in trouble; he had to act. His brother chanted a spell as Catten stepped out of reach of the tentacles.

Catten could feel the energy his brother summoned as Verbard held his hands out as if he was going to grab something. His brother looked at the monster, then clasped his hands tightly together.

You can do it, brother.

Verbard squeezed something. The monster's screech was ear shattering. It struggled, and its tentacles loosened on the Juegen. They went back to chopping away at the creature. Catten avoided the onslaught, stepping back and knocking over the work table, then stumbling to his knees. From the floor, he felt his brother squeeze even more, and he felt Verbard's strength ebb. Catten sensed his brother's pain-filled mind and aching chest, and directed a thought toward him. *The Darkslayer, brother! Remember!*

An eruption of power came from Verbard as he squeezed his hands and ignored the burning pain in his chest. Dark hatred coursed through Verbard's mind and Catten could feel it all. Verbard's compressed hands glowed like a thousand candles, and his face twisted in a snarl of rage, sweat dripping off his brow.

Catten felt the final inner heave of his brother.

POP!

The creature splattered—everywhere. Chunks of slimy flesh showered the room. Verbard fell to the ground, clutching his chest.

"Happy, dear brother?" Verbard croaked, spitting out a dash of blood.

"No. Your idiot urchlings destroyed the potions." Catten shook his head, extending his hand to Verbard. "I see you still are not completely healed from the Warfield."

"No, I'm not, but the more I use magic, the better I feel. That exercise did serve me for the better, and that is why I did it," Verbard said, out of breath.

"I see." Catten gathered up the chest and placed it on a different table. He pulled out another object—a scroll— and rolled it out. "Take a look at this."

Verbard read over it, Catten could sense his brother feeling better the more he read.

"Do you think it will work?" Verbard asked.

Catten shrugged. "There is only one way to find out."

They cleared off a large circular table in another cavern. Catten grabbed a thick vial from the chest and poured scintillating glitter on the table. It crackled and smoked on the surface. Excitement grew within. Verbard stood behind his brother and put his hands on his shoulders as Catten read from the scroll.

The spell was strong, his words a whisper soon turning to thunder. It took over his body as he read, sucking out the magic within. Catten, though, could feel Verbard's will strengthening him. His heart was bursting, but it was thrilling at the same time. The cavern seemed to shrink and grow before him. A gateway opened in Catten's mind, from somewhere else, somewhere incomprehensible. Something dark and sinister came through it. A brilliant golden flash burst in Catten's eyes. He fell, but Verbard caught him and pulled him up. Steadying himself, Catten smelled sulfur.

He looked at the table. Two black, leathery, bat-like wings flapped gently before him—the wings attached to the back of a three-foot-high imp who looked left to right and rasped with shrill excitement.

"You killed him, Master Oran!" the imp said. "You killed that man that spiked me! Let me eat his head! Where are you, Master Oran? Do you sleep? Are you back in your lair?" Eep the imp turned around. Its big eye popped open wide. It turned back around—then back again, slowly opening its eyelid. The imp had tiny horns on its head and a single, large, orb-like eye over a hawkish nose with flaring nostrils, all of which sat above an oversized mouth filled with white, razor-sharp teeth. Eep had short muscular arms with hands that featured a thumb and three long, black-clawed fingers made for ripping flesh and bones to shreds. Its skin was ruddy, purple, scaled, and knotted. Eep was a one-of-a-kind horror and even the underlings admired him. Catten couldn't have been more thrilled. The legendary imp was now at his command.

Lord Verbard spoke first, "So, Eep, in a unique turn of events, it appears that you are no longer in Oran's service. No need to thank us, it seems he has undone himself, but I think that you can possibly shed some light on things."

Catten knew that Eep wanted nothing more than to tear their throats out. Over the decades, he and his brother had tormented the imp to death. He had always envied Oran's possession of creature, but now the fearless terror was his. Verbard grabbed it by the long, dimpled chin.

"Last time, you came to us with a message about the Darkslayer," Verbard said to Eep. "I want a full, detailed recount of everything that transpired since then and up to this very moment. Don't try to trick us or we'll send you back to your realm in pieces again."

Eep muttered something under his breath then nodded.

Catten clapped his brother on the shoulder.

"Enjoy your new pet, brother." Verbard couldn't contain his elated smile.

On their own, it would likely take months or longer to track down the Darkslayer, but with the imp's help, it would go quicker. Catten rummaged for some wine, then he and Verbard sat down on the sofa and hung on the imp's every word. Eep told them everything about the adventure of Oran, the human detective, McKnight, and the human Royal, Tonio. He did not leave out a single detail and could not even if he wanted to. Catten lay back, drunk with fascination.

11

"**I**'M TRULY STARTING TO APPRECIATE some of the things Oran did, brother," Lord Verbard said while studying the jars of humanoid experiments.

Verbard didn't hear a reply and scowled at the back of Catten, whose nose was down in other studies. He was starting to feel better while his brother was becoming more edgy. In truth, he didn't mind the lair so much. He studied what he could and relaxed, while his brother studied without sleep. So be it.

In the meantime, Verbard had enjoyed the services of the evil imp, Eep—at least until he sent him out on his mission. He had been curious and wanted to test out his new toy's limits. So Verbard had set up a battle. He watched the imp fight and almost kill one of his urchlings in a matter of seconds. He stopped the scuffle just as Eep was about to tear out its throat. He was still tickled, though. Then he told the imp he couldn't kill or maim during the next bout.

Eep had fought all five of the urchlings. The scrap was so brutal it had caught Catten's attention. He was elated at the imp's unyielding fury. He clapped as the imp subdued all of the urchlings.

"Put him in with my Juegen," Catten said, arms folded in his cloak.

My, he is speaking to me now, Verbard had thought. Verbard opened the dungeon gate. *This is going to be excellent.*

The Juegen strolled in. Eep clutched his claws and Catten almost smiled. He slammed the door shut behind them.

Catten's guards pounced at the imp with precision and speed, cutting the imp to ribbons. His brother hiss under his breath. Eep could do little to avoid their blades, as the confines of the cell limited him.

Verbard could feel the imp's anger rise, causing him to clench his teeth. *Take it to them!*

Eep pounded the two armored guards, darting back and forth, and busting their faces. The imp was stronger, endless in energy, and it wore them down. Verbard wanted to scream in triumph, but Catten tore the door open and stopped the bout. Verbard watched his brother and the wounded warriors walk away. He stepped inside and patted the imp on the head. Eep swallowed a piece of Juegen ear and blinked away.

Over the passing weeks, Verbard had learned much about Eep and his magic eye. The magic eye was the means that Oran had used to track down the Darkslayer. Verbard aimed to use it as well. He had to find the man. He cast the spell with his brother at his side, and off Eep went.

A mirror of scintillating colors burst forth before his eyes. In it, they could see everything the imp saw as he flew through the air. It was one of the most fascinating things Verbard had ever felt. His brother's golden eyes were as wide as saucers. Through Eep's eye, Verbard could see the treetops below. Skirmishes in flux. Humanoids jumping away.

The imp moved so fast that he could gather a great deal of information in an instant of time.

Still, finding the Darkslayer would not be easy. The imp knew what he looked like, but finding him for certain in the city of Bone, where they hoped the man would be, would still be an excruciating search. The brothers could only hold the spell so long. It was a strain on them both.

Verbard spent hours looking upon detestable human faces over and over again. He hoped every single one would die in pain or anguish. The more he watched, the more he learned about them. Their wicked practices were similar to the brothers' own, except that they tormented their own. Verbard's kind only practiced it on other races, except when under judgment. Urchlings didn't count. He found it odd that humans took their own kind for granted. Yes, they did good things for one another too, but he couldn't relate to that at all. They were weak. They deserved to die.

The days had become weeks and his patience was wearing thin. Then Eep shouted in his thoughts, *"It's him!"*

And there he was—a hulking figure of muscle tangled up with a dark-haired woman. Verbard almost broke the spell as he tore his silver eyes away.

"Catten," he yelled, "what are they doing with their faces? I hate it when they do that. It's disgusting."

"It's called kissing, I think. Don't look if you don't want to," Catten replied in agitation. "You've certainly witnessed far worse events these past days than this, so quit being so annoying. Be glad we have found the man. See that big tattoo on his back? It must be him."

"I can't stop watching," Verbard cried while squinting his eyes. He mentally commanded Eep to move on, which the imp quickly did. Sighing with relief, he looked at his brother.

Now what is your big plan?

Now that the imp had finally located the Darkslayer, there would not be a problem for him to find him again. He had the imp keep tabs on the man and his companions. The armored Darkslayer never surfaced however. All he saw was just ordinary men. It didn't help that Verbard could not hear what he could see. The spell had that limitation.

He and his brother spent the days mulling over the task at hand. The brute man was no doubt formidable, but was he the same man that carved up their Badoon brigade? The one who chopped Master Sinway's prized warriors, the Vicious, into bits? Eep assured them it was indeed the same man, but they needed more proof.

Verbard was almost jealous of the imp's powers. It was able to see whatever it wanted without even being there. Somehow, the magic allowed the imp to view the world from another dimension. If the imp didn't want to be seen, then it was not. Both underling brothers marveled at it. *If only I could figure out how to do that.* Most likely his brother would, but writing spells was not his thing.

One day, the imp was watching the apartment of the humans. The big man talked with excitement as his skinny friend and two boys watched. One of the boys was a halfling, and he stayed busy scribbling in thick tomes.

"Catten, come here. What do you make of this?" Verbard said.

Catten floated over and stared into the portal. Catten slapped him on the back. "Tell that imp to bring us a tome!"

Verbard hadn't heard his brother that excited the whole trip. "Will do."

The plan was simple. Eep could blink into the apartment and would only have to fly away as he could not take the tome back into the magic dimension. The timing proved to be an issue, however, as the halfling and human boys were almost always in the apartment. There was still some tension in the air, but it lightened. Verbard planned to enjoy his seclusion in the lair. He lay down on the soft velvet couch while listening to the cave water dripping and his brother's pacing footsteps nearby. It wasn't long before he was asleep.

12

WHEN EEP BLINKED, HE COULD feel Verbard watching through his eye. It was as if he was inside his head. It irritated him. He slapped his head and growled. The sparse apartment was dim as no candles or lanterns were lit. It was early in the daytime, and both boys were gone for a change.

Eep crept through the small room. The table, cots, blankets, stove, and cupboard were cold. Things were in good order. In one corner of the room, tomes of various sizes were stacked along with loose parchment, ink, and quills.

He buzzed over to them. Verbard screamed in his mind, *Open a window first!* He did and returned, scratching his head. All the books looked the same. Verbard then said, *Pull one from the bottom.* He did, then straightened the pile and headed for the window.

Eep scanned the room one final time. He noticed a large leather sack underneath one of the cots and pulled it out. He'd begun looking inside when faint footfalls came from just outside the door. He stuffed the sack back under the cot and hopped onto the window sill. He could hear the tumblers on the locks being worked and the lock unlatching as he closed the window behind him just a moment before the door swung open. He was already buzzing away as the thief, Melegal, sauntered in.

The giant, book-wielding bat screeched from the sky, startling the busy early goers below. Then he disappeared into the blazing horizon.

13

TWO SUNS HOVERED, ORANGE AND red, blazing like mirages over the world of Bish. Little reprieve could be had from the sweltering heat, day or night. The inhabitants never stayed comfortable for long. Most of Bish was barren, though its landscapes included lakes, streams, forests, and cities. Life of all sorts was accustomed to the harsh elements of this world. It was either that or give in and die.

Coping with the challenging climate and terrain of Bish was one thing all its races had in common. It kept them weathered, hardy, and ready for the next battle. All races—the good, the evil, and those in between—were locked in an unending battle for survival, whether they liked it or not. It was their fate, and it was unavoidable, for it was the very reason that Bish had been created.

The largest inhabitance in the world of Bish was in the city of Bone. The lone monolith stood in stark contrast to the barren terrain that surrounded its ominous walls. A human-dominated city, Bone boasted over a hundred thousand occupants enclosed by thick stone walls that stood four stories high. Miserable though they usually were, the commoners of its inner districts preferred the interior of Bone to the harsh outlands of Bish. The Outlands offered few comforts to the common man.

Bone was full of corruption. The ruling Royals managed to keep their own brand of order behind the scenes of the treacherous city. Every inhabitant knew that crossing the Royals was to one's detriment. The public executions testified to that. The people did not complain, though; instead, they boasted that Bone was the greatest city in the world. The simple folk simply minded their own affairs — or else.

Among the common folk, many prospered. The slaves, thieves, prostitutes, and executioners did just as well as the merchants, guardsman, farmers, and landlords. At first appearance, a newcomer to the city would think it a grand place to live or visit. But it did not take long for Bone's plethora of indulgences to drag a good man deep into the vileness of its belly. Yet, its self-enslaved people seemed to prefer it that way.

Not all in Bone succumbed, of course; there were those willful ones who enjoyed its pleasures without falling into its soft yet suffocating grip. Just as the Royals were able to enjoy life on the backs of its citizens, others were also able to have fun and make a profit from the weakness of others.

The tavern of the Drunken Octopus was the perfect example of a place where these types of profiteers thrived. The Octopus stood off the beaten path, deep in the narrowest of alleys, far from patrolled districts. Smugglers, slavers, skimmers, adventurers, pleasure seekers, and other dodgy spirits from the city and elsewhere would gather at the Octopus every day, as it was a place where citizens could unwind and do business of whatever sort satisfied their needs and pleasures.

On this particular day, the worn tables of the smoky tavern brimmed over with desperate risk takers, their eyes cold and sunken. Tales spewed back and forth from foul mouths and rotted teeth. The perfumes of shameless women mingled with the smells of unwashed men. Pint after pint of ale was guzzled and spilled on the grimy, oaken floor. Shots of grog were sucked from the bellies of giggling dancers. Uproarious laughter and shouting voices filled the sagging room. Flickering shadows by way of burning torches and candles in wrought-iron chandeliers added to the gloom.

Among all those who sat in the room, one large man's voice bellowed over the rest. Taking slurps of ale and swigs of grog, Venir sat centralized at a table near the bar. His long, straw-blond locks were drawn back, revealing his hardened face, bright blue eyes, and broad grin. He relished the gaze of the long-lashed woman at the table, and she seemed captivated by his handsome face and wild stories. Although he knew most women were more interested in his purse than his tales, he was intent, as always, on holding their attention.

He shadow boxed in the air, almost knocking over a waitress. Despite his impressive stories, not a man or woman believed half of what he said. But true or not, he could spin a yarn. His voice sucked them in. And they liked it.

Only his friend, Melegal, sitting opposite him with a sultry woman on his arm, knew the half of it for sure. Venir had not stretched a word, and had even left out a detail or two.

Melegal was gaunt, quiet, and thin. Dressed in deep gray clothes, he sipped purple wine and surveyed the room. Venir kept rambling on, knowing his friend was waiting for something. The thief leaned forward while another attractive woman played with his graying hair and the floppy gray hat that hung over his ear.

"So, Melegal," Venir said, leaning back in his chair after he finished with his tale of the Outlands. "Is that how you recall it, back at the marsh?"

The thief leaned in farther, speaking loud. "I can't say, Vee. I didn't hear the whole thing. Why not tell it again?"

"A great idea. What do you say, ladies?" Venir said, smiling from ear to ear.

The previously interested female parties at the table began to disperse, looks of disappointment in their painted eyes. It was clear that one particular lady had established squatter's rights on Venir for the night. Seated next to him, this woman, in her revealing red gown, smiled while gazing into his eyes.

"Tell me another story, big man, or the same one. I love 'em," she said, almost slurring.

Venir's blood ran hot as her bare thigh crossed over his leg. He squeezed her knee and leaned back. She made a squeak.

"Another bottle of wine, barkeep!" Venir said. "Make that two. Maybe I'll sample some as well," he added, looking into her eyes. "You really are pretty, you know ... Dresla, you said your name was, right?"

Dresla blushed.

"Hey, Vee, don't you go telling her all that same stuff," Melegal said, then finished off his wine and motioned for more. "You know how mad they get when you're not so nice to them the next day."

"Shut up, Me. Dresla and I know each other plenty well." He held her chin. "I could teach you a thing or two about how to sweet-talk a lady."

"Talking's for blabbermouths," the thief replied as a wry smile crossed his lips. "I let my actions speak."

He squeezed the knee of his own lady, who let out a yelp.

Amid their laughter, the wine soon arrived, along with more grog and ale. The tavern crowd brightened by the minute as the two men flattered their dates with compliments and coin.

Venir began another tale. A new crowd gathered around their table, helping themselves to the drinks. Venir was too caught up in himself to care. He let Melegal handle those things. He was more talk, Melegal more business.

A fine young lute player—Luke—joined their table and played in harmony with Venir's new tale. The slender fingers strummed the strings, drawing more interest from the crowd. Venir soaked it all in as he charmed the crowd with his rumbling voice, his massive arms gesticulating as he recounted tales of epic adventure.

Most everyone enjoyed his storytelling—but not all. Many a bad element lurked within the tavern, looking to take advantage of those with foolish tongues. And Venir knew his lips would draw them out. Anyone in the room would see him as prey if they did not know him. He was counting on this, as was Melegal.

Venir caught the telling look in Melegal's face. The thief gave a subtle nod and leaned back from the table. Something was afoot. It had been weeks since they'd made a solid score. Although to Venir it was just a game—his real concern was his survival outside the city—for his friend Melegal, this was his sole mode of making a living.

Skimming was the name of the game. It was illegal, and it could lead to the dungeon and worse: torture, beatings, or even hanging, assuming whoever caught you didn't kill you first. Skimming was a rare type of inner-city hustle that only the brave and the bold dared undertake. Accepting challenges was not supposed to be a profession, and the playing field was assumed to be even, sort of.

But if the ringer happened to be more than a mere man, as in the case of Venir, they had an edge. Melegal would set the stage, and Venir played it. True, Venir had taken his lumps more than a time or two, but the payoff was worth it. The take from a good skim would last weeks, even months, allowing Melegal to lay low for a while and Venir to feel all right about leaving to fight underlings. Tonight was going to be one of those big nights, Venir sensed, and he was ready. Melegal was too, as his friend complained daily on account of their thinning purses.

As Venir rambled on, he caught quick glances of Melegal sitting with a glint in his eye.

A thrill went up Venir's spine as Dresla ran her long, painted nails over the belly hair beneath his dark blue tunic. He tilted back in his chair, only to have Dresla tip him forward again by tugging on his chest hair and shirt. He had just tilted back again when an abrupt voice cut in.

"Let me help you, blondie!" A loud woman kicked the back legs out from under his chair.

He crashed to the floor, bringing a roar of laughter.

Venir looked up, stupefied, while Dresla stared at a fistful of blond hair from his chest.

"The floor suits you, blondie," said the woman who had kicked his chair out from beneath him. "You can get up now, but you gotta shut up as well!"

Venir gave her a hard look. She was about as ugly a woman as he'd ever seen there before—plain and rugged, a gal of medium build with cropped black hair, but smart-eyed, along with a crooked overbite, pot belly, and black clothes from head to toe. Most of all, she appeared angry.

Propping himself up on his elbows, Venir started to chuckle. "Go back to your stable, girl. I have no quarrel with you."

The crowd chuckled. Her pale cheeks turned pink. "Start flapping those lips of yours again and you soon will," she said with a lisp. "I didn't come here to listen to none of your stories."

Venir gathered himself to his feet. "Listen to me. I'll say what I want when I want. If you don't like it, you can leave. You keep running your mouth at me and I'll drag you right back to the stable you came from."

Melegal chuckled out loud as two more black-clad women closed in on their table, nodding at the first woman and calling her "Sis." Venir couldn't believe that this odd assortment of women were the ones that had taken Melegal's bait. It was going to be embarrassing if he was challenged by a woman. Dresla rose to his side in support, and as she pressed closer, the much bigger black-clad woman grabbed her long, honey tresses and slung her back into her chair, tipping her backward and onto the floor.

"You stay put, miss prissy!" said the heavyset assailant, bringing her foot down onto Dresla's hair and pinning her to the grimy floor. Dresla shot a furious look at Venir.

As a skinny third woman approached Melegal, his date abandoned the table. The black-clad woman perched herself in the vacant chair and stared at Melegal. The tavern's revelers were gathering about now, seeking the cause of the commotion. Venir heard the crowd referring to their assailants as the Motley Girls. *Accurate*, he thought.

"Let her up, fatty!" Venir said with a growl.

The hefty, black-clad woman pinning Dresla down jerked her foot up and stepped back with a confused look on her face.

"Why did you do that?" Sis said. "You listen to *me*, Frigdah, not him!"

"Sorry, Sis," Frigdah said. "He … scared me."

Crossing his arms over his chest, Venir sized up Frigdah. She was much larger than her two sisters, heavy and full bodied, with the face of a child.

Venir heard a huff and looked over at his date. Dresla wiped off her filthy dress, cast Venir an evil glance, and stormed away.

"See what you did … Sis?" Venir asked. "Now my date's gone, and all just because you don't like my storytelling." He took a step forward.

She held her hands up, stepping back. "Easy now, big fella," she replied, winking with obvious inexperience. "But … I guess I could be your date."

"You can handle him, Sis!" a patron yelled.

The tavern crowd roared in laughter.

"Are you kidding me?" Venir said. "What do you want? My patience is about done!"

Oh, here it comes, he thought. Venir planned to make quick work of the woman and then track down Dresla before it was too late.

Sis paused, looking at the gathering crowd. She wiped her sweaty hands on her dark clothes. Venir unfolded his arms and grabbed the hilt of his long hunting knife sheathed at his side. He didn't know what to expect, but he'd be ready nonetheless.

Sis licked her thin, cracked lips. "I want a challenge!"

Cries of elation poured from the patrons' drunken lips like a thunderous waterfall. They began to cheer at the unexpected and somewhat ludicrous announcement. Word spread like fire that the Motley Girls had challenged the cow-kissing loudmouth. The men and women danced in elation as Luke played a daring song on his lute.

"What do you challenge me with, Sis?" Venir said over the noise. "You want me to wrestle you? Or maybe the bigger version of you over there?" He nodded at Frigdah, who was helping herself to the half-empty drinks on the table.

"Not you—him." Sis pointed at Melegal. "We want to challenge him."

"Me?" the thief exclaimed in uncharacteristic bewilderment.

"Him!" Venir said, arms extended wide. "Then why did you kick my chair instead of his?"

"I don't like your dumb stories!"

"Fine. What's the challenge, then?" Venir said, almost laughing at the sudden turn of events. He couldn't remember the last time Melegal had been challenged.

Sis crossed her chest. "Hand stabs," she said. "I want my little sister to take on your skinny friend."

The crowd oohed at this suggestion as the sound of coins shuffled from hand to hand. Luke began the betting runs. A frown grew on Melegal's face. The thief wouldn't even look Venir's way, but kept his eyes glued to the wine sitting before him. Seeing his friend at risk for a change was a welcome sight. After all, why should Venir have to take all the risks?

Melegal preferred not to take on a challenge, but Venir was confident he could handle the hand stabs against this female counterpart—but then, one never knew for sure what an opponent had up their sleeve. Venir began taking bets.

"All right, Sis," Venir said. "I like straight bets, so how much coin are you going to put on this wager?"

"Ten," she replied.

"Ten?" He shrugged. "That's no wager. All this trouble for ten pieces of silver?"

The crowd likewise responded with boos.

"Ten gold talents! And not a talent more!" she said, slapping her gold on the table.

His eyes widened; it was a sizeable sum.

"What do you think, Me?" Venir said, looking at Melegal. "Is ten worth the risk?"

Melegal shrugged, still not looking up from his wine.

"Sis," Venir said, "you and Big Sis over there, clear a smaller table and bring it here. I'll fetch a blade."

"Hold up, blondie." Sis poked his chest. "We'll use her blade. Women get to pick, fair enough? You're a sport, aren't you?" she said with a toothy smile.

"Let's give it a look, then," Venir said.

The thinner sister produced a slender, twin-bladed dagger with a black onyx hilt about nine inches long. She handed it to Venir. He eyed it, thumbed the edge, and stuck it into the table that Frigdah and Luke brought over. Melegal and his opponent dragged their chairs to opposite sides of the table and sat down.

"What's your name?" Melegal asked her, looking up and tilting back on his chair.

"Haze," she said, trying to see what he was looking at. "You ever been challenged by a woman before?"

Venir could see she was flirting, but Melegal kept his gaze away.

"Not under these circumstances. This time of night, I'm usually challenged by women much prettier than you," he said with a scowl.

"You'd be lucky to wind up with a gal like me." She spat on the floor.

"How charming," he said, bringing his eyes down to meet hers.

"You ain't so tough, thief. I know you," Haze said. "You're an urchin like the rest of us. You and your big friend—we remember you."

Venir eyed Melegal, but the thief didn't look his way. He didn't recall the three sisters, but he had no reason to disbelieve their claim. Not wanting to dredge up what they might have in common, Venir hollered over to the barkeep for the rules.

The stocky barkeep with hairy black arms strolled into their midst. His scars and tattoos suggested he'd once been a soldier. He looked sleepy, smoking his long, thin cigar and turning his smoke-reddened eyes toward the table. Venir clasped the shoulder of the man, who nodded.

"Hands flat on the table, both of you," the barkeep said. "When I say go, the one who grabs the blade first gets the first strike … or stab. Whoever doesn't get the blade keeps both hands on the table. When I say go again, the one with the blade keeps one hand on the table and one on the blade. Gets one shot at either of the opponent's hands with the blade. The dodger can only move one hand or the other. Whoever draws blood first wins. But," the barkeep stretched out his fingers wide, "if the dodger moves both hands, it's a forfeit. Are you both clear on the rules?"

They nodded.

Hand stabs were a popular traditional skill practiced among all races on Bish. As a result, plenty of individuals had missing fingers or scars where hands had been impaled. Hand stabs was one of the most exciting and common tavern challenges in Bone. The stakes were always high and there were several hand stab heroes—not those one might expect. Some of the best players had hardly any scars to show. Venir had seen massive brutes from the field take the risk against someone who appeared to be a lesser opponent. But many delicate and defter hands made such grizzled challengers pay.

Haze's hands were rough and calloused, but without scars. He rubbed his chin. Her mysterious, dark eyes kept him wary.

The flickering torch flames seemed to dim as the crowd quieted in anticipation. The odds favored Melegal. Venir let Luke manage the betting for him. He liked the young man. He eased into the crowd for a closer look.

The barkeep drew a loud breath. "Ready?"

14

As the barkeep's voice rang out, the room took in one unified breath.

"Go!"

Haze struck like a snake, snatching the blade first. Melegal's long, slender hands remained flat on the table. The crowd had puzzled looks. The wagering began favoring Haze amidst some grumbles. Even Venir was surprised that Melegal hadn't moved at all.

"You're a righty, I see," Melegal said. "Good for you. I'm a gentleman, now, so ladies first. Take your strike."

Keeping her right elbow down, Haze pointed the blade high above and between Melegal's bony hands. Her brown eyes remained locked on his, confident. Venir glanced at Melegal. He looked bored.

The barkeep settled the stirring room, and Luke waved off the betting.

"Ready?" the barkeep said, silencing the crowd.

"Go!"

Wham!

Like the tail of a whip, her blade pierced deep into the wood where Melegal's left index finger had been. The crowd roared as they saw both his hands still on the table, and everyone fought to get a look at the damage she had wrought. Venir struggled to see through the throng.

"She got him!" someone screamed.

Cheers erupted over the cries of disappointment.

"Hold!" the barkeep said, shoving people out of the way. "Let me see, for the love of Bone!"

The thief's hands were still in place, yet there was no sign of blood. Haze's blade was exactly where the middle knuckle of his index finger had been, but his finger was missing. Venir saw the puzzled look on her face as well as everyone else and then he looked at Melegal, who was grinning.

"Nice try. Fast. But you missed." Melegal untucked his finger from beneath his hand. He tucked it in and out a few more times, and wriggled it around some for the benefit of the bewildered crowd. All of the Motley Girls' dropped their jaws.

Venir rolled his eyes. Melegal was showing off. Well, so be it; it was a flat bet, after all. Soon, he'd have enough to celebrate for a month.

"Round two!" the barkeep called.

Venir pushed his big frame closer to the table. Luke stood by his side, his lute silent. The haggard woman flattened her palms on the table again. Melegal remained in place. Sweat beaded on Haze's brow as she shrugged off encouragement from her sisters behind her.

"Ready?" the barkeep said once more.

Venir clenched his hands into fists.

"Go!"

The woman snatched the blade like a viper. She eyed the thief as more grumbling began. The sound of coins being exchanged drifted in and out of the air.

"Care to try again?" the thief said, grinning.

Venir grimaced. *Get it over with, man!* He bit his tongue. The woman was plenty quick; she didn't need an extra chance. He scowled at his comrade, but Melegal didn't notice.

The room hushed. All eyes were on the woman, and her limber body grew tight. She waved the dagger back and forth like a charmed snake. The bets stayed in her favor. The revelers noted Luke's suggestions.

If he loses a finger, he'll blame me. Venir tried to enjoy letting his comrade take the heat for a change, but it did not sit well with him. It seemed like a bad idea.

"Ready?"

The smoke curdled in the air from the tension.

"Go!"

Wham!

The blade slammed straight into the table where Melegal's left palm had lain. He had tilted his hand up at ninety degrees. Venir heard plenty of gasps among the crowd.

"She missed!" someone yelled.

Angry voices raised as losses mounted. None seemed angrier than Haze. She fidgeted in her chair, muttering curses under her breath. Her rowdy sisters, meanwhile, had faces drawn tight with doubt. Letting out a deep breath, Venir pulled his thick locks behind his head. Melegal was still full of surprises. His friend was completely in control.

The barkeep readied the table for one final round.

"Round three!"

The woman's eyes were focused wide. The room fell silent.

"Ready ... go!"

Haze snatched the blade in her right hand. Venir couldn't believe it. Melegal's palms still remained flat on the table. The Motley sister's exposed arm glistened with perspiration and her brown eyes seemed unable to hold her opponent's gaze. Her hand trembled a hair. Venir was dumbfounded. Ten good gold were on the line and Melegal sat there like a mute. *Why?* He tugged on his ponytail. *He's getting back at me!*

No match had ever gone like this. Everyone knew the rules, but no one had ever witnessed such a loss before, not even Venir. Melegal had turned this challenge into something quite extraordinary.

The barkeep spoke. "You miss a third time, missy, you lose. If you hit, you win."

No one in the room could decide how to bet this time. It seemed they were incapable of calculating the odds. But Luke snatched more coins in favor of the thief. Venir sipped on his grog while eyeing his friend. Melegal raised his brows a couple of times. He didn't know what to think. Maybe his friend had lost his mind.

Still, the pressure was mounting on Haze—and her sisters, who were biting their shirt collars now. Haze was faster than she was smart. Venir could see her going back and forth over Melegal's hands.

Melegal fanned out his fingers on the table. Was he taunting her?

Haze's face turned blood-red.

"Ready?" the barkeep cried.

There was dead silence.

Venir's eyes widened.

"Go!"

Wham!

The blade embedded itself. "A hit!" someone cried. Haze gave a shout of triumph. The room roared, but Melegal never moved. Venir pushed people away from the barkeep. There was no blood. Melegal sat, his hand unmoved. The blade was sunk deep, right between Melegal's middle and right index finger. Haze had missed. She was only a razor's edge away from either finger, but there was not a nick on the thief's hand.

"I can't believe it," the barkeep said. "The man wins!"

While the winners rejoiced, the losers shouted "cheat" from their frothing lips. Luke offered to buy some rounds, but many scowled and left. Grinning, Venir took the gold from Sis, smiling at her scowling face. Haze nodded at Melegal, shoulders sagging, and walked away. Sis and Haze helped the biggest sister walk to the far side of the tavern and sat her down. Only Venir, Melegal, and Luke remained at the punctured table.

"How'd we do, Luke?" Venir asked.

"Embarrassingly well," he said, beaming a wide smile.

"Well, I'm certainly not embarrassed to take their money," Melegal said, "so hand it over."

Luke set down the coins, and Melegal made them disappear.

"Well, Melegal," said Venir, "that was pretty good, I have to say."

"No, that was great," the thief said.

"Indeed." Venir slapped him on the back and poured him a fresh goblet of wine.

It wasn't long before the crowd was nipping at their heels again and they relished every minute of it so much that Venir soon forgot the Motley Girls were still in the tavern. He even forgot about Dresla—but that was only because other suitors came his way.

The night was still young, and danger still hung in the air, despite Venir's lack of perception. The Motley Girls weren't done with the men just yet.

15

ROYAL LORD ALMEN STRODE THROUGH his courtyard and out the portcullis gate. A guard snapped to attention. With his house ranked fourth in the city of Bone, Almen remained a very busy man.

It was the Royals who kept order in the world of Bish, using their power and wealth for both good and evil, and for keeping a grip on the cities. Though they were also subject to the natural order of things, they were at the top of the food chain. The Royal houses in each city varied in ranking and responsibility. The houses were neither purely good nor evil, but in general an entire family leaned one way or the other. In the pursuit of greater power, houses would strive to destroy or align themselves with others. When they were not united by waging war abroad, they waged war games among themselves instead. Their plots and schemes were so thick, insidious, and fluid that an outsider would never know what was happening.

At the time of Lord Almen's birth, his house had ranked tenth, and much of its rise had been due to his singlehanded success. Now, at age forty, he was in his prime—handsome, tall, athletic, and broad shouldered, with thick brown hair and clothed in rare fabrics of crimson and gold.

The guard exhaled as Almen passed, for the slightest discrepancy had cost many sentries a night in the dungeon—or worse. Royal Lord Almen was not a good man, neither were most who shared his exquisite castle. He relished his power over others.

Castle Almen boasted marble, inlaid gold, silver, and gems all worked into spectacular designs and breathtaking artwork. Candles by the thousands of all shapes, colors, and sizes were lit in every room and corridor to set the mood and best accent the decorations.

Each house had its talking point. The Almens had a knack for spectacular design that ensured their name would be held in awe in every other Royal house. It was a practice among their kind to enslave a talented commoner long enough to create a few masterpieces. Then they would dispose of them. No one else could make use of their talent or learn to replicate it. Few outsiders knew what occurred on the inside, for servants stayed within the walls, but a few succulent morsels of gossip escaped.

Royal Lord Almen was rounding the corner toward his study below the castle when he nearly bumped into his half-naked cleric, Sefron.

"What are you doing here?" Almen asked. "You know I don't want you running about my castle unsettling my guests. Your business better be good."

"I apologize, my lord. But you told me that Te—"

"Stop, idiot!" The Royal lord clutched his hand around Sefron's greasy throat, making the cleric's normally bulbous eyes bulge even farther. "How many times do I have to tell you not to use names? Must I feed you to the dogs?" He wanted to flay the skin off the troublesome man. "Do not speak, Sefron. Follow."

He released his grip, but had to restrain himself from slapping the man. Sefron was annoying, but a serviceable man whom he needed. The flabby, middle-aged house cleric scurried behind the lord, dark eyes round like a frightened child's, his naked, pale, and hairless form lumbering to keep up.

A lone, armed sentry stood steadfast by a stone entrance beyond the castle kitchens. Torches were spaced ten feet apart along a sloping, spiral staircase chiseled from the rock. Few but Lord Almen were allowed down here;

indeed, few family members knew or even cared where the lord did their dirty work, for which he retained their unwavering loyalty. Sefron pushed open the thick oaken door at the bottom and closed it again behind Almen.

The room was unlike any other in the castle. Walls of rough sandstone fanned out, forming catacombs that were lit by ample torchlight wavering in the constant draft. Several tables and desks sat here and there, all stacked neatly with papers and maps. Beside one stood a tall, sinewy, olive-skinned man in white cotton robes, studying something.

"Teku, what news?" Almen said.

"Greetings, my lord." Teku bowed. "I have had an encounter with some of the adversaries you inquired about. It seems your suspicions are well founded. The Twelfth House of Bone has been behind recent events. The prisoner was unwilling, though she was convinced after a time."

Almen pulled up a chair and sat down, considering the words. Sefron wheezed behind him and the torches crackled. The Twelfth House was the Slerg family, once the Sixth House of Bone, whose fall had come at the hands of the Almens—his very own hands at that. *The Slergs should have seen it coming.* He remembered the day he took them down to nothing.

Well over a decade had passed since then, and the Slergs had barely been able to maintain their Royal status. Had they not been absorbed into another house, the family line would have become extinct. But they had survived near the bottom and even managed to absorb some weaker houses. He always knew they were still a threat, but so were all the others. He was accustomed to watching his back.

Now the Slergs wanted to get back on top—or wanted revenge. Almen wasn't sure which. They had managed to damage Lord Almen's reputation by exposing a weakness in his family line. Tonio, his most promising son, had disappeared, along with Almen's finest house detective, McKnight. Despite a lack of proof, the Slergs were receiving all the credit, and now it seemed they *did* have a hand in it after all. No one knew for sure what had happened to Royal Lord Tonio or Detective McKnight, but Almen was proceeding with his plans regardless. He would have the Slergs where he wanted them soon enough.

Almen studied the silent Teku, who had been on this assignment for weeks. He was his chief assassin. Teku relied on hand-to-hand combat as opposed to poison, traps, and the like. The man took pleasure in doing the killing himself. Almen admired that.

And even though Teku was as mysterious as a ghost, over the years Almen had come to appreciate him. He trusted him as far as his gold could pay, and that was a lot.

"Anything else, Teku?" Almen was hoping for news about Tonio and McKnight. It still frustrated him that little evidence of their disappearance had surfaced.

"No, Sir." Teku bowed.

"Can I get anything for you or your guest, my lord?" Sefron spoke up, no doubt to shift Almen's attention away from Teku.

"Food and wine for me," Almen said. "Teku?"

"Fruit and water, my lord," he said.

"Have the servants prepare plenty, Sefron. We will be here awhile."

Sefron closed the large oaken door behind him. He pressed his ear to the door, waited, and raced up the stairs. At the top of the steps, he panted as he passed the sentry and entered the kitchen. The heavy aroma of beast stew and wood-baked bread filled the room, as dinner for the fifty-odd family members and guests was being prepared for the exquisite supper of the day.

The women would look ravishing, their lips bathed in wine pressed from the finest slaves in Bish. The men would gorge themselves while blathering on about their reputations and meaningless accomplishments. Sefron loved the romance of it, but Royal Lord Almen would never let the cleric attend.

His stomach growled as he spotted a fresh batch of fluffy split rolls. Almost swooning from the aroma, he grabbed one, then two more, and a small bowl of butter. He gave Almen and Teku's food requests to a pretty, gray-eyed servant girl, who darted away from his stare.

Sefron found a small table where the staff dined, and sat down to enjoy the hot rolls. He hummed in self-delight. It was a benefit of his position as cleric that he ranked above the common staff, and he took full advantage. The girl returned and set down the food, eyes averted. Sefron tugged at her long brown braids, running his pasty hands along her lithe figure, smiling as she trembled.

"It's fine, dear. Go back to your duties," he said with a hungry sneer.

Chuckling, he stacked the two trays of food on one another and returned past the sentry and down the stairs. He hovered near the door at the bottom, but heard nothing.

He knocked.

Teku opened the door, took the trays of food, and closed the door in his face. Sefron scowled and dragged himself back up the stairs and found a spot where he could keep his eyes on the dinner party — as well as the servant girl.

16

IN A SMALL ROOM FOUR floors above the Drunken Octopus, torches supplemented the faint red moonlight that penetrated through two windows. A cot sat beneath each window, and two more between them, each with a green blanket. A coffeepot brewed on the little coal stove that warmed the room. The only other furniture was a tiny cupboard and a wooden table with four unmatched chairs of varying sizes. Though lacking a woman's touch, the room was cozy and full of life.

Lefty Lightfoot sat cross-legged on the floor, scribbling on a parchment as fast as his tiny fingers could fly. Beside him lay several large leather-bound tomes that collected parchments he had already finished. He was a halfling boy, about the size of a human toddler. His blond hair fell over his intent light blue eyes as he blew his locks away. Like most of them, he was the sole survivor of a devastating attack by underlings. Venir, Georgio, and Melegal had taken him in and he'd been their ally ever since.

Survival was the main focus of everyone on Bish, and halflings were no different. Halflings survived by moving throughout the realm in small clans. They were good scouts and woodsmen, and experts in trading, bartering, and sleight of hand. They could talk anyone into buying or trading by pestering them to no end. The only way to make them go away, other than killing them, was to strike a deal. Plenty of fair-haired halflings had perished in pursuit of an ill-advised transaction. Lefty had inherited the trading skills of his clan, as well as other special gifts, and did a fine job keeping his friends stocked with groceries. He brought at least that much to the table.

But right now, Lefty was scribbling down every word as Georgio recounted tale after tale of Venir — the Darkslayer. Georgio's curly brown locks bounced as he recounted in dramatic fervor how he had helped the Darkslayer destroy the forest magi in Red Clay Forest. The halfling listened closely as he wrote.

"So I took out my sling," Georgio said, "and Melegal took out his. We waited to make our move. Then Venir got caught in some vines or something, and the forest magi started casting spells. We struck like cats. No … I mean like panthers. Wait, like eagles, I think. Uh … what does a sling strike like, Lefty?" Georgio asked while scratching his head.

"Hold it," Lefty cried. "I'm trying to catch up. You talk too fast! My hand hurts from writing. Let's take a break and have our coffee." Lefty put down his quill and gingerly massaged his little hand.

Georgio shrugged and heaved a sigh. The excitement of recounting this adventure with the Darkslayer had left him breathless. Lefty grabbed two ceramic cups from the board and filled them.

Smells good, Lefty thought while wafting the aroma through his nostrils. He set the cups down on the table, took a seat by the husky boy, and relaxed. After several sips in silence, Georgio began to hum.

Lefty felt like humming too. Actually, he was ready to race around the room and do anything. He sipped more coffee. Then he began humming, whistling, and singing along.

"Do you like the coffee?" Georgio said, hopping from his chair, and swinging his elbow about.

"Yes!" Lefty jumped onto the table.

"Would you like more coffee?"

"Yes, I want more coffee!" Lefty leaped onto Georgio's back. Over and over, the big boy marched him around. Lefty started to leapfrog Georgio and then Georgio did the same over him. Lefty landed as silently as a cat, while Georgio thumped on the floor like a small black bear, causing cries to come from underneath the shaking floor. The coffee on Bish was intoxicating, and for these boys it might as well have been a kettle full of grog. Lefty lay back and giggled, tears streaking his face.

Georgio did the same then perked up, ran over to the urine shoot, and began to pee. "Ah!"

Lefty kept giggling. At last, he managed to regain some composure, sat on the floor, and leaned back against his friend.

"Lefty, why are you writing down all this stuff? I've never seen anything like it," Georgio said, fumbling through the books.

"Georgio!" Lefty raised his voice. "How come you keep asking me this same question? We can't help it, either of us." He shrugged, palms raised. "Can we? We just have to."

"That's weird," Georgio said.

"It is," he replied, elbowing him and causing a grunt.

Lefty Lightfoot had become obsessed with chronicling any and every event he could about his friends and the Darkslayer. He couldn't help it for some reason, as if he were compelled to do it. He even dreamed about it.

Lefty did enjoy it, though. It made him feel like he belonged. His tomes were filled with tales of the big warrior, many of which made him cringe. He wrote in a language no one could read. Even savvy Melegal had trouble with it. It was halfling shorthand, Melegal insisted. That must be how Lefty kept pace with Venir's blathering, the thief would say, if not by magic. But, given time, Melegal swore to Lefty that he would be able to decipher it. Lefty laughed at him. He might teach Melegal one day. The thief had taught him many things, after all. Melegal seemed demanding most times, but Lefty noticed that the unpleasant thief would crack a smile at his skills from time to time.

"When's Vee coming back here?" Georgio said in a huff. "He got back and now he's been gone nearly two days. What in the world could he be doing in this cruddy city?"

"Girlfriend, maybe?" the halfling said.

"Yeah right! Vee doesn't need a girlfriend. That's the stupidest thing I ever heard," Georgio insisted, finishing off his coffee. "Besides, he can't be having more fun than us!" The boy stood up behind Lefty, meaty hands on hips. "Well, want to come to the stable? I gotta feed Chongo and Quickster." Georgio put on his muddy shoes and headed for the door.

"I'll stay, but hurry back. They'll need some good coffee, and they always show up around coffee time," Lefty replied as he began writing again.

"All right," said Georgio. "I'll go the back way; they get mad when I go through the tavern. See you soon."

Lefty waved, but a queasy feeling started in his stomach. Georgio was a true friend. Lefty just could not imagine what he would do without him. An odd sense of dread overcame him as his best friend sauntered away. Maybe it was just the coffee making him sick. Lefty continued on, finishing the latest tale in his tome.

17

I T WAS ALMOST DAWN AT the Drunken Octopus and only a few other scoundrels remained along with Venir and Melegal. The Motley Girls were present, along with two hefty men slouched over a table. Venir had stripped to the waist for a strength challenge not long after the hand stabs incident. He suspected Melegal had set up the challenge as some sort of payback, but he didn't mind. One of the Motley Girls—Haze—had been paying close attention to Melegal, keeping a keen eye on the thief.

Venir had been challenged by an inebriated local with a big head and bad smile. Someone—he suspected Luke, at the prodding of Melegal—had told the oaf he looked like a girlie in his new bearskin vest. The man was even more insulted when told that his coin wouldn't even earn him a good-night kiss from the likes of Frigdah. Then he was told that he should go back to the farm and feed the pigs.

And Venir had been accused of it all.

The big oaf boasted that he was indeed a farm boy and that he would show everyone how farm boys took care of city boys. That comment brought audible snickers from many in the room. The ignorant fellow removed his vest and shirt, flexed his muscles, and slapped his big belly a few times before calling Venir out. Venir removed his shirt in acceptance. His massive chest, corded arms, and broad back put all bets in his favor. The V-shaped tattoo covering his back drew comments and gasps, and even the Motley Girls looked impressed.

The goal of this particular strength test was to see who could wrestle his opponent out the front door of the tavern. The grubby oaf failed to realize that despite his superior height and weight advantage, he was in over his head. The match went fast, as Venir didn't hold back and tossed the three-hundred-pound-plus oaf right through the tavern wall.

Venir then began arguing with Melegal. Luke moved on and nodded politely to the ugly women, who sneered in return as he walked out through the hole recently made in the wall. Venir got up, tossed his mug across the room, and headed toward the men's room to relieve himself, leaving the gray-haired thief muttering to himself.

After Venir left, Haze sat down beside Melegal.

"Go away," Melegal said.

"Naw." She batted her eyelashes at him.

He rolled his eyes under his floppy gray hat. "Pah! You and me? You're not serious."

"Why? I ain't so bad looking, and you ain't so good looking. So why not?" she asked.

"Cause you're ugly and I don't do ugly. Now go, you're scaring the rats," he said, turning his back to her.

The indignant woman unsheathed her blade. He whirled in a single motion and twisted the weapon out of her hand. It dropped onto the table. He pinned her palm to the table.

"Spread your fingers," he ordered with a cold stare, squeezing her wrist like a vise.

She complied. He snatched up her dagger and moved it over her hand in a blur of flickering steel.

Rat-a-tat-ta-tat-a-tat!

The blade left a clean cut on the outside and inside of each of her slender fingers. He tossed the weapon aside and poured grog over the top of her fresh, bleeding wounds, ignoring her howls.

As tears streamed down her cheeks, he looked her in the eyes. "Now you've had a night with me you'll never forget."

She clutched her bleeding hand, trembling with shock. She sat there like a frightened child. Her older sister swooped over to get her away from Melegal, glaring into his eyes. Haze, though, stubbornly remained.

He just sneered.

"Come on, Haze," Sis said. "Let's go before you get us both killed. We got places to be today, you know, or our bosses will cut our pay, and I need some sleep first."

The lean woman let out a hysterical little laugh, then rose stiff as a board and followed her sister. Melegal waved at Sis, who scowled at him.

Venir sauntered back toward the table as the three women left. He watched his defeated opponent—the self-proclaimed farm boy—ogle the women with one swollen eye closed.

It wouldn't surprise me one bit, Venir thought.

The farm oaf smiled, then shook his head and stumbled back to his table. Sis glared and gestured back at him.

"Hey, what's all this blood?" Venir said with a slur. "And who drank my grog?"

"Don't ask." Melegal got up. "I'm going home."

"Me … did you recognize them? The Motley Girls?" Venir asked,

"Yep," he said.

"And?" Venir folded his arms across his chest.

"They were in the kiddie's hooch with us, I remember. Younger than us. And you know how it goes for girls in there, Vee."

"Yeah, I know. But at least they made it out. They've certainly got something going for them—three sisters, all ugly. You don't see that a lot these days." Venir sat down and poured another drink.

Melegal chuckled. Venir broke out laughing, and in no time his guffaws caused his chair to slip and land him on his back again. On that high note, they ended one more miserable night in Bone.

18

V ENIR WAS RESTLESS AFTER THE night's events at the Drunken Octopus. He did not feel ready to return to his room after Melegal had left. He still sought some passion with Dresla, and thought he just might pay her a visit. Her long lashes, ivory skin, honey-scented hair, and sultry figure had burned a lasting impression into his mind. She was as fine a woman as a man could come by in a place like the Drunken Octopus. The problem was that he had no idea where she lived. His grog-addled mind, though, convinced him otherwise.

The first sun of Bish was not yet on the horizon. Dawn had barely begun. No one was about on the cobbled streets. In any case, the streets in this part of the city were not well traveled even during the day. Venir whistled as he strolled with determination through the dangerous alleyways.

As Venir walked down the narrow street known as Death Hall, he came to an abrupt stop. Several men poured out into the alley.

They were man-urchins, an impoverished breed who belonged to the subservient guilds that did much of the Royals' dirty work. Most were scarred and disfigured, with rotten teeth and rancid breath. These were men no longer suited for common society, but proud of their purpose nonetheless. Murder, robbery, and kidnapping were their forte, and they were efficient despite their disheveled appearance.

Venir pulled out his knife. He cared little for what others had to say about them; Venir was not about to be delayed from the delightful thighs of Dresla.

"Out of my way, roaches!" he said, brandishing his weapon. "I've no time to kill you."

The ragged men were barely ten feet away, armed with the crooked steel daggers of their kind. He felt the gaze of many others on his back, and sensed that they were after more than his gold.

What is this about?

The man-urchins usually operated in small groups, but here they seemed to have the whole guild. He took a quick glance around. They were everywhere. His blood ran hot.

Hearing sharply drawn breaths behind him, he crouched and sprang like a panther, slamming into their surprised faces before they could strike. The flatfooted men tried to move away from Venir's long hunting knife, but it soon found its way deep into two of their bellies. Venir punched another so hard the man's eye burst in its socket. With the butt of his knife, he swung back and cracked another's skull.

Run now, dogs!

But they kept coming.

A throng of tattered men tried to grapple him to the ground. Venir pumped his arms and kicked his legs, determined to keep his feet. He pounded their inferior frames in a relentless fury, eyes blazing. He lost his knife deep in the skull of one.

They tried to match his strength and ferocity, but he only tore into them like a hungry bear tearing at its prey. Their bones broke under the hammer-like blows of his knees and elbows. They were like schoolchildren and he a seasoned warrior.

Venir enjoyed it.

He pressed, not letting up. Each pop and snap of shattered teeth, jaws, and ribs stoked his inner fire. Their rags now looked more like blood-soaked bandages.

"How's this feel?" the Outlands warrior yelled in mockery.

Pop!

"Taste my fist!"

Crunch!

"How's my elbow feel?"

Swistka!

"Ever been slapped before?"

Slap!

"You fight like his mother!"

Slap! Slap! Slap!

"Sorry, you don't have mothers, do you? Say good night, smelly!"

Boom! Crunch!

The man-urchins scrambled over each other like rats drowning in a sewer. They were a far cry from the brawniest Bone had to offer. Two more rushed in. He grabbed their lice-ridden heads and smashed them together. Another he hoisted and heaved like a hay bale into the others. They finally began to back away.

"Is that all you over-tattered whores got?" he said, peering around.

All eyes were on him.

Venir bled from several cuts that began to burn. His blue jerkin and green tunic were wet with blood. *Nothing a bottle of grog won't heal up.* His blood dripped onto the stone road.

Scanning for his hunting knife, he noticed several long wooden darts on the ground. Some stuck out of the prone man-urchins at his feet. Wrenching his blade from one dead man's skull, he noticed the anticipation on his enemies' faces.

What is this?

In his zeal for battle, he had failed to observe the shadowy figures in the windows and on the rooftops above him. He now realized they'd been shooting darts his way during the fray. He reached back and felt several protruding across the broad expanse of his upper back. He felt woozy and his knees wobbled. Bright spots of blue and purple obscured his vision. As he sank in a swoon, he mumbled with a smile, "I'll be there soon, Dresla …" And his face crashed into the red-slicked cobblestone road.

"Great Bish! Me thought that monster wouldna ever stop," one man-urchin mumbled through split lips and a busted nose.

"And who might he be, anyhow?" asked another.

A short, stocky man-urchin appeared and shoved them aside, his face hidden beneath a dark cowl. He strode over to the brawler's body, plucked the long knife from his powerful grip, and tossed it aside. He checked the body and removed several darts. Examining their tips, he nodded with satisfaction. He grabbed the fallen warrior's small belt pouch and tossed it to his men. They poured out the coins, then spat in dissatisfaction at the meager contents.

"Don't worry, boys!" The man's voice was charming and spirited, unlike the rest. "There'll be plenty of gold when we take him in. Now get over here and let's haul away this carcass so you can claim your booty."

They grumbled a cheer as several hoisted Venir's body and trudged away. The rest dragged away their own dead and wounded. Soon the masses of Bone would trample these blood-soaked cobbles, and in no time there would be no sign of the brawl.

As the man-urchins vacated Death Hall alley, two pairs of feet crept that way. A slender, bandaged hand reached down and retrieved Venir's bloodied hunting knife.

"Man, Haze, that man can fight," Sis said.

"He sure can. But what should we do? Follow, or leave him for dead?" Haze asked.

Sis rubbed her pimpled chin.

"Let's see where he goes. Your new boyfriend would be glad to know—and to have that knife."

"He's *not* my boyfriend, Sis," Haze said with a whine.

"Is too! He marked you." Sis winked, grabbed Haze's bandaged hand and giggled.

"Ow!" Haze pulled her hand away. "Oh, shut up. I hate men as much as you do. Now let's follow. And don't talk about my ... I mean you-know-who, till we have to," Haze said, almost stammering.

Sis let out a laugh, her belly jiggling as they followed. Frigdah had stayed behind to tend the needs of the poor oaf Venir had tossed through the tavern wall earlier.

19

V ENIR AWOKE WITH AN AWFUL headache. He reached for his head, but found that his arms had been shackled. Peering about, he discovered that his head, too, was restrained. As he realized where he must be, a sense of dread filled him. His thick neck was imprisoned in the stocks, resulting in his throbbing skull.

His hands protruded to his right and left, red and purple and pinched between the wooden planks. Venir strained within the embrace of the oaken frame, which groaned against his raw strength, but did not give. Again he strained against the cruel device, but to no avail. He pulled his feet up, hearing and feeling the resistance of the steel cuffs. He had no leverage. He was at the mercy of his captors, whoever they were. What did the man-urchins want of him?

Venir recognized the gray slab wall typical of the dungeons beneath the castles in Bone a few feet before him. It was all too familiar and unsettling. He had spent time in his childhood maintaining such facilities for the Royal houses that ruled above.

As an adolescent, he had witnessed the atrocities that happened in such places—sometimes to him. Most Royal houses treated their prisoners worse than dogs. In the dungeons, freedom and mercy ceased to exist. Fear ruled here, a fear he thought he had overcome the day he escaped. The memories sparked something inside.

He pulled and shoved at the oaken frame, which creaked and popped against his force. Every muscle in his thick torso was knotted like iron, and sweat slithered down his body like oil. He heard the distant ring of a warden's keys, and the hard sound of a sentry's soles echoing off the dungeon floor.

Never again!

Redoubling his efforts, the stocks popped and creaked louder. The footsteps grew faster. Venir heard yelling and running now, getting closer as he moaned and writhed like a frenzied bull. Shaking and trembling, his eyes rolled up into his head, red with rage. The will to escape displaced all pain as he wrenched his bleeding wrists through the holes. His neck and ears bled, and blood dripped from his nose under the strain.

He didn't care—he would not be a prisoner of the Royals again. He would die first.

He heaved once more with such force that his eyes bulged from their sockets.

A thunderous crack reverberated in the dungeon, followed by cries of alarm.

The hardened oak frame gave way, splintering over the dungeon floor. Freed from the stocks, he yanked at the shackles on his feet. A blinding white flash exploded inside his head, wracking his body in pain. He snorted in defiance as he wrenched at the links. The metal bent, just about ready to snap. A second flash exploded. He reeled and sank in a heap.

Four dungeon sentries stood around, gaping at the massive prisoner in wonder. One picked up a piece of the splintered wood and shook his head. They had previously seen men and women pick the locks or dislocate the joints in their hands to escape. None had ever torn the thick oak beams asunder with sheer brute force. Not until now. The men gawped at the shattered stock.

"Go and make sure he's out," said one onlooker in a distinguished voice. He brandished a club-like cudgel of white ash that glowed, and wore a dark cowl around his neck. Although his clothes were tattered, they showed the markings of a Royal family.

He had helped to capture the prisoner from Death Hall alley earlier. His blond locks almost covered his eyes as they bore into the sentries who hesitated at his orders. One stepped over to check the fallen warrior on the ground with a shaky hand. A sudden twitch from the man's hulking frame sent the sentries leaping backward like frightened cats.

"Cowards!" yelled the cudgel wielder, shaking it their way and laughing. "He's out, trust me, you worthless lot."

"Apologies, Leezir, sir."

They cast their gazes down, not wanting to draw Royal displeasure. Leezir was not quick tempered, but not known for unlimited patience, either. He loved his cudgel—known as Spine Breaker to his servants—and used it to instill discipline in them.

Leezir sauntered over to the big body and examined Venir. He was nervous, but maintained his poise. Shattering the stocks was bad enough, but not dropping after a direct hit to the back of the head with Spine Breaker was another matter. *How in Bish did he do that?* Spine Breaker contained stunning magic, and he was not happy to have used up two of its charges on a single prisoner. He tore Venir's green tunic from his back and there it was—the V-shaped tattoo.

It's him.

He smiled and stood up.

"All right, boys, he's the one … the Vee-Man!"

20

G EORGIO HUSTLED THROUGH THE DANGEROUS streets of Bone. The smell of the bakeries prompted his quick feet through the early morning darkness. His mouth watered at the thought of all those hot, fresh biscuits that his meager coin could buy.

Melegal never left him many wages for caring for the pony and other menial tasks. He said that Georgio would just spend it on food—which he would. But it didn't change Georgio's mind that the thief was cheap. They always squabbled over pay.

Venir never seemed to pay much more, either. Melegal and Venir would both insist that they were setting his money aside so he could have his own place one day, but Georgio wasn't as stupid as the thief made him out to be. He knew they were wasting his money on other things. He just didn't know what. And so they argued.

Putting it out of his mind—for now—Georgio dashed up to one of his favorite bakeries, startling the baker.

"Oy!" the man said. The beefy man with short sleeves and hairy arms was removing a fresh batch of bread from the large stone oven. Georgio inhaled the fresh-baked aroma and let out a sigh. He rubbed his tummy, thinking about all that coffee he'd drunk.

"Tis the likes o' Georgio, I see. Back for more biscuits, might he be?" the man said, wiping his hands.

"That's right! Do you remember what I like on them?" Georgio asked.

"Hah …" The baker tugged at his mustache. "I think I do remember. O' course, yes, I do. I call it the *Georgio*."

"Wow … a biscuit that's named after me!" Georgio said, now licking his lips.

The baker smiled, reached over the counter, and tousled Georgio's dark brown locks.

"There's only one *Georgio* biscuit, so how could I forget it? Now, let's see …" The baker removed the first batch and placed the pan underneath Georgio's nose. The biscuits were the size of a man's hand, golden and fluffy, warming his face like the morning sun.

"Ah, yes. You'll be wantin' lots o' golden cheese," the man said.

The boy nodded as the man sliced a biscuit open, let the steam escape, and lathered it in cheese.

"And then a lot o' bacon …"

Georgio continued nodding.

"Lots o' butter, plenty o' spicy sausage, lots o' hot pepper, and, eh … what am I forgetting?"

"Pickles and goat mustard!" Georgio said, clasping his hands.

"That's right! Now how many will you be wantin' today, then? Two, might it be?" the baker asked.

Georgio checked his pockets and pulled out three small silver coins.

"Ah, you've enough for two biscuits, I see."

"And some milk, too?" Georgio asked with a shrug.

"Well, fine, then. But then you'll need to come by my bakery later and help clear out the trash, all right? Now take yourself a seat over there. I want to see you eat both o' my biscuits, I do. I could barely eat one if I tried," the baker said, holding his stomach.

"I want to keep one for later," Georgio said.

"It won't be as fresh later."

Georgio grinned as he held out his hands. "It won't be that much later, just when I get back to the stable."

The baker chuckled. "You're a lucky one, you are, Georgio. Not many lucky boys in this city. Here you go, then. Enjoy."

Georgio took a huge bite of his first biscuit and gulped down his milk. Two bites later, it was gone. He stretched his arms, patted his belly in satisfaction, and burped. Then he grabbed the other biscuit, thanked the baker, and skipped off as the baker waved.

"Don't forget to come back, Georgio!"

"I won't," he said, rounding the corner.

The barns were still a long walk from the inner-city bakery, and the smell of his remaining biscuit was bound to attract starving urchlings. Georgio stopped, looked around, and pressed himself out of sight. Not long ago, Venir had given him a special snakeskin parchment for wrapping up his leftovers. It had been a lifesaver on countless occasions, as it sealed in the freshness of his leftover food and kept the aromas from escaping and drawing attention. He wrapped up the biscuit and shoved it into his leather pouch.

The suns had risen by the time he arrived at the stables. The massive brick-red barns loomed ahead. He headed along one side until he found his usual entrance for coming and going throughout the week as he did his chores. Not many traveled there. He had worked in the barns for years and they now felt like a second home to him. He even slept there from time to time.

As he entered, he could hear a lot of stirring in the surrounding barns. They were busier than usual. Still, he thought, it was the time of day when the City Watch and Royal equestrian societies were about. Farmers were also busy with their cows, pigs, and various livestock. Not giving it another thought, Georgio walked along. With no one paying much mind to him, he passed a few farmers on his way into the stables.

He stopped and looked up and down the barn's great hall. It was quiet and dreary, with only a few people in sight farther away. Georgio put his ear to the stable door. Nothing. He shook his and listened again. Still nothing.

Where's Quickster and Chongo?

If they'd gotten out again, Melegal would have his hide. Georgio squatted to get through the small livestock door set into the stable gate, but stepped back instead. Something wasn't right.

A strange silence descended on the stalls He looked to both ends of the barn, and slipped on the jacket he was carrying then pulled it tight—and waited. Finally he heard a snore. It was Quickster. Relieved, Georgio rubbed his growling stomach again. He figured he'd better eat his other biscuit—before Chongo and Quickster were all over him trying to get at the food.

Georgio pulled the biscuit out of his leather pouch, unwrapped it from the snakeskin, and waved it above his head toward the stall door. *This'll wake them up.* He tilted his ear upward, expecting begging or whining, but he shrugged as he only heard the pony snore.

He rolled his eyes as he opened his mouth while a cloud blotted out the light from above, darkening the interior of the barn a bit. Even as he bit into his biscuit with vigor, he felt cold, almost like a shiver. After devouring the biscuit, Georgio let out a loud burp, brushed the crumbs from his hands and licked his buttery fingers. Shaking off the cold shivers, he headed through the small stable door.

"Bish, Chongo, I can't believe you didn't tear that gate down for my biscuit," he said. "You—What!"

There was no Chongo. Instead two men stood before him, one a slender individual in a broad black hat with matching black clothing. Georgio's blood went cold at the sight of the other man—the scariest man he'd ever seen.

Georgio's body turned taut as a bowstring. The man clad in black reminded him of the detective in the stories he'd heard from Venir. *Mc ... McKnight?* And if the slender man was McKnight, then the other man would have to be ...

Tonio.

Staring at the monstrous man, Georgio recognized Tonio as the same powerful warrior from an encounter months back. But now the ghoulish man was a menacing sight. Georgio's mind raced, trying to comprehend why these men were here. *They're not dead?* He tried to back out the small door through which he'd come.

Tonio stepped forward and pulled Georgio up by the scruff of his neck.

"Ow!" Georgio cried.

Tonio hoisted him with one arm and dangled him in front of McKnight.

"What do you want with me?" Georgio asked, trying to control his panic and knowing he probably didn't sound like it. From his elevated position, Georgio noticed Quickster, the shaggy gray pony, still snoring in the corner.

"I want you to give your big brother Venir a message, boy," McKnight said.

Georgio turned his face away, covering his nose. "Who's Venir?"

Tonio squeezed his neck even harder, and Georgio felt his face turn beet red.

"Don't play games with me, you fat little lout," McKnight said, brandishing two steel daggers. "Any more crap and I'll have Tonio snap your neck, if I don't slash it first."

Georgio's eyes widened. He'd had nightmares about that all too often. He was brave, but he was still just a boy. He kicked and flailed to avoid the blade.

McKnight stepped back, twisting the black hair of his goatee. "Drop him, Tonio. He isn't going anywhere."

Tonio did so, and Georgio scrambled behind Quickster, peering at his captors over the pony. Quickster kept snoring. On the other side of the pony, McKnight began flipping his daggers in his hands, making them flicker like candle flames.

"Fine, boy, let's start again. If you don't want your throat cut, deliver this message to your friends …"

No. No. No. Georgio clutched his throat behind the pony.

"Tell Venir if he wants his canine returned alive, he has exactly two days to turn himself in at the Royal Almen House. Alone. Tonio will meet him outside the gates. I'm sure he'll be surprised to see Tonio alive. And tell Melegal I've killed his filthy donkey, and that I'm coming to kill him. Got it?" the detective asked.

Georgio nodded, peering over Quickster's shaggy belly. Never before had he so hoped that Melegal would appear. And where was the big-time hero Venir when he needed him?

But no one magically appeared. It was up to him to defend Quickster.

Slipping his hand downward, Georgio felt for something under the hay behind him, up against the wall—the long sword he'd been given by Venir, which they'd agreed to keep hidden there in case of trouble—like this. Georgio looked up just as McKnight hurled a dagger straight at Quickster's exposed belly. Without hesitation, Georgio flung himself across the pony like a shield and caught the blade square in his back. He screamed, pain burning in his back.

It's … only a dagger. But, Bone … it burns! Wait … Melegal … told me about this. Poison!

Georgio's throat swelled shut as the stable around him turned black. McKnight's confused face came his way, but he couldn't move. And then he began to fade away into the darkness.

"What on Bish did he do that for?" McKnight said. "Sacrificing himself for a stupid donkey! Dumb boy!" McKnight looked at Tonio then shook his head. "I'm beginning to doubt the boy would have been able to remember my message, but who's going to deliver it now? I'll have to do this another way. Bone! The boy's dead, Tonio. Dead! To save a donkey! Outrageous!"

McKnight kicked the hay. The pair stood there, uncertain what to do next. They had spent weeks spying and planning their revenge on Venir and Melegal. They had even managed to corral the Darkslayer's mount. And now this … thwarted by a runt who thought more of a donkey than himself.

"Drag the boy out of the way, Tonio. And kill that blasted donkey," McKnight said. "We'll think of something."

Keeping his eyes closed, Georgio could still hear everything—and he already felt better. Even with the dagger still embedded in his back, his blood had stopped burning, and his throat no longer felt swollen. His healing powers had kicked in.

His head still thundered, but he was clear enough to hear Tonio approaching. When Tonio's footsteps stopped and Georgio felt a hand on his leg, he opened his eyes and smashed his boot heel into Tonio's nose. McKnight cursed as Tonio stumbled back a few steps.

Now what? Think!

Quickster stirred—finally. As McKnight approached and Tonio righted himself, an idea flashed in Georgio's mind. He kicked Quickster right in his pony parts. The beast catapulted to his feet, bucking in a frenzy. Burying himself in a corner of the stall, Georgio watched as Quickster ricocheted around the stable as if on fire.

The pony barreled through McKnight and smashed Tonio into the stable gate. Georgio's hand shot out and he pulled his long sword from underneath the hay. Despite lingering pain, he charged at McKnight, who was scrambling to his feet and aiming a poisoned dagger at Quickster.

"No!" Georgio swung his blade at McKnight's back. The detective whirled at the last moment, deflecting the blow. The blade bit into McKnight's left shoulder.

"Bone!" McKnight shouted.

As Georgio's mind raced for what to do next, Quickster bolted toward the small door and squeezed through. Georgio dashed after him. He was almost clear when he felt something powerful grip his leg and yank him back in.

Tonio.

Georgio whirled and brought his sword down with both hands, but McKnight caught his wrists and twisted the long blade free. The blade fell to the ground. Tonio kicked Georgio in the belly, dropping him to both knees with an *oomph*. Georgio sucked for air, feeling the dagger still lodged in his back. He looked up at McKnight and frowned.

Georgio's jacket was red, yet not soaked with blood as McKnight would have expected by now.

Reaching down, McKnight tore Georgio's clothes open around the blade then yanked the dagger out. Georgio screamed. McKnight gasped as the wound began closing.

"Mmmy sssword!"

McKnight jerked his head to the right to look at Tonio. Had he just spoken? The words were almost unintelligible, but Tonio had indeed said something—a rarity since the ravaging of his body. In his hand, Tonio held the boy's long sword, and his split face had even managed a smile.

"Mmmy sword!" Tonio whipped it through the air as if writing across the sky, his face looking more alive than ever. The tempered steel blade gleamed in the early light, its brass pommel glittering with jewels. McKnight knew the sword to be Tonio's prized possession from his rite of passage in becoming a warrior. It was as fine a forged sword as could be found in the city of Bone. As McKnight saluted Tonio, the boy struggled to his feet, and McKnight kicked him back to the floor.

"What *are* you, boy?" McKnight demanded.

When Georgio said nothing, McKnight took out a small knife and cut an X into his back. Georgio felt that the wound bleed a little, then close almost as quickly as it had opened. His back burned like fire. Tears streaked down his face. He wanted to scream but could not.

"What *are* you?" McKnight asked. "Magical? A wizard ... or maybe a lycan? Tell me! Or I'll slice your throat."

"I'm ... I'm a ... regener. I heal. It's natural, no magic," he cried then pinched his lips shut.

Oh no!

Melegal and Venir had always warned him to say nothing about his healing power. But then, he never imagined he'd face having his throat slit. He began to wail and covered his throat with a hand.

"Ah ... I see!" McKnight said. "You've had your throat cut before, haven't you? And it didn't kill you. But it scares you, doesn't it? Not being able to breathe? Hmm ..."

McKnight tipped his hat back and paced about the stall, scratching his chin. Georgio knew the man wanted to find out more. *Why did I have to tell him that?* Venir had always told him there was plenty on Bish that Georgio would have to learn about the hard way. Melegal had also told Georgio that his secret healing ability had value. So, if McKnight figured that out ... *I'm in trouble.*

With a dagger in each hand, McKnight walked over and knelt at his side.

"Now I have the dog ... and a healing boy as well. This will certainly get your big friend's attention, won't it?"

Georgio just looked away.

"This will be more than just sweet revenge," McKnight said. "I can profit from this as well. Oh, I can't wait to see their faces, and I might just have to tell them myself."

Georgio swallowed as McKnight stood and clapped Tonio on the back.

"All right, Tonio, let's take the boy with us. See if you can knock him out somehow."

"To ... Castle Almen?" Tonio asked, sounding to Georgio almost like a child, except for the hoarse voice. "I have ... sword."

"Yes, you do," McKnight said. "But, no, Tonio, not to the castle yet. Let's first complete our mission. Then the castle will be at our feet. I promise you that." McKnight stuck his daggers back into their sheaths. Tonio walked up to Georgio and slammed the pommel of his sword into the back of Georgio's head. Everything went black—again.

21

MELEGAL WAS SOUND ASLEEP IN his bed when a shocking clang caused one red eye to pop open. He stuffed his face back into his silk-covered goose-feather pillow. Another clatter brought him up in his cot. *I'm gonna kill the boy!*

"Sorry, Me," Lefty said as he retrieved an iron skillet from the floor. "Did that disturb your eternal slumber?"

Melegal sent one of his boots careening towards the halfling's head. The tiny boy ducked beneath it. The aroma of eggs and the warmth of the burning coals had done nothing to mellow Melegal's dour mood.

"All right, Lefty," Melegal said, standing up and yawning. "You're not stupid enough to wake me unless you need something. You may be a loudmouth, but you aren't clumsy. What's the deal?"

Lefty said nothing as Melegal reached for the boot he'd thrown and then sat down and put both boots on. Melegal and Lefty had gotten to know each other well enough over the past few months. No sense in beating around the bush. And he knew the look in Lefty's wide blue eyes.

"Well?" Melegal said.

The boy's hands shook. "Sorry, Me. I tried to wake you with the smell of breakfast, but you were pretty beat. I've never seen you sleep so deeply before."

Melegal rubbed his eyes. "Humph. I guess I could sleep because Georgio and Venir aren't around. Have they come and gone already?"

Again Lefty said nothing, so Melegal went over to the small table where a steaming plate of food awaited him. He sat down, grabbed a fork, and dug in.

"It's good, Lefty. Where's yours?" he said through a mouthful of food.

"I'm not hungry. I'm worried."

"Why? Where's Georgio? At the stables? I can guess where Venir is," he said.

"Georgio left for the stables early this morning, before you got in. I figured he would be back by now. He's never missed Venir. You know how he gets about his big brother."

Melegal rolled his eyes as he chewed. "I know, I know. So, he's been gone little more than half of today while I've been asleep. He's been gone a lot longer than that before."

"I know. But something's wrong, Me. Really wrong."

"What makes you so sure?"

Lefty jumped onto the table, disturbing nothing, and pointed to his feet. Small damp pools spread around them.

"Ugh! Get them off the table!" Melegal said, picking up his plate. "Is that sweat, or did you step in something?"

"I'm a halfling, see?" Lefty stood on one foot and held the other. "My feet always tell me when something's wrong. They're sweating so much that something must *really* be wrong. I'm not playing you, Me, I swear." Lefty held up his tiny hands in surrender.

The thief studied the boy's feet. They were disproportionate in length, smooth and slender, with thick pads underneath like stuffed leather. Even he had trouble hearing the tiny boy's footfalls—being so light that the old wooden floor never creaked beneath his feet. But as enviable as the thief found many of the halfling's characteristics, he had no desire to be a halfling.

"How long have they been sweating?"

"Since just after you got in."

"Do you think it could mean Venir's in danger?" Melegal asked, pushing the empty plate aside.

Lefty looked perplexed. It was no doubt hard for the boy to imagine Venir in danger. "I guess so," Lefty finally said, "though it seems pretty unlikely."

"Oh, it's likely. Venir gets into trouble plenty. Haven't you paid any attention to the stories you've been recording?"

The boy's eyes lit up like flames while he combed his tiny fingers through his thick, yellow hair. The boy had difficulty facing fear or dealing with bad news. It always made him withdraw. Even when writing down many of the things he was told, Lefty often had to take a break when his innocent mind became overwhelmed.

Melegal gripped the boy's shoulder. "It's probably not as bad as it seems. Take a deep breath. We'll go look for them and ease your little mind."

"All right." Lefty jumped off the table and scurried for his gear. Melegal washed down the last crumbs with a swig of coffee and rose.

"Tell you what, Lefty. To save time, you go to the stables. You have a better idea of how Georgio does his rounds. *First* make sure Quickster is all right—and he'd better be. I'll see what I can find out about Venir. I doubt he's far, but he could be in a dungeon. Sound good?"

"Yes!" the boy answered, pulling on his cloak.

Melegal waved as the boy jumped out of the little window and descended the bare wall like a spider. Lefty vanished into the streets before Melegal shut the window. The thief shrugged, poured the last of the coffee into his mug, and drank it down before he walked out, locking the apartment behind him. He had no intention of going anywhere to find his friend, but he would at least make some inquiries downstairs. The halfling had been convincing enough.

Quickster better be fine. Eh … Georgio probably choked on one of those biscuits he's always eating. Melegal chuckled. *Venir must be with a woman — maybe one of those Motley Girls. It wouldn't surprise me a bit.* No matter, Melegal wasn't going to let that spoil his day.

As he headed downstairs, Melegal noticed the sun setting through the windows. He took a seat in a corner near a crackling fireplace and let his new day begin on Bish. He had a feeling it would be a great day, Lefty's portents of evil aside.

22

J ARLA, THE FORMER BRIGAND QUEEN, hadn't sleep well last night — and hadn't for years. She was tormented by her own hatred and anger. She sat alone in her memories on a sandy bank between the trees of the Lush Lakes of Bish. A breeze blew her long, silken black hair over her scarred and haggard face. Her body, once spectacular and shapely, had succumbed to the ravages of stress and time, and now felt weighted down and soft. Her eyes, though, remained bitter, blazing blue gems beneath a furrowed brow that creased deeply between her eyes and up her forehead. Many who had known her as the powerful Brigand Queen would not recognize her today. Even those who had known her as Jarla their royal captain would not know her now.

Not long after the fall of Outpost Thirty-One, Jarla had inflicted merciless vengeance on those who had wronged her. She had trusted those men. She'd fought alongside them for years. They gorged themselves in blood-filled battles and were showered with glory, but they weren't the men she thought them to be. She had saved them many times with instinct and skills they didn't have. They became jealous — and her good character didn't see it coming.

They took her one day. Her own trusted inner circle of men had pinned her down and defiled her. Beaten her. Broken her. Then, they'd laughed at her. She'd crawled away from Outpost Thirty-One stunned, heartbroken, and humiliated. She never cried, but she survived, disappearing from the clutches of the outpost.

Soon enough, though, Jarla had showed up again, with different men and the underlings — and they'd mutilated every single living man at Outpost Thirty-One, good and evil, beyond recognition. She'd enjoyed every bit of it. Had even found some of her former tormentors and castrated them, and laughed as they were dragged away by the underlings.

Her revenge had only darkened her heart, and her problems had only begun anew. She was yet without her armaments from the mystic leather sack — her precious bracers, axes, and helmet. With those armaments, Jarla's power had reached its zenith. But they'd been taken from her by another man.

Venir.

He was brash, handsome, and cunning. She had melted in his iron arms. He was like no other she'd met before. But when she betrayed him, he'd sworn he would kill her. She knew he would. It was only a matter of time.

Bringing herself back to the present, Jarla used some cloths to wipe down her burnished bronze armor. Wearing only a long white shirt, she waded waist deep into the soothing waters of Lush Lakes deep in southern Bish. She pulled off the shirt and scrubbed the sweat and filth from it. She let it soak as the shining waters settled around her. Jarla looked hard at her figure in the water, which was fuller, her chest more prominent, but less appealing, and her scarred face sunken and worn. She was once a beautiful and proud woman that was the envy of them all, but the hazards of Bish had taken that from her. For a moment in those waters, she saw herself younger and happy, but the image faded. She smacked the water and cursed, then grabbed up her armor and shirt and stormed naked up the beach and into the forest to her fire.

There she sat, uncertain what to do. She always came here to wander. It was here that she had come years ago and found the large leather sack on the forest floor. She remembered that *clank* the moment she'd picked it up and emptied its contents — to be reborn as someone else.

That power had consumed her.

She remembered the years that she terrorized the south with exploits of daring and wonder using the armaments. Piece by piece, she'd taken back from men what they had taken from her. Turned her small band of brigands into an army and destroyed Outpost Thirty-One — the most powerful outpost in Bish — only to run scared for years from Venir, who now wore her mystic mantle.

Venir and his men had kept her on the run for days and months. They had been relentless, chopping her brigand army into bits and pieces. Jarla had ridden her beloved Nightmare, the dapple gray warhorse, to the brink of death one day as Venir and his men closed in on her and the few of her army that remained. Those remaining few had sacrificed themselves for her as she hid deep beyond the Outlaw's Hide, waiting for her certain death.

It never came.

Venir never caught up with her, so her inevitable death by his mighty axe had been delayed. She never knew what happened. He'd abandoned her to herself. Just like a man. She couldn't even count on one to kill her.

On the brink of starvation, she had staggered into Outlaw's Hide, her life without purpose. Had given in to its simple pleasures, carrying on without shame. For years, her wine-induced state had allowed her to survive. During those tainted years, she had cared for no one but herself — until a startling dream had awoken her from intoxicated slumber, causing her to run out of town screaming in terror. *Venir is near*, the dream had whispered. Her paranoia would not let her rest. The dream had sobered her. She had to face him. She was a big girl, and facing her fears was better than dying from them. Deep down, she hoped she would wrest the armaments back from him. So she set out alone, armed and ugly with strife, determined to fight one last glorious battle against her former lover, Venir … the Darkslayer.

23

M ELEGAL'S CORNER IN THE DRUNKEN Octopus was cozy and discreet this time of day. The dingy windows and shabby curtains curtailed the blaze of Bish's late-afternoon suns. The stone fireplace blazing beside Melegal added warmth in the damp corner. He liked the seclusion; it gave him a feeling of solitude that he craved amidst constant activity.

Sipping wine and cleaning his nails with a tiny knife, Melegal sat in thought. *The halfling boy worries too much.* He was glad to have peace of mind away from the rest of the group for a change. He was even glad that Venir was out for a spell — though he found it odd that the man had not yet returned.

The past several weeks had begun to take their toll on Melegal. Sharing a cramped room with a big man, a big boy, and a tiny one exhausted him. It was far from the dream he'd envisioned for himself at this stage of his life. He scratched his dimpled chin, wondering what it would be like if not one of the others ever returned. He finished his wine and chuckled.

The past few weeks had taught him more patience, but they had tested it as well. The last thing he needed to do was go on a wild goose chase. He told himself he was going to spend the day making good use of the booty they had scored. A half-empty plate of potatoes and roast, along with two bottles of decent wine, were a good start. Even with his roommates gone, Melegal was not without companionship.

He stroked the thick fur of the massive black cat sitting on the table. The cat was as big as a wilderness bobcat and just as mean. Thousands of cats ran the streets of Bone, but none like this. It was the king of cats if there ever was one. The table shook as the cat's belly rumbled like a tiny thunderstorm. The animal was a mystery to him. The cat seemed to have come with the tavern and had been there as long as anyone could remember. As far as the owner and the patrons knew, the Drunken Octopus was named after the powerful feline. Indeed, Octopus could eat and drink just about anything, including the cheap grog.

Out of everyone that ever came in the tavern, Octopus only let Melegal touch him. The cat sprawled across the table. As it yawned, it stretched out and flexed its four fat paws, all the size of a normal cat's head. Each black-padded paw had eight long, pearl-colored claws that looked like they would cut glass.

Smiling, Melegal remembered the time when a city watchman had come in with his canine companion, a Rottweiler. Octopus had torn the dog with his thick claws, deep into the bone, leaving the once-proud dog in a mangled mess on the floor. No dog had ever entered the tavern since.

The feline rolled onto its back. Melegal studied another of its odd features. The feline's eyes were milky white, almost the color of its claws. The thief could see only a faint outline of its pupils and irises within, but as best as he could tell, the cat was blind.

"You are one mean, crazy kitty, Octopus," Melegal said, dropping some chunks of beef and cheese into its gaping mouth. "But you know what I like about you most? You can't talk."

Melegal was enjoying the peaceful moment — until more patrons began filling the tavern. The sound and smoke built up anew as the locals unwound from their daily labors or woke themselves up from the previous night's lecherous behavior. Melegal sat, eyes alert, with his floppy gray hat hanging over the side of his face. A scowl emerged. Octopus would be gone soon and so would the best part of the day.

Cats certainly weren't the most popular creatures in Bone, but they kept the rats away. Most people treated them with disdain as they tended to overrun things from time to time. Sometimes tavern customers complained about the cat, but it was to no avail. None had ever been able to capture the beast.

Octopus was smart, fast, and dangerous, and when he left, people stepped out of his way. A single scratch from one of his claws could puff a man up like a pillow for days. Melegal had seen that happen a time or two.

Luke sauntered into the tavern and made small talk as he peered around, looking for familiar faces.

Oh no, Melegal thought. *It's "Mister Happy."*

Luke always appeared to be bright and refreshed, dressed in white and beige colored clothes that were more exquisite than those of the typical brethren in the tavern. The curly-haired blond man was charming to all. People knew him to be quite the entertainer and liked his company, which was odd since Luke wasn't a true local. The lute player, though, took full advantage of his popularity.

Melegal scrunched down at his table, pulling his hat farther over his face. *Please don't come over here and blather about something meaningless.* He figured if he was unpleasant and terse, the young man might go away, but he often didn't. Melegal didn't mind the man trying to make a living off him so long as Melegal got his share. He just didn't like the small talk. Out of the corner of his eye, Melegal saw the red and maroon painted lute in one hand and a bottle of wine in the other making its way over.

Great. Well, free drinks at least, Melegal thought as he sat up and pushed his hat back.

"Hello, Melegal," Luke said in a soothing voice as polished as a Royal diplomat. "Do you care if I join you?"

Melegal opened his hand over the sleeping cat. The man eased out a chair from across the table. Octopus's eyes opened then slowly closed. Melegal continued to rub the cat's furry belly. The handsome musician sat down in the armless, heavy wooden chair and set his lute down on the table.

Luke scooted his chair back, clearing his view of the room's entrance again. "That was quite a time last night. A very nice score I might say, and I thank you for including me. Melegal, I have never seen a man move like that before. I mean, how on Bish did you do that?" The lute player stretched his arms out wide. "That skinny freak you took was baffled. I was baffled. I still am, actually."

Melegal smiled at the thought of the hand stabs contest. It certainly had been one of his better moments. He found himself wishing that Billip would have been around to see that one. Billip would have had a fit if he bet against Melegal that time.

"A drunken thief never tells, Luke," Melegal said. "Now, let's fill these glasses while we still have the coin to enjoy."

The man obliged, pushing a fresh glass goblet into Melegal's waiting palm. As Melegal warmed up, he began discussing some details of other skims he'd pulled off.

Luke was all ears.

As he talked, Melegal studied Luke. He enjoyed testing one's powers of observation and quickly learned his lute-playing friend was great at reading other people. He found Luke's presence relaxing, as the young man always agreed with what he said. The young man appeared to be a good person who'd grown up in the seedier side of some town. Even Melegal didn't know where the man was from, but you could bet good coin that he knew where everyone else was from. The man could just tell. Melegal liked that quality — they had that much in common.

"So Melegal, where's Venir?" Luke said, craning his neck about. "Usually you can hear him roaring about some ridiculous adventure this time of day. Do you think he was able to track down the raven-haired beauty or did he run off with those Motley girls for a tussle?"

"Probably with those wretched gals, knowing him," Melegal replied, leaning back in his chair.

"If that's true, then that's an adventure I don't want to hear about. Hah!" Luke said, slapping his knee. "Seriously, though, is he going to be coming around? No offense, but it's just not the same without him here. His stories are what drew me back here to begin with. They make for good ballads, and I wanted to play some of them tonight."

Melegal could tell by Luke's wide blue eyes that the young man was sincere, but he didn't have anything to offer him. Melegal was at a bit of a loss as well, as the hours that passed without Venir, Georgio, and Lefty began to feel ominous, but he just shrugged.

"I'm sure he'll be here soon," Luke said, tuning his lute. "You know he can't go a full day without taking an opportunity to talk about himself."

After another hour of small talk, the Drunken Octopus was burgeoning with activity. Melegal heard a rousing scuffle near the entrance. *Must be Venir.* Whoever it was seemed to be rubbing the locals the wrong way.

Curses and shouts of outrage came forth as many were pushed back toward the fireplace. Chairs toppled over. The usual patrons didn't take to strangers of any kind, so whoever it was had made quite an impression. If you made trouble while you were around the tavern, then you wouldn't be sticking around. He couldn't wait to see who was causing the commotion. Strangers were among them tonight, that much was clear.

Not Vee. Would have heard him by now and no one would be making such a ruckus about him.

Maybe the city guards — but they never came this deep into Bone.

Things grew quiet.

A path opened, leading to the corner of the room where Melegal's table sat. He caught sight of two men removing heavy dark gray cloaks and tossing them toward the fire's hearth. One of the men donned a wide-brimmed black hat, and the other man, a tall stone-faced individual, appeared to have been split in two and sewn back together again. As Melegal's heart sank, he heard Luke gasp at the sight of the monstrous man.

It can't be!

"It's good to see you again so soon, Melegal," McKnight said, tipping his hat.

Melegal swallowed his shock and maintained his cool composure. "I wish I could say the same, McKnight."

Luke cocked his head, eyes wide. Melegal hoped that Luke recognized McKnight's name from Venir's stories and had sense enough to leave. Instead, the bard only stared at the stone-cold face of the man behind McKnight.

Melegal cast another glance at the golem-like presence of Tonio. The ashen man was positive proof that Venir had indeed split him in half. *So why is he still alive?* How Tonio still lived, Melegal did not know, and he had no desire to find out, either. He pushed his foot out until it hit Luke's leg. Luke failed to notice the subtle nudge to run.

Yes, the tales are true, Luke. Now go!

But the lute player still went nowhere. He just hunched down into the chair to avoid Tonio's hollow stare.

Melegal adjusted his hat and eyeballed the man once more. Luke didn't notice. *Too jolly for your own good.*

McKnight poured himself a glass of wine. The cat's eyes opened toward the two strangers and the fur rose on its back. It sounded like a tiger growling, and the ferocious cat coiled back on its haunches. The puffed-up feline looked as big as a dog, eyes glowing at Tonio. Its white claws dug into the table and it hissed loudly, but the seemingly half-dead Royal with the contorted face paid no mind to the black ball of fury. The gaunt brown eyes remained fixed on Melegal.

As the detective set the bottle down, the cat sprang between the looming men. The bard flinched as the cat disappeared from the room. *At least the cat will live.* Luke shifted in his seat.

The swarthy McKnight sniffed the wine. "Is this what you were giving the cat? No wonder it left. This wine isn't fit for a dog, but bottoms up!" He hoisted the glass and took a big sip, then wiped his mouth with a filthy handkerchief. "I have bad news to celebrate with you, my old protégé," McKnight said.

Melegal sat expressionless, heart racing, hands ready, an escape already planned. He couldn't believe that he was facing a man he was sure he'd killed months ago, yet here he was, alive and well. *How? How? How!* A storm of questions entered his mind. Had they gotten Quickster? Venir? Lefty? What could it be?

"Well, McKnight, whatever news you have, I am sure it couldn't possibly be worse than the fact you are *alive,*" Melegal said, noting that the room's bustle had picked back up. "But I must admit, I am very curious why you have come back to life just to tell *me.*"

The detective stroked his mustache. "Oh, the smug little rat has forgotten his manners. After all I've taught you, still you show no gratitude. Of course, what could one expect from an urchin? First off, where is your big friend? The news pertains to him."

So they don't have Venir! Melegal thought relieved, but didn't show it.

"I don't know," Melegal said.

"Strange. He's usually here, from what I've heard," McKnight said, scanning the room.

Melegal just stared at the detective.

"Well, I will go ahead and fill you in." McKnight fanned himself with his black hat. "You see, our task for the Royal Almen family was to track down your friend and bring him to justice. He tried to kill Tonio here." He thumbed in the Royal's direction. "And he committed other crimes against the Royal house. As you know, according to the ways of Royals, I can't return empty-handed when given a dire request such as this. Rather than being taken in, I would be cast out. Better off dead than condemned to the life of a Royal exile."

Melegal was well aware of Royal ways. Luke remained wide-eyed.

Leave already!

The bard glanced his way with a funny look on his face.

Melegal squinted at him, adjusted his hat, and shrugged again.

McKnight spoke. "I have made some assurances that your formidable axe-wielding friend doesn't evade my efforts any longer. I guess I can allow you to relay them to him."

"Why don't you do that yourself? I can't guarantee that I will see him anytime soon, you know. It could be days or even weeks, knowing him."

"Well, Melegal, I don't plan on letting that beloved pet of his live that long. I don't figure he is accustomed to leaving town without him, either."

If they had Chongo, was Quickster in danger as well? That would explain why Georgio had disappeared, and now maybe Lefty, too. Was McKnight about to reveal that he had them all?

The air thickened, dread surfacing. He stared back into the detective's probing eyes. Luke sweated, picking his lip, but unable to find words.

Don't say a word, Luke.

But the bard grabbed his lute.

"How about a song, fellas?" Luke smiled in good cheer.

Shut up, you fool!

Melegal kicked Luke under the table again.

But it was too late.

Melegal's blood turned cold as Tonio's dagger burst through the front of Luke's neck. The bard's eyes glassed over as the Royal laid the limp body down on the table. The Drunken Octopus cleared out as the scarred warrior wiped his blade on the dead man's back.

Melegal could feel Tonio's hatred as the young Royal's sneer of satisfaction bore into him. He felt cornered, uncertain, and couldn't even glance at Luke's corpse.

"Well, Tonio, you didn't have to do that, but I guess that leaves more wine for me," the detective said as he readied another glass. "And I would like dibs on the lute. Any objections?"

Tonio picked up the beautiful red lute and began to pass it to McKnight. The detective reached over, but the Royal pulled it away and smashed it against the stone hearth, tossing the splintered remains into the fire.

The whole room was empty. The commoners, apparently, were smarter than Luke had been.

"I guess that's an objection," McKnight said, shaking his head in disgust. "So, where does that leave us, Melegal?" McKnight reached into his chest pocket. "Oh, a funny thing happened after we took the two-headed dog. A boy came by and left us this."

McKnight tossed something onto the table. Melegal looked down, slumping in horror at the sight of what lay in front of him. It was a boy's finger, pudgy and greasy—just like Georgio's. The gruesome sight caused his eyes to water with rage. He was ready to cut McKnight into ribbons. His sunken cheeks reddened as he hissed through his teeth, "You are going to regret doing that, McKnight."

"Oh, I wouldn't let it bother you. The boy grew back another one. It was something I had never seen before. Such a boy will fetch a fine price, wouldn't you think? Every time I cut one off, another grew back. See."

The cruel man tossed several more of the boy's blood-clotted fingers onto the table. Melegal's heart sank at the thought of what his friend had gone through. He felt numb and empty inside. "You are twisted, McKnight. And you won't live through this. Once Venir finds out, he will kill you and that rotting Royal you are with. I'll … I'll find the boy … somehow."

McKnight seemed to be relishing Melegal's torment. "You only have so long to save the boy, rat. You and your big friend, that is. Now, I give you my word that if you bring your friend outside the gates of Castle Almen, I will release the boy. That doesn't mean someone won't come after him again, but I will release him to you. All we care about is Venir. I will settle my score with you later."

The detective gave a signal that only the likes of him and Melegal knew. It was a thief's guarantee, and Melegal knew his former mentor would keep his word.

"I will give you until dusk tomorrow to have your friend at the gate. If he shows, I will lead you to the boy. Agreed?"

Melegal nodded. He had no other choice. He felt cornered, and for the first time in a long time, at a loss for words.

"If he isn't there, then the boy's free time will be up shortly thereafter. I will see to that. He will fetch quite a price, indeed. Now I will leave you with Tonio while I depart. I can't have you following me. Not that you could, but I will take no chances. See you soon, little rat." McKnight turned to leave, but then whirled around. "One more thing. Your donkey is dead."

Melegal was convinced. He watched as his enemy tipped his hat, turned, and sauntered out of the empty tavern, wine and all. Tonio stood before Melegal, gazing at him with a complacent look on his face, arms folded across his chest. Melegal just stared back, unblinking, waiting for the man to leave.

As he waited, Melegal wondered which one of them had cut the boy's fingers off. *How painful that must have been.* As he looked into the compassionless face of a once-proud warrior, Melegal could see little other than the man's grayed skin, but he sensed that something did burn deep inside, like a furnace of hatred that gleamed in the back of Tonio's deep brown eyes.

Melegal was sure that revenge was the only thing actually keeping the young man alive.

About an hour later, Tonio left the tavern. So there Melegal sat, never feeling more alone. A headache throbbed under his furrowed brow.

He looked down at the table where Luke's blue eyes stared up at him in frozen horror. The fingers and a thumb of the boy he had bickered at so much over the years now lay scattered before him.

And his beloved pet Quickster was dead.

Melegal fought back tears. He couldn't remember the last time he'd cried. He sat there, dumbfounded and helpless. Venir was nowhere to be found. No one was, for that matter. His sly and calculating mind for once didn't have a plan, a response, or anything. Panic was overwhelmed his thoughts and he had no desire to move. Just as he began contemplating whether or not he would just be better off if he jammed his dagger into his head, the Motley Girls returned.

24

Faint sobbing echoed off of the dungeon's damp stone walls. Cold water drops fell from the low ceiling of a torch-lit corridor, creating thin streams along the muddied pavement. The glimmer of torchlight against the ruddy walls faded as the corridor sloped and wound deeper—toward the sound. At path's end, where only extinguished torches hung from the walls, a steel-barred door loomed, allowing the sobbing sounds to find escape into the corridor's dank air. Outside the door burned a small torch, flickering its last moments of light.

On the other side of the steel bars, a big, brown-haired boy, half-naked and shivering, huddled in a corner against the cell's cold walls. Fresh blood streaked the walls and ground—and the boy's body.

With a rumbling stomach and wide eyes that darted back and forth, Georgio pressed himself harder against the walls as large, red-eyed rats prepared to nip at his feet and hands.

Between sobs, over and over again, Georgio muttered, "Save me, Vee. Please save me." Then the last of the torchlight expired.

25

Lefty moved unnoticed through the busy streets of Bone. His large, sweating feet evaded the muck and grime as if they had noses and eyes of their own. He was worried that Melegal was not heeding his warnings. It didn't take him long to reach the large barn where he hoped to find his best friend. His trek seemed to take hours as countless horrific scenarios paralyzed his thumping heart.

He pulled his cloak tight over his shoulders and slid in through a side door, taking several glances around. The old barn filled with stables had its usual signs of life at the busier end facing the heart of the city. His own path seemed abandoned by comparison. The enormous barn intimidated him whenever he traveled it alone.

Lefty was never comfortable with large beasts, sometimes not even with dogs and cats. Good thing for him, he could outrun almost anything. Once, a young bull had set its sights on his plum red vest and chased him over a stable gate and into the mud of grimy pigs. Panic had almost cost him his life as the jaws of the brainless animals jerked up and down. If Melegal hadn't pulled him out, he'd have been dead. The thief had followed it up by slapping him silly.

That very day, the thief had begun instilling principles within Lefty to set his mind right in any situation. Lefty, though, still had trouble coping with reality. The thief would reiterate over and over, "Sometimes you just have to act and not think. Better to die doing something than doing nothing."

The lesson raced through his mind as he drifted like a shadow down to the stable where he hoped to greet Georgio. Standing just outside the stable door, Lefty listened for the boy singing or Chongo's low rumblings. He pressed his keen ear to the stable door.

Nothing.

The small door built into the stable was open with hay scattered about. *He must be moving Chongo or just out picking up eats again.*

Lefty took a deep breath, nudged open the door, and peeked inside. Quickster slumbered without a sound near the back. He stepped inside. As he cleared the door, a strange scent filled his nostrils, something sweet and familiar. He paused as his spine tingled. A light rustle stirred beside him as he turned. Something powerful gripped his face, covered his mouth and jerked him off the ground.

"Shhhhh. Don't be squirming, or I might hurt you," a rumbling voice whispered in his ear.

Lefty couldn't reply as his face was squeezed so tight that his lips couldn't move. He tapped the rough, meaty hand that engulfed his face. The powerful hand set him down and released him. He couldn't believe his eyes as a blood-red bushy face stared down at him with a smile.

It was Mood, the king of the Blood Rangers. Lefty stared up at the massive dwarf in awe. Indeed, the dwarf was a giant compared to him, standing near six feet tall and broad as a door. Mood closed the small door then knelt down.

"All right, little feller," Mood said. "Go ahead'n ask me why I'm here," he said as he puffed on his thick, aromatic cigar.

Something bad had happened if Mood was here.

"Wh-What's wr-wrong? Wh-Where is Georgio, and-and Chongo?"

The fair-haired halfling couldn't make out the expression on the giant dwarf's face, but he could see a glint of green in his eyes and detect concern in his voice. "I don't know where the boy is. Chongo, I know. He calls for me in distress and that's why I'm here."

"Chongo can do that?" Lefty said. "He must have a really loud bark. I didn't hear it."

The dwarf chuckled. "It's no bark, just a connection I has with the pooch. See, Chongo is a special breed that is reared by us Blood Rangers." He poked Lefty with his finger.

"Do they all have two heads like Chongo?"

"No, just Chongo. How he got two heads is another story, but you can ask our friend Venir about that. Something 'bout a silver fish."

Lefty shook his head. He didn't recollect a silver fish in any of Venir's wondrous tales. Of course, no one believed in legends of the giant dwarven Blood Rangers, yet here their king stood.

"You listen," Mood said. "I need you to help me. We'll go rescue Chongo, but I can't do it alone. Dwarves ain't liked here, and giant ones are no exception. Pah!" He spat in disgust.

"What did you do that for?"

Mood's face darkened. "I always do. Dwarves built this city like all the rest. Long time ago it was, but we know the ins and outs here. We let the humans live here. We don't like this life, but the Royals like control, and show no gratitude. Don't like us around. City of Bone's the worst."

"So, what do you want me to do?" Lefty realized his tiny fists were balled up as he asked the question.

"You help me get Chongo. I'll guide you. We'll get the pony out of here too. Whoever is behind all this, they're dangerous. Chongo's in much danger. Will you help?" Mood clamped his massive hands on Lefty's tiny shoulders.

Feeling strength stir within, Lefty knew he would do anything to help. He nodded. "What about Georgio? Where is he? We have to find him!"

"One thing atta time, boy," Mood said rising. "We get Chongo, then I think we get the boy, too—at least that what I be feelin'. Someone's after Venir, I'd say. Very bad. They tryin' to trap him. Maybe the boy is with Chongo. We'll see."

Lefty had never felt so nervous, but he was willing to do anything to save his friend. He could feel the big dwarf's gaze heavy on him. Something in the bushy man's voice let him know he could do it. His best friend was in peril, so Lefty had to do something.

"Are you ready?" Mood asked.

Lefty took a deep breath and lifted his chin. "I am."

<h1 style="text-align:center">26</h1>

T HE TIMING OF THE MOTLEY Girls' appearance couldn't have been any worse. The sight of the sisters only darkened Melegal's already distraught demeanor.

"What on Bish do you three trolls want of me now?" he asked.

The women smirked at him from where they stood at the bar—clearly unable to see Luke's corpse or Georgio's fingers lying on the table in front of Melegal.

"We know something," Haze said.

He rolled his eyes. "I can't imagine the three of you actually *know* something. Please, delight me with what that might be."

"Fine, smart pants," Sis said, her pimpled face turning red. "If you're too dumb to see we have something important you need to know, then we won't tell you."

"Hmph!" Frigdah muttered, standing next to Sis, arms crossing her big chest as she nodded like an imbecile.

Melegal was losing his patience. He started to get up, but Haze walked forward and tossed something onto the table. His eyes widened.

Venir's hunting knife.

"Where did you get this?" Melegal said.

Sis wagged her finger at him. "Oh, so now you want to hear what we have to say, do you? Well, it's gonna cost you, smarty pants."

"Yeah, smarty pants!" Frigdah shouted as she sauntered over and picked up the bottle of wine.

She took a big swig, looked down at the table, and spit out the wine. She jumped back, tripped, and smashed into another table. That's when Sis and Haze walked up and noticed Luke's stiff body and the pudgy fingers scattered on the table. The two sisters pulled their daggers out as they looked at the table in terror.

"Why'd you kill the lute player?" Sis asked.

"And cut off his fingers!" Haze yelled.

He couldn't believe how stupid they were, but it did give him an opportunity.

"Oh, him," Melegal said. "I asked him where Venir was and he wouldn't tell me."

They stared at him, eyes wide. Looking at one another in confusion, they began shifting back and forth on their feet.

"Now, can you tell me where he is?" Melegal said, even louder.

Sis and Haze's faces looked aghast, no doubt uncertain of his claim of killing Luke, but their fear didn't overcome their lips.

"He's in Castle Slerg!" Frigdah shouted. The big woman rushed through the tavern, bottle of wine in hand, and out the door.

Melegal folded his arms over his chest. "Is that true? Remember, your life depends on it." He nodded toward the body.

Haze rubbed her bandaged hand, staring at the fingers on the table.

"I don't think you killed him," Sis said.

"Maybe I did, maybe I didn't. Now tell me what you know of Venir."

The two remaining sisters looked at each other. His voice was convincing. He knew they were in over their heads, but he needed help, and if it cost him some coin, so be it. Still, they seemed to want to help, and he had no idea why. They had a tough exterior, but they were women, and something beyond their greasy hair and ragged clothes seemed to compel them to help him. Their shared past intrigued him as well.

Sis sighed and elbowed Haze. "Tell him."

After Melegal had the corpse removed, the atmosphere of the Drunken Octopus seemed more back to normal. The two women sat and relayed the details of Venir's battle in Death Hall. Melegal believed them, as they weren't smart enough to tell such a detailed lie. It wasn't very common to have such assistance in Bone, but the Motley Girls, despite their unpolished exterior, seemed to be good people.

Of course, the news about Venir did not help matters. Georgio was still missing, as was Chongo. Quickster was dead. Men he thought were dead lived again. The key to saving them all was Venir, and he had been taken prisoner for an unknown reason. He pondered all this information for a long moment. Haze and Sis sat before him, eyes wide, lips shut, waiting.

"Do you still have friends inside Castle Slerg?" Melegal finally asked them.

"Yes," they said in unison.

"Will you go and find out what you can? I will pay. I need to know something fast, so if you aren't up to it, let me know. I can only give you a few hours at best."

Sis got up. "If we help you and your friend, you better not be mean to my sister anymore. You owe her for what you did to her hand. We shouldn't be helping you out because of that, but we owe you. You don't know it, but we do."

Melegal raised an eyebrow at her. He had no idea what she meant. "Tell me all about it later then. And Haze ..."

She looked at him, waiting to hear his apology, but he couldn't bring himself to say it. He looked down at the table and then back up at her. His eyes must have told her that he didn't mean the harm he'd caused her. Haze smiled a big, toothy smile and got up to follow Sis out of the tavern. Melegal couldn't believe how desperate he had become. *Where in Bish is Vee?*

27

HIS BRAIN POUNDED IN HIS ears like some stampede. Venir remembered a blinding flash when he was mere moments from breaking free. Now he was in yet another cell, much larger than the last one. This time, though, his head was surrounded by sand, and it appeared that the rest of him was buried in it. He couldn't believe it. He was in the man box.

He wouldn't be going anywhere without help. Long ago, while cleaning dungeons for the Royals, he had seen prisoners buried in the man box. It was a clever contraption. Little more than a large, rectangular crate, it was used not only to secure prisoners, but to interrogate them. The prisoner was strapped to an upright plank inside the crate while a massive iron vat filled with sand was raised overhead on chains and pulleys. Then the sand was poured over the prisoner, making any movement below the neck impossible. The captors would then use vermin and poisonous or flesh-eating bugs to torment their prisoners or interrogate them.

Venir recalled stinger gnats consuming wailing faces, crimson scorpions popping cherry-sized welts onto cheeks, and onyx woodpeckers drilling holes straight through ears, eye sockets, and even skulls.

His stomach knotted. His body was completely immobilized; he was helpless to defend himself.

No. No. No!

All he could do was try to talk himself out of his situation. He'd been a prisoner before, but this situation was extreme. His body ached from the gritty sand rubbing into his wounds. He shuddered as he thought about his face being mutilated beyond recognition. He blocked it out and waited.

The dungeon was quiet. No other moaning or breathing or voices could be heard. The sound of dripping water and scurrying rats was it. He was alone in the dimness. As the minutes passed into hours, he catnapped off and on while his keen senses remained on alert.

He had no idea how long he had been there, maybe a day or more. The faces of the busted man-urchins filled his thoughts. He finally fell into a deep sleep filled with long-buried memories …

She stood before him as she had so many times. She was unlike any other woman on Bish. Dark, radiant, and seductive, her hair draped itself like a pelt of black silk over her broad shoulders, framing high cheekbones scarred from a strange twist in her life. Her smile was playful, rueful, and vengeful as her azure eyes bore into his body, weakening his knees.

Taller than most men, her tanned, athletic body was extraordinarily raw and powerful. She was the Brigand Queen whom he had sworn he would kill and had not. She had been his greatest lover and then become his ultimate betrayer.

He had yet to overcome her power over him. Every so often, something would remind him of her — a fleeting gesture, a moment on a battlefield, a hint of perfume, the shift of a shapely shadow.

Fighting side by side, they devastated their enemies. It fueled their insatiable passion for one another, which had found expression on countless nights in her tented quarters.

He had been the brave young warrior, but he had lacked the foresight of a wiser man. She was not who he imagined her to be. She was fascinating, but also evil, damaged, hateful, and merciless.

Despite the clear signs of danger, Venir remained blinded by her allure. His pride had almost cost him his life, but he had survived. Yet, so long as she lived she would haunt him. He could not shake it, though he had sworn he would get her one day.

He stood before his enemies as the Darkslayer, Brool in hand, the eyelets of his iron-banded helmet glowing. He rushed headlong through clutches of orcs, ogres, goblins, and kobolds that guarded their Brigand Queen. Blood covered the ground like rainwater as Brool carved into his enemies, blow after blow. Bones were shattered, bellies gutted, skulls crushed under his boot in a sea of rage and fury that the brigand army could not resist. Limbs, heads, and bowels lay scattered across the ground, yet still he could not kill her.

All around him was death, but never hers. He could not catch her. Whenever he got close, the underlings were there, distracting him from his mission. The underlings that he had spent a lifetime pursuing and destroying chunk by chunk, kept him at bay, kept him always from obliterating his one last haunting memory.

Jarla …

His eyes popped open. A dungeon door screeched open and clanged against the stone wall. A pair of hard-soled boots echoed his way. He feigned slumber. He could hear light breathing now, and sense a steady gaze upon him. *Jarla?*

"Come now, Venir. I know you're awake," said a familiar voice. "You always were a light sleeper."

It was not her. It was not a female at all. Venir forced his mind to awaken from the effects of the dream. His thoughts raced to put a face to the voice.

"I don't have endless patience, Venir. Shall I send in Creighton and Hagerdon?"

"Leezir!" Venir snarled, his eyes still closed.

"Ah, you do remember me. Or us, shall I say. It's been fifteen years, maybe more. And my, you've grown! From urchin to warrior in the blink of an eye. Quite impressive."

He could feel Leezir's breath on his face. Finally, Venir opened his eyes and stared into Leezir's pudgy, pitted face.

"Are the Slergs now in the business of enslaving overgrown orphans?" Venir asked. "I have no quarrel with you, Leezir, so what is it you want?"

The cleric stepped back and smiled. "Easy now. I know you had a horrible past here, like most children, but you survived. And in a strange roundabout way, it seems you've remained in our service, however unwittingly."

Wary of the mind games the Royals liked to play, Venir said nothing. It was times like these he needed to be strong and silent. It increased his chances of escape.

"You might recall the Royal braggart Tonio you thrashed in the Chimera months back?" Leezir asked. "We set that up, you know. We rather hoped you would kill him. It's been months since he was last seen, but he just may be in the safety of Castle Almen. I suspect this is what they want other interested parties to think. Are you with me so far?" Leezir twirled his grubby fingers through the sand below Venir's nose.

"I would be if you let me out of this man box. Otherwise, I have nothing to say."

Venir didn't remember the Royals' demeanor as softened as it seemed now with Leezir. It was hard to believe Leezir was still with Castle Slerg. Venir had never had a full conversation with a Royal as a teenager, but they were always condescending.

Despite his past and his contempt for most Royal families and their methods, they weren't all bad. He even had friends among them as a soldier from the Outlands. But the Royals in Bone were something else.

"You'd only escape and kill my sentries, if not me," Leezir said. "But I didn't bring you here to punish you, Venir. If I had, you'd be dead already. I brought you here to help us."

"Not interested," Venir said. "Let me out."

Leezir's nostrils flared. Common people did not make demands on Royals. The man scooped up a handful of sand and let it pour to the floor.

"You're good-natured, Venir," Leezir said, pacing around the man box. "A man of your word. Dutiful. Loyal. You were unlike the other children in the castle. You were raised right. So, if you just give me your word, I know I can trust you."

Venir said nothing.

"There was a reason you escaped the first time, you and some others," Leezir said, fingering his dark cowl. "Castle Almen was below us back then, you see, and we had a growing alliance. But then they deceived our family and almost destroyed us. Many children died during that battle, but you few escaped. We were very lucky to escape with our lives ourselves."

"I'm all teary-eyed, Leezir. Let me out and I'll give you a big hug," Venir said, his voice echoing throughout the dungeon chambers.

Leezir chuckled. "You're one of a kind, Venir, and we want your help. The day has come for the Slergs to take revenge on the Almens. I will pay you well."

Venir raised an eyebrow, surprised at the rare offer. And though he had no intention of accepting it, he needed time, so he decided to play along. "You'll pay me how well?"

"First, your freedom. Second, ten bags of gold and a bag of rubies. All you have to do is complete a simple task," Leezir said.

"What?"

"First, tell me what happened to Tonio."

"I don't know," he said, picturing the moment months earlier in the Great Forest when he had cleaved the man in twain.

"Come now," Leezir said. "Certainly you can give more assurance than that."

"It's safe to assume he's dead. Now what do you want of me?"

"To kill more Almens." Leezir slapped his palm with a white cudgel—no doubt the infamous "Spine Breaker" Venir had heard of at one time or another.

"I'm not an assassin," Venir said, all the while wanting to grab the cudgel and bash the man's brains in.

"But you are a mercenary."

"I don't kill for money," he said, but the thought of killing Royals for money was tempting.

The man lit another torch. "But you'll kill for survival. So you may like to know that they're coming for you. They assume you've killed Tonio. They won't let that go."

Regret sank into Venir's heart. He should not have returned to Bone. He knew better.

"I got word and pulled you off the streets just as they closed in," Leezir said. "They were so close that you're lucky to be alive. I mean, really, did you think they'd just let you off the hook?"

"I didn't figure they knew who I was. There are lots of people in this city."

"But few who cross an upper house of the Royals." Leezir rapped his cudgel against the wall. "When they want to find someone, they do—trust me. I don't want you to kill them if you don't have to, but you'll have to be the bait. I'll keep it simple."

"What do you have in mind?"

"Go about your business. They'll come for you. I'll have my eyes ready. When they close in on you, you close in on them. It's only a small strike, but it will weaken them. If we survive, you get paid. Do we have a deal?"

The clang of the dungeon's door resounded through the surrounding empty cells, interrupting Venir's thoughts. Two men appeared dressed in brown and red Royal garments with sheathed swords at their waists. Leezir's tattered clothes and dark cowl seemed out of place beside them as he raised his hands.

"Stop right there, Creighton, Hagerdon!" Leezir said. "You have no business here. This is my prisoner. Go!"

The two identical men looked at each other and laughed. The twins stood over Leezir, both tall and wiry with brown hair pulled back into ponytails. Their green eyes were arrogant, but jittery as they surveyed Leezir and Venir with sneers. Venir's blood rose. He still recognized Creighton and Hagerdon after all these years. There was a moment of silence.

"Ah!" Venir finally said, shattering the awkward quietude. "Your acne's finally cleared, Creighton. And you've worked off your baby fat, Hagerdon. Seems you two ladies finally hit puberty."

"Urchin!" Hagerdon shouted. "You dare speak to me like that!"

"Out of the way, Leezir!" Creighton pulled a dagger from his boot. "I'll carve out his mangy eyes and snip off his tongue!"

Leezir raised Spine Breaker and they stopped before him. "One step from either of you and I'll bust your chests in. Got it?"

They backed off.

"Got that, girls?" Venir said.

"Why is this vagrant here, Leezir?" Hagerdon said. "We don't need him! Let him go so we can give him a good thrashing."

Venir's laughter echoed so loudly that it sent the rats scurrying. His past with the Slerg brothers sparked bitter memories. Young Royals training as soldiers had always used enslaved urchins— such as Venir when he was a child—as practice dummies. The brattiest Royals would thrash their weakened and starving opponents over and over again, without mercy.

It was all for show, and a great joke among the older Royals and soldiers. As Venir had always been taller and bigger boned than Creighton and Hagerdon, the twin teenagers had enjoyed proving their prowess by beating him with their wooden swords.

Then, at their formal coming-of-age ceremony, with the whole Slerg family and their honored guests in attendance, Venir had faced the twin Royals in his rags with just a small club to fend off their large mahogany bludgeons.

The goal of the battle for the twins was simple—to disarm and humiliate Venir into submission. Venir had even been ordered to cry out and beg for mercy. He'd also been told to make the battle interesting or he'd be whipped. He was neither defiant nor defeated, but wanted it over with. The twins, adorned in leather chest plates, arm braces, and helmets, had something different in mind. They'd tried to kill him.

When the whistle had blown, they came at him with routine jabs and taunts. Venir made a game of it for a bit then gave some ground. As he lowered his guard, expecting a simple shot to the body, the brothers leaped on top of him and began beating him like he was some rabid dog.

The other urchins watched the scene in horror. But the brutal assault turned as quick as it had started. Young as Venir was, he was fearless. He had survived much already and was not about to let the twins snatch away a life so hard won.

Desperate for survival, the young warrior tore into them like an enraged ape. Hagerdon was swinging his club when Venir's fist struck his belly. An audible *whoosh* followed, and Hagerdon's club clattered to the ground. The urchins screamed in joy, to the horror of the Royals, and the sentries began cracking whips at them.

Creighton caught the side of Venir's face with his club, but Venir stood unfazed, spitting a bloody tooth into the Slerg's face. Creighton charged. Venir ducked and delivered an uppercut so hard that the boy's teeth rattled as he dropped with a yelp.

Venir spun toward Hagerdon, who was regaining his feet. He grabbed Hagerdon by his hair and punched him several times in the belly. The boy's eyes rolled into his head as he swooned, and Venir let him flop to the ground. Then Venir snatched up the long mahogany club, poised to attack Creighton if he rose again.

It was a mistake.

The Royal sentries descended from all directions, ordering Venir to drop the club. Blinded by fear, he swung at them.

Chaos broke out as he whirled among the surprised sentries, like a bludgeoning tornado. But a senior sentry soon stunned him with a blow from his spear shaft across the back of his head.

None of the slave children ate for a week after that, but for some reason, Venir was allowed to live. He always sensed that Leezir had something to do with it, assuming it was because Leezir also enjoyed the twins' humiliation. It wasn't long after that episode that Venir escaped.

"Do we have a deal?" Leezir gazed into his eyes.

Venir nodded while looking into the eager green eyes of the twins. "Thrashing, eh?" Venir said. "Well, drop those little swords on the floor, then. Come, you two warriors don't need those to take me on, now do you?"

"Shut up, Venir," Hagerdon said. "You know we don't need these. We've been preparing for this for over a decade."

They dropped their belts and blades without hesitation. The twins removed their shirts. They were in fine shape for city warriors. The lesson he had taught the two young miscreants long ago had apparently benefitted them. They were fit, as soldiers should be.

They turned their backs to him, a gesture of insult. He was amused as they warmed up, stretching and shadow boxing in the corner of the dungeon.

Leezir opened the end of the man box and sand cascaded onto the floor. Leezir loosened the cords binding Venir to the plank.

After rolling his shoulders a couple times and flexing his chest muscles, Venir stepped out and strode up behind the twins.

"Ready to dance, girls?" he asked.

They continued their routine without turning at first, whirled in perfect unison, trying to catch him off guard.

"Sweet mother of Bish!" Creighton cried.

Both of them leaped backward at the sight of his hulking frame, eyes wide with alarm.

"Get him back in the box!" Creighton yelled.

Venir took a menacing step toward them, and they shuffled behind Leezir.

"Stop him, Leezir!" Hagerdon said, cowering behind the cleric.

Leezir chuckled. The two grown men looked like cubs in a lion's den, hiding behind their mother. They avoided Venir's burning gaze and stared down at the floor. Having rarely seen his entire body in a looking glass, Venir could only imagine what the twins saw. His bronzed body was no doubt a solid mass of brawn emblazoned with battle scars—compared to their somewhat calloused hands and overly primped fingernails. He was far more now than a mere man. He had endured countless battles with foes in places they'd never dreamed of—and he'd survived. They backed away from his presence.

"Leezir, get him out of here," Creighton said in a quavering voice. "We don't need him. Get him out or we'll have to kill him."

Venir closed in. "You are the ones to die."

"Hold on, Venir! Deal's off if you kill them," Leezir said, cudgel at the ready.

"Fine, I'll just beat them till all they can do is breathe."

"Guards!" they hollered. "Guards! GUARDS!"

"Shut up!" Leezir said, seething. "Idiots! Stop interfering with the plan!"

The twins tried to back away. Venir pursued them, determined to tear them apart. Once again, the cleric cut him off and guided him away. Venir wanted to crush them all, but he kept his cool, not wanting to be trapped in this castle any longer. He backed off as the twins eyed him with looks of relief.

"The exit's this way, Venir," Leezir said. "Let's get you out of here before I lose my patience with them as well."

Leezir guided him through a dimly lit corridor beneath Castle Slerg.

"Look, Venir," Leezir said along the way. "Like it or not, they're coming after you. Be on your guard. We'll be watching. You can either kill them or be captured, but if you leave Bone, don't plan to return … ever! They'll protect their reputation. It's you or them."

"Doesn't sound like I can stick around either way."

They reached a secret entrance that led into the sewers below.

"Go," Leezir said, then turned and disappeared back up the tunnel.

Entering the sewer, Venir found it hard to believe that the Royals were still after him. It might all be a lie. There had to be something more to this business—there always was. Melegal wouldn't be happy when Venir broke this news, but there'd been no mention of Melegal, so he was probably fine. Venir had certainly had it with the city, but the Outlands offered him little rest.

I'll go elsewhere, then.

28

As Venir waded through the sewers beneath the streets of Bone, his mind was troubled thanks to the recurring dream that haunted him … a chronic reminder of unfinished business. Jarla, the Brigand Queen, who had become less of a priority over the years, was now on his mind again. It was almost five years since he had snatched from her hands the sack that contained the powerful weaponry and armor that had transformed him into the Darkslayer.

His mouth turned into a scowl at the memory. She whom Venir had trusted had betrayed him. She had planned to kill him, or have the underlings do it for her. Her dark blue eyes still played seductively in his thoughts whenever he encountered another woman with features that resembled hers. Thick, silky black hair, a tall sensual body, long fingers, or even intoxicating perfume—any of these could trigger unwanted memories of her. But the last time he glimpsed her eyes, they had held only hatred for him.

It had also been a critical time for the world of Bish as Jarla had helped bring about the fall of the key southern stronghold, Outpost Thirty-One. He witnessed how Jarla had rocked the southern borders with her five-hundred-strong brigand army of men, orcs, gnolls, and kobolds. They had been such a force that even the Royal garrisons stationed throughout the area were troubled by them. The Royals had not anticipated that Jarla's horde was in cahoots with the underlings, a foul and unlikely alliance. The combined force of two thousand underlings plus the full brigand army had overwhelmed Outpost Thirty-One.

One thousand Royal soldiers inside the outpost had been cut off from aid. If not for a few brigand exiles who managed to warn them in time, they all would have been obliterated. Those were the hard-fought days when Venir made his first appearance on the battlefield with his new armament. He had never forgotten it. He felt he had somehow missed something. So, as he waded through the foul sewers beneath the city of Bone, he retraced his past. He wasn't alone in his hunt for the Brigand Queen. His closest comrades had been at his side in the southern cities as well. Billip the archer, Mikkel the mauler, Slim the healer, and Chongo remained by his side in those dark years.

The small group had hunted the renegade brigand army all over the sweltering south. One by one, or group by group, they tracked them down and caught up with them. He had driven his friends to the limits chasing down the evil woman. Tempers flared, disagreements mounted, and after a year of pursuit, they separated. He and Chongo kept after her scent, but then the underlings cropped up here and there, taking him from one trail to another. His pursuit of Jarla had finally ended.

Venir emerged onto the streets of Bone. Feeling impatient and abused, he was at his limit with this troublesome brood that would never leave him alone. He didn't know whom to trust, but as far as he was concerned, the fewer Royals, the better. Let them have a go at him if they liked. He and Brool would be waiting.

It was dusk as he approached the Drunken Octopus, hoping his companions were waiting inside.

29

LEFTY'S MIND RACED THROUGH MOOD'S instructions again and again. It was up to *him* to free Chongo and bring him back to the stable. The halfling boy didn't have any idea how he was supposed to pull this off, but the massive dwarf reassured him that his plan would work. Lefty couldn't help but feel doubt. Still, he wanted to help Chongo and find Georgio. All the while, he could hear Melegal's voice in his head. *"You have to push through it without thinking so much. Get tough. Shut off the doubt. You are better off trying to live than waiting to die."*

Lefty paused inside a doorway that led to another large barn. According to Mood, the barn now housed Chongo. One last time, Lefty thought about what he had to do, then pulled his hood over his head, complete with dirtied hair and face, in an effort to pass for an urchin. He hunched over and waddled inside.

Unlike the run-down and barren barn he had just come from, the barn he entered was quite orderly and clean. It was bustling with activity of the city watch, Royals, and their servants. All of the colors and banners were in full flux of the early day. He heard the excited shouts and whines of the steeds from all directions. Lefty had never ventured inside any of these other barns before and it was another new feast for his eyes.

Beautiful horses trotted up and down the massive stable courtyard. Lefty quickened his pace, staying close to the gates and jumping at the sound of snorting mounts along the way. He felt out of place and small.

He passed many other horses being attended to by their pitiful stable hands. They were working hard to please their house lords. The Royals all seemed to be preoccupied with seeing which Royal could make his servants miserable.

The men and women of the Royal houses were clad in the unique clothes of their house colors to distinguish their equestrian hobby. He'd never encountered Royals of any sort during his stay in Bone. The women in particular seemed very beautiful to Lefty. Their clothes left little to the imagination as the designs seemed to enhance their athletic and graceful figures.

It seemed to Lefty that Chongo would not be anywhere in this barn, but Mood had assured him that he was.

Lefty stopped, mouth open, watching the gaudy scene, but the sound of loud voices yelling in his direction snapped him from dazing. Several black and white horses trotted his way. Large men yelled, warning everyone to get out of the way. Lefty stepped back to avoid being trampled then turned his back as the horses thundered by. He got moving again.

He grabbed an abandoned bucket and brush and pretended to limp past the stalls. He hoped no one would call for him as the Royals seemed to enjoy finding someone to pick on at every opportunity. So many people were shouting that he felt as if they were yelling at him, but he never turned his head or paused.

There were hundreds of stalls in the barn. He hoped the dwarf was right. How the dwarf knew Chongo's exact location was beyond Lefty, but he trusted Mood. The mindful, tiny boy counted the stalls as he limped in and out of the traffic. *Thirty-one … thirty-two …*

It felt agonizing after a while.

Lefty's heart thundered and sweat beaded all over him. He never sweated, except for his feet, which were now caked with mud. If he were caught, he'd be in grave misfortune. Mood had also told him that the stalls were marked, but the dwarf didn't know the mark on Chongo's stall—only where the stall was located. Lefty looked at the small mark on each stall—small flags bearing the colors and insignia of the Royal house. But not all the stalls bore a mark. Mood had figured that Chongo's stall probably wouldn't.

Lefty continued his countdown amidst the busy barn. The flags marking the stalls became less frequent as he neared the southern entrance. *Sixty-eight.* He stopped in front of an unmarked stall door. The interior was concealed by a high gate, unlike the rest. Much like Chongo's stable from the other barn, this one had a small door built into the main gate. This one, though, looked to be locked. Mood had cautioned him against just climbing over the gate, as it might draw suspicion. Lefty would have to pick the lock.

He pulled out a small, soft-leather cloth and unrolled it, revealing several small metal tools. Melegal had given them to him and instructed him on the basics of locks. Lefty wiped his sweaty hands on his cloak, took out a slender tool, poked it into the small keyhole, and felt around the mechanism. It seemed complicated, but within moments he had it unlocked. *Hah, take that, Melegal.* He looked over his shoulders, grabbed the bucket and brush, and disappeared inside, closing the door behind him.

It was dim within, but he saw Chongo lying on the ground. Lefty shuddered as fear sunk in that the giant dog might be dead. He was unaccustomed to the dog not covering him in saliva as soon as he entered. He noticed that the dog had been tethered to the ground with ropes and stakes. Its belly rose and fell. *Thank goodness.* He cut the tethers away, freeing the furry two-headed dog.

The dog, though, still lay there quietly. Lefty tugged on its ears.

Nothing happened.

Oh ... what is wrong? He wondered how they got the big dog in there to begin with, but he would have to figure that out later. As he stared at Chongo, Lefty noticed several darts stuck in various places all over the dog's body. He plucked them out one at a time.

A few minutes later, the dog stirred, then its nostrils widened as it snorted. Finally, Chongo rolled up on his massive, lion-like paws. Lefty soon felt hot snorts on his face that he wiped off on his cloak. The pooch's paws stamped in excitement. Lefty wrapped his arms around one of his big necks while the other head licked him like a bone.

"It's good to see you too, Chongo!" he whispered, tears rolling down his cheeks.

Lefty looked around the stall again. No sign of Georgio. His heart sank. *Oh no.* From the inside of his cloak, Lefty pulled out a sack big enough to hold a pumpkin.

Inside the sack was an odd-looking fruit shaped like a pear, but pale blue in color. It seemed to glow from within as Lefty held it out in front of him in wonder. Mood had told him that the fruit would do what was needed, even though the dwarf had said nothing else. Lefty was ready to see what would happen.

He extended his hand toward one of Chongo's mouths and waited. Both heads sniffed the blue fruit, and one head growled a bit in warning. The other paid no mind and gobbled down the fruit. Lefty waited.

Nothing.

He checked inside the bag. No more fruit. Now what would he do? He sat down.

The dog seemed to be his robust self, just like any other day. Minute after minute passed. Lefty didn't know what to do. He looked over at the big dog and stood back up when he noticed a change.

Chongo was shrinking.

It was really slow at first. The back barn wall seemed to be growing. The farther the dog shrank, the dizzier it made Lefty. One moment, the big dog was staring down at the little halfling boy, and in the next, Lefty was staring down at a miniature dog. The puppy-sized animal sat down on his haunches, tongues out and twin tails whipping with excitement.

"Wow!" Lefty couldn't believe his blue eyes.

Then he remembered what Mood had told him. "Hustle out! Magic don't last long! Put the pooch in the sack and beat your bitty feet back here!"

Lefty grabbed the sack and tried to pull it over the dog. Both heads nipped and growled at his hands. Frustration and panic set in after several moments. *Just act,* he told himself. Dropping the sack, Lefty snatched up the snapping dog. The dog was still plenty big and heavy in his arms, but it didn't bite him. He pulled his cloak over the dog, headed out of the stable through the door, closing it behind him, and limped away. *What if he grows back while I'm carrying him?* he thought. *What will they do? They'll kill him. Kill us! And what if someone sees me with a two-headed dog? What will I tell them?*

He kept his head down, filled with uncertainty as he limped back the way he came. The dog nuzzled his heads into his chest and shivered. He had just crossed to the other side of the barn when someone stopped him.

"Let me see that puppy, urchin," a little girl's voice demanded.

He froze. *Crap!* He kept his head down and waited, squeezing the dog in agitation as one of his heads popped out. The little Royal girl, who looked about nine years old, walked up to him and studied the dog. She was a pretty young lady, really, with straight black hair and chestnut eyes. She wore black riding pants and a matching vest over a long white shirt. She reached out to stroke the pup's exposed face and it growled. The other head sniffed around and popped out.

"He's got two heads!" she cried. "Whose dog is it? Where did he come from? Tell me!"

The bratty little girl was causing a commotion. Lefty looked around. Another Royal walked up to check out the situation. It was a young lady, maybe twenty, wearing the typical riding garb of the other women with lighter tones.

She knelt down, palm exposed, and Chongo sniffed her. Her voice was soft when she asked, "Whose dog is this, child?"

He began mumbling and shuffling so that they could not understand him.

"This boy is an idiot. He cannot speak," the little girl said. "I want that dog. Find its owner and buy him."

"Oh, shut up, Elizabeth," the young lady said. "You would just neglect it like you do everything else. Now go find our mother and I will wait for you here. And then we shall find the owner. Perhaps there is a litter."

The little girl stuck her tongue out at her sister, but did as she was told and ran off screaming for her mother. The young lady petted the dog, much to Lefty's liking. Whoever the lady was, she smelled good.

"It seems we have more than just a two-headed puppy, here." She tilted Lefty's chin up with her painted fingernails, and gasped as she held his tiny head in her hand by his cheek, his eyes widening at the sight of her warm, beautiful face.

"What is your name, halfling?" she whispered.

"Lefty," he said, then regretted it, but he couldn't resist her.

"Lefty, I am Rayal. I don't know what you are doing here or whose dog this is, but you better take it home quickly before my sister gets back. She always gets what she wants. So go."

"Oh thank you, thank you, thank you! I will do anything for you one day. You are beautiful like a rainbow. Thank you!"

He smiled at her one more time, leaving her blushing as he disappeared.

Rayal had not seen much outside of the city of Bone, but she did know a lot about the different races. She wasn't sure why she'd let the halfling go, but whatever was going on with the halfling and dog was much more important than the chronic whims of the Royals.

Elizabeth soon reappeared. "Where did they go? I couldn't find Mother. Where are they, Rayal?"

"I am sorry, little sister, but the owner caught up with them. He took the dog. I asked if there was a litter and he said no. Then he took the boy away for a beating because he is the one that let his dog loose in the first place."

Elizabeth looked satisfied with the answer even though Rayal could tell she was miffed. "Well, at least that little boy is getting a beating. If he lost my dog, I would flay him alive."

"I am sure you would."

Whack!

Elizabeth kicked Rayal hard in the shin. "I think you are a liar!" Elizabeth ran off before Rayal could catch her — to choke her to death. Curiosity consumed Rayal, though, and she followed Lefty out of the barn. He and the dog had caught her fancy.

30

V ENIR SMASHED A TABLE. THEN a chair.

He had snapped at the sight of Georgio's fingers lying on the tavern table. Rage and guilt rose as he trembled while the thief recounted his encounter with Tonio and McKnight. Venir bellowed so loudly that the walls shook. Melegal was not the only one that cringed. Two of the Motley Girls—Sis and Haze—stood back for fear of their own lives, Venir having arrived just as Frigdah ran off. The rest of the tavern remained clear. No one wanted to rile the big man.

The past day had been bad enough. Venir had been looking forward to returning home for a drink and a bath despite his problems. Instead, he ran into an ugly woman in the tavern doorway and then his friend with even uglier news. One problem had now become three.

Looking at Melegal's sagging shoulders deflated Venir's confidence even more. He didn't bother explaining where he had been or why he looked like he just crawled out of a bloody hole; he just wanted to get to the bottom of this. He forced himself to take a deep breath and exhale. It didn't help.

"How long has it been since Tonio departed?" he asked.

"Maybe an hour, if that?" Melegal said.

"Any ideas?"

"No," Melegal replied, chin down.

Venir sat down, shaking his head. Never in all of his life would he have ever imagined being in the center of so many torrid predicaments. It was one thing to fight and hunt enemies all across the Outlands, it was quite another not being able to find or fight them at all.

Anguish rose in his chest as he stared at the fingers lying on the table. His young friend had been tormented on account of him. The blood of Luke was fresh on his mind—another senseless death because of him.

Emptiness overcame him and his reddened skin began to regain its tanned color. Life seemed to drain from him. All of this had happened on account of one bar-room scuffle, but there was more to it than that. He was a pawn, a Royal pawn. For most of his life, he had seen how the Royals, good and bad, played such games with men. Up to this point, he had been able to avoid them, but now there was nothing he could do. He felt useless.

Venir stared at his comrade and knew that Melegal was feeling the same thing—doubt. Venir reached for a wine bottle, and guzzled it down.

"Tomorrow at dusk, huh?" he said. "The Almen gate? I will be there."

Melegal said nothing for several seconds. He looked at Venir. "A lot can happen over the next day, Vee. We have to try and find the boy first. I can't imagine they would kill him, seeing how *special* he is."

Sis stepped up. "Do you fellas still want us to help?"

Venir looked at her then over to Melegal, who nodded. "All right, girls," Venir said.

They both grinned like goblins, seemingly overjoyed for some strange reason. The way they looked at him and Melegal told him they were sticking around one way or another.

Octopus, the cat, jumped onto the table out of nowhere . It was an odd moment as the massive cat sniffed the fingers as if they were laced with catnip.

"Melegal, get that cat away," Venir said.

The black cat puffed up and rumbled when the thief tried to take the fingers away. Octopus's white eyes widened as if the fingers were a feast of fish or tuna. The cat snatched a finger in his mouth, then jumped off of the table and bounded out the door. Venir slammed his fist on the table.

Haze cleared her throat. "If the cat likes that finger, it might be that he'll lead us to the boy. We'll follow him. And don't worry, we won't lose him; we see him all the time. Plus, I know cats. "

"Go then!" Melegal said. "Go before you lose him. Check back here in a few hours and let me know if you have any luck with that cat or anything else."

Haze tossed Venir his knife as the women ran out the door. The men stayed put, gathering their thoughts.

"Let's head up to the room, Me," Venir said. "I'll get cleaned up and fill you in on where I've been. Maybe Lefty will show up by then. Anything can happen the way this day has been."

"You can say that again."

Once upstairs, the room felt dead without the presence of Georgio's busy lips and the comforting scent of Lefty's hot coffee. Instead, a cold stove awaited Venir with nothing fresh to warm his darkening mood.

He stood within the room watching Melegal pace. One of the two boys was almost always in the way somehow, but not today. The leather tomes, parchment, ink, and quills were stacked snug in one corner of the room. Venir shuffled around as if he was hoping to find a shred of evidence where they could be. In frustration, Venir washed up a bit then sat down on his cot.

"So," Melegal finally said, "where have you been?"

"Well, you aren't going to believe this, but here goes. And be ready, because you aren't going to like it."

The thief frowned, slung his hat on the table, and sat down. "Just get on with it."

The room brightened a bit as Venir got caught up in telling another story. Then he remembered the halfling was not there to record it, and he toned his voice down a bit.

"Here is the short version, Melegal. I left the tavern to find Dresla. When I was cutting through Death Hall, I was jumped by a whole gang of man-urchins. I was dropping them like hot coals when they feathered me with juiced darts. Now this is the part you will hate. I—"

"You woke up in the Slerg dungeon."

Venir's eyes widened in surprise, but when he remembered that the Motley Girls had his knife, it came together and he got back on track. "Yes, I woke up in a stockade, got knocked out trying to escape, and then I woke up in the man box."

His friend's face scrunched in concern, and he pushed himself back in his chair.

"The next thing I know," Venir said, "I am talking to Leezir the Slerg. You remember him, of course?" Venir paused as he worked himself up with the tale again.

Melegal motioned with his hand for Venir to continue.

"So, Leezir tells me the whole story of how he and the Slergs used me as a pawn to take out that brat of a Royal, Tonio." He motioned a chop with his hands. "I didn't tell them I chopped his arms off and split him in half, so I guess they don't know he is still alive—although with Tonio and McKnight skulking around, they'll know before too long. Anyhow, they're trying to take down the Almens and want my help. He also told me that the Almens are on to me, with bounty, because they can't find Tonio, so I need to be ready."

The thief buried his head in his arms on the table.

"Leezir offered me ten bags of gold and one bag of rubies," Venir said.

Melegal's head came up, eyes bright, chin raised.

Venir raised his hands. "Like that will happen."

The thief shrugged.

Venir became more animated as he chewed on some stale bread and spicy jerky. "Then those idiots Hagerdon and Creighton showed up and wanted a tussle, but my full-grown size scared them." Venir smiled. "You should have seen their faces when they turned to confront me, Me. They looked like frightened children!"

Melegal smiled back, then gestured his impatience for the rest of the story.

"Turns out they want me to help them kill more Almens." Venir stood up and sauntered around the apartment. "The Slergs seemed different. Leezir was very easygoing, and he and I bartered for my release. At this point, I'm ready to try and kill them all like underlings. Whoo. What a mess." He ran his hands through his blond locks.

Venir felt guilty for enjoying his tale, but it was what it was. Flee or fight was his option, and he wouldn't flee without the boys and dog. There was a time when he might have, but those times were long past. The hard man had grown a soft spot—and in this case, it might prove fatal. Venir grabbed his backpack that contained the large leather sack while the thief grabbed a few other items of some use.

"Here's the deal," Venir said. "You take the back way out and I'll head out the front door. Let's try and meet at the other place within a few hours. If I'm not there, that means they got me." He tied his knife scabbard along his thick thigh. "I don't know what McKnight and Tonio have in mind, but they need us for some reason. Some sick matter of honor is my guess. If the Almens get me first, be sure to let them know. " He grabbed his friend's shoulder. "Find my boys, Me."

"I will."

Venir's face darkened into a nasty grin. "Don't be surprised to find out that me and Brool tried to take them all down, either." He slammed the knife in his sheath and left.

31

L EFTY HURRIED THROUGH THE BARN where he'd left the dwarf. He was trotting with the dog in his arms when it lurched. Chongo began to grow. *Oh no!* He ran as fast as he could in a panic, only twenty-five yards from the stall where Mood was waiting for him. Lefty was terrified that he would be seen and captured. The dog was now bigger than him. He strained with all his might, but it was impossible. He collapsed to the ground.

"Oof! Geez, Chongo, get out of here. Find Mood," he said, breathless.

The big dog was off and running to the stable. Lefty looked around to see if anyone had caught sight of them, but the run-down barn was barren of people. He got up, dusted himself off, and headed for the stall, almost skipping.

I did it! Melegal will be amazed when he hears this.

He entered through the open stable gateway then closed and secured it behind him. The secret passageway lay open before him, however Mood, Chongo, and Quickster were nowhere to be seen. But Lefty couldn't just leave. *I've got to find Georgio.*

He closed the secret passageway. It was his choice, and he knew both the pony and dog were in good hands now. Lefty decided to head back to report to the thief. His sweaty feet were soon moving again over the cobblestones inside the city of Bone.

In all of his excitement, he failed to notice that someone else wasn't far behind him.

32

M ONTHS HAD PASSED SINCE JARLA the former Brigand Queen had set out on a mission of self-redemption—the pursuit of her former lover and now archenemy, Venir. She had headed north from Outlaw's Hide, careful of her identity and inquiries. The trek had proven difficult. She had grown soft over the years from living in pointless revelry.

She was a far cry from the strong soldier she'd once been. Her shambled armor had once shone bright in the suns. Now all of her clothing was in tatters. People paid her little mind when she passed.

Queen? Hah. She could hear them laughing though they knew her not.

Still, people kept clear of her glare. Her terse questions carried authority, which made the weaker more willing to comply. The once wicked but beautiful queen walked with a degree of humility. Those that chose to cross her with force fell at their peril.

Regaining her gallant warhorse Nightmare was her first objective. Like a fool, she had lost her steed, her most trusted friend, in a night of games and unwanted pleasure. She was ashamed, almost embarrassed. If anyone on Bish cared for her, it was Nightmare. She had to get her back. She hoped her steed would forgive her.

The dapple gray was a commodity and companion that she parted with at the lowest point in her life. If she were to live just one more day, it would have the purpose of nothing more than saying she was sorry to the horse. She had walked on blistered feet mile after mile and day after day with that simple purpose in mind. When her bloody feet finally stopped, she was in Two-Ten City.

Two-Ten was an open city full of all races. The best of the worst resided there. It was a border town between the barren Outlands and green forests.

As she advanced into the city, Jarla saw a shabby building in the distance. Caravans pushing cheap commodities came and went. She wiped the dust and sweat from her eyes. She wasn't going in there.

As Jarla stumbled along, she thought of when she'd lost Nightmare. Over a year had passed since she'd succumbed to a formidable orcen soldier by the name of Brandoff. He was as cunning with cards as he was with a sword. She was overconfident, figuring the orc to be as stupid as the rest. He showed her otherwise. He was a better cheater than she.

She paid for it. She lost her warhorse and the rest of her pride. Today she would regain at least one of the two, or die.

Brandoff had always spent time with his minions in the inhuman folds of Two-Ten City in a tavern called the Ogre's Nest. It was anything but a typical tavern. It was a barn that sat outside the edge of the notorious city. If the orcs and ogres had ever come up with one single brilliant idea in all their lifetimes, it was turning a barn full of stables into a tavern.

The orcs and ogres rode right into the tavern, stabled their mounts, and went to their reveling. It was the perfect place for their kind. Shoveling was in constant flux, however, as the less-gifted orcen and half-orcen children were tasked with keeping the place clean. They did a poor job. Muck and grime were piled everywhere.

The Ogre's Nest was the only place of its kind on Bish. If you weren't part orc or part ogre, then you were not in there. The other races couldn't tolerate the smell. Smoking wasn't allowed, either. Even the orcs knew fire would burn the entire place down. They smoked just outside. It made them feel civilized.

For illumination, they filled jars with the lime-yellow glowing tail sacs of the gargantuan lightning bugs. The bugs were as big as a man's head and the juice glowed brightly for weeks on end. They were not easy to catch, but the children always seemed to enjoy doing so. The task kept them busy at night while their older brethren played cards, drank, and indulged in pleasures not fit for human eyes.

On this particular night, Brandoff the brawler sat listening to his filthy comrades. They swapped stories about his incredible exploits on the battlefield. Brandoff embellished them with tales of all the women he had conquered in his life. His audience lapped it up. They all heard a shrill whistle followed by a horse neighing in the back of the tavern, but it wasn't as interesting as Brandoff's tales, so they ignored it.

The orc fighter was bigger than the rest. He was almost six and a half feet tall, muscular, and heavyset. His scarred face and head were covered with a coal-black beard and long braided hair. A broad and sweaty swine-like nose flared above his canine teeth. His jutting chin smiled at himself most of the time. His brown eyes were smaller than his kin, darting and intelligent—uncommon of their kind. He wore thick, black-studded leather armor about his chest and sported matching bracers. His arms were long and corded with muscle—and hair. Only the half-ogres were his match, but they had no part of him and he none of them.

Like most orcs, he was mean, bullish, proud, fearless, and tough. He was the talk of the tavern. Ugly orcen women sat on the bed of rotten straw, hanging on his filthy words. The entire tavern sang and tussled, serving each other with pleasure and without shame throughout the night.

The tavern was the most uncivilized of them all and the scene was overwhelmed with debauchery that would make the seediest trollop from Bone blush. No woman from any other race would be caught in the Ogre's Nest.

As she entered, Jarla's stomach soured at the sight and smell of it all, but she held her head high and strode in. Silence deepened over the tavern with each passing step. When she reached Brandoff's table, all that could be heard was the sound of a dripping keg behind the bar. Jarla felt their yellow eyes on her. Their breath was hot on her back. She wanted to leave, but it was too late to turn back now.

Nightmare.

She pulled her dark hair from her face and said, "You owe me a challenge, orc."

33

T HE VOID WAS A PLACE in the universe where a great deal of immortals could be found. As the infinite beings pursued the endless vat of space, they all came across the Void. It was here that Trinos hoped to find the meddler who had diminished her sparkling gem of Bish.

Her fury over the matter seemed to move her across the black, star-laden expanse with the speed of a thousand dawning suns. Much was destroyed in her wake, past and present.

Her trek ended in front of the great mouth of blackness. The Void was a dark monolith that could swallow moons, planets, stars, and galaxies as easily as a giant swallows a gnat. There it was, larger than anything else in the universe she knew. Her concerns seemed minute in its ominous and foreboding presence, and she lost all track of why she was there for a moment. She was not alone.

Scattered all about the edges of it were tiny glimmering snowflakes that resembled stars. They were immortal ones, such as herself, that gathered here. It was the one place they all became curious about from time to time. At first, it seemed to only be a few. As the depth of space continued, the few began growing beyond all she could see. Each had something discernible from the others. One just had to know what to look for.

She knew they were there for a variety of reasons, such as study, discovery, companionship, or curiosity. There were darker reasons as well. The immortal ones struggled with their tedious and meaningless lives, and every so often, one of those glimmering snowflakes would float into the black space and disappear forever.

Suicide.

They didn't call it that, but Trinos did.

They had tried everything imaginable within their power to test the inner sanctum of the Void. Everything that went in, no matter what the size or substance, never came out again. Some were even so brave as to tether others and lower them inside, but none of them were ever pulled back. It was as if you lowered your fellow over the cliff into a foggy mist, and once you lost sight, the rope went slack and they were lost forever.

Trinos scoffed for a moment as she remembered another time when they'd tried to enclose the Void. It had worked out about as well as trying to put an ocean in a fish bowl. So many immortal beings with no answers, some resigned while others lived on. She would rather live.

She scoured the Void for a burning red flake and soon found it. Scorch teetered close to the edge. *What is he doing?* She wasn't going to let him go anywhere. She wanted answers for his transgressions and she was determined to get them.

34

L ORD ALMEN SLOUCHED OVER HIS desk within his exquisite bedroom chamber. It was one of his favorite places within the safety and confines of his glamorous castle. He rummaged over parchments and ran his long fingers through his thick locks of dark brown hair. The papers were nothing more than ordinary business. The more important records were kept within the realms of his devious and calculating skull. That was what his father had taught him. *If Father could see me now.*

Despite the stern countenance, he was poised, even in moments when a great deal was about to happen. He stretched back his broad shoulders, thinking about his most recent orders. Lord Almen was looking forward to another triumphant day.

He stood up and strolled over to the bay window overlooking his grand courtyard. A whimsical smile crossed his face. Below, his soldiers prepared to venture into the city on new business.

"I know that smirk," a woman said from his side.

He grinned at the strong and pleasant voice that he knew so well. She wrapped her arms around the waist of his black, terry cloth robe.

"You do, do you?" he asked. "And might I ask what that might be?"

"It means you are thinking about last night and this morning, dear husband." Her voice was like the purring of a kitten, turning his smirk to a smile.

"My dear wife, you couldn't be more right, as usual." He turned and pulled her soft body into his, then kissed her. His kiss was one of his finest qualities, she always said, but it was she who had no equal. Her hungry lips aroused him, but he pulled away. She was bewitching to him sometimes — tall, slender, elegant, and beautiful. Her auburn hair was wet and hung just below her neck. Her amber eyes were like a cat's, her nose small and pointed. She loved him, and the feeling was mutual, though there were things he loved more that he'd never admit to.

She had little idea of the havoc he wreaked behind closed doors. All that seemed to matter to her was the glory of being an Almen. What she did know, she never let on to him about. He was fine with that. She was his loyal wife and friend. She gave him the companionship he needed. She also maintained much of the politics and display as the matriarch of the castle. She had been with him a long time, and knew when he was up to something. She just liked to play with that knowledge — another fine quality.

Her smile, though, suggested she had different playful things in mind. She was hard to resist, but more pressing matters had to be attended to first.

"My dear, I am needed elsewhere. Do forgive me?" He hugged her and kissed her neck.

She pouted, but he knew she understood — she always did. "Of course, my love," she said. "But it will cost you."

He felt her soft kiss on his cheek and watched the sensual sway of her hips as she strolled away.

"Enjoy the markets, my dear," he said, biting his lip.

"I will." She turned back toward him in the doorway. "Dear, do you happen to know when Tonio will return? I miss him. How much longer must he remain serving in the outposts?"

As seductive as she'd just been, now he fought the urge to slap her. The question was warranted as a mother, but out of line as a wife. His nails dug into his palms. She was the only person he hated lying to. She had put him on the spot, though. He walked over and grabbed her hands, looking deep into her eyes.

"I have word that he is doing well and will be gone only a few more weeks at most. Be patient, my love, and focus on those others that need your spoiling."

"As you wish." She nodded and walked away.

After returning to his desk, Lord Almen grabbed a sharp letter opener and jammed it into his desktop. He didn't know if she'd believed him or not. He hoped she didn't ask again. What would he tell her next time?

As knowledgeable of current events as the Royal lord was, he had no idea if Tonio was even alive — or McKnight for that matter. Lord Almen assumed Tonio lost or dead; he just had not proven it yet.

Teku had been busy gathering the facts of Tonio's likely demise, and even Sefron had assisted. The Royal lord now questioned his own judgment by risking an alliance with an underling called Oran. He couldn't help but think the underling might have betrayed them all. Nothing ventured, nothing gained, to be sure — but at what cost?

Almen was only mere hours from a reckoning. It was time to put more of his enemies to rest.

35

MELEGAL GLIDED OUT OF THE back stairwell and headed toward the dim alley below. The suns had diminished over the horizon, leaving only a black corridor before him. He considered taking a few rooftops first, but that would require more time and he needed all the extra time he could muster.

Despite the deterrents his former mentor had offered, Melegal was still confident he could locate his finger-growing little friend. He didn't count on the aid of the Motley Girls, but they could at least serve as a possible distraction to his enemies, perhaps drawing attention away from himself or Venir.

Looking down into the dark pathway, Melegal considered that Venir had his own way of doing things, much different than his own. Still, they both were plenty savvy when it came to dealing with the complexities of the deeper secrets of Bone.

He dropped ten feet down onto the narrow road without a sound, and stared onto the main street in the distance, allowing his sight to adjust. Nothing seemed unusual so he moved on, his mind a torrent of thought.

For most, this hunt would be in vain. The city was enormous and crowded. People kept to themselves if they wanted to stay out of trouble. The myriad streets, alleys, catwalks, and building tops would have a newcomer lost within minutes. The colorful and flamboyant banners that marked off the districts did help, but not every portion of the city had an assigned district.

It was easy to get lost on the monstrous roadways that crisscrossed between the walls, seemingly in straight lines, but with deceptive twists and turns. Those who could afford it often traveled on horseback or pony so they could at least see the road signs above the crowds. Personally, Melegal thrived in the mess. It was easy to disappear in when one needed to.

He treaded, gray as a ghost, over the hardened road, feet missing puddles of muck along the way. He could see activity toward the distant end of the confined alley. Cats, rats, and other rodents were busy hunting in the grime. The sounds of arguing and pleasure were heard from the tiny apartment windows scattered just above him.

There was always risk of a swarthy purse cutter to challenge him. It wasn't likely, though, as they all knew him. Anyone else was open game. He was halfway up the alley when an ominous figure stepped out of the shadows a dozen feet before him. He froze, his spine tingling in alarm. Scented oil filled his nostrils, mixed with something else. This wasn't a common cut purse. It was someone dangerous.

Melegal squinted, making out the tall image before him. The man was olive-skinned and wore long, white robe-like garments and high-strapped sandals. He didn't appear to be carrying a weapon as his arms were concealed behind him, but whoever it was had something to hide.

His nerves burst like sparks in his veins. He remained still, calm, waiting for his assailant to act. *Must be an assassin. Dangerous. Not from Bone.* He breathed in through his nostrils. *Kitchen spices.*

Melegal stared at the assassin.

Evade. Evade. Evade

No sooner had he thought it than twin blades flicked his way. *Son of Bish! Get to the street, Melegal. Disappear.* He backpedaled while dodging the two blades that licked toward his neck like serpent's tongues. *Man, he's fast. Can't get pinned at the back wall. Must parry, dodge, run … or be dead.*

The man pressed inward with his two long butterfly knives dancing in a foreign cadence. The long arms and blades fully defended the alley against Melegal, slipping past the attacker.

Whistling cuts sliced over Melegal's ears and under his chin, over and over again. His shoulders and feet shifted between stabs and undercuts like he was a fencer. The flurry came at him from all directions. He never took his eye off the man. The assassin's white smile was confident. It was only a matter of time before he cut the thief to ribbons. Most men would have been dead seconds long gone, but Melegal was far better at dodging death than most would presume.

Dozens of cut-and-thrust combinations executed to perfection came his way. He dodged the blades like a fish in water. Sweat furrowed on the man's brow, his breath labored. Melegal's own lungs were on fire. He fought the urge to place his hands on his hips and rest.

The strange man stopped his assault, nodding at Melegal. *Not so easy to kill, am I?* He wanted to make a run for the wall and scramble up to the roof, but the man was too fast. The assailant angled around, then lowered the tips of his knives near the ground.

Melegal felt cornered for what seemed to be the tenth time that day. It didn't sit well with him. It was tight situations like these that he went out of his way to avoid. Now he had no other choice. *Pull out the Twins. No time for games. Wish I hadn't taken that last drink. Pull one out, or both? One! Both! One! Both!* His pride caved to survival and he drew two black-hilted and razor-sharp short swords. They would be a quicker match for the heavy butterfly swords.

Melegal always considered the twin swords use to be an inferior option of defense opposed to running or talking himself out of a dangerous situation, but it had come to this—a brutal last ditch effort to save his life. Yet it still felt like surrender to him. He'd rather avoid the heavy hardware. He was still overmatched, but some swordplay would buy him more time. *All right girls,* he thought, twirling the twin blades, *it's time to play.*

The ring of clanging metal filled the alley as the assassin laid into him like a conductor of death. Melegal parried like a defender of life. The heavier blows of the robed man beat down the lighter blades over and over again. Melegal's cherished swords popped right back up with their own ferocity. His clothes were sliced here and there, but his blood remained in place. *Can't kill what you can't hit.*

The sharp clangs came quickly, over and over, both men pressing for the advantage, back and forth, ducking, dodging, and jumping like skilled acrobats trapped in a cage of vipers. Melegal's arms grew heavy. *Oh, man, this is getting old. Gotta try something new. Arms feel like fire and lead.* He labored for breath, a thin film of sweat glistening over his hands. *Too much booze. I should have stayed in bed.*

He avoided grappling swords with the larger man. The man wanted to suck him in and cut him down. The fighter whirled before Melegal, tireless and cold. Melegal wanted nothing more than to gouge out the man's eyes, but he couldn't take the risk. The butterfly blades banged down over and over, jolting his arms as he struggled with his grip. It was only a matter of time.

Then the assailant backed off, winded. Melegal kept his guard up. He eyed the man, whose mouth opened to reveal filed teeth. *Now why would you do that to your teeth? Oh, yeah … he's an assassin. Better not bite me. I don't want to die by biting. I won't be buried with bite marks. Gotta get out of here.*

Melegal waited while the man backed farther away. *What is he up to now?* The man took off his robes. *Pervert.*

The man stood before him, a polished figure of slender corded muscles and white tattoos, garnished with an array of throwing knives. Melegal's hopes of survival sank to his toes.

Along the man's colored forearms were bracer-like contraptions. *Son of Bish!* Melegal recognized the dart launchers that many warriors coveted, but could not afford. *I knew I should have gotten some of those.* He could not dodge them all. "I assume you are hired to kill me only, not capture me?" Melegal asked.

The man nodded, checking his dart contraptions.

He's got the drop on me. I'm looking at dodging about ten poisoned darts. No way. Not in this condition.

The alley seemed to shrink before him. His path barred, he was unprepared and overmatched. The dart launcher was a powerful weapon, fast and accurate. He had seen one work before and this man had two of them. Retreating was his only option, but it was a terrible plan. His last moments on Bish would be spent in a meaningless alley of muck. His life would end as meaninglessly as it began.

Melegal lowered his blades. *It's just as well. I'm tired of the hassle. I wish I could have helped save the boy, though.*

The assassin took aim. The man had a throwing blade ready to go in each hand as well.

Not leaving anything to chance. Melegal pulled back his shoulders, chest out. *This is it – my final move.* Melegal bent his knees while loosening the grip on his swords. A familiar sound caught his ear. He cocked his head.

"Eh?" the assassin said, casting a bent ear over his shoulder.

I hope that's what I think it is.

Melegal listened.

Whirl …

Whizz …

Whop!

The assassin's chin buckled into his chest. He dropped to his knees. A large sling bullet echoed off the cobblestone. Melegal ran before it hit the street. He hurdled the man like a giant greyhound before the assassin could blink.

At the end of the alley, Melegal spied his tiny, sling-wielding hero. "Run!"

And Lefty did, a few paces ahead of Melegal.

Don't look back, Melegal warned himself. *Go legs! Go!*

He cut around the alley corner as a barrage of darts imbedded into the stone walls where his body had been a fraction of a second ago. A dart caught one man in the ankle and another in the hip. Both men stiffened and face planted into the street.

Melegal ran past the halfling as the boy turned to find him. The halfling had no trouble keeping up, though. *I can't believe it,* Melegal thought over and over again.

"Who was that, Me?" Lefty yelled from behind.

"Don't know," Melegal said, tears streaming down his face.

"Good shot, huh?"

"Greatest shot ever!"

After wiping his eyes, Melegal turned and saw that Lefty was grinning.

Rayal lost the halfling when he burst from an alley, chased by a very thin man. Then the man passed the halfling and they were both gone. Two innocent men dropped dead before her and a crowd began to gather. She peered down the alley, and soon a dark man stepped out, rubbing his head.

Her blood turned cold. They must have been running from him. She wanted to run too. No doubt her little friend was in danger, but there was little she could do. Her trek back to the barns was long and lonesome as she thought of adventure.

36

THE MOTLEY GIRLS WENT TO work. They began by bullying, abusing, coercing, and beating any local cut purses or alley snipes they could find. While Haze was off following the cat, Frigdah and Sis worked over one particular street rogue.

Sis slapped the man's cheeks while her stocky sister held him in a headlock. The beggar was young and ferret-faced with snot streaming from his nose.

Sis grabbed his greasy black hair. "Did you see the men I described or not? And no more of that forked tongue of yours."

He rolled his beady eyes. "You know, Sis, you are about as pretty as you are friendly."

"Oh … is that so? Why, thank you!" Sis punched his belly.

He groaned as he sagged.

She leaned over and stared deep in his eyes. "Did you think that was friendly, little rodent? Because that is how I likes to be friendly."

"No … uh … no surprise that you hit like a man," he said, still groaning.

Sis nodded and Frigdah ramped up the pressure. His head became purple. Sis pounded his belly over and over. The bigger sister finally let him loose. He fell, gasping for breath and clutching his stomach. Sis knelt and put a knife to his throat, then whispered in a hiss, "All right, you've made it pretty clear you know something, or you wouldn't be acting up like this, boy. I've no time for games. Tell me what you know or Frigdah here is gonna put a hole in that hungry belly of yours."

His eyes widened as Frigdah pushed the tip of her blade into his gut. He sobbed. "I-I-I … know the men. They killed some of us just for watching. I don't want to die." The man balled up on the ground. "They've been back and forth between here, the south gate, and the odd district. I've only seen them go back there once. I didn't follow though. Usually the one with the black hat just hangs around, watching the streets, and then moving on. Those men scare me, so I hid from them the last few days."

"How long's this been going on?" Sis asked.

"Weeks at least."

"Anything else that might help?"

He shook his head. Sis lifted his chin with her blade. He flailed his hands.

"All right! All right!" he cried. "They ain't the only ones. There are others. Royals and the like. Men like I've never seen before armed to the teeth. Please just let me go. I swear if you do, I'll disappear and never let my curiosity get the better of me again."

Sis and Frigdah both looked around.

"They here now?" Sis asked.

"Probably."

"All right, boy. One more thing—those two men, where do you think they headed last?"

"Towards the south gate. Don't know where. "

"Off with you then. Not a word—and here." She handed him two coppers.

He looked at the coins, then tossed them to the ground and ran away.

Sis crouched along the wall, not sure what they had committed themselves to. She and her sisters were survivors, almost as fearless as they were rugged. Still, she didn't want to get caught up in the Royal games again. Frigdah's belly growled beside her and she realized she was hungry too. Her meaty sister pulled out a stick of salami and half a loaf of bread from underneath her baggy clothes. Frigdah broke apart the food and handed some to Sis.

"Gee, thanks," Sis said, looking down at the bread and meat, but not taking it. "Just what I wanted—sweaty food."

Frigdah shrugged and ate.

Sis turned away. The minutes grew long as she waited for Haze to return. She hoped Haze hadn't run into trouble. But what if she had?

Sis needed to find out. "Come on," Sis said. "Let's go."

They moved through the darkness toward where Haze had been headed. Sis kept up a brisk pace, her nerves on edge. In the back of her mind, she felt that someone or something was watching them.

Something was definitely wrong.

She stopped, listened. All she heard was her sister's heavy breathing. She turned, facing Frigdah, and put her fingers to her lips. Frigdah drew in her breath and held it. *Why is she so dumb?* Frigdah's eyes widened in alarm, and something hit Sis in the back.

Smack!

She whirled, dagger raised, and saw Haze's grinning face.

"Bone!" Sis grasped at her chest, ignoring Haze's chuckles. "You skinny tramp! Don't do that anymore. You know I don't like it!"

"I found Octopus," Haze said.

"No surprise, cat lady," Sis said. "You probably sniffed him out. Now on with it."

Her gangly sister often spent time looking for strange cats of a unique pedigree. When Haze came across some of the unique litters, she made decent coin. At the same time, Haze could protect those litters from less noble and caring cat hunters.

"C'mon," Haze said, waving for them to follow her.

Haze ran through the alley's twists and turns into a place that even Sis didn't know. She stood alongside Haze, staring at an ancient archway long forgotten. Deep inside the archway stood a heavy door. Haze pulled Sis and Frigdah inside.

"Listen," Haze whispered.

A deep rumbling came from the other side of the door. Sis recognized it as the purr of Octopus. Sis climbed onto

Frigdah's big shoulders and peered through a tiny opening at the top of the entryway. The big, eight-clawed cat sat deep inside a dim corridor that ended at another door. Sis jumped down and tested the door. *Locked, of course.*

Studying the keyhole, Sis caught Haze motioning at her out of the corner of her eye, but Sis also heard faint footsteps approaching. *Someone's coming!*

Sis pulled out a corkscrew-shaped tool and shoved it inside the lock. She gave it a twist.

Nothing.

The footsteps grew louder. She wrenched the tool again. Still nothing. The footsteps were way too close for comfort. Grabbing Frigdah and Haze by the arms, Sis pressed herself along the wall, deep into the shadows.

A few seconds later, two men passed by the doorway without pause and continued on. Sis exhaled, then stepped forward and wrenched the lock one more time. It broke free. The cat now sat in front of the door at the end of the corridor. Even from where she stood in the dim hall, Sis could see that the door was solid steel, with not a single crack around the edges.

37

D ETECTIVE McKNIGHT SPIT AND CURSED when he discovered Chongo was gone. Tonio looked all over the stable, tossing hay and trying to help the detective locate the dog. He didn't understand why McKnight kept hitting him with his hat and yelling at him. The dog might help them in their plan, but Tonio just wanted to kill Venir. He didn't understand why he had to wait—and why they needed the dog so badly, and why McKnight was so mad at him and raving about "ransom."

Revenge Tonio understood, but not ransom.

"Someone had to have seen something," McKnight said. "Melegal could not have done this. Impossible!"

"Should have killed dog," Tonio said. "Dead dog can't run."

"Shut up, you imbecile! I'll do the thinking," McKnight shouted in his face.

Tonio grasped for McKnight's neck, but the detective ducked away.

"Don't yell at me!" Tonio said.

The swarthy man backed away, nodding. "Fine. Tonio, go and check on the boy. Put your cloak back on and don't be followed. I am going to try to figure out what happened to the dog. I will catch up with you there. I won't be far behind. And don't screw it up!"

Still feeling anger at how the detective treated him, Tonio stepped toward McKnight again.

McKnight put his hands up and shook his head. "It's no time to get emotional, Tonio. We have revenge to enact. Venir … remember? Just go!" McKnight waved him off.

"Venir … yes." Tonio walked away. He knew, deep down, that he was not a dolt. He was a Royal, after all. He remembered that … but his mind just didn't seem as sharp as before.

Venir's fault.

He had to concentrate on everything now, and it wasn't easy. He just wanted to kill Venir and go home. Even as he left the stables, Tonio had trouble remembering home—but his mother … she was the one he remembered the most. He felt something warm—and good—when he thought of her, but he didn't know what that was exactly.

Tonio's mood turned dark when he reminded himself where he was headed and why.

It was all because of Venir.

And when he thought of Venir, something inside him burned.

McKnight remained in the stables, checking the floor over and over, but he couldn't make out much of anything because of all the hay. The impressions seemed to suggest a child had been in the room. Maybe a small dog, too. Outside of the stable, though, he'd found no tracks from any size dog at all, just a child's. It was a mystery. The halfling boy could have been behind it, but how would he have known where to find the dog? It was not possible, other than chance.

Donning his cloak again, McKnight decided to head back to the stable from where they'd taken Georgio—and Chongo. But first he'd give this barn's courtyard another quick study. He looked and listened—and finally discovered something of interest. Earlier in the day, a girl claimed to have seen a boy carrying a two-headed puppy.

Puppy?

It didn't make any sense to McKnight, but it was too much of a coincidence to ignore.

He shook down those he could, but no one could confirm the story. Frustrated, McKnight stormed back to the stable from where they'd taken Georgio. He stepped inside the stall, looking for a sign, but it was as if nothing had ever been there. Someone had covered their tracks well.

"Blast it all to Bish!" McKnight threw his hat to the ground and screamed, causing several roosting pigeons above to burst from the rafters.

The savvy man from Bone stood there, unsure what to do. *Stay or move?* He could not decide.

38

V ENIR WADED THROUGH THE STREETS, paying no mind to those he jostled. Others steered clear of his hot glare. Curses and daggers were poised for his back, but when he turned, they found silence and sheaths again. A drunken group of revelers stumbled into his path. He knocked them to the side and tossed one through a window.

Leezir the Slerg had warned Venir they were coming for him, but he was only worried about the boy and Chongo. His thoughts were haunted by Tonio's arrogant face. What had he done?

As for the rest, let them come. He could still feel gazes on him. Whether they were friend or foe, or just someone of interest, he didn't know. He was ready regardless. Underlings or Royals … he'd kill them all. He kicked a crate and slipped deeper into the city.

Venir knew the city as well as any natural-born citizen. Over the years, Melegal had managed to talk him in and out of places only the uncommon kept. The thief had spots he liked for them to hide in as well. They'd hidden supplies here and there for when they were on the lam time and again.

One place the thief regarded with esteem was an old castle in the city of the Royals that had all but been forgotten long ago. Melegal swore it was his place of birth, but the castle had obviously been long gone before he came to be. Figuring that claiming the place was easier on his friend than dealing with the reality that he didn't know, Venir never disagreed.

Venir arrived in an area that was little more than rocks and rubble. It lay just outside the edge of the Royal district. Its secrets and history were now long buried, and its riches lost to time. Partial walls of some rooms still stood and stairways started here and there. Many vagrant families appeared to reside within the grounds. The once grand castle was now nothing more than ruins and refuse. It made good hiding, Melegal had said. Their spot was a spire, almost three stories tall, still standing amidst the grounds.

A narrow, spiraling stairway of odd, grayish marble made its way into an abandoned tower. Venir headed to the tower's top like an alley cat. Inside was a small room under collapsed, gabled roofs. Birds and rats scattered at his sound, but some remained. He looked out from a window opening, the stonework of which still held. The rogue once told him this was where his father looked on the grounds and people below. It was still a great view of the city.

Castle Almen looked magnificent not so far away. Its lights shone in the hundreds among its common grounds and rooms. The rest of the district's castles were illuminated the same. Some were lit by fire and gas, and others by magic provided by the wizards of Bone. Most wizards were among the Royal families. A few managed to protect their prospective investments and homes to a reasonable degree.

Venir watched the activity below. His eyes were sharp at night, but he had something else that would make them even more acute. He removed his backpack and unrolled the large leather sack within. He paused before reaching inside. He pulled out Brool, his cherished hand-and-a-half axe, kissed its blade, and murmured, "Soon, brother … soon." The shield was next. He pulled out the helm, its spike glimmering in the moon's red light, and put it on.

Greater awareness swept through him, his senses sharpened like razors. The details were clearer in the night and he could see farther and with greater clarity. The images were still dark, but he could detect more movements deep in the shadows that easily would be missed by the naked eye. Sounds were amplified, almost annoyingly. In the Outlands, there weren't as many distractions, but in the city, sounds of the usual discourse were overwhelming. He tuned it out, focusing on a single source.

The magic in the helm was powerful. His overall sense of awareness was improved and he needed that edge to find Georgio. He focused on his memory of the boy's voice and image minute after minute. The troubled warrior hoped his plan might bear some evidence of the boy's whereabouts. After long minutes, though, it did not. He thought of Tonio, the arrogant fool whose folly had gotten him into this, but there was nothing there, either.

More man-urchins lurked in great numbers nearby. Castle Almen seemed to bustle with more armored men than usual. They were gearing up for something, but he doubted so many men were coming after him.

And still, no sign of Georgio.

Venir tore off the helm and dropped it. He noticed someone standing there.

"Miss us?" Melegal asked.

"I knew you were there. I heard you moments ago," Venir said, looking at his friend and Lefty.

"Funny, but we've been here for hours."

"Now's not the time to split hairs, Melegal." He walked over and hoisted up Lefty. "I'm glad you're back with us."

The boy's smile was sheepish. "Me, too. I'm sorry, Venir, I didn't find Georgio—but Chongo and Quickster are fine."

He almost dropped him. "Really! How did that come to be?"

"Well, I went to the stable and Mood was there …"

The boy recounted the whole tale of how he encountered Mood, rescued Chongo, and saved Melegal from certain death. It was a quick recount, but accurate. The thief confirmed it all with grudgeless nods of confirmation. The thief's time with the halfling boy had apparently been well spent.

"So, did your fancy helm find anything?" Melegal asked.

"No, but I say it's time to have at them all." Venir grabbed Brool. "Let's find those fiends and let loose on them. We'll carve Georgio's location from their black hearts if we have to. We've got the jump on them now. Let's go!"

Melegal stepped into his path. "No, let's wait. We'll do what you say, but let's be more subtle, Vee. They are bound to secure Georgio if he's not with the dog. We still have plenty of time to track them. McKnight and Tonio stick out like sore thumbs around here—although somehow they've managed to not alert anyone at Castle Almen. You know Lord Almen would have taken action by now if he knew they were around. So, hey, it might take some coin, but we can get them quietly. But from here on out, we stick together. Agreed?"

Venir looked at his friend. "Fine, but we gotta be moving. I have to feel like I'm doing something. And Brool stays out." He put the shield and helm back inside the sack, stuffed it into the backpack, and shouldered it on. He covered Brool's blades and spike in a heavy cloth and slid it between the backpack and his shoulder blades. Plenty of people were armed in Bone, but Brool was a menacing attention-getter and there was no need for that right now.

The thief rolled his eyes and the three of them treaded down the stairs in hopes of catching a break and locating Georgio.

39

OCTOPUS PUFFED UP AS HAZE and Sis approached. Frigdah stood guard at the outer entryway. Sis stayed back while Haze tossed the cat a treat. The big feline sniffed it, reluctant to drop the boy's finger from his mouth, and growled. Sis wanted no part of a cat scratch and nudged her sister. Haze started purring, something Sis had heard her do many times before. The cat sauntered over, rubbing along Haze's skinny legs. Sis stepped to the steel door. It had a handle, but no lock. She pulled. It creaked, but did not budge.

"Haze," Sis said in a quiet voice. "Get Frigdah down here."

Haze whistled, and Frigdah's hulking silhouette lumbered through the entryway.

"Frig," Sis said, "I can't open it. Fetch me somethin' to pry it open—or knock it through with something. Be quick, though."

Frigdah pressed her broad shoulders against the door, and the metal groaned, but did not budge. Sis punched Frigdah in the arm and received a funny look in return.

What is she thinking now? Sis thought. Yes, Frigdah was a big woman—over six feet tall and every bit of two hundred twenty pounds. Sis had seen Frigdah's thick forearms slam down a bigger man's in contests before. She was the muscle of the Motley Girls among other things, but she wasn't someone who could knock down doors.

Sis punched her again. "What are you doing? You're not going to bust through it! So get going and find a pry bar of some kind. Time's a wasting!"

"But—"

"Go!" Sis said.

Frigdah turned, head hanging, and walked back out. Sis ran her fingers over the edges of the door and the walls that encased it. She banged on it a couple times. They were at a dead end. She hoped her sister found something useful, and soon. She wanted to find the boy and go. She had no desire to trifle with the Royals.

A rush of heavy footsteps came their way. Octopus sprang away, and Haze scrambled flat against the wall. Sis turned just in time to see a large figure rush toward them. She dove out of the way just as she heard a familiar voice yell, "Gangway!"

Frigdah crashed into the door, shattering the hinges and knocking it flat with a loud *whump!* And Frigdah kept on going into a torch-lit corridor. She finally stumbled and fell. As Sis rose, Frigdah rolled down a spiral stone staircase. As she rushed forward, Sis heard a few *ooff's* and *oww's* before it sounded like Frigdah came to a full stop below.

Octopus ran past Sis, a fuzzy black streak, and disappeared down the staircase. Sis waited with Haze at the top of the stairs, then heard a groan as Frigdah crawled back up to them.

"Geez, Frig," Haze said, "wha'cha been eating these days?"

Stumbling to her feet, Frigdah pulled a large flask out with a meaty hand and sucked it down. "Whatever I can get my hands on, I guess. Did I do good, Sis?"

Sis put her hands on Frigdah's big shoulders and looked her dead in the eye. "Yeah, Frig. But next time you better warn me before you almost trample me."

"Sorry," she said, smiling.

Sis slapped her on the rump.

40

IN THE DARK AND DANK cell, Georgio lay curled up, sobbing. His tummy kept rumbling, and he was cold, miserable, and scared. Everything was black thanks to the last of the torches finally dying. He could not see his own hand, but he could hear and feel plenty. Roaches crawled under and over him. The rats nipped at his flesh and he wailed in pain. He'd never killed so many living things before, but he knew that numerous rats and bugs lay crushed on the floor all around him. He felt exhausted and he could fight no more.

Still the vermin came. He was in agony.

"Vee … where are you?" he mumbled.

A few minutes later, Georgio heard what sounded like someone pounding on a door somewhere nearby. His heart thumped with fear. McKnight and Tonio were coming back. What else would they do to him? What would they cut off?

But … what if it was Vee or Melegal coming to save him?

He listened and heard nothing. Hope faded as he cried again. There was a loud crash. He sat up.

"Vee?" Georgio tried to stand, but could not. Odd sounds and someone grunting and groaning, followed by some unfamiliar voices caught his ear. Torchlight flickered through the small window in the door. It might as well have been the sun, but it brought no warmth. The rats scurried away and a sense of relief assailed him.

But something was wrong. He didn't hear Venir. He drew himself into the corner and shivered.

Then came a loud *clatch!* —and the sound of metal hitting stone. The door swung open as he shielded his eyes. A blur came his way and he heard a squeak followed by a crunch. He blinked several times to let his eyes adjust, and then saw that Octopus had a large rat crushed in his mouth. A few steps behind the cat, three strange, ugly women hissed at him to come with them fast.

He didn't move.

One finally came toward him and shook him with her warm hands, but he balled up even tighter, and kept shaking.

"Haze, give him a shirt or something," said the woman who had shaken him.

Haze took off a heavy cotton sweater and tossed it to the other woman.

"All right, boy, my name's Sis," the woman said as she leaned closer. "This is Haze, and that's Frigdah. We're sisters. You're safe now. We're going to take you home—back to your friend Venir. He's been looking for you."

Georgio relaxed a bit, then sat up and tried to stand. "Vee?" he croaked through dry lips.

"Yes," Sis said, rubbing his cold arms.

Haze stepped forward and put a canteen to his lips. The water tasted good—and cold.

The big cat crawled onto his lap.

"Octopus," Georgio mumbled. He gained strength as the water refreshed him and the big cat licked the blood off his hands. Haze and Sis stood him up and put the long sweater on him.

"Please … please get me out of here," Georgio cried. "Take me to Vee. Please."

Tears welled up in all the women's eyes. Georgio didn't know who they were, but he figured they must be on his side.

"All right, Georgio. We're going. Do you want us to carry you?" Sis asked.

He raised an eyebrow.

"No, I'm … a big boy," Georgio said. "Let's hurry before they come back."

Frigdah led followed by Sis, Georgio, and Haze. Frigdah and Haze each held torches as they all headed up the damp, moldy stairway. They had almost reached the top of the staircase when Frigdah stopped. It was quiet for a moment, but then raspy breathing echoed from above, along with shuffling of feet.

Georgio squeezed Sis's hand and began trembling again. Terror struck his heart, and tears streamed down his face. "I don't want my fingers cut off again!"

The shuffling feet and breathing grew louder as someone approached, barring the way to freedom. In the dimness atop the stairs, a man stood before them, slowly removing a tattered cloak. The women all gasped at the shirtless figure standing before them, then stepped backward, shielding Georgio.

There Tonio was—ghastly, tall, and powerful in the flickering torchlight. One of the sisters whispered a curse. Tonio sneered, his split face even more terrifying in the torchlight. Georgio's would-be rescuers drew their blades, hands shaking, but still standing their ground. Georgio saw the hilt of his own sword strapped to Tonio's back, but the giant man didn't draw it. He just looked at them all and smiled.

"Don't let him get me!" Georgio turned and tried to run back down the stairs, but Sis held him tight. Tonio just waited, arms across his chest—and then he came toward them.

"Sisters!" Sis said. "Gimme those torches now. Haze, guard the boy and be ready to run."

Sis slipped off her shabby cloak, then snuffed out the torches. In the near darkness, Georgio could see that Tonio had stopped on the steps above them. Georgio held onto Haze, watching and listening.

"Wrap his legs," Sis whispered to Frigdah. Then Sis yelled, "Let's go!"

All three sisters battle-cried and Georgio was jerked up the stairs.

Ahead of him, Sis lunged forward in the darkness, blade first, and took a stab at where she no doubt hoped Tonio's throat would be. Tonio's fist crashed into her jaw, and she staggered into the wall.

Frigdah grabbed onto the man's legs and squeezed them with all her might. Tonio hammered blows downward, but she didn't budge. Haze pulled Georgio tight as they watched the horror of it all. Sis recovered, tackling Tonio while he was still off balance. The three thrashed about for several seconds as Tonio struggled to break free from their desperate clutches. Cries of pain and anguish rang in Georgio's ears. He could barely see what was going on.

Sis cried out, "Haze, get him out of here!"

Haze jerked on his arm, but Georgio was too scared to budge. The thin sister hoisted him over her shoulder and ran up the stairs.

Tonio pummeled Sis and Frigdah with jarring fury. The man grabbed at Haze's nimble legs. He caught her ankle and jerked, and Georgio tumbled hard onto the stairs.

The big woman, Frigdah, bit Tonio in the calf, but the violent man still managed to grab him and Haze by the hair, pulling them into the fray. Tonio head-butted Frigdah with Haze's head, knocking Haze out cold. Frigdah, though, still held onto his legs like a leech.

Georgio wailed, kicking and screaming.

Tonio pulled a knife from a small scabbard on his hip and stabbed at the big woman clutching his legs. The blade plunged deep into her shoulder. She screamed, and lost her grip.

Georgio closed his eyes as Tonio raised the blade for a killing blow. Then he heard a growl and a scream—from Tonio.

Georgio opened his eyes to see Tonio's face and throat catching the full onslaught of thirty-two claws ripping into him like a furry black tornado. Octopus's white claws tore deep into the man's eyes, nose, and throat. Tonio roared in pain. He grabbed the cat by the scruff of the neck to try and pull him off with his free hand, but Octopus only tore up his face more. As Georgio kicked at the demonic man, Tonio tried to stab the cat.

Sis finally recovered and launched herself onto Tonio's arm, pulling it down with all her might. Georgio saw an opening and flew up the twisting stairs without a glance back. The screams and yells echoed along with screeches of the savage cat.

He just kept running.

On the stairs, Tonio's body began to bloat from the wounds suffered by the cat's claws. He could feel the effect spreading like poison through his system. Using both hands, he finally tore the cat from his bloodied and shredded face.

As soon as the creature hit the steps, it scurried upward. Tonio continued his onslaught on the women, leaving them in a battered and bloodied heap on the stairs, all unmoving. He recovered his dagger and limped up the stairs after the boy.

Georgio had no idea where he was. Thoughts of freedom from the terrors he'd faced caused him to try and get as far away as he could. He couldn't have cared less where he was going, at least until he stopped to catch his breath.

Looking around, he couldn't believe his eyes when he saw Octopus running toward him.

"Octopus," Georgio said, gasping for air. "Did … Did you come to find me?"

The big cat rubbed across his legs and bounded off, only to stop a few dozen feet up the street, apparently waiting for the boy.

"All right, I'll follow you, but I hope you're going home."

The big cat cut in and out of several alleys that Georgio didn't recognize. After several minutes, things became familiar, and his fears of Tonio were left behind.

Never in his life would he have imagined that people could do such terrible things to him, but at the same time, he was starting to get used to the fact that he had a hard time dying. He clutched at his right hand where Tonio had cut off his fingers, still in disbelief that they had grown back. He actually couldn't wait to show Venir.

Georgio wasn't far from the Drunken Octopus now, and once in sight of it, he ran full speed to get inside the tavern and find Venir, or Melegal. If they weren't there, then he would head up to the apartment where he was sure Lefty would be—that was if Lefty wasn't out looking for him too.

Seeing a gaping hole in the Drunken Octopus's wall, Georgio jumped through and found himself amidst a crowd of activity. No one gave the boy any notice as he navigated the tavern floor, but Georgio didn't see any familiar faces. Without waiting, he headed up the stairs, floor after floor, to the top where they lived. The door was locked, so he knocked.

No answer.

Over and over he knocked until he convinced himself they all must be out looking for him. He rubbed his growling stomach. Hopefully, the barkeep would let him wait for their return and feed him in the meantime. He headed back down the stairs and crept behind the bar unnoticed.

The smell of cooked food wafted into his nostrils from the kitchen behind the bar. Someone had some meat-and-vegetable stew brewing, along with bread in the oven. He forgot about everything and ducked into the back.

A rugged woman in her sixties stood by the oven, and saw Georgio right away. She looked over him. Georgio remembered meeting her once before, but he didn't know her name. She said nothing, but nodded toward him, then sat him down and fed him. She kept about her business and left the hungry boy to himself.

After stuffing himself full, Georgio left the kitchen, satisfied as if all his troubles had gone away. He rubbed his belly as he sauntered into the tavern. Once again, he made his way through the smoke-filled and crowded room until he reached the fireplace. The warmth on his face was welcoming and inviting, and he lost himself in the fire's glow. He let his eyes fall shut as he relaxed and sleep pressed in on him. Moments passed and he opened his eyes, blinking a few times. He looked to his left and then his right—only to lock eyes with McKnight.

41

THE ROYAL FAMILIES IN BONE often battled in the shadows when in conflict. The clever infiltration of a castle would allow one to usurp another. Assassination, blackmail, marriage, and bribery were often the sources of those insidious struggles for power. Vows were broken, and families split as a result of desperate survival from oblivion or being cast out to the streets or even banished from Bone all together.

There were other ways, more forceful ways, to weaken another house from the outside rather than within. Every Royal castle had at their disposal specialized men and women that battled in the dark streets and alleys from time to time. They waited, then tracked and trapped the careless and overconfident smaller groups of exposed or weaker Royal families in the alleys, striking quickly and leaving a bloody message in the streets.

And they covered their tracks well.

These cadres consisted of skilled and seasoned soldiers, the most trusted guards of the Royals. They had been hardened from wars and skirmishes all over Bish. Some had even fought at the Warfield, the most renowned battlefield in the world. Their peers respected their prowess. They lived as Royals, given creature comforts and status within the castles. They were the overseers of the training and security affairs of the family. They were called the Shadow Sentries, and they enforced fear throughout the city—but Leezir wondered if the mighty Venir had even the smallest place in his heart for fear of these deadly fighters.

From the rooftops, Leezir watched Venir and his two companions pass by along the dark street below.

Be ready, warrior.

Not long after Venir and his friends had passed, a trio of Shadow Sentries—from Lord Almen, no doubt—slipped quietly along the street as well, their black armor blending them into the shadows. Leezir cupped his hand behind his ear.

Bone! They're wearing ghost armor.

The Almen House was apparently taking little risk. The armor was proof of that. It was rare—black-dyed braided cloth, woven with tiny rings of steel and brass by magic. It was as effective as a full suit of chain mail, but light and quiet like clothing. Leezir grimaced as the Shadow Sentries brandished swords, daggers, axes, crossbows, spears, and the like. He had seen their work before. They were cunning as assassins, ferocious as panthers, and as merciless as hobgoblins. Now they sought a lone man—their mission to hunt down and kill Venir.

Thankfully, Leezir wasn't alone in his monitoring of Venir. The man-urchins also kept watch on the streets. The ambush was set with Venir and his companions as the bait. Leezir felt he had little choice other than to use Venir as a pawn to draw out the Almens. The man had been doomed from the moment he returned. At least Leezir was giving him a fighting chance.

His trap was ready to be sprung.

Leezir's man-urchins crouched deep in the nooks and windows, eager to strike. In the dimness below, Leezir could see his own men poised to lash out at the Shadow Sentries. He had the numbers, but the ragged man-urchins would be pressed to overtake the legendary soldiers below. The darts of his man-urchins would be of little use against the ghost armor. They would have to rely on their overwhelming numbers to take them. *Cut their throats and run*. It was all Leezir wanted, just to chip away at the Almen forces a piece at a time. Licking his lips as he rubbed his hands together, Leezir prepared the signal.

42

Venir, Melegal, and Lefty had traveled on foot, crisscrossing streets and alleys the best they could to try and shake down any information about Georgio—and also to draw out the assailants Leezir had told Venir about. Lefty urged Venir to return to the Drunken Octopus. Venir had never heard of sweating halfling's feet, but the boy seemed convincing enough. Melegal reminded Venir that the Motley Girls might have returned to the tavern and have something of use to share. It felt like the entire city was against Venir, and he was uncertain where to go. He was itching to kill something, but he had to find the boy.

Melegal and Lefty stayed busy behind Venir, keeping tabs on their pursuers. Venir could feel man-urchin eyes everywhere, from all around and even above on the one and two-story rooftops. The man-urchins posed little threat to Venir or his friends. The Shadow Sentries, though, were a different matter.

Venir pulled Melegal and the halfling out of sight. "This is getting silly, you two!" Venir whispered through gritted teeth. "I am ready to get on with this. I need to get the drop on them. Did you get a count, Me?"

"Over a dozen man-urchins are posted on the roofs for certain, and the ground-pounders of Castle Almen account for at least three or more. I don't think they can take us," Melegal whispered.

Venir glared at him.

Melegal looked away from his gaze and said, "I think they're trying to cut us off."

"Georgio is near, I swear it!" Lefty cried.

Venir clamped a hand over Lefty's mouth, then knelt down and gazed into Lefty's watery blue eyes.

"Listen," Venir whispered. "If the Royal dogs make their move before we get back to the tavern, you two take Georgio's charge. Don't let them catch you, and don't worry about me. I don't have the stomach for killing men normally, but I've had my fill of these Royals screwing around. It's time Brool and I taught them a lesson. Besides, I don't need anyone else being caught up in their clutches."

They both nodded at him.

Venir's voice was strained as he said, "You must find Georgio. Otherwise, this madness may never come to an end."

There was silence. The air was thick. A sense of dread filled the alley.

Venir didn't know what the limitations of his friends were in this kind of situation, but they were about to be tested. The farther away from him they could get, the better. This fight had to be his alone. Doubt filled his belly. He had no idea how many pursuers were coming. Battles abroad on Bish were one thing, but fights in the city were an entirely different animal. You might live to fight another day, but the Royals would make you pay. Victory only led to temporary salvation.

Venir stood up. "The plan is to check out the Drunken Octopus and then the stables if we get split up. I will have to catch you at one or the other. Are we good?"

"I'm good," Melegal said.

"I'm good, too," Lefty said.

"Me," Venir said, "take us through."

43

THREE SHADOW SENTRIES CROUCHED IN the middle of the filth-ridden alley called Death Hall. It was just where Leezir wanted them. At the other end, Venir and his two companions entered the alley. The three Shadow Sentries headed for Venir and his friends. Leezir put his fingers in his lips and blew.

A loud whistle burst forth, echoing down the corridor.

The three sentries were swarmed by figures that appeared from behind building corners, out of windows, and up from of sewer grates. The man-urchins closed in fast. A dozen of them surrounded the three sentries, who now stood in a defensive triangle. Two sentries wielded swords and daggers, while the other held two wicked hand axes.

Leezir felt glee, but as he looked toward the other end of the alley he noticed that five more Shadow Sentries had appeared. Venir was cut off at his end. The Shadow Sentries had them all boxed in.

As the screams began, Leezir felt a chill—he'd underestimated the Royal force. His gut feeling told him that the sentries not only hunted Venir, but him as well.

So be it! I'll take as many as I can.

Blood spilled into the murky sewers. He summoned Hagerdon and Creighton forward to stand with him. He glanced toward Venir, just thirty yards away and now sporting a helmet and shield. Venir stepped into the charge, wielding a giant axe the likes of which he had never seen before. Venir's friends disappeared into the alley's shadows and did not reappear. Leezir's attention was drawn away from Venir when he heard screams directly below him.

He looked down. His man-urchins were in the fight of their lives with three Shadow Sentries. Leezir barked commands at the man-urchins. Six of the ragged men overwhelmed one sentry and dragged him to the ground, cutting at his limbs and throat with everything they had.

But the sentry did not go down easily.

He poked holes in the bellies and skulls of the man-urchins before they finally ran his dark heart through. Leezir cheered along with Hagerdon and Creighton.

The other six man-urchins, meanwhile, kept the other two sentries preoccupied with their numbers. They darted in and out, cutting at the sentries from every direction. The Sentries cut down the inferior urchins with critical blows.

One man-urchin managed to jump onto the back of a sentry—only to have a dagger driven into his skull by the other sentry. Leezir grimaced. Even as the other six man-urchins joined the fray, the disfigured men looked reckless in their attempts as they charged forward in anger and desperation, their curved daggers and cheap iron swords no match for the finely forged weapons of the sentries. One man-urchin fell to hammering hand-axe blows that chopped him from head to toe like a sapling. Leezir cringed at the sight.

"Oh!" Creighton said behind him.

The black sentry grinned up at them before screaming as a dagger was jammed into the back of his thigh. The sentry chopped off the attacking man-urchin's hand with one of his axes and brained him with the other. Leezir didn't like where this was going. The other sentry was fairing quite well as his sword and dagger seemed to be steadily chopping Leezir's men to bits one finger, hand, ear, or arm at a time. The gruesome scene left men howling in pain. The cobblestones were slick with blood and they were all covered head to toe in it. Leezir shook his head. *They cut my urchins down like sheep.*

Death Hall was filled with roars of rage, throes of death, cries for mercy, and delight in killing. Leezir and his men stood captivated, staring down at the gory display. In the world of Bish, dying in battle was usually the only thing you were ever remembered for and even the outmatched man-urchins would receive their posthumous accolades for this day, if anyone survived the fray. Leezir would see to that.

The two sentries had almost finished their business, whirling their blades and axes with devastating accuracy. The remaining man-urchins dragged the merciless men down under sheer numbers and weight.

It was a valiant battle on both sides, but the man-urchins managed to pin down the crafty mens' arms while their brethren stabbed the sentries to death. It was the victory that Leezir had been hoping for, but the price was high. Only a handful of busted and crippled man-urchins remained at his disposal.

Meanwhile, two sentries coming forward from the district end were about to eliminate those few man-urchins and then fully ensnare Venir, who was in the fight of his life at the other end.

Leezir considered cutting and running, but his thirst for Almen blood was too great. The twin brothers waited for his order, their eyes darting between him and the fight. He knew they wanted an Almen or two.

"Ready the bows!" Leezir shouted at them.

Each brother had been carrying a heavy crossbow that was loaded with a barb-ended bolt. A line of specially made silk rope hung by their sides, running all the way up to their barbed crossbow bolts, where the rope had been tied off on small eyelets at the butt end of the bolts. The special roped bolts had been designed for fishing for large game in the lakes that littered the land, but there was little purpose for them in the city. The twins were a creative pair and had recommended another use for them.

Leezir liked their plan.

Steady as rocks, Creighton and Hagerdon zeroed in on the two Shadow Sentries below. The darkness made the shots tough from over fifty feet away, and their ropes were not much longer than that. Leezir waited until the last man-urchin had fallen or fled, then dropped his hand. They pulled their triggers.

Clack! Clack! Thwk! Thwk! Thunk! Thunk!

"Bone!" a man cried in pain.

"Bish!" a woman screamed in astonishment.

The bolts hit their marks with great accuracy, popping through the ghost armor and puncturing clear through the man's and woman's shoulder blades, sticking out the back.

"Nice shots, boys!" Leezir said.

The brothers grabbed the ropes and pulled them tight. The man and woman dropped to their knees, screaming in sheer agony. They grabbed and chopped at the silken cords, but their swords and daggers did not work on the odd fabric of the ropes. The green-eyed twins tugged harder at the cords, causing the bolts to grind and tear at bones, nerves, and muscles within. The sentries leaned forward to ease the pain, but the Slerg boys kept the pressure on.

"We have to act quickly," Leezir said. "Give me those cords, boys!"

They did as they were told. Leezir wrapped the cords around his hands, pulling them taut, and began the tug of war with the warriors below. The sentries tried to pull him from the rooftop, yelling in agony.

"Grab my waist, you two halfwits, and hold me on this roof!" Leezir yelled from beneath his black cowl.

They secured him while he braced his feet against the roof wall. He muttered a spell. Magic surged inside him as the words of power erupted from his lips, shaking the roof below them. The silk cords sparkled and burned in his grip. The cords burned away slowly from his hands and fell onto the ground, freeing the man and woman below. Each end of the ropes slowly crackled with fire, but began to gradually pick up speed.

The sentries looked at each other, then at the strange fire. They scrambled to stamp the fire out.

It didn't work. The ropes kept burning.

Leezir laughed above them. They spit on it, even bit the cord, but the rope burned even faster, like a candle wick. One tried to rip the barb out from the other's back, but time was running out.

"Watch this," Leezir said, smiling.

The wick burned in a flash from one end to the other, the protruding tips of the barbed bolts glowing red hot as the wick itself. The sentries screamed so loudly it echoed throughout the alley.

Boom! Ka-boom!

Red chunks of flesh and bone filled the alleyway as the bodies of the sentries exploded in an arc of mutilation and carnage.

"That was amazing, Leezir," Creighton whispered.

"I know," Leezir said.

Still, Leezir himself couldn't believe they had been fortunate enough to wipe out five Shadow guards. Certainly, Venir would take out a few more, and though it wouldn't be enough to stop the Almens, it was still weakening them a piece at a time. Now Leezir had to decide whether or not it was worth it to aid Venir or watch him perish. No way could one man handle five Shadow guards. At worst, he would see to it that Venir was honored somehow. He also had to make sure more Shadow guards weren't coming, so he decided that he better play it safe for now.

"Let's go, boys," Leezir said. "Our work is done here."

"Don't you want to see the fight?" Hagerdon asked. "I want to see them kill Venir. He's a fool!"

"And risk being caught?" Leezir said. "Stay if you want, but those Shadows will be coming for us as soon as they are done with him."

The brothers shrugged and followed Leezir over the roofs and out of sight.

44

V ENIR STRAPPED ON HIS SHIELD, buckled his helmet, and grinned, Brool clutched tightly in his grip. Venir was ready, a stark contrast between the man that was there moments earlier. Melegal was uneasy as he saw Venir's countenance turn dark.

It was time to flush them out, however, and Melegal and Lefty walked into the alley just ahead of Venir. Three Shadow Sentries emerged from their rear and headed for them, but then a host of man-urchins slipped out of the alley's darkness and waded into the sentries.

Might make it out of here yet, Melegal thought.

Five more Shadow Sentries appeared in the darkness ahead of them. Melegal barely heard them move. *Ghost armor. I need a set of that.* He hadn't expected so many. His heart sank. He glanced at the man-urchins as they fought three of the sentries, then back at the five that glided toward them.

Could Venir handle five Shadow Sentries? Alone? Melegal wanted to stick around, but Georgio needed help.

Three of the five sentries brandished long, barbed spears that would prevent anyone going over or around them. One stood in the middle and two more held close to the alley's walls. Two others stood inside of those three, stout and formidable, one wielding a finely forged battle-axe with a razor-sharp edge that gleamed in the night, while the other carried a pair of short swords of similar work. They were the close-range fighters who chopped men to bits while the spears pinned them down.

Melegal shuddered and sank back into the alley. "Hey, Vee, five armed to the teeth," Melegal whispered. "Don't hold back." Melegal took another hard look at Venir.

His friend, though, was no longer there. It was someone else, someone far more dark and dangerous. Clutched in Venir's grip, Brool hung by his side. Under the helmet, Venir's blue eyes smoldered like fire in the night. Still, Melegal wondered if he might see his friend alive again.

"Yeah, Vee, go get them," Lefty said and he rushed past.

Melegal slapped Venir on the shoulder. "Sorry I can't stick around to see this. Maybe next time."

Venir didn't respond as he stepped fully into Death Hall. Melegal smiled as he heard gasps—their enemies catching first sight of the Darkslayer.

Melegal moved through the darkness and Lefty floated nearby as his shadow. They crept into an apartment window and slipped through the building on the feet of kittens, continuing through one building after another, padding over surfaces without a sound. Even the rats remained undisturbed. The pair had played this game a few times before, as Melegal had found that his tiny protégé seemed able to catch-on to all of his tricks. He led the little boy in and out of windows, stepping over slumbering faces. He was certain Lefty would rouse someone or something, but he never did. Through doorways, across balconies, and over rooftops, step for step, Lefty stayed close behind.

Lefty was light, and that made for great silent walking. Melegal envied that, and though ginger for a man, he himself had to be more cautious. Still, his experience allowed him to move unhindered and without slowing down.

Finally, Melegal stopped to catch his breath. They had made it over a few city blocks. The wider streets opened up to where the tavern awaited them. On the main drag, merchants prepared for the sunrise of the new day. Melegal stood on a rooftop balcony and watched the front door of the Drunken Octopus. He wasn't sure what to do. He looked down at Lefty's worried face and sweating feet.

Lefty tugged on Melegal's cloak and whispered, "My feet have never sweated this much before! I swear Georgio is in danger close by."

Melegal could feel something amiss in his own gut. He thought he heard something and scanned toward the tavern door. Shouts and a crash came from inside. He hoped it was Georgio causing such a stir. A handful of patrons rushed out the door. Voices shouted in anger and pain from inside, catching the wary attention of the early merchants, who gathered to see what the commotion was.

Georgio's curly brown head appeared through the hole that Venir had recently made. Lefty gasped. Relief washed over Melegal.

Georgio scrambled out in horror.

Lefty began to cry out to his friend, but Melegal clasped both hands over the halfling's small mouth. Melegal's hope faded as a dark figure in a hat exited the hole right behind Georgio.

McKnight ... again.

The detective strode forward, slinging blood from his sword and dagger. McKnight turned and pursued the boy. Hatred bubbled in Melegal's mind. It was time to take care of McKnight once and for all.

Melegal grabbed Lefty's chin and looked into his eyes. "Catch up to Georgio. Take him to the spot in the barn. You remember the spot, right?"

Lefty swallowed and nodded.

"Let McKnight follow you and Georgio into the barn. Then wait for me. And if McKnight gets too close, just run." He let go of the halfling. "You can do this!"

Lefty nodded, then climbed down the wall and out of sight. Melegal followed, but headed a different way. McKnight would track Georgio down. The barn wasn't too far away. He only hoped Lefty would find his friend in time and take him to the prearranged spot. Lefty had proven to be very capable in following Melegal's orders so far, but desperation could be treacherous. Even if the boys didn't make it to where they were supposed to go, Melegal was still going to deal with McKnight, one way or another. He just hoped it was his way.

45

Lefty's sweaty feet splashed over the streets as if he were running on water. He was nervous, almost in a panic, trying to catch his friend. His feet hardly touched the ground. He ran like a deer through the streets and alleys. Those that saw him jumped aside in astonishment. Some thought they were seeing a ghost. Quick feet were a rare and magical gift among only a few halflings, and Lefty was one of them. It only took him a couple of minutes to find Georgio huffing and puffing in exhaustion in a nook not far from the barn. The boy's head was down and he was mumbling when Lefty skidded to a halt by him.

"Georgio! It's me, Lefty!"

When Georgio looked up, Lefty stepped back in surprise. His friend sported a large, bloody gash over his cheek, and blood covered his ragged clothes. The gash, though, did seem to be healing, and Georgio's face lit up a bit as he realized who was talking to him.

"Lefty, I ... I can't run anymore. He's ... McKnight's going to kill me. I can't take it anymore," he cried, then lurched forward.

Lefty caught him and hugged him. "No, you won't die!" Lefty said. "I'll protect you. Melegal is right behind me—and Venir isn't too far away—but we have to get to the barn. Let's go!"

Georgio stood up with a groan. Lefty pulled him along, but the boy could barely trot. Lefty's heart was racing, fearing that any second McKnight would step out of the shadows and take them both out. Street after street, they plodded through the crowd until they finally made it into the barn. All seemed dark and dead quiet. Of course, in any of the stables a man could be lurking behind the gate, but they pressed on.

The spot that Melegal spoke of was a small stable near the one where they kept Chongo and Quickster. It didn't have much of a gate and offered little concealment as it was just a few planks spaced more like a fence. A faint red dot the size of a coin could be seen on the fence.

Georgio crept in as Lefty grabbed some rocks gathered on the ground and hurled them at the pigeons above. They scattered in flight by the dozens from the open roof and rafters above. Melegal never told Lefty why he had to do this, but just told him it every time they talked about an emergency situation. The curious halfling figured it was just a signal, nothing more, nothing less. He also wondered if all the stories of hangings Melegal had witnessed on those rafters were true as he stared up at them, noticing some old ropes that still dangled here and there. He shuddered from the haunting thought and closed the gate behind him. He and Georgio huddled inside together. Neither said a word as Lefty tried to comfort his trembling friend the best he could. It wasn't long before he was trembling as well.

When McKnight saw the plume of pigeons burst into the air, he knew he would soon have the boy. He confidently moved through the streets near the stable. His pursuit was almost over. He would regain his station among the Royals.

His vengeance on his former apprentice, Melegal, would be complete as well. He smiled to himself. All of his suffering was coming to an end and Melegal's was about to begin. Oh, the fun he would have using his resources to see to it that the former urchin would never be able to rest in this city again.

He wondered what price the regener boy would fetch in the slave markets. It would be enough of a fortune to start his own Royal line. He almost began to whistle. Finally, he could plan on the oft enjoyed indulgences of the city once again.

Melegal managed to clear the barn's roof and slip down into the rafters after Lefty scattered the birds. *"Good boy!"* he thought.

The boys had made it to the spot and all was in order as he wanted it to be. Melegal tucked his hat into his pants. He grabbed two strands of climber's rope that he had planted there long ago, now dusty, but still undisturbed, and looped the rope around his feet, tethering himself to the rafters. *This better work.* He eased himself deeper into the rafters and aligned himself with the stable in which Georgio and Lefty huddled, completely unaware of his presence.

He pulled out a concealed dagger with a two-handed hilt and an extra-long blade, placing the flat of its sharpened iron between his teeth. *This better work.* He pulled himself into a crook between the roof and high wall, tied his feet tight to the long rope that was secured onto a higher rafter, and jumped to grab another rafter to wait for his prey. He strained to keep still as he hung suspended over the barn's ground thirty feet below.

He had seen trapeze artists before, and remembered how they'd swung. It had inspired the idea to set up this trap for a day like this. Closing his eyes, Melegal breathed deeply through his nostrils and thought about what he was going to do … for the first time. Focusing on the single moment that he had executed in his thoughts hundreds of times, he knew he was ready. Still, he had his doubts. *This better work.* He exhaled, opened his eyes, and waited. Moments passed.

Someone entered the side barn door. Melegal saw the trademark black hat. It was McKnight. The detective crept in and paused, craning his head back and forth. By now, Melegal's acute ears could hear Georgio's heavy breathing below, so certainly McKnight would too.

As McKnight crept along, Melegal's hands began to ache from hanging onto the rafter so long. *Get on with it, man!*

Melegal could only see the detective's wide-brimmed black hat and little else. The hat seemed to tip left and right, not honing in on where Melegal wanted him to. McKnight now stood almost directly below him, and the hat tilted upward in his direction.

Don't look up. Don't look up! Melegal almost said the words out loud as his heart pounded. The dagger began to slip from his mouth. *Listen for the boy, you fool!* Melegal's fingers burned. McKnight seemed content to linger for the moment.

Melegal's body quivered. *Can't hold it much longer – move, you fool!* The detective seemed to hear something and finally headed where Melegal wanted him to go. McKnight stood right in front of the red dot. *This better work.* He let go and grabbed the dagger from his teeth. He could hear the wind in his ears as the ground rushed up to meet him. McKnight's back was in his sights.

This better work!

As he led Georgio over to their hiding spot in the stall, Lefty heard McKnight's footsteps. Georgio squeezed his hand so hard it hurt. *Whatever Melegal has in mind, it better happen soon, or we're both dead..*

Georgio sobbed over and over, "Where's Vee?"

Then McKnight's face came into full view above the small gate—a menacing figure stroking his mustache. Lefty felt helpless. Was this "spot" of Melegal's the place he'd sent them to die? And where was Melegal?

The detective looked elated at their horror, and he pulled at the gate. Lefty's eyes widened as a silent shadow descended from the rafters.

McKnight noticed and began to turn. "Eh?"

Wham!

A blade exploded like a blooming, bloody rose from McKnight's black chest, knocking him through the gate into the stall. Georgio dove onto Lefty. Lefty peeked out from underneath the boy. McKnight stood on shaky knees, blood oozing from his mouth and chest, and behind McKnight hung Melegal, head down.

Lefty could hardly believe his eyes.

Melegal twirled the detective around and faced him eye to eye.

"That … that was my … idea," McKnight croaked through bloody lips.

"And it worked. What a wonderful teacher you were," Melegal said with a sneer.

McKnight's eyes widened in frozen horror as the detective realized he faced a death he could not escape.

Melegal drew closer and whispered in McKnight's ear, "This time, there will be no body to come back from the dead. I'm feeding you to the hogs. Mmmmm. They just love the succulent meat and marrow of the men of Bone. You remember, don't you?"

McKnight crumpled slowly to the ground. Melegal turned him around and removed his dagger, smiling bigger than Lefty had ever seen. The monster of all back stabs was complete.

Mindful of the thief's lessons, Lefty and Georgio's claps were silent as Melegal gave an inverted bow. Georgio scrambled up again.

"What about Vee?" Georgio said. "Where is he? Isn't Tonio still out there?"

Melegal got out of the ropes and scratched his head. Lefty looked at him.

"You two stay here," Melegal said.

"No!" Georgio cried. "We're coming too!"

But Melegal was already running away.

46

V ENIR STEPPED OUT FULLY INTO the alley, facing his foes. Some of the Shadow Sentries gasped while others stepped to the rear, heads looking back and forth at him and one another. He couldn't see their faces through the armor they wore, but he could see their wide eyes and smell their fear. They already knew that some of their number would soon die at his hands.

It made him hungry for their blood. He smiled to himself.

The sentries murmured as they raised their weapons. One of them said, "He is only a man," but the voice seemed uncertain.

Besides, Venir didn't feel like a man. He felt like a killing machine. He chopped Brool through the air before them. He knew their kind—cruel and dangerous. One mistake on his part could be fatal, but he didn't care. It was time to end this and save Georgio.

Venir rushed in, catching a spear tip on his shield and knocking it away. The others flanked him with their axes and swords. He was a burst of motion, swinging left and right, keeping them at bay. They were reluctant to get too close, Brool's ferocity barring their way.

From the corner of his eye, Venir caught sight of someone rushing at him with a spear. They were quicker than he'd thought. Venir parried, then jabbed Brool's spike through the sentry's chest. Snarling, Venir ripped it out as another sentry came in with a sword at his now exposed back.

Too late, Venir twisted away. The blade sank into his back a couple of inches. Pain exploded in his mind. There was no time to be cautious. Hesitation would kill him.

He let the fighting machine inside him take over. His rage flowed. His instincts ignited. Brool became a living part of him, exploding into action and cutting off the sword arm of the sentry who had injured him. The sight of the sentry screaming on the ground softened the attack of the others—a major mistake on their part. Venir pressed into them like a landslide of sharpened steel. Their senses could not keep up with his movements.

The injured sentry tried to retreat, but Brool cut clean through his armor like paper and left him with bleeding stumps. *Two down, three more to go.* A spear tip sank deep into his thigh. He didn't care, determined to render them all into dog food. Deep in his mind, he knew time was running out.

Two men with spears and an axe man surrounded him. The spear jabs kept Venir in constant motion. He swatted their jabs away, time after time, but he was still cornered. One spearman tried to turn him around, hoping to expose Venir's back to the axe man. Venir knew what was happening, but he had to keep his front guarded.

The battle-axe of the sentry ripped into his back, tearing his chainmail away. Venir fumbled his shield. It clattered to the ground. They seized the moment and rushed in. He scrambled out of the way over and over again—snatching up his shield at one point—but he couldn't keep it up. He had to attack.

They barked out commands to one another, and Venir roared back. He'd had enough.

A spearman glanced toward his yelling comrade, giving Venir a small opening. Venir dashed in. Brool's long spike punctured the man's throat, and he ripped it out, gleaming in triumph.

"You fight like ferrets!" Venir shouted. "I've only two more to sink my metal into, so enjoy your last moments on Bish, boys!"

The battle raged on as the alley grew slick with blood. Clangs of steel echoed down the corridor, awakening all within the block. No one ventured out to see, though. The two remaining Shadow Sentries maintained their ground, fighting in desperation. Venir began to feel woozy from the blood loss. He had been gashed and stabbed from head to toe.

He pressed the sentries, blocked their jabs, and batted away their blows, but they seemed to be getting the best of him. His arms felt weary. Their blows on his shield became lighter and less frequent. And they gasped for breath. He reached deep inside.

Gotta get through this … gotta save Georgio.

The two sentries attacked in unison, spear tip stabbing high and low while the battle-axe attacked in the middle. Venir squirted between the weapons like a ghost, distancing himself from the swinging axe that cut toward his belly and leaving him in the clear to attack the exposed man.

With all his might, he swung into the spearman's back, ripping clear through his torso. The bewildered man fell in two. *Only one to go.*

He turned on his final assailant who just stood there waiting with his battle-axe. Something was wrong. Venir whirled as another sentry burst from a side alley wielding a sword. Brool's razor edge severed the man's arm in the middle and drove deep through the side of his chest like a machete cutting a watermelon. The man somehow slunk away, spewing blood into the alley. Venir's arms dropped, nearing exhaustion.

The helm screamed, *Move!* He tried to duck under the battle-axe as it closed in on his throat. It clanged off the helm. Pain blinded his sight as he hit the ground and rolled away. The remaining warrior pressed his attack, but Venir somehow blocked it. He couldn't feel or see anything, so he just chopped back. His arms ached, his nerves were on fire. His axe loosened in his blood-slick grip. He felt the end approaching. The last sentry was clearly the best of the lot, waiting to catch Venir at his weakest.

The man had accomplished that much.

Venir could barely remember why he was there. *Got to save Georgio.* The sentry came for him again. With both hands, Venir made a desperate slice at the man, catching him off guard. The sentry leapt back, stumbling.

Venir had some breathing room. His ringing head began to clear. His chest heaved from labored breath and the dawn's first light showed on his blood-soaked face.

The lone sentry stood before him, with not so much as a mark. The sentry's face had an expression of astonishment as if he were looking at the living dead.

Venir grasped his mighty axe in two powerful hands. The Shadow Sentry gripped his as well.

"Who are you, warrior?" the sentry asked through parched lips.

Venir's gaze burned back at him. The Sentry shrugged, still standing between him and the alley's exit. Venir charged him, axe slicing the air. Nothing was faster.

Blood and flesh scattered before his eyes. The man cringed under his raw power. The shaft of the man's axe split in two. Venir cut off one hand, then the other. The man stood limp, gaping at his gushing forearms.

Again he asked from blood-thick lips, "Who are you?"

Venir brought Brool down with such force it cleaved the man in two.

He shook the blood off his axe as he said, "The one you should have left alone."

In the distance, the sound of more men came his way. Weak and aching from head to toe, he limped away. *Got to save Georgio.*

47

L ORD CATTEN HAD SPENT MANY hours studying the leather tome Eep had fetched. The mind of the underling was hard at work trying to decipher the shorthand writing of the halfling scribe, Lefty Lightfoot. Catten's clawed hands hadn't stopped scribbling since the tome's arrival.

The sharpened features of his gray, rat-like face contorted from time to time. A plethora of discoveries about the surface world caused his golden eyes to dance in delight and rage from time to time. The unusual book in his hands was a treasure without equal. The mystery of the Darkslayer began to unravel.

Verbard stood quietly by his side, assisting his efforts for a change. "Brother Catten, do you mean to tell me that the large leather sack Eep pulled out from under that cot is the single thing that could resolve our horrendous predicament?" he rasped while clenching his hands and teeth as if he wanted to wrench the life out of something with his bare hands.

"Indeed," Catten muttered, sticking his nose deeper in the book. His nails riddled the table as he read. "The acquisition of that sack would not only be the permanent demise of the troublesome Darkslayer, but it might be a tool we could use for our own gain as well. I cannot believe we were so close!" He slammed his fist down. "And now we have to wait for another chance. Coming across the book itself was hard enough, but getting that sack will be tougher."

"Any ideas?" Verbard asked.

"We can have Eep wait for a chance to snatch the sack. If we don't get a chance in the city, then we will have to track Venir into the Outlands." He slapped the book shut. He sat up and ran his nails along the rows of jars. "If we are patient, I think we can have it all once the man heads to the Outlands, but if he wears that armament, it will be a trying fetch. I think Eep can get to him while he sleeps … maybe. If this man is but ten feet away from the filled sack, Eep shall have it!"

"Yes, and to think we will not even have to engage the man ourselves. Surely Master Sinway will be overwhelmed by our success."

"Indeed."

Of course, Catten had no interest in pleasing Master Sinway. No, the sack would warrant the power to usurp Sinway. Catten caught his brother smiling right back at him. "Verbard, even though we understand where the armament comes from, we still do not know much about it. It seems too easy," he said.

"There is only one way to find out." Verbard summoned Eep. The timing couldn't have been better. He and his brother watched through Eep's eye as the Darkslayer carved a host of Shadow Sentries into bits in a dark alley of Bone.

"I am certain that I want Eep to be successful at his task, brother," Verbard said.

Catten could hear the awe in his brother's voice as the two of them watched the Darkslayer kill the last sentry. "I don't want to be within fifty yards of him, either, brother."

His hatred was mixed with reverence as he watched Venir stumble off in the early morning darkness. Even Eep expressed his malice for the man that had skewered him and used him as a lightning rod.

Catten laughed at the imp's thoughts. *It seems the imp hates the man just as much as we. He couldn't be in better company to kill the man and take the sack.*

Catten would have to wait for the right opportunity, but they were getting close.

48

M ELEGAL STOPPED ON HIS WAY to the barn door. He signaled to Lefty that someone was coming. He and the boys ducked into the shadows and waited. A few seconds passed and Venir came limping their way.

"Vee!" Georgio cried. "It's Vee!"

Melegal's heart stirred as the limping man ran to embrace the boy. It was a long hug filled with blood, sweat, and tears. Melegal was glad to see them both alive. Lefty sobbed from behind him then ran over and jumped on Venir. All that gore didn't seem to bother them. As Venir stood up, a boy in each arm, Melegal could see in his friend's eyes that it wasn't over yet.

"More sentries are coming. We have to go now," Venir said.

"How much time?" Melegal asked.

"Several minutes, maybe more. I can't be certain. Let's just go."

"Not yet, we have to dispose of something first. Follow me?"

Heading back into the stall, Melegal looked hard at the corpse of McKnight as Georgio and Lefty stripped the man down. The detective and Melegal went way back. McKnight had mentored him. And tormented him. And tortured him.

Still, McKnight had been the closest thing to a father he ever had.

Melegal hated him.

"Now what?" said Venir, looking around.

Melegal's voice was flat as he said, "To the hogs."

"Then you're gonna need this." Venir held out Brool.

Melegal had never held the weapon before. He'd never even considered it. But he wanted it now. He wanted to make sure McKnight never saw life again. He grabbed the blood-slickened armament. It was much lighter than he'd suspected. He had never even swung an axe before. He stood over the corpse, and brought the blade down as hard as he could.

Chop!

It was so easy.

Chop!

It was good.

Chop!

Never come back.

He swung hard. *Chop!*

His arms quivered.

Bastard!

Venir pulled Melegal's shaking body away.

They carried McKnight's limbs to an inner pen that had a large opening to the mud holes outside. Venir kept watch as Georgio and Lefty helped Melegal toss the parts over the rail. The boys watched in horrific wonder as three big hogs devoured the man in bone-snapping chomps. It made Melegal's spine tingle with delight. His dark expression eased as satisfaction flowed through him.

Back in the stall, Melegal pointed to McKnight's garb and belongings. "Get all those things, Lefty, every bit."

They hid in the stable and enjoyed a moment of peace and seclusion. The enormous barn was still silent when the rising sun's light entered through the slits overhead. Melegal rummaged through McKnight's clothes as if he were looking for something in particular and then he began tearing off strips of cloth and dressing several of Venir's wounds. The warrior was gashed and punctured from head to toe, most of the wounds amazingly cosmetic. Venir's leg was the worst, but a tourniquet would not be required. His comrade was either lucky or invulnerable.

"It astounds me you are still alive," Melegal said.

"I could say the same for you … and Georgio." Venir rubbed Georgio's curly head with his blood-caked knuckles.

"I'm not the one who plays with glass all the time like you do," Melegal said. "So how did you survive that fracas back their? Did you tell them one of your stories?"

The stable erupted in uncontrollable laughter. Even Melegal couldn't help but laugh at his own comment. Anguish turned to a deep sigh of relief, but it didn't last. They heard a rustle of men in the distance. Time had run out.

"Melegal, get some supplies and meet us outside the city," Venir said.

"No. I'm staying." Even as the words left Melegal's mouth, the warm stable became cold.

The boys' eyes got big.

Venir gave his friend a worried look. "Me, what about that assassin and those Royals? They aren't done with you or me. It's not safe here."

Melegal sighed. He felt different now. A weight had lifted from his chest. He didn't need Venir anymore. He stood by him as he said, "Vee, this is my home. They never wanted me. They want you. That assassin won't get the drop on me again. The Royals will forget about me. I'm not the one that killed one of their own."

Venir stepped away like he was bitten, shaking his head, but Melegal was not like him. He was loyal to a point, but not to a fault, and his fate was better served in his own hands for a change. The thief barely noticed Lefty's tiny hand tugging on his own.

"What?" Melegal said, jerking his hand away.

"You have to be with us," Lefty pleaded.

Georgio began to cry.

It made Melegal uncomfortable. "You can stay with me if you like, Lefty," Melegal said. "You don't have to go."

"Oh no," Georgio said. "He's coming with me. He's my friend and I'll take care of him!"

"It's his choice, Georgio," Melegal said. "It's much safer for him here in the city than it is out there. I'm just trying to help."

It was a sincere offer and an honest one as well. Lefty had a big decision to make.

"I'm sorry, Me. Thanks, but I'm not leaving Georgio's side," Lefty said.

Melegal knew Lefty couldn't leave Georgio. Lefty wasn't like him. Melegal knelt down eye to eye with the halfling boy, and put his hands on both of his shoulders. "It's fine, Lefty. I understand. You just remember everything I have taught you. You will need it out there."

"Will you take care of my books while I'm gone?"

"Yes, and I will require something of you."

"What?"

"Help Georgio take good care of Quickster. Make sure that Georgio doesn't eat Quickster's food and that he feeds him more than he feeds himself for a change."

"Speed it up, girls," Venir said. "They're still coming."

Tearful laughs burst through both boys' lips. Melegal grabbed the blue-bladed dagger from McKnight's belongings and tucked it into Lefty's belt. "You'll need this eventually. I don't know what kind of steel that is, but it should serve you well."

Melegal got up and turned toward Venir. "Where will you go now, Vee? And for how long?"

Venir had shed his armament and managed to somehow look human again.

"We'll catch up with Mood, Chongo, and Quickster, and maybe head north for a change. I have a feeling that Lefty and Georgio might enjoy seeing the city of Three or Hohm. There aren't too many underlings up there to distract me … hopefully. I am sorry you can't come along. I just hope the smoke clears for you soon. I assume Tonio is still out there somewhere. I don't think he can go home in his condition, but he knows a lot about us. Me, we really aren't safe here. You should come. We can start over, elsewhere."

Melegal just shook his head. "No, this is it for me. You can find me when you return. Who knows, maybe I'll figure out a way to solve all of our problems." He tapped his dark, floppy hat.

He and Venir clasped arms.

"Maybe," Venir said. "So be it then."

Melegal let them out through the secret passageway. Just like that, they were out of sight. He nodded his head as he closed the door. Mixed feelings mounted within. He didn't know if he was happy or sad. He didn't know if they would ever be back again. Lost in thought, Melegal almost forgot about the approaching sentries. He gathered McKnight's belongings.

Hah, they'll never catch me. He smiled. Then he remembered Tonio. He frowned and disappeared.

49

L EEZIR OF CASTLE SLERG WAS elated with their success in the decimation of Castle Almen's Shadow Sentries. He, along with Hagerdon and Creighton, had headed back toward Castle Slerg, making the city trek through the first light of day in the shadow-filled alleys.

The green-eyed twins nudged one another back and forth, bragging about the gruesome onslaught they'd inflicted on the Almens. Even Leezir couldn't wait to share the tale of their spoil. Leezir tolerated their foul lips with a keen ear, but his thoughts were on Venir. He couldn't help but wonder whether or not that man would actually survive the swarm of sentries who had been on him. Even from a distance, it had seemed unlikely the massive warrior would fall.

Creighton and Hagerdon bickered back and forth over who would possess the axe from his fallen hand. *Foolish boys,* Leezir thought. Venir was more man than the two put together and then some. Venir had proven that when he was just an urchin.

Leezir headed home in haste, hoping to reach their castle's sanctuary before traces of their involvement caught them in their own snare. The evidence of dead man-urchin bodies would lead the Almens back to the Slergs. He was sure of it—unless the other man-urchins managed to drag off their kindred in time.

Weakening Castle Almen gave Leezir a thrill. He was almost skipping at the thought.

Then he heard something.

Twing! Twing! Twing! Twing!

The twin brothers lurched before Leezir, each clutching a long dart deep in their throats. He watched, unable to move as the young men spun around. He could see the darts clean through their necks.

Assassin!

He couldn't move. The twins' heads dropped. Their bodies twitched and fell to the ground with a thud. A dark figure in white robes stepped out of the shadows. *Now what!*

Leezir turned to take cover.

Twing! Twing!

He screamed as he fell to the ground, face down in the muddied alley. His back burned. Someone stepped over him and rolled him over. He saw a face, but didn't know the man, although his filed teeth made Leezir think of underlings for some reason.

The man kissed his dart-launching bracers. Leezir looked at all the knives strapped inside the man's robes and shivered. Was the assassin going to cut his throat? He could still move. It hurt everywhere. The poison was in him. Thanks to an earlier spell, it moved slowly, like lava.

The olive-skinned man stared deep into Leezir's eyes. Then Leezir felt a long blade on the skin of his throat. Leezir caught the assassin's eyes one more time and managed a whisper. "Freeze."

The man froze where he stood, his eyes darting back and forth. Leezir slid out from beneath him, fighting the pain. The magical suggestion he'd empowered had saved his life more than once, but this was his closet call ever.

Leezir groaned in misery as he pulled out his cudgel, Spine Breaker. This could only be another one of Almen's goons, but Leezir wasn't so easy to kill. Leezir would see to it that the Almens never underestimated him again.

He brandished the cudgel under the assassin's nose. "This is gonna hurt."

Sweat glistened over the assassin's muscular back. Leezir called on the cudgel's power; it glowed white hot in his grip. He swung at the man's hunched back.

Crack!

It sounded like a small bolt of lightning struck in the alley. The man's vertebrae shattered into fragments. The second blow had the same result when it landed on the man's skull. The assassin lay dead like a wet sock in the alley. Leezir fell to his knees, holding his sides, wincing in pain.

He mustered the strength to try to save Hagerdon and Creighton. He reached deep in his reserves. His hands glowed, burning the long wooden dart from Hagerdon's throat. The man coughed blood, but was still alive. The poison hadn't taken in Hagerdon either, since he had received the same precautionary spell as Leezir. Creighton was not so lucky. His neck had bled out. Hagerdon knelt by his brother, fingers in his hair, sobbing, as Leezir stripped the assassin down. He poured oil over the man, and with a word, the corpse burst into fire, turning the man to ash in seconds. Hagerdon slung his brother over his shoulder, and they headed for home.

Leezir's man-urchins stopped them along the way with dire news—Castle Slerg was no more. The Almens had ripped it asunder, inside and out. Some Slergs had escaped, but only a few.

Leezir and Hagerdon were now renegades without a Royal name. Leezir might be branded an outcast, but he swore he'd live on.

50

TONIO HAD ABANDONED THE MOTLEY Girls in pursuit of the boy that escaped. The claws of the black cat had torn deeply into Tonio's half-dead skin and inflamed it. His body had puffed up beyond recognition and he could barely see through his watery eyes. Staggering and moaning in misery through the streets, he gave up the search for the boy.

Dawn crested. He longed to be home again. He could still remember it well. It was where she would be. It was the time in the morning when his beautiful mother would be walking the wall of Castle Almen.

Just outside the castle wall, Tonio stopped, a tall unsightly figure bringing sharp gasps from passersby. He waited for her to walk along the wall, hoping she would cast a glance his way. He remembered those walks with her. It was something he still clung to. She'd only made those strolls with him.

And then she came along … with two sentries at her side. She wore a silk gown that Tonio had bought her as a gift. She was a stunning woman, one that he felt his father, Royal Lord Almen, was not fit for. He didn't like how his father treated her.

She peered over the wall and scanned the people below. The merchants that bartered outside the castles waved in reply. She was always liked by the people. She was gentle, not harsh, but also silent and strong. She waved and talked to those below. He moved into her line of sight.

She caught his eye. His heart moved as he waved his scarred and bloated arm at her. She recoiled and turned away. The castle's exterior ground sentries came after Tonio. He yelled for her, but his thickened tongue would not allow words to form. She turned back once more, and he could feel her gaze, but then she was whisked away.

His heart emptied.

As the sentries closed in on him, Tonio scrambled away, busting through the markets in rage. The City Watch came. He bludgeoned two of them to death with his puffy fists. People screamed in terror. He ran. Tears filled his eyes over rejection from the only person he'd ever loved.

Tonio stopped and waited. Hearing the pursuit of the City Watch, he contemplated letting the watchmen carve him to bits. Their blades could not stop him, though. He felt little pain and bled little in his condition, yet his heart ached. He fled back to the stairs where he'd left the Motley Girls.

The three uncomely women lay still, bruised and bloodied. He shook them all, only managing to stir the one called Sis.

"Ew …" she mumbled, looking up at him. "Just kill me, monster. I got no fight left."

Tonio dragged her down the steps by the hair of her head. The open dungeon door awaited him. He sat her up in the corridor outside the dungeon, leaning her against the wall.

Tonio stepped inside the cell. He stripped down to his trousers and tossed everything else outside. Then he threw Sis the heavy, cast-iron padlock. He stepped back inside the dark room, out of view, and sat down.

He would never go home—could never go home.

Sis struggled to her feet, but didn't peer into the dungeon. She closed the door and secured it with the padlock. She heard a muffled sob, and then she heard no more. The monster, or whatever he was, had given up, and that was just fine with her. She gathered his belongings then spent the rest of the day rousing her bludgeoned sisters. They left the dungeon corridor and thought of him no more.

51

THE OGRE'S NEST WAS STUNNED. Orcs and ogres alike gawped in confusion. If Brandoff the brawler was caught off guard, he did not show it. Instead, he tugged at his small black beard, then slugged down more mead.

"Well, it's Jarla the Brigand Queen," Brandoff said in his deep, garbled tongue. "Did you enjoy being defiled so much by me the last time that you want defiled some more?"

Loud laughter erupted and spread like fire throughout the barn. The orcen women turned their noses up.

When the laughter subsided, Jarla pointed at him. "I claim that *you* cheated on our last challenge and that you owe me another match."

Roars of outrage burst from the lips of the armored orcs. Hands went to hilts, and steel was brandished. She wouldn't be surprised if a sword burst through her back. Every orc cheated, but calling them a cheater was a matter of honor. A mug of mead caught her in the chest, splashing her face. She didn't move, hands on hips.

"Queenie, go away. I won't tell you one more time. There will be no challenge here or anywhere. I will say, though, I am tempted to toss you over again like the last time." Brandoff stroked his goatee as he stood up and walked around her.

She would have shuddered at the memory, but she blocked it out.

"I am flattered that you enjoyed me so much that you came back all this way for more. My prowess speaks for itself. Even the human women cannot resist Brandoff the brawler!" he shouted, opening his arms wide and bringing roars of triumph that shook the rafters.

"Your prowess lasted as long as a wink," Jarla shouted in his face, "and I've known dwarves that are larger."

Brandoff gulped at the statement. His brethren were wide-eyed and the orcen women snickered. More laughs followed. Orcs and ogres always liked a good joke.

He swatted her on the butt, almost knocking her down. "Get out of here, wench, or I shall have you chained with the beasts."

Her blue eyes shined with outrage. He didn't have anything to lose, but she could tell he was not confident he could beat her twice. Why else would he let her go? He waved his hand in her face. He gave a signal and his colleagues began to drag her away.

She had to do something. *No!* Somewhere a horse nickered. *Nightmare is near!*

She screamed as loud as she could, "COWARD!"

It grabbed everyone's attention. Serving trays fell from fingertips with a clash. They all took a closer look at the woman. She'd hit home.

Brandoff's grin turned to a scowl.

The word *coward* in the world of Bish was a potent one. It carried different weight among the races, but among them all it was a great insult. They had different ways to deal with it. When it came to the orcs, their pride would never let them walk away from *that* word. It was the worst insult you could call an orc, and it was often followed with a fight to the death. Honor and dishonor had meaning on Bish.

Tables were dragged away as the center of the tavern was cleared. Brandoff stood in the middle of the floor, facing her. She was a striking woman, standing over six feet in height, but she paled in front of Brandoff. He was two hundred fifty pounds of muscle covered by thick layers of fat. She seemed an unlikely threat, and she felt like one too.

Brandoff pulled out a heavy sword that the orcs had designed, called the "fang." It was a big machete-like blade with a fang at the tip above the blade. She had seen her own brigands use these weapons to shatter bones and bust open the heavy armor of Royal soldiers. Brandoff eyed his own, fingering its fang.

Another warrior tossed his at her feet. She picked it up, checking its heft and balance. She couldn't remember the last time she'd fought with a sword, or any weapon for that matter. The fang was not even meant for a man's arm, let alone a woman's. She closed her eyes. *Nightmare.*

The level of excitement and tension raced inside her. Bets were placed, none in her favor. Instead, they bet how long she would last. Jarla's stomach was in knots and she had to fight back the urge to vomit. Her brow became feverish. She readied herself in a defensive stance, watching as Brandoff chopped and flipped his broad blade with skill and ease. It was clear that he aimed to finish her.

"Last chance, queenie! Are you sure you wouldn't rather have another defiling in the hay as opposed to a certain death?"

"I'd rather die, you pig," she said.

"Then so be it!" He rushed in, his fang flashing before her. She froze as the blade plunged her way. *Move!* She ducked out of the way. Her heart raced, and her body became alive. *Nightmare.*

She stepped around the circle, keeping her distance, her sword held in two hands above her head. Brandoff seemed to toy with her as he lunged, testing her. The powerful orc brought down a series of blows that sent shocks through her arms, numbing her hands. Over and over, he banged down on her blade. The orcs and ogres bellowed as they gathered around.

She eyed his mocking face as she parried over and over again. Sparks flew from their clashing blades. Every time he struck, she almost dropped her weapon. One mistake and he would cleave her in twain. He was just waiting for the opening.

She couldn't let him have it.

Jarla shuffled her feet, gasping for breath, almost falling to her knees from the last blow. Her wrists ached, her chest labored. She couldn't keep it up. The orc looked determined to kill her. She tripped over a mug someone tossed behind her. Brandoff's fang came down as she struggled for balance. It glanced off her blade and sheared skin from her arm. She cried out in pain.

The room erupted.

Her arm was soaked in blood. The pain almost made her black out. Her horse neighed. *Nightmare!*

Brandoff came to finish her off, raising his blade high. Deep inside her, something exploded. She screamed as she stepped under his swing, whipping her blade upward between his powerful legs. He roared in shock as she split off his privates, dropping him, genderless, to the floor. Brandoff the brawler's life as he knew it would be forever changed … if he managed to live through this. He wallowed in the horrifying misery of his castration — and began to die. His brethren watched in silence.

"Stupid orc," Jarla muttered. "Now," she said with authority, "get me my horse."

A path cleared before her that led deep into the back stable. She sobbed aloud as the dapple gray stamped its feet then rose on its back hooves. Nightmare's stable appeared to be the cleanest in the barn. A pitiful-looking orcen girl with red hair and a disfigured eye smiled at her. Jarla hugged her mount's neck, tears streaming from her eyes. She began to feel like her old self again. She bandaged her arm then saddled her steed, mounted, and trotted out of the Ogre's Nest. Jarla the Brigand Queen had returned.

A tiny portion of her army followed.

52

THE OUTLANDS OF BISH MADE up the majority of its landscape. Hot, barren, and dry during blazing days, the Outlands were often chilly and crisp during the night. Traveling long distances over the course of weeks and days was extremely dangerous in the Outlands, as the landscape seemed to change under the different shades of night.

North, south, east, and west bearings were not what travelers always relied on. The suns and moons rose and fell at different times on occasion. Their beacons were always full and round with light, and days and nights could be longer and shorter regardless of the season. Oft times this was nothing noticeable, but days that were longer than most could be devastating for the unwary traveler.

Bish's unique elements made even the frailest of the races hardy and durable survivalists. It was never safe to travel long in the Outlands, but it was the best way to leave your enemies and past behind you. Venir's small party trekked northeast over the wasteland of sand and stone toward another city.

A normal trip between Bone and Three was three to five days on horseback. This was one of those times in Bish where the days and nights were long. The days were quickly becoming weeks between the two cities. Blasts of hot wind and dry sand parched and cracked their lips.

Georgio's thoughts drifted toward death as he questioned leaving the sanctuary of Bone. He no longer had a home, it seemed. He felt as if he would perish in the desert. He was thirsty, exhausted, and hungry. He didn't know which was worse, the dungeon he'd escaped from, or the endless days in the heat.

He rode on the back of Quickster, with Lefty huddled at his back. He worried about his friend, who had barely managed a word in two days. He looked back at Lefty from time to time, but the halfling had a weak look in his eyes.

Up ahead, Venir walked beside Chongo and Mood. They looked like three giants, not bothered by the miserable conditions. Georgio wanted to be like that, but he could barely even stand. The men took care of him and the halfling. He was grateful. They gave him hope. He just wanted to get as far away from Bone as possible. Wherever they were going, it had to be better.

As nighttime came, Georgio and Lefty curled up under the bellies of Quickster and Chongo while Venir and Mood took turns vanquishing ravenous and enlarged rodents, poisonous millipedes, scorpions, and snakes. Mood would eat the millipedes and tell stories, laughing. The sickening sight only made Georgio feel worse. Everything was bad and there was nothing he could do to change it.

Venir hadn't said much to him other than, "We'll be there soon." Soon never came and Georgio felt as if he was the cause of all the trouble. Was Venir mad at him? The only person he saw Venir talking to was Mood. It made him uneasy.

As they trudged along, he realized there was no water left. Nor food. He bit off his sandy fingernails, watching them grow back, only to eat them again. Sleeping was as exhausting as staying awake. His nightmares came over and over again. Lefty was now tied to Chongo's saddle, unmoving. He frowned. *The City of Three is a myth and the big lout has brought us out here to die.*

He was dreaming of McKnight cutting off his fingers again when he was suddenly awakened.

Venir's broad grinning face looked down at him. "Georgio, we're here."

Georgio rubbed the sand and grit from his eyes and looked forward in bewilderment. If there ever was a place he didn't possibly believe existed, it was this city. Before his very eyes, a majestic city sat in the distance with a backdrop of a colorful green and blue mountain range behind it. Green pastures surrounded the city, which looked to be enclosed in part by high alabaster walls of cut rock and marble.

Unlike the foreboding appearance of Bone, Three was more welcoming and pleasing to the eyes. He noticed a blue skyline that seemed brilliant over the mountains, and the clouds looked even more white and numerous than what was seen back in Bone. Though they were still miles away, the colorful spires on the castles within shone like burnished chrome armor. It was beautiful.

Streams of water came down from the mountains, some ending abruptly at rocky edges and cascading into waterfalls and ponds, and other large streams that flowed into the city. He licked his cracked lips. Venir told him this city was unlike Bone. It had more than just humans. Dwarves, halflings, striders, and mintaurs lived in and frequented it as well. He couldn't wait to see them. The best of the best contributed to the city of Three, but just like any other, it had its problems and odd characteristics as well. "Mood, I guess this is it for now. Thanks for the escort," Venir said.

Mood's nose crinkled. "Pah, it's just another filthy city. I can smell it from here. You do what you gotta do. I'll wait with Chongo at Dwarven Hole for you. I'm due back. You know, I'm still the king, for all it's worth."

Venir laughed.

"Did he say he's taking Chongo? Why?" Georgio asked.

Venir sighed. "I told you already. He can't go into the city. There is nowhere safe for him in there. He is safest with Mood for now. Besides, Chongo needs special care from time to time and only the dwarves can do that."

"All right," Georgio said, pouting as he hugged the big pooch who was busy licking him like a dog treat.

He looked and saw Venir cradling his tiny friend in his arms. His heart fell when he saw the look on Venir's hardened face. He began to cry as he walked over.

"Is he dead, Vee?"

"He's still breathing."

Venir's words didn't comfort him. Lefty was wrapped in a blanket like a child, gaunt and lifeless. Raspy breaths came from his cracked lips. Georgio didn't want to lose his friend. Not now.

"Can they help him in there?"

"He's pretty sick. The desert flu takes time to heal from." Venir knelt down and faced him. "You have to be strong for him. Now let's get moving."

Georgio didn't want to move. All of his worries and fears swarmed back. The bright city before him dimmed. Death still lingered in his life. He crawled onto Quickster's back and they trudged along.

53

THE ORCS LIVED IN CLANS scattered all over Bish, making settlements wherever they felt like it. They were a strong, stupid, and fearless race just a few notches above the underlings in terms of evil. Their evil nature consisted of being nothing more than a loud and filthy nuisance among the rest of the world. They were intolerant of the ways of other races, feeling themselves superior, but what they mustered in force never blossomed into any kind of threat. They were limited in intelligence and magic. It hindered them from ever doing anything strategic. They fought more amongst themselves than the rest, so largely they were ignored.

A gang of roughneck orcen boys had worked their sweaty, snotty, piggish faces into quite a lather. The ugly children played harsh games of sport together in the field of grass and dirt as if it were war. The piggish-nosed, heavy-browed boys and girls whacked and tussled each other with the virility of grown men.

Their ruddy skin was tanned from long hours of play in the sun. They pulled each other's locks of coarse black and brown hair with passion and roars as they struggled for the prize. There was no discrimination between the sexes, either, as private parts seemed to be open game for quick kicks and rabbit punches. They laughed, slapped, spit, and elbowed each other with little concern for safety. Fairness was not considered. Despite their flaws, lack of grace, and culture, they were still pretty darn tough and they liked to prove it.

A large, sewn-up cattle hide stuffed with tender meat was the orb of delight that sailed high in the air. Over and over, it crossed the suns and into the hands of the orcen children. The two teams played keep-away with that leather orb as if their lives depended on it. Victory came when the other team succumbed, either by force or surrender. The biggest and strongest children of age would wear all takers down to a point of exhaustion or dehydration, then gut open the orb of meat and celebrate with his or her team. It had ended that way for centuries.

The ugly, skinned-up face of an orcen boy crinkled as he searched for the prized orb that had been punted high into the sky. He lost it for a moment in the red sun's haze. He shuffled his feet when he saw it coming down. The boy's arms stretched out as he licked his lips, his eyes wide. Catching it, he turned to run over his pursuers, but the child hesitated as he ran his filthy hands over the orb.

A loud snorting erupted as he gazed on the orb and saw the bloodied head of one of his teammates instead of the usual orb.

Stamping his feet, he screamed, "Ugh! Ugh! Ugh!"

Pursuit stopped as he tossed the head to the ground. The rest of them gathered, looking at the head and one another. Then a sound caught their attention. They looked into the sky.

A loud buzzing noise filled their tiny ears. A creature hovered over them, holding their prize. It tore into the orb's contents with its short powerful arms and three-taloned hands. A wide row of razor-sharp teeth ripped into the red meat. A large, evil eye gazed down on them, and the creature's leathery, bat-like wings flapped like a hummingbird's. Whatever it was, it was eating their meat and it was going to die.

Eep was surprised as the orcen children pelted him with rocks while screaming ugly names. It was the opposite of what he was used to. Terror was replaced by anger. They had to be the most ignorant creatures in this world. A rock struck his eye, then was followed by another, dropping him bewildered from the sky.

Before he knew it, the children were bashing him with sticks and stones. *This can't be happening.* Blow after blow they came, kicking, punching, and beating him with rocks. He thought of Verbard and Catten—all of the cruel tricks they pulled on him. The thought sobered him up.

He tore the children apart one by one. They fought back, not noticing that they were piling up in heaps. Gashed faces and bellies abounded, some nearly torn asunder like children's toys. They tried to tackle him and bash his brains in. He was too fast and powerful. It wasn't long before he prevailed. He looked around. Not a single orcen child lived. Not one had fled.

Eep brushed his claws off. He took a large bite out of an orcen boy's leg as he looked around. He would give anything to do that to the underling lords. He spat out the flesh, wiping his mouth. "Yuck!"

They fight better than they taste.

He buzzed off to the nearby village and killed all the rest. He had a mission, but saw no reason why he couldn't have some fun along the way. He just couldn't help himself. *Gotta be me.*

54

V ENIR'S THOUGHTS WERE HEAVY. GEORGIO, who felt like a brother, had almost died. Lefty had almost died too. It was all on account of him. It tore at him. He knew nothing about raising children. He did know that the city of Bone was a poor choice for doing it. He didn't feel there was any place fit for children in all of Bish. Underlings ran loose in the south and treachery was afoot everywhere else. The somewhat safe harbor of the city of Three was the only option he could think of.

Three was by far the lesser of evils when it came to larger cities. It offered protection far less ominous than those massive rock walls that surrounded Bone. Instead, tall cut block walls of alabaster stone and marble guarded the occupants.

Spires of shining metal and sparkling jewels shone in all directions. The streets were clean and the city felt cool as the backdrops of waterfalls and the mountains' shade provided for a greener and more serene atmosphere.

The people in the fairer city cleaned up better as well and the districts were less confusing to navigate than their previous home. With fewer people, the crowds were more amiable and not as guarded. The humans were all about, but dwarves and halflings contributed to society as well.

Venir knew where to take Lefty when they arrived. The ailing boy was taken to the House of Clerics. They wore soft pale robes, spoke in whispers, and represented many races. Venir paid them well for their services, thanks to Mood. It took more than a handful of gold, a small fortune, but in two days Lefty was back on his light feet, eyes wide with astonishment.

As Venir led them through the city, and they brushed against other races, he noticed tears rolling down Lefty's cheeks. The boy must be thinking of his family and the Vicious that had slaughtered them. Those same creatures had almost killed Georgio. Venir and Brool had put a stop to the Vicious, turning them into dog food. He swore he would never put the boys in danger again. At least now he felt he had them in the right place.

"Why do they call it the city of Three, Vee?" asked Georgio, his eyes alive with excitement.

"You'll see," Venir said. "We're almost there, but before I show you, do you want to eat the most delicious food in all of Bish?"

"Yes!" they said.

Food flourished in the city of Three, more so than any other city on Bish. The waters that surrounded it made for great catches of fish from the mountain streams, and the surrounding land was fertile and green with grass and gardens for leagues in all directions. They found a tavern that Venir was familiar with, stabled Quickster, and settled in.

"I can't wait to eat," Georgio said. "Everything smells great here."

Venir smiled as the scent of fresh meat and other delicacies seemed to ease all their nerves.

"Anything is better than more jerky and hard biscuits," Lefty said.

"You boys are going to like this place. It has the best food around," Venir said.

After the food was brought, the boys ate like pigs. Venir spared no expense for them, buying soups, fish, chicken, and many other items the likes of which they had never tasted. Their noses sniffed everything and they commented incredulously with every bite. The other patrons didn't seem to mind their boisterous behavior, either. When Venir had his fill, he made his way around the room. He felt a bit awkward. The dwellers were more polished than those of the Drunken Octopus, and he stood out like a sore thumb—just like the last time.

The tavern inn was called the Magi Roost because it was owned and run by an actual mage, one whom Venir knew well—quite well. At the bar, he surveyed the crowd as he sucked down a large mug of ale then called for another. His nerves finally settled. The staring faces didn't bother him so much.

The men and women were certainly more fair and polished, but their ways were still the same. Royals were afoot as well—not as pompous and overbearing here as in Bone, but still dominating among the locals and other races. Just like back at the Drunken Octopus, fireplaces blazed in every corner, but the contests and gamblers' feats were less obvious.

As for the magi in the city, they primarily made up the ruling class. The Royal houses had many in the positions of heads of state and their odd ways seemed to keep things in order. Whereas the leaders from Bone ruled with strict intimidation, the leaders in Three ruled with more subtle abilities that were not feared or spoken of in any way. The people knew what not to say, and didn't, and that kept them safe.

A woman with a figure as intoxicating as a bottle of ancient wine approached Venir. He drained his third pint, licking his lips. She was the most welcoming sight he had seen in years. Her full red lips seemed like bright cherries against her pale alabaster skin. It stirred him. Her locks of curly red hair cascaded over her broad shoulders. She wore a jewel-adorned green dress that accented every feature of her flawless figure. Venir's heart pounded inside his chest. She smiled at him, filling his mind with passion—but her hard slap across his cheek told him there would be none of that.

"You've been gone too long to even *think* about me again like that, Venir," she said as some from the room chuckled around him.

"Then you shouldn't dress like that, Kam." He looked her up and down. "Slap me all you want; it just reassures me that I'm not dreaming,"

Kam glared at him. "You smell horrible and you're filthy, so if you are going to stay in my place, you better get cleaned up."

"Ready for my company already, are we? Well, then … I'll do it right away."

As he was sucking down another drink, Kam eased her hand onto his shoulder. Her touch and perfume drew him in. He wanted to take her.

"Don't be so sure, big man," she whispered in his ear.

A shock of magic jostled him so hard that he spilled his drink all over himself, almost dropping the mug to the floor. The whole room laughed.

"Ah!" He groaned. "Glad to see you still got that same fire burning for me, red. Notice I didn't drop my mug, either." Venir shook the mug while watching her voluptuous figure saunter away.

"Get cleaned up," Kam said over her shoulder. "Then I'll be back and you can tell me why you are here."

He wanted to grab her in his arms and kiss her. He couldn't wait a moment longer. He got up from his stool to follow.

Georgio and Lefty ran up to Venir.

"Who was that?" Lefty asked. "She was beautiful."

"Yeah, really pretty," Georgio said through a mouthful of pasta.

The moment passed as Kam disappeared. He could feel himself breathe again. "Kam … She's an old friend. She'll be back and she can't wait to answer anything you ask her. Now finish up. I'm taking you to see why this is called the city of Three."

They headed down the broad streets, block after block, until the roads narrowed and became quiet. The sweltering heat that had consumed them in the Outlands was blocked as the spray of mist caught them from time to time, and the sounds of the thundering falls roared in the distance. The farther they went, the fewer pedestrians they saw. They were now in a part of the city that was unlike the rest. It reminded Venir more of Bone. They rounded another corner and there it was.

"What is that?" Georgio whispered in awe.

"Those are giants, Georgio. Three of them in all." Venir had only seen them a few times in his life, but every time it got him. Stone statues of three massive men standing almost twenty feet tall loomed before them, intimidating and grim looks enhancing their size. The detail of the marble stone was so lifelike that Venir could have sworn he could count every fiber of hair.

Lefty ran his deft fingers over the hairs on the toes of one statue. "Ooo."

All three of the giants stood, hands crossed on their chests, armed with swords, axes, and hammers. The large garden in which they stood seemed small, and the beautiful trees that surrounded them seemed more like huge mushrooms. Not a single soul was present except for the man and two boys who stood staring upward.

Lefty finally broke the calm. "Are they who the city was named after, Venir?"

"Well, yes and no. You see, those giants are some of the builders of this city from long ago. As the legend goes, they made a deal with the magi here to protect it. The problem is that giants aren't very smart. So the magi tricked them by turning them into stone so they would be here if ever needed."

"That's mean," Georgio said.

"It sure is, but it's only a legend." Venir rubbed the boy's shoulder.

"Lousy legend," Georgio said.

"Do they have names?" Lefty asked.

"No."

"Is that really true? Are there really giants on Bish?" Georgio asked.

"Yes."

"Have you ever seen one, Venir?" Lefty said.

He thought about it. He had never seen one, but the world offered plenty of evidence. Mood had told him there were giants. He never understood how something so big could be so hard to find.

"Well," Venir said, "I see three right now that look pretty real to me."

The boys just shook their heads.

"So, if the city's not named after the three giants, then where did it get its name?" Lefty said.

"Oh … well, I almost forgot that part. Follow me." Venir climbed up the giants. Georgio and Lefty looked at each other then followed. It didn't take long to reach the top. Venir pointed toward the sounds of the pounding water. In the distance stood three massive waterfalls, each over two hundred feet high. People worked and played all around for mile after mile as they looked into the clear cool basin of water the falls created below the city. Venir remembered those cool waters—and Kam's wet body at his side.

"Wow!" the boys said. "Can we go down there, Vee, please?" they pleaded as they hopped up and down.

"Georgio, you are gonna have to take a bath somewhere so it might as well be there. I just hope that water will work on your dirty little hide."

"It will! It will!" the boy cried. The excited pair rushed off.

He sat down and took a moment to enjoy the peace while the boys splashed and played in the water. Watching them, Venir laughed and felt a sense of calm. Eventually, though, underlings, Royals, and the rest of the wicked entered his thoughts. He became uneasy again.

"Let's get back," he finally said.

They headed into the city, leaving the giants to themselves. He looked hard at their massive faces as he left. He always felt a connection with their stoic expressions. It seemed a cruel way to live, trapped like that. He felt trapped himself.

Venir managed to settle Georgio and Lefty in at the Magi Roost. Then he cleaned himself up and even shaved his grisly face. He couldn't stop thinking about Kam. She was the one woman he'd always gotten along with. *Why would such a woman ever fool with me?*

He stared in the mirror of his room, not remembering the last time he even looked at himself. He had changed. Hard lines of a soldier etched his tanned face. He smiled. At least no teeth were missing. It could have been worse. He could have looked how he felt inside.

He was far from the man Kam knew. He was more serious than lighthearted these days. He wasn't about to let that stop him from tossing her over his broad shoulders and taking her up the stairs like he used to, though. *Those were the days,* he thought, then grinned as he headed downstairs with thoughts of her wine-red lips dancing in his head.

Evening had settled and the city of Three stayed particularly dark in the moons' shadows from the mountains, but there was warm inviting light everywhere, inside and out. The Magi Roost's décor seemed a good reflection of the owner. Blazing fires, ample torches, and candlelit chandeliers were warm and inviting for all comers and goers.

The rough voices of battle-tested dwarves spoke of grim adventures to the sophisticated and common folk. In the background, music came from a band of string and percussion players with long locks of braided hair. The hands of halflings and humans strummed and snapped their instruments with passion and fire.

Mugs and goblets of ale, mead, and wine sloshed about and the patrons indulged themselves in conversations inappropriate for fair ears. Kam provided specialties from all over Bish, drawing strangers in every night. She told Venir she liked that.

He liked it too. Unlike Bone, the seedy elements of desperation and need were not so prevalent, but they were there the same, just not as easy for the common eye to detect.

The city of Three's ruling Royals had a different philosophy of governing things. They didn't isolate themselves within their majestic and fortified castle walls, but instead they openly mingled with the citizens—to a limited degree. Some Royals even opted to live among the commoners as it was considered goodwill by the people. In fact, it was merely a very subtle way of keeping an eye on things.

Kam, the vibrant tavern owner, was one of those Royals, and she had chosen a path that wasn't well accepted within her family. Venir liked to hear stories about her bickering siblings and how she found the life of formality and luxury boring and pathetic. She had once told him how she'd taken on the endeavor of the Magi Roost. It was where he'd met her for the very first time. He was incorrigible and charming, but he could never get her to admit it.

Venir took his place at a table between a stone fireplace and a large window opening that gave full view of the active streets. He enjoyed the peaceful setting as a buxom waitress with a plunging neckline leaned forward.

"Can I get you something?" she asked, tossing her curly auburn hair.

He leaned back in his chair. "What did you have in mind?"

"Drinks? Food? Whatever pleases you, handsome," she said with a wink.

"I'll start with a decanter of mead and a plate of hot food—steak and eggs," he said, winking back.

"As you wish," she replied.

As she walked away, Venir admired her round hips and firm legs swaying with her tight skirt. He shook his head. There were many women of that sort around and a man had to be careful which one he dangled with. The ways of the women in Three were not as straightforward as they were in Bone.

Three wasn't all that it appeared to be. Much of what he saw was less than reality. The use of magic was heavy, but not apparent. Illusions were used to make things look better than they really were. It took a long time for Kam to get him to understand that.

Perceptions remained skewed as long-lasting spells were cast in efforts to keep up appearances. If they were forgetful, which sometimes they were, the walls and ornaments would quickly fade. Even their clothing would in some cases appear filthy and ragged, but in some instances the foul smell of a finely dressed gentleman would quickly give him away as something he did not appear to be.

The gorgeous women that strolled about were not as they appeared, either. They managed to apply the appropriate spells and cantrips to enhance their figures, hair, and clothes to the fullest. Usually in the morning, their glow was gone. Venir had woken up to more than one or two surprises.

The food and beverages embellished the reality as well. Delicious and exotic drinks were salted and peppered with mystically tainted herbs and grains that made one drink more and more. The city of Three was not what it seemed, but not because they had something to hide, more so because they liked to keep things nice. It made for good order and kept lawlessness under control.

Venir had finished his savory meal and mead when Kam arrived. Unlike most of the women in the room, Kam was everything she appeared to be. Her thick red hair was pulled back on the top of her head by a flat golden tiara. Her face was radiant, her skin soft and pale, and her beautiful green eyes twinkled from her teardrop face. Her small nose, high cheekbones, and delicate features distinguished her as a Royal as well. She now wore a tight and revealing long-sleeved tunic of red silk with a short brown leather skirt beneath it. High, brown suede boots came up to above her knees. Venir's mouth began to water as she sat down across from him.

Her full red lips were pursed to speak when he blurted out, "Come to bed with me!"

Kam's eyes widened as she blushed. All eyes were on him and her, it seemed. Keeping her chin up, she replied calmly in a polished, red-faced refined voice, "Listen, you lout, one more remark like that and you will be leaving. You haven't seen me in years and all you can think to say is 'Come to bed with me'?"

Venir felt ashamed—almost.

Her words came at him, accented, full and effective, as she continued, "You haven't seen me in years and you don't even ask how I have been, or have the sense to comment on my hair or my clothes or my tavern." She paused.

Venir didn't care. He could watch her talk all day.

She pointed his chest and said, "You just sit down, ogle my waitresses, ogle me, and then blurt out words like an ogre!"

She crossed her arms, blocking his view of her splendid chest and forcing his eyes to meet hers. The audience of listeners was waiting to see if he had anything to say.

"I am sorry, Kam," he said, speaking with polish. He wiped his mouth with his napkin and sat up straight. "You have a wonderful place here. The service is very, very pleasant, and the food and mead is just as savory. You look like a queen. That tiara really goes well with your hair. I really like your outfit. It is very exquisite and it is quite fetching on you. You are absolutely the most beautiful woman I have ever seen." He paused.

She looked around, then back at him.

"Now will you come to bed with me?" he said.

Laughter erupted around them and the tension evaporated. Kam just smiled then said above the crowd, "No!" But her eyes told him maybe.

The people went back about their business.

"Do you always have to strut in here and make an impression?" Kam said lowering her voice.

"I don't mean to."

"Liar."

"All right, maybe a little, but it's harmless."

"For you maybe it's harmless, but for me it's costly."

"What do you mean?" he asked as he put her hand in his, rubbing it.

"Oh … don't act like you don't remember the first time we met and you managed to run off some of my best patrons. They still talk about it, to my disdain, I might add." She tried to pull her hand away, but he wouldn't let her. "They always have to talk about the burly roughneck who came in here and trounced Fogle Boon. Every time the story gets taller about that night. It's taken me years to convince people that it never happened, but someone always comes in here and reminds everyone that it did. And now here you are!"

"Who's Fogle Boon?"

"Don't play stupid just because you look it, Venir. I know better." She scowled at him then snapped her fingers in the air. A waitress ran over with a lavender bottle of wine and half filled her goblet.

Kam sipped then continued, "I mean, I had just been running the Magi Roost for a few months and you came strutting in here, all burly and big mouthed while making a complete fool of yourself. All the lowlife sorts saw nothing but a bull's-eye for their amusement and profit. I tried to help, but for the life of me …" She smiled. "I couldn't help but see something that I liked."

He loved hearing about himself almost as much as he loved hearing her talk.

"What happened then?"

She huffed. "Oh, geez, you are going to make me say it all again, aren't you … you big rogue?" She took another sip and licked her lips.

"Yes! But you have to tell Lefty later. He will want to write it down. He's my chronicler."

Exasperated, she replied, "What? The halfling is writing down your silly stories? I can't believe that. It's ridiculous."

Venir motioned, wide-eyed, for her to continue as he took another big drink.

"Don't get carried away with that mead now," Kam said. "I'm pretty sure she gave you the strong stuff. She's tricky like that."

"It's good … now on with it." He slapped the mug down on the table. The waitress filled his mug as well as his eyes. Kam glared at him, tapping her long painted nails on the table. He shrugged.

She took a deep breath into her full chest, much to his delight, and began, "So I am heading down from my room to check up on things as the girls had sent for me. I don't like seeing anyone, particularly travelers, getting hurt. The girls tell me about this overbearing handsome hulk of a man that is as big as he is loud who is causing a commotion."

She took another sip. "Naturally I had to see you for myself, and there you stood by the bar. Blond, handsome, smiling, and telling stories while you were trying to make friends with everyone in the room. Normally characters like you I don't give a second thought, but there was something in your deep blue eyes and rumbling voice that made me curious, and I had to listen.

"The tavern was packed and you bandied about a full half head taller than the rest, getting into unwilling people's business. It drew the attention of the likes you had clearly never dealt with before and the contests were soon on." She stared into her goblet.

"Don't stop, please, Kam. I just don't seem to remember the whole thing so well," he said, faking a serious look.

"And lucky for you, I do. Before it was too late, the girls and I tried to guide you out, but their magic cantrips didn't seem to affect your mead-addled brain, which was a first. We all knew you were strong willed and were going to be hard to get rid of, but we never expected you to be so …" She paused. "So … formidable."

Venir smiled.

Kam's voice became sultrier with every word, drawing in more ears. "And there you stood, overlooking some tables where they were locked in the mind grumbles, asking what everyone was doing. And not long after that, every thief and cutthroat came after you like cats to milk."

Venir filled her goblet again, all ears. *Sleep with me,* he chanted in his mind. *Sleep with me. Sleep with me.*

But she kept on talking. "But your curiosity and pride were to your detriment as you managed to annoy the night's heavies who were used to ruling the Roost around here. I watched your confidence grow as you were successfully set up for some small victories and quick coins when along came Fogle Boon." She paused. "The Tormentor."

YOU are tormenting me with those beautiful lips.

"Now skimming in Three isn't the same as skimming in Bone or elsewhere. If you get skimmed here, you're just considered ignorant for admitting to it, so you take your losses and go. Fogle Boon wasn't setting you up for coin; he was setting you up for humiliation. The tavern only had room for one big shot and that was him."

Venir interrupted with a finger. "Hey, where is that waitress? I'm empty."

The story, food, and mead managed to take off a lot of the edge that had been building up for days, and Venir was beginning to feel himself again.

"Don't overdo it," Kam said, "or you will forget the story *again.*"

"Maybe I want you to tell it to me again, then. It *rolls* off your tongue and into my heart so well."

"Settle down, *big* man. We'll get to that later," she said with a wink. "I remember the scene, right over there by that fire." She pointed with her lips. "And Fogle Boon, a man not even half your size with a head just as big, sits down at your table for a challenge. You laugh at him and ask him if he wants to arm wrestle." She shook her head.

"Well, we all knew that Fogle Boon, the most *dominant will* in the room, was eager to teach you a lesson. He just gave you a deceptive little smile and laughed. I'd seen big men take on small halflings before, but the differences between the two of you couldn't have been more vast. You were in a white cotton shirt, bulging at the seams, and I could see that tattoo through it on your knotted back."

He could hear the excitement in her voice.

"The bets were quiet, discreet, and quick, as you could not have known who you were up against, but nothing was in your favor. I just hoped you would walk out of here and not be carried, because Fogle Boon was notorious for having killed a man like you before. You both sat there smiling, confident, and proud. Another mage cast the cantrip while you both locked your eyes and waited for the wills to connect."

She took a sip and wiped her lips.

"Normally, mind grumble matches last maybe a minute or two before someone yields and breaks out, but the opponents of the Tormentor were usually undone in seconds. The crowd was quiet and tense, and there was a lot of snickering going on all around. It was clear when both of your wills locked as your faces grew taut." She paused.

"What?"

"I was just making sure you were still listening."

"I couldn't stop listening if a dozen orcs were breathing down my neck." He winked.

She blushed and continued on, "The first few seconds brought sweat to your brow like raindrops, but Fogle Boon's head was bone dry and just as white. *Ten* then *twenty* more seconds passed and the people started to stir in alarm, astounded you were still locked in. No one had even gone *thirty* seconds with *him* before. Then the betting became intense to see if you could go ten more and make it to thirty. And you did!"

Venir hadn't noticed the small crowd that surrounded them as Kam retold the story. Her voice was distinct as well as alluring, and her enthusiastic crescendos sucked them in like she was a singing gypsy.

"Now the people were talking and word was spreading, and minds were signaling that Fogle was fighting over thirty. But then someone said, 'He's just toying with the ape. It'll be over soon, you'll see.' But you made it to *forty.* You were snorting like a wild brush hog and breathing heavily like the fever was on you, but you still hung in there. *Fifty* seconds took and people started cheering for *you!* I don't think either you or Fogle heard a thing, but I know he sensed he was in for a fight and he turned it on."

Someone in the crowd gulped behind Venir.

"You could see it because suddenly his face reddened and a tiny blue vein rose across his prominent forehead and at *sixty seconds* gone your nose started bleeding something awful."

She stared at him. "Do you remember all that blood, Venir? I don't think you would have bled less if someone had cut your nose off."

He shook his head and motioned for her to continue.

"All right. All right!" She waved her hands. "Now over a *minute* had passed, and you both were sweating and shaking. You began to pale, and I was certain that the blood loss and Fogle were finally wearing you down. You slumped down in your chair. I thought you were dying. It scared me to death."

Her voice rose and she spoke faster. "Fogle must have sensed that, too. He went for the throat. You shook *violently* in your seat like a possessed man and began to stammer and stomp. Then your bloodshot blue eyes popped open. You screamed a bloodcurdling scream the likes no one has ever heard. Your eyes rolled up into your head. Blood covered your shirt and dripped on the floor. I swore I could hear your mind roar when it happened."

She took a big drink — they all did.

"What happened?" someone shouted.

"Something amazing! I don't know how else to explain it, but it looked like a giant invisible fist smashed Fogle Boon's nose straight into his face with a nauseating *smack!* Blood sprayed and the crowd screamed in bewilderment and horror, and Fogle Boon's eyes opened wide as he fell back to the floor and lay still like a poisoned rodent. We thought he was dead, but his heart was clearly pumping blood out of his body and onto my floor. The stain is still there, by the way."

Everyone, it seemed, looked at where a large dark spot stained the floor's inlaid stones.

"You could always put a nice rug over it, Kam," Venir said.

"Ha. That would just cost me money. Anyhow, everyone looked at you as Fogle's men took his limp body away. Your white cotton tunic was soaked in sweat and blood. Your rugged face was no longer sun-browned, but ashen. Your eyes were blazing like a rabid wolf's, and you were shuddering. It was a pitiful sight and my heart went out to you."

"It did? Aww …"

"I felt bad for you! That was all. I didn't want someone dying in my bar. Your big grave would be costly," she said.

He nodded.

"The people settled over the rules of the bets and trying to decide if it went the full two minutes, longer or shorter. The girls and I grabbed some towels and covered you up with them and tried to clean you up. Your body was ice cold, but after a few minutes, color came back to your face and you looked at me and said, 'You sure are pretty. Can I have a kiss?' I said, 'No,' and then you asked me if you could have a drink instead. I turned to fetch it and you pinched me on my rump."

"Now *that* I remember!" Venir said.

The audience laughed and patted him on the back and congratulated him as if he had just completed the feat again.

Kam's eyes showed him fondness. "That was one amazing event, but I enjoyed the one from later on far better."

"Me, too. It was certainly more memorable."

"So, *Venir*," she said, rubbing his hand, "are you going to ever tell me what you saw when you locked with Fogle Boon? I know how those battles go. You see things like dreams and flashes."

"I can't really say for sure, Kam. It was the first time I ever did a mind contest. I have seen so many things it's hard to tell the difference sometimes. All I can say is that Fogle Boon played the wrong hand and I must not have liked it."

Kam pouted a bit. He knew she couldn't stand not knowing. She always wanted to know more about his inner man. He didn't understand why. She always told him that men tended to darken as the world of Bish wore them down, but not him. That was why she put up with him. He didn't mind.

"So, Kam, whatever happened to Fogle Boon, anyway? Did he ever come back to the Magi Roost again?"

"No and neither did any of his cohorts. That was a lot of good business you cost me that night. He was my best customer."

"You know that people have been pouring in here ever since."

"It's not the same. Fogle Boon wasn't the most charming man, but he kept things in order. Ever since he left and you left, it's been without character. It's like the greatest night that could ever happen here already happened, and no one thinks something that exciting could ever happen again."

Venir clasped her hands in his and said softly, "I bet we can achieve another great thing."

"No doubt you want to try."

"We—"

"Stop," she said, pulling her hands away. "I don't have time for old flames, lover boy. I have things to do—" Her words dropped off and she gave a puzzled stare behind him.

"What is it, Kam? And don't act like something urgent has happened and you are needed elsewhere. I know how you girls cover for each other whenever a man gets too close to getting his mitts on you." He didn't want to stay up all hours of the night trying to woo his former love. His needs needed met.

"It's not that, Vee," she said, still looking over his shoulder.

"Really, I suppose it's something else more ridiculous then. Look, Kam, it's been a long time. I really can't explain how badly I want you. *Soon. Now.* "

"Stop. It's not that. Really," she said, her eyes still looking past him.

He tossed his hands in the air, and slumped back in his chair.

"Remember when you were asking me what happened to Fogle Boon?" she said.

"Yes."

He rolled his eyes and tipped the decanter to his lips and drank until he found the bottom..

"Well, if you really want to know, you might want to turn around," she said.

"Why would I do that?" he said drawing his forearm across his mouth.

"Because he's right behind you."

55

"**I** BET YOU DIDN'T EXPECT TO see me here," Fogle Boon said.

Kam studied the serene face of the mage. The scholarly man gingerly pulled a chair alongside their table, sat down, crossed his legs in good manner, leaned back, and stared Venir directly in the eyes. She swallowed deep. Venir's hard gaze met the man across from him with a curious look.

She didn't know what to think. Time seemed to stop as she looked back and forth between the two, but more so, on the man she thought had disappeared. He made her very nervous.

Fogle Boon was adorned in a set of green and white robes, laced in extravagant patterns that only magi understood. His small frame and slender shoulders seemed mismatched compared to his large head with small enigmatic features. His shoulder-length hair was thick, black, and wavy. She remembered it as being short, the transition more pleasant.

His clasped fingers were large and refined, decorated with rings of expensive and mystic designs. His countenance was bright and intelligent, and his pale blue eyes shone like sparkling waters. Something was different, and she tensed up as he opened his mouth.

"I am glad to see that you recounted the story of my downfall so well, Kam. I found it rather enjoyable, despite my upending," he said without taking his stare from Venir.

Was this the same bitter little man who never once tipped a waitress, offered courtesy, or courted a woman? She looked to Venir, who sat there, arms crossed over his big chest, seeming bored.

Her mouth was dry as she said, "It is good to see you, Fogle. I must say that I am very surprised. Your timing couldn't have been less predictable."

Fogle chuckled, something Kam never recalled him doing.

"Ah … well, word gets around, and so long as I am not dead then I am not likely to miss out on any pertinent news. I knew this man had arrived. I have been waiting for his return for quite some time."

Venir shifted in his seat.

This Fogle Boon was different from the man she'd known. He was similar to Kam in the sense that he was a Royal rebel of sorts, but more renowned. His tight lips, which spat dissatisfaction in the past, now were soft in tone. His pale skin had color and his face was more pleasant to look at. She did a double take. *An illusion may be afoot*, but she sensed nothing. She poured him a glass of wine, and he nodded, almost smiling.

"Let me get to the point," he said. "I am not here for another contest."

She let out a deep sigh.

"But I am here to talk to this man. May I?" Fogle made a subtle motion. It as an arcane gesture that would initiate a spell of privacy. .

She nodded. "Venir, he is going to give us some privacy."

Venir sat up. "Works for me. I've always wanted to do this."

Fogle Boon muttered rapid words. In one instant, the tavern's customers saw a big man and a small man with Kam, and in the next moment, they saw a curvy painted trollop wooing two burly, dwarven statesmen. The illusion concealed their conversation as well and no one seemed to even notice the change because of the power of Fogle's spell. As for Kam and Venir, the setting had not changed at all.

The illusionist continued with his voice down. "After our contest, my mind was crushed for weeks. My head was splitting in pain and no healers could soothe it. Finally, I awoke at home with some clarity of the situation. I had lost. I lost to a warrior that appeared to have little intellect. When I was younger, I had lost to a man well beyond my years, but I was barely a teenager when that happened last. Ever since then, I'd only gotten better and better. I'd never lost again."

He fidgeted with the rings on his fingers as he bit his lip.

Kam couldn't believe her ears—a Royal wizard, admitting defeat? It was no wonder he'd cast the illusion.

Fogle Boon's voice brightened. "Much like you, Kam, I had tired of the tawdry chores of living within the confines of the castle walls. They limited me." He ran his hands through his thick hair, resting his elbow on the chair arm. "I wanted to test my will against people from all over, so I left the castle and did my part with them on the outside. It was challenging to meet other minds from all over, but I still did not have an equal. I came to the conclusion that my intellect could survive anything, and from the comfort of your tavern, I lived out my adventures." His beady eyes gleamed. "I felt I was invincible and no one could prove me otherwise." He paused.

Don't stop talking now!

As if he heard her thoughts, he went on. "Then this man ..." His hand leaped out. "He came in one night and got my dander up. As soon as you came in the door, Venir, I just wanted to crush you. The women were making fools of themselves all on account of your long straw hair, sun tan, and bulging muscles. My colleagues and I laid it out, like we always did, but the plan was to make sure that you left a babbling fool not fit for orcen conversation."

All you had to do was leave him alone and let him drink, if that's all you wanted. Men!

Venir chuckled.

"My plan, or rather my pride, almost proved to be my undoing. Not only did I almost die in the process, as well as you, mind you ..." He winked Venir's way. "... but I lost all confidence after my recovery. I was bitter and broken." He slumped in his chair, painful memories in his expression. "My reputation among my colleagues had been damaged. Slowly, month after month, year after year, I became my old self again—back to the same old tricks and full of excuses. It wasn't long before everyone was patting me on the back and telling me how great I was again, but I knew they didn't really mean it."

Fogle sighed. He lifted his head up to Venir again. Kam rubbed her knees.

"I couldn't really admit that I lost to you. My pride would not let me. I ignored my thoughts and finally one of my colleagues reminded me of something I'd said. I think it was in mockery, but nonetheless I said it."

He took a long pause.

Say it, for the love of Bish! Kam thought.

"I said that if anyone ever beat me, I would follow them to the bottom of Bish and back again."

Venir broke out laughing, but Kam didn't think it was funny.

56

MOOD'S BLOOD-RED BEARD BRISTLED IN the stiff winds as he knelt down and scratched at the dirt. He sniffed a grimy substance that was smudged between his thick fingertips. The scent was peculiar and pungent. It was exactly what he suspected. The king of the Blood Rangers had his enemies just like any other warrior on Bish—and he was hot on the trail of one.

He whipped his hand axe into the ground. This enemy had managed to elude him over the decades. Mood had hunted underlings, ogres, bears, winged lizards, clawed harpens, striders, lycans, and beyond, but not with the vengeance he had in his heart for this creature.

Mood tugged at his beard. His eyes watered as he remembered so many scenes of slaughter. His kinsfolk, women and children alike, died not far from here. He should have saved them the last time, but he was with Venir, fighting the underlings elsewhere. He could still picture their bodies strewn and crushed on the ground.

He couldn't let that happen again.

Venir would be coming this way, and he didn't want him to cross the giant alone. It was too dangerous. Underlings were one thing, this giant was another. This was his fight.

"Smell him, Chongo. I need you for this one," he whispered in his low rumble as he twitched his fingers under the mastiff's left snout.

Chongo's heads snorted in acknowledgment and his paws began to stamp in excitement as the pooch realized a new hunt was on.

Days had passed since their departure from Venir and the boys at the city of Three. Mood and Chongo had headed southwest toward Dwarven Hole. There they would await Venir. Mood and Chongo had been companions even before Chongo had become Venir's pup. The mastiff-faced dog, with a long pelt of soft golden fur, was part of a special breed on Bish raised by the dwarves. Chongo was a dwarven dog, similar to retrievers and mastiffs bred to hunt and guard. They were large, usually bigger than a normal dwarf, and were excellent swimmers, amazing trackers, and unrivaled in loyalty. The dogs chose their masters and served them faithfully all of their lives, which was the case with Chongo. Mood scratched his ears as he rode atop him. Chongo's snouts snorted at the sandy ground.

Mood was glad to have such a special companion along. Chongo was a part of Mood's clan, but he was also the top of his breed in character and training. The dwarves called them Setters, and they were only born with one head. Chongo had been born with only one head as well. It was after his adventures with Venir that he'd gained another head as well as become as big as a small horse. Both of those heads made Chongo the greatest tracker in all of Bish as far as Mood was concerned, and he was determined to put Chongo's great snouts to use. Mood never had the advantage before when hunting the giant. This time would be different.

He was still miles from the massive holes in the surface that led down into Dwarven Hole. The midday suns made for excellent light in the barren landscape that led over the rock-filled terrain marred by massive boulders and leafless, knotted trees.

In some places, the boulders seemed piled hundreds of feet high, and others seemed to have been smashed together by some unearthly force. The terrain made great hiding places for bandits and ogre clans, as well as the fiercest wildlife on Bish. Mood was worried as they moved, avoiding detection from the harsh races all around them.

Mood continued in his thoughts. Executing justice in the land warranted swift, cunning and deadly efforts. He chewed on a cigar that he could not light for fear of detection. His nerves were boiling. He couldn't fail his people again. His green eyes flared like emeralds beneath his bushy, blood-red hair as he again smelled the unforgettable scent on his fingers—his greatest foe, Horace the hill giant.

57

V ENIR LAUGHED AT FOGLE BOON so hard he almost fell from his chair. "You aren't going to follow me anywhere, little man. Stay within the comfort of this fair city. The bugs will eat you alive out there."

Kam twisted her auburn hair as she contemplated the wizard's sudden want for adventure. Even she'd never considered it. Most mages shunned travel and adventure, preferring to build their skills with practice and plans. It was a mental discipline with them that developed through tests, trials, and training.

"This is not normal, Fogle. Why?" Kam asked.

He looked at her, eyes pleading. "Purpose, Kam. I have no purpose."

She actually felt sorry for him.

"After I healed, I seethed and my pride guided me nowhere. All I wanted to do was regain my reputation as a powerful mind. Then it dawned on me." He lifted his arms high. "Who cares? I am just like all the rest. I already beat everyone I could except for this man. I let the conclusion of that battle humble me. I saw some of what this man faced and survived." Fogle gritted his teeth. "And I knew that there was more to my life than passing trials and winning contests. I've passed! I've won by all the standards set by my peers and colleagues! This man showed me that there is a world full of new challenges, and only he can take me there!" He pointed at Venir's chest.

"You can call me Venir, you know."

"I know, I'm trying … *Venir*."

Kam chuckled. Men like Fogle Boon tended to treat other people like inferiors and didn't dignify them with names.

"Well, Fogle, I think what you are proposing is nonsense," she said.

"Me, too." Venir slapped his mug on the table. "Another round."

"No," Fogle said.

"Where's the waitress?" Venir whipped his head around.

"They can't see us," Fogle said.

"Oh, well, are we done with this?" Venir asked. "It's your life if you want to come along, fine, but I'll not be risking my neck for you." Venir stood up and sauntered over to the bar, breaking the spell and startling the crowd with his sudden reappearance.

The two magi sat and looked at one another. Kam didn't understand Venir at all—neither of them, for that matter … both of them running off, facing death. Fogle's shell of a body didn't look like it would last a day in the sun. He must have lost part of his mind.

Stupid men.

"Fogle," Kam said, "will you tell me what you saw in that man's mind that shattered you?"

There was a moment of pause. "Underlings," Fogle said. "That man *really* hates underlings."

"How do you know?" She leaned in.

"I thought I had him in the lock and decided to take him down permanently. I tried to bury him under a horde of underlings. The image of the terrifying creatures usually shakes people, but in his case it enraged him, and in an instant, I was in the fight of my life." He shuddered.

She felt a chill, remembering the bloody scene.

"Oh … well, Venir hunts underlings for a living, you know," Kam said. "So, if you want to meet underlings face-to-face, then you'll soon get your chance."

"He's a mercenary that hunts underlings? That is odd."

"He's … the Darkslayer," she whispered.

Fogle sat up, eyes wide. The underlings were a hot topic in the northern cities as their resurgence in the south was an ever-growing cause for worry. Most conversations about underlings included the Darkslayer.

"Venir was there when Outpost Thirty-One fell," Kam said. "He is the one who helped save the ones who could be saved."

"I can't believe it. It's funny how these things happen. So he is more than some brutish lout of a man after all. That is good to know, though it lessens my humiliation very little. How about some wine then, as it seems our mutual friend has gone out for a stroll?"

She looked around. Venir was nowhere to be seen.

"Suits me."

After the wine came, Kam listened to Fogle and told him what she knew of Venir and underlings. She liked this new Fogle Boon, and hated the thought of him going out with Venir and dying. She told him what she understood about the fall of Outpost Thirty-One, as well as information about the two northern cities, Three and Hohm, and how they no longer trusted Bone. He didn't seem surprised when she told him it was the Royal soldiers of Bone that rode out against the remaining soldiers from Three and Hohm—an ultimate betrayal.

Men and their grudges. At least Fogle Boon no longer had one.

The underlings didn't occupy the outpost, but they controlled it. She didn't understand that, either. Venir told her it would take a massive force to oust the underlings. The Royals would not agree to commit troops to the task as they could not agree who would control the key outpost. So Outpost Thirty-One sat, abandoned on its grand forest hilltop. She told Fogle how Venir planned to return and take it back one day. Fogle Boon seemed impressed.

Fogle departed early in the morning and Venir returned to her table. She was glad to see him. His charming smile covered his heavy scars. She felt his warmth, and liked his eyes on her, liked the way they made her feel like the only woman on Bish. She missed that about him. It stoked her fires as he took her hand.

"Are you ready for bed now, big man?"

"Am I ever," he said, tossing her over his shoulder.

She giggled.

58

T RINOS'S CONVERSATION WITH HER NEMESIS, Scorch, was as unpleasant as it was surprising. She approached with hostility the other infinite being, who drifted on the edge of the massive black void. Scorch seemed preoccupied with other things. He ignored her efforts for conversation, not seeming to either understand or care.

She touched him. The contact put a jolt of new reality in her universal body. So long had it been since she had contact with anything alive that she had forgotten sensation, and was suddenly overwhelmed. It got his attention, too.

What? Scorch asked.

Why my world? Trinos returned.

She heard his thoughts with clarity. She did not agree. She would not be satisfied with his remarks. As Scorch tried to move away, she stayed with him. She did not know why she pursued her interests as she did, but she felt the need for some satisfaction. All Scorch would communicate was, *What difference does it make?*

Scorch stared into the void, certainly contemplating something. Would he pitch himself into the everlasting blackness? His demise would be fitting, but she didn't want to see him go. After all, he'd made the last few moments in her existence more interesting. So she made him an offer.

Return to my world with me, and within its realm, let's settle this. You can always leave.

Her offer seemed to intrigue him. He drifted back her way. She felt something stir inside him. Conflicted and dangerous thoughts when he agreed. *What is that?*

59

H ORACE, THE HILL GIANT, WAS frustrated. He was unable to shake his adversary, the giant dwarven king, Mood. The stocky giant was hidden by magic high in the rocky outcrops of the barren Outlands, many miles south from Hohm's Marsh. He ground his teeth and waited.

Over the decades, the giant had encountered Mood and his clan. He loved to taunt them then disappear. It was the way of giants. Giants waded in and out of the realm of Bish and into another realm of their own. They were bound by the world and bred by magi long ago. The monstrous brutes were careful.

The giants were an aloof race—far more aloof than intelligent. Men had managed to acquire their services from time to time by crafty promises that often were not paid. The giants kept to themselves for the most part after those times, but they would forget their folly over the course of decades and be tempted by their worldly wants once more.

They desired to fit in with the rest, be smaller so they could enjoy the things in Bish that were abundant, such as food, wine, and women. Their men were few and their women far fewer. Many times, the magic of men would size them down from their astounding height to the size of a man—a very large man.

Men would give them their fill of pleasure then trick them into giving service that often brought them a shattered life of slavery. They built and destroyed cities among countless other things. The giants were strong, and amiable, but shortsighted, lacking in common sense, and reckless in their desires.

Horace, though, was different. He was crafty, cunning, cruel, and cold. The bitterness in his black heart came from his stature. He only stood ten feet tall, a runt among his kind. They shunned him.

He hated them.

He had the same desires and was more prone than most to act on them.

His size was abnormal, but his mind was not right, either. The hill giant was moderately insane, lacking care or consciousness, and he tended to unleash his fury on smaller things … such as the giant dwarves.

Horace's massive head was ugly, with long braids of brown hair that hung to his thick neck, brooding black eyes, and a broad nose. Coarse hair covered him from head to toe.He had a foul mouth full of curses and rotten teeth, and a square jutting chin, bearded black.

He wore priceless baubles of gold and silver, and hooped earrings adorned his lobes, plus he sported a buckled belt, and rings that would fit on a warrior's biceps. His muscles bulged under his grizzly bearskin vest. Pelts and hides of beasts wrapped his legs and arms like trophies as skulls rattled around his neck. He was worshipped by ogres, a race he adored, and despised by the dwarves, whom he hated.

Now he found himself in a quandary as his efforts to escape the Blood Ranger were becoming more and more in vain. He could not be seen or smelled by the common nose or eye, and he relied on that advantage for survival. Horace could smell and hear the beast that accompanied the dwarf; it was an unfamiliar scent.

The giant had not seen his pursuers, as he was wary to keep his distance from their relentless pursuit. Magic somehow aided the snout of the beast or dwarf. There would be no avoiding the conflict today. The hill giant gripped a massive, studded mace. Its oaken shaft was nearly six feet long and thicker than a man's leg. Its head was a ball of black metal studded with welded steel. The weapon was impossible for a mere man to swing in combat, but Horace eagerly flipped it around like a child's rattle in anticipation.

He pondered moving on all together, to somewhere else, as his kind could and often did, but his arrogance and hatred would not allow him to be hounded any longer. Besides, he hated Mood and his Blood Rangers.

Horace liked staying on Bish too, and saw no reason to leave its comforts. The giants wouldn't want him back anyway. No, he would wait for the dwarf and the beast. He had a trap in place. He pictured the look on the dwarf's face then laughed to himself.

60

VENIR WAS HAVING SECOND THOUGHTS. So he spent his time trying to fast-talk Fogle Boon out of following him into the Outlands. Every time he placed an example of the menaces of the land, Fogle implored him to know more. He had never been asked so many questions in his life.

There he sat in the Magi Roost, surrounded by people he was quite fond of. Kam, Fogle, Georgio, and Lefty seemed to be in harmony with the rest of the room. It was Venir who felt out of place. He had put the boys through too much. He couldn't do it again.

Kam cast him a glare. He deserved it. He'd duped her into taking the boys while he was away. She didn't mind it so much as she let on, though. The boys always talked about the glimmering pools and the fascinating web-footed water cats. Georgio had brought one home, but it was gone the next day.

Venir told his stories as he watched them. Lefty's deft hand scribbled away as Fogle looked over his shoulder in amazement. The mage had been trying to pick up on the halfling's shorthand and seemed to be doing well. Lefty checked Fogle's notes and gave him a nod. Venir finished his latest tale, bowed at their applause, and stepped outside for some fresh air. It was midday, but the horizon in the south was overcast. He was itching inside. Ready to go.

When he returned to the table, a long piece of steel rod was on it. "What's this?"

"Do it, Vee." Georgio said with his fists bunched.

"Do what?" Fogle and Kam asked.

"Bend the bar," Lefty said.

"Hah! He can't bend that bar. No man can," Kam said.

Fogle was silent on the matter.

"Can too," Georgio said, then stuck his tongue out at her.

Venir picked up the hefty rod of steel. It was as thick as his thumb. He put the bar over his monstrous shoulders, grasping it at both ends, and pulled down on it. It bent slightly then straightened.

A new crowd gathered.

Venir looked at Kam and Fogle, doubt in their eyes. He didn't like it. He pulled down on the bar again. He pulled it around his bullish neck with all his might.

The steel groaned.

He roared. He didn't hear the excitement in the voices around him, only the blood rushing in his ears. His veins popped out under the strain, muscles corded like snakes bulged out. He gave a final heave as the steel crossed between his fists, and let out a blast of breath.

He pulled the loop of steel off his neck and put it on Georgio. The crowd applauded.

"What did you think of that?" Venir asked.

"Amazing!" Kam said.

Fogle applauded.

Georgio started tugging at his tunic, "How did you get so strong, Vee?"

"Ah … you know this one, boy," he said, rubbing Georgio's curly brown head.

"I don't, you big brute," Kam said, running her leg up and down his.

He had two urges, but he opted to tell the story. He settled in.

"My village sat on glimmering streams that boasted the best fishing in all of Bish. I remember the day well. A gentle breeze cut through treetops and swooped over the waters that were cascading over river rocks and tamping down the reeds along the bank. I waded between the banks with my fishing pole, casting over and over in a particular spot. I was only ten years old and fishing like a veteran of thirty years. I was good. I was trying to hook a fish the likes of which I had never seen. It was a silver fish! Or so I thought.

"My father and grandfather recalled the time they had seen one skipping up and down the streams like a spawning trout, its thick scales as bright as polished silver. They told me it contained mystical powers.

"There was nothing more I wanted to do than catch that fish. I wanted to make my family proud. Chongo was there too, treading water like a duck. He kept spooking the fish, sending it farther downstream. He wouldn't shut up.

"I followed that fish all day. I couldn't let up. When night hit, it was gone and I collapsed on the bank. The next morning, the fish was there again. I don't know where I found the strength, but I cast on.

"The fish settled in a deep part of the stream. I wanted him so bad that I could taste him. I could just imagine the look on my family's face when I brought him home."

He smacked his lips.

"And that's how you got strong, by catching a special fish?" Georgio asked.

"Patience, boy, patience." Venir winked at Kam. "I remember my father telling me to avoid the dark spots in the streams, but I didn't care. I wanted that fish. He was very far away, just hovering over the black water. I cast over and over. My arm tired. I crept farther in, my feet slipping on the rocks below.

"It was just ten feet away. It was the most magnificent fish I'd ever seen. It was over two feet long and slender, and its fins waved at me slowly, in rhythm with its tail. Its mouth opened and shut over and over again. I had the best bait, but nothing worked. It just hovered there in mockery.

"I inched closer. Chongo barked like a dozen hounds behind me, but I didn't listen. Something caught my foot. Whatever it was held me fast, but I still kept casting with my rod.

"Before I knew it, I was sunk down to my chin, and still sinking. Something was pulling me under. I'd never been so scared in my life.

"The water began to swirl around me. I splashed around like a fish on a line. I was pulled under. In that clear water, I could see the fish. I could almost touch it, but my arms were too tired to lift. Its silver eyes stared at me. I could swear it smiled.

"I was drowning. It seemed like every day of my life raced through my mind. Then it hit me. I wasn't going to catch the fish. It was catching me.

"I looked at it one last time. It was almost touching my nose. I looked below. A dark hole was there and silver tentacles crept out of it a dozen feet from my toes. I yelled, bubbles bursting out. I pulled out my grandfather's knife and thrust at that fish. I struck it behind the gills. I grabbed its tail and drove the blade in deeper. I swear it screamed.

"Silver blood streaked the water. Something pulled me by my neck. Somehow, Chongo dragged me to shore, but I had passed out. When I woke up, I saw the fish lying on the ground beside me. I had no idea how long it had been since I'd eaten, but I was starving. I wanted to take it home." Venir paused.

"But I couldn't resist it. I tore it open with my hands. Chongo and I ate every bit of that raw fish."

"Ewww," Kam said.

"Even the scales," Venir said. "It was the most delicious thing I ever tasted in my life. Every ounce of strength I'd lost was gained back immediately. I felt like I could do anything. When the fish was gone, I cried. I knew no one would believe me, and my dad would be mad that I'd been gone.

"I'd been traveling two days back up that stream when my father and grandfather found me. I thought they'd be mad, but they hugged me instead. They were crying, too. I'll never forget that. I told them what I'd done. They just looked at me funny.

"I started crying all over again. My dad settled me down. My grandfather held out his hand. Inside it was a large silver fish scale. Then Grandpa said, 'We believe you, but nobody else probably will. Leave it between us.'" Venir saw that Georgio was asleep as he finished the tale. So, Venir spent some time with Fogle and Kam stirred the groggy boys and led them away.

The reserved mage quaffed down several drinks. Finally, Venir, tired of his babbling, had to carry the man home. He found it strange that Fogle could be so careless, but the illusionist said, "Sometimes it's the only way I can stop my mind for a while."

Venir didn't entirely believe him. He had used a similar excuse. Fogle expressed concern that he might not ever get a chance to return to the pleasures of the city again. Venir made it clear that no drinks would accompany them. Venir said, "Treks in the Outland are different than these city-borne ones. You can't leave your wits somewhere else out there."

Fogle said he understood—then passed out.

The day had come to leave. Georgio and Lefty were heading to the lakes when Venir told them good-bye without them realizing he was actually leaving the city. Kam watched him go with tear-filled eyes. The marauder and mage made their way out of the warm folds of the Magi Roost unnoticed to all others, and Eep's eager eye watched them.

61

A TALL FIGURE STOOD OVER THE *face of a cliff, hurling the bodies of his slain underling foes into the abyss below. He was a striking young man, adorned in a set of short, dark blue robes that glimmered in the moonlit sky. Hammered dark steel bracers wrapped his forearms, shinning dimly in the moonlight. An ornate metal amulet of similar alien design and work hung on a thick metal chain over his broad chest. A slender, six foot long oaken staff shod in matching dark metalwork lay on the ground near his side.*

His broad shoulders and corded arms heaved body after body below. The hot wind blew his long mane of cropped auburn hair, and his steely eyes squinted in resistance. He was diligent in his task, focused, and a smile filled his tanned face in triumph.

The young mage was barely twenty years old. In one second, a band of twelve underlings thought they had trapped him on the edge of that abyss, but the armament he procured from the large leather sack had time and again magically unleashed the fury of a dozen lightning spears that ripped through their black chests like snapping bow strings. Most of them died. The ones that didn't would perish in the abyss.

Fogle Boon woke up in a feverish sweat. "Grandfather!"

62

T HE ROCKY HILLS CLIMBED HIGH into the mists above the world of Bish. Horace waited as a large two-headed dog approached him from below. The dog might be able to smell him, but it would not be able to see him before it was too late. The giant's magic blended him in with the rocks and terrain, like a massive piece of cut stone.

The dog walked under Horace's enormous studded mace disguised as an outcropping of boulders. The killing blow came down on the dog, crushing it like an egg and driving the big body hard into the ground. He hammered it again and again until its body was unrecognizable.

"Come on, dwarf! It's time you shared the fate of your dead pooch!" the giant said in a voice so deep it rumbled like thunder and echoed over the rocks. "If you are scared, I understand, but at least your dog was brave. He didn't last much better than the rest of your kind. They pretty much turned out the same, all those bodies of your women and children. It was a horrible sight—did you see it? Do you remember it? Ha, ha, ha!" His baritone laughter rumbled on.

Nothing moved. The wind was not even blowing as his nose twitched in the air. He filled his large hairy nostrils again. He looked at the smashed animal below him. Instead of the dog, he saw antlers and hooves. He squinted, then peered around warily and began backing up the mountain.

THWHIP!

"ARGH!" Horace yelled out.

A heavy harpoon-like crossbow bolt punctured his heel. He looked down to pluck the barbed bolt from his heel and noticed a line hooked to the bolt.

"You're tethered, Horace, which means you ain't leaving this world for yours ever again. I am gonna kill you!" Mood yelled from somewhere deeper in the mist.

"You won't kill me, Mood. You won't get close enough. I smash your head like a tomato, red beard, so bring it on. I wait." Horace cast his head around then pulled on the tether. He wanted to rip out the bolt, but that would cripple him. He wasn't going anywhere and that was just fine. Fighting the dwarf didn't worry him, as the Blood Ranger was no match for his power, but he wouldn't be careless.

The sound of barking dogs came from behind him. He whirled, smashing the rocks with his mace. A two-headed dog leaped away and circled him at a distance.

"Two heads on a mutt? I never saw that before. Nice trick, Mood. Pah!" He spat while swinging his mace down at the dog like a hammer, shattering the stone to fragments. The two-headed canine charged in and out, but he was far from worried. The dog couldn't hurt him. Not much on Bish could.

He beckoned for Mood. "Here, dwarfie, dwarfie, come on so I can kill you." He sniffed the air some more. "Come on, Mood. I know you have been thinking about me all these years. How many of your kind did I kill? Hundreds, thousands?" He laughed, loud and powerful. "So, king, where were you the last time I killed your flock? As I recall, one of those children was yours and—"

"Time's up, Horace!" Mood shouted.

Two razor-sharp hand axes flashed his way. Horace just laughed.

63

FOGLE BOON DID NOT MIND the foot travel over the barren lands in Bish as much as he thought he would. Even the heat was welcoming. He had never spent much time outside the city. Still, he didn't understand why they traveled on foot rather than on horses. Venir insisted it was safer that way. He didn't see how.

The thought of meeting a giant dwarf and a two-headed dog kept Fogle's imagination running wild. Setting foot in Dwarven Hole would be a tale in itself. Venir told him he might not like it there, but he didn't care. He just kept his cowl tight and did his best to keep up.

Venir's determined gait never slowed. The helmeted man looked like a myth as he carried his great axe at his side. He didn't understand how Venir wore the armor in the heat. *I guess that's why he's the Darkslayer and not me.* He was far from fit for this travel, but he wouldn't let the warrior know that.

It seemed Venir loosened up as soon as he left the city. *This must be his comfort zone.* Fogle was glad. He had never been in a real fight before. Not even with a lizard or an insect for that matter, and Venir said they were quite big out here. He couldn't tell if the brute meant it or not.

He shuffled to keep up from time to time, but Venir paid him no mind. It was clear that Venir was on a mission, something that only the Outland survivor could understand.

Fogle wasn't without a companion, though. He'd brought his pack-bearer, Ox, who was a mintaur—a stocky man-like creature with a horned ram's head and hooves instead of feet. Ox stood just over five feet tall, was muscular, clothed like a man, and had a long leather rucksack filled to the brim.

Fogle spoke with Ox in his language, but Ox didn't have much to say. It was good having him along, though. The sleepless mintaurs were a hardy race, small in number, peaceful, and one of the few that the dwarves liked. He had been in the service of Fogle Boon since he was a boy. Ox worked for him, as well as protected him. Fogle had no better friend. The sack on Ox's back carried everything he needed. He would have been lost without his magic necessities.

The illusionist brandished a broken five-foot staff. He had shown its ancient workings and iron shod to Venir. The man had told him it was just a stick and it might come in handy for firewood. That had offended Fogle, but not for long. The staff was more than just a stick. He kept it with him when he memorized his spells early in the morning. He stayed prepared. Every day, he felt as if it could be his last. Adventure had a different meaning out here.

They traveled far in good weather the first few days, with barely an encounter. A few pesky brigand orcs came their way, but Venir brandishing his axe intimidated them and they ran away. Venir and Ox stayed on guard the whole time, even while Fogle slept. He couldn't help it. He had to rest his inner self. Venir didn't allow for fires at night, but it wasn't cold. His blanket saw to that. A simple spell kept the creepy crawlies away, but his dreams stayed.

Something foreboding was near. He felt it every time he woke. He looked around. Nothing.

64

W*HAT NOW, MASTERS?* E*EP ASKED* in Verbard's mind.

Verbard nodded at Catten as they watched the Darkslayer and company trotting over the barren surface. He and his brother had abandoned Oran's lair. Verbard frowned. He liked that place.

They had just finished their trek and now they were hidden in caves northeast of Dwarven Hole. Verbard had hoped to already have acquired the armament from the leather sack.

Catten said in a hiss, "The foul man even sleeps with it on."

"He keeps it close. Wouldn't you?" he replied.

"We have to try something."

He made a risky decision and Verbard commanded the imp, *Grab the backpack with the sack inside the first chance you get!*

It was another issue that had not yet been overcome. Still they waited.

65

M*OOD CHOPPED HARD AND FAST* at the skin just above the giant's kneecap. Chunks of flesh peeled off as Horace screamed. Horace backhanded him, knocking Mood hard into the rocks. He groaned, clutching his chest as he struggled back to his feet. He shook off the pain. It would take more than that to stop him today. He wasn't about to let the giant take any more of his friends.

Mood yelled as he rushed back in, ducked under Horace's mace, and chopped into the hard skin. His arms ached, but he pumped away. Horace knocked him from his feet and brought his mace down. Mood rolled away as stone skipped across the shaking ground. The ten-foot giant stared down at him. It seemed like an impossible task to defeat Horace. The giant showed no pain and didn't slow.*Think blood beard. Think!*

Mood had to make his cuts count. He wouldn't get many more chances. One solid blow from Horace, and he was done for. Chongo leaped onto the giant's back and Mood rushed in.

The giant grasped Chongo by one of his necks. The dog's bites did him little harm. Mood cut hard and deep into the back of Horace's leg. He heard a yelp of pain.

He chopped again. Blood started to flow.

The giant screamed as he let Chongo go. "You are going to die, dwarf. You can cut me all you like, but it won't be enough. I will crush you like your children!"

"We'll see about that, stupid!" Mood cut Horace on the inside of his upper thigh, almost rendering the giant genderless.

He pressed on.

Stepping and dodging, Mood's twin axes sliced deep gashes into the giant's thick hide. The Blood Ranger inside him took over. Nothing could stop him now. Every chop hit its mark like a venomous snake bite. Horace's tree-trunk legs bled all over. The giant hammered down two-handed strikes with his giant mace. Rocks shattered like glass under the blows. The ground tremored. The terrain became loose. He slipped. Horace brought his mace around, catching him flush on the shoulder.

His axes flew from his grip.

He spun to the ground. Breathless and in pain, Mood turned his head in time to see the mace coming down on him.

"Hah!" Horace yelled in triumph.

Wham!

Mood rolled out of the way as lances of pain shot through his busted shoulder.

Wham!

He kept rolling. Chongo jumped over him, barring the giant's path. Horace laughed some more.

"What's the matter, Mood? Shoulder busted?" The giant rubbed his own shoulder.

"Yes, stupid! It's busted. Stupid luck of a stupid giant!"

"I'm not stupid, you are!"

"You're stupid, all right. You are bleeding pretty badly. It just hasn't reached your senses yet, beast. You're gonna be off your feet any moment now, and I'm gonna cut you up."

Horace glanced at his legs, thick with blood. A look of worry crossed his face. Mood had shredded the giant's tendons around his knees and legs. The giant staggered back, slipping in his own blood, and dropped like a stone. He roared and tore at his clothes in an attempt to stop the bleeding.

"Mood, stop this bleeding and I swear I will never come back. I promise you that!" he yelled. "Giants don't break their promises! You know that!"

Mood was silent, in memory of all those Horace had killed, and watched the evil giant suffer.

"Brothers, save me!" Horace cried out over and over again. The giant's cries for help continued. If other giants heard his call, they did not respond.

It was the most pitiful sight Mood ever had seen. The giant bellowed out in misery to end his suffering through healing or death. Mood didn't think he deserved either. He would let him suffer forever if he could. After several hours passed and the day turned into night, the hill giant died. Mood sobbed, not for the giant, but in memory of all those who had fallen. Mood had his vengeance and many lives would be spared in the future. His heart was still heavy when he patted Chongo on the head.

"I never could have done it without you, boy."

Mood and Chongo spent hours slowly dragging the behemoth to the bottom of the rock hill and into a small forest nearby. He stripped the giant of all his belongings and skinned the giant from head to toe. He carved him up like stag meat. He then prepared a spit and fire, lit a cigar, and slowly roasted pieces of the evil giant's flesh. Chongo stayed by his side over the next few weeks, chewing on the bare giant bones. Mood consumed every bit of Horace the hill giant.

"They don't call us Blood Rangers for nothin'."

66

V ERBARD BICKERED WITH HIS BROTHER as they waited for Eep to fulfill his mission. They argued about how they would bypass the ogres that were mining deep into the caves they sought. The pair could have bypassed the creatures easily enough, but a battle with a host of ogres was not a wise decision. Verbard wanted to go for it, but his brother was adamant they would not.

The ogres mined minerals, gems, and metals like obsessed beasts. Oft times, they skirmished with the dwarves over territory. Ogres were lousy miners, but they could swing a pick all day. It was a sound that Verbard became quite uncomfortable with over the passing days.

He observed the tireless ogres. Their hulking seven and eight-foot frames lumbered in and out of the tunnels, pushing massive carts or carrying boulders. Their picks were bigger and heavier than the underlings themselves. Their powerful swings struck the hard rocks that showered sparks and rung like thunder. They chanted in bellows as they worked in horrific harmony.

The adventure was becoming tiresome. Verbard had to destroy something. They needed to get moving through the pass. He looked over to his brother, whose nose was in a scroll. *No guts.* Three or four ogres would have been manageable, but over two dozen was suicide.

He didn't care. He began chittering some words. Catten stirred from his studies, but Verbard felt nothing. He was a shadow now and he drifted without notice into the mines below. *This should do it.*

It didn't take him long before he returned to his brother.

Catten's golden eyes bored into him. "What have you been doing?"

"You will see," he said under an unbreakable grin.

Catten shook his head and turned away.

The next day, an ogre erupted from deep inside one of the tunnels. Large chunks of gold, silver, and rock-sized gems spilled from its massive arms.

The underlings watched the scene below them, transfixed.

The ogres stormed into those tunnels like bees in a hive. One after the other came in and out, carrying all the precious elements they could. Verbard clapped his hands while Catten scratched at his chin.

The ogres danced all over their camp and even burst into song. Verbard clasped his hands. He delighted at the broad grins full of yellow, rotting teeth under protruding brows and bright dream-filled eyes. The amount of booty they collected from their tunnels was inconceivable, but the ogres' capacity for reason didn't account for that.

Confusion filled his brother's watchful eyes. *You'll see.*

The ogres stopped work to celebrate. They piled up their hoard. They celebrated with a feast of raw bear meat and horrendous homemade grog. Verbard wanted no part of that bilious drink. It was known to paralyze men.

"What is this, Verbard? Some sort of stupid distraction?" Catten said with a hiss.

Verbard pointed downward at the ogre bonfire, the revelry ringing clear.

Catten lurched forward as one ogre smashed a large chunk of gold into another grog-drinking ogre's head. The camp burst into thunderous laughter.

Here we go.

Another ogre followed suit with his massive gem. One launched a silver rock at his brethren. The ones who did not have any of the treasure laughed the hardest.

Chaos blossomed. It would take more than a few shiny rocks of gold or silver to hurt an ogre. As soon as those objects contacted them, they got in on the bludgeoning too.

Catten hissed. Verbard chuckled.

The ogres began to massacre each other. Noses were broken and bleeding, teeth shattered, and bones crushed. They were out of control. One ogre in particular was terrified as he could not stop striking himself in the face with the two copper rocks he had picked up in self-defense. Over and over, he bashed his own skull until he could stand no more. So confused they were that they didn't know who was friend or foe.

The madness spread like a virus. The confused ogres eliminated themselves with the colorful booty they'd gathered. Verbard was thrilled with his cursed illusion. Many of them were knocked out and many others died at their brethren's hands. After a long sequence of violent events, the survivors came to their senses again. Broken bones and headaches abounded.

"I have had my fun, now you should have yours." Verbard pointed to his albino urchlings and Catten waved to his Juegen warriors. The creatures charged into the camp. The ogres were far from ready. The Juegens' curved swords sliced like whips in the air as they pierced the hearts and necks of their massive foes, some prone and others feeble. The Juegen guards' were relentless as they carved into their massive foes as if they were giant children.

The albino urchlings ran up and down the backs of the brutes like scurrying rats, stabbing and jabbing them in the eyes, ears, nose, and throat with their clawed hands. Blood ran everywhere, the horrific sight of slaughter and mutilation one for the ages.

Lord Catten nodded.

One lone ogre escaped and hid for days. It had the wit to utilize its free hand to cut off the hand that held the rock it was hitting itself with. It was a small part human, and despite its ignorance of the fact, that was what saved it. Its broken face and bloodied stump for an arm began to heal. It headed back to the mining camp.

When it got there, the ogre saw many bodies of its fellow ogres buried headfirst in massive holes, with their legs protruding from the ground, which was littered with severed heads. Vultures gathered by the hundreds to feast, and the underlings that had afflicted them were long gone.

The gold, silver, and gems had only been rocks, after all.

67

JUST BEFORE DAYBREAK, VENIR, FOGLE, and Ox began preparations to break camp. Venir sauntered out of the way to relieve himself in a glen nearby. He stuck his axe in the ground, surveying their surroundings. Ox stood nearby, packing the wizard's sack. Fogle Boon kneeled on his pillow, deep in meditation. Venir began to pee. *Almost there,* he thought. A strange chill ran down his spine. He crooked his ear.

Fogle Boon shouted, "Venir! Ox! Something is afoot!"

Venir cut himself off midstream. A familiar buzz hit his ears. He whirled the mage's way. Ten feet from Fogle Boon hovered a stocky bat-winged creature holding Venir's backpack. *That imp!* They charged at the intruder, but the imp flew into the air. It bared its razor-sharp teeth at him, then buzzed high above and out of sight. He looked back. Brool was still stuck in the ground.

"Was that what I thought it was, Venir?" Fogle said. "That imp or something like it that you told me about?"

"I think so."

Venir pulled Brool from the ground. His shield and helmet still lay near, but the bag that held them was clearly gone with his backpack. He didn't know what to think. One thing was for certain—underlings had to be near. They had been watching him all along.

After several moments, Fogle asked, "Now what? Will your weapon still work, disappear, or what?"

"I don't know." Venir grabbed what gear he had left. "I guess we'll find out soon enough. In the meantime, let's keep going. Whatever is going to happen is going to happen."

Fogle's wizened face lit up at the statement. "I guess so."

<h1 style="text-align:center">68</h1>

WEEKS HAD PASSED SINCE MELEGAL'S roommates had departed. His face grim, Melegal sat on his cot within the apartment and tried to let the serenity soak in. The first few weeks had been bliss, in the absence of Georgio and his halfling counterpart. Their chronic attention to his comings and goings had become wearisome. Now, no one asked a thing about his business.

Night after night, he did as he pleased. The women, the wine … it was what he was used to. He was a typical greedy thief, living large. The splendid city of Bone was his playground.

But his old indulgences didn't have the same flavor as before.

He looked over to the table where the halfling's tomes sat, save for the one that had gone missing — which Melegal had discovered well after Venir and the boys had departed. Melegal had almost solved the puzzle of Lefty's shorthand. He had spent more time on that than anything else the past few days. Plus, the missing tome ate at him. *Where could it be?*

He stood up, cracked his neck, and stretched. He sat back down, and looked around. The cupboard was bare. The metal coffee carafe sat cold on the coal stove that had not been kindled in weeks. It had never seemed so empty. Even the time between Venir's visits had not been so desolate.

The boys had spoiled him. He smirked at the odd thought. Even Octopus never came by these days. It was Georgio who had fed the cat scraps of chicken gizzards from time to time. Melegal considered that they would not return soon, if ever. *Why would they?*

"Maybe the city of Three is better for them." He stood up and circled the room. *Georgio probably isn't feeding Quickster. I'll give it a few more weeks.* The sound of heavy footsteps interrupted his thoughts. He stopped and listened. Heavy knocks came from below. More boot steps came and someone barked orders.

Knock-knock-knock!

His door shook from the blows. Melegal waited, knowing full well whoever was on the other side had no idea whether he was inside or not. *Probably the City Watch harassing folks,* he told himself. He opened the window.

CRASH!

Melegal turned as the door splintered. *Who on Bish is that?* He dashed for the window. He was in grave danger. Something hit his body and shocked him from head to toe. He writhed in pain and screamed. The apartment dimmed. More pain lanced through his core. *This is it. Agony … forever.* Darkness came as he collapsed to the floor.

<h1 style="text-align:center">69</h1>

VERBARD WAS ELATED AS EEP snatched the large leather sack from Venir's camp. *Yes!* Everything was working. A return home was near. He couldn't wait to get the sack and see what power lay inside, even without the mystic armaments. *Well done, imp!*

Just beyond the passage taken from the ogre camp, he and his brother looked into the spectrum of magic. Eep's eye showed them much. The old, worn leather sack, stitched up with thick cords, hung tight in the imp's claws. Catten stood shoulder to shoulder with Verbard, a loose expression on his face.

"What now? Kill the man? Leave?" Verbard asked.

"You still want the man dead, don't you?"

"Absolutely," Verbard said.

There was nothing he would rather have. A delicious victory was at hand.

The imp soared like an eagle across the blazing sky. A thrill went through Verbard. He could almost feel the wind rushing past his ears as Eep sang some happy song. Verbard savored every flap of Eep's wings as he beheld the rough terrain rushing past. The imp's flight was smooth and soundless, almost serene.

But then the scene became erratic. It seemed like Eep was doing something with the sack. The imp screamed and jerked back and forth. The picture spiraled before Verbard's eyes, and the ground rushed up from below. Nausea overcame him as he watched in confusion. Something had befallen the imp.

"What is happening?" Catten shouted.

Verbard tried to steady himself before the swirling image. His knees weakened.

The imp made no reply. It seemed to be struggling for its very life. Something stirred in the mirage. Verbard and Catten jumped clear out of the way. When Verbard looked up again, the image had faded.

Eep was gone.

"What was that, brother?" Verbard asked.

"I don't know, but it wasn't human. Find out!" Catten said.

Verbard scowled. He wasn't happy, either, but he didn't need his brother breathing down his neck. Verbard made preparations and tried to summon the imp's eye.

Nothing happened.

He tried again. Nothing.

Catten howled in fury.

70

THE SUNS BURNED LIKE FURNACES as Venir walked alongside his companions. He held Brool tight in his grip. Underlings had to be near. They must have been behind the imp's thievery. Still, he opted to continue on toward Dwarven Hole. Over the sand and rock they went with nothing being said.

The silence was as agonizing as the sun when Fogle Boon gasped. "Venir!"

"What, Fogle?"

Fogle just stood there, staring at him.

Venir's grip was empty. *Bone!* The axe, helm, and shield were gone. So comfortable to him they had become that he hadn't even noticed their disappearance.

"Bone!" Venir said.

The hulking man stood with nothing more than his chain shirt, trousers, boots, and his grandfather's long hunting knife. He felt both worry and relief, but his first instinct was to find another formidable weapon. He gripped his long hunting knife by its carved bone hilt, then looked at Fogle Boon and Ox and shrugged. He couldn't let them know the panic he was in. If underlings were near, he had no way of knowing now.

"Can you handle these ventures without that gear?" Fogle asked. "The odds don't seem to be as favorable as before. How do you expect to scare the orcs off with that knife and … well … me?"

Venir smiled. "Well … I guess we'll just have to be careful."

Ox walked over and offered him one of his three hand axes.

Venir took it, and tested its blade. "It'll have to do."

71

EEP BUZZED TOWARD THE HORIZON in victory. He sang an ancient imp song that shattered the eardrums of the wilderness creatures below. Oh, how pleased Lord Catten and Verbard were going to be when he returned. Still … he hated them both, but at least Verbard let him have some fun.

As he flew farther away from the men the bag grew heavier. Maybe the flight was longer than he'd anticipated.

He studied the thick sewn seams that pulled the sack together. As far as he could tell, it was an ordinary sack. His arms and wings began to strain from the weight. He had carried men before and dropped them to their deaths. Why was this sack so heavy? He pressed on.

Eep knew his curiosity was getting the better of him. He ignored his orders and opted for a peek inside. He switched the sack from claw to claw, loosening the neck as he did so. His shoulders began to ache under its weight when he heard a *clank* inside. The bag rustled. He looked up and away as he reached inside. His short arm searched all boundaries of the sack. He could feel the bag's interior. Everything seemed to be as it appeared — a simple, overly large leather sack that was empty.

Grunting in frustration, he rasped, "Stupid heavy bag." He tried to withdraw his arm from the neck of the bag, but it held fast. Pain seized his clawed fingers. Something bit them. Something had hold of his hand. It was chomping off one of his clawed fingers!

Screaming in shock and rage, Eep tore free, and with a howling yank, he withdrew his bloodied now two-fingered hand. A bloody stump was in the middle.

Hissing in rage and shock, he thrust his other arm in the sack. Something grabbed hold of his arm, trying to pull him inside. Eep pulled back. Whatever was holding him let go, freeing Eep's arm. He hissed again and shook the sack. Nothing fell out. He looked back in. A ruddy knuckled fist smashed into his eye. He howled, let loose of the sack, and tumbled out of the sky.

Thud!

Eep rolled over on the ground. Standing up, he popped his shoulder back into place and fluttered his wings. He rubbed his throbbing eye and let out an awful screech. Whatever hit him had hurt. He was going to hurt it back. He clenched his empty claws, and looked around.

The sack was gone. "No!" he rasped.

He looked for it. Twenty yards away it lay on the ground before him, but it was not alone. He recoiled.

Another imp stood over the sack, waiting for him. The imp was almost the same three feet of height as Eep, but built like a man, corded with muscle, thick ruddy brown skin, oversized hands and feet, a large mouth, a single large eye, and a row of small horns above his brow.

The guardian imp was different from Eep in many ways, as it had a face like a man, was without wings, and seemed to be layered with hard, flat patches of thick, stone-like skin here and there.

Jealousy rose in Eep's gut. He hated it, but did not fear it. He was going to kill it. He was the most powerful imp of all.

The other imp made no sound as it pounded its hardened fist into its hand over and over. Eep attacked without hesitation. Zooming in flight, Eep headed straight for his enemy and blinked away before he got there. The other imp's eye widened in puzzlement and then it howled in astonishment. Eep reappeared behind its back and ripped his claws into its backside. A pale, thick blood rose to the surface.

The somewhat smaller imp whirled in attack and hammered Eep's body with a rapid succession of blows that staggered him. Each painful blow had the force of a mallet. His ribs cracked as he spat dark blood. He writhed under the blows, then tore himself away and flew into the sky.

There he hovered over his nearly unscathed assailant. Now Eep had a busted nose to go along with his missing finger. He shook it off. Verbard and Catten had put him through worse many times before. He dove straight into the fray again.

Eep ripped and slashed the small man-like imp with speed and cunning that overwhelmed it. It fought back like a seasoned fighter and counter-punched blow after blow. Oily blood seethed from both bodies until they were covered in it. The smaller imp grimaced in pain. Small chunks of its flesh had been torn and bitten from its body — and it was weakening.

Although exhausted, Eep had the edge. The other imp became slow as it gathered itself off the grimy ground over and over again. It rasped from its small mouth, raised its fists up to its chin, and waited for the next attack. His prey was done.

Flying high, Eep dove down, and blinked away. The small imp looked around and saw nothing. Moments passed.

Eep appeared behind the imp, then grabbed and pulled it defenseless into the air. It tried to wrench itself free, but wasn't quick enough. Eep dropped it over one thousand feet onto the jagged rocks below. The fall didn't kill it, though, just busted its arms and legs so that it could no longer walk or raise its arms.

Eep hovered over it and spat on it. He hissed. Burning with rage, he dropped beside it and tore the helpless creature into pieces.

It was over. He tossed one of its legs away and shook off the flesh and blood of the other imp. The little terror clasped his bloody claws together and licked his lips. The imp hovered over to the sack. He picked it up and opened it up, peered inside again, and saw nothing. *Yes. Mission completed.* Something shined, deep down inside the bag. *Treasure?* A thrill went through him.

Mesmerized, he looked deeper into the sack.

Urk!

A large hand grasped Eep's neck, choking him. He fought for his freedom, but could not escape its powerful grip. An identical imp from moments before — just way bigger — grasped Eep, squeezing his neck, nearly popping his eye out.

The imp — what Eep figured to be some sort of guardian of the sack — stepped outside the bag. It was twice as big as the other imp and every bit of six feet tall. Without hesitation, it punched Eep in the face over and over again. He could hear the wet painful smacks in his ear holes. He was helpless as it pounded him into the ground. The cracking sounds of his bones burst in his ears as he screeched in pain.

Eep groaned as he looked up at another of his kind. "You can't kill me forever, brother," Eep mumbled. "I will heal and have vengeance,"

The guardian imp stepped on his back and grasped his wings. *Oh no, not that!* The guardian roared in triumph as it ripped off Eep's bat-like wings. Eep howled in pain and horror, not knowing which present pain was worse. The giant imp dragged Eep's broken body back inside of the sack. The greatest horror on Bish was gone. For now.

72

A BUCKET OF COLD WATER BROUGHT Melegal to his senses. Numb from head to toe, skull throbbing, he tugged at the cords that bound his hands to a chair behind him. Squinting, it appeared that he was in a library of sorts, no longer in use for anything more than common storage of unwanted baubles and artifacts.

Large, colorful candles burned bright, bringing an eerie illumination to the room. A dozen or so candles sat scattered along bookshelves and walls. It was all familiar. Melegal had spent many hours in similar chambers as a child, scribing and delivering meals to those who made plans and kept their secrets within such concealed confines. A chill entered him.

He closed his eyes and ascertained his predicament. A hundred faces raced through his mind as he tried to piece everything together. He thought of everyone he'd seen in the hours and days before he was captured. *McKnight? No, can't be!*

And who had awoken him? Why was he even here? He had to escape.

Melegal heard his captor still behind him, now whistling an annoying tune. He smelled sweat and heard the naked footsteps of a heavy-set man that seemed winded from only a little exertion. Almost a minute passed before the character finally appeared before him. The man—obviously a cleric—was pale, flabby, and disturbing, wearing only a tiny breech of cloth around his waist, as well as Melegal's own floppy, dark-gray hat on his head.

Bone! Not my hat!

"My name is Sefron," the man said, licking his lips. Sefron wiped the sweat from his bulging eyes with the floppy hat. The creepy man with pasty white skin wrung his sweaty hands. "And you would be Melegal—a thief, a one-time servant of the Royal houses of Bone, an urchin. Do you deny any of this?"

Melegal didn't move; he only stared hard at the man.

Take off my hat, you sweaty pig!

"Well … I see you don't care for conversation," Sefron said. "We have our ways of convincing you that it would be wise of you to speak. Actually … I have my ways."

The foul cleric came face-to-face with his prisoner. The smell of Sefron's rotten breath made Melegal want to gag. He didn't move.

This fool's not my captor. Have to be patient. Find out what's going on. I can always kill him later. Easily.

A door behind Melegal swung open and the cleric jumped back as if someone had taken a swing at him. Sefron knelt on the ground.

A deep, rich voice spoke. "What are you still doing here, Sefron? I told you to wake him and leave."

Almen? This is not good. Melegal listened closely.

"I am sorry, my lord! He has only been awake but a moment," Sefron said, groveling on the floor.

"Cleric, shut up! And take off that hat!"

"But—"

The end of a spear poked the cleric in his fat belly. Sefron squealed like a wounded pig, making a scene as if his leg had been cut off.

Good. A bit more merciful than I would have been.

"Drag him out," Almen said, still behind Melegal.

Two Royal household sentries came in and did as ordered without hesitation.

"Close the door and stay outside," Almen said.

After a few more moments, Sefron's wailing could no longer be heard. There Melegal sat, trying to get the feeling back in his numb fingers.

The Royal lord walked in front of the thief and placed the hat back on his head. Almen pulled up a chair and set it down in front of him. The man was tall, handsome, and broad shouldered. His clothes were exquisite, typical of leading Royal household members. His long brown hair was pulled back behind his ears and his brown eyes were sharp, intelligent, and intimidating.

Melegal remembered him as the father from the dungeons where Venir had received lashes from his son Tonio. That was when all the trouble started. This was Royal Lord Almen, of the Third House in the city of Bone. Melegal got the feeling this man should never have been trifled with.

I should have listened to Venir and gotten out of Bone when I had the chance.

"Thief, I will make this clear once," Almen said, his voice commanding as he leaned forward. "We are going to have a conversation. If you do not engage in the conversation, you will die where you sit. Do you understand?'

"Yes," Melegal answered, fully convinced the man's words were true.

"That is good," Almen said, sounding more diplomatic. "Now, I pride myself on the gathering of information, which as *you* well know is common within the walls of Royal castles. Over the years, I have had many assistants, and one in particular has gone missing. His name is McKnight. Do you know this man?"

"Yes, I know him."

"Good, good. Then you know that he was in my service. What else do you know?"

Melegal held the man's gaze. How much did this man know already? He didn't want to call his bluff. He worked his fingers harder. "The last I saw him, he was having dinner with the swine."

Royal Lord Almen chuckled. "Yes, I heard something like that too. So, it is unlikely he will be returning to my service, which is disappointing because he was skilled, enough so that he went unnoticed by my spies for some time upon his return to Bone. But he is gone—and that leads me to you." He pointed at him. "One thing that Detective McKnight did for me was recruit talented servants. He talked about it with me from time to time. He also gave me a list. Many years ago. You were on it."

I was?

"He said you could read and write with a deft hand. I believe he also spent time with your kind and tested them with other things. Is this ringing a bell?"

It was true that McKnight had singled Melegal out at one time and began a secret tutelage of sorts, but Melegal and Venir's escape had brought that to an end. The detective had tracked the teenage Melegal down, and for a few years, the street urchin had been his protégé. It had been as if McKnight was preparing him for something more than just stealing in the streets. But he didn't like McKnight. He had gone his separate way, and McKnight had hated him ever since.

"Yes." Melegal considered himself lucky that he didn't sweat. If he did, Royal Lord Almen would know how nervous he was.

This is not good.

"That is good. Now, McKnight was a loyal servant of mine for decades and his services will be greatly missed. I need a suitable replacement. That is why I brought you here. The replacement, assuming he or she is worthy and loyal, will have all of the pleasures and privileges typically bestowed on their predecessor. Do you understand everything that entails, Melegal?"

Are you serious?

He understood, indeed—to have everything a Royal could have without being a Royal and be able to enjoy it all behind the scenes. Was this what McKnight had tried to prepare him for? And if so, why him?

An inner struggle churned inside Melegal. He hated the Royals and their cruel and twisted ways. His thoughts went to Venir and the boys, and he wondered if he would ever see them again. Certainly from this vantage point, Almen's arrangement would benefit them all. Melegal would be able to protect his friends. Then he considered the fine food, wine, and beautiful women he could indulge himself in daily. It was an offer he saw no reason to refuse, not a man of his ilk. *What kind of greedy thief would ever say no to this?*

"Yes, I understand."

"Then will you take my offer?"

There was only one answer to the question. Yes—or die. He would be bound to Almen or dead. A slave again.

A slave with benefits. Lots of them.

An *offer* from a Royal such as Almen was only made once. Melegal knew what he was getting into, but he was getting older and he didn't want to live off the streets forever. "Yes."

"Excellent."

The Royal lord stood and walked to the door. Melegal felt relieved already.

"I shall have my guards unbind you," Almen said.

"No need." Melegal stood up, hands unfettered.

"Impressive, Detective Melegal," Almen said, walking over to the thief, and looking down on Melegal's head.

Melegal kept his eyes on the Royal lord's chest. *Now what does he want?*

"I have another question for you."

"Of course." Melegal wiped his hat. He needed to have it washed.

"Have you seen my son Tonio?"

Again, he didn't want to call his Royal lord's bluff. Lying to this man would not be a good idea. "Yes."

Tonio had not resurfaced since the last time Melegal had seen him. How much did this man already know? He met the Royal lord's eyes, ready for the next question.

"There have been rumors that my son is near. I want you to see to it that those rumors disappear."

"Of course, Lord Almen."

"Now let's get you cleaned up. Follow me."

This was a bad deal, but what choice did he have? He thought of his friends and wondered about them. He had to play along. How hard would that be? Dread filled him with every step he took. He followed the Royal lord up into the warmth of the castle. Sefron was hanging around, pestering the servants, men and women who had been broken. A sick urchin was chained to the kitchen floor, peeling potatoes.

Why did I do this? Death now seemed the better choice.

73

C ATTEN SIMMERED WITH RAGE FOR days. It was clear the imp was gone, and along with it, so were his plans for a quick and easy path for the destruction for the Darkslayer. His brother was no less unhappy, but his suggestions to return to Oran's lair were preposterous.

Catten hissed, "We will not return to the lair!"

"Why not? We might find something else of aid! There is no need to be hasty!"

Catten's disdain for his brother had only increased after the imp's sudden demise. He could have killed him, but he knew Verbard wasn't to blame. Catten wanted to go home, but didn't feel his brother did. The pair had exhausted themselves with scenarios about what had happened with Eep, the leather sack, and the man, but ultimately there was only one plan that would find the truth. They had to track down the Darkslayer the old-fashioned way.

"Let's just do this. We can't avoid this fight forever," Catten said.

Verbard's silver eyes popped open and he sighed. "Agreed."

Catten led the party and headed north, avoiding eyes during the day and making haste at night. It was a shame the Current didn't run farther north. If it did, things would have been easier.

Being on the surface bothered him. The Darkslayer would come for them. *We better find the troublesome man before he finds us first.*

74

F OGLE BOON TRUDGED ALONG, KEEPING the backs of Venir and Ox in his sight.

Dwarven Hole must be an eternity away.

He was slowing them down. Ever since the imp had appeared and taken Venir's sack, things had gotten worse. Fogle's feet felt like they were on fire. Seeing Venir waiting for him to catch up made him feel embarrassed.

"Fogle, how are your feet?" Venir said with concern in his voice.

"See for yourself." Fogle flopped down, wincing as he pulled off his boots. Red sores and blisters covered his heels, pads, and even his toe tops. Venir grimaced. It only made him feel worse. "Maybe I should cut them off," Fogle said.

"You'll live. We aren't too far from Dwarven Hole—a few more days maybe. If we make it, the lady dwarves will patch you up right. You'll like them; they are excellent with their care. A little man like you will be like tending a babe," he said with a wink.

"I don't share your enthusiasm." Fogle shook sand from his bloody sock.

"You will when you meet them."

"Can't wait."

"Well, stay put, because there are ways in this wasteland to heal those feet, but the streams and grass I need are scarce. I can lance those blisters, coat them in the stream's clay and mud, let them sit overnight and they'll callous quickly … make your feet tough. Me and Ox will make a stretcher if need be, but we have to keep moving."

Venir was sincere, but Fogle Boon still didn't care for it.

"You try to put me on a stretcher and I might as well be dead, and I am far from that," Fogle said, tugging his boots back on. It only made the pain worse.

"If you're almost dead, we'll just bury you. You did have Ox bring a shovel, didn't you?"

Fogle heard Ox's goat-like laughter.

A smile cracked over Fogle's dry lips. "I did have him pack one, and all along I thought it was to help you dig down to the Underland."

Venir laughed, but there was something dark behind the man's eyes. Fogle remembered the story of when the underlings had buried Venir as a boy. He grew silent and sensed an awkwardness overcoming his burly comrade. He laced up his boots as the warrior walked away. Ox followed along as if something was amiss.

Fogle gathered himself. Staring into the Outland furnace of nothing, he wondered why he'd gotten into this. Only a fool would follow another into the Outlands. He'd left his life for this adventure. He shook his head, leaned on his staff, and shuffled ahead. They had walked for hours when Venir finally stopped. Fogle stood beside the warrior, peering ahead.

"What is it?" Fogle asked.

"We are being watched."

75

JARLA, AGAIN WORTHY OF THE title "queen," carved her way through Bish to track down Venir. She had little idea where to start, but she knew where to call to find out. She was every bit the assassin that she was the soldier, and she kept things that tied her to her prey. When Venir departed from her, he left his clothes. She had retained them all these years.

It was nothing more than a leather jerkin she had kept, but it was enough. She took it to a female enchantress and bartered payment. The enchantress spent hours inside her forested bungalow, executing a spell that would locate the wearer. Jarla and her gang waited outside. She felt in control again. Her confidence was growing.

When the red-haired enchantress emerged, she held a small globe before her and Venir appeared within the city of Three.

Jarla cackled. She took the fiery orange globe from the flame-haired enchantress, who demanded payment. The brigand queen laughed in her face and nodded to some of her brigands. They dragged the woman kicking and screaming back inside.

Jarla now possessed the small globe of magic. It was charged with only two more uses. She would see to it that Venir did not escape her again.

Another use of the globe several days later showed Venir leaving Three with two companions. Then, after a few more days had passed, she used the last charge and saw her former lover traveling west with the same two companions. Venir, though, didn't appear as she'd suspected he would.

Before it vanished into nothingness, the magic orb helped her get close enough to Venir's current location to use her powerful spyglass. This was it. She was eager to see the man castrated by her sword.

She and her men, made up of men, half-orcs, dog-faced gnolls, and a kobold, waited in the distance. They rode light warhorses, and were armored in brigand leathers, and equipped with swords and spears.. Her stomach knotted at the sight of Venir. She called to her men, who rode up alongside her. They trotted toward Venir and his two friends.

76

"BISH!" VENIR EXCLAIMED AT THE sound of hooves thundering in their direction. A billow of smoke followed in the wake of the riders.

"What is it? Underlings?" Fogle cried.

Venir almost started to laugh. "No … underlings don't ride horses, especially not in broad daylight. We'll know soon enough, but whoever it is knows we are here. And there is nowhere to run without mounts. Whatever tricks you have up your sleeve, get them ready, Fogle. This is what you came for." Clutching at the small axe in one hand and the hunting knife in the other, Venir felt naked.

Fogle's eyes were wider than he had ever seen. The mage huddled behind him, crafting his spells. Ox stood at Venir's side, axes bared for battle—giving Venir a little comfort.

The horses formed a line twenty paces away. Something was strange about the motley band. Brigands like them wouldn't normally travel so far north. Then a helmeted figure trotted forward on a powerful dapple gray steed. The woman's raven-black hair billowed in the hot wind. Sweat rolled down her long, tanned—and savory—legs. A scent wafted through the air.

Venir's eyes blazed as he yelled, "Jarla!"

Fogle Boon stopped what he was doing and peered over Venir's massive shoulder. The woman took off her helmet and dropped it to the ground. Fogle sucked air between his teeth. Jarla just gazed at Venir with hot blue eyes over her scarred cheekbones. He said nothing as she basked her bronzed figure in the sunlight a bit longer.

She was the last thing he expected to see. She was still a striking and powerful woman. Fogle Boon whispered, "Sweet mother of Bish! What an amazing woman!"

Venir lost himself for a moment. He returned her gaze. Her smile told it all. She had him. He didn't like it. "Looks like you are ready to die, witch!"

Jarla laughed a bit. "No, blondie, I came here to kill you. And by the looks of things, it's going to be easy." She pointed to Fogle and Ox.

"Oh … it won't be easy," Venir said. "Now come down off that horse and let's finish this."

"Return to me my armament, and I might let you live."

Venir chuckled. "If I still had it, I wouldn't be facing you with these pig stickers, now would I? It's gone! Now move on or die, wench!"

Jarla's face was stone, believing of his words, but he could see they had little effect on her plans for him. And the sound of her voice had awakened all he hated about her.

"You should know better," Jarla said. "I'll carve you up with my blades. I was always the superior fighter. You are little more than a brute with a toy knife and axe—how pathetic."

"By the looks of that rump of yours, it doesn't look like you've been fighting anything other than a jug of wine," Venir said, regaining his composure. He knew how much she despised his humor.

"Lout! I'm gonna cut you into ribbons." She reared up on Nightmare. "No! We all are!"

He pressed on, hoping his taunts would buy the mage time. "Well, if you wait any longer, the rest of your hair is likely to turn gray, so you better get after it, hag!"

Venir could have sworn one of the brigands snickered. Jarla's face filled with rage. She wanted nothing more than to trample him, but she wouldn't risk that horse of hers.

Jarla seemed to stammer for words. "Have it your way, you … you buffoon! Make a line, men, and let's run them down like filthy curs. Then this blond dog will bark no more. Attack!"

The brigands turned their mounts and fanned out in two ranks, lining up one behind the other. Jarla stayed back behind her men, sword ready, awaiting the slaughter, her eyes gleaming with the look of victory.

He knew what they were doing. He had done the same with the brigand army. The riders were prepared to run one after the other right over Fogle, Ox, and himself, grinding their crushed bones into the rock and sand. They would be easy pickings unless, as Venir hoped, the mage had something up his sleeve. He braced himself for the charge.

The brigands cried aloud as they spurred their horses. The sound of hooves galloping came their way from thirty lengths.

This can't be it.

Twenty lengths.

Take all you can.

Ten lengths.

I'm waiting.

The column of horses collapsed. Nests of large rattlesnakes burst from the ground. Panic overtook the men and beasts as the snakes struck everything moving. The riders tried to control their frenzied mounts. Many brigands were bucked to the ground, trampled, or snake struck.

Jarla yelled, "It's an illusion, you fools! Regain yourselves!"

The words did little good. Venir moved into the fray. Fogle Boon stayed guarded behind the protection of Ox.

Jarla noticed Venir coming her way and turned to a black-bearded brigand archer, still mounted, arrow nocked in hesitation. "What are you waiting for? Shoot something, fool!" she screamed.

The wiry brigand pointed his bow dead center on Venir, who was caught up in the skirmish on the ground, but the archer didn't release on his clear shot, drawing Jarla's fury further.

"Shoot that mangy dog of a man!"

Shifting his sight in a fluid motion, the brigand pointed his bow toward her and replied, "Fine!"

Thwack!

Jarla turned Nightmare in the nick of time. The arrow's shaft caught her horse between its saddle and hide. Nightmare bucked, throwing Jarla to the ground. Chaos consumed Jarla's army as yet another surly brigand turned on them. He was bald, dark-faced and bearded, as big as Venir and swinging a studded club like a stick. The brute smashed other brigands' clavicles and broke thigh bones like toothpicks while singing a song of battle.

The remaining men were little match for the archer that lanced their throats and chests with unfailing accuracy while the big, black brute crashed through them like they were children.

Fogle Boon watched from behind Ox, who fended off other brigands. There must have been twenty in all. The mage pursed his lips together in an inaudible whisper and pointed toward a large, dog-faced gnoll that broke free of the melee. It barreled over the sand straight toward the helpless man. A tiny, red missile the size of a nail appeared before Fogle's eyes and he flicked his hand as if he were tossing a dart. The red missile hovered slowly toward the gnoll, who broke off his charge and turned the other way. The missile hovered before its wide eyes, blocking its path.

Zzzzzit! Zzzzzit! Zzzzzit! Zzzzzit!

The magic projectile zipped in and out of the gnoll's body in rapid flashes of light, searing blood and bone, and drawing a bloodcurdling scream from the helpless creature. It fell, smoking, and dead as the terrain beneath him. Fogle grinned.

Jarla regained herself and sat again on her bleeding mount. She could have easily ridden off, tried to trample them, and left, but instead she squared up her mount on Venir, who stood splattered in fresh gore before her, his battle lust still hot in his eyes.

They stared at each other as he spoke. "Get off your horse, witch!"

She dismounted. The other brigands backed off. Clearly, a score was left to be settled between the two, so no others needed to die.

"Clearly you have turned the tables on me again, Venir, but you are not as well equipped as when we last parted."

Venir might no longer have the magical armament that Jarla herself once possessed, but he had managed to gain a gleaming broadsword to complement his hunting knife. He shook the blood from both blades.

Jarla withdrew her long sword. It was polished, sleek, and of the high quality only the commanders of the Royal armies possessed. It was a superior weapon compared to the blade her held. He noted the scars and hard lines of time in her face. She had bested him long ago in bouts at the campsite—and he hadn't swung a sword in years.

"Drop the knife," Jarla said. "I have only one blade. You are smart to wish to face me with two blades, but no matter. I'll carve you up either way."

Venir sheathed the knife. The tension of the moment seemed to billow within the hot air. The woman looked magnificent and powerful in their presence. Her charisma had once garnered his respect somehow.

But she had betrayed him. Slaughtered his friends. Allied herself with underlings. For years, he'd sought revenge before giving up the chase. Now he could have his vengeance. His nerves boiled over the painful memories. He was ready.

Jarla moved in, cutting and slashing with the precision of a seasoned fighter. He parried her efforts blow after blow. Steel rang aloud as the two shuffled back and forth. The men and brigands formed a circle around them. Jarla's long sword licked out time after time, faster and faster, only to be countered by his reflexes and instincts.

She's still quick.

Her strong sword arm did not fatigue from the assault. Her thrusts came faster and closer. He swiped his heavy blade back and forth, batting her efforts away. She broke off. It surprised him.

"I see you are too scared to attack me, blondie. You're afraid, aren't you?" she said winded. Her breasts heaved up and down.

Clear your head, man! She's trying to kill you.

"You don't know what to do without your big axe, do you, lout?" she said. "Now come on! Be a man and fight me. I'll cut you down quick, I promise. I might even save your humorous tongue and hang it from my neck." She ran a finger down her neck. "As a memento."

Truth rang from her lips. He did not feel the same without Brool, but he knew all he needed. He beckoned her forward with his blades and grinned. "Come now, that wasn't your best, was it, Jarla? I think that chicken fat under your arms is slowing you down. Sit down, take a drink of some wine—"

She clipped his ear as he ducked under her blade. He spun away and caught her with the flat side of his blade, stinging her rump and bringing a yelp from her lips.

"Man, this is gettin' good!" one of the brigands said.

Even Ox's eyes were enthralled by the battle.

Jarla came at him again, slice after slice. The audience had trouble watching the moves, but the banging sound of the blades helped them keep track of the attacks. It was clear she wanted to take off his head. He didn't know why she hated him so much. *She* was the one that betrayed him. Why would she come all this way to kill him?

She's crazy!

His corded arm was pressed to match her speed, but his sword was weightless in his powerful arm, unfailing and getting faster.

The rust was coming off.

Venir parried her thrusts with ease. One after the other, he seemed to grow quicker. He turned the tables. *Thrust. Stab. Cut. Thrust. Stab. Cut.* She parried and ducked in desperation. He pressed on. She was running out of breath as he banged away.

Clang!

Knocking her sword clean from her grasp, Venir closed in and punched her hard in the stomach. She dropped to her knees, head down, defeated. It was as if his punch had knocked both the wind and will from her. After several gasping moments, she managed to speak. He held the sword at her neck.

"Kill me, Vee. I have nothing to live for. You win. Kill me," she croaked.

He paused and stepped back, wary of a trick, then stuck his sword in the ground.

She sobbed, and rolled to the ground, wailing, "Please just kill me!"

"Kill her, Vee! Wha'cha waitin' for? She's evil," the big bearded black man said.

"You ever kill a woman, Mikkel?" Venir said.

"No," he answered.

"Neither have I, and I won't today."

"Kill me, you coward!" Jarla screamed. "I can't live with the thought of yet another man humiliating me!"

Jarla sounded hysterical, broken, and lost. All the men could see it, and it made even their hardened spirits uncomfortable. She had no purpose. It had been kill Venir and live, or fail and die. Now she was failing to do either.

"Venir, just leave her to rot in the sand. She doesn't even deserve that," Billip added from beneath his black beard, bow and arrow poised to strike her.

"You!" she blurted. "You shot my horse! I'll cut you to pieces if you do it again. I'll slice your—"

"Shut up, foul woman! Your horse is fine—and I was aiming for you," the wiry archer snapped back. "I've had enough of your mouth on this trek. I'll have no more or I will kill you myself … woman or witch."

The brigand queen seemed to gather herself among the men, then stood up, tall and prominent, and carefully went to check on Nightmare. She stroked her steed's mane.

"Billip and Mikkel," Venir said, "how did you manage to make it up here and not be noticed?"

"I guess 'cause we weren't as memorable as you, stud," Mikkel said, laughing.

Billip laughed too. "She didn't have any idea who we were. She just showed up at the tavern and ordered us to follow. It shocked us that she was alive, and when we asked her where we were going, she just said, 'We'll know when we get there.' Her other men filled us in on the details, though, and seeing as how she didn't know or remember us, we figured we'd better be around to bail you out."

"Yeah … bail *you* out!" Mikkel agreed.

Venir wondered what his next move was with Jarla. All the hatred he had for her was gone. Something felt … bigger inside of him. It wasn't compassion or mercy. He didn't know what it was. Maybe Fogle could give some insight.

"What do you think about the woman, Fogle?" Venir said. "What should we do with her?"

Fogle's face showed careful thought before he made his reply. "She is broken, Venir. I see it in her eyes. I know it. She is a threat no more. You have won."

Jarla's hot eyes bore into the mage. She glared at Venir. "You won long ago, Venir," Jarla said. "I just could not admit it, not to a man, and I hate you for it. The scrawny man is right. I am a husk, nothing more. On my word, I have no fight left for you."

"But the rest of you dogs will taste my steel if you *ever* cross me," Jarla shouted. "Don't even look my way if our paths cross again. Understand?"

"Don't worry, we won't," Billip fired back.

"Get on your horse and go—and hope you don't cross our path, woman," Mikkel said while motioning with his club.

Jarla mounted Nightmare and Venir tossed her sword up to her. "You'll need that again soon enough to defend that attitude of yours," he said. "If I ever see you again, it will be too soon."

Jarla spurred Nightmare away without hesitation along with the men she had remaining.

"Man, Vee, she might be mean, but she is a fox," said Mikkel.

"I have to agree," Fogle said.

Billip shrugged in unity.

"Still, Vee," Mikkel said, "How can you just let her go after her alliance with the underlings and what she did at Outpost Thirty-One? She's dangerous."

"She has enough to worry about. The Royals won't ever forget her transgressions. She'll have to lay low. As long as she doesn't raise an army, she's a renegade, nothing more, but she's a survivor, too. Now we've got mounts and more weapons. You want to head to Dwarven Hole with us?"

As he said it, Venir watched Jarla gallop away. The warrior felt some relief. Her image would no longer haunt his memories. Still, deep in his gut, he knew it wasn't over. The two of them shared something no one else ever had—the mystical armaments—and somehow it would keep them bonded forever.

"Why not?" Mikkel said. "It's been a while since I tussled with the dwarven ladies. I remember that last time I went there—"

"We aren't going *there,* Mikkel," Billip said. "That's all I heard about up here—you and this woman, and you and that woman. Can't you think of anything else to talk about?"

"Nope, can you?" Mikkel said.

All the men had a chuckle.

"What do you say, Ox?" Venir said, "Awfully quiet over there."

Ox, the mintaur, had no words, as always, but his eyes were fixed south where unusual storms seemed to be gathering. The sky blackened over them, and the winds picked up.

"What on Bish is that?" Fogle shouted above the increasing wind.

Massive tornados twirled in the distance. Lightning lanced over the sky. Thunder cracked, the likes they had never heard before. A sea of darkness swirled before them.

"Let's ride to Dwarven Hole! Else that storm will take us!" Venir yelled.

They mounted up and charged away.

77

TRINOS AND SCORCH LANDED. THE world of Bish trembled. The wake of the world's newest arrivals sent tremors of change throughout the lands. Trinos had no intent to molest the world she'd created, but her presence had ramifications, though subtle, and change still came. The infinite pair set themselves up for a life on Bish.

They agreed to be neutral in their prospective dealings. They also agreed to limit their power, storing most of it deep beneath the surface, where only the two of them together could ever acquire it again.

Still, they were the most powerful beings on Bish.

Trinos was overcome with compassion for her creation and its creatures. She hadn't realized what she had inflicted on others for her own entertainment. She was moved to try and teach them to somehow survive amiably with one another. She challenged herself to bring something better to the world with her power, charisma, and beauty. She would change her form to blend in with whichever race or creature she was trying to sway. She found a new purpose in her life.

Scorch was overcome with exhilaration from the feeling of having great power at his disposal that he could use for his own purpose and not be judged. He had little care for the affairs of life on Bish. Instead, he seemed content to meddle whenever and with whomever he deemed fit, and he planned to enjoy it.

The unique pair agreed to meet from time to time, and when the time was right, they would depart again. But the world of Bish that they now claimed as home also claimed them. It would not be long before its harsh elements beset them, little by little, day by day, and they, too, would be changed forever.

They were flesh and blood now, mortal—yet as invulnerable as they desired. They had powers and intelligence beyond what the rest of the realm had, yet they would be challenged with the willful and self-serving fiber of the relentless world and its demanding races. Bish was unique within the universe.

78

THE STORMS THAT BESIEGED THE land made travel slow for the men. It was rare weather—the rain, whipping winds, and thunderstorms slowed the trek to Dwarven Hole to a walk. Ox guided the mounted men, checked the unstable ground for sinkholes, and led them through slippery rock passages prone to flooding and avalanches that were known to drown and crush even the most experienced of travelers.

The weather was indeed rare—sudden and odd in appearance to the extreme. Venir felt out of his element. The grim faces of the other men told him he wasn't alone. He struggled with more than that, though. He wondered if his time as the Darkslayer had come and gone forever.

The others seemed to avoid him, not sure what to say. They chatted among themselves, behind his broad back, with uncertainty of their mission.

He was determined to get to Dwarven Hole and they were with him. There was no other direction to go. The rain and wind were endless, beating on the men day in and day out. Anywhere with a ceiling would be better. He just needed to get out of the rain. Maybe some warm dwarven ale would help. Maybe that would ease his spirits and loosen his tongue.

The weeklong journey seemed to take months, but they finally made it. The weather had returned to normal— hot and barren—a full day before they arrived at the home of the dwarves. Relief filled the men's voices. They rode toward a canyon in the distance. It grew larger with the trot of every hoof. Coming along its edge, they peered down and across the massive natural barrier, like an inverted volcano. Fogle cleared his eyes, staring into the deep chasm.

It was one of many holes that housed the dwarven cities, over a mile long. Looking downward, it seemed as deep as it was wide. The inner walls were carved-out stone homes, roads, and aqueducts. Massive bridges of iron ore and rock crisscrossed at every level, defying reason. Busy bodies of thick men and women moved in harmony along its roadways like hairy ants. The sight was spectacular every time Venir saw it. It was organized, yet unexplainable by words. It was something only the dwarves could do.

"Well, boys," Mikkel said, breaking the silence, "I am ready for a hot bath and a dwarven massage! You coming, or am I getting it all to myself?"

"I can't believe it," Fogle said. "I have heard about this. Impressive, indeed. Tell me more about those dwarven women, Mikkel?"

"You're in for a treat, mage," he replied.

The pair was the first to disappear over the steep edge that spiraled down along the walls into the city. There were no guards posted—there was no need. If they didn't like someone, dispatching them was not an issue. Only a fool would rattle the anger of a city of dwarves. Their catapults were always available for crushing any nuisance that came their way. Venir had seen many unwelcome guests launched from deep below through the air onto the Bish terrain. Some survived, but most didn't. It was a sight to see.

He followed the men down below, but didn't feel any better.

79

"**W**HAT IS IT, BROTHER?" VERBARD said.

The unknown force had them both reeling. Catten took a knee, feeling sick.

"Remember the change we felt in the Warfield?" Catten said, steadying himself on one knee. "I have felt it again."

Verbard was quiet for a moment, round silver eyes unblinking, then he hissed.

"I have felt something similar. It makes my aura seem to ebb in and out, as if it isn't reliable. The last time, I felt complete control, but now, not so much. I feel uncertain. You?"

Catten nodded. "It's more physical than mental, still unstable, but very faint. It is as if something we cannot see is changing in the landscape." He took a deep breath and groaned as he got back on his feet. The weird feeling passed. Catten put his hands on his head then nodded. It was all there.

Underlings were intuitive creatures that relied on the magic from Bish more than any other race. Most underlings probably did not notice a thing, but Catten felt like a chunk of power had come and gone, only to come again. He summoned energy that surged in his belly. It was his and his alone. He let the moment pass.

The underlings trekked over the landscape between Dwarven Hole and Hohm's Marsh. The wet and treacherous storms didn't bother Catten. He delighted in them. His brother drew his robes tight and cast a spell that deflected the cutting rain.

Spoiled and soft. He concluded that even though Eep had come to a great demise, Catten still had the same mission—seek out and destroy the Darkslayer once and for all. He wanted the man's head.

He did not come this far to fail. He must have the sack. It drove him onward. The tome told him all he needed to know. The Darkslayer was just a man. His skin and bones could be seared alive. Catten had the hunter's edge.

After days beneath the lashing storms, Verbard spoke again, "We can be patient and wait, or we can draw him out. We know this man hunts us with or without the magic armaments. I say we try to draw him here if we don't find any evidence soon."

"Maybe … maybe," Catten said.

He had an idea. He grabbed large rocks and piled them up. His energy was steady as he spoke mystic words. He focused on the image of the Darkslayer. Everything he knew about the man came to mind. The stones brightened then dulled again. He wiped his brow.

Verbard chattered to his albino urchlings, who gathered the stones inside their knotted arms. As they traveled, they placed the stones where Catten ordered as he floated along.

The stones were magic wards. Only certain creatures would set them off. Something similar to his pursuers coming within proximity would let him know to investigate. The vast landscape made it difficult to spread the wards where the man and his friends would go, but it was still better than tracking the man alone. The wards were another edge the underlings had over the other races. It was one spell that served their methods of guerilla warfare quite well.

It will have to do.

80

"W HAT'S GOING ON WITH YOU, man? Why ain't you runnin' that loud mouth of yours?" Mood said.

Venir pet Chongo at his side. It had seemed like he had to wait forever for Mood and Chongo to return to Dwarven Hole. He had been worried. It had been more than a month before the dog and giant dwarf returned. It only increased his doubt.

Everyone marveled at Mood's story of his battle with Horace the hill giant—everyone but Venir, as he feared that Chongo could have been hurt badly or even killed. The other men didn't really believe there were giants at all on Bish, until the Blood Ranger pulled out the giant's booty. Playing with jewels, rings, and necklaces that would fit over their thighs or heads, they no longer doubted that giants walked Bish. It made the dwarven king much easier to forgive for Venir.

Chongo wagged his tails in rhythm to the steady dwarven tones that beat in harmony in the massive canyon.

Venir was tired as he stared back at Mood's bushy red-bearded face. "I think I'll be going soon," Venir said. "It's been weeks, and the storms have subsided. I have things to do."

"Have you invited the others, or were you and Chongo planning on sneaking out like you always do?" Mood asked as he lit up a fat cigar.

"Don't know. I'd rather go it alone," Venir said, frowning.

"You're a stubborn man. Since these storms started, the blooming world is agitated. The underlings are crawlin' everywhere like cockroaches," Mood said, stomping an ugly bug under his boot. "They're staying south, but there are some here, above us. You know, the ones we think are looking for you. Crafty, that pair, and powerful. Methinks they are the same ones from the Warfield." Mood grabbed Venir by the shoulders and looked him in the eye.

Venir, though, struggled to meet the dwarf's stern gaze. He didn't want to hear it.

"You can't handle them alone if that is what you're thinking. Not now, and not without that bloomin' axe, neither," Mood said. "Wait it out. You can't find them if we can't. Not even with Chongo. Believe me, we have been trying. Best we can figure, they are waiting on someone—and that someone is you."

It was quiet for a moment, then Venir asked, "I'm making you dwarves edgy, aren't I?'

Mood shrugged and handed Venir his lit cigar. "Well, maybe Billip and Mikkel are doing that on their own. Did you have to drag them in here? They're wearing out their welcome. Our women adore those men, and my smaller brethren are gettin' fed up with the hospitality. They can't play nice forever. Settle those boys, or it's gonna be the catapults for them."

"I'll take care of it." Venir took a long drag on Mood's cigar. It made his head light. He started to grin. He knew full well that his friends were getting carried away with wine, romance, and the amply built little women. Even dwarves could get jealous.

Mood snatched his cigar back. "Gimme that. It'll make you blind."

The two men peered up into the city. After weeks of hard rain, water rushed like waterfalls over the walls, and the suns blazed overhead. Venir felt guilty. Ever since he'd arrived, the dwarves had been busier. Forges blazed and soldiers marched everywhere. It couldn't all be on his account. Were the underlings about to invade Dwarven Hole or was it someone else?

"On top of that," Mood said, "something has been running around the past few days. An intruder. We can't find it, can't see it, but we smell it. It's driving my men crazy. And my men are drivin' me crazy." Mood shook his head and scratched. "It's been quiet, whatever it is, hiding, but it's foreign. Everyone thinks that you people have something to do with it."

"Ahem," Fogle Boon said with Ox in tow. They strolled in tailed by Billip and Mikkel. They were all geared up. "Don't worry, Mood," Fogle said. "He's not leaving without us. Billip already caught him packing Chongo's saddle. We've been watching, though this came on a bit more suddenly than we expected. Why is that, Venir?"

"Yeah, Vee! Why are you trying to roll on out again like this? Why you always got to do that?" Mikkel's deep voice was filled with aggravation.

Venir shrugged a bit, palms open in wry guilt. "Follow me."

They all headed back under the surface where they had been staying in Dwarven Hole. Venir's gear was laid out and he picked up his backpack, unbuckled its straps, and withdrew a familiar large leather sack. They all gasped in bewilderment.

"How long have you had that?" Mikkel asked with excitement.

"Since last night."

"Why didn't you tell us? Where did it come from? Did you open it?" Fogle asked, eyes wide with excitement.

"No," Venir said. He clutched it in his grip. It was *the* sack. He ran his fingers along the sewn edges. "I have no idea where it came from, but maybe it had something to do with that intruder. What do you think, Mood?"

Mood sniffed the air. "Nope." He sniffed again. "Maybe. Awww, I don't know. Methinks maybe you're right. Magic. That'd explain lots."

"Why not open it?" Billip asked.

"If I do, I don't know if I'll end up running out of here like my head's on fire. Besides, maybe one of you should try."

Fogle took a step his way then stepped back. "Clearly it sought you, as always. Now open it! The suspense is killing me."

Tension filled the air with enthusiasm. Even he couldn't help but be filled with nervous excitement. "All right, but first, in case something happens, I have to ask something of you all."

All their shoulders sank. They all motioned and said in their own way, "Get on with it and open the bag."

"Mikkel and Billip," Venir said. "You two owe me. You can't come with me. No matter what happens, I want you to stay close to Three and check on the boys—but not Kam so much."

"What! I'm not doing that! We are going after underlings like the good old days!" Mikkel said as he whirled his studded club Skull Basher around.

"No!" Venir said. "Give me your word on it. I gave you mine."

"You already have our word, begrudgingly, but I'll make sure Mikkel keeps it," Billip said, cracking his knuckles.

Mikkel got in Venir's face. "I'll keep it. But you're stupid for not taking me and Skull Basher. I don't care what's in that sack—you need us."

"Now open the sack," Fogle said.

Venir nodded. All eyes were on him as he pulled the strings loose. His skin became cold and clammy. What if it wasn't in there? What if it was nothing? He took in a small breath and reached inside.

81

Corpses of dwarven bodies were buried face first and legs out, every hundred yards from the Outlands into the northern edge of Hohm's Marsh. Over two score of the hardy race were stretched and strewn across the expanse. They did not have the skill or size of their larger brethren, the Blood Rangers, and they had never needed it more.

The albino urchlings did the tracking and digging while the Juegen took care of the slaughter. The magic of the underling lords was more than enough to give their bodyguards the surprise and edge they needed. The dwarven warriors weren't ready. The Juegen fighters' twin blades carved and cut open the dwarves in the dead of night.

Magic concealed the attack, and before the dwarves knew what hit them, they were left for dead. Their armor and skills were no match for underling steel forged by magic. The underling lords were sending a message. Their deeds caused rumors of destruction to spread in all directions around them.

It was what they wanted.

The city of Hohm was afflicted with fear. Its people felt as if an army lurked within the massive green reeds of the marsh, and in the caves that littered its landscape. As the days spread into weeks, the talk of war increased. People came and went through the marsh and its swamp-slickened roads, as they always did, only to see corpses of shredded residents here and there. Death invaded their peaceful solitude. They blamed the cities below them for what befell them, rather than take action themselves. It was their way and it played right into Verbard and Catten's hands. They would do anything to draw the Darkslayer out.

"More dwarves will be coming for us soon enough, Catten. We can't keep this up much longer," Verbard said as he watched his albino urchlings shovel more dirt into the graves of misshapen dwarves.

"Let them come. The more dead dwarves the better, especially those Blood Rangers." Catten hated the Rangers. For centuries, they had been a thorn in his kind's side. There were barely a hundred of them, but they always kept an ear on the underlings. Many plans had been foiled by their strange and brave kind. If they could take down more of them, as they had in the Warfield, it would be great. "I only wish we would be around to see it. Our summoning was excellent," Catten said.

Hohm's Marsh was miles long and deep, filled with swampy waters and massive willow trees, tea green and golden. Enormous reptiles, slick with mud and scaled in blended colors, crawled here and there. It was the only way in or out of the northeastern city of Hohm.

Thousands of humans along with other races populated the foreign city. It was an intricate and self-sufficient city, but not accommodating by most people's standards. Its people and leaders were content to keep to themselves and they liked it that way. A single road, vast, rocky and wide, was the only dry stretch of land that curved through the marsh. Its waters were clean, not foul like most, and its creatures tranquil. The constant fog left it still and eerie. Many travelers often disappeared there.

Still, great danger was deep in its belly, ancient and foul, as like anywhere else on Bish. Most people feared to take anything but the trail through. There were other ways. It was the perfect sanctuary for any who needed privacy and seclusion.

Catten's head throbbed. He and his brother had spent days summoning something powerful from deep within the marsh. Catten looked up at the monster they'd dredged up, and his black heart filled with delight. It was massive, slimy, and capable of eating three men in a single bite. It was a simple creature, not unlike others, just ten tons of it. He could imagine its enormous jaws swallowing dwarven men whole. *This will keep the rodent dwarves entertained.*

"If the man is with the dwarves, he'll be flanking their line," Catten said. "We've spent weeks setting wards. He will have to cross them and we will strike."

"If there are others with him, who takes whom? And what if he doesn't come?" Verbard asked.

Catten rubbed his chin. The Darkslayer was unpredictable and liable to show up where they least expected it. He was indeed dangerous, fearless, and willful. The man would come. He had to.

"Just focus on him. The rest are of no concern. We'll bury them like the rest, if there's anything left," Catten said.

Verbard chittered in laughter beside him. Magic or no magic, the Darkslayer would not escape again.

82

A LL EYES WERE WIDE AS Venir reached deep into the weathered leather sack. He never knew which item would come out first, but he'd always known it as soon as he touched it. Something, though, was different within and his heart thundered. *What is this?* He let go, then grabbed again. It wasn't something he'd ever felt before. Drawing his hand out from the bag's mouth, he heard Mikkel sucking air through his teeth. He held the item before his eyes. *A girdle?* Gilded around blackened leather, ornate copper and bronze markings crossed over the girdle's unique centerpiece.

"That's strange," Venir said.

He glanced at the others, who looked confused as well. It looked like any other girdle used in battle, broad in the front and buckling in the back. Venir ran his hand over it. It felt cold to the touch.

"Put it on, man! Or else I will," Mikkel said.

"Fine then." Uncertainty crept in on the large man as he swung it over his shoulder. He set down the sack and buckled on the girdle, then stood straight as he pulled his shoulders back. "There. Happy?"

"Feel any different?" Fogle asked.

They were all ears.

"Well … I think I do," Venir said. His belly warmed. He felt good, better than he'd felt in weeks.

"Like how?" Billip asked.

"Like I can crush an underling's head with my bare hands," Venir said as he clenched his massive fist and punched his other hand.

Smack! Smack! Smack!

The sound resonated with more and more power with each blow.

"Pull out something else, man," Mood said. "This is exciting!"

Venir shoved his meaty hand back into the sack and pulled out the next item. "Helm," he whispered.

It was the same helm, but the metal was darker now, almost black, and the ornate markings, copper, and brass seemed to gleam brighter than before. The spike on top glistened of bright steel. The helm's patterns tied in with the girdle's—a matching set. In comparison to its predecessor, the helm seemed more polished and refined. Something had changed. He couldn't wait to put it on his head.

"Don't put it on," Fogle Boon warned.

"Yeah, I don't want to see you running out of here like a flaming ogre as you usually do," Mood said.

Venir smiled. He could feel color filling his rugged cheeks, and he couldn't wait to see if Brool waited inside. He set down the helmet and reached inside. Everyone's jaw dropped as he pulled out the final armament.

"Brool!" they all whispered loudly.

Venir held the mighty battle axe before his eyes. He couldn't believe it. It was as if a long-lost friend had come home.

It was the great battle-axe, the hand-and-a-half axe, as he liked to call it. But it had changed as well. The rich, red-oak shaft was now a deep ebony oak in color. The massive twin blades and spike were no longer the titanium dull gray burnished metal. The axe head now gleamed bright with steel like that of the finest forged in Bish. It no longer appeared as the rugged devastator that he swung with ease, but instead it was purified and refined, every bit as menacing as before, if not more so. His burning blue eyes examined the length of the massive weapon from spike tip to shod as exhilaration filled his body.

"How's it feel?" Mood asked, his green eyes wide.

"Stand back and we shall see!" Venir said.

The others moved out of the way as he began whirling. The balance was as perfect as before. The heft seemed even lighter. A furnace inside him exploded.

He tested his weapon with two-handed little chops and slices. A film of sweat gathered on his brow as he went into a trance. He burst into a furious motion, whirling the blade like a storm of lightning around his body.

His companions stepped farther back.

He wanted to cut through something. He had to. The sound of the twin blades whistling through the air was all he could hear as he wove a pattern of destruction around his body. He couldn't take it anymore. He rushed over to one of many thick posts supporting the room and with a single two-handed stroke cut clean through it.

"You're gonna fix that!" Mood shouted.

Mood's booming voice jarred Venir from his haze. "Sorry, Mood," Venir said. "I just got carried away. I'll fix it when I get back."

"Is there anything else?" Fogle asked.

Venir had forgotten about the shield. He knelt and reached inside. Nothing. He stepped back up.

"I guess the girdle will have to do," Venir said.

"You leaving right now?' Billip asked.

"Oh yeah … it's time to slay the day!" Venir said. "I'm getting Chongo ready. Fogle Boon, it's time to go. Meet me up top." Venir couldn't wait to leave. Whatever awaited him, he was ready for it.

"Hold on!" Fogle said. "You aren't running off anywhere without this."

The mage produced a leather strap with an amber gemstone hanging from it. The small man was careful to step around Brool as he tied the strap around Venir's neck.

"What's this for?" Venir asked.

"In case you run off, I can find you, or we can," Fogle said. "Who knows what will happen if you put on that helmet and even smell an underling. I can't have you leaving me high and dry."

"That's a good idea, Boon, you gotta watch him! He's always running off in the middle of the night or even during battle," Mikkel said as he rubbed Venir on the head. "I'll say this though, Vee, I hate to have to miss out on the next encounter. Skull Basher likes being in Brool's company. Nothin' but smashed underlings and dark blood. Carve the Bish out of them, brother!"

"Yep, you never know," Billip said. "Anyhow, we'll be on our way after we say our good-byes … to the ladies."

Mikkel and Billip grinned as they slapped Venir on the shoulder and headed out.

"Make it quick!" Mood bellowed down the hall after them. "As for you, Venir, you need some armor. You don't even have a shield now—no way of protecting yourself. I'll grab you a vest of dwarven scale and then we *all* will be on our way."

Venir hadn't expected Mood to come along. Then he remembered the dwarf had told him countless dwarves had been torn apart and stuffed into holes. The Blood Ranger would want to avenge them. Venir must have been the cause—something to draw him out into the open. How many more had suffered for him and the sack? Dread overshadowed his excitement. He had to get this over with, but he didn't want them to come along.

83

I N THE DAWN, MILES NORTH of Dwarven Hole, two men, a dwarf, and a mintaur traveled on the backs of horses and a giant two-headed dog. They had managed to hold the warrior down long enough to gather supplies and come up with a plan. In some haste, they all left before Venir got away.

Wearing the magic girdle and clutching Brool—but keeping the helm in the sack for now—Venir led atop Chongo's massive back. The big dog swayed with the rhythm of his twin tails as they headed farther away from Bone. The party traveled close to the western edge of the world of Bish, where the great mists threatened to engulf them.

The world of Bish was unique, the land surrounded by endless mists and seemingly bottomless cliffs that no one was known to return from—or come from. No creature or fowl of the air was ever seen to venture there, either. The world's inhabitants avoided the rim altogether. Lately, though, things had changed. Folks started asking questions and seeing things in the mist.

Venir's group traveled for days in the hot winds that blew down from the north. Flanking the small dwarven army, they marched dead center toward Hohm's Marsh. Somewhere ahead, underlings waited—likely the pair that Mood suspected … the ones from the battle at the Warfield.

Dwarven scouts on stout ponies came and went from their group, updating Mood, king of the Blood Rangers, to their discoveries. They were not far from Hohm's Marsh now. The bodies they found, of all races, became more frequent and the stories more horrific.

Fogle Boon was appalled.

The man has yet to face pure evil. "Be ready," Venir told the mage over and over again. Fogle Boon muttered along, his face taut, his narrow eyes focused.

Venir simmered at the stories of destruction. He felt responsible and it weighed him down. He wanted to get it over with … alone. His reckless nature began to take over, and he considered leaving them in the night, but something interrupted his plans.

Krowwww-ak!

The odd sound passed through his body like the crackling thunder from a nearby storm.

Krowwww-ak!

Mood lurched up in his saddle and came to a quick stop.

"What in a hairy orc's hide is that, Venir?" Fogle stated.

"No idea. Never heard that before," Venir replied.

"It's a balfrog!" Mood cried.

"What's that?" Fogle asked.

"A toad the size of a mountain." Mood rounded up the dwarven scouts on each of their flanks. A look of worry crossed the dwarf king's face. Venir had never seen that look before.

"A toad? Is that anything we need to worry about?" the mage asked, as if in relief.

"No, but it's somethin' I got to worry about. Me kin don't know what a bloody balfrog is. Methinks I'm the only one to survive a battle. It's been centuries. I go to help kill it. I know how."

"Why don't they just leave it alone?" Fogle asked.

"Man, didn't you learn about us in the Hole?" Mood said. "We don't retreat. We are as hardheaded when faced with an obstacle as an ogre, just a lot smarter. I got to get up there. Last time, over a hundred dwarves died before we got him down. That thing has a hide thicker than steel, and up close that croak can kill you. It also has three tongues strike like monstrous snakes and it'll eat'cha in a wink."

"You need us?" Venir asked, shaking Brool.

"No, you keep your course. I'll catch up." Mood barked some orders to his scouts and headed off at a gallop on his horse toward Hohm's Marsh, his thick, blood-red hair billowing behind him. "WOOO-HAAAAA!" Mood bellowed.

Venir wished Mood had taken the others with him.

"I don't like how things are going all of a sudden," Fogle said. "Things seem to happen pretty fast on these ventures with you. Mind if we pause and I cast a spell?"

Venir pondered the man's wisdom. "You are your own man. Do what you think is best. Seems you have been around long enough to realize the kind of trouble I'll get you in."

"That's true."

The mage dismounted along with Ox, who brought the large rucksack with him. The mage procured a scroll then sat down cross-legged.

"Don't disrupt me," Fogle said. "And don't let *anything* else disrupt me, either."

Ox stood tall nearby and Venir turned his back, peered north, and waited. Venir could hear the faint mumblings of the mage, minute after minute, and saw something in the distance come into focus. He held his hand over his eyes, blocking the suns, for a clearer look. Close to a hundred yards away, he swore he saw himself, Chongo, Fogle Boon, Ox, and their mounts. Venir turned.

Fogle stood behind him, his large head showing bright eyes and a wide smile. "You like it?"

"What is it?" he asked.

"It is a phantasm, or mirage rather, of our images. It will mimic us from ahead and should fool anything. It'll take away their opportunity for surprise while giving us one."

Venir nodded. "That's really something. How long will it last? We still have a decent journey ahead."

"It will last continuously, or until someone comes in serious direct contact with it, or kills me."

Anything would help, but it wasn't the wizard's fight. Then again, maybe it was everyone's battle—the struggle against the underlings, against oppression, for freedom. He didn't know. Still, Fogle and Ox gave him an edge he didn't have before. Maybe it would make a difference.

Melegal tended to be the best planner in the city, but not in the Outlands. The pair had relied more on skill and improvisation as keys to their survival over the course of their years.

How many weeks had passed since he'd given thought to his friend? Venir assumed he was doing well, but still wondered if their days of venturing for profit had come to an end. Only time would tell.

"Fogle, I can't hold off from this fight much longer. If you are going, be ready. In any case, I need to be ready. Who knows what is in store for me? Maybe nothing, but I can't put it off." Venir pulled out his sack.

"Just wait," Fogle said.

"No. If there were any underlings within the next few miles, Chongo would have sniffed them out. Trust me, Chongo can track anything, especially those dark little fiends." Venir scratched the heads of the big pooch.

"At least wait until we get on our horses then," Fogle said.

Ignoring Fogle, Venir took out the helm. The spike on top and ornate markings gleamed bright in the rising sunlight. *Ready or not, underlings, here I come.* He strapped the helm on his head and waited. It fit just as before. The metal was cold on his forehead. Unlike with the girdle, though, he felt nothing new.

Fogle observed the man as his entire identity seemed to shift into something else. The powerful warrior seemed as if he'd been molded out of metal as the thick rings of dwarven scale mail blended in with the girdle of magic and metal. The girdle, axe, and helmet were clearly unique and as a whole gave the hulkish man an invincible appearance.

The wizard rode along his side. "Well, do you sense any underlings or do you think you will?"

Venir took a deep breath and exhaled. "No, I don't know if I can track them any better, but I am sure I can kill them."

"Do you feel anything at all? Anything different from before?"

"Hmm …" Venir scratched his grizzled chin. "I feel better than I have felt in a long time. I feel good. Free. Strong."

"Great, just keep a clear head and let's get a move on. Hopefully, some of your enlightened perspective will rub off on me."

84

T HE BALFROG BATTLE WASN'T ONE to be short. The stout dwarves would keep going until the last. Assault after assault, they faced an immovable object that stood near three stories in height. The balfrog was enormous, brown and ruddy like a toad, but scaled in armor like a dragon.

The dwarves, heavy in artillery, armor, and weapons, had little effect against it, yet they tried something new time after time, only to end in death. Little did they know that even though help from their king was on its way, they would pay the price en masse before he could attempt to save them.

Lords Catten and Verbard heeded little of the battle, still waiting in hopes the Darkslayer would show. It was the day after the dwarves first collided with the balfrog that one of Catten's mystic wards was set off. Several miles south and farther west at the eastern edge was an area they had only placed a few. He knew exactly where to go.

"Brother, our time has come!" Catten said with an excited hiss.

"Indeed, let's make haste," Verbard said.

Catten focused and chattered with excitement. A door of black space appeared before him. "I'll go ahead and set up, then beckon you through."

Verbard nodded.

Catten chittered again then glided upward. Black robes blowing against the wind, he flew from sight. It felt good to be so close. Faster and faster he went, mile after mile. He floated down to the ground a few miles from the ward that was triggered in the south, and waited a moment. *Maybe I can take him. Kill him myself.*

He summoned more energy and another black space appeared from nowhere. He reached his hand through.

Miles away, where his brother Verbard waited along with the Juegen and albino urchlings, Catten's hand appeared before them and waved them through. They stepped through the space one at a time. The door closed behind them and they reappeared on the other side.

"How do you feel, Catten, after that much effort?" Verbard asked.

Catten breathed heavily and felt tired, but his voice was still strong. "I have plenty left, but you better be ready for this next task. If indeed he comes, he'll come fast."

Catten found one of the many rocky steppes typical of the Outlands to set their group on, giving them a good view of the open land south of their position. Far off to the west, mist surrounded their world. He gave it little thought.

Verbard spat orders to his albino urchlings. The hunched and hulking pasty-white little underlings sniffed and snorted in a disgusting fashion. They scurried on their arms and legs and headed down over the rocky steppes, disappearing without a sound.

"This is it," Verbard said, his silver eyes glowing in the night.

"This better be," Catten replied.

85

THE SMALL PARTY MAINTAINED THEIR course toward Hohm's Marsh with haste. Fogle shifted in his saddle the whole day. The sound of the croaking balfrog became louder every mile they traveled. Venir felt as if he'd let another friend down. He wanted to be there with Mood. He needed to fight something.

The suns began to set, but stopping was out of the question for Venir. His hunt was on and his steely determination would not be deterred. He had almost forgotten about the man and mintaur behind him. They had been quiet all day long.

Venir reined in Chongo and came to a halt. The pair stood like statues, shadowed in the sinking suns' light. His mind sparked. Gears tumbled in his head. He felt a powerful presence.

"Underlings are near," he whispered.

Chongo's four ears perked up. The breeze, though, was upwind, giving the underlings the advantage of scent.

"Fool," Fogle whispered, "keep moving! Our shadow image is well ahead of us. It should draw them out and conceal us back here."

Venir didn't move. He fought the urge to run ahead. The helm didn't have the same command as it did before. He still had control. Fogle's words registered, and he spurred Chongo along. Fogle sighed behind him.

86

THE WIZARD'S MIND AND HEART pounded. When Venir stopped and said "underlings," Fogle forgot everything else. Venir didn't seem to move for an eternity. Fogle felt like a sitting duck. When the iron warrior started moving again, Fogle finally found his breath.

And his memory.

Be ready. He motioned for Ox to ride along his side and began talking to him. Ox soon reached into the backpack and pulled out a three-foot-long metal rod, similar to a tent stake, but longer, and kept it ready with him.

Onward Fogle trotted into the unknown. The light on Bish dimmed the farther they went north. The mists of the rims were like massive black clouds. He was in no-man's-land. He had never felt farther from anything all of his life. *What in Bish am I doing?*

Venir still seemed in control. An eerie black glow shimmered around eyelets of Venir's helmet. It made Fogle's fingertips tingle. At any moment something would strike.

87

IT WAS DARK WHEN ONE of the albino urchlings returned to its master with news. All of the urchlings descended down the steppe at Verbard's command. Verbard rose from the ground as he raised his hands to cast his spell. Below him, still on the steppe, Catten saw the small party of men coming their way in the distance. And there was the Darkslayer—helmet on his head and axe in tow.

Catten's eagerness was replaced with uncertainty. *How?* He closed his eyes. *It doesn't matter.* His brothers power joined with his. Elation raced through his bones. *Ah, that's better.*

The knotted urchlings and his Juegen guards disappeared. He sensed them and knew within moments they were gone. He waited. Powerful spells were ready in his grasp. A rainless storm rumbled above.

The Darkslayer approached, and soon Verbard would be going home.

88

VENIR ZEROED IN ON THE creatures that crept up on Fogle's phantasm ahead of them. The helm was doing what he hoped. He knew they were underlings, just not the everyday kind he usually encountered—but he'd seen albino urchlings in the past, and he'd heard tales of Juegen underlings, like the two ahead. He wanted them—all of them. Brool warmed in his grip. His helm seemed to smolder, beckoning him to take action.

He looked back at the nervous face of the illusionist. Fogle pet his horse, while Ox sat on his like a statue. Venir tugged at Chongo's reins, and the dog frothed at the mouth, ears folded back.

Venir's lust, however, was not overwhelming, and it gave him some relief to know he wouldn't go berserk as he had before. He maintained his focus. He watched far away as the heat pattern of the creatures came upon their phantasmal trap.

Fogle Boon whispered, "Venir, you still with us up there?"

"I am," he said. His head ached, however. He needed to move — or go insane.

"Remember, we don't appear where we are. Just wait," Fogle reminded him.

"I will," he said. It was killing him, though.

"I need to start casting something else. Stop and get off Chongo, like you are checking something. I assume they can still see you, but they'll see the dog either way."

Venir did so. They all dismounted. The projection ahead stopped as if they were getting ready for something. Behind Venir, Fogle Boon muttered a spell on the long metal rod he'd had Ox procure then tucked the rod under the horse's saddle. Venir went through the motions as if they were setting up camp. He peered ahead.

Lightning streaked across the sky, and thunder cracked like splintering trees. A blast turned their phantasms into a smoking pile of ruin. Another blue bolt flared down, shaking the ground and lighting the sky. Smoke and dust billowed up.

The underlings rushed into the smoldering pile of ruin. Their white-clawed bodies and flashing swords burst into the crater. He couldn't wait any longer. Five urchlings scampered on the ground, plus two Juegen. He was ready to take them. He leaped back on top of Chongo and charged forward, holding Brool high in the air.

"Yah!"

89

E LATION FILLED CATTEN'S BONES AS he looked upon the smoldering scene below. Coming back down to the ground, Verbard shook his fists in triumph as the urchlings and Juegen rushed into the smoke. The golden-eyed underling could imagine one of his bodyguards bringing the head of the Darkslayer, while another brought the axe. His homecoming couldn't come too soon. His plan had worked to perfection. *Yes!*

He and his brother floated down, dark forms in the smoke. Nothing must have been left as he heard no screams. Something else moved as the smoke shifted away in the wind. The figures of the men and their mounts shimmered as claws and blades ripped through them without a sound. Urchlings snarled in confusion.

His brother looked back and forth. "An illusion!" Verbard yelled.

Catten gawped. His hands grew numb. His brother grasped his robes as something flashed in the distance. It was too late.

A streaking barrage of green bolts ripped through the black sky. They punched through his robes like nails and drilled deep into his skin. The force knocked him from the air as he howled out in pain. He'd never felt anything like it before. His blood was on fire and he lay writhing on the ground. Who had done this? He focused and felt another powerful magic presence. It seemed familiar.

Above him, Verbard summoned a protective shield around them. Another barrage of green missiles ricocheted away into the black sky. Catten fought the pain as he regained his feet.

"Brother, how is your damage?" Verbard shouted, hands raised and pointing outward.

Patting out the tiny smoking holes in his robes, Catten said, "Pah! Only painful, burning, somewhat refreshing, but nothing compared to what I am going to do to that human." Catten licked his split black lip and rubbed his dislocated shoulder. He stuck his fingers in the holes of his chest. The wounds cauterized. The scars would take centuries to heal.

The Darkslayer headed toward the crater. Magic spread like an inferno inside Catten and he let it loose.

90

"O H MY!" WAS ALL FOGLE Boon could say as one of the underling magi in the distance fell from the sky. *My plan worked!*

After telling Ox to dismount from his steed, Fogle took his enchanted metal rod in hand and slipped it under the saddle of Ox's horse. Fogle then had the mintaur hop up behind him on Fogle's horse. A second later, Fogle reached over and slapped Ox's horse in the rear. It galloped ahead, stopping behind Venir and Chongo. From behind, Fogle spurred his own horse forward.

Did I kill it? There was still the other one. He held close to the mintaur as he looked ahead. The sky far away and above brightened. *Oh no!* His heart sank as cords of lightning wrapped around the dark silhouettes like serpents. His hair stood up on his head from the energy. *This better work!* The underlings arms lashed out before them.

Szzwham! Szzwham! Szzwham!

White bolts of blinding energy bore down on Venir. Fogle squinted in the brilliant light. The streaks curved away from Venir, then toward Fogle. Ox yelled as the lightning came their way. He hung on and closed his eyes.

Ka-poom! Ka-poom! Ka-poom!

In front of them, Ox's horse was blown into chunks of charred flesh. Fogle lost his grip and fell hard to the ground. Simmering flesh rained down around him. He'd lived. *It worked.* The display of power Fogle Boon had just witnessed was more than anything he'd ever beheld or even heard told. He didn't have any plans left. He was down to nothing. *Certainly those underlings don't have more.*

In the distance, he swore he could hear the underlings scream as they dug their nails into their skulls.

91

V ENIR DIDN'T NOTICE AS THE lightning seared past his head. He was somewhere else. He was someone else. He was the Darkslayer.

Ahead of him, several figures stepped forward from the smoking ground. He could feel their evil presence. He despised them. He reined in Chongo and hopped off.

He slapped Brool's blade against the palm of his hand. "Come on, you black-metal Juegen dogs! Let me skin that scale from you and rip out the worm inside! Who is going down first?"

He was confident. Strong. Ready. The ringing in his head was replaced with a rush of battle heat.

The two black-plated Juegen underlings flanked him as the white muscled urchlings pursued Chongo. Venir waited, flexing his muscles and feeling them bulge beneath his thick scale mail. He could see the Juegen's colorful eyes underneath their black helmets. Their curved swords glinted in the red moons' light. He looked down at them. His grip was white knuckled. The Juegen paced around him.

The first Juegen came in swinging. Venir caught the blows on his axe blade. He jabbed Brool's spike toward the Juegen's maw. It ducked under and slashed him across the belly, then rolled away as Brool bit into the ground where it had once stood. Mood's scale mail saved Venir's belly from being cut wide open. He groaned. The underling was faster than he figured.

He felt something cold at his back, and whirled in time to swat at the other underling warrior. It rolled away with ease, but not before clipping his calf. One at a time they came, darting like dragonflies, as fluid as gazelles. Brool pulsed in his hands, wanting blood. He wanted it, too.

His own blood dripped to the ground. The tiny lacerations burned like poison. Chongo yelped and barked nearby. He couldn't let that distract him. He felt an underling lunge for him from behind. He turned as something painful stabbed his back. The underling sprang away as he struck.

Clang!

Venir clipped it upside its helmet, knocking it to the ground. The axe was alive in his hand as the other Juegen came in a headlong rush. He anticipated its move, swinging Brool full force into its side. Bones crushed inside it. Its black-plated armor saved it from being cut in two. The blow knocked the fiend to the ground, breathless. It chittered as it regained its feet. The other came along its side. Neither underling seemed to be harmed. Now they mocked him.

Venir wiped the sweat from his brow with his bloody forearm. He missed his shield.

They came at him again. It took all he had to block them. The sound rang back and forth as he battled their blades away. The magic metals clashed. Sparks flew. A deep gash opened in his thigh.

He lunged at his attacker … and missed, over swinging the mark, as the underling blades cut across his armor. He backpedaled, the next blows raining in like a swarm. Using his axe's shaft to parry and its bottom shod to counter was all he could do to save himself from getting cut to ribbons. The Juegen stayed close to the warrior, pressing their advantage and getting a slice of the Darkslayer here and there.

Blocking out the pain, Venir focused on what he needed to do — destroy the little underlings. Parrying and side-stepping blow after blow, the Juegen finally seemed to slow from his efforts. One stepped back too far.

Bang!

Metal clashed on metal. The massive axe's edge put a deep dent in the underling warrior's helmet, almost knocking it down.

Bang!

He swung into it again, this time turning the Juegen's helmet sideways. It backed away, trying to remove its helmet. He turned as the remaining Juegen jabbed his way. Venir raised his arms up high. It raised its swords in defense. Brool crashed downward, shattering the blades and glancing off the Juegen's armored skull. Weaponless, it tried to pull out a dagger only to have its hand sliced off for the effort. Venir chopped into the foul thing over and over. Its armor held, but its body did not. It was a mutilated mess of black flesh and metal.

The other one howled. The remaining Juegen had managed to remove its helmet, ripping its face half open in the process. Its black visage was torn, teeth filed, eyes black as coal, and it chittered in fury. It charged with its dripping blades. It sprang high into the air, arms wide, cutting at his head.

Venir jabbed Brool's spike straight through to the back of its head.

Crunch! Rip!

"Now that's more like it," Venir said as he twisted the axe out in satisfaction.

It wasn't over, though. Chongo barked and yelped. The massive dog had guarded his backside all along, fighting off the albino urchlings along with Ox. One crumpled white corpse hung from Chongo's maw. Two other mangled corpses lay on the ground not far from the big dog. One urchling, though, was trying to rend Chongo's second head to pieces. Ox, meanwhile, was in the midst of fighting off the remaining albino.

The white fiend bit deep into one of Chongo's jugular veins.

"No!" Venir yelled.

Blood flowed from one of the dog's two necks. The urchling fighting Ox jumped over Ox's swinging axe and charged at Venir, its bloody claws ready. He was furious as it came at him. He sliced the foul urchling clean through the torso. Two halves fell to the ground. Blood thickened on the dirt beneath his feet.

Venir stuck Brool in the ground as Ox chopped at the urchling sucking on his dog's neck, but the mintaur's axes had no effect on the creature. Venir limped over and grabbed the smaller urchling by the nape of its neck. Its jaws opened wide, freeing Chongo.

The creature's claws tore deep into his skin.

It had hurt his dog. He would kill it.

He wrapped both of his bloodied hands around its muscled neck, and squeezed. His arms bulged in strain. The screaming urchling's pink eyes seemed to burst from its head.

"Rrrrrrrr!" Venir gave it more effort. Its neck felt like tree roots. He squeezed harder. His strength grew. It had hurt Chongo. Then in one final squeeze … *Snap!* Its neck broke.

Venir tossed the urchling away and collapsed to the ground. He crawled over to where Chongo lay.

The big dog bled heavily, the gash in his neck severe. Chongo had sacrificed himself to protect his owner. There was little Venir could do now.

Venir grabbed his beloved pet by the other neck. "Chongo …"

He thought he heard one of the underlings cackling above.

92

T HE NIGHT SEEMED TO COME to a stop as Catten studied the carnage below. Verbard's chest heaved. All of their bodyguards were dead. He'd thought they had him, but the Darkslayer got faster as the battle went on. Catten felt helpless as his Juegen were pounded into the dirt and sand.

The man seemed stronger and more elusive than ever.

The Juegen and albino urchlings were more than a match for twenty men, but one warrior had destroyed them all. Catten rubbed his hands together. His busted shoulder felt more painful than before. The wounded Darkslayer beckoned toward him and his brother over and over from below. He wanted to throw everything he had left at him, but not just yet. Verbard hovered by his side, running his hands through his thick, black hair.

Then there was the formidable wizard below, hanging back and waiting for his chance. It wasn't something Catten had expected. He'd had no reason to. He could feel the wizard's power. *Impressive for a human!*

Catten rubbed his ailing chest. Should they focus their attacks on one or both? He shared his thoughts with Verbard. *It's worth a shot to go after both*, Catten thought. His silver-eyed brother only shook his head and sighed.

93

V ENIR'S TEMPLES THROBBED AS HE stared at the two underlings high above. He didn't know if the pain was because of the helm or all the yelling he'd done. The underlings' heavy black robes billowed in the wind. Something shimmered before the underlings as one floated before the other. The underling magi were black in the night, but he could make out their faces now. The weight of their gold and silver eyes was on him.

He didn't know how, but he felt hesitation from them. He checked on Chongo and Ox. Ox's body looked like he had fallen in a den of wolverines. The mintaur had suffered deep wounds from the urchlings, but his efforts had saved Chongo. The mintaur finished stitching the gash in the large dog's neck. Somehow, Ox got the bleeding to stop. One dog head licked the other that hung down, almost lifeless on the ground.

Venir stroked the wounded, panting head. "You're gonna make it, boy."

He looked over at Fogle Boon. The mage still sat on horseback, eyes trying to make out the underlings above. The man mumbled something as he gripped his staff. He noticed the smell of burnt flesh in the air when he realized Ox's horse was gone. He had no idea how that happened.

The illusionist had a whimsical look on his round face when he turned to look at him. "I'm out of ideas."

Venir was too. "At least you live."

The mage didn't have a scratch, but he slumped in his saddle. "Now what?"

Venir shrugged.

Long, quiet moments passed. It was possible that more underlings were coming, but he wouldn't let the two above out of his sight. Frustration set in. Venir's head throbbed and his body ached. He started gathering stones. He emptied all their packs on the ground, and looked for anything he might find to hurl at the underlings.

He pulled out a sling from his backpack. It was one of Georgio's. There were smooth sling bullets as well. He loaded one and drew back his arm. The sling whirled away, whistling in his ears. He let it loose. The bullet flew straight and true then bounced away before colliding with the underling's face. It didn't even flinch.

A scroll fell from Fogle's pack. He said with excitement, "Venir, bring me that scroll."

Venir picked it up and came his way. "Now's not a good time to read," he said, handing over the scroll.

Fogle Boon got off his horse and piled up the stones and bullets. The wizard sat down and unraveled the scroll. When the the man began to read aloud, his eyes rolled up in his head. Something was wrong. Fogle Boon pitched face forward into the pile of stones. The scroll withered away.

"What is it, Ox?" Venir asked.

But the mintaur had no words.

94

FOGLE BOON'S MIND WAS UNDER assault. Everything turned dark. Someone ancient, evil, powerful, and mysterious was crushing the light of his conscience. He was locked in a mind grumble with an underling.

It was killing him.

He fought back. Light deep inside his mind still burned. He had to keep going. He protected the tiny bit of light and fueled it with his thoughts.

He stood in a black room, a lone candle flame wavering before him. Nails were being driven into his head.

A dark shadow prompted him to blow out the flame. It would ease his pain. It would be easy.

His will waned, and the candle dimmed. The pain started to ease.

Fogle struck back, and the flame brightened again. Something recoiled in rage. His relief was temporary. Assault after assault came. He watched the ones he knew or cared for tormented and destroyed over and over again. He witnessed himself being cut to pieces, limb by limb, and tossed into burning fires.

His brilliant mind was twisted inside out, trapped in a maze of endless terror. He fought his way out time and again. It went on for days, it seemed. He had no idea of time or reality. He had to break free.

He defended his very life. Everything felt real. His skin was flayed from his back. Urchlings devoured his flesh.

It isn't real, he told himself again and again. He had to fight back. He had to believe in himself, or die. The overwhelming challenge ignited the warrior deep inside. He fought back.

95

VENIR STAYED BUSY THROWING WHATEVER he could at the underling magi. Everything bounced away, though. He wanted a straight fight, but he'd never encountered two powerful wizards at the same time. It was alien to him. The underlings were a patient race who could wear him down. All the power in his grip would serve him little if he could not take the fight to them on the ground. But what could he do to an enemy that would not come down to fight him?

Hours passed as a fog rolled in. Fogle Boon sweated in a trance, and Ox covered the man with a blanket. The bookish mage seemed as if he were about to die. The wizard's body shuddered and convulsed now and then. With the magic of the helm, he could still see the underlings through the thick of the fog, but his head ached. Still, he feared to take it off and lose sight of them.

"Uhhhh!" Fogle gasped.

Venir and Ox jumped as Fogle lurched forward.

"Uhhhh!"

It was well past midnight when Fogle Boon's eyes finally snapped open. Blood trickled from his nose and a bitten lip. The man's eyes were sunken and milky.

"Shades of the dungeons," the mage said. "I was not going to give in, not again."

Then Fogle slumped over into a deep sleep.

96

V ERBARD WAS CONCERNED NOW. HIS brother had failed to take over the human with his mind. He should have done it. It should have been over the moment it started. He had contemplated helping out, but that would have left them defenseless. He waited, unable to see the Darkslayer below, but he could still sense him and his power. He couldn't risk lowering his shield for a moment.

The warrior below was deadly accurate with every weapon and rock he threw. There were other things Verbard could do, but not without leaving Catten unprotected. The standoff was truly one of a kind. The moments of silence were deafening, other than an occasional cackle from Verbard and the thunderous croak of the balfrog in the distance.

Catten snapped up at his side. Verbard grabbed him before he fell from the air.

"Verbard ... brother ... get us away from here ... now," Catten said.

Up they went, higher in the air, far from harm's way.

"What happened, Catten? You could not take this man!" Verbard said.

Catten held his hands over his eyes. "He has faced the same man we now do—the Darkslayer. He survived it, absorbed it and turned it on me. One moment, I was ready to crush him, and in the next, the Darkslayer was bearing down on me. I had no choice but to break it. A few more moments and I would have been through."

"Now what?" Verbard said. "Certainly we can take this man by other magical means! Let's let loose again."

97

V ENIR COULD SEE THE TWO figures high in the air, distant specks. He didn't know if they were worried or waiting. He needed Fogle Boon to bring them down. He needed to get help for Chongo. It was late in the morning when the mage recovered and babbled for an hour.

"How much time has passed?" Fogle asked.

"It's the next morning," Venir said.

"Great Bish! That's all? It seemed forever. Where is he?"

"Up there, way high. Both of them. Got anything we can use? We need to get them down."

"I know this—they want you dead. Period. It's why they are here. It was at the forefront of his mind. They won't go away, and I assume you won't, either. Oooh ... Give me some food, Ox? I'm starving."

Ox fed Fogle, who seemed to regain his strength. "You know, those two have a lot of power," Fogle said. "I don't see how we can survive if they decide to strike us down. They can. They can strike down a small army if need be." He wiped his hands on his knees, dusted them off, and stood up. "They don't think they can kill you, though. It's what holds them back. They have tried before and failed. Every time they have you dead to rights, you wriggle out of it and turn it against them." He picked up pieces of the withered scroll. It turned to dust in his hands. "They are trying a new tactic. They want to wear you down—test your limits."

Venir didn't like what he heard. "I need a straight fight. Can you make that happen? Can you make anything happen?"

"Well, they can't float forever," he said.

It was true. The underlings' spell would not last forever. They had to eat and they had to come down and rest. They would have to hide when they did. Venir would be able to track them anywhere on Bish now, but he would get hungry and tired too. Still, he was determined to be there whenever they came down, wherever that might be.

"Fogle Boon, I am going to track them as long as I can. So long as I have all of this," he tapped his helm, "I am meant for it. I always have been."

"It's an insane mission. You will never get a wink of sleep without help."

"It shouldn't take forever. I need you to stay with Chongo. Mood will return, I am sure of it. I have not heard a croak in a while. I'm sure he's coming here. It's been good with you, Fogle Boon." He pulled out Fogle's amulet and stuck it back under his vest. "I'll keep this with me at all times in case I don't come back soon."

The underlings moved away. Venir had to follow. He had to stop them somehow. He had never been closer. Step by step, he vanished into the burning horizon.

98

MOOD AND COMPANY ARRIVED AT the battle site a couple of days later. "Great Bish! What happened to Chongo?" Mood asked.

Fogle filled him in and Mood was grieved.

"Mood, what happened to the balfrog? Did you slay it?" Fogle asked.

"Indeed," the dwarf said.

"How?"

"Well, I let him eat me."

"What?" he exclaimed. "You let him eat you? Are you being serious?"

"I am. He sucked me in with his three forked tongues. Then I gutted him inside out," he said, chopping his axes. "No air in there, but I can hold me breath a long time. It took me hours to gut him out, but I burst free. Next time, I take you with me, wha'cha say?" he said with a nudge.

"Is that dried frog guts I smell? It's foul."

"It sure is, little man. So, we going after Vee? Me kin will take care of Chongo and get him back to Dwarven Hole."

"I guess so. I've nothing better to do. Hold on," Fogle said.

Mood fired up a cigar.

The wizard began his casting, holding in his palm a small dart that twirled fast at first, then slowed down to a stop. Northeast was the direction it pointed when it rose.

"Why's it rising?" Mood asked.

"Every inch up is every few miles. So I'd say he's only twenty miles away. We've got some catching up to do."

Fogle couldn't believe the man had chased the underlings that far already. He must have been running. The muscled juggernaut had strode away on foot, big axe in hand, helmet glinting in the suns. How would the man last in the sun?

"We gots the horses, so let's go then," Mood said. "Eh … mage, is there any way to know if he's alive or dead?"

"No," Fogle said.

They headed closer to the edge of the world, where the mist loomed. Mood checked for signs of the man, his face showing deep concern. He was unable to find a single trace of the man passing through.

Fogle questioned his magic. The outright disappearance of Venir bewildered him. What he'd thought would be a two-day trip became ten. They might have been going in circles. He wondered if the mist had something to do with it.

"I've never come this close to the mist before," Mood said.

The mist went up as high as the eye could see. It still was miles away, how many they could not tell, but they had no desire to approach it, either. A ledge formed, but they were not tempted to peer over it. Many had peered over and been fine from it, but many more had been drawn into it, never to return. It was the most foreboding thing in all of Bish—the utter unknown, as foreign to the races as the Underland to an eagle.

As they trotted along, the needle rose again then floated ahead. It stopped and fell on a pile of rocks. A horrifying feeling sunk in their bellies. The rocks were large, almost too big for a man to move.

"What do you think? Should we move them?" Fogle asked.

"We? Little man, you ain't movin' nothing. Me and the mintaur can handle this," Mood said in a gruff voice.

Rock after rock, Mood and Ox strained to carry each boulder away. As each rock thudded to the ground, a sense of dread filled the mage's chest. As the last big stone was moved, Fogle saw a shallow grave covered in dirt. The dart hovered above it. Ox and Mood cleared the dirt away. An outline of a body was covered by a thick black cloth. It appeared to be lying on its side.

"Shall I do the honors?" the dwarf asked, reaching forward.

"No … let me," Fogle said as a chill raced down his spine.

Fogle Boon tore the dark burlap cloth away. He jumped back in alarm, startling them all. Nothing was moving but them, though. They got a clear view of two bright, colorful eyes glossed over in death. It was an underling, no doubt. It must be one of the two Venir sought.

Mood pulled the corpse from the grave and set it down. The dead underling mage indeed seemed to be one of the two they'd fought. Venir's hunting knife was still deep in its back, the tip poking clear through its chest. Fogle's amulet was tied around its neck.

"He killed one of them; the crafty human actually did it. But how? There is no sign of him anywhere," Mood said in awe.

Fogle spent hours contemplating what had happened over a fire and some stag meat that Mood had brought along.

"Do you think he entered the mist, Mood, or followed the other one in there?" he asked.

"No." Mood tore a big hunk of flesh from the leg. "We are going to keep looking for him. Someone is bound to see him. He's too big and loud not to show up."

"Do you think he is dead? I just don't know."

"I don't," Mood grumbled. "He's hard to kill, that man. If he got one of them, I'd say it's likely he's bound to get the other." Mood spat. "If he ain't already."

"I agree, but too many mysteries remain." Fogle couldn't shake the feeling that he would never see his friend again.

"Were you born yesterday?" Mood said. "That's how it is on Bish, you know."

"I just like having some answers," Fogle said, staring into the mist.

"Well, startin' tomorrow, we begin trying to find you some. Rest knowin' that our friend is still out there doing what he does best—huntin' down and killin' underlings."

Fogle wasn't so certain. He stared out into the expanse, thinking. Venir—the Darkslayer—had become a shadow that didn't want to be found, alive or dead.

Series 1 THE BOOK 3

THE DARKSLAYER

Underling Revenge

CRAIG HALLORAN

1

T HE STANDSTILL HAD BEEN GOING on for days, ever since Venir parted ways with Fogle Boon. North, south, east, and west no longer mattered. Wind, rain, or fire would not stop him. No, he was on a mission, the same one he had been on for years. This time, if he completed it, he thought it would be over. Alive or dead, this would have to end it.

His canteens were empty and had been so for a day. He needed a stream, an oasis, a raindrop … anything. He dug his hunting knife into the dirt of a small chasm where water must have once flowed. The dirt was soft and full of gritty pebbles. He dug out the dirt with his hands, making it a foot down before the damp sand and dirt began to show. He scooped out the wet mud, placed it in his cowl, and squeezed it. Wet drops dripped into his eager mouth. The best ale in Bish wouldn't have tasted any better. He gave it a go a few more times and then sunk down in the shade to rest. The water helped a little, but his stomach began to groan again. How much longer did this battle have to go on?

Venir was accustomed to suffering in his life, but the past few days had been a strain indeed. He had been reduced to little more than a deranged tracker—a madman of the wilderness—ravenous for the blood of some underlings. His head had a steady ache, something he seemed to be getting accustomed to. He could sense those underlings: their moods and their contempt, hatred, and fear of him. One hundred scorned women couldn't have hated him more than the pair that evaded him in the sky certainly did. Fogle Boon had told him they would eventually come down, but Venir began to doubt that the citified mage—who had never seen an underling—would know anything about them. He rested.

Dawn had long ago broken, and Venir knew he was in for another long day. The underlings were determined to drag him over the most treacherous of terrains. They were moving again; he could feel it. He looked out ahead where jagged outcroppings of rocks and briars awaited him. He could make out two specks that stood out against the bright sky. It was the underlings, waiting for him to sleep, stop, or fail. He carried his shell of a body over the hard ground, Brool still hanging in his grasp. He wished they would do something, anything. He couldn't figure out if they were trying to flee or lead him to a trap. He looked over and saw the Endless Mists, miles in the distance. He stared, shook his head, turned, and moved on. He kept moving forward, step after step, watching the underlings move away slowly. He lost sight of them in the sunlight. His brain groaned inside his helmet.

"Bone."

He thought of Melegal, Georgio, and the City of Bone.And Kam. Only a fool would leave a woman such as that: beautiful, sweet, and seductive. What he wouldn't do to taste her lips again. Instead, he chased the filth of Bish, in the middle of nowhere, outmatched and against the odds. Had Kam been in another life that he only dreamed about now? He trudged on, his belly full of hunger and hate. His single-minded focus was razor sharp on the task at hand. It was not time for fantasies, not time to be soft. It was time to finish what the underlings started long ago.

He had followed for several more miles when the landscape began to slope upward. The ground was slick with shale, leading up into rugged hills and sheer rock-faced walls. It was the perfect place to slow his efforts and force him to drop his weapon and climb. He could see the specks getting bigger. They seemed to rest above the crest of the hilltops.

"Come on, rodents! Come down and fight!" his voice cracked.

There was an echo and a stiff breeze, but that was the only answer he got. He opted to walk around the steep cliff faces, looking for an easier way to ascend toward the top. He could feel their disappointment in his unwillingness to climb. *Let's have some fun.* He set his axe down, felt for some finger holds on the rocky face, and began to climb. *There it is.* He could feel their elation and sense their cold bodies coming closer, floating down his way. He wasn't even ten feet up when he hopped back down and grabbed his war-axe, Brool. Feeling the frustration and anger of the underlings made him laugh.

"Ha-Ha-Ha-Ha!"

He could see the underlings pulling away. They were scared of him, but why? Maybe Fogle Boon was right. Maybe they did doubt they could kill him, but he didn't doubt that they could. He was starving, and what had sustained him this long was a mystery to him. He had to eat, and eat soon. Maybe that was their plan: make him weak from the lack of food and water and blast him away at his lowest point. He found some tufts of grass along the hillside. Pulling grass from the dirt, he tried to chew it as he had seen long-horned goats do before. It tasted bitter. He chewed and tried to swallow. He spit it out, convinced that weeds were for beasts only.

Venir wanted meat, eggs, birds, rodents, or anything he could skin and put on a spit and roast. He'd been a tracker for years, survived in the south and the Outland for days on end, but the terrain he trekked through now offered nothing. They knew that. The crafty underlings were plotting his every weakening step straight into the grave. It made him angry. He pushed himself a few miles along the hilly terrain that now reached as far as he could see. It was new territory for him. As he walked along the jagged hillside he spied a nook in the rock. A nest was hanging over the side, on a narrow ledge just a few hundred feet in the distance.

He could taste the raw yokes of a wild condor on his tongue. A single egg like that would fill him for another day. He scanned the sky. The underlings were as far away as he recalled them ever being since he started chasing them. He made his way up the hillside, passing through the wide crevasses that hindered his sight of the sky above. If the underlings were concerned with his whereabouts, he didn't sense it. Instead, he gauged his position and tried his best to sneak up under the nest that was near the thick branch of a twisting vine-like tree. *A condor perch maybe.*

If he was careful and quiet, there might be a bird in the condor nest as well. The levels leading up to the nest were rocky and steep, but manageable. There were no signs of life in the area, no vermin or other fowl in the air. Venir pulled himself up over the ridge and spied the nest a few more dozen feet above. His hunger was growing at the thought of food. He was ready to continue his climb, but his helmet burned. He stopped and waited, peering up the steep face of the hill, but the sky was not there, just more terrain. He didn't sense anything more pressing than before. The underlings must be farther than he imagined, possibly heading toward another risky path. Now might be his best shot at getting the food he needed, and maybe they needed food, too.

Wary of any changes from above, Venir climbed upward, half-crawling and walking, over the slippery stone. His feet slipped, sending loose shale falling below. He caught himself and pulled himself back on the ledge. He looked at the nest above; nothing moved. Could the nest be abandoned? He'd hate to risk it all if it was empty. He made his way onto the ledge, which was just wide enough to hold his feet on the ground.

A mild gust of hot air came whipping through the hills. He paused and took a breath. No underlings came or seemed to know of his cause. He was fine. *Move or die … of starvation.* Thirty feet away he could see the old branch dangling over the hill. It was thick with leaves, branches, and twigs. He could make out the nest in the hole in the rock several feet above the ledge. He would have to somehow climb up to it. The wild condors of Bish were thirty to fifty pounds of meat. Venir's dry tongue began to water. However, their beaks were more than capable of snapping off a finger or toe. Their wings were powerful as well, capable of lifting a stout dwarf from the ground and knocking him from the ledge. He looked down. He was higher up than he expected. The wind made his sure feet unsteady. He began to dig Brool's spike into the ground with each step.

He shuffled farther along the ledge, getting closer and concerned. Where were the underlings? He looked up again, but the sky offered nothing new, just more sun and clouds shading the ground below him. His head throbbed, his stomach growled, and his ribs hurt. He grimaced as he shook his head. *Let the underlings come; I'm gonna eat something regardless.*

He stood under the nest and listened. The wind whistled through his helmet as he stuck Brool spike-first into the hard ledge. He grabbed some loose dirt and tossed it into the nest. Nothing stirred. Reaching up, his fingers didn't quite make it to the nook's edge. He searched for finger holds, but the slick face of the hill was bare. He looked outward, craning his neck to make out any birds in the sky. The helmet gave him better sight than normal, an extra awareness, but there was nothing to be seen or heard. He couldn't risk the climb. Something didn't seem right. *Now what?*

He looked at the strange branch jutting from the ledge. There were many scattered along the hillsides, growing like leafy arms from the rock. Looking closer, he saw bunched brown leaves, like a hive of twigs that were twisted up along the branch. It was another nest, possibly, but odd. It looked easier to get to, just a few feet out. He traipsed onto the branch, straddling it, his knife in hand. He looked back to check his war axe. His hands felt cold without it in his grip, which was odd for such a hot day. He waited, his head throbbing the same as before, steady like a pulse.

"Man's got to eat," he mumbled, shaking his concerns.

He scooted over the branch like a ravenous animal, peering downward at the long drop before he hit the hillside below. There it was, the makeshift nest, tangled up with the vines of the corded tree limb. *YES!* The branches were a dull gray like the rock, and knotted with rough bumps all over the bark. He gently jabbed his grandfather's hunting knife into the misshapen nest. Nothing moved. He stabbed again, careless of any peril waiting inside. Who cared if something deadly burst out? If it moved, it lived. If it lived, he could eat it. He stabbed again. Nothing.

He turned, stabbed his knife into the limb, and began pulling apart the outer husk of the nest with his hands like a hungry bear. The leaves, moss, and twigs fell slowly to the ground. Inside the nest he saw something shaped like an egg. *Yes!* It was almost as big as his hand, light brown, and somewhat translucent. It wasn't like any egg he had ever seen before, but there were a thousand things in Bish he'd never live to see. An egg was an egg however, and he was going to eat this egg.

"Come to Vee," he croaked, licking his lips, the prevailing dangers all but forgotten.

The air was still, the hillside quiet as he scanned the sky once more: no birds, no underlings, and no problems. He grabbed the egg. It was warm in his palm and felt like it was beating in his hand. His face shined with delight.

He wanted to stuff the entire thing in his mouth. He took his knife and began trying to crack a hole in the top of the shell. His face was bathed in light as the egg burst open, and something cracked beneath him. *BISH!*

2

SOMEONE WAS STROKING HIS BACK, causing him to stir from his relaxing slumber. The feeling of gentle finger nails caressing him up and down his body was stimulating. It wasn't something he had been used to in the past, but he was now. Melegal rolled over on the small wooden bed, staring into the beaming face of a younger woman. Her eyes were soft, and her smile was warm as he ran his hand along the firm curves of her body. Being an employee of Castle Almen had many advantages, and sleeping with the ginger servant girls was one of them.

He held her eyes, sat up, and let her begin rubbing his shoulders. *Ah.* Her hands were rough from her castle duties, but he still liked it. He admired his surroundings: a sparse room, typical of any serving quarters in the castle. This room in particular was little more than a bedroom in a large closet. It suited him just fine. The girl with Melegal was only one of many that he had shared the private space with. It wasn't much to him, but to the women it was, compared to other quarters with stone floors. Melegal forced those memories from his mind. He inhaled a deep breath through his nose and let the woman knead the muscles between his shoulders. He had another busy day ahead, and it wouldn't be long before his mind was no longer at ease.

A few more minutes passed by before he patted the hands that were working out the stiffness in his shoulders. Tension wasn't something he was used to, but it was a part of his life now. The girl slipped off the bed and gathered his clothes. He could see some of the scars on her back from whippings, but none were fresh; he had seen to that. He felt some pity, but not so much as before. He had his own scars, but most he had gotten used to, and she would, too.

The rest of the woman was in fine shape, much more so than the trollops in the belly of the City of Bone. She had tawny brown hair and a slender face. She was clean and mannerly, subservient and accommodating, leaving him to go about his business as he pleased, no questions or badgering for more coin. She straddled him as she slipped his shirt over his shoulders. He liked the smell of her scented hair. Her body was suggesting many reasons for him not to leave yet, but he had to go. She began pulling up his trousers, taking extra care they were a comfortable fit. She looked into his eyes, biting her lip, but he shook his head. He pushed her away, bringing a giggle, and finished dressing. *Why is it so much harder getting out of bed than in it?* He grabbed his floppy gray hat, slapped the pouting servant on the rump, and made his way from the quarters.

Melegal stood in the sub-level of the castle where servants worked, ate, and slept. It was busy in the morning, and dozens of bodies, young, old, and small were working like ants. He used to be one of them, but not anymore. He made his way through a washing room, all eyes averting his. He could see the stress lines and dark circles under the eyes of many young faces. It bothered him, when he knew it shouldn't.

He continued up the stone-faced corridor, toward the door that led up inside the main castle. It opened before he reached the handle, and he lost the spring in his gait. There stood Sefron, face sagging, belly bulging, and bug-eyes watering. *Great.* He scowled as he pushed along his course, but Sefron blocked his passage.

"Where do you think you are going, Melegal? You are not to be going wherever, whenever you wish."

Melegal's hand slipped to a small knife tucked inside his vest. *Fat sicko would sound better without a tongue. A nice red line along his throat would be nice, too.*

"It's nowhere you need to be concerned about. Now step aside before I shove a blade up your nose."

The cleric's face tightened up, but he didn't budge. Melegal averted his stare, but could feel Sefron's watery eyes boring into him, fighting to somehow gain control of him. It left the thief uneasy, staring at the strange pasty man, so he avoided it, to the ire of the cleric.

"You don't belong here, Urchin. You belong behind this door with the rest, slaving at my feet. Stay out of the castle … and I mean clear out. Only return when you are called." Sefron wheezed as he spoke. He always did, especially when irritated.

"Lord? Is that so?" He touched his chest. "I'll have to check that with Lord Almen, I suppose. He'll certainly be upset with me treating another Lord so poorly. Lord Sefron the slimy. It sure sounds good. I can't wait to mention it to him!"

Melegal watched Sefron slink back, eyes flitting with uncertainty. He pressed on.

"As I recall, he wasn't very fond of you questioning his orders. Even for a Lord. Now, what was it he did to you that last time you trifled with me? Hmmm …"

He posed in thought, rubbing his chin, listening to Sefron's breath growing thinner.

"Ah … yes, I remember now. He had you cleaning the muck from the cracks of the elderly Royals! Wasn't that it? That's right, I recall seeing you disposing of several bowls of granny slat—"

"Enough, Urchin! I'll have you drained alive of all your fluids if you ever meddle with me again!"

The busy servants that had been crossing through the hall veered away, eyes on the ground, out of the two men's paths. It wasn't the first of the standoffs between the detective and the cleric, and unlikely to be the last, but they certainly didn't want to be on the end of Sefron's anger. Melegal almost began to laugh as the scrawny cleric's frail chest heaved. He looked the foul man up and down with a sneer. He could never understand why the man wouldn't wear more clothes. The cleric's skin was pale and clammy, his belly soft and hanging over the breach of cloth he wore around his waist. Sefron's pale legs were scrawny and knobby kneed, his sandals slick with grime. Melegal thought Sefron was one of the most disgusting men he had ever seen. He never got used to his appearance. *I'd hate to be his mirror.*

Sefron gave him one final leer and shoved by him, barking at the nearest servant. Melegal didn't stick around to see what happened, either. He breezed through the door and entered the serving corridors that surrounded the main castle floors. As much as he enjoyed jerking the cleric around, he knew he had to be careful. Sefron had displayed talents he lacked in the world of magic, and magic was something he preferred to avoid. The cleric had also been around the Almen family for decades and was favored by Lord Almen for some insane reason. No, Sefron had his uses, just like he did. In the meantime, Melegal felt it best to avoid the cleric whenever he could, but not take any of his slat, either. He allowed himself a smile. He just had to be sure to watch his back, which he was comfortable with.

He pulled back a portion of a blue velvet curtain and looked into one of the main living chambers of the castle. It was just past the crack of dawn. Sunlight began to shine through the stained glass windows above. A serving girl was watering fresh-cut flowers while another dusted. No Royals were around, or sentries either, which was good. Lord Almen insisted he maintain a low profile and avoid conversations with his family beyond passing courtesy. It was a great idea to him, but if a Royal demanded his conversation he had to play along. Hence, he avoided the castle most of the time, as their probing and demanding nature made him feel confined. However, a few simple words such as, *Excuse me, but Lord Almen is expecting me, and I don't want to be late,* seemed to do the trick. But their questions also revealed to him much about them. He stored that knowledge deep under his cap.

He stepped through the living room, marveling at the exquisite design. Paintings, tapestries, and decorations, each of which was worth a small fortune, adorned the room. There was a sofa large enough to sleep ten people from end to end. Melegal always wanted to sit on that sofa, filled with plush pillows and made of cattle-neck leather. He had never even touched it. He walked close to the edge of its seat, fingers twitching. There was just something about that couch that seemed forbidden, like many other things in the castle. *I bet it's never been napped on before.*

"It's a beautiful couch, isn't it Detective?"

Melegal turned, a bit quicker than normal, at the sound of the woman's voice. There she stood, in another entrance-way, arms folded … Lord Almen's wife. He was at a loss for words for a moment, his eyes glancing into hers, then down to the floor.

"Yes ma'am … it is," he said, pulling his hat from his head.

She began coming his way and said, "Would you like to sit in it, Detective?"

"No ma'am. No thank you."

"Look at me," she said in a stern voice.

He obeyed, much to his pleasure. Lord Almen's wife was perfection from head to toe. Her face was soft and elegant, beautiful cat-shaped eyes, and voice that seemed to purr. He didn't feel worthy of being so close to such a beautiful creature. In an instant he locked in every detail of her being. She wore soft leather sandals that matched her painted toes. Her legs were shaven and showed a tanned sheen underneath a dark cherry colored robe that cut off at her upper thigh. A loose black belt around her tiny waist kept the robe from falling open. She held the neck closed above her ample chest, and her teeth were white as snow. He was convinced he would do anything she told him to do, and he just hoped it wouldn't get him killed. She continued.

"Let me give you a command, Detective. Do not ever call me *ma'am* again. If you do, I'll have your skin flayed from your back. Do you understand me?"

"Yes."

"Yes what?"

"Yes … Lorda Almen?"

He looked up and held her gaze, knowing full well she was considering having his skin flayed from his back. Her eyes were intelligent and contemplating, and he began to feel like his days were suddenly numbered. *Oh no, what have I said.*

"Sit down on the couch, Detective. Get comfortable."

He did as she said, but he didn't feel one bit comfortable.

She sat down beside him, crossed her legs, and said, "I bought his from a caravan of merchants from the City of Hohm. Actually, they came into this castle and stitched its entirety together. Very impressive, isn't it?" she said, rubbing one of the couch arms by her side with a delicate and bejeweled hand.

"Yes, Lorda Almen."

"Lorda will do, Detective. Of course, Royal Lorda Almen would have been the correct response, as you would address my husband as Royal Lord Almen. Do you understand, Detective?"

"Yes."

How can a woman smell as good as she looks? It was a trivial thought, but a reflex, as he was getting nervous. He should have remembered how big the Royals were on titles after all the years he had spent working beneath them. Servants often were whipped for less. He needed to get out of here, offer his excuse.

"Of course, I don't care for all of the titles, but it is my role as the head matron of the castle, to see to it that all are addressed properly and according to the common rules of social etiquette. Royal etiquette, that is. So Detective, I suggest that you be very careful how you address me among others. I would hate to see you lose your tongue because of a simple slip of it."

"Thank you, Lorda."

Lorda Almen shifted in her seat, allowing her robes to briefly fall open. He glanced. Her eyes were stern as she gave him a once over from head to toe. *Blast your eyes, Thief!* He didn't know whether to look at her or away, but he held her steady stare. It seemed safest to keep his eyes where he could see hers.

"So Detective," she purred, "can you use your powers of deduction to tell me how much money I spent on this incredibly comfortable couch?"

"Nothing."

"Ah … a quick reply. I like that. Very good, and you are right. I did not pay for it, and nor did my husband. Do you care to consider why we didn't have to pay?"

"Because they were doing you a favor, Lorda?"

"No … it is because after I had them build it, I couldn't bear for them to make another just like it … so I had them killed."

He knew it. He wasn't going to say it, but he knew it. He needed to get out of here, and he didn't want to know any more. He sat still as a stone, her eyes still searching his, testing his reaction. She seemed frustrated that her story hadn't garnered one. He couldn't help but swallow, though. It was time for him to make his exit.

"Lorda—"

"Ah-Ah-Ah … don't speak unless spoken to, Detective. Now come with me."

He didn't want to leave the couch now, and going anywhere else with her was a really bad idea. He hoped another Royal or servant, anybody, would show up and offer a distraction so he could weasel his was out. At the moment though, the castle seemed like a graveyard. It was breakfast time, and they were a long way from the dining hall, and getting farther with every step it seemed.

She led him up a small flight of marble stairs and stopped on the middle landing. An ornate vase of pewter, black, and gold sat on a shelf, filled with fresh white roses. Just above it was a painting. *Oh slat!* Melegal's narrow shoulders grew tight as he began to wring his hat from behind his back. *Let me go. Let me go. Let me go.* Lorda Almen studied his gaze, which had returned back to hers. *Please don't let this be about him.*

"Detective, I am in need of your services, and it is something that is to be kept between the two of us."

He gave her a subtle nod.

"Good … Now the man in the portrait is my son dearest son, Tonio."

The mere mention of the name sent chills down Melegal's spine.

"He has gone missing for many months. My husband assures me that he is in the south, soldiering on a mission, but that is not the understanding I have from my sources. I cherish my husband Almen more than life itself, but he keeps many things from me, protecting me, so to speak."

No … controlling you, so to speak.

"But my son Tonio is special to me. His siblings don't compare, despite their talents …"

Melegal could feel the truth of her words, and her eyes watered as she gazed the portrait with her fingertips. Her sincerity was genuine, but Melegal couldn't understand how she could adore a monster like Tonio. Only a mother could love that man, something he would never understand. Still, her long-lashed eyes suggested there was some good in her, unlike many of the others he crossed in the castle.

"… and this portrait is about all I have left of him," she said, letting out a small sob.

He wanted to jam his hat on his head and suggest she let him be, but the effort might offend her. His hat might be lost, and he didn't want that. It was too risky. He was going to have to stick this one out, despite his discomfort around one of the most powerful women in the City of Bone.

Her voice regained control as she said, "I want you to find out what happened to him, even if the news is the worst. I need to know if he's dead or alive. I don't care which, and I want proof."

Great, maybe I should just go into Lord Almen's study and ask to be flogged to death.

"There was another detective, McKnight was his name, and if you can locate him he may be of some assistance. He was in our service, but my husband has told me that his services had become inadequate and that he found a more favorable replacement ... you."

Are the dead ever really dead these days? Is it possible that if I shovel a giant pile of pig slat that the man will be re-born? Why not; I'll get right on it.

"Again, Detective, I cannot emphasize how imperative it is that you keep this between us. If my husband were to find out he would be upset with me, so I will be grateful for your discretion. A man can gain much when he pleases me."

She ran her finger down his chest to his belt and stopped.

"I expect to hear from you as soon as you find something. I realize that these delicate things can take some time," she paused, "but I am not a very patient woman."

"Yes Lorda."

"I believe my husband is awaiting your arrival, and I suggest you don't be late."

Melegal watched her perfect legs for a moment as she headed back up the stairs and disappeared. *I can't believe this! Why me?* It was hard enough working directly for Lord Almen, and now he worked for his wife ... in secret. He would have avoided the castle altogether if not for the willing serving girls, the good food, and the excellent wine. Now it seemed as if he had escaped from one net only to land in another. He made his way through the busy kitchen, ignoring the stares of the servants. He passed a sentry at the top at a door and headed down the stone steps toward Royal Lord Almen's meeting place. A large wooden door awaited him there. What would the Royal Lord have for him today? It was always something new and despicable. He hesitated.

Knock! Knock!

Lorda Almen was unhappy. She missed her son dearly and didn't believe her husband. She had spent weeks trying to figure out exactly what had happened to Tonio, but to no avail. Now, desperate and angry, she decided to reach out to one of Lord Almen's own. The house Detective Melegal gave her some hope, and she knew he could be swayed. He seemed to take her threats seriously, but they were harmless. She could lie with conviction—as was part of her role—just as naturally as strolling down the hall.

She had told the detective the story of the couch, a tale, nothing more, as the sofa pre-existed her days in Castle Almen. It seemed he had believed her, and that was all that mattered. She wasn't one to commit murder for the simple prize, but she was close to those who were. She made her way back to her quarters and sat down on the edge of her bed. A serving girl was there, cleaning and dusting. The girl bowed and began to dismiss herself.

"Stay. I need my feet rubbed."

The young girl, dressed in a plain gray smock and black-dyed slacks, sank down on both knees, removed Lorda Almen's sandals, and began to rub her feet. Lorda let out a sigh, laid back on the bed, and ran her slender hands through her black hair. It felt good to be the Lorda of the Almen house.

"Now, be sure and do a good job, or I'll have you whipped."

3

MOOD PULLED OUT A CIGAR and lit it up. The aroma was strong, like burning wheat and cherries. Fogle caught a solid whiff and said, "That's not bad. Let me have one; I used to smoke a pipe back home."

"Ho! Ho! Naw, Little Man. This is dwarven smoke, mystic and strong. Ye've got ta have the right blood, dwarven blood, or out you go. The smoke will do ye fine."

The cigar smoke was thick, hanging in the air like a yellow mist. Fogle stepped inside and sucked it in, holding his nose.

"Heh, what are you doing, Little Man? You'll be flying back home if you aren't careful," Mood said, fanning the smoke away with his meaty hand.

Fogle didn't care. The smoke was just what he needed, that and a bath, maybe even a woman, too. He thought of Kam and the last conversation they had. He had never spoken so long to a woman before, not to his sisters or his mother even. He found her splendid, intelligent, and voluptuous. He made sure to burn a mental image of her in his mind: long auburn hair, sweet eyes, a soft face, and her chest swelling behind the laces of her dress. What if Venir were not to come back? Did that even matter? This was Bish after all.

"Mood?"

"Yes, Little Man."

"How did you come to know Venir?"

Somehow, Fogle could see a reflective expression in Mood's eyes. Fogle had never noticed them before: deep, ancient and thoughtful.

Mood said, "Ah, now that tis somethin' I've never spoke of before, or bin asked for the matter. Funny ye should ask. I've been thinkin' about it lately myself. I've been wandering this world for centuries, ain't ever met a man like him but once."

Fogle pulled off his boots and began rubbing his burning feet. Even with a horse, he still did more walking than he was accustomed to on the rugged terrain. He rocked forward and asked, "Really, why is that?"

"It just is," Mood said, letting out a puff of smoke. Fogle Boon swore he saw an image of Venir appear in the smoke. He blinked hard, but the image had dissipated.

"It just is because you haven't known many men, or it just is because of something else?"

"Ha, I've known many men. Fought with 'em and against 'em all over. I've seen the best and worst. Nay, tis somethin' else."

He hesitated before he asked.

"Is it because he's ... the Darkslayer?"

"No, he was different long before that."

Fogle Boon shifted on the hard ground. Mood's words and tone offered a great deal of mystery. The way the dwarf spoke, Venir was just as unique as himself. He was beginning to understand that quite possibly, he could learn more from this dwarf than from any other man. Of all the brilliant wizards who had schooled him all of his life, he began to realize that Mood had more wisdom than all of them combined. The Blood Ranger was more than just a burly body that cut down trees in a single stroke. The dwarf was a part of Bish that no human could have ever lived long enough to see for himself. Fogle wanted to learn more from Mood, and if he had to ask questions all night long to do it, he would.

"So Mood, how long have you known Venir then?"

"Since he was a boy, about tis tall," Mood said, holding his hand up high above his head.

There was more odd silence. Fogle was used to people offering more to the conversation beyond one-sentence answers. Back home, in the City of Three, the men would never shut up. Each man had a story to tell, a menial, boorish yarn of something astounding and pointless they had achieved that day. Of course, he was no different. He remembered a particular story of his own; he had bragged about how he had mastered a spell in a day that took most magi a week. Or, there was the time when he had defeated a senior classmate with a whipping spell. He never would have known how shallow and vain he was if Venir hadn't come into his life. Now the mere presence of Mood made him realize how pointless all the things he cherished were. He felt ashamed.

Fogle spoke in a stronger voice now and asked, "Mood, will you tell me, in detail, the circumstances of how you came to know Venir?"

Mood's head tilted as he turned to face him.

"It started in Dwarven Hole. Tis' there that we breed the dwarven setters, like Chongo. The setters are as ancient as us, going back as far as we know. Chongo was one of a litter of pups, not so much different than da rest. A few months after they're born we take 'em out with us. They're natural hunters, trackers, and swimmers, but they still need trained. They can be hard to break, but that's why ta Blood Rangers train 'em. We can teach 'em things that others can't."

An image the shape of Chongo hung in the air and drifted away. *How does he do that?* He thought about how Chongo, the massive two-headed dog, had looked when he was being taken back to Dwarven Hole for healing. One of the pooch's heads had still sagged near the ground. It had been almost lifeless, it's big brown eyes barely open and its tongue hanging from its mouth. The other head had seemed sad and alone, and the memory saddened Fogle Boon as well. He wondered if one head could survive without the other. Back in Dwarven Hole, Mikkel and Billip had told him that Chongo used to have only one head. For some reason, it had seemed hard to believe. Fogle opened his mouth to speak, and then closed it. Mood's lips were still moving. *I'd better not stop him now.*

"After a few years, the setters are ready. We set 'em free. They can go anywhere they want on all of Bish. They find a master on their own. It kin' be man or beast, but it's nearly always a dwarf. I never seen one not come back to Dwarven Hole. But from this litter, Chongo left and never came back. I thought he were dead; maybe an underling got 'em, I didn't know," Mood finished shaking his head.

Don't stop, Mood; keep going. An odd few minutes passed as Fogle looked around, willing Mood to continue, but not daring to interrupt the giant dwarf's thoughts. The dwarf's gaze was transfixed in the distance still; a cloud of smoke shaped like a forest came forth and drifted away. Fogle was rolling his hand. *Come on!*

4

C ATTEN'S STOMACH GROWLED. HIS MIND ached. Staying afloat days on end was not something he had done before. Now it seemed he had no choice. The wounds he had suffered days earlier from the human mage, Fogle Boon, were almost healed. Yet, he still ached inside. The shock of magic penetrating his skin and boiling his innards had been the first of its kind. He wiped his cracked lips and fingered the black scars on his abdomen. Pain was something he had no desire to ever get used to. Floating beside his brother, he was trying to catch a glimpse of the most brutal and unrelenting opponent he had ever known … the Darkslayer.

Verbard floated at his side, glaring downward at the hills. His brother was determined to take the human apart with another assault. Catten was patient while his brother was not, but his plan prevailed. Wear the man down, starve him to death, and leave not a single drop of water near the ground. Over the past two days they had both used their power and presence to clear any living thing from the man's path. The Darkslayer below was more concerned with them than his own nutrition. What had sustained the man this long Catten could not comprehend, but something powerful and magical must have given him aid. It was frustrating.

He inhaled the stuffy hot air and closed his golden eyes. *Insufferable!* It seemed like the *do or die* mission Master Sinway had put them on was never going to end. Catten wanted to go home and bury himself in the comforts of the caves a thousand feet below. Now, he was out of his element, stuck under the beating suns and in the harsh winds. The smells of the lands began to annoy him, and his brother's chronic suggestions were wearing him down. If it weren't for Verbard, he swore the Darkslayer would already be dead.

"Do you really think this will work, Catten? The man hasn't fallen for any of our tricks, many of which have failed," Verbard said.

"Please Brother, go ahead and try your tactic then. Land on the ground and have your power sweep the man away. When it falters and he finishes chopping you to bits, I'll pluck your bloody ear from the ground and scream into it, 'I told you so'."

Verbard's black brow buckled.

"Pah! We are not so weak. We have the power between us to turn that man into dust. The longer we wait, the stronger he gets."

"I disagree, Fool! We have to wait until he is at his weakest, and then strike. You've seen the man and what he did to my Juegen, your urchlings, Master Sinway's Vicious, and the Badoon. He must be separated from those weapons. He's a man, but with that armament he's something else. We can't land and strike until he is flat-footed on the ground."

Verbard's eyes were molten silver on him, but Catten no longer cared if his brother hated him or not. He was beginning to think he would be better off on this charge alone. He was tired; his magic was coming and going. There were moments when he felt invincible, but they would pass, and doubt would settle in. No, Catten had to play it smarter, not be hasty, but patient and cunning, the way of his kind. He believed he could wear the man down. He had read the tomes about him from the halfling's written hand. The Darkslayer was only a man, a man named Venir, whose record clearly showed that he hated underlings. Catten watched as his brother floated away. The two had been feeding off each other as well. Maintaining constant flight was not easy, but they were born with the shadow walk, and that helped. The greater the altitude, the more difficult it became to maintain. Both of the underlings knew that if they hit the ground the Darkslayer would be there. They didn't have the energy to stay in flight and strike at the same time. They had tried that before, expecting to destroy the man and hit the ground in victory. It hadn't turned out that way, so they stayed airborne, captive to the predator below. Catten had another plan, a clever one. If it worked, they could land and take the fight to the man. One final battle—winner take all—and go home.

Catten felt like he was cooking within his black robes. The two suns beat on his hooded black head, leaving his hair matted and sticky. It was hot, obscenely so, and he missed the cool cave air of the Underland. His skin was dry and flaking, and he felt thirsty for the first time in years. He pulled a small vial from the inside of his robes and twisted the cork out. It contained a clear yellow-green liquid of which he added a drop to his tongue. His mouth was filled with a rush of ice-cold water that he swallowed down in a gulp. His stomach filled, and his mouth tasted of baked meat and sweet vegetables. *Ah … that's better.*

The potion was something his wife had prepared for him, and the small vial could last him weeks. He missed his wife, her beautiful face and fiendish grin. The thought that he might not see her again was a bother.

He looked into the clouds. Their patterns had been erratic, scattered, and swirling for the past few days. It seemed as if the air itself affected the flow of magic, bringing it in a rush and taking it away the same. Now, for the past few hours, things had been steady. The blue cloud-filled sky seemed normal for a change. He felt normal as well. Maybe Verbard was right, and the time was now.

He watched the hills below. A small figure emerged from the hills before his searching eyes. An axe-wielding butcher scaled the cliff like a natural born predator. The man's trek was undaunted as he kept coming after them. Catten pulled his robes tight. *This has to work.* Verbard had gathered himself by his side. Both sets of eyes, silver and gold, were intent on what the man was about to do. Hours ago Catten had set a trap, despite Verbard's misgivings. It was little more than an illusion, but a good one. There was a thick rotting branch jutting from a hillside. Above it was a nest of vipers hidden in the rock. Catten cast the illusion of a nest in both locations. The branch looked to be more like a sturdy limb of a tree with another nest inside.

"He seems wary, Brother," Verbard said. "Perhaps we should go. You'll know if he takes the bait, won't you?"

"Yes, let's move farther away. I'll know it when the time comes."

Catten and Verbard flew beyond the hill and waited. Catten meditated on his mutilation spells in the meantime. It was time the Darkslayer was undone.

5

KAM WAS SOBBING, AGAIN. SHE never used to cry, other than at a funeral or two, but now it seemed to come on all the time. Wiping her eyes with a rag, she rubbed more wax into one of the tables, bringing a nice sheen. It wasn't a chore she often did, but she was sitting at the table where she had last sat with him … Venir. It was early, and no one was about. The boys, Lefty and Georgio, were still asleep. Her serving staff wouldn't be in for a couple more hours. It was the only time she could sit here and think about the last time she talked with Venir, which always made her cry. She didn't really understand why.

She muttered something. Invisible hands tied her long curly auburn hair behind her head, twisting it up in a perfect braid. It was a simple spell she had mastered when she was a girl. She tossed the rag down and had the invisible hands rub her shoulders. She had been polishing the same spot for half an hour. She missed Venir. He brought something she needed, something that other men simply didn't have. His rugged character, charming smile, and crushing arms melted her. His kisses wanted her, and she missed that. The boys he left behind with her were little trouble, but they were chronic reminders of him.

She pushed herself away from the table and walked over to the semi-circle bar of gleaming black wood. Small brass lanterns with mystic yellow lights illuminated the bar from above, a personal touch of her own. The shelves behind the bar offered a wide array of bottles, clear and filled with multi-colored liquids. Wine, grog and other things from all over Bish filled those bottles, and much of it was hard to come by. It served to draw a more reputed crowd and kept the more desperate types out. *What will it be, Kam?*

She twirled her fingers, and a rose-colored bottle floated over to her hand. She lifted the bottle, pulled the cork, and sniffed the bouquet. It was strong and sweet, like honeysuckles mixed with long fermented wine. She filled a tall glass, lifted her chin and drained it. The mead warmed her from throat to belly, the sweet taste of honey and the biting taste of something stronger at the same time.

"Ah! A few more of those and I'll forget all about that man."

Kam didn't care what had gotten into her, but something was missing. A void she could not fill.

"Arses up," she said, draining another glass. Her imagination exploded now with new thoughts, some dark and some light. Was Venir gone, dead? What about Fogle Boon? The morbid sense she had felt when Venir left this time was like a dark shadow in her mind. It told her he might be heading to the grave, facing his final conflict against evil. His smiles had been reassuring, but not warm, not like she knew him to be. The man was racked up in his own personal torment of good versus evil.

"This one's for you, Venir, may Bish be with you."

She drained the remaining contents from the bottle. Now toying with the bottle, she watched it teeter-totter back and forth. It wouldn't be long. Just a few more minutes and she would be ready to deal with the new day. Muckle Sap had a long and lasting effect. It wasn't her best seller, but it was now her best friend. She took the bottle in her gentle hand and walked back into the kitchen. An older woman with short graying curly hair smiled as she walked by.

"Good morning Kam … I see you're about ready for a new day," the woman said in a positive voice.

"Almost there, Joline."

Kam placed the bottle in a crate that was filled with many other empties. *Did I drink all of those?* "Hey, Joline, did I—"

"Yes, yes you did, you lush. I told you that the other day," Joline said as she stirred more spices into a large vat of morning stew.

"Well, you better order some more."

"I already did. Now sit down and have some breakfast."

"I don't have time. Maybe later."

Joline grabbed her with a firm grip as she turned to walk away.

"Sit!"

"But—"

It was too late; Joline pushed her into a seat and poured a ladle filled with stew into the bowl that awaited her. It smelled great! Her tummy growled, and she shoveled a spoonful in her mouth. "Happy," she said with her mouth full.

Joline's long face was warm, round-eyed, flat-nosed and unaffected by her appearance. Kam gave her surroundings further study as she added another mouthful. The kitchen was tidy, and Joline's apron didn't have a speck of food on it. *How does she do it?* She had known the cook for many years now, and she knew her quite well. Joline didn't say much, always focused on serving food, but Kam knew it was time to listen. It wasn't something she was good at.

"I've never seen you so crossed up about a man before, Kam, or anything else for that matter," Joline said, adding some more spice to her breakfast stew.

Kam took in another spoonful, tasting the potatoes, bacon, and vegetables, all mixed into one, along with something else. The Muckle Sap was taking effect, making her appetite seem to increase with every bite. She began to feel stronger. Her mind eased, but she was itching to dig into something else now.

"It's wonderful, Joline, as always."

"You need a clear head! You've been sulking over that brute for weeks. He's only a man; you know you can't count on them for long. Heck, he even left his children with you."

Kam let out a laugh. The thought of Venir having children, a halfling at that, was amusing.

"Now listen to me, Girlie. You have your pick in this city. Men are always courting you. You're even a Royal. You just don't act like one. Get over that big man."

The woman's matter-of-fact words brought a frown to Kam's face. Her eyes began to tear up.

Joline's eyes widened, and she rushed over to her side and wiped Kam's eyes with her apron. Joline started rubbing her hand around in circles on Kam's back.

"There, there, I'm sorry, Kam. Don't get me wrong. That man, Venir, he's a good one. He cares for you, those boys too. He's one of those cut from the better bones of Bish. But Kam, that man's eyes—as blue as they may be—behind them is a fiery inferno. You get too close …"

Joline's kindness opened the dam, and the tears started streaming down Kam's face. She had never felt so confused, lonely and desperate. Nothing had really changed since he came or since he left. It was all the same, except for the boys. Georgio and Lefty brought her nothing but joy … and the reminder of Venir. He treated her better than any other man ever had, listening, touching, caressing … he had even bought her a gift. She rubbed the tiny ruby earring on her lobe. Men didn't often treat women like that, not the way he did.

Kam blew her nose in Joline's apron and said, "I've never known anyone like him. The first time I saw him, he swept me off my feet in a river of blood and was gone. I missed him, but I got over it, a passing fling. But when he came back this time Joline, I felt something like I've never felt before. It was happiness. The man's hard as a rock and stubborn as a goat, but the sound of his voice … his presence … made me happy." She started sobbing again. She couldn't control it, and that embarrassed her.

Joline hugged her, rocking her like her mother used to. It was comforting. Then she felt a hand patting her back. It was soothing as well, and tiny. Something was wrong.

"Joline …" she said, slipping out of the woman's embrace. "Were you just patting my back?"

"No."

Both of the women started looking around.

"Are you sure?"

Joline shrugged, looking all over.

Kam had a funny feeling, and for the moment she forgot all of her troubles. There was pounding out front, coming from of the Magi Roost entrance. It was early for customers, but they would be open soon enough. It was probably just the City Watch. They often gave her updates on any unruly customers they had locked away. There had been several incidents lately. People had been edgy.

"Joline, will you go ahead and open up?"

"Sure, Dear," the woman said, walking away with a concerned look at Kam.

Kam started to look around again; she swore she felt something on her back. She got up, spinning around slowly and looking up and down. When she turned back around, her bowl of stew was gone. *What in the world?*

The kitchen wasn't very large, so whatever was going on wouldn't be easy to hide. Her head wasn't very clear, either, from the Muckle Sap. She walked around the kitchen, beginning to think she should have just stayed in bed. When she got back to where she had been a moment earlier, her bowl was there … empty.

"What!?"

She heard a small giggling voice close by.

"Lefty, where are you?"

A tiny finger was tapping her on the shoulder. She whirled around only to see Lefty's tiny face, eye to eye with her, standing on a table.

"Good morning, Kam. Did I fool you?"

"Yes, you little booger," she said, lifting him into the air. Lefty was as light as a baby, and she couldn't resist tickling him.

"Ew … stop it Kam … that tickles … hahahahaha …"

Lefty twisted away, disappearing into a cupboard.

"Morning, Kam. Can I have breakfast stew? I'm starving!"

It was Georgio, rubbing his pudgy belly, shirtless, with his trousers on, held up by his suspenders.

"Not if you don't get some clothes on. What did I tell you about that?"

"But, I am really hungry, Kam! Just a bite … pleeeeease!"

She re-filled the bowl and handed it to him. "Take it to your room, eat it, get dressed, and bring the bowl back down."

Georgio was filling his face saying, "Mmm … all right."

"Go Georgio!"

He tilted the bowl up to his nose, swallowed the whole thing down, and handed Kam the empty bowl. She was ready to pull every lock of curly brown hair from his head.

"Buuh-urp!"

Lefty was having a giggling fit inside the cabinet.

"Can I have some water, plea—"

"Get out!" she said, shaking the room.

Georgio was gone, and only an empty cupboard remained. Kam's feelings for Venir began to take a turn.

"Men!"

6

THE EGG VANISHED. THE BRANCH that held Venir withered and gave way under his weight. Emptiness filled him, and then he was plummeting downward, screaming while the underlings cackled somewhere above. Venir free-fell about thirty feet and then banged into the hillside, almost blacking out. His fingers clawed at the jagged edges of the hill, rock and dirt cutting into his hands. His feet were kicking, arms flailing, but nothing he touched slowed his fall. He barreled down the hill like a stone, sliding faster and farther toward the rugged ground below.

"Bone!" he cried, but it didn't help. The bottom still neared.

He stopped for a moment, clinging to the face of the hill, clutching at a small finger hold. He pinched at a rock, struggling to pull himself up. His booted feet dug into the hill. His shoulders heaved from the effort to hang on. He could feel the underlings coming now. He peered upward. The branch he had fallen from was a hundred feet above, little more than a withered branch, not what he had seen before. Brool was abandoned up there! The underlings were closing in. He could feel their hatred, confidence, and excitement. He growled from the effort to pull himself up, but there was nowhere to go. He looked over his back, realizing it would be easier to climb down.

He let himself slide a bit, but the combined weight of him and his dwarven-scale armor was more than the loose dirt on the hillside could hold. He slipped and then tumbled down the hill, rolling, clutching, screaming, and snarling. It was a lost cause. He fell like a drunken orc playing King of the Mountain. Down he went, rolling off of a ledge and landing hard another twenty feet below.

"Oomph!"

His head bounced off a rock, cracking the stone and almost knocking him cold. Venir felt woozy, and blood flowed into his eyebrows. He could hear laughter, underling chitter, echoing in his helmet. He looked around through a bloody haze. He was in a ravine. He saw his knife lying on the ground near his side, a fortunate break. He grabbed it, spying the path of the ravine, looking for somewhere to hide. It was too late.

A robed underling landed three dozen feet away. It was dark, bigger than most, gold eyes blazing like an inferno of power. Venir felt like an underling army stood before him. He sensed its power like a man senses an oncoming storm. The hairs on his arms stood on end. His helmet boomed another warning. He turned. The other underling appeared behind him, just as far away. It had round flashing silver eyes, short-cropped black hair, and a twisted sneering face. Venir's hands felt cold and empty without Brool. The knife was all that stood between him and death. *Fight or die!*

He tried to fight the rage that was building inside him, beckoning him to attack, pushing him into the slaughter. *There has to be another way.* The air began to thicken around him. The hands of the narrow-faced underling with golden eyes started to radiate. The girdle around his waist began to throb. Venir saw a stone bigger than his head on the ground and felt the urge to pick it up and throw it. Jamming his knife in his sheath, he grabbed the rock, pulled it behind his head and slung it like a skipping stone. The small boulder sailed straight and true, soaring toward the astounded underling before it ricocheted off an invisible shield, knocking the underling to the ground.

Great Bish!

Venir was charging toward the stunned creature when he felt two cold hands squeezing his heart. He cried out in pain as he fell to the ground. Looking over his shoulder he could see the underling's silver eyes shining like polished coins. Its hands were squeezing something in the air, its face straining with hatred. Venir gasped for air. He was suffocating. He kicked and twitched. Then he couldn't move. Little bright spots started to coat his vision.

The underling he smote with the boulder rose to one knee, its face filled with fury. The underlings nodded at one another, coming closer. One's fingers were clutching with energy and the other looked to be crushing something in its clawed grasp. Venir knew that it somehow had a hold of his heart. He watched them come closer and knew his end drew near. He heard them both cackle, and inside his mind he screamed.

7

"ENTER."
      Melegal took a breath before he did so, opening the door and closing it with a light *clatch* behind him. He stood before an ordinary desk of hand-carved mahogany wood, hands behind his back, hat tucked inside his vest. Lord Almen sat quietly hunched over the large desk, his complacent face in study. The Royal Lord looked foreboding, his chiseled features shadowed by the candle and torchlight. Even seated , the polished man seemed tall; his shoulders seemed to match the breadth of the heavy desk. Melegal had trouble measuring up the man. Almen's stern expression told little of the mind inside, but he always felt like he was in danger when he was near the Royal.

"You seem to be running a tad late this morning. What happened?"

Slat! Let the lying games begin. "Apologies Lord Almen, I had an unpleasant surprise from that cleric, Sefron."

Lord Almen hadn't even looked up at him yet, eyes still intent on the documents before him. Melegal counted the jeweled rings on the man's long fingers. It seemed like the man wore a different set every time he saw him, each ring worth a small fortune.

"Oh, I see. Is it anything I need to be concerned about?"

"No, Lord Almen."

"Good, I'd hate to have to intercede on your behalf again." Lord Almen then looked up at him and said, "I know that Sefron can be a jealous nuisance, but he is of value to this house, Detective … as are you. He does what I expect him to do, so make sure you don't entertain his petty rivalry. It can be deadly."

"I understand." Yes he did indeed. *Stay out of the castle, the place where you are entitled to sanctuary and pleasures you only dreamed of. Avoid all of it on account of a rotten fat-bellied cleric who licks the paws of dogs. I don't think so.*

Royal Lord Almen stood up, tall and foreboding. He walked around to the front of his desk and half-sat on the top. The man was always exquisite, Melegal noticed. Thick brown hair, almost shoulder length, parted neatly in the middle. Almen's clothes were simple and refined, a brown and tan dress coat with squared brass buttons running from chest to waist. Melegal never noticed the man carrying a weapon of any sort, but there was a slight bulge about Almen's waist and chest. *Daggers, knives … oh what could it be?*

Royal Lord Almen's next question had a harsher tone. "Anything else you would like to mention, Detective?"

The muscles began knot in the small of his back. *Does he know I talked with the Lorda? Did she set me up? Did they plan this? Was it a test?* Time was ticking, and a delay in his reply might be fatal. If he could only turn into a rat, he would be more than happy to scurry off into a hole. Without hesitation, he replied and said, "Yes, I had a brief conversation with the Lorda. It was unavoidable."

Royal Lord Almen could not hide his peaked interest as the thick brows lifted on his face. Almen began to stand up, but opted to stay put, uncertain. "I can only imagine what my wife may have demanded of you. She enjoys being involved with my servants. I also realize that her promptings are impossible to say *no* to. But remember Melegal, I am the Lord of this house, and what I say goes as far as you are concerned."

"Yes, Lord Almen."

"So, out with it, Man … What did she ask of you?"

To lie, or not to lie, that is the question. Melegal could feel his palms turn clammy. He pictured a candle in his mind and blew it out. His fingers became dry as a bone. *I might as well be dead anyway.* "She showed me a picture of your son, Tonio. She asked me to find out if he was alive or dead."

Melegal couldn't see the anger in Lord Almen's face, but he could feel it.

"She also asked me not to mention it to you." *There, have some truth for breakfast, Royal Lord. How does that feel?*

Oddly, Melegal didn't feel any better. Instead, he expected either the Lorda to pop up or Lord Almen to scream for the guards. He briefly wondered what his head would look like decorating a castle wall spike. Lord Almen's stoic expression leered down on him as the man stood up, fists clenched. Melegal felt himself breathe as the man walked back behind the desk and sat back down, causing the chair to creak. His back was still as tight as a spring in the growing silence. *Well? Say something! Do I live or die? Can I at least have breakfast first?*

Lord Almen leaned forward on his desk after a few long moments.

"So … my wife still misses her dear boy, Tonio. Hmph. This isn't good news, Detective, but telling me was the right thing to do. Of course, I am curious as to why you didn't tell me this at first. It makes me wonder if you weren't holding it back to begin with."

"I was merely reporting the events as they occurred, Lord Almen. I pride myself on being accurate … and wise." Melegal could only imagine what would happen if Lord Almen didn't buy into his tale. He thought of Venir. His burly body guard gave him security on occasions like this. It was a stark moment, all alone, not an ally within the city. *The lout used to always be near when I needed him.*

Lord Almen was needling his strong chin, eyes cast upward at the support beams. Melegal noticed something odd up there, a glimmer of steel. Lord Almen caught him looking as he cast his eyes away at the ground. He noticed Lord Almen's hands stretching out, reaching for something underneath the desk, a weapon, perhaps. Melegal allowed a gentle bend in his knees even though he had nowhere to go.

"Come closer, Melegal. I have something I would like to show you … a prized possession."

"I would be honored," Melegal said, taking a step forward, using his toes to feel for a false bottom under the floor. *Plenty solid — No strange holes in the desk — looks to be clear.*

Lord Almen rested his fist on the desk and opened it up. A small brooch of pewter, gold and steel now sat on the table, with a small insignia of Castle Almen on it. Melegal instantly knew what it was; it was special.

"This, Detective, will gain you access to many places in the city. Some protection comes with it as well. Take it, and don't lose it."

Melegal picked it up and slid it beneath his clothes, saying, "Thank you; I won't lose it."

Lord Almen nodded.

"Now, as for my wife, go ahead and entertain her quest. I've already charged you with making sure that not a word is mentioned of my son, Tonio. I've heard nothing; you've reported nothing, which is what I expected. But … can you find him, or do you already know where he is?"

Melegal had no idea, and he didn't want to know, either, but he was pretty sure where he could find out something.

"No, I have not seen him, and I don't know where he is, but I can take a deeper look into it."

Lord Almen's voice lowered, "Find my son, or evidence of his whereabouts, but limit the search to Bone. Don't approach him, just keep me informed. As for my wife, avoid her. If she catches up with you, just lie. I'll handle the rest."

Melegal didn't care for how the man said the last words, but he would go along with anything just to get out of there.

"Yes, Lord Almen."

"So, is there anything else you would care to report? Any other encounters while you were strolling about in my castle?"

Only that your serving girls would make some of the finest whores in Bone, which I'd like to thank you for, but I'm not.

"Nothing else, Lord Almen."

"Good. Now, have you had the good fortune of tracking down any of the remaining Slergs?"

Ah yes, the unfortunate Slergs, possibly a whole deadly handful of them at most. Whatever will you do Lord Almen? "The man-urchin guilds are quiet, Lord Almen. Activity is infrequent at best. It seems the elimination of the Slergs was quite thorough," Melegal said, remaining perfectly still.

Melegal was already aware that Lord Almen knew he was once an urchin in the service of Slerg Castle. As a matter of fact, Melegal had been able to readily identify many of the Slergs that Lord Almen had captured after their raid on that castle. It had been the same night that Melegal dispatched his former mentor, McKnight, and the last time he had seen Venir, Georgio, Lefty and Quickster. He had found a good bit of satisfaction in seeing there a few Slerg faces that had tormented him when he was younger. There hadn't been that many left to begin with, but the handful of prisoners managed to name the few that were missing. The twins Hagerdon and Creighton had escaped, and Leezir. Venir had a deal with Leezir, one that the Slerg would never have to repay now that Venir had left Bone, but Melegal had an interest in trying to collect Venir's debt. *A purse of gems, I believe.*

Lord Almen's tone was harsh as he said, "So, you have nothing, not a trace after two months. I am beginning to wonder if you are taking your charges seriously, Detective Melegal. Perhaps I should find someone better suited."

Melegal remained calm.

"Lord Almen, I know these streets better than anyone, but they are vast, and I am only a single man. I have been focusing more on gathering information on the other threats to your great throne. The Nippert Castle's latest plot I had delivered straight into your hands. The slaving guilds had shaved you many servants before I had their injustice undone. I apologize for my failure with the Slergs, but it is due to the pressing matter of more imminent dangers. I will find the location of the remaining Slergs, and your son Tonio, as soon as I leave your castle doors."

Lord Almen's expression did not change, but he sensed the man's agitation. At this point, Melegal would say anything to get out of the room, which seemed to be shrinking with every breath. *Just dismiss me. Let me go.*

"I am well aware of your successes, but my expectations are high for managing my affairs. The next time you come, you had best bring better news. You are dismissed."

Melegal made a slight bow and made his way for the door. *Finally!* He grabbed the handle and just as his thumb began to press down on the latch, he felt something powerful around his throat.

"*Urk!*"

He was being hoisted from the ground, by his neck, like a small child. A pair of strong hands were squeezing his throat. His toes were inches above the stone floor. *How!?* But he had a more pressing matter to be concerned about. He couldn't breathe.

8

J OLINE MADE HER WAY BACK to the kitchen, with an unsettling look on her face. "We have customers … er … rather a customer."

Kam was leaning with both hands on the table; her head was starting to ache.

"Anything you can't handle? I'd like to lie down."

"Well, I'm not sure I can handle this one. Pretty unpleasant and demanding. I think I better get some more food ready, and quick." Joline got out of her way and continued with her baking, oven doors opening and dough rising. Kam had a feeling it was going to be a long day.

Kam made her way out of the kitchen and back behind the bar. Back in the corner, not far from a monumental granite fireplace, sat a lone figure. The Magi Roost was filled with ample light from its windows and cantrip-lit steel chandeliers above. The figure in the back seemed to have avoided the light and was somehow shaded in darkness. Kam could see a sword and scabbard on the table. The figure wore a dark gray cloak, and she could make out a head of short dark hair. It was mysterious.

Time to be hospitable.

With every step the figure became more ominous. Kam didn't often feel nervous in her tavern, but now the tips of her fingers tingled. She prepared a defensive spell in her mind. She was only five steps away when a long slender hand made its way to the hilt of the sword.

"No need for that, I'm the owner … just here to serve. What will it be?"

"Food and wine, Prissy, and no chit chat," said a voice as cold as water from the bottom of a well.

A woman!?

Kam was getting an eyeful now. The woman had thick black hair that looked like it had been cut with a knife. Her face was battered and bruised, with dark blue eyes, and a scowl.

"We have everything here, can you be more specific … we aim to please," Kam said, rubbing her head and neck.

"What's the matter, did your boyfriend bang you too hard into the bed board, Prissy?"

Kam fought back her retort. She didn't like this woman; something sinister and vile lurked behind her eyes. Still, the woman's voice was polished, commanding, and refined. The woman's words carried authority, not as much as hers, but authority nonetheless.

"What will it be? Fine cuisine, wine, clear water or slop and dishwater. I have it all."

The woman's hand slipped from her sword.

"Heh … I'll take whatever that is I smell, and that rose-colored bottle on the top shelf."

Kam nodded, turned, and walked away. She had a feeling the sooner she got this woman fed and out of here, the better.

"And bring me some cold water, too … Prissy!"

9

T HE UNDERLING MAGE LORD HAD the Darkslayer right where he wanted him. Squeezing with all his might, Verbard could feel the man's beating heart cringing in his hands. Concentrating on his mystic grip, he watched the man in the distance pitch forward with a groan. The Darkslayer's heart was hard, like a throbbing rock, in his glimmering palms. His spell was a powerful one, the same one he had used on the creature from the current at Oran's lair. He had the man where he wanted him, putty in his hands, while Catten was recovering from the other side and closing in on the man. His thoughts screamed in delight.

All Verbard had to do was hold on and let his brother take care of the rest. Verbard's eyes were elated coins of silver as the Darkslayer kicked and screamed on the ground. The man looked like a fish out of water. Verbard squeezed even harder. His hands were clutched together as if he were holding a glowing ball the size of two fists. His fingers and lightly furred forearms were corded with strain. He let his mind—filled with cold hatred and fury—enforce his efforts. The heart was pounding like a galloping horse, but it was beginning to slow. The man was writhing over the rough ground in a fitful seizure.

Yes, Brother, he soon will be gone. Kill him with me! Let's finish this and go home!

Verbard felt his brother's reply, another surge of energy developing on the other side of the man. He wanted nothing more than to torment the man, bind him and flay him, cut off his fingers, toes, hands, and legs one by one. He wanted the man who cost his kind so much to suffer every day for a thousand years. It could be done.

He could feel the rapid heartbeat begin to slow now, and the man's spasms and screams started to subside. *Yes!* He had the man, paralyzed, suffocated, and catatonic. He took a quick breath and exhaled. It all seemed so easy. He watched as his brother's golden eyes flickered with power, mystic energy shimmering around him, hands black with fire. A black javelin of energy formed in Catten's hand. Verbard watched as his brother threw it into the man, piercing the man in the leg. The prone man didn't even howl. Another javelin followed, penetrating the metal scale armor, and driving deep into the man's chest. The Darkslayer lurched up, black fire in his eyes. Verbard took a sharp breath. The man tried to cry out, but the effort was without sound. He pitched forward, bloodied hands clutching at the javelin jutting from his chest.

Verbard could feel the heart weakening now as the black javelin kept boring farther into the man's body. Blood was spilling to the ground in sizzling drops. The pain the brothers inflicted on the man must have been excruciating and unbearable. It made Verbard feel good. He could feel the man dying in his grasp. *He is mine!* Verbard's mind squeezed harder, determined to squeeze the heart into a bloody pulp. His own chest began to burn from the effort now as the old wound from the Warfield was flaring up. He needed this man's heart to stop. He needed the man to die.

Catten walked over and plunged another mystic javelin through the man's back. Blood erupted from underneath the Darkslayer's helmet. *That should do it,* Verbard thought. His own strength was fading. The energy of the spell was not without its limits. He had to hang on just a little longer. Something shuddered beneath his feet, and rocks and debris began to fall down the hill side.

Thoom!

Verbard almost lost his footing as the ground quaked. He still felt the beating heart in his hands. He hung on, sweating profusely and gasping for air.

Thoom!

He watched his brother Catten, who began looking around in wonder. The sound that shook the hillside was getting closer and louder.

Thoom! Thoom! Thoom! Thoom!

The sound stopped. Verbard didn't. *Thump-Thump.* The Darkslayer's heart was still beating in his hands, but he didn't know if the spell was weakening or if it was a man. He watched as Catten floated high off the ground and began taking slow turns in the air. His brother's golden eyes were searching. Whatever the strange source of the sound was, it didn't have him worried. The Darkslayer was his only concern, and the Darkslayer was almost dead.

Verbard watched his brother rise out of the ravine. His own heart skipped a beat as a massive face appeared in the sky. Verbard could not hide his alarm as a hand the size of a door swatted his brother Catten to the ground like a tiny bird. Above him, standing on the edge of the ravine above, was a giant.

"No!" Verbard hissed. He fought to maintain his focus on the spell. He backed into the hillside, crouching down, hiding from the giant above. *How!?* The figure was so big he needed time to get a full look. It was a man, thick, hairy and corded, wearing ordinary trousers and a heavy tunic that blended in with the hillside. How could he have missed the giant? Had it been here all along? There was nothing extraordinary about the giant, other than the fact it was more than twice as tall as a man. The giant's hair was pulled back in many brown braids. Its face was hard and bearded. It wore no armor and had no weapons. It was just bigger than the hillside. Catten had no time to deal with the giant … he had more important things to do. "You're on your own, Brother."

The giant was reaching down in the ravine now, trying to catch his brother. Catten was flattened on the ground, rolling over and scrambling to recover. The giant's monstrous fingers were just a few feet away when Catten let out a blast of lightning. The giant jerked back its hand and howled like a thunderstorm, shaking the branches above. The giant was studying its scorched hand, its face twisted in anger and pain. Its brows crinkled as it tried to clench its inhuman hand that was now red with peeling skin. It bellowed like a hundred ogres gone mad. It also stepped down into the ravine.

Verbard kept up the pressure. His brother would have to battle the giant without him. *I must finish this!* Still the man's heart beat in his clutches. *Thump-thump.* He could not get it to stop. His chest and mind were burning from the effort. His silver eyes were flashes of lightning, and his forehead was dripping with sweat. *What would it take to kill this man?* Verbard could see the brute lying face down in the ground, blood seeping into the stone. The spiked helmet was cock-eyed on the man's head, the metal scale armor was seared and red with blood. *Die, Human, die!* But doubt was beginning to settle in. He thought he might have to try something else. Farther down the ravine, his brother Catten had his hands full. The giant filled the ravine with its gargantuan back, its arms slapping in the air, trying to smash the miniscule underling. Catten was floating high above again, summoning tree roots from the ground to ensnare the giant. Massive roots burst from the ground, growing around the giant's legs like serpents and dragging it to the earth. It slowed the giant, but Verbard swore the giant's bellow was a laugh as it tore the roots and trees clear from the ground. Catten launched a series of emerald green missiles into its eyes. It roared now, slinging a tree at the underling. Catten flew upward, now cackling, himself.

Verbard needed his brother to distract the giant a little longer. The heartbeats were becoming weaker. His own chest felt like it was about to collapse, though. Blood trickled from his mouth as his sharp teeth dug into his lip. *More, more, more!* He summoned everything he had left in him. His grip almost enclosed the white light inside it. *Just a few moments more! Come on! Die, Darkslayer! Die!* The light inside his palms was gone. The rock hard organ became a sponge in his clawed hands. *Thump.* The Darkslayer was done.

10

MELEGAL WASN'T ACCUSTOMED TO THE feeling of helplessness, that or surprise. As his toes dangled from the floor he could only think of one thing. *Escape!* It didn't seem within his ability at the moment. Instead, he was a toddler, in the grips of a man. He didn't twitch, flail, or kick. He wouldn't give his adversary the satisfaction. *Think or die!*

A hard voice spoke in his ear.

"Almen didn't become the 3rd House of Bone on account of mercy, Detective."

Melegal could almost feel the man's lips on his earlobe. He could smell peach cider on his breath.

"I've wrenched bigger necks than yours for less. Your results had better be more meaningful the next time. You have potential, Detective, but I am not convinced. Time is running out."

Melegal couldn't agree more. How had such a beautiful morning turned so bad? He thought of that savory serving girl and swore if he survived he'd have her again. He thought of Quickster as the blood stopped running to his head. He had spent most of his life avoiding situations such as this, and here he was imprisoned by it, all because of Venir.

"Mercy is something you need to remove from your life if you want to live, Detective. I've no time for compassion among my staff. Do you understand?"

He couldn't breathe, but he could understand. Somehow, he managed to let his blue face nod. He felt another tight squeeze before he was released. He dropped to the floor, but didn't fall to his knees. He gasped for air, once, but not twice. He said, "No mercy, Lord Almen." Then he opened the door and walked away.

Melegal ascended the stone steps three at a time. He didn't notice the smell of the fine breakfast casseroles and coffee. It was something he had gotten accustomed to, but now all he could think of was escape. The kitchen was busy with several hands hard at work, not taking any notice of the thief of Bone. He went on his way, not casting a glance anywhere but ahead. The castle was large, but he padded his way through it like a cat. If other Royals and their ilk crossed his path, he'd find another one. He was determined not to have another conversation with anyone else in the castle this day.

As far as he knew, the castle had one main entrance that everyone used. It was the smart defensive thing to do, but Melegal had come across other entrances. There were always other entrances. He passed some stern-looking sentries as he slipped on his hat. *I should have left you on.* The Royals and their particular manners were a nuisance. It was just more meaningless etiquette from the vilest of people.

Melegal could see the small portcullis ahead, opening into the streets of the City of Bone. Two more sentries barred his path, but they stepped aside. *Buffoons!* As he passed them, the morning suns shined brightly in his eyes, and the foul air of the city seemed to cleanse him. The air in the castle had gotten stiff. In ten more steps he disappeared into the city. He needed some wine.

The farther he got from the castle, the better he felt. The sounds of the busy streets and shouting merchants were like music. His uneasiness and fear began to quell. It took some time to get there, and it seemed to be farther away than ever before, but when he arrived he felt at home. The Drunken Octopus welcomed him with empty tables and an extinguishing fire. A few sour faces at the bar paid him no mind, nor did the others that were slouched over on the tables. A burly fellow in a mottled jerkin was tickling a chubby dirty blonde that sat on his lap. The smell of sour wine and other putrid things made Melegal's stomach growl.

He found his spot in the corner, back to the wall, with the fireplace on his left. A scrawny woman with a shaven patch of black hair showed up, wiping her greasy fingers on an oversized apron.

"Gruel and wine."

She tossed two logs from a metal cauldron into the fireplace before she limped away.

The tavern wasn't quiet; there were snores, creaking floors, and the sound of a happy drunk man and giggling woman, but it gave him some peace. The rock of the fireplace at his side was warming up now, and the fresh tinder began to crackle. It wasn't long before the serving girl dragged herself back and set down a steaming bowl of gray stew and a bottle of purple wine. He slid over some steel and copper coins. The frown on the girl's long face almost turned upward before she trudged off. Melegal's time to sulk had come. The muscles in his back began to ease.

Lord Almen had surprised him. How such a big man had managed to sneak up on him from behind without so much as a sound he could not figure. Melegal rubbed his neck. He could still feel the man's strong hands crushing his throat, cutting off his air. He took a long drink of wine, then another ... and another. He still could feel the metal of the man's rings, five in all, on his skin. He tried to picture himself in the room, tried to imagine how Lord Almen had done it. The man was tall, with a medium build, at least two hundred twenty pounds, and like a ghost he had crept up on Melegal, blindsided him, and startled him. Melegal had his talents. He was an excellent thief. However, what Lord Almen had done was beyond him. *Magic, it must be.* But his instincts told him it was not. Lord Almen was no mere Royal. He ran his mind through the events a hundred times. *Extraordinary.*

The wine and gruel were beginning to warm his belly and lighten his dour mood. He couldn't forget the feeling of those hands closing around his neck. The Royals weren't all fat-bodied wine bags. They were taught skills and talents, beginning in childhood, from the best instructors in Bish. Melegal had witnessed much of that in the castle while he was working as an urchin. The children were drilled every day, each talent drawn from their spoiled and unwilling bodies. Melegal's spying and curiosity had even learned him a thing or two. So what exactly was Lord Almen, so poised, placid, and discreet? *Could he be an assassin?* Absolutely, the Royals of the City of Bone kept close quarters with them. *I better be more careful what I drink and eat around there.*

He shoveled in another mouthful of gruel that was bland, hot, and filling. *Another spoonful should do.* Melegal fanned out his fingers, giving them a studious look. Hanging around the castle seemed to have fattened him up. His usually slender fingers seemed a tad meaty. *Too many biscuits with honey. I must have had two this week.* He swallowed another spoonful, washed it down with some wine, and leaned back in his chair. *As long as nobody talks to me this next hour, I'll be fine.*

It was his time for meditation, something that was self-taught. His mind had been rattled. It was time to regain his mental composure. He closed his eyes, pulled his cap over his head, and blocked out all sound. He pictured himself in a room with many candles: dozens, hundreds, thousands. They were white, unlit, and in a dark room. The candles were sitting on the ground, encircling him like a pin wheel that spanned out as far as he could see. He pictured himself sitting there in the middle of all these candles and using his mind to light each candle in order, one by one, spinning as he did so.

He breathed quietly through his nose as the candles flared to life, one after the other. The light did not brighten as the candles lit. The darkness stayed the same. He was careful not to light any candles out of order. He made sure they remained lit as he went on to the others, as well. He faltered, noticing a black spot of extinguished candles nearby. He blew out all the candles with a gentle breath and started all over again, one by one, round and round. He didn't count them. He just lit them until they were all alight, as far as his eyes could see. He hovered over them now, watching them stretch a hundred feet all around. When he was satisfied, he quit.

He opened his eyes and saw the waitress taking away his gruel. The fire beside him was blazing with life. Judging by the light of the two suns, only thirty minutes had passed. He felt better, refocused, and wanting to use his crafty mind to get out of this jam. The Royals would never let him go, not now. He either had to make the best of it, or get out of town. In the meantime, he had to play along, and playing along was actually something he enjoyed.

The Drunken Octopus was one of the most run-down taverns in Bone, but it was one of the most entertaining as well. It was entertaining for a thief anyway, as Melegal watched a variety of Bone dwellers plying their trades. The people in the Octopus were a cut above the common ilk, more brazen and desperate than their neighbors. They tended to live in the tiny apartments that outlined the streets, coming to unwind from a brutal day of hard work. It had merchants with colored clothes with armpits stained in sweat. The wenches were painted like parakeets. The make-up they wore did little to cover their flaws, but in the dark who would notice.

Things got busier the later the day. It was about this time that Melegal had preferred to saunter down from his room and ply his own trade—being nosy. As the room filled to about half capacity he checked for new faces and old. There were regulars who he knew like close friends, but they didn't know him. Then the others came, to make a shady deal, or succumb to the eager lips of a willing wench. Men and women that didn't want to be found would come and go. Hard faces and pleasure seekers mingled, swapping services, bribes, inducers, and information. Melegal was amazed at what he came by, just from listening, but nothing caught his interest.

A man and woman, in dusty boots and weathered cloaks, sat a few tables away. Their heads were close, each casting a glance over their shoulders every once in a while. They spoke in low voices, but Melegal was watching their lips, picking up on their words. The woman had short braided hair and a pink split lip, and the man was big-headed and lazy eyed. He could see weapons concealed beneath their clothes, but that was nothing out of the ordinary, as only a fool would come to the Octopus unarmed.

Melegal caught the eye of a wench, half-clad with painted pink toes. She sat down by his side, draped her arm over his, and started rubbing it gently.

"What will it be, Handsome?"

He could smell her perfume, and it was as resistible as pickled eggs. She was fair for a woman, a bit grubby, young, and playful. She showed a pair of splendid legs with skinned up knees under her skirt, but that was about all. He slid a few coins over her way.

"Just drink with me and I'll let you know what I want as we go."

"Whatever you say," she said, scooting closer, twirling her stringy hair and rubbing his leg.

He didn't mind her proximity, instead he talked and she acted interested. All the while he focused on the man and woman adjacent to him. They were busy being careful of spying eyes and burning ears. The table wench would be a distraction for him as he pretended to laugh at his own jokes. Melegal talked, and she was a natural at playing along. He told her a story about himself and Venir, long ago.

Melegal noted more details from the pair he was spying on. The woman was rugged from long travel or hard work. He supposed she would clean up nice, though. She had delicate fingers, but dirty nails. She was running them over the man's arm. They drank ale, a pitcher that had been filled twice. She spoke to the man and he grumbled at her words. The man was big, not muscular, but formidable. The man had a big oblong head, saggy cheeks, droopy eyes, and a small chin. The man's fingers were big and stubby, always rubbing his chin and the back of his head.

They're nervous over something.

The pair weren't any more out of place than anyone else, but Melegal knew they were out of their element. It was interesting.

"What shall I call you tonight, Handsome?" Melegal's companion said.

He patted her knee and gave it a squeeze.

"Venir will do." *Why not?*

"Ooh … I like it, Venir."

Melegal recommitted to his task. Reading lips in a busy bar wasn't easy. The couple wasn't talking so much as waiting. Something told him they had something he needed to know. The woman, whoever she might be, had something to hide. Besides, he needed to bone up on some of his skills. This was how he usually found marks for his skims, and it had been awhile since he had done one. *You don't need to be doing this, Thief. You've got bigger things to do.* But the other side of him would say, *The Bish with it all; you're dead anyway. Steal some coin!*

The wine and the wench were beginning to soften his position. It could put him at risk. He didn't have any back-up, either. It had been a long enough day already. *Maybe I should just go upstairs and call it a night.* But night was when he did his best work. He noticed the cloaked woman talking again, and he had a clear shot at her thick sun-dried lips. He saw her saying, "…the platinum and emeralds aren't worth this." Then the woman's round eyes caught his. Melegal shot her a wink, and she didn't like it. *Just being friendly, no need to scowl.*

The woman tapped her companion on the forearm and nodded his way. The big man with offset eyes leered over at Melegal. The man ran his hands through his tuft of blonde hair, continuing his glare. *Frightening and ugly. Certainly stupid, too.*

"You ever seen this pair before?" he said to the wench.

She looked over at them and said, "Nope."

Melegal fought the urge to look away from the man. He had no reason to. *Just a little longer and the man will come unglued.* Both the man and the woman were staring back at him now, their faces turning dark. *Go ahead, get up and tell me more.* The big man did. The man towered over six and a half feet tall. He could see a heavy sword under the man's opened cloak. The woman sat still, poised, hands inside her sleeves. *Something's in there.* As the man walked over, he could hear the floor boards groan.

The man, rough as could be, was younger than he expected, dirt covering his youthful face. Melegal could see thin pale yellow eyebrows. Something about the man reminded him of Georgio. The man's voice was monstrous when he spoke.

"You being too nosy over here. You been watching us for a while, and we've been watching you. You want to die, Tiny Man?"

Melegal remained calm. The man's hand fell to fat-bladed dagger around his belt. He had a good feeling the young man knew how to use it. He was corned at the moment.

The wench by his side spoke up first.

"Get out of here, you lout! The man's free to look where he wants. But I prefer it was at me," she said, pulling his chin over her way.

Melegal nodded.

"Thief," the man said, "keep your eyes and ears somewhere else, or I'll take them both."

Melegal felt a formidable presence before him, but something else about the young man bothered him. He couldn't let him get away.

"I am sorry for the trouble, fellow, how about I offer you some more to drink … ale isn't it?"

"No thanks," the man said, beginning to turn away.

"Something for your lovely companion then, wine to sweeten her lips perhaps—"

The man was snarling as he whirled, shoving the table into Melegal and his date. She squealed as she was pinned to the wall, screaming. *I knew I should have gone to bed!* Melegal slid under the table, dagger raised to stab the big man's toe.

11

V ENIR WAS UNAWARE OF ANYTHING except excruciating pain. His heart felt like it was being ripped from his chest, and his massive lungs were vacant of air. He didn't know if he was standing or lying on the ground. All he knew was the searing pain of a white hot poker was jammed through him. The next one that came was even worse. His whole life seemed to have been nothing more than pain and anguish, and he never got used to it. All he could do was what he always did, hold on.

Gone was the ravenous hunger and throbbing in his head. It was all replaced by something more extreme, scathing him all over. He couldn't feel his fingers that were curled up like knotted branches or his legs that thrashed in the grasses. He had visions of the underlings that surrounded him, a nightmare that left him feverish. One had come and the other had gone. He felt one's fist in his chest and then the pain, the pain of a hundred spikes being driven in his head. How much longer could he hold on?

Just as Venir felt the pain beginning to subside, it came again with fury. Hatred was battling hatred now … his against the unseen force that held him. He had to hang on, or die. His face was purple from suffocation, and his body was leaking blood. Sometimes with pain came numbness, but the pain lived on. Inside his chest he felt his heart giving in. His heart's *thump* registered in his ears. He tried to look around, but only the bright sky and shadows remained. If he had the strength to move, he would, but where would he go. Unlike all of the other times he had faced death, this time was different. There was no blacking out at the end, only pain.

He thought of nothing; time was suspended; his life was sublime. The hatred of two iron wills remained intertwined until the bitter end. He would not let the underling win. He could give in. His mind roared one last time as his heart stopped. Everything went cold as the sky turned pink. The squeezing inside his chest remained. The world around him was mute. His eye lids opened and closed a few times before they closed again for good. If he had taken one of these underlings with him, it wouldn't have been so bad. The grip inside his chest went slack.

Thump-Thump.

Hot blood began course through his veins.

Thump-Thump … Thump-Thump …

He lived. He sucked hot air into his lungs and followed with painful coughs. He was breathing, his color returning from white to a bronzed tan. The sound of the living crashed inside his ears. An underling was screeching nearby. He tried to roll over and stand, but he was weak, like a newborn babe. *Get up!* Struggling, he flipped over onto his back. The javelins of black light were gone, but not the searing pain. He could see the underling that had assailed him now. Its silver eyes were clear as the sky; its face was contorted with anger as it clutched its chest. It looked injured, but Venir was wary of a trap.

He felt the ground shake beneath him as he sat up. Debris was rolling down the hillside and a human-like sound roared from behind him. Venir hated to take his eyes off the underling, but he couldn't help himself. He turned. A man the size of a tree towered underneath the suns. The monstrous man was swatting at another underling that moved through the skyline like a ghost. He was stupefied. His jaw dropped while his heart continued to race inside his chest. He was coughing again when he turned back toward the underling that was dragging itself away. He had to kill it, but he could barely move. He found his knife lying on the ground and gripped its bone hilt. He squeezed it, but he couldn't feel a thing. He just hoped he had enough strength to not let go. The silver-eyed underling was getting farther away, shuffling through the ravine, but slowly. *Catch him! Kill him!* It was easier said than done, but he began to crawl over the dirt, every inch of progress filled with agony.

Behind him, the giant and the flying underling were exchanging blows. The ravine shook as branches, rock and debris were scattered as if by a tornado. He ignored the bellows, pushing himself over the shaking ground, coughing and spitting. It hurt, but he was alive, and as long as he lived, more underlings would die. The silver-eyed underling stopped and turned on him, hissing in its own arcane way. The grasses and bushes on the ground came to life, clutching at his arms, legs, and knees. *Brool!* But his weapon was gone. He didn't have the strength to pull the weeds away as they pulled him to the ground. *Bone!* He tried cutting with his knife, but the blade seemed as dull as a stone against the growing brush. He locked eyes with the underling once more, but it just stared, its chest heaving underneath its gaping mouth. The underling chittered at him again, dark blood trickling from its hawk nose, and teetered away. The foliage encircled his arms and legs, pinning him to the ground, tightening around his body. Exhausted as he was, he tried to rip free, snapping some of the vegetation just to have it replaced by more. In moments he would be engulfed and suffocating again. He sat up, pulling the living ground away. He didn't know where the strength was coming from, but the girdle encircling his belly was warm.

THOOM!

THOOM!

He looked back down the ravine; the giant was coming back in retreat, crushing everything in its path. It was flailing its hands, swatting at the swarm of birds that now filled the air. Hundreds of rock peckers were jabbing their long hard beaks into the giant's head. Venir could barely make out the giant's bellowing face as the flock of birds covered it like a swarm of bees. He watched in awe as the giant pulled handfuls of the crushed birds away, but more kept coming.

Venir could see the underling nearby, muttering its spell, controlling the small red-feathered army. The underling was oblivious to him now, golden eyes intent on the giant alone. If he only had a crossbow, a spear … anything at all, he would kill it. Exhausted, he fought with his entangled menace, grabbing hold of the roots and ripping them from the ground. The underling mage above caused a stir within him. He was still weak and aching, but his limbs were starting to regain life. *Snap! Crack!* More of the tangles were tearing away. Maybe the spell was weakening; he didn't know. *Keep fighting!* His helmet was starting to burn again, strengthening his limbs.

The giant was only a few dozen yards from crushing him. One way or another he had to move. The giant began pulling chunks of the hillside and throwing it in the air like a maniac. The underling floated higher and out of harm's way, but the giant noticed. It scooped fresh rock from the ground and slung it hard into the air, showering the underling with small boulders. Venir couldn't believe his eyes.

It worked!

The underling fell forty feet from the sky, bouncing off the hillside, over the ravine, and landing between him and the giant. Venir could feel the vines and foliage still encircling him, and he let them be as he watched. The underling scrambled to his feet, but the giant turned back on it. The rock peckers that consumed the giant's face darted away and began to disappear in the horizon. It was giant versus underling, and the angry giant was coming fast. It raised its fist high in the air and smashed it into the ground a split second too late as the underling leapt clear of the life-ending blow. Green and blue energy encircled the underling's arms as it blasted a streak of energy into the giant's belly. It fell to one knee, and the underling blasted it again. The monstrous creature groaned, but still it came, backing the underling Venir's way. *Keep coming.*

The underling cast a glance back his way, but it didn't seem to notice him beneath the brush that surrounded him. He could see its eyes though, bright gold, evil, demented, drained and exhausted. Venir's head was on fire now. He wanted to scream, but he held it in. He might never get another shot like this. *Come on, Giant, bring him closer.*

The giant was moving slowly now, staggered by the mystic power. Its face was grimacing in pain, flaring with disappointment and anger. Venir marveled at how much it looked like a man, so much like the statues in the City of Three. Now the mighty creature was felled by one of the smallest of races, an underling. The underling pulled something from its robes, a translucent silver globe. It chittered with wicked intent as it blew the hand-sized bauble the giant's way. The underling stepped back, several steps from Venir now, and watched the globe float down the giant's path. It was like a tiny bead when the giant wrapped its hand around it and laughed.

BOOM!

The ravine shuddered as the giant's hand exploded. Large chunks of flesh showered, blood speckled the air, and the giant pulled back a bloody stump, wailing in horror. The sound of the mortified giant was deafening, but Venir could still hear the golden-eyed underling cackle.

Kill or Die!

All Venir saw was the laughing underling's back. He didn't notice the foliage tearing off his skin as he began to rip through it. The underling was still laughing when he struck. He could feel the blade punch through the chest bones and heart of the underling. He shoved the knife hilt deep into the underling's back and lifted the screaming underling from the ground. He gave his own bellow of victory, but he made little noise. He lowered the limp body to the ground. The golden eyes of the underling were frozen in death. Its blood no longer pumped or oozed from its mouth. Venir looked up the ravine where the other underling had gone. The burning in his head was gone now, but the sounds of the giant were not. He looked up just in time to see the biggest hand he ever saw swat him in the face.

12

"LEFTY, DO YOU HAVE ANY idea why Kam was crying?"

Lefty sat cross-legged on a small twin bed, twitching his tiny fingers at a feather. The goose feather from his pillow lifted in the air, twirled, and drifted back onto the pillow.

"I did it!" Lefty exclaimed.

"Wow, you really did do it, Lefty! That was incredible!" Georgio was thrilled yet unmoving as he lounged on his twin bed. The bed seemed too small for him, and Lefty's seemed too big for him, but anything was better than the floor inside the Drunken Octopus or a bed of hay at the stables.

Lefty leaped from his bed and onto Georgio's, his blue eyes filled with glee.

"I can't wait to tell Kam! She'll be so proud of me!"

"Yeah, hopefully that will make her stop crying. Why does she cry , Lefty?"

Lefty looked up at the room ceiling and then back at Georgio.

"I think women do that when they get old."

"Ah … now that makes sense. She is getting old."

The apartment where they lived now, above the Magi Roost, was like a castle compared to anything else they'd ever stayed in. The ceiling was high and adorned with several sky lights. There were three bedrooms, and the one Lefty and Georgio stayed in was the smallest. It had a dresser, two beds, and a couple of chairs along the wall. It was nice and colorful, and they still had ample room to play. Clothes that needed washing were scattered on the floor, and some small toy soldiers stood on the dressers.

A large smile grew on Georgio's chubby face when he sniffed the air.

"I think it's coffee time, Lefty!"

"Yes!" Lefty clapped.

They both hopped off the bed. Lefty was the first to dash outside their bedroom door. The main chamber was filled with the finest décor. A kitchenette, sofa, table and chairs welcomed them. A fancy hand-woven rug covered most of the oaken floor. The chamber had windows too, with curtains, some thick and others sheer. There was a huge desk made from black walnut sitting in the corner, with scrolls, vials and other things of the mystic around it. It was where Kam spent time teaching Lefty some skills with magic.

The coffee was bubbling on the stove. As Lefty grabbed two cups, Georgio grabbed the pot by its metal handle. It was burning hot.

"Georgio, get a potholder!" Lefty exclaimed.

"Hah … I don't need one."

The metal was like fire in his hand, and sweat formed on his brow. He held on, filled both cups and set it back down. He looked at his meaty hand and then showed Lefty. There was a thick red line from the pot's handle, but in a moment it was gone. Georgio rubbed his hands together.

"I'm getting tougher. It doesn't even hurt as much."

Lefty shook his head and said, "Man, I wish I could do that."

"Well, at least you can learn magic. I can't. I'm not smart enough," he said with a little frown.

Kam had tried to teach Georgio some, but it was a lost cause. It just wasn't in him. It wasn't in just anybody.

Either you had it, or you did not. Georgio didn't care that much, though. All of that concentrating hurt his head. As long as he could eat and nap as he pleased, he had no need for magic.

They both sat down on the couch and looked out the window. They could see the mountains and cascading falls in the distance. They spent most of their free time at the falls and even had made some friends. The water here was the most refreshing in the world of Bish. Georgio never knew that such a wonderful place could exist.

Now came that time of the day when the boys would have to tackle some chores. Georgio patted his full belly, content to wait for the coffee to kick in.

"Lefty, do you ever miss Melegal?"

Lefty took a sip and gave him a thoughtful look.

"Yes."

"I don't. He's cruel."

"Ah … you don't mean that."

Georgio slugged down the steaming coffee and went back over to the stove.

"Yes I do. He liked you, but he didn't like me."

"He just didn't act like he liked you," Lefty said, as he played with the hairs on the top of his toes.

Melegal had worn Georgio out with meaningless chores. The thief would starve him for hours that seemed like days if he didn't get his work done. He made him treat Quickster like a Royal stallion. Georgio didn't miss the chronic brow beating and cursing, either. He didn't miss being Melegal's scapegoat. But, he did miss Venir.

"Lefty, who do you miss more … Melegal or Venir?"

Lefty shrugged.

"I don't know. I miss writing Venir's stories, but I miss all the things Melegal taught me, too. It's different."

Georgio returned back to the sofa, sinking into its maroon cushions. It was beginning to seem like Venir had been gone forever. He still simmered inside that the big man had left without saying good-bye. He had cried for days after that. He wanted his hero back home.

With the coffee fully consumed, the pair began whistling and doing their meager chores. Lefty picked up the clothes, made the beds, and dusted the room. Georgio took out the trash and headed to the stables next door. It was just like old times, except Melegal wasn't around.

"Lucky me," he said, shoveling out some of the manure in the back of Quickster's stall. The quick pony stood there, staring at him with a blank look.

"What Quickster? Why do you always stare at me? Go eat!"

Quickster didn't move, continuing its odd stare. It made Georgio uncomfortable. It was as if Melegal was still watching him, waiting for him to do something wrong. It wasn't long before Georgio was sweating, and his tummy began to growl. He took a sack of apples that was hanging in the corner and fed one to Quickster. The pony nickered, turned away, and lay down in the corner. Georgio watched the gray pony's furry black stomach rise and fall as it quickly went back to sleep.

Georgio took a bite out of his green granny apple and sat down in the hay. The sour taste made him think of Melegal. He forced it down and smacked his lips.

"Ugh," he said, grimacing.

The apple would curb his hunger. Kam wouldn't feed him any more until lunch, and he hated to wait. Kam told him he couldn't just sit around and eat all of the time, but he didn't understand why. She wouldn't give him any money, either. At least Venir and Melegal gave him money. It had been a long time since he had a savory Georgio biscuit. His mouth watered at the thought. That was one thing he missed about Bone.

"You ready to go?" a tiny voice said from outside the stall.

Georgio dusted off his hands as he stood up, closed the stable door, and latched it.

"You bet, Lefty. I'm starving. Let's go skim somebody."

13

A HEAVY BLADE BURST THROUGH THE table, inches above Melegal's head. The wench was screaming as the tavern's clamoring began. Melegal was ready to strike his dagger into the man's boot when someone pulled his assailant away.

"Leave him be, Brak! Sit down! I can handle myself!"

Bodyguard?

Melegal got a better look at the legs of the big man's cloaked companion. She wore low-cut boots. A jade-colored tattoo ran up her sensual calf to her thigh. A short sword was strapped to her waist, her fist wrapped along the hilt, finger nails painted in jade as well. Melegal caught the faint aroma of her perfume. It wasn't bad.

The table lifted from the ground as the big man pulled his blade out.

"But, Mah!" The woman slapped the man across the cheek. There was a snicker in the room.

"Do as I say!"

"Fine," the man said, stuffing his knife back into his belt.

Melegal watched as the man pushed back the table. His wine and goblets were knocked over, and the wine was dripping everywhere. He slithered back into his seat, clothing unscathed.

"You owe me a bottle," Melegal said.

The man's face had a dangerous intent, his big fists turned into white-knuckled balls. The waif of a waitress came over and ran a soppy rag over the table. He felt the wench at his side scooting back. He patted her knee under the table, then focused on his business at hand.

The cloaked woman passed the waitress some coins.

"For the damage," she said, motioning to the wary barkeep. The barkeep nodded back. Melegal got a better look at the woman. Her sandy hair was full of grit, and her skin was rough. Her face was stern and streaked with dirt and sweat. Her calloused hands tipped him that she knew how to use a sword and do many other menial things. *Merchant guard?*

She looked down at him, glaring and speaking in a harsh voice.

"Why were you spying on us?"

"I wasn't. Now, how about my bottle of wine?"

"Yes, how about our bottle of wine?" the wench said, leaning her chest into him. Melegal didn't have much need for the woman now, he'd been caught, but he might as well play it through. The cloaked woman didn't even cast a glance the wench's way. She dropped a few coins on the table.

"We'll be going. Come on, Brak."

Melegal caught the man staring at him with his blue offset eyes. The man seemed enormous and childish at the same time. The woman he was with looked to be in her thirties. Why he called the woman *Mah,* he didn't understand. *She must have raised the bastard.* The man stooped as he stood, as if he head was too heavy for his shoulders. He was barrel-chested, but the muscles in his arms weren't fully developed. The man had soft hands, too, and he kept rubbing them over his thick tuft of blond hair. Melegal didn't know whether to feel uneasy or not, but he got the feeling the man could snap another in two if he wanted. It had been a rough morning, best to let them go. The pair turned to walk away, but the wench had something to say.

"Ahem … Miss, me and Venir were drinking wine much finer than these coins will buy."

The woman and her son whirled at the wench's words. Their faces were filled with avid interest. At the same time, they stepped forward. He was uneasy now, and his hand slipped to a blade inside his vest. The man's big body, clenched fingers, and bared teeth seemed to push him deeper into the corner.

Now what? It's only wine. It must be something else, though. The man and woman had them trapped in the corner.

The woman remarked, "Did you say — Venir?"

The wench, Velvet, nodded her head. Melegal noted the look of surprise on the man and woman's faces. Was it Venir that they had been waiting on all along? Why?

The woman pulled up a chair and sat down. Brak stood tall, arms crossed over his chest. Melegal got the feeling he wasn't going to be going back to bed anytime soon.

"Is your name Venir?" the woman asked.

Melegal saw no reason to lie; it was pointless. He just needed to figure out her game.

"No. That's the name I gave Velvet here," he said, stroking the woman's hair. Velvet smiled.

"Where did you get the name, Rogue?"

"I'd be curious to know yours first, Lady?"

The waitress returned with another jug of wine and more goblets, filling Melegal's first, then Velvet's.

"Fetch my bottle, Girl." The woman sat quietly for a moment. Melegal sipped his wine. "My name is Vorla. Now, what is yours?"

"Melegal."

"Fine Melegal, now tell me, where did you come up with the name Venir?"

"I've heard it around. It's just something I like to use from time to time, in case I get into trouble."

Vorla and Brak seemed to be hanging on his every word. He could tell them anything now, and they would listen. He refilled Velvet's goblet. She twirled her hair and whispered enticing things in his ear. Vorla didn't seem to mind, intent on more questions.

"Do you know Venir?" she said, pulling out a small purse and setting it on the table with a jingle. "I need to find this man. I made the search this far, but the well ran dry. I've talked with many patrons and they said that he lived here and others said that he did not. Help me find him and this bag is yours."

If that bag had been full of the platinum and emeralds she was talking about, he'd have given up the golden brute's location. His ears told him the bag was mostly steel and some silver. *Still, every little bit helps.* Not that it mattered. No matter what he told her, she would never find Venir. She had learned enough already, and Velvet's slip only managed to make things worse.

"Hmmm … the truth is that I am not one to spread rumors. But, I do know many things. Velvet, be a dear and go. I'll catch up with you later."

Velvet started to object, but Melegal's scowl set her back. She re-filled her goblet and stomped away.

"Now, tell me more about this man that you seek, Vorla. What does he look like?"

Oh, why not? Might as well enjoy something today. Besides, what would this woman want with Venir?

Vorla remarked, "Venir is a big tawny headed man …"

Yes.

"… with almost more mouth than muscles …"

Ah … you're wrong there, more mouth these days.

"He has a V-shaped tattoo on his back …"

She seems to know him well.

"… and he's very handsome."

That's a matter of opinion.

"… a storyteller of sorts … rowdy like an overgrown child …"

But I'd say you must know him quite well.

Brak was staring a Vorla, now hanging on her words, as if she was telling a story he had heard a hundred times before. It was strange, seeing the man hung up on a story like that.

Melegal ran his fingers over the rim of his goblet, contemplating what to say next. Venir had many enemies, and few other friends that he knew about. It was time to lead this couple elsewhere, because he had so many other things to do, and getting caught up in Venir's affairs wasn't one of them. He'd had enough of that. A bitter taste formed in his mouth. He just needed to say something believable.

"Very well, Vorla, I'll allow I do know something of this man. I have seen him before, but it's not customary to give people up in the City of Bone. Sure, it happens, but blood money can come back to get you. Coin doesn't last forever, at least not in my case. A bounty often lasts just long enough to see the squealer dead."

The woman's plain expression started to brighten. Her full lips began to part into a smile. Brak stood, unmoving, like a statue, glaring at him, his eyes filled with a dangerous intent. Melegal couldn't help but feel that if he said something wrong, the man would snap again and try to throw him through a wall.

"Melegal, I've nothing to hide. I knew Venir long ago; we worked guarding merchant trains together." She sighed. "Well, that's not true. He guarded the merchant train. I was part of the merchant family. He was the most fearless man I ever saw, young and brave."

Melegal noticed a quiver in her strong voice. The truth was in her eyes. So what did she want with him now? *Merchants are loaded. This could turn into a good thing.* He looked deep into her eyes. She began to speak again.

"I need a good man. I have a job, and it pays well. I was just hoping he was still around."

She's lying now. She's better than most, but not good enough for me.

"So, do you know where he is?"

Whatever she really wanted now didn't matter. Venir was gone, at least from Bone he was. He couldn't ever come back. Melegal was certain of that. He wasn't sure if he liked that or not, but he was getting used to it.

"Vorla, I cannot prove it, but I am certain this Venir you knew … is dead." Melegal's own stomach churned at the words. *It is possible, I suppose.* An odd feeling of guilt crept over him.

Across the table he noticed a great degree of sadness in her eyes. Brak looked at her with confusion. She was fighting the urge to choke, and managed to regain her composure. Brak's stance had softened as well for some reason.

"What makes you think so?"

"I hear a lot of things. Venir used to live here, but he hasn't been seen for months. It was my understanding that the Royals had a bounty on his head. Royal games, you know. He must have got caught in the middle of something. It's only safe to assume he's gone."

Vorla's face drew up tight and she gave him an angry look.

"If that is all that you have to offer, Rogue, it's not worth my gold."

"But we had a deal."

"No … no we didn't. You didn't help me find him. Let's go, Brak."

"No Mah! He's lying!"

Well, I guess I am. At least I hope I am. I think.

"Good luck finding another good man. And don't be a stranger the next time you visit Bone," he said, hoisting up his goblet.

Brak's face filled with anger. Melegal didn't really understand why. Still, the tension was beginning to increase, not to Lord Almen levels, but something dangerous was in the air, nonetheless.

"Don't call me that, Brak," she said with a furrowed stare.

"Why did he call you that? Mah?" Melegal asked, easing his fingers around his chest blade. "Is that something bodyguards call the merchants? It sounds like he's family, a brother or cousin maybe?"

Vorla was silent, and a look of exhaustion came over her face. Her shoulders sagged. Her brown eyes began to swell. Melegal decided it was time to excuse himself. He was ready to go. He'd had enough tantalizing drama for the day. He finished his wine, grabbed the jug, and stood up.

"Sorry for the news, but leave the past in the past. Your friend Venir is gone."

He almost believed it himself. He felt even worse for having said it again. It was as if he were betraying his best friend, the very same friend who was the whole reason he now worked for the Royals he had spent his entire life trying to escape.

Brak had a dumbfounded look as Melegal headed around the table Vorla's way, with Brak watching every step that he took. He was almost clear of her when she spoke again.

"Brak is my son."

Melegal stopped and stared at the big man. It wasn't possible. He was too old, and she was too young.

"Adopted son?"

Brak bristled.

"No, birth son."

"Huh, well how old is he?"

"I'm fourteen," Brak added.

Fourteen going on twenty five. She must be feeding him ogre food. The pair as a mother and son was unnatural. Melegal had never seen a fourteen-year-old boy that big before. Georgio was big at twelve, but this boy was huge. *She must be lying. The boy is just too stupid to know his own age.*

Vorla grabbed his sleeve.

"Rogue, how certain are you that Venir is gone?"

Melegal shrugged.

"It's just the most likely scenario, but I am certain you won't find him in Bone, not alive anyway."

Now Brak went over to Melegal's chair and sat down, sulking. Vorla rubbed his thick hands in hers. The pair seemed hopeless and lost. It was as if they had traveled across half the world to move into a new home, only to find it had been burned to the ground. He wondered why she insisted on Venir so much. He had been a more than capable soldier for hire long ago, but that time was long past. Melegal shrugged. He had things to do. It was time to track down Tonio and the Slergs.

As he walked away, he could her Vorla saying, "I am sorry, Son, but it looks like your father is dead."

14

V ENIR WAS SMASHED INTO THE hillside and sliding to the ground. His helmet was the only thing that saved his face from being crushed. All he saw were bright spots: pink, purple, and blue. He heard a pain-filled roar coming from the giant. His vision was blurred, but he could make out the giant trying to staunch the bleeding of its stump. That was fine. All Venir wanted to do was get away.

Starving, beaten, and broken, Venir didn't have any fight left. His helmet no longer urged him along, but his ears still rang from the giant's blow. Every ache and pain was still amplified. He rolled himself off of his belly and sat up. He had been knocked twenty feet from the underling he had killed. He could see its crumpled corpse lying on the ground with the hilt of his knife still buried in it. *Where is the other one?*

He needed help, and water. He couldn't ever remember being so thirsty. What had sustained him this far he did not know. He noticed the backpack straps on his chest. He had forgotten it was still on. He figured after the entire fracas it would have been gone. *Good.* The giant was stomping the ground, saying something loud and awful. It was making words with its huge lips, but they seemed so long it was impossible to understand. Whatever the giant was doing, it was the perfect time for Venir to get out of there.

He pulled off his backpack and reached inside, fumbling for something that might help, a sling maybe. He was so delirious that he tried to drink more water from an empty canteen. He swore he could taste something, but there was nothing but air. He started laughing.

"Ha-Ha-Ha-Ha … *cough!*" He wasn't going anywhere, except maybe to sleep. He saw the giant more clearly now as the suns shone over its monstrous shoulders. The grimacing giant began packing dirt into its stump. Beads of sweat were dripping off its head like rain drops. Venir had a crazy idea … that sweat might be water. He would do anything for a drink of something. It was a brilliant idea, for a delirious warrior.

"Hey Giant! Give me some sweat. I'm thirsty over here," he said, wagging his canteen in the air. His throat hurt from the effort, but he wouldn't be deterred.

"Hey! Get over here!"

The giant cast an evil bloodshot eye his way. It gave him a bothered look, like he was a rodent raiding its camp. It looked at its stump of a hand, and it was all packed in with ground, gravel and blood. It gathered its full height and pounded its chest with its good fist.

"Thatta boy — come on, gimme a drink … Giant."

His words were barely audible. The giant took a step his way. Its face was horrible, like one of those ridiculous carvings in a castle room. Its brown eyes expressed its murderous thoughts. Its face was contorted now, looking more like a monster than a man. The clear and present danger began to awaken in Venir. Fear began to overtake his lack of reason. Now, the idea of drinking giant sweat seemed his worst idea of all. *This must be it.*

Venir started rummaging in his backpack, desperate to find anything that might help. He found his sling, but there were no stones.

THOOM!

The giant took a step over the underling.

There was nowhere for Venir to go. He could barely move, and the giant would close the distance in two-steps if he tried to run. He dumped out all of the contents of his backpack.

THOOM!

The giant loomed over him now — face filled with pain and rage — its furious yell echoing down the ravine. Venir felt his skin crawl as the giant lifted its boot from the ground. His eyes darted at the contents of the backpack, scattered on the ground. There was nothing he could use to save himself. A sling, canteens, rope, a tinderbox, and a stitched-up leather sack. Feeling only sadness, Venir pulled the sack up to him, like a frightened child hiding behind a blanket. Oddly then, Venir felt a compelling urge to crawl inside the sack.

The giant's bare heel was now rising high above him.

I'm sure I won't fit, but why not try?

He reached his hand inside. There seemed to be plenty of room. Then he felt something sturdy and solid in his grip.

The giant's heel was beginning to come down. *Move or die!*

He yanked something out, screaming as he thrust upward with all of his might.

"BROOL!"

Venir sunk the spike in deep, through the flesh and into bone. The giant howled in fury, hopping away, grabbing at its foot. Somehow more alive now with Brool in his hand, Venir wasted no time standing around. He charged.

The giant wasn't ready for that.

Brool sung in the air and cut off the giant's big toe.

The hillside shook as the giant roared out with pain, grabbing hunks of the ground and hurtling it Venir's way. Venir was mangling the giant's foot when several small boulders knocked him from his feet. Winded, he crawled back to his knees, waiting for the giant to deliver the death blow at any moment. Instead, he saw the giant limping away, leaving a bloody trail on the ground. Down the ravine it went, not looking back, and then it was gone.

Venir rolled onto his back and laughed. The moment was short-lived. His belly resumed its groans. The rest of him was in bad enough shape without the metal of his scale armor heating up in the sun. He crawled over to a shady spot to rest. He could hear his ragged draws of breath. *More busted ribs, probably.* His nose was broken and dripping blood. He fingered the spots where the javelin had cut through his armor, searing it as well as his skin. The underling magic was gone, and only the pain remained. He sagged into the hillside. *Where's that other underling?* A massive shadow fell over him from above. It was a cloud.

Rain! Please Rain!

Bish had rain, just not very often in the Outlands. Rain had saved him before. He'd do anything to be drenched once more. He looked up and noticed the clouds above, some white pillows and others almost black. He thought there was a rumble in the distance, but that may have only been the giant.

A giant! Where on Bish had the giant come from? Mood had told him of such men, and there were other legends as well. He thought of the stone statues in the City of Three. "Those giants were once real," the seers would say, and now he believed. He thought about Georgio, Lefty and Kam. It seemed unlikely he would ever see them again. The likelihood of going anywhere right now seemed limited. Besides, he had left them because he wanted to be left alone. Too many people had suffered or died on account of him. He didn't want that burden anymore. *Melegal has probably never been happier than since I've been gone.*

He held Brool out, probably his only remaining friend. The dark axe had a dull glimmer in the daylight. The giant's blood was still thick and wet on its spike. A shiny red blood drop looked delicious on its tip. It was wet and thick, like red dew on a giant flower. Venir ran his finger over the axe's tip, catching the blood on his finger. It slid like mercury and settled in the middle of his palm. It was cool, almost cold. Venir's mouth would have watered if it weren't so dry. He needed something to quench his thirst, anything wet would do.

He sucked the blood out of his hand, swished it around and swallowed. It tasted bad, but at least his tongue was wet. The blood slid down his throat like ice water, landing in the pit of his stomach and catching fire. Venir felt like his stomach was going to explode. It churned inside him like a nest of awakening snakes. He convulsed on the ground. His vision began to darken. Now, he was not only sick, but blind, too. He lost consciousness. A host of vultures began to circle above.

15

THE THOUGHT OF VENIR HAVING a son baffled Melegal. He wanted to laugh at the absurdity of it all. For all he knew, he and Venir could each have a dozen bastards, but based off the type of women he and Venir kept company with, it wasn't likely they could prove such a claim. Not that it mattered. It wasn't his concern. He kept moving, though, as fast as he could in the crowded streets of Bone.

There were families in Bone and Bish, large and small, mother and father, husband and wife. Melegal wasn't born to such a privilege. He was one of the sordid lots, a bastard, probably sold by his mother after she had been impregnated by a lout. That was the most likely case, but he replaced those thoughts with his childhood fancy as he made his way through the alleyways of Bone.

Bish was a hard place to live, and children had it the worst. Urchin boys and girls knew they had fathers, but didn't care to know which ones. If they gave it much thought, they just figured they were better off not knowing. Melegal emerged from an alley and took greater notice of the small and dirty faces littering the streets. There were many, but they weren't out looking for their fathers, like Brak was.

He made his way out onto the main street where Royals were toted along in carriages pulled by horses. The City Watch maintained its presence. The merchants stood before their shops and stands, trying to wave the passing Royal carriages down. Beautiful ladies adorned in exquisite clothing were scattered in and out of the shops here in the nicer part of town. They were accompanied by their sentries and other servants as they gossiped, ate, and shopped on slave-made coin.

Melegal stopped and spat. He hated this place, preferring the darker corners of the City of Bone. There was only one way to get to where he was going though, unless he trudged through the sewers. He had to cross Main Street, or as they called it, the Royal's Roadway. Melegal stood back in the shadows, several feet from the street, listening to the sounds of the women, horses, lies and barterers. Carriages rumbled by while others stopped at the sound of a bell that hung on the outside that was rung from within. Gorgeous, ugly, fat and rich women stepped out and berated the efforts of anyone that tried to help. Melegal wished it would rain. The City Watch was thick and active this time of day, beating any beggars or urchins away from the Royals. The City Watch wore dark brown uniforms and flat black caps with short bills. Each carried a club and a curved scimitar sword. Thieves were quickly dealt with when they got caught. Children could lose fingers and toes, while adults lost hands and feet.

Melegal leaned against a wall, head down, eyes up. He watched to see what others could not. A little black-haired boy maybe eight years old pinched a tiny gemstone from a lady's inlaid dress, and disappeared. A watchman clubbed an old man that got too close to the main road while another man with feverish eyes snatched a box of cakes from a carriage. A small bunch of urchins dashed and leaped into one of the large fountains that decorated the main corridor. The City Watch dragged the children out by the hair of their heads, while a Royal sentry chased a ragged man down the alley and was never seen again. One royal woman screamed when a platinum wig was stolen from her head, and another cried out when she noticed her bracelet was gone.

He watched all of this action take place in less than an hour. He shook his head. He never understood why the Royals didn't just let their servants do the shopping for them. *Stupid custom, like the rest.*

It was time to go. Melegal made his way out boldly onto the street. It was the first time in years that he had done so. He traversed his way between the carriages and carts, head down, hands in his pockets, each step a hair quicker than the last. He didn't feel like running today.

"Stop, Rogue!"

He was caught now, busted for having crossed the street. The Royals had some silly name for the crime, but he didn't recall it. Two of the City Watch cut off his path, then two more rushed up from behind with watch sticks ready. He was surrounded.

Great! I guess running's not even an option now.

The City Watch consisted of large and beefy men with dishonest looks in their eyes. Melegal could see the tobacco bits in between their teeth. One spit juice on his toe. He stood still. Any sudden moves or snide comments would garner him a clubbing.

"I'm just crossing the street, minding my own business, sirs. I'll be along in a moment."

He knew they didn't care if it was true or not. The City Watch found nothing more fun than a legal mugging in broad daylight.

One had three chevrons on his shoulder sleeve, while the others had just one. He was the biggest and oldest, reddish brown hair spilling out from underneath his cap, a small booger dangling in his hairy nose. He sounded more like an orc than a man when he spoke orders to the others, gruff and condescending. The watchmen nudged Melegal a step back with their clubs.

"A girlie man like you should know better than to cross the Roadway during the high time. What do you think, boys? This little man looks like a thief to me."

You are smarter than I imagined. Good for you. He could hear one smacking his club into his meaty hand from behind him, another lifted his stick onto his shoulder. The hardwood clubs were straight, three inches thick and almost three feet long. He'd seen a City Watchman break a man's thigh with one. The muscles between Melegal's shoulders started to knot. He allowed a gentle bend in his knees. *Don't blow your cover. Talk your way out, Thief!*

"Sirs, I'm merely tracking down my sister. She's not all there, giddy and troublesome. I'm just trying to spare—"

"Shut up!"

One grabbed him by his cloak while another slammed a club into the backs of his legs. Melegal fell to his knees.

"I think I heard a jingle. Find his purse, boys."

Melegal tried to squirm away, but the men were overbearing. One wrapped a club up under his chin. Melegal's belly caught the full force of another's fist. He had completely lost his ability to avoid harm today. Such was the way of Bish. You didn't go unscathed for long, no matter how sly you were.

Rough hands were rummaging through his clothes. He heard his purse strings snap. The sound of his dagger being slid from its concealed sheath caught his ears.

"He's armed, trying to assassinate a Royal, I'd say."

"Heh, heh ..." said another.

What made the City Watch so effective all of a sudden? This can't be happening. I should have waited until dark. Will this day ever end ... with me alive?

"Assassin? We hang or quarter assassins. See how much coin he's got."

He heard his coins clinking in their grubby hands. He knew the value by the sound of each one.

"It's a pretty hefty purse."

"It's assassin money. He's here to kill someone."

Melegal wanted to remind them that assassins only got paid after the job was done, but the club wrapped around his throat prevented that. *Play possum and slip away.* Melegal's body went limp.

The one holding him smelled like rotting cheese and spoke with a very deep voice.

"Uh ... boss, I think he fainted. You want me to lock him up?"

The red-haired City Watchman was biting a small gold coin.

"No ... just choke him to death now. And make sure no one will hear him scream."

Bone!

16

"I T'S NOT MY TURN, IT'S your turn," Georgio argued.

"No, it's your turn, not my turn."

"Lefty, I did it last time and you said you'd do it this time. I don't want to go again."

"I assure you, Georgio, I was the bait the last time. This time *is* your turn."

Lefty watched as Georgio looked up in the air, his pudgy face a mask of concentration. Deceiving his friend on these deeds was becoming more difficult. Georgio was getting smarter, but his best friend wasn't ever going to be smart enough to catch up with him.

Georgio was rubbing his chin and giving him the eye.

"I'm not so sure about that, Lefty. I mean, it was just a week ago that I did what I'd done, and we haven't done a skim since. I'm thinking this time you gotta go."

Lefty looked up in his naive friend's face. There was a stern look underneath Georgio's curly brown locks. The boy was determined to not be duped so easily, not this time anyway. Lefty hopped up on a wooden crate in the alley, put his hand on the boy's shoulder and looked him in the eye.

"You know Georgio, come to think of it, I'm not so sure about it, either. I'll tell you what though. Since *we* can't remember exactly, I have an idea."

Georgio gave him a sheepish look and said, "What?"

"I'll give you twenty percent more of the take, and I'll buy you a batch of honey biscuits."

He watched Georgio lick his lips at the sound of the mouth-watering biscuits. It was one of his friend's weak spots.

"What do you say, *Best Friend*?"

"I want a slice of ham, too!"

Oh my, he's bargaining with me … not good.

"No, forget about it. I'll just do it. It's more for me this way, and less for you," Lefty said, hopping the crate and heading down the alley.

Georgio jumped at his heels.

"No wait Lefty—I was just kidding. I'll do it!"

Lefty erased his sly grin before he turned back around.

"No, that's all right. You've been taking too much risk. You are right; it is my turn."

Georgio reached down and shook his shoulders.

"No Lefty, it's all right … I'll take the risk. I'm bigger than you and all. Let me do it this time, please."

Lefty made the effort as if he were giving it serious thought.

Melegal would be so proud. Never do something if you can get some buffoon to do it for you.

Of course, duping his best friend bothered him, but he told himself it was just for practice. There would be bigger game to play as he got older.

"Oh, all right, Georgio, this time it's a deal. But next time I'll do it."

"Thanks, Lefty," Georgio said, shaking his hand.

The two boys headed to the end of the alley and sat on the corner of a storefront porch. The City of Three was laid out much like any other, just better maintained. Unlike in the City of Bone, the City Watch here was less visible. The urchins and beggars didn't roam the streets in hoards. Things were safer and more civil in the City of Three. Lefty spied the tall towers that were scattered against the skyline, like giant shiny candles. The towers hosted the Royals and wizards, he had been told. He was told the wizards had the towers so they could keep to themselves. Lefty wondered if that was what was really in there. He was tempted to climb up and take a peek.

Lefty would do anything to go inside one of those towers. He had begged Kam for weeks, but she was adamant, telling him 'No!' Of course, what she didn't know, he wouldn't tell. For the time being he was happy being in the softer confines of the City of Three. Almost everything was an improvement over the City of Bone. The people smiled and didn't smell like the gutter. When the people weren't working themselves, they took time at home or for leisure. There was a good showing of all the races, the best of what they had to offer, whether it was food, wine or art of some sort.

Lefty and Georgio took a moment to help an ancient dwarven woman across the busy street. She had a thousand winkles in her face, a tiny shine in her eyes, and a thin wispy white beard. She sounded like an old man when she talked.

"Here, have a cookie, boys."

Georgio took it from her knotty hand as she trudged along. The cookie looked more like a rock than anything else. It was burnt, brown and flecked with shiny morsels.

"Taste it, Georgio," Lefty said.

Georgio bit into it with a crunch then began to spit it out, tossing it on the street saying, "Yeck!"

"Well, what did it taste like?"

"Like baked dirt."

Lefty started to giggle.

"Come on, I've found our mark."

Georgio followed Lefty a little farther down the street where the two settled near a dry goods store. A pair of men of the common sort were unloading cases of glass bottles filled with wine. Lefty took note of the men, each dressed in a clean pale blue uniform that signified their merchant class. He noticed their nails were not dirty, and along their waists each carried a knife, as opposed to a sword or dagger. The balding storekeeper stood by in a gray shirt and black apron, eyeing the wagon as people passed by. He held a club in his hand that he rattled off the back of the wagon from time to time. Some people looked. Others hurried on.

Lefty gathered Georgio by his side and pulled something from his pocket.

"Ah ... not this one again, Lefty," Georgio said.

Lefty tossed a small, stuffed leather ball in the air. It was stitched up with twine and was much bigger than his tiny hand. Georgio watched as Lefty tossed the ball in the air and caught it behind his back ... on his bare foot. Somehow, he tossed it over his back with his foot, and into the awaiting hands of the frowning boy.

"Come now, Georgio. We haven't much time. They're almost finished."

"Ah ..." Georgio said, tossing the ball back.

Lefty noted the storekeeper was paying them no mind. The stores and streets were busy in the morning. Horse-drawn wagons and carriages passed by, driven mostly by humans or dwarves. The ram-faced mintaurs pushed wheel barrows and carts, unloading thatches of wheat, and barrels of ale and barley. Lefty inhaled the aroma from the flowers of the florist shop nearby. There was nothing like planning a skim on a busy morning in broad daylight.

Lefty flung the ball hard at Georgio, popping him on the nose.

"Ow!"

"Pay attention; it's almost time."

Georgio slung the ball back, high over his head.

Lefty backpedaled, climbed a post, and snatched it from the air.

Georgio was rubbing his nose when he slung the ball back at him again.

Lefty watched as the store keeper signed off on something and counted out a variety of coins. Shaking the men's hands after he handed them over. *Perfect,* Lefty thought.

The merchants secured the wagon and climbed into their seats. They had pleasant smiles on their faces, chatting back and forth about where to eat. Lefty wasn't even looking when he grabbed the leather bean-filled ball coming at him from the air. *Here we go.* One of the traders lashed the horse on the back. The wagon lurched forward and in a moment the traders were rolling his way.

Georgio was jumping up and down, waving his hands.

"Hit me! Hit me!"

The horse drawn wagon was coming at a trot from behind the big boy. Lefty hurled the ball over Georgio's head. The big boy turned to try and catch it, tripped and fell in front of the wagon.

Crunch!

"Ow!" Georgio screamed as the wagon jostled to a halt. The boy was pinned between the wagon wheel and the ground.

"Whoa! What on Bish happened?" said one of the merchants. Both of the men jumped out of the wagon and came to Georgio's aid. Georgio lay there, grimacing in pain, pinched between the wheel and the cobblestone ground.

"Hess, lead that horse back," one man ordered.

The other nudged horse backward, freeing Georgio.

"You all right, Boy?"

"Ugh!" Georgio cried. "It hurts, hurts bad. Somebody call a cleric."

Lefty dashed over and held Georgio's head in his lap saying, "Somebody call the Watch, hurry!"

The two men looked at one another with alarm in their eyes.

One said, "No need for that. Let us take a look."

Georgio groaned aloud.

"He needs healing! I must report this to the Watch to get healing!"

Both men looked worried. A small crowd began to gather nearby.

"Tell you what, Halfling, I'll give you coin for a healer. Just stop crying for the Watch."

Georgio's eyes were rolled up in his head as he said, "It hurts sooo bad. You have to get the Watch. I'm dyin'."

"Friend," Lefty said, "can you stand? We must walk."

The men helped Georgio to his feet. Clutching at his side, he fell back down again. He rolled in the street. The men were looking around, the worry in their faces beginning to grow. One of the men shoved some coins in Lefty's hand.

"That's more than enough, Halfling. Will you just go?"

Yes! "I suppose so."

The two men got back on the wagon, snapped the reigns and were off.

Lefty felt nothing but glee as he watched them go. He helped Georgio from the road and back into an alley. Georgio sat down, his back against the wall, still groaning.

"Ow! Man, that hurts, Lefty! I wish you'd try it sometime."

"I would, but I don't regenerate."

Lefty counted the coins in his palm. It was a tidy sum, at least a week's worth. It was almost too easy of a skim, at least for him anyway. The mere mention of the City Watch turned the men to ghosts. If the Watch arrived, the men would be tied up for hours, maybe a day, waiting for the Watch to decide whether or not they had to pay. If they were uncertain what to do, then they would have to see a magistrate and that could be costly. The traders and merchants made their living by staying on the move, no delays. They always decided it was better to pay up front rather than risk a whole day's wage, or disgruntle your customers. Any missed shipments would allow another to take your customer away. The mercantile business was a cutthroat business.

Georgio pulled is shirt up to look at the wheel mark along his rib cage. The bruise was black and blue, but Lefty could see it beginning to fade. He could see the pain in Georgio's grimacing face. Tears were running down his cheeks. He felt ashamed suddenly.

He sat down by his friend, patting him on his back.

"You feeling better?"

Georgio spit blood from his mouth.

"Yeah, a little. Ugh."

"I'm sorry, Georgio. Next time, I'll figure an easier skim."

"You better."

After a few quiet moments Georgio got back up.

"Gimme my money, Lefty. I'm hungry. And you're buying my first round of biscuits."

Crap, he remembered.

Lefty counted out the coins, placing them in Georgio's beefy palm.

"This better be all of it."

"It is." It wasn't.

Lefty didn't even notice the man standing there when they turned to go.

"Well, well, you two have quite a skim running here," the man said in a haunting voice.

Lefty and Georgio froze when they turned around and saw the man.

"I don't think you should be skimming, unless you have permission from the Thieves Guild," the man said in a voice like a sheet of ice.

Georgio wrapped his arm around Lefty, trying to back away with him, but there was nowhere to go. They were surrounded.

17

H IS MOUTH TASTED LIKE BITTER apples. Worse, his body felt like it had been trampled by a stampede. His stomach ached, but it was full and sustained. It was midday now, and Venir realized he had been asleep quite a while. The last thing he remembered was the giant's attack. He didn't recall drinking the drop of blood, but his ravenous hunger and thirst were gone now, and his battered mind was clear. He managed to stand up with a groan, but dark purple spots appeared in his eyes. He was woozy.

He found his backpack and gathered his gear, stuffing it inside. Brool was a comfort in his hand, and the helmet no longer throbbed. He walked over to the underling corpse on the ground. He could see the steel blade jutting from its chest, golden eyes affixed towards the sky. He rolled the dead mage over and grabbed the knife by the hilt. It was ice cold. He pulled his hand away. Suddenly wary, he looked around, in the sky and down both ends of the ravine. Sensing nothing living was anywhere near, he wrapped his big hand around the blade again. Goosebumps rose on his skin. *Blast!* There was still powerful magic working inside the underling. He let go. Uneasy now, he stood and circled the robed creature. He had heard of underlings rising from the dead before. This one was powerful. If the stories were true, certainly one like it would be the type to do so. He should chop the creature to bits, scatter its parts, and bury them. His hunt wasn't over, though. One more was still out there. It would want revenge. Venir would need some bait, and maybe the corpse at his feet would be the advantage that he needed.

Grabbing the underling by the leg, he began dragging it through the ravine, following the giant's massive tracks. He couldn't help but be curious to see where the giant would go. The underling was light, like a child, but he had no desire to carry it. Touching the foul creature repulsed him. Besides, he had nothing but the greatest contempt for them, their magic and all.

He plodded over the ground for at least an hour, stopped and stood inside one of the giant's footprints. He was astounded how he could fit ten of his footprints in one of the giant's. He'd actually seen a giant, fought one and lived. He couldn't wait to tell a story in a tavern about that. That fantasy seemed like an impossibility now.

He doubled over and fell to his knees, clutching his stomach.

"Ugh!"

His burning belly reminded him of drinking the giant's blood drop. His feet were aching too, swelling in his shoes. His scale armor tightened around his chest. The giant's blood was working some ill inside him. When he waved his hand in front of his face, it was like an illusion, there and not there, traipsing across his eyes. He strained his eyes, kicked at the ground, and screamed. He shook for a few more moments and lay still. The last thing he heard was the sound of thunder and rain. The last thing he felt was his fingers turning ice cold.

18

H E FELT EMPTY. SOMETHING INSIDE of him was gone. His chest felt like it had a knife jammed inside it, but it was not there. It didn't take Lord Verbard long to realize that his brother Catten was dead. Verbard had been staggering away on foot, after trying to kill the Darkslayer. The man had been in his clutches; beating heart and all … and he had failed. The failure was costly … now his brother was gone. He was alone. Wheezing, he fought to suck air between his teeth. His Warfield wound caused him agony. His cold skin was sweating, and his fine line of fur glistened with sweat. Now, for the first time, the suns above seemed to be baking him inside his dark cloak. It was something that had never bothered him before. He had been outside and playing in the dirt long enough. Now he wanted more than ever to go home, but he could not. Only death awaited him there.

Verbard kept hiking through the brush along the bottom of the hill. He had no strength or desire to climb, or find safety in the high ground. No, he would distance himself on foot as best as he could from the Darkslayer. His magic was drained. He had little means left to defend himself. It would take time before he had enough energy to pick up on the quest again, but did he want to?

He reached inside his cloak, pulled out a crystal vial, and drank.

"Ah …."

He felt a burst of energy. *Thank you, Brother. You always told me I would need that someday.* He was still empty inside, though. His brother was gone, along with many of their future plans for the Underland.

Looking ahead, he saw little more than difficult terrain. His feet and legs were strained. He couldn't remember walking so far or so fast in centuries. He couldn't even remember if he ever had. He was feeble and vulnerable now, for the first time in his life. He was the brash one, bold and daring, the risk taker his brother was not. Now, he was reduced to scurrying over the ground of Bish like a rodent, fighting for a scrap of food to survive.

He was climbing down a steep slope when he slipped, fell, and rolled over and over like a log before stopping at the bottom. He sat up and noticed all the scrapes and cuts on his formerly smooth and pristine hands. His bony knees were skinned, too, and his feet were developing sores. His thick black finger nails had dirt caked under them, and his robes were dusty. He stood up, flapped his robes, and kicked the loose stones on the ground.

"Pah!"

He stood, robes billowing in the wind, wanting to cry out. But to who?

Now what, Verbard? Your brother is dead. The Darkslayer lives. You can't go home. Now what!?

He screamed and walked onward. He knew the Darkslayer would be coming soon.

19

K AM OPTED FOR PEELING POTATOES with Joline rather than drink for the rest of the morning. It wasn't something that she normally did. This time in the morning she would normally be up in her room getting ready for the day, but the thought of leaving Joline alone, with a scowling sword-bearing woman in the midst, didn't sit well with her. She couldn't shake the unsettling feeling that hung in the air. It didn't help that the morning seemed to be creeping by, either. It would be at least another hour before more help arrived.

She jumped when there was a knock at the back kitchen door.

Joline gave her a funny look.

"I'll get it. It's just a delivery."

Kam decided to check on her only customer. She muttered something mystic, a protection spell. The hairs on her arms rose and fell, and she tingled from head to toe. After the magic passed through her she felt her anxiety begin to settle. She rubbed her shoulders. She could handle this. In all of the years of running the Magi Roost she had survived many unpleasant encounters. But, this time it was different. There wasn't a room full of tavern dwellers she knew would watch her back — this time she was all alone.

She stepped out of the kitchen and slipped behind the bar. She grabbed a rag and began rubbing the glassy black surface. It was pointless; the black wood was spotless, without a single smudge. She eyed the woman in the corner. The woman sat there with her face cast in a shadow, but Kam could still feel the woman's eyes burning into her. There was a presence in the air, cold and chilling, like the feeling she got before watching a public execution. It had been a long time since she had seen a man hung, but it was the same feeling nonetheless. The feeling of death was in the room.

Come on Kam, gut it up. This is your house. Get the woman away. She found herself wishing the boys were still around. Despite their behavior, she still adored them. They gave her comfort. She frowned. No, this morning she would have to face her fears alone. Taking a deep breath, she headed over to the woman in the corner, with the rag still in her hand.

"Don't you have something to do?" the woman said, eyes down on her drink.

"Do you need anything else?" Kam replied.

The woman looked up at her with an icy blue gaze.

"What I have will do. When I need more, I'll let you know."

Kam fought the urge to walk away, but she held the woman's glare. It was clear the woman was of a notorious ilk. The City of Three's inhabitants were clearly defined by their language and demeanor. The travelers that came through were of the business lot and visiting sort. Hardened people of ill repute were not comfortable with all the pleasantries of this city. They preferred the darkness or very little light. This woman was a dark smudge on a sheet of crystal clear glass.

Kam placed her hands on the table's edge and leaned over.

"There won't be any more."

"Is that so, Prissy?"

"It is."

The woman held her cup with both hands and took a sip, then set it back down.

"I like it here," she said.

Kam's fingernails began digging into the table. *Now what?* She had the feeling that she may have just opened up something she could never close again. *I should have just left her alone.* She studied the sword on the table. It had the distinct markings of a Royal smith. *Stolen or found.*

The woman caressed the scabbard with her long fingers and said, "It was a gift, an honor. I used to be a soldier."

Kam pulled back a chair and took a seat.

"Interesting, and who did you serve?"

The woman's face darkened.

"I don't serve anybody now! Get up from my table, I didn't ask for company, just service!"

The black haired woman was making Kam angry, and it was clear the woman was getting angry as well. Kam was pretty sure she was outmatched, but something inside her didn't care. She was going to stand her ground.

"It's my table," Kam said in a stern voice, "… and I want you to leave. You don't belong."

The woman began to draw up, like a cobra about to spring. Kam was certain the woman was going to reach across the table and rip her eyes from her head. The woman withdrew and tossed her booted feet on the table and leaned back in her chair.

Bone! Kam was furious now. *Savage whore!*

"I suppose you're going to call the City Watch now, eh … Prissy?"

Kam had thought about it, but for what? The woman hadn't done anything aside from being dirty and unpleasant. Calling the City Watch on such a frivolous matter would be an embarrassment. Perhaps she was the one being unpleasant.

The woman sat with a crooked smile breaking across her thin lips as Kam got up. When she turned and walked away, the woman's eyes felt like daggers poised at her back. She went in the kitchen and returned with a plate of crackers, spreads and cheese, an onyx cup, and another bottle from the bar. She set it all down and sat, smiling as she refilled the woman's cup along with hers.

"Let's try this again. Welcome to the Magi Roost. My name is Kam, what is yours?"

The corner of the woman's maroon lips turned up.

"It's best I didn't say."

Kam got the feeling her idea wasn't the best idea after all. She raised her glass anyway.

"To the woman with no name then?"

The woman raised her glass in return.

"I'll drink to that … after you."

Bone!

20

VENIR AWOKE IN A STREAM of water with a hard rain splashing in his face.

"Yes!" he yelled. *Bish!* He clutched at his busted ribs. The pain remained.

The sky was black with clouds, drenching him in hot rain. It felt great, being wet again. He scooped water from the stream he sat in and drank. He couldn't remember water ever tasting so good. The sour taste in his mouth was washed away as well, so that his belly was no longer ill. He sucked in another mouthful and slung off his backpack. He removed the canteens and refilled them, then stuffed them back in his pack and drank the fresh water again.

The dirt and blood on his skin and armor was washing away with the stream. The underling corpse was lying on the ground like a soaked sack of rags, water drops bouncing of its golden eyes. Venir gathered his pack, grabbed the underling by the foot, and started dragging it through the mud. The load was heavier now, but he was moving at a brisker pace than before. He had to keep on going; certainly the other underling was out there. Another hour passed before the rain stopped. The black clouds had moved farther north, and the blazing suns were back.

Ahead, the mist still waited, higher than the eye could see. It was impossible to tell how far away it actually was, but it was close. He could see the outlines of birds in the distance, cutting through the sky. He still followed the faint traces of the giant's steps. Steam was rising off of his boots, and the leather was becoming tight and uncomfortable. Venir had an urge to take them off, but he knew his feet would be blistered after a few miles travel. He shifted inside the scale armor that Mood had given him. It was pinching his skin now. *Blasted suns! Blasted land!* He kept moving, trying to decide whether or not to shed it.

The hills he had climbed before were in the distance now as he looked back. The helmet was hot from the sun, but he didn't sense anything abnormal. He checked the sky, shook his head, and kept on going.

The terrain had changed; it was flat with bigger rocks and busted shale. The ground was cracked with baked mud, and insects now crawled the ground. He would have devoured those insects hours ago, but now he didn't feel the need. Birds pecking for worms in the drying mud fluttered away at his approach. Shadows were being cast from the circling vultures above.

"Maybe this is my last day after all. So be it."

He let go of the underling's leg and stopped. He scanned the ground as he walked around. The giant's tracks were gone, vanished. Venir retraced his steps over one hundred yards, running his hands over the dirt and crawling on the ground, but it was as if the giant had never existed.

"What in the world of Bish?" he said, tugging at his chin.

As the suns were beginning to dip in the distance, Venir decided this was the place he would make his stand. He went back to the underling and touched the hilt of the knife, but it was still ice cold, so he jerked his hand away.

"Blasted magic fiend!" Venir sat down and began tugging off his boots. It took some effort before he finally slung them off. His feet were raw, but they didn't appear to be swollen or sickly. He figured the hot sun must have shrunk the leather. He wiggled his toes and sat in the quiet before he tugged his boots back on.

From around his neck, he pulled out the amulet that Fogle Boon had given him. He suspected his friends would be along any time now, but he wasn't so sure he wanted to be found. He had caused them so much harm over the years that you would think they would learn to stay away. He took the amulet off and put it around the head of the underling. *Finding a dead underling is safer than finding a living me.*

Venir walked over to a stone half his size, bent over, wrapped his arms around it, and felt his girdle warm around his waist as he lifted it. He strained with the effort, but he pulled it off the ground like a stone half its size.

"Ha!" he said, strength coursing through him as he tossed the stone several feet to the side and watched it bounce off the ground before coming to a stop. It should have taken nothing smaller than an ogre to lift that rock, maybe two. He patted his girdle with new found appreciation and awe.

Venir wrapped up the underling in its cloak and set it in a rut, then gathered rocks from all around that were too heavy for a normal man to carry and piled them over the underling. A few hours later, the underling was buried under a cairn of huge stones. If it came back to life, it would have a hard time getting out. There were enough stones to bury a horse. Now, all Venir had to do was sit, rest, and think. He did regret leaving his grandfather's knife inside the underling corpse, though. He pulled a smaller blade from his sack, something he had been meaning for years to give to Melegal. It was half the size of his grandfather's ancient blade. *It'll have to do.*

He sat down and leaned against the cairn with Brool stuck in the ground at his side. It seemed like he and the axe had been together forever, but it had only been five years. They had survived countless battles, slaughtered multitudes of underlings, and survived. He felt it had all led up to these final battles, that one last clash with the underlings would free him and his friends of his troubles.

Darkness soon accompanied him with only the sound of the wind. He dozed on and off through the night, underlings and giants now tormenting him in dreams. He lay as still as a rock through it all, unflinching. When the light returned again, so did his starvation and pain. All he could do was sulk and wait for the other underling to come for the bait.

21

T HE CLOUDS WERE STREAKED LIKE rows of corn, dark gray with seams of blue bleeding through. The air was damp and chill, and the wind was picking up. It was another one of those moments on Bish that was abnormal, filling the air with uncertainty. The storms and tornadoes that had overpowered the lands weeks ago had settled down, but something remained. Something still lingered that couldn't be explained. Sometimes it was good, and sometimes it was bad.

Verbard looked at his shaking hands. They were small, but big for an underling. Short black fingernails came to sharp points, like the ends of picks. The gray skin was almost translucent beneath the thin layer of soft rat-like fur. They were cold, not the cold from the caves of the Underland, but rather cold from climbing high in the mountains. He rubbed them together and they began to ignite. He could see a warm red glow coming from his hands, a jolt of energy made its way through him, filling him with warmth.

His wheezing stopped, and the aching in his chest had subsided. Pulling his cloak tight around his body, he moved on. A drizzling rain splattered off his cloak, but it was followed by a torrential down pour. He hissed, pulling his cloak tighter around his chest. It never rained in the Underland. Still, there was something refreshing about the sound of the rain pounding into the ground around him, a peace he had never experienced before. It lasted less than a few seconds.

Verbard couldn't see where he was going as he continued to slosh through the muddied ground with his head hanging down. He fought the need to keep himself dry with a spell. He needed to save all the magic he had for fighting. After another hour of walking, he sat down under a spiny-leafed bone tree. He took note of its white thorns that hung dripping drops of water like venom on his face. *How long does this rain go on?* There was an ear-splitting crack of thunder nearby. Bright flashes of light were everywhere. *I have to keep going. He may be near.*

He had left the Darkslayer incapacitated, crawling like a cripple over the ground. The man had proved the most determined and resilient of all foes. Now Verbard was fated to face him alone. He got back up and leaned against the tree with a great feeling of emptiness settling inside of him. His brother, Catten, was gone.

"Brother, of all the times I wished you dead, now was not that time."

He and Catten had been raised in magic together since birth. There had been centuries of study and daring between the two. It was absurd that one of them should fall at the hands of a human. His head rolled from side to side in his hood. *Impossible ...*

CRACK!

A blast of lightning hit the ground nearby, shaking the ground and knocking him from his feet. He pulled himself up out of the mud.

"Heh-Heh."

It felt good, like an awakening. He thought of his brother Catten and made his decision to not let him die in vain. He thought of something else. It was possible his brother could be saved, or part of him at least. He would have to survive first, regain some strength and calculate his plans. In the meantime, he'd have to keep walking.

He walked on, oblivious of time, plotting his scheme, unaware of his feet that were now skimming the ground. Another half-hour went by before he realized his toes hadn't been touching the ground. He chittered a joyous sound that even he had never made before. Feeling the return of his strength, his heart began to beat like that of a horse. The storms and rain began to subside. He felt the power of Bish renewing inside of him in a wave of energy.

"YES!"

Verbard's doubts began to wash away along with the mud on his cloak. The gleam in his silver eyes had returned along with something else. His everlasting hatred of the Darkslayer ignited inside of him like a forest fire. He floated higher in the air, above the hillsides, through the clouds, where he basked in the rising moonlight. Night had come. In the darkness he would rest, and tomorrow he would see to it the Darkslayer was finished once and for all. If he could retrieve his brother, he could save a part of him. A thought struck him as he basked in the light of the two red moons. It was something he had never considered before.

"Maybe my brother was going about this all wrong. Maybe there is a better way, an easier way," he said, clasping his fingers behind his back as he walked through the sky. He burst out in a fiendish chitter.

"Vengeance shall be mine!"

22

" **W** *HAT!?*"
He couldn't say the word. The City Watchmen's club was wrapped around his throat just below his Adam's apple. *Not this again!* The pressure was building in his neck. He could feel his eyes bulging. Melegal watched four rough faces begin to close in. They were big men, callous, and rough as stones. There was little chance anyone was going to intervene on his behalf. His head jerked back as he was lifted from the ground.

"He's a light one, Boss," the one choking him said.

"Not much of a fighter by the looks of him, either," said another.

The red haired leader balled his fist up and drew it back.

"Yep … now lift him up higher so we can all get a shot in. Let's see how much of a beating he can take before he chokes to death. I bet he dies after the first blow."

He could hear them chuckling now, loud and obnoxious. Deep inside of him a fit of anger began to climb out. He had taken enough torment in the past day. His gray eyes dimmed. *At some point you have to put an end to it.* He found the eyes of the red-haired sergeant.

"What are you looking at, you little rat?" the man said, drawing back his fist.

Make it hurt!

Melegal brought the sharp point of his boot in the man's nose.

Crack!

The watchman cried out, holding the dislodged nose on his face. Blood was oozing between the fingers of the man's hand.

"Yer gonna get it now, Boy!" one said.

Melegal grabbed the stick around his neck with both hands and used it to kick his legs over his head into his captor's face.

"Argh!" the man cried out, letting go of his club.

Melegal landed on the ground like a cat, brandishing the club in his hand. He twirled it around a few times and said, "Come and get it, ladies."

The other two watchmen rushed in, clubs swinging.

Swat! Swat!

Melegal struck each in the hand, their clubs falling to the ground. He whirled and cracked the one that was behind him hard in the head.

"Ow!"

The other two were standing still, rubbing their hands.

"Go ahead, pick up those clubs so I can knot your heads."

They didn't move, staring at their boss instead. The man still held his nose in one hand, club brandished in the other.

"Yer gonna be buried for this!"

Melegal felt the blood rushing through him. He felt a tad unglued, ready to battle. It was different, but good.

"Am I now? Will you be the one digging my grave, then?"

The man came rushing in.

"You bet!"

Whack!

Melegal busted him in the knee. The man dropped to one knee.

Whack!

Whack!

He busted the man in his broken nose again and cracked the one behind him as well. The other two guards just watched with gawping faces.

The red-haired leader swung again. Melegal side stepped the swing.

Whack! Whack! Whack!

The man's club fell from his hand. A knot rose on his head, and his other knee was shattered. He fell to the ground, spitting in pain.

"Get him, you two bastards!"

They reached for their clubs on the ground only to have their heads drummed with Melegal's flashing black club. They tried to fend off the blows, only to have their arms numbed and wrists busted.

Melegal spun around, counting all of the men who writhed on the ground. There were shouts nearby, and more City Watch were running his way. He stood in the middle of the fray, dusting off his clothes.

No blood, ah, there's some … good … Bone!

A button was missing on his shirt sleeve. Now he was surrounded by half a dozen more members of the City Watch. One, tall and rangy, with five chevrons of a sergeant, lowered a longsword on him.

"You won't get out of this alive! Come with us if you want a quicker death. If not, me and all of my men will each chop a piece of you."

Melegal held out his palm, where a piece of metal glinted in the sun. The watchmen blanched.

"Er … sorry Detective. I didn't know."

"You didn't ask!" Melegal said, waving the brooch of Lord Almen in the man's face. "Now, have these dogs shackled in the nearest Watch dungeon. I'll deal with them later, a long time later." *Eh, so much for working under cover.* News of the new Almen detective would be all over Bone in an hour.

"Yes Sir!" the sergeant said, stepping away. Melegal could see the fear in his assailants' eyes. The red-haired one still managed a sneer. Melegal slung the club into his nose as he walked by. The surrounding City Watchmen stepped out of his way. He rubbed his brooch on his vest and stashed it. *It's good to be Melegal.* He took his time crossing the Royal Roadway without looking behind, and back down the alleyways he went.

The vastness of the City of Bone was not easily explained. It was circular and miles wide. Some of the overlooking apartment buildings were several stories tall, and the castles that overlooked them were much higher. Every year more children, beggars, and thugs crowded the roads and alleyways that streamed away from the castles. *More money for the Royals but less food for you.* Melegal brushed past a sordid lot of ragged fellows that stood drinking stale ale from buckets. One stepped in his way and found the tip of a dagger at his throat.

"Sorry, Sir … apologies. Not paying attention, that's all."

The gang of men stepped back from the narrow road, eyes averted as they began passing the bucket around again. Melegal kept going. *Drunken robbers, a disgrace to thievery.* He tucked his dagger up under his sleeve and placed a toothpick in his mouth. He turned down one alley, then another, walking like a ghost over the slick cobblestones. The alley seemed to darken as it narrowed. He thought of that assassin that had almost cut him down months ago. It sent a shiver down his spine. Was that man still out there, looking for him? That assassin had all but vanished. It was another unknown. Lord Almen hadn't mentioned the man, but Melegal suspected Almen had hired that man. *Who else?* He reached for another dagger at his side and fingered the pommel.

He leapt over a large puddle of muck and dodged a bucket of slop being poured from the windows above. Something splashed on his clothes that smelled like rotten eggs. *Mother of Bish! Filthy vermin, if I were Royal I'd hang them all.* He kept going, taking out a silk handkerchief, wiping off his cloak, and tossing the rag away. His hands fell to his hidden daggers as another group of men were coming his way. They wore thick woven clothes and carried hammers, saws and big wooden tool boxes. They slowed at the sight of him, pressing closer to the left side of the alley, avoiding his gaze, calloused hands clutching at their tools.

"Gents," Melegal said as he passed by.

They muttered something and hurried along.

Not everyone's a thief. Someone has to work.

Loud shouts and cries were coming from up ahead. The pounding of metal on stone and steel was getting louder the farther he went. The alley merged into an open stretch of road filled with hardworking men and women milling about. Whips were snapping in the air followed by a rugged harmony of bellowing voices making demands. Piles of rubble were being carted away in wheel barrows by wiry teenagers and durable women. Their long faces were filled with oily sweat. Melegal frowned. Back breaking work was something he'd always been able to avoid, even as an urchin. His deft hands and sharp mind kept him from the grind. The mere sight of these haggard people made him long for his cozy cot.

Men were churning cement, filling massive urns that were hoisted three stories high. More men awaited them from atop the scaffolding, pulling in the load, with spades and trowels ready. Melegal watched as they spackled in the cement and laid the stones. His mouth began to water. He slipped out of the hot suns and into the shade underneath the scaffolding. His presence didn't garner any stares. The workers were too miserable to care about trespassers and the slave bosses too eager to punish. Melegal made his way to a small rickety building of wood on the edge of the construction site. He stopped and listened at the open doorway. He stepped inside.

It was a single room, dark and windowless. The furnishings were sparse: a chair and table sat in the corner and a slanted table on the other side. There was a hatch in the floor, open, with a wooden stairs leading down. He felt a rush of cool damp air on his face as he stepped on cat's paws down into the darkness.

It was black, but there was a tiny glimmer of light far below and the sound of trickling water. He paused at the landing twenty steps down from where he started. *Only twenty more to go.* He closed his eyes for a long moment.

When he re-opened them he could make out the edges of the stairs and the rock-cut walls that surrounded it. He noticed additional light reflecting off the bottle floor, and he could hear the faint sound of voices as well. He made his way down the rotting stairs without squeaking the timber. There was only one way to go, toward the voices and the wavering light. He took ten more steps and stopped. An armed sentry was ahead, armored in leather, with a longsword hanging from his side. The average-sized man was leaning against the wall, talking back and forth with the gruff voices beyond him. Melegal could hear small feet splattering water over the moisture-slickened floor. They were coming his way. He climbed over the rail and hung from beneath the stairs.

A small boy emerged, two full buckets of water pulling down his narrow shoulders.

"Move it, Urchin!" the sentry said.

The slouching silhouette of the boy carried on as his haggard breath labored up every creaking step.

"Hurry up, Boy! You got ten minutes to make it back, or it's the lash for you!"

The child had made his way up about eight steps when Melegal reached up and tripped him. The water splashed down the stairs, followed by the clonking buckets. Melegal heard the boy let out a desperate sob as the sentry stormed over. Melegal maintained his position of seclusion beneath the steps.

"No you didn't! No you didn't!" the angry sentry said.

The boy was trying to brush the water back into the bucket. Melegal's stomach turned into a knot as he could make out the fear and desperation in the boy's face. The sentry stomped up the stairs, lash held high. The boy curled up into a ball.

"This is gonna be a lot of lashes, Boy. I don't even think I can count that high."

The sentry went up another step. Melegal reached between the stair planks, grabbed the man around the boot and pulled it out from under him. The man yelped, arms flailing in the air before he crashed down the steps. The man groaned as he rolled up, shaking his head. Melegal stooped behind him, dagger ready.

The man said, "What in the B—"

Whack!

Melegal struck him hard in the back of the head with the pommel of his blade. He caught the man as he pitched forward and laid his head down on the steps. The man was out cold, and he swore he felt his skull crack. *Good.* Above him the boy trembled, eyes still shut. Three sets of boot steps were rushing his way, with shouts. He tucked two small blades behind his palms and crouched back into the darkness.

23

L EFTY WAS KICKING IN THE air as a pair of rough hands hoisted him up by the neck.

"Let him go!" Georgio cried, as two goons pinned his arms behind his back. Another punched him in his face and then in the belly.

"Shut up, Children. If you draw the Watch it'll be worse for you."

The man who spoke was bearded and heavyset, not much taller than Georgio. His clothes were colorful and baggy, silk and cotton. His cuffed boots shone as well as the trinkets around his neck and pudgy fingers. The man had a full head of curly light brown hair. His brown eyes were soft, and his countenance was as harmless as a toy merchant's, but his voice sent shivers down Georgio's spine.

"Let him go—"

Whack!

"Ah, ah, ah," the man said, pinching Georgio's lips shut. "You don't want my friends to poke a hole in the halfling now, do you?"

Georgio could see a knife being held underneath Lefty's belly. He shook his head.

The man patted him on the head saying, "Good, good boy."

Now the men were holding Lefty upside down and shaking him.

"We can't find the money, Boss," one said.

"Eh ... well let me take a look."

The man ran his soft hands all over the dangling halfling, with no results.

The frumpish man who boasted of the Thieves Guild rubbed his chin.

"Hmmm ... pretty good."

He grabbed Lefty by the throat and pinched his Adam's apple. Lefty squirmed and twisted. The man held out his other hand and caught the coins that flew out of Lefty's mouth. The man forced his finger in Lefty's mouth, turning him green. Another coin popped out.

"Very good, indeed," he said.

Georgio's face turned red. *There go my biscuits!* He'd gotten run over by a cart for nothing now.

"Give us back our money!" Lefty cried.

The man swatted him hard in the face, drawing blood in the crack of the halfling's mouth.

"What did I say about the noise, Child? Do that again, and I'll cut your throat."

Georgio broke out in a cold sweat and began to sob. The words went through him like a hot knife. He sagged on his weakened knees, tears filling his eyes.

"Look Boss, you scared him good."

"Is that so?"

The man walked over and tilted Georgio's face up by the chin.

"Tell me, Boy, where do you come from?" the man said, his voice persuasive, his eyes glinting and hypnotic.

Georgio shook his head.

A blade whisked past his nose.

"The Magi Roost!"

The thief stepped back and said, "Interesting. I know this place. There are many wealthy patrons there. Hmmm."

The man paced back and forth in the alley, hands behind his back, flipping and catching a coin.

"All right men, take the halfling back to the nest and await my word. I'll take the boy with me."

Georgio saw the alarm in Lefty's face as they gagged him and started to drag him away.

"No!" Georgio cried, trying to pull away.

The man's powerful hand grasped him by the nape of his neck.

"Don't do anything stupid, Boy, and your friend will be fine. It'll cost you … well someone … though."

Georgio puzzled over what that might mean as the man pulled him along. Still, he didn't know which would be worse: Lefty being kidnapped, or Georgio having to explain to Kam how that had happened. One thing was certain; he and Lefty were in for it.

24

H E COULDN'T TELL IF IT tasted good or bad. He didn't even know what it was called. He kept chewing, biting into something hard, and spitting it out. He picked the small seed off of the ground, pinching it between his fingers. He took another bite of the porous and watery blue bulb, chewed some more, and swallowed. He rubbed the seed between his fingers, thinking that he wanted more, before dropping it onto the grassy ground. He stepped back as the ground began to quake. It split open and a tree burst forth, first the trunk, followed by the branches and then the pale blue leaves. The fruit burst forth on the branches like blossoming flowers. An odd feeling went up his spine. Scorch's work had just begun.

Scorch didn't yet have the words, but only his thoughts mattered.

That seems good. I wonder what seems bad.

Scorch had remained in isolation since he arrived on Bish. He was uncertain whether or not taking Trinos up on her charge was wise. He felt confined and listless. He tried to remember what or who he was before. He thought something on the roughshod world would remind him of that, but it hadn't come yet. He wasn't sure if it was a new start or an imprisonment. One thing was certain: he didn't belong here. He sat and watched a wagon train winding over the grassy terrain. From the distant hillside where he sat alone, he could clearly hear the people speaking and singing. Song birds chirped in the air, and the insects that crawled and flew made sounds of their own. Scorch's keen ears were growing accustomed to the new sights and sounds on Bish. They picked up on the danger lurking nearby. A lusty group of orcen robbers and highwaymen readied an ambush nearby. *Why would Trinos make such ugly and smelly creatures?* It was one of those many moments Scorch would watch with contemplation, trying to understand the world in which he now lived. The unsuspecting humans kept rolling along, livestock in tow. It looked like their last day on Bish had come.

Scorch watched the attackers charge from behind the rocks and down the hill. He was callous to all of the blood that splattered over the grass as the heavy blades fell. *Interesting.* It was time his new life on Bish began. He took on a dangerous form and bounded down the hill toward the mayhem at the caravan.

25

H E WAS SITTING ON A stone with his knuckles under his chin. Brool was stuck in the ground at his side. A gentle gust of wind ruffled the straggling hairs under his helmet. He inspected the holes in his scale mail, rubbing his finger in the fleshy wounds left by the underling's mystic javelins. The one in his backside was as bad. His skin was hard and dry with thick scabs all over it that were charred and black. He had been picking at them for over an hour, fighting the urge to take the armor off. He was pretty sure the dwarven mail had saved him though, by somehow absorbing the mage's power.

One underling down and one more to go. It was a singular thought that kept running circles in his head, reminding him that he actually hoped this was the last underling. He twisted the bracers on his wrists and sighed. He had never felt such anticipation like this about any fight. He got up and stretched his arms high.

"Bone!" The armor was still pinching into his skin. It was bad enough that he had been slashed and poked over a dozen times in the past two days, but now his own armor seemed to attack him. He plucked Brool from the ground and began to twirl it around.

"Cut, thrust, swipe! Cut, thrust, swipe!"

He stuck the war-axe back in the ground.

"Slat!"

He sat back down and pulled a canteen from his backpack. He now kept the backpack looped on his arm out of a healthy caution born of the times he had been parted from it and from the sack. He drank. The slug of water was warm, adding little comfort to his dried throat. Just thinking seemed to hurt. His eyes were bloodshot and weary behind the slots of his helmet. He was more stiff and achy from head to toe than he could ever recall feeling in his life. If that underling was coming, he wouldn't be catching him at his best, which he felt had come and gone. He felt like an old warrior that had survived one too many battles. He swore if he survived the next encounter he would go home.

Now that he had stopped and had time to think, reality began to settle in. He had left a beautiful woman for the taste of blood and dirt. He still felt he was doing the right thing, leaving his friends behind and out of harm's way, but maybe there was another choice, another path, another road. He had been tracking paths with keen eyes for years, but maybe he had missed one. Still, all of the pleasurable images had faded in his memories, had receded back so that right now, his mind was full of vibrant recent memories of his battle with the underlings.

Might as well build a fire.

He didn't want to take a chance that the underling would miss him. He started picking twigs and tree needles from the ground. The land was sparse. Loose rocks and rugged brush was all he came by. He pulled some from the ground with his hands. The roots weren't deep, but they spidered out a good distance along the ground. Some wilting bone trees were nearby. They were eight to ten feet tall, sparsely covered with ghostly white leaves. He took Brool and chopped them down. The massive blade chopped the narrow trunks into kindling.

Ten minutes later he was warming his hands on a small blazing fire. The suns were still an hour above the horizon, so it was still hotter than two red-headed whores outside, but the fire kept Venir company. The crackling fire was a friend, alive and breathing. His mouth watered for ale. He stomach rumbled for bread. *One more fight and I'm going home.*

The darkness covered the land now as the suns dipped and the moons rose. Venir sat staring into the fire, the rock grave of the underling at his back. An orange hue illuminated his haggard face. The vibrant warrior was gone, only a shell remained.

His grumbling didn't sound natural.

"I'll give it till morning, then I'm gone. Blast these underlings! Let someone else kill them!"

He strapped his backpack fully onto both arms and then lay back against it on his elbows, staring at the eerie moons rising over the distant hillside. He closed his eyes. He was in a deep slumber when his head began to throb. He dreamed of a pair of cloaked underlings coming his way, eyes brighter than fire, arms wrapped in energized snakes. Venir lurched up from the ground, snatching his axe and rolling to his feet. His pulsating head aroused his body like strong coffee. New energy surged from head to toe. Every hair on his arms rose, and his vision was as razor sharp as an eagle's. He spied in the sky a billowing black shadow that hovered before one of the glowing moons.

"Come down and play, Underling! I have a message for you!" All of Venir's thoughts about his friends receded completely when he slashed Brool in the air. Suddenly, he was hungry for vengeance. Brool was alive in his hand, its razor's edges gleaming in the night.

"Are you scared, Underling!? Why not come down? My axe will comfort you!"

Venir could feel the underling's contempt and hatred. It was strong, maybe more so than the other's had been.

"Come, Vermin! I'll make a nice stone grave for you, just like the other's!"

The underling was closing in; its eyes were blazing silver dots in the sky. Thirty feet high and fifty feet away, it stopped. Venir could feel its eyes boring into him. It was the one that had tried to crush his heart in his chest. Venir's heart ached at the thought. He didn't want to go through that again. Venir picked up a stone and threw it, only to watch it ricochet harmlessly away.

"Come! Fight!" he cried.

Venir noticed a thin silver lining catching fire along the underling's robes. He picked up a murmuring from high above inside of his helm. The hairs on the nape of his neck stood up. He was surrounded by something invisible and smothering. One second he was standing and in the next he was lifted from his feet. He swung wild in the air, trying to strike what had lifted him from the ground, but he didn't feel a thing. It felt like a soft cushion had scooped him up and begun carrying him away.

"NO!" he shouted, legs kicking in mid-air.

The underling was coming closer now, hands fanned out, fingers manipulating his direction like a puppet. All of Venir's strength and anger did him no good fighting the unseen hands that held him. He squirmed and thrashed like a suffocating fish, but it was to no avail. He glided now, back toward the endless wall of mist in the distance.

What is it doing?

The underling, Lord Verbard, was walking on the ground now, twenty feet away, and still manipulating Venir in the air with unseen hands, pushing him back. The underling stopped by the stone grave. A twisted smile crossed its evil face. It seemed to anchor its feet to the ground. It began pushing the air in powerful motions, howling with glee.

Venir was sailing backward now, ten feet above the ground. The underling was diminishing in the distance. Venir's head burned like fire. He could sense the triumph in the underling, like nothing he ever felt from them before. Its fear was gone. All it felt was a triumphant glee in the revenge it wrought. Venir felt envy and fury as the mist began to thicken around him. One second the underling was there and the next the entire world he knew was gone.

He felt the wind rushing through his hair. All he knew was that he was still going backward. How far he had gone he did not know. He could see nothing but the thick white mist. His axe was hardly visible before his eyes. The throbbing in his head began to subside, but another series of thoughts ate at his brain.

Where will I be?

There were no suns nor moons along the horizon. No up or down. He had heard stories of cliffs that dropped off deep within the mist. He had known of people that had gone in, only to never return. In his mind he still felt the underling's presence, but the force that surrounded him began to subside. He was slowing down. Suddenly, there was a total disconnect with the underling inside his head. The difference was day and night, a prolonged burden lifted. He felt freedom from any underling presence in his mind, something he hadn't felt in five years. With the underling's presence, the unseen hands that held him disappeared, dropping him in midair.

Venir's heart pounded with elation that the invisible clutches that had held him were gone.

"Yes!"

He prepared himself for the hard landing as he fell, but he kept going. He was in a free fall. As the seconds passed, his fear of the inevitable began to grow. He continued to fall.

26

T HE LAST THING KAM NEEDED was another drink of Muckle Sap, especially with an objectionable patron. It was one of those rules that she had made for her staff: too much fraternization with the customers led to trouble. It was early though, so no one else was around except Joline. Of course, it was her rule, and she could break her own rule … if she wanted. Besides, she felt compelled to appease the unpleasant woman across from her. She tipped her glass and drank.

The woman with the chopped up black hair gave it a moment before she took a drink of her own. Kam folded her arms over her chest and cocked her eye.

"How is it?"

"It's good. The best I've had in years."

"Try it with some cheese."

The nameless woman helped herself without a word. Her fingers were long and scarred, but proficient with the proper etiquette of eating pleasantries. The woman's rugged appearance defied her manners. What Kam had fed her was delicious stuff, the kind that made uncouth pallets grunt. It was not so with this stranger, therefore she'd had the best food before. *Who is she?*

Kam shifted in her chair as she spread some jelly on her bread. She was full, but it was good manners to eat when company ate. She had no idea what to say to this woman. It wasn't like her to be nervous. It was clear the dark woman wasn't going to offer anything, either. She chose her words with care.

"So, are you settling in or passing through?"

The woman just stared, blue eyes as hard as sapphires.

"Look, Prissy—"

"Kam—call me Kam."

"Very well, Kam. I'll be moving on …"

She felt like she could breathe again. *Thank goodness.*

"… just not right away."

The tightness in her chest returned. *Please don't ask for a room.*

"I'll be needing a room and a stable."

Slat! The Magi Roost had one vacant room. She took another sip.

"So how long do you need to stay?"

The woman shrugged and said, "As long as I have to."

Kam smiled, saying, "Well, I know a great place."

"I like it here."

"The Magi Roost is full," she lied, taking another sip.

The stranger washed down her food and wiped off her mouth with a napkin. Her fingers ran across the scabbard on her sword.

"I don't believe you … Kam." Kam propped her elbow on the table and leaned toward the stranger. *This is my roost, and I'll decide who stays and who goes!*

"I don't care if you believe me or not."

"Is that so?"

The woman had a witchy look in her eye. Either the woman was teasing, or she was about to take a swipe at her. Kam was a good judge of character, but in this case she couldn't tell. *Where are my customers? Someone should have come in for breakfast by now.* Resisting the urge to look around, she confronted the woman.

"Look, Lady, I decide who stays. You won't be. I can tell an honest face when I see one, and yours isn't one."

She readied her spell and her tongue began to tingle. For a moment, the woman's face remained as cold as stone. Then the woman's face softened the ever slightest and so did her grinding tone.

"I'm sorry, Kam. It's … it's just been a rough road. I feel out of place here. It's so nice and I'm so filthy. I smell, and my clothes are a tattered mess. I-I can't say who I am. I'm not trying to deceive you. I just can't say my name. Really," she pleaded.

Kam leaned back, astonished at the woman's words. The sour face had somehow turned to gold. The woman was bewitching enough, but Kam's gut wouldn't trust her words, no matter how sincere they sounded.

"I'm sorry, Miss, but it's odd that you can't give a name. I don't do business like that."

The woman's hand lifted from her sword, hiding her face in shame.

"I know, I know. It's just that I'm an outcast. A lone one at that."

"You don't have anybody?"

"Just the sword, and it's not even mine. It was my husband's, a betrayed soldier, now dead."

The woman began to sob, hiding her watering eyes in her cloak.

Kam refilled the woman's goblet and said, "So, what brings you here?"

The woman wiped the tears from her eyes and took a long swallow.

"I need to hide … to change," she stammered. "You know what I mean. I was told the City of Three was the place to go. I was told to come here."

Kam tried to hide her sympathy by fiddling with her goblet. She searched the woman's pleading eyes. She shifted in her seat as she wiped her hand on her short dress. The City of Three was known for its illusions, but what this woman was asking for was extreme. *Is she talking transfiguration? She cannot be.* But she sensed the worst, based off the desperation in the woman's voice. What this woman was asking for was a dangerous thing, indeed.

"Well, you came to the right city, just the wrong tavern. This place is full of magi, wizards, sorcerers, and the like, but if you're talking about what I think you are … then you need to seek help elsewhere. I don't deal with things like that."

The woman stiffened.

"I was told that your patrons do."

The stranger was right. Any one of many were connected enough to see such a task through, however, it wasn't the kind of business that Kam wanted the Magi Roost to be known for. As far as she knew, it wasn't, until now. She rubbed her palms on her dress.

"What my patrons do is their business, and I don't need some nameless stranger harassing them. My customers come to unwind."

"That's not all … I hear," the woman said as she leaned forward on her elbows.

"Maybe what you heard is wrong. How could you possibly know if you have never been here? Maybe you bribed a liar. Have you considered that? The people have tongues of silver in this city. They'll sell anything, especially to a desperate woman like you."

The woman let out a chuckle; her feeble expression had vanished only to be replaced by something even more sinister than before. Kam's headache began to reassert itself. Her heart started pounding in her chest. She placed her fingers on her temples and said, "I think it's time that you go."

The woman gave her a hard look as she finished her drink. Kam began to sense another presence in the room. The woman stood up. She was tall, more so than Kam expected. Kam's heart jumped when she reached inside her cloak. She noticed more blades along her belt as well, and legs as long as a man's. The woman opened a small purse and dropped some coins on the table.

"Very well, Kam. You win. I'll leave, but you better hope I don't have to come back."

Kam stood up to face her, pulled her shoulders back, and said, "This isn't the kind of place for those kinds of people. You'll have better luck deeper in town, but you won't hear where from me." Glowering at her, the woman strapped on her sword belt. Kam had never met a woman so commanding. *Please leave. Please leave. Please leave.* She couldn't take her eyes off of the woman, though; she was too scared to even blink. *Where's a really big man when you need one?* It wasn't something she thought would do her much good, but any kind of back-up would do.

"You are a pretty one, Kam, bold too. I hate that in a woman."

Before she could respond, the woman had turned and was walking through her doors. She let out a sigh of relief as she slumped back down. She clasped her jittery hands together. *Tears, boys, and now a butcher of a woman. What could make the morning worse?*

The tavern door swung open.

Oh no, she's come back! She shot up from her seat, magic words dangling on her lips. Georgio came running in, as white as a ghost. *Thank goodness!*

"Slow down, Georgio!"

The teenager dashed behind her and squatted down.

"What are you doing? I'm in no mood for games, Georgio!"

"But ... but ... they've got him!"

Another figure stepped inside the door and closed it from behind. He was short and heavyset, dressed in fine, loose-fitting clothes. He made his way over with grace that belied his girth. His light eyes and skin went well with his baby soft skin. His face was calm, and his voice was as pleasant as his walk.

"Hello, Kam. It's been a long time," he said with a bow.

The sound of the familiar voice aroused the butterflies in her stomach. It had been a long time indeed since she had met with Palos, son of the master of the thieves' guild.

You've got to be kidding me.

27

THREE FIGURES RUSHED BY MELEGAL as he remained hidden along the wall at the bottom of the stairwell. They smelled like fish and rice. One stopped and stood with a long dagger in hand. The biggest one had an ugly club, and the third held a lantern.

"Hey Boy, what happened?" the skinny one said, kneeling by the unconscious sentry. The other shined the light on the boy, who was still curled up and shaking on the steps. The big one with the club spoke first.

"Uh ... I think he slipped and broke his head, Sis."

The one with the lantern shined it back in the fat woman's face.

"Is that so, Frig? Well ... it's a good thing we brought you along to tell as that."

Melegal could see the dumb look on the woman's face turn into a smile. *What an imbecile.*

The skinny woman then added, "Duh! Stupid."

Frigdah frowned.

"Uh ..."

"Just go gather up that boy, Frig. Let's figure out what happened."

The slender one kneeled by the sentry, checked, and shook him hard.

"He ain't waking up, Sis. He hit his head hard ... real hard. There's blood, see," she said holding up her hand.

Melegal wanted to laugh at the sight of the Motley girls. *It looks like Bone has three new detectives.* He waited, wary of the lantern light. *Come on, girls. What else you got?*

Sis shined the light on Frigdah, who was carrying the boy back down. With her hand on her hip she said, "All right sisters, just settle down. We got ourselves a situation." Sis spit out some juice. "Haze, get those buckets and refill 'em. Frigdah, settle the boy down, and get ready to send him back up."

Melegal watched the extraordinary gang of three hop to it. Haze dashed by him with Frigdah carrying the boy from behind. When Sis held the lantern's light on the sentry, he could see the dire expression on her illuminated face. He heard her mumbling.

"Poor boy's gonna get a whipping something fierce."

He saw her shoulders sag as she walked by. Like a mouse, Melegal followed.

He followed Sis around the corner, every step inside of her shadow that was cast from the light that glowed from up ahead. Two burning torches outlined the wall, casting shadows on their worried faces. He could see Haze and Frigdah standing beside a large stone-carved fountain with a burbling spout of water in the middle. It was an Everwell. Melegal had never been this close to one before. Sis stopped and he froze, hunkering down, head twisting about. Melegal pressed himself along the wall. He could smell the stink of her feet. He noticed a hole in her boot with a long black toenail jutting out. The other boot was missing a heel.

"Hurry up, Haze. Get that boy going. We're gonna have some problems explaining this up top. I'll take the boy up with me and tell them what happened, but you two are gonna have to look after the well."

Yes, the Everwell; worth more than gold to the Royals.

The Everwells were scattered around the city, hidden in a network of ancient corridors built … another time long ago. It was Melegal's understanding that the water never stopped, flowing free as the rain. It was the elixir on which the City of Bone thrived. How else could such a big city survive in the Outlands? The Everwells were little known to the city's miserable citizens. The Royals saw to that. They controlled the water, therefore they controlled the people.

All of this water and still the people die of thirst.

Frigdah set the boy back down on his feet.

"I think he's ready to go, Sis."

Haze put a bucket in each of his shaking hands. She patted his head and gave the child a toothy smile.

"You'll be fine, Boy. Just take the water—"

"Don't coddle him, Girl! Boy, get up them stairs and hurry back. The sooner you get it over with, the better," Sis said so loudly her belly jiggled.

The boy sobbed as he walked by, staring at the steps as if they were a guillotine, careful not to slosh more water on the ground. Sis headed toward the Everwell. Melegal began to feel the cool mist of the waters on his face.

"You want me to go up, Sis?" Haze asked.

"Nah … just gimme a drink."

Melegal stepped from the shadows and raised up behind Sis.

"I'll take one too."

Sis whirled, swinging the lantern at his head. He ducked under it and kicked his boot heel in her belly.

"Oooph!"

She fell breathless to the ground, clutching her stomach.

Haze charged him, knife slashing in the dim torchlight. Melegal caught her wrist and twisted it away with a clatter on the stone floor. He caught the astonished look in her eye.

"You!"

"Yes me, now sit down," he said, sweeping her legs and knocking her off her feet.

Frigdah charged three steps, snorting like a bull, and then came to a sudden stop as he held his blade in the meaty side of her neck.

"Crap …" she said, eyes darting to her sisters.

The Motley girls remained still. He could see the tension in their pasty faces.

Sis sat back up, holding her stomach, and pushed herself up against the fountain.

"Haze, looks like yer boyfriend missed you."

"Shut up!" Haze said with her lips drawn down. She started to get up.

"Stay put."

She stopped.

Melegal eased his blade from Frigdah's neck.

"Good. Now, back off, Biggie. Just get down on the ground."

Frigdah flopped to the ground, lying flat on her belly.

That's one big arse.

"Get over here, Idiot," Sis scolded.

Frigdah crawled over to her sister's side. Haze scooted over as well.

You never knew who on Bish you might need, so Melegal kept tabs on everyone, just in case. Now, he couldn't help but take note of the hapless women he had previously taken pains to never see again. He shook his head as they cast wary glances at each other then back at him.

Haze was the most normal of the bunch, wearing steel hooped earrings that hung past her chin. He could almost see the bone beneath her thin pale skin. Frigdah's girth was still formidable, even for a man, bigger than the other two sisters put together. Her face drooped above her chins. Sis was stout, pie-faced and adorned with red pimples all over her forehead. He couldn't determine which was worse: Haze's over bite or Sis's under bite. *A marvel.*

He almost sighed.

Frigdah's belly rumbled aloud.

"Quit it," Sis said with a nudge.

"Sorry. Can't help it."

Melegal shook his head.

Haze said, "What do you want, Melegal?"

"Yeah," Sis said, "… what is it? We know yer working for them Royals. You come to make us slaves again … Traitor?"

He didn't show it, but the word stung. *Slave is more like it.*

"I have a simple request, and I'll pay."

The women all looked at each other, their disheveled faces lighting up.

"We're listening, Thief," Sis replied, as they all leaned forward.

"I need to know where the man … Tonio is."

"Who?"

"The man with the split face … the big one who kidnapped the boy."

Their faces darkened as they all bristled and sneered.

"We'll never tell," Sis retorted.

28

V ERBARD SLUMPED TO THE GROUND, relief flooding over him. There he sat, quiet in the moonlight, staring at the glowing fire several feet away. He was tired, but not as tired as before. The magic he had used to vanquish the man was something different, not all his. He reached inside his robes, pulled out a small scroll, and unrolled it. When he had read it just hours ago, it had been a complicated series of mystical symbols and words, but now those words were gone. His brother had been right: scrolls could come in handy.

The telekinesis spell was powerful, not something Verbard would ever have taken the time to remember. He never would have thought that such a passive spell could give him such delight.

Now he sat by his brother's tomb, accompanied by the whispering wind and the crackling embers of the Darkslayer's dying fire. Verbard couldn't remember ever being so tired before. Exhaustion was not something he was accustomed to. He could hear his heavy breath as he allowed his eyes to close. He began to drift into sleep.

He lurched up, staring into the mist. The Darkslayer was coming, but where from?

"No! It can't be!"

His silver eyes scanned the mist. He saw nothing. His instincts couldn't shake the thought that the man was still coming. He closed his eyes, summoning magic, focusing on the living, but there was nothing. The Darkslayer was a ghost, an apparition in his mind, something that would haunt him for a long time. He pulled his robes around him and began walking around his brother's tomb.

"Dear Brother, who would have thought I would figure something out without you?"

But he had. All along, he had never needed Catten for anything more than a sacrificial lamb. *Silly.* He knew better. He grabbed one of the small boulders and tried to lift it. It didn't budge. Verbard cursed. At the moment, his body was little stronger than a male child's, and not much stronger than one with full rest. The telekinesis spell would have been perfect for this task, but that opportunity was lost. How would he get his brother's remains out of there?

His clawed fingers rummaged through his robes. A few small vials rattled in his palm. He held a rod in his hand. It was a heavy piece of wrought iron, with a fist on the end, less than a foot long.

Interesting.

It was a trophy from a human wizard he had defeated long ago. It was something that had been used on him, but that he had never had need to use. *No, that's no help. What else?* He reached deeper inside his pockets; he had stored much in there, so much that he had long forgotten many of the things he carried with him. His robes had mystic pockets that allowed him to store a great deal and do other things as well. There was nothing, however, that would help him with his present situation.

He put another small vial to his lips and drank the sky blue fluid. He was filled, and his thirst was quenched, but he still felt weary. He placed the cork back in the vial and stuck everything else back in his robes, except another scroll. He needed rest and protection. With the twirl of his finger, he made the scroll unroll in midair and remain suspended before him. He began to read out loud. His face lit up and his eyes seemed to glow. Some of his words were whispers, while others were quite loud. He stopped as the scroll withered in the air. He waited.

Over an hour went by before something popped up from the ground: a mantis-like creature, almost twelve inches tall, emerged from the dirt. Its insect head tilted back and forth, looking up at him.

"Spread out and warn me of any trespassers."

The insect creature made a clicking sound. Hundreds more of the creatures crawled from the ground and took flight in every direction. In a moment they were out of sight. Verbard sighed, lay back, and soaked in the darkness of the night. His thoughts drifted to home and to his pregnant monster of a wife. He was actually beginning to miss her fanged and unpleasant face. If he could figure out a way to get his brother out from under the rocks, he could return home. If not, did he dare go back? After all, as far as he knew, the Darkslayer was gone.

Dawn was breaking when the tug of the mantis creature startled him from his rest. He cracked open his eyes and turned his head from the glaring sunlight. He crawled into the shadows on the other side of the rocks, yawned, stretched his arms, and felt restored. His gray skin seemed to shine under his thin pelt. The magic he commanded had returned, and he felt in control once again. He picked the mantis up in his hands.

"What is it?"

The insect made several clicking sounds, its mandible jaws opening and closing, its pinchers gesturing.

Verbard nodded and frowned.

"I see."

He crushed the mantis in his hands and dropped the remains on the ground.

Apparently, that wizard and Blood Ranger were approaching. *How?*

They were not far away, either. Verbard summoned more of the mantis hoard. He ordered them to cover his tracks and also those of the man, and to erase all traces of the fire. The creatures swarmed all over as Verbard rose from the ground. In moments, the land around the tomb looked undisturbed by man, beast or insect. He floated northward, letting the insects be his eyes. He was curious to see what his enemy's friends would do. When they arrived, he would be ready. If necessary, they would die.

29

B OUND, GAGGED AND BLINDED BY a sack that covered his face, Lefty's body jolted as he was hurried away. Panic seized his thoughts along with something else. *Do something or die!* Melegal's words spoke inside his head somehow. *Don't panic.* He let his ridged body go limp. The rough hands had him secured over a knobby shoulder. *Focus. Where did that man say they were taking me? 'The roost'? No, 'The Nest'. That was it! A hide out of some sort.* Melegal had told him about a place in Bone like that before. What else had the thief told him?

Count the steps to know how far you go.

Smell the city. Listen for sounds you know.

It was all a blur, though, as his tiny hands fidgeted with the tight leather cords that bound his wrists. *Almost there. 212 steps. 220 … 230 ….* The smell of ginger was in the air, the shouts of playing children in the distance.

A door slid open as the host of men stepped inside and slowed down. The sunlight he felt warming the cloth sack on his head — that smelled like potatoes — was gone. It was darker; the warm shadows from the daylight were no longer on his back. He was jostled, bumping up and down. *265 … I'm going down steps. Bad, very bad!* A smell like dry mold hung in the air, and the sounds from the street were gone. *Do something!*

His wrists hurt from the effort, but they were free now. The sack was still taut around his neck. He didn't know whether to strike or pull the sack off. Fear of the unknown below began to rise inside him. The thought of never seeing light again rushed the blood through his body. He had to act. He listened to the man's breathing and tried to picture his face. He reached out and jammed his tiny thumbs in the man's eyes.

"Aargh!" the thug screamed, as he squeezed Lefty by the waist.

He pushed his thumbs farther into the man's head. The man wailed, dropping him. He landed like a cat, removing the blinding sack as he did so. The man that had held him was holding his eyes and screaming now.

"Get him! Get him now!"

The stairwell was pitch black, however. The thieves preferred the darkness. It was a lucky thing for Lefty. He pressed himself along the wall and crouched, still as a stone. The men grumbled as they crowded inside the stairwell. Some were ahead of him and some were behind.

"Come on, Little Boy. You ain't got nowhere to go," one said, his foul breath only two steps from his face.

"Shut up and listen, Fool," warned another.

The corridor became quiet, but Lefty could hear their breathing and rustling clothes, and the sounds of daggers being scraped out of sheaths. *Don't panic. Don't panic.* The men were moving to cut off the upward stairs. There was only one way to go, down, but he was determined not to go that way. *Think! Move or die!*

The thieves' excited panting began to subside. The smell of sweat filled the air. For a moment, the stairwell became dead quiet. A pant leg rustled, brushing past his nose. Lefty clamped himself onto it and bit the thigh as hard as he could.

"Yee-ouch!" the man cried. "Get him, he's on my leg!"

Lefty let go as another man dived on the bitten man's legs. They crashed down the steps.

"Get off of me. He's gone!"

Lefty tried the same tactic on another who let out a scream.

"Where is he?" said another.

Lefty crawled up the man's back and wrapped his legs around the man's throat.

"I'm right here, behind you, Fool!"

Smack!

A fist crashed into the man's face whose shoulders he was on. He noticed something else, too; he could make out pale red shapes in the dark. *I can see!?* He could, just like his father had told him one day he would. It almost made him feel like hair on his chest had begun to grow. He leaped off of one man and kicked the face of another.

Swoosh!

A blade clipped his hair above his ear. He dashed under another man's feet and jammed his heel on the toes. The man cursed, swatting at his feet, slicing his own dagger across his leg. Chaos began to erupt as the men crawled over one another.

"Someone get a light!"

Whap! Whap! Whap!

"Stop hitting me," one man groaned.

Lefty watched from the top of the steps as the mass of men wrestled amongst each other. He rubbed his eyes. "Wait till I tell Georgio." He slapped his hand over his mouth.

"Did you hear that?" one said.

They all stopped, the outline of red bodies turned on him.

"He's up the top of the stairs!"

They came rushing up in a stampede, but Lefty was out the door and gone.

265-264-263-262-261 ... 250 ... turn ... 243 ... turn ... 236 ... 220 ... turn ...

It wasn't long before he could hear the children playing and smell the ginger. He knew where he was. It was time to get back to the Magi Roost. *135 ... 131.* He shimmied a pole and climbed onto a store rooftop. The rooftops were littered with birds, clothes lines, and gardens. He ran along the edges, climbed down gutters and back over walls. *Gotta tell Kam!*

He was across the street from the Magi Roost, dusting himself and looking around. A woman with a scowling scarred face was trotting her big horse his way. He started to cross, staring at her angry face. Something seemed familiar about her, and he paused. She dug her spurs into the dapple gray beast and veered his way.

OH MY!

Lefty leapt out of the way, feeling the horse tail whip his face as they thundered past. He clutched his heart as the woman galloped away.

He was shaking now. Everything began to soak in. He wasn't sure, but he felt like he had almost died, twice. He looked up and down the street. The coast was clear. *No horses. Whew!* He looked over to the Magi Roost and saw that the door was closed. Then he heard screaming voices coming from the inside.

30

F OGLE BOON'S CONFIDENCE HAD BEEN shaken once in his life. Now it was twice. Venir had been right in saying The Outlands was no place for him. Death was much easier to come by here, rather than in the City of Three. He was out of place in a strange land, following a dwarf that was built like a mountain. He felt captivated by the Blood Ranger's composure, certain and fearless, as Mood cut out the eyes of the underling. The scene was eerie and disturbing. He wanted to withdraw, but could not. He knew those eyes, those golden eyes, from the battle of wills from days before.

Mood waved his hand, filled with the eyes, in front of Fogle's face. The golden eyes were brilliant and staring, with an unnatural glimmer deep inside.

"Tis the one you said ye battled?"

Although uneasiness settled over him, Fogle couldn't tear his eyes away.

"Why did you cut his eyes out?" he said, shaking his head.

Mood looked at the eyes, then back at him and said, "I've never seen ones that were gold before. That was one powerful underling. They'll come looking for him. His eyes have magic and power inside."

Mood squeezed the orbs in his hand, his face straining from the effort. Fogle turned his head half away, fully expecting the eyes to pop. Mood opened his hand again. The eyes were there, solid as stone, gleaming in the sun.

"Can you burn them?"

"No, not here, wizard. There is a place, hot like an inferno. Tis' too far, though. It's best I take them to Dwarven Hole and bury them."

Fogle Boon swatted at a huge green-eyed fly that landed on his shoulder, and said, "Am I to take it that this underling is still alive? Can he still be brought back?"

"Yep," Mood said. "Here, you take them?"

Fogle Boon reached out, and then pulled back his hand.

"They don't bite. It's dead. Take ''em. Dis way, ye learn about yer enemies."

Fogle took the underling eyes in his hand. They were smooth like pearl stones from a river, hard like marble, and cold like metal. They still looked alive in his hand; the black pupils were wide, trimmed in brilliant gold. They had the heft of a fortune in coin, rare and desirable. He knew there must be some power within. Still, he felt nothing. He studied them and nodded. If there was magic in them, it wasn't much, if anything at all.

"Here, you take them?"

"I think ye should swallow them."

"What? I won't do that."

Mood laughed and took them back saying, "Suit yourself, Little Man."

The Blood Ranger began dragging the corpse of Catten over ground, and then seemed to think better of it. The red-bearded dwarf sat down, took out a metal file and began sharpening his axes. He caught Fogle staring and shrugged.

"Might as well chop him up and burn him."

Ox the Mintaur showed up with a stack of branches in his arms, dropping them to the ground. The ram-faced man was as expressionless as ever, barely a word spoken since the last battle. Fogle couldn't have been gladder that he had brought Ox along. Ox was the only true friend he had kept, most of his life anyway.

Ox was striking a flint rock with a steel knife, but the wood was damp from the earlier rains.

Fogle walked over and said, "Let me help."

Ox stepped away, handing him a branch. Fogle Boon reached inside his robes and pulled out a black satin pouch. He took a pinch of red shavings out, dusted the branch, and tossed it on the pile of wood.

He pushed the mintaur behind him and said, "Stand back."

Ox took two hooves back, peering over his shoulder. Fogle picked up a rock, dusted it with the shavings as well, and tossed the rock on the pile.

Fffroosh!

The pile burst into a brilliant orange flame. It felt good having a fire that couldn't be doused by the rain.

"Hrumph!" Mood snorted.

The timing couldn't have been better. The suns had set, and a chill now hung in the air. The clouds above were black, and he knew it was going to rain. That last rain had already soaked him to the bone, and he never remembered being so wet and hungry.

Ox was pulling items from his big travel sack, preparing a small tent of sorts. He watched as the mintaur hammered stakes in the ground with his short powerful arms and stomped the final blows with his hoofed foot. Fogle stared up at the rising moons, each a pale yellow, with dark clouds passing by. He wondered about home, the City of Three, and how far he was from there. He was in another world now. He felt ashamed for having sheltered himself for so long.

Fogle chewed on some stiff strips of beef, peppered with lemon and lime. He washed it down with some water, but his scrawny belly was only a tad full. He pulled the amulet out that now hung around his neck. *Maybe I should give it to Ox or the dwarf.* The radiant green gem twinkled before his eyes. What was Venir thinking? Why did he leave it? Why not take it? He wanted to understand.

Venir was a grim man, not the man he locked horns with so many years ago, but something else. He looked out into the mist. The mist was smoky in the distance, a fog that never rolled in. He wanted to distance himself from it, fearing it would creep in and overtake them in the night. It seemed to move, but never did. What was in there?

"Whatcha thinkin', Little Man?"

Fogle tilted his big head up in Mood's direction and said, "Do you think he's after that other underling, or that maybe he's in there?"

Mood turned all the way around, breathing in deeply through his nose. Fogle sniffed at the air, but caught only the smell of burning wood and his own sweat. Mood kept turning, searching the ground, and walking around the stone grave. *What is he doing?*

"I don't know. Something's not right here. There's no tracks, not man er underling. I don't smell nothin'. I should smell somethin'. Even the rain don't kill a scent. It's what ye human's call peculiar, I'd say. Something's been here; we know that. He was here, but left no tracks. Humph."

"Could something have snatched him away?"

Mood gave him a worried look.

Fogle sat down and pulled his knees to his chin, facing the fire. Where was Venir? Should he search for the man, go home, or go elsewhere? Mood sat down on the other side of the fire, where his read beard blended in with the flames. Mood looked like something born of the ground of Bish, an element, a mystery. The Blood Ranger looked like he could dig a hole through a mountain side with his bare hands. How had he gotten crossed up with him, the King of the Blood Rangers? Fogle rubbed his once gentle hand over his face. It had a beard now that covered the side of his face, his chin and neck. He had never worn a beard before. He looked over at the dwarf again. *I hope I don't look like that.*

Another whiff of smoke caught his nose. He lay on his back. Just when he thought Mood had forgotten their conversation about Venir, Mood continued his story.

"I've tracked about everything on Bish and found it, but I had a hard time finding Chongo, even though I took another dog with me. After a few weeks I found him in a village, a human village. Ho, Ho! I couldn't believe me eyes. A dwarven setter with a man, a boy at that! Venir couldn't have been even ten years old, but the dog, Chongo, was fine. He told me so. So, I let him be, and checked on them now and again."

Mood stretched out his legs and spat a bit of cigar leaf in the fire. A blaze of green shot up, filling the air with a comforting smell.

"Venir was a good boy, but a different sort, not like the rest, taller and quicker than the others, acted like a hunter, a born one, fished like a king. He had a head full of that goldish hair and eyes as blue as the sky. Then something happened one day that I don't care to admit."

Fogle saw him looking right at him now, his lips no longer moving. *What?* Fogle just nodded.

"Ya see, I would just scout him, stay away and all. Dwarves like me don't like to be seen. One day, Venir and Chongo snuck up on me."

Mood was pointing his finger right at him.

"But dont'cha ever tell anyone I ever told that, er I'll chop ya ta bits. Not even Venir; I made him forget." Mood blew a pointed smoke ring in the air and winked.

Fogle nodded, the intent was perfectly clear. Mood leaned back again.

"Bish is full of a lot of strange things. No sense in trying to explain it all. It just is. But, when the boy found me I began to wander. It wasn't long after that when the bad thing happened. Chongo called for me. It's not a bark or yelp, just something else. If the pooch is in danger, I'll know. By the time I made it to the village, I was too late. They were all gone: dead, smashed, buried. There was a couple of underlings left carrying shovels and digging them holes. Ya see, that's how they frighten you men, burying you alive, face down, with legs sprouting out like weeds. That way when they're found, everyone is scared ta death. That and all the blood and limbs scattered about. I hate that smell, the smell of a child's spilt blood."

Fogle could feel a lump in his throat and a chill in his spine. Mood's voice made it seem all the more real. He had heard about the horror of the underlings before, but he had always figured it to be exaggerated, believing his intellect was more able to see through such exaggerated things. Now Mood had proved Fogle's stupendous intelligence was wrong.

"I brained both of those wicked creatures. The hairy little black fiends even saw me coming, I wanted 'em to. I found Chongo not long after that. The pooch had begun digging a hole where the legs of the boy were sticking up from the ground. I grabbed a shovel and started helping Chongo dig. It seemed to take forever; one shovel full after the other. The boy's legs were white, like all the rest of the legs were. I finally was able to drag him out. I listened to his chest, but there was no beat there, or so I thought. Then his chest heaved, and he coughed. I slapped him on the back a few times. He opened his eyes fer a moment and passed back out."

Ox walked over and placed more wood on the fire. The mintaur sat down between Fogle and Mood and began brushing the metal shoe on his hoof. The rough brush Ox used made a rhythmic sound that seemed as natural as the fire. It was one of those things he hadn't even noticed before, that his companion wore the same shoes as a horse. Fogle rubbed his calloused feet some more. *Hooves, I could sure use those now.* It gave him an idea.

"… I spent the day and night digging all of the others out. None of the rest survived. I spent two more days diggin' all of their graves, proper like. Venir slept through the entire thing. I was glad, too. I didn't want 'em to see what happened to his family. It was bad, Human. You ever saw what underlings do to others?"

Fogle shook his head.

"Hmph, well I've seen it all. I've only told ye a bit, not the whole horror. That ain't nothin' fer boys ta see. The next day he woke up, scared at first of me. But Chongo was there. I told 'em who I was, that I'd help him. We had a burial of sorts for his family, without the bodies of course. There wasn't much left of 'em anyway. I expected him to cry, many men do at times like that, but he didn't. Quiet he was. I knew he was thinkin', about what I didn't know. Then he told me. He says 'Can you help me find them?' and I said I could, but he better know how to use more than an old knife when we caught up with 'em."

The moons were bright whenever they made their appearance through the clouds. Fogle thought he saw something else along the skyline, a figure, like a ghost. Mood looked over his shoulder, head turning the same way.

"Clouds can show ye funny things durin' times like this. Pay ''em no mind."

Mood's words did little to qualm Fogle's worries. There was still an underling out there, or was there? When he looked back up, the clouds had moved on. *Don't go to sleep without a plan, Little Man.*

31

IT TOOK SOME TIME, BUT things began to sink in. The smells, the heat, the anger and discontent, all of these things she had created. It had never occurred to her how they might actually feel, living and breathing it every second of every day. Her mind became restless as a new wave of feelings washed over her every day. It was confusing at first, but Trinos enjoyed it. As she wandered more, the harsh world began to settle in. It wasn't as pleasant as she expected, rather morbid in many cases—more darkness despite her bright lights.

Trinos wondered if Scorch felt the same. Was it wise to abandon their universe to live in this little world? What purpose would any of it serve? Was her creation better off as it was or in the world beyond? She did not know. Was she better off than she was before? What was different? Which was better, and which was worse?

"Get out of the way, Hag!" someone said as a wagon rushed by, splashing mud on her clothes.

Trinos wiped the muck from her face with a rag. She was pressed in with a throng of people that were begging to enter the City of Bone. Its high rock walls seemed enormous, which was an odd feeling for her. The portcullis was right in front of her, iron metal hammered out into gaping jaws. It reminded her of the Void. Whatever went in … didn't come out.

She was being shoved forward now, dingy fingers pushing into her back and the smell of rotten mouths breathing on her neck. She could feel the desperation surrounding her, the coldness of Bish's mankind.

"Come on you old bat, move on. Bone ain't got need for you," a younger woman said, shoving her with an elbow.

Trinos got a good look at the young woman's puffy face and frizzy brown hair. She didn't like the brash behavior, or the craw wrought of foul language and disrespect. It would take little effort to destroy the girl, and the urge was there. A forceful shove knocked her sprawling to the ground. Muddied feet were stepping over and on top of her. She could taste dirt in her mouth and the tang of blood from a split lip. Perhaps she should have taken the form of a man, rather than a wizened old woman.

"GET OFF ME, YOU WRETCHED PEOPLE!"

The people stopped, looking down at the source of the noise. Trinos rose to her feet, dusting off her humble robes.

"Did that hag say that?"

"Who said that?"

"I've never heard anything like that!"

Some of the faces were staring at her in wonder, while the others were looking around. Trinos smiled. Then a pie of manure hit her in the face.

The buxom girl with frizzy hair was pointing at her and laughing.

"Get back on the dirt, Granny!"

They were all laughing at her now as she wiped the stink from her face. *Be neutral. Don't be involved.* But the girl was slapping her knees, pointing and calling her more names.

"Granny! Granny! Granny! How's that cow pie taste, you old bitty!"

They were all in on it, treating her like some animal for their entertainment. Trinos clenched her fists and stared the loud-mouth girl down.

"Well … it looks like Granny here wants a tussle. I've never beat up an old one before." The girl spit in each of her hands.

Trinos had seen enough.

"THIS IS MY WORLD, FOOLS!"

The power of her voice blew the crowd back. Many dropped to their knees.

The boisterous girl's hair stood straight up on all ends. Her stare was frozen in a gape at Trinos, who stood looking down on her. A tear ran down her cheek.

"Sorry … Ma'am …"Trinos fought the urge to end the girl's existence right then and there. She clenched her fist and said, "Move away!"

The crowd began to cower, heads down and backing away.

"She's a Royal!" someone screamed.

"Leave her be, or she'll kill us all!" said another.

Now that's more like it.

Trinos entered the city of Bone unmolested, and was gone.

32

BACK IN SCHOOL HE HAD been smooth. The words had rolled from his tongue like sweet honey to the young girls' ears. Yes, Palos might not be the same lady killer she knew from the halls of school, but the man still had his charm just the same. Kam could feel his eyes pawing over her clothes, and she blushed. He was the man all the girls had wanted back then; notorious, shameless, and indiscreet.

Palos was the legitimate son of the Master Thief, Palzor. He also had many known sisters and brothers, all rumored to be from different mothers. Palos's family was known to be from the Guild of Favors who controlled the slavers, smugglers, and whores. Yet, none of that was ever proven to be a fact, only suspected. Kam had known much of him when he was a young man. He was small, lithe, and clever-tongued. He was a trickster and juggler, a singer and heart-stealer. She began to perspire from the scent of his cologne. It was one of the most delicious things she ever smelled on a man.

"It's good to s-see you, too, Palos," she said, pinching her shirt together above her breasts.

It was odd watching him stroll inside her tavern with his eyes wandering around. His slim waist had been replaced by a thickened belly, and crow's feet had landed by his soft eyes. Despite the man's unusual girth, he still carried himself with a great deal of charm.

He walked over, placed her hand in his, and kissed it.

"Kam, you have always been magnificent, a beauty unlike the rest, but now … I can't find the words, but I'd give a moat full of gold to find them."

She wanted to stand, but her knees felt weak. His eyes had undressed her, and his words had melted her. He had always had that effect on her. She didn't mind. *It's the Muckle Sap. Pull your legs together!* She started to rise. Palos had her by the hands, his soft palms pulling her to her feet, face to face with him. She felt his arm wrap around her waist, holding her tight. She held his gaze, unable to break his stare. It had been months since she'd been with a man, and she'd tussled with Palos before. She remembered it well.

"Kam!" Georgio shouted.

She glared at the boy.

"What?"

"He's got Lefty, Kam!"

Her weak knees stiffened as she shoved herself from Palos's grasp.

"Is that so, Palos?"

He reached for her hands, but she jerked them away as he said, "I'm just holding him, Kam, scaring the boy. I caught the boys skimming in The Quarters, quite adeptly I might add."

"Georgio! Is it true you are stealing?" she said, eyes searching for the boy who had crawled under a table.

"Lefty made me do it!"

Lefty! The boys had no business in The Quarters. Getting caught by the City Watch was one thing she could handle, but working without the consent of the thieves' guild was another. The guild was known for their lack of tolerance for other thieves. The guild was tight, had its own caste system in place. Like the Royals, they had houses of their own, just not so many. The guilds were the notorious insiders of the Royal families, each aligned with one or another, working for favors. But, unlike the Royals, as a whole the thieves guild was loyal to the master guild. That one was at the top and oversaw them all. The ruler of the master guild was Palzor, King of the Thieves, making Palos the Prince of them all.

"Where is the boy, Palos? You need to release him now," she said, struggling to keep her temper in check. It was one thing that the boys were stealing, but quite another that one was being held against his will.

Palos hoisted his leg on a chair.

"Ah Kam, how about some wine first?"

"Where is my boy, Palos?"

"Interesting ... I didn't know you had any children. Did you bear the boy under the table, too? I'm interested in the halfling most. How did you come upon him?" he said, taking a seat.

Kam didn't like the shift in Palos's tone.

"The halfling and the boy are dear friends of mine. If anything unfortunate were to happen to them, I'd be quite upset."

Palos was balancing himself on the back legs of his chair, hands folded in his lap, toes not touching the floor, when he laughed.

"Easy Kam ... now how about some wine? I am your guest here, and it's been a while, so please sit down. Is that a bottle of Muckle Sap over there? Let's finish it ... together," he said with a twinkle in his eye.

His voice left her calm and at ease. His suggestion loosened the muscles that had been knotting in her back. She fixed her auburn hair as he teetered back and forth on the legs of the chair. His chubby face was handsome and harmless, like a child's. She felt compelled to please him. She grabbed the unfinished wine bottle and started to pour.

"Kam," a timid Georgio said from underneath the table, "he's got Lefty and he put a knife to my throat!"

She turned on Palos, eyes blazing hot.

"You what?"

Palos raised his palms up.

"Easy now, I can explain. I was just trying to scare them, is all. There are many urchins running around. I can't sort them all out. I don't know who is who. You realize there are things that I have to keep under control."

Kam allowed a surge of energy to course through her, empowering her words.

"Get me my boy!"

The chandeliers shook. All four chair legs clopped back on the floor, Palos's face visibly shaken. He stood up.

"I will, but things still need to be sorted out. I need some reassurance—"

"You will get nothing ... Rogue!"

Her voice was no longer human, and her face lit up like the embers of a fire. Palos took two long steps backward.

"Kam, you don't want to upset the Guild of Favors. You know better ... I'm just doing my job. My coming here was a favor. I could have done worse to the boys. It would be wise of you to settle down."

It had been a bad morning that suddenly got worse. She had heard enough and seen enough for the day. No man, beast, or underling was going to tell her how to feel. Palos had picked the wrong moment in time to cross her. Any other moment in infinity would have been better. But now, Kam's personal cosmos was going to collide with him.

Palos was still backing away, hands patting the air before him, a sheepish smile on his face.

"I tell you what, Kam; I'll get you your boy. This time ... no harm and no foul. But you'll still owe me a small favor. Deal?"

Georgio was white-faced underneath the table, holding his ears. Kam was laughing, her face magnetic and hysterical. Palos eased his right foot backward, hips starting to turn.

"I don't need you to get the boy. He is already here!"

Palos looked back over his shoulder and there Lefty was, hunkered down by the doorway.

"Impressive," the man whispered under his breath.

Kam pointed her index finger down toward the floor. She muttered faint mystic-filled words. A long fiery snake burst from underneath the planks and slithered Palos's way. What she was unleashing felt so good; it was just what she needed.

"Your illusions won't work on me, Kam. Now, let this go, you are taking it too far ... really," he said as the snake licked at his boots.

"It's no illusion — FOOL!"

Palos had his hands on his hips as the burning red snake coiled around his leg.

"Hah ... certainly it is."

His face changed dramatically when his clothes and hair began to burn.

"Gagh!" he cried, swatting at the coiling snake. Frantic, he ripped off his pants and slung them to the floor. They burned into a pile of ash. The snake slithered back his way, striking at his naked legs. It hissed and struck, backing him toward the door. It was quick, but the hefty Palos was quicker.

Palos hissed back. "Kam, you'll regret this! You owe me a favor, and I will be paid!"

The hefty man jumped clear through the window. The flaming snake pushed through the tavern wall like it wasn't there and disappeared after the prince of thieves.

Kam didn't bother to watch him go.

"Lefty! Georgio! Get over here — NOW!"

33

T HE CITY OF BONE WAS a maze compared to all of the other cities they had traveled. It was difficult to discern a street from an alley, and honest directions were hard to come by. The foul air was another assault that misguided Vorla's senses. Regardless, she and her son, Brak, pushed their way through the busy city streets, drawing the attention of others. A group of children darted back and forth, shouting and pointing at her son.

"Big face!"

"Droopy eye!"

"He's got a bird's nest on his head!"

Brak shrugged it off, growled, and shoved them aside. They scrambled away, tongues hanging from their dirty faces, and fingers making unpleasant signs. It had been like this since they entered the city. The city was full of many odd things, but something about Brak made him stand out.

The City Watch was the hardest to get by. They didn't let just anybody in Bone; it wasn't some vacation town. Vorla didn't have any trade or commerce to offer, and she didn't want to part with her gold. People asked a lot of questions about Brak, and she found it easier to explain he was her brother, rather than her son. They took him for a useless dope and recommended she go back home. She wasn't going to be deterred from her mission. It took some convincing by her, alone in the guard shack with one of the men. The City Watchman didn't look half bad, and it had been a while, so she left him with a smile. Vorla and Brak had been searching the city ever since.

"I'm hungry, Mah," the man-boy said.

Not again.

"We'll find something soon, Brak, and stop calling me Mah."

"Sorry, Mah," he said again, looking around at all of the tall buildings.

The surroundings made her uncomfortable, too. If smaller cities made her uneasy, then Bone would soon make her insane. The open plains and farms were much more to her liking. The food was much better in the country, too. Her stomach started to grumble.

Brak stopped her in the middle of the street, forcing her to look up at him.

"I want more of those biscuits and goat milk. Can we go there again? Please?"

She couldn't help but smile as she placed her rough hand on his big face. She had no idea how to get back to where that place was, however.

"Certainly Son, now just you stay close behind."

She walked on, determined not to ask questions of any more rude passersby. Brak followed, holding his tummy like a five-year-old. His big foot caught on the back of her boot and her foot slipped right out of it and landed in an oily puddle.

"Brak!"

"Sorry, Mah."

She jerked off her sock, sniffed it, rung it out and put it back on.

"No stink?" her boy said.

She jammed on her boot.

"No!"

Every day of her life had been an adventure with Brak. She only had this one child, because after him she had vowed she would never have another. She didn't think she could, either. The baby boy had swollen her belly like a pregnant ogre's, making her gain more than one hundred pounds with him. And he had been so hungry, always hungry. Her nipples ached at the memory.

It had taken Brak two years before he could walk, and he had weighed fifty pounds by then. Her poor aching back had finally felt better after those days of carrying him were over. Oddly, once he got moving he didn't go very far, always staying near her side. It was hard though, making enough money to keep him fed and always having to find new shelter as they traveled. It was the farms that took them in and kept the boy working and corn fed. It worked out well. Despite Brak's girth and height, he worked slowly but steadily throughout the day, as tireless as the rising suns. The other children made their fun of him until Brak popped one boy in the face. The boy didn't wake up until the next week. After that, Brak and that boy became friends. This pattern repeated itself each time they moved on.

Brak pulled the carts, while Vorla did all of the other chores. A farm seemed like a good place to raise him as a boy, but his unnatural size always began to raise some questions. Rumors were that he was part orc or ogre, which was absurd, but even the peaceful farms had their gossiping crones. Vorla never hesitated to put them in their place, reminding them she had spent the night with all of their men a time or two. She told them she'd be happy to do it again if she had to. It shut them up.

Then it had happened, a few months ago. Brak woke up in the middle of the night shouting, "I must find my father!" Vorla calmed him down, but Brak, who slept little, did the same thing the next night and the night after that. Brak told her that his father was in danger and he had to help. It was absurd to say the least. Her son, now fourteen, didn't have an inkling of what his father looked like. It had been a long time, and there had been many men, but Brak's father she remembered as if she had just seen him ten minutes ago.

It was then that Brak started urging her to leave. She had no desire to leave the country and take him farther into the world out there. She had seen much of the wide world and survived, but much was lost. Brak, slow-tongued as he might have been, remained persistent. Then Vorla asked him what his father looked like, for she had never described him in the slightest detail before. She would never forget that day when he described the father he saw in his dreams.

"He's got long hair, colored like mine. Big muscles, sometimes a happy face, and other times angry. His eyes are like blue suns. His skin is tanned like yours, Mah ..."

The description was accurate, but he could have seen many men like that. It wasn't common to see a man like that, but it wasn't impossible, either. Of course, no one at any of the farms had matched that description. But Brak wasn't finished.

"... and he's got paint on his back that looks like this." Brak held his index fingers up, forming a V in the front of her face.

They packed up and left the next day. The journey started near the Lush Lakes, to Two-Ten City, through numerous outposts and finally, the City of Bone. It didn't make sense, but often on Bish, many things never did. Every day, Brak would tell his mother something he knew about his father, Venir. It was ridiculous, but she knew her son's words were true. Venir was in danger, but she remembered him to be a man where peril was always near. She had always liked that about him.

She finally found a food stand and ate some cheese while watching Brak devour enough for three bellies full. He didn't eat like he was starving; he took large bites that he slowly chewed up and swallowed down. The boy knew how to enjoy a meal. He grunted, "Mmm ...Mmm ..." and those sounds made her want to be a better cook. But, watching him eat was often a long endeavor. He ate jerky, sausage, gruel, biscuits and gravy, three people's worth, and he took his time. Sometimes it took him an hour to finish a meal, but sometimes that would last a whole day.

Vorla finished off her biscuit, washed it down with some sour wine, and stuffed some jerky and hard biscuits into her pack. She paid a woman and man, both dingy and peppered with flour on their arms and aprons. She wasn't going to compliment them on the greasy food, and she didn't give them a single coin extra. The humpbacked older woman counted out the coins in her shaking palm and dropped them in her pocket. The man, ugly and fat, stood with his hands on his hips and spat. The people in Bone were strange and uncompromising. Vorla had never felt such dark presences in the world. The people in Bone acted like you owed them for more than what you paid for. *Greed.* It seemed like every face she met was marked with it.

"Come on, Brak. Let's go."

"All right."

It was time to get out of Bone. She considered heading to the City of Three, a place she had heard was a much better place to be. Any place would be better than Bone, she was certain of that. In truth, she didn't know what she was doing. She was on a mission to find a man she hadn't seen in over a decade. She had traced him to this city. As far as she knew, he was dead, but the rogue she met may have been lying to her. She found it hard to believe that Venir wasn't alive. He seemed too crafty to fall.

"Hey Mah, where are we going? We need to find my father. He's in danger!"

Vorla stopped, turned, and put her hands on her son's face. Brak had the rugged features of a man, with soft skin and gentle eyes. One eye was noticeably lower than the other, and they seemed small on his over-sized head. She ran her hands over the thick patch of blond hair on the top of his head. She looked deep into his eyes, the same color of blue as Venir's, just different. There wasn't much else about her giant boy that resembled his father, yet Brak was who he was: the son of Venir.

"Brak, have you had any more dreams? You haven't said much lately."

Brak took her hand in his, looked deep into her eyes and said, "Yes."

She got a chill. He sounded just like Venir; at least she thought he did.

"Tell me more about it then," she said.

"Sometimes I see him, sometimes I don't. He's in pain, lost, angry. He fights, never really winning. I see things he sees sometimes, I think. I don't know. Scary things, dangerous," he said, his baritone voice started to quaver.

She hugged him and could feel his big body trembling. It hurt her that her boy was suffering alone with this. It also made her angry at Venir. For whatever reason, he was at the root of all of this. She wished Brak just didn't care, but for some strange reason he did. He needed to find the father that he never knew.

"Brak, are you sure he is alive?"

"Yeah, Mah," he said, nodding his head.

"All right, Boy, then we'll keep looking. Just don't sob anymore. Grown men don't cry. You're too old for that."

"I'm not a man though."

She pulled his face in close and said, "You are a man, Brak. You walk like a man, and talk like a man, so you have to act like a man. People will think you're slow if you don't."

"All right..."

Vorla led them back through the streets, back to where they came from. That rogue would have to know more. If he knew Venir, then that meant other people knew him as well. Besides, Venir was too hard to forget with his stories and all. She would find that thief or someone else and get the truth from them. This journey was wearing her down, and she wanted to get it over with.

Brak followed on heavy feet as she tried to retrace her steps back to the Drunken Octopus. Her feet ached. They must have walked miles since they left there. They cut through a narrow alley like so many from before. It dead ended, which was odd because most turned from one place to another. Brak was looking up at the high walls that surrounded them; a few small windows with closed shutters were up there, nothing else.

"Mah, I don't like this place."

"Me, either. It looks like we'll have to go all the way back."

"Yes, but it won't be as easy to get back as it was to get here," another voice said.

Vorla whirled around, ripping her short sword from her sheath. Two men blocked their path just over a dozen feet away. A pair of crossbows was pointed at their bellies as well. *Thieves! Blasted slat-ridden city!* More faceless men filled in behind the two, brandishing knives and axes. The two in front seemed the most formidable. They wore grimy clothes and steel jewels. Their faces were haggard, starved, and their eyes were desperate and jittery. She could see where one was shaking and fighting to control it.

Brak stepped in front of her, but she pulled him back.

"What will it be? I have nothing."

The one on the right with a steady hand and feral eyes licked his lips.

"Oh ... everyone has something. That sword is something. Both of them. And your earrings, too."

"Call the Watch, Mah!"

"Shut up, Brak!"

The thieves started to chuckle, low and wicked.

"Boys, they are lost ain't they? Ain't no watch down here ... *Mah*!"

"That sure is one funny name for a woman," one said.

"No stupid, that's no name, she must be the big fella's mother. She's a pretty one, too."

Vorla could feel Brak begin to bristle at her side. Any second, he would lunge and be shot. She grabbed his big arm, holding him back. She whispered through her teeth, "Be still."

Her boy's hand went for his sword.

Clatch –Zip!

She felt something burning in her belly. She reached down and pulled up a bloody hand. A crossbow bolt was jutting from her stomach. It hurt. He knees buckled, and she sagged to the ground. She could see the nervous thief, looking at her, wild-eyed with shock. The other men froze for an instant.

"Mah!" Brak screamed.

But it sounded like it came from miles away. She saw her son tear his sword from his sheath and charge.

Clatch –Zip!

A bolt punched into him. The thieves went for their other arms. Brak's sword was chopping up and down as the bodies were scrambling. The pain inside her began to ease. She reached inside her cloak and pulled out a pouch. *Kill them, Son! Kill them all! I'll miss you ....* Vorla's sight went black ....

Brak sat at the end of the alley with his dead mother in his lap. He was wailing, his face drenched with tears and his cloak soaked with blood. A crossbow bolt protruded from his shoulder, but he didn't feel it. He paid no mind to the half dozen bodies that were mangled heaps in the alley, either. He wasn't sure how they got that way, and he didn't care. His lamentations echoed in the alley, and the dogs of Bone of began to howl as well. His mother was dead, and he was abandoned and lost.

34

T HE AIR BECAME COLDER THE farther he dropped. The tips of his ears were frozen. An icy chill wrapped around him like a blanket of snow as he continued his free fall. Venir had never felt such cold, only the blazing hot suns. He had fallen so far and so long that his ravenous hunger, once forgotten, began to grow. His aches and pains were only enhanced with the cold. The Mist wasn't darker or lighter, just smoky and white, the way it had always been.

He screamed, but there were no echoes. He listened for any source of life, but there was only the whistling in his ears. The fall, the everlasting journey into the depths of the unknown, was maddening. It was a foe that he couldn't see or attack, one which kept him in a suffering grip. He lost track of time. *Wait and die. Wait and live.* He preferred the foremost. He was convinced he had been falling for hours, maybe days. Suffering, aching, starving. *This is no way to live.* His fate on Bish was not what he expected. A fall at the Warfield was what he would have preferred. *Better to die.* He pulled out the small dagger he had only just strapped on his belt and held the tip to his belly.

35

" A H ... THAT'S GREAT, SO YOU do know where he is then."
Sis's face scrunched up, her body tightening like a ball.
"Yeah, so ... we still ain't telling you, Big Shot. That man's a monster. Find him yerself!"
Melegal juggled two small knives between his hands. Haze's cat eyes watched his every move intently. He whipped one through the air at Sis, but Haze snatched it from the air as Sis dived away.
"Pretty quick, Woman, but your missed the other," he said, looking down at her legs.
A dagger was stuck in the ground, inches from her crotch. Haze scooted back, tugging the blade from the ground, flinging them both back his way. He pulled them from the air with a single hand and tucked them away.
"Now, women, seeing how you all know where the man is, I am pretty sure one of you will tell me."
"No we won't," they all said, except Frigdah who was picking her nose.
Great.
Three stubborn and stupid women weren't anything he cared to deal with, but he had to. Nothing was going his way today. First it was Sefron, then Lorda Almen, followed by Lord Almen, then Venir's bastard son and an unpleasant interlude with the City Watch. Now he had the Motley Girls to deal with. It was time to turn on the charm and bargain, not that they deserved it.
He smiled, squatted down, and spoke softly.
"All right then, girls, why don't you just tell me? I'll pay. I can get you better positions, out of this hole."
They didn't say a thing, holding each other's hands instead.
"Come on Haze, certainly there is something I can do for you?"
He noticed the bony woman was breathing hard, her eyes enlarged. She shook her head a bit. Her sisters looked at her and then him. *Come on, Girl. Say something.*
She choked out a word.
"No."
Melegal spun a large gold coin on his fingertip.
"Hmmm ... well, how about you then, Fatty. You can buy a lot of food and wine with this, and I've got many more."
Frigdah licked her lips saying, "Uh ..."
"We ain't taking yer gold, Rich Man, that's it!" Sis spat. "Leave us alone, or kill us!"
It didn't make any sense that these women would go to so much trouble covering for a single man. It was agitating him. *Idiot women!* But then he remembered Tonio's face: split, twisted, and scarred. He remembered watching the man plunge a blade through Luke the Lute player's throat, as casually as a child stepping on an ant. He had seen the man chewed up by Chongo and split in half by Venir. The memory gave him an inner shudder. That day, in the Octopus, had been one of the worst days of his life, until today. What did they see in the Royal that he hadn't?
"All right, so tell me why you fear this man so much?"
Haze spoke up.
"He's mean and evil."
Sis followed up.

"He kills women and boys."

Frigdah dumbly nodded her head.

"He's a bad, bad man."

Melegal put his hands behind his head, twisting back and forth.

"Have you girls ever seen an underling?"

They all recoiled, shaking their heads.

"I have. I've fought them and killed them. I can handle Tonio, but you have to tell me where he is."

"No," Sis said, "he'll kill you. He'll kill us all."

Fear. It was something even gold or Royals couldn't control. Melegal had seen people commit suicide from overwhelming fear. Fear of torture. Fear of humiliation. Fear of starvation. Fear of failure. He was going to need something more powerful than fear in order to get these women to cooperate.

Melegal straightened the floppy cap on his head and locked eyes on Haze.

Show me to the man. Take me to the man. Tell me where the split man is.

He felt his mind begin to glow. A gateway inside his head opened up and let out an eerie power. It felt good, a satisfying control, like a man breaking a horse for the first time. Melegal lapped up the exhilaration, feeling himself take control of the minds before him. Haze's face turned from a guarded grimace to a transfixed gaze. The other women eyed him with muted disbelief.

He could feel the thoughts and fears inside their heads. They were children that wanted to please him, but they were fearful of the consequences. He looked upon Sis's pimpled chin. *Tell me where he is.* The woman's chin dipped. He looked back at Haze, who wanted to tell him something, yearned to please him. He knew he could ask her to do anything: sleep, step, steal, and maybe even kill. He had to be careful what he said.

He glanced over at the brute of the three, the mind of a child, trapped in a brain the size of an apple. *Where's the man, Woman?* Frigdah started to drool and sway. He scanned them all again, his thoughts tugging at theirs, casting and reeling like a fisherman. He could feel the nibbles, the small bites, but fear kept them from taking the bait. *Tell me, please tell me where the man called Tonio is.*

Haze's thin mouth cracked open, the ever slightest. Sis lifted her hands towards Haze's mouth. Melegal felt the mystic tether between them begin to thin as his frustration set in. He could feel his heart beating in his chest. Sis's hand had almost covered Haze's eager mouth.

Melegal's words rushed out with the force of a geyser.

"TAKE ME TO WHERE THE SPLIT-FACED MAN IS!"

The women rocked back, hands clasping their ears, bodies curling up into balls.

Melegal was shaking a tad himself, his mind was hazy, and the floor seemed unsteady.

"Whoa," he said, putting his hand on his forehead.

The women were shaking their heads and breathing heavy. Sis was clutching her heart, Frigdah her stomach and Haze her head. He could feel he had control of them, their feeble minds putty in his hands. They all looked at him, all faces as blank as stone. One by one, they got up and headed for the stairs.

"This way," Haze said.

Melegal followed, saying under his breath, "My, oh my."

The guard lay still at the bottom of the stairs. What was Melegal going to do about him?

"Stop."

They each obeyed.

He had to think about this.

"Sis and Frigdah, tell the guards about that man who fell. Do what you would normally do after someone falls. Haze, you take me another way out of here to where Tonio is."

Haze led him back down the corridor past the well and beyond. The catacombs under the streets were endless, but Haze navigated them as if she was born there. It was black, but he could hear her footsteps and feel the wispy edges of her clothes. It wasn't long before they came upon a ladder leading up, consisting of iron rings in the stone. They emerged through a small manhole that opened out onto a backstreet.

Clouds filtered out the bright sunlight in the dingy quadrant where they now stood. Melegal was surprised to discover they were on the other side of the Royal Roadway, not too far from the Drunken Octopus. Haze led him through the city, careful to avoid any curious faces. The people had distractions other than the mission of the two. *No one cares what we do. Nor do we care what they do.*

Haze was a proven navigator. She knew the streets as well him almost. Melegal was more than familiar with the territory, taking note of a few short cuts she missed, but she showed him some others as well. An hour went by before they were walking down a backstreet that was lined with alcoves and doors. Melegal knew the place, but it had been a long time since he had been there. It was another abandoned part of the city with no food or commerce. It was little more than stone walls and rusting gates that fought the decay of time.

"Are we close, Woman?"

"Yes," she said, treading over the ground as if her footfalls might unsettle a trap.

A hard drizzle had begun, making Haze pull her clothes around her tighter. Melegal noticed that under the woman's clothes she had a curve or two. Maybe she wouldn't be so bad if he just focused on her legs and not her face. She stopped and turned, almost catching him off guard.

"Ahem … what is it?"

"This is it," she said, stepping halfway into a brick-layered alcove.

Melegal stepped inside, and then her hand brushed against his. He turned, staring into her gray eyes. There was fear behind them still, and something else.

"Don't make me go down there, please! I brought you here. I did what you said. I don't want to ever see that man again."

"I have no intention of letting him out. I only need to make sure he is there."

Haze's face loosened up. Melegal could feel the grip he had over her earlier was gone. She could go whenever she pleased.

The rain started coming down harder now, and the two of them stepped inside the dripping alcove. Melegal stood before a doorway with steps leading down. A busted door was propped up against the wall. Haze tried to grab his hand, but he jerked it away.

"What are you trying to do?"

"Nothin'" she said, sticking her hands under her clothes.

"So, he's down there? What else is down there?"

Melegal knew what it was: a solitary dungeon, a place where the worst criminals were holed up and starved. That's what the bards' songs told, but these holes had been abandoned long ago. This was an ancient prison block, now a place of decay and superstition. There was nothing to be found; things could only be lost here.

"He's in a locked cell at the bottom."

"Is there a key?"

"Yeah, but it's in the sewer. Sis saw to that. She wasn't gonna be the one that let that man go anywhere."

It hardly concerned him; Melegal never met a lock that he couldn't pick. He didn't have any intention of opening it up, anyway. He took a deep draw through his nose. There was only the smell of mold and decay, maybe a dead rodent as well.

"Is this where you found the boy?" he asked.

"Yes," she said. "Is that boy all right?"

"He is," Melegal said, staring into the blackness. He had thought little of Georgio, if any at all. Still, the thought of the boy's fingers being scattered on the table unsettled him. How much that must have hurt, having your fingers cut off one by one. Then he remembered what he had done to Haze, cutting hers one by one. He took a glance at her hand, but it was behind her back. She noticed him looking and blushed.

The rain was steady now, splashing on the stones, making it difficult for him to hear anything else. He took a step down the stairs. Haze grabbed his arm.

"Don't touch me again, Woman," he said.

She still held on to the back of his shirt sleeve, a determined look in her eye as she said, "There is another way for you to prove he's in there, but you can't let him go."

Melegal stepped back up on the stoop.

"This better be good. If not, I will go down there and let him out."

"No, no," she said waving her hands in front of him. "But, it will cost you."

"I already offered to pay; was I not clear?"

"You were; you were, but I want something else, plus the gold."

Melegal folded his arms across his chest saying, "Tell me what you have in mind then, and I'll think about it."

Haze licked her lips and ran her hands through her hair. Her eyes were shifting toward him, toward the stairwell, and back out to the rain. He had a feeling she was about to run at any moment. He touched her hand, speaking softly again.

"Come on, Haze. What is it?"

Her hand was trembling in his.

"It's a sword. We have Tonio's sword."

Melegal squeezed her hand. *Yes!* Something was going his way for once today.

"All right, Woman. Name your price."

She looked at him, eyes unblinking, and her mouth coming close to his.

"I want you …"she said with a shaky voice, "and thirty gold."

"Which do you want first?" he said, taking a step closer.

"You," she said, looking up into his eyes.

He could barely make out her face, thanks to the dark enclosure and the rain. Sometimes, you had to do what you had to do.

36

"SO HOW DID VENIR SURVIVE when the others didn't?"

"That, I don't know. But, like I said, there was somethin' different about the boy. I spent a long time with 'em after that. I taught him to track and fight, and he was good at both."

"Maybe it was the Silver Fish?"

"Ah, I see he told you that story as well. He told me that one as a boy then, too. I never figured it for being true. I've never seen a Silver Fish before, and I've seen a lot of things."

"Like you said, things happen on Bish."

Mood rubbed his beard and gave him a nod.

"I told him stories, too. He seemed to like that, said his grandfather used to tell 'em those, too. He said he missed 'em. Every day he asked me when we'd catch up with the underlings. I told 'em sometimes it takes a lot of time and we'd catch 'em when he was ready.

"The problem was that I had things to do, and I couldn't be raisin' a human boy. I's King of the Dwarves, you know. Even I had to go home now and again. Dwarven Hole was no place ta raise a boy. He needed to be among his own, so I sent him to Bone …" Mood said, shaking his head as his voice filtered off.

Fogle Boon felt a great deal of sympathy for Venir. After all, his own father and mother still lived, and he had many brothers and sisters. He tried to picture them slaughtered or buried. It was something he had even joked about before. Now, it didn't seem so funny. What a sheltered life he lived. He had it so much better at home than most people on Bish, but he never knew it. His brothers and sisters were the same. For the first time in his life, he now felt like he was truly living.

Another thing entered his thoughts, a dream he had many nights ago; his grandfather Boon, a staff-wielding wizard, battling underlings by a cliff-side. He looked over and saw a piece of that staff jutting from the sack Ox carried for him. His grandfather, an old geezer by his standards, had given it to him several days before he disappeared. He had hardly known the man or paid him any mind. A rambling fool was all he was to him, who talked about nothing he ever cared to hear. The only ones Fogle ever listened to were his teachers and some of his friends. It was strange though, how his grandfather left. The family didn't even seem to mind. Fogle remembered most everything, and the last thing his grandfather had said to him was still clear in his mind.

'It's more than just a stick. Don't be an idiot and lose it.'

Fogle had wanted to throw it away ever since, but every time he started to, the old man's haunting words convinced him to keep it.

Fogle rubbed his face; he was getting very tired now. He forced himself to his feet and headed for the tent that Ox had set. It was time to get ready for tomorrow. He rummaged through his sack and pulled out a small, leather-bound book that was not much bigger than his hand. He opened and closed it. *One.* The book got bigger. He did it again. *Two.* It grew one size bigger. He opened and closed it one more time. *Three.* The ancient book sat heavy in his lap, thousands of pages of knowledge within. Almost everything he had ever learned was inside the massive tome: spells, notes, ideas, strategies, colleagues, a family history, and more. This tome was his best friend.

He opened it up, but was unable to see much with the firelight. He muttered a cantrip and his eyes filled with light that beamed down on the pages. *That's better.* His hands ran over the tiny words and turned the pages like a pianist. He was looking for a spell, something that might give him hooves, or something similar. The truth was, there were hundreds of spells in the book, and he hadn't tried them all, only a few. To his shame, it was his Grandfather Boon's book, and after all of his years of adding to it, he had never gone back and took so much as a look at what his grandfather had to say. He had time now, though.

"I smell something," said Mood, who had snuck up behind him. "Can you see anything else with them lantern eyes?"

He looked up at Mood, lighting up his face. He could see the fibers in the blood-red beard, bound together like straw. He looked up in the sky, but the light from his eyes only went a dozen feet before it faded in the black night beyond.

"No, I need a stronger spell for that. Maybe I can try one tomorrow."

"Be ready," Mood mumbled, rubbing his face, as he went back to the fire.

Ready? How could he possibly be ready for anything out here in the wasteland? Every day it was a challenge just knowing which spells to remember and which ones not. It was far easier to stick with the ones that you always used and lock them in for the next day. New ones took more time to memorize, and chewing up the morning and losing more sleep wasn't something he wanted to do. His feet weren't doing much better though, aching with every step. Why he couldn't ride his horse over the rocky palisades, he didn't understand. Chongo would have been great to have. All of the walking was ridiculous. He needed to find a better way.

He thought about the underlings floating across the air. *Now that would be something.* He thumbed over the pages, back toward the front for a change. The words were tiny, which he found odd because his grandfather had such a big hand. If you were a stranger to magic, the words would be something you could not read. Magic had a language of its own, filled with marks and signs, nothing close to the common course. It was a cumbersome task, but Fogle Boon thrived on it. It was his passion. Again his thoughts went to the underlings. From what he had been told, the underlings had no need to write any of their spells down. To them it was a discipline that came from the inside. He wondered how that could possibly be true.

He rubbed his radiant eyes and yawned. He lay just outside of the tent and stared inside the canvas doorway, concentrating on locking in the spells he had already learned. That was easy, but he left out a few. He could always add the new ones on the morrow. He looked up in the sky once more, wondering if what Mood smelled was up there. He muttered something that made the light in his eyes go out and his spellbook begin to shrink. He pulled the broken staff of Boon from his pack to sleep with, and pulled a blanket over him. The sound of Mood and Ox sharpening their axes by the crackling fire put him to sleep.

37

S HE HAD DRONED ON FOR over an hour, chewing their ears off, spanking their behinds. Just when Georgio thought it was over she was in both of their faces, yelling, her cheeks flush red.

"That man, that's Palos … he's the prince of Thieves around here! He says that I owe him! I OWE HIM! Do you know what that means? Do you, boys!?"

Lefty shrugged his tiny shoulders.

"You owe him?"

Georgio couldn't believe Lefty said that. He tried to shrink into the sofa.

With her eyes blazing like the suns, she grabbed Lefty by his shirt, picked him up off the couch, and shook him like a doll.

"Yes! Yes halfling, I owe him! What—I don't know, but he'll be back. Men like him always come back."

Lefty's tears streamed down his face and she dropped him on the couch. Georgio was quiet by his side, eyes on the floor, crossing his feet back and forth.

"Venir! That blasted bastard, it's his fault!"

The boys didn't look up as she stormed away.

SLAM!

The entire room rattled as they both lurched upright and looked over at the entrance door. They heard Kam stomping down the steps.

"Whew!" Lefty said, wiping his brow. "I never thought that was going to end. I've never seen her so mad before."

Georgio's face was pale. He began biting his nails and shaking his head.

"I'm never doing that again, Lefty. That guy, that Palos, he's bad news. Are you all right; are you crying?"

Lefty wiped his blue eyes and grinned saying, "Oh gosh no, but those tears always get Kam off my back. Women get melted when they see them. Melegal told me that."

"I need to try that."

Georgio had never felt so bad before. He had been through worse, but guilt wasn't something he had ever suffered from. It had been one of those days, a bad one for sure. They got caught skimming, then robbed with a knife to Lefty's throat. His eyes began to water. He shouldn't steal anymore; he would have to do more chores. His stomach growled. He was hungry, still hungry. He heard Lefty coughing by his side.

Lefty was doubled over, his hand shoved in his mouth. Georgio ran over, slapping the gagging halfling on his back.

"Lefty, what's wrong? What's wrong!?"

Georgio pounded harder and harder, knocking the tiny boy from the couch onto the floor. Lefty was on all fours now, retching.

"Stop hitting me Georgio," Lefty said with a red face. "I'm all right."

Georgio was mortified as he backed away … Why was his friend eating his hand? He turned away as Lefty made a nasty sound.

"Blecht!"

Georgio looked back and saw stuff coming from Lefty's mouth. He put his hand over his own mouth and tried to tear his eyes away, holding his stomach. It was horrifying; whatever was happening to his friend was hideously horrifying.

Lefty had his hand out, hacking bile into it filled with shiny gobbets of silver and gold.

Tink. Tink. Tink …

Lefty's purple face let out one more final retch and more coins spilled from his mouth. They lay on the floor and in his hand, coated with saliva. Lefty looked at him, and he looked at Lefty and the coins.

"That was stupidness!"

"No, *stupendous*," Lefty corrected.

"Oh, yeah, stupendous."

Lefty showed him a grim smile and said, "Could you please get me a towel, and a glass of water?"

"Sure."

Georgio was back in a moment. Lefty gulped down the water, beat his chest, burped and drank some more. Georgio made a face as he tried to count the coins on the floor. They were bunched in a glob of saliva, but it looked like a lot, over a handful anyway. Lefty took the towel and began to wipe down the coins.

"Want to help?" the halfling said.

"I guess," he said, sitting on the floor and crossing his legs.

It was a hoard, a tiny hoard, but a hoard none the less.

"Lefty, how'd you learn to do this?"

The halfling gave him a look.

"Ah … Melegal."

Georgio grabbed Lefty by the collar and squeezed his neck.

"Ulp!"

"I want my share, and I want my biscuits. You almost got me killed out there."

Lefty couldn't hide his shock. The tiny boy wiped off a bunch of coins and placed them in Georgio's hands.

"I'm sorry, Georgio. I over did it, I guess. It won't happen again."

Georgio was counting his coins, a glimmer in his eye. The metal felt good in his hands, and he could smell the honey biscuits already. He stuffed the coins in his pocket and patted it.

"Ah, I guess I'll be all right. I still want those biscuits you owe me, though. Kam probably won't feed us again until tonight. She said we couldn't leave, either. Boy, she sure was mad," he said, running his fingers through his locks of hair.

Lefty patted him on the back and said, "I'll sneak down and get you something. It's the least I can do. In the meantime, how about some coffee?"

Georgio jumped up, "That'll do. I'll warm the stove."

"I'll grab the pot."

"You grab the beans."

"I'll grind them into dust."

The pair slapped hands, in a synchronized manner, singing a childhood song. Georgio rapped his hands on the table, while Lefty snapped the pot's lid open and closed to the rhythm.

"Coffee pot, coffee pot, high on the hill.

Coffee pot, coffee pot, I need a thrill!

Up the hill we take it, Down the hill we go!

Drink it! (clap)

Don't spill it! (clap clap)

Sip it. (clap)

Don't gulp it! (clap clap)

Coffee makes me grow strong.(clap clap clap)

Coffee speeds you up (clap clap clap).

All day long. (CLAP CLAP CLAP)

An ogre can't catch you and a bugbear too,

But if you steal my coffee, I'll ram my sword in you!"

It wasn't long before the smell of roasting beans filled the room. Georgio was fanning himself as Lefty watched the blue fire under the pot.

"Keep your fingers away from that pot, Lefty. The last time you burned it, trying that magic and all," Georgio commented.

"Ah, but it's such a simple spell. Kam does it all the time. She warms up the coffee pot and makes it just right. I've almost got it anyway; I just need a little more practice."

Georgio's head peeked up from the sofa and he said, "You need to practice getting me something to eat downstairs. I'm about to eat my shoe."

"Why don't you try your toe nails? They're long enough."

Lefty ducked under a pillow that soared his way.

"How many times do you have to miss before you stop?"

"I don't know. Hey Lefty, you never told me how you got away from those thieves. What happened, did they let you go?"

Lefty hopped over onto the couch, his face a wide smile.

"Georgio, they grabbed me, stuck a sack over my head, tied me up and carried me off. I was terrified," the halfling said in a shrill voice.

"Well, what happened then?"

Lefty looked up at the ceiling, scratching his head, then he looked back a Georgio.

"They said they were taking me to their Nest, and down the stairs I went, carried on this burly fella's shoulder. It smelled so horrible down there that I almost vomited in the bag that covered my face. I got my hands untied and bit the man on the ear. No wait … I poked him in the eyes. He dropped me into the pitch black."

Lefty became an animated puppet as he re-enacted his abduction and escape.

Georgio stared at Lefty with his enlarged brown eyes and bit his nails, saying, "Keep going."

"I pressed myself along the wall, and they all came after me, but it was so dark they couldn't find me. I really don't know what I did to get way, but I did. I ran under their legs, up the stairs, back the way they had carried me, and I had found my way back here when I heard the screams and—"

Lefty stopped and lurched upward.

"Oh my!"

"What? What is it, Lefty?"

Lefty's blue eyes were glazed over, giving his face a dumbfounded look.

"That woman."

"What woman … Kam?"

Lefty shook his head.

"No, the woman that tried to trample me in the street, I think I know who she was!"

"Lefty, what are you talking about? I didn't see any woman but Kam and Joline."

Georgio knew that look in his friend's eye. It was a fearful look, but calculating as well. He asked his friend another question.

"How are your feet?"

Lefty pulled them up; his bare feet were covered with dried mud.

"I should have noticed this before. It all happened so fast though, I didn't think about it. Something was dangerous, or someone. Either those thieves, or that mean-looking woman on that terrible horse."

Georgio shoved the halfling, saying, "What woman?"

Lefty was almost afraid to say it, but he did.

"I swear that was Jarla, the Brigand Queen."

Georgio gasped.

Lefty was fidgeting and drinking. He needed his tomes, the ones back in Bone. He hoped Melegal had taken care of them. He drummed his fingers on his head. Georgio was lying on the couch, his eyes opening and closing. *Take a nap.* He waited a little longer, and the boy was out like a light. The stew he had swiped from Joline's kitchen, with Joline's assistance, had hit his friend's spot. The busy morning had caught up with Georgio, but not with him. His day had just begun.

The Brigand Queen. It was one of the first stories he had recorded. He remembered it well, as Venir tended to be very vivid about the details. It had caused Lefty to wince sometimes while he wrote. He had left some of those details out, though. Some of those things, people didn't need to know. But the woman, the evil woman that betrayed Venir, he knew. In his mind, he could still see the words he had written.

A beautiful face, marred by men, scarred by time, and filled with enough hatred to fill a lake. Silky hair as black as coal.

Deeply tanned, perfect thighs, eyes as blue as an early night sky. Then the horse, Nightmare. A dapple gray snorting steed that trampled through armies with bloody hooves.

He shivered as he finished off his coffee. Lefty was terrified of big beasts, except Chongo. Horses he avoided. He put a blanket over Georgio.

Why is this woman here? Is she looking for Venir? The armament? Lefty had a lot to think about. Should he tell Kam? *She's already upset enough for today.* Of course, the Brigand Queen would have a price on her head, wouldn't she?

And what about the thief, Palos? Lefty had to admit, he was fascinated by him. Kam had told them to stay away from such people. The Prince of Thieves and the Brigand Queen, both in the same city. Despite the sweat between his toes, Lefty slipped out, leaving Georgio all alone.

38

MELEGAL BUCKLED HIS PANTS WHILE Haze caught her breath and pulled on her clothes. She was shaking a bit, looking back at him, her eyes seeking his, and then looking away. The rain began to subside. He pulled his hat from his pocket, pushed back his hair, and put it back on. He didn't feel half bad having done what he did, until he noticed that glow in her eyes. He had the woman in the palm of his hand, but that could be troublesome.

"Bring the sword to the Octopus tonight."

She straightened up, pulled back her hair and shoulders, and wiped her nose.

"Thirty gold."

He waved her away.

"You bring the sword. I'll bring the gold. Now go!"

She looked at him, hurt.

"Ain't you coming?"

He laughed saying, "The suns are coming back out; I can't be seen with you."

"Arsehole," she said, darting away.

"You got that right," he said, watching her go.

It was odd; the woman didn't really bother him. He expected the regret to be there, but it wasn't, he even considered giving her another go … one day … maybe. *It's gotta be dark, very dark.* He turned toward the doorway. A flux of rain water was running down the stairwell. He headed down.

The mold on the walls turned slick, and water drops plopped down from above. Earlier, the steps had been dry, but now they were damp with silt. He let his eyes adjust. The stairwell was still pitch black, but he detected the faintest of outlines. When he looked back up, the mouth at the top was gone, taken away by the spirally bend in the stairs. He felt like he was a mile down already. His rubbed his cold hands together. If that man, Tonio, still lived down here, could McKnight be alive, too? *No!* His mentor was dead, consumed by the swine. He had chopped the man up and fed the bits to the pigs. Still, anything could happen in Bone.

On silent feet he headed down the winding rock stairs. Everything was as Haze had described when it bottomed out forty steps below. The sounds of dripping water echoed from everywhere. He cupped his ears with both hands and held his breath. *Listen.*

The sounds of rats' claws scratched on stones beyond a metal barrier. Reaching out, he touched a cold iron door. There was a scurry of rodents on the other side. His fingers found the edges on an opening at the top of the door, barred. *Ah … a window.*

There was a rustle of clothes. His heart began to race. He waited, the pounding in his chest too loud for him to concentrate. He exercised his breathing. Another minute went by, then two. The silence returned, no rats and no rustle. *Use your nose.* He inhaled slowly, in and out. There was a strange odor he couldn't identify. *Rot, rust … dirty toes?*

The darkness in the stairwell covered him like a cape now. He swore he heard something. He must have. Possibly it was the rats running over rotting clothes. Above, the rain became heavy once again, sending the stream of water in more of a rush, filling the landing, raising water about the soles of his boots. He wondered if the heavy rains could drown a man inside these buried cells.

Melegal had to decide whether or not he needed to see Tonio in order to be sure he was alive. Would the sword do? Should he tell Lord Almen where he thought his son was? Let Almen send someone else to find the proof? It was a bad idea. He didn't want to give the Royal Lord any reason to choke him again; the next time might be the last. He would have to see for himself if Tonio was in there.

He reached into his pants pocket and pulled out a satin pouch. It was soft with something hard inside. It was an item he had taken from McKnight's clothes. He had never seen the need to use it before now. He wiggled his finger in the mouth between his purse strings, closed his eyes, and dumped the purse's object into his other hand. He gripped it tightly. The warm metal of a small coin was in the palm of his hand. *Just a little, Melegal. Just a tad.*

Turning his head away, he opened a crack in his fist, between his thumb and index finger. There was light, radiant as the sky, a thin beam was all. His pupils shrunk as he squinted. *Careful.* The coin had blinded him once, the day he first discovered it. It had taken two days to be able to see again, another week before the spots went away along with the headaches.

He shined the beam of light on the door. The iron was thick, the hinges large. There was a padlock with a big key hole, almost the size of his finger. He could pick that lock if he had to, he was sure of it. *Interesting.* He kneeled down, inspecting the lock. It was unique; a key for that lock would have been centuries old, he guessed. He'd never seen one like it before. He had an urge to pick it, just to make sure he could.

He saw the water rushing under the door now. A rat squeezed out from underneath, red eyes glowing in his light, and scurried up the steps. When he eased the light up the door, the entire space seemed to glow, revealing the colors of the green mold, the yellow slime, and the brown and black stone patterns underneath. There were stains: blood, most likely. A torch was mounted on the wall. There was a small, square, barred opening in the metal, with a sliding door that was almost closed.

He closed his hand over the coin and cupped his other hand to his ear once more. He heard nothing, but his instincts assured him there was something. He reached up and slid the portal open. It screeched. It might as well have been a cymbal crashing in his ears. *Fool!*

He crouched down and waited.

Idiot, nothing's in there but rats and roaches. Stupid Motley Girls.

He let more light spill out, running it back up the door. His heart leapt in his chest.

Bish!

Two eyes separated by a jagged scar were burning into him. In his hurry to shut and cover his eyes, he dropped the coin.

The man sounded like something else as it cried out in an inhuman voice.

"GO AWAY!"

WHAM!

It was Tonio, alive and kicking the door, rattling the hinges. Melegal saw spots. If he opened his eyes, he would see the light, so bright it was clearing the muck from the walls. With his eyes still closed, he searched through the rushing water, feeling for the coin.

WHAM!

The sound resounded up the stairs like a gong.

He felt the coin, snatched it up, jammed it into the purse, and clutched it to his chest. He heard heavy footsteps sloshing through the water on the other side. Tonio was screaming.

"GO! GO!"

Melegal stayed, hunching over the steps, soaking in the darkness. *Settle down. He can't get through that door.* He listened, hearing the sound of Tonio balling up in the corner. He had the urge to toss the coin inside, shut the portal, and lock it shut. Maybe it would destroy the man! But no: if an axe couldn't do it, then certainly a bright light wouldn't fare much better. *Pah! He lives, that's all the matters.*

Melegal dashed up the steps, back into the rain, chest heaving. He understood why the Motley Girls never wanted that man out again. Those eyes were like nothing he'd ever seen: cold, dead, and angry. Tonio's fate wasn't up to him, he hoped to assure himself. But, what would Lord Almen do? Or Lorda Almen, for the matter? Who should he tell first?

Just get the sword first.

Maybe he didn't have to tell either one of them that Tonio lived. Head bowed, cloak tight, he navigated through the rain, a maze of thoughts in his brain, a dead end after every turn. Maybe it was time to get out of Bone, once and for all.

39

HE WATCHED AND WAITED. UNDETECTED, he hovered high in the sky watching the man and the dwarf below by the fire. Verbard, as powerful as he might be, was wary. The Blood Ranger had the eyes of his brother, and was the one that concerned him the most. Months ago, at the Warfield, he had witnessed what those rangers did to the Badoon Brigade. He had watched his brethren cut down like saplings, falling into piles only to be trampled by dwarven boots. The Blood Ranger would be the hardest to kill, but it could be done.

The mage offered another concern. This same mage had surprised him and Catten a few days ago, blasting into them from the distance. Catten had locked into a mind grumble with the man, and somehow the battle had been a draw. Verbard didn't see how that was possible. *My brother was weak. Perhaps he deserved to die.* As Verbard hovered in the cover of the clouds, he watched with interest the mage's glowing eyes below. *Interesting.* He noted the spellbook resting in the mage's lap. *That could be useful.*

Verbard reached in his robes, searching the inner pockets. There were over a dozen of them, each filled with as much space as a backpack. He didn't care to carry many things, unlike his brother, so most of his were empty. He was certain that his brother's pockets were full. *I'll be needing Catten's as well.* There were things his brother had that he could use. Inside his own robes, he pulled forth another vial and sniffed it. *This will help.* He focused on all of the things that he wanted: the eyes, the spellbook, and Catten's robes. He would only be able to get one of the three, but the eyes weren't possible. The potion wouldn't work on something that still lived. *One drink should do it.*

He watched as the dwarf stripped down his brother, tossing the robes aside. Catten's naked body lay cold on the ground, unmoving as the dwarf raised his axe high. Verbard winced with every dismembering chop. Through the bond he had with his brother, he felt himself burning as the dwarf tossed each limb onto the fire. Sweat began dripping into his eyes. He wondered if he would come to such an end. Suddenly, his own death seemed more imminent, and he felt old. He pulled his robes tighter around his body. All of his life had been spent with his brother, century after century, a single day without end. Now, for the first time in his life he would have to face it on his own. A great void grew inside of him as he watched his brother's body burn. *I'll make them pay, Brother.* The foul smell of his burning brother filled his nose. He fought the urge to retch. *I'll scatter their limbs and feed them to the dogs. I'll flay every man and dwarf I find.* His chest heaved as his clawed fingers drew blood inside his palms. He took a deep breath.

The distant fire reflected in his silver eyes. His thoughts were on his next move. He knew what he had to do. He had vanquished the Darkslayer on his own; surely he could handle what was left. *Brother, if you could only see me now.*

Below, the dwarf and mintaur sat in the quiet, watching the fire dwindle away. The moons sank, and the suns began to rise. Verbard was ready. He drank the vial. He stared at the small spellbook that was tucked underneath the sleeping mage's arms. Verbard closed his eyes, reached out, and grabbed it. He could feel the leather, the thickness of the tiny tome. When he opened his eyes, there it was inside his clawed hands. He chuckled as he tucked it inside his robes and saw the mage bolt up from the ground.

40

L IFE IN THE C ITY OF Three offered freedom that the young halfling could enjoy. He could go anywhere he wanted: the lakes, the stores, and the races. It had everything, as long as you were cared for. Lefty had Kam to thank for that. Still, as time went by in his life, Lefty felt compelled to do things out of the ordinary. His curiosity about the acquisition of things drove him onward. He didn't realize this was the nature of a halfling, though. No, his family, now long gone, had not been around to guide him in this world. To some degree, he was still alone.

He was backtracking now, heading back to The Nest, where his captors had failed to secure him. Now that he had been to the Magi Roost and back, things didn't seem so far away, either. It was early afternoon, and the suns were at their zeniths; many shopkeepers were seeking the shade after working early in the morning and enjoying lunch. It was the time of day when business slowed to a crawl and storekeepers took snoozes.

Lefty wiped the sweat from his face with a handkerchief. He was hunkered down in the shade of a smokestack on a rooftop. It was hot and humid, and the mists from the three waterfalls in the back of the city drifted in his eyes. He could smell grilled fish and chicken in the air. The scent of baked bread and the sugar of pastries watered in his mouth. Now he waited, eyes closed and listening for familiar tones. It would have been easier to concentrate if there was a breeze. *Everything's good but the heat,* he thought, as he stretched his legs.

He leaned his head over the building's rooftop and spied the alley below. He was sure it was the alley he had emerged from earlier in the day. It led to The Nest, the rogues had called it, the base of the thieves' guild, he assumed. He was so very curious. Palos, the prince of thieves, had left an impression on him. Something about the pleasant demeanor of the rogue still reminded him of Melegal. He thought often of the man, who was the only reason he cared to return to Bone. He didn't like being cooped up in that tiny room at the Drunken Octopus. That was too much, even for him. It was good to feel safe and free again. It was easier to breathe in the City of Three.

The City of Three had halflings, too, but not many. As soon as Lefty got to know some, they were gone, moved on or chased from the city. One family had even asked him to come with them, but he couldn't and wouldn't leave Georgio. He had made the choice of who he was going to stick with. It was the ones that were willing to give their lives for him, and him for them, that mattered most. Still, he wished he had another halfling to talk to. Something was still missing from his life.

He rubbed his eyes and thought about what he had seen in the dark hall during his abduction. The warm images of the other thieves were still fresh in his mind. There were other things, too that he didn't understand, like sweaty feet and lightning speed. It came and went. Melegal had taught him things that he picked up with ease and Kam taught him magic. His deft little hands allowed him to replicate her writing as well as her own. Reading was easy, and writing a snap. He wondered if that was all normal for his kind. No one had ever told him that.

It was warm where he sat, and a breeze began to freshen up the stagnant air. He could feel some of the mist from the falls now. The longer he sat, the heavier his eyes became, and he was fast asleep ….

It was dark when Lefty awoke. A smell of burning tobacco was in the air, sweet and fruity. He looked around. He didn't feel any heat from the chimney stack, but the smell was strong and near. He blinked his eyes, a hazy red bulge was in front of him. He blinked again; it seemed to be smoking something.

"Enjoy your nap, Boy?" a rough voice said.

He froze as the figure in front of him shifted on the ledge of the building. It was short and dumpy, not much bigger than him, just a lot heavier. Whatever it was, it was smoking a pipe. Lefty's heart was pumping hard inside his tiny chest as two sets of boots stepped from around the side of the chimney and surrounded him. *Run!* He sprang straight up, fingers gripping the lip of the chimney. In a second he was on top and leaping away. A single hand snatched him by the ankle, jerking him in mid-air, whipping back his neck. He hung upside down, looking at a familiar buckle.

"He's quick, just like I told you," Palos said, hoisting him in one hand.

"Quick indeed," said the unfamiliar voice that spoke earlier. It sounded like a man, but different, more like the men from his own village. *A halfling?*

The figure walked over to his dangling head, eye to eye with him, only upside down. Lefty's vision had focused in the light, the infravision gone. The halfling man had a pie-face, big round eyes, a head of curly brown hair and a beard, no moustache. The man was almost three times the girth of him. His clothes were loose and refined, similar to Palos. The pipe he smoked had a long stem with a narrow chamber and bowl. His breath smelled like fruit, ale and tobacco. It reminded Lefty of home.

Palos flipped him right side up, catching him under his arms, setting him down on the roof, still holding him tight. "Be still, Boy, and no harm will come to you, or the others," Palos said.

Others? Georgio? Kam? Be silent. Listen. It was what Melegal had taught him. He nodded his head and felt Palos' strong grip release him.

"Sit down," the halfling man said. Lefty did so.

He looked up into the faces of the two men and the halfling now, each expression non-threatening. The other man with Palos, one that he had escaped from before, had a busted nose. Palos had changed clothes from earlier in the day, his face much more serene since dealing with Kam's flaming snake. The halfling man's expression was as warm as a village elder, a wizened face full of stories and adventure. Still, Lefty could see the deadly intent deep behind each of their eyes. He looked down, hands between his knees.

"What is your name, Boy?" the halfling man said.

"Lefty."

"Is that all?"

"… Lightfoot," he said in an audible mumble.

"Ah … no wonder you move so fast. I've known Lightfoots in my time. A very rare and unique breed of halflings Palos, especially these ones with blue eyes. Look at me," he pointed to his face, "heh-heh, two-eyes like pools of mud, much like the majority of all of my kin."

The halfling chuckled with delight and kneeled down beside him.

"… as for me, my name is Gillem … Gillem Longfingers."

Lefty's eyes immediately went to Gillem's extended hand. It was as big as a normal man's, unnatural with a halfling's palm and extra-long fingers. He could feel the warmth and strength in Gillem's when he placed his hand in it. The fingers reminded him of Melegal's, smooth and slender.

"Nice to meet you, I think," Lefty said.

Palos pulled over a box crate and sat down along with them, while the other man was leaning on the chimney side. Lefty was feeling jumpy, but his feet didn't sweat.

What's this all about?

"I told you, Gillem."

"Aye, and I had my doubts, Boss, but you were right. Shame on me," Gillem said, sucking on his pipe.

Palos continued, "Pretty impressive, Boy: you escaped my men, found your way home, and tracked us back again. Where'd you learn to do that?"

Lie! Lie! Lie! It was all that Lefty thought, but the eyes of Palos and Gillem told him that he wouldn't be fooling them. It was a test perhaps. What would Melegal have him do?

"I used to live in the City of Bone before I came here."

Palos and Gillem looked at one another and back at him.

"Interesting … I didn't think they let halflings in Bone," Palos said.

"I'd say, I mean, I've never been there," added Gillem. "How long were you there, Boy?"

"Not long, less than a year."

"Did someone from Bone teach you stuff? Clever stuff?" Gillem asked.

He felt pressure mounting between his eyes all of a sudden, more so than before. He didn't want to nod his head, but he did.

"Man or halfling?"

"It matters not, Gillem. He's been taught and he stands to be taught more."

"Agreed. All right then, Palos. The boy looks good by me. This is your show. Your decision is mine."

Lefty was beginning to shake now. A tremor was going up and down his spine. He didn't know what to make of his situation. A shroud of danger had enveloped him. For the first time in the City of Three he felt all alone.

Palos's tone then changed from that of the friendly neighbor to a venomous serpent.

"I've caught on to your skimming these past few weeks. Such matters don't escape the guild, no matter how small they might seem." Palos pulled a curved dagger from his belt and began whittling on a block of wood. "You've crossed the line. Kam is your keeper, and she has crossed us as well. You owe us, your big friend owes us, and she owes us. Favors, that is. Whether Kam likes it or not, she owes me."

Lefty didn't like the look on the man's face. It suggested something more than a favor, something he didn't yet understand.

"I've got a lot of men, Lefty, all over this city. Kam may be of Royal blood, but she has no authority over my kind. If something bad was to happen to her, the guild would be the last place they looked."

He looked over at Gillem, but the halfling man was expressionless as Palos spoke.

"And I bet you'd hate to see anything happen to her or that boy you run around with, either. Why, you'd both be orphaned if she died in a fire as her place burnt down."

He couldn't hold back the tears. His belly was full of fear as visions of his friends dying swamped his thoughts.

Palos' acidic voice was now as polished as stone as he spoke softly, "There, there, Lefty. You can make this all go away. I'm willing to make you a deal."

Lefty heard the man's words, but shook his head.

"Listen, this is going to be easy. An opportunity of a lifetime. I'm gonna let you work off your favors," Palos said.

"Give ''em a moment, Palos," Gillem said, patting him on the shoulders.

It took several moments before Lefty could pull himself together. He pulled out his handkerchief and blew his nose.

"Feel better now, do you?" the halfling man said.

Lefty nodded and said, "What do I have to do?"

"You'll work for Gillem."

"How long?"

"As long as it takes," Palos said, handing him the wooden block that now showed the face of Kam. "And don't tell her or your friend about us."

"When do I start?"

"That's up to Gillem."

Lefty looked at Gillem and noticed a glimmer in the halfling's eyes. It made him uneasy.

Gillem pulled him up and said, "Go home to your friends, Lefty. Not a word. I'll be in contact. I think you're gonna like the work I've set aside for you. Now go!"

He didn't have to say it twice. Lefty bounded to another rooftop and out of sight.

Gillem and Palos watched him go.

"He's a good one, that one," Gillem said.

"Not for long," Palos added with a chuckle.

It had been one of the worst days Kam had in years, maybe ever. Even the busy tavern couldn't keep her mind off all that took place in the morning. To make matters worse, Lefty had been missing all evening. Maybe she had yelled too much at him and Georgio. They were only boys, and they didn't understand life all that well yet. Now, for some reason, she felt more determined than ever to keep a closer watch on them.

She had work to do, though. The Magi Roost was in full swing, and a couple of workers hadn't reported in for duty. She wondered if Palos had something to do with that, and with Lefty's absence as well.

"Joline!" she yelled.

"What!?" the woman cried, nicking her finger with a knife. "Ow. What are you yelling for?"

"Lords, I don't know. I'm sorry," Kam said, taking a deep breath, closing her eyes, and making a quick mental count to ten. "Keep Georgio busy, and I don't care if he peels a thousand potatoes. He doesn't go anywhere without me, and that includes upstairs."

Georgio whined, "But Kam, I'm already tired of these stupid potatoes. I'm exhausted. I want to go to bed."

"Well, you should have thought about that before you started skimming people. Of all the stupid things."

"Well, I eat a lot, and you don't pay much for our chores."

Kam drew back her hand. Georgio flinched. Joline did as well.

"Easy Kam!" Joline said, stepping in her way, holding a wet rag over her bleeding finger.

The looks on their faces shocked Kam. *What am I doing?* Georgio looked mortified as he picked up a big red potato and began peeling it as fast as he could. She felt the tears coming on again as Joline put her hands on her shoulders. She wanted to run and hide.

"I'm so sorry, Jo," she sobbed. "I'm sorry, Georgio. I don't know what's come over me. That woman and Palos! Something about them just messed me up, and now Lefty's gone. He's probably run away, and it's all because of me ..."

Her world was upside down for some reason. Nothing so extraordinary had happened, but it seemed like it. Her thoughts seemed plagued with disaster. If she could just get away, just for a while, it might help.

"It's all right, girl. Running a tavern and raising two boys isn't easy. You go on now, go and get some rest. I can handle things out there. I'll send someone out to round up more help. We'll get a full staff tonight," Joline said.

Kam was shaking her head.

"No, I can't rest, not until Lefty is back. I'm just gonna have to work through it," she said, her voice shaking. "Georgio, you don't have peel all of those potatoes. Just a couple buckets more, to help Joline out."

A wave of nausea overcame her. The room started to spin. Her knees wobbled.

"Oh my," Joline cried.

Kam was sagging in the woman's arms now.

"Georgio, bring her the stool!"

Kam could barely make out what the woman was saying. She felt hot and weak. She was sitting now, and Georgio was fanning her with a rag. Joline put a cold wet cloth on her neck and put her lips on her forehead.

"My, she's burning with fever. All of the stress has given her the sweats. Come on, Georgio, we got to lay her down."

"Is she gonna be all right? Why is she so pale?" the boy said.

"She'll be fine as long as we act quickly."

Kam didn't know where she was. Half a dozen faces surrounded her, but she didn't recognize a single one. She was saying things, and she didn't know what. She wanted to get up, but she couldn't find the strength, and then she didn't know if she was sitting up, standing or lying down. Whatever had befallen her, it was like she was in a miserable, strange nightmare without an end in sight. She could see distorted images of Georgio, Lefty and Venir. Palos and that foul woman were there, too. She moaned. Fogle Boon was there, and his head had swollen like a watermelon. It seemed like she was in a new world now, one where everything was wrong. She tried to open her eyes, anything to get the spinning nightmares to stop. Nothing helped. It just kept going on and on and on.

41

"**M**OOD, IT'S GONE!"

Fogle Boon was upright, scrambling in the light of the cracking dawn. He felt cold and lost, and his stomach filled with nausea. He thought about that imp; could the imp have returned and taken it?

"What is gone, Little Man?" Mood asked.

"My spellbook is gone! Disappeared. Did you see anything at all? Hear anything?"

He couldn't hide the desperation in his voice as he emptied his packs onto the ground. Ox was at his side, rummaging through the pile as well. That spellbook had everything he knew about life, and more for him to learn.

It wasn't possible that it had just slipped away. Someone or something had to have taken it. He went through the catalog of spells in his mind. They were ready, but not all. He grinded his teeth and dug his nails into his big head.

The two horses they rode began to snort and stamp their hooves. Mood was looking around, head turning side to side. Then he saw it, floating down from the sky, an underling, one of the two from before. Mood stepped out in front of them, a crossbow his hands.

"Stay behind me!"

Time seemed to stop until the underling landed. It hovered in the air, robes flapping in the wind, its face threatening and evil. Fogle had never seen one up close before. The creature was small, but scary, like a nightmare come to life. He could sense its power too, ancient and incomprehensible. Then the worst of all things happened. It spoke.

"Eyes, give me the eyes!"

It was a hiss of sorts, raspy and distorted, as well as suggestive.

Clatch-Zip!

Mood's bolt sailed straight and true, then bounced away from the underling's unchanged face.

"Nothin' for you, Underling! Death is certain though," Mood said, snatching the axes from his back.

"A bargain, Ranger," the underling said.

Mood shook his head.

Fogle stepped alongside him.

"What sort of bargain?"

"Your spellbook for the eyes and robes, and you can leave alive."

It was a no-brainer for Fogle Boon. He would hand over anything for his spellbook, especially when it wasn't his. He gave Mood a pleading look, but the stern-faced dwarf just shook his bearded head.

"I have to have that that spellbook," he whispered.

"Have you ever bartered with an underling before?"

"No, have you?"

Mood was silent. The underling stood there, calm, sinister, and quiet. Fogle weighed his options. An attack could lead to the destruction of his book. Losing the battle could mean his own death. And where was Venir; was he dead as well? Had the underling defeated him? Then there was the matter of the robes. He hadn't even bothered to touch them, fearing a curse of sorts, but they must contain something valuable, something he could have used as well. It seemed like it was another one of those *Fight or Die* situations, as Venir would say. He didn't want that.

Fogle found it hard to speak up in the midst of a dwarf that seemed to have over five hundred years of experience on him. Likely, the underling had at least that much as well. He felt small among the other races, almost like he was invited to a dinner because he was to be the entertainment or the main course. Yes, things were different in the land beyond the cities—harsh and uncivilized. Despite the knee-buckling tension in the air, there had to be room to reason. Fogle still had ample confidence in his capabilities to do so. Ox by his side, he turned to Mood, hand out and said, "Let me have the eyes."

"I don't know what yer up to, Mage, but it better be good," Mood said, handing them over.

He was trying his best to hide his desperation, but his hand shook a bit when he took them. He nodded, sending Ox over to gather the robes of the dead underling, Catten. The black robes looked heavy and ordinary, but were very light when he received them. The material was foreign to the touch; a faint silver lining of arcane symbols could be made out, as well. He knew what he held would be worth a fortune in the City of Three. He noticed the silver begin to burn in the underling's eyes as it shifted in the air, lips turning tight.

"What are you doing?" the underling demanded in its raspy voice.

"I'm just trying to decide which is more valuable, my spellbook, or these robes ... or the eyes, for that matter. I'm sure it would all fetch quite a price where I come from."

The underling chuckled.

"Heh, heh, heh ... Fool, you would not be able to use the magic of an underling. It's as worthless to you as your book is to me. Of course, if you prefer that I try to take it from you I'd be more than happy to remove your skin from your bones, just like your former comrade, the Darkslayer."

"Let's kill him," Mood said, stepping forward.

Fogle held his hand out. As unsettling as the thought was, he wasn't convinced. It was true that underling magic would be useless to him, but as for Venir, he needed to know more.

"Interesting, Underling, and what proof do you have of that? After all, we have the proof that your brother died, but you show us none that ours died. Can you prove that? I can only assume that you have a trophy of sorts? We at least have these eyes and robes."

Fogle was almost in a trance now, the words flowing from his mouth like a dream with him being in a distant land. Standing face to face with an underling so powerful that its single thought could blow up a horse, he was bargaining with the creature, the vilest of them all, and he was holding his own. It seemed if he ever returned home, he would have a tale to tell that would shame them all, recounting the days he had mind-grumbled with one underling and bargained with another. His chest began to swell, until the underling spoke again.

"My patience is limited, Human. Each second puts you in graver danger. The eyes and the robes for the book. My offer will not remain much longer. The only other option is death."

The underling's hissing words weren't perfectly clear, but the intent was. Standing around waiting to call the underling's bluff was not going to get him the results he needed. It didn't matter if Venir was alive or dead. But still, he had to know … something.

"What are ye thinkin?" Mood said, the irritation rising in his voice.

Fogle kept his voice down and said, "There is nothing to gain at this time. I must have my book. It means much to me. The underling's items are worthless to us. Besides, these underlings are as susceptible to reason as are we. He has self-preservation to be concerned about, too. We make the deal, and we can all part ways freely."

Mood shook his head, but said, "Get his word, then. Every race stays bound by its word."

"You think that's true with underlings?"

"It's worth a try."

Fogle took a few steps forward and the underling raised its arms. He rose his, motioning a sign in the air. The underling did the same. A truce was made for wizard kind. Fogle began to get that renewed sense of power from the underling he had sensed before. His stomach began to turn in knots, and his feet seemed to waver on the ground.

"Here is what we want, Underling."

"My patience is oh so thin," the underling said, clenching his hands. "Out with it, then."

"First, tell us where the Darkslayer is."

Fogle's neck tightened like a bowstring as the underling hovered up a little higher; his silver eyes coming alive like lightning.

"You are impudent, Human! We will exchange, nothing else!"

"Surely you can guide us to his remains. If not, your word that you will take no aggression on us after the exchange."

"I grow weary of your demands! Pah, but I agree. As for the man, you learn nothing from me!" Verbard said, waving Fogle's spellbook in his hand. The tips of the underling's fingers began to blaze like fire.

Fogle took in a sharp breath. There was nothing to gain here. He knew the underling would not budge. He could feel that he was only a few seconds from seeing his own book destroyed. He had to have his spellbook back. He summoned a bit of energy and let go of the eyes and robes. They hung suspended in the air, the eyes above the shape of the robes, floating like an apparition. Slowly, he let the objects drift the underling's way. His spellbook was floated his way as well. He kept his mystic grip tight on the items, his mind using tendrils that engulfed the objects. His book, he could see and feel, was the genuine thing, not a trick from the crafty fiend. He noted every crease, dings in the cornered brass, a smudge of spilled ink, and a darkening of leather from candle wax. It was his and his alone.

The underling reached out and grabbed the robes. Fogle could feel the power of the underling, tugging at his mind on the other side. He now held his spellbook in his grasp, and hugged it tight between his chest and arm. *I will not let go!* He felt the underling's invisible tendrils still hanging on, the strength of the creature remained ready to rip it away. He felt the underling's claws, once burning bright, now cold and clutching at its items. He let go of them.

There was a tug at his chest, a pulling of the book, causing him to stubble forward and fall. In the next instant the force was gone. He looked up from the ground as the underling floated away, disappearing into the sky. He wasn't sure if he heard a cackle or not. He didn't care.

I have my book!

He rolled in the dirt, hugging his book, shouting with glee, and staring in wonder at it. He opened the book, scanning page after page. It was all there. Nothing had changed. He wiped a tear from his cheek. He had never felt joy that could make him cry before, only pain. He marveled at how much a single book meant to him, and vowed to never part with it again.

"Ye happy now, Little Man!"

Fogle looked up into Mood's battle-hardened face. He could see the cracks hidden behind the red hair that surrounded his eyes. He didn't understand why the dwarf seemed so unhappy.

"I have the book and we live. What is your problem with that?"

"I'm in no habit of letting underlings get away."

"I'm in no habit of dying, or seeing the same happen to Ox or you. We are fortunate to have the book. It could have taken it all if it wanted."

"Bah … you men don't get it, do you? You can't bargain with evil. Evil wins every time. The only way to beat it is to destroy it. Venir understood that. Didn't he tell ya that?"

Indeed he had. Fogle remembered it well. He had heard the entire *take no prisoners* speech, finding it to be utterly ridiculous. He had been taught that reason and compromise would always serve him well. So far in his life they had. He followed Mood's eyes up into the sky. All traces of the underling were gone. He got up, headed for his tent, and recited a spell. His spell book glowed and disappeared.

"Now what, Mood? Do you want to try and find Venir, or go after the underling?"

"Ho! Ho! Now the little man wants me to track an underling, too. Can ye cast a spell on us so we can fly after him?"

"Well, actually, yes. But that's not what I had in mind. Remember that amulet I gave Venir?"

Mood nodded.

"It's in the underling's robes."

The smile that broke out on Mood's broad face was brief. Something beneath them began to shake. The ground started to crack open and something huge was emerging from the opening. Mood's words ran through his thoughts again, with much more meaning this time than the last.

You cannot bargain with evil. Evil wins every time.

Verbard was relieved. He had been relieved when he dispatched the Darkslayer, but now, with the return of his brother's eyes, he was even more satisfied. He could even return home if he so wished. Still, he was exhausted from the trek, and the impudent human had tested his patience. With the robes and eyes back in his possession there was no need to fool with them, but things had already been underway, before the bargaining had even begun.

He chuckled to himself. He had been ready to fight for what was his, but he didn't like the risk. Before he set things in motion he had prepared something else. Removing a scroll from his robes, he had read off an ancient spell. The scroll had dissipated when he finished. If he timed everything right, the elemental would be arriving to destroy the man, mintaur and dwarf at any moment.

Why do all the work when you don't have to?

42

H E WAITED, ARMS CROSSED AND hunched over the table. A waif for a waitress showed up, offering more wine. It was the one Venir always hated. The warrior had been right, the woman never seemed right, spilling the wine almost every time she tilted the bottle. Melegal shook his head and waved her away. The working class was filling in now, men and women covered in grit and smelling like pig oil. He swore not a one of them was clean, only him, but he didn't feel clean, rather dirty and wet instead. A man in filthy trousers and a rope belt pitched another log in the fire, staggered, and bumped his table. Melegal snatched his goblet off the table before it spilt any wine.

"Ss-sorry, Sir, I didn't see yer table," the man said with a slur, belching, then stumbling along the floor.

Nearby, a woman was dancing and singing on a table. Her blouse came loose as she wiggled her skirt in front of the men, hopped down and straddled one. The men let out a raunchy cheer as the woman made her way around the table, kissing them all. Somewhere a banjo played, but it was cut short from shouts and hurled objects of disdain.

"Get out of here, Troubadour! You don't want to end up like that last one!"

The troubadour, older with graying hair and a garish face, tipped his cap, bowed, and exited. It was the oddest of things for Melegal: Luke the lute player was gone, dead as a toad. He didn't even know where the man was buried: no place for the body, no friend for a funeral. No, the City Watch wouldn't have come to drag him out, either. There was no justice here. The body was probably dragged off and sold to somebody for disposal. He could only imagine where: the sewers, the cadaver caves, or the everlasting incinerators. Bone's greatest secrets lay down there. It was another place he dreaded to go, alive anyway.

The stone fire place was hot on the left side of his face as he rolled his shoulders. A group of men, unlike the usual kind, came in. Brawny and armed with swords, they each donned a brand on their cheeks that had little meaning to Melegal. *Thugs.* Plenty of hard cases found their way into the Octopus now and again, but not so often. These men, scarred and unpleasant, were determined to find a table, most of which were now full. He ran his hands over his vest and pants. *All there.*

One of them grabbed his unpleasant serving girl by the arm.

"Ale and grog for all of us, Wench," he said, shoving her away. She struggled to gain her balance before falling to the floor. They all laughed as she crawled away.

Melegal rubbed his head. Everywhere he went, something agitating followed. *I should have locked myself in the room.* It wouldn't be so bad right now if Venir was there. There wasn't the same kind of order in the Octopus since he hadn't been around. And what about the woman, Vorla, and the man-boy, Brak? He wondered if he should have done more to help them. If Venir had a son, would he even want to know? *Strange boy, stranger father.*

He was so deep in thought that he almost didn't notice that the gang of thugs now shadowed his table. One man pulled up a chair and sat himself down. He had a meaty face with an unkempt head of black hair, sideburns and a thick moustache. His sleeves were rolled up, revealing two corded forearms and butcher's hands. He licked his lips as he talked.

"Say, you wouldn't mind if me and my men took your table now, would you?"

"I am expecting company, besides, I don't think you want this table," he replied, matter-of-factly.

The man grunted, "Huh, and why is that? Can you talk to tables?"

The gang of formidable men laughed along with their leader. Each was fingering the pommel of his blade. All eyes were intent on Melegal.

He let out a slight smile and said, "Yes, as a matter of fact I can."

"Really, and what did the table say?"

"It told me it didn't like arseholes ... you in particular." Melegal rubbed his hand over the table and patted it, saying, "Now, now table, that's not very nice to say to an ugly stranger."

The man leaned back, his face filling with a dangerous look.

One. Two. Three. Four. All bigger and tougher than me. The odds have never been better.

The man's hand dropped down to his knife.

"I've asked ya nice. The last man that made me ask twice found himself stuck on the end of my blade. I don't think you want that."

Four blades are probably more like it, all in the back I imagine.

Melegal noticed the other patrons going about their business like he and the men weren't even there. Nobody was coming to his aid. It was unusual. Even in the Octopus, the regulars tended to look out for their own. Their current disinterest in his predicament could be attributed to one thing, the new stink he had from working for one of the Royal castles. To them, he was better off dead than alive. He was pretty sure about one thing, though. *These men don't need many reasons to kill me.* It had been a bad enough day. He thought maybe he should go, but his pride didn't see it that way. He rubbed the brooch tucked in his vest. *Maybe ... Probably not.*

Melegal sat up straight in his chair and edged forward.

"Let me ask you a question. Have you ever heard of the Warfield?"

The men looked at one another then back at him. One's fingers slipped inside his clothes, while another slipped a dagger into his hand.

"I have. What's that got to do with anything?" the leader across from him replied, slipping a wide bladed dagger from the sheath. It was stained with blood, the metal workings showing signs of age and rust.

Melegal looked deeper into the man's eyes and said, "Have you ever been there? Better yet, have you ever been in a battle there?"

The leader shifted in his seat, fingers rubbing along the edge of his blade. The others were spreading out now, enclosing the table, blotting out the light.

"I've been there, and I've fought and lived," the thug retorted.

Melegal saw the man's eyes flick up to the left before settling back on him. The rest of the thugs cast more glances among themselves. *Liar. He's no soldier, never has been. A killer, maybe.*

"Well you see, there's something we have in common. I've fought there, too. I fought underlings, I did: mages, Badoon, the Vicious and the like. My, you could have filled ten barrels with all the blood we spilled. You ever see underlings bleed? The blood is reddish black, mostly black, though. Slick like oil, not sticky like men's. So—"

"He's lying!" "Look at him, he ain't fought nothing but hunger all his life."

"Just beat him or kill him, Jeb! I wanna sit down! Shut the rat up!"

Melegal began to stiffen at the remark. How many more times would he be called that today? The seated leader, Jeb, pulled back his shoulders, but his eyes had a wary look now. Melegal's words were convincing, and Jeb leaned back. Now the tension was real. The thugs, stupid as they may be, were dangerous. They had survived this long on weaker prey and desperate wits. Melegal always knew with distinction when the moment came to run, fight, or die. In this case, for some unusual reason, he was in the mood for a fight. Reason wasn't going to work on these men today, if any day. They were willing to be wounded or die just to have his table.

"It's time for you to move on," Jeb said, jerking his thumb over his shoulder. "If you move quick I'll let you live ... too slow, we just cut you down. I don't see any Warfield warriors to help you out, either. Maybe you've been there, but I don't think you ever fought a single thing. I'll give you to five."

"I'm impressed you can count that high."

"Three, then. One!"

The men pressed closer to the table. Melegal didn't bat an eye.

"Two!"

The calloused hands across from him were white to the knuckle on the hilt of the blade.

"I challenge you!" Melegal shouted, bolting up from his chair.

43

HE HIT SOMETHING HARD, AND all of the air burst from his lungs. Something bit into his side. Venir lay there like he had just been thrown from a third-story window. He was now a piece of pavement where there was no road. He didn't move; he couldn't, and he wasn't sure that he wanted to. There was one thought crystal clear in his mind. *I stopped!*

It was dark, and he wasn't sure if his eyes were opened or closed. He wasn't sure he wanted to open them if they were closed. What would be there when he did, more mist or something else? He began to shuffle around, still fighting for his breath. The ground was cool, as compared to the cold that had been rushing around him for what seemed to be forever. The feeling in his extremities began to return, pins and needles, the pain reminding his brain he was still alive. He opened his eyes.

Mist. More mist. He cursed out loud. But, at least he knew he was somewhere. He clutched at his side. There was blood, but the wound wasn't bad. He felt around his feet and found his knife. He felt the ground; it was packed dirt or clay with loose soil on top, brown maybe. The mist swirled in patterns around his hand as it moved the dust. He could see something; it wasn't much but it was something, a road maybe.

Venir craned his neck, closing his eyes. There was a gentle wind brushing over the fine hair on his ears, nothing more. He listened for minutes, desperate for a sound, any sound. *Nothing.* He felt some excitement as he stood up. The ground beneath him gave him new life. *Brool!*

He had forgotten about his war-axe, not that there was much need for the thing. He had lost it before. He ran his hands over his armor, his helm, the girdle and backpack. *All there.* He got on his hands and knees and began crawling around. It was better than standing, as this way he could see more around him, almost two feet. The mist didn't seem as thick down here.

"Ah!"

He wrapped his hand around the bottom of Brool's iron-shod handle. He hefted the thing. It was cool, not warm like he was used to. He took off his backpack and opened it up. He pulled out the leather sack, putting the axe inside. It disappeared in the black depths of the bag. He unbuckled the strap from his helmet, pulled it off, looked at it for a moment, and then closed his eyes. Nothing changed. There was only a chronic dampness that hung in the air. It felt good though, the odd wind blowing across his neck. He dropped the helmet inside the sack, and the girdle. He figured the new coolness would feel even better on his wounds without the armor. He unstrapped the sides of the scale mail and slipped it off. It was refreshing. He lay back on the ground, stomach rumbling, but he didn't mind as he let his limbs thaw.

As he lay there, he considered doing something he had never done before. He wondered if he could put Mood's dwarven armor in the sack. All these years, he had never tried putting anything else inside out of fear he might lose it or the magical armament.

"It's got to end some time."

He stuffed the dwarven armor in the sack and let go. He pulled the ties closed, then opened them back up. He reached inside. He pulled out and axe, girdle, and helm, but the dwarven armor was gone.

"That was stupid," he said, gripping his hair in his hands.

He felt bad, ignorant and useless.

"The Bone with it!"

He stuffed the rest of his armament back inside the sack and stuffed it in his backpack. He was lost, and if his gear was lost then so be it. What difference did it make? He stuffed his small knife in his sheath and pulled on his backpack.

"Time to move on."

Venir walked and walked, step after step, mile after mile … never hearing or seeing another thing.

44

"A CHALLENGE! SOMEONE'S MADE A CHALLENGE!" A distant patron shouted.

In moments, the tavern was abuzz. The thugs were forced back as a crowd began to gather around the table. It wasn't something that Melegal would typically do. He wasn't even sure why he'd done it, but now it was done.

Jeb the thug bristled in his seat and then snorted. The rest of his men were glaring at him as well. Now, it was more than bullying a man from his seat, but it could be a costly endeavor as well.

"I'll pick the challenge then," Jeb said.

"I say we let the tavern pick," Melegal said, as a raucous cheer filled the room.

There was nothing like the energy of a challenge, and one so early in the evening was rare. The barkeeps loved this type of business in Bone. In moments, every gambler within a quarter mile would come around. More casks of ale would be tapped, and the wine would flow into thirsty gullets like a river. Coin and more coin: men of business made a lot of money on men like him, which was why the Drunken Octopus put up with him and Venir for so long.

"Somebody bring the cards!" Shouted a big bald man with mutton chops in a brass-buttoned ruddy red coat.

"Girls! Where're my girls! I need 'em all," the barkeep said. The barkeep, a heavyset man who appeared as dimwitted as a cow, began shoving his way through the crowd. He wore a gray apron; his thinning black hair was combed over his balding head. He looked tired, but moved like a soldier charging up a hill. It was the kind of energy that only greed could build.

"Out of my way, idiots!" the barkeep said. "You!" He pointed at Melegal. "You called them out, so what's yer terms!"

"This table, and the banishment of these men, plus five gold for the trouble," he said.

"All of this over a table?" The barkeep's smoky eyes looked over at Jeb and his men.

The thugs stood there, hands on hips, big grins on their faces. The barkeep held his hand out and wafer thin woman, older than the wood on the floor, placed a burning cigar between his fingers. It made Melegal think of Mood.

"Hey Sam, I've got the cards!" A man said, pushing his way through the crowd. It was a younger man, brown hair pulled back in a ponytail, with a dish towel draped over his shoulder. He resembled the barkeep, Sam. "Here you go D-D ... er ... Sam."

With a pitiful face, Sam snatched the leather pouch from the younger and even shorter man. Sam, as most all knew in the City of Bone, was what all the barkeepers were called. The barkeep and tavern owners were a guild of their own. Sam, of the Drunken Octopus, had been doing it a long time. Running an establishment such as his was hard work, sometimes dangerous, but very lucrative as well. For the most part, the tavern owners let things be. A natural course always seemed to flow, but tonight, the thugs presented a different challenge. A group of such men could unsettle that balance, and their presence could turn the profits sour. Melegal trusted that Sam was onto this, and not out to get him killed because he now worked for the Royals.

"Make way! Make way!" Sam said, pushing through the crowd, stepping up on a two-step stage that made a rickety sound. His son, the bus boy, pulled an easel out from under the stage and placed a shelf-like board on it. Sam glared at the squat boy who stood there. The boy caught his eyes and jumped away. Sam stretched his stubby arm high and began waving the leather pouch in the air for all to see.

"It's been a while, patrons of Bone! A long time since the deck has been shuffled. A challenge, thugs against a rogue," he said, pointed the men out.

The crowd was enamored; Sam's strong voice was that of a circus master, bright and bold. Melegal could see the eager faces, their curious stares passing from him to the thugs. The smell of sweat began to grow as the entire room, as hot as it was, began to warm up another notch. The familiar sound of exchanging coins tinkled in his ears. He loved that sound of metal touching metal. Melegal had never skimmed, found, or stolen a coin he didn't like. He fanned himself with his cap and ignored his opponents' pressing stares.

"Now, take a look—a look at these men. One just as dangerous and brave as the other. They fight for the greatest of things, a cozy spot at the Octopus's table. The challenger has sat there for many, many years, unmolested like an 80-year-old man. He would rather have his throat cut, face smashed, or ribs pulverized than give up his favorite wenching and sipping spot! A proud one is he, crafty and greedy, too!"

There was a roar of applause, surprising Melegal. Frowns and worry began to crease into the thugs' faces. Melegal knew almost every single face in the crowd, their name, trade and addiction. It was good, good to know that after all, for some reason, the dwellers were behind him. They could have shouted out his name, but didn't, not that it mattered. It seemed that home-court advantage was on his side. Melegal listened to Sam, who would have full control of the bets. Sam would ham it up and have his pockets filled full by the end of the fight.

"… And who is this bony, gaunt, unhealthy man going to face? Men of a different breed, of the likes not often seen in here. Look at that man," Sam said, pointing at Jeb, "… he looks as strong as a bear and has the face of a heartless killer. His companions, one just as fierce as the other, are the kind who run the streets or run you through …"

Several voices let out audible gasps, raising a smile above Jeb's nodding chin.

"… Their hands are strong from years of swinging iron, no doubt. Look at the scars, badges of honor left from the ones they felled. How I'd hate to be the man foolish enough to challenge any one of them on a night like this …"

It was true, any man would be a fool to challenge a group such as this. Thugs, which was what they were called, were a sordid lot. They could be anyone from anywhere. A soldier, a mercenary, a brigand, a former City Watchman, or even an outcast member of the thieves guild. For the most part, they were swords for hire, doing the dirty work of local merchants or even the City Watch. They came in small gangs, singling out competition and drubbing them senseless until they moved on. They were guilty of all sorts of things: kidnapping, rape, torture, and mutilation. Strength in numbers and intimidation were their operation; being a pain was their game.

"… Here we have all the cards. Ten in all. All sorts of challenges and no two alike."

Sam pulled the cards from the leather pouch, flashing them one by one in the air. They were as big as his hand, colorful and stiff. He began to shuffle them as the women stepped onto the stage, six in all. They were painted, faces, nails and toes, sheer and silken sashes showing flashes of perfumed skin. The women batted their eyes and blew kisses to the crowd. One was short, like a child, another with hair hanging to the back of her knees. Another's hair was blonde and frizzy, with the worst mouth and manners in the entire city. They stood alongside Sam, welcoming the cat calls and whistles.

Sam shouted above the crowd. "All right, settle down everyone. It's time to draw!"

45

H E PACED AROUND THE BED, how many times he didn't know. His tiny hands were twiddling behind his back. Lefty's heart had sunk when he made it back to the Magi Roost. Kam was lying on the kitchen floor, surrounded by many distraught faces. He never imagined such a beautiful woman could have looked so bad before. She was sick, really sick. He thought of the sickness, the desert fever that had overcome him on his way to the City of Three. It was a horrible thing, but it seemed whatever she had was worse.

All of a sudden, his brief disappearance wasn't such a big deal, but her survival was. A man, tall and lean, wearing exquisite robes, scooped her up and loaded her into a white carriage. The horses galloped away, leaving him, Georgio and Joline standing in the dust. That had been three days ago, and yesterday Kam had been returned to the Magi Roost where she now lay in her bed. The man who had taken her had brought her back.

He'd said, "She'll be fine now. She's exhausted, but the fever is gone."

As quickly as the man had come and saved her life, he'd been gone. It was very mysterious, with almost no explanation at all. Georgio kept asking who the man was, but all Joline would say was, "Family." A couple of other hands came by, too, helping Joline keep things in order downstairs. Lefty wondered if they were different, too. They were certainly charming and attractive, as was Kam.

Her breathing was light, but strong. He could feel the air from her nose as Georgio sat at her bedside rubbing her hand. Her face was frail, her color that of a pale pink rose, and she trembled and moaned from time to time. Lefty took the washcloth from her head, dipped it in a basin of water, wrung it out, and returned it to her head.

"Do you think she'll wake up soon?" Georgio said.

"Ssshh … don't be so loud. You don't want to wake her up before she's ready. Remember what Joline said."

"You're just saying that because you know when she does wake up, you're gonna get it."

"Am not!"

"Are, too!"

Kam stirred, brushing the rag from her head.

"Ssshh!" they both said.

Kam resumed her slumber, and Lefty tucked more sheets around her.

Georgio stood up and said, "Come on Lefty, if were gonna stay up all night, we might as well make more coffee."

Lefty glanced at Kam, kissed her on the cheek, and followed Georgio from the room, careful to leave a slight crack in the door.

Georgio was reaching up into the cabinets when Lefty jumped in the way. "I'll do it. You make too much noise."

Lefty felt so guilty. He had started all of this. Kam had worried herself so bad over him she became sick. She had cared for him and he had repaid her with betrayal. He felt a good bit homesick now, not for the forest, but for

Bone. Melegal and Venir had protected him there, but it seemed there was only so much Kam could do. Now he was in even deeper trouble.

"Come on Lefty, it won't be so bad when she wakes up. Maybe she'll even have forgotten it all," Georgio said as he sat the steaming pot of coffee down on the table. "You can have Gillem tell your story for you. She'll take it well from him. He's such a nice guy. I'm glad you met him."

For three days he had been lying to Georgio, and when Kam awoke he'd have to lie to her, too. Gillem had shown up at the Magi Roost the next day. Lefty had already told Georgio and Joline that he fell asleep on the roof, which was true. Gillem had embellished that version and had them eating out of his hand. He recalled how that subverted conversation went.

"So I'm up there, just waterin' the flowers on my roof. You know how those sun daisies get. Stubborn little ladies, they won't come out if you don't sprinkle the roots. Ah … where was I … ah yes … the boy. I almost tripped over the tiny fella. Even for a halfling he's a tiny one, and there ain't many of us around here to begin with. He certainly wouldn't be hard to miss.

So, real careful like I nudge him. BING! He leaps like a fawn on top of the chimney, nearly teeters off, runs the ridge on them long toes and froze. Heh, heh, heh … my oh my, I didn't know who wuz more surprised to see who. It took a bit of convincing, but he came around. I asked him if he was lost, and he said no. I asked him what he was doing on my roof, and he said he didn't know. I asked him if he had a home and if he knew how to get there — he told me. I told him I was gonna check it out. I'm glad to see the boy is all right and all."

Georgio had sat gawping at the entire lie, but Joline had been less than convinced.

She said, "It makes no sense, the boy being on your roof and all. Boys get into trouble, any fool knows that. Lefty, I want to know why you wound up there. You better tell me now, that way I can soften the blow when Kam returns."

Lefty had been certain his ruse was up then. Gillem laughed at that comment, like an old grandfather tickled at the simple misunderstanding of a grandchild. The halfling man, round face full of a troubadour's charm, and a voice as warming as a smoldering fire, had taken over.

"Now Woman, I agree a hundred percent, and as sweet and concerned as you are, let me ask you something. Have you ever seen halfling boys raised before?"

Joline shook her head no, but her body suggested she wasn't offended.

"Perhaps I can explain. Yah see, there's a reason you've never seen or heard of a halfling being raised before. You know why? It's because they can't be raised. They raise themselves. Sure, you feed them and clothe them when their wee little, but it ain't long until they're on their own, doing their own thing. Whatever their role is, they figure it out.

"One father might be a blacksmith, but the boy won't have nothin' ta do with that, instead he'll be a farmer, a tailor, or a miscreant. Nay … raising a halfling would be like raising a bee. He's just gonna be what he's gonna be, ain't no changing that. Now this one, he's hit that age. His curiosity is high, and he does things, goes places, and he doesn't know why. It's still gonna take some time for him to figure it out. But don't get me wrong though, he still needs some mentoring and family, you just can't force it on him."

It all made perfect sense, the nods of Georgio and Joline seemed to confirm that. Joline had even let out a sigh of relief. Even Lefty had been almost convinced, despite knowing that the whole account Gillem had given them was a bald-faced lie. His parents had told him no such thing, and they told him everything. Yet, it seemed only he knew that, and even though he wasn't sure of it, he was pretty sure Gillem knew it, too. But, he played along.

Lefty sat swishing the coffee in circles inside his mug. He felt tired, exhausted rather, something he had not ever encountered before. He said, "Georgio, do you miss Bone?"

"Ah, sort of. I mean, I miss Venir and Chongo, and those biscuits Luga made for me. Those were the best! The food here is great, but there's nothing that compares to 'The Georgio'."

Lefty swore he heard the boy's tummy rumble.

"I kinda miss the stables, too for some odd reason," Georgio said.

"Do you miss Melegal?"

"Hah! No way, not that guy."

"Really?"

"Yes … well, mostly yes anyway. He never said anything nice to me, not once. He'd pay me sometimes and steal it back and try to tell me I lost it."

"He did not."

"Did, too!"

Lefty put his finger to his lips and said, "Ssshh!"

"So," Georgio said, "do you miss Melegal?"

Lefty shrugged. "Yeah."

"Why? He's mean," Georgio said, slurping his coffee and wiping it on his sleeve.

"No he isn't, he just makes things hard on you. It's for your own good, I think. You just think its mean. I think that's how he teaches us things."

Georgio laughed and took another drink of his coffee.

"He's a mean teacher, then. I miss Venir. He's never mean to me. He knows how to smile and tell story. He lights up a room. Melegal scares away the fun."

Lefty was shaking his head as he said, "See, Venir scares me."

"What? That's silly. You're scared of everything, Lefty, even your own kind. I see how you look at Gillem. He's harmless, and you act like he's a ghost."

"I do not. What do you mean?"

"You bounce on your toes and your eyes dart around. You keep wiping your nose on that handkerchief," Georgio said as he drained his cup, walked over to the couch, laid down, and yawned. Lefty was stunned at his friend's accurate recount of his nervous actions. If Georgio took notice of such things, then certainly others could detect his nervousness as well. Now he understood what Gillem had meant when he'd said, "You got to act yerself." It had never made any sense, until now. Now though, the only thing he wanted was for Kam to wake up. He had no one but Georgio now. He wanted to tell him about Gillem and Palos, but Georgio wouldn't understand, and would certainly tell Kam. He was tempted to shake her and tell her himself. Then he had an idea.

"I'm gonna check on Kam."

Kam was still, breathing her only movement. Lefty ran his little fingers over her hair, and then nudged her shoulder. He did it again, a little harder this time. She didn't move, resting like a beautiful corpse. He whispered in her ear the whole truth about Gillem and Palos and the pact he had made with them. When he was finished, he felt better. *I just hope when she wakes up she doesn't remember any of that.* He turned to walk away and heard a rustle. When he looked back behind him, Kam was sitting up in her bed. He froze. *Oh no, I'm gonna get it now!*

Georgio's curly head raised up then flopped back down in the cushions as he answered with a muffled, "All right."

46

MELEGAL WAS FAMILIAR WITH EVERY card in the deck, all of which he had no desire to play. Most of them were of a physical nature, as the challenges tended to be brutish games. He could feel the eyes of Jeb and his men on him now, but he kept his eyes in the deck.

Sam held up a card with the standard of the tavern on one side. They all were like that. Then he turned it around; it was black. He handed it to one of the girls, plain and busty with pigtails. Each other girl picked a card from the deck and held it face-down to her chest. Sam put the remaining cards back in the leather pouch and held out his hand. Each woman set her card face down in his palm. He shuffled them, pudgy hands swift and deft, hard to follow without a trained eye. He fanned the cards out again.

Sam sauntered among the women as he spoke.

"Ah … here we are, patrons. The time has come. Each girl shall draw a card and place it on the board. That card represents one of the challenges, BUT the black card represents the woman, as fine she may be, who gets to pick the challenge." Sam sniffed one trollop's ginger-colored hair, and slapped another on the rump, bringing a squeal of delight. Then he stood out on the end of the stage and faced the challengers.

"Now men, it's not too late to back out," the *boo*'s came down like rain, "… but I wouldn't advise it, 'cause if ya did, the challenge would be trying to drag your sorry arse out of here!" The patrons let out a roar. Melegal was still, and the thugs just nodded and sneered. "All right then, let the drawing begin."

Sam fanned the cards out in his hands. The girls lined up in a row in front of him. The one with the foul mouth and frizzy hair drew first, rubbed it on her breasts and held it up high. It was a picture of the two fencing swords crossed over a bleeding moon.

"The Quick Fence!" Sam said, to the delight of the crowd as the strumpet set the card along the back board.

Good, Melegal thought.

The next girl, tiny as a boy, but saucy as the rest, drew next. The card pictured a bear wrestling an ogre on a pile of bones. The crowd cheered.

"The Grapple of Giants!"

Not good.

The next wench, more comely than the rest, with long legs and lashes, held up the next card. It was black.

"Ah!" the crowd said, nudging one another and clonking tankards together. It was this woman who would decide the fate of the game.

"I see Velvet has the controls of your destiny, men. I'd be telling her how ravishing she is if I were you," Sam said.

Good. It was the wench from earlier in the day, the one that had sat with him during the encounter with Brak and Vorla. Melegal caught her eye, and she smiled at him, as well as the rest. He had no way of knowing what was on her mind; he just hoped he hadn't offended her somehow. A vengeful wench could be troublesome if you crossed her one too many times.

Velvet placed the card on the shelf, bent over, lifted her skirt and got back in line. Shouts and whistles of delight came from the men.

The next woman, taller than most men, pale as ghost, with the figure of a plank, drew next. She held it up as if the weight of the card was a strain on her arms.

"Ooooh!" the crowd said.

It was a picture of a hatchet stuck in a man's head.

"Hatchet Catchin'!"

Not bad either, he thought. Whoever won the flip of a coin got the first toss. It was a game Melegal had only seen one time before. Both men had been drunk, and their misses had ended up in a draw.

"Two cards left!" cried the barkeep.

The last woman, rounder than the rest, took it and held it high over her hive of red hair. It pictured a rope tied around the waist of two burly men.

"The Tug!"

It was simple game, two men each trying to pull the other from his feet. Balance and power were the keys. Melegal didn't care for his chances against such heavier foes, but it could be done.

So far, most of the cards weren't much in his favor. Most challenges tended to favor more formidable men, but there were some games of skill as well, such as Hand Stabs. It seemed however, most of them were still in the deck.

"One last card!"

The last woman took it from her hand, a smile on her face. She held it up revealing a picture of a gauntleted fist smashing a wall of stone.

A cheer rang out.

"Iron gloves!"

Oh great! It was always a crowd favorite and the crowd had a major influence on these sports. There was nothing better than watching two grown beat the crap out of one another with metal gauntlets. Melegal glanced at Jeb, whose arms crossed his chest, head bobbing.

I'm sure there are other taverns better than this. The Chimera for one, maybe the Dirty Mongoose. His loose neck began to tighten. He found Velvet's eyes for a fleeting moment, catching Sam whispering harsh words in her ears. She nodded. *I need a new body guard.*

"Quiet! Quiet everyone!" Sam said, puffing his cigar. "It's time to let the Lady Velvet choose."

That's when more chanting began. The desperate and beleaguered faces of the thrill seekers would suffer a whipping in order to see a fight like this.

"Iron gloves! Iron gloves! Iron gloves!"

Melegal questioned his judgment. His pride could prove costly, and he knew it. Now that he was a Detective for a Royal House he could have called in favors, but that would compromise his need to operate in the shadows. Instead, he chose to gamble. He had been counting on hand stabs, knife tossing, coin stacking or something of the sort. Not one card seemed to favor his skills. He was pretty sure Sam had a hand in that. Either the barkeep wanted him gone, or the barkeep knew there wouldn't be much to gain playing the games he normally won. *Fat bastard's as crafty as me.* He could have used Billip right about now. The archer would have covered his back and purse.

"Quiet, everyone!" Sam yelled, gesturing the woman's way.

A hush came over the crowd as Velvet opened her mouth to speak.

"I choose ... IRON GLOVES!"

The roars, stomping and clapping began. Chairs and tables were dragged over the planks and in a moment the center of the tavern floor was cleared. Only a circle of crowding bodies remained. An old woman appeared on stage alongside Sam. She held a pair of bloodstained chainmail and iron plated gauntlets in each unsteady hand.

"Aye, listen up now. The challengers have a choice. They can name a champion if they like, assuming the champion doesn't refuse. Now, you man, are you to fight, or is it to be one of your men perhaps?"

"Nay, I'll fight for myself," Jeb said, spitting at Melegal's feet.

"You then, vested rogue, do you call on a champion then?"

He remembered the last time he was in a fist fight. He'd been an urchin on the losing end of a bludgeoning, one of many. It hadn't been long after that when Venir had come around and put an end to all of that. Today, there was no such man to bail him out. It was just another hurdle in a long and dreadful day. He cast a glance into the blood-thirsty crowd and noticed a few new ones had surfaced. Haze, Sis and Frigdah were there, too. He was tempted to call on the big one, Frigdah. *I bet she could mop him up.* He almost said something, but the drool on her chin and her blood-shot eyes suggested it wasn't a good idea. *Worthless sot.*

"No!"

"Then it's time to let the match begin!"

Melegal and Jeb stepped inside a ring of living inebriated flesh and bone. Sam stood between them.

"Here are the rules. You can only strike with the gloves and the gloves alone. No knees, elbows, head-butts or tackling. Hands! Nothing else of the sort or you'll be disqualified. Got it!"

Both men nodded.

"As for the gloves, you can use a fist or fingers, it doesn't matter. Whatever it takes until the other man yields or falls out cold! Shirts off, men! And drop your metal."

Melegal rolled his eyes. This was a part he had hoped would be overlooked. He slipped a dozen coins from his purse and shoved them into the hands of a bookie he knew. "On me," he whispered. The man nodded and disappeared. Haze was by his side now, a concerned look in her eyes as she looked over his shoulder. A cheer rose from the crowd. He turned around.

Jeb stood half-naked, pumping his short powerful arms in the air. He was meat, muscle and hard bone, with a block jaw and a broad chest of thick hair. He looked more like a grappler than a brawler, but his biceps suggested he had thrown a thousand punches or two. It was clear that the man had been trained in combat sometime in his life. Some ugly white scars were bald under his hairy chest, and a long white gash ran across his shoulder and neck. There was a brand on his arm, a symbol of certain fighters. This man had fought in Two-Ten City before, in the Pit. *Great.*

The coins were singing in Jeb's favor. The women began to catcall Jeb now as they hung on his gang's arms, squealing with delight. Jeb punched the air a bit as one of the men rubbed his shoulders. Sam tossed the iron gauntlets over to one of the other men. Jeb shoved his hands inside and punched his fist into his hand. The chainmail made a rattling sound, like tiny bones breaking. The man took a swig of grog, swished it around his mouth and swallowed.

Melegal pulled off his vest and shirt in a single motion and handed them over to Haze. His pants looked too large on him now, as the belt that held them up was tight around his waist. He felt cold as every eye in the room looked upon him. You could see his bones where there was no muscle, only tendon. He was pale and chicken-chested, his stomach sunken in from the looks of starvation. There wasn't a single hair on his chest, only scars, some small, others large. His elbows were knobby, as were his shoulders. His hair seemed longer than it had before, as if it was the only living thing on his body. When he moved, a thin, tested layer of muscle rippled underneath his pathetic skin. When he felt Haze's hand run along one of the scars on his back, he fought the need to twist away.

"Somebody feed the man before he fights!"

"Don't let the wafer die hungry, too!"

The room was an eruption of laughter. Even Sam, always business-like, seemed amused. Velvet the whore had wrapped her arms around one of the thugs, a mocking smile on her lips. He snatched the gauntlets that were coming his way from the air and slipped them on. Their warm and heavy metal bit into his skin. They had been made for a bigger and heavier man. He squeezed his hand inside; his bony hand could do little inside the slack. The old leather within was tattered and dry. He squeezed his fingers into a fist, open and closed. His palms began to perspire and stick to the leather. *Loosen up. You can do this.*

Sam spoke up, "It's almost that time! Just one more thing to do!"

Sam walked over and patted Jeb down. Melegal knew the man had no other weapons, but he looked covertly for other things: poison, powder, acid, or anything else the man could put on his gloves. Sam was careful, keeping the men away, his own men-for-hire anchoring the corners. Jeb was lathered up now, 210-pounds of meat and muscle. It was clear that Jeb liked his chances. Melegal listened to the betting. The odds ranged from 10-1 to 3-1 in Jeb's favor. Time was another factor taken in consideration, too. How long did they think Melegal could last? Still, Melegal had his fans, too. Many had seen the things he had pulled off before.

Sis walked up to him and whispered harsh words in his ear.

"Don't be losing the gold you owe us for the sword, Skinny."

"Don't be stupid and bet the sword," he retorted.

Sis nodded with her jaw jutted out, taking a slug of her ale and said, "Don't worry about the sword. And just so you know, I'm bettin' against yah. I hope that man tears ya to pieces."

Haze pulled Sis away saying, "Will you shut up. Your courage-building never works."

Sis shrugged. "Whose tryin' to build any courage? Heh-heh."

By this time Sam had walked over and begun to pat him down.

"Don't hurt 'em Sam!"

"Yeah, we can't win our money if you knock him out before the fight is over!"

"Somebody feed the man!"

"If he lives, I'll buy him a meal with my winnings!"

Sam said as he patted him down, "Take your hat off, Skinny Man."

"Ah," someone cried, "let him keep the hat; it'll hold his brains in."

"No hat," Sam said.

Oh great. Melegal slid it off and stuffed it in his pants pocket.

"That'll do," Sam said.

Looks like I'm gonna have to do this all by myself.

The Drunken Octopus was at an all-time high it seemed, making the sound that Melegal had come to adore so much over the years. A bunch of sots watching others suffer at the end of their miserable day. They all were sure they'd be winners tonight. The capacity level crowd was rumbling, shouting and jeering for the fight to begin. Men and women were standing on the bar top, chairs and tables, shoving one another and spilling more ale. A jug of wine sailed across the room and shattered against the wall.

"IRON GLOVES!"

"IRON GLOVES!"

They chanted, shaking the chandeliers.

Sam's pudgy face was dripping with sweat now as he wiped his face on his apron and shouted, "LET THE FIGHT BEGIN ON MY SIGNAL!"

The room quieted to a violent rustle.

Melegal squared off on Jeb, iron fists hanging at his sides, just a body length away. The thug stood a couple inches taller, sneering down at him.

"ONE!"

The air in the room tightened.

"TWO!"

Jeb drew his knotted arms back. Melegal lifted his gloves before his face. *Make it quick.*

"THREE!"

47

T HE SUB-LEVEL OF THE CITY of Three was unique. Unlike the sewers filled with rats and waste in the City of Bone, it was another network unto itself. It spanned only a fraction of the city above, and was only forty feet down, but there another world opened. The best and the worst of people lived, thrived, and failed there, just as well as in the world above. It was called The Nest, and Gillem Longfingers was headed there.

Gillem had cut his way through the City of Three and headed through the alley door where Lefty had escaped days earlier. It was pitch black as soon as he closed the door behind him. He was down the steps in moments and standing on a wooden platform that floated on water. A faint green light was near. A small lantern with the tiniest beacon glowed at the end of a roughly hewn gondola-like craft. The waters surrounding the craft reflected the dim light with a yellowish hue. The tiny boat rocked as Gillem slipped inside. He began rowing two small oars, whisking the craft away.

He had a hundred things playing inside his active mind. Foremost in his thoughts was the halfling boy, Lefty, his latest charge. It was good to be around one of his own kind, especially one with such potential. Gillem had mentored halflings before, but none of them had ever exceeded his expectations. Still, when it came to stealing, they were much better than humans, and the other races, for that matter.

The underground river flowed in a variety of directions. The channels were split by man-made docks that hovered on buoys over the water. Taking the wrong channel could be dangerous if not fatal. The inhabitants of The Nest wanted it this way: unsafe for visitors and favorable to privacy of the highest degree.

Gillem looked up where a myriad of shiny stones winked in and out like stars in the night. Someone had put them there long ago, when the city was built above and the waterways were designed to filter into the city below. As these shiny stones guided him to The Nest, he was reminded of his childhood, night fishing on a canoe, looking into the starry sky. It made him feel old, though, and so did being around Lefty. He saw a lot of what he used to be in the boy. He frowned. *Too bad for him.*

The sound of creaking pipes and flowing water could be heard from above. The waters from the three massive waterfalls outside of the city all flowed through channels and enormous pipes underneath the city. It was here that the water was pumped up into the public fountains and reservoirs. The shiny stones above were placed along the copper pipes and girders that supported the streets. Gillem understood their meaning and layout, even though it was dwarven. The lights were maps and signs, making it easy for workers to find their way back and forth without any light. Still, the making of it all was a marvel he would never fully understand.

Gillem rowed through a stone archway, one of dozens that interlocked the channels. More light began to welcome him from the opposite end. It took about two dozen strokes before he was through. His back began to ache from the effort, something that had never happened before.

"Oh my, a back ache?"

He wanted to rub it, but that could wait. He was home. He turned the craft around to face the underground port city so he could gaze at it. The city was a row of waterfront buildings running along a monstrous boardwalk. Tiny boats like his were docked all around it, many much bigger, but most were as small as his. Torches were burning along the boardwalk, and light filled the glass panes from the dingy buildings in the background. It had been more than thirty years ago, the first time he had come down here as a young man. It hadn't been Palos that brought him, but rather Palzor the father. The first time he saw it he was far from fascinated, filled with dread instead.

He sighed, shook his head, and rowed on until he pulled into a slip, tied the boat off, and hopped up on the dock. It wasn't long before familiar voices were coming his way.

"Aye, Gillem!" one man said.

"Gillem! I'm buying; my gal had twins above!" another commented.

"You gonna be at the games tonight!"

He waved and nodded, offering the usual handshakes and smiles.

"I'll be there," he said.

There were just over five thousand people down here, and he was pretty sure he knew them all by name. They all knew his. He was a lieutenant under Palzor, and one didn't become that without making a name for himself. As he strolled onto the boardwalk he was greeted by more enthusiastic nods and glances. He reached in his vest pocket and pulled out his pipe. A mintaur, a bit taller than he, walked over with a small pouch and a slender burning stick. Gillem reached inside the pouch and pinched the moist tobacco between his fingers. He sniffed it and took a moment to let the rich aroma fill his nose. He stuffed it into his pipe, put the flaming stick to it, sucked in, puffed at the smoke, and nodded to the mintaur. The ram-faced man bumped elbows with him and walked on. Several pipe-smoking dwarves who were fishing along the docks tipped their hats to him as he went by.

He cut down an alley, noting the gigantic chimney-like construction that was the center of The Nest. Small tufts of smoke were billowing out of the stack as it plunged upward into the darkness. He crossed another street into another alley. The traffic of people began to thicken. The Nest wasn't just full of thieves. No, many other things happened beneath the City of Three. The mintaurs and dwarves were a big part of the city's construction force. They worked hand in hand, day and night, keeping the belly of the infrastructure in order.

Men were still a ruling lot, and not a one could be trusted above, but down in The Nest, the thieves' code prevailed. Violating the code down here could mean a quick and easy death, but everything above was fair game. There was a brotherhood at The Nest, one hundred rogues strong, of all races, from all across the lands of Bish. If you came of your own free will, you were safer here than anywhere. But, it wasn't the kind of place where just anyone would want to stay. Gillem had taken over a decade to get used to it, and some days, like today, his discomfort and paranoia returned. He popped every knuckle on his long fingers as he stood outside of Palos's home. *Poor boy; poor little Lefty.*

48

"I'VE NEVER HEARD A MAN cry so much before, have you?"

The City Watchman shook his head saying, "No, I don't think I've even heard a woman cry that much."

There were three of them in all, hardy men of the City Watch. They had been all but dragged into the cramped alley by the distraught locals. It was places like this they tended to ignore, but seeing how it bordered on the district lines, they felt an obligation. The sound of the wailing man was disturbing, and on gentle feet they headed down the alley to investigate. The wails would come and go, like that of a wounded bear, loud and raw. Each carrying a watchman's club in hand, they headed deeper down the lane. The buzz of flies caught their ears. When they reached the end, there it was, a litter of dead men. They had all seen wounded and dead men before, but nothing like this. The sight turned their veins to ice. Each body looked to have been chopped in half a dozen times. One man's face was sheared off between the skull and eyes. Another man's leg had been cut off. There was blood everywhere. One man's entrails had been ripped from his body and strewn from one wall to another. Two of the City Watchmen retched.

Not far away was the wailing man, with wet blood coating him from head to toe. A dead woman was cradled in his arms, and a gory sword lay on the ground behind him. All the watch could do was look at one another dumbfoundedly as they eyed the man. For twenty minutes no one said anything, and then the investigation began.

"So now what?"

"Eh … grab that crossbow over there and cover that man."

One of the watchmen did so, eyes never leaving the sobbing form of Brak. The man-boy wasn't paying them any mind.

"These dead are thieves, Sergeant. I can tell by their clothes. Look at this arm," the man said, as he held up the entire appendage. He was the only watchman that hadn't retched. He seemed more enamored by the scene than disgusted.

"Will you put that thing down? I can see they're thieves."

"Well, I say the less thieves the bet—"

"MAAAAAAHHHHHH!" Brak moaned.

All of the watchmen jumped, one of them plugging his fingers in his ears. A small crowd of people had gathered behind them. The crowd's confidence seemed to build as they began to fill the alley with speculating voices.

"You!" the sergeant said, pointing at a local. One man pointed to his chest. "Yes, you. Go to the nearest station and tell them we need a carrion wagon. Move!" The man disappeared. "As for the rest of you, you better be gone before the wagon comes, or I'll arrest you." He pulled out his watch stick and added, "Or beat the tar from you!"

"Shoot that moaning murderer!" one shouted back.

"Yeah!" the crowd added, bunching into a small mob.

"Turn the crossbow on them," the sergeant said.

"Hey, we didn't kill no one. He did!" one man pointed towards Brak.

The sergeant added, "How do I know that? For all I know you are behind the whole thing. How could one man kill five? Huh? Can you tell me that? He musta had some help, wouldn't you say? You look awfully suspicious to me. Come over here. I've got some questioning to do. How about we take you down to the dungeons and wring the truth out of you?"

The sergeant smiled as the little mob quickly dispersed. He walked over to the moaning man, whose entire face was streaked with tears. Brak looked like his mind was only on one thing, his dead mother. The sergeant pushed the gory sword farther away with his foot. Brak paid it no mind, only sobbing and rocking his mother.

"He's wounded," the sergeant said over his shoulder, "look at the bolt sticking out of him."

The other watchmen nodded with a look of awe.

"So, what do we do, Boss?"

The sergeant looked at Brak and at the corpses, as well as all around the alley.

He shook his head and said, "Looks like these two strangers were getting robbed. The woman fought and died. It looks like self-defense. Maybe if I can get the man to talk he can tell us what's going on."

"But Boss, he couldn't have killed five armed men, could he?"

"You ever been to war?"

"No," one said.

"Me either," said the other.

"Well, I have. I saw a man kill ten before, saved my life and many others. He fought like a wild beast. It was the scariest thing I ever saw, and he was on my side. Sometimes things snap in a man and he goes berserk, twists into something else, completely unimaginable. Seems to me this big fella here went berserk."

"Want us to grab these weapons?"

"Get 'em all, and check their pockets, too. Might be we have an early payday."

Brak was oblivious to the men around him, the lancing pain in his shoulder, and his dripping wounds. All he knew was his mah didn't move; her frozen eyes stared at the darkening sky. He had been with her every single day of his life, fourteen years, and now she was gone, and he was lost and alone. Why he cried and moaned he didn't know, because he had never done it before. Now, more than ever he wanted to go home, take her home, back to the country. Maybe she could come back to life there.

He clutched her body and wiped her hair from her face, smearing it with his blood. He began wiping her face with his cloak, but it did little good. He pulled her close again and a pouch fell from her hand. He picked it up.

"Boss, did you see that?" one of the men nearby said.

"Yeah, I saw it. Get the crossbow ready."

It was the first time Brak paid the men any mind at all. They looked old, ugly, and dangerous, much like the ones that had killed Vorla. His heart began to race again. He pulled her closer, and then he noticed their uniforms, like on the guards that had helped his mah, and he settled down a bit. One of the guards, bigger and older than the others, sheathed his sword.

"Man? It's gonna cost you to bury this mess. Give us the purse and I can make it all go away."

Brak sat in silence, rocking his mother. The words he heard, but didn't comprehend.

"Trust us, Man. We can make this easy or make it hard."

Why was the guard calling him a man? Why did people always call him names that he wasn't? His mah had told him he was different, but most of the time he didn't understand what she meant. He had become a man suddenly, without the opportunity to grow up. Man-child.

"Can you help my Mah?" he said.

The man looked at him funny.

"Huh?"

"Can you help her?"

"Sure, sure we can. Just let me have the purse."

Brak squeezed the bag of coins tight in his hand and then tossed it to the guard. The watchmen all had bewildered looks on their faces.

"Now, help my Mah!"

Things started to turn fuzzy in Brak's mind. The guard he was talking to got a big smile on his face when he saw inside the purse of coins.

"Very well, pick her up and follow me, then."

Brak picked up Vorla, and the men had to tilt their heads back to see his face once he was standing. The watchmen went over and gathered his sword and his mah's.

If they were going to kill him, he didn't think he minded. He stayed still.

"Is this really your mother, Mister?"

Brak nodded.

"Strange," the man said, shaking his head and putting Brak's sword back in his sheath. The man sheathed Vorla's sword, too and peered at her face. "I am sorry about your mother, Son. She was a pretty one. Follow me."

Brak followed, his head downcast, with no ideas about anything. His mah had always taught him to listen to his elders, never explaining that could be a bad thing.

The head watchman said, "Wait for the carrion wagon. Tell 'em nothing, if you want your share. I'll explain when I get back."

"Leave the purse with us!" one said.

"Shut up! I'll be back like I said!"

Brak carried his mah, gazing into her face, not making a sound, oblivious to the staring faces in his midst.

"You can't be lugging your dead mother around, Son. You're gonna have dispose of her body. There's nowhere to bury her around here, either. You're gonna have to have her burned."

"What? No!"

"Hush, Man, there's no choice. It's either this or you'll have put her on the cart with all those you chopped up. At least this way you can see her go."

Fresh tears were running down his cheeks as he followed the man he didn't know. He noticed hot air blasting on his face and looked up. An open iron gate was in front of him, tall and thick with twisted bars. Inside a desolate facility the pair went, and down a wide set of stone stairs. Brak could hear the sound of a thousand roaring fires ahead as blood and sweat dripped down his face.

The watchman stopped and said, "Son, I can do this if you want me to."

"Do what?" Brak stammered, holding his mah tighter.

"Ah ... this is it, where the dead go ... into the inferno."

"You burn them like wood?"

"No choice. I've done it a hundred times at least. It's not something a man should get used to, but you do. It's better than the sewers, or being eaten by the dogs. There are people that pay to eat people, too. Your mother could end up with them. I don't think you want that."

Brak had never imagined such a thing, but now images rose in his mind that were crystal clear. He stepped forward and said, "No, I'll go."

"All right then. Tell you what, get whatever you want to keep of her things, and say your good-byes. I'll ready the chute," the watchmen said, his gray bearded face moist with sweat. The man set his pack down.

Brak watched the man's face become illuminated for moment in orange wavering light, as he rounded a corner.

Brak set his mah down and ran his hands over her clothes. Whatever she had, he put it in his pack. He kneeled beside her and looked into her eyes one last time before he closed them.

"I'm gonna miss you, Mah ..." he said with a last heavy sigh. His sobs renewed.

He took her sword off last and looped it over his shoulder. He picked her up and walked around the corner. The heat jumped another fifty degrees. He'd never experienced such heat before. It was intense, like a sun stuck in the ground. Squinting, he headed toward the black silhouette of a man. The man wasn't alone; another one with long leather gloves, goggles and a heavy apron was at his side.

"Set her here, Mister."

Brak set her on a long metal slab that was hooked to a network of chains. The man in goggles began pulling at the rattling chains, hoisting the woman up with the slab. Brak looked over at the giant-sized rectangular opening. It was bright orange and yellow, but he couldn't see the roaring flames. He stepped toward the retaining wall that housed the fire below.

The watchman grabbed his arm and said, "You can't look in there, Son, it'll blind you. Just watch her go. It's time to say your last good-byes."

When Brak looked up again, the slab was moving over the edge of the fiery pit. He heard metal gears winding up, and the slab began to tip forward. He heard nothing as she slid from the slab and down into the fire. He screamed.

"Whatever goes in never comes out. Sorry, Son. Life's a Bish."

49

T HE SMELL OF HOT FOOD filled his nostrils, but it was nothing compared to the kitchens above the surface. Coarse voices could be heard mixed in with delightful giggles. Gillem erased the grim look off his face with a broad smile as he pushed his way through a pair of swinging doors. No more than ten men and women were scattered about a dimly lit tavern room. He made a quick wave as a few hands raised a glass to him and back to their lips. A staircase awaited on the other side of the room. Up he went, meeting a gruesome-looking man with a crooked nose who towered over the top of him. Crooked Nose Man was standing in front of a closed door, two shortswords strapped on his hips. Farther down the balcony, another man nodded at Gillem. This man was holding a crossbow over the rail and dangling a toothpick from his mouth.

Crooked Nose Man uncrossed his arms and cleared his throat before saying, "Welcome, Master Gillem."

He nodded and said, "What kind of mood is he in today, Thorn?"

"Most of the ladies just left, so I'd say right now he's pretty good. Want me to check?"

"Nah ... I'll take my chances," he said.

Thorn opened the door and stepped aside so Gillem could enter. *I hope the tramps didn't disappoint him.*

The master suite was divine in comparison to everything else in The Nest. The room was designed around a marble fireplace mantle and a dining table with a dozen chairs. Candles with the girth of a man and half as tall were lit and scattered around the room. He could smell the freshly cut flowers that bloomed in crystal vases. The carpet was of royal fiber, hand stitched by the finest urchins of Holm. Paintings, rare and picturesque, decorated the walls of the room. A rack of weaponry stood shining in the corner. Everything was refined, perfect, and exquisite, even by the highest of Royal standards.

Gillem sat down at the long table where goblets and a carafe of wine awaited him. The fire roared with life, toasting him from his head to his toes. He admired a great sword that gleamed over the mantle. It looked unnatural to him: six feet of gleaming superior steel. How could any man possibly wield such a thing? But according to Palzor it had been done. In the middle of the table were dozens of neatly stacked columns of silver and gold coins. His mouth watered. Wiping the sweat from his brow, he moved down another seat, away from the fire.

Gillem helped himself to some wine and waited. He could hear the rustling of sheets from behind a nearby door, and a pair of light footsteps hitting the floor. The door opened, and a short pudgy man in a fluffy maroon robe and matching slippers stepped out.

"Ah, Gillem, I thought I heard someone come in. Welcome back," Palos said.

The tightness in his chest began to ease. It seemed the past few days had been good ones. The coins on the table were evidence of that.

A woman with dark and mysterious features emerged, wearing a shear black slip and nothing else. She tiptoed up, wrapped her arms around Palos from behind, and sucked on his ear.

"Ah ... that's the spot, Dear. But I've got company; Master Gillem is here."

"Hello, Master Gillem," she said, "would you like me to send for some of my girls?"

"No thanks," he said, puffing on his pipe.

"Later perhaps?"

"Perhaps."

"Oh, leave the man alone, Woman. He just got here," Palos said with a happy look on his face. "Now, be a bad girl: go back in the bedroom and wait for me."

"As you wish, Master Palos," she said in his ear as she slipped through the door and closed it behind her.

Palos pulled up a chair and sat down across from Gillem. The man's hair was a mess, and his eyes were glassy and wide. Gillem pushed him over a goblet of wine. Palos gulped it down.

"Ah … now, she knows how to make a man thirsty, and hungry. Thorn! Thorn!" he yelled.

The main door opened and Thorn's form filled the doorway saying, "Yes, Master Palos?"

"Food! Now!"

"Right away," the big man responded, closing the door.

"So Gillem, tell me about things: the boy, the Magi Roost, and Kam." Palos began to drift into thought. "Kam … she is a bit of perfection, isn't she. I'd love to nuzzle my face in those perfect breasts once more. I was so close, Gillem, so close … but she evaded my charms," Palos said, his hands gripping the air in front of him.

"She is a beautiful lady. It'd be a shame to see her go before you got another try at her."

"Pah … those Royals are hard nuts to crack sometimes, but when they owe you a favor, they pay up. Kam's family owes us no favors, though. This halfling, Lefty, should help with that. Tell me the latest, and remember, things have been good, I'd hate to have any bad news today."

Yes, I'd hate that, too.

"Kam's sudden fever was remedied by her family. Within a day she was back home. It was a good break, giving me time to set things in motion quicker. The boy is coming along fine. He's tentative and fearful, but I'm hardening him up."

"How so?"

"I've been applying palm root to him."

"Why?" Palos said, as Gillem refilled his goblet.

"It's keeping the woman down. The longer she's out, the more he worries. I'm giving him tasks under pressure and worry. Besides, without her around it's easier for me to mentor him. That strange fever was a good thing. I'm getting a stronger hold on him each day. In time he'll toughen like leather, and worry no more. "

The fire reflected in Palos's gazing eyes. Gillem knew what the man was thinking. He didn't like him using palm root, which was something Palos didn't understand or care for. Gillem had a gift with herbal toxins, a halfling legacy. The palm root was dissolved in the bucket of water by Kam's bed. Gillem had been sneaking in there to add it from time to time. The wash cloth would fill with the stuff. One application would knock a human out for a week or more. The trick was that halflings and dwarves were immune to it.

"Palm root," Palos mumbled, his voice trailing off as he stared into his goblet. Palos's eyes met his.

"It seemed necessary, Sir. It's working fine. The woman could be out for good, if you asked."

Palos rubbed his head and said, "No, it's fine. I'd rather she was knocked out than dead. I couldn't possibly relieve the miserable world of such a fine woman as that. Her breasts are magnificent, as beautiful as the rising suns." Palos rubbed his finger under his chin, eyes closing as he said no more.

It was an awkward moment. Gillem intervened.

"Ahem." Palos's eyes snapped up as he shifted in his chair. "Ah … where was I? Oh … I would just give it another week Gillem, no more. I don't need her family getting too concerned. They have the power to find us out. Those magi are nothing short of the most arrogant creatures in the world. They might turn a blind eye to trivial matters, but they can still be dangerous. They only tolerate us because of all the dirty work we do for them. We've been running their errands forever it seems, finding every ingredient needed in order to cast their little spells."

Palos was waving his arms in the air in imitation.

"We've stolen and smuggled every ounce of their special needs for centuries: parchment, skin, bone, roots, herbs, minerals, organs, dung, fruit, hair, ink, powders and so forth. They haggle as fiercely as us, but in the end they pay well. Shaking down the merchants is a workload too: bribing the guards, stealing keys, starting fires. Ah … Gillem, I miss the days when you tutored me, running the streets and taking whatever we wanted. Now, I stay confined, Prince of the Underground, while my father advises from above. Such an inheritance this is, with enough water and gold to drown a giant."

Thorn stepped inside with a tray of food and set it in front of Palos. The crooked-nosed man's eyes flicked back and forth to the piles of gold and silver.

"It's about time, Thorn, now get your greedy eyes off my gold. That's for me, not a dumb arse like you!"

Thorn slammed the door behind him.

"Buffoon!" Palos said, stuffing a roll into his mouth. "But you gotta have them. No telling when assassins might be about. Now where was I?"

"You were talking about missing the streets and your inheritance. Can I remind you that you will be the King of the Streets above one day, like your father?"

"Ah Gillem, I could slap you. You know my greedy heart doesn't want to wait. I want it now!" he said, slamming his fist on the table. His face turned full of fire, then back to its warming charm. "Oh, I guess I can wait … a little while longer. Now, back to the boy … What is your long-term plan? I can't have you spending too much time with him. We still have recruiting to do. Our numbers are getting thin. The Royals just beheaded eight of our brothers a few weeks ago."

Gillem had friends among those men, and Palos did, too. They were a family, but they didn't mourn the consequences of their risky actions for very long. There were no graves or funerals for thieves. It was the incinerators for them. If there was one thing Gillem feared, it was dying on the end of a noose. The spectacle of the men's tongues hanging out and their feet twitching had burned a vivid impression in his mind. He wasn't required to watch hangings, but he always did. It was like watching his own death. He hoped he wasn't leading Lefty to a similar fate, but for now he had no choice.

"I'll work him on the streets; keep him with me as often as can be. He's fast-learning, this one. He already knew how to pick a lock, even has his own tools. You've seen the skims he's already set up," Gillem said as he rubbed his long-fingered hands together. "I'll be able to keep recruiting up there, too. There are plenty of hapless humans running around. There's got to be some talent in some of them."

"Mmmph … good Gillem, good," Palos said, washing his food down with more wine. "Keep me informed, every week. If Kam wakes up, let me know immediately. I can't believe the woman had the gall to attack me. The favor she owes me in the meantime is the boy; she just doesn't know it yet."

Gillem's stomach crawled, the way the man said it.

"Find something else we can use against her while you train the boy, too. Until the next time, Gillem," Palos said, his eyes flickering from the stacks of coins to his.

"Until then Master Palos," Gillem said, adding four gold to one pile and three silver to the other as he walked away.

"I'll expect more than that that next time, much more."

Gillem heard the man scoot his chair across the floor and slam the bedroom door behind. He left for the city above, his heart heavy for the first time in decades. Lefty Lightfoot's life was being staged for him. The halfling would be a bound prisoner of sorts. It was a sad feeling. *The boy would have been better off in Bone.*

50

H E WAS LYING DOWN NOW, or so he thought. He tried to sleep, but didn't know if he was. His dreams were intertwined with nightmares. Everywhere was white mist, no day, no night, just mist. Even his thoughts and memories seemed fogged by it. Venir could have sworn that he was dead, but his aching body and groaning stomach suggested otherwise. He never could have imagined that life could be so everlastingly miserable.

He rolled onto his stomach and rubbed the ground. He was pinching something like dirt in between his fingers. Other sounds began to echo in his mind, birds and water-like sounds. He got up and tried to follow, but nothing was there. The sounds came and went as he trudged onward, following the echoes only to have his hopes fade time and again. *Move or die.* There didn't seem to be a difference now.

He thought he was moving upward; a gentle slope seemed to slow his pace. The farther he went, the steeper it became. A new energy surged through him when the mist seemed to become brighter. He stumbled over something. *A rock?* Another one tripped him along the path. The new footing was different. Boulders began to crop up everywhere. He sat on one of the rocks, pulled out his canteen, and took a drink.

"Yes!"

He felt something around him now. A monolith of rock seemed to loom in the mist before him. He headed straight for it. It was there! A thrill rose inside of him. He was climbing like a mountain goat now, his powerful legs straining against the ever steepening grade. Upward he went, yards, miles, leagues. His fingers and feet slipped as he fought for foot holds. He slipped down time and again, only to fight his way back up. He kept going, knowing no mountain could be too tall to climb.

A blood curdling roar froze his blood. He didn't realize he stopped breathing. His body was immobilized. The unexpected sound rang in his ears. Another roar came, louder than the first and shaking the ground. Shards of rock began slipping down the jagged hill he was climbing. He found himself hanging on to a cleft in the rock when his ears started ringing with the sound of massive wings beating somewhere high above him.

WHUMP! WHUMP! WHUMP! SNORT!

Another roar followed, closer than the last one. Something whooshed through the mist over his head. He pressed himself into the mountain. It roared again, now farther away. The roars began to fade so that Venir could hear his blood rushing behind his temples. Every instinctual thought told him not to follow that sound, but he did anyway.

51

A TEN-FOOT-TALL SHAMBLING MOUND OF ROCK and dirt emerged from the ground. It was shaped like a man, just two tons heavier. The horses were already galloping away as Fogle Boon prepared a spell. The fear inside him caused the words of power to falter on his lips. Mood was yelling.

"Get away from this thing!"

Mood stood between him and the living rock pile, axes crossed before him. Ox the mintaur stood by his side, his own hand axes ready. The brave figures in front of him seemed insignificant as the elemental creature blocked out the rising suns. The ground shook as it stepped forward.

Mood dashed in, taking a swipe at its knee, rock debris scattering from the blow. The creature roared as it struck, hitting the ground hard as the Blood Ranger dove between its legs. Mood was chopping it from behind now, causing the elemental to turn away.

Fogle rubbed his hands together as he formed a spell on his lips. It was coming, mystic power flowing into him as from an opened dam. He caught a glimpse of Mood getting punched flat to the ground. He raised his hands up and let the spell go. A burst of brilliant white light formed between his hands in a ball of swirling energy and shot forth in a jagged bolt of lightning. It blew a hole in the center of the elemental, bringing forth an enraged moan. The elemental turned on him, its black eye holes dark and angry in its shambled face.

Fogle Boon staggered back. His head was dizzy as he tried to recall another spell. He moved backward on quivering legs, stumbling as the elemental's steps shook the ground. Fogle Boon was frozen with fear. His spell should have destroyed the monster. *It can't be!* If that spell couldn't do it, then he didn't know what would. *Move or die.* That's what Venir had told him, but he couldn't move. Instead, he watched in fascination as the elemental rambled forward. Two powerful arms were dragging him away. It was Ox. *Pull me faster, Ox!* He could barely think, and his tongue clove to the roof of his gawping mouth. *Is this how I die? Run, Ox. Save yourself!*

The elemental was closing in. Ox let Fogle go. He fell back onto his elbows as the mintaur rushed ahead. All he could do was watch. The elemental, with a gaping hole in its chest, clamped its rocky hands around the chopping Ox, picking him up like a child's doll. Fogle watched in horror as he heard his friend's bones cracking inside the elemental's grip. Ox's eyes bulged out from the sockets as his ram face cried out like a dying sheep. Ox, his servant all of his life, was nothing more than a rodent to the elemental. Fogle shuddered as the elemental slammed his friend horns-first into the ground. The mintaur was dead, his body no longer humanoid, but a bloody pulp of flesh.

"NOOOOO!" Fogle Boon screamed.

Mood was on his feet again, limping toward the monstrous hulk. His axes began to carve out the backs of the elemental's knees. Fogle Boon gathered to his feet, stared at the mangled body that was his friend, and summoned everything he had. *You will not die in vain, OX!*

His mind became as sharp as a razor as he recalled some words of power he had never used before. The air began to swirl around him, fluttering his robes like flags in the wind. His mind intertwined his brilliance and emotion into a single focal point. He raised his arms above his head, and a sphere of scintillating color ebbed above him. The elemental knocked Mood to the ground again.

"OVER HERE, CREATURE!"

The elemental whirled on him and charged. Fogle Boon let it all go. The rush of the entire realm of magic at his command was exhilarating.

The sphere shot out like a boulder from a catapult. It smacked straight into the rocky body, wedging itself inside the gaping hole in its chest.

"FOR OX!" Fogle shouted as he clapped his hands together.

The sphere exploded in a burst of black energy. The elemental was blasted into gravel that scattered like drops flying from a rock dropped in a puddle. Fogle Boon could feel the rain of tiny rocks all over his face. *That felt good!* He could still feel the energy inside him, simmering like a bad temper he had never let out. His grandfather Boon had told him,

"It's not what you know, it's what's inside you that matters most."

There certainly was something inside of him, and it felt good letting it out.

He looked around and saw a pile of rocks moving. *It's gathering itself.* Mood emerged from the element's rubble. Fogle sighed. The giant dwarf was covered from head to toe in brown soot with little evidence showing of his red beard. The big figure limped over to him.

"Are you all right?" Fogle asked.

Dusting himself off, Mood said, "Aye, I'm well. That was somethin' else you did, Mage. I've fought an elemental before. It takes time to whittle one down, but you did it in no time … impressive." Mood started looking around. "Where's yer mintaur?"

Fogle didn't see the busted body at first. Then he noticed a pair of hooves sticking up from under the dirt. A great feeling of sadness settled over him when he realized he would have to dig his friend out.

Fogle nodded and said, "He's over there. It was awful, the worst thing I have ever seen. That monster squeezed him like a piece of ripened fruit." He started to tremble, and his eyes teared up. He closed them and turned away from Mood.

"Tis a shame. I like them mintaurs. Much like us dwarves, with hooves and horns. He gave his life for ya. No better kind of friend than that."

Mood's words sunk in. Fogle Boon had never been really sure what the mintaur was to him, besides a servant he had all his life. Never once had he called him friend or even thanked him for what he did. He just suspected that was what mintaurs did. In the end, Ox had given Fogle Boon the only thing he ever had … his life.

"Would you like me to dig 'em out and bury him for you?" Mood asked.

"No … I'll bury him. It's the least I can do."

"I'll fetch the horses, then. They won't be too far away." Mood limped away.

Fogle Boon got on his knees and scooped away the dirt with his hands. It didn't take long before he had Ox outlined. All of the dirt did a good job coating all of the blood on Ox's smashed form. Mood returned with the horses just as Fogle picked the broken body up from the ground. The mintaur was even heavier than he imagined. It was like carrying water-filled saddle bags, and he could feel Ox's parts sloshing around inside his skin. On unsteady legs, he headed for the stone grave where the dead underling once laid. He set Ox down inside it.

"I'm gonna need your help with this next part, if you don't mind."

"Sure," Mood said.

"What do you do with your people's dead?"

"We carry 'em back to Dwarven Hole. We've got tombs there, deep in the ground. Funerals are important to us. Dwarves that die in battle are highly regarded, and most prefer that to aging to death. That's why we like to fight so much. Of course, we all live a pretty long time, anyway."

Fogle nodded and began picking up some of the small rocks and filling them inside the tomb. Mood worked on the bigger boulders. After a couple of hours it was done.

"It's a good burial, better than most get," Mood said.

"I don't even know if Ox had any family. If I met them what would I say?"

"He died saving your life. They'll be honored by that."

They both stood in silence, the wind whipping through their hair.

Fogle spoke. "What now, Mood? Are we going to track Venir, or that underling that crossed his words?"

"I'll not be following that underling into any dark holes. We lived. He ran. No sense in crossing that one again, not without Venir at least."

"Where do we start, the Mist?"

The King of the Blood Rangers didn't say anything. Instead, he stood staring into the mist. It was the most mysterious thing he had ever seen, endless and penetrating. The longer Fogle looked at it, the more lost he seemed. He felt small in its presence and wanted nothing more than to get away. It made him long for home, the City of Three. What was the right thing to do? What would Ox have done to find him? Would he have the courage to do the same?

52

M ELEGAL DUCKED UNDER JEB'S RIGHT cross. As another punch flew at him, he had little trouble dodging away. The man's eyes gave away everything he was going to do. Still, Melegal was no brawler. He was way out of his comfort zone. *Don't get hit.*

Across from him, Jeb was worked up.

"Come on, take a swing!"

Good, use your breath.

The crowd was booing and yelling obscenities now. They wanted blood, but he was determined not to spill his own.

"Fight him, Chicken Man!"

Jeb rushed in with a flurry of punches. Melegal simply held up his iron gauntlets, batting the blows away. Still, it stung his delicate hands inside the over-sized armor. His hands were hot with sweat inside and he could smell the funk, like the sweat of a hundred rotting men. *Gonna need a lot of soap.* He kept his eyes on his opponent's. *Here he goes.* Every attack was telegraphed ahead by those eyes. *Drop the shoulder. Upper cut. Blink hard. Body shot. Snort. A haymaker's coming.*

Jeb's face was full of frustration. Melegal could see how hard it could be to fight something you couldn't touch.

"Come on, Girl, fight like a ma—"

Smack! Smack! Smack!

Melegal loaded Jeb's face with three striking jabs, cutting open Jeb's cheek. He scored first blood. The crowd went wild. A thrill went through his spine. People were cheering him on, and he liked it. He shook his loose hands. *That hurts!* The gauntlets were cutting into his knuckles where the leather was long gone.

Jeb wasn't dazed for long. His eyes were still sharp and focused. He crashed his gauntlets together and came on, fists lowered. Melegal stabbed him in the mouth, rocking back his head. The man came on like an angry bull. The crowd screamed just as Jeb stepped into another mouthful of iron. Still, Melegal felt like he was stabbing a rock. *Knock him in the chin, Fool!*

When Melegal got distracted by the sounds of coins clinking in his favor, his opponent slipped in and almost snapped his own head back. Melegal dodged just in time. *Slat!* Jeb pressed on, eyes wary, but full of fury. Blood was dripping from the man's face, and his busted lips were beginning to swell. The circle of people surrounding them seemed to get tighter as Melegal continued to step away and jab.

Melegal was surprised at how heavy his arms were getting. Every fiber of muscle started to knot in his back and shoulders. Jeb began swinging again, landing heavy blows on his arms. Melegal winced as he balled up and danced away. The iron gloves were up above Jeb's chin and his punches became more persistent. The man's lower body was open, begging for a heavy blow, but Melegal didn't have that kind of strength. He side-stepped an uppercut and drove his fist into the man's kidney. Jeb groaned, punched out, and backed off. A series of boo's followed.

He punched into the man's stomach again. The man was rugged and hard though, every bit the solid soldier he appeared to be. The man's iron gloves stayed up, a bloodied grin on his face.

"Take him, Jeb. He can't hurt you!"

It seemed true. The man had forty pounds on him, if not more. Jeb was a fighter and a good survivor who had made it this far. Melegal's alert eyes didn't blink. He knew the man was planning something.

Jeb stepped back and beat his hairy chest with a mailed hand.

"Come on, Coward!"

Jeb beckoned the roaring crowd by rolling his fists in the air. Melegal edged closer. *Keep that chin out there.* The thug leapt inside at him, a flurry of punches coming his way. Melegal twisted away, heavy handed blows landing along his back and ribs. The punches that landed hurt as they cracked into his side.

"You got him!"

"Finished him!"

Melegal slumped over, clutching at his side, shuffling away from the flurry of Jeb's iron fists. He could see the man's eyes light up as he came in for the knock out. Jeb's jaws were clenching as he dropped his shoulder.

SMACK!

Melegal hit Jeb in the chin with everything he had. The man wobbled backward. A collective gasp filled the room. He waited for the man's eyes to roll up in his head as he fell to the floor on his arse. Jeb grabbed his blood smeared chin, shook his head and howled.

Slat!

Jeb hopped back on his feet, laughed, and came after him faster and stronger than before. Melegal had given the man his best shot, but the man's jaw was as sturdy as a dwarf's. He let on a flurry of jabs, cutting into the man's face, but the man shrugged it all off like rain drops. He felt something hard glance across his bony ribs, causing him to suck the air in his teeth. Then he felt like he was being beaten with a giant meat tenderizer. Something hard slammed into his ear, and the sound of the cheers was gone. Blood was dripping in his eyes and a snarling figure stood before him like a wolverine. Melegal had been beaten by many things, many times before, years ago, but he didn't remember it feeling like this. The thunderous blows were painful, like mallets used to drive spikes. His body quivered, and his strength left him. He tried to cover up, but he ended up falling down instead, blacking out as soon as his head hit the floor.

He woke up to the smell of coffee, followed by a great deal of pain rippling through his body. Opening his eyes ached, and one was swollen shut. He was in his apartment, lying on his cot. At Melegal's table sat a woman, Haze, stroking the black fur of a muscular feline, Octopus. He tried to sit up and say, "What are you doing here?" but his jaw was too stiff. He let out a muffled grunt, forcing his feet to the floor. It felt like his muscles were tearing inside of him.

Haze came over to him and said, "You need to be still. You don't want to tear the stitches."

What? Stitches?

He started with his face. He could feel three rough bumps over his face, two long and one short. It didn't feel like too bad of a job though. They were tight, done by a deft hand.

"The scars won't be bad, if any at all, depending on how good a healer you are."

Melegal realized his shirt was off as his fingers tested the welts and bruises along the rest of his body. His ribs were sore, and his back felt broken. He wriggled some looseness back into his jaw. He was starving and had an awful headache.

"Coffee," he managed to say.

Haze poured him a fresh mug as Octopus rumbled on the table. The cat had been spending more time in his apartment lately. Melegal had seen to it that the cat had a way in through the window. He had nothing there to steal. His belongings were elsewhere now. Besides, the apartment was a difficult place to get into. Only someone that really wanted something would try, and Melegal didn't have anything that people wanted. He was sure of that.

He took the coffee from Haze and had a painful sip. Still, it was good coffee, almost good enough to give him a reason to live.

"So what happened, and how did you get in?"

She sat back down at the table and started stroking the cat again. Her shoulders were pulled back, a small smile on her lips. He knew what she was thinking, that he somehow owed her one, but he would put an end to that. He wouldn't have her roosting in his nest for long. She tossed her greasy black hair with a whip of her thin neck. Her eyes were flickered with pride.

"It was a good fight until he caught you. He was good, even better than I thought. Turns out he's used the iron gloves before … many times. I think the fix was in on you. They don't like you here anymore."

He rolled his shoulders and said, "Octopus does."

"Hmph … maybe so. Anyway, as I said, it was a good fight. But when he clipped you good, there was nothing left in you. POW! Your eyes rolled up in your head and that man was all over you. I don't know how you kept your feet so long. The crowd was so loud a chandelier fell from the roof. Of course, a pair of midgets was hanging off of it, but it made for a great effect."

"I'm glad you enjoyed it."

Haze waved her hands at him and said, "Oh no I didn't. A lot of people didn't. Seeing you get beat to death is hard to watch. I thought for sure you would either be dead or have a cracked skull. That man, Jeb, he tried to stomp on your skull, but Frigdah covered you up as the bouncers pulled him away."

What?

"What? OW! That tub of lard laid down on me. You didn't stop her." He didn't know which hurt worse, saying it, or imagining it.

"She's hard to stop. Don't worry though, not too many people were laughing. Well, I mean, not everyone was laughing that is. At least not us, anyway." Her eyes darted away from his.

It was the most humiliating thing he had ever heard about himself. *Shielded by a fat woman, twice my size. I'm sure she'll want some gratuity, too.* He forced himself back onto his feet. *Good, they work.* His chest tightened as he patted down his pockets. *My hat's gone.*

"Here it is," Haze said, twirling the cap on her finger. "I took it out when I was looking for your key. The barkeep told me where your room was, but I already knew."

He walked over and snatched the cap off of her finger. He noticed his key lying on the table. He folded it inside his cap and tossed it onto the cot.

"You're welcome," she said.

He gave her a look.

"How's the coffee?"

"I'm still drinking it, aren't I?"

Haze was beginning to bother him, not because she was there, but because he didn't seem to mind her being there. She was all smiles now.

"Where's the sword?"

Haze pointed to the corner by the cupboard. Something was wrapped up and bound in cloth. He picked it up, undoing the bindings. There it was, scabbard and all. When he pulled a portion of the blade free, the steel shined in the dim light. The jewel-encrusted hilt was unlike any he had ever seen. He had never held it before, but it was clear to him it was special. It was the gift that Venir had given to Georgio, the blade that pierced the hide of the Vicious at the Warfield. It was funny how, if not for Tonio's longsword, Venir would have been dead. Now that blade was about to play another big part in his own life as well. He could still feel Lord Almen's strong grip around his throat. Hopefully, this sword would put an end to all of that tension.

"Sis and Frigdah already took some money from your purse. They said to tell you they lost a lot betting on you, and that you'd better understand. The rest is all there."

Melegal could feel the bulge in his pocket. There wasn't much left, as he had bet a lot on himself, too. Now he was broke and vanquished from his brothel stoop. He was no longer wanted in the Drunken Octopus. That message was clear. He wasn't ready to go anywhere yet, still, he had another place to go.

"I'm gonna need some salve for these wounds, too. Do you know where to get some?"

Haze's eyes brightened as she stuck her small chest out and said, "I know where to get the best there is."

He tossed her his remaining coins and said, "Good, will you get me some?"

"I'll be right back," she said, backing her way to the door. It was clear that she was all too ready to grant him another favor.

He waved at her as the door closed.

Good!

Grabbing his coffee, he reached down and stroked Octopus. The big cat yawned, its eight pearl white claws fanning out before it tucked them back underneath its chest. Melegal wasn't sure why the cat chose to keep company with him or why he allowed it, but seeing how he was short on friends these days, Octopus was as good as any.

"Octopus, why did you let that crazy woman in here? Am I going to have to get a dog?"

The cat rumbled on the table, the hairs on its back rising up.

"I was just teasing."

He sat down at the table and thought as he peered outside the small window. It was pitch black outside, close to midnight he supposed. He had been out awhile and hadn't even felt the woman stitching his face. He recounted the events of the day and tried to determine whether or not the nightmare was real. *It felt real*, he thought, as he shifted his swollen jaw.

"How was your day, Octopus?"

The cat was silent as its chest rose and fell without a worry in the world.

"I see. How I envy you, feline. Well, let me tell you about mine," he said, and he stroked the cat's furry pelt. "I woke up in the throes of passion with a succulent servant girl in Castle Almen. It was a promising start, but then I encountered a bastard of a man named Sefron. You would like him even less than I. He's fat, dirty and slimy, almost like a slug with arms and legs.

"Then I had the pleasure of meeting Lorda Almen, as picturesque a woman as could be. She bent my ear and told me to locate her son, Tonio. You remember him don't you?" he said, stroking the yawning cat.

"Then it was off to Lord Almen's study. Yes, the man gives me my charges and decides to throttle me before I even get started. He's dangerous, that one, possibly the most dangerous man I ever met."

How did that big man sneak up on me? ME!

"Ah … so I come back here, oddly enough, to be confronted by a voracious woman, Vorla. It seems my eyes jostled her ginormous son Brak, the supposed son of Venir. You should have seen this boy, fourteen years old and the size of two men. I think Venir would be proud of that one …"

Venir … if he had been there tonight, things wouldn't have been so bad. He took another sip and licked the salty scab that was building on his lip.

"Hmmm … then I get mugged by the City Watch on the Royal Roadway. I track the Motley Girls down into a dingy hole and throttle another guard. Things were actually looking up at that point. Then Haze leads me to the dungeon that houses Tonio."

He paused and looked around before he whispered to the cat.

"Don't tell anyone this, Octopus, but I romped with the skinny hag and she wasn't half bad. I almost enjoyed myself. Ahem … anyway, down a dripping stairwell I go. I put out my coin of light, well McKnight's actually, and there he was … Tonio. That evil bastard is alive! His eyes were as terrifying as anything I ever saw."

A candle-lit lamp was flickering nearby, and he got up and closed the window. He shivered and pulled a blanket over his narrow shoulders. "I must be getting old. It's too hot in this place to be cold."

He went back to drinking his coffee and stroking his cat.

"And now here I am, back in my home, after getting every bit of slat beat out of me."

He took another drink and went to lie down on his cot. He closed his aching eyes.

"Oh Octopus, how many more horrors will tomorrow bring?"

53

T HE ORCS WERE CHOPPING AT everything moving, and men and women were screaming in the heat of battle. Scorch just stood nearby, watching the carnage with interest. He looked like a mere man, refined like stained glass, dressed in little more than a traveling cloak and common clothes he had created for himself. He was fair-haired and blue-eyed, but not like that of common men, his features were more vivid and colorful.

A female screamed nearby, catching his attention. A rugged-faced orc was dragging a woman across the ground by her hair and another one was pulling away her clothes. *Perhaps this would be an ideal incident to intervene in.* He approached the orcs on casual feet, oblivious to the chaos that surrounded him. One of the orcs charged at him, a long blade high in his hand, and stabbed it deep into his bare chest. The blade sunk inches deep before it stopped. It was an uncomfortable feeling for Scorch, at worst.

The orcen man began to back away, eyes wary and uncertain.

"Huh … What man is this? He does not bleed!"

"I'll make him bleed," offered another.

The next orc punched the woman down, her body lying limp at his feet, and then stood up, pulled his sword from his sheath, and charged. "I bet my orcen steel can cut his throat!"

Scorch pulled the long knife free from his chest. It didn't seem like anything he had much need for, but given the situation it would do. The orc rushed in, sword slashing at his throat. As the orc's accurate sword thrusts passed right through Scorch, the orc's black eyes were filled with marvel.

"My sword!" it cried. "It won't touch him!"

Scorch took the moment to jam the knife inside of the orc's bewildered head. There was little thrill in it for him. He found the orcs repulsive and annoying. He decided it was time to eliminate them, but resorting to the use of their own violent nature was not his style. No, he would use something a little more sanitary to rid him of the vermin.

The orc that stabbed him was yelling something loud, and more began coming his way. He disintegrated the one that was yelling with a single thought. The others stopped, their ugly faces filled with fear. One of them exploded, followed by another. Blood and guts went everywhere. He didn't like that kind of mess, either, but he liked the results. The rest of the bandit orcs were running now, but he managed to disintegrate a few more to smelly ash before they were gone.

He noticed the blood and guts on his cloak as he looked around. The humans, whose form he had taken, were nowhere to be found. With another thought he changed his clothes, garnering a simpler and plainer set of robes and sandals. He stepped around the wagons and found the humans all huddled together, sobbing, quivering, with most eyes turned away. Why were they afraid of him?

A man stood there, tall and long-limbed. He held a spear before him, the tip quavering in the air. He said, "Are you here to kill us, too?"

Scorch felt something else now. He could sense the awe and fear in them. He liked it. He liked it a lot. He felt something else. As effortless as all of the carnage he reaped seemed, still he felt ever so slightly drained. Then he spoke his first words on Bish.

"No, I'm not here to kill anyone."

The man's voice was shaking when he said, "Well, maybe so, but you seem awfully good at it. Are you a mage?"

"Something like that. And what are you men?"

"Just a family of merchants, moving along with a caravan. We were down to our last guards when you showed up."

Scorch began to find himself becoming bored. It seemed these people didn't have a lot to offer. Still, it wouldn't hurt to learn more about them and their customs.

"So what do you merchants do?"

They all had funny looks on their faces now, but they seemed to be warming up to him. Most all of them had begun to stand up.

"Er … we take supplies to the city, make trade and such? We have wheat and barley?"

"What city are you taking these items to?"

"Hohm City."

"Well then, I believe I shall accompany you to Hohm City. Is it an interesting place?"

The man said, "It's the most interesting place of all, if you ask me."

Scorch climbed onto the seat of one of the wagons and said, "How do you drive this thing?"

54

THE SMELLS OF THE CITY didn't sit well with her. Her creation had many things that seemed to be like chaos run amok. It didn't even seem natural. Her universe, despite its enormity, was clean. The filth created by other worlds was hardly something of notice, if it was even noticed at all. She didn't recall her own world, in which she originated, as being a place so wrought with filth.

Trinos did find some things that she enjoyed with her re-established senses that she was becoming accustomed to. Freshly baked food had an effect that was much of a surprise. She sat straight up on a stool at an outdoor eatery, a fresh piece of pie on her plate. It was wonderful. Her mug of tea was good as well. For hours she sat staring at the people that surrounded her. Almost every one of them was coarse and cold. Most of their garments were in tatters and wrought with grime. The children had little more than a stitch of clothing on, and every little face was tired and dirty. The children came to her begging for coins or scraps of food. The proprietor of the eatery, an older man with a long moustache, stayed busy whisking the children away with a switch.

A carriage passed her by and stopped farther up the street. Two guards in hauberk armor and open-faced helms came down from their seat. The men were clean, and their armor and uniforms were impeccable. One of them opened up the door, and two women in colorful attire stepped out. A smile crossed the face of Trinos. That was something more along the lines of what she had in mind for her world.

Urchins rushed toward the women, pleading and crying for anything of value. The elegant women greeted the children with curses that would blush a whore. The sentries beat the urchins back with the horse lash, catching many of them across the backs of their legs, but some on the fronts of their faces. The children wailed as many more men appeared, dressed in uniforms of brown and gray. The City Watch began clearing the street of urchins with methods of their own. All the children cried as they scurried or limped away, depending how injured they were. One of them was knocked out cold and hauled away. The women scolded the City Watch and then continued on to go shop as soon their own children came forth. They were laughing at the urchins, pointing fingers and making unpleasant comments. This was not at all what Trinos had in mind!

Her world was filled with both good and evil, she knew that, but it wasn't as easy to watch up close. These beings were her creations, and for some reason she didn't like seeing them abused. She had gotten involved once already and made quite a scene. Should she do anything now?

"Sir," she said, pointing at the Royals, "what can you tell me about those people?"

The storekeeper jumped to her side and pushed her finger down.

"What are you doing, Woman? Don't point! Don't point at a Royal, or at the City Watch, for that matter. You'll get us both killed." The man was nervous; his head was looking around, trying to find any unwanted eyes. It was clear to Trinos that her comments posed some sort of danger. She saw little reason for him to suffer.

"All right then, just tell me about those women. Are they Royals?"

She already knew the answer. She had even spent time among them before, but her memory, it seemed, needed refreshing. She felt a great deal of detachment from her creation, like a mother who had lost the purpose of raising a child.

"All right, just don't point. A woman like you don't want to draw too much attention to yerself, especially when you are new to town," he said, his face blushing.

"What do you mean?" she asked.

"Well … y-y-you're beautiful, radiant, of the likes I've never seen. I mean, I've never given anyone a free meal before, but with you, I cannot say no."

"Free meal? You mean, you desired payment." She paused. "Oh … I see."

She had forgotten that she had made a change since she arrived. She had been a wizened old woman, but that hadn't suited her. Instead, she had opted for something else. She had chosen to be striking: platinum-haired with eyes the color of shards of blue ice. The stares she drew stopped people in their tracks. She donned the hood on her garment and let the eatery keeper finish.

"Anyhow, I can't figure how you entered into this city without being taken in by the City Watch. A woman like you would be a high prize for the Royals. I can't help but think that you are in danger."

Trinos tightened the strings on her cloak. She noticed the man staring at her figure, his eyes running over her chest and down her legs. She had paid the man little mind before, as distracted as she was by everything else. His heart was racing, and his wanton desires glimmered in his eyes. Still, there was shame within the man, something that pulled him back, something good within.

"I appreciate your food and the concern. Have you any family?"

"Yes, er … well no and yes. My wife died not long ago. My sons were killed by the City Watch," he said with a distant voice.

Trinos sensed his lust turning into regret all of a sudden. She realized she needed to pay more attention to these things.

"It's a hard place, this City of Bone, isn't it?"

"I can't rightly say, I don't suppose. I've never been anywhere else."

She reached in her pocket and pulled out a small stone that was almost the size of the nail on her finger. She held it before his eyes and said, "Take it."

He snatched it from her hand saying, "Don't do that in broad daylight. You'll get killed." He looked around, but people were too busy to notice. He took a quick glance in his palm and whispered, "A diamond. I've never touched one before."

"Can I have some more pie and tea?" she said.

"Lady, you can have all that you want," he said, scurrying away.

It felt good, making that man happy. For the rest of the stay she sat, ate, and watched. She came to know the eatery owner as Murad. He filled her ears with everything that he knew, from his childhood on. Through him, Trinos learned that her creation had become more intricate than she ever would have thought. One lone man whose own survival had very little meaning became a very important source for her. The City of Bone needed some changes, and with the simple man's knowledge, she had a better idea on where to start. It was time to go.

"Where are you going, Lady?" he said, wringing his hands in a wash rag with a great deal of sadness in his voice.

"To the castle," she said, pointing to the white and bronze spires that jutted into the moonlit sky.

"Will you ever come back for more pie?"

"No. Fare well."

Trinos was walking away now, unhindered by fear or anything else, for that matter. No, it was time that she began to straighten things out. Creating a world was one thing, telling it what to do was another. Behind her, she could hear Murad sobbing as he cried out,

"But it's dangerous up there. You need to stay away from those castles and Royals. Once you go in, they'll never let you out of their sight!"

55

IT DIDN'T TAKE LONG FOR Verbard to return to Oran's lair. He felt a sense of relief that he hadn't felt in months as he slumped down into Oran's massive couch. He was certain he had never appreciated such comfort before, even though he had. His battle against the Darkslayer gave him a new perspective on things.

He clutched at his chest. The teleportation scroll had taken a lot from him. It sapped him into near unconsciousness as he arrived. It was something else his dead brother, Catten, had provided. His brother's robes, now crumpled in his lap, had more pockets inside them than his own, and he had many. Finding the scroll in the second pocket he searched had been fortunate. One day he would have to take the time to empty the rest of the pockets and find out what else his brother had hidden from him.

The coolness of the cave was revitalizing. The weeks above in the blazing suns had dried out his bones and covered his hands and face with grit. Even his dust-coated robes, once a brilliant black, looked like nothing more than common garb. He fanned and dusted them off, but found that he didn't have the energy to continue.

The burning green and blue candles that outlined the cavern walls added a radiant glow to all of Oran's ghastly jars. Verbard's silver eyes took their time as they went from one jar to the other, gazing at the faces of dwarves, men, orcs and others who had all been drowned with expressions of endless horror. He shook his head. Oran had been an ally long ago, but the underling cleric's desires had become different from his own.

He found himself staring at the pickle-jarred face of a black-bearded dwarf. *If only the Darkslayer's head was in there instead.* He still hated the man, as he hated all men, but ten times worse. The trials he had faced in the Underland to prove himself had been harsh, but they were nothing compared to this last adventure. He rolled his brother's eyes in the palm of his hand. The golden orbs still had life in them, but they were cooling. He held them up to his eyes; let them stare him back in his face. He could sense his brother was still there, the pupils almost seemed to dilate in the faint glow of the candles.

"Brother, we did it; The Darkslayer is vanquished and we can return home," he said, but his tone was hollow and unconvincing. For some reason, he felt as if he was the one that should not have survived. It was his brother, the planner and tactician, who had spear-headed their quest all along. His brother had talents and powers that he did not, but he had his own special abilities as well, maybe survival was among those. He set Catten's eyes down on a table by the couch. "But first let me take my rest."

He sighed, stood up and walked around, his hands wringing behind his back. He was safe, his journey complete, yet he was agitated.

"Ah … what is this?"

A wine rack, a person wide and ten feet tall, was in his midst. He pulled one burgundy bottle from the rack and blew a thin film of dust away. There was a label in the common tongue of the humans. He checked another and another. All sorts of wines and liquors from all of the races were there. "Impressive, Oran. What a lush you have become. All of those years, drinking alone … Tsk, tsk. My, you've got two centuries' worth here."

Just below his waist he spied what he needed. He squatted down and pulled out a long black bottle with a mushroom cork.

"Ah … underling port, my favorite," he said as he grabbed a small fish bowl of a glass. He wriggled his finger and the cork pulled out, hovering in the air. The fragrance enriched his senses. He had filled his glass more than half full when he noticed something else; a box made out of wire mesh sat on a dark pine table behind the sofa. Dozens of insects of all sorts were sitting inside in their garden of dirt, rock, water and sand. A jar of fine powder, like crushed pearls and salt, illuminated the side of the wire mesh box.

"I haven't seen one of these in over a century."

He took a large pinch from the jar and sprinkled it over the insects. The mantises, crickets, grasshoppers and the like came to life and started crawling around. A strange music began to play, like tiny violins in a forest. It sounded so good that Verbard began tapping his foot. He finished his glass in one drink and poured another.

"An insect box and all the port I can drink. I think it's time to celebrate."

It wasn't long before the tightness in his chest began to subside. He let his thoughts escape somewhere else, home perhaps. He gave his mate some thought. The underling woman had been a pregnant beast when he left, and when he returned he wondered if his children might have been born. He wasn't sure if he was ready for that yet, all of the ceremonies and the like.

"Maybe I'll just stay here a while longer," he said, covering his mouth to yawn. Exhaustion had set in from his fingertips to his toenails, and in seconds he was fast asleep, oblivious to the fact that he was not alone.

56

"Is it ready yet, Wizard?" a gruff voice demanded.

Fogle gave Mood another frustrated look. His face was strained with concentration, while the Blood Ranger King's had the fiery look of an inferno. The giant dwarf's oversized hands were clutching in and out at his sides as he paced. Fogle rubbed his scrawny neck, and then buried his nose back in his spellbook.

"I'm almost done writing, Mood. Writing spells onto scrolls is much more difficult than it looks. Go smoke another cigar or something," he said, looking back up, "and keep your distance. I can't be getting confused."

The big dwarf gave him a dangerous look that caused him to take in a sharp breath. Fogle would be more wary of how he addressed a king from now on.

"I'll look fer some more grub, I suppose," Mood said as he walked away.

"Shoo," he said, wiping his brow while mumbling, "… and good riddance."

"I heard that." But the dwarf kept going.

Fogle Boon sat cross-legged by the stone pyre. The wall of mist was still over a hundred yards away, but a fog seemed to be rolling in from it. For the past two days he had been writing one of the spells from his grandfather's spellbook, one that he had come across over a decade ago and thought utterly ridiculous. How little he had known then compared to what he knew now. Wondering if any of these spells had even been tried before, he drew in a deep breath, regained his focus, and began writing anew.

His lithe hand was steady on the parchment as he wrote. Every symbol he copied had to be exact and perfect. A small wooden box, similar to a craftsman's toolbox, sat beside him full of scroll parchment, ink, quills and an assortment of tiny drawers and bottles. His wizard's kit had most everything he needed for his spells, but not for his grandfather's. No, his grandfather's spells required many other sorts of things.

He wiped the drops of sweat off his face with his sleeve. *Almost done.*

Unlike his own spells that he could memorize, recall and cast, his grandfather's required a different discipline. To save time, he could have just read each one from the spellbook page while casting it, but that would erase it forever. Without the proper spell components, such as an albino cat's hair or a powdered orcen toe, it wouldn't be possible to memorize these new spells. Instead, he had to re-write each spell in its entirety on a scroll. Each was so long it would make a bookkeeper's hand ache, but his hand was just fine. He could write days on end if he had to, and his pace was faster than normal. He shook his hand, waving the feathered quill back and forth.

Two hours later, the writing was finished.

"Are you done yet, Wizard?" Mood's sour voice had returned.

"Almost, now get the rope."

Mood did as he was told, pulling a coil of rope from one of the horses' saddlebags. Fogle reached inside his wizard kit and grabbed a tiny jar. After twisting off the metal cap, he dabbed his fingertip into the silvery oil. Setting the jar back inside the box, he rubbed the oil on the scroll he had written. He made a few intricate symbols on the parchment and whispered a word that ignited the oil on the paper. His face was bathed in silver light for a moment, and then the light winked out on the scroll.

"Is it ready yet?" Mood said, tossing the rope by his feet.

"It's ready," he said, picking up the rope as he stood up. It was climbing rope, beige, layered with fine cotton, and inlaid with twine. It wasn't something he was accustomed to using; even as a child he had never tied a person up during play. There were many rope tricks that the magi liked to play, but rope spells were not his forte. He had never desired to study the more passive arts of wizardry.

"I suppose yer gonna be wanting me to tie it to me now," Mood said.

The plan had already been discussed, but it was more Moods' idea than his.

"Here, tie it around your waist," he said, handing a length over to him.

Mood wrapped it around his waist, grumbling something in dwarven, and then secured it with a knot. Fogle tried to do the same. His fingers fumbled, and Mood had to come to his aid. "Can't even tie a simple knot I see, silly human."

Fogle wasn't embarrassed though; instead, he held up before him the scroll he had just written. "Be silent now, and hold on to the rope," he said, wrapping his free hand around his side of the rope.

He took a deep breath and began to read. As the fog rolled past his knees and the suns rose behind his back, he let the magic of the words flow from his lips. The words came fast, twisting his lips and turning his tongue. Once he got going there was no stopping. He didn't notice the bemused look on Mood's face. He tried not to think. Writing was so much easier than speaking. The words he pronounced were even foreign to him, and each annunciation was stranger than the one before. This was why wizards rarely read spells with the tongue. The mind could do things far quicker than the body. Memorization and trigger words were their usual practice.

Fogle felt his stomach twitch as the mystic power filled him like water fills a glass, then flushed out of him in a spiral. The parchment in his hands began to dry up and wither away, like the ashes of a fire. His throat felt dry, and his tongue was swollen and burning.

"Well Little Man, did yer little spell work or not?" Mood said as he stood at his side, still holding the rope. "You look like a sick dog."

Fogle tried to answer, but only a mouthful of spit came out.

"Son of a Bish! Take a drink," Mood said, handing over his canteen. Waving him off, Fogle opted to drink from a vial in his magic kit instead. The clear liquid was pasty, sticking on his tongue like honey, but tasting like salt. "Er … ulp … Ah, that's better. I hope I never have to do that again," he said, rolling his neck and tongue.

"Can we get on with this? And explain how this works again. I've never heard of no *endless rope* spell. We dwarves got our own spells and —"

"I don't see any dwarven magi here, and this is what you agreed to." Mood's remarks over the past two days had worn him down. The loss of Ox still left parts of him numb. "The rope will keep you tethered to me. Our knots won't untie, either, unless we do it. It'll go on a long ways, miles maybe, I don't know. It's supposed to be never-ending. Just don't take the knot off. Tug on it whenever you can't see me… I'll feel it and tug back." Fogle shrugged.

Mood held his hand up, waving him off.

"Fine, I get it. Off I go, then."

They headed toward the mist, each towing his horse. Fogle checked over his shoulder, making sure their camp didn't leave his sight. The fog was rising over it now, but the rising suns were still clear.

"I'll wait here."

Mood had remarked that the coil of rope was more than 100 feet long. As he walked away, the coil of rope between them unwound. It didn't seem like Mood had taken more than twenty steps away when he disappeared altogether. The rope was still unwinding. A naked chill ran down Fogle's spine. He pulled his horse farther back from the wall of mist. Fogle couldn't shake the eerie feeling that there was something very unnatural about the Mist.

Mood thought he had been everywhere on Bish, even the Underland, until today. The Mist was entirely new. He looked back toward Fogle Boon, but only the mist was there. The step of his boots was cautious at first, short and uncertain. He took a deep snort in his nose and found himself in a new, strange, and tasteless world. For centuries Mood had treaded the world with absolute certainty, but now, for the first time in his life, he felt like he had no idea where he was. He tugged on the rope. A moment later it was tugged back.

Venir. If his friend was in here, it was an absolute certainty he was lost. He crunched over the hard ground until he heard a faint howling of the wind. Something or nothing was ahead; another void in space that was different from where he stood now. He had senses other men did not. He could see, taste and hear things like a wild animal in the woods.

"Sweet Mother of Bish," he whispered.

He could see his foot hanging over a ledge. His keen eyes guided him as he walked along it, putting one foot in front of the other and fighting a feeling of despair that had begun to set in. He reached inside his pouch, grabbed some stones, and tossed one over. More than a minute passed, and he heard nothing. He hurled another one through the chasm, hoping to hear something land on another side. Only the mist, the silent white mist was there. He ran his fingers through his beard. He felt a tugging around his belt. He tugged back and turned around.

He wasn't one to worry, but what if Fogle Boon was attacked, the rope cut or gone slack? Without the suns or moon, a landmark, water, or any life, how would he find his way out? He was certain that whatever came too far into the Mist wasn't coming out. If Venir was in there, he was on his own, at least until they figured something out. Hand over hand he pulled his way back out of the mist. It seemed like heading out took much longer than heading in. He had counted his steps, but he was well past that amount now. He felt confused.

"What in all of Bish!" he said, as he stormed ahead.

He kept on going, wondering when the suns' light would emerge. What if Fogle Boon's spell had not worked? What if the underling had come back and the mage was dead? Such thoughts were not common among his hardened kind. Dying in battle was honorable, but dying from being lost was … unheard of.

57

VENIR DONNED HIS HELMET AND forged up the hill. The roar he heard and the flapping of wings began to fade the farther he went. He could have traveled for hours or days, he did not know. He was desperate to feel or hear anything, something living, other than himself. Maybe the helmet would help him find something, for he couldn't trust his own instincts and ears anymore.

He swore he'd kiss an underling if he saw one at this point. All of his anger had burned for decades over the evil creatures. Something inside of him made him feel obligated to kill them all. It wasn't something he ever understood, or cared to. It was just what it was. It didn't matter to him anymore, and he wasn't sure why it ever had. He stubbed his toe on a rock, cursed, and stopped.

"Where'd that come from?"

His foot began to throb. More jagged rocks and boulders jutted from the steep hillside that he climbed. The loose rocks under his feet were becoming more secure. He stopped and closed his eyes. There was a hum in his ears, natural like the silence of a cave. There was a beating of wings somewhere far ahead or above. He fanned the mist before his eyes, but it went nowhere. He resumed his climb, focusing on the sound of beating wings, heavy and slow, as if from a dream in a faraway land.

Sleep. How long had it been since he had indeed slept. He knew nothing but moving on in hunger, anguish and pain. He had no idea how he was sustained. Had it been hours, days, months, or years since he had been on the move? It felt like a day or two, but his mind suggested something longer. Again, the thought of his reality was intertwined with a dream or a nightmare. Was he dead or alive? Did the underlings have him captured or imprisoned in the Underland far below? He did not know. *Move and live … or die.*

WHUMP! WHUMP! WHUMP!

The sound drummed in his head from time to time, but it seemed to be getting stronger. Venir had never heard a roar like that before. Many beasts roared, but not like a dozen lions in one. Whatever type of monster it might be, he was all too eager to face it. Anything would be better than what he was dealing with now: a tortuous journey that had no end in sight.

He was clawing his way up the hillside when he grabbed hold of something else. *A vine?* He ripped something from the ground and held it close to his face. It was a root from a plant of some kind. He pushed upward and was crawling across the boulders when felt something slick and soft under his hands. *Moss?* It was moist and silky. He tongue began to swell inside his mouth. *There must be water nearby.*

The steep incline of the hill began to subside, and his footsteps began to find softer ground. The mist began to thin and green grass mixed in with the rocks. He could see his boots now. He held his hand out from the utmost point of his face and it was still there. He picked up his pace and stepped over a large piece of driftwood. The mist seemed to dissipate and become damp, more like fog, and it left a taste of water in the air. *WHUMP! WHUMP! WHUMP!*

He crouched down. The beating wings were closer now than before, almost as close as the first time he heard them. He could make out a line of brush ahead and swore that he heard a trickle of water from a stream or brook. Still, everything was haunting. The assault on his senses that were dulled by the time in the mist was an awakening. There were sounds, tastes, feeling and smells. *I hope I'm not dreaming.*

His heart began to pound in his chest. His temples thundered the way they did before battle. Fighting the need to surge into the unknown, he slowed his pace as he passed through the brush and foliage. The mist was more like a heavy fog now, and it seemed to be lifting. The ground beneath his feet had turned to grass, leaving the rocks and rubble long behind him. *WHUMP! WHUMP! WHUMP! CRUNCH!*

It sounded like a flying beast had landed on a pile of logs nearby.

THOOM ... THOOM ... THOOM ... SNORT!

The ground under his feet trembled as he crept forward, every hair on his body standing up. Venir's breathing became loud and heavy, but he couldn't help it. He unslung his pack, pulled out the sack, and reached inside. There was nothing there! A streak of fear raced up his spine. His shoulder was half inside the bag before he grasped hold of something. He pulled something out. "Brool," he whispered.

SNORT! THOOM! ... THOOM! ... THOOM! ...

The snorting beast was coming his way. Venir remained still; his muscles were as rigid as a statue's. His arm was still in the sack, searching the vast empty space inside. *I'm gonna need some armor.* Nothing else came out. *Blasted bag!*

THOOM ... THOOM ... Thoom ...

The beast was moving away, but the suffocating tightness was still there. He had been ready to die and get this insane journey over with, but his need for survival kicked in.

"The Bish with it!"

Venir charged ahead, emerging from the mist. Toward the beast he went, war-axe raised high.

58

MELEGAL SLIPPED OUT OF HIS apartment, leaving Octopus and Haze to themselves. He had Tonio's sword, wrapped up in some cloth. He headed for the main floor. He had spent half a day recovering and letting Haze dress his wounds, now it was time to move on. He was ten feet into the main tavern floor of the Drunken Octopus when he realized he should have taken the window. His body ached so much that he didn't have the climb in him. He glanced over to his table where Jeb and his gang now sat. Velvet was sitting on the thug leader's lap, arms draped around his neck, whispering and pointing his way. That's when the snickers and foul remarks came. He averted his eyes.

Sam the barkeep barred his way, hands crossed over his chest.

"Ye got three days left on rent," the man said with a guilty look in his eye. "I suggest that be the end of it. Hole up with yer friends elsewhere."

Melegal let out a short little laugh, side stepped the barkeep, and continued on. He could feel eyes burning into his back as he headed through the door. The outer districts were onto him. They didn't want his kind hanging around anymore. There was a constant battle between the commoners and the Royals, a silent war of sorts. Melegal worked for the other side now, the one that always won. He took a long look back and moved on. *They can have it.*

One by one he lit the wall lanterns. A soft glow filled the room. McKnight's apartment was a bit bigger and much nicer. The studio had a wooden framed queen bed, a small sofa, and a table and chairs that matched. A rug covered most of the wood planked floor, and a fireplace was in the corner. It had taken a lot of doing for Melegal to find his former mentor's hidey hole, but all of the pushy questions he asked had led him here. It wasn't above a tavern like his former home, no, it was part of an array of decent apartments a few blocks from Castle Almen. Things were much safer in this district, and the City Watch was always nearby.

It was here that Melegal had already moved his own possessions and added a few as well: Lefty's Tomes, thick, leather bound and heavy, sat on the edge of a coffee table's corner. His short swords, the Sisters, were sheathed and hung on the bedpost nearby. Melegal had even filled the chest of draws with his own clothes. A high-backed leather chair faced the fireplace. An empty bottle and goblet sat on the end table at its side. Melegal walked over and stirred the ashes in the fireplace. A black stitch of heavy cloth was the only evidence of what had been consumed weeks ago. It was from another one of McKnight's wide-brimmed hats.

Melegal set Tonio's sword on the small dining table and pulled a bottle of wine from the cupboard. He rubbed his head and closed his eyes. The stress from his employer was wearing him thin. Wondering if this was how it all began with McKnight, he found himself staring at a cock-eyed picture on the wall. It wasn't something one found among the merchants on the streets of the City of Bone. No, the artwork rivaled that of what he had seen inside a few castle walls. He first assumed the detective had stolen it, but the evidence suggested otherwise. A chest sat below the painting, filled with paint, brushes and other supplies. By the looks of it, it hadn't been handled in years, or longer. Still, it appeared McKnight had another talent after all. The colorful painting of endless fields filled with white cottages basking in the sunlight being overtaken by a shadow, well, it suggested something. He took a drink.

His fingers played along the cotton fabric that encased Tonio's sword. How long should he wait before he shared it with Royal Lord Almen? He had little desire to confront the man, seeing how he had become unpredictable. It didn't help that the man was inherently dangerous. The Royal had snuck up on him like a giant shadow and crushed his neck like a kitten's. The feeling of helplessness still lurked inside him, becoming quite the motivator. Did McKnight have the same feelings, in Lord Almen's "service"?

There was a mirror over a wash basin. He checked the new stitches in his face. Haze had done a fine job, and her skill with a needle was appreciated. With the salve he had applied, he should be able to take them out in a couple of days. He wasn't sure how Lord Almen would react to his scarred face. It would only make prying eyes uncomfortable and raise questions. Still, he had a feeling withholding any information too long from the Royal would catch up to him. Lord Almen seemed to know everything. Melegal wasn't comfortable with his uncertainty.

Decisions, decisions.

He started a fire, grabbed a blanket, covered himself, and eased back in the chair. For now it was time to drink, rest, and burn. He tossed another one of McKnight's hats into the blaze.

"Burn memories, burn."

59

THE CITY WATCHMAN LEFT BRAK with a few coins in his hand. There was a sorrowful look in the guard's eyes, but he didn't notice. He was lost and empty inside.

"You look like a man, so act like a man," was the last thing the guard said before he departed.

Brak walked through the busy streets, bustling through people with a blank look in his eyes. The sounds, sights and smells were muted by his sadness. He had his heavy sword strapped to his hip and his mother's hung over his drooping shoulder. The watchman had pulled the bolt from his shoulder and patched it up. It ached now, but not more so than his heart.

The past fourteen years of his life he had never been alone, but he was young and strong. The young of the world were resilient survivors who seemed to escape the most meager conditions or learn to live with them. Brak would have to be no different, but at least he had an advantage: he was as big as a man, just not quite as smart.

Night began to fall, and the shops began to close. Faces became drawn up as he headed down the streets. His belly began to groan, and all of sudden it was easier to deal with death than hunger. The coins the watchman had left him with were a meager few. Slowly, the reality of being swindled by the watchman dawned on him. He remembered the purse that had dropped from his mah's dead hand, and much more money being in there.

"Aw," he said in aggravation. He should have had all the money. He needed that money to find his father. Where was that place that they had last looked for the man? *The Drunken Octopus.* He decided to head back there.

As the streets began to clear out, he tried to find someone to ask which way to go. Everyone scurried by, avoiding his desperate stare. He found himself rambling down the Royal Roadway. Ahead, the massive gate was closed like a titan's mouth. The City Watch stood along the wall, with fire pits glowing on their faces. The watchman who had "helped" him had warned him to avoid the guards at the wall. A couple men brandishing spears turned his way. He looked around, not realizing that he was the only one in the roadway. He sauntered from the street, but he could hear the heavy boots of the men as they approached.

"You there, come over!"

Brak didn't like the tone of the man's voice.

"Stop!"

The man's commanding voice froze his legs. It was normal for him to follow the voice of authority. He turned and caught the stern faces of the watch. Their body language suggested an intent to murder, even more so than that of the thieves that had killed his mother, Vorla. He turned and ran.

"Stop! Stop, Rogue!"

Something clattered over the cobblestone road, sliding underneath his toes. A spear had fallen short of the mark. Brak darted down a narrow street and cut down an alley, his heavy feet splashing over the muck. He kept running, letting the shout of voices and the sound of hard footsteps spur him to greater speed. A group of men stood barring his way ahead, but they were different than the watch, ragged and brandishing steel blades. He froze, caught between the mob of filthy men and the rushing City Watch. He didn't know what to do. He was trapped.

The throng of man-urchins rushed by him and blocked the path of the City Watch. The watch now stood still in their tracks, spears reared back. There were only two watchmen and over a dozen of the ragged-faced men. Brak stood, unmoving, chest heaving.

"Get out of our way rodents!" one of the City Watch shouted.

There was a mocking snicker among the crowd. Every ragged arm raised a dagger high in the air and screeched. Brak didn't stick around to see what happened next. He ran on and turned down the next open alley.

Something dropped over his head, and he sank to the ground. A weighted net had a hold on him. He thrashed inside, arms and legs kicking with futility. He was certain that the City Watch had him, but instead, it was something worse. The man-urchins were dragging him, ragged and foul smelling men, barefoot or sandaled. He could feel the harsh cobble stones tearing his clothes and scrapping his skin as he was dragged through the puddles of filth.

He began to scream.

Clunk!

Something slammed into his head. He screamed again, only to see a metal club crush him between the eyes.

"He's a heavy bastard," one said.

Still, he fought for his voice and yelled again.

Whap!

Bright lights flashed inside his eyelids. He wasn't out, but his energy was sapped. He lay still, clutching his hands to his chest.

"He's quit now," the one with the club said.

Indeed he had. Terrified, Brak let himself be taken deeper into the belly of Bone.

60

HER LONG SILKY BLACK HAIR was now a network of short braids on top of her head. The brownish color was unnatural as well, but only she would recognize herself. The mirror revealed the deep disfigurements of her once-beautiful face: white lines like the veins on a leaf scattered beneath her eyes. She could still see the faces of the men that had pinned her down, held her at knife point and showed no mercy when they carved her face up and defiled her over and over again. They had laughed as they left, saying no man would have her after that, and for years they were right, but not for the reasons they supposed. She hated all men for what a few had done to her. The scars on the outside had faded over time, but her inner scars still burned. Rape and torture were common in the world of Bish, but the humiliation of a powerful Royal officer was not. Jarla was never the same after that, a dark shadow of her once-proud self.

She ran her fingers over the scars on her half-naked body, remembering all the battles she had fought ever since she was a young woman. A jagged gash was still prominent along her belly, from her first battle in the field. An orc had ripped open her chainmail with a battle axe, causing excruciating pain that was intoxicating at the same time. She hadn't noticed death's shadow as the roaring beast raised up his axe to brain her. Instead, she had plunged her longsword hilt deep into its stomach and tasted her first blood.

A porcelain basin of water was underneath the mirror, and water flowed freely from a brass spigot. She liked that about the City of Three, the abundance of water that washed the filth from the streets. She must have bathed every day for a week, enjoying the common use of tubs. There had been a time when she had all but forgotten the finer things in life, had lived in the field of battle, caring only for spilt blood. Then she found herself lost and humiliated, serving in taverns, doing what she must for coin, food, and sanctuary. She was disgraced, a fallen Royal, discarded and forgotten.

She began rinsing the blood from her hands. She rubbed her hands together, letting the blood and water drip down the drain, and then took a towel and some soap and scrubbed until not a single red speck was left and the drain was clean. She wiped her hands off of on a white towel, inspected it, and hung it back to dry.

She turned around and faced a man in an exquisite leather tunic. He was sitting upright and bound in a chair with his head slumped over in his chest and his long blond hair dangling down to hide his entire head. His chest rose up and down in a wet and sickening wheeze. A puddle of blood had formed beneath the chair. She found little comfort in the man's demise.

She sat on the edge of a bed and smoothed out the long sleeves on her white cotton shirt. It was soft, like animal fur, a new skin for her. If she was going to hide in the open from now on, she was going to have to change a few things. Running her long fingers along her dagger that lay silent on the bed, she looked over at the man dripping in the chair. He was a big man, arms and chest thick from years of swinging steel. She had come across him in the tavern in which she now stayed. The sight of him had washed every desire for a fresh start from her mind. He was Cider, a Royal Almen commander, one of those who rode out with her from the siege of Outpost Thirty-One, abandoning duty. The man had not only been one of those who defiled her, but he had betrayed the rest of his own kind as well.

Her words were like polished silver when she spoke.

"How do you feel, Cider?"

His head raised up few inches as he said, "Disappointed."

The lone sound of his deep voice turned her blood hot.

"Why is that, Cider?"

"Because, I came to bed a beautiful whore and got stuck with an ugly slu—ULP!"

She began laughing as his face turned purple, but her knuckles were white on her blade. She wanted so badly to chop off his face. Cider had been a trusted friend back then, a fierce soldier of Castle Almen. For half a decade he had galloped along her side. She had been blind-sided by the cruel nature that most men hide. His was one of the worst of all.

Cider began coughing now, and more blood dripped to his chest.

"I wouldn't laugh much more if I were you. Those holes I put in your stomach wouldn't like that. Maybe saying something nice will heal the wound." She got up and set a jar full of salve on the floor and slid it between his tied up feet. "If you were to apologize—FOR RAPING ME— I might even use some of this on your wounds."

Cider's head rose up and searched for her face. The candles in the tavern bedroom were dim, but the fresh gashes in his face were clear, as was the bloody collar around his neck. It was a magic device that choked the man if he tried to scream or yell. It was another one of those luxuries that weren't so hard to come by in the City of Three. Cider was older than she, by a decade, rugged and good-looking as well. She had looked up to him like an older brother, but that was all. Maybe her lack of interest had been what sparked aggression in him, and in many of the other men as well.

"I'll not apologize to you, Witch. You got what most women want and what most women get. You're the one that thought you were so much better than the rest, but we showed you, didn't we?" A smile crossed his split lips that matched the sparkle in his blue eyes. She rammed a dagger up under his chin, skewering deep into his brain. His eyes filled with horror, fluttered and closed. She yanked the dagger out and noticed the blood on the sleeve of her shirt.

"Bone!"

Men had done nothing but ruin her life, and now her clothes. *Slat on a transfiguration!* She was what she was. *I am the Brigand Queen!* And if the men still wanted to capture her, so be it. Still a wanted woman with everything to hide, Jarla rinsed out her shirt, gathered her belongings, and rode from the City of Three. She was just as lost when she left as when she got there, but maybe she could find more Royal bastards to kill in the City of Bone.

61

H E EMERGED FROM THE MIST. The unexpected visual sensation blinded him. His nostrils filled with a hundred scents, each of its own fragrance. The air was hot and wet as his hungry lungs sucked it in like a swimmer coming up from deep water. Venir held his hand over the eyelets of his helmet to block the light and let the bright spots in his vision subside as he relished the sudden heat of the suns on his back. He took his time turning around. Behind him, the mist was a few dozen feet from kissing his face. He kept turning, closing his eyes, and when he opened them he looked out over the landscape again. He cocked his head.

"Bish?"

There was nothing familiar before him. Not one rock, tree, hillside or river. He had traveled along the mist before, and was very familiar with the Outland terrain. Now, the mist had led him somewhere else, somewhere more vibrant and alive. The bitter landscape of the Outlands was gone and replaced by rolling green hillsides and groves of trees a mile high. He squinted as he peered into the bright blue sky. Two familiar suns, burning globes of orange and red, hung in the distance.

The world of Bish is shaped like a thick coin. The mist hovers on the edges of the coin, and anyone who steps off the edge falls down until they reach the other side of the coin. Now, Venir was on the underside of Bish. He just didn't know it.

His stomach growled as the scent of cooked flesh wafted into his nose. Another roar came, the same as before, louder than the thunder of a storm. Venir's hunger was erased by fear as he squatted down. He was so enthralled by the picturesque landscape that he had forgotten about the monster that led him there.

A black bulk was hunched on all fours, lapping up water from a tranquil river that looked miles wide. Its scales shimmered like broken black coal, and its tail thrashed back and forth, fanning a pattern in the grassy embankment. Venir had faced similar long-necked lizards before, but this one was much bigger, and it had wings. *How big is that thing?* It was hard to tell.

For some reason, he looked down at his hand. It rested in a patch of green clovers, each as big as his thumb. He flinched as a flock of white birds soared over his head, bearing down on the lizard. The birds were big, each the size of a forest eagle. He watched them land on the back of the lizard. Now they looked no bigger than white flies on a pile of shiny slat. *That thing's huge.*

Venir had heard songs about giants, and now he had seen one. He had heard songs about dragons, too. *This must be one.* His stomach was rumbling again, and fatigue wrapped around him like a cool blanket. His grip on the hilt of Brool began to slacken as he yawned. The last thing he saw was the citrine eyes of the dragon as its long neck stretched his way. He caught a glimpse of a stone bridge expanding over the river behind the creature. He felt the dragon's steps shaking the ground as it came his way, but he couldn't shake the sleep that consumed him.

62

FOGLE BOON WAS ALMOST ASLEEP when he felt a tug and noticed a shroud coming his way from the mist. He smoothed out his disheveled robes, gathered his feet and stood back up. He felt the taut rope in his hand. The figure became more hulking by the step. *Venir?* He couldn't say for sure in the light. The mist and fog began to break away from the bushy face of Mood. He could have kissed the dwarf. It had been a long day.

"What were you doing in there, drawing a map?" he said.

Mood shook his head, staring up into the sky, a blank look on his face.

"Well, did you see anything? I mean you had to have seen something; you've been gone all day," Fogle added.

Mood said nothing. Instead, he just ran his thick fingers through his beard and drank from his canteen, then wiped his mouth on his sleeve.

"What have you done, Mage?" Mood said his gruff voice.

He shrugged and said, "I don't know what you mean. I've done nothing but sit here since you left."

"Pah!" Mood spat and began staring into the sky. He pointed his arm in the air and retorted, "When I left, the suns were rising, and now the moons are full? Explain it!"

Fogle looked up at the yellow and orange lights in the sky. Nothing seemed out of the ordinary about them. He said, "All right Mood, so the moons are out. What did you expect? You've been gone all day."

Mood stormed right up on his toes and began breathing down in his face, reminding him of the elemental that had crushed Ox. He had the distinct feeling that same fate was about to befall him. *He's delirious! Don't move, Fogle! Be still … be silent!*

Mood yelled in his face.

"I wasn't gone more than an hour! Madness it is!"

Fogle felt like something sucked the marrow from his bones. *Impossible!*

Mood turned and walked away toward the fire. Fogle felt his heart start inside his chest again. For minutes, he watched from a distance as Mood sat by the fire, grumbling to himself. He summoned up his courage, walked over, and sat down as well.

"So … what did you see in there?"

"Mist thicker than soup … and nothing else." Mood shifted on the ground as his green eyes glinted in the fire. "There's no sound, er taste, er wind in the air. The only thing I could smell was myself. The cliff they speak about was there. I supposed that's what it was."

Fogle didn't want to ask it, but he did.

"Do you think Venir could get out of there?"

Mood shook his head and said, "No … not without this rope anyhow. I didn't even go in that far, just a few hundred steps, maybe a few more. Without this rope … I don't think I could have made it out. Not after even just a hundred steps! Pah! I've been in dangerous places before, but nothing ever shook me up like being in there."

"Something's got to be in there, though."

"Yeah, something … I just hope it's not Venir."

Both of them stared into the mist now. Fogle Boon felt a sudden compulsion to get as far away from there as possible. He snapped his fingers and the rope unknotted from their waists. Slowly, like a snake, it began to coin itself up.

"How long's yer trick last, Mage?"

"We can use it many times. Mood, what are we going to do now? I'm at my wit's end."

Mood started a new cigar.

"I say's we go back to Dwarven Hole. I can send out some scouts to help us look abroad. I need to see if anyone of my seers has knowledge beyond this mist. What about you, Human? You gonna stick it out with me, or go home?"

Home, the City of Three, and the finest women and wine in Bish. There was no other place that he would rather be, but he had left for a reason. He had questions about Bish, and about himself. His foresight told him that only "life and death" adventures would reveal the answers he sought. Besides, he was getting used to being out in the wilderness. His experiences with the arts of survival were changing him. He was getting physically, mentally, and mystically stronger, and his confidence grew daily. For some odd reason, he thought his grandfather, Boon, would be proud.

"I'll stay with you. I want to find Venir. And that underling, too."

"Ho, ho … you want to be a Darkslayer, too? Now that's something else. Well, I'm not tracking that underling. The blasted thing about killed me, and I've seen 'em kill my kin before. Be careful watcha want for, Little Man."

Fogle didn't regret what he said. If Mood was trying to make him feel foolish, it wasn't working. It didn't encourage him, either. He would heed Mood's warning. Still, something about that underling festered inside of him.

He held up the coil of rope.

"Ye can keep it," Mood said.

He took it over to his horse, put it in his rough sack, and grabbed the broken staff of his grandfather, Boon. There were so many incoherent things that his grandfather Boon had told him, one of them being *There is more out there.* Of course there is, he had thought so many years ago, but he hadn't cared at the time. He tapped the busted staff on the ground. It must still have some power; why else would Boon have given it to him. He put it back in the sack.

"When you want to go?" he asked.

"Might as well be now," Mood said.

"I have another spell I want to try, so do you have anything of Venir's?"

Mood stood up, his face as grim as ever in the firelight.

"We've got the knife that was in the underling. Whatcha gonna do now, Wizard?"

He gathered the knife and handed it to Mood and said, "What's the hilt made from?"

"Bone."

"Can you shave a piece off?"

"Yes. Can't you? 'Fraid of cuttin' yerself?"

Fogle Boon produced a thumb knife from under his robes. He shaved the side of the hilt, but nothing was produced.

"Ah … gimme that," Mood said, snatching it away. The Blood Ranger produced a blade of his own. "How much you want?"

"Just some heavy shavings."

He watched as Mood peeled a piece that rolled up the edge of his blade.

"Perfect," he said, holding out a small jar. Mood knocked the curled strip of bone inside. Fogle grabbed his kit, opened his spellbook, muttered, and lit up his eyes.

Mood huffed as he rambled away saying, "This again? I'll be looking for monsters. You do what you must. Just don't take too long."

He stuffed components of feathers, oils, ground up insect shells, and wax in the jar and shook it up. He studied and memorized a new spell, one he had added to the spellbook on his own. The mystic words were now coiled up in his mind, waiting to be unwound. *Tomorrow then. First, rest.* He lay down and slept.

It was bright morning when Mood kicked him.

"What?"

A heavy boot punched his thigh again.

He swung his arm saying, "All right." Mood was standing over him, hands on hips. He moved faster.

"I'm going. Just a second and this will be done."

Mood slung himself up on his horse and began to trot off.

"Hold it! You've waited this long, what's a minute more?"

"A minute I ain't got and —"

"Fine—GO—but you'll wish you hadn't. Besides, I need you."

"For what?"

Fogle shook up the jar and poured it on the ground. He focused on the image of Venir and with a word the spell inside his mind uncoiled. He watched as the ground began to bubble, boil and sparkle like chipping flint stones. From the ground something began to grow and take form. He shuffled back and bumped into Mood.

"What is it, Little Man?" Mood said with a twinge of awe in his voice.

He stepped back beside the dwarf and waited. A bird-like form almost eight inches tall appeared. It was ebony in color, with a hard sheen to its frame. The bird had the face of a hawk, black-beaked and white-eyed. A row of jagged feathers rose on its neck as it stretched its wings. It had the wing span of a much bigger bird, and its under-feathers were streaked with white. Its legs and talons were black, but ringed with tiny gray stripes.

It flapped up into the air, soaring high. Fogle lost sight of it in the bright light of the two suns. He summoned it back. A black dart dived down from the air, the wings flapping a few feet from his outstretched arm, where it perched itself. The small hawk had little weight, but a menacing look.

"Strange feathers for a bird," Mood said, rubbing his chin.

The onyx hawk's feathers were hard and sharp, like and insect or bug. It looked more like a statue than a living thing.

"This is my familiar, Mood. I call him Inky. His feathers aren't the normal sort. I gave him a thicker shell, more like a hornet. He's tougher, no need for food and water, just my own version of something else. Back in school they taught us to use familiars to retrieve things and deliver messages. All of the other familiars were too easy to kill: rats, dogs, cats. Most magi don't mind, but I didn't like seeing my familiars die, so I created him, just bending the rules a tad," he said, as a thin smile turned up on his bookish face. "Inky was the best. He's hard to find and kill."

"Strange … so what's he supposed to do?"

He pulled out his thumb knife and said, "Can I have a piece of your beard?"

Mood drew up like an ogre.

"Are ye mad!? No dwarf cuts his beard! Ye'd be better to try and cut off me leg first!"

Fogle wasn't ignorant of all customs; he was just raised not to care.

"I just need a hair, or something. The bird can find you that way, in case I'm not around."

Mood snatched the thumb knife from him and shaved some hair from his arm.

"Feed it to the bird … please," he said, sticking his arm out.

The onyx hawk gulped it down like a worm.

"That's it. Go Inky!"

Inky spread its wings, flapped away, and disappeared into the mist.

"You actually think that thing can find Venir in there?"

Fogle didn't. The bone from the hunting knife didn't seem like much of an attachment to tie the spell to the man. Normally, blood, skin or hair was used to track something with magic such as this. Sweat or a strong personal attachment might work, too. He sighed. He hated to see Inky go. The creature wasn't real, but it wasn't indestructible, either, just hardier than most. If anything, the bird might help eliminate the possibility that Venir was in there. That seemed to be the most likely case.

"I'd say he has a better chance than we do," he remarked

"What if it don't come back out?" Mood inquired.

Better it than me.

"You worry too much, Mood."

"What if it gets killed?"

"I'd know. So as long as it lives, we have hope."

They both got back on their horses and headed south. Fogle Boon kept his eyes away from the Mist. Maybe it was time to quit worrying about Venir altogether. After all, it seemed that the man wanted to be alone. *I wonder how Kam is getting along.*

63

THE BLACK DRAGON LOOMED OVER Venir, its foot-long fangs dripping with saliva, its long serpentine neck grazing back and forth over his body. Its nostrils sniffed and snorted at him like a dog's. Venir didn't stir. His body and mind remained in a deep sleep. The dragon had three claws and one thumb on each hand, more man-like than lizardish. A thick fingernail capable of tearing through steel gently poked his body. It snorted at him again, stirring Venir's hair that spilled from underneath his helm. Its neck coiled back like a serpent's, and it began looking around. Its big face snapped back over him.

It grabbed him with its short humanoid arms. They seemed small compared to the rest of its body, but they still held Venir like a children's doll. The dragon's black wings stretched out fifty feet wide. The suns illuminated the leathery membrane of skin that formed them. The wings began to beat and pound the air like a storm as the dragon rose from the ground. In moments, the man and beast were high in the air, while Brool lay alone on the ground below. Over the rushing silver-blue waters of the river the dragon went. It crossed over hills, valleys and small mountain-like ranges. The leaves of the treetops below were green, brown and yellow, and many trees were of an unknown variety.

In the distance, a fortress jutted from the ground to the sky. It was monolithic. Cut rock formed the stones that built its walls over ten stories tall. It resembled the City of Bone, except it was more like a Ziggurat, not just a perimeter wall. The dragon landed outside of its walls where an iron portcullis was open, rusted and twice the size of Bone's huge gate. Vines thicker than a man's leg crept up and over the massive fortress. The rest of the exterior was crumbling and coated in moss. The land that surround it was lush with overgrowth, and any evidence of civilization was centuries gone.

The dragon set Venir down, roared, and launched itself into the sky. *WHUMP! WHUMP! WHUMP!*

It disappeared into the light. The suns crossed over the sky and dipped below the horizon. Venir lay still as a rock; only the rising and falling of his chest gave evidence he was alive. The pale yellow moons cast an eerie shadow over his unconscious body.

A man appeared in the gateway, black and enormous. He was clothed in a commoner's tunic, fingers and neck adorned in gems and gold. The giant stood over fifteen feet tall, and his face and decorated earlobes were long. His black brows buckled as his merciless eyes fixed on Venir. The giant kneeled down, scooped him up like a rodent, and took him inside the fortress.

64

IT WAS A MORNING HE dreaded more than any morning before. A pig pen would have been a more preferable place than Castle Almen. The beautiful palace that he had come to admire so much might as well have been a dungeon. The comforts he had sought all his life were here, but now they only made him uncomfortable. Melegal kept his head down and eyes forward as he headed up the stairs from the servants' quarters.

No one seemed to pay his presence any mind. The servants were brisk with their tasks. He slipped past a few of them in the corridor and made his way into the castle's main halls. There was more than one way to Lord Almen's place below the kitchen. Still, the shortest distance was the way he had passed through the last time. *Lorda Almen, please, not today.* He shifted his floppy hat on his head as his eyes darted all around. It was quiet in the main chambers; the expected rumbling of voices in the dining hall was vacant. *Good.* He was early, and he knew Lord Almen to be early as well. In three long steps he strode past the sofa where Lorda Almen's gracious figure had entrapped him before.

There were voices, female voices, coming from the kitchen. *Lorda!* He was stuck inside the corridor. Turning back was the only way out. After he turned, he noticed two figures in the sofa room. *Slat!* It was a servant man and one of the Almen siblings. He didn't slow, just continued down the corridor and ducked inside an alcove under a stairway. Lorda Almen's voice was getting stronger. Another woman was with her, a younger woman, almost as striking as Lorda herself. Melegal knew of her, but not a lot. She spent much time with the Lorda, though.

He pressed himself against the wall inside the alcove. A three-legged cherry chestnut table with a huge vase full of fresh flowers was the only thing between him and the hallway. It was a lousy place to hide, but it would have to do. He propped Tonio's sword in a dim spot on the inner side of the alcove. *She can find me, but not the sword.*

From behind the small table he heard the women's laughter, tranquil and fluid. Melegal's heart was in his throat. *Calm down!* They had stopped; their robed legs were turned and facing the sofa room. *Go in! Go in! Go in!* More chatter and laughter broke out. It was something about a spree on the Royal Roadway and last night's dinner at another castle. *Shut up and go, wenches.* The conversation continued another ten minutes. *Interesting, I must remember that.* The women's gowns almost hid their feet, but they had turned back his way. Their slippers were as quiet as dust on the floor as they stepped down the corridor. *Almost here.*

He could see the women walking hip to hip, arms around each other's waists like mother and daughter. Again they stopped less than ten feet away. Melegal felt his heart freeze when the younger woman spoke, "Lorda, have you got word back on Tonio? It's been so long, and I fear something terrible has happened to my beloved."

You got that right.

Lorda's voice was soothing when she said, "Oh, Rayal, you are so sweet. I am sure he is fine. He's a soldier now. I've known men to be gone for years. You knew that. Are you lonely, Dear?"

"Lonely is an understatement," she said with desperation in her voice.

"I see, so you've been holding out all of this time. Such a charming woman with men following her every curve. Rayal, you can't be expected to hold out for him."

Don't take the bait.

"No, it's not that. I just want to be crushed in his arms again and gaze on his handsome face once more."

Oh no, you don't want to do that, Lady. Be careful what you wish for.

"I knew my son was wise when he chose you. You are strong, Rayal. You'll make it through this," Lorda said, as her feet shifted in the direction of the table. "Ah, the smell of tiger roses, my favorite."

He could feel Lorda Almen hovering over the table and smell her fragrance as she inhaled the rose petals.

GO UPSTAIRS! GO UPSTAIRS! GO UPSTAIRS!

His brain began to tickle as he continued with the suggestion.

Their feet shuffled, turned and headed back down the corridor.

"Rayal, come and do some gardening with me today. I would adore your company. Let's go upstairs and change."

"Oh, Lorda, I am so sorry. I have to take my little wench of a sister to the stables today, for her weekly lesson. I just love to watch her torment the urchins. She's such a monster."

Lorda let out a pleasant laugh and said, "I see, little Elizabeth is still a blossoming thorn."

"There's no changing her course, it appears. I can't even beat a good deed out of her."

The two women were laughing now. Lorda added.

"She's an odd little wafer. The last time she was here she told me a story about a two-headed puppy you hid from her."

What's this?

"Oh … she did? When was this?"

Surprise, she's seen it, too. Melegal's mind began to spin another direction.

"The last time you brought her by. I told her she must have been seeing things. Two-headed dogs … ha, I've never heard of such a thing. Yes, my little Elizabeth is such a little liar."

Good recovery.

"Is she now?" Lorda asked with a hint of doubt.

"Did I just hear someone mention a two-headed dog?" a loud voice sounded from the stairwell above.

Lord Almen. Son of a Bish!

Melegal's blood ran cold. If Lord Almen caught him here, his life would be over. Melegal's knees began to ache. The long period of squatting had strained his thighs, and he could feel his body tremble. It didn't help that everything else from hair to toe was already aching from the contest the other night at the Octopus. *I'm way off my game.*

"Ah … my handsome husband has arrived. I see you haven't lost your touch for eavesdropping on women's gossip. It's no wonder you are so good with us ladies."

Melegal could hear Lord Almen's leather-soled feet coming down the marble steps. The next thing he saw was Lord Almen's feet joining in with the group. He heard Almen's lips peck his wife's lips.

"So, what do you two ravishing women have to say about two-headed dogs? My ear couldn't let such an interesting story pass." he said, his polished voice just short of a demand.

"Aw, it's just a little girl's tale. There are no such things here. Now, Rayal must be going, and I have some gardening to do. Of course, you heard that already. Rayal, can you see yourself out?"

"Yes, Lorda Almen."

"Don't be silly, Rayal. It would be my pleasure to escort you out, and you must tell me this tale of Elizabeth's. I find such stories fascinating."

Melegal watched all their feet walk away, and then grabbed the sword and stepped from his pitiful hiding spot behind the tiger roses. Looking both ways, he headed down the corridor and into the kitchen. Three women servants were there, paying him little mind as they worked like ants to clean up the kitchen. He sat down at a servants' table. A pitcher of milk and a plate of biscuits greeted him, but he wasn't hungry. He was nervous. *Make it short, Melegal.*

65

VENIR'S EYES PEEKED OPEN. BARS. Steel bars. A rough-hewn stone floor complemented the rest of his surroundings. A thrill rushed through his arms and legs. *I'm home!* He had woken up and thought he was back underneath the City of Bone. He sat up, rattling the chains that bound him to the floor. Something wasn't right, though; it was different. The smell of rot and mold wasn't there. The cell was illuminated by a strange torchlight high above, beyond his reach. The eerie illumination revealed something more: he wasn't alone. Another man was in there, chained and huddled in the opposite corner of the over-sized cell. The man appeared to be venerable, his skin and hair blending in with the gray walls. The old man seemed oblivious to Venir's arrival.

He realized he was pinned inside a cage, steel bars rising twenty feet high to the left and right. There were others in the adjacent cages. There were dwarves, orcs, and gnolls, but mostly men. It couldn't be Bone, but somewhere else. *The dragon?* How had he gotten here? Venir didn't remember a thing. He ran his hands over his body and found nothing but his shirt, trousers, and boots. A metal brace was clamped around his neck, connected to a long chain that was mounted to the floor. He stood up and walked.

If he was imprisoned, it was the biggest cell he had ever been in, thirty feet wide, deep and tall, something not meant for a typical man, but something else. A giant, maybe. He pressed his face to the outer bars. There were more cells to his left and right, as many as eight, maybe ten more. The other figures sat in the silence, their eyes fixed on something else or closed. It was that odd quiet so many had before the guillotine fell, or the noose stretched the life from their necks. Venir rubbed his throat.

The smell of food drifted into his nose. He'd been so busy marveling at his prison that he hadn't noticed the tray of food at the foot of the cell's door. A roasted bird the size of a turkey was there, along with a loaf of bread and a metal carafe of something. Venir's mouth began to water. He looked over at the man in the corner. The man's eyes were peering at him now from underneath busy white and gray brows.

"Eat," the figure's eccentric voice said. "The food is good. The comforts are not."

Venir's eyes went from the food, to the man, to the food. He made an impulsive decision. He fell down on his knees, tore the leg off the bird and took a big bite out of it. It was good, and there was nothing extraordinary about it. He gulped down a few more meaty bites, then put the pitcher to his lips and drank. The water slid down his throat. He pulled off a hunk of bread and stuffed it in his mouth. His growling stomach became more satisfied with every bite he washed down. His senses had been on full alert, but now they seemed to relax. The world he was in was real, hard, cold, and tangible. The strangers in the prison only confirmed that he was alive and not in some odd fantasy world. Maybe it wasn't Bone, but it was real.

"Goodness, you ate that entire pheasant."

Venir whirled around. The old man in the corner was standing over him, green eyes bright with cunning and curiosity. The old man wore nothing more than a short-sleeved set of ragged blue robes. His forearms were corded with muscle above his bony wrists. He had a chiseled face underneath a stiff white and gray beard. The older man seemed younger than he appeared as he spoke in a fluid voice.

"I guess a big man like you needs to eat a lot. Still, I've never seen one consume the entire bird before."

"It was good," Venir said as he rose from his knees, licking the greasy bird from his fingertips. "You wouldn't happen to have a napkin, would you?"

The old man looked like he had swallowed a fly. He started fanning his hands in the air and said, "Oh my, oh my … was that a joke?"

Venir allowed himself a smile as he shrugged.

"BWAHH HA HA HA HA!" The old man was clutching his belly as he dropped to one knee on the floor. "Oh, my sides are aching … I'm too old for this," he said, as he kept on laughing.

With a belly full of food and the sound of another human voice, Venir began to feel like his old self. His head was clear, no longer throbbing with the incessant need to kill. The chronic fight for his survival had subsided as well. The guilt was gone. Wherever he was now, his friends were not. The farther away from him, the better off they would be. Despite the shackles and the surrounding bars and gates, Venir felt free.

"Say, Old Man, when you finish, maybe you can tell me where I am?"

Hack. Hack. The man had his hand on his knee, while the other clutched his head.

"Sure …, sure, just give me a second." The man took a wheezy draw in his nose. "Whew! I can't remember the last time I laughed. So, do you have a name, Stranger?"

"Venir. And yours?"

The man blinked, raised and eye, pinched his finger and thumb on his chin, and gave pause. A few odd moments had passed when the man snapped his fingers.

"Boon … but I haven't been called that in a long time."

Venir remained silent as his blue eyes searched the man's face. Fogle Boon had mentioned his grandfather before, but the man had little resemblance to his friend. Fogle had a large oblong head that sat on a skinny neck and narrow shoulders. This older man stood tall and broad, with a formidable way of carrying himself.

"You know," Boon continued, "I'm not used to looking up to many fellas. I'm pretty tall myself, but by a man's standard you are quite large." Boon reached out and squeezed his arm. "A brute … heh, heh."

Venir looked at the metal collar that was secured around the man's neck. A long chain kept Boon secured to the floor as well. He noted some other things. The large cobblestones on the floor seemed absent of any filth, much unlike the prison holes he was accustomed to. It just didn't seem natural that an area of incarceration would be so tidy. He grabbed the length of chain and began to pull.

Boon's eyes lifted as he bit his tongue and rubbed his bearded chin. He said, "I don't think you can pull that out. Those chains were meant to hold more than just men."

Venir paid him no mind as he tugged away. The rope of chain had links of steel thicker than his thumb. He squatted down, dug his boots into the crevices between the cobblestones, and began to really pull.

66

HE FELT LIKE HE WAS in a dungeon, chained, but without shackles. The walls of Lord Almen's study below the kitchen were closing in. Melegal had followed the man's scowling face down the stairs, every step as uncomfortable as the last. He had the feeling that the Royal Lord was not in good spirits today. He stood straight, one hand holding the sword, the other behind his back. His hat was still on.

Lord Almen was leaning back in his chair, speaking with an irritable tone. "So, Melegal, have you brought me a gift?"

His throat was dry when he replied, "No, Lord Almen, evidence."

"By the looks of you, it looks like this *evidence* was hard to come by. Such marks on a man's face can draw suspicion, as well as many questions. Make sure you avoid my family, detective. But, it is good to see you putting your back into the job. I'll be very interested to hear what you have to say." Lord Almen leaned forward, and his body seemed to rise up in his chair. "Every bit of it."

"Yes, Lord Almen," he sputtered, once again feeling an invisible vise begin to squeeze his chest.

"Well, out with it! Let me see what you have and hear the tale behind it. I don't have all day to watch you stand like a slack-jawed crane."

Melegal unbound the leather cords that held the cloth around the sword. He set the object on Lord Almen's desk and stepped back. Eyeing him, Lord Almen peeled the cloth off Tonio's sword. There it sat, scabbard and hilt, with tiny encrusted gems twinkling in the candle light. He could see Lord Almen's eyes flicker and enlarge. Something about the sword disturbed the man. There was a moment of weakness in his eyes, as if he didn't have things under control.

Lord Almen picked up the sword and pulled half the glimmering blade from the scabbard, asking, "Where did you get this?"

This was the part Melegal hated … the lying. He didn't mind lying, but getting caught in one by Royal Lord Almen would equate to nothing less than torture before death. He could feel a noose tightening around his neck already. *To lie, or not?*

"I took it from the people who led me to him."

Lord Almen slammed the blade in the scabbard and stood up.

"He lives?"

"Yes, and I have seen him myself. I can take you to him—"

"No! Tell me where he is! What is he doing?"

"He is below the grounds of the old prison, locked behind a solitary door, in part of the old city."

Lord Almen was silent, his stern face covered in shadows. Melegal knew that a hundred thoughts were racing through the man's mind, his death probably being one of them. He also got the feeling that Lord Almen didn't want his son alive. He must have been telling Lorda something else over the past few months. *Will he let his son live or have him die?*

"How did he look?"

"Terrible. Unnatural."

"Hmmm, was there anyone else in this prison?"

He's wondering about McKnight. "No, Lord Almen, just him."

Lord Almen stood before him, eyes glaring, and said, "So tell me then, how did my son come to be locked up in a remote dungeon in Bone?"

Believe me! Believe me! Believe me!

His head did not begin to tingle or warm. He was certain that Lord Almen knew more than he let on. He had to be careful. It was impossible to know what Lord Almen was thinking. He was certain that Lord Almen knew McKnight was dead, and suspected him, but how much more did he already know? Maybe he already knew where Tonio was. His stretched story was all on him.

"I combed the streets, asked a lot of questions, and shook some people down. Some thugs in the Drunken Octopus accounted for his presence."

"Interesting, seeing how that is where you live."

"Yes, well it's a popular place for troublemakers, like me. It seems that Tonio and McKnight were working together, trying to find someone, a man with a bounty on his name."

Lord Almen turned away and sat back down.

"Continue."

"I made a challenge for more information," Melegal said.

"I take it you won?"

"I lost, bad, but that was my intent. They had the numbers and wouldn't have told me a thing. I took my beating then followed them later. A pair of them led me to Tonio."

"I see," Lord Almen said, "and if I were to confirm your story with these men, where might they be?"

"Still at the Octopus I suspect, just ask for Jeb," he said.

No doubt you won't like him.

Lord Almen ran his fingers through the thick locks of his brown hair. A crease of concern grew on his brow. Melegal was certain the man was about to call him out and have him throttled or whipped. Lord Almen was very specific about the time he came and the schedules he had kept. For all Melegal knew, he had a dozen detectives working for him.

Spotters! Yes indeed, how the Royals loved to use spotters. A simple bribe would garner good information or bad. Melegal began to suspect that there had been a spotter in the Drunken Octopus watching him all along. Still though, spotters weren't entirely reliable. They didn't always see the things they said they did. Melegal began to realize he needed to be even more secluded in his affairs. *Maybe I'm a rat after all.*

He watched as Lord Almen rubbed his face and inspected his nails. The man sighed again and again. *This is unusual.* Melegal swallowed just as the Royal Lord looked back up at him.

"How secure is my son, Detective?"

"Very, unless the thugs let him out."

"And why did they lock my son up instead of kill him?"

Let the lies buy you time.

"My suspicion is that they tried and failed. They trapped him somehow … I presume."

It was all such a bad lie. He tried his best, but only produced his worst ever. If anything, he wished Lord Almen would cut his tongue out. It was serve him better in the long run. *How did I get into this? Venir and that brat, Tonio! A simple skim gone out of control!*

Lord Almen stood back up and said, "Come with me, Detective."

Melegal didn't like the sound of Almen's voice. A chill filled the air. Melegal wanted to ask the Royal Lord where they were going, but his tongue clove to the roof of his mouth. Lord Almen led the way, and Melegal cast a glance back inside the study. Tonio's sword was the last thing he saw as he closed the door. Following the powerful vulture-like man up the stairs, Melegal shuddered within himself. He had never walked within the castle with Almen before. *This can't be good.*

67

BRAK'S DREAM WAS A VIOLENT and bloody maelstrom. Everywhere, he saw his father's image among carnage and death. His dreams were vivid, almost more so than the real world. He could see, smell, and hear things as if he was in the room with them, watching the events unfold. The dreams changed from one scene to another, but in every one his father's peril was just as real as in the last. He could see himself standing in the midst of Venir's fray, trying to bring aid to his struggling father, only to see him washed away in a tide of blood.

Something kicked him in the head, disrupting the dream. He was hit harder the next time, his ribs sore to the touch.

"Get up, Sluggard!" a rugged voice said.

He rolled up on his hips and allowed his vision to adjust. A pair of small lanterns sat on a hapless table in a dingy room. He suspected he was in a dungeon, even though he had never been in one before, except in his dreams. There were several figures about, all dressed in rags from head to toe. These were the men that had taken him by force, dragging him through the streets and down into the sewers. Somewhere between there and here he had blacked out. He could feel a knot throbbing on the crown of his head. He tried to reach for it, but his hands were bound behind him. He tried to speak, but he was gagged.

The same ragged man's foot was about to lay into him. He closed his eyes as he cringed.

"Stop it! He's awake, isn't he?"

A man, shorter and stockier than the rest, lumbered over his way. A dark cowl hung around his neck. A rough hand grabbed him by the face and pulled out the gag. Two pale eyes met with his, leaving an uneasy feeling in his stomach. The others in the group began to bristle.

"Watcha gonna do with him, Boss? He's too big to feed."

"Yeah, let's eat him. I'm hungry."

Brak was frightened now. The thought of being eaten made him sick to his stomach. He tried to fight back the tears, but the drops streamed down his cheeks.

"Interesting, very interesting indeed. Somebody bring me a chair!"

Two of the man-urchins fought to bring one over, both dragging it across the floor. Scowling at them, the man sat down. Brak kept his eyes on the man's feet as he started to shudder.

"Easy, Boy, no one is going to eat you. I would never do that to the son of the one called Venir."

Brak's sagging head pulled itself up to meet the gaze of the man.

"Ah … so it is certain, then. Good, very good. I had my doubts, but something in your eyes reminds me of your father. Interesting how things turn out."

Brak had no idea what the man was talking about. He didn't care, either; he just wanted out of the City of Bone. He let his head fall back down.

"Brak is it?"

He didn't move.

"I'm sorry about your mother. She was a pretty one."

Something began to stir inside Brak, anger and sadness mixing together.

"You avenged her quite well—scared the slat out of me, along with the rest of us!"

The other men grumbled in acknowledgment.

"You took that sword of yours and butchered those men like dogs. You father would have been proud … a chip off the old anvil."

Brak was pulling at his bonds now. Were these men part of the same group that killed his mah?

"Save your energy, Brak. We had no part in your mother's death. We arrived too late. My agents failed to inform me of the pertinent news."

Brak still didn't comprehend a thing.

"In the tavern, I understand you had a conversation with a man, a rather thin and unpleasant man. We've kept tabs on that one." The man ran his eyes up and down him, scratching his head. "Amazing … Boy, are you really only fourteen, as I have been told?"

He hated it when people asked him questions like that. Still, he nodded.

"Hah! That Venir's got something special in his seed! The boy looks like giant-spawn!"

The dull room brightened with the seedy chuckles.

"Let me tell you something, Boy, and if you behave, I will tell you more about your father."

There was a pause.

"Did you hear me? Speak up—I'll not be feeding a giant boy that acts like a mute!"

His throat was dry as he said, "Yes …"

"Your father and I had an arrangement—so to speak—but he didn't really have a choice. You see, a bunch of men were coming for him, and I warned him. If he chopped them down, I'd owe him. It's a political thing really, something a boy from the farms wouldn't understand. As it turns out, Venir did his part and killed them all."

Brak was all ears now.

"They were a dangerous sort, more so than that City Watch coming to harass you. No, these men were killers, like your father, but without a code."

"Code?" Brak asked.

"Ah, that's two words. I can't wait to see you put it all in a sentence. Yes, a code. I've known your father since he was about your age. Even then he was different. He wasn't one to do things for personal gain … like the rest of us. No, he just did what he had to do to survive. Anyhow, I gave him my word. He did his part. I've searched months to find him, but now he's gone. You already met his counterpart, Melegal, but never trust a rogue."

The man leaned back in his chair, causing it to groan.

Brak watched as the man needled his chin with is fingers, and then he resumed looking back down. He wanted to hear more about his father and this Melegal. Brak had learned little from his mother, Vorla, about his father. He always felt like she held something back from him. Somewhere in his adolescent mind her reluctance had made sense, but it still made him mad.

"What do you want with me?" he asked, raising his eyes to meet the man's.

The man cocked his head and said, "Well, I'm not sure, but I will tell you this, you won't survive out there much longer without some help. As a matter of fact, it would be better for you if one of my men just slit your throat. A quick death is better than a long miserable life."

Brak's heavy shoulders began to shudder and he found it hard to breath. He wanted his mother. He wanted out of this city. He looked around, but there was nowhere to go. He was bound, helpless, and crying.

"Ah … get him some food! A lot of it, too!"

The man pulled his chair closer to him and said, "No more of that crying now, Brak. Your father never shed a tear, even when I, er … they took the lash to him."

Brak's body stopped and his tears dried up.

"Now, you can stick with me, for now, and see how it goes, or you can … well, you can't really do anything, but get thrown in the dungeons to die. I'll teach you how to survive and fight, and you just do as you're told."

One of the man-urchins returned with a plate of food and set it on the table. Brak could smell the cooked roast and baked bread. He licked his lips, and his tummy groaned.

The other men snickered.

"I see you're pretty hungry, Brak. Oh, and by the way, my name is Leezir … Leezir the former Slerg. Now stand up."

Brak did so.

"So, do you agree to our arrangement Brak, or do I turn you over to the City Watch? And before you answer, remember, your father was a man of his word. Can I expect the same from you?"

He nodded.

"Excellent, now as I promised, I will teach you how to survive. In Bone, in order to survive, you must fight. Let's see what you can do without three feet of steel in your grasp. If you want that food over there, you are going to have to fight them. They win, they eat. You win, you eat. Simple, right?"

Two man-urchins stepped between him and the table with their hands clenched into fists. One was punching his fist into his hand. A chill washed over Brak like a bucket of ice water. He fought the urge to pee. All he wanted to do was run away.

Leezir whispered in his ear, "Don't hesitate when I cut you lose. Those two are just as hungry as you." As soon as the knife slit his cords the man-urchins charged.

68

HE TURNED RED AND PURPLE, his muscles bursting underneath his shirt like tree roots. The chain held fast as Venir listened for the groan of twisting metal. He roared, throwing more weight and back into it. His teeth were clenched while sweat was pouring from his brow and blue veins rose under his skin like snakes. He tugged away ten seconds more; hoping for the sound of snapping chains, but it never came. He let go, gasping for breath, chest heaving, and arms trembling.

He noticed Boon breathing heavily at his side. Beads of sweat had lined the man's wrinkled forehead. The man had a look of surprise in his face when he caught his eyes.

Boon said, "I thought you were going to explode. For a moment, I even thought that chain might snap. I've never seen a man pull so hard before, and they all pull. There was a minotaur in here once, but not even he could break it. I swear, you almost did."

"Even if I did, there would still be nowhere to go. The door would be impossible." Venir thumbed in the direction of the barred cell door. The steel was thicker than his wrists.

"The door is unlocked."

"What?"

"Yes, and you can leave any time. There just isn't anywhere to go. Let me show you something."

The man stepped behind him. Venir felt something sliding from the metal collar on his neck. Boon waved a pin and bolt in front of his face, and smiled. The older man reached behind his neck and removed a similar pin and bolt.

Venir walked over to the cell door and pulled it open, then turned back around.

"Why don't you leave? Or escape?"

"There is nowhere to go, Venir. If you leave, that dragon will only find you and bring you back. I have tried to leave, but the dragon is immune to my little tricks. My powers are limited as well, the giants saw to that." Boon smiled at Venir sheepishly.

Venir looked up and down the corridor. Its girth reminded him of the stables in the City of Bone. It was strange indeed that there were no guards about.

"Bring me back to where? What is this place?"

Boon said, "You are inside Giant's Home. That's what I call it, anyway."

"Where on Bish are we, Boon?"

Boon's shoulders slumped and his chin dipped as he let out a sigh. He mumbled, "I hate this part."

"What was that? You hate what part?"

Boon's eyes rose back up to meet his and he said, "You are not on Bish, not as you know it. You are where the giants go, on the underside of Bish."

"And what if I want to get back to *my side of* Bish?"

"Heh, heh … Venir, I wouldn't worry about that. No, you probably won't live to see the light of another day," Boon said in a morbid voice.

Venir's battle heat came on him as his survival instincts began to catch fire. The surrounding bars and cells of the prison began to fade before his eyes. He saw now that he was inside a damp dungeon. The chains and steel bars were gone, replaced with slick stone, mold, and stagnating muck. The cavern was large, but not enormous. Wrought-iron candelabra hung from the stone above, where a few candles burned. A foul stench began to fill his nose. He looked down at the tray of food that he had eaten. It was the skin and bones of a fat river rat. The metal pitcher was there but filled with something else, milky and thick. The loaf of bread was hard and molded in parts. He held his stomach.

"Sorry Venir, but you had to eat. You are going to need your strength if it's going to be an entertaining fight."

Venir lashed out, hands clutching at Boon's throat. Boon stood his ground, and Venir's hands passed right through him.

"Bish!"

Boon was on the other side of the room now; arms crossed over his chest.

"Venir, I am not your enemy. I am a prisoner as well. The giants have us all. They brought you here to fight and die."

"NO GIANT BROUGHT ME HERE!" His wild instincts were taking over, like those of a trapped animal. He dove at the illusionist again. Boon was gone and standing elsewhere when he spoke.

"Venir, save your strength. If you live, you can fight another day, but I must ask you, how did you get here, then?" Boon said.

Venir's emotions began to subside. Something honest about Boon's words settled in him. He had been more than willing to die in the Mist, not so long ago. At least it sounded like he had an option.

"Fine! If you must know, an underling threw me into the Mist."

"Where?"

"Leagues south of Hohm, north of Dwarven Hole."

Boon stood at his side now. Venir poked him in the chest, knocking him back two full steps.

"How did you get from the Mist to here?"

"I walked … for an eternity."

Boon had a bewildered look on his face when he said, "So, a giant didn't bring you here?"

"No, but I stabbed one who fled into the Mist. That's where I got thrown—"

"You are the one who stuck Gorfelm! You!?"

"I suppose."

BRAWWWWWWWW!

It was the sound of a hundred battle horns that blasted the interior of the walls. Venir couldn't help but cover his ears.

BRAWWWWWWWW!

"Venir, I am sorry, but your time has come. I must go, but tell me this, where on Bish did you come from last? I've missed my home a long time. "

"Your grandson Fogle, too?"

"What? How did you know that?"

BRAWWWWWWWW!

"You'll only find out if I live."

"I am sorry, but that is unlikely," Boon said with a sigh.

Something unseen assailed Venir, and his eyelids grew heavy. "Just find my pack!"

He rubbed his eyes and staggered. His eyes fluttered and closed as he collapsed to the ground. Boon shook his head and disappeared from the dungeon.

69

V ERBARD WOKE UP FEELING REFRESHED. He stretched out his arms and yawned. The insect box was still playing along with cave drops plopping into the Current. He looked over at the empty bottle of underling port and rubbed his hands together. He was thirsty, and cave water wouldn't do. *Maybe I'll try something different this time.*

"I wouldn't get too comfortable if I were you," an icy voice said.

Verbard's silver eyes almost emerged from his head and his fingernails dug into his palms. *NO!*

His feet floated off the ground as he spun in the direction of the voice. A male underling stood with his leg propped up on a storage chest, wearing black underling mail. The intrusive underling's eyes burned like copper ore. A pair of longswords was strapped along the underling's back and waist, as was a bandana of knives. The underling was as tall as Verbard, thick-shouldered and round-faced. His hair was cut only a half inch from his head. A pair of silver earrings were hooped in his ears, and a matching medallion hung around his neck. It was Kierway, one of Master Sinway's own sons.

Verbard replied, "What a pleasant surprise, Master Kierway. How can I be of some service to you?"

How did I miss you? Verbard was distraught in his error. There had been no evidence of anyone else in Oran's lair. He had checked. No other barges or canoes were about, only his own. Still, there could have been another entrance, and there were other means of traveling the current.

Kierway's thin black lips curled up over his sharp teeth. The intruder rolled Catten's eyes between his palm and fingers. Verbard was uncomfortable at the sight of that. He began to focus on snatching them from the underling master's hand. He kept a spell in mind as he watched Kierway's lips begin to move.

"I see your brother, Catten, is vanquished. I can only imagine how worthless you must feel without your brother. Are you sad, Verbard? Is that why you came here, to drown your sorrows?"

Verbard hated Kierway. Catten hated Kierway. Kierway hated them. Master Sinway's son was not the formidable user of magic that they were. Instead, Kierway was given other gifts in order to compensate for his weakness. Master Sinway was known for gloating over the underling mage brothers, much to the public shame of Kierway. A dark rivalry had loomed between the three for centuries, but Catten and Verbard's exploits forever cast Kierway in their shadow. The loss of Catten put Verbard at a disadvantage. To Kierway, he was vulnerable.

"Carrying out your father's orders has a price, but completing them is worth all the glory."

Kierway stiffened at the remark as his clawed hand began to linger near the hilt of his sword. The underling son's failures were well known in the Underland, his ego only matched by his incompetence in the field. It was so bad that his own father, Master Sinway, had to remove him from the field altogether. Now Kierway was little more than a stooge near the throne.

"It seems your brother is the only one that paid a price ... Verbard," he said, staring at the eyes. He then began juggling them one handed. "I like your brother in this state; he's not as annoying."

Kierway stopped to stare tauntingly at Verbard's glowering face. Verbard let his hatred of the underling grow as a tendril of power reached his fingertips.

"YOU are hardly one to mock my brother's demise! I'd set those eyes down if I were you!"

Kierway allowed for a chuckle with a short chirt. Two figures emerged from one of the surrounding caves.

Verbard made a sharp sucking sound through his teeth. His blood ran cold. Each figure was a hulking mass of muscle underneath a thick layer of ebony skin. Their evil countenances were intelligent and cunning, and their nostrils flared on their feline faces. Their clawed hands looked like black spear tips as they clutched in and out. The legends of death were back. *The Vicious! How can that be!?* He almost didn't realize that both of his hands were glowing now, the light reflecting from all of their faces. If he was going down, he would take Kierway with him. He raised his arms up.

"STOP VERBARD!" Kierway yelled.

The underling mage hesitated. His eyes darted back and forth between the two Vicious. They stood quiet. He lowered his hands.

"I didn't come to kill you!"

"Why else would you come? I'm not used to welcoming committees. Out with it Kierway, or I'll let it loose!"

Kierway held his hands up, palms out and said, "Relax, Verbard. My father sent me to track you ... and assist you."

Underlings were notorious for lying to one another. It was something they all thrived on. The appearance of the Vicious was compelling, however. Truth or lie, the conversation was buying time.

"How long have you been here then, and how did you come to know this place?"

Kierway said, "Just over a week. I know a surface entrance. As for Oran, he and I have had an alliance for centuries, and his banishment did nothing to tarnish that. I even helped him out with his pickling business from time to time." Kierway pointed toward all the odd jars. "It was a good excuse for me to exercise my steels, and it gave me something to do. There is nothing quite as exhilarating as plunging one's blade through the other races. It's just so ... satisfying."

Verbard knew Kierway's exploits well. He had been the underling that trained the Juegen guards for centuries. His skills were better used in the field as a fighter than in command, though. He had pushed his men onward like blood-thirsty hounds, causing many unnecessary deaths. His father had no choice but to pull his reckless son from the field. He also knew that the only thing in the room faster than Kierway's blades was his mind.

Kierway began strolling around the room.

"So, what of Oran? Has he perished?"

"Yes."

"Hmmmmm," the underling son said, slapping his hand on his hilt.

"So, what is it that you came to assist me with?" Verbard hissed.

"My father wasn't confident of your mission. He shared this with me, and I offered him my services. He agreed. I must confess though, I didn't expect to see you alive. The Darkslayer needs to be taken by steel, not mag—"

"The Darkslayer is vanquished! By my power! My brother's power!" Verbard began to rise from the floor. Kierway's impudence had worn thin. "I had the man's heart in my fist! I crushed it! You, Kierway, you will never know anything as great as that! Now, don't waste my time with your charades and stories about steel! I DON'T CARE!" The last syllables shook the room. Kierway backpedaled into a shelf full of jars. The Vicious coiled down like cats ready to spring, their feverish yellow eyes waiting for their master's command.

Verbard's head bumped into the cavern ceiling as he looked down on them all, but he wasn't finished.

"Do you think the Vicious could help you kill the Darkslayer? Did your father not tell you that the man chopped the last pair into bits! He tore through your precious Juegen like rag dolls! Did you not hear that? And you thought you came here to help me? My brother!? Why would we need a fool like you, Kierway? WHY?!"

Kierway clutched his longsword hilts, his body taut, and his face full of rage. Verbard could feel his fellow underling's anger building within. The rivalry had sparked into a full blown feud.

Pull them out Kierway! Pull them out!

Their eyes burned into each other's for another long moment. Each underling was eager to kill the other, but that was not what they had been ordered to do. The order was to kill the Darkslayer, or never return home. As far as Verbard was concerned, the mission was complete. He noticed his brother's eyes now sitting on the ground. They zipped into his palm, garnering a hiss from Kierway.

The standoff was over. He allowed himself to float back down.

"Now, Kierway, I shall return to the Underland and gather my glory. I am sure your father will be pleased with my exploits once again."

The underling son's thick arms were now crossed over is chest. He said, "Aren't you forgetting something? The Darkslayer's head, perhaps?"

"I have my proof."

"What about the man's axe, is it in the folds of your robes? Up your sleeve? Where is your proof, Verbard? Without that my father will skin you alive!"

Verbard floated toward the barge, and with a single thought he was sailing home. He could still hear Kierway's voice echoing down the tunnel.

"He'll skin you alive. I can't wait to see it!"

It could happen and probably would. He wanted to run, but they would only track him down and kill him. The Darkslayer had to be dead. The Mist was not something one could escape from; even the underlings knew that. He pulled his brother's eyes from his pocket and said, "At least there is something left of you. I don't think there will be anything left of me."

He sat with his robes billowing in the darkness as he made the long awaited journey home, empty handed.

70

Almen couldn't help but enjoy — to a mild degree — the amount of pressure he was putting on his newest servant, Melegal. The rogue's eyes were not as piercing and intelligent as before, instead they drifted and flickered. Melegal's confidence was being shaken. His frail-looking body moved a bit slower and was a tad hunched over. Breaking in a new man was one of those pleasures that Lord Almen relished.

Lord Almen could barely hear the man's footfalls as they made their way down the gallant halls. The pair walked by a few sentries, Melegal a few steps behind as he ignored their nervous eyes. How many had he broken over the years to serve his will? He couldn't recall, but only the most worthy ones lasted long.

As they made their way toward the utmost end of the castle, he stopped beside a door. It was nothing extraordinary, a large wooden and brass-hinged door inside of an archway of stone. He pushed on a handle and the door swung inward. A torch was lit at the top of a dark stone stairwell that dropped into the dark. A cool draft of air tickled the fine hairs on his ears. He nodded toward the torch. He noticed Melegal's hand seemed to tremble when he grabbed it. *A nervous little rat now, isn't he.*

Lord Almen knew much more than he let on. It hadn't been long after Tonio, Oran and McKnight departed that his sources procured more information. Troves of coins and jewelry could buy a man all the information he needed in Bone. Magic was a precious resource, too, however, he preferred to be cheap about it. Grunt henchmen like McKnight, Melegal and even Teku's services weren't so hard to come by. Still, they were valuable assets. It just seemed that often, in their line of work, they didn't last long. Almen was careful not to overdo it on his investments.

Now, an assassin and a detective were down, and for the time being Melegal would replace both. The rogue was a work in progress, but just as capable as the others, if not more so. There was something that Lord Almen liked about Melegal. He was a survivor, a cunning mind behind hard gray eyes. It was clear that the skinny man preferred using his razor sharp mind over his body. It could make him a formidable ally and adversary. Plus, he was the comrade of Venir, the scourge of the underlings.

It was a chuckling thought, the day Oran the underling cleric had exposed his thoughts about the warrior. Lord Almen hadn't been able to help but be curious as to who the man was. It had taken some time, but he had found out by courtesy of a chunky City Watchman. It had been in those dungeons, months ago, that his son, Tonio, had demanded to punish a man who had embarrassed him. Lord Almen remembered the rugged brute chained in the dungeon, no more scared of any of them than he would have been in a den of kobold babes. No, the man with the V tattoo was savage, elemental, and frightening. Almen had been tempted to take the man into his service then, but he had respected his son's need for revenge. He had let the opportunity pass, to his regret.

Now, he had discovered that Venir had been carving his way through Bish and the underlings for quite some time. The tales of the two-headed beast were true; many soldiers had seen the man on the beast before. At the same time, Venir was a link to his betrayal at the gates of Outpost Thirty-One. It had been Almen's men who betrayed them all to the underlings.

It had become his goal to see to it that all of the survivors of the fiasco at Outpost Thirty-One were dead. He had decided that it was time to raise the bounty on Venir's head. When the man had returned to Bone, it hadn't been long before he had tracked the swilling fool down. He had sent his shadow sentries after him, only to see all of them cut down. It had been at that point when Almen decided maybe Venir would serve him better alive. If he did not, he would die. It was a common fate for the pawns of the Royal games. So, he forced the services of Venir's friend, Melegal. His newest detective had no knowledge that he was only a worm to catch the bigger fish.

Now, what his deranged son had begun, he was left having to finish. Moving the pieces into place was only the beginning of the fun.

He stood at the bottom of the stairwell now, and a heavy steel door barred the way.

"Go ahead; knock on it, three times only."

Melegal rapped his knuckles on the door. He could see the thief's face as the torch flickered on his apprehensive expression. The man was ashen. *Good,* Almen thought. *Nothing breaks a man like fear.*

He could hear the latches and bolts being pulled out of place. The sounds of metal hinges rubbing together made an awful racket as the door swung open.

"You first, Detective."

71

T HE MAN, VENIR, WAS A mystery to Boon, the long lost wizard.

"He's formidable, I'll give him that," he said, as he rummaged through a large storage room. A long-legged spider was spinning a web in a nearby corner. The insect was as big as his chest. Boon paid the creature no mind.

Boon's alert eyes searched through the piles of arms, armor, clothing, and other gear. He pushed up the sleeves on his blue robes, revealing his corded forearms. The wizard was built more like a lumberjack than a mage. The piles of junk he scoured were over ten feet high. He was making his way to the top of one when he slipped and tumbled to the bottom, crashing over the trove. A smelly breast plate of leather armor was covering his head.

"Orc plate, disgusting," he said, tossing it away. "Bloody giants will take anybody, it seems."

Boon had grown accustomed to talking to himself over the years. He was a loner and had been so pretty much all of his life. If it weren't for the spells he spun, he probably would have quit talking altogether. He had discovered when he was young that most people only enjoyed talking about themselves, and that he preferred not to encourage them. Now that he was trapped on the underside of Bish, he missed all of those pathetic conversations. The people that arrived here didn't last for long, and the giants didn't have much to say, either, other than complaining to one another about the top side of Bish. He had heard it all. Tossing a dented shield from one pile to another, he grumbled, "Bickering giants, collecting people and discarding their toys. Running them through gauntlets and watching them die. What a pathetic plan, snatching people and tormenting them like wild animals."

He renewed his ascent up the pile and began digging around. The giants could have tossed the man's backpack anywhere. Why was he even bothering? The man was doomed. Certainly a backpack would not save his life. Nothing could. Still, Venir knew his grandson, Fogle, a name he had thought he would never hear again. The warrior had also survived the Mist. All of the others, including him, had been brought to the underside of Bish by giants, against their will. They'd been snatched in broad daylight just as often as in the night. He huffed.

Then there were the illusional chains he had shackled the man with. Venir had almost ripped free of the spell, and Boon had a headache to prove it. He had almost passed out from maintaining it, but the brute had let go, and not a moment too soon. Venir was stronger than he had realized, unnaturally strong. Boon had shackled powerful creatures before, even a minotaur, but only Venir had come close to snapping his chains.

"I don't know too much about you, but I've a feeling you have a chance. Now, where is that backpack?"

He rummaged through plate armor, hauberks, cuirasses, and helms. Ancient clothing that had been deteriorating for ages crumbled over his fingertips. He searched and he searched, but time was running out. He hated to see the man die. He wanted to learn more about his grandson, plus he found the man's conversation funny.

"Gotta find something—the giants must be beat!"

He grabbed a great sword, and chucked it away. A helm with three horns, big enough for two heads was kicked down the pile. He was buried to his knees in rust, dried blood and old sweat.

"My, what if it isn't here?" He shrugged. "I've nothing better to do."

BRAAAAAAWWWWNGGG!

"No!"

Boon kicked his way down the pile and headed for the door.

"I don't see how that backpack could have helped, anyway."

It ate at him as he headed down the massive corridor. He wanted to believe in something. There had to be a way back out. *If a man can get in, a man can get back out.* Still, he wanted to know what was in that backpack.

"Oh well, there will be plenty of time to look later. Venir … huh … I wonder if I'll remember his name tomorrow."

72

B RAK CRINGED AS THE TWO man-urchins rushed him. In a split second he was overwhelmed and screaming for his life. All he could feel was knotty hands driving into his ribs and taking his breath. He was scared. A pair of fists punched him in his jaw. He tasted blood in his mouth as he writhed on his back.

"Stop! Please, stop it! Please!"

They didn't. Instead their blows came faster and harder. He caught glimpses of the faces that assaulted him. The rags that draped over their faces had come loose. Unlike the other man, Leezir, their faces were pitted and scarred. One's eye drooped, and his teeth were crooked and smelled of rot. The other's face was chewed up with a flat nose full of large blackheads. Both had wiry hair, and lice fell from their jolting heads. He had never seen such ugly men before, a nightmare come to life. It only intensified his panic. He tightened up into a ball and pissed himself.

"Fight, Brak! Fight or you will DIE!" Leezir was shouting in his ear, while the men continued on without relenting.

Blow after blow came, but they began to subside. He was coughing now, making it hurt even more as he cried out, "Please STOP! Please, I didn't do anything! I'm not hungry!"

Leezir said, "What are you two stopping for? Are you winded? My men tire from fighting a man that doesn't fight back! Hapless bastards!"

"He's hard, Boss. It's like hitting a bag of sand. Can't we use clubs or something?"

Brak saw Leezir swing a large white club at the head of a diving man. The other was doubled over, clutching his sides as he backed away.

"Impressive, Brak. These two men are tired from just beating the slat out of you. Perhaps I shall bring in two more. You two—on your feet!"

Another pair of man-urchins now stood by the table with the food.

"Please, don't let them beat me. I don't want your food. I just want to leave," Brak begged, wiping the spit and blood from his mouth.

He could see Leezir's face fill with fury. The man got right up in his face and said, "Your father would have ripped these men in two when he was your age. You're bigger than my men, much bigger than your father back then, too, yet here you lie on the floor like a big baby. You just got the snot beaten from you by two grown men. You can still speak and beg, but you can't FIGHT!?"

Brak looked up at him, wiping the blood from his dripping nose. "I don't want to fight," he whined, tears running down his face. "Just make them leave me alone … p-p-lease."

He was answered with a hard boot in his stomach.

"I'm tired of hearing you cry like some overgrown toddler! Look at those men, Brak! It was men like them that killed your mother! It was men like them that tried to kill your father! WOULD YOU NOT FIGHT THOSE MEN TO SAVE YOUR MOTHER?"

He stirred. Holding his stomach, slowly he began to pull himself from the floor.

"Yes Brak, you have to fight if you want to save yourself or someone else."

Brak took in a breath, wincing as he stared down on the man-urchins. They were menacing despite their ragged clothes, black toe nails sticking out from one of their boots. His jaw was sore, and his eyes were beginning to swell. Still, he could not hold back tears as he raised his fists. The men laughed at him.

Leezir just rubbed his head and said, "Fine. This experiment is over, boys. Get the clubs and beat him until he dies."

Brak could only watch in horror as the man-urchins took up the huge clubs. They all pulled the ragged cowls from their heads, revealing their ugly faces. Their eyes were dark and full of cruel and murderous intent. They came at him.

"Let's crack his skull," one said.

"You take the head; I'll bust up the rest."

"Farewell, Brak. Better to die now than suffer a day longer in Bish. You're welcome," Leezir said, heading for the door.

A sense of abandonment began to renew itself inside him as he watched Leezir go. He turned his watery eyes toward the men with the clubs. He knew they were going to hurt as he backed away, but there was nowhere to go.

"This is gonna hurt …" one said. "But don't worry; it won't be long before we knock you cold. You won't feel a thing after that."

"Except maybe the sound of your skull breaking open and your brains spilling out," remarked the other.

Brak's heart began to race. He didn't feel a thing now as he just watched the men's aggressive approach. One was whooshing his club in the air; the other was loose and comfortable, head weaving back and forth. At him they came.

Brak pulled his arms up as the first one swung at him with a wild blow. The club bounced off the back of his tricep, bringing forth a gasp. He didn't want more of that. He grabbed the club, drew the man closer, grabbed his arm, and caught a blow to his chest from the other man. He winced, but didn't let go.

"Hey, what are you doing? Let go!" the man-urchin cried as Brak squeezed his forearm. Brak didn't know what he was doing; he just didn't want to be hit again. His fingers squeezed the man's scrawny arm, pinching the bone and drawing a cry of pain. As the other club pounded into his back he slung one man into the other.

Whap!

Both men fell to the floor. As the pair of men scrambled to their feet, he grabbed one by the hair and the other by the collar. A sickening sound followed …

Smack! Smack! Smack!

… as he slammed one face into the other, again and again. He felt the bones in their faces giving in. The man-urchins sagged between his hands, broken and lifeless. The other two came back and brought their full weight upon him, tackling him to the ground. One pinned his arm as the other stomped on his hand. He screamed as he punched the one stomping on his other hand in the gut.

"Ooomph!" The man fell down, gasping for air.

He wrapped his arms and legs around the other man and squeezed him hard. He didn't know what he was doing; he just wanted the fight to stop. The man's eyes were bulging from their sockets and his face began to purple.

"S-sstop, can't breathe—"

Crack!

Something hit him hard in the back. It was Leezir, wielding his cudgel, a smile growing behind his black cowl. He said, "That's enough, Brak! I think you've broken the man's arm, or ribs. Fight's over … you won! Now eat!"

He looked around with wary eyes. No one else was moving, except him and Leezir. Fighting now for short draws of air, he regained his feet and staggered over to the table. He looked at Leezir, who gave him a nod. He dove in, savoring every bite despite the tears he couldn't stop shedding. He chewed on.

Leezir joined him at the table, watching with avid interest.

"Impressive, I'll say that. You are strong, Boy, very strong, like your father." Leezir laid his white ash cudgel on the table and pulled off his cowl. He was pleasant looking compared to the rest, his pale eyes and sandy hair softened the man's rigid interior. "Just so you know, Brak, I was going to let you die, but you survived. You fared as well as could be expected. So, now that you know what you have to go through to live, it's time to teach you to fight."

Leezir set Brak's swords on the table. Brak continued to eat, licking the greasy meat from his fingers.

"You know how to use these," Leezir said.

Brak shrugged. His mother had taught him a few things over the years, but they hadn't practiced much. She had always seemed unhappy when he played with the blades, so he hadn't pushed himself, hating that tight look she made with her face.

"Brak, you stick with me and you'll learn. That's a better offer than most orphans get. It's perhaps not the kind you are accustomed to, but you'll have a family," Leezir said, looking at the groaning figures on the floor, "and that's better than no family at all."

Brak didn't know if the offer was good or bad, but it sounded good to him. He also didn't have much of a choice. The truth was he didn't want to travel alone in the city, or anywhere else, for that matter.

"Will you feed me?"

"Yes, you'll be fed."

"I eat a lot," he said with his mouth full.

73

S EFRON'S PASTY FACE WITH ITS triple-chin was the first thing Melegal saw peeking around the door. All of Melegal's worries were replaced with disgust. As the door widened open, he could see and smell more. The smell of blood, rot, and fear filled his nose. He knew that smell, the scent of torture on the horizon. *Blast it! I'm a fool!*

Sefron bowed as Lord Almen walked through the doorway. Melegal followed, avoiding the sneering cleric's gaze. He swore he could feel the man's eyes jamming knives in his back. He tried to moisten his dry throat with a swallow as he scanned the cruel devices that he passed by. Rusting shackles dropped from the ceilings along with assorted blades and whips that hung along the walls. He noticed his hand was clutching at his vest. *Stay calm, Melegal.* He lowered his hand to his side and felt the comforting bulge of his blade. He took a long silent breath into his nose. *Why is he bringing me here? This can't be the end.*

Lord Almen stopped beside a bloodstained table that held branding irons and screw devices for thumbs and feet. Sefron shuffled alongside the tall Royal, wheezing behind a gap-toothed grin. Both men were staring at Melegal. Sefron reached around the table and grabbed a lash that was hanging on the other side. Melegal heard the door creak shut in the distance, followed by two pairs of booted feet. Two sentries emerged from around a standing stockade, holding a woman up.

"Is this the culprit?" Lord Almen asked of Sefron.

"Yes, Lord Almen, she is the accused."

Melegal took a closer look at the disheveled figure. She was young, her hair a long mop that covered her eyes. She was in servants' clothes that were now torn. She raised her head. *No!* It was the servant girl he had tussled under the sheets with days ago. Her face was bruised and swollen, and her lips were cracked with blood. Her eyes met his.

"I didn't do it, Melegal," she said with little breath. "That wicked man lies. He tried to force me on him. He *urk!*"

The sentry jerked the collar that bound her neck. The young woman's face began to redden as her eyes bulged. Melegal turned away. Sefron was smiling at him.

Lord Almen said, "Is this true, Sefron? Did you accost one of my servants?"

The cleric was as composed as ever when he said, "No, my lord. The woman was rummaging in the upstairs quarters. She was very suspicious when I questioned her. I called for the sentries, had her searched, and found this on her person."

Sefron held up a gold earring with sapphires surrounding a white pearl.

"That is from the Lorda's box," Lord Almen said.

"I didn't take it my lord! I swear I did not take it! He lies!"

The pressure began to build in the back of Melegal's head like a vice. The set-up was clear, but why?

"Lord Almen," Sefron said, "I did not conduct the search. It was this pair of men, long-standing servants of Castle Almen."

"Is this true?" Almen said in the general direction of the sentries.

"Aye, Milord."

"I see. This is a serious crime, indeed. Death is in order—"

"NOOO! Please, I didn't take it, my *ulp*—"

"As I was saying, death is in order. However, even servants can make mistakes, and I am feeling merciful today. Let the lesson be learned with as many lashes as she can stand." Melegal noticed Lord Almen looking is way. He held his gaze. "Sefron, let's let Detective Melegal handle this one. After all, it is a detective's duty to discover these indiscretions, is it not?"

Sefron tossed him the lash. The sentries dragged the sobbing woman to a post and chained her to it. They tore the remaining clothes from her back. Melegal could see the smooth skin on her back, not a single blemish, scar or freckle. He could still feel her soft alabaster skin on his fingertips, and now it would be turned as rough as grated cheese. He could feel all of the eyes on him as he stepped forward with the lash.

He had been whipped many times when he was young. Since, he had done everything possible to avoid the lash.

As far as whipping someone else, it wasn't something he'd ever considered. He'd kill them first. Now, however, there was no choice. He was put in the impossible position of ruining another person's life.

He stepped behind the shaking girl, the lash held loose in his hand.

"Detective, keep at it until Sefron says to stop. I want to make sure she is never tempted to steal from this castle again. This is a better option, so spare her life."

He heard the servant girl say, "It's all right Melegal, I won't blame y—"

Crack!

She writhed and wailed.

"Again!" Sefron yelled.

Melegal drew back.

Crack!

"Again!"

Fresh welts rose on the woman's soft back and blood dripped down around her waist.

Crack!

She was screaming and flailing without control, but Melegal didn't hold back.

"Again!"

Melegal added one more thing that he was going to do in his life: Kill Sefron.

He was a slave of the castles again.

74

"**Y**OU'RE ON, VENIR."

The voice was familiar, but not as tranquil as before. Venir sprung up on the balls of his toes. His head was full of cobwebs, but the heat of the coming battle began to burn them from his mind. He found the voice and the face. It was Boon. The older man's hard face seemed poised for some kind of battle, but he had no weapons or armor, just a stern look. Still, Venir got the feeling the man would and could fight anything and had done much of that before, even for a mage.

"Where am I?" he said, looking around.

His surroundings were vast. Polished stone walls of gray rose at least fifteen feet high inside the corridor where he now stood. The corridor was wide, big enough for two trains of horses. There were no such tracks on the dirt-covered ground, only ruts. The ground was otherwise smooth in most spots. This was another odd place that smelled of death and decay, but was otherwise bright with light. He looked up and realized there was no ceiling, only the passing light of the suns. At least, he thought so.

Boon said, "It's a maze."

"A what?"

"Surely you have been in a maze before, Venir?"

Sure he had. Tombs, catacombs, sewers and streets, all were a maze of sorts.

"I can't say I haven't been, but this looks more like a corridor … for giants."

Boon rubbed his knotty fingers up and down his dark blue robes and shifted back and forth on his feet. "It's a corridor of death with more twists and turns than your guts have. For every horror you survive, another will replace it. It's the end of your journey, Venir. I'm sad to say it, but at least you know what to expect. Most of the others that come through don't get that privilege."

Venir glowered down at the mage.

"No need to thank me," Boon added.

Venir smiled and Boon did too.

"Hah. Another illusion, I'd guess?"

Boon shook his head.

"No, but I am. I'm up there, actually," Boon said, pointing above his head.

High above the walls was another platform where men and women were standing. They were giants, one and all, leaning on the rail or gripping it with fists as big as his head. Some of the faces were grim, others hardy and jovial. The only difference between giants and men was their size, but far away as they were, they seemed to be normal-sized. He knew better because he could see the image of Boon, much smaller than the others, sitting on the rail, waving down at him. Then, he noticed something else, and his smile expanded as large as a field. A giantess with the most enormous breasts he'd ever seen was looking at him. *I'd crawl into the Underland for a closer look at those.* A fleeting memory of Kam scowling interrupted his thoughts, and something else.

"This is no time for lust! You're about to die! Snap out of it!"

Venir realized Boon's image was waving in his face.

"Huh?"

"Get your wits about you! That's pretty much all you have to go with."

Venir looked down and only saw his bare toes on the dusty ground. He patted himself down. All he had were his pants and cotton shirt.

"Not exactly what I had in mind to face my death in. Got anything with a shine to it?"

"BWAHAHAAHA!" Boon laughed.

He's insane, Venir thought, looking up. He saw Boon whispering in the ear of one of the giants, who let out a thunderous bellow. The others joined in, a booming laughter of what seemed to be a thousand voices.

"They liked that," Boon said, clutching his side, "… but no. However, you might find something shiny in the maze, if you live long enough."

Venir looked down the length of the corridor. He could see a break in the walls farther ahead. It was the same behind him, with a break on both sides of a dead end. He looked back at his toes and wiggled them. It didn't make much sense that they hadn't left his boots on.

"Yep, no boots. I never saw the point of it myself, but it's a tradition with them," Boon said, scratching his nose.

"So tell me, did you have to go through this maze?"

"No, I was brought here for a different purpose, I suppose."

"Being?"

Boon shrugged. "No idea. I just do as I'm told."

"Don't you want to leave?"

"Hmmm … maybe … But, I don't think it's possible to go back, not with Blackie out there."

"Blackie?"

Boon's eyes brightened as he answered, "Yes, the dragon. He serves the giants, but you don't need to concern yourself with such things. You need to focus on what lies ahead."

"Why should that concern me if I'm about to die?"

"True." Boon needled his chin hairs. "Venir, I looked for your backpack. I had no luck with it, but out of curiosity, what was in it? There is still time to look for it, you know."

Venir noticed that the big bodies of the giants were getting restless above. His time was coming up. Strange sounds began to catch in his ears, echoing from down the corridors: shuffling, rustling, growling, and the like. There was a sound of a gate grinding open in the distance.

The battle heat came on him even stronger, washing away the sluggishness from whatever had put him to sleep. The blood coursing through him began to warm him like the rising suns. A fight was coming. He clenched his fists. Boon's image came closer. He didn't trust the man, but it seemed Fogle Boon's grandfather was all that he had.

"I'll tell you if you agree to help me however you can."

"Agreed."

"Your word on your grandson, Fogle?"

"Yes, yes, my word on my own grandson. I wish we had more time for you to tell me how you met."

"You never know," Venir said rubbing his hands into the dirt. "All right then, my backpack has some common gear and an old leather sack."

Boon gawped and his fingers tickled the air as he demanded, "Tell me about the sack! Does it have heavy stitches?"

"A patchwork of them."

Boon licked his lips.

"Is it magic?"

"Aye."

Boon's eyes were transfixed on Venir. A familiarity grew between them.

"I can't believe it," Boon whispered.

BRAAAAAAWWWWNNGGG!!!

"NO!" The mage shouted, "Venir, live as long as you can. I must go!"

The image of Boon drifted away, and Venir stood alone.

<h1 style="text-align:center">75</h1>

HER HEAD FELT LIGHT AND full, like a stuffed feather pillow. Her faded vision began to sharpen around the image of Lefty Lightfoot. The look on his face was one of kindness tinged with guilt, shock and fear. He was the last thing she remembered thinking about.

Kam pulled her knees up to her chest and said, "Come over here, Boy." She patted the quilted blanket on her bed. Head down, Lefty made his way over. *He's never looked so sad,* she thought. She reached over and poured a glass of water. Her arms trembled as she tried to pour it.

"Here, let me get that," Lefty said, hopping over. He filled the glass and handed it over to her.

"Get up here, Lefty, and tell me what's going on. How long have I been asleep? I feel like I just woke from the dead." She hoped the water would take the rattle from her voice. She noticed the loose rings on her fingers and felt her face. She ran her fingers through her hair. "Bish, I must look terrible."

"KAM!"

She dropped her glass at the sound of Georgio's bellow, but Lefty caught it before it even spilled a drop. Georgio dove headfirst over the footboard and crushed her legs.

"Easy Georgio!"

The big boy froze; his big brown watery eyes were wide. They melted her within.

"Ah … come here and give me a hug. You too, Lefty."

Within moments she was soaked with tears. The heavy sobs coming from the boy shook the bed and she found herself sobbing heavily as well. She didn't understand what could have gotten into the boys. It was as if they hadn't seen her in weeks. It was a good feeling she felt though, something she hadn't felt in a while.

She tried to pull away from Georgio's strong arms that were crushing her waist. Georgio was almost as big as her now. She said, "All right, all right you two, I need to breathe … let me go please."

The hands loosened around her and the boys sat back. Both of their eyes were puffy and red, as if they had just come from her funeral. An eerie feeling began to settle inside of her. She looked at Lefty, but his innocent face still seemed as if there was something to hide. She grabbed Georgio by the hand and asked, "How long have I been asleep?"

Georgio looked at Lefty, who was looking down on the bed.

"Uh … I think two weeks, maybe not quite —"

"Two weeks!" She was on her feet now and heading through the door.

Lefty was tugging on her hand saying, "Kam, you must rest. Everything is all right. Joline can explain it all. I'll go and get her."

Everything was in place in the apartment, even the coffee smelled good. *Two weeks?* It might as well have been a year. The Magi Roost would be a wreck without her. *Palos!* The fiend of a man would be up to something, she could feel it. For all she knew, he might have hoodwinked the place. She noticed Lefty was still pulling at her arm.

"Kam, please, sit down," he urged.

"Lefty, let go, I'm fine!"

Her body began to quiver as her legs failed from underneath her. Someone was propping her up and then easing her down onto the couch. She tried to move and speak, but she couldn't find the words. *I need help. This can't be happening.* A dozen faces of Lefty and Georgio swirled before her eyes. She felt herself spinning and then nothing else.

76

FEELING SMALL BETWEEN THE EXPANSES of the corridor, he ran and jumped as high as he could, reaching for the upper rim of the wall. His fingertips grasped several feet short of the lip. He landed on his feet and ran his hands over the surface. The walls were smooth, solid like stone. There wasn't the slightest finger hold. He didn't even think Melegal could do it. He looked up. About a dozen giant faces watched him with interest. He could feel their eyes following him as he treaded down the corridor, to the north, south, east or west, he did not know.

Something emerged from one of the openings in the wall ahead. It was a pair of kobolds, of all things. Their little bodies were barely four feet tall. Tiny horns rose on the heads of their dog-like faces with reptilian skin. One held a spear, and the other grasped a short sword in both hands. They approached, long tongues flickering as they hissed from their mouths. Venir strode toward them, towering like a giant before them. The corner of his eye caught something else along the corridor. The bones of beasts and men were piled along the wall. The flesh sagged on some of them, and the others seemed to be picked clean. The kobolds, like hungry hounds, must have devoured them.

I'm gonna make it farther than this.

"Kobolds, Pah!" he spat. "You rodents better consider yourselves lucky that Mikkel isn't here!"

The pair of vermin stood their ground, taunting him with their weapons. Venir was ready to take their toys away and stab them in their necks. He was twenty paces away when he fell. That weightless feeling from the mist was back. The battle heat caught fire, and his arms shot out like crossbow bolts. His fingers caught the lip of the pit, sliding as they fought to grab hold of something firm. Below his dangling feet was a pit full of steel spikes. Its victims were many.

Legs kicking for traction, Venir fought his way up onto his elbows. Something jabbed him in the forearm. A small spear dangled in the meat of his flesh. Snarling, he ripped it out. On the other side of the pit, the Kobold was preparing to throw another. He pulled himself out of the pit and rolled to the side, barely dodging another spear that sailed past his neck.

The fires inside him were a burning hot furnace now. He ran over to the spear and snatched it from the ground. Something else approached from behind him. The ground shook beneath its feet as it charged his way. *A minotaur!* It was seven feet tall and carrying a great sword. Its bull-like face snorted. Its hooves pounded the ground as it barreled his way. The chasm of the pit between him and the kobolds was far, but Venir ran toward it. He sprinted and leapt from the edge of the pit. He was in mid-air when he threw the spear into one kobold's throat. He landed and rolled away from the other one, which stabbed its sword at his chest.

Venir got up to one knee, deflected the tiny humanoid's swing with his forearm, and punched it in the face. The stunned creature dropped its blade just before Venir hurled it screaming into the pit. A sickening sound followed as it was impaled on one of the long spikes.

On the other side, the minotaur stood for a moment like an angered beast, its powerful hooves digging into the dirt, and then it began to pace, sweeping its massive sword back and forth. Venir snatched up the short sword, hunkered down, and gasped, "Go ahead, jump, you two-legged cow!"

The minotaur stomped, roared, turned, and thundered back from where it came, out of sight.

"Slat!"

Venir was pretty sure it knew another way around to find him. He sucked in some deep breaths and checked the wound in his forearm. The puncture was nasty, but the muscle wasn't torn. He looked up, but there was no applause, only the stoic faces of the giants.

"Are you disappointed — arseholes!"

Don't forget the booby traps.

He found the tiny footprints of the kobolds in the dirt, and followed them. *You can't be too careful when you're trying to survive.* Two sets of tracks led into the opening from which they had emerged. There was no other way to go but follow another wide corridor to the left. He followed the footprints another fifty feet, and they disappeared. It was as if the kobolds had been lowered from above, dropped like rats into a maze. More gaps in the walls could be seen ahead, along with more piles of bones. He noticed the canine teeth of a gnoll's skeleton lying against the wall. He kept his shoulder to the wall, his eyes on the ground. Venir feared more pits could be anywhere, and other traps as well. It was one of those times he could have used Melegal. Detecting traps was not his forte, killing was.

He poked the gnoll skeleton's figure with his sword. The weapon seemed like a toy in his hand. His lost hunting knife would have felt much better. The claws on one of its feet were still intact, a potential weapon. It might help, and the dead gnoll's chain mail armor looked like it would fit him just fine. He knelt to get them. The sound of a bull crying out echoed from somewhere. He couldn't tell if it was close or far away. He started working faster.

He ripped the head and arms from the gnoll in order to tug the chain mail from its carcass. A foul smell of rotting fresh caused him to gag. The chain mail had preserved some of the flesh. Venir began to realize that this gnoll may have been eaten recently, just a few days past. Blood red and bloated larva-like bugs almost as big as his fingers were still eating what was left of the humanoid. He recoiled when one bit deep into his hand. He smashed it. Red gooey juice squirted out.

"Blast!"

The armor was worthless to him. It would take at least an hour to get all of the bugs out. The sound of the minotaur was getting closer, or was it something else. A strange clicking sound caught his ears. He knew it. His heart pumped faster. Only one thing made that clicking and clacking sound. He squeezed the small sword in his white-knuckled grip.

Striders! Bone!

77

HE WAS BACK, BACK IN Lord Almen's secluded study and ready to stab a knife into his skull. The Royal Lord sat at his desk, toying with Tonio's sword. Its keen edge was razor sharp, without the slightest knick on it. The Royal was testing the balance in his right hand, cutting the air with short pen-like strokes. *Say something, or kill me.* Melegal could hear the air filtering in and out of the hairs inside Lord Almen's snobbish nose. It was heavy, annoying, and getting old. So was standing for an unnecessary and prolonged amount of time.

The past few days had been horrible enough: beating an innocent serving girl had left him numb. A fresh callous began to harden around what was left of his humane side. He wondered if he would feel much worse the next time. He was shaking his head inside his mind. Doubt was assailing his thoughts. *Enough!*

Melegal spoke.

"Have you decided what you want done with Tonio? Does it involve me? I've got Slerg business to attend to, unless you have changed my priorities."

Lord Almen looked at him like a hawk that was ready to snatch a mouse.

Go ahead, kill me.

The man's thin lips under his high cheek bones began to rise up into a smile. For a moment, Melegal thought it was the last smile he would ever see. Lord Almen stood up, sword in hand, tip pointed his way. A gentle bend found its way back into Melegal's knees. *You won't catch me off-guard again.*

Lord Almen replied, "What do you think I should do with my son: bring him home, or kill him?"

It was a shocking question. *Kill him!* His son deserved nothing less than death. He was one of the worst that the Royals had to offer. Of course, Melegal had to wonder where that came from. *Like father, like son. Hmmm … Kill him, and then kill yourself. Even the living dead can dream.*

"Your son didn't appear to be worth saving. I saw no humanity in him … only a danger of the most unpredictable sort. Whatever he is, he's more monster than man."

The tall form of Lord Almen glided over and bounced the tip of his sword on his chest. The slight pressure of the blade began to dig right where his heart was pumping like a frightened rabbit. *Just do it, or let me leave.*

"I'm sure it would break his mother's heart to see him so, but still … I am curious."

Curious what the Lorda will do to you when she finds out you turned him into a monster. I'd like to see that. Almen turned away and began slicing the blade back and forth over the floor. Melegal could tell the man was having trouble dealing with this dilemma. If Tonio could be controlled though, it would be a formidable weapon in his hands. No doubt he would want to have another powerful ally under his control. Who could be more loyal than his own son? Still, it didn't seem like a reasonable option.

Almen leaned back from his desk and stuck the longsword into the stone ground. The man's tight lips seemed to take forever to part as he said, "I tell you what, Detective, I don't think I am going to be the one to decide his fate. I think I will leave that to his mother."

There was a long silence, but that was better than having a sword rammed through his chest.

"Tell me your thoughts," Almen demanded.

"I think you are very wise. Shall I have someone send for her, Lord?"

"Ha!" Almen laughed as he came over and put his hands on Melegal's scrawny shoulders and squeezed. "No, I'll be leaving that honor to you … Melegal."

"Me?" he said, the pitch of his voice going up as Almen's fingers dug deeper into his shoulders, somehow causing him to twitch with pangs of pain in his neck and arm.

"Yes, you. Not only are you going to tell her that you found him, but you are going to get the honor of telling her how you came to find him. You'll be certain to leave out the entirety of my part in this." Lord Almen chuckled. "I must warn you, Lorda is very perceptive, so make sure your lies are good ones."

Lord Almen let go, pulled the sword from the stone, and sheathed it. He tossed it to Melegal.

"Here you go. You'll be needing this. Good fortune on your quest."

"Uh … what about the Slergs, Lord Almen?"

"See to my wife first, and if you survive you can go after the Slergs," Almen said as he sat back at his desk. "It's your day to be the hero or the goat, depending on how you sell it."

Melegal nodded, backed away, and opened the door. When he closed it, Almen was hunched back over his desk. He made his way to the top of the steps and took a deep breath. *What did he mean, 'survive'?*

He grabbed some dishtowels as he passed through the kitchen, to conceal the sword. A hundred lies were running through his mind. It was the first time in days he felt like he had some control, but to what end? The Lorda was no fool. The slightest bit of mistrust of him would relieve him of his head. As he made his way down the corridor, two sentries were coming his way, carrying the bleeding and sobbing serving girl back to the kitchens. She looked away from his gaze. He could see the gentle hand that had been so deft at caring for him days ago. The pair of sentries gave him seedy smiles when they went by. Melegal felt hollow. *Gotta move on. Put it behind you.* His hatred for all things Royal refilled him. Sefron was shuffling his way as well.

"And where do you think you're—"

Melegal lowered his shoulder into the sap of a man, knocking him to the ground, and kept going. He could hear the foul cleric yelling obscenities, but paid him no mind. He headed up the stairs, past the portrait of Tonio, without a solid plan in his mind. *I'm gonna die anyway, but not before I take that bastard and some more with me.*

78

As FAR AS BOON COULD figure, he had been living on the underside of Bish for years, maybe even decades. He had stopped counting after it began to seem pointless. He wasn't going anywhere. Now, as he watched Venir battle for his survival, he shook his head. It seemed that brutal contests such as this would be beneath the giants. They had proven to be obsessed with them, however, and he didn't understand why.

He found the giants fascinating, but short sighted. They could do everything that men or underlings could do, with power beyond his own dreams, yet all they did was doddle and twittle with their days. It was as if their minds were as small as that of a man's, regular brains hosted inside barren cave-like skulls. *Big, tricky, and stupid.* He sighed.

All the giants had focused their eyes on the man below, wanting to catch and discern every desperate movement. Their lazy eyes glimmered with anticipation. He had seen that look before, that sporting hope that someone might survive their game. Of course, none ever even came close, but then again none had made it much farther than Venir. He just wished he could somehow help the man fighting for his life below. But what could he do.

I need the sack.

Rubbing his lips and short fuzzy beard, he peered back and forth between the giants and the man. *Do they have the sack?* It wasn't likely they would pay attention to such a small thing. They were more obsessed with ornaments of jewels and metal. The giant man beside him held the rail, clicking the wood with a gold bracer that would fit around Boon's neck. He didn't understand the value of that.

The sack … where is it?

Boon couldn't go anywhere while the fight transpired, they wouldn't allow it. He would have to wait until Venir was dead. He was torn, wanting the man to live, but also wanting to continue his search for the sack. It had to be his key to freedom. With a numb heart, he watched the man fight on. It was only a matter of time before it would be over. He sighed. *All but the giants are doomed.* He felt ashamed.

79

Dwarven Hole was a marvel. It was a network of iron and stone bridges and stairways that crossed, twisted and spiraled down the mouth of its tunnel and into the ground. Every time Fogle Boon thought he began to grasp the purposes of its internal makings, something else turned his mind inside out. One bridge in particular spanned well over a mile without an arch or steel cable to hold it. There was nothing artistic or beautiful about any of it, only the fact that the sound structures stood in defiance of everything he understood. *It has to be magic,* he thought. But it wasn't.

He stood on a terrace looking across the massive hole in wonder. The grim and hardy faces of the dwarves moved in a steady cadence all around. Their short stout frames moved with an intent gait that reminded him of how others worked with song and rhythm. Fogle had hardly spoken to any of them, being a stranger in their land, but they didn't seem to mind him, either. He had visitors, though. The pleasant faces of their women were appealing when they stopped by. Still, he preferred to keep to himself. He found himself wondering about Kam and how she was doing.

"Ya still trying to figure it out, Wizard?"

Fogle flinched.

"How do you do that?"

"It's what I do, now come on. We got places ta go."

Mood had taken him to many different spots of late. There were ceremonies, meetings, and even the King's chambers, an abandoned throne room of sorts. It was big: more than a hundred yards long and just as wide. Solid pillars make from a variety of rock, minerals, and ore held up a ceiling way up high. At the end was the King of the Blood Rangers' throne, one ton of molded gold, rich with gems as big as his eyes. Mood told him he had never sat in it once, but the big purple cushion seemed to suggest he had.

Now he followed along another mind-scrambling trek. One wide corridor straight as a rail, and another that was narrow and twisting like roots. After he traversed up one set of stairs, he found himself traipsing down another. He was grateful for the small torches that burned with light. Even so, it was a labyrinth to him, a challenge to his brilliant mind, but Mood explained how it made perfect sense. Still, the Blood Ranger insisted he never travel outside of his quarters alone. Fogle was sure he could make it back, but the dwarf insisted he shouldn't try.

His legs became tired on these journeys, but he had gotten used to working through his weariness as he trudged along. Mood stopped at the foot of another door, simple in design and made of wood, and pulled the metal ring. The door swung open without a sound. Fogle fanned the air in front of his nose. The smell was unexpected.

"What is that —"

"Sshh. We can't be waking him if he don't want to be woken," Mood warned.

The room was dimly lit as he peered inside. It was a cave, filled with rows of stables, each big enough for a horse. There must have been a dozen of them, but he didn't see or hear any beasts.

Fogle whispered, "Wake who?"

Mood didn't say another word as he took a long burning torch from the wall and headed down between the stables. The light was dim as Fogle tried to catch a glimpse of anything inside the stalls. There was nothing, not even a single strand of hay. Mood stopped and looked inside that last stall. He heard something rustle inside the stall, something big. Mood nodded him over. *What special thing does he have to show me now? A winged horse? That would be impressive. No, probably a winged goat, knowing the dwarves.* He stopped at the stall's edge and looked inside. Deep sadness fell upon him. It was Chongo. Venir's beast was no longer what it had been.

80

CLICKING THEIR MANDIBLES, THE STRIDERS rounded past the wall. The mauls on their ant-like faces opened and shut with a stomach-turning sucking sound. Their nut-brown bodies were like that of men, but they crouched down on two very long legs. Each held a barb-headed spear longer than a man. Venir tensed as they both poised to throw, but they clacked their mandibles back and forth instead.

Striders were not an evil race, just dangerous hunters. Venir had fought with and against them before. Their ant-shaped faces were dark and smooth, with coal colored eyes like men. They were fast, long-legged and slim-limbed. Their extra-long legs had two sets of knees and thick muscular thighs. Their feet were long and narrow. The pair of striders wore leather armor chest plate as well as arm, knee and shin guards. They were prepared. Venir wasn't.

Venir waved his short sword at them and took a step forward. One strider drew back. The other lowered his spear to meet the charge. *Slat!* He couldn't decide whether to run or charge. The closet strider beat his chest with his fist. Venir's fighting instincts over-loaded his reason.

"So be it then!" he yelled.

Venir charged, raising the short sword high in the air. The inadequacy of his weapon didn't matter anymore; he just needed a part of his arm that could cut and stab. The strider closed in on him with the speed of a panther, its spear lowered like a lance. The other remained at bay, spear hoisted high over its head, its mandibles clacking away.

Clang!

Venir swatted away the tip of the spear that jabbed as his heart. He plunged his blade into the strider's belly, only to see it twist out of harm's way. Venir squared back up on his opponent, determined to work inside its body. He ducked away in time to avoid a metal tip jabbing at his neck, deflecting it to cut open his cheek. The strider had drawn first blood, and both creatures yelled like a pair of busted horns.

For whatever reason, Venir again felt like he hadn't fought in years. His reflexes seemed aged and slowed. He spit blood. *Stop thinking so much!* He kept his head on a swivel as the striders flanked him, their spear tips licking out at his legs. Venir's blade slapped away at the spearheads as he dodged in and out of their trap. Every strike at his person became closer and deadlier. He knew they wanted to immobilize him and pin him permanently to the ground.

"Gah!" he cried, as a spear tip took a chunk of flesh from his side. "Bone! This is getting old!"

The striders were patient and cautious, content to wear him down. The sword in his hand seemed useless against their long spears designed for creatures as big as elephants. They had plenty of room to work those spears, too. If this were one of the countless crowded alleys of Bone, the fight would be child's play, or if he only had Brool.

He flung the sword at one, causing it to duck. When it did, Venir jumped on its spear, fighting to rip it from its grasp. It howled as he kicked it in the side of the face with his bare heel. It wouldn't let go. The two of them rolled back and forth together, grappling over the ground. The creature held strong, with its long black fingers wrapped around the spear shaft like coiled snakes. Venir's back was on the ground. He held one end of the spear, and the strider stood over him, pulling the other end away. The shaft began to bend.

Snap!

The shaft broke in the middle, leaving Venir with half a spear in each hand. The creature lost its balance and fell. He tossed both pieces over the wall. The other strider was bearing down on him, screeching with fury. The tussle on the ground had cleared Venir's head, and now the strider seemed to slow down. He sidestepped the pointed head of the spear and punched the strider hard in the throat. He heard something crackle as it dropped to its knees with its mouth clutching open and closed. He grabbed at the spear, but the creature's grip remained firm.

Out of the corner of his eye he caught the other one diving for the sword. Venir ran and leaped on top of it as soon as its hand grasped the hilt. Venir's dense weight drove the lighter creature to the ground. The strider was pinned beneath him, wriggling like a man, but striders were known for their speed and skill, not their strength. Venir wrapped his muscular forearm around its neck.

"How's this necklace feel!?" he said, cranking it up.

The mandibles clacked in a flurry of desperate signals. They began to slow. Venir spied the other, still prone on the ground, kicking at the dirt. It rose up, one hand on its throat, the other still clutching the spear. Blue veins rose along Venir's arms as he increased the pressure of his choke hold. The strider shuddered, arms and legs flailing, until its neck snapped with a loud pop. Venir jumped away as a spear sailed over his head.

The remaining strider dropped to its knees, clutching its busted throat, mandibles clacking for air. Venir picked up the short sword, walked over, and rammed it through its throat. It fell face first to the ground. Venir wiped the blood off his face as he fought to catch his breath.

He noticed loud, bellowing exasperation above. He picked up the spear that was stuck in the ground and waved it in the air, its tip pointed at the giants. He thought he saw one of the giants clapping, but heard nothing.

Venir stripped the armor and gear from one of the striders. The leather breast plate was too small, but he could strap thigh and shin guards over his triceps and forearms.

"Better than nothing," he said, adding the short sword back to his arsenal.

He followed the striders' tracks on the ground. He turned the corner and could see another intersection. Following the tracks, he stopped just short of the corner and listened. Hooved feet trampled the ground on the other side of the wall. They seemed so close at one point, only to trail back off like distant thunder. Venir kneeled down and ran his fingers over the impressions in the dirt. They led to a dead end farther down the intersection. *Maybe that's where they were dropped in?* He shook his head.

As he was facing the dead end, he noticed he could head straight to his left or his right. Nothing looked disturbed. There wasn't even a rotting corpse. Maybe no others had made it this far. One thing was for sure, he wasn't ready to fight a minotaur. It was something he had never faced before.

"Blasted beast is as big as an ogre," he said.

Hugging the wall and even brushing its cool surface with his shoulder, he headed up the corridor on his right. His side was burning. He looked down and noticed it was dripping with blood. He pulled off his shirt, stretched it around his waist, and tied it off to try and staunch the bleeding. *It'll have to do.* He headed forward, battle heat building with every step. Venir had a feeling this place was filled with booby traps. He heard something scurrying across the ground from somewhere ahead. It was coming faster, getting closer and louder. He froze.

A wave of rats—hundreds of them—were coming his way. The sea of black, white, and gray vermin filled the corridor. Most of them were as big as cats, if not bigger. Their high-pitched squeaking chilled his brains.

Seeing all the gray teeth gnashing below yellow eyes, Venir realized there was only one thing to do. He backtracked at full speed, the vermin nipping at his heels. He had seen rats devour men in dungeons before. It didn't take them long to pick a man clean once they started. He felt the shivers behind his pumping knees down to his toes. Facing the minotaur seemed like a better way to go.

The rats were almost on him when he ran past the striders he defeated before. *The pit, get to the pit.* He sprinted past the walls, winding through the corridors, certain of where he was headed. One dead kobold was still on the ground. The pit loomed ahead, long and foreboding. He could hear the rats screaming for his flesh. He ran on, jamming the spear in the ground and using it to vault over the expanse. Pain jabbed into his ankle and his side as he landed at an awkward angle and tumbled hard to the ground. He looked up and watched the rats devour the kobolds. The rest of the frenzied hoard of vermin were spilling like water into the pit.

The rats weren't alone, however. Something else had been following along their path. On the other side of the pit it stood. It was humanoid and wearing a gray cloak. Its face was hooded, but it wore boots and pants like a man. Its hands were gray and hairy, with long black claws. It reminded him of the Vicious, but it was a little different. A longsword was strapped along its back, where a pink, rat-like tail whipped back and forth. It pulled down its hood to reveal its face. Venir's skin crawled at the sight of the were-rat, a female one at that. *I wish Melegal was here.*

Another sound shook him to his core.

"MAAH-ROOOOOO!!"

There it was, seven full feet of horns and brawn was coming his way. The minotaur's hooves shook the ground where he lay. Venir glanced over his shoulder. The were-rat stood with her arms across her furry chest, tail slashing back and forth. The screech of the hungry rats in the pit was like a nail being driven into his ear hole. Venir shook his head. *Die fighting!*

"So be it!"

He lowered his spear at the minotaur and charged.

81

P *OW-POW-POW …*
Every blow shook his bones. Everything hurt from his lips to his toenails. The fight, or lack thereof on his part, seemed to last forever. All he could do was feel a heavy fist rise and fall on his face, and he was helpless to stop it. He wished his heart would give out, but he didn't have one, didn't need one, not to do his job. Right now, something was doing a better job than he ever had … on him.

… Pow-pow-pow …

The pounding stopped. He could see his tormentor moving away from behind the swollen lid of his eye. He wanted to tear the creature to shreds, but Eep the imp could not move … yet.

There was a gap, a tear in the fabric of the dimension. The burly imp, the guardian of the sack, was heading for this tear. The dimension was filled with stars and a network of crossroads. A thousand different colors of candle light painted the landscape. It was similar to Eep's own magic realm, smaller but deeper. He wanted to explore, find a way out, but he had no wings or power here, just his flesh and bone.

Eep screeched, his tongue lashing out, as the guardian imp headed for the black tear in the sky. His rage burned and ignited fires in his limbs. He swam in the midst of the star-glazed sky. He was moving, willing himself toward the toes of his opponent. The guardian imp was moving faster toward the void, arms cutting through the eerie sky like it was a frog in water. Eep knew he could catch him, because he was the fastest thing he ever knew.

The bigger imp's knotted arms reached upward into the gap and began pulling it through the tear. Eep caught a glimpse of the world he knew, bathed in the glow of its decadent cruelty. He missed the world he hated so much. He swam hard through the sky, stretched to grab the guardian's toes that disappeared into the brilliant blue sky above. The tear in the sky sealed.

"NOOOOOOOOOO!!!!"

82

L *IES! LIES! LIES!*
They had to come easy or else the Lorda would know — Melegal was sure of it. Her beautiful eyes penetrated his fabric like a flame catching cotton. He could feel whatever veil of protection his slippery tongue provided wouldn't be enough. He expected joy and elation when he delivered the sword; instead he was assaulted with a barrage of probing questions. It was a mental inquisition of sorts. He felt his conviction of sharing the partial truth was what kept him alive. Now, he felt a great deal of respect for the ravishing Lorda Almen, who was every bit the complement of her husband. *They're meant for each other.*

Melegal walked alongside a black carriage pulled by two black horses. His head felt as heavy as an anvil. Two heavily armed sentries adorned in decorative cuirasses and small ornate helms walked alongside as well. Two more were driving the horses.

"Stop here," Melegal said. It was a sunny morning in the City of Bone, and the abandoned prison from the old ward didn't' seem as full of despair and gloom. He pointed to the archway that led down to the cell that held Tonio. The black alcove was the last place he wanted to go. *Nothing but pure evil to be found down there, fools.*

One of the sentries grabbed a small block of steps from the back of a carriage and set it down beneath the carriage door. The door swung open. The Lorda stepped down, dressed in a garish green cloak with the hood draped over a portion of her head. She spied the unpleasant surroundings and held a black silk handkerchief to her nose. The sentry bowed as he extended his hand. She was off the steps and on the street in two ginger steps. The man saluted and pulled the stool away.

Melegal bowed his head as she approached.

"Lorda," he said, bowing.

His eyes lifted up to her eyes and over her shoulder. The steel springs of the carriage groaned. *Who is this?*

A leg of partial plate armor stepped out onto the street. The carriage door obstructed his vision of the behemoth that had emerged. Melegal could see the top of a man's forehead. The big man closed the carriage door and stood like a statue. He was bald, blue-eyed, and big. He was an older man, maybe fifty, his face scarred and hard like a soldier of one hundred battles. The sight of the man left Melegal more restless than before. He felt small now, like he did when Venir and Mikkel were around. *He's bigger.* The dark gray metal of the man's partial-plate armor gave the illusion that he was as big as an ogre. The man's hard stare caught Melegal off guard, forcing him to look away.

The sentry walked over, his shadow falling over him and Lorda, and said, "It seems dangerous. I prefer you stayed back at the castle. Are you sure you want to do this, Lorda?"

The man's polished and pleasant voice seemed out of place with his grim exterior. Melegal found something odd about the man.

"Absolutely, Gordin," she said, brushing past Melegal and looking into the archway. "Is this the place?"

"Yes Lorda," he said, avoiding the body guard's doubting gaze.

"Then lead the way," she said.

Melegal hadn't taken a full step when a powerful hand grabbed his cloak and pulled him up to his toes. "No tricks, Rogue, or I'll break your neck, and if you survive that, it will be just the beginning."

"If I live, I doubt I'll be feeling anything after that. Besides, I'm not the one you need to worry about. The one down there is where I'd place my concerns if I were you, Bodyguard."

The man's droopy eyes became more vibrant and alert as Gordin shoved him forward. Melegal stepped inside the archway and said, "Your hounds may want to bring some light along, Lorda."

All eyes fell on her. Melegal stood his ground, watching her lips in reply.

"Mind your tongue, Detective. It's as easy to fall out of my favor as into it."

"Apologies, Lorda. I just wanted to get their blood up. It will be needed."

She seemed to pale at the sound of his cold words. *Good.* But her curiosity over the demise of her son would not be deterred. *I warned them.*

Two sentries surrounded him, torches in hand. Their fires were lit, and Melegal stepped down into the stairwell in the brightened gloom. One sentry followed him from two steps behind. The Lorda followed the sentry. Gordin her bodyguard took her back, with the remaining sentry with the other torch in the rear. Their breathing seemed exceptionally loud to Melegal's ears. His own was hardly a vapor, but his heart was pounding in his chest. *Stupid idea.*

They all crowded on the landing now, the metal door locked and alone in their midst. Melegal could still envision the tormented face of the man, Tonio, behind the bars in the door. Of all men, this was the last one he ever wanted to see again. They all waited, heads cocked, as the torchlight flickered on their eager faces. The sentries all dripped with sweat; only the Lorda's face was calm. Silence and their own heavy breath greeted them.

Her voice seemed uncomfortably loud when she said, "This is it, the cell where my son is held?"

"Yes," he said. His hand trembled slightly as he slid open the portal window. No one seemed to notice but him.

"Is there a key?" Gordin said.

"I'm the key," Melegal said, pulling out his tools. "Shall I unlock it?"

Lorda grabbed a torch from one of the sentries and held it to the barred window in the door. She pushed up on her toes, her head barely clearing the bottom of the small window. "I can't see anything. Gordin, take a look."

She handed the torch to Gordin. His face looked like an over-sized goblin in the orange light. He looked down inside the small window. Melegal inched back, palms rubbing the pommels of his daggers tucked in the back of his pants. *Here goes.*

"Hmmph …" the massive body guard said. "I see nothing." Gordin peered deeper into the window. "Smells foul, like dungeon rot."

Melegal felt Lorda's heavy gaze fall on him.

"You're sure he was alive, Detective," she said in a shrill voice, "not dead?"

Melegal nodded. *It's a matter of interpretation, I suppose.* Still, he should have heard a rustle or something by now, but the heavy breathing and the jangling gear was disrupting his skill. *Amateurs.*

Melegal almost gasped as Gordin stuck the torch through the bars. "I don't see nothing Lorda, just some puddles and …" he took a deeper look inside, "… rats. Big ones, too. I wonder how —"

BANG!

Gordin's arm was pulled inside up to the shoulder, his helmet slamming hard into the metal door. Everyone jumped back. The sentries fumbled for the swords in their sheaths.

"HEY!" Gordin yelled, fighting to pull his arm back through the portal.

The big man gave a grunt, his face darkening, spitting through his lips. A tug of war between the man and what was behind the door ensued. Melegal saw the light of the torch inside expire. Gordin's face became a mask of anger and pain.

"Tonio! Tonio! Stop, my son! It is your mother!" Lorda cried, slamming her hands against the door.

The sentries stood at her sides, their weapons of little use in such close quarters.

"Blast you, Thief — open this door!"

A moment in time seemed to freeze as Melegal got a closer look at their horrified faces. Not a one of them had any idea what to do. They should have listened to him. *Fools!* His mind ran over a dozen scenarios. What was it Lord

Almen had said? *Be the hero or the goat.* He put his slender hand on his cap and concentrated. A smile grew inside his head as his mind began to glow, tendrils of energy racing through a network of thoughts.

"Hurry up, Detective! Rrraahhh!" Gordin bellowed.

"Just one more moment!" he said.

"Tonio! Tonio! Tonio! Listen!" Lorda cried, pounding on the door.

Melegal let his suggestion go …

83

VENIR STOPPED INCHES SHORT OF a great sword ripping out his throat. The minotaur's swing took a chunk out of the wall instead. He countered with the spear, jabbing at the creature's abdomen, tearing a piece of flesh from its side. The creature backed away, stamping its hooved feet on the ground. Venir poked at it, backing it farther down the corridor. It was as if the minotaur had never faced an experienced fighter before. It snorted, its massive arms knotting as it brandished its sword.

Swoosh!

The decapitating chop soared over his head like a stroke of lightening, forcing Venir to the ground, belly first. He rolled left. Debris burst from where the sword chopped into the ground. He rolled right, dodging the next powerful blow. Venir caught the minotaur in the belly with the butt of his spear. It was like hitting a wall, but the man-monster backed off, blowing snot from its nose. Venir was on his feet, winded and squaring up again. He blocked out the pain in his leg as he shuffled in a circle. The broad hairy chest of the minotaur rose and fell with normal effort. It was an elemental thing, a tireless beast bred for destruction. The spear and short sword were slippery in his grasp now, unlike the sure-handed grip he always felt on Brool. Boon had minutes earlier all but given his existence good-bye. That seemed likely now. He couldn't remember the last day when it hadn't.

Go for the hands!

The minotaur chopped at him with short strokes, keeping him off balance and shifting away. The long blade of its sword could chop a pony in half. One cut could be fatal. Venir found himself being forced back toward the mouth of the spiked pit full of rats. From the corner of his eye, he saw the lycan mere-rat girl poised to spring across the pit.

Venir dashed forward to his left. His path was cut off by a resounding chop into the ground. Venir jumped over the blade and dashed farther down the corridor. He was almost back to where the journey had begun. He took a peek over his shoulder as the beast-man renewed his approach. He didn't want to go too far. There was no telling what was around the next corner. The rat-woman still stood on the other side of the pit, sword now drawn, waiting with a pink glimmer in her eyes. He labored for his breath, braced himself, and decided to face his fate head on.

He beckoned with his sword and spear once more. The minotaur's head reared up as it roared and charged. Venir braced himself; timing was everything. Twenty steps away, the creature lowered its sword level to his chest. He dropped the sword and lowered his spear, its unwavering tip steady, extended six feet before him. Venir eyed a bead on its heart as he braced himself for the impact. Ten steps—five steps—

The minotaur's chest collided with the spear, its barbed tip right on.

SNAP!

The spear shaft shattered like a twig. The great sword still came down, cutting through the meat on Venir's shoulder. Man and beast's bodies collided as the minotaur bowled him over. Venir scrambled to crawl out from underneath five-hundred pounds of monster. It clutched at his legs. Venir kicked it in the face with his heel. The effect was minimal as it rose to its feet again. It clutched at its chest where the spear was buried. Red blood ran over its black-furred chest.

"MAH-ROOOOO!" it bellowed.

Venir couldn't tell if he had hit a vital spot or not. It was not a man, but a beast. His own shoulder was on fire, and his left arm dangled at his side. His eyes roved for the short sword. It lay on the ground beneath its feet. He wiped his hair from his eyes and closed them for one second. *Bone!*

The minotaur charged, head down, horned head catching him full in the chest and driving him into the wall. Venir never would have guessed the thing could have moved so fast. The force knocked the breath from his lungs as he collapsed and slid down the wall. Things inside his body were broken. Pain was replaced by numbness. His head rang and dark purple spots were all over. He looked up just in time to see the beast raise its hoof to stomp the slat out of him.

84

THERE WAS A WAY OUT. There always was. Eep had seen things in his mystic life that the common mind of mortal beings couldn't comprehend. He just never gave it any thought. The complexities surrounding his life were beneath his desires: search and destroy. Still, he was a survivor, and if he were to continue his life of letting blood and onslaught, he would have to find a way out of this world.

He crossed one bridge only to find himself on another. He stopped and looked over its edge and saw himself looking down at himself. He sat down and bit at his black-taloned hands. He was in another world within a world. His own world, the dimension of magic from which he was summoned, was still another. He pondered this. Unlike his world, he could not see out of this one. All he could see within the space were bridges and roads, all of which seemed to go nowhere. One of them had to go somewhere.

"I must find it," he hissed.

He reached behind his back and scratched at a bloody bump where his wings once were. If he were home they would grow back. He snorted. His tiny black heart beat with anguish and fury. Head down, he slugged over the bridge and down the steps that looked to lead to a bright inferno. There was no heat, just a bath of brilliant cold light, no flames, just bright flickering lights. Sticking his claw inside the spectrum, he felt something soft to the touch. The entire area wavered under his stroke.

"Ah ..."

The sack had walls after all. He just had to find a way to tear them down.

85

SOME OF THEIR BELLIES LAPPED over their belts. Massive tankards of ale had been sloshing around and spilling onto their beards. Boon noticed the intensity building in the air from the battles below. The giants — one and all — were engrossed by the scene. How many battles had Boon watched like this, knowing the end, the inevitable outcome? The tension would build as they all watched for the guillotine to fall, the drop floor to open beneath the noose, or the moment before the man screamed as he was quartered by a team of horses, and when it was over, the giants would remain as stoic, odd and cheerless as they had been before it started. Why did they do it?

They hated men. Men were craftier than they were. Men tricked the giants time and again, and this was how the giants avenged themselves: snatching men, dropping them in the maze, and watching them suffer. It was pointless.

Boon shifted on the rail. He didn't want to watch, but was compelled to do so. The man had been valiant in his efforts, brave and honorable. It stirred something inside of him: that old feeling he had from the times before, when he had battled underling after underling during his own personal war. His hands opened and closed into fists at his side as he ground his teeth. He had been the giants' stooge, a personal pet of sorts, helping them as needed. He was more fortunate than the rest, but he hated it. Times like this he felt really bad. He had felt much worse though, after he lost possession of the sack decades ago. He had become little more than a drooling and rambling madman of sorts. He couldn't relate to others anymore. No longer fit for society, he had read from a scroll, and then a giant came and he wound up in the Under Bish.

He had an inspiration. He glanced up at the giants, their faces intent above their bearded faces and big noses. Glee filled their eyes over the formidable man who was about to die. Venir was his only attachment now to his humanity. A reserve of strength flared inside him. *Am I a man, or a giant's imbecile?*

Boon didn't have his spellbook, but he still had powers. The giants were aware, as they sometimes used magic, too. He had even taught some of them how to harness it. As long as he didn't write any spells down, they let him be. Still, he had some that he kept to himself, written in his mind where they could not see. Many other spells had been committed to his memory, where they had remained for years, even decades. He always figured if the underlings could do it, he could do it. It was sorcery, a discipline of its own kind.

He focused. One spell in particular — that the giants often allowed — might be of a different use to him today. His thoughts began running through the courses of magic. *Focus.* In the back of his mind, he couldn't shake the feeling the giants would catch him. They caught everything else. The thought of them squashing him like a bug revealed itself in his thoughts. The magic began to die down inside him. *Be brave, Boon!* He took another glimpse at the battered man down below. That old fire inside him began to burn. *Fie upon the giants!*

All fear was cast aside as a wave of magic coursed through his mind. Eyes intent on the struggling warrior, he unleashed the spell. His hands trembled as the magic finished running through him, sapping his strength. He gave it all he had and was glad for it. He tilted up his sagging head. The giants hadn't noticed his efforts; all eyes were transfixed on Venir. He could see their grins beginning to rise on their faces. Boon hoped his efforts were in time. Either way, he'd get caught and most likely die inside their bone-breaking hands. *Or in the maze? At least I know what to expect. I just wish I could have held that sack one more time.* He shrugged and looked back over the rail.

86

F OGLE COULD HAVE SWORN MOOD'S green eyes were watering when the big dwarf turned away. He rubbed his sleeve across his face. It was a depressing thing when his lifelong companion, Ox the mintaur, was squished like a rotten fruit. It was another thing seeing something once vibrant now living as a husk of what was. He took a tentative step forward, but a growl arose from the two-headed dog.

"Just gimme a sec," Mood said, producing two purple fruits.

Mood stopped a few feet away and rolled the treats toward the beast. The dwarf then stepped back and lit up another torch inside the stable. Fogle got a better eye-full of Chongo, and despair filled him.

Chongo had been one of the most vibrant things he had ever seen. Now, the beast's thick red-brown coat was matted and mangy. The dog lay on its side; it's once lustrous undercoat now only a thin patch of hair. Neither head touched the fruit, nor gave it so much as a sniff. One head was still a healthy brown, trimmed in black lines with its red tongue hanging out. There was a blank look in its eyes, sadness, as it licked the other head on the left.

The other head of Chongo was pitiful. Once the more robust of the two, it would have licked the bark of a tree if it thought the tree would pet it. Now, it had whittled down to what seemed to be half the size of the other. Its once bullish neck now seemed too thin to hold up even the shrunken second head, which sagged onto the straw floor. The fur around the second face was mostly gray, with a little brown. Its eyes were closed, and the rest of the head was unmoving.

Fogle dreaded his next question.

"Is he dead?"

He heard Mood release a heavy sigh through his nose. *Oh no.*

"No … he still lives, just not very much."

"What happened?"

The giant dwarf walked alongside the other head. Chongo bared his teeth and his throat began to rumble.

"Ssssh, Boy, it's just me. Ye know I won't hurt yer brother," Mood said, as he slid down along the dog's healthy head and managed to put its wounded head in his lap. He tried to put the fruit in the dog's healthy mouth, but Chongo turned toward his brother. "That wound, the one the underlings inflicted, was graver than we thought. My kin told me the dog kept bleeding, long after our healing, but them was just soldiers who're used to less mortal wounds, not a woman among them, and Chongo's not like most dogs. He's different. No one thought the bleeding would ever stop; it only slowed, despite all they did. When they made it back to Dwarven Hole, the bleedin' stopped, but the damage had been done."

Fogle wasn't sure if a dwarf could sob, but the sudden jolt in Mood's body suggested that one might have.

"What damage?"

Mood's meaty hands were scratching behind Chongo's healthy floppy ears as he replied, "They told me he lost too much blood in his mind. His second brain began to choke and die. There's no one around here that can heal something like that. I've seen many falls from it before, mostly on the battle field. We usually put 'em out of their misery when they can't speak or eat, but it's the family's choice. Just a tough way to live, not being able to feed yerself."

It was deep. Fogle had seen a few men in such a condition, but never were they put out of their misery. He had an older cousin, a mage like him, who had failed to pronounce a syllable on a powerful spell that had turned his mind inside out. All the man did was shake and drool. The City of Three was renowned for its healers, but even their efforts had failed. Fogle never did find out what became of his cousin, and had never given the man another thought until now.

As bad as Chongo looked in his starving condition, the other head looked far worse. Fogle tried to imagine what it would be like to have a dead head on his own shoulder. If that were ever the case, he was sure he would insist someone cut it off. Now didn't seem like the best time to suggest that, however.

Mood continued saying, "I never expected this. When we got back here, I thought I had it all figured out …"

"Figured what out?"

"Finding Venir … I was sure that Chongo could find him; they are bonded, but now I fear that without Chongo's help he may be lost forever."

"You still think he's in the Mist, don't you?"

Mood nodded.

We still have Inky, Fogle wanted to say. Of course, deep inside he knew his creation was of no comparison to such a magnificent living creature as Chongo. The massive dwarven setter was a legend in his own right, much like his master. Now, with the pitiful sight of both Mood and Chongo, it began to sink in that Venir might be forever gone as well. He thought of Kam. *How did that happen? Shame on me.* Mood's mutterings saved him from further selfish thoughts.

"I know yer depressed, Boy, without yer brother. I know ya miss em.'"

"What's the plan then?"

Mood huffed.

"I plan to keep up a search. One never knows. Still, it's gonna be harder without Chongo. It just doesn't seem right, Chongo without Venir. They need each other, like fish and water. This pooch has got to get better."

"Maybe we can find someone else that can help. A druid maybe."

"Sheesh … you are out of your mind. It would be easier to find Venir than a druid. Trust me, I've looked before."

"Did you find one?"

Mood rolled his bearded neck from shoulder to shoulder and said under his breath, "Yeah."

Fogle knew that the dwarf was holding something back when his broad body began to stiffen.

"So, what are we waiting for?"

Mood was silent.

"You know where one is, don't you, one that can help Chongo?"

"Aye," he said in a solemn voice, "But druids are tricky, and slippery as salamanders. Catching one won't be easy."

"Catch one? Can't we just pay one to come here?"

"Do you know anything about druids, Wizard?"

"Just that they can heal almost anything."

Mood wrapped his arms around Chongo's bullish neck and said, "That's only a small part of what they can do. Ye better hope ya don't learn about the rest. Now, leave us be."

Fogle had a funny expression on his face.

"Go on now, Wizard. You can wander the hole alone. If ya get lost, me people will get ya found."

Fogle gave the dog and dwarf a final look and walked away.

As he approached the door, he heard Mood add, "We leave tomorrow. Don't fergit to close the door, either."

Tomorrow? What have I become, an adventurer? Ha! But he had, indeed. Fogle left the odd stables feeling taller. An uncertain path was about to open ahead, and he was ready to test out the strength in his new abilities. That raw power he had felt against the elemental, he wanted to feel that again. The ability to wipe something out with a single thought filled him with elation. He hoped one day he could return to the City of Three as a great wizard.

He began to wonder if Venir could beat him in a mind grumble now. *I wouldn't mind a rematch.* Such thoughts were what got him into trouble in the first place, and now they brought back his grandfather's words, which hung in his mind now. The old man Boon had said,

There is always someone stronger than you. You don't want to meet them, either. Remember that if you want to live … long.

He found himself sweating on the long winding trek back to his room. He grabbed his sack, pulled out his spellbook, sat on the edge of his huge bed, and crossed his legs. It was comfortable. He thought of the hard ground that awaited him out on the plains of Bish, where the beating suns would be waiting, too. He realized that he didn't have to do this. He had enough stories to take home with him now. Still, something inside of him was pushing him forward. This is what he had asked for. He opened his spellbook.

One. Two. Three. Keep it simple, Fogle. Stay prepared and live. Get sloppy and die.

87

VENIR JERKED AWAY, CATCHING THE descending hoof in his unwounded shoulder. It should have caved his face in, but for a few more seconds the Darkslayer was going to live. The left side of his body felt like it had been beaten with a meat cleaver. His bones were rattling around his core. He staggered to his feet as the minotaur gathered itself for another charge. He growled, letting his will to live take over. Using every bit of the fight left in him, Venir ran for the short sword and snatched it up.

"Finish me off, then! Let's go!" he bellowed, brandishing the blade.

His entire chest was wracked with pain. He didn't care. The short sword shook in his grip as he spat a mouthful of blood to the ground. *Let it end.* At least he wouldn't die at the hands of an underling. The creature turned and snorted. The spear was still deep in its chest, and an angry look was in its eyes. Venir braced himself on unsteady legs one last time.

His blue eyes flared when he said, "Come on." It hesitated.

It's getting weaker, Venir thought. A strange sensation overcame him. His body became rigid, and his stomach turned to mud. The minotaur looked up at him, snorted, mooed, and charged. Venir braced himself for the impact, but something was off.

Crunch!

He looked down as the beast crashed into his knee.

"WHAT IS THIS?" he said, his voice sounding like thunder.

SWAT!

His enormous hand caught the beast in the face, knocking it off of its feet and slamming it into adjacent wall.

"HA!"

He realized his head was almost at the top of the wall. The sword, his armor, and his clothes had all grown as well.

"YES!" he said in a booming voice.

The odds were better now. He felt the strength of a hundred men coursing through him. He saw the minotaur pulling itself up on its legs. Venir jabbed his giant short sword into the roaring beast's heart, pinning it to the ground. The creature still fought on, but its efforts began to fade as Venir stepped on it and ripped the sword free. The blood gushed out, and then gushed no more.

He looked up, and the giants no longer seemed so far away. Boon sat on the rail. The sorcerer saluted and winked. Venir saw the mage mouth the word "Run" just as he was hit by a giant's fist and fell over the rail to disappear into the maze.

"Hey! Hey you!" A female voice barked in his ear.

The rat-woman had crawled up onto his shoulder. Her furry face was hairy and exotic. She yelled, "Don't hurt me and I'll show you the way out!"

"Pah, I've got giants to kill," he said, pulling himself up on the wall.

"Don't be a fool! You won't stay so big much longer, and then what will you do?"

She had a point. Above, the giants' faces were filled with fury. They were still twenty to his one, but he was out of reach. He had pulled himself on top of the wall now, and was looking down in the maze. There were monsters from all walks of Bish below, screaming and screeching at him. The maze was an endless network of walls and corners. Boon was right; there was no way out of there. "All right Rat Lady, I'll follow."

She hopped down onto the wall. It was six feet wide, but Venir had to tight rope his steps. His massive strides gave him little trouble in keeping up with her, but she was quick. He couldn't believe how big the maze actually was. There must have been miles of twists and turns. So far as he could tell, he must have been placed at the center. Despite his current size and strength, a feeling of horror still crawled in his belly. He owed Boon a debt of gratitude.

They made it to the outer wall of the maze. Venir could still see the giants pointing and shouting his way. He wondered if they would come for him or send something else. He jumped off the wall and almost landed on the rat-woman.

"Watch it will you! Now come on!"

He pushed through a door. She was running down the corridor at full speed. Venir still ached all over. His wounds hadn't healed, but the bleeding had seemed to stop. His perspective within the walls of the Ziggurat had changed. The halls were lifeless, cold and unattended, but the décor reminded him of some of the castle walls in Bone.

She yelled up at him, "Will you run!"

He could barely hear the words coming from her tiny voice. He ran, and in a second was almost on top of her. She jumped onto him, her sharp claws digging into his skin. She was on his shoulder again.

"Sorry about that," she said in his ear.

"Where to?"

"Just keep going straight and out those doors … way up there!"

It must have been a giant's mile or more. *How big is this place?* He kept running, but it was agony. His ribs felt cracked, and his lungs were burning. He was certain his shoulder was busted. He barreled down the corridor. He had no desire to stay here any longer. The maze was a certain end for any man.

"You got any idea where to go once we get out of here?" he asked.

She yelled in his ear, "No, but there are some places I can hide."

"You can hide? What about me?"

"Hey, I only said I could get you out of here. What you do after that is up to you."

There had to be some type of life between the mist and the ziggurat. Venir had seen a bridge and a river. A black dragon was there as well. What if he fell asleep again? It had already happened twice before.

"What is it that causes the sleep?"

"Oh that. Well, that's a spell that the sorcerer would cast. I don't think you have to worry about that anymore."

"But it happened when I walked out of the mist."

"Did you see a dragon? Blackie? Wait a minute, did you say you walked out of the mist?"

"Yes."

"Where did you come in from?"

"Leagues south of Hohm City. An underling dropped me in there."

The rat-woman's pink and black eyes were as wide as saucers. "I didn't think that was possible, to cross the mist and all."

Venir came to heavy oak double doors. They were too big for a normal man to open. As a giant, he had no problem lifting the bar and pulling them back. Open fields greeted him as far as the eye could see.

"Drink from the river to stay awake," she said. The rat-woman darted into the weeds, waved, and was gone.

It was strange, wherever he was. He was outside now, but lost. The ziggurat at his back must have been fifty man-stories tall. He looked back inside the fortress once more. The place was devoid of any pursuit, but certainly the giants would be coming. *Move or die.* He jogged along a road, hoping it would lead to the river, checking over his shoulder every so often. The suns were setting behind the giants' home. The need for rest and food began to overcome him. His wounds were clotted, but his body ached from every heavy step, and the battle heat was subsiding.

He wondered if Boon would survive; he could use some more magic assistance right now. And what of the rat-woman who had so quickly come and gone. Maybe he was better off without her. Those lycan girls were full of tricks, and leading him here might yet prove to be one. As he continued his trot down the path, he began to wonder if any of what he was doing was real at all. The cobbled road turned to stone and sand. It wasn't long before the shape of the ziggurat was a speck behind him. The mist was even farther in the distance.

"There has to be somewhere else to go."

His eyes roved over the landscape in all directions. It was all the same. There were sloping dales and abundant trees, but no other signs of life. He looked at his hands and could no longer tell if he was as big as a giant or normal sized. Everything was an unnatural mess.

Whump … Whump… Whump … Snort!

He crouched down. The skies had darkened, and the moonlight was hidden by the thick rolling clouds. He wondered if that dragon was looking for him. *Bone.* He waited, but no other sounds came. He continued down the path of the fading road, the short sword gripped tight in his right hand, his left arm almost dragging the ground. Sleep and exhaustion were settling over him as he trudged along. The last time he fell asleep he had awoken in a maze, the time before that in a dungeon. *Keep going, Vee, or die.*

88

F*AINT. F*AINT. F*AINT.*

Melegal repeated the suggestion in his mind. Lorda Almen's knees gave out as she swooned and fell backward. One sentry dropped his torch as he caught her, while the other dropped to his knees and attended her.

"Blast you, Rogue, open the door now before my arm's ripped off!" Gordin yelled back over his shoulder.

Melegal dropped his leather satchel of tools to the ground and withdrew something else. His bony hands were wrapped along the hilt of his two-handed dagger, the same one he had used to kill McKnight. He rose up on his toes as Gordin turned to yell at him once more. The struggling man's face turned ashen.

Melegal raised his arms above his head, and the dim blade flashed red in the torchlight. Gordin's big sweaty face turned white and he had a look of death in his eyes. Melegal plunged the dagger down into Gordin's exposed neck. He could feel the sharp blade of the dagger sink deep into the muscle and into the spine. Gordin's eyes rolled up in his head, his lids shut, and blood oozed from his mouth. The big body was lifeless and banging into the portal. Tonio seemed determined to pull the dead man through. Melegal stood captivated by the morbid scene.

He wrenched his blade free and knelt back down behind Gordin's sagging legs. The guards were still attending to Lorda Almen, oblivious to the silent murder that just occurred. Melegal grabbed his tools and began picking at the ancient padlock. His mind was flowing with energy now, his body moving as fast as his thoughts. He had a superior feeling he could do anything he wished right now. The padlock popped open.

"Take her back to the carriage," one of the guards instructed the other.

Melegal hurled the lock into the speaking man's unsuspecting face. The other sentry turned on him in time to catch a blade in his throat. The man collapsed on the landing, blood flowing from the hole in his neck. Now the other man was ready, a longsword swinging through the dark. Melegal side-stepped the clumsy blow and slashed the man's wrist.

"Gah!" the man's sword clanged on the ground.

Melegal closed in, two daggers at the ready. *Cut, cut, thrust! Cut, cut, thrust!*

The sentry gawped as steels made a pin cushion out of him. Melegal continued to whittle the dying man down to a bloody stump. Something angry inside him pressed the torment on. In a moment it was over, and his chest was heaving.

Melegal looked around at the mess he had created. *What madness is this? What have I done?*

There was silence in the chamber now. A feeling of horror crept over him as Gordin's body was released and sliding down the door. He slung Lorda over his shoulder, backed up a few stair steps, and surveyed the surroundings. It wasn't his style, slaughtering men like hogs. He shrugged. *So be it!*

"Come on VENIR, let's get out of here!" he shouted, racing up the stairs. He was over halfway up when he heard the door slam open.

Someone yelled from down below, "*VEE-MAN!*"

Come and get him, Tonio!

Melegal burst up the remaining stairs and charged through the archway. The bewildered sentries drew their swords.

"He's killed them! He's killed them all! I'll put her in the carriage, you hold him off!"

"Hey! How do we know … ulp!"

Melegal wasn't paying their comments any mind. He threw open the carriage door and tossed Lorda Almen inside.

"VEEMAN!"

A chill went down his spine. He had enough sense to grab the reins as the horses tried to bolt.

Tonio stood in the archway now, a ghastly sight. A jagged scar ran down from his head to his torso, and his eyes were a smoky evil yellow. The man looked even fouler than Melegal remembered. The once proud Royal warrior's skin was caked with dry dead skin that cracked and drifted off in the wind. Melegal expected that at any moment the man's body would fall apart. It didn't. Instead, the man slammed into the first sentry and tried to tear his screaming head off. The other sentry chopped into Tonio's side. Tonio turned on the sentry, twisted the sword from his hand like a child's toy, and punched him in the face. Melegal didn't stick around to see what happened next.

"Eee-yah!" Melegal cried, whipping the reins and driving the horse and carriage over the roadway. He dared another glance back over his shoulder. Tonio was dragging one of the men back through the archway. *Poor bastards.* His plan had been a bad one, but it had worked. Now he had Lorda Almen in his clutches. He had to decide what to do. Did he take her home or somewhere else?

Someone had lied. There was no Vee-man to be found. Tonio dragged all the bodies down the stairwell to the landing and stripped them down. He had been sure the big one was the Vee-Man, but when he pulled off the armor he only found a bloody back and no V-shaped tattoo. It made him angry, and he had an uncontrollable fit.

He didn't remember doing it afterward. He remembered something else. *Mother.* Had that really been her calling for him? He had heard so many things inside that room he couldn't tell what was real. An aroma drifted into his nose, the smell of tiger roses. It was what his mother liked and what he liked for her. Had she come for him? Did she still care for him? He peered up into the stairwell, watching for the suns to go down. The bright light blinded his eyes. He would venture above when the dark came out; it had become his bedfellow.

In the meantime, Tonio sat at the bottom steps and donned Gordin's armor and bastard sword. He felt hungry, but not for food. There was little hunger in him after months of solitary confinement. Any pangs he had, the rats fulfilled. He could eat; he just didn't have the desire to. He'd had nothing to live for before, feeling his mother had forgotten him. Now, it was clear she had come for him. He checked the gash in his side. It wasn't bad, just a rip through the muscle to the bone. No blood was lost within him, and he was absent of pain.

He held the torch over his scaly hands and started picking the dry flesh off. Smooth gray skin was still underneath his shell. He ran his fingers over the scar than ran a jagged course down his face. He held Gordin's dismembered head in his hand and gave it study. The face was similar, but not the same.

"Venir," he said in his raspy voice.

That was the man who had caused it all. He needed help. What was that other man's name?

"McKnight," he croaked out.

There was a carriage and a man on top. Was that McKnight or Venir? The image was blurry. Maybe Venir had his mother now. Someone had said Venir was here. He needed help getting his thoughts sorted out. McKnight could help with that, if he could find him, or should he go home?

He searched the sentries' clothing for money and loaded himself up with all the weapons he thought he needed. He had trouble deciding what to do. His mother could help him, would help him. He had to find her. He had to find Venir and kill him.

"Rrrr-ah!" he growled as he launched Gordin's head into the wall with a nasty smack.

He watched the darkness blot out the light above and headed up the stairway. The clouds had rolled in overhead, and it began to rain. He stepped out into the street and wandered.

89

WHEN KAM AWOKE SHE FELT feverish. Her white night gown was drenched, and the blankets on her goose feather bed were damp. She also felt like emptying her already empty stomach. She couldn't recall the last time she had felt so ill before, but this had to be the worst.

"Lie down, Dear, lie down," Joline said, stepping into the room, a fresh pitcher of water in her hand.

"No, I'm all right," Kam croaked. "Just get me to my feet."

Joline's pleasant face was stern as she walked over, fluffed up her pillows and gently shoved her back into them. "Take a few drinks first."

Kam ran her fingers through her matted hair and thought how dire her need was for a comb. How terrible she must look now. She had to get past Joline and find a mirror before anyone else saw her.

Joline pressed a crystal glass to her lips and said, "Drink this and I'll fix the rest of you. Don't you worry; no one's been coming around to see you. Everyone's got plenty to do, but lots of people are asking."

Guilt was beginning to overtake her strange fever feelings. Her customers and workers depended on her, and she might as well have been dead to them, and what about Georgio and Lefty? Who was watching over them? The last thing she remembered was Lefty leading her out of the room by the hand. Something was wrong with that boy. He had seemed strange.

She drank. The cool liquid was more than a common glass of water, something Joline whipped up for customer hangovers. The taste of mint and other spices seemed to perk her up, but only a tad so.

She had a dozen questions on her mind, but she only had the strength to ask one.

"Where are the boys, and how long have I been out?"

Joline was keeping herself busy, straightening up the items in her bedroom.

"*Joline,*" she said with growing irritation, "Answer me!"

The woman turned around with a flustered look on her aging face. Joline was tired, too. Still, she answered, "Another week you been out, and the boys are just fine. Georgio is staying close, helping with the Roost, and Lefty is spending time at Master Gillem's flower shop."

"Master who?"

Joline seemed excited as she sat down on the edge of the bed and grabbed her hand. Her friend added, "Yes, Gillem is a halfling that has taken to Lefty like a long lost uncle. The boy's never been more accountable than since Gillem came along. I must tell you Kam, you would like him, and he's full of the most pleasant stories and delivers the most beautiful bouquets of flowers." Joline pointed toward the dresser. "See those over there? Those are from Master Gillem."

Kam was more than impressed. The flowers were beautiful, and the vase was filled with many of her favorite kinds. She said, "They are wonderful. Did this Gillem bring them in here?"

"Oh, lords no, I'd never let a man see you looking like this." Joline paused under her glare. "I … uh, well Lefty brought them up. He's been looking in on you. He feels awfully bad about your sickness and all, acts like he's the cause of it."

Kam set the glass down on her nightstand and said, "Maybe he is."

"What?"

"I tell you, something is strange with Lefty. This can't be some coincidence. I'm smarter than that, and you should be, too."

"Ah, I think you need more rest K—"

"No, I don't need more rest! What I need is to find out is what is wrong with me! There's that terrible woman,

Palos, Lefty, and this Gillem. All of this is not ordinary. Things like this don't just happen all at once." She grabbed the glass off the table and took another swallow.

"Everyone goes through a rough patch, Kam. You've just never had so much to deal with before."

Kam wanted to slap the woman. She was certainly smart enough to know better than most. Her family had taught her that much. Things happen for a reason. Something causes them. She wasn't stupid, and she wasn't about to let someone play her for a fool. Palos was behind this; she was sure of it.

"Get those flowers out of my room!" she yelled.

The look on Joline's torn face began to sink into her heart. She had never screamed at Joline before. She felt ashamed and began to cry. She sobbed, "I'm sorry. I'm so sorry, Joline. I just feel so bad."

Joline squeezed her hand and said, "Dear, you've been sick a long time. It's worn you down, and it's a lot of stress. You've been going through something for the first time that a lot of women go through."

Kam wiped her tears on her blanket and said, "What?"

"Dear girl, we are pretty sure why you have been sick, now."

"Who's 'we'?"

"Just me and your mother."

"My mother's been here?"

"Of course, several times."

Some relief began to flood over Kam. She hadn't spoken with her mother in a long time, but it wasn't because of a falling out. They were both just busy, independent women. She asked, "What did she say was wrong with me?"

Joline ran her hands over her belly and said with a pleasant smile, "You're pregnant, Kam."

She felt like her world had come to an end.

90

"I CANNOT BELIEVE THIS! WHY WOULD you do something so foolish? Why didn't you tell me? You could have been killed!" Lord Almen's face was a mask of fury, and his voice was barely under control.

Lorda Almen stood her ground, stepping between the Royal Lord and Melegal. The detective had been listening to the argument go round and round for the past fifteen minutes. She knew Lord Almen was acting, but it didn't feel like it.

"I'll have you flogged, Detective! You had no business taking my wife on wild chases—"

"He is at my command as well!" Lorda yelled. "If I say go, he goes. What is yours is mine, Dearest, or has that changed?" She crossed her arms over her chest, glaring at her husband.

Lord Almen stepped forward and gripped her shoulders.

"It changes when you have evidence of my son's return and you don't inform me. It changes when you send this man on a quest without my knowledge. Our trust is sacred, but only when you don't break our bond. Lorda, you can do what you will with your servants, but not mine!"

Melegal was helpless as the man shook the woman like a doll. He knew the Royal Lord wanted to do nothing more than snap her pretty neck, or did he? *He's convincing. I'll give him that.* He wondered how much abuse the woman had been through, if any at all. Her eyes blazed right back into his as she tore herself away. Lorda screeched as Lord Almen caught a handful of her hair and jerked her head back. A look of remorse appeared on his face and his tone softened.

"I cannot let you go, Gail, you know that. You are my life, my everything. I would rather suffer the lash myself than see an ounce of harm come to you." He ran his free hands over the rings on her fingers and the jewels across her chest. She bunched up and pulled away, but he held her tight, staring deep into her eyes. "Have I not gone to extreme measures to get you what you want? Have men and women not suffered at my hand in your tribute. Did I not kill—"

"Stop!" she interjected, easing back into his arms. "I know all you have done, but there are things a mother must do as well. It's not something you would understand … you are a man."

"I am your man."

Lorda smiled and closed her eyes as he pulled her entirely into his arms.

"I know, but you must trust my instincts. After all, they led me into your arms."

You gotta be kidding me. Ten seconds ago they were ready to kill one another. Melegal shifted on his feet, his eyes all over the secluded dining room, on everything but the two of them. It was a room he had never been in before, but Almen had brought them both there after she came around. The pleasant setting did little to quash the queasiness in his stomach. After Melegal had woken her up, he'd had time to tell her about his version of the slaughter by her son, Tonio. He had spun lie after lie, but felt he had been convincing enough. The hardest part had been explaining the blood on him and her. As careful as he had been with his cuts, he couldn't control the spray. His agitation had cost him on the last man. He blamed the blood on the valiant sentries that fought Tonio as he carried her free of the skirmish. Her eyes were still lazy, her sharp mind not yet intact. He thought she had bought it.

He had sent word to Almen through a sentry and made sure her arrival was kept discreet. Lord Almen had arrived shortly after that and dragged them away from the back courtyard.

Melegal was counting the panes on the glass windows when Lord Almen caught his ear.

"My dear, did you not even see a glimpse of our son? Or hear his voice?"

Lorda gracefully twisted herself from under her husband's grasp and said, "No."

"Yet, you believe this man's words? He seems to be the only witness."

Melegal's heart sped up a tad. *Hero or goat. Who cares? I'm dead either way.*

Lorda's defiant voice was back. "I'm not some idiot! I am certain this man saved my life. What reason would he have to betray me? Betray us? It would be utterly fatal. His nuggets couldn't possibly be that big."

Hah. Thanks, Lady. It might behoove you to know that my nuggets are bigger than I even realized these days. Lord Almen's eyes bore into him like a hawk. He had a look in his eye that unsettled Melegal in the core. He wasn't sure how smart Lord Almen really thought he was, but he was certain Lord Almen knew he was much smarter than him. He was positive the man was a few steps ahead in all things, except today.

"It's just suspicious. I have never known you to faint before."

"Nor I of you, but it can still happen. If you saw the look of horror in Gordin's face, you might have been spelled as well. It's the last thing I can remember." She shivered as goose bumps rose along her slender arms. "Poor Gordin … he was ever so loyal."

"Like a dog, that man. His loss will be honored, but maybe he is not lost at all. Maybe he survived. He was a most formidable fellow."

No. He's dead. All of your sorry arse bastard men are. And if I don't pull this off, I'll be joining them. Lord Almen's brown eyes seemed to be trying to penetrate his skull. Lorda's expression was pleasant, thankful and warm. *I've fooled one, but can I fool two?*

"Do you think it's possible?" she asked.

"I've already sent men to secure the location and look for Tonio. My best men will be out there finding answers to your questions."

"I want to go back. I must see for myself."

Not good! Melegal was hoping to have more time to set the scene. Before returning to Lorda, he had contacted some urchins. The roving little bandits would pick the bodies clean and haul them off. There was a market for dead bodies in Bone; there was a market for anything, dead or living.

Melegal's body went cold when Lord Almen replied, "Perhaps you are right, my dear. Finding our son should be something that we do together." He kissed her on the forehead. "Get what you need and meet me at the carriage. I'll gather some more guards and Sefron. If anyone can sort out what happened there, it's him."

Slat!

"Er … any objections, Detective?" Lord Almen asked, his hawkish face as penetrating as ever.

"None, Lord Almen, your wishes are mine," he said with a slight bow.

"Good, because I want you to come along. I would like you to run us through what happened."

I would like to run you through, too. Definitely the goat! Slat!

He pulled his fingernails out of his palms and escorted Lorda to the carriage.

91

HE FOUGHT TO STAY AWAKE long enough to find a safe place to sleep. Venir couldn't remember ever feeling so tired before. He wanted nothing more than to fall into the cushions provided by the tall grass, and slumber. He knew that if he fell asleep, he would wind up back in the ziggurat. He didn't want to go back. As bad as he wanted to escape the mist, he wanted even more to avoid the giants. This place, wherever it was, was not where he was meant to die.

The dull glow of the orange moons seemed to hang in the black sky forever. It was a soothing light that beckoned for him to sleep. He kept on going, even as each step seemed to make him more tired than the last. The eerie silence of the land only increased his desire for a long, undisturbed rest. It also increased his want to go home. Maybe vengeance had been his path all along. Maybe the destroyer of underlings was what he was meant to be. What kind of man had he become, that lived and did not hunt underlings? He wanted to sit down and think about things, but would not. He had to escape.

He traversed from meadow to meadow, and not a single living creature appeared. No crickets, no hoot owls or bugs crawling over the ground. He was starving, and his side and shoulder were aching, but his surroundings were devoid of anything fulfilling to staunch his hunger or pain. What had the lycan woman said? "Drink from the river to avoid the sleep." He remembered seeing a bridge, a river, and a dragon, when he first emerged from the mist. The river was the biggest he had ever seen. It had to be somewhere nearby. He closed in on the mist, so he thought, but it seemed just as far away as before.

He looked over his shoulder from time to time. The giants had not come, but certainly something must be coming for him. He was used to being hunted now. The underlings had made a point of it. They sought his death. The silver-eyed one had finally managed his undoing. It had picked him up like a leaf and sent him sailing helpless into the mist. He should have died in there, but he had only survived to die at the hands of another tormenter, the giants. Now he had survived that, only to face dying in his sleep or inside a dragon.

The moons began to dip, and the suns began to rise. A wet breeze ruffled his hair. Venir ran his fingers through his beard. The blonde mat of hair hung inches below his chin. He hadn't noticed it before. How long had he been down here? There was something damp in the air that made him pick up his agonizing pace. The landscape of rolling hills began to fade, and groves of small trees sprouted up in the distance. Venir could taste it now: something wet, something cold.

He ran for the gleaming stream of sparkling water ahead, thinking his thirst would be unquenchable. He ran and ran, but the distance didn't seem to close. *Keep going!* He had a feeling he wasn't a giant anymore. Everything was beyond what he imagined, like the Great Forest of Bish. What he wouldn't do to be there, to see its massive leaves one more time. He spurred himself on; he had to be getting closer. A different garden of vegetation began to crop up here and there, filled with mushrooms, daffodils, ferns and dry gullies. Abundant life was here. It was real; he could smell it.

He fell down the bank, dropped his sword, and crawled on his hands and knees to the river, where he plunged his face in the water and drank. He reared up and laughed, splashing the water around. This moment of joy and triumph was something he had not felt in a long time. It felt good. His stomach began to rumble anew. His instincts ignited. There was something living in the river, close by. He could feel it.

"Fish!"

92

E EP'S CLAWS DUG INTO THE dark tapestry that was made of the sky. He was the only tangible thing he had felt other than the guardian that had been pummeling him in the face. He pushed his claws deep into the fabric, but it led to nowhere. There had been a rip; he had seen it before, one that the guardian passed through that led into the other sky. It led back into Bish, it had to.

The imp allowed his clawed feet to dig into the ceiling now. He walked along it, feeling for some kind of opening or hole. He knew he was inside the sack, and it had limitations, so he walked on, eye alert for the return of the guardian.

He hissed.

Something began to shudder underneath his clawed toes. He hissed again, tongue lashing out, his head swiveling back and forth on a muscular neck. His hands clutched open and closed. He opened his jaws wide and chomped his teeth. If he could only sink his teeth into the guardian, he could get free. Everything around him seemed to shake inside the void.

Eep gasped.

He watched as a hole opened again, far in the distance, and the guardian stepped back through, its eye immediately searching him.

"NO!" he screamed.

The tear in the sky was too far away. If he only had his wings he could have made it. The hole began to close again as the guardian began swimming his way. Something else within caught his eye. A train of objects were passing him from nearby. He couldn't tell what they were, but they were moving toward the rift. He swam for them, arms and legs pumping in the air, like a frog in water.

"NO!" he shrieked.

The guardian was almost on him now. He could almost feel that other imp's fists of granite hammering into him. He caught hold of something and swore he would never let go. The guardian had hold of him now and began to flail away.

93

T HE ANCIENT PRISON WARD WASN'T that far away, but the carriage ride was still long and miserable. It was midday, and the soft leather seats inside were more like sweating pillows. The rain had come and gone, and the humidity was unbearable. Lord Almen had insisted that both Melegal and Sefron accompany him and his wife inside the carriage.

Across from him, Sefron's twisted stare was transfixed on him the entire trip. The cleric's bald head was beaded with large drops of sweat that trickled over his scrawny naked chest. As the horses rumbled onward, all Melegal could think of was how badly he wanted to gouge those bulging eyes out. Sefron had set him up, forcing him to whip a delightful servant girl.

At Melegal's side sat Lorda, proper and elegant in her changed clothes. She dabbed a handkerchief on her neck as the sweat rolled down her cheek and between her breasts. Lord Almen sat beside the foul cleric, saying few words. Melegal hated Almen now — his imposed liege — almost as much as Sefron. He had promised himself he would kill one, but the other he wasn't so sure he could. Melegal wasn't a killer, or was he? *Three are dead by my hands just today. What has become of me?*

He kept his gaze fixed outside the window. There were ten sentries in the company, all in chain mail, strapped with swords and some carrying halberds and pikes. The crest of the Almen house was nowhere to be seen. This mission would only draw the attention of the other Royal houses. Melegal could only wonder how much this little bit of information would be worth to him if he survived the day. *At least they'll be too slow to catch me.*

He allowed his eyes to glance over at Sefron. The flabby man wheezed where he sat. Still, the cleric caught his eyes and a slight smile formed on his cross mouth. If Melegal had any reason to survive until tomorrow, it would be to kill Sefron. He wanted vengeance, and he also had a personal need to see someone so sick and perverted undone forever.

The carriage came to a halt, and Melegal was the first one outside. The hot suns were refreshing compared to the rolling sweat box he had just escaped. Lord Almen and Lorda made their way from the other side. As Sefron's sandaled foot emerged from the carriage, Melegal closed the door.

"Ow!" the cleric said, recoiling back.

Melegal moved on, catching up to the Almens. Sefron exited from the other side of the carriage. The ragged breathing of the cleric was now accompanied by a limp. Melegal couldn't help but notice Sefron grimacing with every step. *Good!*

Another half dozen sentries of the Almen house had already secured the area. *Sixteen men and then some. Great!* Melegal was regretting his impulsive fit of carnage.

Lord Almen engaged himself with one of the sergeant-at-arms.

"Any news to report?"

The sergeant-at-arms was grim, almost sick-looking in his weathered face.

"Lord, it is nothing the likes I have seen before."

"Oh, I am sure that it couldn't be much worse than the battlefield. Is there anything else that I should expect, other than some corpses?"

"It's just that—"

"Let's go! I must see!" Lorda Almen demanded, shoving her way past the sentry and through the archways.

"Lorda, wait!" Almen said, hustling after her. "Sefron — Detective — what are you waiting for? You," he grabbed the sergeant-at-arms, "come with us!"

A long series of torches now illuminated the long and winding stairwell. It did little to comfort Melegal, who knew that he was pinned in. If any of them were able to figure that it was his blade that cut their throats, it was all over. He had many blades with him, most too small to notice, but one was rather long and difficult to conceal. A simple search of his person could easily reveal the truth.

Melegal took his time, staying behind Sefron for the duration of the downward trek. The cleric kept making nervous glances back over his hunched shoulders.

"Be careful not to slip," Melegal said, "it's a long hard fall."

"Why don't you go on ahead then," Sefron said with a sneer.

"Oh, I'm in no hurry, and I would hate to break your fall."

"I bet you wuh—"

A blood curdling scream resounded up the stairwell. It was Lorda. Melegal dashed past the cleric, shoving the man into the wall. Lord Almen was right on his heels. The pair, along with the sergeant-at-arms, was on the bottom landing in seconds. Lorda rushed into Lord Almen's arms and buried her face in his chest, sobbing with hysteria.

"He couldn't have done this! He couldn't have."

Another sentry at the bottom of the stairwell was pressed along the wall, his nervous face looking back and forth at everyone. He started to speak, "I tried to warn the Lorda, Sir—"

The sergeant-at-arms cut him off and began pushing the cell door closed. Melegal grabbed it with his hand and looked to Lord Almen. Sefron managed to huff his way to the bottom of the stairs. Melegal peeked inside the cell and felt himself turn green. Lord Almen and Sefron both caught the look in his eyes.

"Sergeant, escort the Lorda back atop." He gathered her in his arms. Her face was a blank, her limbs without feeling as the sergeant managed to lead her back up the stairs. "Open the door, Detective."

Melegal pushed the door open with a gentle bang into the other side of the wall. Sefron was the first through the doorway, followed by Lord Almen and himself. The entirety of the cell looked as if it had been painted with blood. Something had hacked up all of the bodies as if they were wood. Limbs looked like they had either been sheared or torn from their sockets. Fingers had been bitten off and bodies punctured over a dozen times. It looked as if someone had tried to chop the men in half, from head to hindquarters.

Melegal fought the urge to retch, and would have if he were not equally pleased with joy. *No way they'll be able to pin any of this on me.* The expressions on Lord Almen and Sefron's faces were once in a lifetime. Melegal would never forget their looks of astonishment and horror that could not be hidden. After a long moment of silence, Lord Almen gathered himself and stepped out of the cell.

"Come, Sefron," he ordered.

"But your Lordship, I have an investigation to do."

Melegal slipped out of the cell as well, intent on dissuading the cleric from finding the truth. He knew the cleric would do anything to find a way to pin it all on him. He knew, because he would do the same in the cleric's place.

Lord Almen added, "There is no need for that now. I have come to my conclusion. Detective Melegal, it seems you have saved my wife from the clutches of a monster. You will have my gratitude."

Sefron gawped.

Melegal bowed his head a bit and said, "I only did what you would expect me to do, my Lord."

Melegal didn't look back as Almen said, "Come with me Melegal, we have much to discuss. Sefron, meet us up top and be quick about it. No diddling with the dead, either."

He could feel Sefron's raging eyes burning into his back. The vindication was delicious. If he could fool Lord Almen, could he fool them all. Lord Almen stopped him just over halfway up the stairwell with his large hand pinching the nape of his neck. His voice was almost an inaudible whisper.

"I had my doubts about you, but you have been vindicated. Enjoy all of the rewards my wife might offer, but do not forget who you serve. Do not slip."

Melegal nodded.

"Are you certain that was the work of my son?"

"I only saw it unfold; I didn't stick around for the results."

Lord Almen's next word was said with a slight bit of admiration.

"Remarkable …"

Lord Almen had been certain that Melegal had spun a tale, but all of the evidence proved him wrong. The man had indeed dragged his wife out of the killer's den. That killer was his son, a monster that he didn't understand. Tonio had been deranged when last they parted, but now his child was living on the edge of madness. His son might have killed his own mother. It was unthinkable. The two adored each other more than he and the Lorda ever did. The bond between mother and son was something that he never cared for. Now, his son ran the streets of Bone, a butchering murderer. He had to find him and have him put down. The Lorda would also want that now.

"Sergeant, see to it the cleric doesn't drag away any parts of the dead. Grab all of the men's gear and bring it back to the castle. The bodies are to be burned, and no one is to know of this."

"Yes, Lord."

Melegal was thrilled. Less than fifteen minutes ago he had been certain that he would be caught. Now, Tonio of all people had become his salvation. Maybe this would garner a room in the castle. Maybe it would give him another week of life. For the first time in months he felt like he had something to look forward to, so long as the dead didn't come back to life. In the back of his mind he knew anything was possible. Tonio had proved that.

He fought back the smile that wanted to rise on his face as he entered the carriage and sat beside Lorda. She placed her hand on his knee and told him thank you several times. *Hero!*

Sefron was furious. He had nothing; the thief had tripped him up. There wasn't anything his desperate searching could do. The bodies were mangled and beyond use. It would take months to figure out what had happened. Still, he was fascinated that Tonio was on the loose. The deranged man had become something else, something evil that he admired. Perhaps he could turn that against Melegal. He hated detectives and their kind. They always were trying to get into his business, and he had to make sure no one ever figured out who he truly served.

94

A SOUND STARTED VENIR FROM HIS slumber. He wasn't sure what he heard. He was barely able to tell the difference between reality and his dreams. He had been dreaming of many things since he slept in the Under Bish, things that came and went.

He listened, but heard nothing. His eyelids were half closed, two slits blocking out the daylight. He sniffed the air; an odor of charcoal was faint and then gone.

Thump!

He felt his body shake from inside the muddy hole he had bedded himself in like a pig. Slowly he pulled the leaves and twigs from his face.

Thump!

Tiny balls of mud were falling loose like an avalanche on the other side of the bank. Venir's heart began to thunder behind his breast. Danger was near. He felt a strong desire to make a dash for the river and swim. He sat up, head peering around. There was nothing to see from his mud hole. He crawled over the grit and through the mud and peeked over the lip of the gulley.

Thump!

He didn't make anything out. The suns were rising into his face. He held his hand over his brow but it didn't help. Whatever it was, it was coming. He felt it was close. It was monstrous in size possibly, the kind of thing that could swallow him in a single gulp. The sensation in his fingertips was tingling now. The numbness of his slumber was wearing off. His alert senses had been dulled, but now they were sharpening like knives scraping the stone. *Wake up!*

Then he saw it. A huge man taller than the trees, walking up the bank from down river. They had found him. The giants had come. If he had only woken up sooner he could have taken his chances swimming the river. Like a fool he had rested instead. *Bone!* He hunkered down inside the trench. The river was only thirty yards away. His best chance was to slip inside the river. *Maybe he won't see me. Just wait for his head to turn.*

THUMP!

The giant was getting closer now. A cloud blotted out the sunlight overhead and moved on. The light was there, gone, and back again, except the cloud wasn't a cloud.

WHUMP!

WHUMP!

WHUMP!

SNORT!

Venir's joints locked up, and a sliver of ice coursed down his spine. The dragon swooped downward from high above, breast scraping the trees nearby, then up and out of sight. Venir envisioned himself swimming, only to have himself snatched from the water like a fish snatched by a hawk, a huge hawk with scales, black ones. He got down on his belly and low crawled toward the water. *No choice. Swim or die.*

Clank!

He crawled over something buried in the mud. He tugged at it, the leather texture familiar to his fingers. It was the sack. Venir didn't even think as he opened it and reached inside. Something wriggled violently in his grip. He jerked his arm out just in time to watch Eep the imp's mouth open wide and bite off the fingers on his hand. The pain raced up his arm and pierced deep inside his brain. He wanted to scream, but bit into his lip instead as he slammed the imp into the ground.

"Die human!" it screeched.

Venir saw its eye fixate on the shadow in the sky above. It hissed a laugh, its serpent tongue licking its nose, his lost fingers dangling in-between its razor sharp teeth. The imp gulped and swallowed.

"Death comes for you, Darkslayer!" Eep blinked, disappearing from his grasp, leaving Venir alone with his two bloodied finger stumps.

THUMP!

Slat!

He plunged his arm back into the sack and felt a hard rim of steel. He drew out his shield. The ornate banding was a welcome sight, like a lost friend that had returned home. *Helm,* came out next. The warm leather chinstrap fit snug under his chin. The next object he drew from the sack was the most welcome of all. The shaft of the axe in his bloody hand made the loss of his fingers seem insignificant. Only the tips were gone from his lower fingers, but his hand still held the axe just as tightly as it would a sack filled with gold. He felt inside the sack again, but there was no girdle, nothing else.

"BROOL!" he yelled, holding it up high over his head.

The dull sheen of steel glinted in the light of the two suns. Venir's mind was tickling with fire underneath the awareness of the helm. If it was his time to perish, then this was how he wanted it. He was ready to meet his fate, without fingers, or toes for the matter; as long as he could swing steel he would be just fine.

"Come on, Giant! Come on, Dragon! I'm ready for you!"

The giant stepped into the mouth of the trench. It towered over him, close to twenty feet tall. The black dragon was circling in the air from high above, its yellow eyes like sparkling gems filled with fire. The giant's face was set in anger. It had a strange tilt in its stance. Its voice was as deep as Dwarven Hole as it spoke.

"YOUUU!" the giant said, pointing his stump of a hand his way.

Venir noticed its toe was missing as well. It was the same one from the ravine; the one that had fought him and the underlings.

"ME!" Venir shouted back, holding his war-axe over the blades of his shoulder.

The giant's brows deepened over his nose as it sucked in its breath to speak.

"HOW ... DID ... YOU ... GET ... HERE ...?"

Venir didn't want to talk; he wanted to fight. Still ...

"I came through the mist, where you did!" He shouted.

The giant was considering his words.

"IM ... POSS ... I ... BILE .... ONLY ... OUR ... KIND ... CAN ... CROSS ... THE MIST."

Venir eyed the dragon in the sky and then focused back on the giant. The giant's gaze remained transfixed on him with a murderous intent. The hostility was clear in its voice. Yet, it hesitated.

The giant took a deep draw of air into his nose as it stretched out its arms. It clutched its fingers in one hand and looked at the stump on the other.

"YOU ... HAVE ... OUR ... BLOOD! ... WE ... WILL ... HAVE ... YOURS!"

Venir rolled his shoulder. It was feeling better. The heat of battle was running its course through him, making him stronger and more alert. The giant was two steps from him, unmoving, his big brown eyes fixated on the axe. Good, Venir thought. It knew he could hurt it. The giant reached over, grabbed a tree in its hand, ripped it from the ground, and came at him.

The bottom roots of the tree smashed into the ground as Venir backpedaled away. The giant growled, swung, and busted a man-sized crater into the ground. The enlarged man was quick; his tree trunk descended over and over like a hatchet. All Venir could do was back away from each blast of dirt that shook him from his feet. The sound of the cracking wood and splintering branches was loud, but the giant's voice louder still.

"ONLY TIME ... LITTLE MAN! YOUR BLOOD WILL NOT SAVE YOU!"

The giant's words, steps, and swings were coming faster. Venir didn't follow the meaning of 'your blood', but he had no time to consider it.

CRACK!

The next blow snapped the tree in half. Venir scrambled to his feet and made a dash for a grove of trees. The giant's hand knocked a massive scoop of dirt from the ground, clipping the heels of his feet. Venir scrambled up and dove behind another tree. The sound of the giant's angry grunts was softened by the leaves and branches. He pressed his back to a gray trunk and fought for his breath. There was a moment of silence followed by the sound of the rustling leaves.

Venir had the sack draped around his arm with the shield. He was determined not to lose it again. His fingers he could live without, but not the armament. He looked around the trunk. The giant stood at the edge of the grove. He could hear it laughing.

"NOT SMART. COME OUT, AND I'LL MAKE YOU A DEAL. SURRENDER AND I'LL LET YOU LIVE. I'LL TAKE YOU BACK HOME. YOU'LL LIVE LONGER INSIDE THE MAZE. IF YOU MAKE IT OUT AGAIN, YOU CAN GO BACK TO BISH."

Venir knew little about giants. He had doubted their existence until recent events. Yet, he saw no reason to take the aloof race by their word. Legend said men had tricked them before. Maybe he could, too. He would do anything to increase his chance of survival and get what he wanted more than anything: to go back home. Still, he was glad to be alone here: his fate would be his, and his alone. He waited.

"NOTHING. YOU HAVE NOTHING TO SAY?"

Only the billowing leaves offered an answer. *Think or die!* Well, come to think of it, maybe he wished Mood was with him. The Blood Ranger knew all about giants, especially how to kill them. Mood had told him that the best way to kill them was to get in close.

"FINE THEN ... I'VE GOT ANOTHER OFFER FOR YOU."

He heard the giant whistle. A black shadow hung over the sky.

WHUMP!

WHUMP!

WHUMP!

SNORT!

Above him, something began to suck the air from the grove. *What's it doing?* A roar of fire shot from the black dragon's mouth, engulfing the tree tops in flames. Venir moved away from the fire and the giant. Another blast of fire came, scorching the other side of the grove. The entire top of the grove was ablaze, a fiery inferno that dripped down the trees like lava.

The air was getting thin, and Venir began coughing. Above him was only smoke and flame; the intense heat became unbearable. The burning wood was turning to char and ash, filling his nose and lungs with sooty smoke. He fell to his belly and began to crawl. Burning branches were falling around him now. He had never seen fire that could burn something so fast. It was unnatural.

Venir couldn't handle the thought of being cooked alive. He needed to get out. The smoke was thick, and the flames were bright. He couldn't discern a direction to go. The hairs on his arms began to dry up and curl.

"No!" he cried and coughed.

He could still sense the giant nearby. He pulled his shield in front of him and charged. The small forest was collapsing around him now, fiery branches bouncing from his shoulders. He couldn't see or hear a thing as he burst free of the clearing.

SWAT!

It felt like it had the last time the giant hit him, only worse. He flipped head over heels more than once before crashing into the meadow. The thick grass did little to cushion his fall. He lay still, sprawled out on his back, Brool clutched in his bloody fingers. His shield was still strapped to his arm. He did not move.

Venir coughed and fought to suck in more air. His watery eyes could barely make out the naked sky. He felt the ground shaking beneath him. *Get up!* His body didn't want to move. *GET UP!* He saw the giant's face first, then its hand. He pulled his shield over him just in time to catch the full force of its fist. The blows kept coming, smashing him deeper and deeper into the ground. There was nothing Venir could do but take it. He felt one shoulder give way, then the other. Pain began to bite into his innards as his ribs broke. The next blow knocked out a mouthful of blood. His mind cried for the giant to stop, but it didn't.

<h1 style="text-align:center">95</h1>

"SWING! SWING! SWING!" A HAMMERING voice cried. "Stab! Stab! Stab!"

Brak was pouring with sweat. His arms felt like they were made of iron. He didn't know how much more he could take, the agony of it all.

"FIGHT!" the man screamed in his face. He chopped at the man, a sluggish blow. He winced.

Smack! Smack! Smack!

The wooden sword rang his head like a bell. He collapsed to the ground. He knew what was coming next.

"Oooph!"

The kick to his gut was fierce. He fought for a breath of air only to find the boot tip attacking his stomach once again. It was torture. His life had been nothing but torture since his mother died. He tried to fight, but all he did was defend his own life. The sound of the wooden sword clattered across the stone.

"He's a dolt! A brainless brute like his father! I can't knock a lick of sense into him. Leezir, this experiment is over. I'm done!"

"Not so fast, Hagerdon. I think you have underestimated your efforts. He still lives, doesn't he? You beat him harder every day, yet he stands up for more."

Hagerdon looked at Brak with a sneer. Brak could see the contempt on the man's face. Hagerdon the Slerg was unlike the rest. His face was clean and charming, a polished marble stone in a rat's nest. It was clear the man had been bred for life above the ground, not below it in the damp and filth. Leezir seemed to be the more civil and adjusted of the two, however.

Brak watched as Hagerdon drew a long sword he called a rapier. The man's brown locks of hair bounced as he thrust and cut in the air, making patterns that Brak's eyes could barely follow. He knew the man didn't care for him.

It had something to do with his father, based on what he overheard. Even the rotting bandaged faces of the ragged man-urchins had more civility to offer.

Hagerdon made him uneasy. He was always restlessly watching his back for Hagerdon when Leezir wasn't around. The Slerg was very reluctant to be his mentor, or friend for that matter, leaving him to wonder what his father, Venir, had done.

"What do you expect to do with him, this overgrown turd? He's too big to steal and too stupid to fight," the wiry man said. "Hah!" Hagerdon executed a thrust, stabbed a rotting apple on the table, and flicked the apple into Brak's unsuspecting face.

Leezir hopped from his chair.

"You don't believe what we told you, do you? This man …er, boy … chopped a throng of men into dog food. With a bolt sticking in his arm! His father would have been proud that day," Leezir said, poking Hagerdon in the chest. "You would have been frightened chicken."

"Pah!"

"Pah, hah! Those men he took weren't amateurs or urchins. They were of the guilds — nothing to snivel at."

Hagerdon slammed his blade back into its sheath.

"He was distraught, a temper tantrum gone awry. He simply caught them off guard, is all."

Leezir rubbed the sandy hair atop his head.

"You are a fool. So be it. I've a feeling he'll save your arse one day. Now, get back on with it. See, he stands."

Brak wiped the apple from his face and rose to his feet with a groan. He ached from head to toe. Lumps and bruises were scattered all over his body, and his muscles were sore and tender. He looked at his new family, trying to fit his mah's face in among them. It didn't seem right, nothing did. His simple life had been overturned.

The men, the Slergs, always talked like he was a painting on the wall. He didn't say much, just listened and kept his mouth shut. His mah had always told him to do that when she wasn't around. It wasn't that he didn't know what to say or have anything to ask, he was simply too scared. Fighting and eating were pretty much what his life had boiled down to. *Mah.*

"Pick up the club, you big, pig-stupid urchin!" his tormentor said, picking up the wooden sword from the ground.

One thing was certain; Brak didn't like the name-calling. It was getting old. His mah had told him to just ignore it when others called him names, and walk on. He had never liked that; he always wanted to bust name-callers in the mouth. He wanted to bust Hagerdon in the mouth. The man was arrogant. His voice reminded Brak of the whining farm wives who complained about his sluggish effort. They would say, "I've seen three-legged cows move faster than that," or "My cat knows more words than he does." The muscles in his back began to knot. His youthful face gave away the painful memories.

"Ah, look Leezir, he's going to cry again. I can't train a swordsman that cries. I can beat the Bone out of one, though."

Rap! Rap! Rap!

Brak was lit up on his head and hands. He didn't move and didn't wince.

"Block, you idiot! He's the stu—"

"SHUT UP!"

Hagerdon raised his wooden sword just in time to prevent his skull from being crushed. The club deflected downward, catching the man in the shoulder. "Blast you, Br—"

Clonk! Clonk! Clonk!

Brak didn't stop swinging as wood smacked into wood. Hagerdon was on the defensive now, struggling to find a place to escape. Brak chased him down, swinging hard and fast at Hagerdon's every twist and turn. A look of desperation appeared on the cocky Slerg fighter's face. Hagerdon leapt over a small table as the club smashed through it. The man-urchins and Leezir were scrambling out of Brak's way. The room was small. Hagerdon had nowhere to go.

Brak kept pounding away at the man's stick. He saw the look in the man's face as each blow jolted his arms. He liked it.

Hagerdon dashed away from one of his wild swings that caught one man-urchin in the chest, driving him wailing to the ground. It felt good, hitting something back for a change. He was in control, his lust for battle had risen to the surface, but his fury was growing. He cornered Hagerdon again and began wailing away at the man's weakening arm. Something poked him, first in one leg, then in the other.

"STOP!" Leezir screamed. "STOP BRAK! STOP HAGERDON!"

Brak stepped back. Something was burning in his legs. He looked down and saw blood streaming from the thighs of his pants. Hagerdon had his rapier out, blood dripping from the point. The man's hair was matted with sweat, his face flushed red, and his chest heaving. Leezir had stepped between them, his white ash club glowing.

"I think that's enough for today," he said with a worried smile.

Hagerdon slung his sword across the room and exited through the door with an angry scream.

Brak sat down on the floor.

Leezir turned to Brak, looked down at his legs, and said, "He could have killed you, you know."

"I'm sure he wishes he had," Brak said.

"I agree." Leezir kneeled down and inspected Brak's wounds. "Hmmm … these legs look pretty bad, Brak. You won't stand much of a chance training tomorrow if you can't walk."

Brak shrugged.

"I can fix that. Do you want me to?"

Brak shrugged again.

"I'll fix it, but tomorrow you will have to do as he says."

"I don't like the names."

"Well," Leezir laughed under his breath, "I think Hagerdon understands that now. Still, this time, you caught him off guard. That won't happen again. You can expect the worst and best from him between now and whenever. But at least we know this much."

Brak looked up at him.

Leezir slapped his shoulder saying, "You've got the heart of a fighter. Let us teach you how to use it."

"What about finding my father?"

Brak had had many dreams lately, but he had kept that to himself. The face of Venir would come and go, screaming in pain and fury.

Leezir's voice was cold.

"You aren't ready for that yet, and you still owe me."

Brak's head dipped. He was certain he would always owe the Slerg.

96

H E HAD SURVIVED. HE HOPED Venir had, too, and wished he could have made an escape with him. Boon was proud, though, of having the guts to help the man stay alive. After the giant swatted him like a rodent he thought for sure he would die. He hadn't. A simple spell had afforded him a cushion that protected his body from a painful break. Still, the force of the landing had been enough to black him out. The cushioning spell had only lasted a couple of instants.

He blinked, but it made little difference since he had no light. Most of the time he couldn't remember if his eyes were opened or closed, as if it mattered. It was frustrating; the man named Venir had become like family in the few moments he had spent with him. He and the warrior had something in common … the sack. Boon knew the sack might not free him, but it could give him power if it chose to do so. He longed for it. It was near; it had to be. It was the only way that Venir could have survived the mist, wasn't it?

Boon gave Venir's prowess much thought. The man was strong, like a tiny-sized giant. And that tattoo … What was that tattoo all about? He had heard the giants murmuring about it, saying it was special, something about giants' blood. Maybe it wasn't a tattoo after all, but a different mark of an ancient sort. Regardless, unlike the others that came and fell, Venir had make quite the impression. They wanted him dead or dragged back to be finished in the maze. Boon had a feeling, though: if any man could escape the Under Bish, Land of the Giants, it was Venir.

This is ridiculous! I cannot scratch a single thing! I can't even scream for water … Blast!

He missed talking, but the giants had seen to it that he wouldn't be talking to anybody anytime soon. Instead, Boon was immobilized in a metal cocoon. He couldn't see or move a single appendage. All he had was a tiny nose hole within a body-tight steel sarcophagus. He tried to look on the bright side of things: at least he lived. He could smell and hear things, too.

The giants were restless, and had been for quite some time since the warrior left. It was good, good for him; he knew the man somehow lived. Maybe he had been wrong about his chances of leaving. Maybe his confidence had been lost long ago with the sack of mystical armament. The more he thought about it, the more he realized he hadn't tried very hard to escape before. Now, the brute warrior was doing something he hadn't even bothered to dream about.

Boon wanted to escape now, more than anything. A fire had been ignited within him. It wasn't possible, though. The giants kept him closely guarded. They liked having him around to be the delegate to the other races.

I'll bide my time. It won't be long before I slip their minds.

The giants made it clear that they weren't going anywhere. Their breathing was heavy, and they smelled like drying leaves. Wherever they went, they carried him along, like a cherished figurine to decorate the mantle.

Boon wasn't sure how much longer he could take it.

Fie upon you, stupid giants!

97

"**I**F YOU CAN SURVIVE THAT, YOU CAN SURVIVE ANYTHING!" the giant said, walking away. Venir didn't hear a word of it. The only thing he heard was his blood spilling on the ground. Everything hurt, and his body twitched with convulsions. His limbs felt twisted. Blood filled his mouth, drowning him. Fighting the agony, he tried to force himself on his side. He was doing it, but he didn't know how he was. His mind rocked and reeled, and yet he couldn't block his suffering out. It seemed to get worse with every raspy breath. A blood bubble burst outside his nostril.

His eyes were almost swollen shut, and his face was smashed. He turned his head and coughed reddened chunks onto the ground. It felt like an entire lung had been torn inside him. He couldn't feel his legs, but they must have been dislocated or broken. In the back of Venir's mind, all he could think about was the Warfield. It was the place he preferred to go, to fight and die and perish into the sands before a host of bloodthirsty warriors. Instead, he lay dying in a place of the unknown, lost and as forgettable as the first rain drop.

He could see the giant looking back over its shoulder, laughing as it strode away.

"LITTLE GNAT! HAH … HAH … HAH!"

The black dragon was by its giant master's side, like a scaly black dog whose tail whipped back and forth.

CHONGO! What bothered him most about dying was that he would never see his dog again. Chongo had never left his side, so why had he left Chongo? *UNDERLINGS!* The foul little black creatures had gotten what they wanted, separated this fool of a warrior from his dog and his world. His giant dog? He had failed his friend. Perhaps he deserved to die, alone, in a land that no one knew existed. Venir shuddered violently once more and lay still. *Suffer and die.*

FLASH!

The brilliant white light exploded in his skull, sending tendrils of cleansing white hot power coursing through every busted bone and torn fiber in his being, setting his veins on fire. He could feel and hear the crackling sounds of his bones mending. Energy washed over him, pouring from his helmet like a bucket filling from a waterfall. Venir had felt like slat for days, weeks, or even months, but now he felt like something entirely new. His eyelets burned with smoldering black light. He rose to his feet with Brool clutched fiercely in his grip. *Let's try this again!*

Venir sprinted for the giant, face red with rage, heart exploding with fury. The dragon's long neck twisted around, and when it saw him, it reared up and roared, lashing out with its tail as Venir closed in. As the tail swept over the ground, Venir hurtled over it to chop into the side of the giant's knee.

"R-R-R-RAAAAHHHHHHHH!" the giant yelled.

Venir's biceps worked his axe with bone-jarring ferocity.

CHOP! CHOP! CHOP!

The giant's leg was dangling by skin and muscle just below the knee, spurting blood like a busted pipe spurting water, all over Venir, soaking him and gushing to the ground.

"NOOOOO!" the giant cried, falling to the ground. "NOOOOOO!"

Venir tried to wipe the blood from his eyes.

The black dragon's tail lashed out.

SWAT!

Venir went skipping across the ground like a river stone.

"BONE!"

He was on his feet again, shield lowered and Brool ready. The dragon, Blackie, reared up on its hind legs, looming almost as tall as the giant, and then it roared and charged his way, shaking the ground.

"Come on, Snake!"

The dragon's hands reached out, claws ripping at his head. Venir brought Brool down, clipping the back of its hand. Blackie roared again and began stomping its big clawed foot at him. He and Brool were smaller and quicker, the giant razor whirling and biting into the dragon's skin. Venir sheared off a section of meat and scales, igniting a frenzied roar from the beast. Another stroke of steel split the skin between the dragon's toes.

WHUMP! WHUMP! WHUMP! SNORT!

The dragon's massive wings expanded, and it lifted off. Venir was unrelenting, cutting a nasty gash across its armored belly before it escaped into the sky. It sounded like the world was going to end when it roared. Now it hovered twenty feet over Venir's head, eyes intent on his death. There he stood in the field, smoke from the burning grove rolling across his features, the wind of the wings drying his blood-soaked hair. Then it came, that sound that came as all of the air around him was sucked away.

This is it!

He thought of all the bodies he'd seen dropped in the furnace back in Bone.

He raised his shield just as the stream of fire came, and he screamed in defiance. His scream lasted a while, but the fire lasted longer. The heat was a hundred fold what he expected. The blast of fire rained down on his shield and splattered like molten lava onto the ground. It was agony. Venir swore his blood was boiling on the inside of his smoking skin. He couldn't breathe; he could barely think. The fire stopped. Chill bumps rose all over his arms and legs as the daylight's hot air turned cold. Coated in wet giant blood, Venir was smoldering like a wet towel in the baking suns, but he was alive.

THOOM!

The black dragon dropped from the sky, its reptilian jaw open wide like a fanged door. Venir could see the beast no longer had the fire behind its bejeweled eyes. The magnificent dragon was reduced to little more than a flying lizard. Its head and tail rolled back and forth in contempt.

It hissed.

Venir laughed.

It charged.

It was fast for a cumbersome beast, but Venir was faster. Brool cut its striking tail. It recoiled. Venir whirled and drove a spike into its nose. It tried to pin Venir to the ground, only to lose a part of its toe.

The dragon's armor was hard though, like a shield of stone. Venir's muscular arms were jolted like a black smith hammering iron with every blow. Brool's keen edge was digging in, chipping at the scaled armor like wood. The dragon recoiled and struck. Venir jumped and chopped. The dragon's tail and snapping jaws both struck like frenzied snakes. Venir battled on, ducking, diving, and chopping like a man possessed.

The dragon swatted him to the ground like a rodent with its hand. Its jaws dove down where he lay, filling with a mouthful of dirt as Venir rolled away. He drove his axe's spike deep into the beast's shoulder. It recoiled back, roaring as if it had never been hurt before. Another roar came, so loud Venir felt his legs go numb.

SNORT! WHUMP! WHUMP! WHUMP!

The proud beast rose from the ground again, its long neck sagging as it soared away, across the river and into the mist. Venir fell down to the ground, trembling and thirsty. His chest heaved. His body felt busted and broken again.

His instincts fired a warning. Where was the giant? His eyes followed the trail of blood that smeared a path in the tall grass.

The giant was propped up against the bank of the gully nearby, its head dipped into its chest. Its leg had detached and lay like a log, a bloody stump at one end. Venir limped over the giant's way. The leather belt that held up the giant's pants was strapped like a vise around its leg. One glazed eye opened up as Venir approached.

"COME … TO … FINISH ME … HAVE …YOU … LITTLE GIANT?"

Venir could hardly talk.

"Not if you tell me how to get out of here. Otherwise, your other leg is coming off … and then some," he said, waving his gory axe before the giant's bloodshot eye.

The giant closed his eye and sighed.

Venir wondered if the giant man had expired all together. He poked Brool's spike into its toe. The giant's head rolled back like a lazy dog.

"THEY WILL BE HERE SOON."

"Who," he yelled.

"MY BRETHERN COME!"

Venir raised his axe.

"Well, then they will be coming to bury their dead brother."

"NOOOO! STOP!" the giant tried to shout, but its voice was weak. It held out its giant hand while slowly its head swiveled around. "HUH … YOU CHASED OFF BLACKIE. HE'LL BE BACK WITH HIS BROTHERS. BETTER YOU HIDE, OR GO BACK TO OUR HOME. DRAGON WILL EAT YOU ALIVE. ONE PIECE AT A TIME. YUM."

Venir sliced the skin beside the giant's big toe.

"OWWW!"

Mood had told him about giant lies and tricks, but the thought of more dragons coming coiled fear along his spine. Venir walked over and stood alongside the giant's head. His helmet's spike was almost level to its shoulder. Venir never felt smaller as he rose up on his toes to speak.

"Last chance, Giant. Tell me how to get back to Bish, and I'll let you live." Venir's eyes still burned like blue fires. "Anything else, and I'm going to chop you up one piece at a time!" he screamed into its ear.

"ALL RIGHT, I'LL TELL."

"Give me your word on the truth."

It sighed.

"YES."

"Out with it," he said, banging the flat of Brool's blade on its chin.

"CROSS THE RIVER. STAY ON THE THAT SIDE, AND FOLLOW IT DOWN STREAM INTO THE MIST."

Venir felt as if the sky was closing in on him. Not the mist again. His stomach fluttered. Still, if the mist was the only way in, then it had to be the only way out.

"I heard no river on my way in and smelled no water."

The giant's neck rolled over, its blood shot eye twitching back and forth.

"THE RIVER ONLY LEADS OUT, NOT BACK IN. STAY CLOSE TO THE RIVER."

The giant groaned, sighed, and let its head slump down. Venir could see a stream of blood emptying from its stump and into the river. He looked at what remained of the fingers on his hand. He shrugged. It wasn't so bad; they were only halfway gone. It wasn't his drinking hand, anyway.

He was relieved to find the sack still wrapped around his arm. Scanning the sky, he took a deep breath and dropped the armament back into the sack, slung it over his shoulder, and headed into the river. He kicked along with the current until he made it to the other side, and then walked, checking the skies now and again as he made his way toward the mist. Taking one last look at the setting suns, he wondered what had happened to Boon and the rat-woman. As he stepped into the mist, certain to keep his toes wet, he walked on and on.

Before long, Venir wasn't sure if any of his adventures in the Under Bish had ever really happened at all.

EPILOGUE

K AM LOOKED DOWN AT THE bump on her belly and watched it disappear. It was good, being a mage. Her magic made it easier to hide things. She pulled her auburn hair back in a bun, slipped on her clothes, and headed downstairs into the tavern. It was early; the light of the two suns was only just peeking in through the ruffled cracks of the curtained windows.

In the weeks it had been since Joline informed her of her pregnancy, her own resiliency had become stronger. Joline said her face radiated with energy, and the concerned patrons of the Magi Roost affirmed those opinions as well. No one knew she was pregnant, except her mother and Joline. What she did wasn't any different than what most magi could do during a pregnancy. Some hid it for reasons of vanity, others for their own personal concerns.

A host of voices could be heard from down below. One was a baritone man, big, black and bald. He had arrived during Kam's illness, a friend of Venir's sent to keep tabs on the boys. Mikkel's jovial voice and bright smile were just what everyone needed during some of the tavern's darkest hours, the time when everyone had been anxious about Kam's comatose state. She looked down over the rail onto Georgio's wide-eyed face. The boy sat on a bar stool, his chin propped up on his elbows, hanging on Mikkel's every word.

"… Boy, that ogre had over one hundred pounds on Vee, this much taller," the man motioned with his arm raised high above his head. "Farc was like a living nightmare in flesh and brawn. I've seen Vee in a hundred scrapes before, but fighting an ogre with his bare hands was just stupid. But our man Vee would do anything for a fight. He just laughed at the beast …"

Kam leaned a little farther over the rail. She could see Georgio fidgeting in his seat as he drank from a tankard of ale. The boy wiped the white froth on his sleeve. *What?*

"GEORGIO! What are you drinking!?"

The boy began to shrink in his seat. Mikkel's big hand was smooth as the tankard disappeared underneath the table.

"I can explain, Kam. Apologies! It's just some of my recipe," Mikkel reassured her.

Kam was storming down the stairs, Mikkel's admiring eyes intent on every one of her steps. Her belly wasn't the only thing that got bigger. She pointed her finger up into Mikkel's face.

"He's a boy you idiot, not a customer!"

"He's so big though; a little mead won't hurt," Mikkel said.

"It tasted good," Georgio said.

Kam locked a mind grumble in on the boy. Georgio's face turned ash white. His words were as feeble as a baby's as he said, "I'm sorry ... *sniff* ... never again." She inlaid a suggestion before she let him go, and Georgio slumped over the table. His face was beaded with sweat.

Suddenly, Georgio scurried out the front door, yelling, "Lefty, where are you? We've got chores to do!"

She turned back on Mikkel, whose eyes were full of surprise as she poked his chest, and said, "Do that one more time, and I'll crush your brain like a grape. Do you understand?"

"Yes Kam, yes Kam. Again, I-I apologize." She had never felt so strong. It was like something grew inside of her that gave her more strength. She liked it.

She studied Mikkel's perplexed face. She knew his intentions were harmless, but she had already seen enough evidence of Venir's bad influence on the boy. Still, boys grew up fast in this world, and she couldn't protect him forever.

"You hungry, Kam?" Mikkel asked, in all sincerity.

She hadn't realized her hand had drifted down to her belly. *Careful girl.* She felt like she could eat a cow, however.

"Sure, but I'll have Joline whip up something for me."

Whack!

The front tavern door swung open, and Lefty, Gillem, and a stout wiry black-haired man named Billip entered, followed by Georgio.

"Ah ... good morning Kam, it's great to see you on this beautiful day," Gillem Longfingers said.

"Aye ... couldn't agree more," Billip responded, twisting his goatee.

"Absolutely," added Lefty with a smile as wide as the room.

She paid no mind to Mikkel, who was shaking his head toward them as he stood by her side.

They all stopped a few feet inside the doorway.

The arrival of Mikkel and Billip couldn't have come at a better time. The boys, especially Georgio, had taken a shine to them both. Billip and Mikkel were hardened men, cut from the same cloth as Venir, and they were men of their word. They had proved that much within a few days of their arrival. They knew all about running a tavern, too; she hadn't been busier in years. Without Venir around, the boys needed some type of men to look up to, and it was clear that Venir trusted these men.

It was sad still, trying to figure out why Venir insisted on them checking on her and the boys. It was as if he knew he wasn't coming back. She had no sense of what had happened to the man; she only had what he had left her inside her belly. She couldn't tell if she despised him for it or not, but one thing was for sure: whether Venir was there or not, he kept things interesting.

"Er ... is everything all right, Kam?" Lefty said, walking over and reaching for her hand.

She jerked it away, "Yes, I'm fine."

Lefty withdrew, looking back at the men.

The halfling boy hadn't seemed right since her sickness. Gillem Longfingers, as charming as the halfling man could be, couldn't be trusted. No man that charming should ever be trusted. She still swore Palos had something to do with it; she just had been too busy to bother figuring it out. The guilt that had once been in Lefty's face was now gone. He was no longer the playful boy she knew him to be, but more of a crafty sort. Every week he acted more like Gillem. She told herself that was how halflings were, that it was for the best.

"So Lefty, how many flowers did you deliver yesterday?"

"Oh, it was awful. Master Gillem ran me until my heels gave out," he said, in a semi-dreadful voice.

Gillem stuck his thumbs in his belt and said, "Tis true; I work the boy hard. It keeps him out of trouble. That's how we halflings do it. He's not to be running the streets like a wild urchin, getting into all kinds of mischief."

Georgio shoved his way past Lefty and Gillem, almost knocking them both over.

"Excuse you, Boy," Gillem said, puffing his pipe.

Georgio glared back at the thief and took his place on the stool behind Kam, arms crossed and head down.

Mikkel reached over and rubbed Georgio's curly head. "Chin up, Boy. We've got some mintaur games to play later. You got to be fired up. Of course, if you'd rather pick daisies than swing steel, I'm certain Master Gillem can arrange that."

Georgio eyed Lefty and pounded his fist into his meaty hand.

"Naw, I'm good."

Billip cracked his knuckles, gave Kam a short bow and said before he exited, "How about I go stir up some business?"

"Thank you," she said. It was like this, now; a family was growing all around her, as well as inside her. She took comfort that she still had control over the one inside her, and that it let her know that Venir would always be with her.

Eep was home in his mystic dimension, for now. All he did these days was watch the world of Bish destroy itself, without his help. It left him clutching his claws with jealousy and rage. All he could to was dream that someone or something would summon him soon.

Verbard stood, shoulders back, chin up, as he faced Master Sinway, who sat looming on his jewel-encrusted throne like a giant. The black robes of the Master of all underlings spilled to the floor, where they resembled a ruffled void. The silver-eyed underling Lord cared little now for that warning Master Sinway's son, Kierway, had given him. Upon his arrival he felt nothing more than welcome. He was getting the kind of treatment he had become accustomed to over the centuries, the kind of awe that he relished.

Master Sinway's voice was quiet, but the power was still there.

"Verbard, your recount of your journey is fascinating, almost believable."

He felt his chest begin to tighten as his anger began to swell. *How dare* –

"The part about you living and Catten dying was the hardest part to swallow, but here you are, alive, with your brother's eyes in my palm."

Sinway was rolling the golden orbs of his brother's eyes like a child's toys between his hands. "So, you felt the Darkslayer's heart in your hand, did you? It beat like a racing horse, you say? I know that spell. It's a serviceable one …"

The iron eyes of Master Sinway locked onto his. He felt his thoughts being invaded, a black light probing his mind like a sickness. He wanted to fight against it, but could not. He had nothing to hide. He had to catch his breath as he was released.

"… no doubt it should have killed the man. Yet, it did not. It's a fascinating account, Verbard, and I hate to say it, but I have no choice but to believe it all."

Verbard allowed himself a slight bow.

Master Sinway twirled Catten's eyes in the air, the orbs hovering as a shadow of his brother formed.

"I miss your brother, though. Perhaps he can be resurrected. Would you like that, Verbard?"

"I confess, I could not have succeeded without him, he —"

"Is that so? It seems you were better off without him. Maybe it was he that held you back, not you holding him back?"

Verbard wanted to believe it, and had believed it at one time, but his brother deserved some of the credit.

"I can't say, but my brother has always been my best ally over the years. It would do us both a great honor if he were to come back. I prefer to leave that decision to you; it is and has always been yours to decide, Master."

"Now you are beginning to sound like your brother, Verbard. It doesn't suit you."

Master Sinway made a sharp sound with his mouth. A hulking Vicious stepped from the shadows. Its feline face and muscular body were like those of a statue carved from black marble. He watched as the golden eyes sailed through the air. The Vicious snatched the pair in its claws and slipped away and out of sight.

Master Sinway leaned forward, hands clasped, elbows resting on the throne.

"Smile Verbard, the Darkslayer is gone. I felt the effects not long after the two of you left here. The human race is on the run; the villages are once again filled with fear. The Royals have gotten careless, fat, and lazy. Our time has come. The underlings will take over the land of Bish, one city at a time."

Verbard allowed himself a smile as the fire behind his silver eyes began to glow. He had heard this speech many times before, as the scales tipped back and forth. Something now hung in the air of the world of Bish that had never been there before. Whatever had held the underlings back before, no longer held them back now. They were hungry dogs that had been chained too long. Now they were truly free to hunt on their own. The Darkslayer was gone.

"I am ready, Master!"

"Go home, Verbard; celebrate your victory. I'll keep you informed."

Home. Lord Verbard had little desire to see his ghastly wife. The beastly pregnancy was not something he could stand. No, he made his way to Catten's home, to pay his respects and comfort his brother's widow.

"You can't be serious?"

"Aye, but I am."

Fogle Boon stood at the foot of the Nameless Mountains. He could see the clouds rolling over the icy peaks that were thousands of feet above. He had never been cold before, but a shiver of ice coursed through his veins. He could see a glimmer in Mood's eyes. He was certain the King of the Blood Rangers was insane. He had to remember why he came: to help Chongo and find Venir. He was beginning to think that becoming an adventurer was a stupid way to live his life.

"I didn't think anyone lived in those mountains. I thought it was too cold."

"This is Bish," Mood said, as he led his mount up the base of the mountain, "there is something always livin' anywhere and everywhere."

"Why would a druid live here? I thought they lived in forests."

"What makes you think there ain't a forest up there?"

Fogle Boon held his hand up to his eyes and said, "Because I don't see any trees."

"Ho! Ho! That's because you aren't looking hard enough. Come on."

Fogle followed, pulling his robes around him. He had heard the stories of how the underlings lived below these mountains. The mouths of their caves were yawning open nearby, and he half expected to see the evil race come pouring out.

He said under his breath, "I guess it's safer above them, than below them."

"What's that?" Mood said.

He heard that? "Nothing," he said.

Up the mountain they went, like two flies on a jagged wall, trying to find a druid that could heal a dog that could find Venir, the man who was key to it all.

Series 1   THE   Book 4
DARK SLAYER

Danger and the Druid

CRAIG HALLORAN

1

Venir's fingers ached with every step. The imp had left his mark, a painful one at that. Despite the healing provided by the armament during his battle with the giant, the remaining stubs below his missing fingertips were misshapen and dark, like the wounds he suffered at the hands of the Vicious he battled at the Warfield. Those memories seemed like a lifetime ago, a hundred years. He thought of Georgio, the boy who could heal from such things. He hoped the boy was safe.

He sat down at the edge of the river, facing forward, or at least where he thought was forward. He dipped his blackened fingers in the cool water while he stared across the expanse. There was little to note: blue-gray water as far as the eye could see and a rolling fog floating over the top of the waters. The view across the river was much better than that he was surrounded by: Mist. It surrounded him just like before. His wet hand was shaking as he rubbed his face.

"Bone."

How much farther did he have to go to get back to Bish? The farther he walked, the more time escaped from him. Doubt assailed his mind. Boon the Wizard had told him how much the giants lied, tricking men as men tricked them. Had the giant lied, leading him down a path of death through starvation or exhaustion? He scooped up a mouthful of water, catching a glimpse of himself. His face was haggard, his hair wild and his beard almost reached his chest. He punched his fist into the water and spit.

"What manner of madness is this?"

WHUMP! WHUMP! WHUMP! SNORT!

Every fiber of his body stiffened. The sound had been ongoing since he followed himself into the mist. The image of the black dragon invaded his mind. He pictured rows of giant razor sharp teeth outlining a gaping red maw with an orange furnace burning down its throat. His entire body began to warm as the battle heat spread out to every fiber of hair. He reached over, clutching his leather sack, and craned his neck. Nothing. He sat, the sound of his labored breath filling his ears as he cupped his battered hand behind one ear. He remained still for another hour or minute, he did not know. The flapping of wings had been coming and going. Bedeviling. He remembered fangs as big as his forearm and fire as hot as anything he'd known. He splashed more water on his face. Sometimes it sounded like one massive beast, other times one hundred. The sounds came and faded, leaving him to wonder if they were real or just more tricks of his imagination.

"Come and get me then!" He reached into the sack and withdrew Brool. The axe was warm in his grip, tingling what remained of his fingers, taking the bite from the mangled flesh. He rose back to his feet. "We got to get out of here." He could have sworn the axe replied … *Indeed.*

Again, like so many times before, he donned his helm and shield and walked, one foot splashing on the edge of the water, the other on the soft bar of sand. The helm did little to amplify the sounds of the waters, and his vision was just as obscured as before by a field of feathery cotton that remained in his path, never ending. Venir had walked another mile or two when he began to stomp and rave. Madness was creeping into his thoughts, mixed with festering anger, frustration and rage. He swung and screamed, growled and howled. Not even an echo greeted him.

Onward, forward, unrelenting he walked, jogged and ran. His legs were heavy, and his weakening body begged for rest, sleep. He lay down with his legs in the water, and in a moment he was dreaming of walking along the endless river in the mist.

He snored.

SNORT!

He jerked up, wiping his nose, just as exhausted and weary as before. *Was that me?* The sounds of dragons came again. He replaced the armament into the sack, only to don it again and again. His mutterings and ramblings became more frequent as he conversed with the living and the dead. He laughed, cried, sobbed, lied, thirsted, drifted and starved. Yet somehow he was sustained.

"HELP ME!" he begged and pleaded.

"FIGHT ME!" he raged.

"KILL ME!" he dared.

None replied.

The water that sustained him never quenched his thirst, and the tiny minnows did not fill him. *Kam?* Who was she? *Bone?* Where was he? Venir was losing. Bish's ultimate survivor was being whittled away by forces he could not smell, touch or see. A fighter through and through, Venir moved on without day, night or hope, only instinct. His aching legs carried him on, step by step, mile after mile, league after league.

Plop.

He stopped, head whipping around. His mind muttered. *What was that?* Nothing. He grumbled and continued on.

Plop.

"Huh …" Venir clutched at the stringy hairs in his beard. The sound was nothing like anything he'd experienced before in the Mist, foreign to his mind and senses.

Plop.

Whatever it was, it was ahead of him. A vision formed in his mind of a smooth stone being dropped from a pier into a lake, and then the vision became a drop of rain water dripping from a rooftop into a puddle of mud. Something was going on in the Mist somewhere; it had to be. The tricks his mind had been playing on him were getting old, and his maddening visions must come to an end. *Move or die.* Someone had told him that once.

Plop.

The sound might as well have been a war-hammer smiting him in the ear as the clarity bore into his brain, screaming, maybe warning him that something was out there. He leaned forward, creeping alongside the wet bank, his foot no longer splashing in the water, angling for the next sound. Another twenty steps … *plop* … thirty steps … *plop* … ten steps … *plop plop* … his heart raced … five steps … fifteen steps … thirty steps … nothing. A hundred steps more he counted … nothing. Had he missed it or passed it? He did not know. He punched himself in the head and fell to his knees. He punched himself again and rushed into the river.

"This is hopeless!" He screamed at the top of his lungs.

Venir's feeble mind was breaking. He clutched the sack inside filthy and once powerful hands. He had once been a cunning and crafty warrior so long ago, before the sack. The armament within changed his life forever. The power within changed him, hardened him like stone, not so much as a man but as a minion, a killing machine, a menace to evil. He didn't ask for it, but he had it and hungered for it. He exacted vengeance with it a thousand times, but his hunger was never satisfied. *Underlings.* There was a time in his life when for every ten he killed he wanted to kill a hundred more. That fire and fury was no longer there. All purpose was gone.

Plop.

He turned back towards the bank. Venir swore the sound was only thirty feet away in the mist.

Plop.

Head down, he dragged his dripping wet body onto the bank, hauling the sack out of the water behind him. The plopping sound was steady now, so close he felt like he could touch it. There had to be something, anything out there making that noise. He had to find its source. He left the river on foot, the giant's words still lingering in his mind. *Follow the river.* He had done that. The giant must have lied to him, and there must be another way out.

Plop.

The river was his only friend and ally, and he had left it. He looked back one last time, watching its silent waters flow, realizing he would never see it again. He realized something else: he hated the giants.

Plop.

Without fear or hope he wandered back into the mist.

<h1 style="text-align:center">2</h1>

IT WAS PITCH BLACK BEHIND Castle Almen. A delivery depot stood in the view of a shadow pressed into the gloom. A glimmer of pale moonlight reflected in a puddle in the cobblestoned road a few feet beyond Detective Melegal's nose with drizzling rain shimmering the image. For months, on and off, he had crouched in this very spot, alert to the comings and goings of the castle. At his back was the encompassing wall of the City of Bone, nearly five stories high, a monolith of rock, imprisonment and safe-haven.

His mind gave an inward sigh as his skinny knees began to ache. More than thirty yards ahead of him, a secured wagon rumbled over the road, making its way downward into the dock below the castle. He saw hapless faces, small and dark, pressed against the bars of the windows: urchins, some with talent, others without, all scraped off the streets to serve the unforgiving Royals. His heart didn't skip a beat at the thought of what awaited them, knowing full well he had little more advantage than them. He now—the mighty Detective of the Royal Almens—was little more than a slave himself.

He rubbed his knee. *I'm not old enough to ache.* Yet he did. The memory of himself as an urchin—kneeling in silence, hour after hour, inside the castle, either holding a goblet of wine or a candlestick during another one of their pompous and overbearing ceremonies—swelled the anger within him. The fate of those children would be no worse or no less, but he no longer cared. Without him realizing it, every ounce of compassion had been almost entirely driven from him by none other than Lord Almen, complimented by his Lorda.

A pair of rats crept over his toes where he hunched inside a nook within the city's giant wall. Each sniffed the cuff on his pants. *Looking for a crumb, are we?* Melegal's steely gaze scanned the backside of the castle's reinforcements, noting three heavily armed sentries with halberds dragging in the urchins while another half dozen stood watching from a stone balcony, wearing steel helmets and clutching small crossbows to their chests. All eyes were on the wagon when he made his move.

Jab. Jab.

Two dead rats were skewered on the end of his razor thin dagger's blade. A thin smile formed on his tight lips as he slipped up into a standing position along the way. *I still got it.* Indeed he did. There was little room for error working for Lord Almen, and his training—something forced upon himself, by himself—came from fear and necessity. He studied the two rodents for a moment before flicking them away. *The Rat.* His deceased mentor McKnight had called him that, many times. The image of McKnight's face was permanently etched in his mind when he drove his double hilted dagger in one side and out the other. He had figured life would get much easier in Bone for him after that, but it had only become more complicated. Vastly so.

He stood in the solitude of the drizzling rain, careful to look away from the castle lantern's glow, pondering his demanding charges. Lord Almen wanted results every week when it came to tracking down the Slergs and any others that crossed his path. Every week, death and torture had been led by Melegal's hand. He'd never had much taste for blood, considering it nothing more than leaky filth that would stain your garments. Now, drawing it had become routine and numbing. *Results. Results. Results!* Lord Almen demanded them, and the tall powerful man would have them. Not in all of his life had Melegal been intimidated by another man, but Lord Almen had managed to shake his core.

As the wagon disappeared beneath the castle, another one emerged, driven by a slouched over silhouette of a single man, drawn by a single work horse, filled with barrels, crates, sacks and other misshapen things. No sentries escorted them out. *Same time every week.* Melegal craned his neck. He could hear the murmured greetings of the sentries on the upper balconies changing shift with their fellow guardsmen. This was what he had been waiting for. *Tonight's the night.* He tucked his dagger away as he pulled his cloak tighter around him and slipped along the shadows of the wall.

The wagon, unlike many this time of night, did not have the glow of a lantern on its backside. The sound of the hard wheels rolling and the drizzling rain comforted Melegal on his trek through the darkness. The driver led the wagon another fifty yards past the lower wall courtyard and into a wide alley that ran between the walls of Castle Almen and Castle Kling.

The area between the two was vast, large enough for three wagons, but not heavily guarded. It was unlikely that any rogue or rebel would attempt to traverse into the private outer corridors of the castles. Many heads had been spiked, and many necks had been stretched for even the mildest of trespasses. And the last city-wide rebellion had resulted in live bodies being catapulted, on fire, over the walls. Melegal was still a boy when he witnessed that. He remembered it being one of those rare moments when he and his fellow urchins were laughing. The lashings were worth it for some sick reason that day.

His fingertips were tingling. He watched and waited for his chance to dart from the wall and into the alley. If the Kling or Almen sentries saw him, crossbow bolts would pin him like a cushion. As his keen eyes scanned the ledges of the upper balconies, his keen ears listened for any artillery sounds. The wagon was rolling deeper into the alley, loud and lonely in the night. Usually a head or two would peek out from above. Melegal waited as the wagon disappeared from his sight. *Move.*

His black shadow dashed over the cobblestones, through the moonlight and into the alley. He waited for his heart to stop pounding in his ears and then moved on. It was another fifty yards to the end of the alley, where the wagon had stopped. Before Melegal caught up, it had lurched forward again. From the darkness he watched as the sentries, one from the Klings and another from the Almens, exchanged words before returning to their posts. The lanterns on the guard shacks and on the main street offered ample light to the corridor. No chance he'd slip by unnoticed there. He had to move quicker. He focused as he crept to the end of the alley and peered around the corner.

Look up. Look up. Look up.

His mind illuminated, and his hair tingled. He slipped behind the Kling guard shack stationed on the corner of the castle wall and rounded to the other side. The sentry was staring straight into the sky as he spun around slowly on his heels. *Perfect.* The wagon with its cargo was heading into the bowels of the upper city districts, passing underneath the colorful district banners that sagged down towards the ground. It wasn't the only traffic, either. The roads, though not as busy as daytime, still thrived with workers and commerce. Melegal walked backward into the road looking upward, and it wasn't long before he, the sentries and small passing groups of people were doing the same. *Fools and followers.*

"Heh-heh …" he said, rubbing his cap, before turning back after the wagon.

Block after block, turn after turn, he kept his eyes glued on the wagon. A full hour must have passed before it stopped. Something was moving. Melegal crouched along the wall. *Yes. Finally. Tonight is the night.* The silhouette of a robed man emerged from under a heavy canvas. The person rolled off the back and fell onto the street as the wagon rolled forward. *Hah.* Melegal smiled as the figure rose to its feet with a groan and rambled forward. He followed, closing in on the lumbering figure block after block, turn after turn. The smell of fish oil wafted into his nostrils, the sounds of wheezing filled his ears, and vengeance filled his heart as his hand clutched around the hilt of his dagger. The feverish eyes of Sefron the cleric peered back over his hunched shoulder from time to time, but Melegal kept himself concealed in the shadows. *Where are you going, Fatty? I've got a surprise for you.*

The man he hated, Sefron, was little more than twenty steps away, and the urge to slip his dagger into his neck consumed him. He had more disdain for Sefron than he had for McKnight and Lord Almen put together. He respected them as much as he hated them. The creepy cleric, filled with sickness, driven by defiling, had nothing redeemable to offer anyone as far as he was concerned. Lord Almen felt otherwise, but Melegal was determined to prove him wrong.

Don't lose him. Focus.

Another hour of cat and mouse was played in the drizzling rain until Sefron cast one final glance over his sagging shoulders and ducked into another alley. Four seconds hadn't passed when Melegal crept around the corner and found himself staring down a long and empty corridor filled with an overwhelming smell of excrement and fish oil. *He has to be here.* He pushed his cloak up to his nose and followed the alley to a dead end. No doors, no ladders, no windows and no Sefron. The cleric had disappeared … again.

"*Sunuvabish*," he exclaimed under his breath.

An eerie voice from behind him replied, "No, son of a whore is more like it."

Melegal ducked and rolled as a long blade ripped through his cloak.

3

S NOW AND ICE.

"Rah-OOOR!"

A wooden club slammed into the ground where Fogle Boon's mirage had stood. The image shimmered and faded as an ogre, covered in furs, with hairy white arms and an unforgettably ugly face, grunted in alarm. It raised its club high once again before bringing it down in the same spot, sending shards of ice along the icy path. Fogle Boon's teeth were chattering as he fought to form the words of power for his spell. *Blasted cold! Where is Mood?*

The ogre — a full eight feet of bulging brawn and belly — snorted the air. Its yellow eyes widened on a head as big as a barrel of ale, which turned his direction. Fogle Boon felt so cold on the inside, and now his veins turned to ice as the ogre stormed his way, heavy steps thundering into the ground.

Fogle fanned his frozen fingers outward as he shouted, "KRYZAK-SHO!"

The power warmed inside him. Four radiant darts of energy slammed into the ogre's chest, drawing a howl of agony. *Not good.* The angry ogre was still coming. His spell had misfired. A single syllable from his chattering teeth had slipped, and a barrage of needles designed to enter the face and pierce the brain had simply bored into the thickset muscle and bone of the massive humanoid. The effect would do little more than leave a scar on the monster's smelly hide, but Fogle didn't have time to worry about that now. *DUCK!*

The ogre swung over his head as Fogle rolled through the snow, fumbling inside the pockets of his robes. He grabbed a small rod of steel and thrust it before him, catching the next blow that glanced off a field of energy of bluish hue. Fogle's fragile arms shook under the force, loosening his numb fingers along the rod. *Focus, mage! FOCUS!*

He clutched the rod in two shaking hands now as the ogre pounded away. His body shook to the core. It gave him some idea of what actual fighters went through. He had previously only heard them discuss melee. The spell within the rod only had so much it could take. The transparent field of magic was chipping and cracking like the shell of an egg. He caught his first close-up view of the ogre as it snarled in his face. His razor sharp mind noted the large canine-like teeth, jutting chin and protruding brow. Its expression was evil, cruel and without compassion. The smell of salt and manure didn't mix well with the pure cold air he was growing accustomed to. The smell was pungent and unrelenting, and his eyes watered. The humanoid continued to pound away, not a mindless beast, but a cunning creature that was going punish him before it ripped him apart and ate him. Fogle screamed.

"MOOD!"

His shield was fading, the fragments falling and dissipating in the air like blue crystals. There was nothing he could do at this point to save himself except cry out for help. His arms began to sag because his joints ached. *I don't want to be an adventurer anymore!* He wanted to say it, but he didn't have the wind to say something that long.

"Mood!" he managed, as the next blow punched him deeper into the snow, wracking every joint in his bony body.

Futility. Fatality. He was going to die. Any second now, the next blow was bound to smash through and crush his skull. It made him more mad than fearful. A stupid beast was about to crush his brilliant mind. Even worse, he would die a virgin. He seethed.

"MOOD!"

It was too late. He never thought about his own family until this very moment, and all of those years of studying, ignoring the social pleasantries of his kind. The fun oh-so-many had and bragged about, he'd passed on for knowledge and power. And all for what? To be squashed like a bug without his own seed ever sown or spilled.

"MOOD!" *BONE!*

The ogre raised up its stubbed club one last time as the last shards of magic faded away from Fogle's shield. The ogre showed a growing leer of triumph. Anger and shame swelled inside Fogle, raced from his mind and into his booted leg. *If I can't procreate – this mindless bastard shall not either!* He launched the heel of his boot into the beast's harry crotch, drawing a howl of alarm. Fogle fell back in the snow, exhausted, laughing and muttering.

"No celebrating with your ugly counterpart tonight!"

The ogre snarled with rage as it raised its club once more. Fogle's eyes widened as the club reached its zenith and began its downward arc. *Well, if you can crack my skull you can crack anything.*

Slice! Somewhere a hand axe began to sing.

Howling, the ogre reeled backward.

Slice! Slice! Slice!

A streak of blood splattered across Fogle's face and robes. He noted the warm syrupy feeling and the smell of boar's blood. He'd seen Mood gut one back in Dwarven Hole. There was a sickening sound, like an axe chopping into a rotting log, as he managed to force himself up on his elbows.

There was Mood, standing over the dead ogre, ripping his axes from its skull. The Blood Ranger was coated in dark blood, unlike that of his hair and beard. He was big and grizzly, his emerald eyes blazing like fire underneath his bushy brows. His head shifted left and right above his thick shoulders, wild and frightening. Fogle still wasn't used to it, the Blood Ranger's odd way. But, the King of the Dwarves was the only friend he had. Fogle let out a trembling sigh, and his warm breath fogged, reminding him of how cold he was.

"Yer going ta need a bath, Ogre Bait," Mood said, slinging the blood from his blades into the snow.

He managed to sit all the way up, happy that his cold arse was still a part of his living body, and to say, "Me? Look at you, Ogre Slat."

Mood glanced over his shoulder, checked the blood on his clothes and laughed. The dwarf was coated in blood from head to toe. "Hah!" The husky dwarf walked over and pulled him up off the ground like a child. "Never seen that before."

"What? Ogres? That's the seventh one we've fought since we've—"

"Tenth!"

Fogle gave a quick nod of his head. "I see, so the tenth since we've been wandering these mountains. What are you talking about? 'Never seen that before'?"

"Never seen no wizard kick an ogre in the family jewels before!"

"Is that so?" he replied, rubbing his hands feverishly together. *I hate this cold.*

"Aye," Mood replied, "saved your life, it did. I's coming over ta bank, too late, certain ye was gone."

"Where were you anyway?"

"Killing ogres, Wizard. I thought you could handle them by now."

"I thought I had back-up!"

"Ye did, er ye'd be dead," Mood stated. "Ho! Ho!"

Fogle's teeth were chattering again.

"What are you so ho-ho about?"

Mood lit up a cigar and said, "Ye did good. Saved yerself. Fought till the end. Venir'd a liked to have seen that. I like it. Glad you still be."

The ancient Blood Ranger's words warmed him, leaving him with a sense of pride, unlike his old kind, but the new kind, something good. He reached out his two quivering fingers.

Mood smiled and said, "A smoke, eh? … Well, ye've earned one this day."

"How about a fire, too?"

The fire was warm, but Fogle was still cold and miserable as his victory, albeit a small one, did little to warm his spirits. Now here he was, traversing icy mountains filled with avalanches and monsters, all to help find a man that he hardly knew. Mood had led him on ice cold feet in and out of crevasses, caves and over the tops of mountains for weeks on end. Every step was just as treacherous as the last, and if Mood saved him once on this trek, he'd saved him over a dozen times.

He shivered as he rubbed his hands over the fire and said, "Mood, tell me more about your dwarven women."

Mood's bushy red brow perched in the firelight as he asked, "Whatcha want to know?"

He didn't want to ask any questions at all. He had always assumed he knew everything he needed to know, but when it came to women, the subject was as foreign to him as the Nameless Mountains.

He pulled a thick woolen hood over his head and blew out a long puff of white breath.

"I was just reflecting on the colorful stories that Mikkel and Billip shared. I was wondering if what I heard was true, or if it was more of the same ole' orc's slat men like to tout."

"Hmmm …," Mood tugged at his beard, "I see. Yer sounding more like an adventurer now. Ho! Ho! That's grand. Almost dyin' gets many men thinking about women, children and such."

Fogle glowered at the Blood Ranger. *Answer my question.*

After a long moment Mood sat up saying, "Oh. Ah, well, dwarven women are frisky sorts, so I'd say what ye heard was true. But, don't be disrespectful of them. They'll get you back. Kin of mine once woke up hanging naked by his beard over top a pile of hot coals."

Fogle cringed as the image formed in his mind.

"And another kin with his—"

"That's enough. I get the picture. Be nice and courteous. I got it. Ah … Just forget it."

Fogle stood back up and headed for his tent.

"Don't worry, Wizard. I'll have my wives take care of your needs when we get back," Mood rumbled.

The offer, as generous as it sounded, didn't seem quite right. Fogle turned and said, "Would there be any unmarried ones available instead?"

Mood slapped his knee and said, "Ho! Yer a funny one. An unmarried dwarf! That's silly."

Fogle pulled the flap of his tent open.

"See ya in the mornin'."

He entered, sat inside the darkness and muttered a spell. The canvas of the small tent began to warm and glimmer. *Ah, that's better.* It was a small cantrip, not powerful but effective. He'd been using it on and off, trying to get used to the cold, but the icy air was barely tolerable. *Inhospitable!* Mood told him he'd need to toughen up, but he wasn't Mood. He was a scrawny man with frozen toes. He sneezed, pulled out a cloth handkerchief and blew his nose, remembering something he needed to ask Mood. Reluctantly, he peeked his head outside in the cold saying, "Mood, do you really still think we'll find a druid up here? I've almost lost track of the weeks."

Mood was gone, the fire was out and only the petite figure of an alabaster woman clothed in a snow white fur toga remained. Behind her was a pack of large wolves, shoulder height, with saliva dripping from growling teeth. *Not possible!* Fogle rubbed his eyes as she turned to face him. Two pink eyes, buckled in anger, ran over Fogle as a sudden chill raced through his spine. She was the most beautiful thing he'd ever seen, and she scared him.

Her voice was haunting and powerful as she spoke:

"You killed my ogres … now you will die."

4

TWO BABIES COOED IN THE nooks of the underling Lord Verbard's arms: one with emerald green eyes like his mother, the other with golden eyes like his uncle. Verbard snorted lightly through his nose, and the two underling babes clutched at his chin with their sharp little fingernails and sneered.

A seductive voice from behind him breathed in his ear.

"Glad to be back among your family, I see. Aren't your babies so adorable, Verbard? Were they not worth the all the suffering I put you through?"

The green-eyed one was tugging at his finger when he cleared his throat and said, "Dearest, I'd rather walk barefoot on the sun-scorched land above for another year than spend another single moment with your over-pregnated hide."

Her fingernails tugged into his shoulders as she squeezed them and replied, "That's my Lord. A heart like a rock and a tongue like a forge. Oh … how I missed it." She snickered as she came around him and scooped up the babies, draped in midnight-colored cloth. "Now, now, little ones, we can't have you getting too attached to your father. That would make you soft and weak, like humans."

Verbard's silver eyes glimmered under his mate's playful and penetrating smile. Her rose colored eyes, long silky white and black hair and gossamer slip stirred the blood within him. Her figure weeks earlier was a monstrous thing unworthy of an ogre. *Ghastly.* He shuddered at the thought, for he'd never be able to shed the horrific image from his mind. His passion didn't come as easily as before, but in a few decades he was certain he would overcome that. His mate, now back in her prime, was hungry and lonely, but his new duties from Master Sinway kept him on the move, much to his relief.

Two underling women entered his den and took the children away. *Not what I had in mind.* His mate wrapped her arms around his neck as she slid her lithe frame onto his lap. *Not again.*

"Lord Verbard, there is one way to escape me: you only need to impregnate me."

He groaned and hissed under his breath.

"Your urgings are getting thin. Perhaps it is not me you long for, perhaps it is my brother that you miss."

He studied her eyes, hypnotic and unmoving, capable of hiding the darkest secrets about any mental inquisition. No, she would never reveal what he suspected, not that he cared, but somewhere within he did. He shoved her from his lap and floated away, robes dragging across the black marble floor.

"I've responsibility."

Her hiss was cut off as he flicked his palm, slamming the doors shut behind him.

Things had changed for Verbard in the Underland. His kin — brothers and sisters one and all — treated him differently than before. He and his brother Catten were of the highest order, well regarded and feared, but it had been his brother, the more astute politician, that garnered the majority of their admiration. Now that had changed. Verbard was not only feared, but now admired as well. He liked it and all of the additional pleasantries that came with it. After all, it was he who had rid his people of the pesky but formidable menace, The Darkslayer.

Everyone bowed or nodded as he passed them on the streets of the city. The underlings traveled on foot, along narrow black roads that led up and down the caves and around the spires in the bowels of Bish that hung up and pointed down in cones. Commerce: fruit, meat, some cooked and some raw, were skewered on sticks. The smell would rot an urchin's nose, but to the underling pallet it was quite salivating.

Verbard paid his greeters little mind as he made his way to Master Sinway's Castle, which overlooked the Underland City. There was no need for a road to get there, but there was one. A crossing of sorts. It turned around the hard rock like a coiling snake, defying the odds of engineering, instead consisting of magic entwined with minerals and glowing with the bluish hue of the underlight. Verbard had no need for roads, unlike most underlings, as he sailed upward to the mouth of the cave castle entrance and proceeded through a portal over thirty feet in height.

There were guards, at least a hundred, if not a thousand, how many he did not know, but he often wondered. No challenges came — though his heart did beat a little faster — as only a fool would challenge the Master inside his own castle. He knew where to go. *Through the iron doors to the iron throne.* He hated iron. It was such an ugly color and a tasteless metal. The rat-like fur on his arms began to rise as he proceeded, remembering that last time Master Sinway's iron-irises almost bore out his mind. He saw no need to challenge Sinway any more, not without Catten. Besides, he had done it more to piss off his brother then to challenge the master. *Ah Catten, tis not the same without you.*

He floated by the humongous iron doors, landed at the empty throne and kneeled. He hated this part most of all: being there at the appointed time and waiting. He was careful to shield his resentful thoughts. He thought of death instead, death of mankind above. His body began to relax.

Little more than an hour had passed when the air began to shimmer around him. Verbard opened his eyes and fixed them on the floor at the sound of cave dog nails clicking over to the sides of the throne. The cave dogs weren't alone; another strong presence was there. *The Vicious?* He had not seen one in months, but he did care. The mystic bodyguards of Master Sinway were not something he was comfortable around. It wasn't a fear of them, but rather his lack of command over their power.

"Rise, Verbard," a voice as ancient as the ore of Bish spoke.

He rose to his feet and found himself face to face with a Vicious: smooth black skin wrapped over a body of corded muscle, sharp teeth bared in a grin over crossed arms. *What is this?* His underling heart, as black and fearless as it might be, began to pump quicker in his chest. Its black eyes with white pupils met his, boring into him as if he were some kind of meal. It leaned a little closer, almost touching his chin. Verbard didn't like it, but as he brought up the energy to defend himself against it, it backed away, stepping alongside the arm of the throne.

Sinway looked to be smiling within his deep black robes, iron colored eyes gleaming in the dark, fingers needling his chin. The cave dogs, four in all, grey with matted hair, sat four feet high, to the tops of their heads. The fearsome beasts looked ready to tear him apart at a single command. His heart pumped faster still. *Let them try and eat me. They'll be worm food in an instant.*

Master Sinway's voice echoed softly as he spoke.

"I know it isn't customary of me, Verbard, but relax. I didn't bring you here for slaughter, instead for celebration," he said, snapping his fingers.

Verbard's heart flinched as his ears popped. A fine table of hardened wood appeared, encircled by chairs wrought in gold and silver. A vat of wine and pewter goblets were the centerpiece. His silver eyes flitted between the display and his master. *What is he up to?* He stepped back, bowing, as Master Sinway eased his way over to the table and sat.

"Underling Port, isn't it?"

"Yes, Master Sinway."

Suddenly, Verbard felt like a boy, helpless before his father, or grandfather, both of which had creative ways of initiating punishment. He swallowed hard and hoped his robes hid it.

"Sit and drink with me," Sinway said. "We've much to talk about."

He moved to the table, sat and picked the goblet up in his hand. He could smell the port, full and rich, salivating to say the least, and if he ever needed a drink to ease his tensions it was now. He was in uncharted waters with the most powerful underling of all.

Sinway cracked a smile as he hoisted his glass and said, "Drink Verbard, vanquisher of The Darkslayer. Drink and be fulfilled."

The Vicious, lone and dominating, had slipped behind his chair as the cave dogs surrounded the table.

You first, he wanted to say as he brought the cold rim of the metal goblet to his black lips. *Poison is such a cowardly way to kill me. He could at least tell me what I fouled up this time. Bottoms up, then.* He drank. Sinway let out an unsettling chuckle as his world was turned inside out.

5

C LONK!
White spots burst into his eyes, and pain lanced back into his brain. Georgio's legs wobbled as he fell hard onto his butt. He clutched his stomach and head, fighting the urge to retch, fuming at the giggling sounds of halflings followed by Mikkel roaring in his ear.

"BOY! If you don't cut that out, I'm gonna skin you!" the large black man said, jerking him back to his feet. "That's not what I meant by using your head, Stupid!"

The little giggles ensued.

Georgio tried to shove Mikkel away, saying, "Get off me." He turned and faced off with his opponent, a mintaur, ram-faced and horned, and a full five feet of fight. He stood taller than the hooved creature and sneered down at him.

"Get him, Georgio," Lefty cried, sitting on top of a wall nearby, eating an orange pear.

The halfling wasn't alone. A small brood of halfling children, all barely two-feet tall, were scrambling around with sticks, attacking one another in joy, screaming aloud and laughing. It had been like this all day, hot and annoying.

"Wrestle, Boy!" Mikkel said, shoving him forward.

The mintaur charged, rounded horns catching him under his chin and driving him onto his back. He wrapped his arms around the mintaur's waist and fought to regain his feet.

Mikkel huffed in his ear.

"No! No! No! That's not what I taught you. Get up! Escape!"

He grunted, twisted and forced himself upright only to be slammed into the dusty ground again.

"Oooooh!" the audience exclaimed.

Georgio fought to suck the air in through his teeth. His lungs were thinning, and his own sweat was stinging his eyes.

"COME ON! GET UP!"

He clawed at the dirt and screamed in frustration. The mintaur was tying his legs in a knot, and the pressure was beginning to hurt.

"Are you just going to sit there and let him break your legs? Huh? Do something or die, Georgio!"

It wasn't fair. He was a boy, or a teenager, but the mintaur was a man, older, smarter and more experienced. He wasn't ready to fight. He'd been training all morning, and he didn't want to any more.

"Come on, Georgio," Lefty cried again, "you can do it!"

"Aye, Boy, ye' can do it."

Gillem!

Ever since the older halfling had arrived, Lefty had never been the same. Georgio hated Gillem. Something inside him began to boil over, and his ears began to steam. He cast an angry glance at the little cheerful pie-faced man, sat up and began wailing on the surprised mintaur's face.

"Stop it, Georgio! You'll break your hands!" Mikkel warned.

They didn't break. They hurt, but he didn't care.

Whap! Whap! Whap! Twist!

As the creature loosened its grip, Georgio seized it by the horns and twisted. The mintaur's neck was like iron, not meant to be broken, but it happened. The creature cried out like a sheep, thrashing left and right. Georgio held onto the mintaur, his stare never leaving Gillem.

"RRRRAAAAAH!!!"

He hoisted the mintaur over his head and tossed it to the ground at Gillem's leaping feet, scattering the tiny children like flies.

Georgio was heaving in the silence as all eyes, man, halfling and mintaur, looked on him as if he had gone berserk. The mintaur snorted, breaking the awkward silence, shaking its head as it regained its feet. Lefty was pale. Mikkel held his hand on his head, mouth agape, while Gillem dusted off his boots and lit his pipe with a nod. Georgio wanted to shove that pipe down the man's throat.

"Very impressive, my boy," Gillem said with elegant cheer. "Did you children see that? Georgio the strong one!"

The little halflings looked at him wide-eyed, then burst into applause and cheers.

Georgio shook as his eyes began to water. He covered his face and ran.

Mikkel slapped the mintaur on the shoulder and said, "Sorry about that."

The ram-faced man patted the big man on the back, nodded, gathered his gear, and departed.

"Same time tomorrow then?" The mintaur waved.

Lefty was numb: smiling outwardly, but in turmoil inwardly. He'd never seen such fury on Georgio's face before. It was frightening to see his once cheerful friend so grim. He felt responsible. He didn't know why, but he felt responsible somehow. He looked over at Gillem, who was handing each of the children a copper talon to spend in the markets. In a moment their existence in the small proving grounds was vacant, leaving only Lefty, Gillem and Mikkel.

"Think I'm pushing him too hard?" Mikkel asked of Gillem.

"Never."

Mikkel's smile broadened.

"Maybe I'm going too easy on him."

"Seems likely," Gillem winked. "Very well then, I'll see you two later on I assume, but if you don't mind, try to stay away for a few days. Georgio loses his focus with all of you halflings running around."

"You're the boss, Master Mikkel."

Lefty was silent as Mikkel walked away. He was sad, too. He didn't see enough of Georgio as it was with all of the demands of Gillem and the guild. His own thief training was intense, even rigorous at times, but he liked it. He liked Gillem, too.

"Don't worry about yer friend, Lefty." Gillem said, stroking his long fingers across his back. "He's getting to the age of puberty. Young men start acting strange, is all."

"What's *puberty*?"

"Er ... nothing you need to worry about for another decade er so. Now follow me."

"Where are we going?" Lefty said, hopping from the wall.

"First, we have some stealing to do. Then, it's time to pay Palos his dues."

Lefty's chin dipped as Gillem passed him by.

"Georgio, slow down," Kam ordered.

The teenager stomped through the kitchen, his face turned away.

"Don't you dare walk through my tavern looking like that: a frowning, sweaty little dirtball — get back here."

He stopped with his back still towards her. Kam wasn't in the mood for another of Georgio's fits. She couldn't relate. She looked over to Joline, her confidante and full-time "boys growing up too fast" sitter. Joline's pleasant face mouthed the words, *Be nice.*

"Hungry?" She asked.

Georgio turned and gave her a sheepish look.

"Yeah."

When wasn't he hungry? Georgio was a big boy going on big man. She was taller than most women, but now Georgio's head was up past her chin, and that was big for a fourteen or fifteen year old. At least, that's how old she thought he was. Joline put a steamy bowl of soup and half a loaf of barley baked bread on the table before him.

"Thanks," he mumbled before shoving in a mouthful from the loaf.

She pulled a stool beside him, grabbed his chin and lifted his eyes to meet hers. She loved his big brown eyes and his thick mop of brown hair. He'd be a handsome man one day, any day now at the rate things were going. Some of the waitresses had already expressed keen interest in him, batting their eyelashes, brushing against him, everything but removing their amply-filled blouses before his innocent eyes. She shook her head.

"What?" he asked, frowning.

"Oh nothing. You know, I'm starting to miss those chubby cheeks of yours. Are you sure you're getting enough to eat? Joline, bring him some more food: cheese and milk, lots of it."

"Huh?" both boy and woman replied.

"Eat, it's good to have a belly full for your nap."

Georgio gave her a funny look and said, "Are you right in the head, Kam? You're acting strange."

It was a fair question. For the most part she was feeling as good as ever, strong and fearless, but busy. Deep down she had come to accept that Venir was gone. He was hard to forget, but without Georgio and Lefty around so much, it was getting a little easier. She wiped his mouth off with her apron.

A waitress came inside the kitchen: a few years older than Georgio, long legged and pretty, her bright eyes attaching themselves to him.

"Pardon me," she said, smiling. "Need some frupp steaks, onion skins and deer broth, Joline. Hi Georgio."

Georgio stopped chewing, grinning from ear to ear. "Uh … hello …"

"Get your arse out there and wait tables!" Kam blustered.

The girl's face turned ashen as she said, "Sorry Kam," and scurried out the door.

Kam squeezed his face in her hands and said, "Don't be anywhere alone ever with my girls. Do you understand me? Not ever!"

"Sure, Kam. But what's the harm in it and all?"

She summoned up her energy; the rims of her green eyes began to glow.

"Never."

Georgio had a bewildered look as he shook his head.

"I … Said … Never!"

He nodded over and over.

"Good. Now, tell me what is wrong, and don't lie. Be honest; I need to know. Is Mikkel being too hard on you?"

"No."

"Are you still mad at Lefty?"

"No."

His eyes flitted, though. Even she had a hard time with Lefty. Her sickness, so sudden and strange, by all account might have killed her. Little Lefty, for some reason, seemed to know more than he let on. Call it women's intuition, but something was no longer right. Not after that encounter with Palos, the prince of thieves. She was certain that their encounter was far from over, but what that had to do with Lefty, she didn't know. She kept her eyes open. Billip and Mikkel were very helpful look-outs.

"Is it one of my waitresses? Do you … uh … have feelings for one of them in particular?"

"No Kam! Can I just eat and go? I mean, thanks and all, but I'm not hungry any more. Can I please go? I've got chores to do."

"Just tell me what's bothering you. Don't be hard headed. I don't want you stomping around here anymore, so let's fix this and be done with it. Tell me, Georgio!"

"NO!" he yelled, jumping out of his stool.

As Kam drew her hand back, Joline wrapped her arms around her with a hug and said, "Georgio, go and do what you have to do, but don't you ever do that again."

"Pah!" he said, storming away.

Kam was shaking. "Did he just yell at me? At me? I'm gonna kill him!"

Joline squeezed her even harder. "You'll do no such thing, Kam. The boy's growing up and missing his friends something terrible. You don't see it so much as I do, being so busy with little Erin and all. Now take a deep breath."

She inhaled and exhaled deeply.

"Oh my," Joline said.

"What?"

"Looks like you've got a hungry baby to feed," Joline said, glancing down at her chest.

Kam's breasts were soaking through her blouse.

"Aw, I hope Georgio didn't see that."

"I'm thinking he did," Joline giggled. "No hiding those things. Now get up there and feed that baby."

Kam muttered a spell—concealing her clothes—before she cut through the tavern and made it up the stairs. Her chest was aching. *Someone's awfully hungry.* As soon as she opened the door there was the awfullest scream. *Oh my!*

6

(The Past: 5 years earlier, after Venir escapes the Brigand Queen)

THE COLORFUL BANNERS OF THE Royal houses of Bish flapped above the massive wooden walls of an ancient fort. Outpost Thirty-One was one of a kind, the only structure in Bish built from the massive trees of the Great Forest. Yet these trees had not been cut down. Their hard dark woods were rare, fallen specimens, carried by giants long ago. They had been gifts to the good men of that time.

Such was the story passed down over the centuries. None knew if it was true, but none cared, for such was the way of most men: self-centered, cold, and focused only on the present. The fort complex sat high on a forested hilltop in the southern lands of Bish. It was a perfect square, with outer walls twenty feet high. The gates in the opposite corners of each wall faced north, south, east, and west, from which straight, gravel-filled roads ran. They were busy roads, which made Outpost Thirty-One a strategic foothold that maintained order and protected key commercial trade routes in this region. All of the subordinate forts scattered throughout the south were commanded from here.

In the burning midday haze the fort appeared like a majestic castle, blending in with its surroundings among the distant hilltops that gazed upon it. Many unwanted eyes now stared at Outpost Thirty-One, for the outpost was the subject of their siege. The underlings and the brigand army had cut off all the roads and laid waste for miles around. All human communication throughout the southern lands of Bish was halted. Many would have agreed that the Royals had it coming, but when it came to defending against an underling assault on the upper world, the proclaimed Royal superiors of the selfish human race were Bish's one and only hope.

Jarla's brigand army was busy taunting the confined Royal soldiers, sending kobolds close to the southern gate to deposit the mutilated torsos, heads, arms and legs of the fallen. The tiny horned humanoids cowered behind small wooden shields, but occasionally an arrow from a vengeful archer would pierce their small bodies, adding to the stinking heap of flesh and flies that lay baking in the suns.

Deeper south in the forest was the large beige tent that quartered Jarla, the Brigand Queen. Alone inside, she was studying maps and battlefield notes. Her beautiful face—now scarred and twisted from a fate she'd been unprepared for—was drawn in a tight frown. Unlike most women on Bish, she was a born warrior. She stood taller than most men, with strong shoulders and arms that were sinewy from years of battle. Her jet black hair was tied back, revealing deep blue eyes over her tanned face and scarred cheekbones. She took a deep breath and exhaled, bit her thin red lips, and flung the table over. Everything she had planned for years was about to unfold, yet everything was wrong. She cursed, spat, and drained a glass of wine. *Venir!*

Not only had he stolen her magic armament, but he had also embarrassed her by escaping her camp, slaughtering her commanders, and evading the underlings' bounty on him. Her alliance with the underlings had never been on solid ground; now it was falling apart. She wanted to break the alliance and disappear. She had even felt her grip on her army loosening not long after the young warrior slipped from her side. She spat at the thought of his cocky grin. But, the worst was he had taken her precious, powerful weapons, or they had taken him? For the first time in years she felt vulnerable, rather than invincible.

Nevertheless, she was not ready to abandon her loyal brigand army, who had taken her in when others would not. As for the underlings, they were her best vehicle to take revenge on the Royals who had ripped her life asunder.

She had once been one of them, a Royal household member and a rare soldier, rising to become a trusted leader. She clenched her teeth; how naïve she had been not to see it coming. Men were men, after all, and Royal men were the worst. They took what they wanted, willing or not, and made it their own. She, too had been taken, against her will, and she had never been the same. She wiped her dry eyes and sneered. Her hatred burned like a hot iron. It would have to do.

She was on the cusp of extracting her revenge. Outpost Thirty-One would fall. But then what? She sensed in her gut that Venir would come for her. With the mystic arsenal in his grip there wasn't much she could do to stop him. She only hoped she would live long enough to see the outpost destroyed. She was almost certain the underlings would ensure that.

Stepping outside into the light of the two burning suns, she walked up a rocky hill and grabbed a spy glass from a kneeling orcen sentry. She peered at the great outpost, taking mental note of the defense arrangements underway. The outpost should have been taken by now. She knew Venir was in there, and it left her uneasy. They had tried to catch the man, but could not. He and his comrades were far fleeter than her cumbersome army.

She slung the spyglass at the orc, returned inside her tent and called for her commanders. They discussed how the siege might take weeks or months now, thanks to Venir's warning. She had to remind them that she had people on the inside of the outpost as well. They snickered. The day of her reckoning had come.

A small group of scouts were still outside the walls of Outpost Thirty-One. The three men were outlanders of repute, even among the Royal soldiers that had dealt with them over the years. It was no coincidence that they had been the ones who had given the troublesome news of the underling invasion.

Dusk had settled over the thick green forest that surrounded the outpost. All around the fort were steep ravines that served to drain the heavy rains. They also created vulnerable points where foes could creep undetected right up to the complex. Deep within a ravine, the three men crouched with eyes and ears intent on finding any comers. Skirmishes had been breaking out day and night. Shouts of pain and terror, blended with the sound of battle, came and went as the thick foliage muffled the noise. It was difficult to tell who was winning, but the trio sensed that it was only a matter of time before the fort was stormed.

They had already encountered three underlings earlier and five the night before, but the foul creatures had been no match for Billip's deadly arrows. He possessed a special short bow and arrows that were a gift from an old Royal soldier in the fort. The man's son, who was to inherit them, perished at the hands of the brigand army. It was clear to Venir that Billip relished the rare quality of this bow. The archer made good use of the power and accuracy, grinning each time he dropped an underling with an arrow straight between the eyes or clean through the heart. His comments to the archer irked Mikkel, who cared little for his friend's success. The big man wanted the first crack at the underlings himself.

"Come on, Vee," urged Mikkel in his deep voice, loading his heavy crossbow. "Let me take the first shot. He can't shoot better than me and Bolt Thrower."

Venir had witnessed Mikkel's long bolts impaling two underlings at a time. The problem was that once they were fired, there was no time to reload. Mikkel would charge like a bull into the fray with the massive studded club he called Skull Basher. Mikkel was the only man with less patience than him when it came to fighting.

The archer cracked his knuckles and chuckled, always calm amid chaos. Indeed, the only one cooler was Melegal, but the thief cared little for venturing in the Outlands too long. That man was more disposed to the comforts of the city.

Smaller than his comrades, but hardy and weathered, Billip twisted his goatee with calloused fingers.

"You can't hit one to my five, Mikkel—you know that." "I don't need to!" the man jumped in his face, club high. "I fight like a man. Skull Basher will take ten to your five any day—you know it!"

"Yer an idiot," Billip retorted.

Venir stepped between them.

"Do we have to do this every time?"

"Yes!" they both insisted.

Venir shook his head.

"Mikkel, you know the drill. Billip sets them up, we flank them."

"And if he misses? I get hit with one of his arrows!"

"That's never happened," Billip replied in irritation.

"It almost did."

Billip jumped in his face.

"It almost didn't! It wasn't my arrow, and you didn't get hit! That was three years ago! Let it go!"

Mikkel kissed his club and pointed his sausage-sized finger at the much smaller man. "It better not happen. If it does, you better hope it kills us … or Skull Basher and me are gonna smash you."

Billip rolled his eyes and walked away.

Their bickering was part of the preparation for combat. The competition between them kept them focused. It was what Venir wanted. The two racked up body counts faster as a team than alone, though neither would ever admit it. He loved their spirit and looked to them as older brothers, but they were comfortable with his lead because he had instincts they lacked. The fearsome threesome had become a force to reckon with over the years, but their notoriety was not always well received. They were sometimes considered common bandits as each had his own needs to satisfy.

The men had exited the storm drain, and were once again headed down into the plunging gulch. They navigated the rugged terrain like mountain cats. No leaf rustled in the inert heat. Sweat stinging their eyes, they tried to suppress the sound of their own breathing. Even the panting of Venir's little dog Chongo was undetectable.

Venir watched Billip and Chongo break off toward the far side of the ravine, communicating with hand signals and soft tapping on leather chest plates. The dog's ears perked up at the sound of those signals, and he responded in accord. They took their positions, waiting minute after minute in the thickets. Venir would glance back from time to time, only to see heavy sweat dripping from Mikkel's silent face. He contacted Billip.

Nothing, the archer's white hands signaled back.

Venir's gut told him they needed another accurate volley tonight. Things were just too quiet this time out. His mind began to wander as he wiped the sweat from his brow.

He felt an urgent tap on his shoulder. He looked forward. In the dimness he almost didn't notice the bowman's urgent signaling. Underlings were coming. Billip was trying to make out how many.

"What's up, Vee?" a deep voice asked behind his ear.

"We have company."

A white grin flashed in the darkness.

"How many?"

Venir shrugged his heavy shoulders. The blood of battle began to pump through his veins. His stomach started to knot, and his mouth became dry. He clutched Brool, his war axe, and waited.

Five, was signaled.

He acknowledged and readied himself. Mikkel leaned his club against a tree, taking up position with his heavy crossbow. Venir checked the buckles on his chainmail shirt and lifted his newly acquired shield. He was amazed at its lightness, despite the heavy metal banding and engraving. He studied his great axe and smiled. Its oak shaft was warm in his hand, almost living.

Only a few days ago he had wrangled the magic weapon. He had given little thought to how it now came to be in his hands. The large leather sack it came in was a mystery. When Jarla reached into the sack it contained two smaller axes, a lighter helmet, and metal arm bracers. Yet, for him it had yielded the large helm, shield, and a war axe unlike anything he ever imagined. He remembered the moment she was about to kill him. He smiled a tad. The shock and fury he saw on her face when the mystic arsenal came to his aid had been glorious. Grasping the weapon and feeling the power surge through his hands almost made him laugh, it was so delightful.

Someone tapped him again, snapping him out of his thoughts. The count was now ten.

"Better put on your helmet," Mikkel said, putting on his own metal skullcap that sloped down the back of his neck.

The warriors didn't like to wear armor unless they anticipated a skirmish—or full battle, as in this case—and even then they still opted for lighter armor than most of the Royals around the fort. Venir hadn't yet bothered to extract his helm from the sack. He felt no need for it and feared it would obstruct his vision. And so far the situation hadn't been too risky.

Twenty underlings!

The archer's fingers and elbows were frantic.

Fifty paces. Moving fast. Now what?

The sudden change of circumstances demanded a decision. Venir had been setting up ambushes by letting small underling squads move between them, but this was no small group. It seemed that the underlings had become privy to their tricks and that larger numbers now made those impossible. That tactic would cut Billip off, leaving the archer overwhelmed without an escape route. Indecision began to churn in Venir's belly. He had to decide whether they should retreat while there was time. They could make time to alert the rest of the fort as well, or fight. He wanted to fight, but wisdom prevailed.

Run, Venir signaled Billip.

Hit and run? Billip returned.

When facing a larger force, scouts needing to buy time would drop the point men of the enemy's front line with bolts or arrows. This slowed the enemy and made them more cautious until they could ascertain the strength of their assailants. It also provided critical extra time for a hasty retreat. But twenty was a large group of underlings. Venir didn't want to alert them to their presence. There could be still more underlings as well.

His keen eyes detected several dark silhouettes in the distance. Billip was signaling again for a reply. The underlings were armed with small round shields and curved swords, similar to the bulkier tulwar swords of men. It was a heavier force, and judging by their additional weapons and armor, a full-scale assault was underway. The axe burned in his grasp as the underlings approached, but he made his decision and signaled back.

Run!

Venir could make out the shape of Billip and the smaller shape of Chongo creeping back up the ravine. The archer's arrow was nocked along the shaft of his new bow.

Clatch – Zoop – Thunk!

Mikkel's heavy bolt ripped through the air, clean through the neck of an underling and imbedding into the chest of another. "What are you doing?" Venir said, shoving Mikkel's crossbow down. "I said *run!*"

"Sorry, Vee. I must have missed that," Mikkel shrugged. "I thought it was *hit* and run."

Venir knew better. Mikkel wanted the first kill, and Billip was moments from releasing a few arrows as well. The pair couldn't have cared less about the risk. Their passion to kill underlings took over reason. All three were guilty of this affliction.

Billip began his own onslaught. Two more underlings found their throats punctured with feathered shafts, their warnings gurgling in dark blood. He watched as their hit proved to be a mistake. The underlings scrambled up the ravine like hungry wolves, and thick webs began to form, spreading over the trees, surrounding them from behind and cutting off their escape. In an instant they were trapped.

"Helmet on," Mikkel reminded Venir, picking up his studded club.

Venir felt foolish for a moment. The webs had grown further up the edges of the ravine, trapping the archer and his dog below. He groaned. The underlings had the jump on them.

Venir opened the leather sack and pulled out his helm. Its eyelets had an eerie glow that unsettled his stomach. How would they make it out of this jam? The odds were against them. A superior force approached, and they had nowhere to run or hide. He had a single burning thought: *kill all you can before they kill you.* Oddly, when he pulled the spiked helm over his blue eyes for the second time in days the odds of survival seemed to shift back in his favor.

As he strapped the thick leather chin strap under his grizzled jaw, he felt a heightened sense of awareness he hadn't noticed before. His mind became razor sharp, intent on the task at hand: to find and decimate the underlings. He felt he could handle the score of them alone. Excitement rushed through his body, tingling from fingertip to toenail. Better yet, his vision, far from being obstructed as he had feared, was enhanced. Not only could he see the underlings, he could feel their presence … it was awesome.

Dusk had passed, and the thick forest was almost pitch black, which made battling the creeping underling warriors more difficult. The cave-dwelling creatures could see as well at night as in daylight, an advantage shared by only a few other races. But the men on Bish had no such ability, except now for one man.

Venir's head peered around, and he could make out the details of the landscape before him. *This is good!* He noticed the warmth of the bodies of Billip and Chongo not too far in the distance, and then he saw Mikkel's worried look.

"Vee," the man whispered, "what are we gonna do now? I hate this dark. Can you see them?"

"*Yes,*" he said in an unfamiliar voice.

Mikkel fell silent for a moment.

"You better be able to see them, 'cause I'm following you."

Venir tapped his helm.

"Trust me, then. It's time to take them head on, no choice."

"Sounds good."

"Stay close, and watch out for those webs."

Quiet as shadows, the two slipped deeper into the ravine. In his hunger for battle, he moved faster than normal, and a big hand had to nudge him back. The underlings were holding their positions less than thirty paces away, but the thick vegetation kept the pair out of sight. Concealed on the ridge of the ravine, Billip waited, not moving a muscle, his bow aimed on his next approaching target, his brow and hands slick with sweat. Venir knew the archer's fire would offer them scant protection once combat began. It would have to be enough.

He motioned for Mikkel to stay put, then crept alone toward the underlings. He heard the man mumble in protest, clutching his club from behind. Like an iron panther, he crossed the forest floor. He came within ten paces of the oncoming underlings. He squatted before them like a tree trunk as they came, slow and quiet. Hadn't they seen him? His blood rushed in his ears. He could see, hear and smell every sickening aspect of them. Now they were five paces away. He didn't budge, legs tense, ready to spring. He almost gasped as the underlings passed by. They hadn't even noticed him. The underlings' colorful eyes were dim sparkles in the dark as they glanced back at him and moved on. He couldn't believe it. He couldn't resist their exposed backs, either. His hatred overcame all reason.

There was a flash and a whistle in the air as Brool ripped out the backs of two underlings in one swipe. They dropped lifeless to the ground as the third underling whirled to attack. A whizzing arrow struck the back of the underling's head, pitching it forward. He could see Mikkel's white teeth coming his way as the battler charged along his side.

"Let's do it, Vee!"

He felt the underlings swarming from all directions, chittering loudly, shields low and curved blades high. It raised his fervor more. Underlings surrounded him and Mikkel; their slashing blades were quick and deadly. He parried in broad sweeps, holding the smaller race at bay. The underling blades slashed and licked at his skin like razors.

"Hit 'em Mikk!"

"Bashing time!"

Mikkel burst into assault, his first overhead blow smashing an underling's shield and arm. As the fiend howled in pain, Skull Basher's studs caught another's nose with a sickening smack. Mikkel whirled to block the third one's slash, but too late. The underling punched a hole deep in his thigh, sending him down with a groan. The black warrior's blood flowed, but the man responded by bringing his club down hard and fast, pulverizing the underling's skull like a ceramic vase.

Venir heard his friend scream. He dodged as he jabbed his spike deep into the leg of a charging underling, ripping muscle from bone. He eyed the two other underlings that flanked him, and slammed his shield edge into one's chittering mouth, slicing through the neck of the other. Venir charged the other two hobbled underlings and hacked them down like saplings. As he turned, he saw Mikkel break the other arm of his first victim, then bust its ribcage like a crate of melons. Six underlings were dead now, but more were coming. *Let them come*, he thought.

"You all right?"

Mikkel grimaced as he tied a cloth around his bloody wound.

"Leg's bad, but I can fight fine. No running away from this."

"Stay low while I check what's coming. We need to get out of here," Venir said.

"Don't go far," the bleeding man said, but he didn't even hear it.

Billip had his hands full. Several underlings were closing in on his superior position. He pressed back into the brush. The high ground was an advantage, but the thick vegetation made it hard to track their small, dark bodies. If not for the occasional glint of their colorful eyes he would have lost them. He relied on his excellent hearing to help pinpoint their whereabouts. He fired away. Their howls of pain and anger gave him relief.

Focus. That ain't all.

His eyes strained in the darkness.

Three maybe?

He had killed one, maybe two, but more still bore down on his position. He heard a painful bellow from Mikkel, but the sounds became muted. Would he have to start swinging steel soon as well? He edged farther up the bank. Dreading the thought of melee, despair crept over him. He knew he was trapped. With nowhere to go, he dug in.

He watched the dark figures continue to press upward through the brush.

One more shot.

He had to make it count. He nocked two arrows this time and drew them back. It was a trick shot he often used to infuriate Mikkel and gamble against Melegal. He had never before considered using it in combat, but now it seemed his life might depend on it.

He took a quick breath and held it, watching two underlings, side by side, moving fast up the hill, shields raised for cover.

Bish! Too far apart!

The shot was difficult. The underlings were tacticians of terror in confined spaces, and darkness was their forte. He knew they thrived in it. Just twenty paces were left between him and his assailants. He had to fire. Sweat dripped from his nose. At least one of them had to go, so he let loose into the nearest one.

His arrows whizzed through the air. One imbedded itself in the raised wooden shield, the other streaked straight and low into the underling's exposed belly, knocking it down the hill.

Yes!

The second underling warrior was closing in fast. He nocked another arrow. The wicked face was upon him and shrieking. Billip raised his bow, blocking the underling's slashing sword, jolting his arms and driving him into the ground.

At close quarters now, the ferocious underling warrior had the advantage, and he had no means to defend himself. He tried to draw his sword as the underling lunged at him. The pommel of the underling's short sword caught him on the head, stunning him, bringing a sharp pain as blood trickled in his eyes.

The underling launched a chop at his head. He ducked just enough to avoid a split skull, but it took a slice off his right shoulder. Gasping in pain, he managed to plunge an arrow into the underling's thigh. It staggered back. Dropping its sword with a hiss, it didn't back down, but beckoned the man for closer combat. He had no desire to wrestle the creature, knowing full well it could tear him to shreds. He'd seen that happen before. Underling fingernails were like steel files. His right shoulder drooped, forcing him to draw his broadsword with his left hand. Billip jabbed at the wounded creature, each futile blow glancing off of its shield. Its leg stopped his upward press as it chattered back in mockery. *More must be coming.* He pressed hard, growling in return, shoving the creature downhill. Chunks of the wooden shield were chipping away, but the skill of the underling was too swift. It taunted and clawed at him in anger.

Reaching the bottom of the ravine, Billip disengaged the creature. His arm felt like lead, and his shoulder burned. He sucked in a deep breath. Exhaustion and frustration beset him as the emerald-eyed underling raised its shield in triumph. A shadow raised behind the unsuspecting creature, drawing a grin on his face. A studded club smashed down on its skull, erasing its wicked grin, shattering all of its teeth. It fell over dead in a pile of its own ooze.

Mikkel was almost laughing as he wiped the gore on the grass.

"It's about time you started fighting like a man, Billip! I didn't even know you had a sword, let alone the strength to use it."

Billip struggled to spit out his words but said, "They're everywhere, and regrouping for another attack. We have to get away. Where's Vee?"

The big man shrugged. Billip could make out the bloody bandage on the man's leg. Their bleeding would hobble them in a further fight.

"Come on," Billip said with a groan, heading back up the hill.

Mikkel grunted and followed.

"If I can get to my bow we can hold them off for a while."

Billip trudged up the bank as fast as he could, pulling Mikkel over the slippery spots. He could hear more chittering nearby. Wherever Venir was, he was on his own now. He wouldn't wait around like a crippled calf to see when he might return. He recovered his bow as they reached a small outcropping of mossy boulders, where they hid.

He could see the walls of web billowing at their backs. He turned cold. *Nasty.* This spot would have to do. But it gave better cover, so for the moment they were safe. He checked his wound. A nasty sliver of meat was taken off of his right shoulder. His leather armor saved it.

Maybe armor isn't so bad.

His jerkin sleeve was soaked to the cuff. The men patched each other's wounds, staunching the bleeding the best that they could. Billip's heart thundered in his temples as he listened for the next wave of comers. As the howl of distant battle reached his ears he wondered if they would see Venir or anyone else ever again.

Venir had forgotten the wounded man he left behind. He was hunting now, and his comrades weren't his concern; his enemies were. Gripping Brool's oak shaft with white knuckles, he felt invincible. The helm heightened his awareness. He had questions ... *Why hadn't they seen him?* ... but that could wait. He moved on with caution, over the creek and through the dense foliage.

He wasn't alone; Chongo had found his side. The pair had tracked underlings together for years, and now they both had heightened senses to serve them. The dog stopped, ears perked up. He hunched down. He saw the silhouettes of underlings coming up the mouth of the ravine. *Keep coming, vermin!*

Bloodlust stirred inside him, and his compulsion to kill them was overwhelming. He could smell their oily stench, almost burning in his nostrils. His hatred of these foul creatures that had destroyed his life so many years ago began to boil over. The helm amplified his senses as the eyelets burned blacker than the night sky. He no longer cared what happened to him, only what happened to them.

Destroy them!

Thought and magic intertwined into a focal point and down the ravine he bounded. Rushing their flank never occurred to him, nor did an ambush. He padded over the wet stones and braced himself along their path.

He counted six underling warriors moving up the gorge. Some of them crept in a staggered column, while the others covered the ravine banks to the left and right. Their faint multi-colored eyes glinted as their heads moved, left and right. He heard their low chittering commands escaping their narrow lips.

In place of physical battle prowess, underlings preferred to trap and outnumber their opponents. Their magic, combined with their cunning and callousness, made them a formidable force, and difficult to kill. Their warriors were as big as an average human woman, bigger and stronger than ordinary underlings. Their bodies were hard from decades of battle that gave them strength that belied their smaller size.

Several footfalls away, the foremost underling stopped and gave a signal. Venir watched them turn still and almost disappear. He could see them clutching their curved blades, waiting to pounce. Like a four-legged ghost, Chongo padded down the path. He followed, like a wraith, watching their gleaming eyes focused on the lone dog. Could they really not see him?

The underling in the front, donned in chain mail, hissed at the growling dog. *It's not even looking my way*, Venir thought. His body was bursting, the axe white hot in his grip. He let out a blood curdling yell.

"*RRRAH!*"

Venir sheared the bewildered lead underling's head from its shoulders. The others stared in astonishment as he appeared from the darkness and descended on them like an angry minotaur. His appetite for blood unsatisfied, he pressed his attack like a steel tornado, deeper into the brood. Yelling like a berserker and chopping like a lumberjack, he came down on the next two underlings, hacking their small shields into splinters and mutilating them with splattering swings. They rushed in. His anger rose. Hurling his shield, he caught one in the ankle. A series of cuts and stabs drew his blood before he battled them away. The iron shod of his great axe shattered an underling's chin, and another fared still worse as he jabbed the long axe tip into its throat. He tore the spike out, ripping its neck open.

He was ready for an entire hoard, his mind one step ahead and his body responding in kind. He watched in slow motion as another underling charged toward him, a curved sword in each hand. He leapt right over the bewildered creature, swinging his axe deep into its gaping maw, splitting its face before he descended to the ground. Blood from his gory axe dripping on the ground, he awaited more attackers. *Where are they?* He could feel them.

He was picking up his shield when he saw one scurry away. He cursed, and then scanned the area. Somewhere nearby he heard his dog yelp. He rushed to its aid, finding the shaggy brown pooch ensnared by forest vegetation. *Underling magic!* He had encountered it before.

He felt the hairs on the nape of his neck rise. As he approached his dog, his boot snagged on the vines, tripping him. He watched smaller roots and grasses reaching upward like tentacles, encircling his legs like serpents.

"Bone!" he yelled, tearing and twisting at them. The foul foliage had engulfed the dog entirely, leaving only a trace of muffled whimpers. His skin crawled with the evil presence he felt bearing down on him.

Two dark-robed underlings, armed with small double-shot crossbows, descended towards him from the ravine bank as if on air. He jerked his shield up as the closest one fired at his chest. The bolt ricocheted away, drawing an angry hiss. He heard murmurs echoing somewhere in his helm. Above him he noticed long fingertips pointed his way, glowing red. He had to free himself.

He sliced at the roots with the edge of his axe. To his surprise, the vines recoiled and began to wither at the blade's touch.

"Chongo!"

The other suspended mage fired another bolt into the foliage where the dog was engulfed. Chongo yelped and fell silent. Venir lost control and charged the airborne assailant. It blasted him with a volley of burning red missiles that bore into his flesh. He cried out in agony. The air filled with the stench of his singed skin. The pain strengthened his rage. He kept going, climbing up the bank, jumping up and catching the cloak of the floating figure. He pulled it to the ground. It chittered, trying to crawl away. Its strength was no match for his weight as he crushed into it, bringing a groan. Pinning the little figure down by the arms, he smashed his helmeted forehead several times into its gnashing face. Its evil countenance burst open like a rotten pumpkin as it died. He fumbled for his axe and turned back toward his dog.

The remaining underling uttered something. The air seemed to be sucked away in the gap. Shock waves blew through the trees, bending the saplings, slamming into his body and down his spine as if he were being pummeled by a hundred hammers. He fell to his knees, face dripping blood, unaware of his surroundings, lost. The pain was something he never recalled. His hands and feet were numb, burning, cold and limp.

Somehow he got up, stumbled towards his pet and fell just close enough to reach the snare with his axe's spike. He could see the bonds disintegrating as the dog lay prone, panting and bleeding.

Rising up on one knee, he found himself between the dog and the lone underling mage, now hovering twenty paces away. He saw its mouth moving, thick black hair covering its head like a shroud. Raising his powerful arms, Venir slung his axe over his head with a scream. Straight as a spear it sailed, the tip crunching deep into the

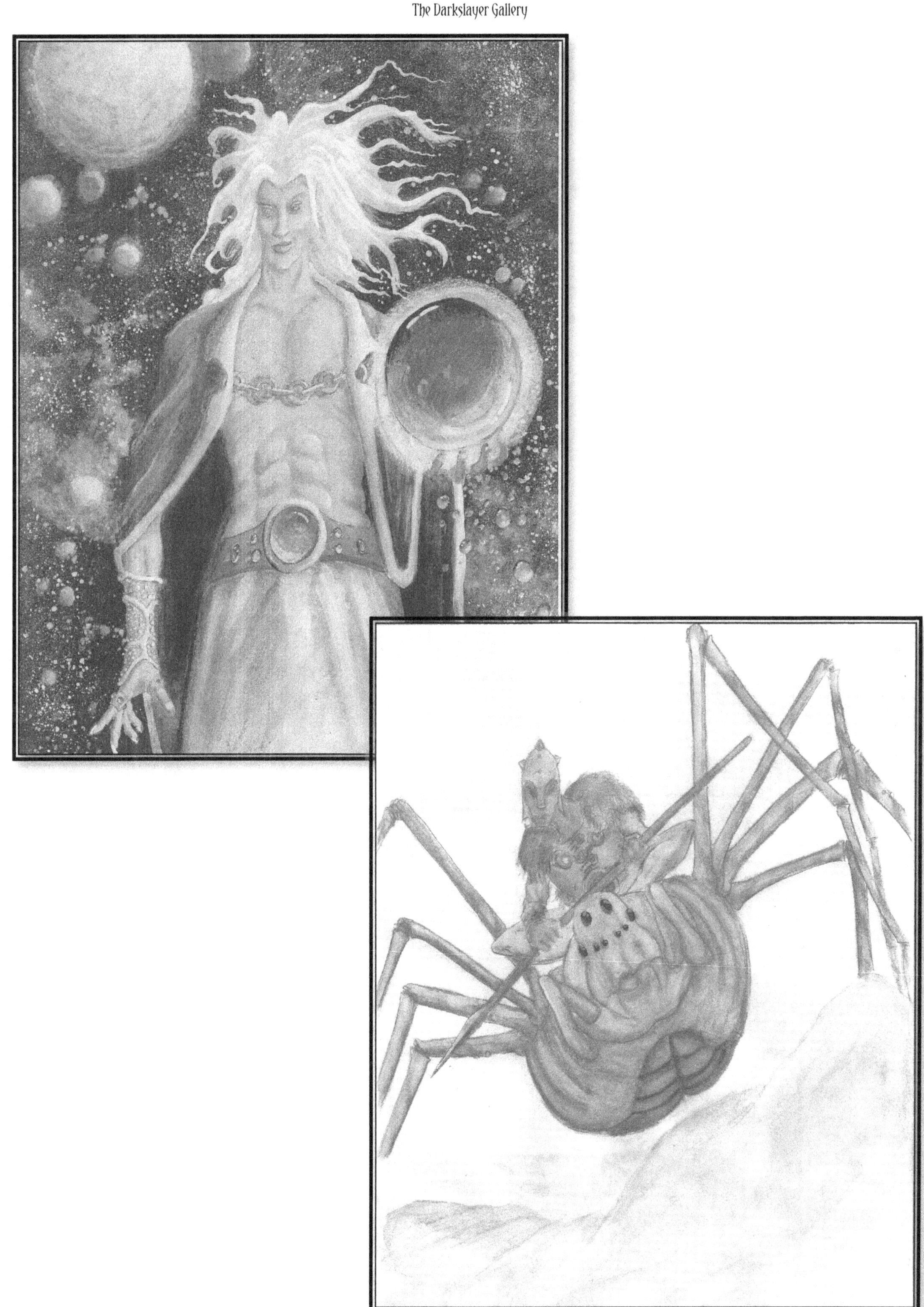

underling mage's chest, driving its floating body to the ground. He staggered over to its crumpled body. The spike was wedged deep into its black heart. Its gemstone green eyes stared blankly at the sky.

He spat the blood from his mouth, wrenched out the axe, and checked for more enemies. He pulled out the wooden bolt from Chongo's hindquarters. He tasted the tip and spat. *No poison.* Unable to feel his legs, but desperate to save Chongo, he lifted the dog in his arms and got a lick in the face as he backtracked up the ravine. The forest was quiet, but he knew underlings were still everywhere. His battered body forged ahead.

Trapped behind a massive rock on the steep hillside, Billip felt his neck hairs prickle. He could see the sweat dripping off Mikkel's body like rain drops as water trickled down the bank. The forest was quiet other than occasional sounds of the skirmish deep in the ravine. His shoulder ached. He craned his neck, but his comrade's ragged breathing hindered his ability to detect approaching assailants. *They could be anywhere.*

He had fought underlings often over the years and knew their tactics well, but it did little to quell his terror. Unlike Venir, whose hatred for underlings blazed as pure as the suns, his was still like all other men on Bish. Billip's hatred for cave dwellers was at times surpassed by his fear of them.

Glancing at Mikkel, he managed to make out the whites of his eyes. The big man was nodding his head. Billip kept his arrow nocked, bowstring straight, resting his shoulder while his friend clutched his club.

Several feet above the forest floor, two cloaked underlings floated undetected in and out among the trees, their clutching hands motioning in the air with intricate patterns. A soft blue glow wavered in their palms.

Where are they? Billip thought.

He scanned what he could, oblivious to the floating figures in the trees. He was certain if he could not see them, they could not see him. Not far from his hiding spot, his ears didn't detect the faint whisper of an underling chanting through its thin black lips. His instincts told him something was going on; he just did not know what.

The low hum of tiny wings caught his ear, and he crouched down as the sound grew. A plague of mosquitoes had found its way among the rocks where they hid. The whining of their buzzing wings increased inside his ears. It seemed as if every mosquito in the ravine began swarming around the men.

What is going on?

The mindless insects consumed the men in a frenzied search for human blood. He could see them, tiny and large, gathered all over Mikkel, who brushed at them in frantic alarm. He could feel them sink their needles into him a hundred times and drink his blood. ***It has to be magic...*** his mind reasoned. He choked down the urge to run. He knew they were being flushed out. *Don't panic.* Tiny welts appeared on his corded forearms as the insects tapped into his veins. Mikkel was covered from head to toe, tormented by the little fiends. Billip tried not to flinch, but his will was tested beyond the limit. He could see Mikkel biting his lip and covering his nose. It was time to act. He mouthed and gestured the words to Mikkel.

Run. Flush them out. Find cover. I've got one shot. Go. The tortured man turned to face down the bank. With Billip readying his bow, the larger man charged out from behind the rock and down the ravine like a maddened bull. Through his swollen eyelids, he caught a flash of light blasting into his powerful friend, who fell down in a scream.

There in the trees.

Down below, he could see the brawler's silhouette engulfed in a mysterious blue flame, drawing forth a sound of searing skin. Mikkel fell to the forest floor, screaming before rolling out of sight.

He wondered which fate was worse, the bugs or the fire. Only Mikkel would know now, but he thought he'd prefer the fire. A smell of charred insect bodies and smoldering hair drifted in his nose. He feared his friend might be finished. Billip heard a throaty laughter below. Mikkel appeared, rising to his feet, only to fall backward as a small crossbow bolt struck his belly. He lay in a singed, motionless heap, Skull Basher still in his hand. Billip couldn't believe it. He scanned the trees; he couldn't let his friend die for nothing.

He replaced the arrow he had nocked, drawing another from his quiver. It was unique with blood-red feathers, a blue-black shaft and a ruby-like arrowhead. The old warrior who had given him the bow assured him he would know when to use it. *That must be now.* He nocked the special arrow with his mosquito-covered hands. He took aim in the trees, scanning back and forth. The arrow tip twinkled as he did so. Maintaining his poise, he searched for any sign. Nothing showed of their concealed assailants. His eyes moved with the arrow, left, right, up and down, but the whining flurry of insects piercing his arms, neck, face, and eyelids was distracting him. As he swept up and across the ruby arrow tip flashed.

He swept it down.

Nothing.

Then back up, and it flashed again.

He lined up the tip so that it glowed steady in light. A silhouette began to form in the tree tops. It was an underling, floating near the upper branches of a willow tree.

Got him! Center mass. An excruciating surge of pain dug into his shoulder when he pulled back the bow string, but he let the shaft fly.

Twing! Zip!

A streak of hot red light punched straight through the sternum of the hovering underling and out of the other side.

Bulls' eye!

The underling still came toward him, chittering with rage. Had he missed? No, he knew he had hit it, yet it came. He fumbled for another arrow, brushing the ravenous insects away. As the underling began descending toward him, a look of horror crossed its features. The underling began to glow, eyes and mouth catching fire from the inside. Suddenly, it exploded in a bright red flash. A cloud of black ash filled the air. Billip crouched back down, noticing the mosquitoes losing interest in him as well. He wiped the creatures away, and gathered his thoughts. *Got to check on Mikkel!*

He ventured down the ravine, bow ready. Another shadowy figure descended on him from above, and he dropped his nocked arrow. He clutched after it as the cloaked underling drifted toward him. Terrified, he watched it touch the ground and crumple in a sagging pile.

Billip inched closer and noticed his red-feathered arrow lodged deep in its brain. Shivering at the sight, he marveled that the arrow had somehow found two targets from his single shot. *Powerful magic, indeed.* Did the same apply to the bow? He reached for the arrow, noticing that the feathers were now blackened and dry, its magic spent.

He slid down the ravine and soon came upon Mikkel on the ground; his breathing was shallow and raspy, lips caked with blood. The man groaned as he sat him up. He put his canteen to Mikkel's lips.

"How is he?" an eerie voice said from behind.

He turned and saw a startling figure of muscle and metal splashed with gore. *Vee?*

"Not good. I haven't seen him this pale since his wedding. We need to get him away from here."

The sounds of battle grew louder all around them. A full-scale attack must have begun.

Venir handed Chongo over to Billip and hefted Mikkel over his shoulder.

"Agreed—let's move … they'll be on us in no time."

The thick webs peeled away as Venir's axe sliced through them. Gasps of pain escaped labored lips from behind him as they treaded back up the ravine. He was exhausted, body wracked with pain. Holes had burned in the mail that covered his belly, singing his flesh to metal. The men reached the bottom outpost wall and entered through the same steel storm drain they had been defending. He locked it down as they headed inside the bowels of the outpost.

Three stout Royal henchmen in scale armor guarded their path, but moved aside with wary glances. Venir could see debris falling from heavy activities above. He led the way upward through the wide tunnel of rock and soil while the sounds of chaos grew. Dim light filtered in at the far end where a steel ladder led twenty feet up through a man-sized hole.

A lanky figure in pale green terrycloth robes and ankle-strap sandals descended the ladder at a brisk pace, hopped off the final five steps and rambled towards them. It was a tall man, near seven feet in height, his narrow face light-skinned and boyish beneath short sandy hair. His voice was soothing, somewhat childlike, his light blue eyes showing a wisdom and compassion that was rare on Bish.

"I knew you would be here."

"No surprise you knew that, Slim." Venir said.

Slim was a man who had answers and seemed to know more than most men, despite his youthful appearance.

"I know you. You never miss a party," Slim said, raising his eyebrows. "Mikkel looks bad." The boyish man began inspecting the brawler with his fingers, motioning his hands downward.

Venir lowered Mikkel to the ground and started to take off his helmet.

"Leave it on," Slim gestured. "You're not out of the woods yet."

The young man noticed the archer's load.

"Ah, it's my favorite pooch … how sad."

He laid his long slender fingers over Chongo's hip.

"Be still," the man whispered.

Venir could see Slim's face twist in agony for a fleeting moment before returning to normal. He grunted.

"Ah," the cleric said with a smile as Chongo licked his face. "That wasn't so bad, was it, Boy?" Slim then turned back to the man laid out in the tunnel and said, "Now the big man. Hold him still, you two."

Venir pressed down on Mikkel's shoulders and watched the young man work. He couldn't believe their good fortune. Slim always reminded him of a young Melegal, except more friendly, something the thief resented. Billip helped him pin down the listless man's powerful arms and legs. *Here we go.*

The long-limbed man grabbed the shaft of the small bolt lodged in Mikkel's belly. The iron warrior's mouth and chin were covered in spit and blood. Slim's slender lips muttered a fast cadence of words, and as he spoke, power radiated into his glowing and elongating hands. The bolt blazed in his hand like a furnace poker as he extracted it inch by inch. The warrior screamed and writhed. The smell of burning flesh filled the tunnel as the charred bolt turned to ash.

Mikkel groaned, his light eyes flitting open and closed. The cleric placed his hands on the man's hard belly and gashed thigh. Again, Slim's face distorted in anguish, but this time he aged before their widened eyes. The wounds closed, and it was over as fast as it had begun. Slim gasped for air, his now withered face full of hard lines and cracked teeth. Venir thought Slim looked like the oldest man he'd ever seen.

"He'll be all right," the cleric said in a ragged voice. "He should be able to walk in a minute, but he's not up for fighting for a while." Slim stood up, hunched over, and cracked his skinny neck. "Ah … man, sometimes I hate this." "What's going on up there, Slim?" Venir asked, looking at the shaking ceiling above. "They need to know that the underlings are bringing more forces now."

"Too late; it's over. Outpost Thirty-One is already lost. And if we don't get moving, *we'll* be lost, too."

His and Billip's eyes met as Slim continued.

"You don't want to go up there. It's overrun. I'll fill you in."

Slim stretched out his long arms, and Venir watched the older face slowly regain its youthful vigor. The young man now inspected Venir's wounds and began chatting in the quick.

"Here goes—the brigands stormed the east gate. Three hundred Royal horsemen rode out to battle them, or so we thought, but they just kept on riding, giving the brigands clear access to the outpost. I'm not sure which Royal general it was, but he clearly betrayed the rest. It won't be long before all the gates are compromised and we're up to our elbows in underlings. Now, we've got to go back out that way." Slim pointed his long index finger toward the south grate where they had just entered. "No choice."

Venir saw Billip's dumbfounded look. It was a heck of a story.

Mikkel groaned and sat up.

"Man, my stomach hurts. What did you do, Slim?"

"Saved your life, that's all. The tummy ache's a side effect. It'll go away," Slim said, patting the man's charred head.

"Thanks," Mikkel muttered as the healer helped him onto his feet.

"That's a heck of a haircut, Mikkel!" Billip said with a faint chuckle.

"What?" The warrior reached for his head, feeling the singed remains of his black hair. "It might grow back," Slim said with a shrug, "one day. Let's go."

"Wait," the archer said, tugging the man's robe. "We need a plan. And I can't even pull back a bowstring."

"Man, what did you guys do out there? And what's with all the bug bites? That's gross!" He said it with his face drawn, hands on his chest. "You got whipped by a bunch of little underlings, didn't you?" Slim now ran his ginger fingers over the archer's shoulder, then reached into a pouch and pulled out a small jar and applied a pasty blue salve to the wound.

Billip's face lightened up.

"What's that amazing stuff?"

"Pigeon dung."

Billip's face turned sour.

Slim had a childish grin and said, "Just teasing, it's a little something I whipped up. I haven't named it yet. Good thing your wound was only cosmetic. It's just a little make-up to match your cheeks. You'll be fine."

The chuckles came, but were hollow, none more so than Venir's. He wasn't so sure he could get them safely out of there.

Billip rolled his shoulder, releasing a brief smile, cracking his knuckles. Touching the scar that had already formed over the wound, he said, "It's closed up!"

The healer slapped his tender shoulder, bringing a grimace.

"And don't worry about the scar. Get a nice tattoo over it and the ladies will love it, especially the orcen ones."

The tunnel was silent for a moment as Venir watched all eyes draw on him. Other than Slim, the bunch looked ragged and beaten. He wanted to collapse. His belly burned. His body ached from head to toe. It seemed there was no other way out. One choice, *Fight or flee.*

"Let me take care of you, Big Man. That's a nasty mess in your belly."

Venir's voice was harsh.

"No, let's go."
The cleric stepped out of his way.

Slim tried to convince the sentries at the outer grate to come along, that remaining would be to their immediate peril. They laughed. They were hard and loyal men who would not abandon their duty. The soldiers made it clear they would rather die than run, wished the men good fortune and turned away. Closing the storm drain behind them and then sealing it shut, one yelled out.

"Bish be with you!"

Now the men stood in the forest, listening. Venir could hear the rising crescendo of bloodshed ringing in his ears. He could picture the underlings and the brigand army spilling inside the outpost and blackening its interior. The gates were compromised. The shouts of Royal orders were silenced by magic, missiles and manslaughter. Plumes of fire and smoke filled the sky.

It was clear that the onslaught was overwhelming and no Royal man or beast would survive. A great chunk of evil would follow the valiant soldiers into the bloodied ground, however. That seemed clear judging by the roar of the fighting above, but it would not be enough.

Mikkel was nodding his head.

"What's the plan?"

"The last plan was to get word to the northern cities for assistance," Slim said. "So let's head that way, or else I'll go alone."

Venir said, "No, we go south. They won't be looking as hard there. The northward route will be the most heavily guarded. The underlings will be thick for miles."

"The underlings will be everywhere—period!" Mikkel retorted.

Slim had something to offer.

"I have magic that should conceal us all. But, I don't want to use it until the last possible moment. It won't last long. We're going to have to move like the wind to get clear. I've got other ideas, too. Are you with me?"

Having ventured with Slim before, Venir had some idea of what he had in mind. He wasn't keen, but they had little choice other than to trust his magic. It could do more than heal.

"I'll take the point. For some odd reason they can't see me. The rest of you should be fine. I just hope there's nothing worse than underlings out there looking for us."

Slim tightened the cords on his sandals.

"That's grand, Venir. You just gave me another idea. By the way, nice helmet or whatever that is. It makes you look mean ... like Melegal."

Venir barreled down the ravine with Chongo at his side. The others followed not far behind, all thoughts heavy on the downfall of Outpost Thirty-One. Mikkel managed to recover his heavy crossbow as they passed by the ambush site. Venir maneuvered through the thick foliage like a metal apparition, striding through the dark like a bobcat. He could sense underlings were all around, but not close enough to pinpoint. He fought the urge to find them, as the helm's awareness made the battle very compelling. He began to realize that he could lead them all out of harm's way if he could stay focused on fleeing, rather than killing.

Nevertheless, the spiked helm on his brow beckoned him to make contact and destroy the underlings. He had to stop more than once to regain his composure, rather than succumb to the battle lust. His will was strong, but only his loyalty to his friends prevented him from giving in to his reckless desires.

He led them through the forest, minute after minute, stirring little more than a muskrat. His nerves were on edge as every unfamiliar sound seemed amplified. He looked back time and again, but Billip signaled they weren't followed. They were already a full mile down the hill. *Almost free*. He kept them moving.

At this pace the great hill that held Outpost Thirty-One would soon bottom out; they were almost halfway down. He felt something strong ahead and froze.

Slim fidgeted beside Mikkel.

Venir signaled back, *Nothing*.

Venir began moving again. He heard the lanky cleric sigh in relief. Their careful footfalls through the humid, bug-filled forest became agonizing; they had been creeping along for almost an hour.

Again he stopped.

They all went still. *Small underling patrol!* he signaled. *Straight for us. Hide!*

Slim began muttering soft chanting words.

Venir turned to watch. The air around the three men and the dog thickened. Next, all he saw was a small grove of trees where his comrades had stood. The illusion worked.

Venir sunk beneath a thick willow tree. The silhouettes of three underling hunters, armed with light crossbows, stood in a small clearing not far from him, chittering in the quiet.

Venir's bloodlust plagued him like a growing migraine. They were right in his path. He should sheer them like sheep. He quelled the urge with iron will, controlling his burgeoning lust and watching them begin to move on up the ravine his way.

Don't move. Don't breathe.

They passed him and were standing beside the grove of trees that were once men. Venir heard one sniffing the air into its hawkish nose. Venir tightened his grip on Brool.

Here we go.

Another underling shoved its comrade along the way, more intent on the sound of the fracas farther uphill, and they passed onward. The throbbing in Venir's head subsided after another long minute, and he started moving again with more haste. The odd grove of trees followed him. Within the hour they were at the bottom of the hill, safe and facing the open plains to the east.

"Wow!" Slim exclaimed, checking the looks of his tree-like arms and hands. "I can't believe we just waltzed through that nest of evil. Insane!"

They all shook their heads, stretched their limbs, and basked in the red moonlight. Such moments as this didn't often come without consequence. "Now what?" Mikkel said, rubbing his tender thigh.

They all looked at Venir. The outpost had fallen. Good men would die. He wanted to take an army in himself and drive the underlings back into their caves. Mostly, he wanted to find Jarla and make her pay. He swore he would hunt her down and kill her, but now was not the time.

He took off his helm, dropping it into the sack, feeling the warm night air soothe his aching head. He ran his fingers through his thick locks of blond hair.

"Two-Ten City … we'll spread the word as we go."

7

(The Present)

PLOP.

Louder and closer. Venir was blinded to everything but that steady sound. A beacon of death or a beacon of hope, which he did not know, nor did he care. *Move or die.* So be it.

The ground beneath his feet had turned to blackened shale as he treaded steep inclines only to slide downward again. His despair was replaced by anger only to turn back to despair again, but the sound kept coming.

Plop.

What was that sound? It seemed familiar now, like streams that rippled over the rocks where he fished as a child. Those days—singing in the sunlight, sucking down fish eggs and washing in the streams—seemed ancient and impossible now. Blood and body parts littered the water like rotting logs, and his days had been darker ever since, no recourse, no choice. *Fight or Die.*

"URK!" he gasped as his body pitched forward, and then he tumbled downward over the shale, each tiny rock cutting under his skin like broken glass under the force of his momentum. His fingers clawed into the ground. His feet kicked, but he did not slow. He slipped off the edge of something. The wind whistled through his ears as he fell.

SPLASH!

The water was cold, dark and unfriendly. The weight of his helm and axe was pulling him downward as his feet paddled for the top, but he had no idea which direction that was. In the back of his mind he figured he was back in the river and just needed to find the bottom. How deep could it be? He could walk back ashore. He sank. His body began to labor for air, twitching and jerking in the murk. Brool glimmered with life as his lungs began to collapse with death. Drowning, what a pitiful way to go. *Bloody lying giants!* Then again, maybe he should have taken the advice he was told.

He closed his eyes, letting the icing waters slow his struggles, and thought his final thoughts of Kam, underlings and grog. *Ah, but to have at them all once more.* Something burst through the water, wrapped around his body and yanked him out. He gasped for air, writhing against the grip that had his arms pinned to his sides. As the icy water cleared his eyes and ran down the rivulets of his helm, he found himself face to face with another foe. A giant with a boyish face, bald and one-eyed, held him like a child's doll in its mighty grip. The face was pitiful and scary at the same time. Its skull, as big as a boulder, was misshapen at the top, one ear sticking out and the other looking melted on the side. Its breath of seaweed and fish wasn't the most unpleasant he'd encountered, but the split blue-green tongue rolling in its mouth might've been the ugliest. Venir was certain he was about to be eaten.

It screamed in Venir's face.

An army of orcs couldn't have been any louder.

Venir screamed back.

It screamed again, louder than the last, shifting his helm on his brow.

Its grip loosened, and Venir took in a full swallow of air.

"RRAAAWWWW!"

Its brown uni-brow perched above its one good eye.

"Hur-Rah?" it said.

Venir gazed at his foe. A deformed giant with only one working eye was standing knee deep in dark water that was surrounded by a lake shore, encompassed by rocky ridges that jutted from the mist. A cone of mist went up as high as he could see before it stopped again in the clouds. Rocks jutted left and right from the smoky spirals, but near the shores there was green, brown and life. A drop of water, as big as his head, fell in the water beside him.

Plop.

Venir warmed at the thought of the small victory, but it was short lived as One Eye started to carry him away. The one big brown eye stared at him, with admiration it seemed. Venir's head whipped around. *Must escape.* But there was only water, rocks, a mile long shore line, if that, and more mist. If he killed the giant, then where would he go? *Think Venir.*

"Where are you taking me?" he yelled.

Its working eye squinted, and its split tongue rolled as it gave him a curious look and spoke.

"HUNG-GAREE."

Venir gulped as its enormous belly groaned.

8

As MELEGAL SPRANG BACK TO his feet, his short swords, the Sisters, were gleaming in his hands. The leather wrapped around the pommels was reassuring as he crouched and faced his unseen foe. Two small figures, decorated in wooden masks, were blocking his path back into the street.

You can't be serious.

"Coin or death, Whore Bred?" A long steel knife flashed in one urchin's hand as the other flanked him with a notched and rusty longsword. Melegal was in no mood to laugh as the renegade urchins adorned in ruddy red robes and bare feet closed in. They were members of the guild, one of many that bred thieves, liars and whores. *You can't be serious.* This bunch in particular called themselves the Wastrels of the Rose, he recalled, a peasant lot of cutpurses at best. They leaped back as he made a quick lunge at them.

"Come now, children. Run, before I have to skewer you," he warned.

Each masked face turned toward the other before returning their weird little gaze back to him. *I should kill them. Stupidity is a crime, in some cases. How did they sneak up on me, though?* Melegal shouldn't have been surprised, ever, but his focus on Sefron had almost proved to be his undoing. A more formidable stalker might have been successful in putting his life to an end. He'd have to be more careful.

"Coin or death—"

Melegal swatted the flat of his blade on the front of the boy's mask.

"Yes, I know—Whore Bred. Is that the line your guild master has you using when you rob the honest and stupid folk?"

"Yaaaaar!" the other one lunched.

Clang! Melegal smacked the boy's blade from his hands.

The other charged. *Really?* Melegal cracked the flat of his blade on the other urchin's mask, knocking it clear off. The Sisters became a blur of steel in the twilight.

Whap! Whap! Whap! Whap! Whap! Whap!

The pair, one boy, one girl, both ugly and pitiful, fell to the ground clutching their heads as they tried to crawl away. Melegal's booted feet pinned their robes to the ground as he warned them, "Keep moving. Start crying or screaming and the next strikes will be with the edges of my blades. Got it?"

They nodded as their elbows scraped over the pavement.

"Mercy!"

Tears of pain and fear dropped onto the stones below them. It was uncharacteristic for these little thieves to try and take a full grown man like Melegal. They tended to work in small groups, strike fast and bully younger or elderly people, but times were as desperate in Bone as they had ever been. There was a clamor coming from the other side of Bone's massive walls that the underlings were coming, coming to kill them all. Of course, it might have been rumors alone, but there were more desperate people being taken in than ever before. However, Melegal had other things to worry about.

"Tell me something, urchlings. Are more of you nearby? Cause if there are, I'm going to carve a hole in you both this big," he said, making a large circle in the air with his blade.

They both shook their heads.

"Good, so tell me this: how long have you been following me?"

It was the girl who spoke.

"Just a few corners, M-m-master."

That's more like it. Maybe I should keep them around.

"Ah … I see," he said, slowly strolling around them. "Tell me, did you see a man enter this alley before me?"

They both shook their heads.

He kicked the boy in the head. "Don't lie to me! Did you not see a man shuffling like a snail over the ground, a mere twenty paces ahead of me?"

"No Master, I swear!"

"No, no such man. Only you!"

He wanted to kill something, anything or anyone. He touched the tips of his blades into their empty bellies, drawing blood as he grimaced with rage.

"Don't lie to me! Where is the man you saw before me?" He looked down the alley, a dead end one way, a street up the other. He didn't miss anything, not one single detail. Studied the walls, not so much as a portal, ladders, or ledges to climb along, not Sefron anyway.

"P-Please don't kill us, Master. Mercy!"

Melegal's voice was cold as ice when he said, "Why not? You've nothing to live for."

"We don't want to die," the girl said. "We want to live to see the morrow. Please don't kill us. We'll help you find the one you lost."

Stupid urchins.

Melegal sheathed his blades. He knew the difference between a lie and the truth when he heard it, and these pathetic waifs had not lied. But, he was still certain they'd be better off dead. "Pah! Go rodents, and remember: if you cherish the morrow so much, make sure I never see you again." He stomped their wooden masks to splinters. "I'll not forget your faces, not now nor twenty years from now."

He could hear their scampering feet as he headed toward the dead end of the alley and began his search. He was seething inside. Sefron had slipped him again, it seemed. He ran his delicate fingers over every niche he could find. Nothing. That left only one other option, and the thought left him uneasy. *Magic, and maybe he was on to me.* Melegal stuffed his hands in his pockets and began the long walk home. *I guess I'm gonna have to kill him in the castle.*

Sefron took one feverish glance over his shoulder after another as he lumbered down a steep series of narrow steps. He labored for breath and wheezed through his nose as he stopped and looked back over his shoulder. Paranoid. He waited a few more moments, confident his spell worked, before he continued his descent. *Good. Good.*

He was oblivious to the fact that Detective Melegal had been following him, but that didn't mean he didn't take precautions whenever he slipped outside the castle walls. For over a decade, almost two, he had been avoiding the prying eyes of the Royals. A spell he had mastered, an apparition of himself, had unloaded itself from the wagon, hours earlier, and in his guise wandered the streets until it expired. Not just one, but two shades were out there before he made his own secretive trek. If someone had indeed been following him, he would not have known, but that didn't matter. What did matter was that no one, especially not the Almens, knew where he was going or who he was about to see. He peeked over his shoulder again. As much as he enjoyed watching others being tortured, he had nightmares of it happening to himself. A betrayed Almen was as merciless as merciless could be. *Hate 'em. Hate them all!*

As the light faded above him he muttered a quick incantation.

Shazal-ong.

A copper ring on his middle finger came to life with a soft glow as he stood on a landing barricaded by an ancient door covered in rust and grit. A new sense of security washed over him as a pair of rats scurried over his feet. He pushed his way through. A cool damp breeze cut though his clothes and raised bumps over the clammy skin on his neck. He swallowed hard. *Slow and easy.* His frail legs ached. His lungs wheezed. It took another twenty minutes for him to reach the bottom of the slick rock stairs that bottomed out in what looked to be an unfinished room that opened into a cave.

The light from his ring did very little to expose his surroundings, and anyhow, the curiosity that bred a need for exploration evaded his being. What lay beneath the City of Bone was of little concern to him. Humans feared what was beneath the ground, always assuming it was filled with ghouls, trolls or underlings, at least at the subterranean levels. The sewers, almost another two hundred feet above, were another matter, but even those desperate enough to try the sewers never crossed to the deep levels, and they hoped whatever lived in the ground never crossed them. Yet it happened. There were monsters that wandered below. Sometimes they reached the sewer levels, and rarely one would creep into the city, but most witnesses never lived to tell about it.

Sefron wiped the sweat from his forehead with a handkerchief as he waited and waited. The sounds of dripping water echoed from everywhere. He began to pace back and forth on his aching and shaking legs, his wheezing just as heavy as ever. He knew he wasn't late. He never had been, not once over the years. He was in the same place as the last time, a place no one would ever think to look: cool, damp, deep, dark and dangerous.

With a raspy sigh he sat down, allowing his lids to close over his bulging eyes. This trek took a lot out of him, and he was grateful that he only did it once a year. His thoughts drifted to the castle's serving girls. *They'll have much work to do, massaging my sagging old muscles.* His dry mouth began to water.

"Taking a nap, are we?" A sinister voice cut through his thoughts.

Sefron shouted out in terror at the sight of the horrifying face before him. It was an abomination of cat and man: black, twisted and cunning, layered with muscles from its toes to its shoulders. It hoisted him off the ground by the neck with a single hand. Sefron could feel its steel file-like claws digging into his neck as it choked him. The smell of piss wafted in the air as he soaked his robes. The monster, unlike anything he ever imagined, sneered at him with fiendish eyes.

Sefron's legs twitched. His eyes bulged like boiled eggs as his slimy tongue writhed inside his mouth. He watched in horror as the creature opened its large mouth, revealing fangs and rows of razor sharp teeth. He must have failed his master. His time had come, his efforts undone. But he wasn't going to die without some kind of fight. He stared into the eyes of the monster, channeled his thoughts and energy. *Let me go. Let me go,* he commanded. The monster's gaze filled his gut with despair as its grip tightened around his throat. *No! It's not working!* Laughter echoed and began to fade.

9

UNDERNEATH AN ANCIENT SNOW COVERED pine, Fogle Boon's knees shook beneath the ropes of ice that bound him. He had been there for hours, his shivering beyond control, without so much as a sound or visit from his gorgeous captor or her pack of wolves. He strained to hear something, anything, but he could only feel the icicles growing on his earlobes as the howling wind continued to rip through him to the bone. He had been miserable before, but nothing compared to this. *I can't go like this. Not without a fight.* Yet, he still felt his chances for survival dwindling away.

Nearby was Mood, frozen up to his neck in a single block of ice, head down, unmoving. Fogle tried to imagine which was worse, his situation or the Blood Ranger's. *He's probably enjoying this. Bloody dwarf!*

He tried to focus on what magic he had left within him, probing his superior intellect to see if there was anything he could use. His hands were bound, and his mouth was gagged with a dirty piece of cloth that tasted like sweat. He was all alone with his only remaining weapon: his mind. Yet she, whoever she was, some strange guardian of ogres and wolves, was careful not to catch his eyes. Instead, two men as tall as small pines, bearded like dwarves and armed with picks, had bound and hauled him away. Two ogres shoved along the block of ice that kept Mood imprisoned.

It was a long trip that led them deep inside a cavern, a veritable garden where vibrant plant life of many colors was bursting through the ice and snow. Flowers, trees and streams filled with jumping fish were abundant in his field of vision. As spectacular as it was, Fogle was far from impressed. It was still cold, colder than a lich's tit, and all he wanted more than anything was fire and a blanket. He groaned a pitiful sound as his teeth clattered together. He was certain they were about to break like ice tablets at any moment.

Another sliver of fear raced down his spine as the pack of wolves appeared from behind him. Their coats brushed along his knees as they growled and barked in low puffs. He watched the saliva drip from their fanged mouths. *What a wonderful coat you would make.* A fearsome sight, the wolves, each one's back stood almost four feet at the shoulder. He thought of Chongo and wondered if the giant two-headed dog could make quick work of them, or if they would tear him to pieces. Chongo, the reason he was here and freezing in the snow.

As the dogs sat, the two tall men reappeared, one carrying a short log as thick as a man on his shoulder, the other a heavy blanket. Gently the man set it on the snow in front of him, and the other laid the blanket on top of it. They both then stood on either side of the log, arms crossed over broad bearded chests, unmoving. *Nice blanket.* Fogle would have fought them both bare handed for it. He looked up at them, each standing taller than even Venir, eyes straight forward, hairy and scary. That's when Fogle noticed the heavy blades with long hilts on their hips. Bastard swords. The heavy picks they had earlier seemed more adequate to the conditions, the swords more out of place because the roughhewn mountain men looked more like executioners. He swallowed a frozen glob of snot. That's when she came. *Oh my Bish!*

She was back, her pink eyes almost glowing in contrast to her soft skin and snow white hair. A tiara of twigs and small flowers adorned her hair while her toga flapped loosely in the air. She eased her rear end onto the blanket, and without a word the two men lifted her from the ground, holding her a head's height above Fogle's frozen face.

She pulled the rag from his mouth. "Tell me, Wizard, why did you kill my ogres?" Her powerful voice was not as threatening as it was before.

Fogle searched for her eyes, but he could not find them. They looked out above him as if he wasn't there. Deep inside of him a pot of anger stirred. It was one of the stupidest questions he had ever heard. He wanted to tell her that, and less than a year ago he certainly would have, but now things were different. Still ...

"Cah-ca-cause they were trying to kill us," he somehow managed to sputter out.

She looked around, making an eerie sound as she did so, before she made her reply.

"My ogres protect me, my brethren, my haven," her voice rose, "they are sweet creatures to be cherished, not slaughtered."

Sweet and ogres didn't mix, not since the dawn of any timeline. Any fool knew that. This witch, or whatever she was, was crazy. *Be wary of the crazy ones,* Venir had told him once.

"Not in this world. Anyone knows ogres are every bit as evil as their armpits are smelly. What I can't understand is — "

"SILENCE!" she yelled. Her wolves began to snap and pounce. She lowered her palms, and they all sat. "Tell me then, why have you come here? What is it that you hunt?"

"I hunt nothing. We've come to help a fah-fah-fah-friend. We need to find a druid."

Fogle thought he saw her eyebrows perch for a moment and noticed her shifting a little on the log. He started to continue, but she cut him off.

"Liar! Men have no use for druids. I have no use for liars," she said, slipping from the log, her feet landing softly on the snow. As she started to walk away, she made an order. "Chop off his head, and feed him to the wolves. Stab that Blood Ranger in the brain."

The thought of losing his head at the swing of icy steel made his teeth ache. He always figured he'd have a peaceful death in bed. His head was cast down in failure as he murmured his final words, "I guess I'll be dying a virgin after all." Fogle cringed as cold steel was scraped from sheaths. *Freeze and die.*

10

THE INSIDE OF VERBARD'S HEAD twisted inside out. *Poison!* He was certain it was in control. Before him, Master Sinway's image stretched, contorted, swirled into a pinwheel and exploded. The urge to vomit came, but it never played out. Instead, something else happened, very unexpected. Everything came to a halt: his heart, his brain and his breath as he took in his new surroundings. He was back underneath the blazing suns of Bish. He was mortified. *Banished!*

"My, my, Verbard, you almost look as pale as a human," Master Sinway said, standing at his side. "Feeling a tad uneasy, are we?"

Verbard turned his back to the suns, clutched at his sides, and retched, but nothing came out.

"Pah, Verbard, you are not in your body; you cannot vomit. My, Catten would be ashamed. An underling mage vomiting from a dimensional spell. Well, I suppose powerful magic is not for everyone."

Master Sinway floated away, tall and foreboding, but in a different light now. The bright suns brought out features of the underling, who looked like part man, part wraith in his fathomless black robes. Verbard went after him, trying to acquire his senses. He felt nothing: no heat, no air and worst of all, no magic. *I live.*

Master Sinway stopped and turned. His ancient face was magnified in the sunlight: intelligent, cunning and omnipotent. His iron eyes were deeper than a mineshaft, his shoulders broad and his hands gave Verbard the impression his master had broken necks before. His master wasn't one to hide from the suns or the moons or anything above. Verbard had the feeling that — if anything — they should hide from him. Master Sinway's evil countenance seemed invigorated, almost cheerful.

"Have you adjusted?"

Verbard nodded.

"Good then. Try to keep up; I've much to show you and little time."

They seemed to move as fast as thought, in a fashion that reminded Verbard of Eep's eye, but this included more sights and sounds. This spell was powerful, dangerously so, something he'd never imagined Sinway had control of. He felt small. Then, Verbard wondered if Master Sinway was defenseless in his home now. *Who's protecting him? Can he be in two places at once?* His idea was fleeting, as his respect for Master Sinway grew. He looked down as they soared through the sky where a plume of heavy white smoke was building. Dark ranks of creatures became more distinct as they fell closer. He gasped. *How glorious!* Judging by the terrain, Verbard was certain of exactly where they were, but this was south of the Great Forest of Bish, somewhere between there and the jungles. Crops, miles of them, had caught fire, but that wasn't all. An army of underlings, a thousand or more strong, were killing men, women and children like sheep.

He and Sinway stood in the center of a village now as underlings on spiders and on foot decimated human flesh like fresh poultry. A woman's head was tossed through his ghost- like form, and that brought forth a chuckle from Master Sinway.

"When, Master? I beg of you, why was I unaware?" He was very careful of his tone.

A man wielding a pitchfork tried to defend himself from the attack of one underling only to have a crossbow bolt shot point blank into the back of his head by an armorless underling. It was strange, euphoric, being in the center of the melee as all sorts of creatures passed through their forms, screaming in terror and glee. Verbard was enthralled, but he needed his questions answered, too.

"Come," Master Sinway said.

In a single step they moved miles. In a field he stood, once vibrant with full crops, now burned to the ground and converted into a graveyard of sorts. Pairs of legs were sticking from the ground, some clammy, some bloody, some twitching as far as his silver eyes could see. Underlings, diggers they called them, were dragging living corpses from all directions, leaving smears of blood over the green and blackened grasses. Verbard began counting. It was unlike anything he imagined. *Simply beautiful.*

He looked over at his master and said, "There's over a thousand, practically an army of men dead. How? When?"

"Ah, that's the best part, less than a couple of months, not a day more. Consider it a tribute for what you have done, Verbard. With the Darkslayer gone, the small towns and villages are so much easier to burn." Master Sinway whirled slowly over the muddied ground then let his eyes rest back on Verbard. "I assume you have a question? Your eyes do not show the glee I anticipated."

Verbard took in a sharp breath as his chin dipped.

"Master, am I to understand the Darkslayer prevented such carnage all alone? He was one man. It seems unlikely that he could have stopped an entire army. There has to be something more to this force than just the Darkslayer's demise." He hated to say the next line. "I could not be the one to take all the credit. Surely your hand is in all of this." When he looked up again, Master Sinway's broad back faced him.

"Heh … is that humility I hear? From my most impudent and challenging servant of all?"

Verbard began to speak but was cut off.

"Don't pretend to think you are undeserving, even when that's the case. Humility is not your way, Verbard. My, without your brother you've become uninteresting. I don't like it."

The sharp words somehow stung his black heart. Sinway continued:

"Now, come alongside me."

"Certainly."

"Hmmm …" Sinway glanced at him, rubbing his chin, then looked away. "You'll figure it out. Now, as for you observations, yes, you are right, this isn't all because of the fall of our foe. But, it did play a key part. These wretched humans lack the will without his presence being totted. The Royals, our greatest enemy of all, squabble amongst one another and let their world fall to ruin. Without man helping man, well, you see the result."

"So, we burn their crops, kill their people and little more than a few hundred soldiers have been sent to stop us. All dead." He fanned his hands over the crops. "The orcs, dwarves and ogres are naught to be heard from. We've hardly been challenged. Our treks of terror began in the twilight, just to see if your words were true. Just to see if the man would come. He did not. Now, we press into the day and strengthen our grip on the South. In a few more months, everything below the Great Forest will be ours. By the time the Royals make a show of force, it will be over."

Following Sinway over forests, jungles and cities large and small, Verbard could see people in large caravans heading north and other humanoid races moving south. He could see fear, worry and starvation on their ugly faces, and his hatred fed on their destruction. He felt stronger.

"What are your thoughts, Verbard? You've been so quiet. It's unlike you," Sinway said with a twinge of annoyance.

"How many of our kind roam the lands?"

"Five thousand."

"That's a huge force for us. The humans can summon armies as big as ten thousand on a moment's notice. We could be slaughtered," he said matter-of-factly.

Sinway hissed.

"But they have not! They sit, whine and wallow in riches, fighting over the next bauble or glimmer of power. It's an opportunity like none from ever before."

Verbard wasn't so certain. The death of thousands of humans was always a good thing, but the way it came about seemed unnatural. Century after century, underlings and humans chipping away at one another had become a ritual. What he saw now was a slaughter. He liked it, but it seemed too easy.

"Oh so many months ago, Verbard, did you not feel a shift in your powers? A quake, a shimmer, an ebb? It was like the entire world of magic we know wobbled and flipped."

He had, several times, and it terrified him. Had it jolted his master as well?

"Indeed, it almost cost me my life more than once. But, it filled me with power so great I sometimes could barely contain it. Like a rich well of energy deeper than our caves. That feeling was indescribable, but the feeling is still with me, just more faint."

"And you brother felt this as well, did he not?"

"He did."

They were hovering over the mirages of the Warfield now, the place of fight and die. Far below, from the ledge of a giant hill, two pairs of unseeing eyes were watching them: the Nameless Two. From within their cave they could see all coming and going, no matter the dimension. Verbard could not contain his grimace as his clawed hand rubbed the heavy scar on his chest. It ached as the agony of dying settled in. In that moment in the cave, when he and his brother felt so invincible, he'd been quickly humbled by the single thrust of a blade. He winced again.

"Problem, Verbard?" Sinway said. "You almost look pale."

"No, Master." *Just you.*

"Then keep up," Sinway almost spat. "We've little time left."

His master sounded stressed. Perhaps the spell was fading; he could only assume.

In merely a few more moments they were hovering just outside the City of Bone. Verbard had last seen it months ago, a fleeting moment in Eep's eye, but his memory didn't serve it justice. The city of Bone was enormous, black against the shades of the suns, spires and lookouts almost ten stories tall. The miserable place was filled with humans, and all Verbard could think was how much he wanted to see them all burn alive. *That would be grand.*

It was strange though, being so close to his enemies, inside the former home of the Darkslayer. His little black heart began to pound even faster. Why were they here? As they floated closer, the multitudes of people on the outer walls began to thicken. They were coming from the Outlands, in droves, crowding the walls and fighting among themselves.

"Master," he hissed with a twinge of joy, "the exodus is, well … masterful!"

"Indeed, Verbard, indeed. They fled the south like drowning rats, causing their own disorder. The soldiers within can barely depart without trampling their own kind like rodents. They are weak, weary, broken, sick and starving. All coming to seek refuge in the great City of Bone. Hah! They can't even bring in rations." Master Sinway's iron eyes glimmered with glee. "They have themselves under siege without even the necessity of our presence."

"How long do you think their reserves will hold them, Master?"

"Ah, well, they are prepared, but less than a year; I am certain. Hardly a blink for us, but long enough to kill off thousands more of the humans. In a few more weeks they'll be eating their dead."

Elation filled Verbard, and even Master Sinway's satisfaction was abundant on his hardened face. Verbard sensed that his master had been waiting on this for a long time. He pulled his shoulders back, lifted his chin beside his master and observed the deteriorating throng of people. Deep down he felt satisfaction that he had something to do with this. Not his brother, not Sinway nor any other underling. Him. *I rule!*

Sinway turned to him, almost with a smile on his face, his flattened teeth bared. "I've not brought you here just to bask in glory, Verbard. We both know how quickly things can change, so we are seizing the moment. I wanted to share something else with you about this grand city that you don't know."

Sinway gazed down on the city, shook his head and pointed.

"The City of Bone, as men would call it, was not always so," Sinway said, lowering his ethereal self to the ground.

Ugh, Verbard thought as the filthy people passed through him with pitiful looks and wallowed around with screaming babies. Verbard looked up the rock walls, so tall and formidable up close. *Impenetrable.* He wondered who had moved such massive rocks and was certain it was the giants or the dwarves. If Sinway was contemplating attacking it, then they would need many siege machines, a full army of soldiers and all the magic powers at their disposal. Outpost Thirty-One was one thing, but the City of Bone was quite another.

"When I was young, Verbard, the City of Bone was what the underlings called home."

Verbard silently mouthed the words, "What?"

But Sinway wasn't finished.

"The time has come to take it back, and I'm placing you in charge of that."

Verbard tried not to stammer as his nails dug into his palms. *This is my reward. I'd rather eat urchling slat first. Slat on that.*

"It would be a great honor," he bowed, "Master Sinway."

11

K AM RUSHED THROUGH THE DOOR, her nerves jangling with danger at the sound of her baby's screams. A man was in the room, stout and wiry, his face aghast, her baby in his corded arms. The man was patting the baby's back, while bouncing the baby on his knees, his face distraught. It appeared nothing was working to shut off the baby's screams.

The little baby's face was red, its small mouth widening into a gaping hole. Kam's moment of panic subsided as she eased the baby into her arms and allowed the little one to latch onto her breast.

"Ssssh. Sssssh. Sssssh. Your mommy's here, you hungry little thing," she said, taking a seat on the couch. She winced. "My! Easy now, Little Girl, I'm not a cow."

Kam gently rocked her baby girl, Erin, back and forth. She felt Billip's heated gaze on her and looked up only to see his eyes quickly flit away. He was a nice enough looking fellow for such a hardened man, shifty and nervous at times, but she still caught an ornery look in his eyes now and again. He popped his knuckles, looked down in her eyes, then lower and away again. Her cheeks turned a little rosy, which was odd because over the years she'd become calloused to men's wanton eyes caressing her features.

"Eh … Kam, I'm sorry about little Erin getting so excited. One second she was fine, then the next she sounded away like a banshee." Billip twisted his black goatee and added, "Can I get you or the baby anything? Milk … er, I mean tea or some plum juice? I'd be happy to fetch you some."

"No thank you, Billip. I can take things from here, and I apologize. I should have come up sooner. I just got caught up with things down there," she said, shifting away from him.

Billip had been a great help since day one, but she had let herself get to a point where she relied on him, as well as Mikkel, too much. It didn't help that both men, each with his own rugged brand of attractiveness, had been more than willing to cater to her every whim. It was nice, though, having two men that appreciated her in a different way than the City of Three's more scholarly types did.

"Perhaps I should head on downstairs," he said. "I'm sure Joline could use the help. It's been busier than a hive of flying toads these past few weeks. Good for business, but maybe not so much for babies. Poor little gal missed her momma something awful, even if it was for just a few hours. She's a light sleeper, that one."

Billip gave her a quick bow and turned to walk out.

"Billip, what do you make of these crowds? Do you think the rumors are true, that the underlings are taking over the south?"

A nervous look was in his eyes as he said, "There's something going on; I'm certain. Mikkel and I talk about it much, and we've been hearing lots of things, nothing like we haven't heard before, but up here in the North, well it's unheard of. Mikkel's worried — er —"

"Worried? About what?" she demanded, rising to her feet. There was something in Billip's voice that worried her.

"Er, nothing you need to concern yourself with."

"Tell me, Billip. Tell me!" she urged.

He rubbed the back of his neck and said, "I'd rather not; it's personal and all. Mikkel would kill me. Man's honor."

Now it would drive her crazy, not knowing what was being spoken about. She couldn't stand it, but she was certain she couldn't force the man to give in to her every whimsy. Or could she? As Billip stood there, eyes shifting back and forth, she shifted Erin from one breast to the other, taking her time in doing so.

"Billip," she said, parting her perfect full lips, "tell me what is on Mikkel's mind."

He blushed.

"All right! But promise you won't say anything."

"I won't," she assured him, recovering herself.

"He's worried about his boy, Nikkel."

"I didn't know he had a boy. Where is he?"

"Two-Ten City."

Kam felt a mix of anger and shame. Too many people were protecting her for her own good and not protecting themselves.

"How old is Nikkel?"

"About the same age as Georgio."

She wanted to slap somebody.

"Is there anything else I should know? Is the boy with his mother? Are there more children? And what about you, Billip? Certainly you have some children of your own."

He sucked in his breath and said, "None that have claimed me as of yet."

"Why doesn't he just go? Both of you? You don't need to stay around here. Go get Mikkel's boy and bring him back here where it's safe."

"I've tried to tell him it would be well, but we promised Venir."

Kam frowned, and her eyes began to water.

Billip cleared his throat and said, "I'm sorry, I didn't mean to say—"

"It's … it's fine, Billip."

But it wasn't. The mere mention of his name sent shivers through her. Sometimes, down in the tavern, she thought she heard his voice or laughter among the crowd, only to be left with a hollow feeling a moment later. That's why she liked to stay down in the tavern as much as she could, hoping he might swing back in the door, but she'd never admit that to herself.

"You all right?" he asked. She didn't even notice that he was sitting beside her with a hand on her knee.

"Billip, I know what you promised Venir, but the boys will be fine. Don't you think he'd understand?"

"Well, he always was pretty understanding. But, what about you, Kam? And baby Erin."

"Your promise was to take care of the boys. You've done that. Besides, seeing how I am the mother of his child, I think it's fair for me to reserve the right to speak for him in his absence. Don't you think?"

Billip tilted his head as he stroked the long hairs of his mustache

"I suppose, but—"

"Good. Now, I'll bring it up to Mikkel later—"

"No, you can't!" Billip stammered.

"Don't worry, Billip. I'll let him convince himself it was his idea. I'll fool him into asking me."

"Now, that's my kind of thinking. Cunning like a fox you are! Very well, then." Billip got up with a squeeze on her knee. "I'll be downstairs, then."

As he closed the door, Kam let out a heavy sob. She grabbed a handkerchief and blew her nose. Her life had been so much simpler before Venir had come and turned it inside out. Even though she had Erin, she still didn't know whether she was happy or sad.

"Ah, finally," she said, pulling the drowsy looking little girl away from her chest. "I see all of that screaming took a toll on you, you sweet little thing." Baby Erin cooed at the sound.

The little baby girl was sweet, with a thick mop of dark brown hair and light eyes that were opening and closing. Unlike Kam's little nose, Erin's was more broad like her father's, but the rest of her was petite, with little hands and feet topped off by a pink ribbon tied into a long braided lock of hair.

She hoisted Erin up in the hair.

"Whee!"

Erin's eyes widened before she let out a sweet little giggle on the way back down.

Kam felt all of her problems leave her in the moment as she stared into her daughter's bright little eyes. She was in control. Erin was happy. She was happy, but why couldn't she stay happy? She ran through the list.

Venir, Lefty, Georgio, Fogle, Billip, Mikkel … all men.

She nuzzled her baby's warm little body into her chest, patted her rear end and said, "I hope you fall for a much simpler kind of man that me, Erin because I don't want that little heart of yours breaking. They're hard to put back together."

Over by the windows she took notice of a rocking chair that had been a gift from Lefty and Master Gillem. The wood craftsmanship was worthy of the interiors of Royal castles, simple yet distinct. She hadn't used it yet, but the others had, from Billip to Joline. Master Gillem had been nothing but the perfect help in mentoring Lefty, and therein lay the problem: too perfect.

She patted Erin on the back, bringing forth a hearty burp.

"That's my girl." She hadn't lost her soft spot for Lefty, the tiny fair-haired halfling boy, but his not-so-innocent charms had not eluded her. He was hiding something, but it didn't bother her so much as it did Georgio. She kept telling herself they were teenage boys and that teens make mistakes, but that justification was a poor excuse on her behalf, and deep down, she knew it. Some days it was better not to try and resolve any problems at all than to bother with any of them. Some things have to work out on their own. So she told herself.

Outside, she could hear the carriages rolling over the cobblestones along with the usual greetings and pleasantries. Below the window sill was the entrance to the Magi Roost, and she recognized many patrons' voices sauntering in from a day of work in the magical city. Erin had gotten used to those sounds, and before long she was fast asleep. Kam laid her head back, closed her eyes and meditated.

She opened her eyes feeling at rest, with baby Erin still sound asleep on her chest.

Coffee.

Raising her arms up over her head and extending her fingers, she mouthed a silent incantation.

Snap-Snap.

The coals inside the stove fired with life, and the metal canister began to percolate. Two minutes later the aroma invigorated her as she laid Erin down inside her purple and olive colored cradle. She muttered another incantation, and the cradle began to rock and hum a soothing ancient tune.

"Nothing's quite like an invisible baby sitter," she said as she walked over and filled her ceramic mug. "You can thank your grandmother for that. Hmph. She even said it was the same one that I used to fall asleep to, but that was awfully long ago."

She stood near the cradle, sipping her coffee and looking out into the street. *Where is he?* All of the murmurings about the underlings had gotten to her, and the stories she overheard Billip and Mikkel telling Georgio disturbed her. She was convinced that Venir being missing had something to do with all this. *Only he could manage to piss off an entire host of underlings.* She let out a short giggle before she reached down and put her warm hand on his daughter's face. She wanted to Erin to know her father. She wanted him to come home and hold her in his arms. She wanted to kill him before anyone else did. She kept assuring herself that he wasn't dead, but every day made it seem more likely he was. Even Billip and Mikkel seemed to have resolved as much, judging by their subtle advances.

At some point you are going to have to let him go, Joline had begun to say.

But for Erin's sake she couldn't do that yet, and another thing bothered her as well: Where on Bish was Fogle Boon?

12

STRAPPED TO A TREE LIKE a frozen log, Fogle Boon awaited his inevitable death shivering his last moments of life away in utter misery. He didn't even bother to look up into the eyes of the mountain man coming his way gripping a gleaming bastard sword in his hairy hands. Deep down he felt shame, realizing his only friend left in the world was about to die as well. He couldn't, he wouldn't, watch his friend die first. Instead he was ready to go.

Keep your chin up before you die, Venir had said someone told him once.

"Bish!" he managed. His head felt like a block of ice as he raised it. At least he could try to volunteer his life first and maybe give Mood more time. He opened his mouth to speak, one last time, as the blade rose over his head.

"Did you say, '*I guess I'll be dying a virgin after all*'?"

The woman stood there, beautiful and cold, pink eyes filled with curiosity.

"I suppose," he said, then sneezed. "Aw … even that hurts."

Her next question caused his brilliant mind to thaw.

"So, you came up here to lose your virginity … to a druid?"

Fogle took a moment to reassure himself that she had said what she said she had. Lying wasn't his thing; he'd never needed it until now.

"Y—y-yes," he managed.

"Get me my log!" she ordered.

The big men looked at one another.

"NOW!"

Snow fell from the tree, coating Fogle as the big men burst into action. In a moment they had her propped back up before them.

She folded her arms below her ample and pleasing breasts and said, "So, why am I to believe that you—unlike every pig of a man in this world—have not been sleeping with harlots and treating uncommonly good women like whores?"

What a highly uncommon question! Fogle felt some of his inner strength return, and he was going to need every bit of it to pull off the rest of the lie. He was no story teller, but he was going to have to spin one if he wanted to make it through the day.

Here we go.

"I'm not so certain that it is possible to prove whether or not I am still a virgin, but I am, not that it matters at this point."

She kept her eyes away from his as she seemed to ponder his words.

"So, you seek to lose your virginity to a druid? Why? Certainly a common woman would do. What man travels so far to lose his innocence, a man of your age at that?"

Fogle felt his mind begin to smile from one side of his brain to the other. *She's a dolt? Is this possible? Go along with it.*

A woman beautiful, formidable and exotic sat before him, as picturesque as the great falls in the City of Three, and he had her undivided attention. The trick was keeping it.

"As you know, I am a mage of sorts, and I've been told that magic runs strongest in the veins of druids because they are the purest magic users of mankind. I want my legacy to be pure and strong." He bragged. "My mentors shielded me from my physical needs and desires until my time had come. My time is now they said, to find a druid woman, a gift of nature, and offer myself to her. If my seed is strong and she wishes to bear my child, then it shall be a strong, formidable force that even the underlings would fear to reckon with. It's—"

"Shut up! That is the most ridiculous thing I have ever heard. You are a lousy liar, but I still, for some reason," her eyes twinkled, "suspect you are a virgin." She rubbed his delicate chin. "Hmmm. Now, tell me, really, why you have sought me out, or I'll have my men pierce your eyes with an icicle."

So much for that, but at least she admits she is a druid.

"Any chance of being warm one last time before I die?"

She reached over and cupped his face in her ginger hands. A feeling of warmth slowly made its way through his face and down to his toes. Her breath was hot steam on his face, and it had the sweet scent of honey. Feeling the urge to kiss her pale lips, he leaned forward.

Slap!

"Seems you want more than you asked for, Virgin," she said, but her tone was not one of anger. "I'm waiting."

"I'm a virgin, but that's not why we are in these, or rather, your mountains. We have a dog, a giant one with two heads, named Chongo. He's sick, and Mood," he caught her eyebrows perching as she took a quick glance over her shoulder. Maybe he said too much. "…said only a druid might be able to heal him."

Slap!

She could have slapped him a hundred times, and he wouldn't have minded. He was still warm. *She's amazing.* He smiled.

"Why are you smiling and lying?" she demanded.

"I'm smiling because I can feel my toes again and because this is the only foreplay I've ever had," he said, offering a grin.

The fingers on her hand transformed into an array of long sharp sticks that reached over and dug into his shoulder.

"Is this foreplay amusing to you, Virgin Liar? Shall I dig a little deeper into your heart's desires?" she said, squeezing.

"Gah!" he blurted out as the wooden finger punctured through his robes into his skin and began to burn. "No, I swear it! There is such a dog, and that is why we are here: to heal it!" He was getting angry now. "Kill me if you must, but know that you are killing an innocent man! Your ogres, every smelly arsed one of them, needed to die! Oh, why does a woman as glorious as you consort with the likes of them?"

She released him.

"Druids don't pick and choose between the races. We each have our purpose. The ogres are no more good or evil than men."

"That's a bunch of slat! Does the same go for underlings as well? How is your consorting with them treating you? It seems to me that you are about as far away from them as anyone could be!"

She made no reply.

He didn't notice one of the mountain men whispering something in her ear. Fogle just stared into the ground.

"Humph," she said to the mountain man. "Are you certain?"

He gave a quick nod.

Once more, she addressed Fogle, "Describe this dog, then."

Fogle spilled out every little detail, from Chongo's two whipping tails to his large dangling tongues. He told her about the albino urchlings and the wounds they had caused. The druid hung on his every word with a growing look of concern on her captivating face.

"What is your name?" she asked.

"Fogle … Fogle Boon. And yours is?"

"Cass," She replied. "Virgin Fogle, did anyone ever tell you that you are a strange looking man?"

"Not to my face. Did anyone ever tell you that you are the most perfect thing they ever saw?"

"Flattery. Hah, you're as good at that as you are at lying. Cover his face and bind his hands," she ordered, turning away.

"But—"

She was gone. He was gagged, and a smelly sack now covered his face.

I'm not very good at this woman thing.

13

THE MORE VENIR STRUGGLED, THE more the ghastly one-eyed giant squeezed, pinching his ribs to the verge of cracking.

"S....top it!" The creature slurred out of deformed lips.

Venir would have none of that; he wasn't about to be a meal if there was anything that he could do about it. The monster, waist deep in the water, traversed from one side of the lake to the other. Ahead, Venir noticed the mouth of a cave. A black cavern over a hundred feet high loomed. *Not good.* Perhaps One Eye was planning to feed him to something else, or roast his skin in there.

Brool was still wrapped in his tight grip, the shaft warm to the touch, and if he'd get enough wiggle room he promised himself he would slice the giant's fingers off. *Wait and fight.* He let his taut muscles begin to slacken, but the grip that held him did little to subside as they entered the dark mouth of the cave.

The light of the mist disappeared as One Eye sloshed deeper into the darkness. Venir looked back for the glow of the mist, his memory flickering as to what illuminated the mist to begin with. Reason told him the mist should have blocked out the light, yet it provided it.

His eyes strained in the black behind the eyelets of his helm, but wherever he was, it was devoid of walls. How did the giant see in the black, with only one good eye no less? Something began to hum a tune, throaty and strange. It was his captor, whose belly continued to groan like an enormous bullfrog.

There was a loud slosh of water, followed by another that jolted Venir. Wet steps slapped on slick rocks he was certain he was hearing.

"Mmmmm-mah … almost time to eat," it said.

Venir's own stomach growled.

"Great Bish …"

"What you say, Little Giant?"

"I say," Venir yelled, "I'm gonna make your belly sour."

He bit his lip, drawing blood, as the giant shook him like a rattle. Miserable, maniacal and mortified at the thought of being eaten, Venir fought against letting his efforts subside. *Patience.* He glanced up one last time into the hot, rotten breath of the giant that was now shadowed from an unknown source of light. As he twisted around, his eyes beheld something he never would have imagined: a forest, filled with an odd assortment of strange vegetation. Green, purple and white leaves hung from branches of trees that stood taller than the giant. The ground was a familiar red, red clay.

It could not be.

No, it was not the Red Clay Forest, but it could have been, aside from the fact that it was inside of a cave and illuminated by a million speckles of yellow and orange lights that littered the sky. There was fruit hanging in abundance: green apples, purple pears and deep red cherries the size of his hand. The deformed giant stuffed him into the high branches of one of the trees. His big ugly face had a smile as he patted his big belly.

"Hungry, little giant must eat?"

Venir fought the urge to stick his axe spike into its other eye, opting to stick it into the knotted grey branch instead. He crunched into the first fruit that he could grab. It was succulent and filling. *Delicious.* Three bites into it and the only thing left was the core. He climbed down along the trunk and plucked another apple from the branches. Nearby, the giant was stuffing handfuls of the tiny fruit into his big jaws. Venir kept his distance as he ate, Brool gripped at his side. He looked around the wondrous cave and felt just as lost as ever.

"Good? Belly full?" One Eye said, with a throaty child-like voice.

Venir nodded.

"Now we play?"

Venir's mind began its trek back into reality. As his ravenous hunger and thirst were quenched, his strength and sanity began to return. He had a choice: chop the scary looking giant down like rotting timber or let his insane journey in the Under Bish play out. He ran his thumb along Brool's keen edge, drawing blood. *Must be real.*

He scanned his surroundings: trees as far as he could see, the ground covered with soft mosses, thick grasses and beds of flowers. It all had a dim hue, unnatural but not foreboding. He had the feeling he could live here for a while, in peace, not harming himself or anyone. He looked at his twelve foot tall captor and thought of Georgio, Kam, Lefty and even Melegal. He took another bite of fruit.

"What kind of game do you want to play?"

The giant stood up, big eye blinking and hands clapping.

"Name game," he said, rubbing his belly.

"All right, what is your name?" Venir asked.

"No, no, we don't play like that. You have to guess my name. I have to guess your name. See? Fun. Fun like that."

Stupid like that.

"Well then," Venir said as he swung Brool onto his shoulder and began to walk around. "If I guess your name, what do I win?"

"You get to play another game with me."

"No, that's not good." Venir rubbed his aching ribs and sighed. "I'll need something better than that."

"Like what?"

"I need to go home. To Bish, the world above this. Can you take me there if I win?"

"The river will take you there, but it's a bad place. Don't go there."

Venir gawped. The other giant hadn't lied. All he had to do was follow the river after all.

"BONE!" he swung his axe into a tree.

"Hey, don't do that!" The giant warned him, storming over. "No hurt the tree."

Venir ripped the axe out. His patience was lost as he bore down on the giant and stabbed it in the foot.

"OW!" It yelped, jumping up and down. "Why you hurting me?"

Pity and remorse for his action fled Venir as he looked upon the distraught giant's ugly face.

"I need to get back to BISH now! Can you take me there? And remember, if you lie, I'll cut your tongue out."

Leaves and fruit fell from the trees, the giant's ghastly scream was so loud. Venir covered his ears, but now was not the time for mercy. He would have his answers.

"I feed you, Little Giant, and you stab me. You don't play nice."

"Can you take me to Bish or not?"

"Not if you don't play with me first," the giant said, holding his bleeding foot.

One Eye cringed as Venir hoisted his axe over his head.

"S......top it! S...top it! Mean little giant!"

"You'll live, you big one-eyed baby." Venir poked him in the leg with Brool. "And no tricks."

"I take you, you play with me."

"NO! You take me and I promise I'll find you someone to play with. I've got things to do."

"Let me guess your name first."

"It's Venir."

"No! Don't tell me! Drat. You stink, Venir. You worse than the giants that don't play with me 'cause I ugly."

"Are you a runaway?"

"NO!"

Venir shook his head. He didn't have time to deal with this nonsense. He wanted to go home.

"Just take me out of here." One Eye pulled his knees up to his chest and buried his face.

Venir sighed. Perhaps he needed another approach, and seeing how he wasn't starving to death he could exercise a little more patience. He grabbed a purple pear that filled his hand and took a hearty bite. Fruit wasn't ever a steady part of his diet, just an occasional substitute for meat and bread when he was out on the hunt. It was tasty, not juicy like a steak of venison, but just as satisfying.

As his aggravations began to subside, the taut muscles in his broad shoulders began to soften. He stuck his axe in the ground.

"So, Giant, what is your name?"

The big bald head waddled back and forth.

"Nothing."

"Is it Big Baldie?"

The giant grumbled a no.

"How about Dragon Rider?"

His head popped up, his big eye glimmering.

"No like that!"

"Ah … Dragon Crusher, then?"

One Eye rose up from the ground to his full height, arms raised over twenty feet in the air, fists clenched. Venir grabbed Brool and stepped back into the trees. *Oh no.*

"Barton like that!" he bellowed, pounding his chest.

Yes! I've got his name.

"Ah …then it's Barton the Dragon Crusher!" Venir yelled.

"Barton hate the dragons!"

"What about the one called Blackie?"

Barton's eye widened beneath his uni-brow as he flopped to the ground and faced Venir.

"You know Blackie?"

"Yes. As a matter of fact, I clipped his wing with my axe after he tried to scorch my flesh from my bones. I sent him wailing into the mist yelping like a wounded dog."

Barton poked his log sized finger into Venir's chest.

"You not lie?"

"No."

"Baron hate Blackie. Blackie always bring Barton home. That's why I hide in this cave. Blackie no come in here and take me away. Barton safe."

"Barton," Venir said, "you also told me your name."

"Huh … ah, stupid me!" he slapped his head.

"You have to take me back to Bish now, Barton. I won the game."

"No," Barton huffed.

"Barton, do the giants break their word to you?"

It frowned and said, "Yes."

"Does it make you mad when they lie?"

"Yes."

"Well, you're doing the same thing to me. You don't want to be like them, do you?"

Barton got up, scratching his chest, big eye blinking. Venir searched the eye of the giant. It was an odd creature, humanoid, scarred and misshapen, that moved more like a child than a man. Venir felt some sorrow for it, but now was not the time for compassion. Now was the time to find freedom. *Come on, you lout, be honest this once. I don't give a slat for the rest of the time.*

"Barton, you get me out of here and I'll tell you where to find a friend."

It'd be pretty hard to sneak up on underlings with you around.

"You be my friend. I stay on Bish with you."

"Sorry Barton, but I've got things to do there. I can't take you where I'm going. All I can offer is a friend, here, that you can count on. He can take care of you, assuming he's still alive." He lied. Boon the wizard was dead in his mind by all accounts. He'd seen the giants swat him on the wall, and he figured if anything, he'd splattered like a bug. Of course, there was the were-rat too, a sly female of silky gray fur. The question was, had any of it at all been real? Barton seemed to confirm that. But, was Barton real? For all Venir knew, he was still walking along the river. Maybe he was even dead or imprisoned somewhere, for that matter.

"What? You try to give me a dead friend. What kind of friend is that? I'm not stupid!"

Yes you are.

"Either way," Venir placed his fists on his hips, "you still have to take me home."

Barton pounded his chest with his meaty hand, shaking his belly and saying, "I have honor." A large tear dripped from his eye and splashed onto the ground. "I take you home, Venir, little giant."

"Why do you call me that, little giant?"

"Hmmm," Baron rubbed his chin and said, "maybe tiny giant better. You smell like a giant."

Ew.

"I hope not."

Venir didn't understand the entire giant thing. It wasn't the first time he had heard that, and he couldn't help but think there was something to it.

"Hee hee, you funny, Venir. Mean, but funny." Barton had a devious look in his eye. "Uh … Venir, I can't take you with your stuff. Giant magic not like metal. You must leave it behind."

The hairs stood up all over his body.

"*I can't do that,*" he exclaimed.

"Then you have to stay," Barton said, eyeing his axe with a keen interest.

Venir had the feeling the giant was lying and wanted the armament for himself. *Toys to play with for an under grown man.* Not so stupid after all, Barton had shown he had another card to play. What choice did Venir have but to believe him? *Think.* He had an idea.

"Tell you what, Barton: since you are helping me I'll leave it all as a gift, to remember me by."

"Really?"

"Yes, but first, one last game, for fun. I'm going to hide them in the forest here, so they'll be safe. When you get back, you can have some fun finding them."

"That does sound like fun. But don't hide them too hard. Barton has trouble seeing sometimes."

"All right, well can you turn around while I go and hide them? And no peeking."

"Hee hee, this is fun. I'll even count," he said, turning his back to Venir. "One … Two …"

As Venir clutched his axe, he had the feeling now would be the best time to brain the brute. Maybe he didn't need Barton after all. *Gonna have to trust him.*

Venir dropped the armament into the sack along with several fruit. *Why not.* He folded the sack and stuffed it beneath his shirt.

"Well enough, I'm finished."

Barton whirled around, dumbstruck.

"Already?"

"Yep, I made it easy," Venir said, arms folded across his chest. "Can we go now?"

Barton pushed up some branches as he peered deeper into the grove of trees and said, "This will be easy." He looked over at Venir, stroked his hair and added, "You look much better now. You have pretty hair like a girl, but you still make an ugly girl."

Venir bit his tongue. *You still make an ugly giant.*

Barton extended his hand and said, "All right, it's time to go. Hang on tight. I'm not very good at this."

Venir grabbed the giant around the wrist and held on for dear life as he felt his body turn inside out.

14

"**M**UST YOU STILL BE HERE?" Melegal slung his cap onto the mantle where a small fire blazed from underneath. "You keep saying you'll change the locks, but you never do," Haze picked up his cap from the mantle and dusted it off before hanging it on a small nail beside the fire.

He sneered as he pulled off his boots and sat down in a pillowed high-back chair that sat in the corner near the fire. He didn't give Haze a single glance as she pushed a stool beneath his feet. He laid his head back and closed his eyes, tracking every movement of Sefron in his mind. *Magic.* The sloppy cleric had foiled him again, and his head ached for it.

As he ran his bony fingers through his salt and pepper hair he could hear Haze creeping through Detective McKnight's former apartment that he now called his own. A smell of spiced soup was in the air, and he heard a cork being pulled from a wine bottle. His face allowed the ever slightest smile while the fire began roasting his toes.

Haze sat beside him on a much smaller chair, holding out a bowl of soup and a goblet.

"I tell you to leave, threaten your paltry life and there you sit like an urchin offering me more piss porridge. I'm beginning to think your sisters are the brightest of the three nitwits."

He sat up in the chair and sniffed the air.

"They haven't been in here, have they? It smells like the fat one's sweat and armpits."

Haze sat there, plain and serene, quite content among his insults. She'd been like this since the day he diddled her like a trollop: fawning and obedient, like he was a Royal of sorts. Despite his reminders that she was of as little worth to him as a field mouse in a cat house, she stuck around like a stubborn child that wouldn't go home. She had even painted her nails, combed her hair and worn more revealing clothes that offered little more than a pair of skinny legs below a tight little rump. She even smelled good.

"You look tired," she remarked.

Melegal swiped the goblet from her hand, swished it around his mouth and spat it into the fire, bringing a sizzle. Octopus rumbled from his spot on the hearth, his back muscles rippling beneath his black coat before lowering.

"Are you trying to poison me, Woman?" he exclaimed, pulling the bowl from her hands.

She blanched. "I thought you might like something different. I'm sorry. I'll get your usual."

She scampered away to grab another goblet, a look of worry in her grey eyes.

He sipped the soup. It was good, not Royal good, but better than his usual fare. He hated to admit it, but she was pretty good at making soup and some other things, too. He grunted.

"Wine please," he said, handing her the bowl.

"Ah," he sipped and swished, "so much better. What was that drivel you gave me?"

"It's called port. I heard many people talking of it in the city. I thought you would—"

"Please don't think on my behalf, understand?"

"Yes Melegal. I'm sorry. I'll pour it out."

He waved her off and said, "Nay, perhaps I'll serve it to my enemies one day. Port, you say?"

She nodded, a half-smile cracked over his thin pale red lips.

"Never heard of it," he lied.

Haze reached over and touched his feet. Her touch was light as a feather, almost soft enough to tickle.

He sighed.

"Must you maintain this obsession with my glorious feet? Do you miss those days beneath the castles, rubbing the feet and arses of the self-glorifying and vain?"

Without saying a word, she twisted and rubbed, while he drank, frowned and enjoyed.

As much as he wanted to give in to the moment, his mind began running over his checklist.

Kill Sefron. Find the Slergs and have them killed. Do what Lord Almen says. Do what Lorda Almen says. Don't get yourself killed. Kill Sefron. Uncover threats to Castle Almen. Find valuable information and deliver it to Lord Almen. Avoid the Castle. Avoid the Almens. Drink more wine. Sample more port.

"Ah! Easy now, I'm not one of your hooved sisters."

She rolled up his pants legs and rubbed his calves.

"So, Melegal, have you found what you're looking for?"

"No."

Without looking at him she said, "I can help."

"No, you can't help, and quit asking."

"But I found some Slergs," she reminded him.

She actually had helped. He hated that.

He pushed is pants leg down and said, "Yes, but I could have paid any urchin a silver booger and that would have yielded the same results."

"I'm not finished," she said as he stood up.

"My feet are fine," he said, removing his vest and shirt.

She grabbed his arm and pulled him back.

"I'm not talking about rubbing your bloody feet!"

In a single motion he had her wrist twisted behind her back. He made a throaty whisper in her jeweled ear saying, "What are you talking about?"

She pushed her hips back into his and said, "I think I know where the rest of the Slergs are."

He twisted her wrist a little harder and whispered, "You lie!"

He felt her chest begin to heave.

"No, I can prove it!" she squealed.

With his other hand he grabbed the back of her hair and began to pull.

He didn't know whether to believe her or not, but it didn't matter. His blood began to run hot as she let out a soft moan.

"Tell me everything you know, Haze, or I'll take my belt to you."

He saw the goose bumps rise on her neck as she shuddered.

"There is a price, Rogue. Either pay it or kill me," she panted.

"You better hope I don't do both," he said as he pulled her into a small candlelit bedroom and slammed the door closed with his foot.

<h1 style="text-align:center">15</h1>

A SMALL GROUP OF RAGGED MEN carrying small torches traversed the tunnels beneath the City of Bone. Each was wrapped from head to toe in torn and tattered clothes, their faces covered in dirty cowls, some feet bare, the others sandaled. Their soft steps and breathing could barely be heard except for one in the rear, a large one that seemed able to plug the narrow corridor with his bulk. He was bigger, significantly so, his breathing heavy, his footsteps loud. He was drawing the ire of another who continued his complaints from the front.

"Leezir, your giant urchin continues to slow us," Hagerdon said with a sneer in his voice. "It's time to cut bait and run."

"Must you be so dramatic, Fool?" Leezir replied, pushing his way through a massive water pipe that was as dry as a bone. "Can you even count, you moron? How many heads do you see?"

Hagerdon pulled his cowl down, revealing a shaven head in the dim torchlight as he hurried along. They all were shaved now; it was the best way to conceal their identities from the searching eyes above, as well as those below. Hagerdon hated it. He loved his thick locks of glorious hair, and he missed the feeling of painted finger tips running through it. All his leader Leezir could offer him was that he wouldn't have to worry about lice, or dandruff for that matter. He scoffed; he'd never had a flake in his life.

"I know, eight Slergs, but we have an army of man-urchins at our disposal," he said, now crawling over a patch of wet and sticky muck on his knees and elbows. Even worse were the comings and goings of abhorrent stench, but he'd managed to get accustomed to them.

Leezir shook his white cudgel in Hagerdon's face.

"You are such a fool, Nephew! Two weeks ago there were fifteen of us. The man-urchins have suffered even greater losses taking bribes for our cause, and now you, still impudent and young, want to abandon a fighting man who is three in one? Was he not the one who pulled you from your grave a mere week ago when the City Watch had us by the balls? And now you want to cut loose the only redeemable man, er boy, er whatever from us?"

Hagerdon was adamant.

"Yes."

He could see Leezir's eyes blaze like fire underneath his black cowl as he swallowed hard and stepped back. When the cudgel began to glow there was a gasp from behind.

The last few months had been hard. The once mighty Slerg House was being dwindled away. Not one Royal house, not even the lowest on the tier, would give them audience. If anything, they gave them away. Lord Almen would not end his hunt until he was certain every single threat was gone.

Leezir added as he turned around, "It's days like this that I wish it was you who died and not your brother Creighton. He was sensible."

His hand clutched the pommel of his sword, but Leezir was already hurrying down the dingy corridor.

"SLAT!" Leezir screamed from up ahead.

Hagerdon and the rest caught up and groaned at the source of their leader's aggravation. A five foot iron grate barred their path, its iron bars eroding but thick.

Leezir kicked. Hagerdon pulled.

"We're just going to have to go back up top," Hagerdon said.

"Is that so?" Leezir walked up on his toes. "Then you go back and lead the hounds from our trails. I'm sure they won't devour your scent." He smacked his cudgel into the stone walls. "Does anyone else want to go back and face the City Watch or suffer an inquisition of Detective Melegal and his brood of Almen thugs?"

No one said a word, until Hagerdon broke the silence.

"It seems we have no choice but to go another way. Certainly we can double back and find another course or wait until night and take our chances on the streets. Leezir, we can't hide forever down here."

Month after month they had stayed down below, stealing from above like common orphans. The man-urchins did most of the work, but the results were paltry. Hagerdon had his fill of the stink, rot and filth that was now his life. Just one more time he wanted to take a shower, adorn clean clothes and swing his steel in one last battle to the death. There was nothing dignified in living like a rodent, but Leezir, in his obsession to avenge himself on the Almens, insisted on this course. And being somewhat of a coward, Hagerdon followed those orders. Life is preferable to death after all, no matter how slatty it gets.

Leezir let out a long drawn out sigh. His shoulders slouched as he slid down the wall onto his haunches. The others followed suit except Brak, who stood like a golem at the end.

"Perhaps, brothers, Hagerdon is right. Our time may have run its course. Jubilee, dear, have we been followed? And please say your pepper left the dogs from our trail."

A small figure crept forward, naked feet pushing through the grime before taking Leezir's hand.

"Aye Grandfather, I've lost the dogs, ten tunnels since. But my pepper is low. I'm sorry."

He patted her ragged head and said, "Well enough, dear one. And, Taggert, are we still on course to the northern most corner of the city?"

"Aye, Leezir. Direction's good. I'm certain."

"Hmmm … I believe my ears have detected something disturbing," Leezir said.

Hagerdon frowned as he heard something, too.

A sound of barking dogs was echoing down the corridor.

The little girl's eyes widened.

Hagerdon's swords sang from their sheaths.

Rising to his feet, Leezir's cudgel burst aglow.

"This is it, Slergs! We will survive this, not all but some. Brak, today you live or die a Slerg."

Brak was coming their way.

"Brak," Hagerdon said, barring his path, "you oaf, what are you doing? Get in front and protect us!"

Everyone cleared out as Brak waded past them as if they weren't there. There was nothing but stark determination in his close-set eyes when he wrapped his big meaty hands around the iron bars.

"You idiot! Get back there and fight, Coward. There's no doorway to run though there."

Brak's short powerful arms began to pull.

"Heave Brak!" Leezir prompted in his ear.

The massive man-boy squatted down, putting his arms and legs into it.

"*Hurk!*"

Hagerdon couldn't hide his amazement as the metal began to groan.

The yelping of the hounds became louder.

"Pull, Man! Pull and I'll roast you the fattest sow you ever saw!" Hagerdon promised.

Sweat was rolling down Brak's forehead as his big face began to turn red and purple under the torch glow. The bars began to bend, the ever slightest.

One of the Slergs said with astonishment, "It's bending! Bend it, Brak!"

Brak dug his heels into the lip of the grate and tugged. The iron groaned in defiance before giving in to living muscle which had turned to steel. The first bar rolled upward.

"I can't believe it!"

Brak grabbed the next bar and pulled.

"Hurry, Brak!" Jubilee cheered.

The bar groaned and gave way. The hounds became louder in the distance, intertwined with the shouting voices of the City Watch.

Leezir shoved Jubilee through the gap.

"Quick everyone, go through!"

There was little more than two feet of space to squeeze through the bars, but none hesitated. One by one they crawled through, tearing clothes and skin, scraping sides. Hagerdon was the last to go.

"Come on, Brak! Bend one more and join us. The roasted sow is waiting!" he said, his green eyes glinting in the torch light.

Brak reached down and bent the first bar downward.

"What are you doing, you buffoon? You'll get yourself killed! Get over here!"

Brak bent the second bar back down and slumped against the wall, chest heaving.

"No!" Jubilee cried. "Brak, no!"

"Go," Brak gasped. "I'm only slowing you down. Goodbye, Jubilee." He reached through the bars, wiping the tear from her cheek. "Slat on the rest of you."

Leezir stood there, face pressed against the bars, his wizened face bewildered. He shook his head.

"Come on, Jubilee. He's bought us time, no reason to stand around and watch his slaughter. Move with haste now; the Watch may have magic afoot, too."

Jubilee sobbed as they scurried away, her eyes drifting back then out of sight, but Hagerdon remained.

"Here," he said, tossing a knife at Brak's feet. "You'll need that in close quarters, you lout. Stupid like your father, I see. Giving your life for others." Hagerdon added a quick salute. "Maybe what I taught you will give you an extra minute to realize how stupid you are."

Brak sat with a glum look on his face, watching him go.

The barking dogs were echoing with loud ferocity now as Hagerdon bolted down the tunnel, happy to know that Brak, the son of Venir, was about to be eaten alive. *At least I gave him a fighting chance before he becomes dog food.*

"More sow for me."

16

F OGLE AWOKE IN DARKNESS, HEAD aching and unable to move. *Where am I?* He tried to choke down his panic as he struggled with his bonds. He found comfort in the fact that his fingertips were no longer frozen, or the rest of him for that matter. Wherever he was, he was upright, sitting on soft ground of an unfamiliar texture. *Mood.* Was his lone protector with him or dead? Mood had told him there would be days like this when you adventured outside your home, and he needed every detail he could find of his surroundings if he was going to formulate a plan ... to escape.

Mood's advice had seemed silly at the time, weeks ago, but the Blood Rangers' wisdom seemed crystal clear. *If you don't have your eyes, use your ears.* He listened. There was a soft rustling nearby, and the wind was rolling over a canvas, like a flag. *A tent.* He balled up into a knot as something growled, hungry and horrible. A picture of the big wolves with those rows of pointed, saliva-dripping canine teeth appeared in his mind. Hadn't Cass said she would feed him to them?

Use your nose, Mood had told him.

"It smells like dogs," he said out loud. He tightened his lips as something padded by him, brushing fur across the bridge of his nose. He took a deep draw through his nose. "And scented candles?"

Skin, he thought.

It was warmer, much more so, as if a fire was nearby, but the sound of crackling wood was not there. As happy as he was to be able to feel himself again, he could only imagine his situation had gotten worse. The woman, Cass, seemed a little touched in the head. Her voice was eerie, and her pink eyes were shifty. Mood had said druids were tricky, and with this one he was certain she was everything a druid could be: strange, sneaky and magnificent. He thought he could smell her breath.

"Aaaaa-CHOO!" he sneezed.

The wolves barked and growled. He could feel them nipping at his face.

"HEEL!" a strong feminine voice commanded. *Cass?*

"Don't make another sound, Virgin Fogle, or my wolves will devour you," she said, her voice dark, ugly, dangerous.

He didn't care.

"If I'm going to—"

A pair of jaws snapped at his face.

"Egad!" he cried. His body began to shiver at the thought of the canines crunching his bones. *Make a plea.*

He cleared his throat.

"Can I at least glance at you on last time, Cass? At least I can dream I'm no longer a virgin in my last moments."

She made a funny sound. Next, he heard footsteps, like petals coming his way. All of the most wonderful fragrances of nature filled his nose as something soft and plentiful brushed into his face. He swallowed as he felt two petite hands working the knot behind his head and slowly removing his blindfold.

"Happy, Virgin Fogle?" Cass's chest was inches from his nose. A pink gossamer robe adorned her exotic figure. Her skin was perfect: translucent and soft, and her white hair seemed impossibly curly and long. Another wave of feeling washed over him, not the kind he expected to have when he was about to die, but something else quite unexpected ... Lust.

"Hmmm ..." she purred as she got down on her knees and began loosening the bonds around his ankles.

Fogle didn't want to take his eyes off of a single inch of her figure, but he fought to do so. His eyes flitted over his surroundings. A tent surrounded them over the top of a bed of green grass. Six large timber wolves had them both surrounded, sitting, licking their chops and other parts as well. Forty one candles of all shapes and sizes were in the room, eleven lit, flames wavering from a draft. Incense sticks burned from a small mantle made of trees. He never imagined he'd experience that again. Three sheep skin rugs. Fifteen pelts of fur. And in the middle, laying over most of the grass, was the pelt of a silverback grizzly bear. He knew, because Mood had killed one weeks earlier. His eyes went back to Cass. His mouth was watering, no longer dry as he began to thirst like he never thirsted before.

"Virgin Fogle," she whispered in his ear, "you are here for a reason. It can only be, because I too am a virgin."

He tried to find the words to speak but could not as she pressed her finger to his lips.

"I've rejected the world of men, Fogle. They can't be trusted, but I know your words are true." His legs trembled as she pulled him up from his chair. "I want to help you, and I want you to help me. I've waited so long for this."

Oh my!

He searched for her eyes, but he could not find them as she pulled him down onto the grizzly pelt. As his heart thundered throughout this body his brilliant mind fought one last time to regain control. *Druids can't be trusted,* Mood had warned.

"Take me, Fogle," she said, pressing her full body into his.

All of the passion buried inside him exploded as he kissed her.

She tugged at his hair, pulling him down on top of her. He glanced at the wolves one last time and said, "This isn't how I imagined it."

"Me either," she added, pulling off her robe. "Disappointed?"

His smile was as broad as a rainbow.

"No, it's an adventurer's life for me." Her chuckle was low and wicked, but he didn't hear a thing.

Outside the tent, Mood awakened inside his icy cocoon. Nearby, two mountain men were sharpening their blades and chatting. One said to the other, "Shame he won't even have time to enjoy it."

17

FOR THE FIRST TIME IN his life, Sefron saw pure evil. It lurked behind the black eyes of the Vicious that squeezed his life from his throat. He managed a sickening gag as his tongue rolled inside his mouth like a salted slug. His mental pleas to be released quickly gave way to despair as he began to slat on himself.

"Release him," a cool voice said from somewhere.

Sefron fell hard to the ground, both knees cracking on the stone as he fought for a breath of air. He hacked, wheezed and sat confused for over a minute before he managed to compose himself. He pulled his skinned up knees to his chest and looked up.

The black creature, inhuman, cat-faced, a monstrous hulk, was now standing behind a much lither figure. An underling stood tall in his black chain mail, a pair of sheathless swords hung criss-crossed on its back, their gleaming edges keener than the sharpest razor. A bandolier of knives was wrapped around its chest. Its eyes were like copper ore, its hair short, almost shaven to its head. The underling was known to Sefron as Kierway, a black ranger of his kind, he had boasted, and the finest swordsman of his craft. The underling man seemed every bit as formidable as the newcomer, but in a different sort of way.

Kierway had his hands on his hips as he said, "Do you have it, Human?"

"Nay, Master," Sefron said, falling to his knees, "but I am close."

Something flashed through the air, and Sefron wailed in misery. A small throwing knife now protruded from his knee.

"Human, I have ten more of these, you know, some poisoned, others not," Kierway said, juggling three in one hand. "I'm beginning to question your loyalty. Perhaps your needs are being fulfilled above, and you no longer desire what I have offered."

Sefron's arm shot out despite his agony.

"No Master Kierway! I am close. Oh so close. The key shall soon be yours. I know where it is, but I don't have the skills to acquire — YEE-OUCH!"

Another knife buried itself deep in his shoulder.

A cave moth fluttered in the dank air only to be cut down by Kierway's longsword in one fluid motion.

Sefron blinked hard.

"Did you see that, Human? Fast, wasn't it?" Kierway began to saunter around. "My, it's been a long journey, only to wind up here and find out that you have been an utter failure. Hmmm … I can't help but wonder how long it would take me to cut your leg into twenty pieces."

Sefron's blood went cold as he watched in helpless horror as Kierway's swords buzzed in the air like humming bird wings. He had to survive. He would survive. He would have vengeance on all of those Royals who had used him for decades. The City of Bone would be run over by underlings, and he was promised a castle and all the human slaves he wanted of his own. All he needed was the key.

"Y-yes, Master Kierway. May I beg of you, this key, will you share with me what it does?"

"NO!" Kierway said, plucking his blades from Sefron's wounds.

"Ah …," he stammered and groaned as he tried to speak, "But …"

"Time is running out, Human," Kierway said as he and the Vicious walked back into the darkness. "When you get it, we will know. Get it soon, or I shall find someone else to gain the prize."

NO!

Sefron stiffened as he sat up. Grimacing, he pulled out a small jar and applied ointment to his wounds. It burned, sealing the wound shut, but he was used to it. Kierway had stabbed him many times over the years, just not this many times at once. Sefron fought his way back to his feet and began the painful walk back up the stairs. He thought he knew where the key was, but he would need help trying to get it. Who would he have to fool to get it? *Maybe Detective Melegal can be useful after all.*

18

It was a gruesome scene, a man and woman, neither more than a day over thirty, torn and broken in broad daylight. The City Watch, decorated in their brown and gray, mired with hate and grime, remained casual about their business. They had seen death in the streets of Bone before, although this situation was a little more unique than the rest. The dead man, a well-known labor boss of the 14th District, lay in a pool of blood, his head missing.

"I'm telling you, I saw the man twist his head from his shoulders and toss it up on the roof."

"Hrmph," the watch sergeant said, "and what about the woman? How come she's still got her head?"

The residents murmured. They didn't normally fool with the Watch, and answering questions usually got you into more trouble than it was worth, but this time things were different. This time, they were under attack and needed protection, of some sort, anyway.

"The monster hit her so hard with its fist I heard her neck snap like a busted pallet. The man pulled his sword and lunged, but the murderer was much faster. Grabbed him by the neck by one hand he did, lifted him from the ground and squeezed."

Another chimed in.

"The man, the dead one, he was big, too, and the other, picked him up like a child, rattled him in the air, then twisted his head off."

The watch sergeant spit brown juice on the ground and wiped the sweat from his brow on his sleeve.

"No man twisted his head off! That's impossible. That's a cut! Idiots!"

"Did too!"

The sergeant nodded his head saying, "Well, did any one of you get a closer look at this big monster of a man? I'm hearing lots of stories, but not many descriptions. And by the way, where is the man's sword that he drew? Which one of you stole it?"

"The monster stole it, not us!"

The watch sergeant grabbed the uppity man by his shirt collar and said, "Don't talk to me like that."

"I pay my fees, I'll say what I—*oomph!*"

The man crumpled in a heap under the force of the Watchman's punch.

"Any more of you want to discuss your fees?"

The small group backed away, but one remained. An older woman, heavy set with deep wrinkles in her forehead, jutted her hip out and said, "That's ten murders in the past few months, and they not so much as stopped yet. And I hear the other districts got murders, too." She spat juice on the road. "What's you gonna do about that?"

He slid his watch stick from behind his belt and began to slap it into his hand.

"Heads up!" a voice yelled from above.

Clonk.

A man's head bounced off the cobble stones and rolled at his feet. It was the labor boss, his long yellow hair matted with blood.

The woman said, "He kinda looks like you, Blondie. Seems the monster-man doesn't like pretty hair like yours. Ain't it true, all them dead men had straw colored hair? Big fellows, too, same as you, except I think your belly's a bit fuller."

The Watchman gawped a bit, his Adams apple rolling under his chin.

The feisty woman began twisting her fingers in her blonde hair and added. "What about that other man, two roads over, everything chopped up from his neck down to his toes? Wasn't he one of yours?" She cackled, but she wasn't alone. It wasn't often that the citizens got a chance to poke at the City Watch. "It's a shame you all aren't yellow headed, then that monster would be a hero."

The lead Watchman looked up on the rooftop and yelled, "Get down here, Clovis. The rest of you," there were four watchmen in all, "get a cart and take them to the morgue, and we'll give the family a day to claim them." He straightened himself up and said, "You fine citizens of Bone better get your stories straight. Whoever is doing this is a man, not a wight, underling or ghoul. It's just some crazy bastard with a sword that is touched in the head. Lock your doors, don't go fooling around at night. As of now there's a curfew."

They groaned.

"And it starts now. Whoever it was must be close; this just happened less than an hour ago. If you see anyone strange, just whistle. In the meantime—"

Somebody whistled.

"Fine, I was being kind, but if yer going to be a bunch of pigs arses—"

Clovis shouted from the roof top.

"Hey! It was me! Look," he said, pointing down the roadway.

A man stood tall and broad a little ways down the road. A bastard sword stained in blood was gripped in his hands. His armor, partial plate, had the insignia of a Royal, and the rest of his body was draped with a dark cloak with a cowl wrapped over his head.

Most of the crowd gasped, but the woman screamed.

The sergeant drew his sword and yelled, "You're under arrest!" The other watchmen followed suit, swords in shaking hands. Clovis watched unblinking from above.

"VEE-MAN!" the man in the road cried.

"Get him!" the leader ordered. The City Watch charged.

CHOP! One Watchman's head was split in twain.

CLANG!

SWIPE! Another fell, writhing in his blood, screaming for mercy as his entrails were spilled.

CHOP! The third turned to run a split second too late.

The leader fell back on his footsteps, gawping in horror.

Fear managed to pull his tongue from the roof of his mouth as he screamed, "Someone go for reinforcements!"

Only the sound of running feet and doors slamming shut greeted him, then he stood there all alone.

"VEE-MAN!" He slipped and fell as he turned to run. The man snorted a laugh, coming his way on heavy legs with armor and weapons creaking and clanking.

Tonio saw a big man with straw colored hair falling to the ground and screaming something at him. What the man was saying didn't matter, as he assumed they could only be more insults from Venir. He thought he'd killed his adversary, if not once, a dozen or more times, only to see him back on the streets again, gloating and mocking him. His broad face and yellow hair was always mocking and taunting him.

He swung into the man's leg and watched it skitter a bloody trail across the road. He followed up with a deep swing into the man's heaving chest, oblivious to the blade that was thrust into his side. It was a pinch at worst in his deranged mind as he swiped the blood from his mouth, knocked the man's cap from his head, pulled him up by the hair and chopped off his head. Somewhere nearby a man screamed, and he peered up on the roof and gazed at a man covering his mouth, tears filling his eyes.

He looked at the face of his vanquished foe, Venir, or so he wanted to believe, and hurled the head through a window.

"Vee-man!"

Bloody sword in hand, Tonio departed from the scene, still hungry for vengeance. He would kill them all if he had to, and make his mother proud. The once empty streets began to fill as he went, and not one person crossed his path. The whispers of horror and sounds of pursuit became loud in his ears as he disappeared into the tunnels beneath the City of Bone. How many more times would he have to kill Venir before Tonio could return home to Castle Almen?

In the darkness he huddled inside a small cell, a former home of other miscreants that all now were dead and washed away in the sewers. He pulled at his hair and mumbled. He knew he didn't always used to be this way, that he had a home, a mother and father. He had eaten at the finest tables, and beautiful women had filled his bed. Everything was confusing though, distorted, blurry, vague and twisted. He snatched a rat and bit into it.

Where was McKnight? That man could help him, give him guidance to something, but without direction all he had was vengeance on his mind, and he would enact it over and over again until the last Venir was gone.

Bish have mercy on the fair-haired citizens of Bone.

19

"THE BLACK FIENDS FROM THE Underland have come!" a warrior, fortyish, with a beard touched by grey clamored. Mikkel and Billip had the man pinned up against the wall near one of the corner fire places in the Magi Roost. The warrior wasn't any slouch, either. His arms were like hammered iron, and his wounds were fresh, but dried. His eyes were darting back and forth, his cracked lips yearning to speak more, but Mikkel kept his forearm shoved in his throat.

"This isn't the place for spreading rumors," Billip warned. "You'll be moving your bad news elsewhere, or you'll be dead or in the hole."

The Magi Roost was in full swing, and the scholars as well as the racial variety of merchant had gathered a keen interest. The serving girls began refilling goblets, batting eyes and swinging their hips, drawing away the customers' attention. But not all the girls could hide the nervous look in their painted eyes. This wasn't the first time a dark tale of underling hordes found its way behind the walls of the tavern. It was just another one of what had become many over the passing weeks.

"Let me go," the man managed. "I'm a warrior, such as you both, and you know my words ring true. I must tell these people what is going on." The warrior's voice was strong and convincing. "The Royals sit in their towers and castles doing nothing while we sit here like sheep waiting to be slaughtered."

Mikkel and Billip eyed one another. They both knew what the underlings did to men. It didn't help that most of the stories that were spreading around the city were for the most part, accurate. Mikkel lowered his arm from the man's neck and said, "Keep it low, Man, and sit. I want to hear more."

Billip raised his eyes in objection, then directed the man to a table tucked behind the bar in the front. As they sat, Mikkel sat down with a pitcher of ale and one of the waitresses brought over a half loaf of bread and cheese.

"Thank you, men," the warrior said. "I've not had real food in a month, and three days travel to here seemed like an eternity." The warrior said it while stuffing his mouth with bread and washing it down with ale. "Sweet Bish, I swore I'd perish before I ever tasted this nectar again."

Mikkel filled his own mug and said, "Tell us more, and keep it down. There's nothing but magi with big ears in here."

"Maybe underling spies, too," the warrior offered.

"No, couldn't be," Billip disagreed, craning his neck and popping his knuckles.

The warrior shrugged. "I'm crossing over from Hohm, part of a heavily guarded merchant train, not a day any different than before. Over twenty well-armed men bringing in the goods, wagons full of spices, seeds, grain, gold and other things. My face is known here, my comrades as well; you can check."

Mikkel rolled his wrist before leaning back and crossing his arms over his chest.

"It was hot, the landscape full of mirages, and tricks began to play on our minds as the first dusk began. We were setting up camp when the horses began acting funny, snapping and stomping men and one another. I don't know about you, but I've never seen horses bite one another like that before. Then the wind came, a crying howl, like a woman in pain, stirring the dirt and blinding us from seeing anything."

The warrior finished his first mug with a loud gulp and whipped his sleeve across his mouth.

"Ah! So, a storm was all, and we'd been through over a dozen land squalls like that before, so we hitched down what we could and prepared to ride it out. As suddenly as it started, it stopped, and that's when the screams began."

Billip re-filled all of their mugs, itchy fingers twisting at his goatee.

"The second dusk had settled, and our camp was swarmed with dark figures, at least two to our one. Some of them rode spiders. Others walked in the air, like living nightmares. I never could have imagined something so terrible if I had not seen it for myself. The underlings, thick furry little faces and bright gemstone eyes, chittered in elation as they began to chop us down. Webs sprung up in the air, taking my men down like helpless flies only to see their throats cut."

Billip interrupted saying, "So did you stand there and watch, or did you fight?"

The man's eyes narrowed.

"I don't know you, Man, and you don't know me, but I didn't stand around with my sword up my arse. I split the skin and bone of two or more. Either of you two waiters ever seen an underling before?"

Mikkel and Billip nodded.

The old warrior placed a folded up piece of cloth, stained in dark blood, on the table.

"Perhaps you'll recognize this, then," he said, unwrapping it.

Two small bolts of a crossbow lay there, the tips a dark metal and the shafts stained black.

"And that isn't all."

The warrior produced a knife and slid it over on the table. It had two sets of blades and forked edges around the pommel.

Mikkel knew underling steel when he saw it. He tossed a dish rag over all of it. Immediately his thoughts went to his son Nikkel, hoping that Two-Ten City hadn't been over run and his boy slaughtered.

Billip pressed on with more questions.

"So I merit that you killed all of the underlings before you managed your return?"

"Why are you mocking me? Of course I didn't kill them all. I gathered a horse and escaped. Those bolts were in my armor—see—here are the holes." The warrior stuck his fingers in the pierced leather shoulder. "Then, I grabbed that blade from a dead one's grip when I lost my own knife." The warrior rapped his fist on the table and got up. "Pah … you two dimwits wouldn't know an underling if you saw one, but I've warned you." He grabbed the underling weapons and tucked them away. As the warrior reached for the bread, Billip pinned down his wrist.

"You've had your fill here. Now, we've been good enough hosts, so if you want to spread more of your stories, do it elsewhere, Scavenger."

"What? I'm no bloody scavenger. I ought to cut your throat," he said as his hand fell to the pommel of his sword.

Billip rolled his eyes, but Mikkel got up and looked down on the warrior.

"Time to go," he said, taking another step towards the man, "quietly."

"So be it," the warrior said, turning and marching through the door.

Returning to his seat, Mikkel rubbed the back of his head and watched the man go.

"Billip, this isn't good, not good at all."

The archer sat with a glum look on his face, cracking his knuckles.

"Our time has come, Mikkel," Billip said.

"What do you mean?"

"You know what I mean. We need to head back home to Two-Ten City and check on Nikkel."

Mikkel slumped over his big forearms on the table. "Ah … I'm sure he's fine."

He didn't believe that, though. He was worried, and every day got longer and longer as the swirl of rumors of the underlings in the South added more fuel to his concerns. "Besides, we gave Venir our word to keep check on these boys and such. And Kam … she needs our help."

Billip said, "Mikkel, it's time to assume that Venir's gone."

Mikkel frowned. It was too sad to even consider, but it tugged at him anyway.

"Besides, the boys are in good shape here with Kam and Gillem. You've got your own to look after. You know Venir would understand, and you know we can't sit around on our butts when underlings are starting to crawl all over." Billip pushed away his mug. "We're fighters, you and I, and we aren't meant to sit around and watch babies grow. Tell Kam about your boy, and we can both go."

Mikkel sighed. Billip was right. There wasn't a whole lot left that he could do here, and he couldn't sit around and feel guilty all the time. He needed to get his son and bring him back to the City of Three, if need be.

"It's going to be a long ride, Brother," he said, taking a drink. "And the bountiful women will be pretty scarce on the trail." He allowed himself a broad smile.

"Agreed," Billip hoisted his mug of ale, "and there won't be much strong drink to take with us, either, so I suggest we round up a cask and head to the nearest brothel."

He clonked his mug on Billip's.

"Ssshh," he grinned, "Don't be so loud. You don't want Kam and Joline to hear. All of these women have big ears," Mikkel said, looking over his shoulder.

Billip hoisted his brows and added.

"And bigger breasts to boot."

From a balcony above, Kam heard every word. A tear ran down her cheek. She wiped it from her rosy cheek and blew her nose in a handkerchief. Her simple suggestion spell was powerful, a bit risky, but it had worked. She'd managed to have Billip do all the dirty work, and he hadn't even known it.

Before he'd left her room, she had already planted the question to ask Mikkel in his mind. That part had been easy, very unobtrusive. The next part had been a little more difficult, opening Mikkel's stubborn mind to the suggestion. His mug of ale, mixed with a part of hers and a part of his, entwined with magic, had done the rest with a little mental prodding.

The whole process left her exhausted, sad and even worse … lonely. Her fingernails dug into the rail, and her heart began to race as she looked down on the two impressive men. *A brothel. I could show them a better time than that.* She almost felt possessed as she pulled back her shoulders and headed down the stairs. She needed companionship as much as they, and if she went another day longer she might explode. *Why not. It's the least I could do.*

As she made her way to the bottom floor, a loud commotion began to stir among the patrons. Shouts and screaming were coming from outside as she watched Billip and Mikkel bolt from the table and head out the tavern's door. Without even realizing it she was running, squeezing through the patrons as she pushed her way outside.

People were running and screaming from all directions like they were being chased by a swarm of bees. Amid the throng of panic stricken faces she searched for Mikkel and Billip, and that's when she saw them, up the road, facing a small force of unlikely assailants. Her blood ran cold as she cried out their names, but her voice failed to rise above the sounds of chaos.

"NO!" She shouted when a group of patrons began pulling her back inside the tavern.

She saw Billip and Mikkel and a few others one last time, squaring off against the dark skinned and black clad brood of underlings.

20

V ERBARD FELT LIKE HIS STOMACH was in his chest as he rubbed his aching head and his silvery eyes. Across from him sat Master Sinway, broad and serene in his chair, and beside him stood a Vicious, its long clawed hands clutching open and closed beside his throat. Apparently, Master Sinway wasn't taking any chances on their little journey. Master Sinway was exposed, or was he?

As Verbard collected his thoughts, Master Sinway stood up and smoothed over his robes. He didn't ever recall seeing his Master act this way in all of his years, relaxed and poised. Master Sinway's fearsome disposition was gone, but the edge of his iron will was still there. He made a quick chit sound. The Vicious returned back to his master's side, and the cave dogs sat up and padded his way as well.

"Take it all in, Verbard. The charge I have given you is a big one indeed, but all the forces you need are at your disposal. Your time for greater glory has come. You can help us take back the surface world," Sinway said, almost smiling.

He groaned inside. His stomach was still a knot of writhing worms as he fought back the bile building in his throat. He forced himself upright in his chair and tried to assess how much power Master Sinway had. The trip, as marvelous as it was, had left him dumbfounded at Sinway's power. He and his brother combined couldn't possibly have achieved such a feat. He wanted that power.

"Perhaps, Master, I can finish this port? It should help me conjure a plan."

"Have all you want; it induces creativity."

"And you?"

Sinway waved his hand and said, "I haven't the craving. So … Verbard, I'll offer you my wisdom at the moment if you wish. You have questions … ask, or else I'll go."

Verbard took a swallow and felt his tongue begin to melt in delight. The underling port was unlike anything he could have ever imagined. *I could sit and drink this all year, but instead, I have to evict an entire city of humans.*

"I would ask how you would have me go about it, Master. And please forgive me, my knowledge of human settlements is somewhat vague." He hated to admit that, but placing a siege on a human empire wasn't something he would consider to be his forte. His silver eyes went from Sinway's chest to his back, as the Master of Underlings paced the floor like a man, robed arms crossed behind him.

"So long ago it was, Verbard, like a dream, when I lived within the city. The stone walls were not there, nor the spires and towers, nothing but the ground and the waters below, an oasis in the Outlands. Underling Lord Master Sidebor was the Master then, my mentor …"

Verbard let out a short cough at the mention of Master Sidebor's name, the one considered to be the greatest of all underlings. Master Sidebor had vanished at some point in time, no one really knew when for sure, as the new Underling Master kept his matters very private and exclusive. The only remaining trace of Sidebor—so the underling sages said—was the robe that Master Sinway wore. It seemed strange that Sinway chose this moment in time to bring it up at all.

"… who led us below ground. Mankind has driven us from our home, our caves, our water, our structures. They—with the help of wizards, giants and dwarves—drove us from that land. They sealed off the waters and choked the ground, which was once fertile, but is now what they call the Outlands: barren, wasted and dreadful."

It seemed unlikely to Verbard that any of this was true. The lands of Bish always had been and always would be what they currently were. The underlings lived in caves and not dwellings above the ground, as they found the heat and bright light uncomfortable.

"So you ask how I would take the city? By siege? By deceit? Magic? Alchemy? Mayhem?" Sinway goaded.

With his stomach settled, Verbard rose from his chair. "I like the sound of them all. Chronic attrition?"

Sinway gave a little snort.

"Yes, you have observed what we are doing on the outside, Verbard, but we need to begin the pressure on the inside as well."

The pressure in between Verbard's eyes was rebuilding. *Please don't tell me you want me to go inside there.*

"Verbard, I want you …"

He felt his black heart stop for an instant as be began missing his quest for The Darkslayer.

"… to work with my son, Kierway, on this."

I'd rather play in cave dog dung.

"It would be an honor."

"I thought so," Sinway sniffed. "Kierway has intimate knowledge of the City of Bone, as did Oran the outcast. You see, despite our hatred for humans and the human hatred for us, we have many allies out there."

"Certainly, Master, hence the demise of Outpost Thirty-One."

"Yes," Sinway began to smirk, "and being such, we know that men can be manipulated just as easily from the inside as the out. There is a key, a magic relic, something Master Sidebor left behind in his failures when he forced us to abandon our city." Sinway's face formed a deep frown. "I believe it was done purposely. That key possesses many secrets to the city and all of its long buried wonders. Kierway has worked dutifully for generations in trying to re-acquire it."

He began to simmer inside. How many things were going on that he didn't know about? He was one of the most powerful underlings in the Underland, but it seemed he was naive when it came to his kin's plans in regards to the domination of mankind. He couldn't help but wonder how much his brother had known that he didn't. There had always been something between Catten and Sinway that he never understood, until now.

Sinway continued.

"And I'd have you rendezvous with Kierway and help him acquire it, but if you feel there is a better way, then before you move on, I would like to hear it."

Patience. It was the underling way, but the tone in Master Sinway's voice was beginning to shift, reverting to his normal demeaning and demanding self. Verbard was beginning to suspect that it wouldn't be up to him after all on how to take the City of Bone, that once again, he'd be another instrument of his master. He hated that.

"Shall I meet with Kierway first, or shall I begin this conquest on my own … Master?"

Master Sinway removed something from within his robes that Verbard had never seen before: a brass amulet, intricate in its works, with a clear crystal as big as the palm of his hand in the middle. Sinway said, "Take this. You can use it daily, if need be, and keep me apprised of your situation. Keep your reports short and accurate, that's all I require," Sinway finished, setting it on the table. "Now, your time to depart from me is here, and your time for greater glory has come. Follow."

They floated through the castle cave of rock and stone back outside to a ledge overlooking the Underland city. Ranks of underlings stood in formation on a stone plateau below. Soldiers stood, solemn and striking with polished steel spear tips pointed skyward. Some were adorned in armor, others cloaks, crossbows and steels. Albino urchlings were mixed in there with cave dogs, giant spiders and lesser magi conjurers. Badoon underlings headed the ranks, well over a hundred strong, some bald and barren, the others covered in leather, mail and chain. In all, the host looked to be over five hundred underlings strong. It was an army that would bring a new meaning of terror to the world above.

Is this all I get to take over the largest city in the world?

"Your army awaits your orders, Lord Commander Verbard," Master Sinway said in his ear. "See to it that they do not perish, and do not return until the City of Bone is ours once again." Master Sinway departed, leaving him alone on the ledge, staring at his new army. *I'm a fool.* He'd just been handed an army to destroy humans and wipe them from the world, but it didn't seem right. If Verbard ever missed his brother, Catten, he missed him now, as he floated down to greet his commanders. *How did I get myself into this? I don't even have the Vicious. I'm going to have to find an easier way.* But he knew in his black heart there wasn't one.

21

L EFTY AND GILLEM STOOD BENEATH the City of Three's spires. Long and ornate, the clay shingled towers twisted upward towards the sky. Lefty marveled, as always. Gillem was at his side, guiding him through the streets, a satchel of flowers strapped to his back. Again Lefty peered upward, gaping at the smooth surface and long length of the tower, which was part of a different type of castle system than that which held the Royals, much more elaborate and sophisticated than the rough cut rock of Bone. *I've got to get in there.*

"Come, Lad," Gillem said, "stare too long and the magi will come after you."

Lefty followed along Gillem's side, still looking back and up over his shoulder.

"Do you really think they know we are watching?" He asked. "I mean, I've never seen anyone come and go from one of them. How do you know they are even in there?"

Gillem bumped into a woman carrying a package wrapped in decorative ribbon. She snorted.

"Watch it, Halfling," she said, sneering down at him.

He produced a purple carnation with a long blue stem and bowed saying, "Apologies, Miss."

"Oh … well, there's no need," she remarked, reluctantly taking the flower from his hand.

Lefty sauntered along Gillem's side, smiling.

"And some baby's breath to go with that, young lady."

"I, uh, very well. Thank you, little halflings, but be more careful. I wouldn't want anyone to call the City Watch, which I was about to do."

Lefty sneezed as she grabbed the flowers.

"Goodness!" she said.

"Pardon me, Miss ... uh, you were saying?"

She took the baby's breath, combined it with the carnation, and said, "Oh, be careful of the Watch. People don't like how halflings always pester us, but in your case, you've been nothing but pleasant."

Gillem added, "And you are as forgiving as you are lovely, and me and my boy, we promise to be more careful."

Both Lefty and Gillem bowed as the woman smiled before she turned and walked away with a spring in her step.

Lefty felt Gillem Longfingers massaging the top of his head.

"So, Lefty, what is it I've acquired?"

"I must admit, you were quick, but not quick enough. All you got was a silver talent from her pocket."

Gillem led the way, flipping the coin and saying, "Is that all you saw?"

He and Gillem Longfingers had been hard at it the past few days, roaming the streets, selling cheap flowers and gifts while picking pockets and running small skims. Lefty liked what he learned, but he was becoming bored with it all and lonely, too. Georgio would hardly speak to him, and Kam didn't seem to like him anymore. He missed learning magic from her, but with the new baby, Erin, she was too busy. Of course, Gillem saw to it he was busy, too. He just wanted things to go back to the way they were, before he and Georgio met Gillem and Palos.

"Yes," he said, "Is that all you saw?"

Gillem stopped and looked down on him and asked, "What do you mean?"

Lefty dangled a small golden bracelet in front of Gillem's puffy eyes that grew like saucers.

Gillem snatched it from his hand and stuffed it inside his coat in one fluid motion.

"Too many eyes, Boy ... but impressive all the same." Gillem shook his head. "My, you are picking up on this stealing too quickly. Ho! The sneeze, that's brilliant, never thought to use that. Come on now, we've got enough booty to report back to the Nest. Prince Palos will be expecting us."

Lefty tried not to slump as he followed Gillem through the busy midday streets, still trading and selling flowers and carrying on. He hated Palos. The man was pushy, demanding, demeaning and cruel. Palos talked to Gillem like a dog and treated Lefty like an infant. The Nest however, was a little more to his liking, as it reminded him of Bone, but with dwarves and even a few halflings. He thought of Melegal often and wondered how he was doing. He wondered what Melegal would do if he had to deal with the likes of Palos and Gillem.

By the time they made it back to Gillem's flower shop Lefty was droopy-eyed. They gathered their hoard of about six pounds of coins and trinkets of gold, silver and tiny gem stones and slipped through the streets, down the alley and into another underground dock where the gondola waited. He rubbed his eyes as he lit the tiny lantern.

"You've not spoke much today Lefty," Gillem said as Lefty rowed. His shoulders were already aching, but not so much as his heart. Things just weren't right.

"I'm in good order, Gillem. No worries."

Gillem lit his pipe and puffed away.

"Now, no sense in lying to me. Just come out with it, Lefty. You and I, well, our kind need to stick together. The thief's life may not be honorable, but you'll still have to trust one of us in order to survive. That might as well be me. Who else do you have down here?"

Lefty felt himself begin to shrink. *No one.* He wiped his eyes on his sleeve and continued to row, the oars splashing into the dim waters. The trip to the Nest was never as pleasant and soothing as when leaving it, but he had gotten accustomed to the quiet and the calming effects of the surrounding waters. Today however, he wished the trip was already going the other way, for there was no telling what deed Palos would have lined up for them next.

"Gillem, have you ever thought about doing something ... elsewhere?"

He could see a frown form on Gillem's abnormally cheerful face before he replied with the usual zeal in his voice gone.

The elder halfling sighed. "I gave up such thoughts long ago, Lefty. You would be wise to do so as well, and let me warn you, Boy: Palos will decide when it's time for you to go, and he'll have a new home waiting for you."

As they made their way through the final passages, Lefty took a look over his shoulder at the smoldering lit windows of the underground city. His little heart began to beat faster as the smell of decay became stronger.

"Take us over that way, on the other side of the docks. I want to show you something."

The little muscles in Lefty's back bemoaned the effort as he realized he had to paddle farther than he normally would. After a few dozen more strokes, Gillem held his hand up.

"This is good, Lefty," Gillem said, puffing his pipe.

He rubbed his aching shoulders and back. *Thank goodness.*

Gillem motioned at the small lantern hanging behind him.

Lefty grabbed it and held it in front of Gillem.

"These lanterns, did you know they work in water? A little something we acquired from our favorite customers, the magi. Of course, the light is not so bright, and they don't last so long." Gillem peered over the bow and motioned Lefty closer. "Now, go ahead, drop it in the water."

Lefty gave Gillem a funny look and said, "It seems like a—"

"Drop it!" Gillem ordered.

Splash.

"Now watch." Gillem's voice was dead and hollow, smoky eyes obscuring in the darkness.

Lefty got a funny feeling in his feet.

As the green glow of the lantern drifted downward, strange shapes began to take from: bloated men, tethered by chains, hands crossed behind their backs, mouths gaping open as their flesh was separating from the bone.

Lefty gasped and turned away. *How horrible!*

Two strong hands gripped his tiny face and forced him to look downward again.

"It is the Nest or this watery grave that Prince Palos has to offer, Boy! Nothing more, nothing less! Look!"

Terror filled his heart as his eyes remained affixed and frozen open. It wasn't just men, but women, boys and girls, halfling, mintaur and dwarf. He began to shake, but he did not cry as the lantern continued its slow decent into the murk and the illumination of horror expired.

"Take us to the dock," Gillem said as puffed on his pipe.

Like a zombie Lefty moved, his heart pounding, his thoughts frozen. He didn't even realize he was rowing until they pulled alongside the dock. *I'm going to die here.* He looked upward for a sun ray of hope, but of course there was none way down here.

The usual greetings from the inhabitants of the Nest were null. Gillem seemed to be shoving him over the planks as he walked along on numb legs, head hanging down. He felt the others staring at him as if this were his funeral procession. No more games, no more illusions. They all knew his secret and he knew theirs. Palos was the prince and executioner of every man and woman of the Nest. Where were Melegal and Venir when you needed them?

22

HE WAS ON HIS HANDS and knees, eyes squeezed shut, head reeling, trying to figure out how his body had been turned inside out. It was an awful moment, wrought with despair as he vomited all over the ground. Venir could smell the bile, and as malodorous as it was, it was relieving.

"Ha! Ha!" A booming voice laughed. "You are barfing, Venir. Do it again; it's funny."

Venir groaned out loud, wiping the milky saliva from his chin. Slowly he rose to his feet, searching for Barton's voice. There was nothing but white cottony mist.

"Blast."

And no sign of the giant. Another trick perhaps.

"Where are you, Barton? We have a deal," he said, not holding back the anger in his tone.

He felt a pair of hands wrap around his chest and lift him from the ground.

"I've got you, Venir."

The mist was wispy around Barton's big nose, his face fading in and out of his field of vision. Venir could still make out the eyes, one eye as big as his head, brown and dull, the other sealed shut. He tried to wriggle free, but Barton's fingers were like hammered iron.

"You promised to take me from the Mist, Giant! What treachery is this? I'm no farther than where I started."

"You are almost out. I can see your world, Venir. But first you promised me a friend. You tell me where that friend is right now, or Barton will crush you."

Venir's eyes bulged as Barton squeezed. He let out a dry gagging sound, and something snapped, somewhere inside him, piercing his lung with pain. Another rib, he supposed. How many of those could break, anyway?

"Ease up," he managed to croak out, "so I can speak."

Barton's fingers eased around him, but his prison of flesh and bone was still secure. Barton said, "Now tell me, Venir. Barton needs a friend."

Now was the moment of truth. He suspected Boon was dead, but that was the lie he had told Barton: that he knew of a friend who still lived within the giants' stronghold. But what if Barton already knew about Boon and his demise? He was certain Barton would crush his body like a yellow tomato and stomp his bones like glass. There was another option he had not considered.

"Barton, do you know what a Lycan is?"

Barton responded with a fierce shake, cracking his teeth.

"DON'T PLAY GAMES. NO LIKE THOSE PEOPLE."

Bad idea.

"Do you know about a wizard, like me, who lives with the giants and does tricks?"

Barton tilted his head.

"No … but I like tricks. Tell me more about this wizard."

"His name is Boon."

Venir waited for a throttling but nothing happened.

"Can he do tricks for me?" Barton asked, curious.

"Well, he made me as big as you."

"He did?"

Barton set Venir on the ground.

"Do you think he can make Barton small like you? Hmmm?"

"Well, yes, or even bigger if you wanted. Twice as big. Think what you could do to Blackie the next time he came for you. You could break his neck."

Barton began clapping and stomping all around.

"Yes! Yes! Yes!"

The ground was shaking beneath his feet, and his eyes began to pop with every loud clap. "Where is he? Where is he?" Barton demanded, picking up Venir and swinging him through the mist.

Venir felt himself turning green.

"Stop! Stop!" he yelled. "Let me down, I'm going to—*blecht!*"

Barton fell down laughing.

Venir had to fight the urge to pull out Brool and begin whittling the giant down to bits. Instead, he fumbled through the mist, found Barton and jammed his heel into his groin.

"Ow! What did you do that for?"

"Do you want the find the wizard or not?"

"Yes. Yes, Venir. Tell Barton now!"

Venir clutched at his aching ribs and said, "His name is Boon. He is in the castle with the maze. He guards the prisoners that fight in the labyrinth."

Barton sounded elated.

"I know where that is. I go get him now."

Venir tackled Barton's legs and hung on saying, "No! Wait!"

Barton began peeling him off.

Venir said, "Your end of the deal, Barton! Send me back to Bish."

Barton laughed as he picked Venir up by the ankles and dangled him before his eyes.

"You are right, Venir. Barton send you back to your Bish now."

The giant flipped Venir over his back like a pack and began running, jostling Venir all over the place.

"Good-Bye, Venir! And in case you lied, I want you to know I'll come for you and you will never leave the mist again."

"*URK!*"

Venir's neck snapped forward as he flipped head over heels through the mist. He swore he kept going higher and higher as the sound of giant laughter began to fade away. As the icy wind whistled and nipped his ears the snow white mist turned to black. His time careening in the air came to a brief stop. *Oh slat!* The wind whistled through his ears as he plunged into the darkness. He braced his body for what he knew would be a mighty long fall.

23

"WHICH ONE DO YOU WANT, the man or the dwarf?" One Mountain Man asked the other. The other, with a long face and yellow beard full of frost, snickered. "I'll be killing the Blood Ranger; not many men live to tell about such a feat."

The other one, hefty and surly, covered in pelts, frowned as he said, "Nay, I saw him first, so I get to kill him. Or … we both say we both killed him."

Mood, still warm within his icy cocoon, kept his bushy eyes closed.

"So, if we kill him, do you think the other Rangers will come after us?" The taller one said as he tested the edge of his bastard sword.

"They'll never know what happened to him up in these mountains. We'll bury him in the lake of ice. Not even the best trackers could find him there."

The one with the brown beard had a worried look as he said, "I don't think it's a good idea, killing him in cold blood. The Blood Rangers will find out. They say they know anything and everything, that they can find a needle in a snow storm."

"Har!" the other one laughed. "Those are just stories. This one here, Mood, is the King they say, and he couldn't even find a druid. She found him. Blood Rangers, pah. I'd be surprised if he wasn't the only of all of them. Look, he's just a big man is all. There ain't no such thing as a dwarf that tall."

The mountain man nodded his head, a look of satisfaction enlightening his cross face.

It was true; not many men had even seen the Blood Rangers, and if they did, it was most likely only one, in passing. The Blood Rangers came to the aid of man from time to time, but for the most part they kept to themselves in Dwarven Hole. Only for the most treacherous of events in the world did they venture out.

Mood began to feel the icy block biting into his fingertips. *Need to move.* His skin, thick and protective like wool, was turning cold. Not a thing on him was ever cold, not even his nose that usually snorted the air, until today. It was time. *Move or die.*

"Have ye ladies decided whose gonna kill me yet," he rumbled, "because I'm getting tired of ye squabblin'."

The two mountain men whirled, their faces aghast. The brown-haired one's sword slipped from his grip. The men looked at one another, then back at Mood. He could smell their fear. It strengthened him. He let his inner power go.

Both men stepped backward as Mood's fists began to gleam red hot from within the ice. Their jaws dropped as he spoke.

"Fools. Did ya' really think I couldn't find you or your wily leader? I wasn't slaughtering the ogres for fun, even though I enjoyed every bit of it. No, I was drawing you fools out, and now I have you! Ho! Ho!"

The bewildered men raised their swords and charged.

Mood's muscles thickened and bulged inside the block of melting ice. There was a popping sound as shards of ice broke free. With a fierce growl he pulled his shoulders back.

Crack!

Chunks of ice fell to the ground as he shivered and shook his shoulders. In one hand a razor sharp hand axe was free; the other hand was still a block of ice. As the two wary Mountain Men came on, Mood tried to lift his feet and return their charge.

"Huh?"

His feet were still frozen in a solid block of ice when he looked down.

"Ah … who needs 'em anyway. Come on, Fools!"

He failed to notice the Ogre's club rising above his back as a black shadow fell over him and the Mountain Men's yellowish eyes gleamed in relief.

Elation. Euphoria. Exhaustion. Fogle Boon never imagined anything could have been as exhilarating as this. His skinny chest heaved in and out. Her fingernails ran down his spine, raising goose bumps from his toes to his eyelids.

"Everything you imagined it would be?" Cass said, her voice a silky purr.

He was shaking as he nodded, ashamed for doing so, but he resisted the urge to pull away when she hugged him from behind, wrapping her legs behind his waist. It was the warmest and most magnificent feeling he had ever felt: hot flesh, soft and firm in all the right places like a blanket that had so much more to offer.

She nibbled at his ear and said, "I thought you were wonderful. You were so, oh, how should I put it … creative."

He perched his eye brows as he managed to say, "Well, I have given it a moderate amount of thought over the years. Of course, there were never any wolves in my fantasies … or any other creatures, for that matter."

"Not even another woman?" she said, twirling her finger in his hair.

"Hah … well, no I suppose."

Woof!

The timber wolves' ears perched up as they growled and stammered on their paws, the thick fur rising on their backs. There was a commotion coming from right outside. He felt Cass unwrap her body from his and watched her wriggle back into her robes. She made a funny sound, her pink eyes leering at the four massive dogs, and Fogle found himself surrounded again.

"What is that?" he asked, rising to his feet, gathering his nearby robes.

But the druid was gone, the tent flap closed.

"Great!"

One of the wolves, black and dark grey, barked and snapped in his face. That's when he heard Mood's thunderous bellow smashing through the canvas. "HUZZAH!"

Something that sounded like a battering ram slamming into ice rocked the air, followed by the sound of silence.

Fogle's gut began to churn. Something was wrong. He had to do something and help out his friend. He'd failed him once, and he couldn't let that happen again, but how was he going to get past the wolves without being eaten alive?

"Blast it!"

The wolf snapped in his face again.

He closed his eyes, letting his mind peel away the layers of mystic energy that were lying dormant within him. No longer was his mind numb, but rather rejuvenated. Every wizard had power within that didn't require components, wands or scrolls to activate, but just a disciplined and powerful mind that could tap the mystic energies of the world without losing his sanity.

He put his fingers to his lips and whistled.

The wolves barked and snapped, coming closer and closer. He could feel their hot breath as their snouts nipped at his robes.

Just enhance the sound.

He opened the gate inside his mind and let out his reserves.

The whistle went from a feathery twill to high pitched shrill.

The wolves howled upward.

It's working.

Fogle blew harder.

The wolves' ears flattened; their howls looked to be cries of pain.

He could feel the energy within begin to grow into a monster of a force, as the high pitch twisted into the roaring forces of a storm. The sound waves were twirling around him, slinging the pelts through the air, grinding the grasses to the ground. It felt good, cutting it loose like that. He saw the wolves' feet lift from the ground, their bodies twisting in the air. Then the canvas walls of the tent buckled and rose, the stakes that held it ripped from the ground as the final ear shattering sound came.

BOOM!

Fogle's knees sagged, his energy spent, and then he fell to the ground.

Mood heaved himself forward a split second before the ogre's club came down.

Crack!

The blow smashed into the frozen block of ice that imprisoned his feet.

"Thanks, Stupid," Mood said, swinging his giant axe into the ogre's exposed skull. Blood spurted up as the heavy blade penetrated bone and punctured brain. The ogre twitched, sprawled out and stopped moving.

He wrenched his axe free and rolled left.

Swish! A long blade almost severed his leg. He rolled right as the other Mountain Man stabbed at his belly, clipping the outer edge of his gut. His frozen axe crashed into the towering man's legs, sweeping his legs from beneath him.

Chop! The big man howled in alarm, his foot detached, his leg stump gushing blood.

"Curse you, Ranger!"

Quickly, Mood rose to his feet and squared off with the lone standing Mountain Man.

"Yer a fool to trifle with me, Mood, King of the Blood Rangers!" he snorted. "HUZZAH!"

The Mountain Man let out his own cry and charged. High and low his sword point stabbed.

Mood parried.

Clang.

Another thrust clipped the hairs at his neck.

Clang.

He knocked it away.

"Ha, working up a sweat before you die I see."

"The Bone with you, Dwarf!" the man yelled, swiping at Mood's side.

The sword and axe crashed with a terrible sound of grinding metal. The bigger man leaned into him, pressing him downward, eyes blazing with battle. Mood rammed his head underneath the man's chin, rocking his head back.

"I bet that hurt, but don't ye worry, yer not be feeling the pain for long!"

Mood clubbed the man over the head with his half-frozen hand, breaking what was left of the ice block that froze his axe to his wrist. Blood began to spurt from the busted nose on the man's face as he howled in pain.

With both hands free, Mood stepped in for the kill.

"Gah!"

Something seized hold of his feet. He looked down, thinking to brain the man with the missing foot, but instead he watched the ice begin to crystallize and grow up and around his feet.

"Ah, not this again," he said, launching his hand axe into the chest of the last mountain man.

The man fell backward, dead.

He chopped at the ice that was up to his knees now.

"Save your energy, Dwarf," the druid woman said, "and perhaps I'll show mercy on your friend. As for you, however, I think you'll make a nice frozen ornament for me — what in Bish?"

A shrill sound erupted from inside the tent. The druid woman pressed her hands over her ears. She wasn't screaming, but whatever it was, Mood could not hear. He chopped into the ice, trying to block out the foul noise. From the corner of his eye he watched the tent rip free from its tethers and blow away with the force of a gale. Pelts and wolves were flying in the air.

BOOM!

Mood felt like a giant just smashed him in the head. He fell to his hands and knees, struggling to regain his feet. All around him was some form of devastation. The snow was gone from the leaves of the trees; smaller growth was ripped from the ground, and the druid woman lay quivering on the ground, clutching her head. Where the tent once was a man now stood, his big bearded face pale, his bright green eyes exhausted.

"Yer just full of surprises, aren't ya Wizard?" Mood said.

Fogle raked his brown hair back from his face and said, "As impossible as it seems, sometimes I surprise myself."

Mood gathered his other axe from the Mountain Man's bloody chest and said, "So, I take it you're a full-fledged adventurer now?"

Fogle smiled as he looked over at Cass's voluptuous form.

"I guess you could say that."

Mood snorted, pulled a cord of thin rope from his pouch, and tossed it as Fogle's feet.

"Bind her hands, then. It's time to go." Cass mumbled something, but didn't resist his binding.

"Should I gag her?" Fogle asked. "And what makes you think she'll help us?"

Mood procured a cigar and lit it up, saying, "Wizard, ye've whipped her. She'll not be crossing you again. At least not until this deed is done. After that, anything goes I suppose."

As Fogle pulled her up from her knees she spoke.

"My word, Fogle and Ranger, I'll carry out this quest, just don't release that awful sound again. If I had pants I swear I would have pissed them. So take me to Dwarven Hole to see this two-headed dog. I promise I'll do what I can."

It didn't seem right, marching a woman he had just bedded hours earlier through the dangerous mountains like a prisoner. Still, Fogle had been warned by Mood several times already, *Ye can never trust a druid.* He couldn't help but wonder if they all looked as incredible as her.

Mood led the way, dragging a small sled that secured their gear. The Blood Ranger was a determined juggernaut, his thick back and heavy set shoulders unusually broad, with his blood stained axes criss-crossed on his back. Fogle couldn't help but wonder if he saved Mood, or if Mood saved him … again. And where had all that magic and power come from, which had leveled the druid's fragile home?

He looked over his shoulder. To the right and left, a pack of humbled timber wolves followed. For whatever reason, he was glad they were there. The journey home, Mood promised, wouldn't be any easier than the journey there.

He guided Cass forward, his hand pressing into the small of her back.

"Feeling frisky again are we, Fogle?" she said, stopping and somehow grabbing his hands in hers. "Unbind me and I'll make this trip … more interesting." Her pink eyes looked deep into his. "Or just take me as I am."

A flush of red washed over his normally pale face. One thing was for sure, the journey back seemed much warmer than the journey there. Still, a question hung in his mind.

"Are you sure you were a virgin?" he asked.

Mood's gruff voice cut in.

"Of course she weren't no virgin, Wizard. What do ya think she kept those two brutes up there for, protection? Now pull your brains out of your groin and get moving. Storm's coming!"

Cass giggled as he pushed her away and frowned, thinking of the two brutish men that both lay dead, frozen blood mixed with snow. She had not even mourned their loss.

"Ah, don't believe the dwarf. He's just jealous. Of course you are the only one to lay with me, my defiler … er … deflowerer," she said with a hint of discontent.

Fogle just shook his head and moved along. The sky was darkening with his attitude. He wanted to believe one thing, but he knew the truth was another. Was Cass just a common slut, the kind his mother warned him about? Some men could make the most of that, but he was pretty certain that he could not.

24

"D ETECTIVE! DETECTIVE!"

Melegal had been driving the City Watch beneath the City of Bone for hours, closing in on his prey, all thanks to a skinny little bird whispering the Slerg whereabouts, among other things, in his ear. And now, after preaching and disciplining the men of the Watch, all Bone had broken loose. The dogs, loud and slobbery, had gone into a frenzy when a family of sewer cats crossed through the tunnels.

"Shut up! Shut these mangy mutts up before I slit their throats, you buffoons," he ordered, shoving one unsuspecting Watchman from his path. He sucked in some air through his teeth, resisting the urge to kick a dog—choked tight on his short leash—in the throat. He had come to hate dogs, all except one, he supposed, giving the fleetest of thought to the two-headed Chongo.

The men pressed along the slopes of the dank tunnel walls, heads down, eyes averted. A City Watch sergeant straddled his long legs on both sides of the tunnel, peering through a portal that was a little over two feet in diameter. The sergeant was long and stringy, too tall to enter a common door, now bent over almost unnaturally, seeming to be quite uncomfortable. Sweat was dripping from the man's long slender nose as he sucked in his raspy breath to speak.

"I sent my hound, Oggie, in there. He made it back thirty feet or so, let out a bark and yelped." The man shuddered a sob. "That was it. I think something got him. I never heard him yelp like that. It must be those Slergs, I tell you. They better not've killed my Oggie."

Good, one less noisemaker the better. Hmmm. This might work out well for me.

"Well, what are you waiting for? Send in the rest of your hounds. Avenge your beast!"

"But Sir," the sergeant started to speak, but stopped. "*Ulp.*"

Melegal stuck his dagger half an inch up the man's nose.

"This isn't a booger picker, Dolt. Now, shall I give the order again? Am I so low as you that I must order dogs and not men?"

"Apologies, Detective! Apologies!" the sergeant blinked rather than nod.

Melegal withdrew his blade and said, "Shut up and do your job."

The man looked confused.

Melegal warned him, saying, "I'm going to kill you, Fool. Now speak and do your job."

The lanky man nodded his head, turned and yelled down the tunnel.

Don't yell!

"You heard 'em men—Release the hounds!"

Brak loved dogs. He had played with them all his life, all kinds, big and small. Some were herders and others hunters, and now one lay unmoving at his feet, a herder and scout. He could tell by its calico coat. He wanted to cry, but there was no time for that. At least three more were coming, and they sounded different than the last: ferocious and hungry for flesh. He didn't want to hurt any more of them, not innocent animals, anyway.

"I surrender!" he yelled. "I SURRENDER!"

There was a series of sharp whistles, and the dogs came to a halt.

Someone in the background was saying, "Did you hear that? That ain't human."

"Shut up, Fool!" a hateful voice sounded. "Unarm yourself, then, and come forth so we can see you."

Brak lumbered down the tunnel and let out a loud sigh. The dogs, four in all, growled at his side. "Easy boys," he mumbled.

"Any sudden moves and those dogs will tear you to bits."

"I'm not going to do anything," Brak said.

"He's coming. Be ready; it might be a trick."

"Shut up already!" the hateful voice came again.

"I'm tossing out my weapons," Brak said. One knife and two swords, one his, the other his dead mother, Vorla's. He wished she was still here, caring for him. He dreamed of her often, and it was of very little comfort, but it was something.

Slowly, he began to squeeze back through the portal, into the torchlight, where many men with swords and torches waited. He wondered if he would be heading into the furnace to join his mother and so many others. So sad, he had failed in his quest to find his father, Venir.

"Sweet Mother of Bish. Look at the size of his head," the sergeant exclaimed.

In his life, Melegal had been surprised a few times, but even he could never have anticipated Brak's big droopy face popping out into the torchlight. He was at a loss for words.

"Do we kill him?" someone asked.

Everyone moved backward as Brak's form began to slowly fill the tunnel.

"How'd he fit in here?"

"I'm not carrying him out. We'll have to cut him in pieces."

"What do we do?"

Brak's lazy face showed no emotion or expression as he stooped inside the unyielding confines of the corridor. Melegal's thoughts raced to Venir, the Drunken Octopus, Chongo, Lefty and Georgio. Everything good he remembered washed over him as he felt compelled to grab Brak and run. *This is not good for the boy, er man.*

"Detective, shall we gut him?" the sergeant said. "We've still got more pursuit. They've left this one to slow us."

Slap!

It stung Melegal's hand as much as the man's pock-marked cheek, but it felt good.

"Are you doing my thinking for me now? Is your tongue privy to things that I am not? Are you the detective or am I?"

Slap! Slap! Slap!

"Who is making the decisions here?" Melegal demanded.

The truth was, he enjoyed tormenting the City Watch. It was one of the few perks left of his job, better yet he could see to their demise from time to time. The City Watch were not of the Royal families' fabled sentries. They were chattel, nothing more. He liked their disposability.

"Y-you are Detective, Melegal, Sir. Apolo—"

"Piss on your apologies, and shut your ignorant hole. Now …" Melegal gestured to the nearest Watchman, "you two pissants crawl through the hole and see what lies ahead, and take your stupid little dung eating pets, too."

He felt Brak's heavy eyes on him, but he ignored his gaze. *Maybe the young dolt won't remember me. Pah. I better gag him … and blindfold him, before it's too late.*

"You—Wart-face! Blindfold and gag him. Gag him first."

"Y-yes, Detective."

Melegal looked through the portal now, satisfied Brak was well under control. If this man was truly Venir's son, then he had to be careful. Such knowledge would be valuable because Venir was still, for all purposes, a wanted man by the Royals, regardless of Tonio's involvement. He'd watched over Venir before in his own kind of way, and he didn't take much comfort in taking his son in. *It can't be his son. It just can't be.*

A voice shouted from up ahead.

"Detective, there's a grate here, bars, no way through."

There was a lot of barking going on, too.

"Shut those beasts up! I can't hear you, Fool! What's this about bars?"

There was a yelp followed by the man's voice resounding off the rock walls.

"The bars on the grate … er … well they look bent, but there's no room for someone to crawl through, not even a pooch."

As Melegal made his way through the portal, he poked the lone remaining Watchman in the chest with his dagger and said, "Don't lose my prisoner. Fail at your peril."

"Aye, Detective."

That's the same dolt that lost the last one. Run man-child, Run.

Making his way to the men, he ran his slender fingers along the stone corridor. His keen eyes searched for any disparities in the architecture of the walls. He noted none.

"Well," he said, folding his arms across his chest, "step aside, torch bearers, so I can investigate your brilliant discovery."

The men shuffled away, eyes nervous and averted.

"My, well look at this. You've indeed found a grate. A barrier of some sort, agreed?"

They nodded.

"I tell you, it takes more than the brain of a gnat to make such a discovery. I'll be sure to report this to your superiors."

Melegal swooped his cloak around his back and over his knee as he squatted in front of the bars.

"A little more light, please," he beckoned with is hand and pointed.

As the Watchman lowered his torch along the rim, he made a startling discovery. The wrought iron, thick and ancient, had been bent. *Fresh debris. Interesting.* Small chips of stone lay along the edge of the grate's metal rim, but worst of all were the markings. The scratches in the iron were fresh, and he could feel the tiny jagged edges around the bottom bars where something had pulled them out and pushed them back again. He looked back down the tunnel. Through the portal he could see Brak's bulk dimming the torchlight from the other side.

One of the Watchmen cleared his throat and said, "How'd they get through there?"

"Huh," Melegal sort of laughed, rising back to his feet. He'd seen Venir bend bars as thick as these before, but he never saw him bother to bend them back. *Wouldn't that take more energy? My, what a seed he has sown!*

He shifted his hat on his head and motioned for the men with torches to step away from the bars. *Look. Listen.* He closed his eyes and opened his mind to the magic with his cap. It was something he'd been practicing which he was becoming quite fond of. Winding through the darkness of the endless corridors were footsteps, confusion and something else unexpected. Something breathed, evil and luminous, beckoning to him and picking at his mind. Something dormant was now awakened, and it was hungry. *Slat!*

Melegal flattened himself on the ground.

Clatch. Clatch. Clatch. Zip. Zip. Zing.

He was running.

Son of a Bish!

Ignoring the impaled faces of the City Watchmen, Melegal dashed down the tunnel and leapt through the portal. In the next instant, one dog after the other was piling on top of him and yelping in a frenzy.

"Get off me, hounds!"

"What was it?" The alarmed sergeant cried out, ducking along the wall.

Melegal was wiggling his finger through the hole inside the hood of his cloak.

"Just cornered Slergs, is all. It seems they can't find a way out."

The sergeant scratched his head, pushing his back to the wall, while peeking back and forth through the portal.

"Your charming friends are dead, but they died valiantly, discovering a murderous sewer grate. Now, take our prisoner to interrogation. You, Dear Sergeant, will get the glory of continuing this pursuit from the other end."

"Y-yes, Detective."

Melegal tried to contain his inner shivers as he made his way out of the tunnels. He couldn't find the moonlight fast enough. Something was down there: evil, insidious and powerful, and he had no desire to find out what that was. He'd heard stories about hoards of ghouls and other monsters that lived within the catacombs of the ancient ruins of Bone. Now he had an overwhelming fear that he had just awakened something that didn't want to be woken. *I am already having enough trouble sleeping.*

Brak didn't know what interrogation meant, and he didn't care now that he could smell the clean air above the ground for the first time in days. Maybe, just maybe, without anyone one's help, he could escape. Maybe the skinny man called Detective might help. He could dream, dream of many things vast, unnatural and wild, but those dreams had not come lately. The dreams of his father were gone.

25

"**B**ISH!" MIKKEL CRIED OUT AS the multi-bladed knife of the underling clipped his nose.

He ducked and dodged, shaking off the rust, back pedaling back and forth between the two underlings as he parried with his club. It was the fighter's instinct that rushed him back into the battle against man's most ancient of foes. He wanted to retreat, his mind recoiling, the frightening countenances of the underlings boring into his flesh: fearless, merciless and cruel. They came at him, one striking high, the other low.

Get it together, Man!

Clumsily he batted their blows away. How long had it been since he'd been in a fight, anyway? Perhaps it was the old warrior, the man they turned away, who cried out the first warning and charged into the fray. The weathered warrior now lay in a pool of his own blood, face split in half like something had just hatched from his skull. Mikkel couldn't shake the sadness that crept though his skin and chilled his bones.

Bang!

Clank!

Whomp!

Bang!

People were screaming, running in all directions, falling prey to the fearless little hoard that invaded their sanctuary. There were at least ten of them, but Mikkel wasn't making a count. He found himself pinned up against a wagon. The underlings chittered, their rat-furred faces and beady emerald eyes unblinking, cold and bright as they began to whittle him down.

Smack!

Billip caught one of them on the wrist, drawing an angry howl.

That's more like it! Now fight like a man!

The underlings weren't any different than any he'd faced before. Small like women, hairy grayish skin corded in knots, fluid in motion, confident in gait, evil in intent, their jagged blades — cruel tortuous devices — licked in and out like striking snakes. Bandoliers of knives and darts and small swords made an eerie jangle on their hips, and even without that armament the rest of them was just as scary. Sharp teeth that could rend flesh like a wild animal and claws that could shave the bark from a tree allowed the minions of the Underland to kill and hunt at all times.

Out of the corner of his eye he noticed a young woman and her boy trapped beneath a carriage. Two other underlings, blood dripping from the blades in their hands, screeched, rushing towards the helpless prey.

Nikkel!

The reminder of his own son's life and safety tore away his fears, unleashing his dormant fury. Mikkel roared. The sluggishness of his long powerful limbs had burned off, turning his defensive actions into a bludgeoning fury. His club, long, studded and heavy, twirled high in the air a split second before he brought it down with a skull-cracking blow. Parts of the underling's brain oozed from its nose as it fell over, leaving the other's serrated maw of teeth agape as it turned to escape the black warrior's fury.

"Where do you think you're going!" Mikkel yelled, giving chase, twisting back away at the sound of the woman and boy screaming. "Bish!"

There was a thrashing of blood spilling out from underneath the wagon. The underlings were a tangled mass of black flesh and leathers, claws clutching as the woman and boy kicked and flailed. Mikkel caught one underling by the foot and yanked it squealing from under the carriages.

"No you don't!" he said, dropping his club and pulling the underling away.

Dark black finger nails dug into his wrists. Mikkel cried out in pain, releasing the fowl underling that scurried away.

He looked under the wagon. "Bone!" The woman and boy lay dead, throats torn open and eyes gouged out. A swell of emotion formed in his light watery eyes. "BLAST THEM ALL!"

Mikkel whirled around at the growing sounds of chittering underlings. His club, Skull Basher, was nowhere in sight. The cobblestone road he defended was smeared in blood where Billip stood, coated in black blood, brandishing a blood-soaked broadsword. He wasn't alone: a dwarven fighter, stout as a stump of oak, black bearded to his knees, grasped a blacksmith's hammer in his hand. Beside him, another dwarf was on his knees, choking up blood and fighting for his breath.

"How are you holding up, Billip?" Mikkel asked, rushing to his comrade's side.

Billip swayed where he stood; a jagged gash in his pants was soaked in blood.

"I'd be better if I had my bow in my hand. This melee's exhausting. Bloody underlings!"

"Aye man!" The dwarf interrupted. "You'd be better fighting from afar, bow or sword. I've seen one-armed halflings swing better steel than that," the dwarf gloated, "but at least, being a man and all, you tried."

Billip said to Mikkel, "This must be a friend of yours."

Mikkel said, "No, never seen him before, but he seems to know you pretty well."

But the time for jokes was over. The streets were cleared, all of the fighting men were dead as far as they could tell, and the underlings, with superior weapons, armor and numbers, had them surrounded. A dark cloud had descended on the City of Three.

"So, you going to go down barehanded?" Billip commented, wiping the blood dripping in his eyes on his sleeve.

"Just like the day I was born, I guess."

"We dwarves are born with hammers for hands. Here, soft black man, take this," the dwarf growled, tossing his hammer to Mikkel. "You'll be needing it more than me. Now, by Mood's blood red beard, who wants to pummel these underlings!"

"Come on, Dogs!" Mikkel yelled.

Billip remained silent, sword up, eyes forward.

"It's time to crush some skulls!"

The underlings chittered with mockery, small crossbows aimed and ready. Mikkel could see the wet dew of poison reflecting on the bolt's tip. There were many men on Bish that could dodge a crossbow bolt, but he wasn't one of them. All he could do was hope he got one last swing.

Billip muttered at his side, "It wouldn't be so bad if I had my bow in my hand."

"You two ladies run, I'll cover you," the dwarf said. "Those little bolts won't hurt—"

Clatch-zip.

The bearded dwarf caught a slender six-inch dart in his burly arm and fell over dead.

"Slat!"

Every underling bolt in Bish looked to be pointed their way.

Clatch-zip.

Clatch-zip.

Clatch-zip.

Clatch-zip.

Clatch-zip.

Clatch-zip.

Everything seemed to be moving in very slow motion. The bolts, each and every one of them, he swore he could count. Three were bearing down on him, agonizingly slow, all center mass, one left, one middle, one right. If he twisted and turned either way it wouldn't matter. He was flat footed and ready to die. He glanced over at Billip, and to his surprise Billip was glancing at him, eyes wide as saucers. He turned back to look at the deadly missiles, each and every one twice as close as it had been before. *Huh?* Then he heard a familiar voice bellow.

"MOVE, YOU TWO IDIOTS!"

Mikkel dove to the left, Billip to the right.

Whap. Whap. Whap. Whap. Whap. Whap.

The bolts juttered as they embedded themselves in the cart behind him. The underlings howled with outrage, their bewildered faces searching the ground and sky.

"What in the—"

"TAKE COVER!" A woman said it in a convincing and powerful voice. She was gorgeous, radiant, and dangerous all at the same time. Her wavy tussles of auburn hair billowed in the sky. She was no ordinary woman, rather an extraordinary creature, an angry mother whose nest had been disturbed. Mikkel sucked in his breath as he caught a glimpse of her warm glowing face.

"Kam!" he exclaimed.

And she wasn't the only one.

Two men, one robed in pure white, the other robed in a color of blue he had never seen before, dropped down behind the pack of underlings. The one in white, older, hair yellow as a bale of straw, held out a slender long black staff, inches from the nose of an underling. The creature grasped the staff in both hands and tried to yank it away. Mikkel gawped. The underling turned white from head to toe and then its body collapsed in on itself.

"Sweet Mother of Bish!"

The blue wizard scattered a cloud of silver and dark purple dust in the air. The agitated underlings began to snort and wheeze. Mikkel almost laughed as they fell to the ground in writhing spasms, kicking clawed feet over the cobble stones in agony, twitching and lurching like fish out of water until they moved no more.

That's when Kam came. Her wrists were entwined with ropes of white lightening as she unleashed her tendrils of energy. The remaining underlings clutched at the burning energy that wrapped itself like a snake around their necks. The mystic snake slithered inside one underling's mouth. It disappeared for an instant, then the underling's eyes flared with white hot light. Slowly at first, Mikkel watched in astonishment as the energy passed through one ear and out the other. Again it raced, passing in one underling and out the other underlings, boring new holes, faster, gaining blinding speed and fury.

Mikkel shielded his eyes as the brilliant light continued to grow.

FOOMPH!

When he turned to look, nothing remained of the underlings but several piles of black ash. The three wizards, Kam, the White and Blue ones, methodically gathered up the dead underling bodies, hoisting them with unseen hands, guiding them through the air and piling them all together. A crowd of citizens now gathered, murmuring in amazement. The blue wizard, his features ageless, handsome and dark, muttered something unintelligible to the common man. The pyre of black underlings blazed to life and burned green with black smoke rising to the sky.

Mikkel covered his nose, eyes squinting when he noticed Billip standing beside him. They both shrugged as they returned their gazes back to Kam.

A cry rose up from behind the crowd, and each of the wizards faces turned. Someone was pushing their way through the crowd with a dead underling hoisted over their shoulder. A pair of underling blades was jammed in its black-haired skull. As he tossed the underling into the fire, Mikkel could hear the young warrior say, "You missed one."

Mikkel couldn't contain his smile.

It was Georgio.

Someone screamed from a nearby window.

26

HOHM CITY WAS CONSIDERED TO be the most dreary city of all. Tucked in the northwestern most corner of the word, Hohm remained in chronic seclusion from the sunlight. A thin veil of fog rolled over the city and through the streets, bending over window sills and corners, a constant companion of those who preferred the seclusion.

The marsh itself, leagues long as it was wide, kept any curious people or invaders away. The willow tree roots were sunk deep in the mud, but their height rose over a hundred feet in some places. Black backed crocodiles rested on massive lily pads, and swamp toads were as big as a man's head. Every crawling, climbing, murk dwelling creature was ten times bigger than anything you'd ever known. So the people of the City of Hohm said.

Morley Sickle, a man of age, long forgotten by his neighbors, had lived in the City of Hohm all of his life, with no desire to go elsewhere … until now. He had come across a stranger of the most amazing character, weird and undeniable, when taking his wares, a very potent homemade wine he called Jig, to sell in the general store. The stranger, handsome beyond reason, asked to sample his Jig, and they'd been talking almost incessantly ever since. This all started months ago, and it had its benefits … at first.

"Morley," the newcomer said, his tone pleasing and demanding, "tell me, how many pickles do you think are in that jar?"

Morley, pinching the upper bridge of his nose, eyes squinted, tried not to think about it. *I don't give a slat!*

"That's not a number," the man said, raking his fingers back through his long locks of blond hair. "Really Morley, you need to do better than that."

Morley scooted towards the burning hearth in front of the tavern fire, trying his best not to think. If he could stop breathing, he would. He rubbed his bejeweled fingers as he stared at the brilliant gold and precious gems that adorned his hand. They were worth a hundred times more than anything he ever wanted. A thousand times if that. He groaned. What good were they when he was under the steady watch of his unavoidable new companion?

"Guess, Morley. Guess, I say!"

Morley lurched up in his seat.

"One hundred twenty, Scorch! One hundred twenty!"

Scorch grabbed him by the face, perfect hands squeezing his saggy cheeks up on his fear filled face, shaking his head.

His heart was thumping like a drum behind his ears, and a drop of water slipped from his eye duct and ran down along his nose.

"Hah! Morley, there's only fifty one. Fifty one pickles in that jar. But, after you go fetch me four of them, then there will be just …"

Morley swallowed a glob of spit and said, "Forty seven?"

Scorch released him, sat back and slapped his crocodile boots up on the table.

"Of course, you dullard. Now, fetch more jig while you're after it." Scorch snapped his fingers, popping Morley's ears, "and some more of that mossy cheese, too. I love the smell. I don't know why I love the smell of cheese, but I do. Ah yes … cheese, pickles, and jig. Mmmmmm. …"

Morley shuffled away, taking his time as his feet creaked over the floor boards. Every day had been like this, one nonchalant meaningless task or question after the other. But, he dared not think that. *I need to die.* If there were only a way to kill himself without thinking.

"Morley," Scorch chimed, "I don't like what you're thinking. And no, you can't make me angry enough to kill you, either. As a matter of fact, I don't think I can even become angry, but I think I can become drunk."

Scorch hoisted his strong chin up towards the rafters, closed his eyes and slowly brought each of his index fingers to the very tip of his perfect nose.

"Er, well, I think I can be drunk, but still very formidable all the same, unlike your kinfolk. A bunch of sots they are, except the dwarves; now they are good for mixing."

Get the pickles. Get the wine. Get the cheese. He repeated over and over in his mind, casting his glances at the empty tables and chairs of what used to be one of the liveliest places in Hohm. The most colorful men and women thrived in Hohm despite the dullness of its gray atmosphere. The strange fog from the marsh softened the tones and features of everything procured or living. It gave people a permanent sense of privacy, and the Royals, with their own dark and mysterious ways, didn't seem inclined to interfere so long as the people behaved themselves and paid taxes on time.

A man, head shaven, tall and brooding with a jagged scar between his lips, twisted the top from the large jar of pickles and handed him a wooden tong.

"I like the big ones, Morley, much juicer, and don't forget the cheese or the jig."

The sound of the man's perfectly strong and tranquil voice had the effect of a tack hammer tapping on his head. The barkeep returned with a rather large block of greenish and yellow cheese on a plate with a thin layer of white fuzz coating it.

"Ah, it smells wonderful," Scorch continued, tapping his fingernail on the table.

Morley flinched. The sound of Scorch's voice did that. He couldn't control it.

"Thanks, Sam," he muttered, returning back to his table with a plate full of rank smelling cheese, tongue assaulting wine and big bumpy green-blue pickles.

Scorch licked his lips as he tucked a handkerchief under his chin.

"Care for some?"

Morley shook his head.

Scorch carved off a chunk of moldy cheese and stabbed it onto a pickle. Stuffing it into his mouth, he said, "Where is everyone?"

"It's after curfew, the dark of night time. No one can leave their homes during this season. The marsh gets edgy. Dangerous," he said, hiding his trembling hand under the table.

Scorch pointed his fork in his face and said, "Are you certain it's the marsh and that they're not just terrified of me?"

"No," Morley admitted.

"But Morley, explain: why would these people be frightened of me? Am I not as handsome and charming as a man can be? Do I not fight like ten men in one? Did I not vanquish that horrible creature, er ... what was it called?"

"A slog dragon."

"Yes, that ugly thing. Big as a pair of ogres it was. Breath like a sewer. Did that not bring comfort among your citizens?"

If Morley could've bitten his tongue off he would've, but he hated pain and blood, and tongues for that matter. He stammered as he said, "No."

Scorch rapped his fist on the table.

Morley banged his knee on the table.

"Why don't they like me, then?" Scorch said, stuffing an entire pickle in his mouth.

"Because you challenged so many people," he said, thinking *pickles*.

"Such contests are considered enjoyment and profitable by your kind, are they not?"

"Yes." *Pickles. Pickles. Pickles.*

"So what happened?" Scorch said, washing down the remaining cheese with a tankard of jig.

"You won the contest."

"So I did, and that's a good thing."

"But they all died ..."

Scorch frowned as he rubbed Morley's shoulder. "So they did." Scorch then smiled. "But only because I am so ... oh what is the word?"

"Marvelous?"

"Yes! Marvelous. I like that word," Scorch said, standing up from his seat. "Now, let's take a walk in this marsh, shall we? I can't have anything more dangerous than me running around out there."

Pickles. Pickles. Pickles.

It was all Morley thought as he dragged himself along behind the most powerful man on Bish.

27

Dᴉsᴛʀɪᴄᴛ Tᴡᴇɴᴛʏ Sᴇᴠᴇɴ ɪɴ ᴛʜᴇ City of Bone wasn't the same as it used to be. Tucked behind the enormous wall of the north-eastern most hemisphere, it was known as the lost city within the city. Vagabonds and murderers ran the streets, along with the most indecent and dangerous of guilds. The Royals, whose City Watch patrols maintained a presence just about everywhere to some degree, had avoided this place entirely. It was foul, abandoned, the streets broken, store fronts rotting, every other piece of glass shattered and every corner a harbor for violence or deceit to some degree. It was the place where people went when they had given up, the most desperate of all people, which was rare, because quitting was not part of the make-up of the people in the City of Bone or in all of Bish, for that matter. Trinos had made it that way, but things had changed and she didn't like it.

Trinos stood in the street like a magnificent piece of china displayed in a butcher shop. Her platinum hair cascaded over her elegant shoulders. Her deep luminous eyes were probing and curious, her clothes of the common sort in design but woven with materials one could not discern or describe. When she spoke, everything moving or crawling stopped to listen, for when her lips moved it was like watching red porcelain lips pouring wine.

"This is not good," she said, shaking her perfect chin. "I need more able people to continue this work."

A large group of men surrounded her, bowing and nodding in acknowledgment. They might as well have been hairy ogres among a new born child, each as rough in feature and texture as a man could come. Their clothes were little more than rags, but every button was buttoned and every stitch had been stitched. They bore scars, marks, burns and some were even missing one of their murderous eyes, but something was different among them beyond the appearance of their character. They moved with purpose.

Trinos lifted her hand and said, "Find me twenty more able men."

A man with a bent nose and wavy black hair that was combed to one side of his head, his calloused fingers fidgeting with the mismatched buttons on his shirt lifted his head to speak.

"Trinos, all of the men we have are rebuilding the castle. All the rest are our sworn enemies. We've betrayed our own to follow you," he swallowed hard, "and our pleas of compassion have gained nothing more than open hostility. Falcrum died by his brother's own hand, and Valcor was poisoned by his own mother's hand." She had brought food, built shelters, bathed children, and yet still the hostility remained. She had even parlayed with Royals only to be rejected with open mockery and disgust as she petitioned for them to take better care of their citizens. Most of them had laughed in her face while others just gaped at her in fascination. The men, their minds as vile as snakes, had peeled off her clothes before her first toe crossed the door's threshold. When she departed, for the first time in her infinite existence she had been concerned for her safety.

She nodded in a graceful motion.

"I just said find me twenty men, and I shall take care of the rest."

"But where?"

"Anywhere you think you can find them. Now go," she commanded.

District 27 was changing. The old was being used to rebuild the new. The citizens, the most pitiful lot in the entire city, smiled on occasion at the sound of the troubadour that played a small gold-painted harp and sang. The ramshackle storefronts displayed a vase of flowers or two. She liked flowers. And fresh food was being baked nearby, which was necessary because she had become very fond of pie.

Her toes didn't seem to touch the ground as she walked and settled herself on a bench near a dried up fountain centered in what used to be a very active plaza. She peered up into the sky, filling her lungs with air behind her perfect breasts, and pondered the suns she had created. She wondered if Scorch was experiencing the same resistance she was or if he even cared. She could do just about anything that she wanted with material things in her world, but she didn't have that kind of power over the willful people. It was frustrating.

"Men," she said, addressing a hapless looking crew that was working on the stonework of the fountain, "are the repairs complete?"

A young man with blue bags under his eyes pulled off his cap and replied, "Yes Trinos, but if I may: there is no water in this place. It's not run with water since I was a boy, and even then it ran with very little."

She rubbed her hands on her skirt that covered most of her voluptuous thighs and said, "The water is coming, and this fountain will return to its original vitality for all to enjoy." She smiled.

The man stammered, saying, "But the Royals—you can't steal their water! They'll wipe us out."

All of the workers blanched as Trinos let out a pleasant little laugh and said, "It's not their water, Corrin. It's mine."

28

THERE WAS DARKNESS, FAMILIAR SOUNDS and pain. Voices, more than one, like shattered crystal, penetrating the recesses of his hazy mind, speaking in a language he swore he understood. There was wheezing and a bubbling sound coming from his busted face, and when he tried to open his mouth to speak it felt like a stake was jabbed in his head. He tasted blood and gravel.

"What now?"

Venir heard that. He strained to open his swollen eyes. One remained shut, heavy as a stone. The other cracked open the ever slightest, catching what he believed to be a moon's blue light. He coughed hard, and his entire body lurched in pain.

"He lives, so let him live," a voice as rough as rusting iron said. "Times like this we need all the help we can get."

"Blast you and your ideas," said another whose voice was full of irritation. "We've no time or supplies to be tending to some stranger, clearly left for dead. He probably has more coming after him, and it's just more trouble for us, as if we don't have enough already."

Venir heard the man spit and curse.

"We take a vote then," a reasonable woman's voice offered. "It's only fair. Look at the man. He's a fighting man; his size is even greater than Baltor's."

Somewhere, a man who sounded as if he had a mouth full of food complained, "What do you mean? Baltor's bigger than that cripple and stronger than any man. Yellow hairs are weak, like women." He sounded stupid, too.

The woman continued.

"Finish your meal, Baltor. I only meant he was almost as big. Your belly and head are far superior."

Baltor made a sound of satisfaction, but a few others laughed quietly and snickered. Venir wanted to laugh himself, but it hurt to even think about it.

"Listen," another man interjected, "I've drug this lout for three days already. He must be three hundred fifty pounds, and I'll not take him a foot farther. My back's killing me. Let the vultures and wolves have him, I say. He'll not be fighting anything but misery for weeks, maybe months. I certainly doubt he'll ever walk again."

Lazy Bastard!

"I'll pull him," the woman said, "and a good bit quicker than you. You might as well ride the stretcher as well. Those stumpy legs of yours aren't worthy of a dwarf."

"What did you say?" The man said with a sneer.

"Maybe you can ride Baltor's shoulders and get some fresh air to fill that big nose of yours, seeing how you've had it shoved up Caralton's arse—"

"Enough!" The voice of the first man who had begun the conversation interjected. "We vote, then. There are seven of us, and I'll break any ties."

"I want to make a plea for the man's life first," the woman decried.

"You've made your case clear Adanna, and we haven't the time to be slowed any longer. We are days away from the nearest Outpost."

Outpost!

Venir's mind was on fire with elation. Men, women, the smell of stew, the taste of Bish's dirt, a hooting owl, the smell of a fire, crackling embers and the metallic pings of a heating metal pot. He was back, back on Bish, and judging by things he was in the south. If he could only speak or pull free of the bonds that had him strapped to a man-made stretcher.

"What about Outlaw's Hide? It's closer," one man said.

"And filled with orcs and gnolls," the woman responded.

"And men just as well. For all we know the Outpost is wiped out. You've seen the fields. The Royals have fled the south, and no word of aid has come," the leader added.

What are they talking about?

"We don't know that!" she disagreed.

"Silence! We'll vote now! Let me see a show of hands of those who think the man should remain in our care and custody."

The voices were coming from behind his head, only adding to the agony that he could not see them. He was propped up at a low angle, leaving him an unfortunate field of vision as well. It was as if he wasn't there, his fate sealed by a council of accusers that he could not face. Venir's dry mouth and swollen tongue were yearning with thirst. *Water.* Maybe that would loosen his jammed up jaw.

"Humph! Only two votes to care for the man, I see."

SLAT!

Venir began to struggle with his bonds, but he could feel little more than his fingertips moving.

"I'm sorry, Adanna. It seems you and your mother have lost out again."

"Father, this is an outrage! That man deserves life. He's a fighter, I tell you. We'll need him."

"Sit down, Girlie," one of the other men chided. "The man will last little more than a day at most. No man can live without taking in water for more than four days, and I'll not be givin' up any more of mine."

"No, Father! At least loose his bonds and leave him to die with whatever he has left."

"Adanna, let go of me. I'll not leave the man, a criminal so far as we know, to be a prone meat basket and be ravaged by coyotes or bugbears."

"More likely underling scouts will take his head and parade it like the rest in their horrible fields."

Underlings!

Venir's hands clenched in and out, pumping more life into his broken body. After all, it had been an underling that cast him in the Mist. Underlings that slaughtered his family. Underlings that slit Georgio's throat. And Underlings that he lived to hunt and kill. He hadn't made it this far and escaped the madness behind the Mist to fail now.

He heard the scrape of a sharp blade coming out of its sheath. His blood surged behind his temples.

"Someone hold his head down while I slip this into his heart. Baltor, start digging a hole. Rogue or not, he deserves a man-made grave."

The sound of sobbing women was drowned out by his instinct to stay alive. Venir summoned every fiber of remaining strength and heaved at his bonds.

Snap! Snap!

He growled in pain like a wounded beast.

There was a sharp gasp behind him when he sat up, half-blind, and began to rise to his feet.

"Great Bish!" someone exclaimed.

Venir winced as he felt a pair of hands wrap around his waist and steady him.

"Someone help the man!" the father commanded.

"But we voted!" One said.

"Yes!" Another agreed.

Venir got a better look at them now, a well-armed but ragged bunch of strangers. Straightening his knees, he pulled back his bullish shoulders and rose to his full height.

"Eek, he's tall, like an oak."

"But can he walk, or follow? He'll slow us down."

Venir grimaced as he stepped forward.

"Easy, Man," the woman said.

He was trying to say, "Let go," but it came out as, "Wetgrowr."

A man, tall and lean, in trousers, bearded and with a strong chin eyed him with suspicion, the short blade in his hand rapping on his pants leg. He, as well as the rest, appeared to be of a better ilk than outlaws or Brigands, but one could never tell for sure. He spoke with more patience in his voice this time.

"Man, can you speak or not? We don't need some mute that can't sound the alarm tagging along."

"Aye," he said, managing a half-hearted smile. He lived, back in Bish, southern Bish to be exact. "Need g-grog."

"Hah, well some water will just have to do. No grog or ale for leagues, Man, just a ragged bunch of mercenaries scurrying along the safety of the Mist. No safer place than the edge of the world right now; the underlings have seen to that."

A moment of panic seized him as his hands fell to his chest. He groaned. His body tamped from head to toe in agony. Something pinched his insides. Busted ribs and splintered bone. *Suck it up!* The sack, once safely tucked in his shirt, was gone. He looked at his fingers, where one appeared to be dislocated. He pulled it back into place with sickening pop. On his other hand, the left, the tips of his outermost fingers remained blackened and gone.

"Sack," he mumbled.

"I have it," the woman said, "but it was quite empty."

"Smother him with it!" someone said. Venir turned away from them all, looking into the mist that was less than a mile distant. He wanted to be as far from it as far could be.

"Get me my sack, and I'll leave you to yourselves," he said, the weariness still heavy as wet canvas. He could barely stand, and walking more than a dozen feet seemed an impossibility at the moment. Pain was something he'd become accustomed to over the years, but being immobile was not.

The woman that was helping him stand up looked up at him. She was a stocky woman, a short-haired red head with round and caring eyes. She said, "Your injuries are too severe, Stranger. You've a busted shoulder and ribs, and your leg seems to be broken."

The leader handed him a canteen of water, eyeing him with concern. "Don't drink it all."

Venir gulped in a mouth full, then another.

"Ah!" he said aloud, his voice rich and robust once more. "Now that's good water, and I'd kill a hundred underlings for more."

"Man, I should cut you where you stand for drinking all of that."

"Kill him! He's a thief!"

"A big, giant, stinking crippled thief."

Venir laughed. My, had he ever missed the insults of people. He said, "You'll do no such thing, my friends. Not without being dragged into the blood and dirt as well."

They all bristled.

"The fool doesn't have a weapon, and now he threatens to kill us all? Kill the lunatic."

"Will you shut up, Lout," she pleaded to Venir. "My father's not one to be trifled with. He's not one for joking; he's moody."

"Ha, your father must have been fed breast milk from an orc when he was a child. A big fat one with three tits and two teeth at that. He misses her, I bet."

No music could have sounded sweeter to his ears than the sound of steel coming unbridled from their beds. In a moment, four men surrounded him as he stood face to face with the leader, but looking down upon him.

The leader said, "Man, your tongue is as twisted as a serpent's tail. My orc mother had four tits, not three!"

Everyone looked at the leader, then Venir, then back to the leader.

Venir knew they were waiting for their leader to spill his blood. He could feel their fear and anger, but the man before him remained calm, eyes giving him closer study.

"Perhaps, Stranger, if you shaved that beard from your face you might not seem so disturbing. You look like a bugbear's nanny. Of course, I can only guess you are trying to hide the ogre portion of your heritage."

"Good for me, but sad for you, clearly being bred of two-legged swine, but your eyes are still quite dashing," Venir said, stretching out his aching limbs, feeling his knotted muscles begin to loosen beneath his skin.

"By Bish," the leader said, "Venir, is that you inside that busted face and elder's beard?"

"Aye, the underlings haven't gnawed the meat from my bones yet, Hogan. I live."

Hogan came over, clasped his hands and looked up in his eyes saying, "Before, you were almost as big as a horse, but now you are, Venir. It's been ten years since we last hunted together, and I thought for certain you were dead, Man."

The rest of the men and women were stupefied. An older woman, Hogan's wife, handed Venir a small loaf of bread and some wine.

"Ah, you were holding out on me," he said to Hogan.

"You asked for grog. But Venir, where have you been, Man? The underlings are over running the entire world these days it seems," he said, guiding him to the fire.

Venir limped over and sat down. The fire's glare seemed to ignite the coals of his blazing blue eyes as he said, "Tell me more about the underlings."

<h1 style="text-align:center">29</h1>

"How do you expect me to defend myself in these treacherous mountains in these bonds, Fogle?" Cass asked, interrupting his thoughts.

The journey back to the hot ground of Bish wasn't any less treacherous than the journey there. Fogle's razor sharp mind had regained its focus with the help of a few feet-warming spells. Still, his head was clogged and draining with snot, and there was little he could do to control that.

"AH-Chooo!"

Cass stopped and turned, saying, "Ah, poor little wizard has a runny nose. Unhitch me and I can help you with that."

"No thanks," he said, avoiding her irresistible gaze.

She was a distraction now. The seductive swagger of her hips drew his gaze when she navigated the snow as if she was part of the snow itself. And every hour or so she had another comment to say: playful, wonderful, tempting, suggestive and even evil. Fogle had defeated her, though. He was the smarter person and stronger as well, but her power was in what she offered him, a want once fulfilled but not fully satisfied. He was curious.

She stood there, waiting for him to catch up, offering a smile.

"Fogle, you have won. I've given my word. There is no need for these bonds," she said, pleading, submissive. "The Blood Ranger knows this. You know this, and if something happens to me, then who will care for your dog? I would hate to see your journey wasted, beyond you losing your virginity, of course. And there is so much more exploring we can offer one another." She smiled the kind of smile that offered many splendors. "After all, it's going to be a long walk." She brushed up against him, looking up into his eyes, the snowflakes falling gently on her beautiful face.

He tore his gaze away, shoved his way past her and trotted up along Mood's side.

"She's witching, isn't she, Wizard?"

"What do you mean?" he answered.

"Ho! I can hear every little word of yer chit chat back there. She's controlling everything from your head to your groin."

"No, that's not the case," he denied. "If anything, I'm controlling her. I'm just letting her think she's getting control. Ah-CHOO!"

A heavy hand slapped him on his back, almost knocking him to the snow-covered ground.

Mood then said, "Keep telling yerself that then, Man, and you'll be in the grave sooner than expected. Remember where you are; this is Bish, yer never in control."

Fogle disagreed. He was always in control.

"No, I have control over my own actions, regardless of the circumstances."

"Is that so, Wizard? Then tell me, were you in control when you slept with her? Was that part of your plan, or hers?"

"That's different. I was trying to seduce her," he said, immediately feeling like a fool after he said it. Cass had caught up and was laughing along with Mood's robust *ho' ho's*.

"Bish on you both!" he cursed. "You outland peoples are impossible."

He walked away, hiding his blushing face and fighting to ignore the soreness of his icy nose.

"She's right, you know," Mood growled back at him.

"About what?" he shot back. He watched Mood slice her bonds apart.

"She has to be able to fend for herself if needed, and we have a long way to go."

Great! Fogle kept on walking over the frozen and rocky tundra. He didn't bother a glance at Cass when she knelt down to nuzzle with the wolves, but he could feel her pink eyes on his back, stirring the memory of her soft lips pressed against his.

"Whoop!" he cried, as his boots slid out from under him and he crashed to the ground. *BONE!* He tried to scramble back to his feet but slipped again, this time jamming his knee into a jagged piece of rock. Pain jabbed into his flesh, and he felt his anger and frustration swelling. Mood's words were loud and clear in his mind for some reason, *Remember where you are; this is Bish, yer never in control.*

A strong pair of arms lifted him back to his feet.

"Thanks, Mood," he said, limping forward.

"Hah," Cass grinned, "is that an insult or a poor attempt at humor?"

Fogle turned to face her, unable to hide his surprise. She locked her fingers around his and held him tight. He tried to pull his hand away, but her firm grip would not give. A moment of panic surged within him. "What are you doing?" he said, "Let go!" He summoned his energy, but her next words subdued his efforts.

"I am your prisoner," she said, kissing his hand.

A lump formed in his throat. His embarrassment at her being stronger than him, physically, began to fade, and he allowed her warm flesh to become one with his.

Mood stood before them with big meaty hands on his hips, a burning cigar hanging out of his mouth.

"Sheesh, just try in' keep up. I'm starting to miss my home already."

But for the time being, Fogle Boon was in no hurry.

30

"I'M GOING, KAM!" GEORGIO YELLED.

Kam shot back, "No, you certainly are not!"

The Magi Roost was empty except for a handful of people including Mikkel, Billip, Joline, Georgio and herself. The madness that consumed the City of Three the prior day had finally come to a close, and now the morning suns of the new day were on the rise. The underlings had brought not only chaos, but fire to the safe harbor of the city. The damage was minimal at worst, but the impact the presence of the underlings had was devastating. For the first time in decades, so far as anyone knew, almost every window and door was locked.

Georgio rose up to his full height, a young man now, but a man nonetheless, and said, "I can do whatever I want. I have family in the south, too, and I want to check on them. I can take care of myself, and I'll have Mikkel and Billip with me. You can't make me stay!" He rapped his first on the bar.

Kam's green eyes were like burning emeralds, and she was shaking with anger and guilt.

"No you won't!"

"Yes I will!" Georgio jumped in her face.

Her eyes fastened on his, blazed with anger, and she began to mumble a spell.

Joline's perspiring face came between the two of them.

"Enough, you two!" Joline stammered, unable to hide the shock on her face. "This isn't the right way to settle this," she said, voice shaking. "Georgio, you are way out of line, talking to Kam that way. She's only done the best by you."

Georgio sulked and turned away, but Joline caught him by his earlobe.

"OW!"

"Sit down, Boy! And don't make me raise my voice again."

Georgio frowned as he plopped down on the nearest chair and brushed his long curly locks from his face.

Mikkel stood up, mouth beginning to fill with words, drawing Kam's glare. He closed his mouth and resumed his seat on the groaning stool.

I can't believe this. She took a deep breath and rubbed her forehead. Her nose was running. Mere hours ago, she had slaughtered a small host of underlings, yet now she was struggling to maintain her wits against the will of an elder boy. She raised her fingers and a half-moon bottle of Muckle Sap floated her way—and was intercepted by Joline.

"Joline," Kam warned, "now is not the time."

As the older woman's lips parted, Kam snatched the bottle from her hand.

"Don't you dare do that again!" Joline fired back. "I can still turn you over my knee!"

Mikkel and Billip's brows perched.

"I'm hungry," Georgio said.

Kam felt her mind unraveling. Things seemed to be happening all at once: underlings had invaded her city; Mikkel and Billip were leaving, and now Georgio wanted to go. Venir was either dead or had abandoned her and his daughter Erin. She tilted the bottle to her lips and drank. *Pull it together.*

"Kam," Joline said with shock, "you aren't some commoner. You're a Royal."

Kam handed her back the jug and said, "And I just killed a hive of underlings, so I think you can give my bad graces a pass." She wrapped her arms around Joline and said, "And I'm very sorry, too."

The brief awkward silence was broken when Billip offered a suggestion, saying, "I think she still deserves a spanking."

Kam let out a little laugh, quiet and pleasant. Joline started to get the giggles. Before she knew what was happening, everyone was laughing, even Georgio chuckled a little. Still laughing, she pulled him up from his chair and said with tears in her eyes, "I'm sorry."

"Me, too," he admitted, hugging her.

Now that the mood had softened in the room, everyone gathered at a big round table by the largest fireplace. Kam was exhausted. Joline looked exhausted, and for the first time since she knew them, Billip and Mikkel's energy seemed drained. Only Georgio remained bright-eyed as he dug a wooden spoon into a large bowl of Joline's stew. Billip and Joline sat beside one another, shoulder to shoulder. It seemed Kam wasn't as aware of things as she'd like to think she was.

"Now, let me be clear," she said to all, but looking at Georgio. "I don't want you to go, but I can't make you stay, any of you, and," she fought back a choking sob, "I don't like it."

"Ah Kam," Mikkel said, "I'll stay."

"No. No, you won't. You have to get your son, and you'll need help. Bish, this is so hard!" She had always figured that things would be simpler once the formidable men parted ways and the boys grew up, but this was painful. Her heart ached. And underlings, ghastly creatures unlike she ever imagined, were waiting out there. She didn't understand how they had the courage to risk their lives going back, knowing full well what was out there.

"Also," she continued, "what about Lefty?"

Georgio looked away, arms crossed over his chest, frowning.

"Don't you want to say good-bye, Georgio? He's your best friend."

Georgio mumbled something.

"What was that?" she said.

"*Was*—I said!"

"You don't mean that," Kam frowned.

"I do mean that. His best friend is the freakish fingered Gillem now. I swear I don't know why all of you like him. He's evil!"

Georgio started to get up, but Mikkel's stern look sat him back down.

For the life of her, Kam hadn't found a single reason to distrust Master Gillem. She'd been paying attention, but maybe not so much as she thought. After all, there had been more than enough distractions lately. As for Gillem being evil, it was absurd, but Georgio was young, and he and his best friend had clearly drifted since Gillem's arrival. Her sudden sickness and the relief Gillem brought did seem a bit too timely.

"Men," she said to Mikkel and Billip, "is there any reason to distrust Gillem? Do you think he's posed a danger to our dear Lefty?"

Mikkel shook his head and said, "No, he's been more than helpful."

"And not overtly so," Billip said, popping his knuckles.

"Stop that," Joline said, wrapping her fingers around Billip's. "Will you ever learn your manners?" The older woman let out a squeal as Billip wiggled his fingers around her waist.

"I think Georgio's just missing his little friend is all," Mikkel continued, rubbing Georgio's head. "But, it's just part of growing up, and halflings are a different race. They have their own ways."

Georgio shoved Mikkel's thick wristed hand away and said through his teeth, "You are an idiot, Mikkel. And so are you, Billip. If Venir were here, he would know better."

Joline gasped, saying, "Georgio!"

Kam slammed her hands onto the table as she rose, saying, "What has gotten into you, Georgio? You're the one acting evil!" She would have done anything to retrieve her words, and if there were such a spell she would have used it. Georgio's handsome round face was now pitiful and sad. His brown eyes watered, and he began to snivel. She reached over to touch him, but he turned his chair away.

"Everyone ease up," Billip suggested. "Georgio's upset and mad, and he's entitled. Besides, it's not like I haven't been called stupid before. Well, at least I don't think I've not been called stupid, so far as I remember."

But no one seemed to be listening to his words, least of all Kam, who felt like dirt. *Venir. Where is that handsome lout who caused all this?* She dabbed her nose with a dish rag and blew. It was an awful sound.

In the meantime, Mikkel reached over, grabbed a handful of Georgio's curly hair, pulled him half out of his seat and said, "You call me an idiot again and I'll bust your fat little arse, Boy."

Georgio's eyes enlarged like moons before Mikkel let him back down.

"Sorry," he managed. "It's just that, I know Venir is out there, and I want to go find him. Maybe he and Chongo are back in Bone — or Two-Ten City? He has to be fighting underlings. Maybe that's why they're leaving the south, because Venir's slaughtering them like he always does."

Kam blew her nose again. She saw Billip and Mikkel give each other hopeless looks. Georgio was a long way from letting Venir go, unlike the rest of them. If anything, the underling assaults were the result of Venir being dead, not alive.

Joline then said, "We can't be parting ways like this, and I can't stay up all night, either. Georgio, I'll keep tabs on Lefty and Master Gillem. I have to say, no man or halfling should be so charming, and he is a bit too nosy for my liking. I love the flowers, and his words, and the way they trickle from his tongue like honey, but … well … I'll leave it at that. I think we all need to be more careful … times are not as they were."

The roasting fire behind Kam did little to warm her spirits. Her friends were leaving, and like Venir and Fogle, she didn't know if she would ever see them again. She scanned the Magi Roost and was overwhelmed with memories. For over a decade it had been her home, and she knew every inch of its fabric from the creaking floorboards to every glass and goblet behind the bar. It was all a part of her. But it had never been so filled with life as it had been these past few months. She looked at the bloodstain on the floor, one table over, where Venir and Fogle had held their legendary Mind Grumble. She whimpered inside. She wanted him back. She wanted them all back to have things like they were before, even if only for one more day.

"Kam," Mikkel's deep voice interrupted her thoughts, "are you well? You look a little lost over there."

"I'm fine. I just realized that, like so many people, I've never been anywhere else before."

Joline kicked her in the leg.

"Do you think you're going to run off and leave your baby? Or me, for that matter?"

"I'll take her with me."

"You set one foot outside of this city with baby Erin … well … neither of you might ever come back again. I can't handle that," Joline got up, flushed, and rushed off to the kitchen.

Kam felt foolish for even suggesting such a thing, and the looks in the men's eyes were ones of grave concern. Georgio had the most worried look of all.

"Clearly I am the only idiot here," she said, standing up. She walked over to Billip and Mikkel, hugged their backs and kissed their heads. Then she did the same to Georgio. She was numb as she walked away and said the rest: "See me before you go. I'll have something for you."

For now, all she wanted to do was crawl in a hole.

31

THE NEST HAD MANY WONDERS one would never imagine … a secret city beneath the golden thrones above. Not many men, or women for that matter, knew of its existence. Even the highest ranking Royals in the City of Three did not know of the location, nor did they care. But there it was: private, quiet, with as many amenities in its crowded nooks as the world above, except for the burning suns and eerie moons. As a matter of fact, it would be a great place to live, if it wasn't full of thieves.

That bothered Lefty as he hurried alongside Master Gillem with a nervous look in his eye and a rapid little heart pounding behind his breast. The novelty of stealing had begun to wear off. It was one thing to make a few ends meet and quite another having to do it against one's own free will. He rubbed his running nose. Something about the moldy air in the dank city bothered him.

"Gillem," he said, "are we going to see Palos now?"

"Prince Palos," Gillem responded, strutting the streets in a long gait, nodding to all of the cohorts they passed by.

The last few hours had been out of the ordinary. Something was going on, and every crooked spine in the Nest had an urgent gesture about it. Whatever was going on, Lefty wasn't being filled in.

He pulled at the long sleeve of Gillem's cotton white shirt and said, "Will you tell me something? What's going on?"

Gillem rubbed his blond locks with his skinny, man-sized fingers that reminded Lefty of Melegal. "Lefty Lightfoot, now is the time to be silent, follow and listen. Yes, something is going on, but that is no matter to us. We serve the Prince of Thieves, and that is all that matters. He will tell us what we can worry about and what we cannot. Now come along."

Lefty didn't like the sound of that. He rubbed the goose bumps on his arms, but they wouldn't go away, not since he'd seen the trove of bodies in their watery graves. He knew, right then and there, he had to make a change. But how? Palos would kill him, of that much he was certain. The Prince of Thieves had made that perfectly clear on more than one occasion. *What would Melegal do? When will Venir get back?* He had convinced himself he wouldn't need them anymore, but on days like this he was reminded how much he did.

"Come on, Lad. We don't need to make the Prince mad," Gillem said as they entered the tavern home of Palos. Gillem didn't offer a single word to the handful of patrons as they made their way up the steps to the balcony.

There stood Thorn, tall and gruesome, big arms crossed over his broad chest, short swords dangling on his hips, blocking the door to Palos's haphazard throne room. Behind Thorn, leaning on the balcony rail, was the other man, small crossbow in hand, toothpick dangling from his mouth, whose name Lefty did not yet know. The man's mousy eyes fixated on Lefty as he stood up and leveled the crossbow at his chest, winked and turned away. Lefty slid a little farther behind Gillem.

"He summoned us, Thorn," Gillem said with an agitated tone, "so open the door, Cretin."

Thorn let out a little snort as he glared down on them like rodents and pushed the door open, taking his time before he stepped aside. Without hesitation Gillem entered, and Lefty stayed on his heels. A brush of air bristled his hair as Thorn slammed the door closed behind them. Lefty let out a sigh. *Here we are again. How dreadful.* The room was empty of life other than the blazing fire inside a marble mantle made for a Royal, with a great sword hanging over the top.

"Have a seat," Gillem gestured toward the table that was half covered with piles of silver and gold coins among other trinkets and jewelry.

The older halfling pulled out a small sack and dropped it with a clank in front of Palos's chair at the head of the table. Lefty saw Gillem's face bunch up as he drew his long fingers away in slow motion. Two weeks of work was in there, a small fortune, a bag of trinkets and trophies, all gone to where? Lefty couldn't help but wonder where it all went and how Palos could possibly spend it all.

Gillem sat down beside him and poured a goblet of wine.

"Thirsty, Lefty?"

My throat is as dry as a cup of Outland sand.

"No."

"Don't be rude, Lefty. If Palos drinks, you drink."

Lefty crinkled his nose. Wine and ale weren't anything he cared to indulge in, unlike the rest of the populace of the Nest, who took a great deal of pride in swilling wine and telling foul jokes. It was fun at first, until the women came, carousing the tavern and stirring the men into a frenzy of hooting and hollering beasts. Lefty never knew the meaning of the word *appalled* or that such a feeling existed until he came to the Nest. Now he found himself feeling appalled every time he came back. He wondered if Gillem ever felt the same, but the master thief didn't ever seem to be bothered by anything, except by Palos.

Gillem slapped him on the shoulder, causing him to raise his head from the table. The warmth of the fire began to seep into his little bones and fill his head with weariness. Palos's bedroom door creaked open, and there the Prince of Thieves stood in a long flowing black silk bathrobe with a belt tightly wrapped around his rotund belly. Palos had put on a few pounds since the first time they met, but he still moved with grace that belied his girth.

"Little thieves," he said, taking a seat at the table, "literally, and with little purses, I see." Palos snatched up Gillem's sack, tested its heft and tossed it aside with all rest. "Really, Master Gillem, that's hardly a day's work, if that."

Lefty watched Gillem's shoulders draw back. It was double what they turned in two weeks before, if not more, and it had been a prosperous couple of weeks.

"You two wouldn't be holding out on me, would you?" said Palos, like a slithering snake.

Lefty looked into Palos's pale probing eyes that were filled with an unnatural, tireless energy. It was as if the man was too greedy to sleep for fear of a rat snatching a golden crumb of cheese. Gone was the charming man he met above, now permanently replaced by something maniacal and greedy. *I can't do this.*

"Certainly not, Palos," Gillem shot back, his fingers falling to his pockets.

"Oh Master Longfingers, I remember our days when you mentored me. Did we not return with more booty than this little sack?"

"No, we did not," the halfling disagreed.

You tell him, Gillem!

"Huh, it seems you are getting old, Halfling. As I recall, we returned with at least two sacks this size," Palos said, stretching out his arms, fighting a yawn.

"In two months maybe," Gillem said, standing up in his chair. "Lefty and I got this in two weeks. I was a master thief then, I am a master now, and I was a master before you cut your first purse."

Lefty couldn't find his breath. Something was wrong. He had never seen Gillem upset before. He grabbed his mentor by the shirt tail and tried to pull him down, only to be swatted away.

Palos fired back, "Sit down, Gillem! Else I'll have Thorn come in here and skewer you like a fat little pig."

The man meant it, every word; Lefty could tell. He tugged at Gillem again, who to his surprise, sat down with a blank look on his face. It was as if Palos's threat sucked all the life from the vibrant halfling man, as if he was looking at his own grave in the murky waters. Lefty remained still, his little heart the only thing moving, like a frightened bunny, barely breathing.

"Now, Gillem, I'll forgive your little fit this once and even this paltry tithe, but one more outburst like that and you both will die! Understand?"

Lefty nodded along with Gillem.

"Now, Boy, bring me a goblet of wine."

Lefty did as he was told and returned back to his seat. Gillem sat stone faced. Sensing that something was very wrong, Lefty slunk deeper into the confines of his chair.

"So, it seems that our gains are meager, and it's not just the two of you, even though you are the most disappointing." He ran his finger around the rim of his bejeweled goblet. "So you both, at my direction, are going to begin playing a bigger game."

Gillem shifted in his seat, and Lefty sat a little farther up.

"It's called *Ransom*. Lefty, do you know what *ransom* is?"

The word sounded familiar, but he didn't know for sure, and he was too scared to guess. He shook his head.

"Oh … well done, Gillem. What a fine mentor you are, not telling him about one of our favorite challenges."

Gillem gave Lefty a sad look over his shoulder that ran a chill down his spine.

"Ransom, little halfling, has a big payday. Maybe ten years' worth or even a lifetime if you play the game right." Palos's polished and charming tone had returned. "Would you like to learn how it's played?"

Lefty was curious. He nodded his head.

"Good," Palos pulled himself up from his chair and leaned on his forearms, eyes intent on his. "First, you need a target, someone of great wealth and passion. Someone who has compassion and a lot of gold. Like a Royal, for instance."

Lefty nodded.

"You find something of theirs, something very valuable, that they cannot live without. Something that they would die for."

Lefty nodded again. It sounded like a challenge, and his thoughts went to the Wizard Towers whose smooth spires reached into the sky. Something valuable or something worth dying for would have to be in there. Maybe this would be an opportunity, a dangerous one, but something new nonetheless.

"Or someone valuable," Palos continued in a whisper, "like a baby, perhaps."

All signs of life went numb from fingertip to toenail. *Erin! Bish! You can't say Erin!* Lefty wanted to run, to hide, to scream or do anything to avoid hearing what Palos said next.

"Yes, Boy, you are going to steal Kam's baby for me." Palos's eyes flickered with evil, his voice as vengeful as a viper and somewhat deranged. "That witch owes me a favor, and I'll have her groveling on her hands and knees before me, offering me anything and everything I want. I'll shackle her, defile her and make her beg for more." Palos slammed his jeweled fists into the table.

Wham!

"I will have her baby, and she will be my whore!"

Lefty couldn't believe what was happening or why. *No! No! No!* How had skimming led him down this dark path? It was his fault and his alone. Now he was being forced to do the unthinkable. Something bumped against his chair. It was the crooked-nosed Thorn, as tall and dark as a stormy night sky.

"You, Gillem and Thorn shall execute this kidnapping, and mind you, little halfling: fail in this charge and Kam and all the rest of your companions will be strewn across every dark corner in this city by the entire thieves guild."

<h1 style="text-align:center">32</h1>

"IMPRESSIVE, DETECTIVE," LORD ALMEN SAID.

It was a compliment; a sincere one that wasn't layered in an accent that suggested anything otherwise would mean death. Instead, Melegal stood tall, not proud, before the Royal Lord's desk beneath the castle kitchens. It had been almost three full weeks since he was last summoned to the hawking man's private study, which gave him great relief and curiosity as well. Lord Almen, an image of strength and power, looked drained. His vulture-like countenance almost sagged, as if recovering from a sudden illness. It wasn't something one would normally notice, but nothing escaped Melegal's notice.

Lord Almen continued as his ring-clad fingers rolled a strange foreign object over his desk. It was one of the items seized during the capture of the Slergs, perhaps the only thing of value at all. The Royal Lord smiled and said, "This is a great prize: a Slerg weapon, very potent. Have you ever seen anything like it before in your life?" Lord Almen held it before his own face, eyes filled with admiration.

"No, Lord Almen. I'm not very familiar with the various forms of weapons, especially one of such a crude make," he said, staring at the white ash cudgel of the one called Leezir, a man he knew from long ago. It looked like nothing more than a club carved from a trunk of wood and shaved down, smooth at the top with a grip carved out for a handle. It had a strange white hue about it.

"Spine Breaker," Lord Almen said, rising from his chair and toying with the hefty weapon. "Tell me about its acquisition. I've heard nothing about this capture of my foes, and I'd like to have some intimate details."

Almen waved the fat end of the cudgel inches from his nose, like a giant rattle. Melegal fought the urge to step back as images of the battle of the Slergs swelled inside the confines of his mind. *Oh, the sick Lord will enjoy this.*

He cleared his throat.

"The short version, Lord Almen?"

"Yes, but don't leave out the interesting parts. I know there must be some," Almen commented while he poured two goblets of wine and handed one to Melegal.

I better make this good, then.

He thought of Venir, the story teller, the man with as much mouth as he had brawn. Venir had his ways, and Melegal had his own, but he'd never been one to entertain men, as opposed to women when it came to using his tongue.

He took a sip, thinking *Oh, that's wonderful,* and began:

"We had them cornered in the catacombs in the sewers beneath the city, between the Northeast passages and the manufacturer's district. I estimated there were only six of them remaining, trapped between the grates with their only way out being up through the storm drains. I ordered the City Watch to drop the smokers in. We had the lone rain portal sealed, twenty Watchmen, swords and watch sticks in hand, ready to dispense your will by my command."

Taking a sip, Lord Almen nodded for him to continue.

"As the smoke billowed from the hole in the street, the first man came out, arms flailing, coughing. An eager Watchmen cut his neck out with a sword, a bit too eager, it seemed. I reminded the dullards we were to take them alive, not dead. So, I had them sheath their swords."

Lord Almen interrupted saying, "Seems risky. They've been a dangerous lot."

"True, Lord Almen, but I needed to interrogate some of them. I had to make sure we had them all," he reassured the Lord. The truth was, he was hoping the City Watch, one or two at least, might be caught off guard. The fewer the Watchmen, the better.

He whet his throat with more wine. *With grapes pressed such as this I could tell stories all day. Man and babe alike. Delicious.*

"The next man burst through the hole in a black cowl, waving that cudgel, which was glowing like the moons. Two watchmen bore down on him, and there was a clap like thunder." He smacked his hands together with a sharp pop. "One man fell to the ground, in a pile of boneless flesh, and the other gawped long enough to have his head cracked open like a nut."

"Excellent," Almen commented, hands caressing the wood.

"About that time another character climbed from the hole, his swords chopping through a small wave of watchmen like they were wheat. He was fast: punching holes in throats and slicing open bellies like a seasoned soldier. Another thunderclap followed. This time it shook the ground, knocking men from their feet. That's when I let loose your snakes."

Melegal opened up his palms. Two coiled pieces of intricate metal shone dully in the lantern light as he set them on the table.

"I'm not a mage, and I had my doubts, but I did as you instructed me. Dropping them to the ground made the things come to life, slithering like sidewinders over the stone and wrapping around the legs of the two formidable Slergs like whips. After that, it was over."

Melegal finished his goblet that Lord Almen refilled.

"Thank you, Lord Almen. At that point, the City Watch overwhelmed them, beating them like a pair of dirty rugs. Really dirty. But the damage had been done. Four of the Watchmen looked like they had just fallen from a cliff and landed on a pile of rocks. Three more were dead from the one Slerg's steels, two others wounded. Blood and guts smeared the road, until the rain came and washed it away. The only ones left of the Slergs were the two and a young girl."

"And wasn't there another, a giant brute of some sort?" Almen asked, hoisting the hefty cudgel on his broad shoulder.

"We'd jailed him earlier. Can't tell if he was kin or not. Seems too big and slow, somewhat mute." Melegal didn't want to say too much. Brak's fate was not in his hands, but if anything, maybe the man could bust rocks for the rest of his life in shackles. *Better than being dead.*

Lord Almen took his seat, dipped a quill in a jar of ink and jotted something down on a piece of parchment. "So, Detective, how confident are you that there are no Slergs left?"

He didn't shift or sigh, despite his resentment of the question—how in Bish was he supposed to know? He had poured over every last bit of information that the torturers had extracted from the men. No man, under thumbscrews or bamboo shoots, was unbreakable, and in the case of the Slergs, they had a weak line of faith. He could only assume they did not lie when they screamed. He had to be right. Of course, it was expected that he would be—after all, he was Castle Almen's Detective—a position he had come to discover offered a degree of reverence, even from the Almen family. *Right or wrong, I'll be dead one day anyway.*

"Certainly, Lord Almen. Every lice-ridden head accounted for. All survivors in uncomfortable and agonizing custody," he said in a reassuring voice.

"Not too agonizing. I have plans for those who remain."

Is that so?

"Lord Almen, may I ask … Do those plans involve me?"

Lord Almen raked his fingers through his long brown hair, fastened his handsome countenance on Melegal and said, "Of course, Detective. With all the work that you have done, it would seem fitting to let you in on our final farewell to the Slergs. I plan to have you and Sefron work on this little project together, along with my family and other Royal friends of mine."

Melegal could feel the blood curdle in his veins at the mention of Sefron's name. He felt his nostrils flaring like galloping horses, even though they weren't, he still struggled to maintain his accommodating composure. *Great, maybe I'll accidentally kill him.* He had already seen the creepy cleric spill more blood in the castle dungeons than most seasoned soldiers spilled on the battlefield. The sick man enjoyed delivering misery, death and pain.

"Excellent, Lord Almen."

"I think you'll enjoy it. There will be a coming of age ceremony for several fine young Royals. It almost makes me want to laugh, thinking about Sefron's plan for the meddlesome Slergs"

"And that would be, Lord Almen?"

Lord Almen raised a brow and said, "I'm sure you are familiar with the Coming of Age ceremony, Detective?"

"Certainly," he answered. Most urchins that served in the castles were very aware, especially the large and slow ones, like Venir. Melegal's memory of back then was as clear of the details as if it had all happened yesterday. It had been at least two decades since he had seen the last one, the one where Venir had fought the Slerg brothers, Creighton and Hagerdon. Leezir had been there, too. Funny how things happen, he thought. "So, the Slergs will be the contestants against the upcoming youth, I suppose?"

"Yes," Almen said, his face showing mild delight. "It's only for the Almens, and as I mentioned, other friends that lie outside of the constrictions of the Royal Castles. I can't have word getting out of this event, Detective." Lord Almen picked up the cudgel that self-illuminated with pale light. "It wouldn't be viewed favorably among other Royal Castles."

"Understood. Is there anything else?"

Lord Almen hawkish eyes fixated on his.

Please don't ask.

"How are you coming along with the Lorda's investigation of my deranged son ... Tonio?"

Lord Almen hadn't mentioned his son in weeks, and now he was interested again? Melegal had no answers. Except one.

Be bold.

"They say a wild butcher in Royal armament runs the streets. They say he is a ghost or ghoul from below. I say that ghoul is yours, Lord Almen."

Lord Almen gave him a wary look and said, "Is this what you have told the Lorda?"

"She can't be as easily convinced, but yes, I have."

"Can you hunt him down and kill him, if need be?"

"I can on your command." *But I'd rather not. I don't think he can be killed.*

Melegal stood there waiting for the Royal Lord to respond. When his feet began to ache, he asked himself the same old question: *How did that big man sneak up on me?*

Lord Almen continued to jot down more notes.

Melegal waited.

Oh, not this again.

Minute after agonizing minute passed.

"I'll be expecting confirmation of what you believe at some point, Detective. Dismissed."

Melegal backed towards the door and left as quietly as he could. How could he confirm what he believed without bringing Lord Almen proof? *Kill Sefron. Kill Tonio? There has to be a way out of all this.* Up the stairs he went, stride after stride, with the full realization that he wasn't going up, he was going down.

33

O UTLAW'S HIDE WAS A PLACE of wary faces. Venir welcomed them all, however, offering greetings and salutations as if they were all long lost friends, not a stranger among them, yet there were many.

"Hello, Pretty One," he said to a chubby half-orcen woman wrapped in tattered robes and carrying a sack of flour.

Adanna, Hogan's daughter, jabbed his ribs with an elbow. "Will you stop that? You draw too much attention upon yourself. And calling that two-legged sow pretty is sickening."

Venir reached over and tickled her ribs, bringing forth a squeal of delight.

"Jealous, I see."

"Hardly," she said, reaching up to pull the clay jar of grog from his lips, "now give me that. You've drank yourself blind."

Venir dangled the jar high over his head. "And before the night's over I'll have drunk myself deaf as well, but not so much that I cannot enjoy your soft lips crying for more." He slapped Adanna on her rump, lifting her to her toes.

"Lout," she said, slapping him away ... with a smile.

Outlaw's Hide was little more than a tent city, the heavy canvasses large, small and some even grand enough to house a hundred people, others little more than a stick and a rug. There were buildings, but these were few and rotting like fallen logs in a swamp. It hardly mattered. The inhabitants of Outlaw's Hide didn't often stay for long. The Hide was dangerous: even the deadliest criminals and renegades were at risk within its shadowy clutches. Some came and went quickly, others didn't last through the night. Venir wasn't worried about any of that.

Venir tossed his empty jug into a small tent, busting it with a crash. A cry of alarm went up, and angry voices stepped out, a pair of stout men, one as scarred and calloused from battle as the other, hands gripping the pommels of their swords. Venir was whistling as he walked by, paying neither man any mind.

"You're a dead man!" one said, ripping free his sword, its keen edge glinting in the moon light.

Venir stopped, turned and laughed, his big hands falling onto two broad swords strapped around his waist.

The men were almost a head shorter than Venir, yet taller than most men. Their opposing demeanor was criminal from head to toe as they spread apart, both brandishing steel. The murderous intent in their eyes began to fade as Venir's shadow fell on them.

"Did you jackals say something?" Venir said.

Both men made grumbling sounds, sheathed their swords and returned inside their tent.

"That was strange," Adanna said. "Oh!"

Venir hoisted her over his shoulder and said, "Let's give those pretty little legs of yours a rest, shall we?"

Other than an excited sigh, her warm, supple body offered little resistance if any at all.

Venir jostled through the throngs of orcs, men, gnolls, kobolds, dwarves and even striders and halflings as if they weren't there. He was the most popular man in the Hide, and that wasn't good.

Outlaw's Hide, on the southernmost corner of Bish, once small and secluded, was getting crowded. The races at most times were barely tolerant of one another, but now they were almost amiable. It wasn't uncommon to see men and gnolls playing cards, though the dwarves still were intolerant of the handful of half-ogres. The Hide was a reminder of Venir's time spent with the Brigand Army, another secure location tucked behind the jungles, behind the grasses and atop jutting hillsides.

"Venir, will you please put me down? I'm getting sick," Adanna said.

He set her down and took a long look in the sky.

The moons in the sky, both a dull reddish hue, stirred his blood. Hogan had caught him up on mankind's plight and the onslaught of the underlings. The days he thought he was gone in the Under Bish and Mist had turned out to be months, perhaps longer. No, it seemed Bish was upside down. Something was wrong, very wrong. He could tell.

"Are you a'right? You seem lost," the soft woman said, pulling him into their small but accommodating tent. "You've been a bit aloof these past few days." She pulled his shirt off and began running her fingers over his scars.

The underlings. According to Hogan, they were as thick as weeds in every direction, subjecting their terror on every race with extreme prejudice. But humans, however, seemed to be taking the brunt of the punishment. Venir was happy to be living and breathing among men again, relishing every day of life. He was different, his vitality returned, a spring in every step, and brightness behind every word. He feared nothing. His belly was filled, and other needs satisfied. He was ready to live again, and for now the underlings would have to wait. But something in the back of his mind was beginning to ebb.

Adanna pushed him down onto the blankets, straddled him and began pulling her top off.

He reached for her breasts.

"Venir!" someone shouted from outside his tent.

Adanna dived for her clothes.

"Go away, Hogan! I'm—"

"Shaddup, Man. I know what you and my daughter are doing. There's no time for that. You need to come and come now!"

Venir stepped outside, the hot night air bristling on his scarred and naked chest.

"I see you trimmed your face."

"Actually, I did that," Adanna said, stepping out from behind the tent flap.

Hogan shook his head. It was clear he was perturbed by their relationship. "Baltor is coming." Adanna's father waved his hand in front of his face. "Man, how much have you been drinking? You smell like a half-orcen sot. And now Baltor comes, full of fire, wanting to challenge you for Adanna."

"What!" she interjected. "I'm not some trophy whore. I can choose whom I please."

"No you can't!" Hogan warned. "You agreed to be Baltor's mate, and word bound it. Now you've gone and broke your oath."

"I never made an oath, Father! Baltor was there when I was alone. There's not some pact between us."

"Well, the fool does not care, and he's not alone. Venir, he's dangerous. Stupid, but dangerous as a gnoll. And I'd be lying if I said he didn't worry me."

Venir smiled grimly and said, "Let him come. I've fared pretty well against better."

"At least hide until you can be prepared, Man. You're swaying like a tree about to fall."

"Too late," Venir huffed, rubbing his blurry eyes.

Baltor had arrived, accompanied by a handful of Hogan's men and another troupe of outlaws and renegades. Baltor was big, his muscles solid as if he were carved from the trunk of a tree, unyielding. His head was shaved on both sides. A strange black collar adorned his neck, and his brutish body seemed unnatural beneath the face, with a sinister look lurking behind his wild eyes.

"Adanna, come with me!" Baltor ordered, thumbing his chest.

She stepped forward, mouth opening to speak when her father pulled her back.

Venir crossed his arms over his chest and sighed, saying, "What's the matter, Baltor? Are the hairy hind ends of your orcen sisters too much for you to handle?" *hic*

Out loud chuckles erupted from the growing crowd, gnoll and orc among them.

Baltor rushed up and jabbed his finger in Venir's face.

"I'll kill you!" he said, practically frothing at the lips.

Venir, despite his impairment, could see the glazed look in the man's eyes. Baltor, already mighty of frame, was endowed with something else. Mystic herbs, dark ones, most likely. It was something the black markets from Outlaw's Hide sold. He couldn't remember what it was called, but it was pricy, something that the Royals were more apt to get their hands on as opposed to common men.

"You couldn't beat me if my arm was tied behind my back," Venir said, sneering down on the man. He was getting annoyed. Then he heard Adanna gasp.

"You heard him! One hand tied behind his back! A Challenge!"

A fervor arose in the crowd. Venir's big mouth had landed him a few challenges already. All of his talk of dragons and giants had branded him as a bit of a loon, though his stories did sound quite convincing and even caused the oldest of crones to swoon.

Unlike challenges in the more civilized establishments in the world of Bish, Outlaw's Hide played by very loose rules. Anything that sounded like a challenge could be construed as a challenge, which was a strong reason why most outlaws kept to themselves. The mildest of disagreements could be turned by gossiping mouths into the bloodiest of contests.

Hogan reached over, grabbed him by his arm and said, "Are you a fool! Baltor's an induced bull."

"Hah, more like an induced imbecile. I've fought a minotaur, and if anything, he's a sheep, or a cow." *Hic* "You're a cow, Baltor."

Adanna stood in front of him, her round face looking up at him like he was a complete lunatic. "What have you done, you fool?"

Hic "I'm taking measures so that the next time we lock legs there'll be no interruptions." Venir swept her up in his arm and gave her a hungry kiss. "Hold on to that until this is over."

Adanna gawped and turned away.

Venir was being shoved into a circle that had formed, of bloodthirsty men, orcs, gnolls and striders. The dwarves and halflings stood in the front. As he peered around, a brief thought of Melegal came to mind, as the coins began their clinking journey from hand to hand. Somewhere, a one-armed troubadour with an eye patch played and sang a semi-rousing tune on his lute.

There was a day when the underlings came
And the Darkslayer wasn't there to slay the day ...
Instead a loon and bald-headed goon squared off to play a game.
Tis the day when one brute must die.
Bye, bye in Outlaw's Hide
Where the liars and the convicts come to live and die, and
The good ole dwarves mix the grog and the wine, singing
This'll be the place that ye'll die.
Bullslat! Someone interjected.
This'll be the place that ye'll die.

"Right or left handed?" A gruff looking man with a long piece of rope asked. "Ah ... it seems you're right handed," the man said, looking at the missing finger tips on his left, then proceeded to tie off his right arm. He tested the bonds and yelled out, "He's secured."

Venir gave his missing fingertips some study as Baltor paced back and forth like a caged animal, drumming his head with his fists. That's when Venir noticed a series of very tall and large figures looming farther behind the ranks of the crowd. He was beginning to think that maybe, just maybe, someone was trying to kill him.

A tall slender man, long haired and wizened, stepped in the middle of the circle, robed in brown clothes from head to toe. Venir had never seen him around before. The man lifted his hands, and the crowd fell silent.

"You, Venir, have made a challenge against Baltor. One-armed you'll fight until one of you begs for mercy or succumbs to death. Is this correct?" the man said, his voice loud and tranquil.

"Aye," Venir said.

"And you, Baltor, you accept?"

"Aye," Baltor said, his sneering face fixated on Venir's as he smashed his fists together.

Venir couldn't ever recall having fought one armed before. How much harder could it be?

"ONE!"

The rambunctious crowd gasped into a whisper as every eager eye widened with elation.

"TWO!"

34

E XHAUSTION. THE WORD WASN'T SUFFICIENT. Fogle lay in a bed that was little more than a mattress stuffed with feathers and hay that sat on the floor. It might as well have been one of the finest beds and mattresses in the City of Three as far as he was concerned. He was no longer cold, and that was all that mattered. He yawned, stretched, tossed and turned, but nothing eased his jangled nerves. However, he did find great comfort in the fact that he lived. Even if it was in Dwarven Hole.

"One adventure down … no more to go," he murmured to himself.

At least I'm warm. His room, consisting of the heaviest wooden furniture he'd ever used, was uncomfortable. But, a sense of security filled him, despite all of the commotion that occurred outside. The dwarves, a more melancholy than mirthful race, were active. Hammers striking steel were always echoing from within the Hole, along with the sounds of a roaring furnace being stuffed with coal and stoked.

The underlings. It seemed the dark vicious little race of creatures had begun to crop up everywhere. On his travels back, Mood had apprised Fogle of their bloody presence and wicked deeds. The most horrific things had happened to several villages and farm towns south of Dwarven Hole. A longtime safe haven under the dwarven wings had all but been wiped out.

It was there Fogle Boon witnessed mankind slaughtered. For the first time, Fogle had been filled with horror. The people, many weeks dead, coated in flies, rodents, worms and decay had even been buried head first in the ground. Their swollen, rotting, gnawed on legs were the most repulsive things he'd ever seen. Jackals and other animals that fed on carrion had picked many of the bones clean. That was far from the worst of it all. The heads of men, women, and children sagged on wooden stakes, mouths hanging open, eyes gouged out. It seemed the vulture hawks considered them a delicacy. And the smell, so horrible, foul and rotting, had made him retch. His stomach became queasy at the thought of it.

Sitting up, he rubbed his weary eyes. Three days had passed since he, Mood and Cass had returned, and for three days, two of which he hardly moved from his bed, he had done nothing. Mood was absent and Cass as well, but his dreams of her had kept him company. Now he was bored and lonely. What was his next move? Remain, or return home? Return home, or resume his quest to find Venir? And what had happened to his ebony hawk, Inky, that he'd sent into the Mist after the brutish man?

A soft knocking rapped at the door.

His heart raced. *Cass.*

"Come in," he said, returning to his feet.

The door swung open, revealing two dwarven women, laden with heavy terry cloth towels in their arms.

"Yes?" He said.

They entered, followed by a third, a brown bearded dwarven man pushing a heavy cart that appeared to be filled with a giant tub of water. The dwarven man set two blocks behind the wheels, gave him a gruff look and departed. The two dwarven women remained. One added something to the water that made it sizzle, and a pleasant smoky aroma filled the room. That's when Fogle realized that he hadn't bathed in months, perhaps longer. He felt disgusting when the moment he last bathed hit him. *What would my mother think?*

He rubbed the wiry hairs on his bearded chin and began to wonder if he should shave as he watched the little women get to work. The two stout little figures moved with purpose and grace that seemed odd. Their round little faces were smooth and warm, eyes narrow and inviting underneath thick heads of hair pulled up in buns. They wore tight sleeveless robes of fleshy tones that revealed short muscular arms and well-rounded chests and rears. Fogle swallowed as he recalled the conversation he'd been having with Mood, before they were captured by Cass. It seemed the King of the Blood Rangers remembered. Either that, or he just stunk really bad.

"Eh … I suppose you want me to get in?"

The closet dwarven lady didn't respond. Instead, she reached over and began helping him out of his clothes. His rosy cheeks did little to hide his embarrassment as the two silent women helped him step up into the tub. As his first foot sunk into the steamy bubbling water, he felt his eyes begin to burn. *Oh my, that feels good.* A smile broke out on his face as if the last three years of his life had been returned. There was no shame now; his surroundings were as meaningless as the dust on the floor as he sank down into the water feeling like a king. *Ah … I deserve this,* he thought, letting his heavy lids close. Strong fingers began rubbing the knots out of his shoulders, and the other lady dwarf began scrubbing him into a thick lather. All embarrassment washed away. *I could get used to this.*

"Fogle Man-Whore! What do you think you are doing?"

Water splashed over the lip of the tub as he twisted his body around. There stood Cass, arms crossed over her chest, her bare foot tapping on the floor with a perturbed look on her delicate face.

"I, well," he stammered, "I haven't bathed in months."

"So, I suppose it's been so long that you have forgotten how to do it yourself?"

His mind scrambled to find an adequate excuse. *I don't need one.*

"No, as a matter of fact, I'm lazy. And there's nothing quite like the hands of a strong dwarven woman to rub out the icicles you used to freeze my thews and bone. And who are you to reprimand me on my bathing habits? Aren't druids notorious for bathing in nothing but mountain sludge?"

Cass's jaw clenched on her pale face, and her pink eyes narrowed with a murderous intent.

He didn't care. She had brought him nothing but misery the entire journey back, offering comfort only to pull it back. Maybe it would have been better to have remained a virgin, after all. *Ah, but those pink lips are as delicious as wine.* He slunk deeper into the warm watery confines of the tub. "What is it? Have you come to gawk or to torment me more?"

She shoved his head down under the water and pulled him back up by his hair.

"Fool! I've come about the dog, and your thoughts are of yourself, Man Whore Fogle." Cass turned and left, the door slamming behind her.

"Well fiddly-dee," he said, as the wonderful bath seemed to sizzle through skin, muscle and bone. He felt short fingers rubbing the muscles in his knotted shoulders. *Ah …*

Wham!

A door slammed into the wall.

"FOGLE MAN-WHORE! Get your arse out of the water and follow me!" Cass stood in the doorway again, her eyes like burning roses. "The dog is about to die!"

35

T HEY CAME. LIKE A BLACK snake Lord Verbard's army slithered beneath the world of Bish towards the unsuspecting City of Bone. It was agonizing. Verbard stood in the back of the bow of a barge that hosted over fifty underlings. Moving an army, though a small one by some standards, was like pushing a heavy cart through a trail of mud. The barges, six in all—each hosting Juegen soldiers that controlled Badoon hunter squads that minded the mindless albino urchlings and ravenous cave dogs—crept over the black waters of the Current with agonizing haste. As patient as the underlings were, Lord Verbard had no patience for this.

I haven't the faintest idea where to start in the City of Bone. Does anyone? Or, is this Master Sinway's way of sending me on a suicide mission?

Verbard sharpened the tips of his fingernails with a metal file. Nearby, hunkered between the weapons and supplies, a pair of large mangy cave dogs were ripping troll meat apart. Days ago, his army happened upon a handful of the slimy and brutish race. More or less, the trolls were the ogres of the lands below: rare, unsightly and monstrous. One barge had been tipped over during the surprise attack, the underling bodies either crushed or dragged into the dark. Thirty had been lost, his army already diminished before his battle even started. He had taken precautions to avoid another tipping experience.

I hope Kierway doesn't plan a head count. The brat probably will. Perhaps I can gather the details from him. I shall have him do my work for me.

It was strange. Verbard was an underling with nothing more than pure hatred towards the race of men. His hatred stoked fires within him, sparking imagination of inflicting the cruelest and twisted things. After his battle with the Darkslayer, he had had quite enough, but now he was pressed into delivering a siege on an entire human city.

Men will not be ready. Men will die. But at what expense?

He reached down into an unnaturally deep pocket inside his robes, wrapping his fingers around the dry parchment of an ancient scroll. It gave him comfort. He knew something about the City of Bone. He'd seen glimpses of its interior before. Would it be possible to conjure the imp once more? Could he control it without the help of his brother? He tucked the parchment back inside his robes. *Did I ever even need my brother's help?* Verbard's feet shifted beneath him as the barge came to a complete stop. He made his way to the fore, where two heavily armored Juegen stood, pointing ahead.

As black as it was, there were still faint traces of light to an underling's discerning eyes. Ahead, the wide expanse of the Current's waters began to broaden, but a dam of rock and stone had barricaded their way through the next corridor. Were they stuck? Not that Verbard was in any hurry, but it would take a day or more to clear the way. The other half of the army, he hoped, didn't experience such delays by trekking through the caves. It had seemed better to split his forces than to move them all as one. Perhaps he should have split them into three. It seemed that something was intentionally trying to slow them, and it wasn't men. *Trolls.*

"Protect me," Verbard ordered.

The Juegen, covered in plate armor from head to toe, withdrew their long curved blades. Another set, each with a barbed trident in its grip, gathered near as well. A silent word traveled back from one barge to the other. If the trolls attacked again, they would be ready.

Verbard's silver eyes opened, gleaming with light. He stretched his palms upward toward the cave ceiling. Mystic energy filled him, tingling first around his ankles and spiraling upward around his body, through his neck and into his mind. It was arousing his senses, which began to heighten to another level. Something primitive lurked nearby, dormant, maybe lazy, but strong and formidable. He felt it. It was agitated. But where was it?

The Current, a long series of stagnant rivers that did not flow, ran through enormous lakes and tunnels. At the moment the underling army drifted along the nearest bank. The creature, wherever it may be, could be down in the deep, how far Verbard did not know. He channeled his thoughts, pushing them forward, looking for any formidable life ahead. There were some trolls: stupid and hungry, their tiny minds having little purpose at all, but it was clear they did not like the invasion. Verbard released his spell. It was decision time.

Four albino urchlings appeared at his thought. Small and hulking, with large hollow nostrils and ears, they snorted and awaited his command. With a nod they dove one by one into the water, out of sight, leaving a trail of rippling waves above their path. Verbard watched as they emerged on the barricade of rocks, two crawling over the pile, disappearing over the other side. The others began pushing rocks out of the way.

Verbard let out a little grunt. Something was wrong. The normally quiet Current was even more so at the moment. He couldn't afford to lose any more underlings, either.

"Ready the lanterns of the underlight," he commanded.

Light. It wasn't the enemy of the underlings, but it was of many other subterranean creatures. The underlings and other cavern dwellers tolerated each other because they were mindful of not disturbing one another, but in this case, it seemed, something else had already been disturbed.

A faint blue light warmed from at the bow and stern of the lead barge. The next barge illuminated to life as well, followed by the next and the next and so on. The underlings, each and every one, were staring abroad, their colorful gemstone eyes filled with a degree of uncertainty. The only things Verbard could hear were the cave dogs slobbering quietly on the troll bones. Irritation mixed with worry.

Scanning his surroundings, he got his first look in a lifetime at the ecosystem of the Current. Enormous stalactites jutted from the ceiling like teeth, smooth and round in some places, jagged in others. Verbard became anxious. One single formation falling would capsize a barge, not just one, either, but possibly all. It seemed too perfect not to be a trap.

The albino urchlings were moving the rocks from the corridor ahead, but their efforts would not be enough. Some of the boulders were huge, maybe over a ton, and it was going to take more than muscle to move it quickly. It would take magic, a great deal of it, too.

"Fetch the magi," he commanded.

Suddenly, the barge pitched and rocked over the waters. Verbard watched the lake come to life, waves rolling and splashing into the barge. Something enormous emerged, rising higher and higher, towering twenty feet above the waters. Verbard hissed.

"Ready the harpoons!"

It was like nothing he'd ever seen: grotesque, humanoid, more fish than man, coated in weed and sludge. It stormed through the waters, a mindless juggernaut of fins and scales. Verbard summoned a protective spell. *I hope it's alone,* he thought as the first barrage of bolts, arrows, spears, tridents and harpoons bounced harmlessly away.

Waves of water crashed over the bows, filling the barges, as the creature roared like a dozen trolls gone insane and smashed its arms into the ceiling. A stalactite fell, splintering wood and crushing underlings. Verbard shouted out another warning as more trolls spilled out from the mouths of the caves. They were trapped.

36

Gone. Mikkel, Billip and Georgio had all departed with all the supplies they could handle in tow, helped by the shaggy pony, Quickster. That had been weeks ago, and Kam had barely been able to contain her emotions since.

She sat in her apartment above the Magi Roost, baby Erin propped up over her shoulder, as she patted the small of the baby girl's back.

"Come on now, little girl, let it all out," she said with a sniff as she rubbed her watering eyes on Erin's pale blue blanket. She kept on patting, every minute seeming longer than the last. Baby Erin wouldn't sleep without a thorough belch, which meant Kam wouldn't get any sleep either, and sleep had been hard to come by since the underling invasion.

"Oh come on, Erin. I need rest; you need rest," she said, patting harder.

Buuu-urp!

"Thank goodness," she said, looking into Erin's twinkling little eyes as she wiped her baby's mouth. "That's a big girl."

Erin smiled with toothless delight, letting out the tiniest of giggles, melting Kam's heart.

She hugged her little girl tight. She had never adored anything like her baby girl. Laying Erin down in her bassinet, she whispered a word and the gentle side to side rocking began. It was late in the day, the time between work and play, those precious moments before all of the worrisome patrons came to spread gossip and rumors.

Kam lay down on her sofa, pulled a blanket over her legs and closed her eyes, now too tired to cry.

KNOCK! KNOCK! KNOCK!

Who dares! She swung her legs to the ground, hoisted herself to her feet and checked on Erin, who was fast asleep. *Thank goodness.* She swore under her breath as she wrapped a blanket around her barren shoulders. *I'm gonna kill someone.* Joline was the only friend she had left, and the older woman never would have bothered to knock, seeing as how she was the only one besides Kam who had a key.

"Who in Bish is it?" She tried not to yell.

A peppy voice from the other side of the heavy oak door responded by saying, "It's just yer favorite halflings, Master Gillem and Lefty Lightfoot."

She slapped her hand to her forehead. Gillem and Lefty had been hanging around more often now that the other men were gone. They were helpful, in an annoying and pestering way, offering to do things one normally wouldn't want done or showing up during the most inappropriate times. Like right now.

"Go away," she ordered them. "I'm taking my nap."

There was an odd silence on the other side. She checked the lock. *Just leave!* Something about Gillem and Lefty was just plain odd.

"Kam," Gillem said, "we don't want to be any trouble, but we wanted to share a concern."

"Blast," she muttered under her breath. They were both full of concerns and suggestions, like two old hags who knew how to do everything but were too old to work. One day the food was served too hot, the next too cold. The flowers needed more water, and then they needed less. Dwarves should have their own section, outside, and men taller than six feet should always have to sit, not stand. She'd had enough.

"I don't care. If you don't like something, just go somewhere else that you do like, if that is at all possible, you two festering ear aches!"

That ought to do it. She leaned towards the door, brushing her hair behind her head as she did. *Now, please go away.*

Of course, insults only seemed to encourage the halflings to do better.

"Eh, Miss," said Gillem, "er Kam, we don't mean any trouble. It's just that … there's a man, a strange looking fellow. He's, well, he's frightening."

Ah yes, he's probably seven feet tall and rides a rabbit the size of an ox. Little idiots.

"Have Joline take care of it. Now go away."

"But, Joline went to the market."

"Not this time of the day," she argued.

"She ran out of onions," Gillem said.

"And 'shrooms," Lefty added.

Kam outstretched both of her arms on the door and fought the urge to slam her head into it.

"Why didn't you go to market for her?" She asked through gritted teeth.

"She insisted," they both replied.

Their voices were as reassuring as a grandfather's hug.

"Just give me a minute."

"Excellent, we'll be right here."

"No, I'll meet you down there."

"But I'd like to watch Baby Erin," Lefty pleaded from the other side.

Kam shook her head. "Send up two of the girls."

"But yer very short handed down stairs, it seems."

"Get them now!" She said, kicking the door.

Lefty felt like a nest of baby snakes were churning in his stomach as he and Gillem headed back down the stairs. The moment had come, despite all of his attempted delays. *How did this happen? Why me?*

Georgio, his best friend, was gone. He didn't even get to say good-bye. Now, his best friend, who he had put up to so many devious tasks, had left him for the Outlands, leaving him with no one to turn to, not even Kam. His head was aching, and his heart was broken. All he had was Gillem.

He felt Gillem's long fingers squeeze his shoulder, and he fought the urge to cringe. He'd suppressed many things, bottling them all up within, turning his core to stone. He was starting to understand that was what they wanted.

"Yer doing fine, Boy," the halfling man said. "It's almost over."

Lefty nodded, but didn't' agree. If anything it was only the beginning of his career as a criminal, a hardened one, slavery without a personal cause. But he had to do it, so he thought, to protect Kam and his friends. Now they were all gone, and it was up to him. The lives of Kam and Erin now were solely in his hands. He wanted to save them, warn them, but visions of his own horrible watery death froze his tongue inside his head.

While making their way down the stairs and into the main floor, Lefty noticed The Magi Roost hosted few patrons, which was odd for this time of day. He sat down near the bar across from Gillem at a small table made for halflings, thanks to many pushy suggestions. Lefty hated that table, small chairs on long legs, surrounding a round table. Being small was bad enough, but sitting at a small table seemed ten times worse. But it had been just another distraction, not for him or Gillem, but for Kam and Joline. It was a devious game.

"Let's have something to drink, shall we?" Gillem said.

No thanks!

"That would be good," he said.

It was getting easier, the lying, cheating and stealing. His hands were steady, his mannerisms cool, and he swore he even had Gillem fooled. He rubbed his hands on his trousers and combed his fingers through his curly blond hair. Gillem's eyebrow lifted the ever slightest. *Good.* He'd been practicing for days, adding a subtle move here and there, figuring Gillem would think he was nervous. That would be normal with so much at stake, but he could control it, turn it on or off as easily as sheathing a sword in a scabbard.

"We'll get some cheese, too," Gillem said quietly. "It will help settle our stomachs."

Lefty nodded as Gillem motioned one of the girls over. The serving girl rolled her eyes before she made her way over, the sway in her hips gone. It was the one that had been quite fond of Georgio, and she was outwardly sad these days. As Gillem placed the order, Lefty cast a quick glance over his shoulder.

There was Thorn. Tall and leering, the man strolled throughout the tavern poking his crooked nose in everyone's business. Several patrons, including a dwarf, had already left, and more were certain to follow as the dangerous looking man in sheepskin vest and trousers continued to tap his ringed fingers on the metal pommels of his swords. It was all part of the plan.

"That'll be all, Dearie," Gillem said, slapping the girl's rear as she turned to walk away.

In the passing weeks Lefty had been involved with the kidnapping plan that was designed to wear Kam down to a nub. He and Gillem had become the friendliest nuisances in the world of Bish, and it came so naturally. Lefty had even reached a point where he felt no shame in it at all. Kam, as strong and alluring as she was, now showed signs of exhaustion. It was a cold reminder of what he was up to, even though he tried to deny it. Deep down, he'd thought someone would arrive in time to prevent all this, but no help had come. *Maybe Kam can save herself.*

The waitress returned, set a pair of small jugs and a tray of cheese on the table and departed. Gillem tore off a hunk of cheese, dipped it in mustard and ate. Lefty followed suit with a smaller portion, and after many long minutes the entire tray was gone. The cheese did little to settle the gnawing feeling that was growing inside him. The jug of hot tea was of little comfort, either. Something was wrong.

Lefty looked over at Gillem and said, "Shouldn't we send the girls up? Kam's very impatient these days."

"Give it a moment," the halfling man responded, leaning back in his chair, long fingers drumming on the table.

Lefty didn't like the way Gillem said it. There was something he didn't know. It was at that moment he noticed something else: his feet were sweating. *Oh no!* Gillem gave him a funny smile. *What in Bish?* The older halfling looked under the table where his dripping feet were making a puddle on the floor. As Gillem's eyes returned to his, a sliver of fear raced through him. What Gillem said next astounded him.

"You've done well, Lefty. A good student, one of the best, but now the real test begins."

What is he talking about?

"We will go upstairs, you and me, and pick the lock. Inside we shall find Kam, bound and gagged by magic. Baby Erin will be long gone."

Lefty could feel his thundering little heart collapsing inside his chest. *No!* How many days had there been to warn her? How many opportunities had he missed?

"She'll never suspect us, Lefty. She'll never suspect a thing thanks to yer damp feet. Thorn will take care of the rest."

Gillem hopped down from his stool, and on numb legs, Lefty followed.

"Too late to warn your friend now, Lad," Gillem said glumly. "Ye should've done that when you had the chance."

37

T*unk-Tunk-Tunk-Tunk.*

"What is that?"

Tunk-Tunk-Tunk.

Something was pecking on the exterior of Boon's standing metal cocoon. The old wizard had ignored the first several minutes of the strange sound, assuming it to be another delusion of his imagination. But, the persistent sound remained.

Tunk-Tunk-Tunk-Tunk …

"Am I some child's rattle? Another musing toy of a giant simpleton?"

He was talking to himself again. The giants kept a watchful eye on him these days, and he was happy that his lips remained free. His ramblings gave him company, but not freedom. No, the giants were privy to his tricks and his magic, which, for all purposes, was dormant. It had something to do with his cocoon, or sarcophagus; he didn't know what to call it: an upright metal husk with three bars in front of a face hole.

Tunk-Tunk-Tunk-Tunk.

"I'd curse right now if I remembered any curse words! And I know I used to know many!"

His prison didn't sustain him. The giants did. They let him out every few days for a few hours, which he spent strolling around an abandoned study of sorts: no books, just musty furniture for people ten times bigger than him, and a cold fireplace big enough to burn a village. It was there he sat, ate and drank. There was nothing to do, nowhere to go. He didn't even get out to toy with the latest captives, assuming there were any. He thought of Venir, on and off, wondering if the man ever escaped the Under Bish. Could he have made it back out of the Mist? It was of little curiosity to him now.

Tunk-Tunk-Tunk-Tunk …

"This is obscene. I've truly gone mad!"

That's when he heard the flapping and something bird-like landing near where he now rested, beside the fireplace's mantle. He squished his bearded face into the bars in front of him. He swore whatever it was had landed above him on the mantle. *What is it?* Boon shifted his weight on his aching feet, back and forth. His metal cocoon bumped against the stone hearth. It was torture, barely moving an inch inside, left to right, his energy within his frail body already spent. *I must see it!* He put what little weight his meager frame had into it. There was a scraping sound on stone as the cocoon teetered to the ground.

Thonk!

His feeble body paid for it, and his teeth cracked inside his mouth. Warm blood trickled over the wispy hairs on his mustache and into his mouth as his cocoon rolled and rolled before it came to a stop. *Painful and nauseating.* His eyes flitted open. There was a tiled floor, and the sofa's mahogany clawed foot could be seen from the corner of his eye. He was facing the wrong way.

He couldn't muster the energy to speak. He lay still, mentally venting the maddening frustration, trying to block out the pain of his broken nose and cracked tooth. He wanted to know what had been making that noise. He had to find out before the giants came.

Tunk-Tunk-Tunk-Tunk-Tunk …

A sliver of the unexpected might just give him the advantage he needed. He might as well try to escape once more before he died. But for now, he wasn't going anywhere.

38

"THREE!"

Baltor closed the distance in two quick steps, head down, fists up. Venir shuffled on his feet, keeping his shoulders square to his opponent's, eyes down toward his head.

Whap! Whap!

Baltor slugged two right crosses into his mid-section.

The crowd of people roared.

Venir winced as the heavy blows banged into his arm. His thick blood was beginning to burn.

He jerked back from a haymaker that clipped his chin and slid aside from another body blow, catching it on his back.

"Punch the lout in the groin, Baltor!"

"Make the giant fall!"

"Kill the loud-mouth story-telling liar, and drag his carcass back to the Mist where he can hump giants, dragons and such!"

Pop!

Baltor's head rocked back on his thick neck, drawing an angry grunt. The man shook off the punch like a dog shedding water.

"Ha! That all you got?" Baltor spat blood. "I'll have Adanna back in my sack in no time."

There was something irritating about the man. Stupidity combined with arrogance. It reminded Venir of someone, but he couldn't remember who.

"Take him to the ground, Baltor!" Another yelled. "Break his neck! You got the juice! Do it!"

Rolling in the dirt with the powerful man was a bad idea. With only one arm, it would be difficult to subdue Baltor. The man looked like he'd wrestled in the Pit before. Maybe the man had even battled in the Warfield. One thing was for sure: Baltor was as tough as he was mean.

Venir shuffled away, his large hand slapping away Baltor's heavy blows before they got too close. The last thing he wanted was more busted ribs among those that were still not fully healed.

"Come on, Girlie," Baltor mocked, "take a swing! I won't bite after your little sting."

Venir jumped away as the brute ripped an uppercut through the air. A chorus of boos followed him, shuffling around the ring.

Venir paid them no mind. Baltor was a seasoned fighter, quick and powerful. One punch could land him on his back or in his grave. He had to be careful … or not.

"Fight, you cow sticker!" An orcen hag offered.

Venir's dander had risen. Fist clenched, he drew his arm back. Baltor's wild eyes widened as he rushed in and swung. Venir unloaded with all he had.

CRACK!

Baltor stopped dead in his tracks, his nose busted open like a tomato. Time seemed to stop as Venir's fist retraced its path and came forth like a rod of power.

CRACK!

Baltor's jaw broke.

The crowd gawped.

Faces were stupefied.

Baltor's arms flailed in a maddened frenzy, slamming into Venir's body with little effect. Baltor's punishment had just begun.

WHOP!

He lifted Baltor off his toes with a punch to the guts.

SMACK!

He felt the bones in the man's face shatter, followed by the next blow that felled the man like an ox.

POW!

He wasn't finished. His red rage began to consume him. He had a message to send. Baltor kicked and twitched as Venir kneeled down and squeezed the man's corded neck in one hand.

"This," he yelled, "is what happens to bad people! This is what happens to my enemies!"

Baltor's face had turned purple, and his eyes bulged from his sockets. Venir didn't care. The man was a menace. The man was evil. The man must die.

"Remember who you bet against, fools! I AM VENIR!"

Baltor's eyes rolled up inside his head, his last breath spent. Venir rose to his feet.

"Which one of you cut throats is next?" He said it wiping his sweaty locks from his eyes. "Anyone!"

None came forward, and most were gone. Venir took in a deep draw of breath as Baltor's body was dragged away. He looked around at the remaining faces, each face marred with guilt from countless crimes. It was clear his message had been sent, and he was certain someone wanted him gone, someone from his past, perhaps. Or, more underling treachery.

Hogan shook his head and tossed him a canteen.

"Did you have to kill him?" Hogan said.

"No." Venir took a drink and said, "but he was an evil bastard."

Hogan nodded and said, "By Bish Venir, what happened behind the Mist?"

"Giants, dragons and such, I tell you," he said, a fierce grin coming to his face.

Hogan shook his head and walked away.

The tall man who had run the challenge walked over and unfastened his arm. The skinny man, older, was looking down on him, his pale eyes sparkling with joy.

"Slim?"

"It's been a long time, Venir. Where in Bone have you been? Don't you know the underlings have taken over? Where are that axe and helmet of yours?"

Venir was still trying to take it all in. Slim, once youthful and strong, so many years ago, was worn and gray, double if not triple his age. The man's features were wrinkled, his skin spotted, but his voice was still strong and playful like children frolicking under a spring.

"Don't you worry about that," he replied.

Adanna had gathered by his side, arms wrapped around his waist, eyes filled with desire and admiration. Venir's blood was still running hot, but not for her. The mention of underlings, his helm and Brool, had ignited another fire. Something in Slim the Cleric's voice told him the fun was over. It was time to get back to work.

"Go get them," Slim said, his skinny arms pushing him forward.

Venir bristled.

"Easy, Venir." Slim looked him up and down. "How in Bish do you keep getting taller?" Slim asked, unable to hide his astonishment.

Hogan had returned and grunted, "Aye."

"I'm not as tall as you, now am I?" Venir said it looking up a little.

"Well, not yet anyway. Now tell me; I've got to know."

Venir shook his head and said, "I don't know. It just happens." He felt Adanna's warm hand playing with his hard belly.

"I bet I can make him grow some more," she said.

"Sheesh Daughter, is that all ye think about?" Hogan said.

"Only when I'm with him."

"STOP!"

Everyone jumped but Venir at the sound of the loud baritone voice.

A dozen feet away, an ominous figure blocked the pathway. Wrapped in a brown cloak, his face covered by a cowl, the man stood taller than Slim and broader than Venir.

Venir's instincts told him it was the figure he had noticed prowling in the background before the fight.

"What is it you want, you oversized scavenger?" Venir said.

The low and throaty voice that responded wasn't human, more monster than man.

"I have a message for the one called Venir," it said, pointing a finger covered in coarse black hair.

Venir stepped forward saying, "And what might that be?"

The creature unrolled a parchment of paper and spoke:

"You survived my first attempt. You and your comrades will not survive the next. Leave now or perish."

Venir noticed a look of concern growing on everyone's faces as they looked at one another.

"Who's the coward that sent this message?" Venir asked in agitation.

Venir watched as a large harry hand pulled the cowl from its face. There was a gasp behind him. *Can it be?*

"I'm no coward, Venir." The big humanoid's knuckles cracked as it crumpled up the parchment and tossed it at Venir's feet. "You will leave, or your friends will die. I'll break their backs like you broke my son's. I'll rip their arms off and bury them in the muck and mire. I am Farc!" The half ogre pounded his chest. "You have till nightfall." The ogre snapped his fingers. A small army of orcs, gnolls, and brigands appeared from behind the tents, brandishing steel of all shapes and sizes.

"And it looks like nightfall has come," Farc said, following within a rugged snicker.

39

LEGS SHACKLED, HANDS BOUND AND stomach rumbling, Brak sat sulking on the dungeon floor. His stomach, as big as those of two men, let out a part roar, part rumble. It was misery. He couldn't remember ever being so hungry before.

The dungeon, vast in size, was superior in facility to his former home with the Slergs, below the city. The stone walls were gray, but dry. The metal bars that housed his cell were clear of rust and debris. Every day, small children, most much younger than he, scrubbed the blood, filth and slat from the floors. They were small and ragged, their faces gaunt, tired and worn. They looked as hungry as him, but fear seemed to propel their skinny little bones with purpose.

The guards, a handful of them, one just as cruel and intolerant as the next, kicked the children around like aging dogs. Brak would have killed them if he could, but he had no energy. He was dry, his tears gone, his fear replaced by apathy. There had been nothing but hardship for him in the City of Bone. His dreams had brought him to the City. His mother, Vorla, was dead now. Cut down. Thrown on a slab of metal. Dropped in a vat of fire. No more mother. A brand new life of survival and misery had begun.

Nearby, Leezir the Slerg, the one who had taken him in, snored. The man had no words of comfort. No words at all. The other one, Hagerdon, lay on rotting piles of hay, quivering beneath a pile of rags. Both men had been lashed a few days ago. Brak had watched from his cell as the men were strung up in chains and whipped until the blood ran down their ankles. The guards left only the little girl, Jubilee, who wailed like a frightened sheep as her grandfather was whipped again and again till the blood ran between his toes. She was flattened with the hilt of a blade crossing the back of her head, gagged, hauled off into a small metal cage and locked inside. It was the last he had heard from her. He nibbled at the skin on his fingertips. His nails were gone from his stubby hands that looked like they could crush rocks into dust. He tried to sleep, but his hunger pangs had gotten so bad they woke him up, and when he did sleep he didn't dream. The image of his father, Venir, had faded. It seemed that whatever had endangered his father had won. The chains scraped across the stone as he pulled his knees to his chest. His lids turned heavy, his small chin dipped and he fell asleep.

"Detective Melegal," Sefron said, "let us put our differences aside for the sake of the Almen family. After all, what choice do we have?"

You death would be my choice.

Sefron had been both pushy and polite ever since he had been ordered to work with Melegal in setting up the Royal games. He suspected it was only a temporary lapse at best, but Sefron's efforts, for some strange reason, had come off as sincere.

"None, it would seem," he said as they walked down the hall, side by side.

Melegal was uncomfortable and very cognizant of the stares. *A shady stick and a pasty tub of goo. Something for the stupid sentries to gossip about between nose pickings.* The plans for the event were in order. Everything was set in stone, and nothing was left to be done, but still Sefron seemed determined to seek him out. The creepy man wanted something from him. What, he couldn't imagine, but it was important. Ever since Melegal came into service, Sefron's words and efforts towards him had been nothing less than poisonous. Why had that suddenly changed? Was it something Lord Almen had said or threatened? Was the castle Lord so pleased with his efforts in capturing and annihilating the Slergs?

Sefron stopped in the hall. Melegal watched the man's eyes shift back and forth as his snail-like tongue licked over his thin purple lips. It was barely a whisper when the cleric spoke.

"Detective, you and I have much more in common than I realized. We both serve against our desires."

This was new. Melegal never suspected the cleric to have been unhappy with his work. Still, he struggled to keep his hand from his dagger. *One blink. One slice. Ah … must I play this game with him!*

"Go on."

Sefron hunched over, drawing himself near, wringing his hands together. "There is something I *seek*. I cannot *retrieve* it. I cannot find it. A *key* of sorts. It can free us from the Royal powers. Help me find it."

What is this fool blathering about? He shoved in front of Sefron's desperate gaze.

"Say no more, Cleric. I'll not be dabbling with any thoughts of treason," Melegal said as he turned to walk away.

He felt Sefron's fingers on his hand and jerked his arm away. The cleric said, "Remember Detective, it is my word against yours. If you keep this between us I'll remember. If you don't, you'll have regret."

"I've had many regrets, but seeing your head removed from your flabby shape would not be one of them," Melegal said, walking on. "I'll not concern myself with your problems. I have my own. As far as I'm concerned, feel free to find your key and shove it where the suns don't shine. Just don't drag me into it or let Lord Almen find out about it."

Sefron watched the Detective disappear around the corner, and a toothy evil grin crossed his face. The seed had been planted. Now all he had to do was wait and watch it grow. Without even knowing it, Melegal would help him find the key. He was certain his spell had worked, as magic had seeped from his limbs and into the marble floor like mist. He rubbed his hands together and recounted his words. *There is something I seek. I cannot retrieve it. I cannot find it. A key of sorts. It can free us from the Royal powers. Help me find it.* He'd emphasized his words: Seek. Retrieve. Key. The spell was activated with a simple touch. He kissed his finger.

"Not long, Master. Not long." He murmured. "As for you, Detective, once it's delivered you'll be the first to go."

He rubbed his flabby belly, smacking his lips as he waddled towards the kitchen.

"All of this scheming makes me hungry."

40

CHONGO, ONCE A VIBRANT, DANGEROUS and playful beast, was now a husk. Both of his massive heads were down, tongues hanging with a grayish tint above his saggy chins. Fogle Boon felt a wave of guilt. In the days since they had returned he had not even come to see the giant two-headed dog. Needless to say, when he entered its stable, things were awkward, as every eye seemed intent on him. Cass was down on her knees, brushing her gentle hand over Chongo's shedding belly. Fogle noticed the scolding look that she cast his way before whispering soothing words into the dwarven setter's floppy black ears.

He started to speak, but was cut off by Mood's meaty hand. Instead, he crammed himself alongside Mood within the confines of the stuffy stable. The thick-set dwarf, the size of a man, had a sad look behind his bushy red beard. Even within the dim torchlight, Fogle thought he could see watery green eyes behind the red.

There were others, too. He counted ten dwarven women, adorned in soft grey robes with lavender trim wrapped around their plump bodies. Their sweet round faces had intense looks as they held hands and hummed. Still, the body heat, stuffiness and straw-filled air made him uncomfortable. So did the feeling of death that lingered in the room.

He focused on Cass. She lay atop Chongo's back, hugging him with her arms and legs, muttering sounds that were not natural for a human to make. Chongo's diminished body shuddered; the muscle spasms rippling underneath his thinning hair. Fogle felt a swelling in his throat. It was both heads now, one as pitiful as the other. He had to admit: it wasn't easy being a witness to another creature's death.

He sneezed, loud and awful. Everything lurched except Chongo. Cass shot daggers from her eyes.

"Sorry." *Not good, Imbecile.*

Fogle, once again, felt horribly out of place as he rubbed his sweaty hands on his robes. He wasn't one to sweat, even when put to task, but it happened at funerals. *I hope this isn't a long ceremony.* He didn't mean it in a bad way, but rather a sad one. He had no desire to be around miserable people.

He didn't want to hear their sad stories or wipe any tears. *Well, I don't think dwarves cry, so that's good news.* He didn't want to be caught crying, either and wondered if it would be rude if he didn't. He hadn't cried when Ox the Mintaur died, or had he? It seemed like forever ago. He supposed it was only proper that he was present. After all, he had almost died trying to retrieve Cass in an effort to save the dog.

Cass rolled from Chongo's back. She had an exhausted look on her face. He hadn't even noticed this when she was up in his room, earlier. He was only thinking about himself these days, it seemed. He leaned back as she extended her hands towards him.

"What?" he said, more defensive than he intended.

Her voice was haunting when she said, "We need your magic, Wizard!" Fogle cocked his head and said, "For what?"

Cass's beautiful face turned into a pit of anger.

"To save the dog, you FOOL!"

He stood there unthinking for a moment. Why would she think that he could save the dog? If that were the case they wouldn't need her. It was preposterous. He was a wizard, not a healer. He looked at Chongo and chose his next words without thinking.

"He doesn't look like he can be saved. Have you not done everything that you can?"

He felt Mood stir at his side. Cass's eyes became daggers of ice.

"Besides—"

Smack!

Fogle's teeth clattered in his jaw. The slap stung. His face flushed red.

"Idiot Man!" Cass vented. "Do you want me to stick your entrails in your mouth? Did you drag me from my mountains so we could fail? You little wart on a frog's arse!"

Hands up, Fogle began backing away. Mood's big frame stepped between them.

"Druid, tell the wizard what you need. No time fer fussin'. Spit it out, Girl!"

Cass bit her lip as she pulled at locks of her hair. Fogle realized she indeed cared about the life of Chongo. His concerns were hardly important. The right thing to do was.

"I'll help," he said. "But you never disclosed the conditions which required my presence here."

Cass's hands were clenched at her sides. "I thought Fogle *Fool* wanted to save the dog, not play splish-splash with dwarven whores."

"Hey!" Mood said. "Ain't no such thing, Druid. Watch yer tongue about me women. Now get on wit it. This pooch is dying. He's my friend. Ye save him, ta' both of ya."

Fogle's narrow shoulders sagged as he sighed and said, "Cass, what would you have me do?"

She stood there, nostrils flaring, tapping her bare foot and biting her lip. She took a deep breath and said, "The dog has one heart, bigger than that of a horse. I hoped for two, but it only has one. It's poisoned. These underlings, or the albino urchlings, they are poison. The wounds were deep, the blood lost was heavy, but the dwarves did well with that. But the poison, a nasty thing, black and deadly, has made its way to his heart."

How do you know that? Fogle kept his mouth shut, however.

"I can extract the poison, but it will take magic, and mine is limited. I need more strength. I need you, Fogle Boon, to tether with me."

"Tether? I've not the slightest idea what you are talking about."

Cass stiffened. She looked like she was about to explode.

"Is there nothing but stupidity filled in that enormous head of yours? Lock minds with me. Mind Grumbles, you pompous imbecile!"

How would she know about Mind Grumbles? He rubbed his chin. Was Cass from the City of Three as well? Still, he was beginning to understand what she wanted, but it wasn't something he'd ever done with a woman before. He let out a puffy laugh.

"What are you laughing at?" Cass said.

"It's just ... well ... it's one of those other things I've never done with a woman before."

"Great Bish, will I have to show you how to do this, too?" She said it while taking him by his hand.

Cass sat down beside Chongo and laid her small hand on the big beast's belly. Fogle joined her on the ground. Her eyes fastened on his. *My, she's beautiful.*

"Wizard, there is no time for your fantasies." She squeezed the blood from his hand. "This must be done now. Lock with me!"

It was a simple spell, for a mage anyway: two willing minds becoming one. He remembered the last one, the battle with the golden-eyed underling. He'd been suffocated, dying, his awesome will being crushed like an egg. Somehow his battle with Venir had saved him. Maybe this was important after all.

The dwarven women surrounded them like a cauldron of warmth, locking arms and murmuring an ancient tune.

"Get on with it, Fogle. I don't like your sweaty hands."

He looked deep into Cass's eyes.

"*Impre ontu doskst,*" he whispered.

A wave of energy rushed through him like a spring. Cass was drawing from him, a warm hand reaching inside and taking hold. It was strong, but he was stronger. With control, he released his power. He saw her body, spinning, contorting and turning black. She plunged into an abyss and was gone.

Don't let me go, Fogle, he heard her mind say, *or the dog will die and I as well.*

Fogle's body broke out in a cold sweat. Cass's hand was burning like fire, and his mind was being stretched down to his toes. Something tugged at his mind, powerful and sinister. The fight for Chongo and Cass had just begun.

41

IT WAS AN ENORMOUS THING, perhaps the largest living creature Verbard had ever seen, and he had to kill it, or rather, direct its killing. That didn't stop the massive stalactite from dropping into a barge filled with fifty underlings, capsizing the vessel. Of the fifty, it could only be assumed that most were dead, and the remaining passengers were swimming for the shore.

"BAAAAAAAAA-HAA-ROOOON!" the creature roared. It was a hulking bi-ped whose neckless fish head scraped debris the size of boulders from the stone ceiling as it attacked. Another volley of arrows and spears ricocheted off the creature's armor. It raised its leg and dropped its foot on the closet barge.

This is a disaster! Underling magi respond!

Robed figures floated over the waters, a dozen wielders of magic, their clawed finger tips burning with life. Verbard floated behind them, his mind and theirs one.

Burn his head! He ordered.

Lightning. Fire. Energy.

The entire cavern was aglow from the various explosions of power. The brilliant colors splashed across the fuzzy faced underlings, adding an additional gleam to their bejeweled eyes. The creature bellowed a deafening roar as it staggered backwards. It raised the fins of its thickset arms in front of its face as the mire and muck broiled on its grotesque body.

Don't let up!

Whatever it was, it was a force. A stupid unyielding one. Verbard took a quick glace into the fray below. The barges were filled with melee. The underling warriors, Badoon, Juegen and urchlings were at odds with a host of Trolls. Not a single underling screamed when it died, and not a single one yelled when it attacked. Instead, the chitters came in precise hissing commands.5 A single troll was drowning three underlings at once. Another underling, a metal-armored Juegen, was being swung like a club. The surprise was becoming an onslaught.

Verbard felt his own black blood begin to boil as another barge was capsized by the trolls. He wanted to scream. Instead, he did something else. *Enough of this!* He pulled a rod with a fist on the end from inside his robes. It was a two-foot long piece of inch-thick iron, cold and heavy in his hand.

He touched the metallic fist to his lips and muttered an incantation.

Jottenhiem, attention!

A Juegen, covered from head to toe in troll guts, stood at the bow of the barge below him. The underling raised its open hand as it ducked under the swing of a troll that had been rocking the barge.

Catch.

Verbard tossed the rod and watched it fall into Jottenhiem the Juegen commander's eager grasp. The rod burst from two to six feet, a fist at the point. As the troll climbed onto the bow, Jottenhiem rammed its skull with the rod. A flash of light erupted, followed by a notable thunder crack, pulverizing the troll's head, sinking the monster back into the current.

Much better.

Another troll had a pair of urchlings in his hands, beating them together like dolls. Jottenhiem hurled the fist in a streak of black light.

CRACK!

The troll fell back into the waves, dead as a stone, two smushed urchlings crushed in its clutches.

Verbard turned his attention back to the other magi. He could feel their energy ebbing. Ahead, in the dimness of the lake, the creature still stood, a smoking ruin of living scales and searing flesh. It stomped its finned legs and punched the jagged ceilings like an angry child. It should have been dead by now, but it wasn't.

That thing must have a heart a big as a barge.

Verbard's lip curled over his clenched teeth.

I can't invade an entire city with half an army.

Another rock formation fell, crushing one underling mage's skull, knocking it from the air and driving it into the waters.

Follow my lead, magi!

A bubble of yellow energy formed in his hand. A soft blow from his thin black lips sent the warbling globe towards the creature. Another series of the globes followed. *Well done, brethren.* The creature swung at them, catching them on its arms and legs, while other globes stuck like dew to its chest and face.

Now!

Bamf! Bamf! Bamf!

The creature roared out in sheer agony as chunks of flesh blew from its body.

Bamf! Bamf!

One arm fell into the murk.

Bamf! Bamf!

Its entrails spilled out into the water.

And for the finale …

BAMF!

Verbard added another hole in the back of its head. It wavered, mouth clutching open and closed, then splashed full force into the waters and sank.

Verbard sat on the beach holding his head. The trolls, what was left of them, had fled. The rod of smiting he had given Jottenhiem lay at his feet, a charred husk of steel. Sixty seven underlings were dead, two barges sunk, and his siege on the greatest city in the world of Bish had not yet begun. He watched in irritation as the magi levitated one barge from the Current, flipped it over and set it down with a splash. Three barges were ready now. The blockade in the tunnel was almost clear as more magi had begun using magic to remove the boulders.

How? Why?

The entire attack was unprecedented. It left him filled with uncertainty, and he couldn't help but wonder if Master Sinway was behind this. After all, it had been Sinway's suggestion to begin the siege from within.

He rubbed his temples.

"Jottenhiem," he said.

The Juegen commander stood at attention by his side, helmet off, long curved blades gleaming with blood at his hips. "Yes, Lord Verbard."

Verbard rose to his aching feet and faced his commander. Why they ached he didn't know, but everything seemed to ache these days.

"What is your assessment?"

Jottenhiem had ruby red eyes, typical of most Juegen warriors. The sides of his head were shaved, and his rat-furred face twitched with muscles. The Juegen, one of Verbard's longtime allies, was reliable. He spoke in a manner unlike most, deep and less chittering, almost slow.

"A troll trap for troll food."

"We are underlings, not troll food, Jottenhiem."

"It seems some of us are troll food."

"And what to you make of that other monster? Was it hungry as well?"

"I didn't get a chance to ask it."

Verbard turned away and watched as the underlings continued their preparations for the remaining journey.

"What do you make of our invasion of the human city?"

Jottenhiem formed a tiny grin of razor sharp teeth.

"It will be glorious and bloody."

"Assuming we get there in one piece," Verbard snapped. "Take the helm of the first barge and see to it we don't fall into more troll traps! Imbecile!"

Verbard floated away, filled with anger and frustration, but there was nowhere to go. He ducked into come caves. *I need help.* He couldn't shake the feeling he was being set up. Now, he should feel nothing more than elation for the opportunity to slaughter mankind with a single lethal strike. His brethren were almost glowing about it, but why was he not? He was an underling. He despised mankind, but this mission, this golden moment of underling kind, filled him with doubt. His fingernails dug into his palms. His teeth bit into his jaw. Something wasn't right.

42

HELPLESS AND ALONE. KAM'S HANDS trembled as her stomach twisted inside out. Her baby girl, Erin, was gone. She wiped her eyes and nose as she sat at a table inside the Magi Roost. She did not recognize the man that sat across from her, but she'd caught his name, Thorn. His speech was slow, reserved, scary.

"This doesn't have to be difficult," he said in a rugged voice that was far from reassuring. "The ransom isn't what is important. The return of your child is."

The tavern was empty, other than herself, the crooked-nosed man, Gillem and Lefty, who sat fidgeting at the bar. It was Lefty that had come to her rescue, a bit conveniently. His story, sweating feet and all, was convincing.

Gillem, in all his stock and grace, affirmed the history of halflings with sweaty feet in brief detail. Kam had no choice but to believe them, for now.

"As you know, the Prince of Thieves, Palos, my master, has been expecting a favor from you for quite some time …"

Palos. The name inflamed her anger like a hot iron. She knew him to be crafty, beguiling and deviant. No thief could be trusted, him least of all. His honor had less weight than a feather, and his greed was without rival. It appeared the rumors were true. But kidnapping a child, of a Royal, no less? That was as unexpected as it was frightening. Who was she really dealing with? She pushed her fingers through her hair, aware of Thorn's hungry eyes on her chest.

She couldn't stop her chin from trembling as she spoke:

"I owe that man no favors. Bring back my daughter, you dog!"

It was there, the magic, a festering blossom of rage ready to unleash itself. *Kill this ugly bastard!*

Thorn wagged his long finger in her face.

"Now, don't lose control. This is a negotiation, not a discussion, nor an argument. I'm just delivering the terms." The chair groaned as he leaned back. Thorn was tall, heavy boned and sinister in expression. He spoke better than his dull eyes let on. There was intelligent life behind his harsh and haggard expression, cunning and without mercy. "Your choices are limited as well as your time, Mistress of the Magi Roost," he finished, licking his tongue over his lips.

Pop.

Kam jumped as an ember cracked in the fireplace behind the man. She clutched her chest, which was fighting her ability to breathe. Thorn chuckled. It took a degree of self-control to not hurl the man aside. What would she do? Who could she turn to for help? Her family, Royals themselves, would be more than agitated by this attempt. But Palos would not have made such a move if he did not already have something on them. Her family, aloof with politics and position, had made it perfectly clear years ago that she was on her own when she made her choice. She had gladly accepted. If anything, she'd be too ashamed to ask for their help. She'd rather die than hear them say *I told you so,* even at the cost of her life or her daughter's.

"Palos knows I'll do anything to get my daughter back. I could not live without her," she said, her sobs becoming heavy again.

"My master is counting on that," Thorn said, leaning forward, entranced by her trembling curves. "What Prince Palos offers is more of a gift than a threat. It's just difficult to present it in any other way. He desires your company. He wants to bask in the glow of your beauty. I cannot fault the prince in his tastes, they are superb. Captivating." Thorn eased closer. "Even alluring on the darkest of days."

Inhaling deeply through her nose, Kam pulled her shoulders back and let out a slow shuddering sigh. She watched as Thorn's Adam's apple rolled up and down, his eyes filled with fantasy.

"So," she said wiping her nose on a rag, "how long have you and Gillem been planning this abduction?"

Thorn's eyes flicked over her shoulder where Gillem sat, then back to her.

I knew it!

"I've no business with the halfling other than this parlay."

Liar!

She let her energy swell behind her chest, a cauldron of boiling power.

"You know what, Thorn?" she said, unable to hide her simmering green eyes.

"Eh …?" he replied, edging back.

"You remind me of something that crawled out of an ogre's nose."

The vulture-like man stiffened in his chair, his hands falling to his sides.

Kam held out her palms.

"Wench! I'll carve — *oomph!*"

Thorn was thrown from his feet and heading towards the fire.

She felt him fighting against the bonds of her telekinesis spell, fighting to avoid the flames.

"Mercy, you wench!" he shouted.

Her anger swelled her energy. Thorn screamed as he was stuffed into the flames. Harder and harder she pushed. She felt small bones breaking as her power began to crush him like a vice of flame.

"YOU WILL PAY, RODENT!"

Bottles were rattled from the shelves, shattering on the floor. Thorn was wailing, burning and writhing with torment. Someone else was yelling as well. She caught a flicker of movement in the corner of her eye. Gillem was making haste towards the door. She released her hold on Thorn.

"STOP, GILLEM!"

A row of plates cut through the air, one by one, making a bead for the halfling's head. Gillem ducked, rolled, twisted and dodged as the air was filled with the sounds of breaking dishes. Master Longfingers leaped toward the window. Kam reached out her painted nails.

"*Kye-Noche-Liene*!"

Tendrils of white energy whipped out from her fingertips, coiled around Gillem's portly little body and snatched him from the air. He writhed within the coils, his aghast face aglow from the white hot light. She rolled her wrists, layer over layer, wrapping the halfling into a tight bundle. Gillem wasn't going anywhere. She let go. The harmless but steel-strong bonds held the halfling tighter that a bear trap.

Gillem rolled into sitting position, a look of bewilderment in his eyes.

"You fool hot tempered woman! What have you done? Ye'll never get back the baby Erin now!"

43

"So be it, Farc," Venir replied, spitting on the ground. "Your stench is more threatening than your words." The small throng of Farc's Outlaws erupted in a sinister chuckle. Venir, despite his blossoming hatred for his foe, didn't care for the odds. He glanced over at the worried looks on Hogan and Adanna's faces. Farc's threats had them convinced.

Farc snorted and looked up into the sky. The second dusk, a glow of radiant yellow light, was washing over the city. Dusk was almost gone. "Look at this human, men! A cheater. A coward. A liar. A murderer. This is the man who took my young son, barely twelve years old, and broke his neck."

Venir's neck warmed, his face flushed. He reached for the swords at his feet. The sound of steel scraping from sheaths and a bow drawing back caught his ears. He was as flatfooted as a horse was hoofed.

"Adanna, get our gear. Hogan, break down the rest. I'll wait."

Another series of chuckles came as Adanna and Hogan scurried into the tent. The sounds of rattling gear and unpleasant words were exchanged from within the canvas. Venir kept his eyes on Farc's one. The ogre, once as powerful a warrior as a warrior could be, was diminished. He stooped. His left shoulder dipped, and the fire behind his yellow eye no longer burned. Farc, at least a decade or two older than Venir, was in decay. He watched as the ogre wiped the drool from his jutting jaw. Farc's hand trembled as he swung it behind his back.

"Venir, I should kill you now."

"Then why don't you?"

"You know the rules in the Hide."

Outlaw's Hide was a sanctuary for the worst that Bish had to offer. There was a code among all, unless you were an underling: no killing without a challenge and don't rat out your neighbors. There was no judge and no law, but there was an unspoken civil order. Other than that, it was anything goes. Of course, if you were killed, which did happen quite often, there was little to defend you. And if you killed, you were asked to leave, or subsequently killed by a self- appointed militia. But, if you had control, which Farc seemed to have at the moment, you could do whatever you wanted.

"Why not challenge me then?"

Farc let out a gruff laugh.

"Time to go, Yellow Hair."

Venir looked over at Slim, who was biting his nails.

"You coming?"

Slim's wizened face looked around at all the outlaws and said with a shrug, "Well, it's either that or die."

Farc and his men followed as Venir, Slim, Adanna, Hogan and his wife trekked a mile north to the edge of the haphazard city, loaded down with all they could carry. The only things they were missing were the tents, water and rations. He heard Farc's final words:

"I sent the underlings my personal mattock to dig a grave for you. I only asked for your boots in return."

They traveled almost five miles north of Outlaw's Hide and made a fireless camp. The terrain, grasslands mixed with jungle, posed few problems. They all sat, wiping sweat and slapping away mosquitoes, or holding their hungry bellies. There was no food.

"What do you think, Venir?"

"They're gone. They followed the first few miles." He unrolled his blanket that contained the large leather sack. "I'm going to do some scouting." He tossed his borrowed broadswords on the ground.

Hogan cocked an eye and said, "With no weapons?"

"Too much noise." Venir stuffed his sack into a pack that Adanna had given him and slung it over his shoulders. "I'll need your cloak, Slim."

"But I like this cloak. Take Hogan's."

"Too small."

"First you get us kicked out of camp, and then you abandon us." Slim slung it from his knobby shoulders and said with a frown, "Fine."

It was past midnight. Outlaw's Hide was in full swing. Heavily armed and cloaked bodies swaggered through the dusty streets singing or crying out shouts of alarm. Venir swaggered as well, cloak hood draped over his face, a jug of wine swinging at his side, vengeance on his mind.

Where is that ogre!

There weren't too many half-ogres here. The sound and smell of them, a salty mix of manure and urine, would knock you down if you weren't ready for it. Venir sauntered in and out of the tents and shabby buildings, one muck and filth ridden alley at a time. Farc, like most ogres, would prefer his privacy. The big humanoid preferred caves, mountains and high places. If anything, Farc probably preferred the wide open spaces that Outlaw's Hide provided.

Venir took a deep draw through his nose.

"Ah!"

Venir followed his nose towards a ramshackle barn where many beasts for slaughter and burden were stabled. A canvas tent, large enough for a host of people, sat catty cornered to the edge of the barn. There was an inhuman squeal of delight coming from within, followed by a series of heavy smacks on bare flesh. Venir kneeled down inside the shadows between the barn and tent, his keen eyes scanning for sentries. An orc leaned against a pile of logs near the tent entrance, hairy hands draped across its bulging belly. It wiped its mouth and yawned, peering around before it tossed another log on the nearby campfire.

Venir pulled out the sack and withdrew Brool. Its razor sharp edges seemed to hum in the moonlight. On cat's feet he slipped around the back side of the tent and slit open a hole the size of a man. Pulling the edge of the canvas back, he saw the backside of Farc's hulking form, sitting on a stool. Bent over the half-ogre's knee was a squealing orcen trollop. Her dirty blonde hair cascaded onto the dirt floor as she squirmed underneath Farc's heavy wallops. *Please don't be Dolly.*

Venir took a breath and waited, avoiding the lantern light as he stepped inside. The shaft of his axe throbbed in his hand. His murderous thoughts began to consume him. His enemies, one and all, must go. Something beckoned him onward towards the removal of all evil. It was him or them. He took another step forward, axe hanging ready over his shoulder.

"Hrmm," Farc murmured, as his head, the size of three men's, swung back his way.

The tip of Brool met the ogre's temple, drawing blood.

"Sssssh," Venir warned the orcen woman, unfamiliar to his relief, jaw dropped open.

"Who dares?" Farc said in a huff, a nervous twinge in his voice.

Venir applied more pressure. Farc took a sharp draw through his nose.

"Ah … Venir," the half-ogre said, "come to assassinate me like a coward, I see."

"No, I came to get a better look at the orc's arse," he retorted. "Flat on your belly, Wench. Shut your eyes and think about bathing."

The trollop flopped onto the ground, thick forearms covering her head.

Venir flipped Brool's blade under Farc's trembling chin.

"What are you wanting, Venir? You beat me, cripple me, humiliate me, and that's not enough. Now come to kill me?"

"Aye, Farc."

Farc grunted. The half-ogre sat, hands on his knees, head tilted down.

Venir could smell the big humanoid's fear as he watched the blood drip from Farc's temple. *That's it. Sweat it out.*

"Tilt your big head back," Venir ordered, lifting Farc's chin with his axe. "I can't have you crying out before I get this over with."

Farc made an audible gulp. The orcen woman went into a fit of squealing shudders and sobs.

"Any last words, Farc? Care to give that hairy arse another good whack before your body's fed to the other pigs?"

The half-ogre let out a raspy sound.

Venir tilted his head down and said, "What's that?"

"S-Sp ..."

Venir grabbed a handful of hair and growled, "Spit it out, Ogre."

Farc trembled as he managed to say, "Sp-Spare me."

"Say again?"

"Spare me, Venir. Spare my life," Farc pleaded.

Farc's monstrous shoulders sagged. His fingers were lifeless at his side. He was beaten.

Venir pulled his axe away.

"I'll need horses. Water. Rations. Your word, Farc. For your life, this grudge is over."

Farc nodded as he buried his face in his trembling hands.

What was it Mood said? he thought as he departed.

Never trust an ogre.

The first dawn's sun was rising as Venir galloped to his camp.

"Whoa," he said, pulling back the reins on a large chestnut steed. Sliding out of his saddle, he inspected impressions in the dirt and grass. The smell of blood was in the air, something rotting and foul as well. "Bone!"

On foot he dashed over the rugged terrain, pushing his way over the tall grasses and thick jungle of vines and trees. He donned his helm. Wind, blood and death whirled through his senses. A burning sensation raised the hair on his arms. He moved forward, heavy feet smashing down the thick grasses, his head on a swivel, his heightened senses alert for the unnatural. He heard the crickets, an owl, a slithering snake, buzzing flies, but none of the distant mocking chitter of underlings, far or near. He pulled the helm off and dropped it into the sack as he stood on the edge of the meager camp. His blood ran cold.

Dark stains were smeared over the patches of moss and grass. Hogan's head, eyes wide with terror, was lying on its ear in the dirt. The man's clothes and body had been severed in many places and made up into a mound of flesh.

Venir's knuckles whitened on Brool's shaft.

One ... Four ... Nine ... Eleven ...

The underlings were many. The footsteps of two women, Adanna and her Mother, were intermingled with the underlings. It was clear they had no concern of being followed. Venir cursed and spat, fighting his urge to howl.

He heard the frightened scream of a horse.

"Slat!"

Nothing could have prepared him for what he saw as he burst through the brush and into the clearing. A jolt of fear erupted in his spine as he scrambled to dig out the armament.

"Sweet Bish!"

44

M ELEGAL LAY FLAT ON HIS belly on a mattress of feathers inside McKnight's old apartment, exhausted.

A key. A key. What did Sefron mean?

Haze straddled his back, her fingers working masterfully over the knotted fibers of muscle on his back and shoulders.

"You sure are tight for a thief," she said, boring her thumb into the middle of his back.

It felt like the blade of a knife was being driven into his spine. *Outrageous.* He had never been anything less than supple before. Now, under Lord Almen's geyser of pressure, he was as taut as a bow string these days. He felt Haze's warm lips pecking on his knobby shoulders.

"Will you stop, Woman," he said, not a question but an order. "You know I hate that."

"Oh, but I like the little goose bumps it makes on your bony back. It's adorable."

"Rub, you wench! And don't ever use the word *adorable* in my presence again. I've removed tongues for less."

Haze giggled. "As you wish, Detective."

He felt her gyrating her hips in a rhythmic sway as dripped more oil onto his back. *Ah, that's nice.* The scent, something with cinnamon, elated his nostrils, and the warm oil opened his pores like a mild lava. It was one of the best moments he'd had in days. *Why haven't I let her do this all along?*

Melegal buried his face inside a small pillow, trying to envision what the key that Sefron mentioned looked like.

How could a key free them from the Almen bondage? If there was such a key, one thing he was certain of, he would have it before Sefron. The half-naked pasty skinned cleric would have to fend for himself.

He let out a sigh.

"Feeling better?" she said.

"A little," he said, words muffled in the pillow.

If I were a key where would I be? Melegal noted every object from Lord Almen's study beneath the kitchens: A cupboard of maps and scrolls. Two desks, one used, the other abandoned, no chair and four deep drawers. A small armament of weapons in the corner. Nine lanterns. Eighteen Candles. A molding rug on the floor with a hollow spot below that he had noted because of the way Lord Almen always stepped over it. *Hmmm.* Two shelves full of small decorations and awards. Above, wooden rafters. A drop down ladder. The edges of tapestries concealing who knew what. A box, small as a hand. A chest of cast iron as big as a man.

"What are you thinking, Me?" Haze said, shoving her palms into the center of his back. A notable series a cracks followed, continuing up to his neck.

His eyes popped open. "Ahhh … nothing." *Key. Key. Key. Key. Key.*

Seek. Retrieve. Key.

Melegal held his hand on his aching head as he crept through Castle Almen. It was always quietest in the hours before the first dawn, long before the city roosters crowed. In the kitchen, a tiled expanse of wood-fed ovens and long maple tables, he'd wedged himself into the dark shadow between two cupboards and settled in. He could hear mice, a pair, their tiny nails scraping the tiles, small teeth nibbling into a silk sack of corn flour. Exterior shudders creaked from a nearby window pane where the two moons' glow added a gentle light in an otherwise dark room.

Listen, Fool.

Everything was quiet and natural, yet ominous and threatening. It was the time of day none should be trespassing within the walls of the castle, not even the heralded detective. Only the sentries and members of the Royal family roamed at night. It was foolish for him to do so. *Got to find that key.* He rubbed his fingers over his chin. *What am I doing?*

His compulsion was natural. The urge to find something of value, enhanced by magic, suggested by an enchanted mind, only charged the thief's natural tendencies. Whatever it was that Sefron wanted, he wanted it more, even at his own peril.

A sound of heavy footsteps made its way up the stone stairwell. Unmoving, eyes closed, Melegal remained one with the kitchen. The sounds of the sentry alone lent a picture as clear as daylight to his mind: a large man with a hitch in his step sauntered through the kitchen and began to rummage quietly through the cupboards. *Ah, good.* It made things easier. No sentry would dare abandon his post with Lord Almen within his chambers.

The sentry was chewing now, strong teeth chomping into a piece of hard fruit. Melegal could feel a shadow closing over the moonlight that was shed his way, the man's footsteps only a few feet away and passing.

"Hmmm," the man said as he stopped, his boots turning over the floor. "What's this?"

Melegal heard the man pick something up from the table. He cracked an eye open. The sentry held a long kitchen knife, its keen edge reflecting the moonlight. The sentry's head cocked back and forth on his bull neck. *Slat.* Like a beast in the fields, the man sensed something was amiss. Melegal could feel the tension rise in the man. Instincts beginning to fire. Oily sweat beginning to build.

Slowly the man turned, his sword scabbard thunking against a table leg. Melegal felt his heart begin to race as the sentry reached toward the cupboard he hunkered behind. He pulled his cloak tight and dipped his chin deeper into his chest. A heavy footstep landed inches from him.

Burp!

The smell of apples and tobacco wafted through the air, followed by a strange sounding fart.

"Mmmm … that's better," the sentry grumbled, tapping his fist on his chest as he continued to walk by, back towards the stone stair case.

Melegal slipped behind the man, matching him step for step, wading through the funk of odor. *One would think you'd get used to it.* The man was halfway to the bottom when he let out another burst, louder than the last, echoing within the corridor. *The fool could wake the dead with that.*

Melegal's hand slipped down to the pommel of his blade. He eased it from the sheath, making a scraping sound of metal on wood, like a whisper. Ten more steps he followed the man like a shadow, the small torches wavering light against the wall. The sentry stretched his arms high, turned at the waist and farted again. *Enough.* Melegal raised his dagger and poised the tip on the man's broad back as he slipped behind and cradled him like a child. *Sleep. Sleep. Sleep.*

His mind tingled. His thoughts raced. The man swayed. Melegal slid his dagger in the sheath as the sentry's knees buckled and he teetered forward. *Catch him.* He grabbed the man behind his girdle and scooped his arm underneath the man's chest. *Heavy bastard. Blasted chainmail.* Melegal sagged along with the man as they both crumpled to the landing. *Whew.* The man began to snore like an ogre. Melegal rolled the man onto his stomach. *That should do it.* Up the stairwell, the small torches, two in all, offered little light against the black stone walls. He withdrew a pair of steel gauged wires and dropped to a knee. Eyeing the keyhole, he stuck the two thin rods inside and began picking. Melegal was already aware of the mechanisms within as he had heard Lord Almen locking and unlocking the door before. It was a heavy brass key that worked the lock, and turned the tumblers. Still, it was not the average lock. Rather, it was one designed to give the utmost security ... *pop* ... except when dealing with the utmost thief. *Unimpressive.* Sliding the tools into the pouch with one hand, he depressed the thumb lever down with the other. He took a deep breath. *Why am I doing this?* And pushed the door open. *Have I gone mad?*

45

Fogle's feet were anchored on the edge of the abyss. His arms and back were straining against a heavy mystical rope that he squeezed inside his grip. He wasn't the same man now, no longer a weakling of a wizard, but instead a titan of sorts. Inside his mind was another world within, one that he knew quite well.

A woman's high pitched scream echoed behind his thoughts.

Hang on, Cass!

Below him, a vat of vile looking green and black goo bubbled with anger. Little by little it sucked the rope he held, burning the fibers in his grasp. Fogle groaned, digging the heels of his boots into the dirt. He'd been here before. Another world. Locked in a mind grumble of the oddest kind. He liked it, but he was losing control. He cried out.

"Cass!"

No reply.

"Cass!"

He slipped the rope over his shoulder, feeling as if a giant, legs like trunks, filled with muscle, churned back at him from the abyss. Something was pulling back, stronger this time, the weight unimaginable. *NO!* Smoke rose as the rope slipped through his skin, rending his flesh. He screamed. *NO! Think, Wizard!*

He screamed for Cass one last time as he fought to hold onto the rope.

One second the druid woman Cass was there, wrapped up with the wizard Fogle Boon. In the next second she twisted, contorted and plunged inside of Chongo. It was possibly the strangest thing the King of the Blood Rangers, Mood, had ever seen in all of his centuries.

Mood huddled before Chongo's dreary heads, holding the beasts in the nooks of his arms. He could feel the dog's big body shaking, its body writhing with sickening sounds. The wizard, Fogle, sat with his face transfixed on a woman who was no longer there. Sweat was dripping from the man's forehead, his body straining against an unseen force.

"Hold on, Boy," Mood said into Chongo's ear. "Help's coming."

In truth, Mood had never seen a dog or anything so sick before. The beast was well past the point where any other beast would have been put out of its misery. Mercy had come to mind more than once. No animal or man should be made to suffer like that. He could only assume that Chongo held on for some reason. The dog was his friend, and he was his. "I got you!"

He looked over and saw the worried look on the lady dwarven faces. Each one was contorted, exerted, and intense. One had her arms around Fogle's waist, and the others followed suit in a chain from behind. Fogle pitched forward, tugging the entire group with him. Chongo trembled and shook, but Mood held on, feeling that the beast's bull necks were not quite as strong as before. That's when the smoke came. Fogle's hands were burning.

Agony. Never had Fogle experienced anything on this level. Chongo was the furthest concern from his mind. Cass was foremost. He couldn't let her go, not with the feelings he had. Not with so much unresolved between them. He wanted to know. He wanted to know how she felt about him. He wasn't sure how he felt about her. It seemed he was about to find out soon enough because his back was being dragged over the ground towards the acidic burbling of the pit. *Think or die. Isn't that what the oaf said?* All of this suffering over one man, one dog, one person. What was the meaning of that?

More rope raced through his loosening fingertips. *Just win, Fogle. Win!*

He dug down into his belly and began loosening the lid off a kettle of energy. *There it is!* A dormant power lay unused except when his life or another's was in peril. He'd found it when Ox the Mintaur died. He'd found it when he thought Mood was about to die. A bit by accident on both accounts. It had been there when the underling Catten was shutting his brain down. He didn't have the control then, but he was gaining control now. *The Bone with the lid! For Three!* He shoved the deposit of energy over.

Elation. Magic and mind intermingled, forming a coating over his mental body. A shiny coat of metal replaced this skin. His grip became hard as iron. He rolled the rope around his wrist and pulled. The sucking pit of goo let out an eerie wail of anger. Fogle rose to his feet, his face molded in steel, his muscles bulging of hammered iron.

"Cass!"

He tugged. Dug his heels into the turf and pulled backward. One step. Two steps. The pit hissed. Green and black acid erupted in splattering globs, splashing his hardened skin and sizzling into nothing. He took control of his magic, his anger, his will, pulling the rope back, hand over hand, faster and faster. The ground quaked beneath his feet. Something dark and deadly was furious with him.

He called for her again. The rope continued to coil, foot after foot, at his feet. Where was she? He dragged a man-sized gob of something, sticky, green and black, onto the ledge. He rushed over and picked the mass up into his arms, and the world exploded.

One second Fogle's hands were burning, the next they were not. Chongo's entire body writhed with violent seizures that tested the limits of Mood's mighty arms. In the next second the naked flesh of the druid spilled outside of Chongo, coated in a dark green and purplish goo. The smell had the foulness of an underling's marsh. Fogle wrapped his arms around the unmoving woman. The wizard was rocking her back and forth, saying, "Don't die. Don't die, my sweet."

46

S *MACK!*

Lefty reeled as Kam's heavy hand knocked him to the floor. She wanted to kill the little betrayer, but she needed him.

"How could you do this to me, Lefty? After all I have done for you!" She screamed in his face.

The little blond haired boy said nothing, only holding his tiny hand on his reddening cheek. Kam's fists were clutched at her sides. She let her anger fight her panic. What else could she do? Her baby was gone, somewhere deep in the vile underbelly of the City of Three. Thorn, Palos's personal messenger, had been pretty clear on what the Prince of Thieves wanted. He wanted her, more so than gold and power. *Why? Why me?*

She could hear Joline sobbing inside the kitchen. The woman had returned violated and mortified somehow, unable to speak. Her thick gray hair was a mess, and her clothes were torn. The woman fell completely apart at the news of Erin's kidnapping.

"Fool woman. What do you suppose to do now?" Thorn said, grimacing. His face and body were burnt and broken, but there was still pleasure in his face. The rogue still had some control, bound by magic or not. "You've attacked me. Palos will kill you and your daughter for your transgression."

Thorn's mocking laughter was cut off with a wave of her palm. The magic cords that bonded him squeezed around his neck.

"Kam, you must stop this and listen," Gillem piped in, a nervous look in his eye. "We can't help you with your baby if you're dead. Just give Palos — urk!"

Similar bonds held the halfling, the sound of leather constricting around his neck. Kam let the halfling's eyes start to bulge from their sockets, his face turning into a turnip.

"Kam!"

Both Thorn and Gillem Longfingers were choking to death.

"KAM!" Joline shouted again, blocking her view of the men.

They both flopped and kicked on the floor, gagging and coughing for air.

Joline grabbed her face that was flushed and streaked with tears and said, "You are not a murderer."

The words affected her. The urge to tear something apart drained out of her. She released her hold. Gillem and Thorn gulped for air.

"What do I do?" Kam whispered.

"How much does Erin mean to you, Kam?" Joline said softly.

"Everything," she sobbed, "she's all I have left."

Joline gave her a look, and she knew what she would have to do. It was time to make a sacrifice.

She turned around and muttered something in magic. Her mind shimmered, searching for Erin, trying to bring her baby back. Nothing. Her powers, formidable as they were, had limitations in that regard. She had focused more on the aggressive arts, as opposed to the passive ones. She slunk down onto a chair. Her mind and powers were exhausted, and her grip on the two thieves on the floor was beginning to ebb. She needed time to regain her strength. Thorn had already made it clear her time was short.

She looked over at Lefty. He sat on a kitchen stool, his little head downcast, spitting out his nails. What had happened to the once innocent little boy? She cast a glance towards Gillem, the robust halfling, as deceiving as Palos himself. Georgio had been right after all. Gillem was at the root of Lefty's problems. How had the boy seen it and not she? Perhaps she hadn't wanted to.

She cursed.

Still, the responsibility was on Lefty. His deceit had led to all this. Lies and dishonesty would cost them all greatly. Maybe the boy didn't think he had a choice, but there was only one choice when it came to right and wrong. One had to discern the difference.

"Joline," Kam said, regaining her feet, "get me the City Watch. I'm sure Thorn's time would be better served with them."

She twirled her fingers in the air, and Gillem's bonds fell loose. The halfling man couldn't hide the surprise on his face as he quickly rose to his feet, soft eyes flitting back and forth. His long fingers rubbed at his wrists and neck as he said, "Kam, we must hurry. Palos is ruthless. He'll kill Erin and have you anyway."

"Aye, wench, she's probably dead—"

"*Chad-dah kin*," Kam spoke. Thorn's lips and ears sealed shut.

Thorn's newly deformed face had the most panicked expression.

"We can't have him blabbing my plans to the City Watch. For all I know they are bought and paid for. That should keep him quiet for now." She looked at Thorn. "You're fortunate I left you your nose holes. As for you two," she motioned to the halflings, "I guess I don't have any choice. Take me to Palos."

A Gondola. It was something Kam had never ridden in nor known existed before. Small and wavering, the tiny craft cut through the blackness with only the green glow of the lantern providing light. She held her stomach as she shivered underneath a heavy cloak. Behind her, Gillem manned the rudder, his pie face almost hidden in the dark. In the front, Lefty paddled the craft, its small oars moving the craft over the black waters at what seemed to be an agonizing pace.

"How much farther," she asked, her voice echoing.

Gillem replied, "Not much longer, Lass. Not long at all," he said as his voice trailed off.

Erin. How would she save her baby? She was venturing far from her beaten path, below the city, into the unknown, where another world waited for her like an open maw. She had heard rumors of the Nest, but she had given little thought to its actual existence. There had never before been a need to concern herself.

"What is that?" she said.

Lefty gave her a glance. She could see the frown etched in his sad face. What had happened to the happy little blond haired and blue-eyed boy? He seemed so much older now, but filled with despair. She looked away. There was no time for forgiveness now. It was his fault.

"Archways, Lass. We are close," Gillem offered.

She fought against the creeping doom that was seeping into her bones. She had to be strong for Erin. Closing her eyes, she meditated, ignoring the sounds of the paddles dipping and pushing through the waters and the creaking of the boat. She had a few spells left. She always did. One by one she recalled the steps in her mind. Her vault of energy had strength, but it was no longer full. It would take more than magic to escape from Palos. The man might be greedy, but he was no fool. He'd dealt with the likes of magi and wizards before. He wouldn't have gotten to be who he was if he hadn't been privy to their tricks. She thought of Venir. What would the man think if he knew he had a daughter who was abducted? Would he be as angry and vengeful as she?

She tucked her hands up under her aching breasts. *I'm getting closer. I must be.* She reached out with her mind for Erin. *Nothing.* For all she knew her baby was starving now. *Be strong.* Fresh tears began to stream from the corners of her eyes as the passed underneath the arches. *Concentrate.* Everything faded away as she stared at the tiny lantern, stroke after stroke. She closed her eyes.

"We're here," Gillem said.

Kam opened her eyes. A rotting city awaited them on a mound of dirt. A massive brick chimney was in the middle of it all, smoke seeping from a tiny vent hole on the side. It gave the otherwise hopeless and dreary slat hole the appearance of life. Docks jutted out and wrapped around the entire city where faceless men strolled, stood and talked. Light flickered from torch lit lampposts and the insides of haphazard storefronts and apartments. She couldn't believe her baby was here, in the dark and murk, among the city's most notorious ilk.

She glared at Lefty, then back at Gillem.

"Take me to Palos, rogues!"

She ignored the hard and gawping stares as she strode behind Gillem. They would all burn if she had her way: thieves, kidnappers and smugglers, all deserved to die. Many of them would if she did not get her way. She ignored the smell, the rodents and the screams of vile pleasure as they traversed the catacombs of the tiny city's alleys. All she knew was she was getting closer to her baby. *Hang on, Baby.*

Gillem pushed his way inside two swinging tavern doors. She followed, booted feet clomping on the planks, and came to a sudden stop. A dozen men wielding crossbows and knives greeted her: four on a balcony, the others on the main floor, spread out among the tables.

"Have a seat, Woman," one said from the balcony, sucking on a toothpick that dangled from his mouth. "Prince Palos will be with you momentarily."

"Tell that blood sucker I'll see him now!" she yelled.

Clatch – Zip!

Kam cried out. A small crossbow bolt protruded from her thigh, knocking her to the ground. An eruption of pain raced through her leg, and humiliation followed on the snickers of the men. She'd never been cut or stabbed by anything before, but she'd stitched a kitchen wound or two. *Blast, it hurts. I never imagined.* Kam fought to regain her feet. As Lefty reached for her hands she punched him in the chest, filling the room with uproarious laughter.

Two uncomely men dragged her up into a chair and bound her. Her leg was on fire. It was agony. *Help me.* There wasn't an honest face in the room to heed her call.

Then, as the man with the toothpick in his mouth reloaded, he said, "Any more blasphemy towards the prince and the next one will go in your neck. That will leave us to take care of your darling little baby."

47

THE CITY OF BONE. A black monolith shimmering below the burning sky. Georgio wiped the sweat from his brow. *Home.* He sped up his pace, mouth watering at the thought of a stuffed biscuit and milk.

"Slow down," Mikkel said, peering through his spy glass. A look of frustration crossed his ebony face, his big smile many days gone. "Get a look at this, Billip."

"I want to see," Georgio turned back and headed for Mikkel.

"In a minute, Boy," Billip said, pushing him aside.

The journey from the City of Three had been nothing short of harrowing. Wind storms came and went; the nights were longer than the days and of all things, underlings. Georgio had killed three himself, and Billip and Mikkel had killed another twelve, but they weren't without casualties. One mintaur and two ponies were dead. Only they themselves and somehow Quickster still lived.

Billip, skin tanned by the suns, his sharp features hardened by battle, gawped as he peered at the ominous city.

"Let me see," Georgio pleaded. His stomach groaned. He was starving. They had started off with all they could carry, but after that last fight with the underling hunters most of their supplies were left to wither in the dust. He'd had little food in days. He couldn't ever remember being so hungry. It didn't seem possible.

Billip tossed Georgio the telescope, turned to Mikkel and said, "Those people are worse off than we are."

"What people?" Georgio said, "I don't see hardly anything."

Billip jerked the spy glass from his grip and hit him in the head.

"Ow! What did you do that for?"

"Wrong end, Stupid."

"Oh," he replied, rubbing his head as he raised the spy glass back to his eye. "What the in world of Bish!"

There were thousands of them. People. Huddled in a moving mass outside the City. He had never seen that many people in one place before. It was enough for an army. An army without a banner or siege equipment. An army that was starving to death. His belly let out another loud growl.

"You better get used to that," Mikkel said, "because we can't get in there. Bone!"

Billip kicked up the dirt. "Bish!"

Georgio could see the anguish in Billip's face as he clutched at the bandage on his side. Mikkel sat down behind Quickster's shadow and adjusted the sling on his busted shoulder. Georgio felt a little guilt as the two men baked in the sun, clearly in some type of agony—internal and external agony. He, however hungry he may be, was fine. Sure, getting feathered with a few crossbow bolts hurt like the dickens, but the look on that underling's face before he ran them through almost made it worth it.

I got to have a biscuit. So close.

He walked over to Quickster and stroked his think black mane. If the quick pony was thirsty or hungry, he didn't show it. The pony seemed as oblivious to the blistering environment as a stone. "We better not take you anywhere nears those people, Quickster. Those people will turn you into a roast."

"They aren't the only ones," Billip said, tossing a knife into the ground.

"Oh no you don't," he said. "I'm not eating my friend."

Mikkel added, "We may have to trade him, Georgio. It's the donkey or us."

"No!" He wrapped his arms around Quickster's neck. "He's not even mine … he's Melegal's"

Billip jumped up on his feet. "The beast is mine, Boy! Melegal stole him from me!"

"Did not!" Georgio screamed.

"Ah, but he did. What else would you expect from a thief?" Billip poked Georgio in his chest. "He stole my ass!"

Mikkel rumbled in laughter, adding, "You can say that again. Did he steal your tender heart, too?"

Georgio slapped Billip's hand away saying, "He's Melegal's, and under my care. You might as well try to kill me if you want to take him." He ripped his broad sword from his sheath. "And just to remind you … You can't kill me!"

Billip slugged him in the jaw. He dropped to his knees, sword falling from his hand. Then it hit him. He raised his finger. "I just remembered: I know a secret way in!" He fell face first into the dirt.

48

IT WAS BIG. VENIR STOOD in helpless horror, his own marrow running cold, at the sight of one of the most ghastly things he ever saw.

"Bish."

One horse was being weaved into a cocoon while the other's life was being sucked from it. A spider, the size of four war horses, had its fangs plunged deep into the big horse's haunches. The grey mare kicked one last time as its strong and vibrant body was sucked down to a husk. The enormous insect rose up on four of its eight hairy legs and let out a frightening screech that would have run a giant's blood cold. *Run!* His instincts screamed, and he would have if not for something else.

Huddled down in the tall grasses, he strapped on his helm and withdrew his shield. There would be no running from that thing. Hide yes, but run … no. But, that's not why Venir stayed. It was something else: underlings. Six of them rode atop a basket impossibly embedded on the spider's back. The second dawn's light had risen to reveal the gleaming evil in their bright speckled eyes.

His helm began to burn and beckon. *Kill!* The black eyelets began their glow. *Them!* The bond between him and Brool became one. *ALL!*

Venir's muscles bulged; his veins writhed beneath his skin as his blood began to flow like lava. He took no notice of his heaving chest or prickling hairs as he fought to hold his position. The venomous spider glided over the grass, its long hairy legs touching the ground as soft as petals. It was the only barrier that came between Venir and the underlings. In order to kill them, Venir would have to kill it. It was time to fight. It was time for something to die.

As the spider tapped around the clearing on its fuzzy black legs, Venir crept forward. *Attack!* The black body and white-and-black-ringed orb of this spider wasn't very different than that of the sand spider had been. He was certain there was nothing but gooey green guts in there. From a hole on its tail end, spider silk shot forth, spraying and coating the dead horse. It turned again, the red glow of its eight eyes scanning over the grass and jungle. It felt like thunder behind his temple, exploding in his ear. *Attack!* The spider reared up on its hind legs almost fifteen feet in height and screeched once more.

The underlings were making short chittering commands as they tugged at many ropes on the saddle. The spider shuddered and shook, knocking one underling off its back and onto the ground. In the next instant, the spider's front spear-shaped leg pierced the underling in a series of lightning quick blows. Something in Venir quivered.

Avoid those.

The underlings chittered with anger as they jabbed long black rods into the insect, and they crackled with every strike. The spider's feet flailed as it reared and then it dropped and settled down. The underlings had regained control and turned the insect toward him. Venir remained still. His shield was pulled in front of him as he hunkered into the tall grasses and angled himself behind a small grove of jungle trees. Fear and rage intermingled in his mind. The spider was getting closer, each of its steps crushing down on the ground with power. He would have liked to be giant sized again so he could smash the insect under his toe. *Attack!*

Something bounded past him. The spider turned. A cotton tailed rabbit as big as a man stood up in the field.

A giant rabbit? What in Bish?

Spider silk shot out. The rabbit bounded away in a single leap that took it clear from his sight. The spider turned in pursuit, its rear flank exposed. Venir couldn't contain himself. The proximity of the underlings was killing him. *Attack!* Like a metal gazelle he bounded over the grass, closing the gap from him to the spider in two seconds. The spider flinched as he rolled under its belly, grazing its hairy coat. A spear-like tentacle jabbed at his head, glancing off of his shield.

"RAH!" Venir cried, ramming Brool to his knuckles into the spider's belly, then ripping it free with another bellow. An ear shattering screech followed. Spider guts coated him from head to toe, like spoiled milk or a toxic sewer. Something hit him hard, sprawling him to the ground, throwing spots before his eyes. He rolled onto his back as the spider crashed his way. *Move!* He screamed in pain as the spider fell down on his legs. He was pinned to the ground.

"Son of a Bish!" he yelled, drawing the bewildered gazes of the underlings. "Come on, you slat eaters! I've been waiting for this!" Venir raised his axe, chopping away at the spider's flesh with fury, black and green chunks of the beast flying everywhere.

As if they had a single mind, the underlings jumped from their saddle, drew their edged weapons and attacked. Venir sat up, catching the ringing blows on his shield. He chopped the legs out from underneath one underling, dismembering it from the knee. It chittered in agony, crawling away. Venir tried to pull his legs free. *Move quicker!*

The helm beckoned a warning. The underlings were circling behind his back.

Clang. Clang. Clang.

Venir fended off the nearest underling then shoved the edge of his shield in its mouth. *Move!* He flopped to the ground as a blade sliced over the top of his head. He cried out as something stabbed into his leg. He could hardly see from all the goo in his eyes, which also coated him from head to toe. He ripped his legs out from under the spider, rolled over one of the underlings and sprang to his feet.

The underling with a mouthful of busted teeth still fumbled for a weapon as the other three rushed him.

Chop!

One stopped to find its arm.

Stab! Rip!

One clutched at the gaping hole in its chest.

Slice!

The other fell to the ground, black-red blood burbling from its headless neck.

A sharp whistle caught his ears. The last underling, busted mouth and all, had managed a whistle. Brool shot from his arm like an arrow, cutting the underling's alarm short. Venir scanned the area as he wrenched his weapon free. He stepped away.

The spider's spear-like tendril poked at his side. The creature lived, its red eyes full of an evil intent. He sliced away the tendril. Webbing shot from the front and rear of the dying creature as he tried to force its bulk up from the ground. One at a time, Venir cut its legs off. He jammed Brool's spike in its skull.

"That's for killing one of my underlings!"

He whirled at the sound of something he hadn't expected to hear: clapping.

There, among the grasses and the gore, stood Slim. He had the ears of a rabbit sticking up from his head.

"You can't be serious," Venir said.

Slim held his finger to his lips and said, "Sssh ... not so loud." The tall lanky man crinkled his bunny nose and added, "That smells horrible, and it's all over you. We've got to find you a river, a big one."

"Great idea," Venir said, slinging the goo from himself. "We need to find some horses and our women, too. At least you survived. What happened?"

"What happened," Slim said, his peaceful face showing a hint of anger, "is you left."

Venir shook his head. More people were dead or abducted because of him, and he'd only been back in Bish a few days. In trying to prevent one bad thing he'd opened the door to another. He shook his head.

"Slim, it's probably best you parted ways with me. Most people don't fare so well in my company these days."

"Bish happens, Venir. Get over it. Besides, I like you."

"Really? Why's that?"

Slim shrugged.

"Because you kill evil. You're good at it."

Venir took off his helm, surveyed the dead underlings and said with a smile, "I'd be lying if didn't say that felt really good. Hmmm, I say we go and find some more." He chopped his axe in the air.

Slim's ears perked up, and his nose began to twitch.

"I hate to say this, but I think more of those things," he motioned towards the spider, "are coming."

"Any chance you can turn into a horse so we can track these kidnapping fiends down?"

Slim's ears shrunk and returned to normal. An older man, with long earlobes and calming blue eyes, remained. "Not today, but if we live till tomorrow maybe I'll surprise you."

In the distance Venir could see three large black things creeping over the landscape. Killing one spider was one thing, but three? *Run or die.* He looked over at Slim, but the lanky cleric was already running.

49

A KEY. *A* KEY. *A* KEY.
He held the continual light coin in his mouth. It made what otherwise would be a very dark room quite bright. The small, tightly wrapped coin gave off quite the powerful beam of illumination. Melegal had become very fond of it. *I wonder if McKnight knew about this key.* Lighting a lantern or candle wasn't an option. The smell of the burning oil or wick would linger and be a dead giveaway.

Melegal's hands ran up and down every nook and crevice of Lord Almen's office. He'd been inside more than a dozen times over the past several months and noted every detail. He could have done it blindfolded if he had to, but why show off when your life was on the line.

Noting the thin layer of dust on the floor, his keen eyes followed a trail unseen to normal sight. The office, virtually dust free and dry as a husk of corn, still left many signs to his naked eye that was as sharp as a bird of prey's. Holding his chin in the nook between his finger and thumb, he bent down on one knee, eyeing a row of books and baubles on the bottom shelf of a book case.

"Hmmm. ..."

Royal Lord Almen, when he was in his presence, rarely moved from his seat at the desk. Instead, the stoic man always remained in close proximity, never venturing far. In all likelihood, his most precious items were probably there. At the same time, it was likely the desk would be booby trapped. Setting a trap off was one thing, but resetting it was another. Melegal didn't have time to risk it, so he chose to run his search from the outside in.

This is interesting.

He removed the coin from his mouth and fanned his hand up and down the shelf. Tiny particles of dust glittered in his coin's bright beam. Some floated; others remained affixed to their objects. There were golden dragon bookends, precious metal candle sticks, several finely crafted letter openers and so on, but dust coated each and every discarded object of appreciation.

What would the key look like?

Melegal aimed the beam high and low. Its brilliance identified other details that his own eyes in the dim lantern light had missed. Tonio's sword, for example, was placed within a trove of weapons that appeared to have been discarded. The encrusted jewels on the pommel of the magnificent sword reflected with brilliance underneath the cloth Melegal had recovered it in. *The murdering brat.* The thought of the horrifying young man left his blood a little cold. What the monster had done to all of the sentries months back had been something he'd set up, the results more grisly than expected. But he lived.

The room itself, a five-hundred square-foot rectangle, seemed vaster than it first appeared as he shined the light around its edges. Another black case, somewhat ominous in its old mahogany finish, sat along the wall askew. The faintest of scratches could be seen at the corner of the case on the castle stone. A delicate breeze nibbled at his fingertips as he ran them along the back edges.

"Clever."

Indeed. It was one of the better concealed passageways he'd ever encountered.

"And where might you go?" He pulled the case outward, not scraping, but gliding over the stone. A small door, less than his chin in height, greeted him. He pulled on a silk glove, reached down and grabbed the brass knob that jutted out just above his knees. He felt cold metal through his glove. *Interesting.* The mechanism's springs pinged his ears as he twisted the knob and shoved it open. A whoosh of icy air nipped at his nose and ruffled his cloak. Chill bumps rose all over his body.

He ducked down and crept inside. A tunnel, tall and wide as a large man, greeted him like a large mouth. Steps carved from the ground descended in a steep decline before dropping out of sight. His beam of light, not withstanding, reached less than thirty feet ahead. The air was musty, chilly and damp. He rubbed his burning nose. Melegal was accustomed to the tunnels beneath the vast City, but this was different.

What am I doing? Why would the key be down here? Fool, I don't even know what the key looks like. Was this another one of Sefron's games? He took a closer look at things. On the landing where he stood were a staff, a cloak and a pair of curved swords on belts and in scabbards. *Cutlasses. Strange.* Two torches hung on the wall, and there was a peg on the wall as well, and hanging from it was … *A Key!*

It was slender, a hollow head, a row of teeth, as long as his hand and made of dark steel. He wrapped his silk covered fingers around it and removed it from the peg. He checked the brass door knob and the key hole below it. *Nope. Blast. This is either it, or it goes to something down there.* He craned his neck above the steps and closed his eyes. Something was scratching against the stone. There was an ebb, something like breathing, and dripping water. *I'm not going down there.* He stepped back inside Lord Almen's chamber and took a deep breath. His hand clutched at his heart.

No thank you.

He twirled the key in his fingers. It was different, certainly not like anything he'd ever come across before. A human locksmith could have made it, but the design wasn't human. The teeth were more round than square, and the rivets weren't smooth, but rough. How long would it be before Lord Almen missed it? Should he give it to Sefron? Draw a picture? *Yes.*

It was closing in on an hour, time to move. There was no telling how early Lord Almen actually came in. He made his way back through the small door and hung the key back on the peg. With relief he began to pull the door closed behind him.

A disturbance was coming from the other side of the main door in Lord Almen's chamber room. *No!* He could hear voices on the other side. One of them was Lord Almen's, and he was angry. He heard a thumb depressing the lever. *SLAT!* He began pulling the cabinet back into place. *Ow!* He pinched his fingers between the stone and wood from the effort.

"Remove that man's head at dawn! See to it all the sentries are in the courtyard to bear witness. Outrageous! Find his superior and remove his right hand as well. Move, Imbecile!"

Melegal heard another sentry racing back up the steps just as he closed the small door. He could barely hear a thing on the other side. The little door seemed as thick as the stones that surrounded it. That's when he closed his hand around the bright light of the coin. *Bone!* He felt for the key on the post and waited in the pitch black. What to do now.

He'll post two guards for this. Even after he leaves, I'll never get back out unnoticed. To make matters worse, he had a meeting with Lord Almen. He pressed his ear to the door. He thought he heard a muffled voice from within. It was hard to say. Lord Almen, more than likely, sat at his desk, plotted death and brooded.

I'm dead. He let his boots dangle over the first step. *If you can't go up, than you must go down. The only place I'm going is down.*

50

CASS'S SLIM, COATED BODY WAS as stiff as driftwood.

"Somebody, do something!" Fogle cried.

The dwarven ladies removed Cass from his grasp and rolled her onto her stomach. Their strong little hands thumped all over the druid's back while another dwarven woman wiped the goo from her mouth. Fogle brushed his gooey fingers through his hair.

She can't die! She can't!

Death wasn't something he'd come to terms with. Ox the Mintaur had been the first friend he'd seen die, and that had been hard. Seeing this exotic woman—perfect in features and form—seeing her perish would be unfathomable.

"Do something, Mood!" he said, shooting the Blood Ranger a pleading look.

Mood stood, his solemn expression unchanged, unmoving.

Cough!

Cass's body shook and shimmered. The dwarves lifted the woman into a sitting position and continued their heavy taps on her back. Fogle watched her fingers writhe and her arms sling. Her body lurched upright as her head heaved forward to retch. Something vile, muddy, brown and black gushed forth like a geyser from the druid's petite mouth. She stopped, gasped, then heaved again with more violent fury that before. The putrid smelly substance seemed unnatural and endless.

Ew!

Fogle turned his nose away. He glanced over and away again. Something about the exotic nature of their relationship had been damaged. At least he thought maybe it had. *She lives. That's all that matters. Well, I'm certain she'll want to clean herself up. She's puking again!*

The retching and puking went on for another minute. The dwarven women had thin smiles growing on their chubby little faces. Cass had her legs wrapped beneath her, her body sagging into the arms of the women. She pulled her hair away and looked down at the massive pile of vomit she had created.

"That's foul," she said in a meek voice. "Burn it. Quickly."

The women dragged her back. Mood dropped a torch into the bile. It burst into a roaring flame. The fire burned green and orange, the smoke shades of deep purple and pink, the heat not hot but cold. It hissed and squealed in anger, like a living thing in its last hideous moments of life. Fogle shielded his face with his hand from the strange beacon of flame. It was evil, vile and deadly. Whatever poison Chongo'd had in him should have killed him. He looked over at Cass. It should have killed her as well. He felt fortunate to be alive.

The fire let out a final vengeful groan and then extinguished as fast as it started, leaving nothing but silence and an unforgettable smell. Suddenly, Fogle Boon felt as weary as he'd ever been. He fought to keep his eyes open. It was a degree of guilt that kept them open. How much had Cass suffered for the dog, and how much had Chongo suffered for … Venir?

That's when he heard Cass's purring voice speaking in a raspy, not-so-seductive manner. His eyes latched onto hers, and he tried to make out the words coming from her grotesquely coated face. Somehow she was both beautiful and disgusting at the same time as she said, "Come, give your *sweet* a kiss."

Something like a tiny mouse ran up and down his spine as he gaped. Then something huge shuffled at his side. Chongo rose to his feet. Fogle looked up and blinked, eyes growing as large as the moons at what happened before them. The dog's thinning grey coat thickened and darkened to a deeper brown. Its tongues turned pink, its big eyes grew alert. Fogle scooted back as Chongo turned, swayed over to Cass and began to lick the entirety of the muck from her body. She giggled.

Mood's big hand landed on his shoulder, and he could have sworn he saw the dwarf wipe something wet from his eyes. "Don't get too cozy, Wizard." The dwarf gave his shoulder a powerful squeeze. "The adventure has just begun."

"No time to celebrate? I've not even gotten a chance to take my bath."

"Better make it quick. Chongo's waited long enough," Mood said, pulling him up to his feet.

It can't be time to go already. It can't be.

Mood whispered something haunting in his ear.

"It won't be long before ta' underlings take Bish over. We must find Venir. The world's gonna need The Darkslayer."

As if the last few months hadn't been difficult enough.

51

T HE ORANGE FLAMES OF A fireplace danced in her green eyes as she struggled against her bonds. Kam, a proud woman, a little more than thirty, for the first time in her life was helpless. The only thing keeping her mind from collapsing was her baby, an innocent creature even more helpless than her. *What has he done with my baby?*

The rogues had taken her up the steps and set her down inside a lavish chamber. There, she sat alongside a massive table, bonds biting into her wrists, gagged with a dish cloth. High back chairs of precious wood and velvet surrounded the ancient table. Piles of gold, silver and other precious metals were stacked up from one end to the other. There were jewels, goblets, fine china, tapestries, art and statues—the equivalent of a Royal throne room. A great sword hung over the fireplace mantle, shadows flickering on its ominous blade. There was something significant about it, a story perhaps, but she did not concern herself with that now.

Her belly groaned. Her leg burned, but the wound had been bandaged. Still, she had been sitting for more than an hour since the last man left. Her tight bonds had numbed her wrists, and the rag inside her mouth was dry. Her breasts ached. She coughed and sniffed. *Where is she?*

She had tried to move her chair, but the ropes were too secure and the chair too heavy. Instead, she sat there, chin dipping downward before rising against her straining neck. She heard heavy footsteps outside the door, the murmuring of voices. *Come on!* Then they were gone, and only the sound of the dying embers of the fire accompanied her. Her gaze moved to another door in the room, closed and filled with nothing but silence behind. *What is he waiting for?*

The hot flames kept the sweat running down her clothes. Every inch of her body was soaked with sweat. Every inch of her body had also been groped as the cutthroats took their time and turns, bringing her up the stairs. It seemed that all had taken a squeeze, a grope, a poke added with a few lip licking lusty glares. She'd never been violated in any manner before. She had a bad feeling the worst was yet to come.

Be strong, Kam. Be strong. You can survive this. You have to, for Erin.

Everything had been a disaster since Venir left, most particularly her. She'd been falling apart for months. She could not figure out if it was because of him or her. She was a woman that always knew what she wanted, but lately all she had been doing was second guessing herself. *I'm a fool, and now my baby is going to die.* She couldn't help but think that was already a possibility. It was killing her inside. *No!* Her body shuddered and heaved against her painful bonds as fresh tears streamed down her rosy cheeks.

She flinched as something soft and delicate wiped the tears from her cheeks.

"Even in the most disagreeable situation, you are still the most captivating woman I've ever seen," a voice said from nowhere.

Palos!

She mumbled angrily behind her gag.

A sinister laughter followed as she felt a finger running across her lips. The hairs on her arms recoiled, and fear raced down her spine. Had he been there the whole time?

The voice of a gentleman charmer spoke again.

"It's a shame to bind your full and perfect lips. They are the color of my favorite wine, and I can only imagine that they taste all the sweeter."

She thought she had died when he said his next words.

"Welcome to your new home, Kam."

It's all my fault. It's all my fault. It's all my fault.

Lefty sulked within, his mind a place of misery. Gillem was quiet at his side. The tavern however, Palos's home, the prison of Kam, was full of rude comments and raunchy jokes. The things the men said about Kam and Palos were sickening. Vile. Evil. Incomprehensible to his young mind. All he could do was sit there like a mute, helpless and full of worry. There was absolutely nothing he could do.

Gillem, however, seemed content to smoke his pipe and drink ale after ale. His halfling mentor smiled and played along with all the congratulations of his brethren, like a wealthy brother returning home.

"Master Gillem, can you kidnap me one of those?"

"Who carried the left breast and who took the right? Take me next time; I'll carry them both."

"Her back must be strong from carrying all that milk. What meadow did you find her in?"

The master thief just slapped his knee, smiled and laughed. All Lefty could do was wallow within, a silly smile on his face. *Smile and everyone will think everything is all right,* Venir had once said. What would Venir do? What would Melegal do? Kill them? Stab them? Save them?

One of the cutthroats swayed into him, spilling ale on his clothes.

"Watch yourself, tiny one!" the man said before staggering away. "Yellow-headed rodent."

There's must be something I can do. If I could just find Erin.

He'd been concentrating as well. His mind was still at work beneath his thick locks of blond hair. The room was full of rugged voices, each expressing fantasies while the others commented in demented delight. There was no mention of the baby girl Erin, however. That worried him. *Please don't be dead.* Someone in the room had to know where the baby was. They all couldn't keep their mouths shut. What had Melegal told him long ago? *What they aren't saying, their bodies are showing. Watch close and see and hear as well.*

"Eat something, Boy," Gillem said in his ear, interrupting his thoughts. "Blend in. Yer suffering is showing. Palos has little need of you now, so ye act like yer a brother of the guild."

For the first time in his life, Lefty felt the urge to jam a dagger in another living person's body. *SCUM! They are scum. I am scum.* His eyes drifted past Gillem's bobbing head to the doorway about the stairs. It was hard to imagine what was going on up there. A tiny fire ignited behind his heart. It was his fault. He had to fix it. From the corner of his eye he noticed a man he'd not seen before, entering the tavern. A nasty scar went from his chin to his ear, and his left eye was milk white. He gave a quick nod to the crossbowman called Diller, on the balcony, then disappeared back outside. Lefty was certain that no one else even noticed, not even Gillem.

Diller headed down the stairs and had quick words with one rogue and then another. The two men finished their drinks before departing without another word.

"Gillem," Lefty said, another minute after the two men were gone, "may I take a moment?"

Master Longfingers' eyes were bloodshot and blurry from all the smoke as he said, "Er … well, don't go far or be gone too long. And come back with more tobacco."

He still had a heart, Gillem just couldn't let it show as he ignored the halfling boy's departure. There was little he could do to save the woman or the child, and he felt horrible for it. It was not natural for a halfling to do such atrocious things. They were simple people that had a knack for getting into trouble with the other races. Why they were drawn to them, he could not figure, but they offered them things the halfling world did not. And like a curious cat, Gillem found himself plunging deeper into the lowest of wells. He never figured it would have gone this far.

Patience, Gillem. Patience.

Even he'd been cut from Palos's loop. He'd been too close to this one, and the Prince of Thieves was privy to that. It didn't help matters that Thorn had not returned. That would only make matters worse for everyone: Kam, Erin, Lefty and him. It was a dangerous time, indeed. Still, Lefty Lightfoot just might have the stones to figure a way out. The boy could do things that he could not, and his heart was still good. Time, however, would be running out. He'd seen many women come to the Roost but never go, woman or child. So he laughed, swapped stories, smoked and drank. *Farewell, friends of fiends.*

One second there was nothing but a table of gold before her and in the next Palos had revealed himself. His face, still handsome, yet demented, glowered above hers. His image faded out, then solidified once more.

Invisibility potion? A waste of potent magic.

"What are you willing to do to see your baby, Kam?" He asked with hungry eyes.

She looked deep into his eyes that rested beneath two well primped brows and said, "Anything."

The Prince of Thieves flashed a handsome row of teeth.

"I find it hard to believe, but I like what I am hearing. Hmmm."

He kneeled down and tore the pants around her leg wound.

"We can't have this holding back your efforts." She groaned as he applied pressure with his thumb. "Still tender, I see." He grabbed a small jar from the table and pulled the lid off, revealing a light blue salve. He gently rubbed it into her leg.

A wonderful sensation, burning and soothing, filled her as she watched the wound close shut. He began messaging her thigh with his nimble fingers. It felt good, comforting, and her eyes began to roll up in her head. *No. Stop.*

"Relax, Kam. That salve will take away more than your pain." He kissed her knees. "It will subdue your vanity as well. Enjoy."

Her head began to roll along her shoulders as the euphoric sensation set in. She felt something being clasped around her neck. A collar.

"This will keep you from mumbling any nasty spells," he said, lips nibbling at her ear.

She had already made her mind up that she would do whatever it took to see her baby again. Her mind was still her own, but now she was so relaxed, as if she had slipped into a warm bed of fox fur minks. Palos slowly removed her gag and other bonds. She was free. Magic swelled within in her then flowed back again. The next thing she knew there was a goblet of wine in her hand. She gulped it down. It was good. She felt good. She felt guilty for feeling so good. *Focus. You've got to see your baby.*

"When can I see my baby?" she asked.

"Follow me," Palos said. He walked with grace that belied his girth, opened the door across the room and passed inside.

She rubbed her wrists and followed. The blood flowing through her body was almost painful from where the circulation had been cut off, but she felt loose. Palos closed the door behind her.

A large candle illuminated an otherwise dark bedroom. A large four posted bed covered in silk and cotton sheets seemed to await her. She fully expected her stomach to curdle, but it did not.

Palos spoke with the most calming and reassuring of voices. It suggested everything would be fine.

"What was it you were trying to say you would do to see your baby?" he said, dropping his robe and slipping beneath the sheets. *I can't be doing this.*

Part of her wanted someone, anyone, to come crashing through the door. The other part of her didn't.

She pushed her matted hair back from her eyes and took a deep breath. She let her clothes fall to the floor. Palos's eyes enlarged like saucers as she walked over, pulled the sheets from him and climbed onto the bed.

She could see his lips moving but heard nothing. She straddled the man, pushed his hands back over his head and dangled her breasts in his face. She gave them both something they'd never forget as a single tear dropped from the corner of her eye.

52

SIXTY-SEVEN.

Melegal slid his thumb back from the wrapped up coin of continual light and gazed in wonder. He was in a room: not a small dungeon only capable of hoarding a few prisoners, no, this was different. It was another world, capable of housing a tiny village. And that wasn't all. Mixed in with the man-made architecture were strange formations cut from the rock. It was alien compared to anything he'd ever seen in the city, or anywhere else for that matter.

Not at all what I expected.

He shivered. The place was foreign to his sharp senses. He wanted to completely unwrap the coin and let its full illumination blossom. For some reason, all he could think of was underlings. They'd forced droves of people to find shelter in the city. Maybe they were closer than he even expected. Why couldn't they be lying beneath the City of Bone itself? He flashed the beam of light over his surroundings and up the steps. The landing at the bottom of the steps had unlit torches at the ready on either side. *Somebody's doing something down here.*

He scanned his light across the room, noting the intricate patterns on the old tiled floor. There was something sinister in how the mosaic seemed to twist and writhe, the light reflecting as if the tiles were moving. He moved toward the exterior of the room, unable to shake the odd feeling drifting into his shoes. Ahead, an open chamber beckoned, and along the sides was a series of small wooden doors with heavy brass handles that were similar to the one he'd ventured through.

There had to be another way out. *Going back is not an option, Rogue.* But this far underground, where would any of these doors go? *What was this room used for? So strange. So odd.* He made his way along the perimeter of the oval room, every footstep light as the one before. The only sound was the occasional scuff of his boots and his soft breath through his nose. He stopped and inspected the key hole in one of the doors. The opening was large enough to insert the key from the top of the stairs. *Interesting.* He depressed the thumb lever only to meet with resistance.

Hmmm. It might even explain why the upstairs door was not secure as one would expect it to be. *The key!* Maybe that was indeed the key. He checked another door that was the same as the first. Pressing his ear to the door, he listened. *Nothing.* He tried another. Still nothing. He made his way to the open chamber and shined his light inside. *Keys!* Not one, but many, all lined on pegs along the curving wall, each the same as the first, but different. The teeth, similar to those on the key up the stairs, twinkled in the light. Each key head was different: round, oval, and rectangular shapes of some foreign sort, ancient and not of the common customs. Melegal sat down, crossing his legs, at the edge of the chamber. He'd need to think about this.

Trap. It must be. He rubbed his chin. *One. Two. Three. Four. Five. Six. Seven pegs.* He looked over his shoulder and scanned his light over the doors. *Six doors. Threes keys left and three right. Lonely peg in the middle.* Perhaps that was for the key at the top of the stairs, which still begged the question: why was the door at the top unlocked? Even worse, why had Lord Almen come to his study in the wee hours of the morning? Lord Almen would expect him early, but who did he expect before him? He wasn't one to track the man, but such a time of day was odd, even for him.

He ran his fingers over the mosaic tiles on the floor. The grey grout between the small tiles was thin, but solid. On his hands and knees he followed his light along the outer edge of the round room toward the first key on his left. At an agonizing pace his light and hands scoured over the wall and floor, feeling for loose plates or difficult to see holes. It seemed unlikely that such a place would not be protected by something. After several minutes he slid his way underneath the first key. *Good so far.*

He rolled onto his knee, shined the light on the wooden peg that jutted out above his nose and gave it intense study. His slender fingers glided over the tiles around the peg. *I hate traps. Hate them.* He took another long draw of stale air through his nose. *Just do it.* He lifted the key from the peg like a feather. A tingling sensation ran from his fingers to his toes. He rubbed the cold key in his grip. *Good. Now, let's try door number one, shall we.*

The squeak of a door came from nearby. *Slat!* It wasn't upstairs. Instead, it was one of the doors in the main room, a door slowly being shoved outward. Melegal dropped his coin of light into his black silk pouch and flattened himself along the floor. The glow of a lantern filled the room. The door, the closest one to the right, was fully open now. *I'm dead.* He pushed his body backward, slithering over the tiles like a snake, into the shadows of the opposing wall. Three pairs of heavy footsteps clomped loudly over the floor.

Clearly not here to steal anything. He reached his hand down his belly, to the pommel of a well concealed knife. The door clanked back shut. A rustle of footsteps echoed within the chamber. The smell of sweaty men began to linger. *Good. No underlings.*

"Follow me," a husky female voice said.

Melegal could see the lantern moving toward the stairs as he peeked from underneath his cloak. They were well armed, weapons jangling on hips, their strides confident without alarm.

He's expecting them. Excellent. But where did they come from? On silent feet he dashed across the room and caught sight of the two men and the woman heading up the steps before they disappeared around the corner. There was something familiar about the way the woman walked. The way she talked. The shadows in the darkness can remind the mind of many things. *Nah.* He crept from behind, up the winding stair case, from deep in the shadows, straining to hear any words that might help. A door opened. Three pairs of booted feet made their way through. The door closed, leaving him back in the utter black near the bottom of the steps.

Melegal leaned against the wall and fanned himself with his hat. He licked the salt from his lips. *I'm thirsty.* He ran the strange key through his hands. A feeling of satisfaction ran through him.

"Ah …," he clutched at his stomach.

A wave of nausea came, and he doubled over. A feverish sweat broke out on his brow. *What is happening to me?* He began panting for his breath.

The sound of a door opening burst in his ears. Whoever just went in to Lord Almen's was coming back. The sounds of booted feet were rushing down the steps, but Melegal was already on the bottom. Threatening voices began to shout. *What had happened? What am I doing here?*

He shut his eyes and recalled everything he'd already seen with the light. Through the pitch black he bottomed out at the stairwell, stumbled, and dashed through the dark to the last door he had the key for. Without looking over his shoulder he jammed the key in the door and turned. *Click.* A sense of dread filled him as the footsteps closed in. A cry and crash roared out from above. He propped the door open as he slipped off his boot, ran into the alcove, hung the key on the peg, ran back, pulled open the door, rushed inside and closed it. *I should have stayed home in bed.* He screamed, or so he thought he did. Something powerful lifted him from his feet, turned him inside out and hurled him through time and space.

"I saw nothing, Lord Almen," the woman said.

Lord Almen stood inside the alcove, touching each and every key. His instincts had never failed him. He had a sleeping guard in front of his office quarters followed by another coincidence.

He turned to the woman that stood a finger shorter than he and said, "But you did smell cinnamon, did you not?"

"As faint as the dew on a honeysuckle," she said, as the lantern light deepened the scars over her sensuous wine red lips.

Lord Almen walked around the room and said, "No man could have escaped so quickly, but we cannot be certain thanks to these two buffoons that stumbled in the stairwell."

"It will never happen again my Lord," she said, ramming her sword in the nearest man's chest. The other's eyes widened like saucers.

Slice!

Lord Almen hacked that one with his cutlass, biting deep into his shoulder and neck. The floor moaned with life, the tiles shifting and sucking. He watched in morbid fascination as the dead men's blood was sucked into the floor and disappeared. Their bodies withered and turned to dust. That chilling sight never grew old for the Royal. The chamber of death was as deadly as fascinating. He smirked.

"As for you," he said, wrapping his arm around the woman's waist and kissing her neck, "it's been too long, my little black queen."

"Don't you mean Brigand Queen?" She purred.

What happened?

The door handle Melegal had been holding was gone. Part of his mind should have been as well. He patted himself up and down. *Dagger. Boots. Belt. Coins. Knife. Hat.* He couldn't be where he was, though. The room was still black as night, but his ears were on high alert as his fingers found the edges of a wall. He fully expected to be inside of a corridor or tunnel of some sort, instead it was nothing more than a closet and another stone door. He ran his ___ over the keyhole, kneeled down and took a look. *Huh?*

___ ___ door open and walked through.

___ screamed and jumped so high her head almost hit the low ceiling. The startled look on

"W-Where did you come from?" she stammered as she pointed at him.

Melegal shrugged, looking over his shoulder and said, "The bedroom."

He might as well have been a ghost in her eyes, and he liked it. *I don't know what happened, but that really was something.* "Perhaps you should sit down," he said.

Instead, Haze came over and wrapped her arms around him. He could feel her body tremble like a frightened animal in his arms. *Oh, this is good.*

"You're real. That's all I need to know," she sighed.

It was the kind of answer he needed for now, and if anyone should sit, it should be him. *Keys.* There were seven in his life now, one as significant as the first. Great power lay within one, but what power did one have with all seven? He pulled his hat off and tossed it on the peg with a little laugh. He'd managed to dodge certain death. *Not too shabby, Rat.*

Haze filled his hand with a glass of port.

He shrugged at her and propped his feet up, letting the crackling embers warm them and wondering. What kind of power did Lord Almen have? How desperate must Sefron have been to align himself with him? But, how could Sefron have ever known?

"Uh … I missed you," Haze said, rubbing his shoulders.

"Not now, I'm still trying to figure out how I got here."

"But, when did you … I was just in there."

"All in due time Haze, now shush, and relish in my presence."

He pinched the bridge of his nose and rubbed. His heart was still beating like a bunny rabbit's. His moment of doom had passed, but that wasn't all. His obsession with finding the key had moved on as well. Whatever possessed him to do something so foolish? As desperate as he was, he'd never considered breaking into Lord Almen's office, and he was certain Lord Almen would have his suspicions. Still, the keys had his undivided attention now. Where did those other doors lead? Could they take you anywhere you ever wanted to go? And what was with all of those strange markings on the wall, the floors?

The dawn's first light crept in through a small stained glass window over the tiny kitchen area. Its bright light ate at his brain. It was time to get up, but all he wanted to do was go to bed. There was something he had to do, though. *The Time!* Haze squeaked as he jumped out of the chair and grabbed his hat.

"Where—?"

He snatched the bottle of port from the table and headed out the door, bounding the steps two at a time. He had a meeting with Lord Almen at the castle, and he was already late.

53

A FTER ALL HIS YEARS DREAMING of adventure, Morley Sickle'd had enough over the past few months. It was time to kill himself. He climbed willow branches. *Pickles. Pickles. Pickles.* Crawled out on a branch. *Cheese. Cheese. Cheese.* And dove headfirst into quicksand that awaited him below. *Jig. Jig. Jig.* The first moments weren't so bad. The murk was warm and comforting as he sank, ever so slowly, into its awaiting darkness. He could hear nothing save for his own heartbeat. In a few moments he'd be listening to his last. *Peace.*

Elsewhere, Scorch, the omnipotent man, was distracted. Swamp trolls, six in all, had taken them by surprise. Morley's man-sized captor, blond hair flowing over his shoulders, was swinging a glowing great sword he'd procured from thin air. The trolls piled around Scorch, twelve feet of evil and hate, teeth chomping at the man who'd invaded their swamp. The trolls didn't stand a chance, but Morley had seen his chance and fled.

Instinct seized his withering bones. His air supply came to an abrupt halt as he sucked his first taste of sandy bile down his throat. It was awful, choking and dying. Suddenly, life didn't seem so bad. *Help!* The quicksand continued to surge down his throat, burning his lungs, as he swam with utter futility in the puddle. *I'm going to die.* His body twitched and lurched. *Scorch!*

Morley hacked. A deep breath of air filled his sandy lungs. He coughed and hacked more. He was on his hands and knees, his body shaking in pain from his violent seizure. It was pure joy compared to where he was before. The grit of the land was a familiar companion as he wiped away the wet dirt that covered his eyes. The first thing he saw was gleaming steel sunk deep into the ground. A pair of booted feet straddled it.

"Morley, seriously, what did I tell you about killing yourself?" Scorch said, voice tranquil with a layer of agitation.

He tilted his head up. Scorch's gore splattered face was almost serene, eyes glittering like te and spit.

"Morley," Scorch said in his upbeat and authoritative tone, "what do you

"Thank you."

"Ah, now that's better, and you're welcome," Scorch said, squatting down in front of him. "Can you not see now living is better than dying now?"

He spit another mouthful of grit away. Scorch was a manner of man like no other. Dressed in a common tunic of leather, the man made the miserable, fog-laden swamp seem like a palace. His voice was soothing, but pressing, borderline arrogant and annoying. Morley couldn't help but like the man and hate him just the same.

"I suppose."

"Morley, why despise me? I've brought you no harm. I've showered you with gifts and look," he stretched his arm over the surrounding landscape, "I've killed all these evil trolls."

He looked over his shoulder. A troll, grey and green as a toad, lay sprawled along the ground, decapitated. Another leaned against a tree, clutching a gaping hole in its chest, dead. Entrails hung from the branches, and the foul smell of a charred husk lingered in the air. He shook his head.

"What is it, Man? Why don't you like me?" Scorch asked, his voice more demanding.

"I don't understand you." He paused. Scorch gave him a pleading look. "Uh … you read my thoughts. You're too powerful!" he yelled, then covered his face, cowering.

Scorch stood up and said, "Ah … so you want my power."

Morley's dander began to rise.

No! I want to be left alone! I want you to leave me alone!

Scorch studied his nails and said, "I can't do that, Morley."

Why?

"I like you, Morley … and, I don't want to."

Morley felt his mind going numb.

"But, I'll tell you what I can do. I'll make you the second most powerful man in the city."

It wasn't such a bad idea. After all, he had been a jig churning nobody all of his life. Now, other than his peace of mind, he could have anything he wanted: Women. Power. Gold. Women. Besides, Scorch didn't seem to mind what he thought. Of course, he'd gone that route before, only to see a lot of people needlessly die and suffer at Scorch's will and pleasure. It had gotten to him, but better them than him.

"Now you're thinking, Morley. Now you're thinking like those troublesome Royals. So, you ready to clean yourself up and head back to the city?"

Morley nodded. *There seems to be no other choice.*

"Excellent. I'm starting to miss my moldy cheese and pickles."

54

T RINOS SAT ON THE WATER fountain's edge, her sensuous arm dangling in its cool waters, basking in the early sunlight. The fountain bubbled and trickled from the mouth of a large fish, endless and sparkling. Around her were many people, some carrying pots, others clay urns, all nodding or bowing in greeting. Corrin stood nearby, a gangly man of medium height and build, wrapped in a light grey cloak, his fingers tapping on his chest. The man had been a thief and cutthroat all his life, but that had changed now. His purpose had been redefined, but his doubts remained persistent.

"They're coming," he warned. "I told you they'd be coming. You can't just open up a fountain in the middle of nowhere and think the Royals won't find out. Son of a boar! There's a dozen of them!" He shuffled closer to Trinos.

She yawned as she gathered her elegant feet and stood. Stretched out in the light, she saw Corrin gawp at her magnificent framework. He had the look of a child seeing a rainbow for the first time. Of all the men she'd encountered, his mind, though savaged by the brutal world, remained respectful. "I'll handle this. You just see the others to safety."

"Er … safety?"

She gave him a look.

"Right away," he said. "Get your pots and go, rodents! The Royals come to fetch their water. They'll have your hides if they catch you with it. Skin you like hogs. Especially you," he said, pointing at a fat woman that waddled as fast as she could, carrying a full pot of water between her legs. "Yer gonna need more water than that to wash that thick hide of yours, Tula!"

Trinos smirked. Corrin was as effective a communicator as he was crude, and for some reason she liked the way he said things.

Two rows of horses trotted in a direct path toward the fountain. The men atop the mounts wore heavy armor, swords dangling from saddle scabbards. One lone man carried the banner whose gold and forest green colors she'd already come to know. They spread out, cutting off her path from going anywhere else, as well as Corrin's. She gazed up at a large man who was blocking her sunlight.

"Can I help you?" she asked.

Trinos could feel their needs: their hunger, anger and lust. The dark clad men weren't here for negotiations. Instead, they were here for humiliation and with orders to destroy, if need be, all the people she protected. In their sight, not one was worth saving. Six of the twelve men swung their legs from their saddles, dropping heavy boots onto the cobblestone road. Corrin became pale at her side as the formidable group of trained soldiers closed in.

The leader folded his arms over the neck of his mount and leaned forward. He had a thick head of yellow hair and a black mustache. He ran his eyes up and down her body, then flicked them towards the burbling fountain and back to her. He cleared his throat.

"This fountain is not for public use. It is property of the Royals." He took a closer look at his surroundings, his black brows arching. "District 27 is under the watch of the Kling household. You are trespassing. You must go."

The soldier's voice was cool and condescending at the same time, his thoughts wicked, but in control. He'd been with many fine women before, but nothing that compared to her. What did women think of such men? *Pigs.* She smiled and offered a suggestion.

"We are only serving the needs of the Royals. No harm is being done. Come, let your horse and men drink from this fountain of Bish's cooling waters. Perhaps you would like to help serve this purpose as well?"

The man blanched and swallowed hard. His face became knit with confusion. She could feel the others begin to thirst for something other than herself. Their eyes began to gaze over the water.

A feminine chuckle came from nowhere, followed by a clapping sound.

"Bravo, Radiant One. Bravo."

Trinos gasped. The horses stirred. Something humanoid shimmered in the air.

A short haired woman, clad in robes of deep purple with copper trim, appeared a few feet away. She was older, her face crinkled like a sun beaten hag, her eyes luminous and dangerous. Many earrings pierced her ears, and mystic power emanated from her persona. She was hunched over as she looked Trinos up and down.

"My, what a beautiful spell you have woven, Sorceress," she said in a voice as frozen as ice. "I myself may have struggled with such a powerful suggestion. You have all of these dogs' tongues hanging from mouths, and you have their tails wagging. Next, they'll be romping in the waters like children." The woman's bracelets jangled as she lifted her arm and snapped her finger.

Pop!

The soldiers blinked and rubbed their glazed eyes. Trinos cringed. How had this woman evaded her detection? It seemed Bish had surprises for even her.

"I only offered them a drink from my fountain, no spell required."

The woman let out a short laugh as she rubbed her knobby chin.

"A well versed liar too, I see. Hmmm … so tell me where you hail from," the woman said, fondling her platinum hair. "What is your name?"

"Trinos. And you are?"

"Manamis. Lorda Manamis Kling," she said, looking for a reaction.

"Pleased to meet you," Trinos said, extending her hand.

Manamis slapped it away. Her voice took on a more dangerous edge than before.

"Fool! You're about to be defiled and then shackled by these very same men. These pathetic people will be slain and fed to the furnace. You dare try to place your hand upon a Royal? I'll have your hands removed, your tongue cut out, your pretty eyes gouged—"

Trinos fell to her knees. Corrin followed suit, trembling at her side.

"I beg forgiveness, Lorda Manamis Kling!" she cried. "I only sought good—"

"Too late to grovel, you little necromancing whore! Soldiers! Seize her and slay these wretched people! Each and every one!"

Trinos kept her head down, hiding the smile on her face. She saw Manamis's feet shuffle back toward the men.

"What are you waiting for? I said seize … er?"

Trinos lifted her chin and watched the look on the stupefied woman. The men, each and every one, were gone.

Manamis looked like someone was pulling her tongue from her face. Her ringed fingers twitched and grasped in the air. Trinos could feel the woman's power growing, her fingers glowing. Manamis's power was dismaying. Trinos had yet to sense such a force before now. The woman's shout could be heard echoing over a quarter mile round.

"Impossible!"

She whirled on Trinos, hands on hips, as she looked down on her like a mother over a spoiled child.

Trinos's eyes radiated in the reflection in Manamis's sunken eyes.

"District 27 is under my good care, Manamis. Go in peace, and do not return …"

Manamis hissed a reply, "Never! Your illusion does not fool me." The older woman flinched at the sound of horrifying screams coming from above.

Manamis looked up just in time to see the Kling soldiers falling from the sky. Metal and screaming flesh smashing into the cobblestone road was as sickening a sound as there ever was, and they splattered all around the street. Manamis gawped at the gore as the horses reared and galloped away.

"As I was saying," Trinos said, dusting off her hands, "go in peace and do not return, or die in a fashion far more horrible."

Manamis gave her one last look, eyes narrowing like needles before she screeched and disappeared.

Corrin stood up and said, "Think she'll be back?"

Trinos shrugged, "Certainly. She hungers for power. She won't be able to let that go."

"Why not kill her?" Corrin said, examining a nearby pile of flesh.

"She'll have an awful lot of explaining to do. For her, that's worse than death. After all, she might not survive her explanation."

Corrin yelled out, "Somebody get a cart and some shovels. Make it quick, else we'll have a swarm of flies all over." He put his hands on his hips. "What a mess, but I like it. The only good Royal is a dead Royal."

She resumed her seat by the fountain and let out a soft sigh. *Next time, I better be more careful.*

55

Tonio didn't even notice the down pour of rain as he sloshed through the city streets. Tiny rivers were filling the sewers below, forcing him to abandon the sanctity of his rotting abode. The rain splattered on his scarred and split face as he looked up into the sky. The moons were not there. He'd grown fond of them, two beacons that he could trust. Their light gave him clarity.

His mother, Lorda Almen, used to walk with him through the castle gardens at night. She often commented on the moons. Her gentle arm always hung inside the nook of his elbow. He was walking in such a fashion now, down the flooding street, not paying any mind to the district in which he wandered. There was no cause for alarm. Few — barring all murderers and criminals — ventured out this time of night, and the rain made for an even more unlikely reception.

"Mutha," he said. "I come soon home."

He growled. His garbled voice was beyond comprehension. Yet he talked to his imaginary mother all the same. Reflecting on fragments of memory, he tried to explain to her what had happened: a two-headed beast had mauled him. He never contemplated how he now lived. He'd died once, or almost had. He'd been resurrected by an underling, only to be severed in twain by an axe as big as the moon. Spidery men had brought him back. Stitch by stitch, their threads laced with fine magic had meticulously taken his innards and put them back inside him. He told his imaginary mother how his throat had been severed and re-sewn, which was why his tongue was thick as leather. He told how somewhere in there, he'd fought a man with a spider's head to the death. His memories were a blur most days, but today they were good.

He looked up to see where his booted feet had taken him. A sign hanging on two chains swayed in the wind. A monstrous creature of color was painted on the wooden sign: a lion, serpent and goat all on one body.

"Kye-mar-ah."

A familiar feeling swept over him as he stepped inside the entry way. He pushed his way through the heavy double doors and found himself face to face with two men every bit as big as he. He paid the startled looks on their faces no mind as he stood dripping inside the foyer.

A bald-headed man unfolded his meaty arms from his chest, said, "Your fee is triple," and held out his hand. Tony reached inside the folds of his tattered cloak and handed the man a small purse. The two men smiled, parted and watched him pass. There was a familiar smell, sweet and musky. The interior décor was refined and uncommon. The smoky room quieted as he made his way to the bar and sat down.

The red-faced bartender recoiled. "Er … What will it be?"

Tonio looked over his shoulder at a table where a finely dressed and aghast couple sat. The table was filled with bottled wine and steaming food. He tipped his chin up.

"S-Sam get." He dropped a small gemstone on the table.

Sam's eyes popped open as the fire-burst gemstone disappeared under his rag. "Right away."

For several minutes Tonio sat, motionless, while the other patrons quietly made their way out. One by one they rustled by, casting nervous glances his way, before disappearing through the front and rear doors. If he noticed, it didn't show. Sam the barkeep, in the meantime, filled a stone cut tumbler with a bottle of grog. Tonio sniffed it and drank. There was a burning sensation, and he coughed. He snatched the bottle from the counter and tipped it up. Down his throat it poured, one ounce after the other, burning like living fire and filling his belly. He slammed the bottle on the bar.

"More!"

More came, and food followed. He stuffed every tasteless bite inside his mouth and chewed. The steak, bread, cheese, and rice did little to fill him, but the grog and ale offered something good. That's when a strange feeling overcame him. He shifted his big hips on the stool as he turned.

Six Watchmen in brown hats with black bills stood soaked from head to toe, dripping on the floor. A net was stretched out by the two on opposite ends. He heard one of them say, "On my signal, men." Tonio's face offered a jagged smile, and he leapt behind the bar.

The net whipped through the air, its weights smashing into bottles and clearing the shelves as Tonio crawled down the barkeep's alley.

"You missed him, you idiots! Kill him! Kill him now!"

Tonio rose behind the bar and caught the tip of a sword being buried in his shoulder. He ripped his sword free with his other hand, sneered and stabbed his assailant's face. He rolled over the bar and squared up against his attackers. In a rush they came, their steel clashing into his.

Clang! Clang! Clang!

Their arms juttered like bowstrings as he swatted them away. He could feel something now. He was alive within, a swordsman.

Clang! Stab!

One man clutched at his bloody belly, his sword clattering on the floor.

He ducked under another man's blow and cut open the skin beneath a third man's chin. He punched a forth in the nose with the pommel of his sword. The men came on, one at a time, at a speed that seemed too slow to measure.

Cut! Stab! Thrust!

Down they went.

More men spilled through the back door as others screamed and scrambled to the front. His fingers closed around his other hilt, ripping the blade from his sheath, and the swarm of men began to fall even faster.

Chop! Chop! Chop!

Stab! Stab! Stab!

Thrust! Thrust! Thrust!

He was lightning in a bottle of blood. The screams of pain and cries of alarm were a symphony in his mangled ears as metal clashed and chopped through bone. The decorative room was getting a makeover, velvet curtains and polished floors now coated in red blood and grey guts.

One man, stout as a stone, came at him with a heavy war hammer, only to be sliced like a dinner roast. Tonio felt his sense of worth begin to return. He'd been there before, fighting and scrapping among his comrades, but now he was something else. He was powerful. Supernatural.

"TONIO!" he shouted as the men of the Watch ran.

Others tried to drag away their dying friends as Tonio noticed Sam the barkeep shaking with horror. The man's blood-speckled face said it all. The barkeep knew him, and more importantly he knew himself now. Smiling, he showed off his blood-stained teeth as he sat down at the bar, his work done.

"Grog."

Both of Sam's hands trembled as he handed over the bottle. To Tonio's surprise, the barkeep spoke, "Y-You killed about a dozen Watchmen, T-Tonio."

Tonio tilted the bottle to his lips and drank.

"Ah!" He wiped his armored sleeve on his mouth and said, "And I'll kill a hundred more … you included … if I don't find the man called Venir."

56

"SINCE WHEN DO UNDERLINGS TAKE prisoners, Venir?" Slim was filling a small canteen from a drying stream bed. They'd been running for what seemed to be hours, but Slim had reassured him they'd lost any pursuers by now. A simple spell, the cleric reassured him, would throw anything off their trail. The cleric, Venir knew, was very resourceful like that, but he still kept looking over his shoulder from time to time.

As for the man's question, Venir didn't have an answer. The women, Adanna and her mother whose name he did not know, most certainly were dead. If not, the torture would be unimaginable. He sat on a large stone, head down over his hulking shoulders, drawing with a stick in the dirt. He'd tracked the underlings as far as he cared to go. Any closer and there was no telling what he would do.

He huffed. "Since when does anything in this land do what it's supposed to do?"

"Good point," Slim said, standing up and stretching his long limbs. The man looked like a crane in his pale green robes and sandaled feet. "So, you aren't really going to try and rescue them, are you? It would be suicide."

Venir looked up with a grim smile, "For who?"

"Oh, listen to you. Ready to put on your shiny helmet and take on an entire regiment of underlings now, are we? Well count me out. I'll just flap my way north, like everyone else."

"I'd be lying if I said I didn't want to try and kill them all. As for the women, well Adanna stuck her neck out for me, else I'd be dead already. I have to do the right thing."

Slim laughed. "The right thing? Since when is dying the right thing? Venir, you can't do it all on your own. Your weapons can only take this fight so far. It's a thousand to one, not including all the other creepy crawlies. You'll be spider food by dawn."

Venir shrugged. "Anything's better than the Mist. Besides, I had time to realize that's what I do."

"Well, why don't you get serious about it, then?"

He cocked he head and said, "I am serious."

"No, you're being unrealistic. Raise an army and protect this land from the fiends."

The thought had crossed his mind, but that was long ago. Before Brool. Before he became his own one man army.

"I'd rather raise my one axe instead."

Slim shook his head.

"You said nothing lasts forever, what then?"

He looked up towards the suns. They were hot on his face, and it was good. He took a drink.

"I'll become a cleric like you."

Slim raised his arms over his head and said with exasperation, "You lunatic! Clerics don't chop the living up into little pieces. What am I going to do with you? I've walked these lands for decades, even before you were born, but I've naught seen one like you, Venir: half happy, half mad. All at the same time. I don't understand you." He kicked the dirt.

Venir didn't understand himself, nor did he care to. He didn't understand Slim's point of view, either.

"What difference does it make if I'm happy or mad? I'm still going to kill underlings."

Slim responded in a mocking voice, "I'm still going to kill underlings."

Venir slung his pack over his monstrous shoulders.

"Don't go all girlie on me now, Cleric. We've got some scouting to do."

They made their way over the slick greenery of the twisting jungle to a cliff face that dropped off behind the trees. Venir wiped the sweat that stung his blue eyes as he crawled to the rim of the edge. Slim slid up beside him as they peered down. Anger and fear began to churn inside his stomach as he scanned the scenery below. He looked over at Slim. The man looked like he'd just swallowed a crow.

"I'm not going down there," the cleric said, his voice barely audible. The cleric then handed over the small spyglass they'd salvaged from Hogan's belongings.

He lifted it to his eye and soaked in every detail. Down on the plains, less than half a mile away, were underlings. Hundreds of them milled between rows of small dark grey tents. Their shapes and sizes were indistinguishable, but that wasn't all. Venir recognized their different manners. The underling warrior hunters called Badoon were there. They had dark leather armor underneath heavy cloaks. The foulest of creatures, the albino urchlings, were there as well, hunkered beneath canvas shades. Four nostrils flared on their faces as their teeth gnashed, and clawed hands opened and closed as they stood chained to posts. They were the creatures that had most recently wounded Chongo.

A rock of guilt stuck in Venir's craw. He'd convinced himself that Chongo would be all right, that his dog and the rest of his friends were better off without him. He was dangerous. Reality hit him now: as far as he knew, he'd left his most trusted friend, Chongo, to die.

He caught an odd flash of movement in the glass. A half dozen of the giant tarantulas were heading away from the camp in pairs: south, east and west. A pair of floating magi were in tow, each to the side of the basket of underling soldiers mounted atop the spiders. It was a scouting party, and most likely they were looking for him.

"See any sign of the women, Vee?"

He fought the images of the women woven inside a cocoon of webs, every drop of water sucked from their bodies. Perhaps they'd been taken as food for the spiders. He couldn't imagine what else was needed of them. His head began to ache as the suns beat down on his bullish neck.

"No. I think we're going to need a closer look."

Slim's head snapped in his direction.

"We! No, you!"

"Slim, sometimes you just have to decide what's worth dying for."

The slender cleric's jaw fell open.

"What happened to you in the Mist?"

"I realized some things: Living for myself isn't as important as living for others. I've been at war with the underlings for a long time, and that will never end. I've come to accept that. I think I could have saved more lives, but I'd been trying to avoid the battle for years." He pointed his two good fingers over the plains. "I've a feeling they wouldn't be here if not for my being gone."

"Your friends stick with you. You should stick with them."

"It's dangerous being close to me," he said, closing the spy glass.

"Well, you are the Darkslayer ... and this is Bish."

"I guess I am."

"So, what's the plan?" Slim said, rolling onto his back and closing his eyes. "Do you want me to fly over like a bird? Or ... I could turn you into a snake. You could slither right through them? How about a beetle?" Slim's long fingers fidgeted in the air. "They won't mess with a beetle. I like beetles."

The cleric continued on with one ludicrous idea after the other. In the meantime, an enormous tarantula had broken off and was coming their way, along with a host of underlings and two magi. Whatever was going to be done would need to be done soon. It wouldn't be long before the spider began to scale the cliff they overlooked.

Venir punched Slim's bony shoulder.

"Ow!"

"Can you control the spider?"

Slim rolled back over on his belly. His peaceful face bunched up with fear.

"No. I only do that with animals and people. Uh ... that thing's moving pretty fast, Venir. It'll be on top of us in no time. Shouldn't we be going? Or is there something else that you wanted me to do?"

Venir caught movement from the corner of his eye. Something was rushing over the plain from the north, a small cloud of dust behind it. Venir pulled open the spyglass. A pair of underlings were running for their lives on the backs of smaller sand spiders like the ones Venir battled near the Red Clay Forest months ago. His knees burned at the memory, and he still had the scars from the acid-like venom to show for it. Another quarter mile behind them came a host of riders on horses. A banner of deep red, light blue and white led the charge of a few score war horses.

"Slim, look there," he said, handing him the spy glass and pointing.

"I'll be! Royal Riders!"

Venir could feel the thunder from the distant hooves now. He wasn't the only one. The spider stopped, pivoted its eight legs and headed back north. The fleeing underlings on the sand spiders had made the edge of the camp and sounded the alarm. The underling army assembled in moments, rank and file facing the charge. Venir's heart began to pound in his temples. He rubbed his hand on the flat of Brool's blades then slipped it between his pack and shoulders.

"Now's your chance, Slim. Come on."

Venir slipped off the edge and began his descent over a hundred feet down where the open plain awaited him. It was more of a steep grade than a cliff, so he slid more than climbed, scraping up his legs and arms all the way down. He didn't feel a thing. He gazed north. The Royal Riders hand formed a single line formation. A Royal banner billowed in the hot winds at one end and the other. The Royal Riders were a mishmash of elite soldiers from all outposts that represented most all of the Royal Houses. It was good thing.

"Sweet Bish! I never thought I'd be happy to see Royals!"

He flinched as something skittered down the cliff along his side. A beetle as big as his hand hung on the jagged rocks. It was black, with splotches of olive green and white. Two pale green eyes flared at him as two protruding black antennas seemed to make an angry gesture. The black and gold wings hummed to life, and the beetle soared toward the underling camp and disappeared in the light.

"Humph ..."

Another fifty feet down and Venir noticed something else. Something writhed beneath the clay patches of the sun baked plain. Tiny holes opened up in the ground. A funny feeling overcame his senses. Something lurked beneath the surface: spiders, snakes or more underlings. Maybe something worse. The mammoth sized spiders were returning to camp. The small army of horsemen would have a hard enough time with one of them, let alone six. The underlings, he knew, were full of surprises.

He hurried his descent and dropped the final ten feet to the ground. He pulled out the spyglass and watched the odd gait of the giant tarantula. He was still have half covered in the guts of the last one he'd slain. Atop the creature was another basket of six underling riders, chittering and pointing back and forth. The underling magi floated six feet above the ground like shades, covered in robes from head to toe. His mouth became dry, and he wished he'd taken one last drink.

"Bones of the dead!" he exclaimed as more underlings began to pop up from the ground in the distance. Their jewel speckled eyes infuriated him. "Too many underlings, not enough Royals." He found himself longing for a saddle between his legs. *Chongo.* He had to find his beast. He swung the spy glass back towards the riders on the spider. Their faces were turned his way. The spider stopped and turned. His blood froze. *Slat!* The brass on the spy glass gleamed in the dipping suns. He slammed it closed. The spider reared up on its back legs and charged as the underling magi soared his way.

Venir yanked his shield and helm from the old leather sack, along with something else: Mood's scale mail shirt.

"Well Bish blast my eyes!" He pulled it over his head, arms bulging under its short sleeves. He stuffed the sack in his backpack and strapped it on his shoulders. The air went still as he strapped on the helm and felt his blood rise. He could see, smell and hear everything as he stood like a gleaming metal statue in the suns. His powerful legs churned forward like a charging bull, and Brool whistled at his side. One second the blue sky was clear in the horizon and in the next instant the underling magi raised their clawed fingers high in the air. The ground beneath him erupted in white hot light.

<h1 style="text-align:center">57</h1>

M ELEGAL HAD ARRIVED BACK AT Castle Almen in time enough to see the head removed from the shoulders of the sentry he'd put to sleep hours earlier. The gloomy feeling followed him to the meeting that involved himself, Sefron and a very irritated Lord Almen. As usual, he averted his stare, but his tardiness was not to be ignored nor his tawdry clothes and breath bathed in alcohol.

The Royal Lord shared with him a sincere concern, which was odd, about an incident that occurred within the city. He was a scowling hawk when he dismissed him, saying, "I shall deal with you later." Melegal silently promised himself to do his best to see to it that later never came. Without further courtesy, Lord Almen departed, leaving him all alone with Sefron.

Sefron had been a different matter entirely. There he stood, as the cleric sat, inside the confines of a dark but quaint living room. All of the preparations for the Royal Coming of Age games were in order according to Sefron, who rambled on with one detail after the other. The foul cleric with a mouthful of blackening teeth kept showing his tell, to Melegal's chagrin.

"The *key* to this event …"

"… and another *key* moment …"

"Where the guests are seated will be *key* …"

Melegal kept his internal fervor in check. The deceit was confirmed. Without a word, he hit the streets and left Sefron babbling all over himself. *I've found the key to killing you, Sefron. Won't be long.*

The pressure behind his eyes began to ease the farther he traveled from the castle. *For a few more hours I live. How grand!* The merchant class was in full swing as he weaved his way in and out of carts, carriages and burly laborers. There had been a time, it seemed so long ago, when he'd been sleeping in with a belly full of wine and playing footsies with a run of the mill wench. Those days might as well have been ages ago. His simple life as a swindler had changed for the worse. Those memories erupted from within as he stepped inside The Chimera.

Retching wasn't the greeting he'd expected, but that's what he got. A Watchman, barely a man, was vomiting on the floor. Melegal's pale demeanor flushed at the sight of all the blood and gore. It looked like twenty men had been slaughtered on the battlefield, but he could only count half a dozen heads. This wasn't the homecoming he was expecting. Behind the bar was Sam, a stout man with greased black hair and a pock-marked face. Sam was puffing heavily on a fat cigar, nervous, his smoke reddened eyes trying to blink away the horror.

Another city Watchman was jotting down notes on a piece of parchment and nodding in dismay. Melegal walked over and snatched the parchment away, saying, "That will be all, Sergeant." *Buffoon.*

The bigger man whirled in anger, but then caught the brooch pinned on Melegal's cloak.

"You pardon, Detective."

"Take your hounds and get some air."

The man nodded, rounded up his green-faced men and departed.

Sam the barkeep gave Melegal a curious look. He was certain that Sam's memory was as keen as his business sense, so it wasn't likely he'd forgotten his face, no matter how long ago it had been. Sam's eyes lingered on his brooch and then on his eyes.

"Don't ask," he said, pointing to the top shelf. "How about some wine?" He looked around. "White." The barkeep reached below the bar, saying, "The good stuff is down here." He plunked a crystal wine glass on the bar and filled up half the glass.

"Tell me what happened, Sam."

Sam rolled his sleeves up over his thick forearms and said:

"A man came in here, tall and blond, as out of place and ugly as an orc. He was like nothing I've ever seen: face split with a jagged scar ..." Melegal stopped drinking. "... but he had coin, plenty of it. His armor had the insignia of a Royal. He could barely sputter a word, so I gave him some grog." Sam made a sour face. "He smelled like death. We cleared everyone out just before the City Watch came."

It can't be. Tonio's out butchering grown men like children. Can the man be stopped? Are my own rumors true?

Sam kept wringing the rag in his meaty hands, and sweat dripped from his brow.

"Detective, he was that Royal, the one you and your brawny friend tussled with. I thought I'd never see another night like that night."

Slat. The barkeep's eyes flitted to the floor where new planks had yet to blend in with the old. Melegal could have sworn that thunderous crack had broken Tonio's back when Venir slammed him to the floor. Instead, it had only raised his ambitions to a new level. He never understood what possessed that man about Venir.

Sam poured himself a drink and continued.

"Not until tonight, anyway. It was a nightmare gone mad." The barkeep was a hardened man, a retired soldier, but he was choked up when he spoke. "He mutilated those men. Fast and powerful strokes. Even when they clipped him with a blade or stabbed him, he still moved without hesitation, unhindered by pain and showing no mercy."

The barkeep wiped his brow and refilled Melegal's glass.

"What did he do after that?"

"I'd never been so scared in my life, not even on the battlefield. After they were all dead, things got really weird."

Melegal leaned forward, careful not to catch his sleeve on any blood, and asked, "How so?"

"He screamed his name—Tonio. That's when I knew for sure the monster was actually him. Then he asked me where he could find Venir. He said he was going to kill every straw-headed man in Bone until he found him. I've got a brother with blond hair. He shaved his head weeks ago."

"Pah! He is the one killing all those people?"

"I suppose, but he's a Royal, right? Why would a Royal—"

Venir is not even here, and he still causes me trouble. Melegal whisked his blade under the man's double chin. In a very audible whisper he said, "Listen to me, Sam. If you want to live much longer, you will forget Tonio's name. Understand?" He said it while pushing the blade farther up into the folds of the man's chin.

The barkeep croaked in acknowledgment.

"Another thing ... who drugged Venir that night he came back, Tonio?"

"He paid me. I didn't want to do it, but he gave me little choice."

It was probably true; Melegal was confident about that. But it wasn't the first time Venir had been removed from a bar under another's power. Something else was bothering him about the barkeep, though.

"The night of the challenge, you were part of that. Was Tonio acting on his own will? It seemed very uncharacteristic for the Royal to take up matters with a commoner."

"Er ... well..."

Melegal drew a thin red line on the man's neck.

"Yes." Sam stammered. "There are lots of Royal houses here. Their brats come in and make sport of my women and other patrons. But the Slergs and Klings set Tonio up. I already told the other Detective—the one with the hat—the same."

Hah! McKnight held back from Almen. I can't believe it! The Klings have a hand in this. The plot thickens. Dead big hatted bastard had some stones after all.

"Not a word of this, Sam. Because if you think Tonio is scary, you don't want to meet his father." He could feel the barkeep's Adams apple roll over the blade just before he pulled it back and walked out the door. Melegal had things to do. The Coming of Age Games were later today.

The Slergs. All but extinct now. The Klings. The 2nd most powerful house in Bone. And they wanted the Almens dead. This card will be worth something.

He made his way down the street, thinking of Venir, the man behind it all. His son Brak was scheduled to die today, and Melegal had no way of saving him. *Seems the mute galoot won't have the fortune of his father.*

Tonio, a dead madman walking, was on the loose, still seeking vengeance on his missing friend. *Can the impudent bastard even die? Perhaps it's time to reunite him with his gorgeous, succulent and vile mother. I could arrange that today. By the way, Lorda Almen, your son is the murdering bastard. He's in that alley.*

And on top of all that, Melegal knew something else: there was indeed a key that would cut him for the grasp of the Almens. He just didn't know where it would take him. Not that it mattered. *I see no reason to let Sefron live a day longer. Perhaps he'll find his way into the deadly arena as well.*

He removed his hat, fanned himself and made his way into the shade of the alleys. *Blasted suns.* It was one of those days, just as hot inside as out. He noted a grey cat pinning down a large brown rat that was inches from a sewer drain. *Almost.* A small tickle ran unseen fingers up his back as a hooded man in a cloak cut off one end of the narrow alley.

Gaghk! What is this?

He slipped his hat back onto his head and slowed his pace as the big man came his way at a brisk pace, along with a gleaming piece of steel. *Perhaps another course would suit me better.*

He spun back the other direction on the heel of his boot and was greeted by more twinkling sharp steel coming his way. He thought of the assassin that had hemmed him in months ago. The day the halfling saved him. *Not again.* He was pinned in with nowhere to go but up, and that wasn't possible. Or, cry for help. *Blasted thieves!* He whipped out his short blades, the Sisters. *Perhaps I'll scare them away.* The appearance of his blades only prompted a lowly chuckle and a charge.

58

"THIS BEAST IS MAGNIFICENT!" Cass exclaimed for about the tenth consecutive time in a day. "I find it impossible to believe that it serves a man. A warrior, you say? Warriors are hardly known for good character. Nothing but sweat and seed spouting louts that swill too much ale and boast impossible tales."

Fogle rubbed his neck and smiled. "It seems you've already met with Chongo's master then? Hmm … or maybe you're referring to the brutes that kept your tent in the mountains? Maybe your true feelings for big sweaty men are beginning to surface."

Cass shot him a dangerous look from atop Chongo's saddle as they traveled south from Dwarven Hole. Then she turned away. *Please ignore me. The trip couldn't be any more unbearable.* He'd become accustomed to the cool settings below the ground, so the burning sunlight was already wearing him down. He had been picking at Cass and she picking back for the past day. There was little thanks for his part in their efforts at renewing Chongo back to full health. He'd expected some gratitude but was granted only further disappointment. *Women!*

The woman and Chongo led the journey, to where, he did not know. All he could do was watch Cass's sensuous figure sway in rhythm with Chongo's gait. The big dog's thick pelt of brown hair had returned, and its tongues hung playfully from its mouths. Cass was right: Chongo was a magnificent creature, padding across the toasted landscape, stiff black tails whipping back and forth in the air. Without having any idea where he was going, he had a feeling Chongo did know.

"Mood," he said to the giant dwarf that was riding a horse along his side, "do you really think Venir is in the South? I'd think we'd be heading north, towards the Mist, where we saw him last, and let Chongo sniff out his trail."

"The pooch knows where he's going, I figure," Mood added along with a plume of pale blue cigar smoke.

"You figure?"

"Aye. Whether Chongo's tracking er huntin', it's all part of the 'venture."

"Well, what would he be hunting if he's not tracking?"

"Underlings."

Fogle stiffened as he pulled his horse to a stop.

"Whoa. Now, let's go over this, Mood. I want to find Venir. I don't want to hunt underlings." His bookish voice began to rise. "Which is it? I don't want to be prepared for one thing only to be dragged into another. I just want to find the man and go home."

"Ye've forgotten how to use the gray matter in that melon head of yers already, haven't ya? Ye can't be prepared fer everything. You survive with what you got. Now, the land's crawling with underlings. If Venir's in the land, he goes where the underlings go. If Chongo is in the land, it's the same. Chongo will sniff out the black little fiends. If we kill 'em first, it's a good thing. Besides, why you think I brought me kin along? To protect yer eccentric lady? If ye want ta' go home, then go. Ya can drink all yer mother's milk ya want when you get there." Mood snapped his reigns. "Yah!"

Fogle sat as glum-faced as ever while the rest of the party trotted past him on ponies that looked like Clydesdales: ten grim-faced dwarves with notable scars, beards hanging down to their bellies, dressed in chainmail, partial plate and leather armor. Bringing up the rear was the biggest one of them all, a Blood Ranger like Mood, except his skin was dark brown and his beard looked like a burning bush. The dwarf's deep blue eyes met his as he stopped his horse and stared. Fogle noted the two swords that crossed his broad back and the enormous crossbow that hung from the saddle.

I guess we'll be dining with underlings after all.

"Alright, Eethum, I'm going," he said, digging his heels into the horse and trotting forward. *Saddle sore already.*

As he made his way back toward the front, his gaze wandered to the small of Cass's supine back. The woman, pale as cotton linen, chose to wear little more than her abundant hair draped over a tight rose-colored travel tunic woven by the dwarven women. The garment enhanced her excellent features, adding a more rugged tone to an otherwise soft looking woman. As if in a trance, he made his way up beside her.

"Ahem."

She left her chin high, pink eyes forward, delicate hands rubbing two of the massive dog's four ears.

He cleared his throat again.

She glared at him and huffed, "Oh … what is it, Flippant Fogle? Have you come to insult me some more? Make light of my yearnings? Boast about your moments splashing in a Dwarven bath?" She turned away. "Please, *my sweet*, layer it on."

He blushed. *My Sweet.* Had he actually said that? It seemed like the entire world had heard. The strangest thing of all was that he was positive he'd never even used the word in conversation before. He didn't even have a sweet spell component. Once again he found his tongue thickening in his mouth. *Blast!*

He fell back.

"You fool!" she said, whipping her neck around like a striking snake. "Get up here!"

"But, you didn't seem like you wanted to speak with me," he stammered.

"I just spoke to you, did I not, Fogle Fool!"

"Well …"

"And we are talking now, are we not?"

He dipped his chin and shook his head saying, "Yes."

"Then say what you must say. The journey is long, and I don't think the dwarves will be providing much conversation."

Fogle wanted to say everything and nothing at the same time. The woman captivated him like a string makes a cat watch and angered him like a bee stinging a raging bull. *I have no idea where to start. I wonder what Venir would say. Ah … I can't do it. I can blast an earth elemental to smithereens, but I can't spit out a single word to speak to a woman I've slept with before. Speak or die.*

"Well, did I ever tell you that your eyes are as pretty as a bed of pink roses?"

Cass's body lurched as she let out an abrupt chuckle.

Chongo's massive right head loomed his way and growled. His steed nickered and stammered.

"Easy, Boy," Fogle said, rubbing the horse's chestnut neck. He could feel the horse's heart thundering the same as his. *I guess I should have expected the laughter, but I didn't think it would piss the dog off, too. Now what?* He stooped over in the saddle and trailed a little further back.

"I'm still listening," Cass said as she stretched her slender arms in the air.

He noticed a tiny grin forming on the corners of her mouth. *I think she liked that.*

"Er … your hair is more lustrous than the twilight moons. As brilliant in the day as in the night."

She flipped her hair over her shoulders.

"When I see you, I can think of nothing. When I can't see you, I can think only of you." *Oh, that's horrible. Here it comes. More giggles. What will she call me now, Fogle Failure with Pleasing Words?*

She gazed over at him with a twinkling curiosity in her eyes and said, "Is that true?"

He shrugged and said, "I suppose."

"Humph. I like it."

"Well, your bosoms are as—"

"Fogle!"

"What?"

"You've said enough. Speak no more, or else ruin it." She shook her head. "I think I shall savor that nectar that just crossed your lips for now."

She smiled at him, warm and welcoming, before turning away. A great bit of relief filled him. Maybe he was beginning to understand women better after all.

Chongo stopped and hunkered down with a growl. The beast's shoulders rippled with agitated muscle, his snouts bared dripping canines, ears alert. A shadow shot across the sky, blotting out the suns for a moment.

"What in the …," he muttered, turning his head to the sky.

A massive projectile of rock come crashing down to the ground, barreling into the small host of dwarven fighters. Dust and rock scattered everywhere, coating them from head to toe in dust and smoke.

"Mood!" Fogle yelled, "What in Bish was that?"

He could barely see a thing. Out of the dirty mist, Mood pulled his mount along his side, giant hand axes ready to go.

"You take care of yer lady! Me and me men shall deal with the giants!"

"Giants!"

"Aye! Huzzah!"

A battle cry rose up from the dwarves as the tiny army scrambled onto their mounts and forged ahead. Chongo and Cass were right behind them.

"Cass!" he cried out, just as another boulder crashed into the ground ahead. He couldn't hear anything but thundering hooves and bellowing dwarves intermingled with a woman's terrified scream. *Giants and dwarves and druids, oh my!*

59

THE CALL. IT HAD COME after what had seemed like another eternity. Every moment away from Bish was as dull as dull could be. There was nothing of interest where he was, only other creatures as discontented as he, bored, lonely and isolated. He avoided them all, watching the world of Bish, waiting for the call. And when it came, he was thankful, if such a thing was ever possible for the imp called Eep.

He hissed with joy as he said his first words on his return to the main world of Bish, "As you wish, Master."

Verbard, the entertaining one, had recalled him with a summoning spell. He'd grown quite fond of the Underling Lord, despite all the powerful mage had put him through. Lord Verbard didn't hold his reigns as tight as his presiding master, the underling cleric Oran. Verbard respected his needs to kill and destroy and never made him hold back. And now, he was on a mission to kill again and this time his prey was not as typical as he was accustomed to.

Kill! Kill! Kill!

Eep salivated as he zipped in and out of the black tunnels that surrounded the Current. His large mouth hung open with razor sharp teeth waiting to devour his prey, and his powerful taloned hands clutched in and out. He could see and hear everything within a quarter mile as his bat-like wings hummed through the black. The sound came fast before it was gone, echoing over the waters, and when his prey turned, it was too late.

A troll, twelve feet of monstrous mass, stood in the waters, a large stalactite club gripped in its hand. Eep's large orb of an eye opened larger before narrowing as he zipped underneath the Troll's clumsy blow and plunged into its stomach. Eep's tiny earholes were filled with its wails and screams as he blinked his little muscular body—almost four feet of muscle and taloned fury—into the troll's belly and tore it from the inside out. He twisted the troll's innards, gashed its lungs and ate its heart before he clawed his way back out and watched the dying troll sink into the current. *More!*

Troll's blood wasn't as delicious as a man's, and the smell, even to his hawkish nose, was quite awful as he sputtered the gore from his wings. It was the seventh troll he had killed today, and it never got old. He was hovering over the waters now, head looking back and forth, when he heard a voice in his head. It was Verbard.

Eep, return!

His long serpent tongue flicked out when he said, "Yes, Master."

The battle with the trolls and the fish golem had taken its toll on the underling army, but those that traveled on foot reported back they had been unscathed. Verbard stood at the helm of the middle barge, alongside him Jottenhiem, his most vicious commander.

Verbard's silver eyes flickered in the blue lantern light as his clawed index finger scratched at the pale fur on his cheek. He scanned the surface above him, the tunnel once again opening up into a massive cave. Humans. He could feel their nearness. Thousands of them, soft, self-indulgent, weak but irrepressible. Now, he was going to get to lead the first strike into their very heart: The City of Bone. *With no more than 500 underlings, at that.*

"Jottenhiem, you've had more dealings with Kierway than I over the centuries. What do you think his plan will be for me?"

The Juegen commander's ruby eyes flicked to his, a fierce smile turned up on the corner of his mouth.

"Lord Verbard, he'll try to take command by offering assistance. No fighter believes a mage can do what a soldier does. His plans, however, are always kept close to the vest, the true ones that is. After all, what kind of leader would he be if he told us everything?"

True. Regardless of outcome, one underling always held out on the other, and this grand event didn't pose any reason to be any different. But why would Sinway go to all this trouble to get rid of Verbard? Was it indeed possible that he actually wanted to take over the massive human city? He couldn't shake the feeling there was less to it than that.

Something fluttered and landed by his side. Jottenhiem stirred in his armor, but his feet remained unmoved. It was Eep. Verbard reached over and stroked the horned head. *My little equalizer.*

"Seems such a small army to take on tens of thousands," Verbard said.

"They're soft, untrained. They'll flee the city like rats in a flooding sewer. Even if we all were to die, the City of Bone would never be the same. I can already taste victory, and it tastes good."

"You seem ready to perish, Commander."

"All of us Juegen are, but we rarely ever do." Jottenhiem shrugged. "Soldiers are meant to die on the battlefield, necks and elbows deep in their enemies' blood. I can't think of a better way to go than into the belly of the vile men, seeing them wailing and crying, burning through the city as we cut them down." Jottenhiem filled his armored chest with air. "Once it starts we won't stop chopping until we're dead. It shall be so … glorifying."

"Hmmm … I, however, have no plans to see any underlings die in vain." Verbard lowered his voice. "Let me be clear, Commander: our siege shall be slow, precise and deliberate. I'll not be turning our kind loose on a suicide mission. You need to be certain of my orders."

Verbard's fingertips glowed red hot as he held them in front of Jottenhiem's face. The commander's tiny facial hairs began to curl and stink as his face beaded with sweat.

"My orders alone, else you won't be the one to lead the Juegen into any battle."

Stone-faced, Jottenhiem bared his teeth as the tiny hairs on his face burned and drifted away. He managed to say, "Lord Verbard, my allegiance to the one that vanquished the Darkslayer is without fail. I'll do as you tell me and no other. You have my word as the Juegen Commander."

Behind him, Verbard was oblivious to the strange look on Eep's face. His fingers winked out. "Very good. Eep, is the rest of the way clear?"

"Ack … Y-Yes, Master."

"Is something wrong, Imp? You look like you've had too much troll."

"No-No. Troll good." The imp patted his belly. "Yum. Yum."

Kierway rose to his feet as the first half of Lord Verbard's army floated into the gray sandy beach that ran alongside the Current. His knees crackled. He'd been sitting for days if not longer, his only company the Vicious who remained steadfast by his side. He dusted the sand from his hands and made his way down the shore.

"Impressive," he hissed under his breath. It had been quite some time since he had dealt with an army of any sort. Now, before him another two hundred men were at his disposal, and two hundred more should be arriving later in the day. He had been aware of that much, as well as many other things.

As Juegen fighters, underling magi, Badoon hunter warriors, albino urchlings and other Underland horrors made their way on shore, he spotted Lord Verbard and his Commander, Jottenhiem. A briar of envy began to jab at his insides as he watched two of his least favorite underlings approach. Verbard's silver eyes glinted with power in the cave's strange twilight, which cast a faint illumination below the city. Kierway rested his hands on the pommel of his sword and nodded a greeting.

"Welcome, Lord Verbard. I see your journey bode you good will, but I was expecting six ships, not three. What happened? Has it been reported to my father, Master Sinway?"

He could see Verbard's eyes flare as he hung in the air, looking down on him with a sneer.

"I see you miss your father too much, as always, Master Kierway. Perhaps you should take him the message yourself. After all, I know you are not accustomed to handling things without his direct supervision."

Kierway glared back and said, "My father expects—"

"Your father expects to hear about success! Not trivial matters. We've a mission above that needs our direct attention, Kierway. We've a city to take over, whether it be with five hundred or fifty. The siege on Bone begins now, unless of course, you'd rather wait on your father to lead the charge?"

Kierway couldn't have been more insulted if Verbard had pissed on his head. His claws wrapped around the pommel of his sword. No one should talk to him like that and live! He noted the mocking expression on Jottenhiem's face as well. The Juegen Commander and he liked little of one another. He'd better be more careful. *Never send a troll to do an underling's job.*

"I see," he said, opening up his hands, "so tell me then, Lord Verbard, how can I be of assistance?" *Before I have you killed.*

Verbard's robe-covered feet lowered to the ground.

"Other than this army, what is it you wait for?"

"A bigger army."

"Don't dally with me, Kierway. Your father's and my conversations have been deep. I'll have the knowledge that you prefer to hide. What do you have to offer me for this invasion?"

"The key. I've an associate bringing me a key that is a great source of power."

Verbard's features darkened. His silver eyes flared. "Shouldn't this key be here by now? What does it do?"

"It opens up a portal into the city." *The likes that none has ever seen in centuries. As I understand it, as explained by my father, the underlings can travel from the Underland to Bone in a single step. An army with the key would be invincible. So he believed.*

"And when can we expect this key?" Verbard interjected.

"Any day now."

Kierway's heart almost stopped at what Verbard snapped out next.

"Tell me everything you know, down to the last detail. I shall locate this key and make preparations with our soldiers. Kierway, my first wave of destruction into the City of Bone will start soon, with or without this *key*."

60

S HAME AND WINE. THEY WENT well together. Kam sat beside Palos's roaring fire and rocked baby Erin. The troubles of the world had faded, all the hurt and humiliation gone now that her baby was safe in her arms. Never had she felt so strongly about any living thing than her beautiful daughter. The baby cooed as she tickled her nose. Now all she had to do was figure out how to escape.

"Your daughter will always be safe here, Kam, and you as well," Palos said. "It was never my intent to harm either one of you." His fingers continued stacking the coins, row after row, on the table. "And I must say, last night my desire for you at all costs was justified."

The rocking chair she sat in creaked as she hummed a dreary tune. His words, last night and after, meant nothing to her. The words she said to him meant nothing at all either, but it had an impact on him. Palos was in control, for now. She just had to make sure she didn't get used to it. She couldn't be too unyielding with him, either.

"I'm talking to you, Woman."

She continued, her humming only interrupted between sips of wine.

He flicked a coin that struck her on the top of her forehead, leaving a painful red mark. Her cheeks brightened. The collar on her neck restricted. Agony ensued as baby Erin almost slipped to the floor. Her magic, what little of it was left, extinguished, but her burning desire to kill the man did not.

"Must you be such a child!" She was shouting. Baby Erin began to wail. "Now look what you've done, my prince! Oh dear Prince Palos, master of the sewers!"

Palos struck the coins, scattering them across the room.

"Silence that baby, you red-haired witch, else I'll have it washed down the gutters. They make a fine cemetery."

"You wouldn't dare!"

"Hah! It wouldn't be the first time, nor the last." He stood up, pushed his chest out and rocked on his toes. "Kam, you can have a good thing here or a bad thing, but whatever the choice—it will be *here*!" He poked his pudgy finger into the table.

He was a snake. A handsome, charming, chubby snake, but not one to make idle threats, either. *Don't push him too hard. Be strong for Erin.* She hoisted Erin on her shoulder, patted her tiny back and said, "If I had a little magic at my disposal I could keep her more content."

Palos's chuckle was low, insidious.

"You have all the magic you need between those splendid thighs of yours." He wiped a dribble of wine on the sleeve of his robe.

Kam felt her face flush. *Repulsive pig.* "You could at least let me clean myself up. Bathe my child, too." She bit her lip and added more of a pleasing tone to her voice. "Feel free to watch if you like. I just need to bathe."

Palos's eyes became orbs of lust. "I'll see what I can arrange," he said, sandals flapping on his heels as he made his way to the front door. She wanted more than a bath, though. She needed scoured from the inside out. She began to recoil within herself. *I can't keep doing this. I need to get out!* Erin's cries began to subside as she pulled her down and hugged her to her chest. She hummed some more.

Palos yelled from the inside of the doorway. "Diller! Fetch the halflings and some water. Lots of water!"

Lefty sat inside Palos's tavern home alongside Gillem, fingers latched and thumbs rolling backward and forward. It had been more than a day since he fetched Gillem his last batch of tobacco, and his back ached from taking cat naps on the dirty wooden floor. His world was collapsing. *What can I do? I have to do something!* Indeed, he had. He'd scouted a little, but that wasn't enough. He had to do more.

"Gillem," he said. "Can I try some of that?"

The master thief's smoky eyes widened in a moment of alarm before shifting back to normal. "Eh … are you serious? You want some ale?"

"The pipe, too."

"Really?" Gillem said, sucking on the long stem of the pipe before letting it out.

Lefty studied the halfling man's face. Gillem, always energetic and cheerful, was exhausted. His cheeks sagged under his graying brows and greasy head of busy hair. Gillem looked old, which had seemed impossible less than a day ago.

"I've nothing better to do, and I just figured, you have to start some time. And I'm bored. This is killing me. Maybe you can teach me cards, too." Lefty straightened his back and leaned forward. "I've been paying attention to them," he pointed with his lips, "and I think I'd be good at the cards."

Gillem shifted his hips on his stool, head still turned away and surrounded by a yellow blossom of smoke. Lefty felt a tingling on his hands. Melegal had taught him how to draw suspicion from himself. *Don't sit and stare. Be a part of something. Stare from within.* Who would worry about a smoking and drinking halfling, anyway? Besides, he'd already figured out where they kept baby Erin. But she'd been upstairs ever since he found the location. It was pretty easy finding a crying baby, but the suffering sounds were horrible.

"Here," Gillem said, handing him the pipe. "Take a puff, but don't inhale just yet. The tobacco smoke will sink in through lips and gum."

He thought of Mood, Venir and Chongo and how much he wished they were here. Georgio, too. What he wouldn't do to have coffee with his best friend once more. He felt the warm smoke and burning tobacco leaves fill his mouth.

"Hold it."

His jaws were popping out as he nodded.

"Good. Good. Now let it out … slowly."

He blew a long stream from his mouth and said, "Like that?"

"Yes. Good. Now take a drink," Gillem said, replacing the pipe with his mug.

Just as Lefty lifted the mug to his lips he heard Diller shout from above.

"Gillem! You and the boy! Prince Palos wants you now!"

Gillem's eyes flickered with surprise before he turned back and said, "Right away!" He snatched the ale away, adding, "There'll be more time for this later. Come."

Kam's eyes glanced over and away as Lefty and Gillem quietly made their way inside Palos's little throne room. Lefty looked pitiful and Gillem mostly drunk as they both swayed and bowed. Palos, a man below average height, towered over them, hands on hips. She hated the halflings, but for some reason she hated the tiny boy more than the man. *Traitor.* When she got free she just might have to kill him as well.

"As you well know," Palos began, "the prince has found his queen, and she'll need watchful servants for her spoilings."

Gillem and Lefty nodded, wide eyed and eager. Kam sneered.

"The lady's pleasure is ours."

"Indeed," Lefty added.

She caught his eyes for a moment, but the stare seemed much longer. The little halfling had a smug look on his face, something devious. A puppet of thieves. Nothing more and nothing less. Just another male that couldn't be trusted. *What happened to that sweet boy? Where did I go wrong?* She pulled the blanket over Erin's face and snuggled her. *I won't ever let that happen to you. I'm just glad you're a girl. Boys are rotten to the core it seems.*

Palos had a bouncing step as he strolled around in his robes, pale eyes dangerous and full of wonder. He'd been doing more than drinking wine and counting gold over the past few hours. She'd watched him sniff the kind of stuff he smuggled in to ruin the Royals.

"Kam and, er … what is the little nuisance's name?"

"Erin," Gillem added, smiling and teetering up on his toes.

"Whatever. So, they'll need clothes, fine ones. I'll be needing fresh linens, too. One of those cribs or a bassinet, I believe it's called. They'll need bathed as well. Yonder is my tub."

He pointed to a large tub that appeared to be made from dark marble and inlaid with gold and silver. "She and the child can bathe there as soon as the water is fetched." He gave Kam a hungry look. "And there shall be plenty of room for the both of us to carry on."

Kam half-sneered and half smiled. It was bad enough she had to sleep with him, but now she would have to bathe with him, too. *Perhaps I'll drown you in that grand tub of yours.*

"Diller!"

Diller swung the door inward.

"Where is the nanny?"

"She's coming, Prince." He took the toothpick from his mouth. "Coming up the steps right now."

A husky woman shoved past Diller and made her way inside, her hard eyes dropping on the table of gold. Kam didn't like the looks of her. Her hair was stringy, her face worn and haggard. She wore trousers and shirts like a man and her bottom lip was jutted out over her fat greasy neck.

"Who is this woman?" Kam demanded, watching the woman fold her beefy forearms under her saggy breasts.

"Meet my nanny, Kam. She'll be your baby's, too," he said as if she was a member of his family.

"I don't need a nanny, Palos. I can take care of my baby just fine."

Palos made an open gesture with his hands saying, "Why, certainly that's the truth when the child is here, but she won't be all of the time, and that will be most of the time, especially when I want you all to myself!"

The rocker teetered to the floor as Kam jumped to her feet.

"I thought we had an understanding, Palos! I've given myself over to you for my child. We both stay!"

Palos had a cool look on his face as he brushed white flakes from his shoulder.

"A happy servant is a pleasing servant. But an unhappy servant is still a servant. Like it or not, the baby comes and goes as I say. And you'll do good to take care of my needs if you want me taking care of your needs."

"You filthy bastard!" she yelled.

Diller opened the door to bring in a bucket of water and set it on the table. She watched as Palos produced a corked vial with a pale pink fluid inside and emptied it inside the bucket. The wooden bucket rocked and reeled.

"Quick, Gillem," he said.

The halfling man snatched the bucket as he rushed over to the tub and poured the water inside. The water kept pouring, as endless as the waterfalls.

Foolish man! Wasting more magic. The reckless use of magic offered a degree of hope. She was trying to think up a plan when Palos interrupted her thoughts.

"Don't worry, Princess. You'll have plenty of time to clean this filthy bastard up shortly." Palos walked over and peeled back a portion of her robe. She recoiled as she felt his kiss below her ear. He stepped away and said, "Diller, if need be, subdue the woman. Nanny, take the baby!"

"No!" Kam wailed. Baby Erin began screaming as Diller strong armed Kam. The nanny snatched and wrestled Erin away, but the wretched woman screamed as Kam clawed a piece of her face off.

"Oomph!"

Kam folded over on her hands and knees as Diller whopped her in the stomach.

Lifting her chin, Kam watched her baby being carried away. She glared at Lefty and said, "This is all your fault, you little halfling bastard!"

The boy just smiled and shrugged. All her hope fled.

61

THE TASTE OF ROCK AND metal filled his mouth as he gasped for air. Venir clawed through the rock that had just erupted below him as his helm screamed at him to move. Disoriented and aggravated, Venir arose from his rocky grave, his entire body coated in debris and dust. His black eyelets smoldered as his body coursed with energy and rage. The Darkslayer was back, and it was good. He shook off the stinging pain from the lightning and yelled.

"Is that all you have, Fiends!"

He snapped up his shield as a small barrage of black missiles assailed him from the robed underling on the left. *Tink. Tink. Tink. Tink.*

They reflected away and sizzled into the ground.

"Hah!"

Another urgent warning came to his mind. Power coursed from the other mage's hands, sending a streak of energy searing downward. Venir stepped into it, shield first, and laughed. The mage's power slammed into the shield with blue and white energy, rocking him back, his feet sliding back in the dirt before the power faded.

Venir flashed the two underlings a fierce grin and charged their retreating forms.

"Now it's my turn!"

He ran and leapt high in the air. The first creature howled as Venir's fingertips caught the bottom of its cloak and pulled it to the ground. A pair of clawed fingers left a burning gash under his chin as he pinned it to the ground and choked the life out of it in his mighty grasp. The other underling continued its hasty retreat towards the camp and out of sight.

Thwwhip! A cord of web caught his shield. He sliced it away. "Blasted insects!"

The giant spider with its basket full of underling warriors had arrived. Venir held onto his shield as the spider began to reel him in. The monstrous beast's fanged mouth dripped with acid that sizzled the ground, and its beady red eyes were filled with hunger. A javelin glanced off the side of his helm. Another stuck in the ground by his foot.

"I'm going to kill your pet! I'll kill you all! HUZZAH!"

He was an inferno. His mind, metal and magic one. Underling destruction was his game. Venir was his name. And no spider, no matter how big, was going to stop him from slaughtering them all.

Venir charged. Bolts and javelins assailed him, glancing off his armor and web covered shield. He didn't feel a thing. Covering the thirty feet between him and the spider in an instant, shoving Brool down to the handle into the spider's brain. Its enormous body lurched and bucked, tossing the underling riders to the ground before it collapsed. Something sizzled Venir's skin as he chopped more hefty strokes into the huge arachnid's brain. Then he whirled on the scrambling pack of underlings, each face aghast and angry. It fed him.

Two, armored in leathers and chain, rushed up from behind, swords clipping at his sides as he dove over the spider's twitching legs and rolled back to his feet.

"There's no insect bigger than me!" *Keep moving!* Venir still had his consciousness as he parried their darting strikes that clanged from his shield and clipped the dwarven scale mail. He fought on as all of the underlings closed in, waiting for a blinding rage to consume him. One hard chop followed another, faster and faster. His massive iron-willed thews struck in powerful cobra like stokes.

Slice!

Brool removed a yellow-eyed underling's head from its shoulders, black-red blood spurting into the sky.

Crunch!

He chopped the knees from beneath another, while catching a wild sword stroke swinging into his shield with a loud *clang*. Venir wrought death, anticipated every move, weaved in and out of harm's way, every strike a death blow. A taloned eagle fighting sparrows. He cracked an underling's head open with his shield, cutting its attack short. He kicked another in the groin. Spiked another in the neck and cut the last one in twain at the waist.

Venir labored for his breath. His oily sweat mixed with blood and gore, some his, some theirs. Underling bodies were scattered on and around the enormous spider, making up a revolting sight. The stench of baking death was heavy in the air. The fight lasted less than a minute, but it seemed to go quicker. Venir jabbed Brool's spike into the heart of an underling that was twitching nearby.

He ripped it out and said, "Seven's a good start!"

He swung his helmeted head around at the familiar sound of battle. Steel crashed on steel, cries of mayhem and triumph roared inside his helm. He'd never seen so many fighting underlings before. The dusty smoke from horse hooves rolled over the camp with a flair of mystic energy cracking in the air. The fight inside him propelled his legs forward over the wasteland, of his own will this time, not the helm's, yet Venir felt stronger than ever. Today was as good a day to die as any, especially if you were an underling.

Faster!

The tide was turning on the valiant Royal Riders as the monstrous spiders closed in on the camp and sprayed them down with webs and anger. Chittering underlings were still spewing from holes in the ground. Venir's powerful legs lengthened his stride, closing the gap at the pace of a galloping horse. He couldn't get there fast enough, and his black eyelets steamed behind his helm. Ahead, an underling mage reappeared, and he wasn't alone. Ten pale white creatures scurried beneath him, all heading his way on all fours, cutting him off from the battle, where he was certain he was needed. Albino urchlings, nostrils flaring and fangs gnashing, closed in on him with the speed of wild wolves. They were the same vicious beasts that had almost killed Chongo. Venir's head exploded in rage as he raised his axe high in the air and screamed …

62

H EMMED IN LIKE A ROOSTER in a chicken coup, Melegal pointed his blades at the opposite ends of the alley, which was becoming smaller. The big one that blocked his original path raised a club over his towering head while the next man brandished a pair of knives. *Hunting knives. Completely inferior to my blades, but the man's forearms are strung like a fighter's. And there's another one behind him, to boot.*

"Drop those blades before you hurt yourself, you bloody rogue, or I'll have your hands for trophies," the short man in a forest green cloak said. "Hah, a man swinging steel thicker than his arm, now that's a laugh."

Melegal fought the smile of relief that was cracking open on his otherwise stern expression while the other man's baritone voice rumbled.

"Ho! This can't be the man we seek; surely it's an illusion. Melegal would never play with swords, unless he stole them."

Melegal couldn't believe his eyes when Mikkel revealed his cheery face and leaned his club along the wall. Billip pulled back his hood, his crafty features still hard, as he stuffed his knives under his belt and began popping his knuckles. *Oh, how annoying.* But who was the other man? *Soon enough.*

"It's good to see you both," he said, sheathing his swords and bumping wrists with the men. "What are you doing in Bone? And who is that?"

"It's me, Me!"

He didn't recognize the deep voice, but he knew the tone. Georgio's curly brown hair was down past his shoulders when he revealed his hooded face. The extra meat he had carried was gone from his pie face, and his broader shoulders suggested solid muscle underneath. The boy, now a man, was at least a foot taller and fifty pounds heavier than last he saw him.

"Where's Quickster?" he snapped.

Georgio's happy face turned into a frown. "Ah, don't start, he's—"

"My pony's fine," Billip intervened.

"He's mine and always has been!" Melegal almost yelled. "Where is he?"

Georgio wasn't finished.

"You gave him to me."

"No, I gave him to Lefty. Where's Lefty?"

An odd silence ensued.

"What?" Melegal asked.

Mikkel slapped his big hand on Melegal's shoulder and said, "Listen Me, Lefty's back in Three. When we heard about all the trouble in the South, we decided to head back down to get my son, Nikkel. That's why we're here. Stocking up for the final leg."

The four men stood in the alley looking at one another for answers to many questions. Melegal had the most, as he'd not seen Billip or Mikkel since the hunt for the Brigand Queen more than five years ago. But they still hadn't answered the primary question.

"Where's Quickster?"

"Same place you'd expect him to be," Georgio answered.

"I can only hope you're not still eating his food. It appears you've still been eating plenty."

Billip had to hold Georgio back as the man-sized boy came after him.

"You better shut your rat hole, Me! I'll pummel your skinny arse. You can't hurt me, but I know how to hurt you!"

Melegal let out a shrill little laugh. *Slat! The boy's changed, indeed. His threat's far from idle.* "I don't think so, Boy," he replied, making a quick cutting motion across his throat. Georgio's eyes widened and his body softened.

"You're still an arse, Melegal," Georgio said, turning away.

"What is this on your cloak … Detective?" Billip said, grabbing the brooch pinned on his cloak.

Melegal snatched it away saying, "Long story, men. I only have time for you to get me up to speed. How'd you wind up in the City of Three? Where's Venir? And how in Bish did you find me in this pit?" He sat down on a crate that was sitting against the wall. It felt good to sit among old friends for the moment, but time was pressing. "And give me the short version."

Mikkel opened his mouth to speak, but Billip put him off.

"He said the short version."

"Mine will be short."

"Yours are as bad as Venir's."

Mikkel bristled.

"And yours are as boring as Georgio's."

"Huh … what?" Georgio came over, a bit confused. "I tell good stories."

Mikkel and Billip laughed, but Mikkel stepped aside with a graceful bow. "Fine, I just want to go eat."

"Me too," piped Georgio.

"We know!" the three other men said.

Billip began.

"First, fortune favored us finding you, as we weren't even looking for you. Georgio caught you ducking into that tavern. Our ears have been filled with stories about the Yellow Hair Butcher. We were snooping around, thinking Venir might have returned. You haven't seen him, have you?"

"No," Melegal said dryly. "Not since the last time I saw Quickster." *Slat!* A little bit of guilt swelled inside his belly. Georgio had been tormented, for all he knew by Tonio. It would shake the boy up if he knew the foul man still lived.

Billip caught him up on how they arrived in the City of Three to begin with, which was surprising as they were southerners. Melegal found it difficult to hide his amazement as he learned about their liaisons with Jarla on her hunt for Venir and the trip to Dwarven Hole, where they all last parted. The falling out between Lefty and Georgio left him hollow inside. He missed the time he'd spent with them both. Billip told him about Kam, a woman he'd consider the journey to see, and Venir's daughter, Erin. *Spreads his seed like a dandelion.* Then he remembered Brak and his upcoming engagement.

"It's all fascinating, but I've no part in this now. I've got my own troubles," he said, tapping his brooch, rising to his feet and unfolding his arms. "Mikkel, traveling south is impossible right now. A death trap they say. You'd be lucky to make it alive to the Red Clay Forest. The Royals are up to their elbows in figuring out how to deal with the underlings."

"Venir will take care of it," Georgio interjected.

"It wouldn't surprise me if the big lout was behind it," Melegal shot back.

"You better watch what you say about him. He saved your skinny neck plenty of times."

"And he's almost gotten me killed ten times more, Foolish Boy. You too!"

Georgio fell silent, but Melegal continued on.

"I'd say there's a good chance your son fled north. For all you know he's right outside these gates. You're bound to see a familiar face or two if you scour the crowd."

Mikkel landed another heavy slap on Melegal's shoulder, saying, "Good advice, thanks."

"Aye, if we find him maybe we can collect that bounty on this yellow haired butcher," Billip said, his greedy eyes dancing with thoughts of more gold.

"Stay out of that," Melegal warned.

"You'll not be collecting what I can collect for myself. Care to put a wager on the bounty, Melegal?"

I'm an idiot. Should have just sent them away. Billip was just as greedy as was he, but of a different make-up. The man had hunted for hefty bags of underling bounty, so a bounty on a man would give him little to fear.

Mikkel frowned at Billip and said, "I'm not getting into that, Billip. I told you that once already. We find Nikkel! If he's not here, we're heading south. That's what we agreed on."

"Fine. Melegal, for the time being Georgio has led us to the place called The Octopus. We'll be there if you need us."

Perfect.

Melegal's steely eyes were dancing behind his lids.

"That's a pretty dangerous hole during these times. I had to leave, no thanks to a man called Jeb. Beat me silly in an Iron Hands contest."

"What?" Mikkel, Billip and Georgio were all incredulous.

"Took my room and my table, so I've heard."

Mikkel's guffaws of laughter echoed up and down the alley.

"You expect me to believe you fist fought someone? And lived?"

Billip clutched at his stomach.

"I gotta see this guy."

"Pah! Both of you sots will fare worse than I did."

Mikkel was leaning against the wall, bowled over in laughter.

It's good to see some things never change. Georgio was frowning at him as he walked away. "I'll get down there to see Quickster, Georgio. Stay close to those two. Bone is more dangerous than ever now. And there's one more thing that I'd like to say."

"W-What?" Georgio stammered a little.

He wanted to warn him about Tonio, but that might do more harm than good. He changed his mind.

"Go back to Three and live. Stay in Bone and die."

"Aw!" Georgio turned and walked away.

Melegal's mind was already elsewhere.

Keys. Keys. Keys. The Coming of Age games. Death to the Slergs and Brak. Slat. He felt guiltier now that ever. After all, the boy had a half-sister and father he'd never know. *Stay focused. Live one day at a time. Kill Sefron!*

63

A RIVER OF BLOOD STRETCHED ACROSS Bish's open landscape as far as he could see. One side of the bank was an endless sea of underlings; on the other side stood his father, Venir: razor sharp axe in hand, screaming with a maddening look in his blazing blue eyes.

Whack.

Brak jumped up, clutching at his side as the warden kicked him hard in the ribs.

Whack! The ugly man did it again.

"Get up, you big fat headed Slerg! It's time for the end."

His stomach rumbled as he rubbed his blurry eyes. Leezir and Hagerdon shuffled by, wrists locked, ankle chains dragging over the floor. Leezir's head sagged, and his shoulder stooped. Hagerdon, once proud and cocky, wheezed and coughed, his lips thin and pale, almost morbid.

"You won't have to worry about being hungry anymore after this, Boy," Hagerdon said, "because soon you'll be dead."

Leezir didn't even look his way as he watched them go.

The warden and two others shackled his wrists, ankles and neck, like the other men, and hooked him to the prisoner chain.

"Criminy, you're a big bastard!" One of the guards said, looking up at him. "Warden, you ever seen this one standing before? He's like a tree, just not as smart. Heh-heh."

"Shaddup, Morg," the warden said, smacking a lash into Brak's back. "He'll be an easy target for the Royal wretches. Chopped into firewood soon enough. Now get the girl and get 'em moving. I don't want to be late, and I'm hoping to get a look for a change."

There had been nothing but dread and misery in Brak's brief life since his mother Vorla was killed. Each day had been worse than the one before. The smells, the food or lack thereof, his itching skin, the gummy taste in his mouth. His fingertips were bloody.

"Come here, you little wretch!" The guard said from ahead, snatching Jubilee by the leg and dragging her from her cage, kicking and screaming. "Oh … them boys will have great sport of you. Sad for such a weensy little thing."

They were all shackled now, moving forward, Jubilee sobbing and sniffling every step of the way. He felt her tears under his bare feet as he walked over them. Her grandfather, Leezir, got smacked in the mouth for trying to comfort her. It seemed that everyone making their way down the tunnel was broken, metal shackles and chains scraping over the cold stone. Brak thought of his father one last time when they stopped in front of a large wooden door. His stomach groaned so loud it made an echo.

"Shame to see a man fight on an empty stomach. Maybe we should have fed him the girl. She'd make a delicious little morsel for somebody," the warden said, playing with her hair.

Brak could hear noises on the other side of the door. There were many people on the other side, and he had good reason to think they all were going to kill him.

He heard Hagerdon say, "I can only assume I had this coming, but I never imagined my end coming in this manner." He went into a fit of coughing. "Bish give me the strength to kill one Almen before it's done." Hagerdon looked back over his shoulder and said to Leezir, "You got anything left?"

"Just a few rotting teeth to throw at them," the once vibrant, now glum-looking man said.

The guard made his way to the door and talked to another guard through a small sliding wood portal in the door.

Hagerdon turned and offered Brak some final words.

"Brak, I hate to admit it, but I wish your father was here. You'll have to do. You see Boy, on the other side of the door is a death so certain, so inevitable I can already feel the heat blistering my bones in the furnace." Hagerdon motioned to the big door.

"I've been there before; your father's been there before but not under these dire circumstances. Whatever you have left—let … it … out! I deserve what's coming, but you don't. Fight … and die! Just take some of them with you."

Hagerdon fell to the ground as the guard jammed his spear butt in his belly.

"Save your breath if you want to beg for mercy, Slerg."

"And save your breath for your orc-faced wife. I'm sure she'll enjoy it as much as a roasted gnoll's gonads."

The guard lowered the point of his spear again, saying, "Why you—"

The door popped open.

A glow of light and the feeling of warm air wafted over Brak, giving him chills. There was the smell of food and what he believed was perfume. The guards prodded him forward. Bleachers greeted his eyes, three rows deep going up, plank after plank forming a circle. Most seats were filled with the rumps of people in elaborate clothes, chatting back and forth and muttering as a strange silence began to fall.

It seemed like every eye was on him. It made him uncomfortable. There was a wall inside the circle, higher than his head, guards posted every few feet at ground and bleacher level. Below them were small men, plus a few notably bigger, in polished armor, pointing in their direction with shining blades, laughing. They weren't men, more like boys, his age possibly, maybe a little older. There was something sinister in each and every one of them. Cruel, cunning and sneering, young hunters wanting that first kill. Brak could tell each of them was hungry for the glory of his death. One of them, bigger than the rest, spat on the ground, glared at him with steely eyes and said, "I'll be gutting that barrel headed galoot as soon as we finish beating him into a bloody rug. His head's going over the mantle, the big mantle!" The others' shrill laughs pierced his ears. Something about the young man frightened him. His body began to tremble as he hunched down behind Leezir. *Mah! I miss my Mah!*

"Welcome to the Royal arena," Leezir said under his breath. "Your final resting stop in Bone."

64

T HERE WERE THREE OF THEM, taller than trees, throwing boulders like skipping stones at the band of dwarven men. Fogle's horse reared up as they were showered with rock and dust, and another boulder tumbled by. There was no sign of Cass and Chongo.

"Cass!" he cried. "Cass, where are you?"

Ahead, Mood and the other Blood Ranger, Eethum, were closing the gap between them and the giants. A rumbling cloud of dust was behind them, and ahead the band chopped at the giants' knees. Fogle blinked hard. *They're real!* He pictured the statues in the former grand square of the City of Three in his mind. He knew the stories, how the magi tricked the monstrous men into building their city and trapped them. He assumed, like so many other things, they were tales to tell children, legends, like dragons and even underlings. It was time he grew up; he should have known better by now. What had Mood said? "Bish happens."

He pulled the reins on his mount, bringing the noble beast to a stop. A giant's club, a heavy piece of carved wood, came down on the head of a dwarf, crushing it and shaking the ground. Fogle was less than fifty yards away when he summoned the energy inside him and let it fly. Two streaks of coiled energy sprung like geysers from his hands. He spoke the words, harnessed the power and guided it straight into the giant's chest, knocking it from its feet and to the ground with a tremendous thud. A cry of cheers arose as the persistent dwarves piled on.

A wave of nausea filled him as his power winked out. Bright spots flashed in his eyes, and he held his aching head.

"Where'd that come from?" He muttered, fighting for his breath.

The giants, hairy chested men wearing little more than a fur cloth about their waists, stood fifteen feet tall, hammering at everything in sight. The one he felled rose to its feet, angry, and shed dwarves like water before stomping them into the ground. "It's not dead?"

A shadow fell over him.

"Move, Fool!"

A lithe figure knocked him from his horse a split second before a spiked club crushed the beast into the ground.

Cass was on top of him, then him on top of her as they rolled out from under the next devastating blow.

"Do something, Fogle!" she screamed inside his ear.

Energy filled him as he summoned his next spell. This time he opened the gate inside him further and let loose the words of power. A ball of swirling energy, a brilliant red light, formed in his grasp. He threw it at the giant's gaping mouth.

Clonk!

The giant batted it away like a stone, sending the ball of energy into the rocky hillside where it exploded in a brilliant flash of light.

"Oh no," he muttered as the big giant smiled and raised his club high.

"Run!" Cass cried, trying to pull him up. Fogle couldn't move. He watched the giant's head descend back down towards Cass. His razor sharp mind told him it was too late.

Boom!

Knocked from his feet, he tumbled to the ground. Everything was loud and dusty. The giant, bald-headed, bearded and ugly, raised its club once more. Fogle had just enough time to look over where Cass once was. All he could think of was Ox the Mintaur being squeezed to a bloody pulp.

"I'm so sorry," he said, reaching out, but there was no sign of her. The giant's club was coming back down.

He muttered another word of power that added a translucent shield before him. The club glanced off the shield, drawing an angry grunt from the giant. Fogle felt like his elbows were about to break apart when another blow came, then another. It was like when he dealt with the snow ogres, but two tons worse. He'd already spent most of his energy this time. Pinned down and with nowhere to go, he tried to yell for help, but his voice was muffled when the giant raised its booted foot and stomped on him like a snail.

"Go for the toes!" Mood ordered back to his men.

There was nothing that got his dander up more than the hill giants. They were a cruel race that was crafty and cunning. His hatred for Horace, his recently dispatched foe, would never settle, nor would his anger ever subside. Most of the giants were as bad as ogres and trolls most of the time. No exception for most hill giants, either. They treated the dwarves like snacks, and sometimes snatched them and enslaved them like pets.

He hunched down at the sound of a powerful energy that slammed into the giant nearest by, felling it like a tree. The dwarves poured over the giant, axes and hammers chopping into it like a piece of wood.

"Eethum!"

The black Blood Ranger and two dwarves swiped at the flesh on the other giant's ankles. Eethum ducked under the giant's clutching grasp, missed a swing at its wrist with his axe and watched in horror as the giant snatched one mailed dwarven warrior up and crushed it in his hands. The dwarf didn't even scream. Mood heard its bones crack and pop.

"Eethum! Over here!"

Eethum waved his battle axe back and forth over his head, catching the giants' eye. It swung its monstrous head around and roared.

Clatch-Zip!

Clatch-Zip!

Rocking back on its heels, the giant cried out in fury. Two large crossbow bolts, one in its right eye, the other embedded in the bridge of its nose, were buried deep.

"I'll be a halfling's uncle; I missed one!" Mood said, tossing his crossbow aside and charging into the fray.

The giant flailed its arms and legs, roaring like thunder, scooping up dirt and debris and showering everything close by with rocks. The third giant jumped into his path, jaw jutting, both hands coming together and smashing Mood like a fly. His ears popped. His bones clattered, and half a dozen ribs busted as he sagged to the ground. The last time he'd taken a direct hit like that he'd lain on his back for weeks.

"Get up and fight, King of the Dwarves!" he growled to himself.

All he could see was Eethum, hacking with fury into his monstrous assailant's knees. Hunks of skin, fingers and muscles scattered the sky as the giant teetered back and wailed. Mood raised himself up, pulled his shoulders back and charged the one he had shot. It was regaining its composure and closing in on Eethum. Feeling like daggers pierced his chest, he side stepped the giant's charge and chopped his axes into the back of the giant's knees. He cut a tendon and could feel it snap like a bowstring. The giant pitched forward, smacking into the ground and rock. The giant began to push itself up, but Mood scrambled up its back and brought both his blades down with all his might. The first blow cracked open its skull. The second pierced its brain. Despite his victory, his instincts suggested they were losing. Something wasn't right. Weary, dizzy and body wracked with pain, Mood wiped the blood from his face, tumbled from the giant's back and fell face first into the dirt.

65

THERE IT WAS. A SCINTILLATING rainbow of colors encircled a strange view that hung in midair before them. Verbard heard Kierway let out a sharp gasp as the view cut through windows, people, walls and doorways like an apparition of lightning. Jottenhiem's rugged chin hung over his shoulder, his nostrils snorting over the back of his neck. The mighty fighters of the Underland gawped in amazement.

"I've never seen so many humans before," the Juegen commander said.

Kierway swallowed hard. "Nor I, either. But that's just more to kill for me."

"Pah, I'll take ten of those white devils to your five any night, Kierway."

Eep, slow it down!

Verbard ordered, shrugging off a wave of nausea.

"Kierway, what is the name of this human you are dealing with, again?"

It was strange, underlings dealing with men, but it had been done before. Even he himself had indulged in human encounters, though he lamented it. The humans were weak and greedy, as easy to bribe with shiny objects as a newborn taken to mother's milk. It worked on some, but not all, however.

"A shabby man, as pathetic as the rot between an urchling's toes," Kierway hissed. "A practitioner of dark healings, named Sefron."

"And how did you come to know this man? How long ago?" Verbard said in a demanding tone.

"We've always had our spies among them, searching for what my father seeks. That and other things. Didn't you and your brother discuss these things?"

Lies. Verbard held a spell on his tongue that would turn Kierway's eyes inside out. *Save it for the mission.* He fought down his bubbling anger. Everything was wrong. Every gesture of Master Sinway's son made him uncomfortable. His words had been accommodating, but not convincing. Now, he, Lord Verbard, one of the most powerful underlings, had just learned that he was not privy to a secret mission that had been going on for decades, if not centuries, beneath the City of Bone. *And within as well.* He wanted to kill someone. *Save it for the humans.*

"There were many things we didn't share with one another, Kierway, but one thing we did always share was our displeasure of your company. Now, tell me, where does this Sefron reside? Certainly you've been there in some shape or form." Verbard turned his silver eyes on Kierway's tightening face. "Oh, I forgot, you're but a fighter, incapable of hiding from anything but a fight."

"Watch your words, Verbard." Kierway warned. "I've had high ranking heads for less."

Verbard's eyes narrowed as he rose from the ground. "And I've destroyed Underland's most powerful enemy of all. Remember that the next time you shove your steel into sleeping men, crying women and one-armed children, you little gnat. Now answer my question!"

The hulking Vicious bristled behind Kierway's back as Kierway's sword flashed from its sheath.

Clang!

Inches from carving a chunk from Verbard's face, Jottenhiem caught the blow on his sword in a shower of sparks. *Excellent,* Verbard thought, floating backward but leaving up his shield. He twisted the enchanted metal ring. *One can never be too careful. Thanks, Brother.*

Clang! Clang! Clang! Blades licked in and out like serpent tongues as the blows got faster and faster. Single handed, they exchanged blows back and forth, one striking, the other counter striking, the next counter striking the counter strike. *If only they both were on my side. Ah, what splendid devastation they'll wreak on the humans.*

Verbard brought his clawed hands together with power.

CLAP!

The entire cavern shook.

Kierway and Jottenhiem stopped.

"Save your energies!" he said in an angry hiss. "We've more planning to do."

The Juegen leaders sheathed their blades and nodded, iron and ruby eyes still narrowed as they backed away. Verbard could see the tiniest glimmer of sweat on both their brows.

"Castle Almen," Kierway said, snapping his fingers. A pair of robed underlings scurried up with a heavy rolled up parchment that looked to be part paper, part quilt. "A map of the entire city," Kierway said, motioning to the underlings who quickly began unrolling it on the ground.

"That will do," he said, turning his gaze back on Eep's vision.

Almen? Almen! Hah! Was that not the name of the human Castle that had given Oran the whereabouts of the Darkslayer? Underling Oran the Cleric had dealt with these men before and had even kept records of it. Still, there was nothing mentioned of a key. He'd known Oran had previous dealings with Kierway, and as he recalled, it had been the Almens who'd been bribed in taking over Outpost Thirty-One. Perhaps Oran knew of the key, and maybe Eep knew something as well.

Eep!

Yes, Master.

Did Oran ever mention a key to you?

No, Master.

Are you certain?

Yes, Master.

I see.

Verbard felt the spell beginning to drain him. He looked down on the map and focused on the banner that Kierway showed of Castle Almen.

Eep, take us into Castle Almen, and find this cleric. We've little time.

One second the vision spiraled above the castle spires, the next second they were diving through the block, zipping in and out of corridors, lavish bedrooms and servant quarters.

"Slow your foul pet down, Verbard. I cannot make out an image, and my stomach churns with grubs," Kierway said, clutching his stomach.

Eep's eye glided into an arena where the faces of many men sat upright in their lavish clothes and women chatted soundlessly with painted lips and faces.

"There he is!" Kierway pointed.

"My, he is a slug, is he not?" Jottenhiem commented on Sefron's flabby, half-naked form that was eyeballing a man as skinny and rigid as a rail. "Send me in, Lord," Jottenhiem pleaded. "I'm ready to kill them all."

Verbard shifted his gaze to Kierway and sighed.

"This is your liaison to mankind? He's the one to acquire this key, and for decades he's been promising to deliver but has not? I cannot help but doubt your wisdom, Kierway."

The underling Master shot back.

"The key's in the castle. Of that, I am certain."

"How can you be ... certain?" Verbard sneered.

"Because Master Sinway told me so."

I think your father has gone mad. Does he want the key, or the city? Or, is it the key to the city? Doubt subdued his thoughts as he let the scintillating image drift away. The underlings, thousands strong, were overtaking the land of Bish. All he had to do was wreak havoc and destruction from within. But it all still made little sense to him. The humans and the other races were bound to fight back at some point, were they not? Then again, perhaps Master Sinway was right. Perhaps now was the time to strike a blow from which the humans would never recover.

"Kierway, as I can see on the map, I believe the Current leads below this Castle which you are so fond of," he said, his feet now lifting from the ground.

"Indeed, and your point is?"

"The point is," Verbard clutched his fists, "you are going inside that castle to fetch the key. Take all the underlings you need."

Kierway raised his voice, saying, "And what will you do while I'm gone?"

"I'll do what I said I was going to do," his voice rising to the level of thunder.

"I'm leading this underling army into the City of Bone! Death to the humans! Death to them all!"

A thunderous chorus of chitters rose up, shaking the streets above.

66

*T*UNK. *TUNK. TUNK. TUNK. TUNK ...*

It had been going on like this for hours. One peck after the other. Boon, once the mightiest wizard in the lands, so far as he knew, couldn't help but envision devious children outside his metal cocoon, pounding away with hammers.

"Dear me," he cried, but his words of desperation did him no good. The pecking would not stop, despite his angry urgings. He let out a long rattling sigh and resumed sucking the blood from his split lip.

The giants, of all the times for them to be tardy, had not come to his aid. When they did, he'd beg to be dropped in the labyrinth to let his suffering end once and for all. Of course, he wouldn't be here if he'd just let Venir die. The might of the warrior gave him hope for escape from the Under Bish that—for all intents and purposes—he had banished himself to. But the sack, the mystical power it contained, he hungered for once more. With it he could escape, even destroy the giants if that was what it was meant for. Its power, so divine, unrelenting and unending was worth dying for.

Tunk. Tunk. Tunk. Tunk. Tunk ...

"NOOOOOOO!" he moaned, but it kept on going. It seemed there was no escape. If he could will himself to die, he would. Boon was certain most of his sanity was already gone, and it seemed that losing the rest wasn't far behind.

Tunk. Tunk. Tunk. Tunk. Tunk ...

Barton was mad. He ripped an apple tree up, roots and all, and slammed it into the ground. For hours, days, he did not know how long, he'd been searching for the toys that Venir had hidden from him.

"Venir cheated! Venir bad! He make the game too hard!" The one-eyed boy moaned, ripping the branches from the trees. "Venir gonna pay for this! Venir will give me my toys!"

Boon's bloodshot eyes had been staring at the same grey tile—for how many hours he did not know.

Tunk. Tunk. Tunk. Tunk. Tunk …

He'd drifted off to sleep several times, only to be awakened by the same chronic sound.

Tunk. Tunk. Tunk. Tunk. Tunk …

No life was worth living like this. Nothing was worth this. He should have let the underlings take him long ago.

"OH, GO AWAY!" he yelled from an otherwise dry throat. He said it, but he wasn't sure he heard it. All he had to note it was a sore throat, busted teeth and, he was pretty certain, a foot full of broken bones, not to mention that his head still ached from the initial contact he made when he fell to the floor.

Something flustered and flapped, and the chronic tapping was gone. A shadow fell over the room, leaving everything dark. *Finally, they're here. Certainly my punishment won't be as bad as the tapping.* Something powerful snatched him from the floor and shook him like a rattle. Pain erupted in his eyes.

"OW!" he cried, his head smacking hard into the metal. Something was looking at him as his vision blurred and everything went black.

Fresh air, pain and annoyance.

Tunk. Tunk. Tunk. Tunk. Tunk …

"Aghk …," Boon said.

It was bright now, so bright he could not see. The air was warm, no longer dank and moldy as he was accustomed to. Still, the new scenery did little to improve his bleak situation. Something was still pounding on his casing, and his brittle bones ached at every joint. *Where am I now?*

The giants. It seemed likely that only they would relocate him to another place, something more secure. But outside? Now that was hardly likely. *Hmmm ….* He recalled a black shadow falling over the room and leaving a dozen knots on his head, each of which throbbed like a painful cyst. What had befallen him? But the smell of grass was good.

SPLASH!

Panic seized him. *They're drowning me! All the things I've done for them and they drown me.*

SPLASH! SPLASH! SPLASH!

That's strange. Does one usually hear splashing when they're sinking?

A wave of water cascaded over his sarcophagus, icy and drenching. A sound of beating wings flapped away. *Where in all of the Under Bish am I now?* Boon knew little about the Under Bish other than what he'd seen in the Ziggurat. Everything was enormous in scale, odd and strange, the river he knew was wider than the eye could see. There was Blackie the dragon and little more that he knew.

THOOM!

That was a giant's footstep. At least now he could get some answers.

THOOM!

Closer it came, shaking and shifting him.

"GO AWAY, TINY BIRD!"

The voice was unfamiliar, strange and garbled. A shadow came, a glimpse of skin, then the dark again.

"Hello!" he yelled.

He was suspended in the air, a feeling he'd gotten used to, but it still jostled his innards, leaving him queasy. He couldn't remember the last time he'd ridden on a raft in the river, but this felt something like that. Slowly, he heard the sound of skin peeling away from the metal, and for the first time he came face to face with his oppressor. And for the first time in years he let out a curse word.

"Slat."

A large droopy eye squinted and shook him around.

"You in there? I heard you. What did you say, *Smat*?"

Boon realized that his situation, bad as it had been, just got worse. *Barton! Of all the giants, why Barton?* The one-eyed boy man, a giant miscast of sorts, was a trouble maker he'd sought to avoid in all of his time in the Under Bish. Boon knew Barton, but Barton, who was never around the Ziggurat for long, did not know Boon. The giants had seen to that. As far as he understood things, the giant boy man, for lack of a better word, was cursed, dangerous, and maligned. And based off the look of things, Boon didn't see any reason to take him at his word. *Perhaps they'll find me and rescue me.*

"Hello!" Barton yelled inside his cage, his breath as foul as waste water.

Boon sighed. *Perhaps I deserve this.* "There is nobody home. Now take me back to the Ziggurat!"

"Huh!"

"Take me now or the giants will be very angry!"

Plunk!

"Ow!" Boon screamed. Everything inside him shuddered painfully as Barton dropped him to the ground. "You blasted idiot! You're going to kill me! Then how angry will the giants be!"

THOOM! THOOM! THOOM! SPLASH! SPLASH! SPLASH!

Icy water drenched him inside his casing. Barton had run away, leaving Boon all alone.

Tunk. Tunk. Tunk. Tunk. Tunk …

Boon learned one thing: *It's a bird.* The hours kept passing, and the bird kept pecking. *I can't take this anymore. Where are you, Barton?*

Series 1   Book 5

THE DARK SLAYER

Outrage in the Outlands

CRAIG HALLORAN

1

N ERVES OF STEEL. *WHERE ARE they?* Melegal swore he used to have them; even in his own darkest hours, he'd had little fear. Ever since he was a boy he'd been beaten and abused to some degree, but it only reinforced his steely resolve. For some reason, as far back as he could recall, he'd always figured he could wriggle his way out of anything, until today.

The Royal Coming of Age games were about to begin, and every face that sat along the benches was eager for blood. Royals—pompous, arrogant, extravagant, impossible and powerful—loved nothing more than seeing their falling brethren hacked down like rabid dogs. Melegal stood leaning against the wall, inspecting his fingernails, five rows up from the bottom of the arena. *Say nothing. Talk to no one. Avoid all contact. It will be over soon.*

The arena, nothing extravagant but fairly large, was a small compound where the Royal sentries did much of their routine training. The Royals and sentries sat behind a wall that was about eight feet in height, along wooden benches where one was no more distinct than the other. Above them, a dome rested on a network of limestone pillars where sun and moonlight could gleam in through the litany of tiny windows, making for a majestic affect. Other than that, it was a place of seclusion. A safe place from prying eyes and a good place to muffle the cries of death. Melegal clutched his fingers in and out, pumping blood into his lengthy fingers. *What to do?* He felt obligated to be doing something. *When all else fails, listen.*

Lord Almen sat in the first row, broad shoulders pulled back proud as a peacock, looking stately as well as deadly in his exquisite black silk jerkin laced with threads of gold. Along his side and spreading out were another twenty people who Melegal hadn't seen before. More Royals, some gray-headed, others bald-headed, both young and old, each having a smile when Lord Almen had their attention and a sneer when he did not. Staff, young women, attractive and revealing, served wine, food and other pleasantries to the men who gathered around one another like a host of evil colleagues. Melegal wanted to spit. *Blathering men.*

The arena itself had other guests, ones that Melegal knew all too well. Sefron sat alone, near the front of the flock of garish Royals, neck craning back, and hanging on their every word, wearing more robes than Melegal had ever seen him in before. *There is still time to kill you today.* He brushed his fingers over his wrists, feeling the contraptions hidden beneath his sleeves and fighting the urge to launch the darts he'd acquired from the Slergs when he took them into custody. Elation had filled him when he came across them. They were prized weapons, indeed. When the right time and place presented itself, he'd be ready. *I'll feather that laggard's flabby back full of them.*

A pair of heavy double doors were pulled open from inside the arena. The contestants of the Coming of Age Games were pulled inside, heavy chains clanking, to a small chorus of cheers.

"Booooo!"

"You're going to die, you wretched Slergs! You killed my brother," one Royal shouted, rising to his toes and hurling a goblet of wine at Leezir.

Here we go.

Melegal wanted to crawl into a hole, such a dreadful feeling overcame him. He'd been in an arena similar to this before, but on the other side of things, when he was an urchin serving in the Slerg castle, watching his one and only friend, Venir, take ritual beating from the Slerg boys. He'd never forget that day, during another ceremony, when Venir stuck it to the twins, Hagerdon and Creighton. That was the day he knew if he was to ever be free of the Royals, or to live a long life, his road to freedom was through Venir. He fought to keep his eyes away from the men inside the arena. *Don't look. Don't look. Don't look.* He looked.

There they stood, two Slerg men and a Slerg girl, beaten, downcast and destitute, except one, Hagerdon. Fighting a hard cough but known to be quite a swordsman, the man kept his chin up, green eyes still ablaze. *Always hated him and his brother. Such scrappy arses. You'd think I'd be happy to see them go.* Instead, Melegal felt pity. *Venir's bloody seed. The man still makes my life impossible.*

He looked at the man who he should be trying to save, Brak. The man, or boy rather, was a monster by comparison to the rest. Tall, sullen-eyed, big-boned with a tuft of blond hair hanging down past his jaws. He stood still, shoulders stooped, eyes gazing at the ground like nothing more than a common mute. Melegal had at least seen to it that he wasn't whipped, but he swore he heard the man's stomach growl from where he sat.

Melegal rubbed his chin. He could see little of Brak's father in him, other than his blue eyes. *I'm not so sure he's Venir's seed.* But he knew that he was. Something eerie about the man's presence told him so.

He fanned himself with his cap and took a seat a few benches down, all alone from the rest of the crowd. Lord Almen's hawking eyes caught his for a moment. He swore the man was going to kill him any day now. He bowed his chin, turned, and refocused his attention on the inner arena, where six well-armed youths were conducting routine exercises with wooden weapons along the wall.

"Look at that one's head," a haughty voiced boy said, swinging a heavy club. The others all looked over and laughed. "Ten gold says I crack it open first."

"I'll take that, and raise you fifteen more. My, his face is three times bigger than mine," another said, strutting around swinging his wooden sword.

They were all laughing and practicing quick little moves.

"I'm in for twenty. They should have just given us cows and sheep to slaughter. It would last longer."

"But we aren't supposed to kill them," one said, his black hair as straight as an arrow.

There was a pause among the boys and then an outburst of laughter.

"Tell you what," one said, freckled and brown headed, "we can take the little Slerg girl back to our quarters and give her something to feel good about after we've killed what's left of her family. She's cute for a Slerg. Has all of her teeth anyway."

"Not for long," one said, whacking a wooden mallet into the wall.

They chattered back and forth like gossiping women, but Melegal could hear the nervous twinge in their voices. It was their first trial against men, unknown men at that. And even though the cards on the table were overwhelmingly in their favor, there was a wild card, Brak. The bastard son of the unstoppable Venir. And Melegal swore it had been Brak's hands that bent those bars in the sewers. *I hope he at least snaps a few necks before he perishes. Alas.*

The bench felt abnormally hard on his skinny butt as he shifted in his seat the ever slightest. Normally, the skinny thief had ice water in his veins, but now his dexterous poise had been violated. Keys. Sefron wanted them. He'd seen them and taken a trip from one side of the city to the other with them. He'd broken into Lord Almen's office to find them, against his will, something he was certain was Sefron's doing. *I'll never follow the reason behind that.* Now, he was certain that Lord Almen suspected him. *He'll have me dead as a toad sure enough. Wicked Royals.* He clenched his fist. *I've had enough.*

He cocked his chin and watched another unsettling figure from the corner of his eye. Another unanticipated obstacle. A woman, tall, sinewy, with short raven hair and maroon lips sat several feet over from Lord Almen. A sheathed sword lay over her lap where she scowled. He noticed Lord Almen's eyes drifting to hers from time to time. *Interesting.*

Melegal was certain it was the same woman from the chamber room, the one he'd thought looked so familiar. Still, he found himself looking over at her, and she was looking back at him. Dark blue eyes as sharp as razors. Face scarred from injury or mishap. Scowling at him like he was the plaque of the earth. He knew who it was: *Jarla the Brigand Queen.* He scowled right back and turned towards the other notable woman in the room, who was scowling at Jarla. Lorda Almen.

She was picture perfect, legs crossed below her short white and rose colored tunic dress, revealing her sensual calves. The Lorda was a marvelous woman who stood out among the rest of the Royals, her lithe frame feline in grace, her every movement accenting her generous curves beneath her snug but appropriate garments. Melegal could see poisoned daggers behind Lorda Almen's glaring expression on the raven-headed interloper. *Fascinating, even when hating.*

She flipped her dark hair behind her shoulders and locked eyes with Melegal. His heart pounded with new energy. The Lorda had become quite fond of him over the passing months. He'd saved her from her own son, Tonio. He'd killed an innocent man that day, Gordin, a commander of the Almen Castle watch. Stabbed him in the back. Duped the Lorda into believing Tonio was at fault and had gone from being a goat to a hero. His plan had worked, and so far, he lived.

Still, Lord Almen and Sefron he was certain remained unconvinced. But, as time passed, Lorda stayed fond of Melegal and treated him less like a servant and more like a confidante. He'd even walked through her gardens with her once, and her exotic nearness had almost curled his toes. If not for her interventions, he was certain he'd be nothing but charred or rotting bones. He read her full and perfect lips as she spoke to one of her servants who got up and headed his way. *No, not now!*

The servant was a pretty little thing, light hair pulled back in a bun, her servant robes ruffling over the bench as she squatted along his side and whispered in his ear.

"The Lorda would like a moment with you, Detective," she said, bowing, then gracefully walking away.

All the men inside the arena were lathered up in conversation, pointing and goading one another as Melegal made his way over with sagging shoulders. Despite the pleasure of Lorda Almen's presence, she still had her own way of being as demanding as her husband. *Who must I spy on this time?* He glimpsed at the back of Jarla's muscular back. *I can only imagine.* He huddled beside the Lorda, catching the full effect of her arousing perfume. *Perhaps I can swipe a drop or two for Haze.*

"Detective, it is good to see you," she said with a pleasant smile. "I've heard that you and Sefron have worked hard together on this venture. Is that true?"

No.

"I do what must be done in hopes it pleases the Lords."

"I see," she said. "But, are you not the one who brought in all of these Slergs? Tracked them down one by one and saw to it that only these few remain? The cleric had no part in that, did he?" She eyed Sefron, frowned, and returned her gaze to Melegal. "We can never get the fiend from the castle, it seems. All he does is ogle the women and creep up on the girls." She reached over and grabbed his sleeve. "He's a disturbing one, and I can only imagine he's hard to work with."

Ha.

"It is true, Lorda, that I am responsible for capturing these men, and the cleric played no part. He did manage the risky task of inviting Lord Almen's guests and picking out the wine and appetizers for this event. I think he even has a blister on his lips to show for it."

Lorda pulled him in closer, laughing and pressing her soft bosom into his arm, sending a wave of passion through him. He wanted to pull away, but she was holding him fast. What if Lord Almen saw? *Cripes! Just toss me in the arena, why don't you?* But Lorda's servants obstructed the view. Lightning raced down his spine as Lorda Almen's lips nibbled at his earlobe and she whispered to him, "See that black clad whore over there?"

There's only one Jarla.

"Yes, Lorda," he managed.

"Kill her."

There's too much blood rushing to my head. Did she just say —

"Kill her," she squeezed his arm, "… and I'll be so very grateful. Don't kill her, and I'll be disappointed." She let go. Returning to her stately posture, her voice was a cold as stone. "And you don't want to see me disappointed. Now go."

"As you wish," he said, turning his steely eyes way. Jaws clenched, he got up, and his mind started thinking. *Madness! Why me? Kill the infamous Brigand Queen. Watch a friend's son die. I need to at least try to save him. Possibly die in the process. If anyone is to go before I expire, it will be Sefron. I've had it with these Royals.* He took a place on the bench adjacent to the back of Jarla, allowing his hand to slip to one of his daggers. *Let the Lorda think I'm at least going to try. Women!*

<h1 style="text-align:center">2</h1>

B RAK CAST A GLANCE AT the leering faces in the crowd. He looked back down. At his side, Hagerdon and Leezir stood in as bad a shape as they'd ever been in before. Leezir hacked and coughed, a trickle of blood coming from his lips, his breathing crackling and raspy. Hagerdon, battered and bruised from head to toe, eyes almost swollen shut, stood chin up and chest out, glaring at his enemies.

The Slerg fighter's eyes locked on his as he said, "Brak, get your chin up. Your father'd be ripping those chains and whipping their scrawny arses with them if he were here. They're going to take you down. Rip you apart. Take some of them down with you." Hagerdon fell to the ground when a spear butt cracked him in the head. A chorus of laughter followed.

"Shaddup, Slerg!"

Brak reached out to Hagerdon and caught the tip of a spear in his ribs.

"Don't move, Mute! Else I'll poke a hole in you before the fight begins."

He shuffled back, chains jangling at his feet, as Hagerdon struggled to rise. He looked around at the people in the seats in the arena now. One woman was stunning, another one scowled. His mouth watered. He could smell the food that robed servant girls carried to the men adorned in the most extravagant clothes. His stomach sounded like a bullfrog as it growled. He'd do anything to eat again, just one last meal and he'd be happy to die. He just didn't want to die hungry. It seemed like such a sorry way to go.

He glanced over at the young men, most of whom he swore were his age, and something else stirred in his hungry belly. Anger mixed with fear. They'd said the crudest things about the little girl, Jubilee. Things he couldn't even imagine. At the same time, he suspected much of what they said was true. Yet, he had no desire to fight them. He just wanted to leave this place. He just wanted to eat. He wanted to see his mother, Vorla, again.

"Hoy! Big Face!" one of the young men said. "We're going to chop you up and feed you to the pigs! Ha-hahahahah!"

Brak looked down at his toes. He'd gotten accustomed to Hagerdon's insults over the passing months, but these young men's tongues made the Slerg fighters sound like honey.

"His face looks like an orc's butthole!" another one added.

"His head is shaped like a cracked ogre's egg!"

He blocked it out and glanced into the stands once more. A flabby man, odd like a hairless bird, was trying to run his hand up a slender girl's robes. Then he noticed the skinny man with steely eyes, the one who knew of his father. *There's sympathy in the cold man's face.* This awareness brought him more fear than hope. It was as if the man who captured him, the one they called Detective, was looking at a corpse. He couldn't take it anymore.

He pumped his big fists in the air, and his voice filled the arena, "LET ME EAT! PLEASE, LET ME EAT!"

A stark silence filled the arena. Food dropped from the mouth of one man, and a young royal dropped his wooden club.

"I DON'T CARE!" Brak moaned. "JUST LET ME EAT ONCE MORE BEFORE I DIE!" He wiped the tears from his face and fell to his knees. "PLEASE!"

Creighton hissed a fierce whisper at him, "Pull yourself together, you imbecile! Die with dignity!"

Brak didn't know what that meant and did not care. He was miserable, alone and starving.

A murmuring began among the men and soldiers, but it was the one in the middle, the broad shouldered vulture of a man dressed in the most ornate clothes, who spoke first.

"I thought you said he was a mute, Detective Melegal?" Lord Almen said, looking back over his shoulder at the skinny man who knew his father.

The thin man shrugged and said, "I figured he'd eaten his tongue, and why wouldn't I, Lord Almen?"

A small chorus of laughter erupted.

"I see, Detective." Lord Almen let out a chuckle and turned his attention back on Brak. "Hmmmm … Brethren, I say we let this former mute eat. Perhaps a plateful of pig's innards would do."

"Nay, Lord Almen, a spoonful of slat would be better."

The suggestions continued, one after the other, and Brak could feel himself slipping into the ground beneath his chains.

"Get up, Brak! Die on your feet, not on your back like a coward!" Hagerdon said.

He heard one of the Royal youths speak up and say to the onlookers, "Don't worry, my Lords. I'll cut out his tongue and feed it to him. Then he'll not complain about being hungry anymore!" The young warrior ran over and cracked him across the skull with a wooden sword.

Brak's head exploded with white lights. Pain filled his eyes. Yet, his hunger was the worst feeling of all. He looked at the faces of the laughing men and women. Compassionless. Cold. The young man that swatted him pumped his fists in the air to a chorus of praise and jubilation. Brak didn't even wipe the blood that ran down into his eyes. How much more would he have to suffer before he died?

"Get up!" The sentries said, jerking him to his feet.

Lord Almen stood up, raised his arms, and said, "I think we've had enough enjoyment from the mute, er, former mute," he bowed, "but the time has come to let the Coming of Age games begin. We've all been there, when were young, oh so many decades ago that seem like yesterday."

"For you maybe, Lord Almen, you old Griffon!" one of his colleagues offered, hoisting his goblet in the air, then sucking it down.

"Ah … but my locks don't share the same gray as yours, Reginald, you son of a Slerg's milk maid."

Laughter

"But now the time has come for the next generation of our Brood to earn their stripes, and who the better to earn them against than some of our former allies turned enemies, the sacrificial Slergs."

Boos

"The Slergs, each and every one save these four, are no more. The House of Almen has seen to that. Now, the time has come to see them pay for all of their betrayals. First," he emphasized, "there will be death!"

The men with decorative weaponry rattled their scabbards.

"Second will come their much overdue deaths!"

Brak could see their faces bearing down on him and the Slergs like they were nothing more than sheep being slaughtered for a feast. He clutched at his groaning belly. He just wanted it all to be over with. He just wished he could see his mother, Vorla, one last time.

"You!" Lord Almen pointed at Hagerdon. "Step forward. You'll be the first to suffer and die, Hagerdon."

The guards shoved the Slerg fighter forward and pulled the rest of them back against the wall. Jubilee's sobbing started up again.

Hagerdon, busted up with drying blood on his filthy clothes, spoke up.

"Why don't you come down here and give me an honorable death yourself, Lord Almen. I'll even leave my back open for your slat eating — *urk!*"

The sentry yanked the collar on his neck. The Slerg fighter jerked away.

"Assassin!" Hagerdon slipped away. "Sending children to do what you don't have the guts to do yourself. I challenge, blade for blade, until the bitter end!"

Brak never realized that laughter could be so annoying. He'd often laughed at his mother's stories during his short fourteen years of life and at other recountings on the farms, and he was pretty sure that laughter wasn't meant to sound like this. It disturbed him.

Lord Almen, in the meantime, remained poised, hand folded across his lap, a smile forming on the corner of his lips.

"I'll tell you what, Hagerdon Slerg. I'll grant part of your wish. We'll begin this contest not with wood, but with steel." He looked over at the sentries and the young men and pointed. "Give those three blades." Then he tossed something into the arena that Hagerdon snatched out of the air.

A wooden sword. A short one at that, carved as a complete replica of a real one. The Slerg fighter's chin bobbed up and down as he studied his useless blade and shrugged, "Better than I expected. May you burn in the furnace soon, Lord Almen," he said, making an offensive gesture as the three young Royals surrounded him. Brak held his stomach and cringed.

The young Royals wore leather cuirasses, short over their well-defined stomach muscles, round bucklers strapped to their sinewy arms and light swords Brak believed were called rapiers. Each sword gleamed along its ornate hilt. These were all studded with gems and pearls. The young Royals cut the blades through the air with sharp *swish-swish-swish* sounds as Hagerdon shuffled in his chains, head whipping back and forth. The Slerg fighter, taller and broader than his opponents, looked over-matched by comparison in his tattered clothes and wooden sword, but he had the look of a seasoned fighter in his hard eyes, which watched them look back and forth at one another.

"Come on, Boys," he growled, "haven't you ever fought a living man before?"

"Do as you've been taught!" one of the Royal trainers ordered. "You've done this before, now make this man bleed!"

The tallest of the three thrust his rapier forward and darted back again. Then the next followed suit, then the other, each blade coming inches from Hagerdon's belly as he shuffled away. Brak watched their every move. He'd seen these moves before.

Step. Lunge. Retreat. Step. Lunge. Retreat. Step. Lunge. Retreat.

Hagerdon dodged the tip of one blade and smacked away another, just in time to twist, parry and dodge out of harm's way.

"Is that all you little slats have?" he said, wiping the sweat from his brow. "I've seen dogs handle blades better than that."

"Press! Faster!" the trainer ordered.

Step. Lunge. Retreat. Step. Lunge. Retreat. Step. Lunge. Retreat.

They were getting faster. Their blades were getting closer, cutting and poking at his unprotected body. For the first time, Brak was seeing what Hagerdon had taught him about how a sword can easily whittle down an unarmed man. *Sword versus no sword strategy. Run.* But the Slerg fighter had nowhere to run.

The small crowd began cheering in eager anticipation of the first drop of Slerg blood being spilt. Hagerdon was gasping for air, chains rattling and clanking, a most desperate sound. Brak knew the heavy chains were wearing him down. It was just a matter of time. Fighting the urge to watch the inevitable, he nonetheless watched on, feeling like the room was about to explode at any moment.

Step. Lunge. Retreat. Step. Lunge. Retreat. Slice!

The arena erupted in a chorus of cheers as one Royal tore a sliver from Hagerdon's shoulder.

"You got first blood, Boy!" one man cried.

"Finish him!" another said.

The trainer yelled over them all, saying, "Keep up the pace! Don't stop!"

Hagerdon was grimacing underneath his thick head of hair, ducking, dodging and parrying in a more desperate fashion now. His fluidity had become stiff, and his efforts in vain. Brak stood solemnly as he watched the man quickly being whittled down without a fight.

Slice! Lunge. Retreat. Step. Lunge. Retreat. Step. Lunge. Retreat.

There was a roar of applause when the Slerg fighter began to bleed from half a dozen wounds. Blood was dripping from his chin to his belly. Brak couldn't help but wonder if this was the kind of death that awaited him. Not only would he die with an empty stomach, it would have a bloody hole in it, too.

Step. Lunge. Retreat.

Whack! Whack! Whack!

Hagerdon burst in a tornado of blood and tattered clothes, cracking one Royal with his wooden sword so hard he broke his sword arm, drawing a howling cry. For a split second, everyone froze but Hagerdon. He tore the buckler away from one man and whacked the throat of another. Two other young Royals were down on their knees as the Slerg fighter twisted the rapier away from the third and stabbed him in the knee.

"Stop him!" everyone seemed to shout at the same time, but Hagerdon kept on going.

One of the young Royals reached after him and had his fingers sliced off. The trainer pulled his sword from his sheath just in time to try and parry Hagerdon from skewing his heart, but he was too late and fell to his knees wide eyed while the Slerg ripped his blade free. A little blood became a lot as he spilled into the dirt and Hagerdon charged towards his nearest opponent.

Churk!

Hagerdon's eyes widened like moons. A spear burst through his chest. One of the sentries from the stands had hurled the deadly weapon into Hagerdon's back. Brak was face to face with the man as it happened. The rapier clattered to the ground as he fell to his knees and said through blood soaked lips, "That's how you go out, Brak."

Brak shook within his shackles. He filled with horror as he watched the remaining young Royals came over and take their turns at hacking the dying many down. He closed his eyes and tried to ignore the warm blood splattering his face while he clutched his groaning belly.

3

ALBINO URCHLINGS. VENIR HAD ONLY seen them once before. That had been the last time he saw Chongo, and it seemed like ages ago. He'd moved on. He hunted the ones that would have him dead, as did his comrade and his best friend. Now there were ten of them. Teeth gnashing, claws barred, ready to rip him to shreds. The translucent white little brutes were nothing more than muscles, fangs and claws as sharp as razors charging at him full speed and leaving behind them a trail of dust.

Venir was red hot with rage. Muscle, steel and magic intertwined and forged the ultimate fighting machine. Brool was singing in his grip, pulsating with power. The eyelets on his helm oozed with a mystic radiance as he crossed the dusty parallel. Man, monster and mayhem met in the middle.

Venir's bulging arms chopped into the face of the first screaming urchling, dropping it like a bloody stone. The smaller creatures ducked and rolled away from the deadly arcs of Brool's sting. Venir could feel their rage and fear intermingle as he plunged his spike into another one's chest. *Two!*

Something else lurks nearby, the helm warned.

Slat! There's more! Another urchling jumped on his shield, its fangs biting into the rim. Two more clawed and nipped at his feet like starving hounds.

Chop! Chop!

They hungered no more, twitching in their own blood.

A heap of them piled on top of him, tearing into his back and biting into his legs. The scale mail saved him from being ripped to shreds as they tried to pull him to the ground and feast.

"NO!"

He pierced the skull of the one hanging on his shield and slung it to the dirt. *Five!* The little monsters were strong! They latched onto his knees and squeezed him while two more assailed him, howling with bloodlust. He couldn't let these underlings stop him from getting in the larger fight with the Royal Riders.

"Fiends!"

With one urchling hanging on his arm, he hacked into the chest of another. With his shield arm, he grabbed the one hanging from his arm by the neck, squeezed, and pulled it off him. It clawed and scratched like an oversized angry rat in Venir's arms. He reversed his grip on Brool and began stabbing the two that wrestled and gnawed at his knees.

Scrunch! Scrunch!

Eight!

The tongue of the one in his clutches was juttering from its mouth in an awful hiss as Venir crushed its throat and dropped it to the ground. One still hung on his back, trying to rip the scale mail from his body. The air shimmered around him. All the hairs on his body stood up. Venir whipped his head around. *Where is it?* He looked up in time to see the underling hovering ten feet above him, hands pointing downward on him, radiating with power. *Move!* It was too late.

Venir balled up on the ground, back up, head down.

CHA – KAOW!

It felt like lightning was shooting through his nose as everything around him exploded in white hot light.

Slim the beetle buzzed through the effort to coordinate the chaos of an underling army that was under attack. His charge: to find and lead to safety two women who had been taken prisoner by underling hunters. As his black and gold wings buzzed through the air, none of the multicolored eyes that gleamed with evil paid him any mind. He soared over their heads, searching for the prisoners.

The camp, a series of dark grey tents lined up row by row, proved to be a bigger search area than he expected, and it was even more challenging when you were the size of a beetle.

If I were an underling, where would I hide two humans?

As the sounds of battle clashed nearby and the giant sized spiders were making their way back, he noticed every underling was moving except for a handful of guards. Armed with serrated spears and adorned in black leather armor, three underling warriors with eyes like hard sapphires chittered back and forth with one another. Behind them was a large pit with a wooden grate dropped over the top of it. Slim flew over the underlings' heads, dropped to the ground on the other side of the pit, and crawled inside.

His insect senses were aroused at the scent of waste in the air, and his instincts told him he was hungry. *I'm craving excrement. I'm not a dung beetle. Just a beetle.* He crawled down the dirt wall, his black shell with olive and white color blending in as he went farther and farther down. The pit was deeper than he expected, and he noticed hand and footholds dug into the dirt on the other side. What purpose did the underlings have for keeping the women alive? For the most part, anytime underlings came into contract with humans, or any other race, they left them for dead.

Making his way to the bottom, he let his antennas start feeling around. He could see the light coming from the top of the cage, but the shadows below left everything pitch black. He sensed vibrations of movement in the area, and sounds vibrated through his butt and into his head. He couldn't tell if the women were in there or not, but something was. There was only one way to find out.

Here goes.

His shell started cracking. His body expanded, warbled and returned to normal. Slim arched his back and stretched his long limbs. "Ah … that's better." He peered through the darkness where two huddled figures shivered.

"Adanna?" he said. "Is that you? It's me, Slim," he said, squatting down and touching a woman's leg.

She flinched.

As his eyes adjusted, her form took on a more distinct shape. Both of the women's figures became more defined, but there was something unnatural in the air. Slim shuffled back, hands out as an overwhelming sense of evil lurked within the pit. As his heart began pounding in his chest, he mumbled a protection spell. The suffocating shadow of the unknown retreated as Slim stepped forward, summoning more magic, and a soft glow erupted in the palm of his hand.

The two women, Adanna and her mother, trembled as they held on to one another for their dear lives. They were bound together with silky cords, like webs that spiders shoot and something else. That's when he heard a sucking sound, and Adanna let out a heavy sob. The mother's body lurched. That's when Slim noticed red eyes glimmering along the walls and on the women's bodies. Dozens of them popped open all at once. Spiders, bigger than his hands like tarantulas, began to detach themselves from the women and scurry towards him. *Oh my!*

He glanced above. The day's light looked like it was a mile off. He looked down as a spider sped his way, and he stomped it under his sandal. The pit erupted with a sound like squealing rats as the tiny horde of spiders darted at him. Above, the underlings chittered, gemstone eyes peering downward, the soft glow of his hand giving him away.

"Not good," he said, stomping each and every spider he could into the ground. The blood sucking spiders bit into his ankles. "Ow! Dratted bugs!" There was no sense in holding back; the underlings knew he was in there. "Enough!" He summoned more energy into his hands, and both burst aglow in white hot fire. The spiders burst into char as he grabbed, crushed or swatted them away. "How many of these things are there!"

They burned. They fried. They died. One palmful at a time. He burned the webs away from Adanna and her mother and shook them both. The mother was dead. An empty feeling overcame Slim, and Adanna sobbed as he wiped her nose with his robes. "Come on. I have to get you out of here." The buxom woman didn't move, quivering. People on Bish, no matter how hard they were, were never prepared for what the underlings had to offer.

He looked her over. Wounds, dozens of spider bites, covered her in red welts from head to toe. They weren't poisonous, but they fed off her blood. Some spiders were like mosquitoes, and others ate flesh like rodents. A few dozen spiders could easily kill a man as big as Venir if you didn't kill them first. He cupped Adanna's face in his palms and muttered under his breath. He felt his skin tighten as he fed his life force into her, sealing her wounds and charging her blood. He sagged to the ground.

"Slim?" she said, reaching down and hugging his lanky bones. "Are you all right?" she said, pulling him up to his feet.

He leaned on her and said, "I'll be fine in a moment." He looked up through the pit at where the underlings had removed the grate. "But I'm not so sure we have that long to wait."

They came. Two sand spiders as big as large dogs, tan with white ringed tails, scurried into the pit and cast a blanket of webbing above them. There was no way out now.

Adanna squeezed her arms around Slim's waist, looked up, and screamed just as the new spiders made their descent.

4

"FIDDERBAY! FIDDERBAY! FIDDERBAY!" FOGLE BOON chanted as the giant foot stomped him into the ground. His face smashed into the rock and dirt. His body shuddered under the weight as it squished and contracted but did not bust. His bones didn't crack, and his skull wasn't crushed. The magic spell had worked. Fidderbay was an odd spell, made more for trick and fun than anything else, something he'd mastered as a young boy when they played games at school. The Fidderbay spell made you and your attachments soft and porous like a sponge. Still, he could feel the giant's foot trying to grind him into dust. *Think and Live!*

He shifted onto his back, and the giant lifted his boot up. The giant cocked its head as it stared down on him, eyes full of confusion. Fogle tried to yell for Cass, but his mouth felt like it was filled with cotton. The spell rendered any other incantations impossible, but it didn't last very long. The giant raised its club over its head and swung down with all its power. *Please keep working.*

Wham!

The giant struck him full in the chest. All of his blood rushed to his head, fingers and toes, stretching his skin to the limits. It fell like a geyser was trying to burst through his skull, and his eyes bulged from the sockets. His brain screamed, but his body remained intact, retaking its natural shape. Fogle was panting as he started to pat down his chest. *I live.*

He shook his fist at the giant and screamed, "I live!"

The giant roared and rotated back for another swing.

"Bish Almighty," he said, realizing that his tongue, along with the rest of him, had lost its cushiony vitality. He backpedaled, stumbled over a rough stone, and fell. He tried to scramble to his feet only to fall again. *Time to die!*

"Mood!" he yelled, but he knew already the Blood Ranger wouldn't come. "Cass!" But it was too late. The giant leered down on him and swung.

There was noise: wails of battle, mountainous bellows and the sound of rock and bones being shattered. Mood struggled to rise to his feet with the bitter taste of a mouthful of blood and dirt, which wasn't so bad for a dwarf. Especially a Blood Ranger no less. Still, his vision was blurry, and everything was a haze, and he couldn't tell if he walked or ran as he reeled toward the sounds of battle. The giant who had smashed him like a fly was dead, but the damage had been done. Mood, born and bred to fight, had been in some bad scraps before, but this last one got him.

"Eethum!" he yelled, but it came out in more of a garbled sound.

Ahead was another giant, bigger than the rest of the hill giants, one he didn't remember seeing before. The black bearded dwarves hurled spear after spear into its legs, but the giant didn't slow down. They looked like grim faced puppies attacking a man. The giant was big, with muscular trapezoids up to his pierced ears. He swung a hammer like a well-trained soldier, each blow ripping the rocks from the ground and sending Mood's brethren flying.

"Retreat! Retreat!" he yelled, but not one dwarven fighter turned.

The giant snatched one fallen dwarf from the ground, clenched his leg in his mouth, and shook him like a dog.

"No! Blasted giant!" Mood said, fighting to regain his feet.

The giant dwarves unleashed another assault of missiles into the giant's face as their comrade kicked and punched within the monster's mouth.

The hammer came down, crushing the nearest dwarf to a bloody pulp and shaking the ground. As Mood ran, it felt like the inner fiber of his being was tearing apart. He didn't notice his clavicle sticking out from his skin or the ribs jutting out underneath his arms or that his face was blackening underneath his bushy blood-red beard. All he knew was if that giant didn't die soon, he and his brethren would.

He banged his axes together and yelled as loud as he could.

"Come on, Giant!"

The monstrous man stopped and spit the broken dwarf from his mouth.

"That's right! I'm talking to you!" he said as the wind picked up and billowed his beard.

Another sharp clang of battle axes came together as Eethum appeared from underneath a pile of rubble, caked from head to toe in dirt and blood.

The remaining black bearded fighters backed up, dragging their comrades out of the way. The giant stuck its chest out and laughed. It looked more like a man than the others, cunning like a hunter, whereas the typical hill giant was more brute than brains. Mood now realized this wasn't a common hill giant that mixed with the ogres. This giant was something else: the real thing he'd rarely seen before. The last time he battled a full bred, he'd barely survived. No doubt this battle wouldn't be any different.

"AH ... BLOOD RANGERS! HA! HA! HA! WHAT A PLEASURE IT WILL BE TO KILL YOU BOTH," the giant said in a voice that was commanding and full of power. "YOU LITTLE INSECTS WILL NEVER LEARN, WILL YOU?" The giant was twirling its massive battle hammer around like a stick. "I AM TUNDOOR ... HA-HA-HA ... AND I'LL BE CRUSHING YOUR HEADS!" It swung its hammer over his head and slammed it into the ground with incredible force. The ground exploded, knocking Mood and Eethum from their feet as a billow of dusty smoke rose, thick as soup.

"HA-HA-HA!" the giant's booming voice mocked. "I CAN SEE YOU! SMELL YOU! AND HEAR YOUR DYING BREATHS!"

A sliver of uncertainty raced through Mood's spine. The smoke was confusing. One moment the giant was there, the next moment it wasn't. He could usually track a giant blindfolded, but at the moment he couldn't sniff out a single thing at all. Either his senses had been damaged, or the giant was using some of its tricks.

Eh? he thought, a split second before he dove to the ground.

The giant's hammer whooshed over his head.

Mood rolled left and kept going. It felt like a bag of knives was rattling inside his chest. He spat his blood into the ground.

The giant's foot came down inches from his head.

He struck, axes cleaving through skin and deep into muscle.

"OW! THAT STINGS, LITTLE RANGER! HA-HA-HA! TUNDOOR HEALS FAST! YOU'LL NEED A BIGGER AXE THAN THAT!"

5

H E WAS TOLD HIS OLD room, the one he, Lefty, Melegal and Venir had shared, was now occupied by a brood of sordid men. It left him empty. Georgio stood on the stairs looking down inside the Drunken Octopus and wiped his sleeve across his forehead. It wasn't the same. The roughshod tavern's atmosphere was as dead as the candles on the chandeliers. He was used to more activity mid-day. Instead, he, Mikkel and Billip were greeted with hard stares from faces he didn't recall. It was as if the tavern had received a makeover. Mikkel's broad face was smiling as he shoved Georgio towards the bar.

"Move it, Boy. I'm as thirsty as a fish on a hook."

"Aye," Billip said, brushing past him with a greedy look in his eye, "let's eat, drink, and get a room." He cracked his knuckles in front of him. "And let me do the talking. I'm not paying coin if I can find some fool to do it for me."

"Fine," Georgio said, frowning and taking a seat at the bar. His stomach rumbled. "They have good stew, but the bread is always stale."

"Perfect!" Mikkel said.

One table at a time, he scanned the room. Not a face was familiar. But something was. His heart almost stopped as he locked eyes with a man in a wide brimmed hat. *McKnight!* His regrown fingers tingled as he stared at the man whose hat was the only thing that resembled the Detective. This man had a shaggy head of hair spilling out from underneath the brim, and there wasn't a single tooth left inside the mouth of his sagging face.

"Here," Mikkel said, shoving a mug of ale into his hand. "What's wrong with you? You look like you've seen an underling."

Georgio shook his head and took a sip of the bitter ale. "Nah ... just thought I saw that guy who chopped my finger off, is all."

"If Melegal chopped him up and fed him to the pigs, then I'm pretty sure you're not going to ever be seeing him again." Mikkel patted his shoulder, looking around. "So this is where Venir used to stay, huh? No surprise, but you'd think there'd at least be some pretty girls."

Georgio scrunched his face up as he looked around some more. He'd never spent much time on the main floor. Someone his age wasn't allowed, but he'd changed. He took another drink. He felt like more of a man now. A sad one that missed his friend, Venir. He was hoping he'd see him here.

"Say, Sam," Billip said to the pock-faced barkeep, "tell me what you've heard about this Blond Haired Butcher? What's the bounty up to now?"

Georgio remained facing the fireplace on the other side of the bar. It had always blazed with a big orange fire, but now it was filled with long dead ashes. Beside it was Melegal's table, now occupied by the men who had taken over the room upstairs. They slammed their fists on the table and guffawed over a bunch of senseless jokes. A few meaty women kept them company, and they had no shame when it came to keeping the men's attention. Georgio had brushed shoulders with the leader while passing down the stairs. Jeb. That's the name Melegal had said. Georgio laughed at the thought of Melegal boxing him. *I wish I could have seen that.*

"The City Watch is offering a thousand gold for this man's head," the barkeep said, smoking a cigar and twisting the water from a rag.

"A thousand gold!" Billip exclaimed. "For one measly man? Pah, that's a bunch of lies. Last I heard, it was a hundred." Billip twisted the hairs under his chin. "Still, a hundred or a thousand is a lot of money. I could live well off that. For a while, anyway."

Mikkel clonked his empty tankard on the table.

"Another," he said, twisting his large frame in the stool towards Billip. "One hundred or one thousand, Billip, it would all slip through your fingers as easily as sand in a grate. You've never kept a hoard longer than a month, I'd say."

Billip rattled a sack of coins in front of Mikkel's face and said, "I've still got more coin than you. Now tell us, Sam," he slid a few coins across the bar, "you know something else, don't you? I can tell by the look in your eye. I've owned a tavern myself, you know."

Georgio locked eyes for a moment with Jeb, the man across the room who was whispering something into the ear of one of his comrades. Jeb, a stout man with a brawny build underneath his jerkin, seemed like just the kind of person looking for a fight. Something about the man's coarse black hair, mustache and sideburns didn't sit well with Georgio as he watched a larger man, almost as big a Mikkel, make his way across the tavern and take a seat at the bar. He didn't like the look of that man, either. He turned around and folded his hands across the bar.

"I've heard the man can't be killed," the barkeep said, "and he's got a scar that runs straight down the middle of his face."

Georgio's blood ran cold. *Tonio!*

6

"**I**'ve seen such man in here, months ago. A tall one, as tall as you," he said, nodding towards Mikkel, "came in here and stabbed a troubadour through the back. The blood's still on the table. Things haven't been quite right around here since then, if you ask me." He refilled Mikkel's tankard and pointed at Georgio. "Not since that boy's big friend left, that is. Venir. I sorta miss having that big lout around here. He kept things interesting, if not even friendly, so to speak."

Mikkel and Billip looked at each other, then at Georgio.

"What?" he said, trying to hide his trembling hands.

"I think that man, whatever sort of evil he may be, has a vendetta on your friend. Why else would he be going around and killing all the yellow-haired people? He's even killed members of the City Watch. People have seen him do it. The urchins say he lives in the sewers. I've not seen a yellow hair in this tavern in weeks, if not months."

Georgio swallowed hard and rubbed his throat. Maybe that's what Melegal's warning was about. *"Go to Three and Live. Stay in Bone and die."* But Tonio wouldn't be after him. He'd be after Venir, and no one had any idea where Venir was. Georgio slumped in his seat.

"Ewww!" Mikkel said, "I'm not going into any sewers, Billip. Let's drop this nonsense and go find Nikkel. We haven't even checked outside the wall yet."

"Quit nagging me, will you? We'll look for your boy then. It'd just be better if I had some additional booty, is all. Besides, I'm beginning to like it here. Reminds me of the Orc's Elbow."

"Stay if you want," Mikkel said, poking Billip in the chest, "but me and Georgio will go."

"What?" Billip cocked an eye and looked over his shoulder. The large man from Jeb's group was walking away with something cupped in his hand. He took a quick look at Mikkel and said, "That big bastard just lifted my purse."

"Serves you right."

Billip flung his tankard into the back of the man's head. The man crashed head first into a table, Billip's coins spilling everywhere.

Georgio jumped from his stool while men and women erupted from Jeb's table. He could hear blades whisking from leather as they knocked over the tables and charged. Georgio stood brandishing a tankard in his hand. Mikkel right behind him.

"Don't any of you dogs move, or I'll skewer this mutt of yours," Billip warned, holding a dagger at the man's throat. "And you better get your foot off my gold," he eyed one of the thugs, "or I'll add some holes into you."

"Back off!" Jeb ordered in a rugged voice. "Back off, I say." His gang of men pressed behind him, a half dozen in all, one looking just as tough and ugly as the next. Jeb held out two knives with wide blades and brass pommels, waggled his wrist, and stuffed them behind his belt. The rest of his men followed suit. "Now let my man up, Little Man," he added, folding his arms across his broad chest.

"I'll collect my coins first," Billip said, flexing the muscles in his wiry forearm, "or this little man's going to skin this big man like an antelope. Then comes you." Billip nodded at Georgio. "Gather my coins before I let this lout up."

Georgio shook his head, but obeyed.

Jeb snorted a laugh. "Is that so?" Jeb scratched at his side burns. "We'll see about that. Tell you what, Little Man."

Georgio looked up at Jeb and then noticed Billip's cheeks flaring. Billip wasn't small for a man by any means, but Georgio had noticed that he now stood as tall as him. Even Kam was taller than the wiry archer. He scooped up all the coins he could find and retook his place beside Mikkel.

"That's enough, Jeb." The barkeep interrupted. "I'm not having any more of my customers run off. You've run off enough of them already."

"Shut it, Sam, or I'll see to it you'll have no more customers at all. Now let my man up from the floor."

Billip clonked the man's head off the hardwood planks and rose to his feet. Georgio tossed his coin sack over, and Billip snatched it from the air. Jeb's hands slipped back to his knives, and Mikkel was breathing down his neck as the tension began to thicken. Billip cracked his knuckles and popped his neck as he walked over and stood face to face with Jeb.

The brute looked down on him, sneered, and said, "Well?"

"Georgio, Mikkel, look at this man. He's awful pretty for an orc, wouldn't you say?"

"What?" Jeb said through clenched teeth.

"Knock him out, Jeb!"

"Jeb? You're the man called Jeb? The Jeb. The best brawler in Bone?" Billip said, stepping back a half step and holding up his palms. "Oh, I've heard about you."

"Yeah, what about it, Little Man?" Jeb replied with a half-smile.

Billip shrugged, his face turning from fearful to whimsical.

"I heard you beat an old woman with the iron gloves, but judging by your face, I'd say she got the best of you!"

"That's it!" Jeb roared, ripping out his knife and lunging forward.

Billip caught him by the wrist and twisted the blade free in one fluid motion. Billip cracked his head on Jeb's hard chin.

Georgio pounced on the man's legs, sending the three of them sprawling to the floor.

"Stop!" The barkeep screamed.

Someone ripped Georgio free from Jeb's legs, a brute of a man with arms of corded iron, and slung him into the nearest table.

"Bone!" he exclaimed, rising to his feet and wiping the blood from his nose

Billip and Jeb were hammering away at each other, one hard punch after the other. Mikkel picked one man up over his head and tossed him into the other three. The women screamed the vilest of things as they slung whatever they could find at Mikkel.

The Drunken Octopus was in a frenzy now, with everyone fighting for themselves. Georgio jumped onto the back of the nearest man and dragged him to the ground.

"CHALLENGE! CHALLENGE! CHALLENGE!"

Mikkel clocked a man in the jaw whose eyes rolled up in his head as he fell like a stone.

"I SAID *CHALLENGE*!"

Every one stopped, even Billip and Jeb loosened their grips around each other's throats, but their eyes were still hot with rage.

"You'll be paying for all this damage, you fools!" Sam said, standing on the bar and holding a large club. "But there will be no more. No fighting in this place without a challenge. Now you, troublemakers," he pointed to the three of them. "Get back over to the bar, or get out."

Georgio slid off the man's back and headed over. Billip and Mikkel joined him.

"Jeb! You make your challenge. You three, that includes you, Boy, accept or go!"

"Fine by me," Mikkel said, flexing his arms.

All eyes fell on Jeb. The burly man had his hands on his knees, sucking for air, when he pointed at Georgio.

"I challenge the lad then, Sam!"

"Coward!" Billip blurted out.

"I'll say," Mikkel added, holding Billip back.

The barkeep added, "Sorry, but he's in this. Of course, you don't have to accept. You can just go if you want to."

Georgio felt every eye in the tavern upon him.

Mikkel laid his heavy hand on his shoulder. "You don't have to do this."

Georgio shoved his hand away.

"Yes, I do. I'm a man the same as the rest." He pointed at Jeb. "What's your challenge, Man with a Face Like a Goat's Behind?"

The women snickered, as well as a few of the men.

Jeb tucked his thumbs in his belt and laughed out loud as his disheveled men joined in. Georgio's cheeks flushed red. His hand slipped to his sword.

"None of the lad," Jeb said, teetering on his toes, "but I tell you what. I'll let you draw from the cards. But, first you need to make a wager." Jeb looked over at Billip and said, "That purse of yours will do."

"Ah! Stupid Boy!" Billip said, eyeing the sack in his grip. "Fine, I'll put it up, but you're going to owe me, Georgio." He tossed his purse to the barkeep. "I'll be shuffling those cards first, if you don't mind." He extended his hand.

Jeb shrugged.

The tavern's old vitality was rekindled. The fireplace was lit as a trove of new faces filled in from the streets. This was more like how Georgio remembered it. He took a long sip of ale. *I wish Venir was here.*

A woman with long black hair and a sultry voice pressed her body into Georgio's back and whispered in his ear, "Why don't you let me draw for you, Handsome?"

Georgio swallowed hard and said, "Certainly."

Billip just shook his head, shuffling the cards like a magician. "Let's get this over with and draw."

Sam the barkeep hopped down from the bar, dragging his club behind him, and headed towards the middle, where he stood puffing his cigar. "Get over here and draw, Velvet."

The woman kissed Georgio on the cheek as she wiggled her way up to Sam, who fanned out all the cards on the table. Georgio's feet twitched and jangled as she bent over to some *oooh*'s and *ahhh*'s while walking her fingers over the cards.

"I think I'll take … this one," she said, sliding the card from the deck and nuzzling it between her breasts.

The crowd jeered with lust.

"Show um' to us, Velvet!" one man shouted.

"The cards, too!" another added.

She peeked at the card, and her bright eyes began to dim.

What? Something was wrong. Georgio could feel it in his bones.

"Show us the card, Wench!"

She was biting her lip as her sad eyes looked on Georgio and she rose the card up over her head.

A gasp filled the air.

A black card faced them, showing a burning skull with a pair of fencing blades stuck through it.

"The Flaming Fence!" the barkeep cried.

Georgio felt a heavy shadow fall over him as every eye in the room turned toward him and the barkeep added, "Ye might wish to yield unless you want to die."

7

KAM WAS NUMB. HUMILIATION WAS something she hoped she never got used to as she soaked in the cooling waters of Palos's golden tub. Since becoming a captive, she'd been shot with a crossbow and punched in the gut by a man named Diller, and she wasn't sure which was worse: taking the pain or succumbing to Palos's erotic needs. She scrubbed the soapy water deeper into her skin with a wash cloth.

"Lefty!" she exclaimed under her breath.

"What was that?" Palos said, knotting the belt over his long black bath robe.

It was only the two of them now and the sound of a roaring fire underneath the nearby mantle. Things would be much better if Venir was here, but there was no chance the man could come to her rescue now. Nor any man for the matter. Besides, for all she knew, the father of her daughter was dead, even though that didn't really seem possible.

"I said, 'When can I see Erin, Palos?'"

He huffed as he dried his hair with a towel and took a seat at the table.

"It's not even been a day," he said, rolling his pale eyes and pouring a jeweled goblet of wine. "Now, let's take a moment to talk about things, Kam. I think it would be better if we had a fresh start." He poured another goblet. "Come on over and join me for some wine, and let's talk about something different. The past, perhaps."

Deep in the water, her nails dug into the palms of her hands. *Just go along with it. What choice do you have? Just don't make it too easy.*

"Fine," she said, grabbing her robe and standing up in the tub while taking her time slipping it on over her soapy body.

Palos' eyes were every bit as hungry as moments earlier.

"We can talk about the past, but not forever." She walked over, grabbed her goblet, and stood by the fire. Its burning logs warmed her from head to toe. It felt good, revitalizing, almost cleansing.

Palos smiled at her. "Feels good, doesn't it, Kam? The fire, the wine and the touch of a man. I know, Kam. I can tell how lonely you are. You've always been that way. You never wanted to get too close or have the kind of fun the other girls had. You were such a serious person, a dreamer within your own little world. I've wanted you since the moment I first saw you, but unlike the rest of your feminine breed, you never dropped your britches for me." He gulped down his wine. "It just made me want you so much more."

"And, now you have me?" she flipped her hair. "Does that mean there are no more pastures of women to conquer? Is it just a matter of time before I'm tossed dead into a gutter when you don't fancy me anymore?"

He lifted his palms up and said, "Easy. Easy now, Kam. I've promised you that no harm will come to you or your daughter."

"So long as I play your little whore."

He shrugged his satin shoulders and smiled.

"Well, that's one way of putting it, but I want more than that with you, and over time you will see that."

I hope not. She ran her fingers under the choker on her neck. If she could just get it off, she'd turn him inside out with a single word. Her power dwelled inside her, and she'd memorized quite a few spells. But she couldn't hang on to them forever. Still, she'd always have some power. Her sorcery allowed for that.

"So, would you like me to rub your feet now, Prince Palos?" She batted her eyes.

"Oh, I like the sound of that! But don't patronize me."

She strolled over behind him and placed her hands on his shoulders.

"How about I rub your shoulders, then?" she whispered in his ear. She could see the hairs on his neck stand up on end.

"Eh … well, I suppose that would be all right."

She rubbed deep into the supple muscles under his meaty neck. The man, despite his additional girth, moved with the grace of a swan. As much as she wanted to choke him to death, she knew taking the opportunity would only meet with failure and with that would come more time away from Erin. She rubbed harder and deeper.

"Aaaahhhh …," Palos moaned, "it feels so good."

She pulled him back into her chest and said in a soft voice, "After this, can I see my baby? It's nursing time already."

"We'll see. But I'm going to need more of these muscles loosened first."

She brushed her hands through his flaky hair. She remembered when Palos never had a thing out of place. Compared to most men, he'd been divine. And he'd been right about her, too. She was a prude. She didn't do things like the other girls in school, but not because she thought she was better, but more because she was afraid.

"Perhaps I could trim this hair of yours? I think it could use a woman's touch." *You vile and fattened beast.*

"And have my own scissors rammed through my eyes, Kam? I don't think so. Besides, when the time comes, I'll have my nanny do it for me."

"So be it, then." She continued her rubbing, minute after minute as Palos slunk deeper into the chair. *Just relax, Pig.* Getting Palos out of her hair was one thing, but escaping the Nest would be another. There were hundreds of cutthroats out there: murderers, slavers, smugglers and thieves, and if Palos fell, no doubt someone would take his place. And she was certain she'd have Palos's father Palzor to deal with after that. There had to be another way.

Palos's eyes rolled up in his head as she rubbed his temples with her thumbs. *Cocky bastard.* The Prince of thieves was as loose as a goose in her hands, and it made her uneasy. The man had no fear of anything bad happening in his own house, it seemed. It left her feeling more helpless than ever. She scanned the room looking for anything that might assist her to escape. Empty bottles of wine, stacked piles of coins, candle stands, and furniture all of the finest quality. But nothing of a useful sort. The magic Palos had displayed had been tucked away somewhere her keen eyes had yet to find.

"What are you thinking, Kam?" he said, raising goose bumps on her arms. "I can feel you thinking, and frankly it's only making it harder for me to relax."

"I want to see my Erin, that's all. Of course I wouldn't expect you to understand."

He puffed a laugh and said, "Why, because my breasts are not yearning to be suckled?"

Something was uncoiling inside her. Her emerald eyes blazed on the great sword that hung on the mantle. Something about that magnificent sword was speaking to her.

"Don't stop now!" Palos warned, "Or you won't see your baby until the morrow', maybe later."

"Of course, Prince ..." *of swine*

He reached back and snatched her by the hair and jerked violently down.

Face to face, she saw a deranged look in his eyes that was not there a moment ago.

"And if you don't stop thinking of escape, Dearie, I'm sure my servant Diller and his men will be more than glad to suckle that swelling chest of yours!"

She cracked her head on the table when he shoved her to the floor.

"Now, rub my feet, you red-headed cow, and think of nothing more!"

Kam shivered and averted her eyes from his. *He's mad!* One second he was as smooth as a stone in a tranquil river and in the next he was an impulsive maniac with murder in his eyes. It scared her. It was one thing to deal with a wicked person that was sane, but it was quite another to deal with one that might just be crazy. Her body trembled as she rubbed and rubbed and rubbed and her doubt at ever again seeing her daughter grew. All she wanted to do was get her baby to safety now, but trying to do that might cost her life.

Got to save them. Got to save them! Lefty sat beside Gillem at a table full of cards and coins, his blond hair disheveled, trying to hide the weight of the world from showing on his face. He faced the steps that led up to Palos's room and cast a casual glance up now and again.

Diller was there, crossbow folded under his arms, toothpick dangling from his mouth, eyes surveying each and every person below.

But how do I get past that man?

"Drop a card, you little rodent," the man with a skinned up face sneered across from him.

"Oh my," he said, running his tiny fingers through his hair before plopping a few coppers on the table. "Tell you what, Scratch, why don't you drop a card instead?"

Scratch glowered at him with beady eyes and said, "You're a little fool, Boy. Master Gillem, why'd you bring this rodent to us? He's as stupid as he is short."

Gillem sat on his stool, his pie face a humble grin, puffing on his pipe.

"He's learnin,' Scratch. Nothing better to teach a youngling quick than to snatch his coins. And since when did you ever care about someone losing to you? Take all his money you want. It's mine you should be worried about." He slipped a silver coin onto the table.

Scratch grunted as the remaining figure at the table, a black-eyed dwarf with a braided brown beard, shoved a matching silver coin across the table.

Lefty showed his teeth to Scratch and said, "It seems fortune's on the side of the little people. Call or withdraw, Scratch."

The card game they played is called Three. Ninety-nine cards fill the deck. There are nine symbolic face cards, each a different animal or creature, numbered from one to eleven. Each player is dealt three cards face down. One can look at them, bet or withdraw. The highest card wins. In the event of a tie, the deck is shuffled and dealt again, and the pile of bets grows.

Lefty's eyes flicked over all the cards turned over on the table. Gillem showed a rooster and a dog, and had withdrawn. The dwarf who had not revealed his name, as he didn't speak, but grunted, had done the same, showing only a pair of weasels. All low cards. Scratch showed a bear and a ram, high cards. Lefty had a dog and a rat. He rubbed his chin. "Hmmmm ..."

There were three of each animal represented. A rat was the lowest, and the dragon was the highest. No dragons were played, and Gillem and the dwarf had withdrawn. He could feel all eyes on him. *Good.* He looked at his last card again. A lion. Only a dragon could beat it. Out of the twelve cards on the table, only the dragons were loose, and two lions would tie.

"Watcha going to do, Lefty?" Gillem asked, his blurry eyes watering as he stuffed more tobacco in his pipe.

"Ah ... I'm thinking, Master Gillem," he said, scratching his head, "but this is pretty hard."

Wham!

Lefty jumped as Scratch rapped his fist on the table and said, "Think faster, you little turd. I'm getting tired of waiting on you. Gillem, teach him cards elsewhere!"

Gillem glared at the man and said, "That's Master Gillem, you son of a pick pocket! You best remember the order of things around here."

Scratch sulked back in his chair as the roughhewn dwarf stuck a wad of chaw in his mouth.

"Apologies, Master Gillem. I'm just getting tired of his halfling's good fortune, is all. He's fared well for someone that's never played before," he said, pouring more grog into his tumbler.

So I have him fooled, after all. Now all I have to do is figure out how to fool them all. His hand that he drummed his fingers with slid down to his tell. *Do one thing so they think you are going to do another,* Melegal had said. Lefty was beginning to understand all of these little lessons better. He'd been observing all of them, taking notice of what they did with a good hand or a bad hand.

Scratch's tell was that he drank a little more with a good hand, and bit his inside cheek with a bad one. The dwarven man was a stone, however, and Lefty had the hardest time figuring him out. He didn't talk; he grunted. He didn't blink at all. All he did was chew and swallow the nasty tobacco juice. But, come to think of it, on a good hand he could hear the dwarf sucking the juice through his teeth, and on a bad hand he switched his chaw from one cheek to the other. And that left Master Gillem, who, as it turned out, had the easiest tell of all. Or was that just what he wanted him to see? On a good hand, he let out a plume of smoke, and on a bad hand he sucked the smoke in from his mouth and in his nose.

He took another peek at his card. *Better let him win one. This is too easy.*

"What's the matter, did you forget what you got, Stupid?"

"No!" Lefty shot back. "Are you certain you don't want to withdraw Scratch? I've got a pretty fine card!"

Scratch pushed another silver coin across and said, "Let's see it, then."

Lefty added his silver to the pile and flipped over his card.

"Ha!"

Scratch slapped a dragon card on top of his lion.

"Beat you again, halflings!" he said in elation, scooping the small pile of coins his way.

Lefty frowned, chin down, and said, "I'm sorry, Master Gillem. I really thought I had him. I really did."

Gillem reached over, rubbed his head, and said, "That's all right, Lad. You're getting better. But sometimes you need to know when to withdraw and wait for the sure thing."

Lefty nodded, locked eyes with Gillem, and said, "I know. Can I take a moment, go outside, and stretch my legs? Besides," he said, fanning the smoke from his face, "I'm getting a bit of a headache."

Gillem was shuffling the cards. "Be quick about it. You never know when Prince Palos will call. We must be ready."

"Hah! I bet he's having some good fun with her up there! I'd give a mouthful of silver just to watch," Scratch said with a lusty look in his yellow eyes. "Give her a week, and she'll be just as common as the rest of his whores."

The man's cold words felt like daggers in Lefty's back. Kam's situation was his fault and his alone. *Do something or die,* Melegal had always said. He patted his belly. There was something in there he'd been careful to conceal from the rest of the guild, especially Gillem. Magic. He could use some, a little bit at least. And he knew that Palos had plenty of items at his disposal as well. If he could just get in there and get his hands on some, he could help. *If I could just make it back to the Magi Roost.* He fought an inner sob. *What have I done to my friend? If I can't do anything else, I'll at least save her baby.* Whether his eyes were watering from tears or from the smoke, he did not know as he stepped over the threshold and outside.

"Ulp!" A pair of strong hands picked him up by the hair of his head.

He clutched at the hands that held him as he looked into the burnt and angry face of the man called Thorn.

"You halflings are going to die," he said in a garbled voice.

Lefty kicked him in his crooked nose.

"Ow! Blasted Halfling!" Thorn swung him by the head of hair, sending him flying back inside. He crashed into a table and whopped his head on the floor so hard bright spots burst forth. The sound of a sword slipping through the leather filled his ears as Thorn cried, "Gillem! You and this little boy are going to die tonight!"

8

T HE CITY OF BONE. IT wasn't a place Verbard ever would have imagined setting his foot in before. As he walked down a narrow alley followed by two dozen of his men, the feeling he had in his gut wasn't something he had ever dealt with. He reached forward and tapped Jottenhiem on the shoulder. The underling fighter turned, a fierce grin under his ruby red eyes.

"My Lord," he said.

Verbard raised a finger, his silver eyes flickering in the shadows of the midday sunlight. The city smelled far worse than he imagined it. *How do men live in this wretched place?* The underlings were notoriously clean by comparison. There were no slums in the underworld, just caves and caverns filled with creatures united in the working cause of destroying mankind.

"Let me send Eep ahead," Verbard said. "We are getting very close to the people; I can hear them now. Many, many people." He stuffed his fingers in his pockets and secured them on some magic objects. *I have a feeling I'll need all of this. Eep, what is ahead?*

Somewhere, Eep sat on the ledge of a building at the end of an alley, peering downward.

People, Master. Many people, working, eating and waiting for me to kill them. Can I kill them all, Master?

Any soldiers?

No. Just sacks of soon to be rotting flesh. So many, Master. I cannot contain myself. Release me!

Be still, Eep. I have other plans for you.

Does it involve killing more people?

Certainly.

Verbard turned to his commander, Jottenhiem. "Our time to strike has come." He looked back over his shoulder at the small group of underlings.

The swords of the twelve Juegen armored in black plate mail from head to toes gleamed in the dim light. Six badoon underlings in black leather hauberks stood with small crossbows and knives at the ready, and behind them were six magi, fingers glimmering with radiant power, eyes flickering under their hoods. No human could possibly be ready for this. Not even The Darkslayer, himself. A slender smile broke over Verbard's lips. He was ready.

"Let's take as many as we can. There will be no time for burials. On my command, we'll retreat. You know what to do."

"This will be glorious," Jottenhiem said, lowering a full iron helmet over his skull and cutting his swords through the air. "On your command, my lord, and we shall remove the skin from their bones."

Verbard felt a charge of energy surge through him at having his natural enemy so close, as if he were running with a pack of timber wolves who were taking down a tired elk.

I can't believe I'm actually doing this. Yet, it feels so right somehow.

Eep, lead us to the largest group of people.

The City of Bone was moments away from never being the same again.

Kierway, the Vicious, three Juegen and three underling magi departed from the barge and the current.

"Stay here," the underling ranger said with iron eyes that seemed to glow.

Another twenty underlings, well-armed and ready, remained on the barge as Kierway drew his sword and led the way through the dark caverns beneath Castle Almen. Oran had described his dealings with Royal Lord Almen before, and he knew the way inside, but still, the very thought of entering the castle of his enemies was a bit unsettling. It was one thing to strike in the dark of the Outlands that he'd been so accustomed to over the decades, but striking within their walls was another matter entirely. *This should be Verbard, not me.*

He led the way up a set of stone stairs to a man-sized wooden door trimmed in discolored iron. He chittered a command and stepped aside as an underling mage floated up to the threshold. The mage's clawed hands flared with energy as it pressed them on the door.

Kierway noticed all the hungry looks on the faces of his troops. Each was a mask of concentration, starving to be the first to strike a lethal blow on behalf of underling kind. Maybe his father, Master Sinway, wasn't being so frivolous after all. Things seemed natural, as if he was returning to regain his home. *Impossible. But maybe the key will explain what is going on.*

There was a flash of energy followed by a sizzling sound when he found himself staring through the other side of a gaping hole. Warmth and the scent of human sweat filled the air around him. The instincts of his black blood pulsated with new life as a craving for battle consumed him.

"Kill anything that moves," he said, pointing the Vicious forward. Everything tingled from head to toe as he stepped through the door into an uncharted battle ground.

9

Venir felt like he'd been struck by a hundred hammers as he struggled to lift his hulking frame from the ground only to collapse again into the turf. He spit dirt and blood as he pushed his chest from the ground and rolled into the light of the blaring suns. He could smell the charred flesh of the underling that was on his back, a rancid smell like that of a burning skunk as he pinched his nose, fighting nausea and rising to his feet.

He mumbled as he took a step forward, staggering and dazed. Above him, the underling mage let out an angry hiss. Venir's helm beckoned action, but he could hardly move as he fought through the numbness and pain. He glanced up as a coat of webbing fell from the sky. *Move or die.* He slung his shield into the net of webbing and dove to the side.

The underling hissed as the shield carried the webbing to the ground, negating the spell. Venir let out a triumphant growl as he felt life begin to flow back into his fingertips and tried to spit the taste of nails from his mouth.

"What else do you have, Fiend?" Venir said, twirling Brool in the air.

The underling floated backward now, slowly retreating towards the battle at the camp, its yellow eyes burning with hatred. Yet, Venir could feel its confusion and sense its doubt.

"That's right! Your moments left on Bish aren't many. I've returned!"

The webs dissipated as he drew Brool's keen edge over his web-coated shield. Strapping it on over his back, he began chasing the underling down. In the dusty distance, the clashing sounds of battle rung inside his helm, and the wind whistled through his ears. He was gaining on the underling. Somehow, Venir could feel its magic fading as its dark robes dipped and brushed over the barren landscape's stones.

"Ha!" Venir cried, churning ahead, long stride after stride, gaining speed.

Twenty Feet. Ten Feet. Five feet. He dove forward, crashing into the back of the much smaller creature and driving it to the ground. Venir wrapped his fingers around its neck and squeezed. The blue veins in his arms rolled up like snakes as the underling kicked and flailed beneath his waist. Its black tongue jutted from inside its mouth as its citrine eyes bulged. Venir felt the taut wiry muscles in its neck heave then slacken as its wind pipe was crushed in his grasp.

"Eleven!" he said, wiping the sweat from his eyes and rushing for the battle. His long strides couldn't get him there fast enough as the Royal Riders were swarmed and ripped down from their saddles.

"BONE!"

The tide had turned. The element of surprise was gone. The riders were outnumbered three to one, and that didn't include the giant spiders that shot webbing from one side of the camp to the other. Horses nickered and neighed as the hairy black creatures from the Underland cut and stabbed at their thundering legs.

From the distance, Venir saw one Knight catch a spear in the neck and tumble into the fray. Another's head was blasted open by a barrage of mystic red missiles. Venir's inner core burned. A knot of fury needed release as he witnessed the battle unfold, blow by blow.

Seek! The helm urged him. *Destroy!*

Thirty yards. Twenty yards. Ten yards. Brool pulsated with life as he hefted it back behind his shoulders and exploded.

A throng of underlings were pulling another rider from his horse. Venir slammed into them, carving into them like canoes. A giant spider as big as a horse had a rider pinned down, its two protruding tentacles poking holes through the man's plate mail. Venir disemboweled the creature, leaving it twitching on the dusty floor. He was in the thick of the fight, powerful arms chopping left and right, splitting dark faces and cleaving through bone. Brool was humming now, a living thing weaving a path of destruction like black lightening. *Seventeen!*

Venir was bigger, faster and stronger than them all. His mind and the armament merged as one, punching holes into the army of underlings one by one.

Glitch!

Hack!

Slack!

Chop!

Chop!

Stab!

The underling bodies piled up at his feet, yet they kept coming on, in pairs and triples, crossbow bolts careening off his helmet, darts bouncing from his shield. Venir snarled down on them and growled like a savage beast, swinging his war-axe in an arc of death that ripped two underlings' heads from their shoulders.

More! The helm pleaded as black blood fertilized the Outland ground.

Still, unlike before, Venir's vision was clear, his mind concise, his body and armor taking all of the punishment he could handle. He could sense their worry; he fed on their fear, his hulking frame moving as fast as thought, a half second faster than everything the underlings threw at him. He kept swinging; they kept coming. His mind forgot about all of the others engaged in the battle.

The helm's black eyelets smoldered like blazing fires; Brool's black blade was a tornado of steel. *No mercy!*

Venir felt in control, his body as strong as a gale, the helm telling him when to duck, twist and turn, but he stayed on the offensive. *Move and die, Underlings! Run and die! I'll have you all!*

They screamed. With rage. With defiance. With fear. Their evil faces were twisted with hatred as they realized their old foe had returned, his vengeance like they'd never seen before. Still, with gnashing teeth they piled on, blades arcing high and low.

He jabbed Brool's spike through one and ripped its heart out. "RRRRRAHHH!"

In the back of his mind, he remembered the Warfield, the Vicious, and Georgio. The armament had propelled him there and pushed him past his limits to where he had collapsed and died, or almost died. Now, he felt invincible. He should be exhausted by now. What was different this time?

He snapped his head around as a massive shadow fell over him. The biggest spider of them all's eight eyes looked down on him like a treat as a burst of green fluid shot from its mouth. Venir bounded away, the splash of the acid sizzling into his legs. He roared as he scrambled into another wave of underlings. *Slice! Chop! Glitch! Twenty-Eight!*

The smoldering helm screamed a warning.

"What!" Venir yelled, casting an upward glance.

Four magi hovered above, a net large enough for twenty men in their grasp. One second Venir was a blur of destruction. The next, he was a helpless heap, trapped like a fish in a net full of piranhas.

There was no time left. Slim sagged alongside Adanna as the spiders crept down the walls and out of the light. Adanna had screamed herself hoarse as she trembled at his side, her body drained of all the rush of fright.

"Wrap this around your face," Slim said, tearing the sleeve from his robe.

She didn't respond. He covered her head with his sleeve and whispered something in her ear. He could feel the tension in her chest ease as she slipped to the floor. Slim covered his head with his robe as well and huddled over Adanna, muttering another spell, and then he had nothing left. His magic was spent. He let his body slacken in the dim light of the pit. He could hear the clicking and sucking sounds of the spiders as they made their way down the walls. He clutched Adanna tight as her body recoiled.

"Don't flinch. I've got you protected," he whispered in her ear. But he didn't. Not from their acidic or blood-sucking bits. But with something else. A gamble. *I hope they've been well fed today, or else I'm going to be spider crap real soon.* He lay still, huddled over the warmth of Adanna's body as the spiders began to coat them with their silk. The strong creatures pulled him and Adanna apart from one another and covered them from head to toe, one by one.

10

ONCE, HE'D BEEN NOTHING MORE than a common rogue who pilfered in the streets and enjoyed cheap wine. Now, Melegal sat in utter misery inside his calm exterior as the loud and distraught pleas of Brak ran loops in his thoughts. *Pitiful. Sick and pitiful.* Down in the arena, the young Royals were hoisting their swords in jubilation and chanting praises to one another as the sentries dragged the bloody corpse of Hagerdon the Slerg across the floor and out of sight.

Disgusting little wretches!

He shifted on the hardened bench beneath him as they paraded around, wiping the blood from their swords before tasting it. Lord Almen and his cohorts were standing and applauding, offering congratulations to the young men. Melegal couldn't help but be disappointed. This seemed beneath someone like Lord Almen. He shifted his attention back to Lorda Almen.

She bit into some sliced fruit, a catty smile on her face as if nothing in the arena was going on. Her servants fanned her face and wiped the sweat glistening on her brow. She'd made him an offer he couldn't refuse, simply because he had no choice. *Just as wicked, twice as beautiful.* But he still couldn't help but be tempted by what her offer meant. *Kill the Brigand Queen. What an honor! For a fool.*

"Who shall we kill next, Lord Almen?" one of the young Royals shouted up into the stands. "The taste of Slerg blood is divine!"

Melegal's fingers caressed the triggers on the dart launching bracers concealed inside his clothes. How many times had he been tolerated and chastised by their kind as a child? The whippings and humiliation were nothing to be forgotten. He'd seen all the things these young men got into: defiling, lying, cheating and stealing from one another like it was their rightful cause. If part of that lingering sentiment made it easy to watch the Slergs go, then they could all die for all he cared. He'd been a part of their castle up until he and Venir escaped, but he'd never desired vengeance upon them. He'd gotten away and left them alone. Now he sat watching them die, one by one, with nothing but an empty feeling inside. *I hate Royals!*

"Leezir the Slerg," Lord Almen spoke, disrupting his thoughts, "my old foe, come … step forward."

Leezir, now a haggard man, once short and shifty, shuffled forward in his chains, head down and fighting the shivers and a cough. He stood in the middle of the arena and lifted his chin up, his pale eyes no longer intent and filled with power like the man Melegal once knew as the fearless and callous leader of his house.

"Ah, Leezir, it seems your final game is over," Lord Almen said with smug satisfaction in his voice. "You attempted to overtake my castle, yet you failed. And now, I, Royal Lord Almen, noble and wise …"

"Hear! Hear!"

"… now stand willing to entertain your pleas. And …" he held his jeweled fingers out, "perhaps I'll show mercy."

Leezir opened his mouth to speak but was overtaken by a fit of coughing.

Lord Almen chuckled, the others as well.

"Come now, Leezir, certainly you can do better than that?"

A hearty burst of laughter filled the room.

Leezir raised his head once more, his eyes drifting into the stands, taking in every face one by one. Of all the Slergs, Leezir was the most reasonable, and he'd be the last one Melegal wanted to see go. After all, Leezir'd had a small hand in freeing them, which was something Melegal had never make sense of.

Stopping on Melegal, he locked his gaze for a moment, sending a jolt to his senses, before moving on. Lord Almen gave him a casual glance as well.

Thanks for that, Slerg! As if I wasn't a greasy blemish already. Blast, I'm getting a headache. What is wrong with me?

"Lord Almen," Leezir managed with a voice that belied his calm appearance, "you are as vile as a pit of vipers. A snake within the roses. Your black heart is filled with nothing but treachery and darkness. You betrayed me," he pointed into the stands, "and he'll betray the rest of you as well. Mercy, you say!" Leezir spat on the ground. "Pah! You don't know the meaning, you murderer of old women and children in their sleep!"

Hear! Hear! Melegal thought, fighting the urge to applaud. *Remember, never sleep near an Almen.*

Lord Almen's body noticeably stiffened at the resounding truth in those words. His glance drifted over to his Lorda, who now sat up glaring. Sefron gaped, and his lips looked to be mumbling a spell, while Jarla the Brigand Queen sat with her legs crossed, hands clasped on her knee, smiling.

Almen cleared his throat and smiled.

"You've an interesting way of pleading for mercy, Leezir. Perhaps your tactics are why all of your negotiations failed. It's almost a shame to see such a slow-witted family go. I'm sure you'd have made excellent grape pressers," Lord Almen needled his chin in pose, "or grave diggers."

"Let us kill him, Lord Almen!" the same youth as before said.

"Arm the young Royals with their bows," Almen ordered. "I think I've found an excellent practice target."

Leezir shouted back, shaking his fist. "I'll not run like some rabbit, Almen! I've seen this game before. You might as well take me as I am!"

"Perhaps you won't, but I'm sure your … granddaughter will," Almen added.

"Let the child go!" Leezir's face reddened as he fell into a fit of coughing. "She's not guilty of anything. She's only a child."

"Oh, but she is guilty of being a Slerg though, isn't she? And I can't have any legacy Slergs hanging around my castle. As you know, I think we all do, revenge can be such a powerful motivator, and I can't have that kind of weapon scurrying around my city. It's best to end this once and for all. It's for the better."

The young Royals, excluding the one who had lost his fingers earlier, had formed a line. One by one, they nocked their bows. Melegal leaned forward on the edge of his seat. He remembered seeing this game before, played with blunt arrows. He and many urchins had suffered welts and bruises from it, even an eye out or two. He stiffened and frowned. In this case however, the arrows were steel tipped.

"You'll burn for this, Almen! I'm not your last enemy standing, you know. *Cough-cough* There will be more, and your blood will run red into the sewers down below, I swear it!" Leezir didn't struggle as the guards dragged him and the wailing girl into the middle of the arena.

Her high pitched screams were unnerving. Melegal fought the urge to cover his ears. He looked to Lorda, but she had her head turned away in chatter. *No mercy there, either. I see.*

"What about the big one?" one of Almen's' guests asked.

Brak!

Time was running out to save Venir's son. He had no plan, nothing at all. It would almost be better if he dove in the arena himself and caught a few shafts in his chest to get it over with. *Way to go, Rat. If I can't save myself, then how can I save anyone else?* He felt a pair of eyes on him and looked down. Jarla's dark blues probed his, like a cat cornering a mouse. Her nostrils flared, and her lips twitched, standing Melegal's hair on end. She narrowed her eyes and turned away.

Witch! What does she know? I think the Lorda has it right, after all.

"We'll save the big one for last. The main event," Lord Almen said. "Carry on!"

The guards knocked the chained figures of Leezir and Jubilee to the ground and backed away. One of the sentries in the arena began counting down.

"Five!"

They could at least take off the chains.

"Four!"

Melegal could read Leezir's lips as he clutched the girl in his arms. He was saying, *Don't run, Jubilee. Stay close to me. I'll keep you safe.* That wasn't possible, Melegal knew. Every blood thirsty Royal knew that, too, but it was still the right thing to say.

"Three!"

Melegal took a quick glance around. For some reason, he thought Venir would come bursting through the door at any moment, axe high, screaming for the heads of every last Royal.

"Two!"

All of Melegal's hopes fled as Leezir hugged his granddaughter with all his might.

"One!"

Twang. Twang. Twang. Twang. Twang. Twang.

Leezir's body lurched forward, six arrows piercing his back. Cheers erupted from the small crowd as Leezir's hand fluttered and he moved no more.

Jubilee crawled out from beneath him, eyes wide with horror, tears streaming down her face, clutching at her grandfather's face.

"Reload, Lads!"

I can't watch this! Melegal's head dipped down at the sound of the wooden shafts scraping along the arrows in the rest of the bows. The sound of the stretching bow strings clenched the muscles in his jaws.

"One at a time," the soldier said, "Let's feather the little Slerg like a goose, shall we?"

The first young Royal, the one with the boasting mouth, let his arrow fly. Melegal's grey eyes watched with deep remorse as the arrow seemed to sail across the arena in slow motion and hit the wall above Jubilee's fragile shoulder, sending her running and tripping over Leezir's corpse. Somehow, she still staggered back to her feet.

Stay down!

Twang.

An arrow narrowly missed her leg as she screamed.

Amid the rousing cheers and cries, a triumphant and most unnatural sound occurred.

Melegal's back straightened as a snake of ice slivered through his spine. The sounds of groaning metal and snapping chains cut through the arena like a lightning strike. Brak, once huddled and forgotten, was in full motion now. His hulking frame was tearing his metal bonds away like cob webbing, and his big face was a raging inferno the likes of which no man had seen before.

Brak stormed across the arena, slamming into the row stunned young Royals. His blue eyes blazed like a man possessed, and his thickset arms were knotted in fury, hammering at the young men who were awestruck by the raging bull.

Melegal had seen a similar look on Venir before, but this was different, a frenzied beast out of control. *Go, Brak!*

A young Royal's neck was snapped like a branch. Brak bent another one's head back over his shoulder.

Melegal remained frozen in his seat, aware that the woman, Jarla, remained poised as well, her hands falling to her sword as she scooted forward. Melegal held his fingers tight on his triggers as madness overcame the crowd.

"NOOOO!" a guest from the stands screamed, his arm stretching out.

In the arena, two soldiers lay dead, and Brak had his hands filled with their swords, chopping down everything, living, moving or breathing. Big and frightening, he came at them with speed that defied the natural boundaries of man.

CHOP!

He cut one soldier in twain.

SLICE!

A young Royal's head was severed from his shoulders.

A durable soldier in chain armor launched an arrow into Brak's shoulder. He ripped it out, charged, and jabbed it into the soldier's neck.

Lord Almen was on his feet now, barking orders as his precious Coming of Age game quickly became a Royal blood bath. The servant girls were scrambling up the stands, dragging the distraught Lorda behind them. By the time they reached the top, he'd seen two more Royals felled under Brak's devastating blows.

Think, Detective! He scanned the arena for Sefron. The vile cleric was scurrying through a door above, his sagging face agape in terror. *Slat!* Melegal contemplated his move, if he had one at all. The Royal guests, the softer sort, adorned in fanciful robes and far from prepared for battle, scurried around the arena stubbing their sandaled toes. Lord Almen was the only calm one among them as Brak skewered the last young Royal and hoisted the dead young man high in the air on his sword.

"Somebody stop him!" Lord Almen cried. He looked back over his shoulder.

"Detective! Get in there!"

Almen sneered at Jarla and pointed inside the ring.

"You get in there as well!"

Jarla looked at Melegal, and he looked at her. He stood up and made his first step. An impossible thought occurred to him. An urge that felt right, good.

I've had it with these Royals.

Jarla unsheathed her sword and took another look at him.

Melegal's mind glimmered with life, filling his body from head to toe.

Sleep! Sleep! Sleep! Sleep!

Jarla's eyes rolled up in her head as she swooned, her sword clattering on the seats.

"What is this!" Lord Almen said, reaching for the collapsing woman.

Everything was in slow motion. Lord Almen's back turned to him. Melegal grinned from cheek to cheek. *Might as well start at the top.*

Stab!

Lord Almen's expression was one he'd never forget as he plunged his dagger deep in between the Royal's ribs.

"Welcome to my arena," he said, twisting his blade.

Lord Almen's handsome expression paled as he tried to twist free, arms pushing away Melegal's face. He held Almen tight by his robes and pushed the blade deeper.

"Urk!"

Almen's eyes widened in alarm as fear filled his eyes.

"You'll pay for this, Detect …"

Lord Almen's eyes rolled up in his head as Melegal lowered him to the floor.

"But you won't be around to see that, will you?" he said, head whipping around.

Whop!

Brak was in the stands now, arrows jutting from his back and shoulders as he smashed two of Lord Almen's guests into each other and hurled them over the wall.

He slipped his dagger from between Almen's ribs. The man was dead. He couldn't believe it. *I killed him. I actually killed him. Have I gone mad?* The memory of Leezir's eyes flashed in his mind. His cap tingled with alarm.

Slice!

He sprung backward as a sword stroke almost cleaved him in half.

"Murdering coward!" Jarla yelled.

It seemed his suggestion hadn't worked so well. What a willful woman she must be.

As Brak continued to hack the Royals down one by one in a maddened frenzy, Melegal dashed up the stairs and down again as more guards and soldiers spilled into the arena from high and low.

"Bone!"

Jarla's steel nipped at his toes as he bounded past her and down into the arena. Ten more able soldiers made their way into the arena and blocked every door. There was no way out for Melegal unless he took out the angry swordswoman coming his way.

Think!

11

F OGLE'S LIMBS WERE FROZEN AS he watched the giant's club descend.

   Poof!

The giant roared as its club burst into sawdust, and it fought to wipe the plume of grit from its eyes.

Fogle Boon clutched his chest and frantically began to speak. Something fierce had clamped down on the collar of his robes and was dragging him backward over the sand. He tried to think of a spell, all the while kicking and flailing his arms and legs. Something snorted a gooey mist over his robes. He strained to look behind him. It was Chongo.

"Quit flapping like a fish, Fogle!" Cass yelled. "I've come to aid you. You called for me, didn't you?"

"Er … Yes!" he said, gathering his feet.

"Well, here I am. Now get out of the way, will you!" she said, raising her hands above her head, soft pink lips muttering a quick incantation.

Fogle jumped out of the way and fell alongside Chongo as the giant clenched its monstrous fists and charged. Cass's body shimmered and convulsed in a captivating matter as a shadow of life erupted beneath the giant.

It moaned as it sank waist deep into the quick sand that had been solid ground moments before.

Impressive!

The giant's free hand clawed at the ground, ripping it up like sand as it sunk chest deep into the dirt. It seemed the last moments of the giant's life were coming to an end as it sank farther and farther and then stopped when the quick sand began to solidify around its neck.

"Looks like you got him, Cass! Amazing!"

The giant's hand burst from beneath the ground.

"It won't hold him forever, Fogle Fool! Do something, before he pulls himself out!"

Fogle's hands rummaged through all the belongings inside his robes. He wished Ox the Mintaur was there. He'd always kept things handy.

"Hurry!" Cass yelled as the giant began pushing itself out of the hole.

"I don't have anything!"

Two stocky black bearded figures charged into the giant's path and began jabbing at its neck with spears.

"Thank Bish for the Dwarves," Cass said, sliding from Chongo's back.

The giant two-headed dog sped towards the giant, attacking with both heads and four lion-like claws. The giant swatted one dwarf away and sent him spinning over the ground. It snatched the other in its palm.

Cass was rummaging through Fogle's robes.

"What are you doing?" he asked.

"Something!" she shot back, producing a vial of luminescent liquid from his robes.

Chongo yelped as the giant sent the big dog sprawling.

Cass winded her arm back with the vial.

"Don't throw that!"

It was too late. The vial sailed into the giant's mouth and disappeared down its maw.

Cass looked over at Fogle and said, "What was that?"

The giant jerked upright, eyes bulging as it clutched at its throat.

"What's happening?" Cass yelled, stepping backward to Fogle's side.

The giant went into a fit of spasms, its big mouth gulping for air as it released the dwarf from its grasp. The dwarves and Chongo backed away from the giant as it swung away at everything in its path. Fogle watched with avid fascination. The giant was choking to death.

It snorted and gurgled as water began spilling from its mouth. Finally, the giant's head pitched forward into the hard ground with a thud. It moved no more.

Fogle and Cass eased their way over and gazed at the pool of water spilling from its mouth.

She grabbed him by his arm and asked again, "What was that?"

"Oh, just about a year's worth of water rations."

She pinched his face in the palm of her hand and said with a glowing smile.

"I knew that, Fogle."

"I don't think — "

"TUNDOOR's GOING TO KILL YOU PESKY DWARVES!"

Fogle whipped his head around. A giant with bulging muscles from his shins to his neck was inside a dust cloud, swinging a hammer as big as a man.

"Where in Bish did he come from?" he said, unable to hide the fear quivering in his voice.

Cass wrapped her arms around his waist and exclaimed, "We're going to need a lot more water to stop that giant!"

Mood had seen many things in his long lifetime on Bish, and the giants were among those, just not giants this big.

The ground erupted where the giant's hammer came down less than a foot from his feet, knocking him to the ground.

"I CAN SMELL YOUR FEAR! YOU CAN'T HIDE FROM TUNDOOR! HA! HA! HA!"

Mood's boots moved toward the sound of the giant's bellowing voice. There were only two good ways to fight a giant: from a long distance or right up close. As he made his way through the dust, the ground erupted once again. Mood's hand axe lashed out, chopping deep in the giant's hand. He swung again, missing as the giant jerked its injured hand away.

"ARGH! A nice sting, you fuzzy red mouse, but it will take more than that to stop Tundoor. HA! HA!" the giant said, raising its leg and stomping the ground. "OUCH!"

Eethum had struck a nasty blow from somewhere nearby. If Eethum was working one side, Mood needed to be working the other. *Got to get him to the ground!*

WHOOM!

WHOOM!

WHOOM!

WHOOM!

Tundoor hammered all over like an angry child. Mood jumped left, right, backward and forward, each leap as painful as the next inside his rattling chest. The hammering moved away from him as he caught a glimpse of the giant's hairy shin in the dust. He chopped into the giant with all of his might.

Whack!

Tundoor jerked his knee up and let out a deafening roar. Mood thought he was listening to the world coming to an end ...

Whang! In the next moment, he was skipping over the hardened ground. He stopped with a mouthful of grit, two dislocated shoulders, and maybe worse. Everything hurt. The world was rumbling beneath him, and for the first time in three hundred years he felt the urge to retch as his blood trickled down his broken face. He tried to speak, but no words came out.

Got to get up! Must kill that giant!

But all he could do was watch the blurry spots in the dusty sky and feel the land-shaking steps getting closer.

12

"**B**RING ME THE DUSSACKS!" SAM the barkeep yelled.

A hunchbacked woman with wispy white hair teetered into the middle of the room with two knife-like swords hanging in her fragile arms. They clattered on the floor as she turned to walk away.

"Get the oil, too," the barkeep ordered, "you old hen, and don't drop it, either."

She teetered away, waving her hand over her head.

"And a flame as well!"

Georgio stood within a circle of pressing people, Billip and Mikkel both at his back. Across from him stood Jeb, a stout brute with a neck of iron, his cutthroats behind, eyes and lips full of mockery. He didn't like them. They weren't the kind of men who had standards. They were takers: cold, merciless and cowardly. He could feel that in his bones.

"You can walk away, Georgio. There's nothing to be gained by this," Billip said, cracking his knuckles.

"No, I'm going to fight."

"You are not ready! This man, he's a seasoned beast. He'll cut you to ribbons. You pick up that Dussack," Billip squeezed his shoulder, "you're on your own."

Georgio looked down at the blade lying on the floor. It was a wide blade of steel, about thirty inches long with a gentle bend towards the tip. It had a loop for a hilt wrapped in leather that reminded him of half a pair of scissors. It was different, but he'd been training with Mikkel and Billip for a while. How different could one sword be from another?

Mikkel stepped out into the center, his broad shoulders and muscular back heaving. He pounded his chest with his fist.

"Take on a man, Jeb! Fight me instead! He's untrained."

Jeb squatted down, plucked his Dussack from the floor, and said, "All knew the risk the moment you stepped in here. The boy can walk away," he thumbed the edge of the blade, "just leave your purses and go."

"Coward!"

Jeb laughed.

"Your words are talking any thoughts of mercy from my mind. I suggest you talk some sense into your young friend ... or give him a hug before he dies."

Mikkel turned and said, "Georgio, this man is a killer. You don't have to do this."

Georgio pushed past Mikkel and picked up the sword.

A cry of cheers went up.

"Thatta boy!"

"Kill him, Jeb, and cut me a lock of that curly hair!" A surly woman cried.

"Don't kill him, just punish him," a harlot said, "I want to pinch those cheeks one time at least."

Coarse laughter erupted as the bar maids bustled, refilling the tankards of ale. It wasn't often action like this happened so early in the day.

That's when Georgio noticed the sullen look on the face of the woman who had drawn the card, Velvet. It as if she was looking at a dead man. Shoulders slumped, he looked away. He didn't know why he was doing this, but he felt compelled to, as if something inside him was driving him forward. But the words Melegal said had haunted him, *Go back to Three and live. Stay in Bone and die.*

Mikkel put his heavy hands on his shoulders and said, "Stay on the defensive, and wait for an opening. You cut him good, he'll yield. Be patient, Georgio." Billip gave him a final squeeze. "You can do it, Georgio!"

"Aye," Billip said, "you've learned from the best. This man's a thug. One good cut and he'll run."

"Thanks," Georgio said, unable to hide the dullness in his voice. He searched for Jeb's eyes and found them staring back at him. His men were all offering encouragement, pointing and mocking at him. Something about the looks on their faces and the sound of their voices began to charge his blood.

"Ah!" the barkeep's voice cut through the noise of the crowd, "our favorite retriever returns."

The old woman's arms quavered as she handed him over a jar and a candle.

"Come here, young warrior," the barkeep said, dousing a rag in the oil. "Let me see your blade."

Georgio stuck it out. The barkeep coated the blade halfway down with thick oily residue. It had a pungent smell, like the glue used to seal stones.

"Step back," he said, holding out the candle.

"Fire them up, Sam!"

Sam the barkeep stuck the candle under the blade's tip, igniting the blade.

Georgio's eyes widened as he watched the wispy black smoke rise from the orange flames.

The crowd started chanting as the barkeep did the same to Jeb's blade.

"Jeb! Jeb! Jeb! Jeb!"

"Take your places, men!" the barkeep said, guiding them both to the middle of the circle.

Georgio looked up into the face of the man leering down on him with a flaming sword in his hand. *Fight or die! That's what Venir would say.* He pulled back his shoulders and clenched his teeth.

"Let's go over the rules of the Flaming Sword. The Dussack is a cutting weapon, but stabbing is allowed. But you only get one poke."

"Aah! Give 'em three pokes, Sam!"

The barkeep waved the comments off as he allowed his words to arouse the crowd.

"I've seen men slashed to ribbons! I saw a woman whittled down to the bone! No Mercy! A merry old man sliced off his best friend's fingers! Be alert! A woman cut her husband's neck open! Be wary!"

Georgio blanched as his hand rubbed his chest below his neck and his forehead burst into beads of sweat. *Fight or die!*

"And there will be no dancing and delays, Men! The flame gets hotter as time goes on. It will seep down the steel until that handle's as hot as a poker. It will cauterize your skin to the metal. The first challenger to drop his weapon loses. Or the first one to yield."

Georgio could feel the warmth growing in his hands.

The barkeep took a long draw on his cigar and exhaled a plume of smoke in the air. There was a glimmer in his sagging bloodshot eyes as he spoke.

"Ready yourselves, then!"

The room stiffened with tension.

"One!"

"Two!"

Georgio raised his flaming sword.

Mikkel's muscles were as taut at bowstrings as he watched his young friend Georgio lift his Dussack from the floor. Over the past few months, a bond had grown between him and Georgio, who served as a reminder of his own son, Nikkel. He couldn't help but think. *What would it be like if Nikkel were out there, about to get cut to ribbons by a man?* So far as he could tell, Jeb was a cold-blooded killer. His hands clenched at his sides. One poke was all it took.

"Come on, Georgio!" he said with encouragement.

Billip's eyes narrowed at his side, flitting back and forth as he twisted the hairs under his chin. Billip wasn't much of a sword fighter, but he'd fair better than Georgio, who was still swinging steels like hatchets. Whatever possessed the boy to take this fight was beyond him. Maybe it was his fault. After all, he'd been saying for weeks, *You have be a man sometime.* People grew up quick on Bish, and it had been no different for him than any other.

"Put these on the young man," Billip said, filling a bet taker's hands with coins.

Mikkel pulled Billip up by the cloth of his shoulder and said through his teeth, "What are you doing?"

"Gambling."

"On the life of our friend?"

Billip shrugged and said, "I can't help it. I just like long shots. You know that."

"That's sick, even for you."

"It's quite normal; you know that. Besides, I've bet for and against you, too."

"I was a man. That was different."

"It seems our Georgio is a man now, too." Billip brushed his arm away. "Now pay attention."

Georgio was squared up with Jeb as the barkeep backed away. Jeb's round face with the squared jaw leered down at Georgio, who stood chest out only half a head shorter. Georgio's thickset frame was almost as broad, but his muscles weren't developed like those on the hardened criminal across from him. Jeb's body was covered in thick hair. Corded muscles bulged under his heavy jerkin, and Georgio looked soft as a lamb by comparison. Mikkel could feel the fight was going to go bad really fast as all the betting was shifting against Georgio.

"Two!"

Oil from the burning swords dripped to the floor, sizzling on the planks. Georgio's back foot slid back, and his stiff legs began to bend. *Good stance. Be ready!*

"Three!"

Georgio leapt back as the flaming tip of Jeb's Dussack ripped at his neck.

"Move, Georgio!" Mikkel cried as Billip grabbed hold of him and pulled him back.

"Ha! You're pretty fast for a chubby one," Jeb said, clashing his sword into Georgio's and almost ripping it from his grasp. Oily flames scattered and fell, leaving sizzling little fires on the floor. "You got sticky hands, too!"

Georgio wrapped both hands around the hilt, feet shuffling back and forth, shoulders rocking left and right.

Clang! Clang! Clang!

The crowd roared in jubilation as Jeb hammered his heavy blade down, juttering Georgio's arms at the elbows. Mikkel could feel the steel ringing his teeth. *He's a sitting duck.*

Jeb sprang away, cutting his sword in arcing flames back and forth like a sickle.

"Is that blade getting hot on those soft hands of yours, Boy? I've got callouses as thick as an ogre's hide."

Georgio's chest was heaving as he wiped the sweat from his face and said, "It seems you've got the ogre's breath, too."

"Har!" One man laughed so loud he dropped his tankard.

"You're funny for a dead man," Jeb said, lunging forward.

Slice!

The flaming blade ripped a gash in Georgio's thigh.

Mikkel wanted to stop the fight, but it was too late. *Live a man, die a man.*

"He'll be fine," Billip said. "He's got skin as thick as his skull."

Mikkel shook his head. Healing took time, even for Georgio, and no matter who you are, getting cut and stabbed always hurts like fire.

Georgio cried out as Jeb cut his arm. The smell of burning flesh filled the smoke-filled air as the red hot sword tip instantly cauterized the wound.

"Feel that, Boy! Wait till I drive this blade into that soft belly and scorch your innards like coals. Won't that be a fine way to die?"

Jeb swung downward in powerful orange flamed strikes, one after the other, driving Georgio to his knees. Tiny flames singed holes in his clothes and burned dark patches on his skin. His arms began to sag, and Jeb knocked his sword back into his head.

"Let go, Georgio!" Mikkel warned. "Blast your pride."

Jeb was toying with the boy, but now his voice took on a deadly tone as he lifted his arm up for the final strike.

Georgio fought for his breath as sweat trickled in his eyes. His arms and legs burned like they were on fire. Jeb was killing him. But he wouldn't let go of the sword. *Fight!* He hadn't even taken a swing. Was this what fighting was really like? He'd never felt so exhausted before. He could feel the sword heating up in his hand. It seemed every inch of him hurt. He felt like he'd fallen in a bucket of knives. *Take the pain! Fight! Get one piece of him before you go!*

He gathered himself to his knees as Jeb's sword came arcing downward, and then he lunged. Something bit deep into his shoulder, cutting it to the bone.

The crowd reeled with delight as Georgio screamed on the floor, his shoulder inflamed with pain, his body going into total recoil. He looked for his opponent. Jeb was shuffling back, flaming sword in hand, patting out a flaming streak across his belly. *Yes!*

He heard Mikkel's voice booming over the rest.

"You got him, Georgio! Go after him!"

Georgio rose to his feet. As a blinding pain erupted in his shoulder, he moved his sword from one hand to the other. It was hot now. Like the handle of a metal coffee kettle. *Don't let go!*

He staggered forward, his shoulder feeling like an anchor was tied to it, his other arm barely able to lift his flaming sword. The steel was glowing red hot to the end.

Jeb switched his sword from one hand to the other, shaking his former sword hand. He snarled, spit coming from his lips, and charged.

Clang!

Georgio parried, but the jabbing pain erupted in his shoulder. Jeb was slower now, and Georgio felt his wind returning. He parried the next series of blows as Jeb's face became wracked with anger and pain. He locked him up, flaming swords inches from their faces.

"I'm going to gut you, Boy! Yield, before I fill your belly with steel."

"Not if I fill yours first!"

Crack!

He head-butted Jeb in the nose.

Blood flowed over Jeb's teeth and lips as he staggered away.

The crowd cried foul.

"It's a fair move!" the barkeep shouted.

Jeb spat the blood from his face, grimacing as he switched his sword from one hand to the other, then back again. A desperate look was filling his eyes.

"Kill him, Jeb!" one of his men said.

Georgio held his sword up and out and said, "I can do this all day."

It felt like his entire hand was on fire, and the steel was beginning to stick to his skin. He fought the urge to switch hands after one person said:

"He's not even switched hands yet. Jeb's done so three times!"

Jeb charged.

Georgio backpedaled away from Jeb's lunging swings and misses.

"Getting hot, isn't it, Jeb!" Georgio said.

Jeb's sword clattered to the ground as he fell to his knees and cried, "Sweet Mother of Bish! Water! I yield! Water!" The thug was blowing his smoldering hands.

"Somebody piss on the baby's hands!"

Billip strolled over to Jeb with a bucket of water and said, "Ah- Ah –Ah … pay first, then take this bucket and get your arses out of here!"

"Georgio! Drop the sword; you won!" Mikkel exclaimed.

Georgio was stunned. His hand kept burning until it was almost done. He looked over at the barkeep, who nodded, shook his head, and walked away.

He flung the blade from his palm, felt his legs buckle, and then the strong hands of Mikkel dragged him away. He thought he heard someone cry out something about underlings as he started puking in the floor.

13

T HORN SUNK ONE BLADE INTO the plank floor were Lefty was a blink ago. The halfling boy leaped from table top to table top as the big rogue ran roughshod through the tavern.

"Somebody grab that little bastard," Thorn yelled.

The big thief's face was pink and white, the raw skin exposed. It was pretty clear Thorn blamed them for his demise. But it had been Kam who shoved him into the fireplace, not them. Of course, they'd had a little something to do with the fact that he was jailed. Gillem had walloped him over the head, and Kam's spell had silenced him for a while. But it seemed Thorn's corrupt connections had won out. He was free to avenge himself.

"Settle down, Thorn. We've got nothing to do with you!" Gillem said from atop a table. "I'm still the Master here, not you. Sheath those swords or be trialed!"

Thorn lowered his short swords by his side and sneered under his burnt and crooked nose as he walked towards the table.

"The Bone I will, Gillem, you little halfling toad!"

Gillem ducked under the first cut and leaped over the other.

Lefty threw a wine bottle that careened off the side of Thorn's head.

"Blast you two rodents! Somebody grab them! That's an order! They're traitors! They left me behind!"

Gillem leapt to another table and surveyed the room. Lefty watched from behind a chair. There was a shift in the room as everyone got a closer look at Thorn's face.

"They watched the woman burn me and did not come to my aid," Thorn whined. "Had me jailed, my lips sealed by magic, and dragged away by the Watch." He spat. "Gillem, you're not the thief you used to be. Nothing more than an aging mushroom."

Gillem stood his ground, stuck his pipe in between his lips and laughed.

"Is that so, coming from the man who guards a door? One trip up top, and you come back roasted like a log, blaming me."

The older halfling had the room's full attention now. His voice the father of all fathers. A thief among thieves. "How embarrassing that must be for you. And naturally, being the bully that you are, you take the fight to the tiniest man in the room, Lefty." Gillem puffed a smoke ring. "And when you can't manage to lay a finger on him, you come after me, and asking for the aid of your brethren as well. I'm ashamed. Ashamed for you and ashamed for the thieves' guild."

Thorn's swords were quavering in his hands, his knuckles white, his face full of shame and anger.

"Why you little liar! Fraud! You're cohorts with that wench up there! When I speak to Palos, I'll prove it."

The rogues in the house looked back and forth between the two men and each other. Lefty remained still. He knew Palos wasn't going to take Gillem's word for anything anymore. He could tell. The way the man spoke to Master Gillem was often harsh and uncalled for. It was clear to him the Prince of Thieves didn't like that halfling anymore.

"Talk all you want, Thorn. Please do. I'm sure Prince Palos has nothing better to do than hear your petty excuses. It was my plan that snatched the child, and my plan that got the woman here. You come back with nothing but a sack full of blame …"

Lefty looked down at his watery feet on the floor.

Oh no! What's wrong? Why are my feet sweating?

He scanned the room. No other daggers were drawn. *Where's Diller?* He looked up at the top of the stairs. The man was there, toothpick and all, a devious look on his face, but he wasn't alone. Lefty's tongue clove to the roof of his mouth as he tried to yell out.

"… Ha!" Gillem continued, chest out, hitching his thumbs in his pants. "I'm sure he'll enjoy that more than gold."

Clatch-Zip!

Thorn jumped five feet backward. Gillem stood with eyes as big as the moon as he looked down at the bolt protruding from his chest.

Clatch-Zip!

The next one caught him clean in the throat. Gillem swayed left and right as the pipe fell from his mouth and clunked on the table. Lefty caught him as he fell, and searched his eyes, only to find an empty blank stare. Now the only friend he had left in the world was dead. *No! Just like that! How? No!* He looked up and saw the leering face of Palos. Cold and crazy.

"The trial has begun and ended, in the favor of my newest Master, Thorn!" Palos said, handing Diller back over his crossbow. "Now, bring me the halfling boy, and dispose of the other one in the cemetery beneath the water."

No hope. Drained of all vitality, Lefty was limp as several rough hands dragged him up the stairs.

Kam sat, chin dipped, huddled in a rocking chair by the fire, arms folded across her chest, rubbing her shoulders. She was an empty vessel as Palos got up to check the commotion outside.

"Don't move an inch," he ordered, slipping a thin dagger through the belt on his robes and strutting to the door.

Think, Kam!

Fear ruined her hopes as Palos crossed the threshold of the door, his back to her, but Diller, long and sly, stood just outside the doorway, leering at her from time to time. She ran her fingers between her neck and the choker Palos had imprisoned her magic with. It was a wispy thing that tightened like a garrote if she tugged on it.

"Ugh!" she growled.

Time was running out for her; she could feel it. Not only her, but Erin as well. It was only a matter of time before Palos tired of her, unless of course, she played his little strumpet. *No! I'll die first!* She scanned the room. Certainly Palos had hidden things that she could use. He'd just produced a dagger from nowhere. That meant there had to be something else. Paintings, a great sword, etchings in the marble mantle, fanciful rugs over a polished hardwood floor, statues, candelabras and more.

"Hmmm …," she muttered, eyes flicking towards Diller, who at the moment seemed to be enthralled with the commotion on the lower floor. There were marble ashtrays as big as her hand. A poker for stoking the wood and coals in the fireplace. An onyx figurine of a part woman, part fox stood over a foot tall on a pedestal. It seemed there were some things, unconventional things, she could use to bash his head in, after all. She picked at her lip. Then what? She'd still need help to remove the choker, and how would she escape after that? *It can't be hopeless.*

Clatch-Zip!

She jerked in her chair, biting her lip. Immediately, her thigh began to throb, and her heart pounded like a fearful rabbit's.

Clatch-Zip!

She jerked again, more so than the last time. She pulled her legs up and curled into the chair. She heard Palos's words to the men below before he strolled back in, sneering and angry.

"Good!" he said, walking in and taking a seat at the table. "You didn't move. I'd hate to have to cut a toe off, but I've had it done before. Now, make yourself presentable. We're having company."

A lurking figure filled the doorway. It was Thorn. He leered at her like a hungry dog as he stepped inside and took a seat at the table. *I should have killed him.*

Diller followed, chewing his toothpick, dragging Lefty by his collar like a heavy sack.

Kam felt her heart sink. *Is he dead? No, it can't be!* Her nose started to run as the door was closed from the outside. She sniffled.

"Don't start blathering, Kam." Palos took a quaff of wine. "Your little friend is alive, for now. But, I'm sorry to say, it seems Master Gillem has had a most unfortunate accident." Thorn and Diller snickered. "He impaled himself on a pair of crossbow bolts. One of the most bizarre things I ever saw."

Kam's eyes drifted to Palos's. There was nothing but the cold-blooded look of a butcher in his eyes. He enjoyed seeing her suffer. He thrived on his power over people. She could feel it. She looked over at Lefty as Diller lifted him to his feet by the scruff of his neck. The little liar's feet were dripping wet, and his swollen eyes were glued on the floor. She almost felt bad for him. He sobbed. Her heart opened as the boy stood there … broken. She turned away, head towards the burning coals under the mantle. She realized it couldn't have all been his fault.

"Kam, Dear, please come and sit at the table with the rest of the family. We've much to discuss," Palos said, stretching his arms over his head and yawning. "Whew … the hot bath you gave me took a lot out of me."

Slime! She rocked forward, shuffled over, and slid into a chair, head down. She'd never been in the presence of people she actually hated, and now there were three of them. The most hated men in the world.

"When can I see Erin?" she said, trying to hide the quivering in her voice. "You were about to send for her before all the commotion."

She jumped as Palos rapped his fist on the table.

"That can wait! We've business to discuss. It seems Master Thorn has brought a different story forward as opposed to the one spun by the former Master Gillem and his apprentice … er … Lefty."

"What would you know?" she said, the fire rising in her voice. "Both men are liars. What difference does the truth make at this point? You have me. Does it really matter how I got here?"

"Well …"

She sat up and pulled her shoulders back and twirled her hair.

"What does this roasted oaf have to offer you that I cannot, Prince Palos? It seems quite peculiar."

"Why, you!" Thorn said, drawing his swords.

"Stop!" Palos ordered. "Thorn, my woman speaks. You do not. Continue, my dearest. Please."

Diller covered his mouth, eyes glimmering from beyond.

"This ugly fool tried to seduce me. Pawed at me like a hungry lion."

Palos's eyes narrowed.

"I defended myself. Launched him into the fire. It was Gillem who stopped me from turning this lout … that you call Master … into a charred log. I should have killed him." She clenched her fists and shook them at him. "But Gillem had him spared. I melted his lips and ears, a minor incantation, and had him dragged off by the City Watch."

He shifted back toward Palos, who sat slunk forward, eyes glaring at Thorn with suspicion.

"Prince, I never laid a finger on her," Thorn said, his eyes shifting back and forth between her and him. Behind him, Diller lowered a crossbow on his back. "I swear, my lord. She—"

Palos sprang on top of the table. "She was to be defiled by no one, Thorn!" Thorn stood at rigid attention as Palos poked the tip of his dagger at his nose. "Which hand did he touch you with, dearest Kam?"

"Both, my Prince."

"Hold them out, Thorn."

"B-But …"

"Hold them out! Diller!"

She could hear Diller's finger squeezing the trigger.

Thorn lifted his hands, palms up, parallel to the ground.

"Yes, Milord."

Stab! Stab!

Stab! Stab!

Like a striking snake, Palos dotted two holes in each palm.

Thorn's bloody hands quavered in the air, fear and agony growing on his face.

"Easy, Thorn," Palos looked down on him and patted his shoulder. "If the daggers had been tip triggered, you'd be dead from the venom already," Palos said, needling the bronze snake-scaled hilt beneath the fang-like blade as he tucked it away from sight.

"Uh … thank you, Prince."

Palos whirled towards Kam and said, "Is there anything you wish to add, Dearest?"

Kam shook her head. There had been enough blood shed for the day. Another death, even the likes of Thorn's, was not something she cared to partake in.

"Go …, Master Thorn, and patch your wounds. I want both Diller and you to return back to your posts."

"And the halfling, Pal—"

Palos shot Diller an angry stare.

"Er … Prince Palos?" Diller corrected, shifting his toothpick from one side to the other.

"Oh …" Palos said looking down at the tiny sad-eyed boy as he resumed his seat at the table. "Bind him up. Leave him here, and let him mourn the loss of his kindred friend." He drummed his pudgy fingers on the table. "Thorn, I've had a change of heart, given the evidence presented. See to it Master Gillem is given a proper burial. After all, he was my own mentor, and it's possible I'll regret my actions tomorrow, or next week maybe. But remember this, you over-sized rogue. My doubt can be quite deadly."

He's mad! Kam struggled with the fear that coiled within her belly. She ached from head to toe. Somewhere, her baby girl hungered. She could feel it. Within her, she had the power to stop it, but couldn't use it without killing herself. She knew full well what the collar around her neck did: it used her power against her.

"Have a drink, Dearest. You look quite thirsty," Palos said, taking another guzzle of wine, the gentility returning to his voice. "You see, running a kingdom, albeit a dark and secret one, has many consequences, and a ruler like me can never be too careful." He reached over and patted her hand and licked his lips. "But being in charge gives you all the power you want and so many, many rewards."

Kam swallowed hard and gave a slight nod while Diller shackled Lefty with a network of rope like chains made from absidium, a thin metal that was stronger than hammered iron. Lefty stood in silence, narrow shoulders sagging, his mop of yellow hair cast down … defeated. The boy had come to the City of Three like a shining beacon of life, but nervous. Adept in magic, quick-witted and sure-footed, a promising little sparrow—now with both wings broken.

"Where do you want him?" Diller said, pulling Lefty up on his tip toes by his hair.

"Hmmm …" Palos said, looking up from the coins he was stacking. "Well, hitch him by the foot of my tub over there, and don't leave any slack in it, either."

Kam didn't turn as she heard Diller dragging Lefty away. A wave of guilt washed over her. The boy had lost his real family once already, to the underlings. He'd lost his friends from the Magi Roost as well. Now, his third family had betrayed him. *Maybe he didn't know better, but he should have. Blast Venir for leaving those boys with me!*

As Diller started to leave, she asked, "Can I please see my baby now, Prince Palos?"

"Can I please see my baby now, Prince Palos?" he said, imitating her voice.

"I've done everything you've asked of me."

"I've done everything you've asked —"

"Palos!" She rose from her chair. "You gave me your word! Now bring me my baby!"

"NO!" he slammed his fists into the table. "NO! NO! NO! NO! NO!"

She saw a feverish look in his eye, and his steady hands began to tremble.

"Diller!" he shouted. "Bind her as well. I need rest."

He got up, calmly walked into his bedroom, and closed the door.

He's crazy!

Diller was coming her way, chains wrapped around his hands, toothpick rolling in and out of his mouth.

"Alone at last …"

14

T HE MARKETPLACE WAS HUMMING WITH activity as the merchants hoisted their voices high in the air, competing to sell their wares. The people of Bone, hundreds, a rugged lot, were well prepared for anything. They stumbled, rumbled, bristled and hissed at one another, fighting over fruits and metal pots. The pickpockets and urchins were out in full force, squeezing their fingers into tiny crevices and snatching purses one at a time. It was all expected in the course of doing daily business in the harshest city in the world. After all, the citizens of Bone were prepared for anything, so they said, until today.

A woman shrieked. The crowd slowed, heads looking around for the source of the outburst that was suddenly cut short.

KA-CHOW!

Something exploded. A cart of fruit was thrown high in the air. A unified gasp followed as all eyes turned to the sky. There, Verbard hovered, feeding on their sudden fear. Each face was a puzzled knot of confusion. He let them have it.

A frizzy brown-haired woman holding a large melon gawped at his appearance a split second before she exploded. Verbard and his fellow magi floated above chaos, spraying their deadly magic from one street corner to the other. Juegen soldiers, led by Jottenhiem, black armor glistening in the sunlight, spilled from the alley's shadows like a pack of hungry wolves. The census in Bone would be lower this year. Men, women and urchins fell beneath the precise cuts of underling blades. Necks were opened, hands and arms lopped off.

Eep snatched a boy from the ground, black wings buzzing as he lifted him high in the air and dropped him into the fray below. Behind Verbard, another mage summoned his power. The sewers, cracks and crevices began to fill with large ants and cockroaches, insects of all kinds. They scurried over all things living and dead, a terrifying army of another kind.

The badoon underlings, naked from the waist to the shoulders, fired missile upon missile into even the fleetest of feet, sending their bearers reeling to the ground. A heavy man with hunched over shoulders, bolts piercing his back, waded through the desperate crowd, grabbed a heavy rope at the corner, and started ringing a brass metal bell.

Let them come, Verbard thought, silver eyes charged with energy.

As he floated over the chaos where the streets began to slicken with blood, he felt nothing but satisfaction. As Jottenhiem led a wedge of blood coated Juegen soldiers, the humans kept piling up. But fear outweighed their forces, and within moments of the beginning of the onslaught, the entire marketplace was cleared. Like rats, the humans had disappeared into their dark little holes. Only the dead and the twitching remained.

Verbard and his men surveyed their surroundings. The small buildings had every door secured and every window shut.

Jottenhiem put an ailing man out of his misery as he shouted up in underling, "What are your orders, Lord Verbard? We're ready for more!"

Eep, come!

The one-eyed imp hummed to his side with an arm hanging out of his razor sharp mouth.

Scout. Let me know what comes. If anything.

The imp nodded and buzzed away.

Brethren magi! Set fire to everything you see!

The black robed underlings fanned out over the market square, toes hovering over the ground as high as the buildings. All hands, twelve in all, ignited with fire. Verbard could feel the radiant heat of pouring flame erupting from the magi surrounding him. Below him, the Juegen and Badoon decapitated the dead and tossed the heads through the windows.

Excellent!

Verbard rose higher in the air overlooking the vast city and the castle tops that surrounded the walls. He felt small in the presence of it all. Below him, the smoke and fires were growing, but it was little more than a campfire compared to the rest of it all. His strike seemed futile compared to what was needed to take this city. *Suicide mission.* Master Sinway couldn't be serious. There were so many people.

Eep hummed along his side, crunching an arm between his teeth before swallowing.

"A large host of armored riders on horseback come riding under Royal banners."

"How many?"

"Two score or more," Eep hissed, wringing his clawed hands.

An arc of light struck Eep full force in the chest and sent him spiraling downward, his small body disappearing into the smoke. Verbard felt the power of many minds converging on him at once. *Suicide Mission.*

Inside Castle Almen, another battle raged. The human soldiers fought hard but were incredibly slow. Kierway's sword flashed twice for every one of their heavy strokes. He sank his blade deep into the heart of one man and sliced out the neck of another. It seemed he and the Vicious, as well as the Juegen and Magi, had come upon the barracks confined within Castle Almen. Their surprise was short-lived. The humans were well fortified and prepared, barricading the tunnels and sealing the doors. Still, in such an enormous place it would take quite some time to find what they were looking for. That's the other reason the magi came.

"Find me that cleric," Kierway ordered, withdrawing his blade from the armored belly of his last victim.

At his side, the Vicious, the black hulking brute with skin as hard as armor, was crushing the neck of another soldier whose feet twitched above the ground.

It felt good, killing all these men. His natural enemies. His most hated foes. But he was in unfamiliar territory. The walls were closing in as time elapsed. He had to find that cleric and get those keys before the Royals, and their total garrison, cut them off completely. Based off all that he had seen, there must be more than seventy fighting men, if not a hundred, who guarded the castle, and they wouldn't all be push overs.

A mage with bright blue eyes drifted in from the door of another room and beckoned towards him.

Kierway smiled, looked over to his soldiers, and said, "Follow me."

Clatch-Zip!

Kierway ducked as a bolt ripped past his head.

Clatch-Zip!

Clatch-Zip!

The blue-eyed mage was shot down, spilling to the floor in a heap, two bolts embedded in his head. Three soldiers armored in plate mail emerged on the other side of the room, tossing down their heavy crossbows as they drew their bastard swords.

"Bish blast my eyes!" one of them yelled, "Underlings in Bone. I'd never have believed it if I weren't seeing it for myself."

"They bleed the same as men!" said another.

"Attack," Kierway ordered in underling.

The Juegen soldiers rushed in, swords flashing out as they cut into their foes. The men, tall and heavy, leaned into the smaller people. Broad arcing swings came from heavy handed blows as the Juegen shifted and ducked away.

The armored Royal soldiers chopped down, their blades clanging from the stone floor. The underlings shifted their stances, swords licking out like snakes, glancing off the heavy mail of the bigger fighters.

"Put your weight on them. They're small and fast, but we can wear them down," a Royal said, taking a swing into the chest and knocking down a Juegen fighter. The underling rolled back to his feet.

"They don't bleed," one soldier yelled.

"If you can't cut them, stab them!"

Kierway rolled his eyes. The underling armor was as hard as it was light, but it didn't make them invulnerable. He was running out of time. If more heavy soldiers rushed in, they'd be cornered. He needed to keep his small group together. He chittered an order. The Juegen pressed the man left of center, blades licking out like a pit of striking snakes.

Kierway attacked. In one fluid motion, he sidestepped one soldier's swing and jammed his blade backwards into the lower abdomen of the other. One soldier remained, backing towards the door as the Juegen peeled away the armor and skin of the other with their swords. One second three men stood valiantly, in the next only one remained. The soldier glanced at Kierway, a determined look under his helmet.

"You're fast, even for a little one, I'll grant you that—"

The Vicious leapt over Kierway's back and landed on top of the soldier.

Wham! Wham! Wham!

The Vicious punched the soldier's head into the wall, denting the metal and crushing the man's skull.

"Well done," Kierway commented, sheathing his sword.

Another underling, eyes bright like sapphires, glided to Kierway's side.

"I think we've located the man you're looking for," it said, extending its hand.

Kierway gazed at a vision on the underling mage's palm. A vision of Sefron the cleric was there. Brow sweating, belly bulging over his tiny belt, glossy eyes filled with fear.

"That's him. Lead the way!"

Five more heavily armored soldiers spilled into the barracks' front doorway.

"Take them out!" he said to the three Juegen soldiers.

They burst into action, hurling their bodies and swinging their swords into the big men with heavy arms. Their chitters were filled with rage as they tried to whittle the force of men down one by one while Kierway, the Vicious and the two remaining magi made their escape through the castle passages with the sound of heavy boots coming from all directions.

15

WRIGGLING IN THE HEAVY ROPES of the net, Venir managed to get his hands around the neck of one underling soldier and squeeze. The underling's orange eyes bulged out of its sockets while it stabbed into Venir's arm with a dagger. Venir held tight as he and the other trapped underlings were dragged over the rugged terrain.

The underlings thrashed, hissed and howled, their sharp claws stretching through the heavy netting trying to carve off a piece of his hide.

Venir upped the pressure, fingers crushing his victim's windpipe.

"Tell your fiend brother good-bye, you black jackals!"

He felt the underling's throat collapse. The remaining brood surged within their bonds.

"Have at me, then!" he yelled.

Venir wrenched the dagger from his arm and sawed at the cords. His muscles tightened in his neck at a sucking and shrieking sound that froze the marrow in his bones. The underlings were dragging him toward another enormous spider ahead that feasted on a horse and rider. He sawed faster.

All around him, the sounds of battle still surged. The underlings chittered in anger and pain, and the Royal Riders thundered past, shouting battle cries at the top of their lungs.

KA-CHOW!

A wave of energy knocked several from their horses.

"Bone!"

Venir could feel the tide of battle turning. The shock and surprise had worn off, and the underlings, they were a well-oiled machine: quick, efficient and deadly. From all directions, they swarmed the men three to one.

"Cut faster, Idiot!"

Venir cut through one piece of the net, but it would take at least ten more to free him.

Nearby, an underling squirmed closer, clawed fingers grabbing his shield. It began pulling him back, its rancid breath on his ear. In his other hand, Brool was useless, bound up in the netting. Another cord broke.

A Royal Rider cried out, "Retreat! Retreat!" waving a banner from atop a white horse.

"Slat! You cowards!" Venir yelled, sawing faster as the underling tugged harder on his shield, stretching him back.

He caught the rider in the corner of his eye, spinning around his horse, and chopping down into an underling with his sword.

"Over here, Rider!" Venir yelled again.

The man peered through the dust as Venir was dragged right past him. The man pointed at him, saluted and galloped away.

"Bone!"

It seemed it was down to Venir; the remains of the decimated army of Royal Riders was now in full retreat.

"Cowardly Royals!"

He cut through the third cord, then the fourth. Something blocked out the suns. Above, a hairy belly was straddled over him with a man in its mouth. A wrenching sound tore at his ears as the creature sucked a rider down to a husk. He cut the 5th cord and then the 6th. *Got to escape!*

The helm began to burn like fire on his head.

Visions of being buried head first in the dirt leapt forward in his mind. Not that again. Not ever. He cut through the 7th and 8th cords. Being sucked down to the marrow didn't sit well with him, either. *Cut faster!* The feisty underling grabbed hold of the eyelets of his helmet, nails cutting the skin around his eyes. A series of angry chitters surrounded him from everywhere. He looked up. Underlings surrounded him. Weapons raised, gemstone eyes glowing as they began pressing closer. *Saw or die!*

Please don't be hungry. Slim struggled in his bonds, but he wasn't going anywhere. *I've got to escape!* He could hear his heart pounding in his chest. He took a deep breath. The cloth on his face kept his lips from being sealed, and the spell he'd cast allowed him and Adanna to breathe much longer. *Just need enough time to get my energy back, and I'll remove these insects from Bish forever.*

"Mrmph!" he exclaimed beneath the cocoon.

A spider bit deep into his ankle, setting his leg on fire as the sucking began. Slim felt the blood being drained away from his body.

NOOOOOOO!

Excruciating. Slim's eyes fluttered in his skull, each second pure agony. He shuddered inside his cocoon, convulsed, then his body stopped. The pain was gone now. The spider was sucking on his limbs. As ghastly as that sounded, it was a merciful predator after all. Their poison subdued whatever man or beast they got hold of, but Slim's body slackened as a mild euphoria settled inside him.

Don't fall asleep. Don't fall asleep. Don't fall asleep.

Slim had never taken into consideration that he'd be eaten by a spider. He always figured he'd die of old age one day. After all, he was never really one to get in trouble. He just liked to help out now and again. He jerked in his web-made cocoon. A shot of fire raced from his toe to his brain as the spider's fang bit farther down.

That will keep you awake!

Now, the battle of wills began. The mind of a man versus the instinctive needs of an insect. Slim felt all sensation leave below his knees. He meditated on his elements. As a healer, a man born attached to the mystic powers of the world, Slim could draw upon the power of the living. The grass, the trees, the birds, even men. At the moment, the pit he lived in was barren of any living forces other than him, Adanna and the spiders, which made it all the tougher to renew his inner power.

Don't fall asleep, or you're dead, Slim the Cleric!

The spell he had cast to keep air in the cowls over his and Adanna's heads wouldn't last much longer. He'd already felt the air beginning to thin. It was dark and warm where he was, his only company now was the sharp sucking sounds from the sand spider gnawing on his calf.

Sssckt! Sssckt! Sssckt!

The numbness rolled over his waist and into his belly.

Maybe this isn't such a bad way to go. Mmmm …

Sssckt! Sssckt! Sssckt!

He thought of Venir. Adanna. All the lives the underlings had taken. The tiny fire inside his mind began to twinkle.

Got to fight it. Fight or die! Fight or die! Or, become a beetle. Mmmm … Flying was enjoyable.

Slim felt himself sinking deeper into a bath of warm goo. *Maybe the spider won't suck all the blood from me. See you tomorrow, Bish. Or never again. What does it matter?*

The fire in his mind began to dim as his lips twitched with the last word of power he remembered. *I better use this before it's too late. Ah … but just another minute. It feels so nice.*

Sssckt! Sssckt! Sssckt!

Zip! Zip! Zip!

The dagger fell from Venir's hand as a small crossbow bolt punctured through it. He cursed. He'd just cut the ninth cord. Another bolt ricocheted from his helmet, and one stuck in his calf.

"Bone!" he roared.

A spider abdomen loomed over his head, and dozens of underlings had him surrounded. He thrashed like a fish in the net that held him. Brool, still hot in his grip, was useless. His eyelets still smoldered like black fire. He'd never been at the mercy of this many underlings before. They had him.

The spider's face lowered before him.

"I'll make your belly sour, you eight-legged underling!" he said, kicking in the net.

The underlings approached, spears lowered, wicked faces chittering back and forth, a look of astonishment in their eyes. Two of them, heavy laden in black armor, approached with spears. Venir fought harder against his bonds. They cocked their elbows back.

"I see you got big plans for those toothpicks! Turn around and I'll show you how to use them," he said, tugging at the bolt protruding from his hand. "Slat! I suppose this is it."

Venir's mortality began to soak in. He was trapped like an animal. A hundred hunters had boxed him in. He was certain he wasn't going to live a moment longer. He just wanted to take a few more with him, however.

"Fight and die." He looked into the horizon. "So it is."

Venir felt the ground rumble. The underlings' heads snapped up. A chorus of surprised chitters was smothered by the sound of galloping horses. Two columns stormed through the camp. The first Royal Rider plunged a lance into the face of the giant spider. The spider reared up and caught two spears in its belly just as the horses trampled over it.

The underlings dove, rolled and died under the thundering hooves of the horses. The riders raced by, spears ripping through the air. One underling caught a spear clean in the throat. Another caught two spears in the chest.

Venir yelled out, "Get me out of this net you Royal Bas—*urk!*"

As the last two riders rode past, they reached down and grabbed the net, dragging Venir and the surviving underlings behind them. Being dragged by horses was a painful way to go. It seemed the Riders had a harsh death in mind for the underlings as their small bodies scraped and bumped over the rough stones, faces screeching in terror. Venir balled up, trying to keep his legs up as he was dragged roughshod over the dirt.

"Blast you, Royals!" he said through gritted teeth.

Behind him, the underling camp was falling farther away. After a mind numbing mile, the Riders came to a stop. Beasts were nickering and stamping their hooves. Horses, all noble, all good, were never comfortable around underlings. As Venir wiped the dust and dirt that caked his eyes, he saw half a dozen well-armed men standing around him.

"Kill them. Kill them all," a rider ordered, his voice full of authority. A gold crescent stained with blood gleamed from atop his helmet.

"Even the warrior?" another rider said, hoisting his spear.

"No, you idiot! Kill the underlings. Why in Bish would we kill a man?" the commander said.

The remaining underlings fell quickly as the spears jabbed into them more times than were needed. Weighted down under the net, Venir struggled to rise.

"Someone cut this big bastard free! Do I have to do everything around here?" the Commander said, unsheathing a broad hunting knife on his belt. In three quick slices, the net fell away.

Venir rose to his full height and said, "Nice knife."

The Commander snorted under his red-brown mustache that hung past his chin and said, "Nice axe," eyeing Brool and stepping back.

Venir groaned. Everything hurt. He could barely stand. His arms and legs were raw. He looked back over his shoulder.

"Why aren't the underlings pursuing us?" he said, looking around at the remaining Royal Riders. There looked to be about thirty or so of them left, all blood splattered and wounded, some broken.

"They won't be coming. They've got more to worry about than us. Look over yonder horizon," the Commander said, pointing towards the northwest. The sound of Royal Battle horns now carried through the air as the banners of more Royal Riders appeared on the crest of the dusty hills.

"My gratitude, Commander," Venir said, nodding "I didn't figure on any Royals coming back for me."

"Ha!" the Commander said, reaching up and slapping him back. "I don't know where you came from, Man, but we'd all be dead if not for your timely arrival. Those underlings took to you like stink on a pig, but it didn't do them much good. I swear I saw you chop down ten of them. I've never seen a man as big as you move so fast. And the axe." He couldn't hide the incredulity in his voice. "It cuts though bone like butter."

"Underling bone that is," Venir said, grimacing as he plucked the bolt from his calf.

"Let us suture that wound, er … what is your name, warrior?"

"Venir," he said, pushing the other bolt through one side of his hand an out the other. "And I don't need stitches. I need a horse!"

"But you need to stop the bleeding," the Commander said, waving a pair of soldiers over. "Those Riders over there will have the underlings routed. This isn't our first assault."

"I don't care about that. I've got friends taken prisoner in there. Now, give me a horse, Commander!"

"Underlings take no prisoners. No chance they're alive."

Venir glared down on the man.

"So be it!" The Commander handed him over the reins of a big brown mare. Venir grabbed the saddle with his bloody hand and swung up with a moan. The Royal Riders bore down on the underlings from the northwest and ran clean through the underlings' first defensive formation.

"Yah!" Venir said, digging his heels into the horse's sides and galloping away.

"Get back on your horses, Soldiers!" the commander ordered. "It's time to finish what we started! Yah!"

Venir didn't hear a thing but the wind whistling through his helmet as the horse galloped in full charge. The underlings were already scurrying into their black holes, possibly dragging Adanna and her mother down with them. And where was Slim? He didn't remember seeing any beetles on the battlefield. He had a feeling something was horribly wrong. *Got to find them!*

16

"Seize her! She killed Lord Almen!" Melegal shouted, pointing at Jarla the Brigand Queen.

"What!" she exclaimed, freezing in her tracks as the sentries surrounded her.

His mind was still glowing beneath his cap.

"Take her down, Men! Kill her if you have to!" he ordered.

A half dozen sentries armed with spears and swords formed a line between him and her. Jarla's face was a mask of rage as her twisted lips fought to find the right words to say. Hah! Melegal was in charge now. After all, he was the head Detective of the Royal Almen house. And what had Lorda Almen ordered him to do? Kill Jarla.

"A hundred gold to whoever can bring me her head! She's a murderer. An Assassin from the guilds. A defiler from another Royal house."

His words carried. Melegal could feel the power he had over the simple minds of the 'take orders first, ask questions later' sentries. He had her right where he wanted. Jarla the Brigand Queen was fighting for her life. Her blade flashed and parried as the small force of men closed in on her. Left and right she went, cut off from every direction she wanted to go. Melegal folded his arms across his chest and watched as the men began picking the woman apart. But where was Brak? Something blocked the suns' light from the windows above.

Move!

Melegal sprung right.

"Oooof!" He was too late. A mound of man and muscle pounced on top of him, driving him to the ground, knocking the wind from his lungs. Melegal squirmed onto his back only to face the berserk face of Brak. The slumped over figure who had been begging for food minutes earlier was now pure monster.

Do something before he breaks your head apart!

Mindless and savage, the boy-turned-man raised both his fists over his head.

Melegal pointed the dart launchers into Brak's chest and belly.

Have to do this!

Brak brought his fists down with all his might.

Whoof!

Two soldiers almost as big as Brak barreled into him, knocking him to the ground. Melegal gasped for air, crawling on his knees. There was a sharp crack in the air. He whipped around. Brak bent another man's head over his neck. *Slat!* Melegal wasn't going to stick around to see what happened next. The berserker was already wrapping his fingers around the hilt of a sword and charging into the nearest warrior. *Move far, move fast!*

Melegal scanned the room. Two sentries had fallen under the deadly strokes of Jarla's sword. *No!* She moved with the feline grace of a panther and struck with the power of a cobra. A man screamed out as his sword hand was sliced off at the wrist, gaping at the sight of all the blood. Up in the bleachers, another commotion was stirring.

Sefron!

The slimy cleric waddled down the stairs, two men in full armor guarding his back shoulders as he made his way down the steps to where Lord Almen had fallen. Melegal slid out of sight along the wall.

Slat!

For all he knew, the cleric could save the man, and he couldn't let that happen. He couldn't let Jarla survive, either, but time was running out. His nose twitched as Sefron hunched down over Lord Almen's body and began to mutter something. Lord Almen's fingers clutched in the air. Melegal's heart lurched in his chest. *Blasted cleric!*

He stuck his hand out, pulled his sleeve back from his wrist, and squeezed the trigger on the dart launchers.

Zing! Zing! Zing! Zing! Zing! Zing!

Sefron jumped up, squealing like a pig, clutching at the darts embedded in his neck and face. The two soldiers reached out for the ailing cleric, who staggered down the steps, smacked into the arena's rail, and fell over the wall.

Yes!

He turned his attention back over to Brak. The over-sized young man stood in the center of the arena, coated in blood and gore, staring around in wide-eyed wonder. The monster was gone. Only the young man remained. A tiny little figure raced out to meet him. It was the Slerg girl named Jubilee.

"Come on, Brak! Come on!" she said, grasping his fingers and pulling him towards the doors at the bottom.

The two soldiers were over the wall, one helping Sefron to his feet, the other, long sword ready, was heading towards Brak and the girl.

On the other side of the arena, a badly limping Jarla had whittled six men down to two. Blood was running down her leg from a nasty gash on her thigh while she grimaced and parried each and every blow. *She can't survive this. She can't!*

Melegal yelled at the fully armored soldier and pointed at her, saying, "Finish that assassin! I'll take care of the mute!"

The soldier stopped for a moment, then took another step towards Brak and Jubilee.

Melegal stuck his finger out again and said, "Now!"

Sefron screeched out, "Get me back over that wall!" He whirled back towards Melegal, plucking a dart from his face, and added, "Curse you, Thief! I curse you and the womb you crawled out of."

Melegal drew the sleeve back over his other hand and raised it towards Sefron's throat.

"Not if I curse you first, Dead Man!"

The soldier stepped between them as Sefron scrambled over the wall.

A door at the top of the stairs exploded open, and a dark energy filled the room.

Melegal crouched back along the wall. A black creature as big as a man, cat-faced and knotted in muscle, stepped through the threshold.

An underling! It cannot be possible!

An underling with short black hair and eyes like burning iron glided in behind the Vicious, two razor sharp swords unlike anything he'd ever seen hanging in his hands. Melegal was already moving for the door when two cloaked underlings floated inside, fingertips glowing with power.

Run, Melegal! Run!

Jubilee was pushing Brak through the nearest doorway, but it was Melegal who shoved them through. He closed the door and barred it shut.

"Follow me!" he snapped.

Down the corridor they went. Brak stumbled along, arrows still embedded in his back, moaning with hunger. Melegal led them down into the dungeons and snatched some shackles from the wall. They all fought for breath. *Think, Thief!* He had to come up with something fast. He also had to figure out what was going on. What were underlings doing inside the castle?

"Listen to me; we have to act quickly. I need you to put these on Brak."

"No," Jubilee shot back.

"It's the safest way for me to lead you through. We'll be stopped. There'll be questions."

Brak's eyes narrowed, but he couldn't hide the exhaustion on his face. The man had just killed a dozen men as easy as a devious child could drown a dozen kittens.

"Brak," Melegal said, trying to sound calm and not in a hurry. "I lied. I know your father, Venir. I know him well. If he were here, he'd tell you to listen and do as you're told."

"Don't listen to him, Brak. He's an Almen. Almens are liars," Jubilee said, tugging at his hand.

"So are Slergs, Little Dear. And I'm not a Royal." He poked her in the chest. "I'm an overgrown urchin that was once a slave that swabbed the blood from the dungeons in your dubious castle." He slapped the first cuff on Brak. "If we live through this, I'd be happy to describe each and every last detail, but for now, we better go ... or die."

Brak looked down on Melegal as he slapped on the second wrist cuff and said, "My back hurts."

Melegal looked around at the two arrows in his back and said, "Just a couple of scratches. We'll patch you up later."

A chorus of screams was followed by a series of explosions coming from the corridor they'd just cleared.

"Let's move!"

They were all running in step, through one corridor and down another. In one doorway and out the other. A pair of dead Royals lay dead on the floor, gashed and bloody. The sounds of booted feet seemed to be echoing from every corner, and shouts were haranguing out from down the halls.

"Get in here," Melegal said, shoving the both of them into a closet.

Four sentries in chainmail hauberks drew their broad swords and came at him. Not every person knew who he was, as most of his dealings with the Almens had been discreet. Melegal held up his hand and pulled out his brooch.

The men stopped and eyed him warily.

"Detective," one managed, eyes shifting in every direction at once, "what business do you have in the Castle?"

"That's no concern of yours. At the present, mine is self-preservation. Yours is to stop the underlings that are running through this place like jackals in a hen house."

KA-BOOM!

Paintings fell from the walls and vases full of flowers tipped from their pedestals and crashed on the floor. All the soldiers were looking around at one another, their faces turning as white as their teeth.

Melegal continued, "I believe that's from the Arena." He clapped his hands together. "Are all the exits sealed?"

Drat! There'd be no way to smuggle Brak and Jubilee out.

"We'll catch those black fiends yet! Now go!" he ordered. *So willing to listen, those sentries. If only more people did as they were told.*

"Yes, Detective," they said, trotting down the corridor and out of sight.

Melegal opened the closet.

"Come on!"

"Where are we going?" Jubilee asked, her little toes on his heels. "They said all the exits are closed."

"And so they are, as far as they know, but if you have any better ideas, I'd like to hear them."

"Well—"

Melegal grabbed her by the wrist, saying, "Shut up!" as he whisked her away.

"Hungry," Brak said, holding his stomach.

They dashed down the corridor that led them to the kitchen.

Two sentries stood alone at the top of the steps.

"Halt!" one said, lowering a spear at Melegal's chest.

"You men need to secure the arena, Lord Almen's under attack," he said, holding out his brooch.

"We're not going anywhere, Detective."

Leave. Leave. Leave.

Melegal pinched the bridge of his nose. He suddenly had a massive headache.

"Are you all right, Detective?"

Lord's no! "I'd be better if you did as I said. I caught these prisoners trying to escape, but the dungeons are filled with underlings. We need every last man to get them under control, and you two fish faces are standing here letting your entire future fall into ruin. Lord Almen will have a fit when he hears about this."

The sentry poked Melegal in the chest with the tip of his spear.

"Sounds like a bunch of horse slat if you ask me. The last man who failed this post was guillotined, and that man was my brother."

Not good. These sentries weren't going anywhere, even if the Castle was on fire. He had to think of something else, or kill them.

Melegal had opened his mouth to speak when one of the worst sounds he'd ever heard came from down the hall. The sentries' faces drew up in horror. He peeked around the corner and down the hall. A man covered in flesh-eating worms was running his way, his own fingernails digging into his face. Behind him were the hulking form of the Vicious and two cloaked figures dragging the disabled form of … Sefron.

Melegal grabbed the shaft of the man's spear and pulled him forward, slipping behind him in one motion.

"Every man for himself!" he said, shoving them down the hall.

"What the," one man said, falling over the other.

Brak, stuffing a loaf of bread in his face, and a terror stricken Jubilee bounded down the staircase.

They learn fast when death is so close.

At the bottom, Brak and Jubilee were pounding on the door.

"It's locked!"

"Get out of my way," Melegal said, shoving through them and dropping to his knees.

Another painful wail billowed from the top of the stair.

Click. Clack. Click. Melegal's slender fingers worked his tools in the keyhole. *CLICK.*

He shoved the door open, spilling Brak and Jubilee inside. He slammed it shut and locked it. Lord Almen's study was empty and undisturbed. Jubilee ran over to the desk and snatched up Leezir's ash white cudgel. She hugged it and looked at Melegal.

"It's yours!" he said. "Brak, pull open that bookshelf."

"Hmrph?" he said, trying to swallow a mouthful of bread.

"Slerg Child, help him!"

WHAM! WHAM! WHAM! …

The hinges on the heavy door were shaking loose.

Melegal rummaged through the objects tucked away in the corner and wrapped his hands around Tonio's sword and something else he'd noticed before that he tucked into his belt. *What have we here?*

He jumped over the desk and slid behind the open bookshelf. The hammering at the door stopped, but the hinges and fixtures were glowing red hot.

He stepped through the threshold of the tiny doorway and closed it behind him. It was pitch black.

"I can't see anything," Jubilee complained.

Melegal stuck his coin of light in his hand, handed Brak the sword, and snatched the key from the peg.

"Follow to the bottom," he said as fast as he could, running down the steps into the darkness.

Keys. Keys. Keys.

Leaping down the next stairs and landing on the bottom, he dashed across the threshold in the dark. What if the keys aren't there? What if Lord Almen removed them? Were these keys what the underlings were after? Why else would they be here? *Sefron!* Melegal's quick mind was putting things together. It couldn't be a coincidence. Light spilled out into the room. Jubilee and Brak were coming, but they weren't alone. The sound of wood splintering came from above.

Melegal ran his hands over the alcove wall. A cold piece of metal brushed against his fingertip. He plucked them from the wall one at a time. *One. Two. Three. Four. Five. Six. I have them!* He bolted for the last door, unlocked it, and entered. Brak and Jubilee made it to the landing, running toward the opposite side.

"This way, you two idiots!" Melegal screamed.

Jubilee whirled, shining the bright beam of light in his eyes.

"Point that down, and hurry!"

He could hear a fierce snarling coming down the steps. Ahead of him, Brak and Jubilee were moving horribly slowly. *They're going to die and get me killed.*

As they ran past the landing, speeding his way, an underling mage appeared, teeth gnashing, fingertips glowing, the air beginning to shimmer with power.

"Faster!" *They're not going to make it!*

He felt the air begin to split as the mage's bright magic coiled around its arms.

Zing! Zing! Zing! Zing! Zing! Zing!

It shrieked in rage as Melegal filled its face full of darts.

Brak and Jubilee raced into the closet, and Melegal closed the door.

"What!"

The door wouldn't shut. Eight claws had hold of it and ripped it open. There the Vicious stood, tall and nasty. Melegal felt his heart stop. They were dead.

Wham!

Pain exploded the creature's face as Jubilee blasted it in the knee with the glowing white cudgel. Melegal jerked her back and slammed the door shut. Melegal couldn't tell their screams from his as his mind twisted inside out.

17

HOW DO YOU KILL A tree with arms, legs and muscle? Fogle Boon couldn't help but marvel at the man who towered at twenty feet tall.

"Do something, Fogle!" Cass urged him as they both stepped back from the smoke.

WHANG!

He flinched as Cass dug her fingers into his arm and an object came careening towards them, stopped, and settled in the dust.

"It's Mood," Fogle exclaimed, his feet moving faster than his lips. Chongo galloped past him and bared down, growling at Mood's side. The over-sized dwarf's body was trembling as he tried to rise from the ground.

"HOW DID THAT FEEL, RANGER? HA! HA! HA! ARE YOU DEAD?" The giant said as its footsteps thundered closer.

Chongo was barking and growling, the hairs rising on his massive necks, two sets of canine teeth bared. But Fogle had a feeling it was going to take more than dog bites to stop that giant. *Where in Bish did that man come from?* Fogle lurched at the giant's thunderous step. Mood was struggling to rise and mumbling something under his bloodied face and beard. That's when Fogle noticed the bone sticking out of the dwarf's shoulder. His stomach became queasy.

"Cass, shut Chongo up and drag Mood out of here!" he said, fanning the dust from his face.

"What are you going to do?" she said, rushing over to Chongo and swinging her legs onto his back.

"Something! Now go!"

"But—"

"Hurry!"

Chongo bit down on Mood's foot and started dragging him away as Fogle fell to his knees and filled his hands with dirt and sand. He closed his eyes and summoned the little power he had within. Swinging his hands around in big circles, he chanted the words and let the sand fly free.

The dust and dirt lifted from the ground, thickening and swirling. A small sand storm encompassed the giant, and it covered its eyes in the nook of its elbow. Fogle fell back away from the storm. The entire area was nothing more than a swirling white brown smoke. Fogle brushed the dust from his hands. *That should buy us some time.*

"HA! HA! HA! TUNDOOR SMELLS A WIZARD! MMMM … I SHALL EAT YOU AND HAVE YOUR MAGIC! HA! HA! HA!"

Fogle ran, catching up with Cass, Chongo and Mood. *I'm not getting eaten by anything.* What he wouldn't do to have the underling power of floating.

"Now what?" Cass yelled at him.

"We've got to lift up Mood. Send him away with Chongo! Are there any horses or dwarves left?"

"I don't see any."

"Just help me get him up," Fogle said.

"He's too heavy in all this gear!" Cass complained. "I'm not an orc!"

The hairs on the back of Fogle's neck stood on end as everything around them went perfectly still. It was as if time stopped. He turned to look back where the giant was. The storm, the sand, and the smoky air were all gone. Not even the giant remained.

"Where in the world of Bish did—"

"HA! HA! HA!" the giant bellowed as it materialized behind them, war hammer raised over its head, trapezoid bulging on its neck.

"CASS!" Fogle screamed as the giant swung the hammer down with all of its power.

WHAM!

Fogle felt his world coming to an end as Cass exploded into thousands of tiny white, black and yellow butterflies that sputtered and fluttered in every direction.

"Cass!" he yelled as the giant raised its hammer once more. There was no sign of the woman, only a large indentation the soil. She was gone.

"TUNDOOR CRUSH YOU, TOO NOW, WIZARD!"

"NO!" Fogle yelled back, raising his arms forward. "Wizard blast Tundoor now!"

A white hot missile left one hand, striking the giant in the knee.

Tundoor roared.

Fogle let out another and another.

Ssszram! Ssszram! Ssszram!

One missile followed the other, the next bigger and more powerful than last. The magic shards created holes in the giant's leg and tore the flesh from his bones. Tundoor toppled backward, falling hard like a massive catapult stone.

Sweat dripping in his eyes, Fogle fell to his knees and fought for his breath. Smoke was rolling from his fingers, and the magi fires had singed the edges of his robes. A series of heavy booted footsteps rushed past. It was Eethum the Blood Ranger and a pair of black bearded dwarves, axes hoisted over their shoulders. Chongo charged forward, digging and clawing into the face of the reeling giant.

Fogle couldn't make heads or tails of all of the thrashing that was going on. All he wanted to do was figure out what happened to Cass. The butterflies, or at least what he thought were butterflies, were gone, his energy along with them. He spit the dust from his mouth and tried to speak. He doubled over. Retching came instead. *What is wrong with me? Where's Cass?*

"TUNDOOR KILL YOU ALL!" the giant said, face full of anguish as it rose to one knee, hammer swinging into a dwarf soldier that was too slow to dodge. The small man's teeth shattered as his skull was driven into his neck like a nail.

Fogle winced and looked away. *Cass!* He looked around and caught sight of Mood rising to his feet, hand axe dragging in his bloody hand as he staggered into the fray. There was nothing Fogle could do to stop him. He could barely hold his throbbing head up for the discomfort behind his eyes.

"ALMOST DEAD! ALL OF YOU WILL FEEL TUDOOR'S POWER!"

He smashed the hammer into the ground where Eethum was just standing.

"FEEL MY WRATH!"

The hammer cracked a pile of boulders into rubble.

"MY FURY!"

Fogle lifted his chin up and stared. The enormous giant—with jewelry the size of barrels hanging from its ears, teeth as big as Fogle's head, and the maddened look of a bull on its snorting face—didn't seem real. It was something that appeared in nightmares. It couldn't possibly be real. He wondered if his grandfather Boon had ever taken on such monsters before. Boon had at least survived long enough to become old, gray and crazy. Fogle was pretty certain his life wasn't going to last that long. Maybe a few more seconds at best.

Eethum, black-faced and red bearded, went spinning to the ground as the hammer clipped him on the shoulder.

Chongo's claws tore into the giant's chest, but the giant grabbed him by the nape of one neck and flung him away.

This is it, Fogle thought with a sinking feeling.

"TIME FOR TUNDOOR TO EAT YOU, WIZARD. MAN WITH MAGIC TASTE GOOD!" He said, reaching towards him with a hand as big as a cart. "HA! HA! URK!"

Tundoor's eyes widened like big white moons. Atop his massive back, Mood was hanging onto a handful of the giant's hair and chopping into the giant's skull with unfettered fury.

"LET GO! STOP!" The giant cried out, arms flailing back towards the pest that was carving a canoe in his skull. "PLEASE! TUND—"

Mood sunk his axe wrist deep inside Tundoor's head and wrenched it free.

The giant's body convulsed then pitched forward like a toppled tower. His big face crashed inches from Fogle, his eyes gawping in wonder. Mood lay still on top of the giant's back.

Fogle rubbed his aching head. Only he, Chongo, Mood, Eethum and a single black-bearded dwarf remained.

"Does he live?" he asked.

Eethum stumbled over and slid Mood from atop the giant's blood smeared back and lowered him to the ground. He wasn't breathing.

"Well?" Fogle managed to say, despite his dry mouth.

Eethum shook his head.

"Pardon me for saying, but he should be dead." Fogle said, rubbing the numbness in his hands. "We all should be. How did he manage that?"

"He summoned the *Odenson*. Part of the Blood Ranger craft where our mystic blood allows us do things beyond our natural power. Some use it for great feats in contests, others to turn the tide of a battle. But there is a price." Eethum tried to pull the axe from Mood's grasp, but it would not budge.

"What is the price?" Fogle said, managing to rise to his feet.

Eethum eyed him with fierce green eyes and shook his head.

"The Everslumber overtakes him."

"How long is that?"

Eethum snorted.

"The last time it happened, a Blood Ranger slumbered for years."

Fogle gulped. He'd finally gotten used to the ancient dwarf, and now he was gone.

"Now what?" he asked.

"I'll take him home."

"But what about our journey?"

Eethum reached under Mood's battered figure, hoisted him up in his arms, and said, "It's your journey now, Wizard. I have to take care of my king." The Blood Ranger started limping away.

"But, where are you going? What if there are more giants? I can't take them alone."

"Make a fire, rest, gather your resources, Wizard. Be better prepared next time."

Fogle felt like he was the only man left in the world as he surveyed the carnage. Four dead giants lay baking under the suns. The black bearded dwarves, all but one, so far as he guessed, were dead. *Cass!*

He hurried over to the spot where Cass had stood before she was pulverized. He sat down at the edge of the big indentation in the ground and ran his fingers though the dirt. There was no sign of her, but there was blood. He looked over at the hammer the giant wielded. There was a lot of blood on that hammer. *I hope it's only dwarven.* Yet a sad feeling overwhelmed him. He sunk his head in his hand and clutched his fingers in his hair.

"No." he panted. "No. She can't be gone."

Chongo lumbered behind him and was panting down his neck.

"This is your fault," he said, pushing away his nose.

"It certainly is not!" Cass snapped.

Fogle jumped to his feet.

The beautiful druid woman sat perched on top of Chongo's saddle. Tiny black, white and yellow butterflies adorned her long white hair.

Fogle shuffled to her side, grabbed the warm ankle of her sensual leg, and gaped up at her.

"I'm real," she said, smiling down on him. "You're handsome when you smile, Fogle. You should try it more," she said, sliding down into his arms.

All of his passions flooded him when he felt her sensual body slide along his. He kissed her deeply, arms tightening around her waist as she melted in his arms. After a few long moments, she broke way.

"Hmmm … Fogle, you are learning," she said in his ear. "But right now we have more important things to worry about."

"How did you… "

"Burst into butterflies? Oh, that's something for only druids to know. We're about as easy to kill as we are to understand," she said with a bewitching smile.

"It's just us now," he said, stepping away and stroking the big dog's necks. "Sorry, Chongo."

Chongo licked him in the face.

Ugh!

Cass giggled. "He's forgiven you, but it looks like he's ready for the next leg of the journey. You look worried."

Fogle looked around, lost in a world that he didn't understand. Rock, dirt, clay and the suns that always sizzled. His robes, a fine gift, were almost in tatters, but all things considered, they'd held up well. Still …

"I am. I'm used to Mood being around, but he's going to be out for a while. Eethum left me with good advice, the likes of 'Be better prepared next time.'" He began pacing. "No one said anything about giants in the Outlands. Underlings I was ready for, but not giants. Where on Bish did they come from? Why'd they attack us?"

Cass shrugged her slender shoulders. "They hate dwarves."

"Have you ever seen giants before?"

"No. But just because I hadn't seen them didn't mean they didn't exist."

Fogle couldn't even begin to imagine all the things he'd never seen that might exist. Back in the City of Three, there were images of monsters and beasts everywhere: giants, griffons, chimeras, minotaurs, trolls of many sorts and so on. He traveled with a giant two-headed dog after all, so why'd he rule out the possibility of other things?

He looked at Tundoor. The giant's earrings alone were worth a fortune. Who'd forged items such as those?

"I believe those jewels would be too big for my ears," Cass said, "but I like the way you're thinking."

"Huh … oh, well, I think you deserve something a hundred times the worth of those."

Cass brightened at the remark, took a deep draw into her chest and said, "It's just us, you know, and it's going to be dark soon. Perhaps you can tell me more about what I deserve beside a nice fire and under the moons."

He smiled again. "I'll fetch the wood." He scurried away, then came to a stop. He turned back and said, "I'm assuming we're not going to pitch a fire around here?"

She shook her head.

"I'll find a place for the fire. You just fetch the wood. Hmmm …," she needled her chin, "we have to take care of the fallen dwarves."

"No, leave them where they lay. Eethum will send for them soon. The dwarves are very picky about the dead. The family will want to see the place of battle. I have a feeling all of these frowns will be upside down when they see it."

"Then I'll see to it they remain undisturbed. Make haste, Fogle."

Make haste, indeed. My, surrounded by the dead and thinking only of my lustful yearnings for a woman. How can that be? Maybe that's why they say the 'The castles rise and fall between the legs of one maiden or another.' I never understood those perverts until now. Slat. What is becoming of me?

Fogle's weariness returned. He felt his skin sagging over his bones. His head hurt, and his stomach was still queasy as he picked his way over the battle ground. The journey had just begun, and almost everyone was dead. Mood had looked more dead than alive. He looked to the south. Nothing but the barren Outlands, a place where only the cacti, bone trees and red toads thrived. Wouldn't it be better to just let the dog go to find his master on his own? Did the dog need them, or did they need the dog? *Maybe it's time to head back to the City of Three.*

He picked up a few more pieces of wood and headed back over to where he'd last seen Chongo and Cass. They were nowhere to be found. An unsettling feeling overcame him.

Somewhere, Chongo was barking like a dozen hounds.

He heard a harrowed scream. It was Cass.

NO! Not again!

He dropped everything and ran.

18

Verbard could see them now: men, robed and wizened, converging on his location. *Impressive.* The Royals, the guardians of the city, were better prepared for the unexpected than he'd anticipated. Across the skyline the wizards came, one rising up behind the other. Verbard could sense their power and their fear as well. It wasn't likely any of them had even seen an underling before, and they couldn't possibly have imagined one like him. His silver eyes shined as he ran his black tongue across his top row of teeth. *Underling Magi, to me!*

One by one, the underlings rose up from the smoke, heavy cloth robes billowing over their toes. Verbard felt a collective attack coming from the human wizards. They were here, but they were far from ready. The first barrage of energy came. Balls of blue light scorched across the sky, blasting full force into the mystic shield of the underlings and ricocheting harmlessly away.

Follow my lead!

Coils of red energy laced around Verbard as he summoned is power. The air crackled above the streets as he unleashed the first bolt of power, which streaked across the expanse and blasted into the wizards' pale blue mystic shield, splitting shards of magic from its edge, rocking a wizard back. The next bolt hit the wizard again, shattering his shield and sending him spinning through the air. Verbard's next bolt disintegrated the wizard completely. One down.

The human wizards huddled behind their shields together, hesitating. Verbard sensed their weakness and something else. He knew the humans couldn't float as the underlings could. Someone or something else was using power to keep them afloat. Another mind, stronger than the rest, was pulling the strings from somewhere else.

Finish them!

Eep, where are you?

Verbard drifted downward towards the burning building tops. Below his dangling feet, Jottenhiem, the Juegen and the Badoon were clashing with a heavy force of well-armored soldiers that had charged into the market place. The war was on. Men were toppled from their horses, and underlings were trampled under hooves. The keen edge of Jottenhiem's sword split through the skull inside a fallen rider's helmet, and another soldier's head was ripped from his shoulders. Still, Verbard could see that as quickly as the men fell, two more replaced them.

Eep buzzed to his side, rough skin singed and stained with blood.

"You calls me, Master," Eep hissed.

"I need you to find someone, a mage, somewhere nearby. And be quick about it."

Eep was wringing his clawed hands as he said, "You want me to kill him, Master?"

"Just sniff out the strongest source of magic and lead me to him," he ordered.

Buzz! Zip!

Eep blinked out of sight.

A barrage of arrows ripped through the air around Verbard, most bouncing harmlessly away. A row of archers had lined up along the wall, nocking and firing at his chest. He called the lightning within him. A white silver light streaked from his finger tips and passed through one soldier and into the others, cooking their bodies inside their metal armor. Verbard surveyed the battle below with wisps of lightning still dancing along his fingers. Jottenhiem and his men had the soldiers hemmed up in corridors, but couldn't hold them back forever. In the distance, Verbard could sense more forces were coming, and coming fast.

Eep reappeared and hissed excitedly.

"Found him, Master! A fat one. Like a giant grape. Let me eat his belly."

"Is he guarded?"

"By many. Sits on a pillow like a toad. Face is fat and sweaty. Red face ready to explode." Eep pointed his clawed finger down the road over the heads of the soldiers. "I can kill him."

"Perhaps." Verbard took a moment. "Nay. I'll handle this man myself. You, however, are needed above. Go."

Eep blinked away.

Verbard kept his energy ready. It was time he got a better feel for how much power the humans wielded. He sailed through the smoke, a shadow that was hidden from sight, whereupon he spied the man that Eep had described. On a wagon bed sat a man as tall as an underling but ten times as round. Three rows of chins hung beneath his bald-headed face, which was beet red with concentration. Surrounding him were ten soldiers: swords and spears ready, chainmail suits from head to toe, eyes wide and jittering at the sounds of the battle and the colorful explosions that came from above.

Verbard let loose the chained lightning. The searing bolt cracked into one man, passed through the next, then fizzled out. The blood-shot eyes of the fat human wizard in orange silk robes snapped open and locked on Verbard's through the smoke. Verbard felt a force surround him, drawing him closer, downward into the throng of soldiers that waited to chop him down.

He hissed. It appeared the fat wizard was as powerful as he was heavy, like a massive anvil wrapped around his neck, weighting him down. Verbard's straining eyes drifted to an orb which sat in the wizard's lap. It gleamed and swirled with intensity. His silver eyes widened. *An Orb of Imbibing!* He was trapped.

Not only did the orb consume magic, in this case it seemed to be feeding the wizard as well. Verbard was getting weaker, and the man, a useless sot by all appearances, was getting stronger. Much stronger. Verbard wrestled against the forces that were wrenching his power from him. His descent to the ground became quicker.

EEP! EEP! KILL THIS HUMAN SLUDGE PILE!

An arrow whizzed past his nose.

All of Verbard's strength was fading as he descended into the awaiting swords and spears.

EEP! HURRY!

Blink!

The imp was standing on the man's bulbous belly, hanging onto the man's ears, poking his clawed fingers into the man's neck and throat. The man wailed and squealed like a hog on fire.

Another arrow crashed through Verbard's shield and into his leg. He hissed. Yet, the blanket that absorbed his power had faded. His strength renewed. More arrows came, but ricocheted away. He realized it was time to go. He sped through the air, back towards the alley from where they had come.

Retreat! Retreat!

At the end of the alley, Verbard summoned a black dimensional doorway. One by one, the Badoon, Juegen and Magi survivors passed through. Verbard made one final command.

Eep, fetch that orb!

Jottenhiem was the last in line, breathing heavily, slick with blood and ailing.

"We have failed, my Lord."

Verbard gently pushed him through, saying, "Only if we were supposed to succeed."

Behind him, Eep was running his way, his wing broken, the orb wrapped in his hands, a wave of soldiers on his tail. "Wait, Master, wait!"

Over Eep's head, Verbard sent a bolt that slammed into Eep pursuers as the imp jumped through the door. Verbard dove in behind him, collapsing the door as a dozen arrows clattered off the alley walls.

Kierway stood inside the ancient chamber below Lord Almen's study, swords sheathed and clenched fists shaking. At his side floated two underling magi, both of whom he wanted to kill, but he needed them if he was going to get out of this castle alive.

Trembling near his feet was the flabby form of the human cleric, Sefron. Groveling.

"My Lord. Apologies. I've never been to this chamber. I never knew there was a secret door. I was never privy to the study. Please, my Lord, don't kill me," he whined, his high voice echoing all over the chamber.

Kierway slapped him across his face.

"Quiet, you failure!"

Kierway made his way over to the pegs in the alcove and touched them with his clawed finger, one by one. Seven keys, not one. His father, Master Sinway, had only required one, but which one would that have been? It hardly mattered now; they had failed.

The Vicious threw his weight into the door where the three humans had escaped. The creature's powerful talons clawed and swiped, its heavy shoulders shaking the door on the hinges, but it held. The magi, both of them, tried spells and incantations, but the door remained sealed. So did their fate as well. There was no escape from where they stood.

"Enough!" he said. The Vicious and Magi fell at attention. He kicked Sefron in the head.

"Who was this man that took the keys? It seems he knew more about them than you knew? I'm curious: why was that?"

Sefron wiped the blood from his mouth and gasped a sickly wheeze. It bothered Kierway's iron eyes to even look at him. Certainly, he could have found someone better to serve him, but the cleric had been the most willing.

"Melegal is his name. He serves Lord Almen as his detective. He's of little importance. Nothing more than a little rat, is all. *Hack. Hack.* A fool with fortune on his side this day."

Kierway reached over and plucked a dart out of Sefron's face.

"A fool. A fool that has seven keys to our none. A fool who it seems is much smarter than you." He grabbed Sefron by the back of his head and held the dart tip to his bulbous eye. "You will find this man, and quickly." He jammed the dart in Sefron's eye. The cleric let out a howl like a wounded wolf. "Or you'll lose the other eye, as well." Voices could be heard over the top of Sefron's pain-filled wails as he kicked and wallowed on the floor.

Kierway drew his blades as the Vicious bounded toward the landing on the stairwell. One of the magi muttered a powerful incantation, and they were gone.

19

T HE GLOWING FIRE WAS HOT on his face, but Georgio, though exhausted, was all smiles. Sucking down a tankard of ale while chewing a mouthful of food, he felt like he'd reached another plateau in his life. He felt all grown up. He'd survived a one-on-one battle with a brutal rogue, and he'd won.

"That was something," Billip said, shoving a small pile of coins across the table. The older man, grim-faced and wiry, looked as uncertain as he was pleased. Running his fingers through his coarse black hair, he leaned back in his chair and added, "Stupid, but something. I'm not sure what possessed you, Boy … er … Georgio, but I'm certain you've sprouted more chest hairs today." He hoisted his goblet up and drank.

Georgio hardly noticed a word that he'd said. His attention was elsewhere.

"Something?" The dark sultry woman by his side had her leg draped over his lap. "Amazing. That's what I'd say."

Her name was Velvet, the one who'd drawn the cards. Raven-haired, sensuous and captivating. She stirred his blood by running her gentle fingers through his hair and down over his chin.

"And to see such a handsome young man thrash such an ugly brute. I must say, I'm grateful. Jeb and his goons have been nothing but a menace to us girls and all the other patrons around here."

Georgio was smiling all over himself when he said, "Aw … it was nothing."

Billip humphed from across the table, folding his arms across his chest.

Velvet reached down, grabbed his hands and began inspecting them.

"How can you not be burned? Your meaty hands are soft like butter, yet there's not a single scorch mark." She started massaging them. "Are you a mage of some sort?"

"Well, I can't exactly —"

He felt a boot smack into his shin. Billip was eyeing him.

"Ow! Er … I'm from a family of blacksmiths, is all. I've been around the furnaces all my life. Tough hands. It runs in the family." He shrugged.

"Impressive," Velvet purred. "And my hands are from a long line of … well … personal services, and they're all yours. I'm sure you have plenty of bumps and bruises that I could," she squeezed his thigh, "remedy."

Georgio scratched the back of his neck.

"Uh …"

"Alright," Billip interjected with a smile, "can you give me and the young warrior a moment, Velvet is it?" He slid her a coin and winked. "And we could use another round if you'd please oblige, Pretty Thing."

Velvet kissed Georgio on his forehead, shot Billip an aggravated look, huffed, and walked away.

"What'd you do that for?" Georgio said, gawking at the sway of Velvet's hips.

Billip reached over and punched him in the arm.

"Ow! What'd you do that for!" he exclaimed, wiping his face.

"No time for fooling around, Georgio! Underlings! In Bone!"

Georgio surveyed the room. The people, what was left of them anyway, were drawn up as tight as bows. Stories and chatter of the vicious creatures were spreading from one chair to the other. There was talk of a mass exodus that had begun, but Georgio had a hard time believing any of it. And the only thing that mattered to him was getting closer to Velvet. He shrugged.

"I don't see any underlings in here."

Billip punched him again, harder this time.

"No, but you're about to see stars."

"Ha! I'd like to see you try."

Billip's eyes narrowed, his voice as deadly as a pit of vipers.

"You think beating that curly haired slug has you prepared for the likes of me … Boy?"

Georgio gulped. He'd seen Billip angry before. On the trek down to Bone, they came across a nomad band of half-orcs that tried pushing them around. Billip skewered one in the neck with one throw and another in the belly with the other. It all happened in the blink of an eye. "Er … only teasing, Billip."

"Fill your belly. Cop your feel, but we're getting out of here … soon. Mikkel's checking the stories out, and when he returns, we're going after Nikkel." The wary archer looked over his shoulder. "Something about this city just isn't right. The whole world isn't right and hasn't been for a while. Underlings in the City of Three and now underlings in Bone. You're young, Georgio. But I'm telling you, this is crazy."

Georgio was weary again. The fire was soothing, but his spirits began to dull. He could tell by the grim looks on the people's faces that something wasn't right. Normally, the people of Bone, though hardened and somewhat criminal, had a more positive tone about them. Now, they spoke in whispers, under their breath, jumping a bit at every unusual sound. It only made sense. The citizens had never seen an underling before, and according to rumors, no one lived to tell about seeing one, either.

"What's going on inside that big melon of yours?" Billip said.

"Ah … I'm just starting to get the feeling that maybe you're right, Billip. What if the underlings are overrunning the city? What if they've overrun Bish? What will happen to us?"

An uncertain smile broadened over Billip's thick black goatee when he said, "Well, I guess we'll all eventually be buried arses up and heads stuck in the ground. Cheers!" He reached over and clonked his tankard against Georgio's.

Reaching for his mug, Georgio saw a group of distraught men burst inside the door.

"Underlings! Hundreds!" a man dressed as a laborer shouted.

"Thousands!" the other man, thick in muscle and skull, added at his partner's side.

The Drunken Octopus fell silent.

"The entire 21st District is overrun. Burning and mutilated. Thousands of Royal Soldiers are dead."

The short stocky one waved his hands over his shoulders.

"All of their heads are gone. Half eaten most of them. You must flee! They're coming!"

A small quiet group of people turned into a frenzied hoard when the entire room made for the stairs and the doors. Georgio was rising to his feet when Billip pushed him back down.

"What?" he asked.

"We'll go when Mikkel returns."

"What if they got him already?"

Billip's lips twitched as he popped his knuckles.

"We wait. Those fools over there are just creating a panic. I'd say there's only ten at most out there, if that."

Velvet glided back into her seat, trembling, and draped her arms around Georgio.

"Will you protect me?"

He could feel her shivering. Her painted eyes were full of fear. His heart began to swell.

"Sure. I've killed underlings before. Just stay close to me," he said, running his arm across her back.

Billip shook his head as the room behind him began to clear out. Velvet's arms tightened around Georgio's neck as the screaming in the streets began to rise. Something was going on out there. Something bad. Something evil.

That's when Sam the Barkeep spoke up.

"Everyone out!"

His usual expressionless countenance now unfurled as he took rapid puffs on his cigar.

The few who remained didn't waste any time heading out the door. Sam stormed over to the table, smacking his club in his hand.

"It's time to get your arses out of here, too. My tavern's closed."

Billip said, "But we've already paid for our room."

Sam cracked his club on the table.

"Tough!"

20

"**Y**OU TRY ANYTHING AND I'LL scream," Kam said as Diller shoved her towards the tub. "I don't think Palos would be too happy with you accosting me. You saw what happened to Thorn."

Diller shoved her hard to the floor. She kicked at his knee. He slipped past and swatted her hard in the back of the head. His calloused hands were strong. He grabbed her by the wrist and dragged her kicking across the floor. One again, she was powerless in the quick and deadly hands of one of Palo's top men. Still, she managed to bite his hand and wriggle free.

"Ahhhh!" He said, wincing. "You keep struggling, and I'll see the little baby starved, you spoiled wench."

Kam froze, chest heavy beneath her robes as she drew her legs up to her chin.

"You leave my daughter alone."

She smacked her in the face, drawing more blood in her mouth.

"That's the plan, Princess."

Kam fell silent. Numb inside. Her courage dissipated as quickly as it had started. There was nothing she could do. Diller reached down, fetid breath on her neck, groping her body while tying her to the legs of the tub with the absidium chains.

"You sick, wretched pervert. Wait until—"

"Until what? You go ahead and tell Palos." He kneeled down in front of her, elbow relaxed on his knee, toothpick rolling back and forth in his mouth. "Princess, you'll be begging to have me once Palos is through with you."

Her green eyes lit up at the matter-of-factness of his statement.

"Ah … that's right. I hope you don't think you're the one and only pretty thing he's ever drug down here. You certainly aren't the first Royal, and you won't be the last."

She swallowed hard and slunk back.

"Yes," he brushed the back of his palm against her cheek. "It's only a matter of time. No woman can ever satisfy a man like that for long." He laughed, a mocking one. "Then you'll certainly be mine … or Thorn's. Ah … there will be suitors aplenty to bid on you, my dear. But you better hope it ends up being me."

He grabbed her chin. She jerked it away.

"Never," she said with trembling breath.

His knees cracked as he rose to his full height and leered down on her.

"I'm a patient man," he said, walking away, dusting off his hands. "You'll be mine, and fortunate for you, I'm much easier to satisfy than him." He gave her a lusty look over his shoulder. "And I'm sure I'll satisfy you as well, not that it will matter."

Kam fell into a fit of tears as soon as he closed the door.

This is my fault. My fault. My fault.

Lefty gently banged his head over into the clawed foot of the tub.

My fault!

He hit it once more, harder this time. It hurt, but it didn't ache near as much as his heart, which was slipping inside his chest as Kam's sobs became deafening. He wanted to reach out. Touch her. Comfort her. Say how sorry he was, but he couldn't. The truth was, he was too scared. If anyone deserved to die, it was him. And if anyone reserved the right to kill him, it was her.

My fault!

He struck his head once more. *Perhaps I can spare her the effort.*

"Stop doing that," Kam managed from beneath her sobs.

Huddled under the tub, he tilted his head back.

"Don't!" she said, her voice stronger, regaining its fiery luster. "I might have use for that little head, after all."

Lefty sucked up the courage to look up into her eyes.

Tears filled his eyes. Kam, still as beautiful as the first day he saw her, was misaligned. Her glorious auburn hair was a tangled mess, and her high cheek bones were now bruised. A split lip accompanied the dark circles under her eyes, and her polished nails were chipped and chewed. She was a lovely white dove now covered in soot and grime. Her robe barely covered her skinned up features and none of her shame. She'd been through something. Something bad. All because of him.

"Stop crying, you little bastard. I've cried enough for all of your years and mine put together."

"K-Kam … I'm sorry," he sobbed, wiping his runny nose. "I didn't …" Tears streaming into his face, he curled up into a ball.

She rankled her chains.

"I said no more crying, Lefty! Now get up."

He didn't move. He just lay there trembling like a frightened bunny.

Kam leaned back against the tub, pulled her legs under her hips, and tried to make herself more comfortable. She blew the locks of hair from her eyes. *I must look horrible. I am horrible.* And now she'd terrified a boy, or at least someone who looked like a boy, but was certainly much older. She wasn't even sure how long halflings lived, and she had no idea how old Lefty actually was. But he was helpless. Far more helpless than her, or so it seemed at the moment.

All men, no matter how big or how small, are trouble.

Lefty. His haggard little face told it all. He was exhausted, weary, over-run by the dangerous life that one can easily encounter in Bish, especially when you're not careful. That must have been what happened to him. Or, maybe he was just trying to deceive her once more. That grin. The one he'd shown earlier, when Gillem was around. The face stuck with her, leaving an unfavorable impression. But at this point, what did they have to gain from her? Was

Lefty spying on her? Why not let Diller do that? It seemed odd that they'd just leave him here with her. What else would they want from her?

She scooted over, stretched out her leg, and pushed him with her toe.

"Stop crying, you little sot."

He kept on. She shoved him again.

"I'm miserable enough already, so don't make it worse. Now tell me something. You owe me at least that much. Have you seen Erin?"

His trembling stopped as he pulled himself to his knees. Tears dripping from his tiny face to the floor, he nodded.

"I'm s-s-s-soooo sorry! I know it's all … all my fault."

The next question was the hardest for her, but she had to ask it.

"Is she alive?"

Her heart stopped as she watched him gulp and take a breath.

"I'm certain of it."

Kam gasped. She would have hugged him if she could.

"Do you know where she is?"

"I do, Kam. It was the first thing I did, finding that out. Kam, I swear I was trying to think of a way out of this. I really was," he pleaded. "But they killed Gillem." His eyes watered again. "And I was scared they'd kill me and you and Erin. They all lied to me, Kam. They tricked me. The kidnapping. Everything. I never, ever would do anything to hurt you or anyone. I really wouldn't. But, I – I just didn't have a choice. Palos … he's so mean and cruel and scary." He dragged his sleeve across his wet face. "He killed Gillem for no reason at all. I've seen him kill other men, too. And he keeps the dead bodies in the lake. Gillem showed it to me. Told me that was where I'd live, at the bottom of the lake. I've seen them all dead. Skin hanging off of them. It's horrifying. Terrible. I didn't want to be drowned and staring forever up at the living. I'm sorry. I'm so sorry! I just—"

Kam nudged him with her foot and tried to sound reassuring.

"That's enough, Lefty. I'm starting to understand."

Lefty was always a jittery little man, a victim of seeing things that were awfully horrible. She actually was beginning to understand. If she were a little girl in the same situation, what would she have done? *No. I would have made the right choice. He made the wrong one. You're better off dying for the right reasons than living for the wrong ones.* That's what her mother taught her anyway, and she remembered passing that along to him and Georgio a time or two. The question now was, could she trust him again?

"Do you think Erin is well?"

He shrugged his small shoulders and said, "I think so. That old woman, she's not so bad, at least not compared to the rest of them. Just ugly is all."

It gave Kam little relief, but it was better than nothing.

"Well, you're a thief now, right? Can't you undo these bonds?"

"I've tried. This absidium is really tough, like living wire. Master Gillem could have undone it, but I haven't figured out how yet."

Kam winced as she fought the chains that bound up her wrists. The more you wriggled, the more they bit. It was strange that the metal wasn't magic, but it sure did act like it, and Lefty was bound up worse than her. Still, she noticed he could wiggle his fingers and toes. It gave her an idea.

"Do you think you can cast a spell?" she asked.

"I think, but can't you?"

"No, this choker prevents that. If I try, it will kill me."

His blue eyes lit up.

"Maybe I can help. If you lie down, maybe I can get it off."

"No, only magic can unseal it."

"But I don't know any spells. And I haven't practiced in a long time."

"True, but I can give you the words, and maybe you can harness the power."

He nodded. "Let's try."

She looked over at the doors. If Palos or Diller stepped in, it would be all over.

Better try something small.

"Lefty, repeat after me."

She started speaking in a slow and rhythmic series of syllables, very quiet, very easy. Lefty's lips followed her, uttering everything as if she spoke it herself. She chanted faster now, repeating the same phrases over and over.

"Urk!"

The choker around her neck seized up like a python, turning her face red as she kicked and reeled on the floor.

"Kam! Kam!" Lefty shrieked, stretching his fingers out to save her.

The choker was like a living snake around her neck, insidious and in control. All she could do was think of Erin and never seeing her baby's face again. *No! No!* The choker released her. Whatever little bit of magic she'd summoned fled her just in time. Now, she lay on the floor gasping, sucking for air.

"I'm so sorry! I'm so sorry!"

It took more than a minute before she recovered herself. She looked over at Lefty and said, "Lefty, don't worry about me. If you can do anything, save Erin. Escape and free her."

"I have to help you, too. If I take her, they might kill you," he said with such a sad look in his eyes she felt like she was dead already.

"That's my choice, not yours. If I can't save her, then you are the only one who can. It's the only way you can make things right with me."

"But Kam—"

"Promise me, Lefty!"

He nodded his head.

"I promise."

She sat there and let her fate sink in. Palos had her. Without her magic, she was nothing. Just an ordinary woman turned into a madman's whore.

Lefty started retching.

She ignored it. Whatever could possibly be wrong now didn't even matter. *Bish.*

21

GALLOPING ON HORSEBACK, VENIR SWEPT Brool into the nearest underling's chest and shattered another's teeth on his shield. All around him was chaos. The underlings were fleeing. A screeching black army scurrying as fast as they could into their dark little holes. Venir hewed them down, one by one, preventing the escape of all he could. Left and right, they fell under his swath of destruction. He was a black knight filling a moat with their blood.

Kill them! Kill them all! The helm urged him on.

His hatred pushed him further.

Horses, dozens of them, spears and lance tips lowered to the ground, ran over and through one underling after the other. The Royal Riders, the stoutest cavalry in the world of Bish, had the underlings undone. The underling army fragmented. Spiders, underlings, Juegen and magi fled, bled and died. Their bones, guts and entire camp were trampled into the dust.

A desperate underling, fleeing for its life, sent a spear into the rump of Venir's horse. He cried out as the horse bucked and sent him careening to the ground. The underlings, the closest ones that still lived, piled on him, tearing at him, their bright eyes wild for his destruction.

Venir's arms and shoulders ached, and his wounded hand felt like it was on fire. Exhausted, he struck onward, upward, downward, until his arms gave out. His wounds many, he pressed on.

Fight! Fight! Fight! The helm urged.

He couldn't go on much longer.

CHOP!

The last underling fell beneath the weight of his axe, its arm dangling from its shoulder. Laboring for breath, he fell to his knees. He checked his surroundings Every last one was dead or fled.

"Finally," he huffed. Brool was sticky and bloody in his grip as he slipped his blood-soaked hand from the shaft and reached for his canteen. It was no longer there. *Bone.*

It was a macabre scene the likes of which he'd never seen before. Dead underlings in their dark mail armor lay baking in the suns. Stout men had fallen to weapons, and others' skin had been sizzled or melted off by powerful magic. Over-sized spider legs were twitching, and webs were scattered everywhere.

Someone stepped into his sunlight and tossed something on the ground before him. A canteen.

"You owe me a horse," a strong and familiar voice said.

Venir looked up. It was the Commander of the Royal Riders, coated in dirt and blood, leaning over the neck of his horse, a meek but broad smile showing.

Venir grabbed the canteen and gulped down every last drop.

"And some water too, it seems," he said, rising on shaking feet. Then a thought jarred his aching head. "Adanna!"

"Who?" the commander asked.

"Can you begin a search? Two women were taken and possibly a man as well."

The Commander shook his head and said, "I'm telling you, underlings don't take prisoners, but I'll see what I can do." He turned in his saddle. "Men, begin a search. Two women and one male survivor!"

Venir walked a few steps away. He need to search as well.

"You can at least give me my canteen back. I'm sure you can pluck a good one from the dead. Huh, I hope that broad back of yours can use a shovel as well as it swings that axe, Stranger. We've got many good men to bury."

Walking away, Venir tossed the man up the canteen. "And many enemies to burn as well."

The underling camp was a small city filled with rows of dark grey tents that no longer stood. Venir limped to the nearest collapsed tent and lifted it up. A bunch of small black spiders scurried out, and he stomped them into the ground. He had an uncanny feeling. Underlings setting up camps like men. It wasn't normal, not above ground that is, at least in his lifetime anyway.

Searching one disheveled tent after the other, he cursed his luck. And, as far as he could tell, the Royal Riders weren't doing their best to look, either. Instead, they sat tending the wounded and catching their breath. Another hour passed, and Venir had covered little ground. His temper and vitality were wearing thin as he limped from one tent to the other. *Blast, there's so many.*

It was beginning to feel like a lost cause. The underlings didn't often take prisoners, but when they did, they usually weren't heard from again. As the first sun sunk down over the horizon, the likelihood that his friends survived darkened as well. He hoisted up the heavy canvas of the tents, one after the other, his wounds festering and burning. His leg was so stiff he could hardly walk, and the insides of his cheeks stung from where he'd bitten them in battle. He pulled off his helm. The throbbing in his head subsided, but he groaned as the other aches and pains intensified. He eased himself to the ground as exhaustion quickly settled into his bones. He just wanted to sleep. He closed his eyes.

"Warrior!"

The voice sounded like an explosion in his ear and made his entire body flinch on the ground. Everything hurt. It even hurt when he blinked. He rose into a sitting position and looked up at the sky. It was dusk, with little more than a few minutes of daylight remaining.

He found the commander's face. "What?"

"Better come with me. I think we've found who you're looking for," he said in a somber tone.

With the help of a strong armed soldier, Venir made it to his feet and followed the man, who was still riding his horse. The commander led him alongside a deep pit that was too dark to see inside. The smell of death and decay filtered up through it. Another bottomless pit opened up, this one in Venir's stomach, and that old guilty feeling rose its ugly head. All his friends were better off without him.

The commander slid from his saddle at his side, stroked his mustache, and said, "There's more of them. Not as deep, but the bodies were many. No women, though. This is the last one we found." He motioned toward a dog-sized sand spider that lay dead on its back, a pair of spears shoved through it. "That thing was crawling out when we got here. Its belly's full." The man spat. "I've seen plenty of them spiders in my day, but not so many nor so big all at once."

He made his way to the edge of the pit and prepared to lower himself inside.

"Give me a torch," Venir asked, strapping on his helm.

A soldier nearby handed one over, and Venir tossed it down inside. It stuck on a bed of webs and then slowly dissipated as it fell all the way through. The pit wasn't as deep as it looked. He uncoiled a rope, tossed it over the side, and started climbing down. That's when he noted the steps cut into the walls, underling size. Reaching the bottom, he noticed the pit was quiet and rank. When he bent to pick the torch up, the marrow in his bones chilled and the hairs on his neck stood on end.

Sssckt. Sssckt. Sssckt … A sand spider was sucking on the cocooned figure of a man.

Venir's instincts fired. He limped over and rammed Brool's spike dead center into the spider's bulbous body. It detached with a screech and died. Venir shuffled around the bottom of the pit, waving the torch back and forth, but no other spiders were in sight. Three figures were wrapped up in spidery cocoons, one of them stretched out at least seven feet. *Slim!*

Venir lowered the torch along the webs and watched the spider silk shrivel and dissipate.

"I'm going to need a hand down here," he shouted upward. "I've got three bodies!"

He found the cloth around Slim's face and pulled it away. His face was gaunt, and no breath came. "Come on, Slim." He slapped the skinny man's face. Nothing happened. Then there was a twitch behind his eyelids.

He lowered the torch to the next cocoon and pulled the sticky webbing away from another face wrapped in cloth. It was Adanna. Her once lustrous hair was dry as bone, and the skin around her once full figure was tight as sun dried leather and sunken in all places. Venir's chin dipped down. She was dead. Besides Adanna, her mother was gone as well.

"Blast my pride-filled hide," he grumbled.

If he'd only stayed with them, they'd probably all be still alive. Instead, he'd doubled back to deal with Farc. Now Hogan, his wife and his daughter were dead. That guilty feeling renewed the fires within him.

"Nay," he said to himself.

It wasn't him that was responsible. It was the underlings. And he was going to make them pay. Every last one.

Venir sat by the campfire, guarding Slim. His friend looked dead as a tombstone. Above him, the moons had risen, both full and glowing in pale shades of blood. He'd just spent the last several hours shoveling shallow graves for Adanna, her mother and many of the hundreds of Royal Riders. It had been a long time since he'd been part of such a big battle, and the feeling inside his gut told him there were many more battles to come.

He took a deep breath and let out the ragged sigh of a tired lion. The throbbing in his hand made it feel like it was about to explode.

"You're going to need to take care of that wound before long."

Venir looked over his shoulder. It was the commander. The man took a spot along his side and stoked the crackling embers of the fire while he stroked the long ends of his mustache

"Quite a battle," he added, reaching out his hand. "By the way, my name is Jans. Commander Jans."

Venir took the man's grip in his and said, "Venir. Underling Killer."

"Ha! You can say that again. You've got most of my men talking about you already. I've even found myself making a comment or two, and I'm not a man of many words."

Jans ran a cloth over the bald crown of his head and took a deep draw from a sack of wine. Venir could see the hardened face of a battle tested soldier who wasn't like many Royals. Some were good, most bad by his account, but Jans seemed alright. An old soldier who put his trust in steel, more so than men.

Slim moaned. It was faint, but at least he was moving. Venir checked the wound on the man's leg. The spider bite, four holes each as big as the tip of his finger, had swollen the man's ankle to the size of Venir's arm. Slim's head was dripping with sweat. Venir let out a grunt.

"He's made it this long, I'd say in a few days he'll be moving, maybe just not walking," Jans said, "but we'll have to clear out first light tomorrow. You sure you don't want someone to look at your wound?"

"No. I've had worse." Venir shrugged.

"So, what were you doing with these people?"

"Heading north. There are some people I'm looking for."

"They must be important if you plan on traversing these jungles that are thicker with underlings than they are mosquitoes."

Venir shrugged. "It looks like you and your men have survived. Certainly there are more Royals to come."

Jans laughed. "Our days are numbered, and our supplies run low. Almost half of our outposts in Southern Bish are either under siege or over taken." Jans tossed him the wine sack and cleared his throat. "The underlings cut through here like a black storm one night. They burned, killed and destroyed everything living and moving for miles. This batch we just ran over," Jans looked over his shoulder where a pyre of burning underling bodies smoked and smoldered, leaving a foul stench lingering in the air, "is only a small roving force. There are underling armies numbering in the thousands out there. The only things getting us through are that we know our lands better and horses travel much faster than underlings and spiders."

Venir knew it to be true. The jungle-like forests of the south were difficult to march an entire army through. Filled with high hill tops that jutted outward in many places and formed steep cliff faces in other places, the southern lands were a place of sanctuary to those who knew them. As well, the deep ravines and vines thick as trees made it tough for travel.

Venir's face turned grim as he asked, "So, what are the Royals doing to deal with this mess? Still sitting on their thrones and spinning lies to the masses, or are they gearing up for battle?"

"They're fortifying the north."

"And leaving the south to die."

"Well, it's mostly gnolls and orcs these days. But, Venir, without Outpost Thirty-One, any attempts to hold the south are in vain."

Venir let out an angry snort. He still didn't understand why the Royals never attempted to retake their most strategic stronghold in the south. If it had been up to him, he would have rooted the underlings out before the underlings were dug in too deep. Now, it seemed like it was too late for that. Besides, it was the Royals who had abandoned their own kind. Jarla the Brigand Queen, in unison with the underlings, led the fort to its fall. As far as he was concerned, the Royals deserved what they got. But now, more than five years later, the issue had a new significance. Something needed to be done.

"Where were you when that Outpost fell?" Venir asked, taking a sip.

"Twenty-Four. And you?"

"I was there. I was part of that small group that gave the early warning."

Jans's brows lifted as the fire reflected on his oily face. "Ah … I know you, Man. At least, I knew of you. Are you one of the rogues who took down the Brigand Army? Hah! That horde, now that was something the likes I hope I never see again. Orcs, gnolls, kobolds and men fighting as one."

"Under the direction of the underlings."

Jans grunted. "Aye, of course. I think that us and the other races are in the same predicament now."

"Have you seen any evidence of that?"

"Yes, but very little. As much as I hate the underlings, I have no sympathy when they carve down the other scum, either. Bish would be better off without all of them."

Venir felt a little irritated at the remark. As despicable as the other races could be, he still had difficulty dealing with the Royals and their attitude of superiority. As much as he hated to admit it, it was the underlings and the other pesky races that kept the Royal egos in check, at least if that was possible. Now, as these soldiers struggled for a foothold for their own survival, he could only imagine that the Royals were too busy pointing the blame at one another instead of acting. As the underlings gained ground and dug in deeper, he imagined the Royals wouldn't do a thing until the last moment possible.

He put the wine sack to Slim's mouth, squeezed out a few drops that soaked right between Slim's lips, and tossed it back over to Jans. Something about what Slim had said to him a day earlier was sticking in his craw. He'd been fighting underlings on his own for the most part. Now, maybe it was time he added some more people to help shoulder the load.

"So, what are you going to do when you run out of supplies?"

Now it was Jans's time to sigh.

"I can feel it, Venir, deep in my belly." He tapped his stomach. "Time. Our time is running out. We've kept on the move knowing full well if we take a fort and hold out the underlings will starve us out."

Jans took out a wetting stone and began running it across the edge of his sword.

"My men are becoming weary with worry now, as I've run out of answers. All I've been able to tell them is that help is on the way, but no aid has come. We send riders north, but none have returned." He stretched his booted feet towards the fire. "The truth is, I figured this battle would be my last. None of my men had planned to survive, either. It was our choice, our sacrifice to distract the underlings so the rest of the force could clean up." He became solemn for a moment, rugged face looking up into the sky. "The fewer mouths to feed, the better. We die so others can live a day or two longer and have one last belly full before battle."

His words sank in. Jans and his men were unlike most men he'd known.

Jans slapped his leg and spit out a laugh.

"And then you show up, and here I sit, ready to live another day and die on another. I just didn't want to die from starvation, holed up in a fort. And the thought of my own men eating one another didn't sit right with me, either. I've seen that happen before, long ago." Jans's head sagged down to his chest as his eyes got all misty.

"What happened?"

"Oh … I was a boy, my brothers and sisters starving, trapped in Bonehole by brigand orcs that had seized a small outpost leagues northwest of here. My father and mother said they were leaving to gather food, but only one returned. The meat got us through the next few days until the Royal Riders showed up, and I've been one of them ever since."

Venir thought he saw a tear on the man's cheek.

Staring into the fire, Jans finished his thought. "I'd rather burn than ever do that again."

22

BRAK'S STOMACH FELT LIKE IT was being turned upside down in his belly, and he swore his head was spinning on his shoulders, but it all ended abruptly. Darkness. The rustling of bodies and the scent of something wonderful. Baked food. Brak noticed light creeping from beneath a doorway and shoved it open.

"Wait!" the skinny man interjected as he pulled on the back of his pants.

A dozen men couldn't have stopped him from stepping out into the smokehouse, wrapping his blood-stained fingers around a hot blackberry pie, and shoving it into his mouth. The café owner didn't contain his dismay or fury, shouting, pointing and crying out for the City Watch. He didn't care. He ate and ate and ate.

"What have you done? Where have you taken us?" Melegal asked, holding his aching head.

Melegal stood behind Brak, watching the big young man stuff his face like a hungry pig. The baker, a man in a flour coated apron and with coarse black hair down his arms and over his knuckles, drew back a butcher's knife, aiming to ram it into Brak's back. *Drat!* In a fluid motion, Melegal wrenched the weapon from the baker's hand and drove his elbow across the man's chin. He didn't bother to slow the man's fall, just let him collapse on the tiles.

Melegal stepped outside the kitchen into the small store front, took a seat on one of the stools at the bar, and let out a sigh. He was still in Bone, and not only that, but he knew exactly where he was as well. He watched as the citizens of Bone scurried along with unusual activity. It was the time of day they would normally be working, but many of them were packed up. Fleeing from an unseen force. *Underlings.* He leaned against the bar to hear what they were saying.

The streets run red with blood.

The Royals have failed.

Thousands have taken over.

They shoot fire from their eyes and insects from their breath.

Thousands of women and children have been killed.

They are bigger than men and ride on the backs of Chimera.

They cut off my uncle's head and devoured his brains.

Something tugged at Melegal's vest. It was Jubilee: pitiful, with big brown eyes and Leezir's flat nose.

"What do you want?"

"Can I have something to eat, too?"

He looked over his shoulder at Brak, whose face was stained in blackberries and crust as he sucked down a jug of goat's milk. The over-sized young man with the face of a hardened soldier seemed awfully content, almost serene for someone who'd just butchered more than a dozen people. Melegal had seen Venir have his own fits of rage, but he'd never seen anything like what Brak was capable of. *Ew! What he did to those people?* He couldn't erase the thought of the man being bent backwards until the back of his head touched his arse. Or that Brak had almost killed him, Melegal, a moment earlier. He'd never been pinned down by such raw power before. He'd heard the term *berserker*, but before now it had seemed like a silly notion: a man so battle crazed that he'd fight, even without limbs, like a ravenous dog until dead. It seemed the stories were true.

He patted Jubilee on the brown-haired head and said, "Yes. But you better hurry before it's gone."

"Thank you," she said, smiling up at him, "for saving us." She wrapped her ginger little arms around his waist and hugged him.

Melegal cocked a brow over his steely eyes. After all the death, all the horror, the little girl still found a reason to smile and be grateful. He peeled her arms away, saying, "Fond of me all of a sudden, are we? Well, little Slerg, you are on your own now, so get a belly full, and don't ever hug me again."

He set Tonio's sword on the bar, felt the pommels on his swords, *the Sisters*, on his hips, took a deep breath, and rubbed his temples. Underlings. They were actually inside the City of Bone and attacking people. The improbable had occurred. Outside of the city walls were thousands of people who had fled the south to find sanctuary in the north. Inside the city, the citizens were scrambling to find a way back outside. No doubt, the Royals would permit them to leave, only never to return. He reached inside his vest, produced new darts, and reloaded his launchers. *If I'd only used poison, Sefron would be dead by now.*

Though thankful for his escape, he still had immediate problems. Lord Almen. Was he alive or dead? Sefron had come to the man's aid, and Melegal had witnessed his moving hand. *Slat. I should have cut his throat.* It wasn't his style, however, and killing wasn't something he was accustomed to, but sometimes that was the only choice if you wanted to live. Jarla the Brigand queen had witnessed the entire ordeal, and he'd tried to dispatch of her, but she had still been fighting when he'd fled. *Should have just done what the Lorda said and killed her. I'm not sure what possessed me to gut Almen.* He looked over at Jubilee, who was chomping on a biscuit. She had Leezir's eyes as well. Melegal grabbed a loaf of bread and had started picking at it when two surly men walked up, eyeing the food.

Melegal's eyes narrowed as he slid Tonio's sword from the sheath, saying, "Keep walking. This store's closed."

"We'll pay," one man said, licking his lips as the other fidgeted at his side.

"I only take blood," he replied, twirling the sword over his wrist.

The men grumbled and shuffled along.

He stuck the sword in the ground and resumed his thoughts. The underlings had been his unlikely ally in all this. They must have slaughtered all of the living in the arena, which should include Lord Almen and Jarla. They'd taken Sefron prisoner and pursued him. They wanted the keys.

"Ha!"

All this time, Sefron, of all people, had an alliance with the underlings. Sefron wanted the keys for the underlings.

Melegal ran his hands over the hidden inner pockets of his clothing. *One. Two. Three. Four. Five. Six. Seven. All present and accounted for.* He pulled a key out, fingering the topaz gem encrusted in the square head. It was the one he'd used on the last door. Then he remembered something. The Brigand Queen. She had arrived through another door with her men. *How did she manage to do that? Were there more keys? Or did she get there by some other means?*

"What is that key for?" Jubilee asked, crawling up on the bar, her legs dangling over the edge, mouth full of a biscuit and appearing happy as a lark.

"Trouble," he said, sliding it back into his clothes. "Now don't bother me. I'm thinking."

"All right," she said, beginning to hum a tune.

Now where was I? Keys. The underlings want the keys. Which means, the underlings will be coming after me. Slat! He couldn't shake the image of the Vicious, the beastly creature that could rend through stone with its nails. Was that creature coming after him as well? He remembered that the last time he saw one, at the Warfield, the nasty thing had slit Georgio's throat. *Oh my.* That made for two things even he'd hope the boy'd never see again: the Vicious and Tonio. He counted his enemies again. *Kill Sefron. Fail. Lord Almen. Fail. The Brigand Queen. Fail. It's only safe to assume that all live. After all, evil has an uncanny ability to survive. And now the Underlings. Aren't they supposed to be the problem for that brutish friend of mine?* He turned towards his friend's son, whose eating pace was now a slow chew. Brak's Venir-like eyes drifted into Melegal's, leaving a haunting feeling in his gut. Was he sane or a madman?

"Er … Jubilee, uh, how well do you know this man?"

She perched her eyebrows, smiling, wiping the crumbs from her lips.

"Brak? He's good. Nothing like my uncles or my grandfather, who weren't too bad, but still did many things I thought were questionable."

"Is that so?" *How interesting for a little Slerg.*

"Hagerdon said Grandfather Leezir had gotten soft in his age, but I never thought of him as old, not for a man, anyway."

"Hmmm … an interesting observation for such a young person. I'll tell you something else about your grandfather, Leezir. You are right. He wasn't one of the worst, not when it comes to Royals. Not that he had a soft side, he didn't, but, uh … how should I put it? He was reasonable and resourceful, just flawed."

Jubilee dusted the crumbs from her hands and hopped down on the ground.

"Everyone is flawed. If they weren't, then the world would be perfect. But if that were so, we'd be quite bored."

"You are smart for one so young."

"I know. Say, where's everybody going?"

"Why don't you go ask them?"

Jubilee didn't say another word. She just stood and stared at the crowd.

"My back hurts," Brak said.

Melegal turned and looked at the man's grimacing face.

Two feathered arrows still protruded from Brak's' back. Moving like a sloth, he made his way over and rested his arms on the bar.

Melegal looked up into his big face with the thick tuft of hair that was marred with blood. "Are you sure the hurt is not your stomach? You just inhaled enough to fill two cows."

"No …"

Brak's speech was a little garbled, low, and his pronunciations were long. It irritated Melegal.

"… it's in my back. It hurts. Did someone stab me? I can't remember."

"What do you remember?"

"Seeing Hagerdon killed. Leezir getting shot and Jubilee screaming. The next thing I remember, my back was on fire, and I was following you through a castle." He lifted his chin in repose. "Those paintings were wonderful. I'd never seen anything like them before."

A brute with an eye for art. Utterly ridiculous. But what isn't these days?

Jubilee wandered back over and gasped. "Brak! Your back! We have to do something!"

Brak's eyes narrowed on Melegal.

"You said it was just a scratch."

"Well it is, in a manner of speaking."

"Take them out," Jubilee demanded.

"You're the smart one; you take them out."

"Give me a knife, and I will."

"Pah … just get out of the way." He removed Brak's' shackles and inspected his back, needling his fingers around the wounds. Though they were not well defined, he could feel the brutish muscles of an ox beneath the meaty skin.

"If your arms were long enough, you could pull them out yourself," he muttered under his breath.

"What?" Brak said, cocking his meaty neck.

"Nothing." He wrapped his fingers around the shafts. "Now be still. This shouldn't hurt a bit."

Yank!

Brak roared like a savage beast, sending everyone nearby scattering in all directions. Melegal was twirling the arrows through his fingers as Brak whirled on him, snorting with rage, fingers clutching in the air.

Melegal took a step back and said, "You'll be fine. Target arrows. See?" He banged the bloody tips together, showing that they were only pointed, not serrated. "It's what they use to kill baby deer with."

"Or my grandfather!" Jubilee sniped, arms folded over her chest, frowning.

Brak snatched the arrows from his hands and snapped them in front of his face.

"Don't ever do that again, or else I'll break you in two."

"Sure. In the meantime, try not to get shot again. And with that, I think it's time we went our separate ways."

"What?" said Brak.

"What? No!" said Jubilee.

Melegal tossed the girl a small purse of coins.

"Get cleaned up and find a private place to live in this big city. I've got problems of my own. They'll be coming for me."

"The Royals will find us and find you no matter where you go. It's best we stick together. They'll be after all of us now. You know that. You tracked us down."

Indeed, she was smart. Street smart to say the least. There would be no hiding Brak, however. He'd only get bigger and bigger. But it wasn't his problem. And what about the Almens? Maybe none of them had survived. Was it possible the underlings had wiped them out? If Lorda Almen lived, she'd expect him, unless she assumed him dead. But without a body, what proof was there of that? He looked up. Dusk had begun. Where had the time gone? It was as if the last few hours had been lost. Where had the past few hours gone? If they did indeed come looking for him, they'd know where to look first. Then he took off in a run. *Haze!*

23

EXHAUSTED, FOGLE BOON FORGED AHEAD, Cass's screams giving him the energy he'd lacked a moment earlier. So far as he was concerned, she was his woman, as he'd never been with another, and as things would have it, he probably wouldn't live long enough to meet another. Instead, the impulse to rescue her overcame all reason. He ambled over a dusty hilltop on weary legs.

Not again! It can't be!

But it was. Another giant. Cass kicked and screamed like a wild woman in the monster's clutches. But where was Chongo? He could hear the dog barking, the sound as powerful and carrying as a dwarven gong, but the two-headed beast was nowhere in sight.

All around he looked. Nothing, but all he was truly concerned about was Cass.

"Let go!" She yelled, kicking the side of the giant's nose.

It sneezed, getting a spray of snot all over Fogle, as well as on Cass's magnificent face.

She shrieked in fury!

"AAAAAAAAAAAAAAAH!" she yelled, her lungs recharged to their full power.

Fogle stumbled down the hill, his mind racing, trying to figure out what the best course of action would be.

"FOGLE!" Cass cried, "get me away from this behemoth! Now!"

He closed in about thirty feet away, summoned all the energy he had left, and flung a small barrage of glowing missiles from his hand.

The giant grunted and sneered when the missiles struck its leg, fizzled, and extinguished like drops of water being poured on a campfire.

He caught the worried look in Cass's eyes. *I've failed.* His shoulders sagged, and he could barely lift his chin up to face the inevitable death of his lover. *Chongo. Mood. Where are you? We need help!*

Chongo's barks were in full agitation, yet the beast was nowhere in sight. Perhaps he was trapped by more giants, but there was nothing nearby where the creatures could hide. He looked up at Cass, whose struggles were as futile as an infant's in the arms of a man. *She's going to be crushed.* He tried to summon that well of energy he'd tapped before, but unable to find it, he stumbled forward on weak knees and pitched face first into the ground.

Cass let out another blood curdling cry as he rose back to his feet into the blinding light of the setting suns.

"FOGLE! SAVE ME!"

He tried not to look. He didn't want his last memory of Cass to be a picture of her head exploding. He fought the urge to plug his ears. The sickening sound of Ox the Mintaur's bones being snapped and pulverized still rung there.

Chongo was still barking, a little closer now than before.

"Where are you, blasted beast?"

He shielded his eyes from the suns with his hands.

"What?"

There was Chongo: a giant two-headed dog suspended forty feet in the sky, running in mid-air, but going nowhere.

Who in Bish did that? Underlings!

"Look out behind you, Fogle!"

As he tried to twist around on his feeble limbs, something hard and painful cracked him in the back of his head. The lights of Bish went out.

"Ow!"

Fogle stirred. A throbbing headache greeted him. He had no idea how long he'd been out, but night had come, and it was dark, very dark. Unnaturally so. *Where am I?* He blinked and tried to wipe the grit from his eyes, quickly learning he could do no such thing. *Slat!* He was bound. *Cass!* There was nothing. Only his muffled efforts to speak could be heard. He struggled against his bonds once more, only to feel his strength fade from the effort as he slumped over and sucked for air.

Think, Fogle. Use the over-sized clump of brain matter in that over-sized skull of yours. One of the main things Mood had taught him in their many months together was not to panic. *When goininta the unknown, don't ferget ta use yer udder senses, he could hear him say.* Without having anything better to do and no other options that mattered, he rolled onto his back with a sigh.

Blinking his eyes and staring upward, or at least what he thought was upward, he allowed his eyes to adjust. *Black. Still black. Even blacker.* He closed his eyes and slowly drew a long whiff of air in his nose. *Dirt. Mud. Hmmm … a foul odor mixed with salt. Oh … it's bad. Not the scent of an animal.* A chill air drifted through his robes. *Underlings!* An unseen force coiled around him like a python and squeezed out all of his courage. The story came to mind of what underlings did to men way down below, under the ground. Why else would he be here in what must be a cave of some sort? He'd been dragged underground by the most deviant race of all. Mood had said that Bish was now crawling with them—and how easy it would have been to find him after all the commotion they'd caused, battling the giants. And now that they had not a single dwarf in tow, the underlings had struck the weakened party.

He could feel his heart pounding in his ears now. A tide of panic was rising. It only made perfect sense that the underlings worked with the giants, sending monstrous men then springing the trap as the giants wore their prey down. *Chongo was floating, and Cass was being crushed by the last giant. No! She's gone!* He wanted to scream out. He wanted to say he was sorry that he had failed. *Why me?*

A little fire ignited inside him suddenly as a vision of Cass's light vibrant features, sharp and picturesque, drifted into his thoughts. Her slender hips, sensuous legs, pale lips and perky breasts had left a life-long impression in his mind. He swore he could almost smell her. The faint smell of flowers and a twinge of an exotic perfume mingled inside his nostrils. *I'll kill anyone that hurt her! I just need out of here.* He fought against his unseen bonds until, exhausted, he fought no more, slumping to the ground

In the distance, something he hadn't noticed before echoed. A muffled crunching sound like a dog chomping on a ham bone. All he could think of was the giant. He recalled seeing one stuff a dwarf in its mouth and bite down. He winced. *Cass!* He had to get out of there. He had to find her.

He summoned his mystic power into his thoughts and reached out for the minds that held him prisoner. He jerked up off the ground. *What?* Something strong, very powerful, unlike anything he'd encountered before, now mingled with his thoughts. His invading powers surprised it and it was coming, coming for him right now. Merciless, unrelenting and formidable. He clutched at the dirt. *A sharp stone or anything.* Nothing. Nothing there to help him at all but the dark.

"Who are you?" He sat up. "Where are my friends?"

The presence remained. Strong and silent.

"What do you want?" he asked.

Nothing.

He struggled within his bonds. The ropes that bound him did not seem natural.

"Huh?"

He could feel the presence growing impatient, and his wrists began to burn as he renewed his struggles.

The mind intertwined with his let out a frustrated groan.

In the distance, the chomping sounds became louder, like tree branches snapping in a storm. He shivered.

Fogle muttered a quick series of words. Part of an old binding spell. His wrists and legs became undone.

"About time," a familiar scratchy voice commented.

Fogle sat up. *Can it really be?*

"Grandfather?" he said, pushing away a thin veil of cloth that was wrapped around his head. It dissipated like twinkling dust. He rubbed his eyes and allowed them to adjust to the dim light that filtered in through the mouth of the cave.

Before him stood an older man with a long wispy white beard: tall and broad shouldered with forearms as stout and wiry as a pit fighter.

"It is you!" he gasped.

"Aye, Grandson." Boon's eyes twinkled as he reached down and helped Fogle back to his feet.

He gawped at his grandfather, whom he hadn't seen in over a decade. The man seemed a little older, yet his grip was as strong as iron.

"Where have you been?" Fogle asked. "Wait! The giant! Cass!" He began to shuffle around.

"Ah … your woman. Yes, she is fine," Boon reassured him. "Very fine, indeed. Fine like a crystal vase pouring chilled wine. Fine as the hairs on a baby's head. Fine like the scintillating, titillating colors of a rainbow." Boon smacked his lips. "Fine like a —"

"Enough already, I know how *fine* she is," Fogle said, irritated.

Boon looked down and patted him on his head.

"I'm sorry, Grandson. It's just that I haven't seen a woman in an awfully long time, and I'm certain the last one I saw didn't look anything like her. She's absolutely gorgeous."

Fogle shoved his grandfather's hand away and said, "It's Fogle. And she's a druid."

"Interesting," Boon said as he turned and teetered deeper into the cave. "Come on."

"But what about the giant?" he objected, looking around.

"Come on," Boon said, beckoning for him, moving more like a man of his wizened years as he shuffled over the loose footing, holding his deep blue robes up over his toes.

Unreal. Unlikely. Weary from head to toe. Fogle tried his best to assess his situation, wondering if it was real. Then he threw his hands up and swung them down through the air. *Just take what the adventure gives you. Trying to make sense of it is of little help,* Mood had said. "Never mind."

"What was that? Did you say something?"

"No."

Boon motioned for him. "Come along then."

The farther they traveled downward through the tunnels, the more Fogle noticed something. There was no source of light. No torch. No suns or moons. No candles or lanterns. Yet the walls were dimly lit with a soft blue hue. In three long strides, he caught up with his grandfather and grabbed him by the elbow.

"Did you do this?"

"Do what?" Boon said, this time a little irritation in is tone.

"The light. What is making this light?"

"Ah. That's the underlight. Incredible, isn't it?"

"Do you mean *under* as in *under*ling?"

Boon looked at him as if he was stupid and said, "Of course. What else would the underlight be?" Boon jerked his elbow away. "Now come on. Your friends are down there."

Fogle didn't move. He was in a cave, an underling cave, being led downward by his grandfather, who he hadn't seen in well over a decade. Nothing tingled or raced down his spine like a trickle of lightening. His senses had heightened over the past few months, yet nothing told him anything was wrong, but something had to be, certainly. If anything, the moment seemed quite ordinary, and that's what worried him most of all. And now the strange munching sound returned, echoing up the massive cavern which he was being led down. Boon was already moving on. Fogle looked back toward the mouth of the cave. It was gone.

"You'll be lost if you don't follow," Boon said. "Don't be such a baby. You always did worry about everything that could possibly go wrong. You can't control everything, just like that whack I gave you on the back of your head. You should know that by now."

Fogle rubbed the small knot on his skull. That was real. By why had his grandfather hit him and brought them all into this cave?

"Your questions will be answered soon enough. Now come. You're beginning to annoy me."

Fogle followed, one slow step at a time, through an enormous cave illuminated by the strange blue light. As the munching sound became louder, the scent of vegetation and water wafted through the air. One second Boon was wandering up ahead, then the next second he dropped out of sight. Fogle rushed over and found himself standing on a ledge overlooking a strange garden. There were trees whose leaves glowed and bushes filled with bright red berries. A stream passed over glittering stones and disappeared from sight. Boon was traversing a narrow pathway that led into the garden more than twenty feet below. And that's when he saw her. *Cass!*

She was lounging alongside Chongo, a curious and happy expression on her face, watching a giant stuffing something that looked like bamboo reeds into his mouth.

"Cass!" he yelled.

She jerked her head up and waved, saying, "Come down, Fogle! This is the most amazing place."

"But," he started to object, looking at the giant as he made his way down the path.

"Come on! His name's Barton. He won't hurt you. He's a friend."

He made it into the garden, dashed by Boon who'd taken a seat on an oversized mushroom, and embraced Cass. She was the real thing. Smelling like honey and roses as her pale eyes and lips seemed to glow in the underlight.

"I-I thought," he looked away, "I'd failed you."

She grabbed his chin and smiled, saying, "I thought so, too, but it seems fortune found us anyway." She eyed Boon. "Hmmm … now I see where you get your striking looks. Your grandfather is quite … interesting, to say the least."

"I guess you could say that. So, are you well? Did that giant hurt you? I thought you were going to die."

Pulling Cass into an embrace, Fogle got his first hard look at the giant, Barton, who was ripping more of the bamboo reeds from the stream bank and stuffing them in his mouth. One of the giant's eyes was disfigured, an impression of scarred flesh, while the other stared right at him, unblinking, a little deranged.

"You burned Barton with magic. No-No. Barton not like that. Do that once more, Barton smash you good. Understand?" Barton said, balling up is meaty fist and snapping the bamboo within.

"Er … yes," Fogle said.

"Grandfa—Boon," he said, turned his attention aside, "where have—"

"I been?" Boon responded less than a foot from his face.

Fogle flinched, then folded his arms behind his back and started pacing around.

"Don't do that again … and yes, where have you been? What are you doing here? Where did this giant come from? How did you find me?"

"Easy Fogle," Boon said, "you always were as uptight as a dwarf. Just give me a few seconds, and I'll explain. I'm tired, you know. Running from giants isn't the easiest thing to do. It takes a lot out of an old man like me, but I tell you what … It sure feels good to be back."

Fogle folded his arms across his chest and faced his grandfather, saying, "What do you mean, 'running from giants'? Why would they be chasing you?"

"I've been their prisoner, and I've befriended one of their own, Barton. I guess you could say that I'm an escapee and he is a fugitive, and a bushel of men twenty feet tall want to kill us. Well, me at least. Sorry to have to drag you into this."

"Wait a second," Fogle motioned to himself and Cass, "we didn't want any part of this."

"Well, you probably didn't want to be my grandson, either, but you are."

Cass giggled.

Boon slapped his knees and sat back down.

"Now, let's get some rest. We're going to need it for the journey ahead. Say, where's my spellbook? I need to bone up on a thing or two."

"It's *my* spellbook," Fogle said, looking around, "and where is it?" As he looked back at Boon, it was laying in his lap, where the old wizard's eyes glimmered with admiration. "Give me that back." He snatched it.

"Pah," Boon shooed him away, "I still remember it all, anyway."

As Fogle opened his mouth to speak, Boon was already snoring. He looked at Cass, who shrugged and lay down on a grassy bed.

What is happening? Is there anything I can control?

24

VERBARD SAT ON A ROUGHHEWN throne of stone beneath the City of Bone, enjoying the celebration. The underlings had struck a nasty blow to the world above and lived to tell about it. Commander Jottenhiem stood at his side, holding a bottle of underling port up in celebration. Verbard was moved. He'd never seen his kind, reserved yet tenacious, so charged up before. Now they bragged, one underling to the other, of the exploit, and the news spread like fire. Perhaps leading underlings into battle wasn't so bad, yet he still couldn't shake the feeling that something was wrong.

"Some port, Lord Verbard?"

"Certainly," he replied. "I see no reason to exclude myself from this celebration. After all, a handful of us just slaughtered hundreds. Just think what we can do with the entire army."

"I've been wondering the same thing," Jottenhiem said, handing him the goblet. "I think with a thousand more underlings we could take the entire city." Jottenhiem ran his black nailed fingers though his short coarse hair and showed him a fierce grin. "My sword arm is at your will and command, my Lord. I'll take all the soldiers you can give me back above right now. The more dead humans, the better."

"I agree, Commander." He picked up the object resting between his legs. The orb of imbibing. "But they will be ready next time."

"They won't be able to anticipate our strikes. They'll assume it's only a handful, but next time it will be hundreds. Whoever responds first will be wiped out."

But Verbard wasn't listening. Instead, he stared into the orb. The human mage wasn't nearly as powerful as he was resourceful, but the fat man's resources almost cost him his life. The magic in Bish was formidable. More so than he'd suspected. If a few more seconds had passed, he'd have been undone if not for Eep. Plus, the imp had followed his command, retrieving the orb to him. A costly move for Eep. The orb prevented him from teleporting, and Eep had a severed wing to show for it. Now the little horror sat behind the throne, mumbling in anger. Eep couldn't return to his world to heal. Verbard chuckled within, stroking the dark mirror-like surface of the orb. He'd had something to do with that. *It was worth the death of all those underlings combined.*

"We have company, Lord Verbard."

It was Kierway, escorted by the Vicious and two magi.

"Where are my Juegen?" Jottenhiem demanded, hands drifting to his swords.

"Dead, Jottenhiem," Kierway fired back, iron eyes smoldering. "Perhaps with better training from the likes of a true swordsman they'd have fared better."

Verbard rose from his throne, silver eyes flashing like lightening.

"Those are my men! And I'd also know the whereabouts of my other magi. Did they perish as well?"

"They died in battle, taking ten humans at least to their one," Kierway said, eyes flitting back and forth between the two. "And I see plenty of other soldiers missing on your watch as well. I'd judge not if I were you, Verbard."

"And yet I don't see a single scratch on you, Kierway. With so many fallen, I can't imagine how you'd come out unscathed. Yet here you stand, like a babe drawn from the refreshing waters of a cave bath. Pah!" Verbard let out a long seething hiss as he struggled to keep down his rage. "Well," he added, "can I at least see the key that my soldiers have died for?"

Kierway took a half step back, fingering his bandolier of knives.

"YOU DON'T HAVE IT!"

Every underling stopped as the dust and bat dung from the cave ceiling drifted downward.

Kierway pulled his shoulders back as he braced his fists on his hips.

"There were no keys! Only an empty chamber!"

Verbard fought the urge to shove the Orb of Imbibing down Kierway's throat. The underling was nothing but lies and disappointment all wrapped up together.

"Ah, so am I to understand that Master Sinway sent us on a fools run? Is that the case? And what do you mean by *keys*? I thought there was only one."

"No, many. Seven pegs, no keys."

Liar. Verbard resumed his place on the throne. For all he knew, Kierway had the keys. Or, there never had been any keys, and Master Sinway had sent them both to meet their final fates in Bone. After all, Kierway was clearly the biggest disappointment in Master Sinway's family. Kierway was a skilled swordsman, the stoutest of fighters, yet his career in leadership was marred in failure. His bloodlust led to the demise of more underling troops than most army commanders combined. Now, here he sat, paired with the most unpredictable underling of all. *Might as well play this ruse through.*

"And what of this cleric you mentioned? Is he dead … alive? I see no prisoners."

Kierway showed a grin of sharp teeth and lied, "He paid the ultimate price."

"I can only assume you mean he's dead?"

Master Kierway nodded.

"So, let me understand this. There were seven pegs and no keys. The only lead you had was this human, which you now claim is dead. Hmmm … I'm having a hard time believing you, Kierway."

Verbard pulled out a brass amulet with a clear crystal in the center. Kierway took a sharp draw in his nose.

"Of course," he added, "I'm not going to take exception with your thin explanation. I'll let Master Sinway handle that."

Kierway's eyes filled with hatred as Verbard draped the amulet over his neck, clasped his hands around it and chittered mystic words. The amulet felt like black fire in his hands as he let go. The humanoid image shimmered to life between the stone throne and Master Kierway. Verbard abandoned his throne and bowed. Master Sinway's apparition was as real as if he was standing there. Verbard's silver eyes drifted onto the amulet that was warm in his hand, radiating with black power, before turning them back to the all too realistic shade.

"What an unexpected surprise," Sinway said in his powerful voice as he gazed upon his son, "and all this time I thought you were undone. I can only imagine that the delay was because you have taken over the entire City of Bone." Sinway's head glanced around. "But, this hardly looks like the interior of a castle." The Master of all underlings turned his attention towards Verbard.

The iron eyes of Master Sinway were a swirl of copper and black, his expression cold and snake-like. Verbard found his tongue cloven to the roof of his mouth as he began to speak.

"I've led one small force inside, and we decimated hundreds. Among them, Royals and many magi. All ours that went in returned alive, and are now rejuvenated and craving the destruction of the Humans and their vile city more than ever. At this very moment, plans are being laid out for the next strike," He bowed again, "Master Sinway."

"Excellent, Verbard, and now, my plans of conquest shall be even easier with the acquisition of the key. Let me see it!" Master Sinway clawed and clutched at the air before him.

"Master Kierway led a small force into Castle Almen to recover the key," Verbard said as he looked over at Kierway, whose eyes bore into him like lances of fire, "but his mission failed. He—"

"WHAT!" Sinway yelled, his vocal power frightening the bats from their roosts and bringing the buzzing underling army to a standstill. He turned on his son. "Kierway! Is this true?"

Kierway opened his mouth to speak, but Sinway cut him off.

"You are a failure! An imbecile! If you were not my son, I'd have you chopped up and fed to the urchlings. But, your mother insists I keep you around. That you will redeem yourself. Instead, you find another failure, this one grander than all the others!"

In a flash, lightning coiled around Master Sinway's arms and blasted into his dumbstruck son. Kierway was bewildered as the bolts passed through him without so much as a singe. Sinway let out an angry hiss and turned his attention back to Verbard.

Verbard wanted to look away but didn't. *Don't say it! Don't say it!*

"I want that key. You," Sinway pointed at him, "will get it for me."

He glared at Kierway. The underling had smirk on his face.

I knew it. The fool fails, and I now have to bear the full responsibility. Is this what success breeds? Escapades of conquest outside the realm of even dreams. He wondered if he should mention there were seven keys. It seemed strange Master Sinway wanted only one, yet Kierway seemed truthful there were seven. *It will be easier to find one that seven. The best laid plans are kept to yourself.*

Master Sinway turned his focus back to his son.

"As for you, Kierway. You are now at the will and pleasure of Lord Verbard, as is my Vicious."

"No, Father!" Kierway objected as the Vicious took his place along Verbard's side.

Verbard looked up at the Vicious. *Things are looking up all of a sudden.*

"Your life is in his hands, Kierway. Failing me is one thing, I'm your father. Failing him is another. He's not." Master Sinway's image began to fade away.

Yes! Perhaps I'm not being set up, after all.

"Father, a moment!" Kierway said. "I've seen a grand chamber that hosted key pegs. There were seven in all, not one. I assumed Lord Verbard would have mentioned that. I thought you should know."

Bastard manipulator!

As Sinway faded away, his gaze locked on Verbard's as he said, "I only need one, but now I want them all. Get the keys. Continue the assault on humans! And await my next ordersssss …"

Verbard squeezed the amulet with all his might, sneering at Kierway, who snarled right back.

<h1 style="text-align:center">25</h1>

L EFTY BARFED OUT TWO GLOBS the size of eyeballs into his tiny hand.

Kam turned her head away, only to turn it back to him.

"Ew … what is that? Have you got a sickness, too?"

Lefty just stared at the objects in his hand, unable to hide his fascination. The look in his eye worried her. It was as if the halfling was possessed. Perhaps he was. He'd been awfully strange, after all.

"It's disgusting, Lefty. Are you ill or not?"

He shook his head and began polishing the murky color from the stones. A flare of red light lit up the entire room, then winked out.

"What was that?" Kam said, exasperated. *Magic!*

Lefty concealed the gems under his clothes as the front door creaked open and Diller entered. Lefty curled back into a ball, and Kam glared at the man.

"What was that?" Diller said, looking around.

"What?" Kam replied, sneering.

"There was a light. A red one, spilling out from under the door."

Kam didn't say a word. Diller walked over, grabbed the chains that bound her, and pulled her up. He ran his rough hands over her bound wrists, brushed his paw all over her, squeezed open her mouth, and looked inside. She decided right then and there that if she got the chance she would kill him first. He shoved her back to the ground.

"You better not try anything foolish, Pretty Lady. I'd hate to bury your fine corpse," he said, walking away and closing the door behind him.

"Lefty, where did you get those gems?"

The halfling rolled up into sitting position with a playful look in his sagging eyes. He looked more like himself that she'd seen him in days. The youthful energy in his voice returned when he spoke.

"The first time I met Venir, there was this underling. A powerful one …," he looked up, "uh …, yes, I wrote it down in my tome."

"I don't care about your tome."

"Oh … well, sorry, but I found these gems in the dead underling's robes. You should have seen that underling, Kam. Venir cut his head in half with Brool. Really gross. So, I've had these gems ever since, and I know they have power; I can feel it. And I meant to tell you about them, but I was always worried someone might steal them, so I stored them in my stomach."

"In your stomach? You can do that?"

Lefty made a cheerful shrug.

"Melegal said it was a gift. Just like my light feet."

Kam cocked an eye at him and said, "Well, did you ever think to store a key to those chains in there?"

"Huh … no," he said, looking sad.

"What else do you have?"

"Nothing, just these gems. Do you think they can help us?" he asked, holding them out in the palm of his hand.

Kam motioned with her hands to put them on the floor.

"We don't need that glow again. Something you did triggered them before." She shook her head. "I can't believe you've had them in your belly all this time. And you never got sick?"

"No."

"Or pooped them out?"

He made a disgusted face, shaking his head.

Kam's fingertips drifted closer to the gems. She wanted to grab them so bad. Find out what kind of power was within. Underling magi weren't anything she'd ever toyed with before, but she'd been taught that all the mystic powers in Bish came from one source. There must be something within them that she could use.

"What do you think they do?" Lefty asked, nosing closer.

Kam hunched a little closer, too. The gems were a deep red like rubies, and their cut wasn't the quality of gemstones, but more rounded on the edges, similar to river stones. Inside each one was a black swirl, like a tornado that she swore either pulsated or throbbed, like a living thing. Dark and mysterious, it beckoned her closer. Her fingers fanned out over the tops of the stones.

"Don't Kam," Lefty warned.

She bit into the soft flesh of her lip as her fingers curled up into a fist. There was power there. Dangerous. Seductive. Liberating. She could feel her heart pounding faster in her chest as beads of sweat burst on her brow. *Take them. They can help. They will help.*

"Kam?" Lefty said, pushing her hand away.

"What?" she snapped.

"We need a plan. For Erin's sake."

She held her aching head in her hand as she eased away while Lefty tucked the gems back under his clothes. *Erin.* Now wasn't the time to be reckless, but what other chances would she get? What would happen if she and Lefty were separated and she didn't get a chance to get her hands on the gems again? She couldn't let that happen. She had to do something. *Die doing something or die for nothing.* Isn't that what Venir once said? Maybe that was Billip or Mikkel, even Georgio, maybe.

"Lefty, do you think you can get those chains off, or not?"

"I think I can, but it might take a while. Why? Do you have a plan?"

She nodded as she shifted her hips to face him, saying, "I want you to free yourself. If you can do that, you can free me as well."

"But then what?"

"Then I'm going to find out what those little gems can do, and when I do that," Lefty's blue eyes were looking right into hers, "I'm going to use it, if I can, to help you fulfill your promise to me. Whatever power I can give you, or me, you are going to use it to get Erin to safety."

"No Kam! Using magic will kill you," he objected. "I can't let that happen. Maybe you can teach me to use the stones."

She ran her finger underneath the choker on her neck and sighed.

"No, if you could use them, you'd have known already. Lefty, you're going to have to be strong," she pointed at him with her shackled wrists, "for you, for me, and especially for Erin."

"But I mess up, Kam."

"No, you messed up." She poked him in the chest. "Now you fix it. Now you use all of your know how to make things right. Whatever happens, get Erin to safety. Find Joline; she'll know what to do."

The distraught look on Lefty's face left a sad feeling inside her, sadder than the one she already had. How hard it must be to do the right thing when evil had you in its grasp. Now, surrounded by thieves, liars and murderers, she'd asked a tiny boy to somehow save her daughter. She shivered under her robes as she pulled them tight and leaned back against the tub. Guilt washed over her as her chin sagged above her breasts. She could have gone to her family for help. She just hadn't wanted to. Over the years, she'd convinced herself they didn't care for her anymore. But now she was in over her head. *Blasted pride!* Now her daughter had to suffer for it. And she had to trust in a halfling boy who didn't look much older than ten, if that.

She sat there, eyes closed, unmoving, gathering all of her thoughts and plans. What would it take for her and Erin to escape? It seemed every plan and scenario met with a dead end.

The sound of Palos's door creaking open brought her chin up. The Prince of Thieves emerged, arms outstretched over his head, yawning in all his glory.

Disgusting.

"Well, it seems I can't sleep with all the excitement going on," he said, tying the belt around his robe, taking a seat, and pouring more wine. "I just love cat naps, so refreshing, brrrrrr. But Kam, my dearest, I couldn't stop thinking about you. Diller!"

Swift as a ghost, the man entered, crossbow ready, concerned eyes drifting towards Kam, before returning to Palos. "Yes, Palos?"

"Prince Palos, mind you. Now, remove her chains and take this little person to the Quarter. I, well, we, will be needing some privacy. I'm in the mood for another extravagant bath already." He rubbed his skin and leered at Kam as he guzzled his wine. "It leaves the skin so smooth." Lefty and Kam glanced at one another as Diller made his way over.

Kam rose to her feet as Diller unbound her, his hands much lighter to the touch this time.

Palos tipped his chin at her, and he swaggered over and said, "Fetch those warming salts. I want my water to make you sweat. It glistens so well on your body."

I need those stones.

As Diller bent over to unshackle Lefty, Palos said, "Better leave him in the chains. I don't want him wandering around here stirring up trouble. See to it the Quartermaster keeps a close eye on him."

Kam almost dropped the bowl of warming salts when she caught Lefty giving her a wink.

"Enjoy your bath, *Princess,*" Lefty said, tongue hanging from his mouth.

She reached down and grabbed a handful of his thick yellow hair and said in his face, "I should kill you, little halfling Bastard!"

"Alright you two, cut that out!" Diller sat, pulling Lefty away, leaving Kam with a fistful of his blond hair.

"Ow!" Lefty said in an angry cry.

"Get him out of here, Diller! And as for you, Kam, you need to calm yourself and focus on me. Get those salts in the tub. Now!"

Kam dabbed her hand in the bowl of bath salts as Diller slung Lefty over his shoulder. A sinking feeling settled in: that she might not ever see the boy again, or the gems either, for that matter. She tossed a ball of bath salt in the tub, bringing the water to a sizzle. The next one she grabbed was as hard as a stone. She looked at it and almost gasped. It was one of the gemstones. The other was resting in the bowl.

When the door closed behind Diller, she realized she was alone with Palos, but with a glimmer of hope this time.

"What are you gawking at?" he said, disrobing as he slipped into the tub. "Throw in more salt; it's not hot enough, you lactating witch."

I'm not going to live another moment like this. I'm sorry, Erin!

She tossed the rest of salts in the water and let the bowl clatter to the floor.

"Ah, that's better," Palos said, closing his eyes.

Inside her hand, the red stones throbbed. The choker around her neck began to tighten. *Summon it! Do something!* The gem stones' magic made contact with the magic within her and rose her to another level. Kam felt more power than she'd ever felt before. Dark and wondrous. Magnifying the magic within her. Her face purpled, and her knees began to buckle. *Hang on, Kam! Think!* But no words came to mind.

Palos wasn't paying her a lick of attention as she hung back to the side of the tub. The water was all bubbles, fizzles and steams. But any second he was certain to notice that she was about to choke to death. *Think!*

Gems in hand, she touched them to her neck and focused her thoughts on the choker. *Remove this harness from me!* She envisioned it unraveling in her mind. The choker squeezed her neck so hard she swore her brains were oozing from her ears as she fought for her life. One magic force in a fierce battle against the other. Her body a punching bag. She summoned all her anger, all her hate, every bit of desperation, and turned it on the white hot line on her neck. Something inside her mind screamed.

Snik-ting. The choker slackened on her neck, yet remained there, its magic spent. She'd won.

She gasped for air, saying, "Oh my."

Palos turned his head, "Did you say something?"

Kam disrobed, swung her legs into the tub, slid into the bubbling waters, and began rubbing his head with one hand as she pressed her breasts into his back.

"Just a little choked up is all," she said. "It's been a long day."

"Ah … that's better," he said, leaning back into her. "Nothing like being a Prince."

The steam from the sizzling hot water did little to relieve the tension in her taut muscles. Filled with power she'd longed for, only one question came to mind. *What now?* She had her magic. She had more power. But she still didn't have any idea where her daughter was, and she couldn't go blasting her magic through the tavern like a bull gone wild, even though that's exactly what she wanted to do.

"It would feel much better if you used both hands, Kam!"

She tossed the red gems on her robes and twitched her fingers at them. The robes moved, concealing the gems.

I should kill you now. She grasped Palos behind the muscles on his neck. *But I just don't think it would be that easy.*

She dug her thumbs deeper into Palos's supple muscles. The man might have gotten hefty over the years, but his svelte feline muscles were still at work under there. She had to be careful, very careful. The man could overpower her in a second.

She brushed her lips against his neck and said, "Feel better?"

"Without question. My, it's a sudden twist in your attitude. Why so sudden?"

"I just want to see—"

"Pah! Of course. You just want to *see your daughter*," he said, mocking her. "Pathetic. It would be best if you lied about liking it. It would make things better for the both of us."

"I see," she said, kissing his neck. *Bastard!* "Does this feel better?" She kissed it again. *Like kissing swine.*

"You're learning."

As much as Kam longed to see her baby and get her to safety, she'd have to play along a bit longer. And hope her shameful acts wouldn't lead her to kill herself in the meantime.

26

"**O**UTPOST THIRTY-ONE!" Jans shouted, slamming his helmet to the ground. "That's Absurd!"

Venir wasn't surprised at the reaction. He'd grown accustomed to it over the years, seeing how he'd suggested it a few times before.

"It's the only foothold the underlings have, Jans," he argued. "And by the looks of things, I think it's the best choice. You are low on supplies and getting lower on men. No word has come from the Royals."

"You are a madman!" He pointed at Venir, gesturing to his men. Each and every one of the commander's top leaders was stark-faced and glum. "I know you swing a mighty axe, but that's hardly enough to take on an entire underling army. They're thicker than thieves in those forests. Thousands if not tens of thousands."

Venir shook his head. "You don't know that, and I don't believe it. The Royals have done nothing but turn tail and run since the day it was overtaken. One swift assault from the beginning would have gotten it back. Instead, they went back home, hid in the castles, and left all the rest for dead." He looked down at Jans. "You know I'm right."

"That's treason, you renegade," Jans warned. "I'd be more careful what you say."

Venir balled up his fist and started to draw back, but stopped. Now wasn't the time to fight with fists. Maybe, for a change, he could try using words.

"Now is not the time to worry about upsetting a bunch of pouty Royals. Now's the time to figure out how to survive. You can't keep running through these hills and jungles until your horses drop dead. You can't wait for orders from the north. They aren't coming. What you need to do is take care of these men. If we can get into the Outpost, spread the word, then a greater force might come."

"You can't possibly believe we can penetrate an impenetrable Outpost? Hah! It's not possible. Not even if I had another thousand riders. We'd need siege equipment, too. You can't really think we can pull this off, can you? Be reasonable. I say we make a bee line for Bone and don't look back."

Venir wanted to stick his fist in Jans's mouth. Certainly the man realized the Outpost had already been overtaken once before.

"They'll expect that. What they won't expect is battle at the front gate. We only have to take one gate, and I wouldn't be surprised if it isn't as heavily defended as you think. The hilltop's been as quiet as the dead since the Royals departed." Venir lifted his brow. "Besides, I think we can take it back the same way they got in."

"I'm not getting all my men killed."

Venir looked around. The Royal Riders were a proud group of hard riding adventurers who had battled more than a few times in their lives, judging by the looks of them. Battered and weary, armor dented, chinked and gashed, they looked like they were up for another fight or two.

"You men," he said, standing tall, "you didn't become Royal Riders because you wanted to live forever, did you?"

No one said a thing, but the crowed began to stir.

"Do you want to sink your spears into more underling bellies?"

"Aye!" a few responded.

"Have you burned enough of their stinking hides to last you a lifetime?"

"Nay!"

"Are you ready to trample their bones into dust? Stomp their guts in the mud? Or do I have to light a fire under your arses!?"

"Nay!" all of the surrounding men chanted, raising their spears and swords.

"Do we need more forces to show us how to kill the underlings, or do we just need the sound of thundering hooves under our feet?"

"Aye!"

"Are you ready to fight?"

"Aye!"

"Are you ready to die?"

"Aye!"

"But most of all, are you ready to make the underlings pay?"

"Aye!"

"Aye, Venir, I'm with you!"

"I want to stick my spear so far up their arses I poke their eyes out!"

The Royal Riders shouted and cheered. The entire camp bristled with energy.

Venir hoisted his axe high in the air.

"Release the Hounds of Chaos!"

27

T HE DAYS OF CARING ABOUT himself had evaporated over the past few months, now replaced with a strange sense of nobility. *Slat! I'm going to save my woman. Well, a woman. And she's not even that pretty, at that!* Melegal traversed the city streets like a grey ghost, the shadows of the dipping suns quickly leaving the street mysterious and deadly compared to the day time.

Looking over his shoulder and ducking into alleys, the city's craftiest of thieves felt pressed for time. The city had never been like this. The people's faces and voices were full of panic, and a chronic series of alarms was being raised. The underlings were here. He'd seen them. The rumors and stories were so rampant he'd have sworn the entire city was on fire. *This can't be happening,* he thought, running up one narrow set of steps and down another. *Underlings in Bone. Insanity!*

He climbed up the window sills to the top of an apartment building, then jumped across from one rooftop to the other. Huffing for breath, he hunkered down in the shadows of a chimney stack and peered at his building across the way. *Haze shouldn't be in there.* Below him, people were pushing and shoving, gathering their gear and heading towards the gates. He could hear windows being nailed shut and deadbolts sliding into place. Not all of Bone's residents were going to flee. He assumed most would fight to the death before they moved. Still. *I've never seen it this bad before. But I don't see any underlings, either. Oh my!*

For the first time, his steely eyes noticed the smoke in the distance and the flames licking from the rooftops. He'd seen plenty of fires in Bone in his lifetime. Civilian riots were the main cause, but they were small and easily quashed under the boots of the City Watch. This, however, was big: an inferno by comparison. He shook his head. *What in Bish is going on?*

Haze. She'd been nothing but kind, in an odd sort of way, since the first time they met, and he'd almost chopped her fingers off for it. Now, he felt compelled to save her, and for all he knew, she wasn't in any real danger. He wouldn't figure they even knew where he lived. It was McKnight's apartment, after all, the former detective's secret place of privacy. But, the Royals' reach was as long as it was deep. After all, they'd found him once before.

It wasn't likely that with all the commotion the Almens would be focused on him. And if anything, they were all dead. Lord Almen, Sefron and the Brigand Queen should really already be eliminated from his life, after what happened in the arena. He should be a free man. He could, perhaps, return to the Castle and console Lorda Almen. *Who knows, maybe the Brigand Queen is dead.* He grinned. *Now that would be special.* He glanced at his apartment building. Nothing was out of the ordinary. Taking a seat, he leaned back, closed his eyes, listened to the chaos in the streets, and tried to relax. *Give it some time. Just a few minutes of peace and quiet.*

In his lap, he laid a long rectangular case that he'd removed from Lord Almen's study. He gently ran his fingers over the edges. *I wonder if this is what I think it is.*

"What's in that case?"

Melegal's eyes snapped open. It was Jubilee.

"How did you get up here?"

"I climbed."

"You couldn't have kept up with me," he said, hiding his incredulity.

"But I did. Why, were you trying to abandon us? I thought we were sticking together," she said, frowning.

"Little Slerg, just to be frank: yes, I was trying to leave you." He looked behind her. "Where's Brak?" *Maybe he's dead and I won't have the blame for that.*

"Hidden in the sewers. We can go back after him later. Unless he gets hungry again. Then he'll leave," she said, taking a seat beside him.

"We aren't going back after anyone. You are."

"I'm not leaving you, and you can't get away from me. I'm a shadow. That's what my grandfather said."

"Do shadows have wings?" Melegal asked, narrowing his eyes.

Jubilee made a strange face and said, "Uh … no. Why?"

Melegal snatched her by the cuff of her shirt and dragged her across the rooftop towards the ledge, saying, "Because you're going to need them after I toss you over this edge."

"No! No! I'll scream!" she cried.

Jubilee's toes were scraping the ledge.

"I'm not worried; no one will listen. Now, are you going to leave me be, or am I going to have to drop you like rotting cabbage?"

She eyed him, saying, "You wouldn't drop me. I'm a girl."

"No, you're a Slerg," he said, shoving her farther out. "Are you going to … eh?"

He pulled her back. The sounds of heavy boots were coming down his apartment stairs. Three Watchmen emerged from the entryway and onto the street. One wiped his bloody dagger on his pants leg. Melegal felt his heart in his throat. *Haze!* The man shoved his dagger back in his sheath, adjusted the black-billed brown cap on his head, laughed, and motioned for his men to follow. Down the street they went. Melegal gawped at his bricked up apartment window.

"Who lives in there? Your wife?"

"No."

"Your whore then?" Jubilee asked.

"No. Be silent, will you?"

"Well, you look very sad. It must have been someone that meant something to you. So it's either your wife, a whore, or your mother, and it couldn't be your mother because you already told me you were a bastard. So which is it? A whore or a wife?"

Melegal heard, but he wasn't listening. He made his way back down onto the street. Jubilee followed him down, still talking.

"Grandfather says there are only four women in a man's life: his mother, his wife, his whore … Ah." She snapped her fingers. "Your sister. But, it couldn't be your sister, seeing that you were an urchin. So," she proudly said. "It's a whore. Grandfather says there are wives and whores and whores that become wives — eek!"

Melegal wrapped his fingers around her neck and said, "What do you call a woman that is not married. A whore? No. Are you married? No. Are you a whore? No."

"But I'm a sister," Jubilee squeaked out.

"No, you are an urchin now. And not being married doesn't make you a whore. Being a whore makes you a whore. And your grandfather, well, it sounds like he knew a lot more about whores than he did about women. Now shut your mouth and come on."

Melegal was accustomed to seeing the dead, but the thought of Haze covered in blood with frozen eyes affixed to the ceiling caused a feeling of fluttering moths in his stomach. Crossing the road and taking the steps up three at a time, he found himself at the top staring at a busted door. *Please, no!*

Stepping through the doorway, the fireplace was the first thing he saw, its embers cold. A table was overturned, two flower vases were shattered, and his easy chair was turned over. Anything that wasn't affixed to something was broken, except the door to the tiny bedroom. In two long steps, Melegal made it from one side of the room to the other and stepped inside.

Haze lay face down on the bed, unmoving, the sheets red with blood.

He touched her bare leg, noting the bruises on her ankles. Gently, he rolled her onto her back and studied her battered face. She looked like she'd fallen face first down a stone staircase, but she was breathing, barely. Her skinny legs had been sliced and poked. But she was alive.

"Is she dead?" Jubilee said, peaking in the door.

Melegal said nothing.

Jubilee stepped up to the foot of the bed and watched the feeble rising of Haze's chest. The little girl's eyes traveled from Haze's toes to her head. "You do have a sister. I'm sorry. I had it all wrong."

Haze's good eye fluttered open as she tried to say something.

"It's Me. Don't talk. I'll get you some aid, Haze."

Haze's voice was garbled, and she winced as she spoke, but he could still understand what she said.

"No. I'm fine. I've taken heavier beatings from Sis and Frigdah before. Just get me up and find me some wine, water or something. Oooh," she moaned, "face feels like it got hit with a sack of gravel."

"It looks like it, too," Jubilee added.

"What?" Haze looked at the little girl, then up at Melegal. "Who in Bone is she?"

Melegal helped Haze back to her feet. "I'll explain when it matters. I suppose those men were looking for me?"

"Yup," she said, pulling out a loose tooth and flicking it away. "Why?"

Slat! That meant either Lord Almen, Sefron or possibly the Brigand Queen were looking for him. But how had they managed to find his apartment so fast? Very little time had passed since he'd left Almen Castle. But that door, something about that door, the magic portal they sailed through. He was certain it had been later in the day when he arrived than when he'd left. At least a couple of hours had been lost. He led Haze to the living room. "What did they say?"

"They wanted to know where they could find you."

"And what did you tell them?"

Haze managed a smile. "I told them you had a woman in District Seven and you stayed there sometimes. I told them you were a dirty bastard that had a thing for bloated whores. I told them your—"

"I get it," he said, patting her on the backside. "Why District Seven?"

"Just a place where someone I don't like lives, is all."

"Good girl," he said, stopping to take one last look at his apartment.

Haze hugged his side and said, "We had good times here, didn't we?"

Sadly, he said, "Some of the best."

"You're an awfully strange brother and sister," Jubilee added, "but don't worry: I have a nice place you can stay with me down in the sewers."

And the rat returns from whence he came.

28

"HOW MUCH LONGER ARE WE going to wait out here, Billip?"

Since being tossed from the Drunken Octopus, Georgio felt tired and agitated. The entire city, a place he'd become quite accustomed to at one time, screamed insanity. The City of Three was so much better. Now, he sat on a melon crate, twiddling his thumbs.

"Stop fidgeting," Billip said, cracking his knuckles for the 1000th time. "We'll go shortly if we have to. Whatever he's doing, he's taking his sweet time about it. Wouldn't surprise me if he was lost."

That wouldn't surprise Georgio one bit. He'd gotten lost in Bone a few times before, himself.

He looked up at Billip and said, "Do you ever get a funny feeling that things aren't right? I mean, I just don't feel like myself right now."

Billip slid an arrow from his quiver and started scratching the tip in the dirt. "Ah … that's just your young loins talking. That girl, Velvet, got you all stirred up down there. Don't worry, you'll get used to it. It'll show till the day you die. A woman does that to a—"

"No Billip. Not that!" Georgio pressed his hands to his ears, shook his head, and then let them back down. "That's all you and Mikkel talked about coming down here. It's disgusting."

"One day, you won't think so." Billip smiled, then snapped his fingers. "I bet he's with a woman!" His green eyes widened. "Oh no!"

"What?"

"I just remembered. I think his wife lives in this town."

"Mikkel's married?" Georgio asked.

"Used to be. Hmmm … but where in Bone would she be? You should see her. Something else."

Georgio leaned forward.

"Really pretty, huh?"

Billip made a sour face. "Bish, no! She's squat legged like a kobold and as barrel chested as an ogre. Feisty as a hungry badger. I'd rather cut off my arm than spend a night with her."

"She couldn't be that bad," Georgio said, laughing.

"Well, every woman has her graces. Mikkel's woman just hides hers much better than the rest. Like a squirrel hides a nut, that is."

Georgio chuckled so hard he fell off his crate. Billip had the funniest way of putting things. He tipped the crate back up and resumed his seat.

"Billip, really, do you have a feeling that things are not normal? Lefty's feet used to sweat when things weren't right. Right now," he patted his tummy, "I'm not even hungry. I'm always hungry!"

Twirling the arrow in his fingers, Billip said, "Whatever it is, I'm sure it will go away. Now let's go."

"What? Already?"

"I'm not waiting on the brute a minute longer. It wouldn't surprise me one bit if he was frolicking with that heifer," Billip said, slinging his bow over his shoulder and walking away.

Georgio jumped to his feet and followed.

"He said he was going to look into things. Maybe he ran into underlings."

"I don't see or smell any. Now come on. He's smart enough to know where we'll be."

"The stable?"

"Yes, but first, I want to check out the main gates."

"Why?"

"Look around. All the people are gone."

"What about Velvet?" Georgio said, stopping to turn around and look. She'd made quite the impression on him, and he hated to leave her.

"She isn't going anywhere. You can look for her when we come back."

Billip led; Georgio followed. Ahead of him, the man strutted through the alleys and down the abandoned streets, elbows swinging and head on a swivel. Billip looked like he was trying to keep an eye on everything at once. Not nervous by doing so, but casual. Georgio found himself looking around, too, but he didn't notice anything. *Just ugly buildings that should be torn down.* He missed his bed in the City of Three. It was soft and warm. He wondered how Kam was doing. *I bet she's glad I'm no longer around.*

"Quit gawking, Boy. We're almost there."

When they rounded the next corner, Georgio was bewildered by the sight. Thousands of men, women and children now crowded the inner gate. They had pack mules, carts and wagons loaded, fighting and pressing as hard to get out as what he'd seen on the other side to get in.

"I've never seen so many crammed together before. Not even for a hanging," he said.

"Look up there," Billip said, pointing at the top of the wall.

Georgio had never seen so many soldiers before. Where there were normally ten spaced out along the perimeter, there were at least a hundred, if not more.

"There really must be underlings in this city," he said, looking at Billip and all around. "What do we do now?"

"If I had a business set up, I'd be making a mighty profit now!" Billip said, clenching his fists and teeth. "Now I'm missing out. Nothing like a crisis to fill a smart man's pockets. Nothing, indeed. Wouldn't surprise me one bit if the Royals were the cause of all this." Billip eyed the spire of the nearest castle. "No. Wouldn't surprise me one bit at all. Bloody thieves. Come on. Let's lay low in the stable. We aren't going anywhere this way."

"What about Mikkel?"

"He'll figure it out."

Georgio followed on heavy feet, trying to make sense of what was going on around him. Underlings had invaded his last two homes, and that unsettling feeling was only growing in his gut. *Where are you, Venir?*

It wasn't long before the scent of hay and fresh manure wafted into his nostrils, and some of that odd feeling drifted away. The old barn was quiet and dark. Billip slowed his pace, eyeballing his surroundings. Nothing seemed out of place to Georgio, but as he started to speak, Billip cut him off with his hand. The archer slipped an arrow from his quiver and notched it on the string. One thought raced through Georgio's mind. *Underlings!*

Georgio had just slid his sword from the sheath when a stark realization hit him like a pan in the face. Every stall and gate was the perfect hiding place for an … *ambush*. Had he not seen it used for the same purpose? The time had come for him to start thinking fast for a change. *Should we retreat? What about Quickster?* He had to make sure the shaggy pony was well. The hilt of his sword was slippery in his palm as they crept farther into the barn.

Billip stopped and pulled his bowstring back as a stall gate creaked nearby. Something darted across the dirt: black, brown and grey. *A cat*! One moment there, the next it was gone.

Billip looked back at him and gave him a wry smile.

"I almost shot that thing. The poor light can be tricky if you're not careful. I'd hate to waste an arrow."

Georgio swallowed hard and wiped the sweat from his brow. After a few dozen more steps, they stood at Quickster's stall. Billip guarded the corridor, and Georgio swung open the stable gate. In the dimness, he could see the shaggy pony lying on its back, legs upward, knees bent downward, without a care in the world.

Georgio entered, bent down, rubbed the pony's shaggy black belly, and said, "Can I light a lantern?"

"Go ahead; just don't burn down the place. Wait a minute."

Georgio froze.

"Someone's coming."

He stepped out of the stall and looked down towards the end of the barn. A man carrying a bottle was swaggering their way.

"Where'd he come from?" Georgio whispered.

"I don't know. He just slipped out of those shadows."

Georgio remembered the old stable hand who'd always been there over the years. The old man, a toothless dullard with flakes and lice in his hair, hadn't been present when they arrived. It was odd. He usually saw the man most of the time. But this man was different. His gait was somewhat staggered, and his tall frame slightly hunched.

"Looks like a drunkard or vagrant," Billip said from the corner of his mouth. "I'll handle it."

But Georgio couldn't stop watching the silhouette that approached. The closer he came, the bigger he was, bigger than most men, almost as big as Mikkel. *Venir?* He took two steps forward, and that's when he heard it. The sound of a ragged breath, like someone exhaling broken glass. His fingers started to ache, and the muscles in his body froze. It wasn't Venir. It was Tonio.

"You!" Tonio pointed Georgio's way, his voice garbled and broken when he spoke. "I know you. I knew someone would be back. I wait. I find. I kill."

"Sh-Sh-Sh …," Georgio tried to say *Shoot* but couldn't.

Twang!

Billip's arrow plunged into Tonio's armored shoulder. The split-faced man locked his hand down on the arrow, took a swig from his bottle, and yanked it out.

The sound of the shaft pulling from the muscle and bone made Georgio's innards flex.

"Who is this man?" Billip said, pulling back the next arrow.

"T-Tonio …," Georgio said, sputtering.

"Ah, I see. One more step, and I'll add a third to your head," Billip warned, pulling the string back along his cheek.

Tonio dropped the arrow to the ground. Georgio's eyes froze on the half-dead man. Tonio was tall, plated from the waist up in mismatched armor. Two swords hung on his hips; another was sheathed on his back. His jaw hung to the right side of his mouth. In the twilight darkness, his black eyes sparkled, demented.

"Shoot him again," Georgio managed.

Tonio held up his hand. "Tell me where the Vee-Man is, and I might spare you."

Billip said, "Oh, so you are the Yellow Hair Butcher, are you not? There is quite a nice bounty on your head."

Tonio's chin dipped down as he eyed Billip.

"You'll never collect it. Tell me where the Vee-Man is ... NOW!"

Tonio's voice scattered the pigeons from the rafters.

Billip let another shaft fly.

Tonio snapped his forearms in front of his face.

Chink.

The arrow juttered on the metal bracer.

"Impossible!" Billip nocked another arrow and fired.

Chink.

Tonio took another step forward. Georgio took a step backward, trying to blink the living nightmare away.

"Tell me where the Vee-Man is!" Tonio growled, ripping a sword from the sheath on his back. "I remember those fingers, Boy. They might grow back, but your head won't. Not after I eat it."

Twang! Twang!

Billip pinned one foot to the ground, then the other.

"Pah! You'll be out of arrows soon, Little Man."

Tonio guzzled down what was left of his whine and tossed the bottle aside.

"Shoot him again, Billip!" Georgio said, shuffling behind the man.

Billip unloaded another feathered shaft at Tonio's face. Tonio knocked it aside in one fluid motion with his sword, reached down, and pulled the other shafts from his feet. He drew his other sword. "When Vee-Man comes, I'll be eating your bones." He pointed one sword at Georgio. "But I'll be saving yours for last."

"Run, Georgio!" Billip said, backing away as he reloaded.

Twang!

This arrow caught Tonio full in the chest, but he was already running. Tonio's bigger body slammed into Billip, driving him hard to the ground. Billip had his fingers wrapped around one of Tonio's wrists as the other sword hand came down. There was a sickening sound of metal meeting bone as Billip cried out and went limp. As Tonio rose his arm to deliver the next deadly blow, Georgio charged.

"NOOOOO!"

He whacked Tonio full in the chest with the edge of his blade, knocking the man backward. With one mighty swing after another, Georgio drove the monster man backwards. Tonio parried again, again and again, then let out a frightening laugh.

"Tired are you, Young Man? Do not fear, you'll not feel fatigue much longer."

Tonio swung.

Georgio parried. The powerful blow stung his hands. Gasping for breath, Georgio took another swing.

Clang!

Tonio swatted it away like a child's rattle.

"Come, Boy, just lead me to the Vee-Man. His head is all I want. Vengeance I must have for what he did to me. See?" He ran his finger down the face of his nasty scar. "Vengeance so I can rest. Tell, and I shall go away."

Georgio's arms quavered as he rose his sword up. He'd never been so tired before, not even during the challenge. There was quite a big difference between swinging a heavy sword and swinging a Dussack knife. Huffing and puffing, he said, "You won't find him. You'll never kill him. He's gone."

Clang!

Tonio knocked his sword from his hand, grabbed him by the throat, and lifted him from the ground. Georgio couldn't get over the putrid smell of rot and alcohol as he gawped for air, his face turning red as a beet.

"He must come back. I must kill the Vee-Man."

Tonio looked as cunning as he was deranged, horrifying Georgio, who kicked and struggled, but Tonio was too powerful. Unyielding. Unnatural. It was like that final moment with the Vicious before it cut his throat was happening all over again. *I can't let him eat my head. Fight or Die!* He kicked at Tonio's belly harder and harder, but the man was like a statue.

"I wait for Vee-Man. But you die."

He could hear the leather in Tonio's gauntlet squeak as the pressure began to build behind his eyes. *I don't want to die again.*

Clatch-Zip!

Something rocketed past his ear, and he found himself on his hands and knees, coughing. He rolled to his back and looked up to see Tonio reeling, a large crossbow bolt lodged in his neck.

Clatch-Zip!

Another bolt ripped through the air, hitting Tonio in the leg, sending him spinning to the ground. A large man with a heavy studded club started pounding the man into submission. The club rose and fell. *Wham! Wham! Wham!* It was Mikkel.

Georgio reached for his sword and rose back to his feet.

"Who is this man, Georgio?" Mikkel cried out, bringing down his club with all he had.

"It's the Yellow Hair Butcher," Billip said, blood dripping from his mouth. "And the bounty's mine."

Mikkel hit Tonio again, harder than the last. Georgio could see the sweat glistening on the back of the man's neck. Tonio was regaining his feet, a golem that would not be put down, swords still dangling in his hands.

Whack!

Billip hit him in the arm.

Whack!

In the knee.

Whack!

Upside the head, but Tonio kept on coming.

"What in Bish is this man made of?" Mikkel said, laboring for breath.

"Hit him again, Father," an unknown voice cut through the darkness, or maybe that was the torch being carried by a young man, about Georgio's size, who was also holding a heavy crossbow.

Whack!

"Good thinking, Nikkel."

Whack!

"Enough!" Tonio groaned, swords flashing in the light.

Slice! Slice! Slice!

"Argh!" Mikkel roared, dropping his club. Tonio cut deep into his arm, leg and across his belly.

Clatch-Zip!

Tonio stopped. A bolt was planted square between his eyes. He teetered backward and fell to the ground.

Mikkel was gasping for air, blood dripping from his wounds. "Great shot, Boy."

"That's my bounty," Billip managed. The archer was grimacing in the torch light. His arm dangled from his shoulder. "I'll need money to stitch my arm back together. Pah!" He spat a mouthful of blood. "Well ... what are you looking at? I'm about to die over here. Do something!" His eyes rolled up in his head as he slumped back to the ground.

Georgio dashed into the stable and led Quickster out. Mikkel was carrying Billip in his arms. "What do we do?" Georgio asked, worried.

"I've never seen him this bad before. We can head for the nearest castle," Mikkel shook his head. "We'll just have to ask the Royals for a favor."

"What about Tonio?" Georgio asked.

When he looked back. Tonio was gone.

29

"**D**ELICIOUS, SIMPLY DELICIOUS," MORLEY SICKLE said, nibbling on another morsel of food. It was the finest dining he'd ever had. He'd never imagined there was so much that the tongue could experience. "The bread, the roasted meat and those vegetables that you ... er ... what did you do to it?"

"Sautéed'," a prosperous man replied, sitting by his side at an unusually long dining table.

"Yes, yes! Sautéed. Excellent. I'd never known food could be prepared as such before. Marvelous."

"More wine, My Lord?" a blossoming servant girl asked, with hands and face as delicate as the fine cloth draped over his lap.

Morley licked his teeth and said, "Absolutely," while reaching over and patting her on the rear. *My. A man could really get used to this.*

"Are you enjoying yourself, Morley, my friend?" the most dashing man asked from the far side of the table.

It was Scorch. The man who could do anything it seemed, which included making him a Royal.

Morley could feel his face stretching into a smile as wide as a canoe. *It must be this wine!* He couldn't contain it, marveling at the excellent dining hall. The chandeliers, each candle lit, hung twelve feet high in the air. The walls were cut limestone, where the most extravagant painted scenes of landscapes and battles were displayed. His wine goblet was pure silver, and his plates a fine porcelain. He never imaged so much wealth in the world. The Royals did well to keep that hidden from the citizens.

"I am, Scorch, but ... I don't think the rest of us are," he said, sucking down more wine as he eyed the others seated at the table.

"No! Er ... excuse me, no, ahem, Lord Sickle. It's just been a busy day, is all," said one Lord dressed in a tunic and pants as expensive as a suit of armor. On each side of the man, two others were face down in their food, dead. "And, ahem, quite frankly, I'm not accustomed to eating in the presence of the dead." The Lord's head lurked back on his neck. "Not with my brothers, anyway."

"Well," Scorch said, rising from his chair and tossing his long blond hair over his shoulder, "perhaps they should have known better than to interrupt my friend, Lord Sickle. And," Scorch twitched his finger on his nose, "I'm not so sure what to make of your tone, Lord Ashlorn. I sense agitation in your tone."

The satin clad women at the table, five in all, one just as pretty as the next, let out gasps. All except one, quite weathered, almost ancient. She was scraping her spoon on the soup bowl.

Slurp. Scrape. Slurp.

Lord Ashlorn dabbed his forehead on his cloth napkin, shaking his head.

"Forgiveness, Lord Scorch —"

"Lord Sickle is over there," Scorch nodded. "I'm not a Lord. I'm well above this drivel."

"Er ... yes, forgive me, Lord Sickle. But, I must confess, I am somewhat ... uh," he eyed his dead brothers, "frightened."

Morley hiccupped as he waved his wobbling hand at the man. "Oh, phish-posh, Lord Ashlorn. How could I ever be upset with my father-in law? Especially after he's blessed me with such beau — beautiful brides." He reached over and patted the trembling arm of the woman on his right. She was young, barely a woman, hair long and black like a sparrow. Her chin was quivering as she closed her eyes. "Hah. Now that's pretty."

In the other chair on his right, another woman sat, older, full figured, with a frown as big as a hat. She was Lorda Ashlorn, Lord Ashlorn's wife. Morley leaned over, puckered his lips and kissed her half on the lips.

"Heh-heh, I kissed her. I haven't kissed a girl since I was a young man," he said, licking his lips. "And she was as ugly as a mountain goat." He tried to kiss her again and slipped from his chair onto the floor. "She kicked like one, too. Heh-heh."

"SOMEBODY HELP HIM UP!" Scorch ordered, the polish in his voice turned hard as a wetting stone.

Everyone at the table moved, aside from the old woman, whom Scorch resumed helping with her spoon. Morley felt several pairs of hands helping him back up into his seat and dusting off his clothes.

"Thank you," he said.

Every face was stark, leaving him with an uneasy feeling. Before in life, most people hardly noticed him, now they were all terrified of him. Friendly or not.

"Oh, this is ridiculous. I don't belong here," he said, dropping his face into his hands.

"Certainly you do," Scorch said. "You've as a much reason to be here as the rest."

"Certainly," Lord Ashlorn agreed.

"Absolutely, here, let me rub your shoulders. They must ache after that fall," his eldest bride said, showing a slight smile.

But Morley, dispatched as he might be, could still feel their uncertainty. Their fear was mixed with loathing and self-preservation. They only did what they did because they had no other choice. It was either that or die. He snorted. He'd not spent much time around many people, but he'd been an avid listener over the years. The Royals in Hohm City, though not as intrusive as the others, still did not hesitate to exert their will. *Serves them well.*

"What was that, Morley?" Scorch said.

Pickles. Pickles. Hic. Pickles.

"Nothing, I just ... I just want to lie down. I think I'm getting sick."

"Have they poisoned you?" Scorch said. As he did so, all of the knives and forks on the grand table rose up on end.

A collective shiver filled the room. Even Morley, as dull as he senses were, blanched at the sudden height of danger.

"Scorch! Blast you! I've no quarrel with them," he said, watching the forks and knives slowly rise from the table. "Please, put the silverware down. I've seen too many die today. I don't want to see any more."

Scorch looked at him, blue eyes shining as bright as the sky. "But these people don't like you, Morley."

"No, we do like you," Lorda Ashlorn fell to her knees, "You are excellent, Lord Sickle. Worthy of the most high on highs." She clutched the silk of his pants and whispered. "Please don't let him kill us. Please."

The desperation in the pretty woman's voice and face sunk Morley's heart down between his knees. In a matter of hours, Scorch had over taken a castle, wiped out an entire garrison of guards, and delivered unto him everything he could ever hope for: the finest wine, women and clothing a man could find, but in all its splendor he was still not content. All he wanted was peace. *Pickles. Pickles. Pickles.*

The women trembled and sobbed, huddling close to one another while the knives and forks flashed and spun in the air. Every Royal was wide-eyed with terror when their heads weren't hunkered down. All accept the leathery old woman, whose satin sleeve now rested in the bowl of soup she scraped, determined to get every last drop in her mouth.

"She's lying, Morley," Scorch said, his silvery voice as hard as stone. "She wants you to leave. You repulse her. She thinks you are unworthy of the dirt beneath a chair."

"No," the Lorda said, rubbing his thighs, "It's not true, Lord Sickle. I've no such inclination. Your will and pleasure are mine. I assure you. I'll show you."

"Hah! She's a convincing one. Aren't they all?" Scorch said as the knives and forks continued to spin over their heads. "Come now, Morley. You have everything you want now. A beautiful woman grovels on her knees. Your belly is filled, and you've drunk wine pressed from mystic vineyards you didn't even know existed. Yet still, you are unhappy. Why is that? Is it these people?"

"NO!" Morley shouted. "NO! NO! NO!" he slammed his fists on the table. "It's YOU, SCORCH! Why won't you leave me alone!" Morley rose to his feet and began tearing off his clothes. He ripped his shirt off. Scorch replaced it with another. He pulled of his shoes and tossed them across the room, only to see them reappear over his toes. "STOP IT! STOP IT!"

"MORLEY!"

The entire castle shook as Scorch rose from the floor, his eyes flashing with anger. All the Royals who lived were scrambling for the doors.

WHAM! WHAM! WHAM!

The Royals fell to their knees, begging for mercy, waning at the threshold of the secured doors.

For the first time in his life, Morley felt something overcoming his fear: anger. He didn't care what Scorch said, what Scorch did. He could not take it anymore.

"Leave me be, Scorch or whoever you are! Be the curse of someone else. Follow these people! Read their thoughts! Leave mine alone! *Ulp!*"

Morley stood as still as a tree as the whirling knives and forks lowered around his head. The look on Scorch's face was one he had not seen before. Impatient. Dangerous.

"I suppose you would rather die than spend another moment with me; is that it?"

Morley swallowed hard. His sweat dripped into his mouth. Scorch had given him everything he ever wanted, except the power to make his own choice. He couldn't take it anymore. No life like this was worth living. Not like this. He just wanted his old life back. To be left alone to make his jig. He nodded.

The silverware hummed to life, spinning faster and faster, the circle narrowing around his neck. Morley heard a woman scream. He shut his eyes. *Pickles. Pickles. Pickles. Blasted Pickles!*

One eye snapped open at the sound of silverware clattering to the ground. The first thing he noticed as he scanned the room was that Scorch was gone. He let out a strange little laugh, like a man whose sanity had returned after a long absence. He opened his mouth to speak. *No! Don't say his name. Don't even utter it. Don't even think it again.*

Lord Ashlorn was the first to rise back to his feet. Hawking, long-limbed and heavy set the man ambled over, casting quick glances all over the room.

"Is he gone?" the Royal said, placing a heavy hand on his shoulder.

Morley showed a bewildered smile and said, "Yes, I believe so. Ur … Lord Ashlorn, I am sorry for all of the — *urk!*"

Morley felt a dagger being rammed through his stomach and out his back. His knees weakened as his body slid from the blade, and he crumbled to the ground. He could see his brides, young and old, sneering down on him as if he was an old rabid dog. His lips stammered under his nose as he tried to summon his last gasping word. *Scorch.* There was no reply, and he died with the taste of blood and pickles in his mouth.

Hohm City was such dreary place. Devoid of the suns' brilliant light and the moons' soothing glow thanks to the chronic company of mist and fog. No. It wasn't something that was going to be missed by Scorch. But Morley Sickle was. Why the man wouldn't accept all that had been given him, he didn't understand. It was clear though: the people of Bish were a stubborn lot. They would rather die than change.

Scorch made his way on foot through the marsh until he passed through the great pillars that marked the entrance to the road to the city. Before him, a hot dry land of cracked mud and hard ground awaited for miles in all directions. He'd learned enough about it before, when he traveled to Hohm City. The kind folk he'd traveled with had taught him a lot about the lands in the world of Bish that they knew. Certainly, there had to be a better place than Hohm.

"Where would you like to go?" he asked.

A woman, maybe thirty, with light brown hair down to her wide hips, strutted like a warrior by his side. *She's a gutsy woman, big boned, rough-handed and durable. Perhaps she'll better handle what Morley Sickle could not.* Plus, she had a funny way of talking, and Scorch liked that.

"Well, I've been south, as far as the settlements beyond dwarven hole. Met my first husband there, but buried him here." She thumbed the marsh. "Well, not really buried. Just killed him for cheating and dropped his bones in the swamp. He's a troll's booger now. Naw, I says we go to the City of Three. I hear it's really pretty there. That's where most all the nice things come from anyway." She tied her hair up in a knot and swung it back over her shoulder. "Of course, you already knew that, didn't you?"

Scorch smiled.

"Indeed, I did. So, Darlene, do you prefer to walk or ride?"

She set her hands to the hunting knifes at her hips and looked around.

"Well, I don't see any horses. Do you? Besides, I don't mind walking. My mother says my father was a dwarf, but I just think she says that 'cause I'm not very pretty. Besides, with these new boots you got me, I feel like I could walk forever." She scratched her head. "Can you make horses, too?"

Scorch chuckled.

"I can make anything. I just can't make you happy."

"Aw, don't worry about that." She spat on the ground. "I'm always happy so long as there's game to be tracked, shot, fetched and skinned. I'm going to feed you like a mountain king. You'll see. I can shoot a swamp rat cutting through the marsh at fifty yards. I once killed a bobcat with my bare hands. I smashed a boar with a log …"

30

T HE CITY OF BONE. PANIC. Chaos. Confusion. The Royals were walled up in their castles while the soldiers and Watchmen marched through the streets in heavy armor and heavy hands. The underling strike had shocked the very core of the hardiest citizens in Bone with its effects spreading and long lasting. District 27 wasn't any different, but the people there, long forgotten, were not in a panic. Instead, they went about their business, rebuilding one block at a time.

Trinos was perched on a bench facing the soothing waters of the fountain. Her platinum hair was brilliant in the light, along with the rest of her as well. The people who served her had worked hard all day long, and now they sat along the busted roads and dipped bread into soup bowls. A little girl, no more than six, was filling a pitcher with water. Her little smile was as warm as the suns as she curtsied towards Trinos and scurried away. It felt good, seeing people get things done, despite themselves. If only more of them would act the same.

"Ahem … Trinos?" said Corrin, taking a seat beside her.

She continued her gaze into the fountain and replied, "Yes."

"The people, well, they are getting nervous, despite their graces. Frightened, unlike anything I've ever seen." Corrin pulled the cloth coif from his head and held it to his chest. "The Royals are one thing to deal with. But Underlings, well that is quite another. They say they are the most atrocious creatures in all of Bish. Vicious. They eat people as they live!"

The underlings. Yes, they indeed were vicious. After all, she was the one who'd created them for such intents and purposes. Well, they were a loose creation copied from another world. Just a spice to give the boiling pot more flavor. Now it felt odd being among the people witnessing and hearing the testimonies of personal terror. She ran her delicate fingers through her hair then patted Corrin on the knee. The man's grim face brightened a little as he pulled his narrow shoulders back and offered a toothy smile.

"Corrin, tell the people they'll always be safe with me. As for the underlings …." She stopped and cocked her head. Someone close by and coming their way was near death. "Corrin. A man needs aid down Warrow's street. Lead him and his companions to me."

Corrin's heavy lids blinked as he said, "But, we've helped enough —"

"Corrin," she warned, narrowing her eyes.

He nodded.

"As you wish."

Stubborn man. They all were. But Corrin was faithful. Being a man of notorious ilk left his compassionate side as barren as a burned bee hive. But he kept the people working, much harder than they cared for, but as he reminded them, he was merciful compared to the Royals. Even though he really wasn't. They were just better fed and not whipped, at least not that she saw.

She rose to her feet and watched down the street. Four men approached her sanctuary: two young, two older including the one who was near death from his wounds. As Corrin led them from the street buildings' shadows and into the courtyard, she got a better look at them. They were a durable group, not attached to anything like the other people, with an amount of unusual pain and suffering carrying on their faces, unlike the rest of the people.

The biggest one, built like a black marble statue, was the first to glance her way. She saw the whites of his eyes as he gawped and stared. She felt him fight the urge to fall to his knees and beg for her hand in marriage. Yet, his concern for his friend prevented him from doing so.

"This one's wounded," Corrin said, "very bad. His arm's almost chopped in two. I'd say he's pretty much dead already by the look of him. Shall I get a shovel?"

Trinos stepped around the bench and made her way over to the man on the shaggy pony. The wounded man's clothes were soaked in blood, and the young man behind him strained to hold him up.

"Hold him still," she said in a soothing voice.

The wiry man moved his head around the back of his comrades to gaze upon her. "I'll be still," he sputtered, "so long as you stay right there. But I go where you go." He gawped and grimaced, continuing his stare as if he'd seen a woman for the first time.

She laid her hand on the wounded man's bloody shoulder and let her power run its course. The sound of muscles and bones stitching together was sickening. The man lurched up in the saddle. His chin cracked back into the face of the man behind him, but that man held on.

"YEE-OUCH!" the man cried as he gulped for air and blinked a dozen times.

No one said anything. All the men just stood in the courtyard watching her, eyes filled with wonder, lust and amazement. Corrin stepped in front of her.

"Your man is healed. You can all leave now." He held his hand out. "But, I'll be needing a contribution … a big one. It's not every day a man gets brought back from the dead."

"I-I wasn't dead," Billip said, craning his neck to get a better look at Trinos. "I was dreaming, and even in my dreams I've seen nothing like you. Will you—"

"Marry me!" Mikkel interjected.

Trinos let out a polite laugh.

"You are a passionate pair, I'll say that much. But I have other things in mind for the both of you."

Billip slid from Quickster's back and started rolling his shoulder.

"My hitch: it's gone." He opened and closed his fingers in front of his face. "And I feel stronger, more like when I was young." He looked at her and said, "Whatever you have in mind, I'm up for it."

"So am I," Mikkel said, stepping in front of his smaller friend.

"But we have to find Venir!" Georgio objected.

"Venir doesn't have legs like that," Mikkel said, smiling from ear to ear.

"Father!" Nikkel said, giving Mikkel an odd look.

Billip's head snapped at the tall black young man with pale blue eyes and broad shoulders and said, "Nikkel! Where'd you come from? Why, you're practically a man!"

"I've been with my mother for the past few weeks. Made the trek with the merchants." He slapped the steel on his hip. "I worked as a guard."

Trinos took her place back on her bench as the men got reacquainted. They were unlike the rest of the men in the City of Bone: fearless, dangerous and even jovial, they spoke with coarse words and high spirits. They were men who had seen it all. They were just what she needed.

"Come, men. Sit and drink from the fountain," she said. "Corrin, please find them food and goblets."

"But … Eh, as you wish," Corrin said, frowning.

"And fetch some bandages for this man's wounds." She nodded at Mikkel. "Are you well, man of many thews?"

Mikkel almost blushed as he said, "Ah, the bleeding stopped, but I could still use a stitch or two."

With a snap of her fingers, two women appeared almost in an instant, sitting Mikkel down and getting to work.

The other men seated themselves on the fountain's edge, the youngest sampling the waters.

"Billip. Georgio. Mikkel and son, Nikkel. It's a pleasure to meet you all. My name is Trinos, and I'm the caregiver of this District. I could use a few men such as you."

They all stared at her as if they'd never heard language spoken before, except one. The younger man called Georgio. He had other things on his mind, though he still found her fascinating, just not to the point where it bridled his tongue.

"We are trying to find *my* friend, Venir." He glared at the others. "And we were, well, about to leave, when Billip was wounded. But now that you've healed him, I think we can continue on."

"Will you hush your mouth, Boy?" Billip said. "This lady saved me, and I'll not be leaving her side to find Venir. Nor would he expect me to. Whatever he's into, I'm sure he'll be just fine."

"Yeah, be quiet, Georgio, and show some respect to this fine woman," Mikkel said, gesturing toward her with his hand, "whom I'm certain I'd eat my hand for. Pardon me, Trinos, but not in all of Bish has a woman such as you touched her toes on this dirt. I'd fight an army of underlings for you."

It was Billip's turn to step in front of Mikkel. "I'd fight ten armies!"

Trinos smiled. The men's passion rose like waters from a dam, almost blocking out all reason. They'd kill for her, and she knew it. It seemed foolish to think a man would go to such great lengths over a woman, even though it was her. Maybe it was time she put a damper on things. She shifted her face and figure into something less bewitching.

Corrin arrived with two women who set food and goblets at their feet.

"Men, eat and drink," she said, flipping her brown hair over her shoulder.

"Ah," Corrin said, gaping at her, "see what you two did? I hate it when she does that."

Billip and Mikkel blinked and stared, eyeing her less pronounced features. She could feel their thoughts returning back to normal.

Billip clutched at his shoulder. "Mercy. I hope your healing is not an illusion as well."

"Oh, I assure you your arm is healed, yet your vile thoughts, well, they need some work." She eyed Mikkel. "Yours, too. After all, you've a son to set a good example for."

"Uh …," Mikkel said, staring blankly back at her, "yes."

"So, you men have fought many underlings, have you not?"

"Er … well, of course. We've slain a great many," Billip said, pushing his chest out.

"I've slain more than him, Trinos. At least two to his one," Mikkel interjected, flexing his muscles. "He's never fought any face to face."

"What! I've saved you from more underlings than you killed."

Mikkel stood up and pointed in Billip's face.

"One time! One time you saved me. I've peeled those black leeches from your back a dozen times. In the mud. In the water. You're a dead goose as soon as they get within ten feet of you, Billip. You know that!"

Billip jumped to his feet and started poking Mikkel in the chest.

"You're as stupid as a troll with the memory of a slug and the accuracy of a toad. I've seen kobolds that shoot, slat and fight better than you!"

"That's it!" Mikkel pulled off his shirt and snatched his crossbow from Nikkel's hands. "We're gonna see who's the better shot, right here and right now!"

Trinos liked the bravado. The men were fearless and full of fire. It wasn't something she'd experienced much of in the City of Bone. The young men, Georgio and Nikkel, were all smiles as well. But Corrin, his hands fell to the pommels of his blades, eyes and feet shifting around as if the fountain was about to explode.

Billip snatched up his bow and snagged three arrows from the quiver.

"Georgio, take the pitcher and hold it up over your head, yonder."

"I'm not doing that! Go hold it up yourself, you knuckle cracking fool!"

By this time, a crowd of Trinos's people had gathered. She sensed their emotion rising at the thought of the competition. It was the most energy she'd felt from them ever. It shouldn't have been a surprise to her. After all, it was a big part of their makeup. She stepped between them.

"Men, I have no doubt about your prowess—"

"My prowess is bigger than his prowess," Mikkel said, snarling.

"Is not!"

"Stop it, please!"

Everyone fell to their knees, except the newcomers. Even Corrin kneeled.

"Listen everyone! These men, Billip and Mikkel, have slain multitudes of underlings, and they are here to protect us."

Mikkel and Billip's bodies slackened as they looked around and lowered their weapons.

Trinos raised her arms and continued.

"So, treat them as one of us. Fear the underlings no more. Fear the Royals no more. You have food, water, and now, protection." She lowered her arms back down. "Now, rest. We've much work to begin tomorrow."

"What about the competition?" a thickset woman with a head full of curls asked.

"Aye! I want to see them in action!" a man added.

"I've got ten coppers on the bald headed one."

"I'll match that!"

"I'm taking the bowman!"

The wave of emotion began to sway even her as she raised her arms and said, "So be it then! Let the competition begin!"

With that, a red ball of energy appeared in one of her hands and a blue ball in the other, each scintillating in its own brilliant color.

"I call red," Billip said, nocking his bow.

Trinos flicked her fingers up, sending the balls soaring into the night, getting small as lit fireflies as they went.

Twang!

The red ball burst into a thousand sparkles of light, much to the delight of the crowd.

Clatch-Zip!

Mikkel's bolt ripped through the air and disappeared into the night.

"Blast!" he roared

Twang!

The blue ball burst in the dark sky; its shards of magic raining down on the people in tiny light blue speckles.

Billip bowed as the crowd applauded.

Mikkel looked at her with a frown.

"Alright, Mikkel, one more time," she said as two more orbs flared up in her palms.

Mikkel loaded his crossbow as Billip nocked another arrow.

"From the hip," Mikkel said. "You aren't getting a jump on me this time."

"Hah."

Up the balls of energy went.

Clatch-Zip!

The red one burst into sparkles of light not even twenty feet above.

"You shot the wrong one, Mikkel!"

"I didn't shoot it," Mikkel said. *Clatch-Zip!* His bolt sailed into the night, disappearing with the blue sphere as well.

"Well then who shot it?" Billip said.

"I did."

It was Nikkel, standing on the fountain's rim, holding a crossbow.

"That's my boy!" Mikkel exclaimed, thumbing his chest.

"Well at least *he* can shoot. You couldn't hit a frog's arse on a Lilly pad from ten steps."

"I've seen cats swing steel better than you," Mikkel retorted.

Trinos resumed her seat on the bench. All the people were in good spirits, except the young curly haired one. He was glum. *Strange.* Still, she had the kind of men she wanted, including Corrin. She would need them to keep things in order. *I can't always be here.* But that wasn't all she needed them for. Royals and Underlings were a problem. There were other things as well. *They've much to offer, but will it be enough?*

31

C HONGO LED THE WAY OVER the Outlands, tongue wagging, his big faces panting. Cass, as radiant as a beam of light, sat atop his back, her lithe body swaying along with the beast's rhythm. She was still the most fantastic thing he'd ever seen, but now Fogle was bitter. On one surviving Clydesdale pony, he, and on the other, his grandfather, followed her and the dog. Behind them, the giant Barton ambled along, silent, yet disturbing like an avalanche ready to fall. His grandfather Boon had said little, other than restating that they must go. Fogle complied, and that was what disturbed him the most. *Let it be. Just let it be.*

"You look troubled, Grandson. You haven't spoken all day. Care to tell me what's going on?"

Fogle gave his grandfather a disgruntled look and said, "No."

"I tell you, if I were you, I'd be talking with the pretty woman, instead of sulking back here alongside me."

Fogle glared at his grandfather. Every time he rode along Cass's side and started speaking, his grandfather joined the conversation. And her ears were all Boon's, not his.

"Oh … well, you have to realize, I've not been around people very much. As a matter of fact, I'd hardly even said a word in years until your friend, Vuh …," Boon glanced over his shoulder at Barton, who was busy staring at the clouds, "you know who, showed up. He's a funny one. Grim, but funny."

Fogle had heard enough about Venir as well. His grandfather had been rambling on about him and Cass ever since he'd arrived. And when he wasn't doing that, he wanted to stick his nose in the spellbook, which had been his at one time, but he'd given it to Fogle. He could have shown more thanks, more respect, but he didn't want to. *Just be silent, Old Man. Your ramblings give me a headache.*

"The sack. Have you seen that sack, Fogle? The things that it can do. The power that it contains!"

"What?" *This is different.* He saw a lustful look in his grandfather's eyes, like a vagrant thirsty for more grog.

"That staff," Boon motioned with his finger. The broken staff slid from Fogle's pack and sailed into Boon's fingers.

"Quit taking without asking. First my spellbook, now this."

Boon wasn't paying him any mind. His eyes were locked on the staff, living in the past, searching for a future. "It's from the sack."

"Excuse me?"

"Yes, from the sack, something I know quite well. Your friend told me about it, but I wasn't so sure that I believed it. But Barton confirmed what I was told. Your friend wields a power so great," he ran his fingers over the weathered wooden shaft, "I think it could destroy anything in this world."

Except your chatty mouth, I'm certain. He huffed. Fogle recalled his dreams of his grandfather, battling before an abyss and blasting through a coven of underlings. It was that staff he had wielded, with braces and an amulet as well, glowing with gemstones like fire. Boon had wiped them out with a single stroke and hurled their corpses into the abyss like a blood mad warrior. Fogle could see the muscles rippling in Boon's forearm as he clutched the staff like a hoard of gold. There was still much fire in there. Uncontrolled fury lurked deep within.

"I had the power, for years. I hunted underlings, and they hunted me. Back and forth we went until my last battle. The day this staff shattered and the sack disappeared. Gone, like a wisp of smoke." Boon's eyes were smoky and lost for a moment, his wispy white beard blowing in his face. "So many underlings were dead and fled that day. I'd won, so it seemed. Those fiends hunkered back down in their caves and me, hee hee, well, I wandered the world, lost, purposeless, unable to reconnect myself."

Boon's worlds weighed heavy on Fogle. He could feel his grandfather's anguish, so it saddened him a little. Only a little.

"So, what is it you want?" Fogle's voice began to rise. "To re-acquire the sack and resume your fight with the underlings? Is that what this journey is all about? Just to be clear, I'm here to find Venir and reacquaint him with his dog. And then, I'm heading home." He looked back at Barton. The giant, now the oddest thing he'd ever seen, trudged along, scratching the nose on his disfigured face. "You and the giant can fend for yourselves."

"There's strength in numbers, Grandson."

"They are looking for you, not us!"

"You are foolish, Fogle. Much like your father. How many more giants do you think you can handle without the dwarves to aid you? You'd be dead without them."

"Well, as you said yourself, it wasn't likely more giants were near. That they were an initial assault. You said there are not so many."

"The giants will want to avenge the deaths of their kind. Most likely, they will take it out on the dwarves."

"What? Well then we should warn them!" Fogle said.

"Hah! You fool, the dwarves are fully aware of the giants. They've fought them all their lives. Besides, they like it."

Fogle couldn't imagine anyone liking to fight giants. Of course, he couldn't imagine many things that he'd already experienced. How can one prepare for the unexpected? He sighed, wishing Mood or Eethum were still there. "Will you do something for me, Boon?" he asked, looking up at Cass.

"Ah … I see. Go on. I'll stay back. Of course, I'd never have left her side in the first place if I were you."

Fogle trotted up alongside Cass and Chongo, smiled, and said, "How are you doing, uh, Cass?"

"Never better," she said, chin up, eyes forward.

He looked up into the sky that was streaked with white clouds. In the distance was nothing but more dry land, covered in rock, sand and caves. He'd never been this far south before, either, and by the looks of things it was dreadful, judging by the mountains that were east of them.

"So, is Chongo leading, or are you?"

He scratched the big dog's necks and smiled, saying, "He is. His friend is out there; he knows it. I don't see how he could smell it, unless the man is close. But he senses it. Such an amazing beast. Strong and faithful. You can learn much from a dog, you know."

"He looks tired," Fogle said.

"He's not tired; he could walk for days," she said, looking at him like he was foolish.

"True, but perhaps his back could use a rest. I think my pony could handle the two of us," he said, swallowing as he looked at her, "for a little while, anyway."

Cass kept riding and said nothing. For the past few days, they'd had very little contact with one another, which was bad. With all the dwarves around he talked even less. Now, Boon kept talking and talking until Cass was fast asleep, barely taking a breath so Fogle could get a word in with her. As difficult as it was to communicate with a woman, it was even worse doing so with his least favorite elder appearing from out of nowhere. Him not getting close to Cass was like a thirsty man unable to reach the waters of a waterfall. He couldn't take it anymore.

He rode close, his leg brushing against hers.

"What are you—"

He wrapped his arm around her waist and with great effort pulled her into his saddle and held her tight.

"Are you a brigand who snatches women now?" she exclaimed.

"No, I'm a wizard who only snatches the most beautiful one in the world," he said, looking down into her pink eyes.

"I should kill you," she said, sliding in behind him and wrapping her arms around his waist and squeezing him hard.

"Ulp!"

"But I think I'll let you live," she said, brushing his ear with her lips.

Fogle felt the tightness in his back and neck fading away. It was the best he'd felt in days. He found it astonishing how a single woman could turn this upside down adventure upright so easily. *No wonder houses rise and fall so quickly.*

Chongo led, his stiff tails snapping back and forth, large tongues dangling from his mouths. It was strange, following a dog into the unknown and what for. He was pretty sure the dog didn't need them anymore. *Maybe I should let the dog do all the thinking for a change.*

"What are you thinking, Fogle?"

"About you."

"No, I'm pretty sure I know what you think about with me!" She giggled. "What else is going on in that over-sized skull of yours?"

"Life is so different in the wild. I don't know how you do it."

"I was born in the wild. It is my way," she said.

"Do you want to return to your icy home in the mountains?"

"You just got me, and now you wish to be separated from me?"

"Never," he smiled. "I just wondered what your plans are when this journey's over. Assuming we all survive." He tried to turn back and look at her, but she evaded his attempt. "I don't want to be the cause of any harm coming to you, Cass."

She squeezed her fists into his gut, draped her chin over his shoulder, and said in his ear.

"It's my choice, Fogle Fool. My home is where I choose it to be: the mountains, the forest or the Outlands. It's all fine by me. Now my home is here, with you and the dog. Besides, did you ever think that maybe it is me protecting you and not the other way around?"

"No," he admitted.

"And to think, you have far less experience in the wild than me. I've lived outside the cities most all of my years, yet, in less than one, you suppose to know more about survival than me."

"Ah … I didn't suppose anything. I just thought protecting you was the right thing to do."

"Because you are a man?" she said, digging her nails into his side.

He fought against his laugh as her fingers half hurt, half tickled. He squirmed in his saddle and replied, "No, because you're my woman." Her fingers went still.

As they trotted along, she didn't say a word. Fogle was trying to be strong, to say the right thing, without pissing her off. But, so far as he could tell, his chances were usually half wrong and half right. *Oh, Bish. She's gonna hop off any moment now.*

"I don't recall giving you any claim to me," she said. "Did I mutter such a musing to you in my sleep?"

"No, but for crying out loud, I like you is all. And you like me."

"I do? Since when, Fogle?"

"Ah … never mind it then. I'm sure my grandfather or Barton could find better words to say than I. Perhaps I should mumble uncontrollably more," he said, stiffening in the saddle.

Cass wrapped her slender arms around his stomach and held tight. "Oh, don't be so impossible. I'm just teasing you. And it's not as if my wiles are so hard to come by. After all, I did deflower you the first day we met. Do you think I'd have done that if I didn't like you already?"

"Well, those Mountain Men, —"

"Don't mention them again if you know what's good for you. They were protectors, nothing more, nothing less."

But what about the snow ogres? They were an evil brood according to Mood. It didn't seem likely that someone as unique as Cass would take up with such a race. Yet she had, and that was a disturbing thing that stuck in Mood's craw. Something about Cass was odd, dangerous, but he couldn't help but be captivated by her. He knew he needed to be more careful, but it was hard. After all, she was the only woman he truly knew, and he should be wary of that. His memories flitted to Kam. *I bet she's not so complicated.*

"Are you still with me, Fogle? Has a nymph got your tongue?" Cass said.

"No, I just—"

Chongo's ears perked up as the two-headed dog snorted the air and let out a rumbling growl. A split second later, the dog dashed ahead, plunging into a rocky gorge and out of sight. Cass jumped from the back of his saddle.

"What are you doing?" he said.

Cass rubbed her hands together, muttering an incantation. She transformed into a large slender dog with a grey and white pelt that sped after Chongo's trail.

"Wait!" he shouted. But Cass and Chongo were gone. "What did she do that for?"

Boon led his pony along his side and said, "That's a woman for you: unpredictable."

"We'll never catch them on these ponies if we don't get going!"

"Looks like a good place to have an ambush up there. I'd proceed with caution."

"Then you do that," Fogle said, digging his heals into his mount. "YAH!"

He could hear Boon say as he thundered ahead, "Barton, make sure you keep up."

32

"HOW ARE YOU FEELING?" VENIR asked.

"Like my veins are filled with sewer," Slim said.

"Ah … you're getting stronger then. Yesterday you smelled like a sewer, but now, look at you, a full seven feet of Bones and manure, living and breathing like a new born calf."

Slim let out a raspy grumble, reached out his hand, and said, "Help me to my feet, will you?"

Slim was light as a feather as he pulled him up onto his sandaled feet. The man was pale as a wight and skinnier than a post, but he was alive. Venir was relieved for that. Adanna and her mother hadn't made it, and he hadn't told Slim that yet.

Slim was leaning against his side when he said, "They didn't make it, did they?"

Chin down, Venir shook his head.

"How'd you know?"

"I didn't think any of us would make it, but I could see it in your eyes. Your voice. Don't blame yourself, Venir. The underlings did this, not you." Slim patted him on the shoulder, his bird-like face peering around. "Say, where are we, anyway? And who are all these people?"

"Royal Riders, remember?"

Slim shook his head.

"This forest seems oddly familiar. Are we?"

Venir nodded. "Just south of Outpost 31."

Slim went into a fit of coughing and spit black bile. He wiped his mouth on his sleeve and said, "Ech … tastes like a spider's butt. Nasty things. I hate spiders. Never hated them before, but I hate them now." Slim teetered up on his toes, stretching beyond his full height, stretching his fingers into the sunlight that peeked through the branches. "Ah … that feels good. The suns are like warm rainbows. Venir, I was so cold. Colder than I'd ever been before. I never would have imagined one could be so cold. Ah … those beams are a blessing. I'll never complain about the heat again."

An older man, stout in frame but shorter than Venir, walked up and nodded.

"You're a survivor I see?" He extended his hand towards Slim. "Commander Jans. Uh … my, you are tall as a crane. How are you feeling?"

"Better," Slim said, then turned back into the light.

Jans stroked his mustache and said, "Say, I understand you're a healer."

Slim nodded.

"I've got some men that are ailing. Do you think you could help out?"

"Certainly, Jans, but I'm unable at the moment. That spider pretty much sucked out all the power I had left in me. I should be dead, you know."

Jans's grunted.

"So should we all. But today, we live."

"And tomorrow, if you stick around Venir much longer, we die," Slim said, laughing.

"And who gives a slat about tomorrow," Venir added, taking a seat on a log. "I'm not going to give it consideration anymore."

Jans pulled up a log and sat beside him. "Certainly you don't care, else you wouldn't be running to your death at Outpost Thirty One."

Venir shot Jans a glance, but the older warrior shrugged.

Slim frowned at him and said, "What? We're going to the outpost?"

"No, *I'm* going to the Outpost … alone."

"Of course you are. After all, that's what you do: leave everyone behind."

"They need you here, Slim. And you are far from fit to travel. I'm not saying I wouldn't let you come, either."

"Let me come!" Slim threw his lanky arms in the air, smacking them into a tree branch. "I've been here many lifetimes, and no one has ever let me do anything. I'll come if I want, Brute. You need me."

The last thing Venir wanted to do was rile the man. He'd just sent him to his death once, and he didn't care to see it happen again. Three had died: Hogan, his wife and Adanna, since he'd returned. It wasn't his fault, according to Slim, Mood and many, but he couldn't help but feel that way. Still, it was their life, they could choose to do as they wished. And if they wanted to tag along, so be it.

"Fine. Come along, then. I'd be glad to have you."

Slim eyed him.

"Really?"

Venir smiled. "Sure, if you want to do something as foolish as following me to a certain death, then who am I to stop you?"

"Well," Slim sputtered as he pulled his robes tighter, "I'd at least like to know the plan first."

Jans was laughing now.

"Not so eager, are you now. Heh-Heh. You'd be wise to stay back here with us and await the signal … though I doubt it will ever come." Jans tossed a wooden canister he had in his hand at Venir's feet. "We'll be able to see that for miles all around. But," he pointed at Venir's face, "don't you dare use it if you don't open that gate. We aren't a rescue party. We're a stronghold storming army, no thanks to you."

"Hold on," Slim said, stretching his long arms in the faces of the two of them, "am I to understand that Venir is going to infiltrate the Outpost and open the gate from the inside?"

"Yes," Venir said as Jans's nodded.

"Venir, you've lost your mind."

"You're the one who suggested I lead the fight against the underlings. Getting back that Outpost is the best place to start the battle."

"Venir, there may be thousands of them in there."

Venir stood back up and grabbed the canister.

"And there might not be that many. Besides, they won't be able to see me. If it's not possible, I can always come back."

Jans stood up and said to Venir, "You better not waste any time with that, either. My men are exposed down here. We'll need all the time we can get to gallop out of here if you fail and the entire underling army spills out. You've got a day. If not, we're gone."

Venir slung his pack over his shoulders.

"I know." He bumped arms with Jans, picked up his axe, and strapped the helm on.

"What? You're going right now?" Slim exclaimed.

"Why let underlings live a second longer than they deserve to?"

Slim's jaw dropped to the forest floor as Venir jogged into the woods and out of sight.

The hunt. It had seemed like a lifetime ago since Venir had been on his own, hunting the underlings. As he passed through the brush, it didn't matter if it was one or a thousand of his enemy. The only thing that mattered was that many more would soon be dead. He'd had enough of the underlings to last him a hundred lifetimes. He wanted them gone.

He kneeled down, took a swig from his canteen, and checked his bearings. He was near the base of the hill, less than two miles from the actual fort, with no signs of underling activity or tracks for that matter, which was odd. The road that led to the southern gate was overgrown when he crossed over. It was strange. He was certain the terrain would be buzzing with underling activity, yet it was not. The metal on his helm didn't even throb.

He rubbed his bearded chin then renewed his journey up the hill, his mind focused on one thing: vengeance on the underlings. All his life they'd been a jagged thorn in his side. Now, he'd just as soon be rid of them once and for all. And now he was free. Unshackled. Unfettered. Simmering with inner fury. And it was good. Alone, in the woods, war-axe singing in his grip with only the remote sounds of nature filling his ears.

He pressed his large form beside a tree. He heard a rustling sound. Brool was warm in his aching grip as he held it tight to his chest. There were other creatures in the forest that were as dangerous as underlings: razorback bears with claws as sharp as steel, forty foot snakes and ten foot lizards with poisoned bites and tails. Any one of them could kill him if he didn't strike first and fast. A drop of sweat fell from his nose into his beard as a ringed python as thick as his arm wound around the tree and over his toes. Venir shifted Brool's shaft in his hand, point down, as the creature's crushing weight slithered over his boots.

Hurry up! Ringed pythons, all black with bright yellow rings, unlike most of their kind, were not only fast, but fanged and poisonous. Venir knew the slightest tremor in his body could set the thing off. As the serpent slithered on, he noticed a bulk under its scales. The serpent's bloated belly dragged over the leaves, not slowed by the hump. *I hope it was an underling.* Venir exhaled through his lips as he watched the tail of the serpent disappear down the slope.

He tugged at the buckle under his chin and resumed his trek. He noted he wasn't so far from where he'd left the last time as he made his way into a ravine. The water that once trickled in the creek was gone, its surrounding greenery withering and dead. Over the past five years, the lush landscape had been forever changed, now darker and quieter. He tightened his grip on Brool. Underlings had to be near. They just had to be. *Where are they?*

In the dim forest, Venir's keen eyes could pick up what the average eye could not: deer droppings, animal impressions, and critters' burrows hidden within the ferns. He patted his palm on the helm. *This has to be working.* Yet not the slightest murmur came within his iron skull. Certainly the underlings would not have abandoned the Outpost? The Royals would have known about that.

He huddled down in the brush at the sound of rustling in the trees. *Spiders!* He'd seen enough of them to last him a lifetime already. Peering up, he noticed two black squirrels, jumping from tree limb to tree limb. He grunted. *Getting rusty.* He crept up the ravine another half mile before he stopped again. The humidity had the sweat dripping from him like a waterfall. He took another drink. Eyeing. Listening. Smelling everything around him. *Nothing.* It was as if the hilltop was dead.

Pressing through a row of man-sized ferns, he found himself alongside a patch of bright green, black and brown mushrooms as tall as his knees. They were unlike anything he'd ever seen before. Not even the Red Clay forest that was filled with wondrous plant life, or even what he'd seen in the Under-Bish. *This is different.* He'd scouted these forests all his life and wouldn't have forgotten something like this. Backwards he retraced his steps and froze.

The mushrooms began to warble with tiny tremors. Their tops sprouted with strange trunk-like mouths.

Venir's ears felt like they were about to split open as the mushrooms ripped out a howling whine. He pressed his palms over the metal of his ears. *Slat! Madness this is!* His knees buckled, and his stomach churned as he stumbled up the bank and crashed into a pit of mud. Trying to regain his wits, he crawled from the mud hole. The underlings would be here at any moment. On his hands and knees, he crawled up the hill at an agonizing pace. The shrieking sound was agonizing and distorting. His stomach churned as he spit up bile. That's when he noticed movement above him. His enemies were coming, and he couldn't hardly move.

33

PALOS'S APARTMENT DOOR CLOSED SHUT, and for a change Palos was on the other side.
Finally!

Kam let out a sigh of relief and slumped her head down on the table. *I thought he'd never leave.* Quietly, she observed Thorn and Diller bringing in purses of coin and other treasure. Palos always moaned that it was never enough, each and every time. It was sickening. The man had more gold than most Royals and then some. To make matters worse, she'd had little time with Erin, despite every defiling attempt she'd allowed from him. Palos would not let the baby girl stay.

"You aren't broken yet, Princess," he'd said.

Now what? The room, despite its gaudy décor, was comfortable. The fire, warm and soothing with the slow burning Everlogs, was her only source of comfort most of the time. She stared at it for hours while Palos napped, conducted business and so forth. It was there that she planned, conspired and contemplated her next move. She flicked her fingers towards the fire. It roared with new life, hungry for air, the same as the mystic power in her belly. She released her magic, and the fire returned to normal.

Diddling with her choker, she said, "It would be a deserving home for Palos in there." Rising from her chair, she paced around the room. She wiggled the handle on the bedroom door, but it was locked. She couldn't help but think that Palos would have a secret exit from there. After all, sometimes he appeared to be in there for hours, and she swore she never heard him make a sound. He couldn't just be in there doing nothing.

"Think, Woman! You must be smarter than these stupid men!" she whispered to herself. She shifted the gems in her fingers. Their power should help. It had to. She tucked them in a small pocket in her robe. Now that her anger had subsided, she found herself missing Lefty. And now was one of those times he would be quite resourceful. If there was a secret door in here, Lefty would find it. Another thought crept into her mind as well. What if Lefty was dead? She had not seen him in days, and she was worried. No one ever said a word about him, either.

Another hour passed as she wandered around, contemplating her ideas. Her first imaginings were always of Palos dying: drowning him in the tub, choking him to death, casting him into the fire, running a snake of mystic energy through his groin and out his nose and ear holes. There were more passive options as well, such as an illusion that she was there when she wasn't. Would that fool him? She shook her head and beat her hands on the table. She knew very little of what was behind the wall. She had to secure Erin first. *I've got to save my baby!*

Once again, she found herself by the fireplace mantle, this time staring up at the great sword that hung above. It fascinated her. Its blade shone of the brightest steel, its pommel and hilt guard were worked with the most intricate metals. She knew little about weapons and combat, but she knew a fine piece of work when she saw it. Whoever forged the sword must have been as much an artist as a weapon smith. She reached up, touching the blade.

A flood of emotion washed over her.

Free me!

Gasping, she jerked her hand away. *That's not possible*, Kam thought to herself as she watched her fingerprint disappear from the blade.

"I must have imagined that," she mumbled. "A trick of the thieves, maybe."

Her reflection in the sword's blade shimmered, contorted to an image of another person, then faded away. She blinked. Rubbed her eyes. Her reflection was now gone, as well as the other. *That's not possible. Not possible at all.* Her teeth dug into her lip. She reached out to touch the blade one more time, trembling.

Free me! the sword moaned, its eerie voice not discernible as a woman's or a man's.

Kam jerked away. Her finger tips were ice cold, which didn't seem possible from touching a metal object that hung over a mantle filled with burning wood.

She combed her fingers through her hair, trying to decide if the voice was real or some kind of delusion. *Why would a sword need to be freed? Perhaps it's one of Palos's tricks.*

Her gut told her not to touch it again, but she leaned closer. *Here we go.* She took a quick glance over her shoulder, saw the door was secure, and grabbed the great sword by the hilt. A thousand thoughts and images assailed her, standing her hairs on end. The room spun around her. She thought she was screaming as she tried to tug her hand free, but the sword would not release her.

The Quarter was the working quadrant of the Nest. It was there that the worst of rogues, urchins and smugglers hammered crates filled with stolen goods under the stern supervision of the Quarter Master.

Crack!

"Hammer those nails faster, else I'll hammer them into you, Halfling!" said a full blooded orc, snapping his whip in the air for the hundredth time in a day.

Lefty had never worked so hard before. All day and night he worked. His gentle hands were calloused, and his back was sore. So tired he was, he could barely lift a hammer, but he did anyway, somehow ... someway. *How did this happen?* He paused to wipe the sweat from his eye.

Crack!

He didn't even flinch.

"Halfling! No break! You nail! Or I break you!"

Tap. Tap. Tap.

He hammered. Both hands wielding the heavy hammer, shoulders aching. All the others, working near the end of the docks, hammered away with tools no bigger than his. Men, dwarves and mintaurs were there: all had failed Palos at some point, and this was part of the punishment. But all of them, excluding the enslaved urchins, left for the night when each day's labors were done. He sighed. He'd never sighed before in his life he didn't think, until now. Now it was a habit.

Don't quit, Lefty! You've got to free Erin. You owe that to Kam! If he could only get some rest. Clear his head so he could think straight. He was given a few hours a day to sleep, but it always ended as soon as it started. And it was uncomfortable sleeping in these absidium chains he was bound with at all times. The more you moved, the more they constricted. He thought of Gillem. He missed his halfling mentor, who, though bad, had still been good to him, as best as could be expected, anyway. He sighed. He swore it was his fault that Gillem had died, too. He shook his little head. *No! Palos is a madman. I'm going to get out of here.*

Tap. Tap. Tap.

Crack!

"Work faster, you ugly toads!"

Lefty snorted a laugh. The quartermaster was the ugliest person he'd ever seen. A warted toad was handsome by comparison. The orcen quarter master's face was pock-marked and lumpy. His skin was covered not only in warts but also in moles, and his teeth were half missing. Worst of all, he always scowled like he'd just eaten a basket full of lemons. The only thing the orc had going for him was a lash and the frame of two stout men in one. He'd seen the quartermaster snap a chain anchor off the deck. *Every bit as strong as he is ugly. I won't ask what his parents looked like.*

Crack!

"What are you looking at, Halfling?"

"Nothing, Quarter Master. Nothing at all."

Tap. Tap. Tap.

His tummy rumbled. He never remembered ever being so hungry before, either. Had Georgio always felt this way? All he'd eaten the past few days was gruel, and unlike the rest, he wasn't given any honey. He blinked the tears from his eyes. *How can I help anyone if I can't help myself? Ugh, somebody help me.*

34

BRAK NIBBLED THE LAST BIT of meat from a ham bone and tossed it into the corner. His stomach still rumbled, but it wasn't nearly as bad as it had been a few days ago, in the arena. It was just him and Jubilee, basking in the feeble glow of a lantern tucked away beneath the streets of the city.

"Brak," Jubilee said, "You weren't supposed to eat all that. Melegal will be mad. Again!"

"He's always mad," he said, rubbing the hairs on his arms. It was always cool down in the sewers. He preferred the heat. He missed the suns. "And he looks like he has an aversion to food."

Jubilee giggled.

"You're funny, Brak. And 'aversion' is a good word. You're learning," she said, teetering around the dank little room, draped in a dirty blanket that barely covered her arms. "Here's a new one to learn. Abhorrence: detestation, indisposition."

A long look formed on Brak's big face.

"Don't worry, Brak, they all mean the same thing as aversion. Lots of different words mean that same thing. The more you know, the smarter you'll be. That's what Grandfather told me."

Jubilee had led them back to the exact same room he'd been brought to when they met. It was here he'd trained with Hagerdon, Leezir and the other men. It was little more than a moldy storage room with a few chairs and a table, but it was far better than the dungeon. It was the only home he'd known since his mother, Vorla, had departed. Every time he thought of her, the sadness within returned.

"Abhorrence." He paused. "Detestation."

Jubilee nodded, lips beginning to mouth the next word.

"Indisposition."

"And," a cold voice interrupted, "don't forget disinclination, disfavor, *loathing* and horror." It was Melegal, scowling as he tossed a bundle on the floor. "For example, my disinclination festers as I return to a man who always hungers and a girl who cannot seal her tongue."

Jubilee crossed her arms and stuck out her tongue.

"Bish, Brak!" Melegal gaped. "You've eaten the entire ham." Melegal grabbed Jubilee by her shirt collar. "Teach the man what rationing means, you little Slerg. Allowance: apportionment, consignment, provender." Melegal slung his cap against the wall. "Next time we need supplies, I'll send you two dally wiggles to get them."

"A dally wiggle's a ne'er-do-well, Brak," Jubilee explained. "Or a wastrel or a loafer. I had many uncles with that quality."

"Oh, shut up!" Melegal said, taking a seat at the table, frowning as his steely eyes drifted away.

Brak wasn't fond of the man, but he didn't dislike him, either. Despite the man's dour demeanor, he was always relieved when Melegal showed up. Especially since the rogue always promised he was leaving them. Plus, he brought the food.

He reached down and unraveled the bundled sack. It was filled with bread loaves, hard biscuits and dried meat.

Jubilee's quick little hand snagged a baked apple tart that she quickly stuffed in her mouth.

"Save a crumb for me, you brats," Melegal sneered. "Food's not so easy to come by now, with or without money. Especially when this entire city is spooked."

Brak picked up the sack and stood. Bending his bullish neck down beneath the ceiling, he walked over towards Melegal and set all the food on the table.

"Thank you," he said, returning to his seat.

Melegal waved his hand at him in a downward motion, lightly shaking his head.

It was odd. Brak couldn't tell if Melegal liked him or not, but he treated him better than the Slergs had.

"Morning, youngins," Haze said, entering the room and tossing a small sack at Brak's feet. The woman was in much better shape than she had been a few days ago. Her black eye was no longer swollen, but the red in her eye remained. "That's some good stuff there. I had to slip it away from Frigdah while she slept. You'd like her, Brak. She likes to eat as much as you do, but she evens it out with ale and all." She placed her hands on her narrow hips. "Enjoy."

Melegal huffed.

"What?" Haze said.

"Melegal's been lecturing us about rationing. Saying that Brak eats too much."

"Oh, well, I see his point." She took a seat by Melegal and rubbed his arm. "Sorry."

Brak felt guilty. If anything, he ate even more than he used to. He just didn't want to be so hungry, ever again. He rummaged through the bag. A cake of fruit and nuts was in there. He tore off a piece and stuffed it in his mouth. It was good. Not like the pies in the bakery he devoured, but better than dried meat and hard cheese, for now.

"So, Me, have you come up with any bright ideas yet?" Haze asked.

Melegal pulled his arm away.

"No. But we can't stay here much longer. If they're coming after us, which they are, it's only a matter of time before they find us."

"I don't know about that. It was you and me that found the Slergs the last time."

Jubilee glared at Haze.

"And I don't think they have the man power to pursue right now. If anything, they're more worried about underlings than you. Those castles are under full guard. Everywhere."

Melegal pulled out a knife and began cleaning his nails.

"I know that. We can't stay in Bone, however. They'll catch us. The Royals always get their man."

"They never got your friend Venir, the fighting man."

Melegal shot Haze a look. He'd told her not to say anything.

Brak jumped to his feet and banged his head on the ceiling.

"Venir! You said you didn't know my father!"

"Brilliant, Haze!" Melegal said, scooting back in his seat.

The time for silence was gone. Melegal was a liar! And Brak was going to squeeze the truth from his throat.

The last thing Melegal had wanted to do was trigger the rage within the young giant. Brak had almost killed him once already, and he wasn't about to risk it again. But now, as with all things, the truth he'd been trying to hide, for Brak's safety, had surfaced. Melegal found himself within the big man's cross hairs. Big meaty hands and short powerful arms clutched at his throat.

"Easy now, Brak!" Haze squeezed her narrow body in between them. "If Melegal isn't telling you something, I'm sure there's a good reason."

Brak pointed at him.

"He told me my father was dead!"

Slat, where's my hat? It was out of reach. *Soothing words. Be honest. Distract the beast.* "I only said I thought he was dead."

"Well he isn't," Brak said, clenching his fist.

"I've no way of knowing that."

Brak thumbed his chest, saying, "I do! I see him in my dreams. He's fighting, fighting for his life, out there. Somewhere. He must be."

A silence fell in the small room that's only illuminating source was the glow of a small lantern. Brak was convinced that Venir lived. Melegal could feel the truth of it in his bones. If anything, news that Venir lived gave him one thing nothing else could. Hope.

Melegal showed a wry smile.

"Is he fighting underlings?"

Brak shrugged his shoulders.

"I don't know. But I must find him. I want to meet my father. My mother is gone," Brak said, choking out the last word.

Jubilee reached over, grabbed his meaty hand with her tiny ones, and said, "I'll help you find him, Brak."

Haze grabbed the other.

"I'll help you, too."

Brak's head dipped into his chest as he started to sniffle.

Both of the women were eyeing Melegal now.

Melegal, tossing his hands out, said, "I don't know where he is! And I'm not going to look for him. If he's still out there, I'm certain he'll show up here eventually. He always did before."

Haze added, "You always said he'd be wherever the underlings were, didn't you?"

"Yes, Haze. I did. And right now, there's thousands of underlings out there. And they're probably trying to kill him. What are you suggesting, we walk up to them and ask them if they've seen The Darkslayer?"

"What's The Darkslayer?" Jubilee asked.

Brak's face was a mask of curiosity.

"Oh …" Melegal rubbed his head. "…I thought these days were over. That's what the pig farmers call him. He's their hero. He's rousted as many underlings into beds of death as an entire army. The truth is: when's he's got that get-up on, that massive axe and helm, he becomes, oh, disturbing. Dangerous, but dismaying, foreboding, ominous—"

"Vexing?" Jubilee piped in.

"Well, that's not the best word to describe him, but partly. It's rather hard to explain. All I know is you'd better be on his side." Melegal cleared his throat. "Brak, your father, despite his brutish and impulsive intellect … is a hero to many."

The small wooden chair groaned as Brak sat down.

"The Slergs … they told me Venir was a fighter. My mother said he was good. A hero?" He looked up at Melegal.

"Barring all of the ideal characteristics of a hero … yes." Melegal leaned over, grabbed his hat, and put it back on his head. "It's not something you hear very often in Bish, but your father tends to save as many lives as he takes. Which isn't really a good thing, especially if you get it wrong. In his case, so far as I know, his bloodshed's been on the right side of things. Though some sources might disagree."

"So, what happened the last time you saw him?"

I was hoping you wouldn't ask that. To lie or not to lie. Still, everyone was looking at him.

"His last trek was to the City of Three."

"Ooh … I've always wanted to go there," Jubilee said. "They say it's named after waterfalls as big as the mountains. And they have otter cats there. My grandfather said so."

Haze grabbed him by the vest.

"I want to go there! Please, Melegal, take me!"

Melegal huffed.

"And separate you from your stupefying siblings? Your detachment would be overwhelming." He pulled away and stood up. "I'm not entertaining any thoughts of traveling. The Outlands is far from ideal for traveling for a man like me. I need shelter." He looked around. "And even this is better comfort than the Outlands."

"It's not so bad," Brak said, "It's how I got here."

Of course. The young are always so hopeful.

"With your mother's aid, I presume?"

Brak started to rise from his seat.

"Don't be a child, Brak. At least you knew your mother. That's far better than many of us." As Brak sat back down, he added, "Besides, the last I heard, your father wasn't there anymore. He'd gone on to Dwarven Hole. Never to be heard from again."

"Who told you that?" Jubilee piped in.

Such a dreaded little girl. I'll not be getting anything over on him with her around. At least Haze knows how to keep her mouth shut. He glanced over at Haze who nodded without even moving her head. *At least she realizes I'm trying to protect them.*

"Men. Acquaintances. Associates. Colleagues. Comrades. Cohorts."

"I know what that means. When did you see them last? Perhaps they will be willing to help us," Brak said.

That's actually a really good idea.

"They wouldn't want to fool with a little rodent like you. They've their own quests and charges."

Brak stood up and banged his head again.

"Ow!" he rubbed it. "I want to meet these ... *cohorts* ... too."

"I've no idea where they are." *At this very moment. But I can find them. The Octopus.*

Haze opened up her mouth to ask a question when her tongue froze.

"Haze?" he said, "Are you well?"

That's when he heard it. A faint hiss. A hiss he knew all too well. *It cannot be!*

He turned his head the direction of his eyes. Two underlings, bright yellow-eyed, sharp weapons in their grasp, cut off the exit from the room. Melegal's blood ran cold then froze as Jubilee let out a stone shattering scream.

35

S EVEN KEYS. *DOES IT EVEN* really matter?

Verbard twitched his fingers together, igniting them in blue fire.

"Nooo ...," a human mumbled, head down inside his robes.

Verbard touched his finger tip to the man's head, searing the skin as the man cried out, his moans echoing through the caves.

How many humans would he have to torment to find the man he sought? A man with skinny bones. Pale complexion. Salt and pepper hair. Moved like a ghost. So Kierway had said. *So, maybe Kierway had lied.* For all he knew, there was no man, or keys, for that matter. But, he had to find out.

"Human, is there such a man as I speak of?"

The man, a Royal dragged against his will from the Almens' very castle, shook his head. He was a tough soldier, but human. He'd sent in some of his kindred to snatch the man out from the night. It was all part of the wave of terror he'd begun from beneath the city. Underlings, in pairs of two and groups of three and four, spread out in the sewers, striking quick and returning with reports. Above, the humans were in full panic, torn by whether to stay or go.

"No ..."

Verbard jabbed his burning blue finger into the man's cheek.

Again the man cried out in pain.

"You lie, Human. I can see it in your eyes, which you are about to lose."

The man's eyes opened wide as Verbard waggled his burning finger close to them. He knew the man was lying; he could tell. But the man's aversion for underlings was strong. Natural. He was loyal to the humans and a natural predator of the spawn of the underworld. Not all men were like that, but this one was.

"Bring him," he said, floating back through the cave until he found himself in a room with a pit.

Two underling soldiers dragged the Royal soldier by the nooks of his armpits. Inside the deep pit, illuminated by the underlight, were two albino urchlings, fighting over a bone. A human one, still covered in sinew and flesh.

"That," he emphasized, "is the last human who did not cooperate. So, answer truthfully, or be eaten alive. And, just so you know, while one holds you down, the other starts devouring your toes."

The man sobbed, shaking his head, quivering from head to toe.

"He is a Detective. Melegal is his name," the man stammered. "That's all I know."

Excellent. There is such a man. Kierway's words are true. But how will I find the man? It's a very large city. Eep ... to me!

A buzz filled the air, and in a blink the imp appeared, hovering. "Human, tell this creature what you know of this man. Every last detail, starting from the top of his head, down to his toe, and I'll set you free. Maimed. But free."

The soldier looked down in the pit, up at Verbard, and nodded.

"Uh ... uh ... he wears a floppy cap ... d-d-d-dark gray ... that hangs down over the side of his face. Hair more white than black. A dimple in his narrow chin. Eyes like cold steel. Fingers long and slender, almost like a g—"

"Master!" Eep hissed, "I know this man of which he speaks. I've seen this man before. He's the man who travels with The Darkslayer."

Verbard felt his stomach tighten in a knot.

"How can you be certain?"

"It's him, Master. He's the one," Eep wrung his taloned fingers in his hands. "McKnight, the detective, was to dispatch of him that day."

Verbard felt his silver eyes begin to twitch inside his head. The mere mention of The Darkslayer was unsettling. After all, the man never perished. He'd only been banished into the Mist.

"What else can you tell me of this man? How dangerous is he?"

Eep's serpent tongue licked out and around his mouth.

"He's a pest. Nothing more. Just a man. A stick with flesh and bones. I can hunt him and kill him if you like." Eep hovered towards the disheveled Royal soldier and chomped his razor sharp teeth down. "I'd like a meal first."

Of all the things in Verbard's life, the only one that gave him an ounce of security was Eep. The heartless horror of Bish brought him as much security as delight. He thought of his brother Catten, 'the wiser of the two,' most had said. He regretted all the times he'd wanted his brother dead. It was one of those things he'd never imagined possible. Now, without him, he found himself lost. Catten'd had focus and purpose. He missed those glaring evil eyes and all of the conspiracies they'd plotted together.

"Eep, find this Melegal, and you shall have a treat upon your return."

"But, you said you'd let me live!" the soldier said, struggling to rise. The two underling soldiers shoved him down.

"Toss him in the pit," Verbard ordered, floating away from the edge.

The man screamed as he was pushed over the edge. Not a moment later, his cries were cut short.

"Master! I wished to have that one!" Eep screeched.

"Be silent and fill your charge, Imp," Verbard said, floating out of the smaller caves. "Contact me when you find him. Not a hair is to come off his head. I want him alive. I want those keys."

"Yes, Master, but there is something I must tell you, first," Eep said.

"Be gone!"

The imp's black wings buzzed with new life. It zipped away and blinked out of sight.

Verbard looked at his soldiers.

"Dismissed." As he watched them go, he muttered like a curse, "The Darkslayer." Somehow, someway, that impossible man had managed to creep back into his life.

Making his way back to the shoreline, he watched his commander, Jottenhiem, organizing the small army. The Royals would be better prepared for the next strike, but not for one of this size. Not for one that could overtake and fortify an entire castle. Jottenhiem's ruby eyes caught his. He waved the commander over.

"We are ready, Lord Verbard. Master Kierway, I believe, delays our tactics," Jottenhiem said, sneering.

"He'll be back as I've ordered, else, as he well knows, he'll have my Vicious to contend with." Verbard almost smiled as he said it. With the imp and the Vicious under his full control, even he felt invincible. "Despite his shortcomings, he's an excellent tactician. He'll find out which castles will give us the superior advantage."

"It shall be a hard fought battle, my Lord. The castles have many soldiers, hundreds in some cases according to Kierway. And how can we be certain he won't set you up for failure?"

"As it is with all of us, Kierway hates humans vastly more than he hates even me. No, he'll plan this one right."

The thought of overtaking an entire human Castle was both frightening and exhilarating. He couldn't imagine the humans ever having the audacity to occupy the Underland. That was unthinkable. But, with the Current, the underlings could run endless supplies, and within a solid fortress they could hold out forever. Perhaps this was what Master Sinway had in mind to begin with.

Verbard continued. "How are our agents performing beneath the streets, Jottenhiem?"

"Every day we quietly fill their sewers with their own dead. We cornered a small force of men in their own streets and slaughtered the frightened dogs."

"Excellent," Verbard said, stretching out his arms, resuming his feet from his stone throne. "Your efforts are appreciated, Jottenhiem. Enjoy the sanctuary of the caves for now." He looked to the cave ceiling above. "You might not be seeing them again for a while."

As Jottenhiem saluted and sauntered off, Verbard's clawed fingers fiddled with the Orb of Imbibing. "Such a precious possession."

Master, a voice sounded in his head. It was Eep.

Have you found the human already?

No Master. Soon, but I fear there is something I must tell you.

What could it possibly be? If you are so ravenous, have one of those urchins.

Master, I've news I failed to mention earlier.

And?

The Darkslayer, Master. He lives.

Verbard didn't feel the orb bounce off his toes as it rolled down the stone steps of the throne.

"*NO!*"

36

THE CHAMBER WAS ILLUMINATED BY a single crystal chandelier that glowed with the light of a lone candle. It was Lord Almen's bedroom. Inside, the Lord of Castle Almen lay still, gray skinned, the gentle rise and fall of his chest the only signs of life. Sefron rubbed his throbbing eye. Now blinded in it, he seethed within. *Melegal's fault.*

"He is strong, Lorda. I'm certain he'll survive his predicament." Sefron replaced the warm damp wash cloth on Lord Almen's head with a cool one. "He needs his rest."

Lorda Almen was in charge now. Graceful. Demanding. Demeaning. She did not hold back her revulsion from him. But for now, she needed him, and he needed her.

"If he dies, you die, Sefron. Are we clear?"

Sefron couldn't fight the lump that formed in his throat as he swallowed and replied, "Certainly, Lorda Almen. I'd rather die than live with my failure." As Lorda turned away, he couldn't tear his gaze from her legs underneath her garish tunic dress.

I'd die just to run my fingers along those thighs of yours.

The Lorda was perfect. Everything a man could desire and then some. For many long years, Sefron had longed for her, spied on her and fantasized of her. *The Lorda of all Lordas.* There was none like her. She, among the women, was revered and reviled. Most Lordas held true power: Magic. Skill. Poison. Words. Lorda Almen was different. She used nothing to control the wills of men and women but her comeliness ... and cunning.

She snapped her fingers in his face.

"Sefron! You ghastly cleric! Pay attention!"

Sefron shook his head. Her magnificent perfume had unhitched his fantasies again.

"Yes, ahem, my Lorda."

"I need Detective Melegal found and brought to me," she ordered.

Biting his lip, he nodded. She had a fancy for the man who he loathed with all his might. Melegal had foiled him. The rat from the streets had managed to snare the Lorda's attention. Had saved the woman from her own son, so witnesses had said. Sefron never believed any of it, but he'd yet to prove otherwise.

"As you wish, Lorda," he said, adjusting the patch over his eye. It ached to do so. "The City Watch is scouring the streets as we speak, and I cannot rule out the possibility that the man, stricken by fear, fled the castle. He should have defended it. Instead, he's gone."

Lorda remained expressionless, stroking her husband's arm, beautiful eyes in contemplation.

"No, he would do no such thing. He's fulfilled all of his charges with the utmost proficiency." Lorda stared into his eyes. A dangerous intent was there. "If you know something, you'd be wise to tell me now, Sefron." She glanced back at the other men in the room. Shadow sentries, presence dulled by their ghost armor, stood eyes forward and at rest. "If I'm given the slightest doubt you're lying to me, on my word, I'll have you chopped into bits."

"No worries, Lorda. If he lives, I'll find him. The Watchmen—"

"The Watchmen are not capable! Laggards! Over trained thugs is all they are! Hire the Bloodhounds if you must. Just see it done!"

"*The* Bloodhounds?"

Lorda pointed to the nearest Shadow Sentry, then at him.

"Oh ... mercy Lorda—"

Two quick strides, and the tall warrior walloped him in his saggy gut. Sefron couldn't breathe as he fell to the floor, but he could still hear.

"I want that black-haired witch, Jarla, accounted for, too. Dead."

Sefron petted the rug that broke his fall as he watched her sensuous legs walk away. *So pretty. One good eye is all I need.* The two shadow sentries remained as she departed with two others who bowed to her in the hall. After a few more minutes, he clutched at the spread on Lord Almen's bed and rose back to his feet, wheezing.

"Shew," he said, wiping the sweat from his pasty forehead. It hurt to even do that. *Thank goodness I can still heal things.* He scratched at one of the places were one of Melegal's many darts had found a new home. *Find the rat. Trap the rat. Kill the rat.* No lying needed to be done in the 'pursuit of Melegal' department. Lorda Almen wanted him. Kierway wanted him. And Sefron wanted him, too. It wasn't likely any man could avoid all those clutches for long. But the Bloodhounds? That was a reckless call.

He dipped a small cup into a bowl of water and whetted Lord Almen's lips.

"That's better. Can't have you drying out on me."

He did it a few more times before setting the cup back down.

"Bloodhounds," he whispered. "Of all the stupid ideas. Those cretins will foil everything."

The Bloodhounds were a guild of henchmen bounty hunters that every Castle used, from one side of the City of Bone to the other. They were the best at what they did, but the price always ended up higher than the gold you paid them. Lord Almen never dawdled with them. He considered their ilk, "Gormandizing Bastards." Sefron couldn't agree more.

He peeled the bandage back from the wound beneath Lord Almen's arm. He could have let the man die, and wasn't fully certain why he hadn't. He'd managed to stop the bleeding, but Lord Almen had lost an awful lot of blood. Still, he hadn't figured out who had stabbed the man. Melegal had accused Jarla, and it was likely the woman was an assassin. But what about Melegal? Could he have the stones to have done such a thing?

"Fiddle me," Melegal muttered, replacing the warm wash cloth on Almen's head with another cold one. "This will help you rest well as you recover, Lord Almen." He glanced back at the two stone-faced Shadow Sentries. They looked like they could break him in half just by staring at him. "It helps if you talk to them. Sing him a delightful song, if you like," he said, waddling out the door holding his finger to his lips, "I won't tell." *Slat sucking soldiers!*

Down the hall he went, limping and wheezing, carrying one lie on top of the other. It was hard lying to the Lorda, given all of her powerful wiles. But, lacking any witnesses from the torrid massacre that had befallen the victims in the arena, he'd convinced Lorda that Lord Almen had fallen battling the underlings. As for Lord Almen when he awakened? Sefron chuckled. *I'll let the man awaken when I'm ready. But it's my castle for now.*

37

"W INE!" Jarla slammed her fist on the table.

The young man jumped out of his stool, wiped his hands off on his apron, and blinked at her.

"Why do you stand and look at me so stupidly, Fish-face?" she asked, carving the tip of her dagger into the table.

"We've no more wine," he stammered, wringing his hands. "Perhaps—"

"I've never been in a tavern that ran out of wine. Where is it, Stooge?"

The young man crouched behind his hands.

"You drank it all … er … what we had left, that is."

Jarla slung the nearest wine jug at him, followed by another. The man scurried behind the bar. "Get me something! Else I'm going to carve another hole in your nose!" She slung the last remaining jug, and it slammed into the shelves behind the bar with a crash. "Idiot!"

Jarla was rattled. She'd faced death before but nothing quite like what had happened the other day in Castle Almen's arena. Madness. One second, she'd been watching the decimation of the Slergs and in the next, a bullish man exploded in a fit of frenzied rage. Her head ached still from the moment she'd momentarily blacked out. Fighting the sudden urge to sleep, she'd come to, only to see one of the skinniest men she'd ever seen sliding a dagger out from between Lord Almen's ribs.

She picked up her goblet and tilted it over her lips, catching the last remaining drops on her tongue. "Where's my drink, Boy?" She slung the goblet across the room.

Lord Almen was probably dead. He was one of the few allies she still had. They'd served together long ago as soldiers in the Royal forces. He'd taken her under his wing and then some. They'd learned to use each other for their wants and needs over the years. An alliance of great mutual benefit. He'd been the one who financed her Brigand Army from the outset. She dispatched of many of his enemies, and hers as well. But it had been her deal with the underlings that took it to another level. The demise at Outpost Thirty-One. When she'd come to Almen later, she'd been pleasantly surprised that he hadn't even seemed to mind. She hadn't figured that one out. But for some reason, he'd always been there when she needed him, until now.

"Slat!"

That detective had foiled her and escaped. Out of nowhere, the underlings came. One moment she was fighting for her life, spilling blood of the Royal soldiers, then came the underlings and she was overwhelmed. Something had struck from the air. A glimmering black javelin had sailed into her chest, searing through one end and out the other. She'd blacked out, only to awaken in excruciating pain. Alone but alive. She'd crawled over the dead, the slaughtered, the mutilated, managed to make it to her feet, and stumbled through the corridors.

The tavern boy interrupted her thoughts.

"I-I found this," he said, holding a bottle out with shaking arms.

"Grog will do."

He set it down, pushed his sweaty locks back, and backed away.

She scanned the room. The fireplace was dead, and the tavern was absent of all people. She liked that. It was only her and the boy, as far as she knew. She pulled the cork out of the bottle with her teeth and drank. It burned all the way down her throat and into her wounded belly. "Ah."

She wiped her sleeve across her busted lip and recalled her thoughts. Bleeding from a half dozen wounds and wracked in pain, she'd dragged her sword over marble floors in the halls. The sounds of battle had been ringing out from all directions. Distancing herself from the sounds, she'd made it to the garrison, into the lower courtyard, and slipped past the abandoned post out into the streets. She took another swig from the bottle.

"Now what?" she said to herself, tossing her head back.

She was alone again. Lord Almen had given her comfort, sanctuary and pleasure after she'd sought him out, but now that was gone. She reached inside her cloak, pulled out a key as long as her hand, and set it down on the table. The key was crafted with brass and iron with a rectangular amethyst setting. Lord Almen had given it to her, not a gift, but a charge.

She twisted a matching ring that was on her finger.

When the gem twinkled, it meant Lord Almen summoned her. The Key, once entered into any key hole, would take her back to the ancient chamber. At some point, Lord Almen might summon her back into his chambers. But she wasn't going to wait around.

38

"WHY SO GLUM, YOUNG MAN? Are you not enjoying the food?" Trinos said, running her fingers through his curly hair.

A rousing sensation raced from his head to his toes. He panted out his words.

"No. The food's great." Georgio took a breath. "I just want to find my friend, is all."

Trinos set him down on the bench alongside her and patted his knee as she looked him up and down.

The woman was the most beautiful thing he ever saw. Prettier than Kam even, and he felt wholly inadequate in her audience. Small. Miniscule. Her long platinum hair seemed to cascade over her shoulders like a living waterfall. Her light blue eyes changed from green to gold in the light.

"Tell me about this friend. What is his name?"

Georgio swallowed hard as he tried to avert his gaze from the plunging neckline on her perfect chest, but had difficulty doing so.

Trinos flipped her hair forward, smiling as she repeated,

"What is his name?"

"Uh … Venir."

"I like that name. It's a strong one."

Georgio's thoughts shifted back to normal. Excited, as he'd felt for days, he said, "He's the strongest. The strongest man that ever lived!"

"Is that so?" Trinos said, crossing her legs and placing her hands on her knees. "Stronger than your comrade Mikkel?"

"Hah! Venir whipped him once already. He's beat an ogre with his bare hands, too."

She reached over and squeezed his bicep.

"You look like you're going to be a strong one, too."

"Well, I guess so." He couldn't help but smile. "I'm still growing, and I'm already big for my age."

"Uh-huh," she nodded, "So then what do you need your friend Venir for? By the looks of things, you can take care of yourself. And by the sounds of things, he can take care of himself. So why do you think you need him? You seem to be doing just fine without him. I'm certain he'd even be proud of the young man you're coming to be. I know if I were your friend that I would be."

Georgio shook his head a little, scooting back from her. Why did he need Venir? He'd never thought about it that way before. When he looked back up at Trinos, her face was a warm ray of sunshine.

"I don't need him." He felt his heart stiffen in his chest. "I miss him. You see, he's my best friend. He's my hero."

Trinos felt her heart tug inside her chest. Since she'd inhabited her world, she'd found little of the qualities she'd find to be noble: love, loyalty, friendship. It was a hard world, filled with as much good as evil, but the good ones, the defenders of right, had trouble showing it. This young person, not yet fully a man, still blossomed with all the things right in the world.

"Georgio, this Venir, I hope he knows how fortunate he is to have a friend like you. You are a true friend, and I'm grateful to know you."

"Me?" Georgio said, looking at her funny.

She laughed and said, "Yes, you. Your loyalty blinds you from all the other circumstances, and that is a good thing. It can be a dangerous one, as well."

"Why?" he said, grabbing a baked biscuit and stuffing it into his mouth.

"You don't want to be loyal to a fault. If Venir were to do bad things, would you still follow after him?"

"*Phmpf* ... Venir would never do anything bad. But Melegal would. Now, he's bad news. All he does is pick on me, but I'm almost as big as him now," he smacked his fist into his hand, "and I'm going to get him good."

Georgio was a breath of fresh air compared to the rest of her crew. He was naïve, yet weathered. His round face was beginning to chisel, and the handsome ruggedness of a man was beginning to show. He combed his fingers back through the long locks of curly brown hair and dusted the crumbs from his chest. Noting his grubby but otherwise perfect complexion, something puzzled her. He was different. Vastly so from the others.

Reaching over, she dug her nails into his wrist, drawing blood.

"Ow!" he cried. "What did you do that for?"

Holding his arm tight she watched the minor wound instantly heal up.

"I apologize, Georgio, but my curiosity got the best of me. Forgive me."

"Ah ... sure thing. It wasn't nothing anyway. I've had my fingers cut off and even had my throat sliced open, too."

Trinos slapped her hand over her chest and said, "That's awful. When was this?"

He shrugged.

"No so long ago. I was shorter and chubbier back then, but Venir took care of all that. Melegal too, though I hate to admit it."

"What did they do?" she asked.

"Venir has a mystic sack, and inside it he keeps his battle axe that he calls Brool. He went after that underling thing ... some black monster ... and chopped it to bits and pieces. Chongo ate what was left of it."

"Who's Chongo?"

"That's Venir's giant two-headed dog. Anyway, Melegal chopped up Detective McKnight into chunks and fed him to the hogs."

Trinos formed a bitter face. What a horrible thing for a child to go through. Was this her intention when she created Bish? All of this suffering for her entertainment? It all seemed quite dreadful when standing on the ground, where it occurred.

"You don't look well, Trinos. Here, have a drink," he said, holding a jug forth.

"No, I'll be just fine, Georgio."

But she wasn't. Guilt. She felt it stronger than any other emotion she'd felt before. Something knotted in her stomach. Compassion and mercy were one thing. You could act and feel good about yourself. But guilt was an entirely different monster to wrangle. *Perhaps it's a good thing, knowing how they feel.*

Georgio tapped her on the shoulder and said, "Trinos, I'm well. I heal. I've been through some bad things, real bad, but I'm better for it now. This is Bish, Lady. The land of fight or die. And like my friend Venir says, "Every day you live is another day to make the underlings die." He shook his fist at the ground. "And I'm going to kill underlings, like my friend, because they're the source of all the problems in this world."

His strong words not only brought her comfort but relief as well. *Perhaps that is why I've made it so tough.* Something else he'd mentioned seemed familiar. "You mentioned a sack, Georgio. Tell me more about it."

<h1 style="text-align:center">39</h1>

T HE FAST RIDE INTO THE pass was cut abruptly short by treacherous terrain that was difficult to navigate. Fogle cursed. At this pace, there was no way he'd be able to catch up to Cass and Chongo. All he could do now was hope they'd come back, and come back soon. The fragile muscles behind his narrow shoulders knotted up again when he saw Boon opening his mouth to speak.

"Haste is the mother of destruction in a situation like this. We need to be careful," the old man said, swatting a fly from his nose. "There are narrow passes like this all throughout the valley. Havens for underlings and other recreant life."

Fogle didn't turn, focusing on what was ahead instead. Cass was gone, and Chongo was the one that was supposed to be leading them to Venir. *If Mood were here, this would not have happened.*

"On a better note," Boon continued, "Barton will provide much protection. The smaller creatures, even underlings, are fearful of the giants. Their odor scares them. Not because it smells ..."

It does smell.

"… but rather because they are unfamiliar with it. That's why dwarves are such good giant hunters. They can smell them."

Fogle brought his pony to a halt and twisted his back around, glaring at his grandfather.

"Then why didn't the dwarves sniff them out before the attack?"

"They were down wind, as were Barton and I. But they were close, so very close to our path. It's a good thing you came along, or I'd have been back to the Under-Bish."

"The dwarves are dead!" Fogle snapped.

"And the giants are, too. The dwarven people couldn't be happier. There's nothing they enjoy celebrating better than giant soup," Boon smiled, patting his belly. "Makes me hungry to think about it!"

"WHAT?" Barton said, shoving his way through the trees. "WHO EATS GIANT SOUP?"

"Just a joke, Barton. Nothing to get excited about," Boon said a bit nervously, then turned back towards Fogle with a wink, saying, "Oops."

Barton the giant was strange. Harmless like a child, yet threatening as an angry bull at the same time. Fogle had seen what giants could do to a fully grown dwarf. He'd eyed this smaller giant's powerful hands. They could crush him like a squirrel. Still, he pitied the creature. Its large head was stooped over, and the skin was mangled over its eye, keeping it closed, and the jaw was askew. Barton was discarded. Alone.

"BARTON want to find Venir. Barton wants to find his toys, Hee. Hee." the giant said, pulling bushes from the ground and tearing out trees.

"Will you tell him to stop doing that? We don't need the entire valley to know we're here. And what is he talking about now? Toys?"

"Eh," Boon twisted at his beard, "seems that your friend tricked Barton in order to escape from The Mist."

"And?"

"Well, Barton's upset. It seems that Venir was supposed to leave him the contents of the sack, but failed to do so."

"And?"

Boon looked over his shoulder. Barton's back was to them as he chewed on a blue-berry Dackle Bush. "So Barton wants to kill him."

"What?" Fogle was aghast. "Why in Bish are you helping him?"

Boon put is fingers to his lips.

"Ssh. Ssh. Ssh. Don't fret it. I'm sure he won't follow through. Just don't mention Venir's name around him. It upsets him."

"What do we do when we find him?"

"If we find him." Boon corrected.

Clenching his teeth, Fogle dropped his head in his hand. He wanted to take out his spellbook and slap Boon in the face. *Idiot!*

"Don't worry, Grandson. If we find him …"

Fogle shot him a look.

"When we find him, I'm sure I'll have figured out something."

"Just come on," Fogle said, digging his heels into the ribs of the pony.

He'd tried to look for signs of where Chongo and Cass had passed. After all, he should have picked up a thing or two from Mood. There was nothing, though. The dirt, rock, trees and bushes that went up one side of the pass and down the other all looked the same to Fogle. The problem was, he couldn't find his way back, despite all the wreckage Barton had created. *Come back, Woman!*

Because the pass seemed to narrow the deeper they traveled, he muttered an incantation under his breath. A feeling of security enveloped him, easing his mind, but it did little to shield him from the hot suns as he sweltered in his own sweat. He jerked.

Something twirled by his head, a radiant swirl of orange energy that buzzed through the treetops, up one side of the pass and down the other before it disappeared around the next bend. He stopped, looking back at Boon.

"What was that?" Fogle asked, frowning.

"A scout."

"Is that so?"

"Sort of. It's good for finding underlings, that is."

Barton was standing behind Boon and his pony, scratching his bald head.

"Where did the pretty light go?"

Boon bent his head backward, looking up into Barton's face. "Keep your eye up in the sky, Barton, and you'll see another pretty light … possibly."

Fogle lifted his chin upward. There was nothing but blue skies for miles all around. But his mind began racing through the pages of his spellbook. The Scout. What was that incantation from?

Turning his attention back to Boon, he asked, "What does the Scout do?"

Boon's left eyebrow was cocked as he gazed into the sky, his wizened face unable to hide his concentration.

Fogle felt the air around him begin to prickle, and his mouth was suddenly dry.

"I don't see anything," Barton said, in his slow way of speaking.

"Ah ... Yes!" Boon exclaimed.

"What are you doing?" Fogle said.

But Boon was no longer there. Instead, the feeble old man sat tall in the saddle, tanned and sinewy arms raised high in the air. Eyes shut, brows buckled, he pulled his elbows down, then shot his fists back up and shouted in a voice of thunder:

"STRIKE!"

Fogle had both hands gripping the saddle when Boon's voice carried down the pass. Above, it sounded as if the sky had split open. The air thinned around him, and the ponies stomped and nickered.

What has he done!

A black slit opened up in the blue sky, and a roaring tower of flame emerged, striking the distant ground of the pass. Beautiful and terrifying, the orange-yellow-red torrent of flame came down upon the land like a powerful waterfall.

Fogle shielded his eyes with his hands. He could feel the heat on his knuckles and through his robes. As quickly as it had started, it stopped. He took a breath.

Beside him, Boon's eyes were glowing with energy, burning with new life and an old hatred. Pure intensity.

"Let's go, Fogle," Boon demanded, snapping the reins on his pony, "there will be survivors. There're always survivors, but not for long. Prepare for battle, Grandson. Yah!"

40

H E KNEW SOMEONE WAS COMING, but that hardly mattered now. Venir, for all his efforts, was immobilized. He fought it, though. *Move or die* racing through his mind. The cocoon of caterpillars writhing in his stomach did not fade, nor did the shrieking sound of the mushrooms subside, either. Venir dug the mud from his eyelets in the helm as he crawled on his hands and knees up the hillside. It was miserable, the sound, the sweat, everything. Bish proved once again to be full of surprises.

What am I doing?

Straining with tremendous effort, he rose to his knees, leaned forward, and stepped slowly up the hillside. The mushrooms screamed louder and louder with every hard fought step as his mind began to dizzy from the maddening sound.

He screamed, but not even his own voice could be heard. He might have jammed Brool's spike in his ear if it were possible. His tortured mind had a better idea. He tore his helmet off and threw it to the ground.

REEEEEEEEEEEEEEEEEEEEEEEEEEEEEEEEEEEEEEEEEEEEEEEEEEE!!!!

The sound amplified. He'd expected the opposite. *BAD IDEA!* He fell to his knees, fingers in his ears, Brool slipping from his grasp as he kicked and writhed on the ground.

REEEEEEEEEEEEEEEEEEEEEEEEEEEEEEEEEEEEEEEEEEEEEEEEEEE!!!!

The blue veins rose in his forearms as he clutched for the helm. Fighting the madness, his fingers clawed at the dirt, getting him closer, inch by inch, when he swore he heard a chitter. *They were here.* The deep instincts of his mind spoke to him a warning.

Underlings!

A pair of underlings appeared, eyes glinting like blue sapphires. Hunters. Armed with small curved swords, metal bucklers, and wearing odd helmets, they scanned the forest. Venir got his fingers around the chinstrap of his helm and dragged it towards himself. That's when the first underling's eyes locked on his. The underling hit his comrade in the arm, who in turn hissed, raised his sword and charged.

Venir's fingers were numb when he realized he didn't have Brool in hand. The deafening sound sapped the strength from his arms and legs. The first underling was on him, sword high and chopping downward. Venir ran the helm's spike into its chest, bowling the smaller humanoid over. The other's blade hit him hard but glanced off his scale mail. Fighting through the dizzying blackness that was trying to overcome him, Venir grabbed the creature by the leg and jerked it down to the ground. The underling bit his hand, kicked him in the face, and twisted and writhed in his grasp. Venir's grip slipped.

REEEEEEEEEEEEEEEEEEEEEEEEEEEEEEEEEEEEEEEEEEEEEEEEEEE!!!!

Everything was fuzzy when both the underlings pounced on him, claws digging into his arms and face. Venir grabbed whatever he could, holding on for his life. His strength was fading. He reached back and caught the lip of something in his fingers. The underling's helmet. He ripped it off.

The underling jolted to its feet, fanged mouth wide open, clawed fingers inside its ears. It was screaming, but there was no sound other than the high pitched ...

REEEEEEEEEEEEEEEEEEEEEEEEEEEEEEEEEEEEEEEEEEEEEEEE!!!!

Black blood trickled from the underling's nose as it fell to the ground and pitched forward, face first.

Somehow, Venir jammed his bloodied helm back down on his head and secured the strap under his chin. The high pitched wail was dulled, but far from no longer being annoying. *Brool!* Where was his axe? Certainly more would be coming.

REEEEEEEEEEEEEEEEEEE —

It stopped. The screeching stopped. Venir felt the weight of the world vacating his broad shoulders, aside from the ringing in his ears. He retched. Then retched again.

"SonuvaBish ... that was nasty!"

Venir picked Brool back up and skewered the unconscious underling. Ripping the spike free, he put as much distance between him and those mushrooms as he could. Finding a cleft along a pile of moss-laden boulders, he tucked himself inside, gasped for breath, and took a long swig from his canteen. *Better lay low awhile.* He smashed a large mosquito that landed on his cheek and flicked it to the ground.

The underlings. Certainly, the hillside would be crawling with them by now. At any second, he expected to hear the angry mutterings of at least a score of underlings searching for him. *Where are they?* A drop of underling blood dripped from the helm onto his toe. One minute passed. Another drop fell. Two minutes passed. *Something's wrong.*

He closed his eyes. The forest smelled like a rotting log, and even the bugs in the air were thinned. He heard something. The sounds of dogs. And voices. *It can't be!* Human voices? But it was.

"Come on, men," he heard a gruff voice say from the bottom of the ravine. Dogs were sniffing and snorting, paws rustling the dry ground.

"What about the shriekers?" one man asked.

"No need to worry. These are old ones. My, pretty big, too. No wonder that shrieking was so bloody loud. Huh ... dead now. Look at this ..."

Venir slid out from the rocks, craning his neck forward.

"... see, they're dead now. Once they blow, they blow until they're dead. Haha. And so you'll be as well."

Another voice from the small party said, "A comrade got too close to one of those once. A littler one that is. He said that blasted thing turned his guts into worms and his ears ring to this day. Well, he's dead now, so I don't assume he can hear anything, I suppose."

Venir heard the jangling of weapons and boot steps stomping over the dirt. Whoever they were, they weren't trying to hide from anything or anyone. There must have been five of them at most. What on in Bish were men doing outside of Outpost Thirty-One? And where were the underlings?

"Hah," one said, his voice higher than the others, "we got two dead over here."

"Underlings?"

"Come take a look for yourself."

Venir eased his way back down the hill and bunched himself over a rocky outcropping.

"I'll be!"

"Aye!"

"I'm taking their eyes!"

"Fools!" the one that sounded like a leader said, "They'll have our heads. Slat! This is trouble. Nothing but trouble. It's been bad enough up here, but at least it's quiet and the food's hot. Now this." Venir saw a man's arm chop down a sapling with his sword. "Slat on it! They'll have our heads!"

Venir crept farther down the rock edge as the man below smashed the sapling down under his boot. He got a view of the men, who were less than thirty yards below. *Royal soldiers? It can't be!* They were in full view now. He could even see the royal insignia on some of their shoulders. *Bone if it isn't.*

The leader wore a crested metal helmet, a full shirt of chainmail, bracers on his arms, and steel worked shin and thigh guards strapped to his legs. A bastard sword hung in his grip. He was a sizable man, Venir noted, when another one stepped along his side. *Sweet mother of Bish!*

The second man was bigger, taller than Venir and heavier, thick thewed and iron-jawed. A thought of Farc entered his mind at the sight of the man's bald crown rimmed with thick black hair, wearing a leather cuirass that bulged some at the gut. Venir noted the pair of long swords strapped at his sides and the thick coarse black hairs on his arms. *A part orc with Royals? What madness is this?*

The other three men were in similar uniform to the leader, one holding the leash to two large hunting dogs. All bigger than the average man, typical of Royal soldiers, each holding a small buckler and longsword. Venir bit into his lip as he tried to make sense of what was going on. Did these men occupy the outpost with underlings? How many more men would be up there? How many more underlings?

One of the men poked an underling with his sword.

"Don't do that," the leader kneeling among the dead said, "it's dead. Look at the hole in it. Bish! What kind of weapon hit the vermin?"

"Spear."

"Lance."

"Who'd be carrying a lance in these woods, Fool?" the leader said to the smallest of the soldiers.

They all looked at the half-orcen man who stood like a statue with oversized biceps crossed over his chest, chin up, nostrils flared, not paying them any mind.

"Have the hounds got a scent yet?"

The big dogs, both with medium coats of black, brown and white, snorted at the ground. He'd worked with such dogs before. They were excellent trackers and hunters, fast as gazelles. It wouldn't take them but a few seconds to track him down. Unless the armament protected him from dogs, which it wasn't known to do.

"Everyone spread out, and look for some signs. We need to get an idea of how many men we're dealing with before this hunt begins."

Venir remained frozen on the rocks and watched. Less than a minute later, the part-orc spoke. He voice was dry and deep.

"One man. Big." The soldier had his hand in the impression where he'd fallen in a mud hole. "Must be pretty strong to survive the shriekers."

"A mage, maybe?" the leader asked, eyeing the area.

"No mage has ever been that big. Not a fat man, either. Big boned. Wearing armor."

"Seeing how there's only one of him ... er ... it *is* a him, isn't it?"

The big part-orcen man shrugged.

"Could be a part ogre woman. Har. If that were the case we'd've all smelled her rotten crack by now. The flies would be thicker, too."

The soldiers showed a disturbed look.

"What?" the part orc said, chuckling "you men haven't lived till you've made woo-wu with an ogre."

Venir hunched back behind the rocks. All he'd wanted to do was make it to the Outpost wall by nightfall and try to slip in. Now, he was trapped. If he ran, there would certainly be more patrols out there. *There's got to be another way.*

"Let loose the dogs then," said the leader, tipping a flask to his lips, eyeing the hill.

"No, I'm not sending them into the unknown," a feisty voice retorted. "Whoever it is has killed two underlings. It can certainly kill my dogs."

"Fine, keep the dogs leashed, but you'll still be taking the point."

Great! Time's running out!

Turning to flee, Venir sent a small boulder tumbling down the hillside.

All the eyes in the ravine locked on him, and the dogs howled. Swords scraped from their scabbards as the leader yelled, "Cut him down!"

41

"Don't despair, huh."

Lefty kept his head down, ears open, hammering away.

Tap. Tap. Tap. Tap. Tap. Tap. Tap. Tap.

"Huh. You listenin'? Huh."

Lefty peeked over the crate. The quarter master was farther down the dock, lash cracking with rhythm and fear. Still hammering, he glanced to his right. An old dwarf with a short white beard tied off in black and white tails hiding his chin was staring at him with beady black eyes. He looked like he was a thousand years old as he chewed the bottom of his mustache that hung inside his mouth.

"Huh. You seein'. Huh. You hearin' now, too? Huh."

Lefty remembered every face he'd come across, but this one he didn't know. The dwarves he'd been acquainted with, they were always gruff or short, unless of course they were telling a nasty joke. He held his tongue and hammered away. *I don't need any more trouble.*

"Listen to me, Boy. Huh. I knows many secrets. I've been here very long. Huh. You listen, Halfling. Huh," the dwarf said, his voice drawing a few curious stares from the other workers.

"Keep it down, Codger. I have no reason to converse with you. I'm in enough trouble already," Lefty replied, shifting his aching body away. The last thing he wanted was a lash on his back to add pain to his misery.

"You do listen. Huh. Good. Jubbler talk. You listen. Listen good. Huh. Jubbler. Me Jubbler. Else I'll talk louder. Huh."

"Yes. Huh!" Lefty said as his hammer slipped free of his sweaty hands and clattered on the planks. "See what you did?" he whispered, glaring at the old dwarf man as he snatched up his hammer.

The orcen quartermaster was coming back, a whip in one hand a leather lash in the other.

Tap. Tap. Tap. Tap. Tap. Tap. Tap. Tap.

"What was that racket, Halfling? You trying to skim off some work?"

Crack!

Lefty felt the whip's tip licking a foot from his back.

"No. No, Quartermaster. A little slip is all. It won't happen again."

Tap. Tap. Tap. Tap. Tap. Tap.

The Quartermaster was eyeing him when he noticed the dwarf.

"Ho. I see you've found some help, Halfling." The orcen man showed him a toothy grin. "Jubbler will have you wanting to drive those nails in your head within a few hours." The Quartermaster leaned down. "Tell you what, though. Once you feel you can't take it any longer, let me know. I'll be glad to drive the nails in your skull for you."

Jubbler jumped up on the crate, faced the quartermaster and started beating his chest like an ape.

"Huh! Huh! Huh! Huh! Huh! …"

The Quartermaster cocked his arm back and laid into Jubbler with the lash.

Jubbler curled up into a ball as he continued his insane mutterings.

After about ten lashes, the orc kicked the old dwarf off the crate, sending him crashing onto the planks with a thud.

"Remember, Halfling. I'll drive those nails for you," the Quartermaster said, holding his big paw of hand in front of his face, "but I'll be needing a bigger hammer." He turned and farted as he walked away.

Melegal had told him, "People often say, 'Misery loves company, unless you're me.'" Lefty looked at Mumbling Jubbler the Dwarf and couldn't agree more. More people and more problems to follow.

Jubbler rocked back and forth with his arms wrapped around his knees and head tucked in between, muttering, "Huh. Huh. Huh. Huh…"

I am Zorth the Everblade. Mind … Magic … Metal … now one.

Kam's arms trembled as she held the great sword before her.

Once I was a dying man, ages ago, a Royal on a throne of blood and gold.

Kam felt her will intertwined with another. A mind grumble of sorts. She fought against the foreign entity with everything she had. Nothing would control her. No man. No woman. No sword.

I asked for longer life, and a mage did this to me. It was not what I had in mind.

A great sadness filled her as tears streaked down her face. She could feel a cold metal tomb surrounding her, forcing the icy breath from her lungs. Long, cold and lonely Zorth's life in the sword had been.

I am thankful for you, Kam. I've not spoken for so long. I know your dilemma. I can help you if you can help me.

Help. It was the word she'd almost given up on. It wasn't someone who could help her it seemed, but rather something.

"How?" she asked.

Lend me your magic. I need strength.

She could feel the sword's hunger nibbling for her power. An invasion, but unobtrusive. The will of the sword was weak, like a fire lacking fuel.

Free me! Kam, please! the sword moaned inside her head.

She was stubborn. She fought back. She wasn't going to freely give what Palos had temporarily taken. She wouldn't be anyone's slave ever again. If only the sword had a woman's voice and not a man's, it would have been much easier; she was certain. It would be hard to trust men anymore.

"You release me first," she ordered.

"I cannot. I will not. I cannot risk this torment any longer. I implore of you, Kam, a woman who is good, intelligent and mystic. I know you can feel my suffering." The sword whined inside her head, miserable. *"You must HELP ME!"*

Kam winced as the word bit deep into the recesses of her mind.

"I will not, Zorth Everblade!"

Alas, Kam. I mean you no harm. I can help. Give me power, and I shall release you. Such is the word of Zorth. Think about it, quickly, if you will.

Zorth. The name seemed as if it should have been familiar. Perhaps that was only what the sword wanted her to think. The thought of a mind infusion by magic with metal was another thing. As far as she was concerned, that wasn't possible. It wasn't even heard of before. As she struggled, her numb fingers remained frozen to the blade. She didn't like being controlled. She was sick of it entirely. She remembered what Joline had said time and time again. "Sometimes, you have to give in a little before you get what you want." She never liked that saying. She'd been giving way too much of herself lately, and it hadn't helped at all. The thought of Palos pawing at her made her mind recoil.

He is less than the crust between an orc's toes. I'd never let a man such as that within a league of a noble woman such as you. I'll make him pay ... if you let me.

"No, I will make him pay!"

Her anger was boiling over. Strengthening her. Filling her with new power. She wasn't going to have a man to do things for or against her ever again. Her fingertips lost their icy touch as new warmth flowed through her hand.

No Kam! Please! Help me! Free me! I need —

The giant sword clattered to the ground.

"Blast!" she said, flapping her hands as a headache came on. "I can get out of here all by myself!"

In her heart, she knew that wasn't true. She needed something or someone. The sword, however, was nothing but another problem. A big one. How was she going to explain why it wasn't on the mantle? She certainly didn't want to pick it up again.

"What am I going to do now?"

The long blade gleamed back at her, tantalizing like a diamond. The fire's light on the metal reflected and wavered on it like a living thing. She brushed her hair back over her ears, wondering how she could even consider carrying the massive thing out of there. It was the biggest sword she'd ever seen. Shaking her head, all she could think was how badly she needed to get out of here, somehow, someway.

Erin! She wanted to see her baby girl. When Palos found the sword on the floor, he'd be furious. He might not let her see her baby again. *Think of something, Kam.* She'd have to have an answer and have it soon. Her heart jumped as the door knob turned, the door opened, and Palos and Thorn appeared.

42

S TAGGERING THROUGH THE STREETS, TONIO paid no mind to the gawping stares, nor the bolt jutting from his forehead. Something had rattled his mind, making it fuzzy again. A big black man with a knotted club had beaten him like a drum, jarring his skull and his bones. He needed something, but what was it that would help him focus?

"Whoa, Man. Watch where you're going!" a drunken bystander he jostled said.

Tonio leered at him, tall, ugly and scary.

The man rammed his knife into Tonio's shoulder, not once but twice, eyes in full alarm.

"What are you?"

Tonio backhanded the man in the face, spinning him to the ground, and then picked up a jug of wine from the ground and staggered on.

He muttered to himself but couldn't talk. A woman with one good eye and a head full of yellow hair passed out as he yanked the bolt from his head. He groaned an awful sound as tiny webs of flesh filled in the hole.

"What am I?"

Ducking into an alley, he found a narrow set of stairs and went down.

"Who am I?"

He sat down in his suit of battered armor, watching the big rats scurry beneath his feet. He tipped the jug of wine to his lips and drank. It was not long before clarity came. Memories of his mother flashed in his mind. The haughty face of the Vee-Man angered him most. He bashed his fist into the wall over and over, screaming, "What has happened to me?"

There was no answer, and not a single rat scurried. He used to be somebody important, but then the Vee-Man ruined it all. He had to kill him to make things right. He remembered the men back at the stables. The place where it all began. Where the beast had mauled him. And then the underling had healed him, bringing him back less than a man. And what had those spiders done to him? The arachnamen, McKnight had called them. What part did they play in all this? *Mother.* Should he not seek her out? And there was another woman in his life. Significant. Meaningful. *Rayal.* Raven-haired and beautiful.

He hungered, grabbed a rat, and bit into it as it squealed. *Plecht!* He spit it out, wiping his mouth and staggering farther down the stairwell where a sewer grate awaited him. He ripped it from the ground and crawled back in. The sewers, as foul as they were, he could not smell. He washed the taste of rat from his mouth with a swish of wine. Traversing through the corridors, he managed to find his spot. A small cell with many jugs, some empty, some full. He took a seat by his stash, closed his eyes, and drank.

He remembered the boy saying that the Vee-Man was gone. If that was true, then what would he do? Where would he find him? If the Vee-Man wasn't in the city, then where? He was confused. Angry. Without purpose now.

A thought drifted into his mind. *Home.*

"I am a Royal. Am I not?" he said in his raspy tone.

He swallowed down another jug of wine and smashed it into the wall. From now on, he was going to walk like a Royal, talk like a Royal, and take whatever he wanted like a Royal. Rising to his feet, he strapped on the sharpest sword he could find in the hoard he had gathered. He filled two flasks of wine and slung them over his shoulder. He didn't need any more confusion. Why the wine helped, he could not explain, but it did, or so he thought. Without it, his mind was rubble.

"I'm going home," he said. "Whether they want me or not."

And back onto the streets he went, picking his way through the alleys, ignoring the desperate faces, and ready to fight anything that stood in his way. A mile into his journey, he forgot where he was going. *Vee-Man!*

43

E VERYONE WAS FROZEN OR SCREAMING, aside from Melegal. *Move!* His swords, the Sisters, slipped from their sheaths in time enough to deflect a blow that would have split his skull. The underlings were quick and taunting, playing with him, the living shield between the underlings and the others.

"Defend yourselves, fools! They're killers!" he exclaimed, chopping his swords in the air as fast as he could, keeping the underlings at bay.

The dark creatures jangled his nerves. Lithe and fluid, rippling in muscle, with sharp teeth chomping the air, they fearlessly came at him. If they got him on the ground with their sharp claws, they'd rend him to pieces, if they didn't chop him to death with their small curved swords. *Clang!*

He parried one blow.

Clang!

Then another.

He was quicker and taller, but they were smaller and stronger, a better fit for close quarters.

Jubilee was still screaming.

"Shut up, Jubilee!" he yelled.

She didn't.

Clang! Clang! Clang! Slit!

A sword tip slashed through his shirt, cutting him under the arm. *Sheesh! Fast little monsters!* Already, Melegal's arms were tiring. The underlings were cunning and content in their efforts to wear him down. He needed help.

"Brak, have you a sword or not?" he shouted.

Brak remained huddled back in the corner with the women. *Sonvuvabish!* Even Melegal couldn't choke down his fear, but it wasn't his first *Fight or Die* moment, either. If he was going to do something, he was going to have to do it fast. *Think!*

The underlings chittered back and forth with each other and one of them broke off and dashed for the lantern, grabbed it, and tossed it to the ground. Everything went pitch black.

Melegal lunged, driving the tip of his sword into the last spot he saw the underling's chest a split second earlier. A ghastly hiss filled the air as he felt the sword tip plunge through muscle and bone. Clawed fingers ripped into the skin above his eyes. He cried out in pain when a metal blade whisked across his side, but he felt the wicked creature give and die under his blade.

Haze moaned out his name.

"Melegal … help!"

He heard a chop into flesh, chittering and screaming all bound together in commotion. In the dark, they were helpless while the underlings tore into them like weasels in a chicken house.

Panting for breath, blood dripping into his eyes, fighting the burning gash in his ribs, Melegal rummaged through his clothes.

There was a sick chopping sound coming from the corner, and the screams of the women were no more. *Haze!* Jittery fingers found the hidden pocket in his vest, the silk pouch within.

Glitch!

No, don't be dead!

He dropped the magic coin into his hand, letting the light spill out.

Melegal was dismayed. The blood. The wounds. The twitching. He was at a loss for words, his thin lips twitching.

Brak had the underling pinned up to the ceiling with its own sword. The dark blood was dripping on Brak's face. Haze and Jubilee were huddled together, but breathing. Brak was squinting, head turned away from the brilliant light.

"I think you got him, Brak," Melegal said, hustling over.

"Haze!" He grabbed her, shaking her quivering shoulders. "Are you hurt?"

She shook her head. Jubilee opened her mouth to speak but was cut off by Melegal's hand. He looked over his shoulder at the entrance. No underlings. "No more screaming, please."

He helped the women up.

"We need to go. Gather all the gear and supplies."

No one wasted any time.

"I'll get the food," Brak said, while Melegal was gathering the rectangular case he'd taken from the corner of Lord Almen's study.

"Uh, you do that, Brak," he said, turning around to look.

The mangled underling remained pinned to the ceiling.

Melegal sniffed a chuckle. "Seems you have some of your father in you after all, Brak. Well done."

Jubilee hugged Brak's legs. "You saved us."

"All right, enough of that. Let's go," Melegal ordered. "As Venir used to say, Brak, 'Where there's two underlings, there's a dozen more waiting.'"

"Slat," Haze said.

Melegal pulled his blade from the underling he'd killed. Its citrine eyes seemed more alive than dead. People always said it was best to burn them or cut their eyes out, but Venir said that wasn't the case. 'Just chop them up till they move no more, and you'll be fine,' Venir'd said. A bad feeling still hung with him, though. Bone was under attack, and for the first time in months he missed Venir.

"Hurry, we need to leave," he said, leading the way out the door.

It was dark, but Melegal allowed a little light from the coin when needed. He cupped his ears, expecting sounds of underlings. Nothing but the scurry of rats and dripping water. *Better make this fast.*

Jubilee's hiding spot beneath the city streets was adequate but not as far removed from the heart of the city as he'd like. Popping up into the streets now would leave them exposed to any soldiers or Watchmen who were looking for them. To be safe, they'd have to travel farther down below the city.

"It stinks down here," Haze commented, holding her shirt up over her nose.

"Life stinks," Melegal replied with a wry smile, reaching back and grabbing her hand, "you'd think you'd be used to it by now."

She squeezed his hand back. "I'm worried about my sisters, Me." She was still shaking. "I've never seen anything as scary as an underling before. I'm scared, and my sisters are probably guarding that Everwell. They'll die before they abandon that post."

"We can't fret that at the moment. Let's make it topside first. I've got another spot to roost. They'll be fine until then, I'm certain," he said, trying to reassure her.

Bish! All I need is another big mouth to feed. Melegal and his family of big bellied urchins. What you won't eat, they will.

Twisting and turning, Melegal quietly led them through a half mile of tunnels and stood at the threshold of an abandoned door. There were stairways all over the city like this, all part of a long failed infrastructure filled with catacombs. Melegal had learned much about it as he chased down the Slergs. It was another world: dark, dank and lonely. Most tunnels were caved in by dirt or heavy rubble, making it impossible to move farther down. Whole families resided there, the most desperate citizens Bone had to offer. Still, despite the sanctuary, not as many people haunted the tunnels as one might expect. He wasn't sure if that was because of the underlings or something else. He remembered the presence he'd sensed months earlier: powerful and evil, unlike anything he'd ever known. Perhaps that's what kept it purged of more life.

"Put on your cowls," he said, making his way through the door and up the stairs.

One by one, they went by him, up the stairs on heavy legs. Using the coin's light, Melegal took one last look down the tunnels. The bright beam cut through the muck and slime covered walls, giving it an odd radiant shine. He exhaled through his pursed lips. *Ah …*

"Where are we going?" Jubilee asked, eyes bright and curious beneath her cowl.

"Be quiet, and you'll soon find out."

The southern part of the city was humming with activity. Crowds of people were pressed down the main street towards the gate. There was talk of nothing but underlings, unexplainable deaths and misery.

Perfect.

Melegal led them to the barn, taking the side entrance, avoiding all the traffic at the other barns where Royal soldiers were preparing horses. There was shouting, ordering and hollering from the barns next door, but this barn was still quiet and abandoned near the south entrance of the wall. He looked up into the rafters and saw the rope he'd used to kill McKnight. It was eerie.

"You sure didn't do a very good job avoiding the stink," Haze said. "Why would you bring us here, anyway?"

He opened the small door that was Quickster and Chongo's stable and ducked inside. No Quickster. That wasn't a good sign. The little bit of hope he had fled. Maybe they'd taken off.

"Now what?" Jubilee said, plopping down in a bed of hay.

"We wait," he said, closing the small door.

Jubilee and Haze both pulled the cowls from their faces, saying, "How long?"

At least Brak was quiet. The big man moaned like a wounded cow and sank to his knees, holding his belly. His fingers were covered in blood. How had Melegal missed that wound?

"Brak! Brak!" Jubilee jumped and pulled the cowl from his face. His face was grey and pasty, and his eyes fluttered up in his head.

Melegal braced himself behind the man to keep him from falling.

Brak was panting. "It's all right, Jubilee. You … you'll be better off without me. M-More food that way. S-so ssssad, dying and st-still being hungry."

"Don't wail, Slerg," Melegal hissed in warning, "or we'll all be dead as well."

He lowered Brak into the hay and ripped off the man's dirty shirt. The wound was deep and fatal. How had the man made it this far? It didn't seem possible. Brak might be a thick skinned slow bleeder, but time was running out. He looked at Haze, who only had a haunting look in her eyes as she shook her head. The son of Venir was a goner.

44

" VENIR CALLS HIS HAND-AND-A-HALF AXE Brool. It's the deadliest weapon of all. I saw him chop an underling in two with it… more than once. One time, he chopped off a forest mage's head and batted it down the path. It was the funniest thing I ever saw, in a weird sort of way. I'll never forget that." Georgio slapped his knee. "And those Forest Magi won't, either; I'm certain."

The young man kept rambling, and she let him go. I was good to be in the presence of someone more cheerful than dour for a change. But Trinos's mind was racing, recalling what she knew about the sack, the tool she'd created to keep Bish balanced between good and evil. She rubbed her arms and shoulders. An unnatural chill was in the air, raising goose bumps on her arms as a stiff breeze tangled her hair.

"And the helm. It can heal him. Brought him back from the dead—at least I think he was dead—at least once. I saw it for myself."

Trinos wouldn't have thought she'd let such an important detail slip her mind. But it had. In her own crude way, she'd put it upon one man, one person at a time, to use a mystic power that would sway the balance back and forth forever and ever. What a charge that would put a person through, handling such awesome power. Yet, it seemed to do its job. And here sat a young man who'd witnessed it in action.

"Melegal was there. I swore he was crying over my almost dying, but he'd have sworn it was sweat. He's still mean, though. Lefty was there, too, along with Mood and Chongo," Georgio's voice trailed off. He had a saddened look on his face.

"What is it, Georgio? What's wrong?" she asked.

"Ah … nothing."

"No, please tell me."

"My friend Lefty, the halfling I told you about, the one with sweaty feet."

She giggled and nodded. It was another one of the touches from her creation she'd forgotten about.

"He caught up with another one named Master Gillem." Georgio's face bunched up. "Turned him rotten, that halfling did. Always lying and stealing. And no one said a thing about it but me. They were all stupid to it or something. Ah, he acts happy, but I know he's not. Just a miserable little halfling."

"You really care about your friends, don't you?"

"Sure, I guess."

"Georgio, I care about people, too. Perhaps we can bring them all here, and I can help you keep them out of trouble."

Georgio looked around, frowning.

"I don't think Venir would like it here. He likes the Octopus and drinking the nasty tasting Grog. Lefty might like to come back, though, but I don't see how that's possible."

"Ahem," a voice interrupted. It was Corrin, holding his hat to his chest.

"Yes, Corrin?" she said.

"Trinos, ah … well, the people are worried about the underlings. They think we need some … er … fortifications. Some are even talking about leaving, but I don't let them. I tell them if they go, they can't ever come back," he finished with a firm nod.

"Corrin, must you always be so harsh? They are just frightened."

"Yes, I fear I must be," he said with a bow, "unless you say otherwise. And, those men, Mikkel and Billip, well, they're getting frisky with the women."

"And how do you know this?" she said, closing her eyes and raising her face to the sun.

"I can't find any of them, aside from the new boy, Nikkel. He's working with the others, as well should be this one." He tipped his chin at Georgio.

Trinos huffed as she rose. There were many things to consider now that she'd become involved. The people needed protection. They also needed self-control. Georgio, who she liked very much, wanted to leave rather than stay within her sanctuary, and Corrin was nothing but a worry wart. It was a wonder that her world managed to keep it all together, yet it did, and somewhere on Bish, a man named Venir unknowingly had that responsibility now. It didn't seem fair.

"I must leave you momentarily. Get along and behave, Corrin. And Georgio, I hope you're still here when I return."

Georgio was wiping his clammy hands on his trousers, admiring Trinos's beautiful face and tranquil speech, and then she was gone as if she wasn't ever there.

"Huh?"

He looked at Corrin, and Corrin looked at him, both looking around. He'd never seen anyone disappear like that.

"I'll be. Not again!" Corrin said, wringing his hat. "Why did she just do that for?"

"She said she'd be back," Georgio added.

"Sure, and the last time she did that she was gone more than a week. And that's no picnic when these people have to survive without her. They get antsy. And with the talk of all the underlings, it'll be much worse than the last time."

Georgio didn't know what to say. It seemed Corrin had his hands full as he stomped his feet, hands on hips and twirled around. It couldn't be that bad, though.

"We can help, Corrin."

"Who, you and those leg chasing louts? I'd rather you didn't bother. It'll only make things worse. If anyone asks, you don't know anything about Trinos. She often comes and goes. Pah!" Corrin spat on the ground and started walking away, "Just stay out of my way and keep your mouth closed. Blasted responsibility. It used to be so much easier: killing them rather than taking care of them."

All Georgio wanted to do was go and find Venir. He needed to find Billip and Mikkel and convince them it was time to go. As he walked around the District, the only person he could find was Nikkel, who was pushing a load of stones with a wheelbarrow.

"Do you know where your father is?" Georgio asked.

Nikkel shrugged his broad shoulders. It was clear he was growing into a sizable frame like his father. "No, why?"

"I want to get out of here."

"So, go already," Nikkel suggested. "You're a man, aren't you? You can do whatever you want to. Me, I have to do what my father says when he's around, but not when he's not."

Father! With all the commotion, Georgio had forgotten about his own family that resided south of the Red Clay Forest. He wanted to check on them as well.

"Tell Mikkel and Billip I'm heading home, to the Red Clay Village."

"Don't be stupid!" Nikkel said, tossing a large stone from the cart. "Underlings are as thick as a hive of bees out there. Besides, last I heard, the Red Clay Village was gone. Even if your family survived, they wouldn't still be there now."

Georgio fell down on his butt. Nikkel's words stunned him. In all these months, he'd given little thought to his family at all. And now, for all he knew they were dead. He'd given little consideration to them before. All this time, he'd been more worried about Venir than his own family. What kind of son did that?

"You aren't going to cry, are you?" Nikkel said, sitting down by his side. "Father says crying's for women and scrawny little men. He also says 'You're safer dead than alive in this world.'"

"What in Bish is that supposed to mean?" Georgio said, wiping his eyes.

"I don't know. It just seemed like the right thing to say about now," Nikkel stretched back up and resumed unloading the wheel barrow. "Want to help?"

Georgio missed his family. He wanted to see them so bad right now. He wanted to find Venir as well. Mikkel and Billip, as well meaning as they were, weren't the most reliable. And Trinos, as captivating as she might be, could certainly handle herself. Venir had said, 'If you want to be a man, act like a man. If you can't take care of yourself, how do you expect to take care of others?'

Georgio got up and said, "No. I'm getting out of Bone."

45

"WILL YOU GET DOWN?" DARLENE said as she settled her wide hips behind the rocks. "Please?"

Scorch didn't feel the need to do any such thing. Why would he bother to hide from anything? Still, he didn't want to ruin all the woman's excitement by not participating. As Darlene had told him on the trail, 'It's not sportsmanlike.' He huddled by her side, watching her beady eyes shift back and forth under her uni-brow.

"Good," she breathed through her puffy lips, "just be still and quiet while I sort this out."

Scorch locked his fingers behind his head, lay down and closed his eyes. He'd gotten used to this. Darlene was a devoted hunter. She'd killed a boar, a hawk, and a pair of rather large horned rabbits. She'd convinced him she was quite the fisherman, too. Her pale brown eyes were always filled with energy as she tirelessly skinned the bloody meat from the bones. She was truly content with her role in the world, even though the meat she cooked wasn't particularly good.

"Scorch," she said in a harsh whisper as she nudged him.

He popped open his eye and looked at her. It was hot, just like any other day, but Darlene's head was always bone dry. Now, beads of sweat adorned it like rain, and her tanned cheeks were flushed. He rolled over to his belly and peeked over the rocks.

"Hmmm …" he said.

Over a hundred yards below their rocky perch, a squad of small, well-armed grey skinned people were digging holes in the outback ground. They weren't human, but the frightened screams of their prisoners were. Scorch rolled onto his back and closed his eyes. He could feel Darlene's uncertain rustlings at his side.

"Er .. well … um … Scorch … uh, I think those are underlings. What do we do?"

He could sense her heart pounding inside her chest and the fear of the unknown in her sweat. But that wasn't all.

He spoke in a calm and reassuring voice, saying, "We are safe here, Darlene. No worries at all. Just keep an eye on them, and when the moment is right, we will go."

"I guess you're right," she replied, her voice more steady than before. "You're safe with me... Yet," she said, sitting down beside him.

He could feel the intensity of her eyes on him. He re-opened his eye.

"Yet?"

"Um … you see, I can't just sit and watch those people die. It wouldn't be right."

"Why not?"

"Why not!" She grabbed his clothes. "Underlings are evil. All they do is kill people. They torture and mutilate them. I can't just sit here and not do anything. It wouldn't be right."

He propped himself up on his elbows. "But what makes you think those people need saving, and why would you put yourself in peril? You've known bad people, like your husband and such sorts. What if they're just as bad as them?"

"It doesn't matter if they're good or bad." She pulled an arrow from her quiver and loaded her bow. "They're men, not underlings." She stepped over Scorch and took a step down the hill, looking back at Scorch with a smile. "Besides, I've always wanted to kill an underling before I die. If I don't make it back, I'd appreciate it if you buried me instead of them."

Scorch found himself perplexed as he watched her go. The woman, durable and crafty as she might be, didn't stand the remotest of chances. And the men and women prisoners, though not as bad as some people could be, he sensed were hardly worth saving at all. Still, the hearts of the underlings were unlike anything he'd ever encountered. The things they did and were capable of.

Below, as silent as a deer, Darlene had closed within fifty yards of the underlings when she let the first arrow fly. It sailed true, catching a shoveling underling in the throat and knocking it into the grave. The next arrow caught an underling in the chest, piercing through its mailed armor. The black creatures scurried up the hill now, zeroing in on the doomed woman.

Scorch rose to his feet, shaking his head. Darlene was terrified, but she kept on shooting when most people would have fled. Her next arrow buried itself in a tree, and the following in an underling skull. He had to admit she was pretty good with that bow, but her wisdom lacked the same accuracy.

Now, the human prisoners were on the run. *Good for them. She's spared them momentarily from their agony.* At least she'd given them a few more moments of freedom and the hope for escape. But Darlene's daring was only seconds from coming to a chilling end. Once the underlings got a hold of her, they'd rip her to pieces.

Scorch sighed. Was she brave or foolish? If she'd stayed with him, no harm would have come to her. He could have given her anything she needed, just about. So he stood in contemplation, wondering if he'd grant her request to bury her or not.

46

SHARDS OF LIGHTNING BLASTED A pair of underlings that were crawling from the fiery scene. Their bodies sizzled and popped as muscle was charred to a crisp on their bones. The smell was as malodorous as Fogle had ever experienced, so he held his nose under his cloak. The underlings, more than twelve of them, were nothing but remains.

Boon's eyes were filled with energy; his arms were draped over his head, fingertips crackling with power. He was a man possessed, standing in the middle of a smoldering hole on a mission to destroy every black thing that tried to crawl out.

Fogle held a spell on the tip of his tongue, eyeing the ridges and the sky. If there were more underlings about, they would come, unless they were scared. He led his horse by the burning trees and smoking bodies on a direct path for Boon. A moment later, the old man's eyes returned to normal.

Boon took a deep draw in through his nose and said, "Ah, there's nothing quite like the smell of roasting underling in the morning, is there?"

Fogle didn't know if it was a question or not. He didn't know whether to be upset or glad. But he didn't hold back the words on his tongue.

"At least if the giants and underlings are trying to find us, they know where to look."

"I hope so. I'm just getting warmed up," Boon said, trying to shake the radiant wisps of energy from his hand. "Oooh, that felt so good."

"Do it again!" Barton said, stomping the remains of an underling to ash. "Smelly. But bad things always smelly." Barton held his nose, stomping another and another.

Fogle grabbed Boon by his robes and said, "Did you even take a second to think that you could have hurt Cass or Chongo? You could have scorched them as well!"

Boon scratched the thinning white hairs on his head and replied, "Well, no, but I wasn't trying to destroy them. I sent my Scout to destroy the underlings ... not them."

"How could you know if they were engaged with them or not?" he said.

Boon grabbed his wrist. The old man had a grip of iron that Fogle struggled to twist away from, hurting his arm in the process.

Boon then said, "Instinct, Grandson. You worry too much. If they wish to run off, let them. We'll catch up ... eventually. Barton!"

Barton had pulled a pine tree from the ground and begun sweeping the underlings up. "What, Boon?"

"Do you smell anything?"

Barton scratched is head. "Huh?"

"Do you smell anything?"

The giant took a long snort through his nose.

"Just underlings. Dead ones," he said, brushing more of the bodies aside.

"No other giants, then?" Boon asked.

Barton didn't say anything as he swept more piles into the flame, stirring up the dust.

Fogle caught a mouthful of the tiny debris.

"Barton! Quit that, will you?" He shot a look a Boon. "Stop him, will you? He's your child, not mine!"

"Oh, you'll be fine." Boon hopped off his horse, stuck his hand into the skull of an underling, and pulled out its eyes. He rubbed the soot covered eyes on his sleeve. A dark blue color was underneath. Boon's face crinkled up when he twitched the marble like objects in his fingers. "Eh, just hunters, it seems. Hardly any magic in them at all." He tossed them into Barton's fire.

Fogle spat the grit from his mouth and asked, "Do they really have magic in them?"

"Finally, a question worthy of my attention," Boon said, taking a seat on the ground. "Just wait a second. We can't just be sitting around. We may be downwind from the north, but I'm certain the south can smell us coming by now."

"Oh, even if they do, they'll proceed with caution. We have a giant, after all. Even underlings are unsettled by giants, being so small and all. Plus, I'm tired. That took a bit more out of me than expected."

"We need to keep moving. It's risky to stay in this spot too long."

"I need rest!" Boon huffed. "Oh, if it makes you feel any better, I'll procure some additional security. Barton!" The giant swept with a mind of his own.

"BARTON!" Boon tried again.

Barton stopped and turned. His face was scrunched, and his head cocked as he slung a tree onto his shoulder.

"Yes, Boon Wizard."

"Will you be so kind as to keep watch on the south side of the fire? It's possible more underlings will come, and I'd like to be prepared."

Barton started tearing the branches from the tree he carried with his bare hands. Fogle felt miniscule in the presence of the giant's raw strength and power. *How did we ever overcome giants even bigger than he?* He felt a small amount of pride realizing he'd pulled off the incredible.

"Yes, Grandson, they are big and powerful on the outside, but it's better to be big and powerful on the inside."

Fogle combed his fingers through his hair. He realized it had never been so long before. Not even when he was a boy. "What's he doing to that tree?"

"Barton!" Boon yelled up at the towering figure, "What are you doing with that tree?"

With his good eye, Barton looked at them both like they were stupid, and said, "I'm making a club so I can smash the underlings." He slapped the club into the meaty palm of his hand and disappeared through the smoke.

"Feel safer now?"

Fogle sat down and replied, "Actually, I do."

"Good then. Now, what was your question?" Boon looked up into the sky. "Yes, yes the underlings' eyes. I'll tell you all about them. Of course, if you'd read all of my spellbook, most of it you'd know."

Fogle pitched a stick over into the fire. He'd always been reluctant to delve into the works of his grandfather, seeing how he believed, as did the rest of the City of Three, that Boon had gone mad. How could a madman be a great wizard? But even in his own young age, he knew that the dynamic power of magic could erode the mind. It seemed improbable that it could happen to him, so he'd considered such accounts weakness. Yet, here was his grandfather, quirky but in control. He sensed he was in the presence of the most powerful wizard he'd ever known. And for the first time in his life, he decided he would listen. The way things were going, he could stand to learn a thing or two.

"Not all underlings use magic, but they have it. Some can use it, some can't. Those we just killed were hunters. I'd need a dozen pairs of their eyes at least to cast the simplest of spells."

"They hold power?" Fogle asked.

"They can give you a charge if you know how to use it. But you don't want to carry too many of those eyes around." Boon said.

"How come?"

"They're heavy. Like rocks or gemstones. No, it's best to burn them like the rest. The underlings hate that. Seeing their kin burned. It makes them extra mad, and they're mad enough at men already."

Fogle wasn't even going to ask why that was. Even if Boon somehow knew the answer, he was pretty sure he wasn't ready to know. He had enough on his plate already.

"But, if you kill an underling mage, well, then you have some power. For the strangest reason, underlings leave power in their eyes. I collected them like a dwarf hoarding gold." Boon's fingers tickled the air. "Oh how I enjoyed turning their own power against them. Delicious," he said, licking his mustache.

Fogle felt a prickling sensation on his neck.

"What color eyes did you collect?"

"Now, there were all sorts. Of course, underlings, whether it be fighters or magic users, still have a variety of color. But the magic users tend to be the lighter shades than the others. I've seen many colors, some like rubies, others like sapphires, peridots, or an odd violet quartz in color. The oddest I ever came across was rose-colored pink. You ever seen a pink gemstone before?"

"No."

"A fascinating thing—"

"Boon, have you ever seen golden-eyed underling eyes before?"

His grandfather looked like he'd swallowed a bug.

"Aye …" he said with a loathing sound under his breath, "and silver, too."

Fogle felt a chill race up and down his spine. He and his grandfather had more in common than they'd realized.

Boon's eyes were intent, and his voice had a dangerous tone. "Tell me what you know, Grandson."

Fogle grabbed his grandfather by the arm and said, "Why don't I show you instead?"

Boon grunted, a wry smile coming to his lips.

"I like this way of thinking. So be it then, Fogle. Take my mind away."

It was a mind grumble of a different sort. Two willing minds coming together with no concern or conflict, only the sharing of knowledge. The trick was keeping your most closely guarded secrets from coming loose, as it was difficult for invading minds to fight their natural tendency to pry. Muttering, Fogle opened the doorway, and Boon quickly stepped through.

Boon tugged at his mind, strong but not forceful. Fogle shoved back, bringing forth a hollow chuckle. *Show me.* There they stood, two apparitions sharing one mind, one memory of a cataclysmic sort. Fogle showed him the battle he'd shared with Venir and the silver and golden eyed underlings.

Ha! Boon exclaimed. *It cannot be. Catten and Verbard!*

Fogle could feel his grandfather's respect for him building.

A grumble! With the most powerful of underling Lords, and you live?

Barely, Grandfather.

Fogle showed him the rest. The grave of boulders. The underling's corpse. The battle with the earth elemental and the exchange of the eyes for the spellbook.

Fogle felt a tremor of anger rippling through his mind. There was a brilliant flash of light, and his mind was again his own.

Boon punched him hard in the arm.

"Grandson, I cannot tell whether I want to hug you or *kill* you!"

The word kill stung, and the dark look in Boon's eye didn't leave him feeling very comfortable.

"Kill me? Why?" he asked, rising to his feet, readying a defensive spell on his tongue.

Boon swallowed hard before he opened his mouth to speak.

"OOOOOOOW!" Barton cried out from beyond the smoking crater.

Bang! Bang! Womp!

"What now?" All he wanted to do was track down Cass, and now something else had to happen. Fogle dashed towards the sound of the commotion with Boon on his heels. Emerging from the trees, he spied Barton with one hand full of an underling and the other swatting the club.

Wham!

Barton pulverized the underling into a greasy black smear. The bones of the other one cracked in his mighty grip before Barton bit its head off and spit it into the oncoming horde.

Fogle lost his breath. He'd never seen so many underlings before. They were coming from up one side of the ravine and down the other. If those underlings were alive, were Cass and Chongo dead? He felt the strong hand of Boon squeezing his arm.

"Whatever you used to save yourself from the gold and silver eyed underlings, you better unleash it now, Grandson!"

With so many underlings, Fogle didn't even know where to begin. *Cass!*

47

"**C**OME ON THEN, RABBITS!" VENIR said, rising to his full height, staring down on the men. "The first one up will be the first one down!" He whirled his axe around his body. "Any takers?"

The scouts stopped their advance, but the dogs howled on.

"Let your mangy curs loose, you raggedy man! I've not eaten in days!"

The soldier yanked back on his dogs' chains. They fell silent.

Venir had their attention. Their eyes passed back and forth between one another. Even the large part-orc slid a half-step back.

"What! I'd expect better from Royal soldiers. Is there not a valiant one among you?"

He hopped off the rocks. The small band shifted back.

"What about you, Orc? A big one, I see. Looks like your mother was diddled by trolls, I'd say!"

The orcen man's eyes darkened, his canine teeth flashed, but not a muscle moved.

Venir chopped Brool back and forth, low strokes beneath his knees that trimmed the foliage like wheat.

"Awfully quiet for an orc. I'm used to more talk and bravado."

The leader, tall and rangy, made a quick nod with his head. His men, aside from the half-orc before him, began to spread out. Venir's veins were charged with energy as they pulsated under his skin. These men, shady in movement and décor, disturbed him.

"Who are you, Man?" the leader spoke up, lowering his sword.

"Man? Aye, indeed, I am a man! I'm not some slug that crawled from the sewage to cavort with underlings. I'm a killer of such things, along with their cohorts, such as you."

The leader stuck his bastard sword in the ground and said, "You have us wrong. We are not cavorters but slaves. We'd just as well see these vermin skinned the same as you. But we've over a hundred men—"

"And orcs," the orc said.

The leader nodded up the hill and continued, "shackled, starving and half-dead. Mostly depraved. It's better to serve moving on two legs than serve with none at all. There are many of our brethren living with less than that already."

Venir sensed some truth in the man's words. But he was going to need more than that before he lowered his blade.

"Tell me then, Soldier, how many underlings hold that Outpost?" Venir asked.

"Oh, well, now I can't readily answer that, nor my colleagues. Such talk would be treasonous and put all of our heads at the mercy of our masters. No, you over-sized metal shade. I'd rather die that let you be privy to that." The leader pulled his sword from the ground and flicked the edge of the blade. "And at this point, a meaningful death in combat is vastly more preferable than facing the consequences of failure."

Treason! How could any man stand to be accused of treason by an underling? Venir had been deceived before by Jarla. The woman consorted with them. She'd been ready to turn him over to them and collect a bounty they had on his head. It was beyond him how any man could serve an underling, willingly or even unwillingly. Certainly death would be preferred. His knuckles whitened on Brool's shaft, his blood bristled, and the air became hot and stale. The shadow of death hung in the air. The men spread farther apart, blades ready, creeping in.

"Why don't you drop the axe and come quietly, Fool? You cannot defeat as all," the orc said, stepping up the hill.

"Maybe, but I'm certainly going to kill you," Venir said, pointing Brool's spike at the part orc's chest. .

Venir was never comfortable killing men, no matter how rotten they were. It was something he sought to avoid over the years. But sometimes, it couldn't be avoided. He hadn't hesitated to kill the brute Baltor; he'd sensed the evil. But with this group, he was uncertain. He couldn't just kill every man he didn't trust, or like, for that matter.

"Turn the dogs loose," the leader ordered.

Bish! And killing dogs was another issue. He was used to Chongo settling such matters. He shifted his feet down into the dirt.

The orc raised his arm and said in his rough voice, "Perhaps a challenge then, Stranger?"

"No, I like the odds I have at the moment, and I don't gamble with swine."

The orc was buying time. Not only for himself but for all of them. The men, as rugged as they appeared, now lacked the overbearing fortitude of being Royal soldiers.

The orc laughed, his brown teeth breaking into a grin.

"Heh-heh. You've got a sharp tongue for a man. Brassy as a lantern. But a fight is not what I had in mind."

"True," the leader interjected. "Stranger, we've no quarrel with the murderer of our tormentors, but our predicament is dire." He held a hand up. A sign of peace and welcome for some. "I don't want to die any more than my men, or you, for that matter. Perhaps we can sort this out." The soldier pointed up the hill towards the outpost. "And, time is short. The shriekers alerted more than us and them." He chopped a sapling down. "We're only the first patrol. There will be more, and they'll be in no mood to parlay."

Venir didn't sense any such thing, however. The soldiers were still making their way up the hill. The dogs' necks were straining on the leash, claws digging up the loose soil. The threat wasn't there. But something about the man's body language wasn't right. The leader was nervous, more desperate than a moment before.

"I'm beginning to think there are not so many up there as you say. Over a hundred Royals, you say, prisoners? I'll tell you what. How about you name me some names?"

The leader rubbed his leather gauntlet under his chin and said, "How about I start with mine first, then?"

"No, I don't know you, but I've known men inside."

"I see, so you were a soldier like us once?"

"No, nothing like you."

"A mercenary then?"

"A hunter. Now, let me hear some names." He waved his axe in the air. "I'm getting antsy."

The leader said nothing at first, then he began, "Well, it seems unlikely your sort of character would have known any of those honorable men. Perhaps if you removed your garish helmet, one of us would know you?"

"If you knew me, you'd have recognized me already," Venir said, stepping back up the hill.

His mind was beginning to catch up with his brawn. For all he knew, these men only wore the uniforms of the Royals. Only the leader, aside from the orc, offered much talk. At first, he'd thought they might be holdovers from the Brigand Army, but he would've recognized them. They didn't carry themselves with the gaits of soldiers, either. Their movement was not refined or disciplined. Even the dogs seemed more savage than trained. Who in Bish were these men?

"A challenge, Stranger?" the orc said again, sheathing his blades. "You and I."

Venir looked at the leader and said, "I thought you said more would be coming. It seems you have more time than you bargained for." He hefted his axe back over his shoulder. "What exactly did you have in mind, Orc?"

At the moment, Venir didn't have many options. Whoever was running the Outpost would be alerted to his presence soon enough. He seethed inside. His plan had been to slip past the underlings like a ghost. He'd assumed only underlings would be there, but there were humans and orcs, too, the occupants of the Outpost, men and underlings, and only Bish knew what else. The smart thing to do would be to abandon his plan, but then what would Jans's Royal Riders do? It was times like this he could have used a mind like Melegal's. He could hear the rogue's voice in his mind, saying, *Think first, Brute! Fight as the last resort. Fighting only increases your chances of getting killed. The gray matter is what counts, not the red meat that hides your bones.*

"First the terms. I win, you come quietly. You win, you go quietly," the orc said.

Venir countered, saying, "I win, I go in peace and you tell me all that I want to know about what lies within the fort. After that, I'll be on my way."

"Huh," the leader said. "Why you'd care to know is beyond me. Only death and misery are in there. Hmmmm … I think I see. You're looking for someone, aren't you?"

Venir didn't reply.

The leader added, "I'll have my men keep an eye on things up the ravine. Far enough away to only use the whistle call. That way, you don't need to be concerned with any interference. My word on that and my men's as well. Men?"

The other soldiers nodded.

"It seems like a risk. Odd, foolish, even for an orc," Venir said. "Makes me wonder if your situation is as precarious as you say."

"Heh … well, Stranger, the truth is I'm bored. We all are. Might as well make things as interesting as I can in the meantime. You win, it's on us, or me rather. I win, I'm taking you up this hill to suffer with the rest of us." The orc dropped his sword belt to the ground and pitched away a few knives. He unbuckled the straps of his leather hauberk and slipped it from his shoulders. The part-orc was knotted with muscle, but his ruddy skin was bare. He cracked his neck in his hands and smiled, a large canine popping up from the bottom of his mouth.

"Don't get his hopes up," the leader said, leading the other soldiers away. "He'll suffer far more greatly than us. He killed two underlings, remember. There will be a price for that. A leg for each perhaps, but maybe just his ears or eyes. One never knows with them. Fiends."

It was a surreal situation. A subtle churning in his gut made him think of his time in the mist, the unnatural atmosphere that had cloaked him like a blanket. At some point in the mist, he'd become used to what was expected, but now he wasn't certain what to expect at all. *I should just run.* But where? There was nowhere to go, and a host of men depended on him, including Slim. He had to play things out, wait and see where they went. Isn't that what Melegal would do? Perhaps when he won, he could get more information from them.

He shuffled up the hill alongside the rocks, where he'd spied on the soldiers before.

"Where are you going, Stranger?" the half-orc said, eyeing him with intent.

Venir held his axe out and said, "Just disposing of my gear. You don't want it too close. I might get tempted to jam it down your throat."

"Hah! Take that scale dress off, as well. What is that, Dwarven?"

Venir nodded.

"Hmmm," the orc rubbed his chin, "looks like it'd fit me just fine. Can I have claim to it if you don't survive… the hill?"

Venir unbuckled the side straps, slid it off, and tossed it to the ground in front of the orc.

"If I die this day, it's yours."

The orc's eyes filled with glee as he eyed the scale like a mound of treasure. As he did, behind the rock and out of sight, Venir slipped his helm, axe and shield into the sack and stuffed it into his pack.

When the orc turned his attention back to him, he grunted.

"Not often do I see another as big as me, Stranger. Or one so ugly, either. That yellow hair of yours is considered a weakness among my race."

"And every aspect of your race, from your hair to your toes, is considered a weakness by ours," Venir said, combing his fingers through his beard before he put his hands on his hips. "So, Orc, what will the challenge be, then?"

The orcen soldier glanced up the ravine. The other soldiers were out of sight, but their rustlings could be heard. The orc held his long arms up and extended his fingers. They were a good bit longer than Venir's.

"I must say, I never thought I'd get another chance at this game. As soon as I saw you, I didn't want to fight, I want to beat you in a game of Mercy."

Venir would have laughed normally, but this orc wasn't going to be a push over. Besides, Mercy wasn't a challenge he'd ever done before, and it seemed that this orc had, judging by the grin on his ugly face. He looked at the insides of his hands, then rubbed his palms together.

"What are the rules?" he asked, stepping down the hill and coming face to face with the orc.

"Very simple. First one to cry Mercy loses."

Venir eyed the wrists on the orc, which seemed twice as thick as his. *Not good.* None of it was. He was fully exposed. His plan had washed down the gutter, and there weren't any options available other than to fight or die. Of course, he hadn't had to volunteer to be there in the first place. What had he been thinking, "Do the right thing"? *Preposterous!* Yet, here he was.

He asked one final question before they locked fingers.

"Have you ever cried *Mercy* before, Orc?"

"Heh-heh-heh ... not even to an ogre."

48

T *AP. TAP. TAP. TAP. TAP. Tap ...*
Head down, shoulders aching, Lefty resigned himself to his duties. Jubbler had quieted, opting to pick the flecks of sawdust from his hair and eating it momentarily. The Quartermaster made his rounds back and forth, but at the moment he'd moved to the far end and was talking, having struck up a conversation with smugglers departing with goods from the dock.

Any plans he had of helping Kam and Erin were abandoned. He had to find a way out of this jam first, and that wasn't likely any time soon. Tapping with one hand, he toyed with the absidium chains that kept him shackled. He was the only one shackled on the dock. All the others were free. He wasn't sure why they worried about him so much. He was hardly a threat.

Rolling his wrist, he felt the metal bonds slip down past his wrist and onto his hand. He swore there was just enough room to slip his hand free. He jerked his elbow back. The chain constricted faster than thought, pinching deep into his hand, almost turning his fingers blue. His eyes started to water. It hurt.

"Whatcha doin'? Huh. Huh. I saw. I saw that. Bad chains. Huh. Absurduim. Huh. Seen 'em squeeze a head off ... huh ... before." Jubbler gawped at Lefty's hands and patted his own hands together.

"Go away, Jubbler," Lefty said with all the venom he had in his voice.

"Huh."

Whack! He crushed a nail head with his hammer. "I said ... ah, never mind." *Whack! Whack! Whack!*

Perhaps that's what they wanted. To make him crazy. Erode his mind like they'd clearly done to Jubbler.

"Don't despair. Huh. Listen to your elders. Huh. I've been here longer ... Huh ... than you've lived. Huh. Many lifetimes. I know where the smoke is. Fire makes smoke. Huh. Smoke, smokey smoke." Jubbler diddled with his beard as his eyes drifted away. "Smoke. Smoke. Huh. Smoke. I like smoke. Huh. And chicken."

Lefty grabbed two nails and stuck them in his ear holes. It caught the eye of Jubbler, who cocked his head like a curious bird.

"Huh. Why you do that? Huh. Nails don't go there. Huh. Huh. Huh."

"Can you use a hammer, Jubbler?"

"Huh. Yes. Huh."

Lefty handed the dwarf his hammer and said, bowing down, "Would you be kind enough to drive these nails into my ears, so I don't have to listen to you anymore?"

There was no reply. Not a mumble, a grumble, a huh or a sigh. Just silence among the resounding sounds of hammers hammering. Lefty closed his eyes. He envisioned the jabbering Jubbler taking him up on it and whacking him upside the head. *I bet Melegal never would have thought of this.*

"Well," Lefty started, "what are you waiting for, Jubbler? Tack them in."

He felt two gentle hands remove the nails from his ears and heard a soft soprano voice say, "Master Gillem was proud of you, Lefty. It would be a shame to waste your brain. You're going to need it to save Erin and Kam."

"What is the meaning of this, Kam!" Palos's paunchy face was filled with fury. "Have you found a new hobby, polishing swords?" In three quick steps, he came across the room and backhanded her in the mouth. She spiraled to the floor.

"Apologies," she said through her split and bloody lip. "Palos, I was only curious—"

Smack!

He hit her again.

"Silence, you red-headed heifer! Do you take me for a fool?" He grabbed her under the chin and leered into her eyes. "I know you've been trying to escape. I know you plot in your mind. You aren't the first whore to reject my musings."

"I'm sure I won't be the last either—*ulp!*"

Palos shoved her to the floor, both hands wrapped around her neck, squeezing her. She could have bit her tongue, but she couldn't take it anymore. The abuse and humiliation had finally snapped her cord. She forced the words out. "Kill me then, Coward!"

Palos's face became darker.

"Oh no, my pretty. You'll not escape life so easily. Suffer you shall. Suffer you and your baby like you never suffered before! Thorn!"

"Yes Prince Palos," the tall man said, stepping into view.

"I'm here as well, Prince," Diller said, arriving on the other side. "The door is secured."

Kam couldn't muster a spell. The pressure on her neck was too much. What had she gotten herself into? The sword. The sword of Zorth had caused this. *Cursed thing!* She strained against her captor.

"She struggles. Always struggles. I tire of that." Palos kept her pinned with one hand and brushed his hair from his eyes. "It seems she was not broken entirely, as I suspected. Too much fight in the lass." His eyes drifted back towards the sword for a moment then back on her. A blank look came on his face. "What did you possibly think you could accomplish with that sword? Put her in the chair, men, and hold her still."

Diller grabbed her by the hair and jerked her up from the ground. Thorn stuffed the chair beneath her legs, bringing a sharp pain to the backs of her knees. Both men leered at her like hungry dogs as they held her down. Diller winked. *Pig.* But at least she could move her mouth now and wriggle her fingers, too. *Concentrate.*

Palos kicked the sword along the floor with his toe, a milder tone in his voice.

"It's magic. The Sword of Zorth." He looked back at her and smiled, hands clasped behind his back. "One of my most prized possessions, actually. Would you like to hear how I acquired it?"

"No." *I want to kill you!*

Diller grabbed her hair and pulled her face up towards Palos.

"It's quite interesting, really." Palos leaned back on the table. "And you might not believe this, but I came across it honestly."

"Pfft," Kam stated. She wasn't going to believe a word he said. Not that it mattered. She wanted to summon something, but his eyes were all over her. *Stop looking at me.* She only needed a few seconds was all. Why hadn't she prepared a spell earlier?

"It was given to me by my father, a gift. As the story goes, Zorth was the founder of the City of Three. Yes, it was he who led the battle against the giants. It was he who subdued them with this, his magic blade. They yielded to him and his army, and in exchange for their lives, they built this city, which would explain why the towers are so tall and unique." Palos smacked his lips. "All of this talking has made me thirsty." He nodded at Thorn.

The man found a bottle and a half empty goblet, refilled it, and handed it over to Palos.

"Mmmm … now, I must say, this wine is something. I could drink it all day."

Kam snarled, "You do drink it all day, Louse."

Palos wagged his finger at her.

"Oh Kam, you'd be wise to show more interest, because once this story ends, the genuine suffering of you and your child begins."

Kam couldn't fight the lump in her throat as her lips tightened. *I can't let this happen! He's a madman!*

Palos looked at Thorn and Diller, saying, "You see? You just have to know the right words to keep a woman quiet, men. Now, oh yes, where was I?"

Diller tugged at her hair.

"The sword, the giants and the towers. So, the wizards and the Royals wanted the giants to look up to them, not down. But the ruins outside the city show a different thing. Many towers were felled there, busted, broken and overgrown. You didn't know about that, did you?"

Diller and Thorn looked at one another, but Kam didn't say a thing.

"I've been there. Many secrets of the old ways lie hidden there as well as untold treasure, too. I've been there before and even spied a gem as big as the moons." Palos' eyes glossed over, and his hands were reaching out to grab something that wasn't there.

"What happened to the gem, Prince?" Diller asked.

"What kind was it?" Thorn added.

"A ruby as fiery as a dragon's breath. As bright as the daylight suns. Like an apparition, it appeared," his fingers tickled the air, "and like the wind, it was gone."

A strange silence fell on the room. Even Kam found herself captivated by his words. She shook it off.

"The Star of the Rising Suns," Kam murmured. "A bedtime story told to children, the same as giants, dragons and magic swords. Do you dogs wag your tails at everything he says?"

Diller cracked her in the mouth with his knuckles.

She glared up at him and spat a bloody tooth out, saying, "You'll pay for that!"

Diller drew his hand back again.

"Stop!" Palos held out his hand. "I've not finished my tale."

She'd had enough. There wasn't much she could take of this anymore. She had to do something and do it now. *Stay focused. You have to be smarter than these fools, Woman!*

"Oh, please do, Mighty Prince. I've nothing better to do, and your hounds are all ears. Perhaps you can add in the tale of the Dragon Clawed Throne or the Hive of Everwonder. Please spoil us with your tongue."

Diller pulled back on her hair, harder this time.

"Is that all you have, Diller? My daughter's stronger than that."

Diller turned red-faced.

"Palos, my Prince, must I stand for this?"

Kam stretched her fingers toward the small pocket in her robes.

"Be patient, Diller. You as well, Thorn. She'll be all yours after my story is done."

"What?" Kam exclaimed.

"You mean it, Prince?" Diller added.

Palos drained and tossed the goblet on the table.

"I've no need for a battered and toothless strumpet. I've a reputation to uphold. What would my men think if I was caught with her? But for you men, well, she's quite a prize, being a Royal."

"Palos, you Bastard! You mangy dog! YOU'LL PAY FOR THIS!"

He was laughing.

"And just think of when her daughter is fully grown, if I let her live that long. Ha-Ha-Ha. Now, where was I?"

Kam couldn't take it. She wasn't going to live with this a moment longer.

Diller leaned down in her face saying, "I told you that you'd be mine." He stroked her hair and tugged it, too.

She cringed. Biting her tongue wasn't an option anymore. She was going to get her fingers on those gems and let them have it. *Just do it!* Her fingertip touched the first stone.

" … so, you say the tales are not true, Kam, but I'll have you know that I saw the very Star of the Rising Suns as well, and I'll make my trek back one day, much better prepared than last time. But that's not where I was going, however. No, the sword," he opened a drawer in the table, removed white cotton gloves, and put them on. "My father says it's not to be touched by human hands, well, skin rather. It could burn you to the touch."

Her fingers wrapped around one of the gems.

"Which I see is not the case," he said, looking at her, "at least for a woman. But magic has its own mind, all the same. The important part I wanted to mention was that this gift, the Sword of Zorth Morgwaggyn, was a gift to me from my father Palzor, who received it for services rendered to …"

Kam had both stones between her knuckles, the magic surge tickled her nose.

"… your father, Lord Kamdroz."

"What?" she said as a glimmer of light twinkled inside her hands.

"She's got something!" Diller wrenched her wrist. Kam felt all her hope flee as the red stones clattered to the floor.

49

"**I**S HE DEAD?" MELEGAL ASKED.

Jubilee had tears streaming down her face. The child had seen enough death in the past few days. It was amazing she kept it together at all.

Haze wiped her bloody forearm across her head.

"He breathes, but the bleeding is only staunched, not stopped. Just stitched, and poorly at that. If he's bleeding inside as bad as he was on the outside, I don't think he can make it much longer."

All eyes were on Melegal. *What am I to do? I'm no healer … I'm a stealer.* Melegal couldn't ignore the feeling in his gut, however. He had to do something. He didn't want to, but felt compelled to. "Stop staring at me. I'm thinking." He stepped over into the corner and sat down. He'd stitched his fair share of wounds in his time, but nothing quite like this. It was just one of those things where you gave a man some water and let him bleed out and die. *Why me? I just want to leave this place.*

"You can make it, Brak," Jubilee was saying, over and over again.

The man's head seemed monstrous in her tiny lap.

Like a woman tending an ogre.

"We need water," Haze said. "I can fetch us some." She started to get up.

"No," Melegal said, rising to his feet. "I'll go. He needs the likes of you, not me."

As he made his way through the door, Jubilee said, "You will come back, won't you?"

"Of course he will," Haze said.

But Melegal didn't say a thing as he left. *Smart child. Even for a Slerg.*

Dreams. Nightmares. Most experience both. Brak only experienced the latter. He hung on the edge of an abyss, a great fire licking at his toes as he struggled to pull himself up. On his feet, a man hung, long and broad, a bearded face full of fire. It was Venir, his father, hanging on for his very life as he held on for his own. Brak had never felt such weight before, like a cart of heavy stones.

His father was screaming up at him, but he didn't understand the words. All he could do was try to hang on, his strength fading, the pain in his arms and neck excruciating. If only his father would let go, stop screaming, he could save himself. But he knew if he did, he would forever lose his face. He hung on. His father began to slip and fall. Still screaming at the top of his lungs.

The next barn was a stark contrast to the one he just left. It was a hive of activity. Horses were being led up and down the concourse. Royal soldiers were adorned in armor from head to toe. Commands and shouts rang out from one end to the other. *No City Watch, at least.*

Melegal threw a coarse blanket over his head, pinched it below his neck, stooped down, hunched his shoulders, and shuffled forward. *Eyes down, ears up!* From one stall to the other he went, doddering along with a discarded rake he found. All he needed to do was snatch a bucket, refill it in a water trough, and disappear as easily as he came. *Why am I suddenly responsible? He's not my bastard child.*

An urchin stumbled into his path, carrying a metal pail.

That will do. He grabbed it by the handle and said, "Child, is that your stall?"

"Let go of my pail, Hag. I'll be whipped if I stall," the boy said, trying to rip it away. He was quite strong.

"Nay, Child. I shall fetch it for you," Melegal suggested.

"Nay, Hag!"

"I'm no hag," he warned, ripping the pail free from the boy's grasp.

The boy opened his mouth wide. Melegal shoved a large silver talent in it.

"Taste that silver? Hush your mouth. Fetch another pail, and run along."

The boy had the strangest expression on his face as his eyes shifted back and forth. "Ulp." He swallowed the coin.

Melegal snorted. He'd have done the same back in those days. Royal urchins could not have coins, but it would serve him well.

"Go along now. My master's horse is thirsty," he said.

Ahead was a row of troughs where a few lathered-up horses drank. It would have been better to get water from an Everwell, but that was too far away. *What good is a bucket of water going to do, anyway? 'Keep the fever down,' they say. Pah, he'll be dead before I return.*

He waited a moment, along the outside of an abandoned stall. Two Royal soldiers chatted from horseback by the troughs. Four stable hands, men and boys, checked the fasteners on their saddles and harnesses. *Hurry up!*

"On good report, the underlings number in the thousands leagues south, outside the city walls. They say hundreds lie below," one soldier was saying.

"Thousands, you say? By my sources, there are tens of thousands and even more below," the other responded, slapping his comrade on the shoulder. "Ha Ha Ha! My, the tales grow taller all the time. I say we ride south into their belly and they'll never come this far north again. Black fiends. They fight like girls with steel and armor. High time we stopped toying with the brood. The pests are getting annoying. I've lost two of my finest house boys."

"Yes, I lost the same. I thought I was going to have to polish my own boots," the other soldier let out a laugh, "I've not done that since my training days."

The banter. It was that tireless banter that he'd grown accustomed to in his childhood, and he'd never grown sick of it. All the boots he'd shined until his arms were numb. And now, it seemed the soldiers weren't going to move. Their chatter continued.

I've got to move.

Melegal rambled over, a little hitch in his step, and dipped his pail in the water. The soldiers paused their conversation. He could feel their eyes on him as he withdrew the pail filled with water.

"Ahem," one of the soldiers said.

Melegal shuffled back.

"I don't think she heard you."

Why do they insist I'm a woman!

"A fragile thing."

"A husk with skin."

"Deaf. Mute. Rankled."

They were getting under his skin now. *Just go!*

He teetered away, turning his back to them.

"Perhaps it's an underling," one soldier said, leading his horse around and blocking his path. "Show me your face, Old One."

"My pail! My pail!" a little girl screeched. "That hag has stolen my urchin's pail!"

It would have been easier to fetch water in the Outland. *Of all the fool things!*

"Elizabeth," one of the soldiers said, chuckling, "Has your pail been stolen?"

Melegal kept his head down, shuffling his feet, trying to go around. *Seem confused. Sell it, Man, sell it!*

"Dullard!" Elizabeth snapped up at the soldier, "Of course I've been robbed. This hag has stolen my property, and my stable hand is now with a broken arm. Now, I'm shorthanded."

"I'll summon the Watch and have this one arrested," the soldier said, dismounting.

"I'll have the hag whipped now!" Elizabeth screamed.

Of all the ridiculous things. Whipped over this? A child no older than Jubilee, nonetheless.

"I think this matter is better served in the hands of the Watch," the soldier added, "and I'm surprised you are out with all the trouble of late. It's not safe—"

"Be silent, Cretin! I'll have you whipped as well. How dare you address me like your child? I am a Kling! And you are a soldier! A pawn to my whims. It is you who has to worry about the underlings, not I."

The air was ripe with tension. Melegal noticed the man's hand falling to his sword. *Split her skull. I would! Impudent Royals.*

"Elizabeth!" a familiar voice cried out. "Mind your tongue! You are creating a scene, as usual!"

"Stay out of this, Rayal! This old bitch stole my pail, and I'll have her head for that! And this soldier sneered at me! No man does that to a Kling and lives. Now give me my pail!" Elizabeth stormed over and wrapped her fingers on the handle.

Melegal held it tight in his grip as the girl, about as big as Jubilee, tugged away with all her strength.

"Give it to me!"

He let go.

Elizabeth lurched backward and tumbled onto her rear, the pail of water spilling all over her. Everyone fell silent as her face erupted in red rage, except Rayal, who was holding her belly and laughing.

Elizabeth pulled out a knife, raised it over her head, and charged.

"I'll kill you, Hag!"

Rayal caught the girl by the wrist and twisted the knife out of her hand.

"Enough of this, Elizabeth! You've gone too far. Men, apologies for my sister's trepidations. She gets carried away with her evil self!"

Elizabeth took the metal pail and swung it into Rayal's knees.

Bang!

"OW! Blast you, Little Fiend!"

Elizabeth ran away, screaming and pointing. "You still owe me a two-headed dog!"

So that's the one. Now what? He'd encountered Rayal before, briefly, and was certain that she would remember him. Rayal, another beauty, was unlike the typical Royals. Not only did she display strength, but grace and kindness as well. But what if she knew about the treachery at the castle? Melegal stepped around in his own private circle, showing he was uncertain where to go.

"Milady," one of the soldiers said. "Shall I send for the Watch? After all, she did, it seems, take a pail?"

"No, but I am curious why this one hides her face," she said, walking over, "and why she took the pail in the first place."

"Er … Milady, she could have a sickness, or a horrible face."

"A spy perhaps," the other soldier suggested.

Melegal swayed in place, looking down at her booted toes. Her perfume was incredible, just like the Lorda's. *I can't risk it.* He concentrated, sending a tingle through his mind.

"No," she said. "But I've run into the strangest people that shuffle around here in cowls and cloaks. You'd be surprised. Please, men, go about your business, I think I'll be fine. Thank you."

"As you wish," the men said, trotting away, their stable hands in tow.

Melegal let his mind ease.

She huffed. "Now, tell me, Old Woman, are you thirsty?"

Melegal didn't reply. *I can't tell her to sleep, run or look away. The first two would look odd, and the latter wouldn't be enough. Think!*

Rayal turned, picked up the pail, and handed it to him.

He grabbed it, shuffled over to the trough, and refilled it, then started to shuffle back the way he came. Eyes down, feet moving forward, not looking over his shoulder, he continued on. Rayal was right behind him. Melegal could hear not one set of footsteps, but three, trailing close behind him. *Drat! An Escort.*

"I'll be curious why this person is so desperate for water that they'd cross a Royal," she said under her breath. "And there's always something strange going on in that barn over there."

Just as he made his way over to the doorway that traversed between the barns, Rayal said, "Halt!"

Melegal kept going.

"Detective Melegal," she said again, "I suggest you stop."

His heart jumped a beat. *Not possible.* He kept going.

"Don't think to fool me; I'd recognize those delicate hands anywhere, especially those scars on your knuckles."

He didn't slow.

Her voice turned cold. "You are a wanted man, Detective. And with a word, I can have every soldier in these barns coming after you."

Mercy, is there no limit on my pursuers!

50

THE UNDER-BISH. *PREPOSTEROUS.* VERBARD SAT on his throne deep in thought. Eep had filled him in on The Darkslayer. It seemed the man lived after all, but in another world below his. One that he never would have believed for himself. Eep had given him few details, other than the fact that he'd bitten the man's fingers off, or a portion of them rather.

He's no longer a threat. Could he escape the world beyond the Mist? Perhaps, but I cannot worry about that now, without proof. I'll forge ahead and press on. Stay on course.

Eep was still after the keys. Kierway still made preparations to overtake a castle. Jottenhiem kept his men in good order, biding their time. With or without keys, a living Darkslayer or not, he was going to press on. Bring the wretched humans to their knees, one citizen at a time.

Eep, have you found that man yet?

No, Master, but it won't be long. Do you require anything else? I hunger. A quick bite, perhaps?

Stay on course!

At his side stood the Vicious: tall and silent with the musculature of a hairless feline. How many of these powerful creatures did Master Sinway have at his disposal? *How many, indeed?*

"If I had a thousand of you, this would be much easier," he said, rising to his feet and drifting away. He cast his silver eyes above. How many thousands of humans could they take out with one lethal strike? With enough force, could they take the entire city? Eradicate the humans once and for all. If anything, he just wanted to get his charge over with.

Now wasn't the time to second guess himself. No. His plan was sound: take a Castle by force, and have a stronghold. It would work, but Kierway was an important part of that plan. He didn't trust him. No, once the castle was located, he'd send a portion to invade. He would lead a full scale assault on the world of men above first, in one giant wave. The castle would not expect an attack from within.

He rolled his fingers. The orb of imbibing floated from the ground and into his grasp. Then he noticed someone was coming. It was Kierway. *That was quick.*

"You have good report?" Verbard said.

"Castle Almen," Kierway stated, running his clawed fingers over his shaven head.

"Again? Have we not drawn enough attention to ourselves at that point?"

Kierway sauntered up, poured himself a glass of wine, and slumped down on the makeshift throne of rock and stone. "Fitting for you, vastly inferior to the one I'll inherit from my father. But for a lesser family, it will do."

Verbard sneered. "I believe your father was very clear with your role and mine. You are beholden to me, and you'd be served well to remember that."

The Vicious stepped forward and bared its fangs. Kierway remained in place.

"You need me as much as I need you, Verbard. Now, let's set our differences aside. I want to fulfill this quest as much as you."

"Go on."

"Castle Almen. Yes, its access to the Current is now overfilled with guards, but they number less than a hundred. Still, it would be difficult to penetrate that small but heavily defended port." Kierway took his first sip and spit it out. "Pah! Did an urchling make this? I wouldn't let a cave dog drink it."

Verbard's silver eyes flashed. It was his favorite port. "Get on with it, Kierway."

"The strange thing is," he tipped his finger up, "the passages to the other castles are quite narrow, and most castles don't have any access at all to the Current. Most are sealed off, as if no passage was ever there to begin with. It wasn't always so. That leaves us with taking one from the upside in, or from the downside up. Castle Almen, it seems, is the only choice."

Kierway kicked his legs up on the armrest and leaned back with his arms behind his head.

"I say we attack from the up and the down. We have more than enough w —"

Kierway's eyes were full of alarm as he sailed from the throne to the ground. Copper eyes filled with rage, he jumped back to his feet, swords ripped from his scabbards.

Verbard rose from the ground, spikes of energy fueling his claws. He'd had enough of the impudent Kierway, and he didn't have to take any more if he didn't want to. The time to let it loose was now.

"Take him out!" he ordered the Vicious.

The Vicious sprang like a cat, claws ripping at Kierway's feet. Kierway twisted away, sword chopping backward, clipping off a pair of the Vicious's fingers. It did not howl or slow. It pressed on. The edges of Kierway's blades danced through the air, licking across the hardened skin of the Vicious, sending black slivers of flesh into the air. The creature's ears matted down on its head. It wasn't accustomed to fighting a faster opponent.

Curse those magic blades. Verbard watched in amazement and alarm. Kierway was a split second faster than the Vicious at every strike or blow. It was as if he'd fought against one before. *I should have known. What an excellent sparring partner one would be.*

"It's only a matter of time before I whittle him down," Kierway said, shifting, juking and parrying. "I can do this all day, but he won't last that long; trust me."

No. Verbard could see that now. But once the Vicious pinned the man down, it would be all over. *Perhaps it's time to intervene. Good-bye Kierway!*

The fluid motion of the Vicious's body had begun to slow.

Slice! Slice! Slice! Slice!

Kierway rolled his wrists with the rapid rhythm of a drummer, whittling two fingers off. The Vicious was hobbled, chopped and gashed like a wounded dog.

Verbard summoned his power. *Let's even the odds, shall we?* The rock beneath the combatant's feet turned to mud.

"No! What are you doing, Verbard? There is no honor in this!" Kierway cried out, sinking to his ankles as the Vicious closed in.

Verbard waved good-bye.

Kierway's blades chopped and parried, keeping the pressing Vicious at bay. A look of concern formed in

Kierway's eyes, his legs now sunk knee deep in the sludge. The Vicious was not slowed. Its mighty limbs still lunged. Kierway clipped its ear off as the Vicious wrapped one good arm around Kierway's neck and drove him into the mud.

Excellent!

Kierway thrashed like a fish on a line, small daggers from his bandolier rising up and down in his hands, blades breaking on the hardened back of the creature. Kierway shouted a plea with a mouthful of mud.

"I yield!"

Verbard dusted his hands off. He wanted to laugh out loud as the Vicious pushed Kierway face down below the mud. In but a moment, it would all be over. One of his least favorite underlings would be gone forever. Bubbles of mud popped on the surface. Verbard glided back to his throne. *So be it.* Taking a seat, he brought a cup of port to his lips. *Might as well enjoy this.*

"STOP!"

Verbard went numb.

51

BAMF!
        One underling burst into dust.

Bamf!

Another did the same.

Bamf!

Followed by another. The rest of the underlings fled back down the hill, leaving Darlene's shattered body bleeding over the pine needles. Scorch took long strides down the slope, over the slippery terrain, watching the underlings go. Several black heads were running at full charge, one exploding into black dust after the other until they were nothing but fertilizer for the terrain.

Darlene lived, blood trickling over her puffy lips that sucked like a catfish out of water. How disturbing it was to see such a lively person dying like this. She tried to speak, lips struggling to form words. The gashes in her belly and chest prevented the effort.

A shame.

Scorch looked over the bright horizon towards the east. It was still a long walk to the City of Three. He kneeled down, grabbed her bloody hand and smiled.

"I still require company on my journey, Darlene. But I can't have you doing whatever it is you want. Stay close to me and live, drift away and die."

Darlene's rugged frame twitched with spasms. Despite the evident pain within her dying body, she nodded. Relief overtook the anguish in her face as Scorch pulled her up into her sitting position. Her eyes were wild with fire as she licked her lips and wiped the blood from her mouth. Then she began fingering the places where the puncture wounds had just been. She gaped at him. Blinking a hundred times before she spoke.

"You don't have to tell me twice, Scorch!" She lunged over and hugged him.

It was the strangest feeling. He couldn't remember ever being hugged before, but the affectionate gesture was touching. He struggled to peel her arms from his waist.

"That's enough of that," he said in a firm tone, "but my, you are strong as a dwarf, I'd say. There may be something to that." He patted her on the head.

She smiled back.

"I'm strong for a girl." She looked around. "I got five of them, I think," she said, shuffling down the hill and inspecting the bodies of the fallen underlings. "WOOOOO HOOOOOOO!" She hoisted a bloody arrow in the air. "I killed me some underlings! There ain't nothing I can't kill!" She rushed over to all the bodies and retrieved all her arrows, then went for the eyes.

"Stop that," Scorch ordered.

Darlene looked up at him and froze.

"But there's magic in their eyes. We have to cut them out and burn the bodies."

"No you don't. It's time to go."

"But ..."

Scorch felt irritated, and his power ebbed the ever slightest, but he didn't like it. It made him feel vulnerable.

"It is time to leave, and there will be no more of this savage talk. Come Darlene, or not. I'll entertain no more chatter."

Darlene slammed her knife into her sheath, fetched her bow, and returned to his side as he walked about the hill and onto the path they had abandoned. They traveled over a mile before Darlene broke her silence.

"I'm with you, Scorch. You saved me. I'm grateful. I saw what you did, too. Turned those underlings into smoke and dust. Incredible," she said, strutting along his side.

That's more like it.

"But ..." Darlene hunkered down a little as she said it.

He felt that mild irritation return.

"What are you going to do about them?"

Scorch looked down on her. She was eyeing him and the path behind her. She pointed.

A small huddled group fell to their knees as he turned. It was the people that Darlene attempted to save earlier.

"Want me to shoot them?"

"What? You almost got yourself killed trying to save them!" he said.

"Well," she licked her lips, "I was mostly looking for a fight, is all. And I really wanted to kill an underling. Plus, I owe you." She readied her bow and arrow.

"Ask them what they want," he said, combing his fingers through his long locks of hair.

"What do you idiots want?" she screamed, pulling back her bowstring.

"Service!" One man shouted back. "We owe you our lives! We seek only to repay the debt."

Darlene looked up at Scorch from the corner of her eye and said, "Just say the word, and I'll put a red dot in his head."

Scorch could feel their willingness and sincerity. He liked it.

"Tell them they may follow, but they must do as they are told."

Darlene eased the string on her bow.

"Does that mean I can tell them what to do?"

"Certainly, but that doesn't mean they will listen," he said, turning forward and continuing his journey to the City of Three.

Darlene started barking orders.

"Don't get closer than thirty paces!"

"Keep up because we ain't slowing!"

"You get your own food and water! And no singing! Unless I say so!"

52

"**W**HAT DO YOU MEAN HE left?" Mikkel said.

Nikkel rammed the wheel barrow of stone into the wall and dropped the arms down. He wiped his hands on his knees and shrugged.

"He's going to find Venir. He seemed pretty determined. But I just think he didn't want to help out with any of the work."

"Why did you let him go?" Billip said, slipping away from the woman who held his waist. "He's not supposed to go anywhere without us. You should have stopped him! Bone!"

"I'll handle this, Billip," Mikkel said, holding out his arm. "Nikkel, what did he say?"

"He just said he was going to 'get out of Bone'."

"And then what?"

"He left."

"Which way?"

Nikkel shrugged. Mikkel swatted him in the back of the head.

"Ow!" Nikkel pushed his father in the chest. "Don't do that again!"

Billip stepped between them as the fires ignited behind the eyes of both father and son.

"Let's not come to blows—"

Mikkel shoved him aside, hooked his arm under Nikkel and slammed him into the ground. Nikkel fought back, but it was over before it started, and Mikkel shoved his face into a pile of dirt.

"Son, you already had my attention, but it seems I didn't have yours. Do I have it now?"

Nikkel nodded, spitting out a mouthful of dirt. Mikkel lifted his son back to his feet.

"Georgio is my friend, Nikkel. Venir is, too, and he wants us to look after him. I'll need your help, too. Do you understand?"

"Sure, Father. And I'm—"

Mikkel cut him off as he helped his son up.

"You don't have to say it, Nikkel. I want you to stick up for yourself, but don't pick a fight with your father. Your mother, maybe?" He slapped his son on the back. "But me? No, no, that's a bad idea." He squeezed Nikkel's arm. "Don't worry, in due time, you'll be more than I can handle."

Nikkel nodded, pointed down the road, and said, "He was trying to find the both of you, but," he looked over his father's shoulder at the giggling women, "you were indisposed. I'm not so sure that man, Corrin, is too pleased with that, either."

"Ah, it's none of that rogue's business." Billip pushed his woman back. "Give me a moment, Jess." She backed away with a giggle. "As I was saying, we need to retrieve Georgio. The streets are dangerous out there. Blast!"

"What?" Mikkel said.

"He's taken Quickster with him," Billip said. "How long's he been gone, Nikkel?"

"An hour, I'd say."

"I bet he's back to the stables by now," Mikkel said. "We can catch up if we hurry."

"No, don't leave me," a brown-haired woman said, tugging on Billip's arm.

Two other women draped their arms on Mikkel. "We can't let you go! You must protect us."

Billip popped his knuckles. The thought of the stables unsettled him. What if that man, Tonio, had returned? He was inches from his death the last time they clashed. It was possible the deranged man could still be waiting at the stables. At the same time, he felt very compelled to stay back and help Trinos.

"I'm sure he'll come back," he offered.

"What? You can't be serious, Billip. You know that boy's as hard-headed as a bull. We have to go and get him, and my pony Quickster."

"I'll go," Nikkel said. "I can run. I might even beat them back to the stables. Assuming that's where they went."

"Has anyone seen Trinos?" Corrin yelled, storming their way. The man looked beside himself.

"No," Billip said, "we were about to ask you the same."

"Why would you be asking me?" Corrin said, looking at the hungry-eyed women, "…fornicators. Perhaps if you weren't diddling the help, you'd know. But know this," he pointed at the three of them, "with Trinos gone, I'm in charge."

Billip and Mikkel laughed.

"I am!" Corrin stomped his foot. "This isn't a brothel, mind you. Chip in, or get out!"

"You better watch yourself," Mikkel said, pointing his finger down in Corrin's face. "I could break you in half, Little Man."

"Hah! Then you better be able to sleep with one eye open," Corrin said. A pair of blades blinked out of his clothes and back in. "The both of you." He twisted around and walked away.

"Huh," Mikkel said, swallowing.

Billip perked up his eyebrows. It seemed there was more to Corrin than originally appeared.

"If we're going after Georgio, we might as well all go, and make it fast. Daylight is burning."

"Yeah, we'll all go," Mikkel said, putting his hand on Nikkel's shoulder. "I could use the run myself."

Billip saluted the women as they went, saying, "I was sure looking forward to keeping one eye open on them. Eh …"

The women in all directions started screaming. A sea of rats was scurrying over the cobblestones by the hundreds, if not thousands. Mikkel and Nikkel stopped in their tracks, eyes wide, watching the vermin run over their booted toes. He and Mikkel looked at one another as the ground began to shake.

"What in the world of Bish?"

Ahead, cutting off the road that lead south towards the stables, the streets erupted. The stone and dirt bulged from underneath with a popping and grinding sound. The men joined the women with shouts, screams and yells as a monstrous hairy bulk unlike anything Billip had ever seen before emerged.

"Sonuvabish!" he cried.

53

FEAR. IT WAS AN ADVENTURER'S enemy and friend. Fear could drive a man to crawl within himself in despair, which was precisely what Fogle Boon wanted to do right now. Or, Fear could spur action and powers deep within you that you'd never known. That furnace was depleted, replaced with a reservoir of icy stone. *Help me. Help us all!*

"Oh my!" Boon said, his hands charging up like fire. "If you have a helmet tucked somewhere in those robes of yours, you better strap it on. You're going to need it!"

The underlings, they weren't all in one spot, but they were many, black forms scurrying all over, spread out from one side of the ravine to the other. A dozen here, a small squad there, all peeking out from behind the rocks and trees, their gemstone eyes twinkling. Shiny steel weapons glinting in the suns' light. There were at least a hundred, if not more, and almost twenty had surrounded Barton. *Think, Fogle! Think!* He crouched down and huddled in his robes.

Boon let the first blast go.

Ka-BOOM!

Fogle cringed and held his hands over his ears as shards of rock and wood scattered all over.

A shower of debris cut his hand, and a chunk of rock clipped his shoulder, sending him to the ground. He hurt all over.

"I cannot do this without you!" Boon was screaming as a litany of small bolts filled the sky. "HOSLOMAN-DEEK!"

A transparent barricade shimmered with flecks of blue and green, deflecting and vaporizing the underling volley. On the other side of that barrier, Barton swatted at a small horde of underlings with his club and had moderate success. Quick and fast they were, driving javelins into his legs and lassoing ropes around his arms and neck.

"YOU CANNOT STOP ME WITH THREAD," Barton roared, grabbing hold of the rope and slinging two underlings across the ground. "YOU CANNOT HURT BARTON! I'M A GIANT, AND YOU ARE COCKROACHES! HA!" Barton stomped on another.

The underlings retreated, reformed, and slung javelins and shot bolts into his face. Barton shielded his face with his arm and stomped the ground, shaking the trees, and screamed at them all.

"Have you finished gawking yet, Grandson? More come! Come to your senses, Man!"

Death. The thought of if dulled his senses. Thrusting oneself into peril with no future knowledge of the outcome could sap the will of a man. Slowly, he rose to his feet, trying to grasp the chaos around him. How could he protect himself with so many things going on at once?

"Courage, Fogle! Have courage!" An array of bright green missiles burst from Boon's finger tips.

A knot of underling soldiers stormed up the ravine, small bucklers raised. They caught the full force of Boon's missiles and chittered with rage. Some were dead, others twitched, but they were still on the move. Fogle managed to make his way alongside his grandfather, where the air was thin. He couldn't breathe, think or do anything.

Boon grabbed hold of his arm.

"Now is not the time to be idle, Wizard. Now is the time to fight! What is wrong with you? You've fought underlings! You've fought giants! What are you waiting for?"

Fogle flinched. Another barrage of bolts slammed into the magic barricade a foot from his face. The underlings were less than a few dozen yards away. They were the most evil things he ever saw. What if he had to fight them with his fists? They'd cut him into little pieces.

He gave his grandfather Boon a blank look. The strong features on the elder's face were beginning to weaken. The wrinkles deepened, the pressure built. Boon couldn't hold up the barricade much longer. *Just cast something. Anything!*

He closed his eyes, muttering the words to the first spell that came to mind. Magic swelled inside his chest and throat, and something eerie oozed in one side of him and out the other. He opened his eyes and found the oddest expression on his grandfather's face.

"It's a start," Boon said, panting "Now do something with what you have done."

Fogle was beside himself, literally. To his left he was, to his right he was, and behind him as well. Three identical Fogles awaited his beck and call. It was an illusion he'd hoped would throw off the giants when he encountered them again.

Fogle pointed down the ravine with both fingers.

"Spread out and attack."

The three Fogles sprang into action.

I can't even move that fast. Concentrate. What shall I have them do?

Illusions were tricky things. Sometimes they worked, and sometimes they did not, depending on the mind of the other. Much of the time, it had more to do with the minds of others than your own. Fogle concentrated on his vision, gave his idea life, and let it go.

The underlings surged toward the direction of Fogle's apparitions, blades slashing, overwhelming the figures. The first one rose into the air, dousing the underlings with rays of arching light. The second fled, evading underling pursuit. The third multiplied from one to three, then fifteen more, all fighting for their lives against the masses.

"Impressive," Boon shouted. "You've bought us some time at least. But how much?"

Fogle half-smiled, "It's the least—"

Boon's barricade fizzled out. The old wizard shrugged. "Well, it was going to happen, but I thought we'd have at least a dozen more seconds or two."

Fogle took a deep breath. He had regained control for the moment, but Boon was right: the illusion wouldn't work forever, a minute more at the most. "What's the plan, Boon?"

"I was hoping you were thinking of one as I doddered around. My plan however, is simple: kill them all." Boon's hands were on his hips as he took a deep draw of air. "But, I'm afraid I'm lacking the firepower at the moment." Boon gritted his teeth. "Seems I don't have as much juice as I used to."

Fogle started to reply, "I'm not so—"

"RAAAAARGH!"

Barton cried out as he crashed into the ground and underlings piled all over him.

"GET OFF ME, PESTS!"

The giant's arms were pinned to his sides by ropes.

Fogle had to do something. Scanning his surroundings, he noticed his apparitions beginning to disappear. The underlings cried out in triumph and confusion. Some broke off after the apparitions that continued to multiply. There were more than twenty scattered throughout the ravine. He retrieved his pack, withdrew his spellbook, and tossed it to his grandfather.

"Find something in there," he said, making way to help Barton. "And get our arses out of here!"

"Giants are friends of fire, Grandson!" Boon shouted.

Fogle shook his head. He didn't see how that would help. Knowing a better weakness for underlings would have been better.

"HELP BARTON! HELP BARTON, WIZARD!" The underlings were on him like a hive of angry bees.

Fogle's heart went out. The giant was big, deformed, but more child than man. It was torment to watch him suffer such savagery as the underlings struck with all the venom they had. Barton cried out again, sending shivers down Fogle's spine. Barton began to bleed.

Move, Fogle! Act! He's about to die!

Four underlings hoisted a rope behind Barton's neck and yanked his chin back. Three others chittered with wicked glee as they hoisted their javelins back and took aim at Barton's last good eye.

54

V ENIR COULD HEAR THE LEATHER squeak as the bald orc twisted his bracers on his wrists. Venir had a similar pair once that he discarded, never feeling the need. Maybe now would have been a good time to make use of such things.

"I am called Tuuth," the orc said, cracking his bullish neck in his hands. "It's best you know the name of your opponent." The orc bared one magnificent fang.

A fitting name. Venir stretched his limbs one last time. He couldn't have beaten an ogre, not a full one anyway. Yet there was truth behind Tuuth's words. Of course, orcs were notorious liars. Venir couldn't afford to worry about that now. He'd beaten ogres before, Farc and Son of Farc, in mortal combat and won. And if anything, he felt much stronger now than he did then.

Tuuth eyed him.

"No name, huh?"

"My name has many enemies," Venir responded, coming eye to eye with the orc.

Tuuth was rangy and powerfully built, as fine a specimen of his race as Venir had ever seen. Still, the thought of calling out mercy to anyone, even if a ploy, wasn't an easy one.

Toy with him. See what he's got.

Venir looked back up the ravine.

"They won't be near. Heh-heh. It don't matter."

Venir took one last look over his shoulder. Hidden behind the rocks, in the sack inside his pack, the armament was safe. No one could get to it but him. But being without it was disconcerting. *I don't need it. Not for this. I never met an orc I couldn't handle before.* He raised his arms up and spread his fingers out.

"Ready?"

Venir nodded.

He and Tuuth gripped hands. He felt the raw power behind the orc's squeeze. *Bish!*

"You make the count to three, Stranger."

Both man and orc braced their legs in the dirt, arms pressing, but holding back.

"You strong for a man," Tuuth muttered, showing an evil grin.

"One," Venir started.

"Tuuth strong for an orc."

"Two."

"Very strong. Not too late to back out, Stranger."

Jaws clenched, eyes filled with fire, he said, "It's not too late for you either, Orc. THREE!"

Tuuth's hands felt like dried leather and were as strong as vices. He pulled Venir's hands up and drove him back. The pressure built quickly. Tuuth squeezed his fingers at the same time, pinching the bone. Sweat beads burst on Venir's brow. *Blast! What kind of orc is this!*

"Say the word, and I'll make this easy," Tuuth mocked, pushing him backward, crushing his hands.

Venir wanted to tear his hands away, but held on. *Fight, Venir!* Tuuth dug his fingernails into the backs of his hands, drawing blood. Venir fought the urge to scream. He was losing. *NO!*

Blocking out the pain, he shoved back. Tuuth grunted, muscles knotting up in cords. Venir squeezed back, fighting with everything he had. Tuuth's feet slid back over the dirt. No, Mercy was not his game. Not in this case it wasn't. Either Tuuth never sweated, or he hadn't broken one.

"Give up you, Stranger? Ha. Just ask for Mercy."

Venir couldn't find the breath to respond. He put everything he had into forcing the orc's wrist back.

"Maybe if you had all your fingers it would help," Tuuth huffed in his face.

Venir couldn't remember the last time he'd been mocked. It stoked the fires in his belly. Spit frothing from his lips doubled his efforts, legs surging and driving the orc backward. Tuuth's eyes widened as Venir began to bend his wrists backward.

"Harrumph!" Tuuth exclaimed. He jerked Venir's arms left then right. Bullish shoulder against bullish shoulder. The orc gave no more, his thick wrists again forcing Venir's backwards.

"Come on, Tuuth!" The leader said, appearing from the brush. "No man can beat you!"

"What game is this?" Venir managed to spit out. "I'll not be bushwhacked!"

"Peace!" The leader said. "Battle on. My men can't pass on a show like this. We'll keep our distance. Our word, Stranger!"

"Aye," the soldier with the dogs said. "I've never seen Tuuth have a struggle before."

Venir blocked them out. The jeers and cheers had no meaning as he and Tuuth struggled back and forth. Keeping his breath and strength up was enough to worry about. *Bone! What strength!* His hands were killing him. It felt like they would break at any moment. A stone gargoyle didn't have a mightier grip.

"You tire, Stranger! Your chest heaves like an excited woman!"

Venir's wrists were back more than before.

"Ye've got him, Tuuth! Now break him."

Fight, Venir, Fight!

He fell to one knee.

A chorus of triumph burst out.

Tuuth towered over him, leering downward, powerful arms pulsating with life and vitality.

"Say it, Stranger!"

Melegal would kill me if he saw this. All the gold he would lose. Hang on! He must tire! He cannot be so strong!

The soldiers said, "Cry mercy! He'll cripple you! He will!"

"Pride's the doom of a man!"

"Tuuth will show no mercy to the foolish."

Venir's sweat-coated face was red and purple. His wrists were bent fully backward. The pain was becoming unbearable.

"Slat!" he yelled.

Tuuth's hot breath was in his face.

"Give in, Stranger! My patience runs out!"

"NO!"

Venir had suffered so many things. The Mist. The underlings. The Marsh. The Pit. A shallow grave. How could he not survive this? How could he be beaten? His heart was ready to explode in his chest. Big purple veins rose inside his temples. His nose bled, and his eyes rolled up in his head. Was it the armament? *Fool!* Was he weaker without it?

"Do it, Tuuth! Break him!" the Leader cried.

"Say the word!" Tuuth snorted.

Venir knew that he had to hold on. Just a little longer. The orc was soon to tire, he was certain. *Save your strength, Venir. He can't keep this up.* Certainly he'd have a second wind. He always had. But the orc shouldn't.

Tuuth shouted in his ear.

"Last chance, Stranger!"

"For you maybe," Venir spit through his lips.

Tuuth roared, wrenched downward and twisted.

Snap!

Venir's wrist broke. His fingers bent back to the edge.

"NOOOOOO!"

The soldiers jumped and hollered.

"Say it!"

Venir's right wrist was folded up to his arm. He might as well have been stabbed in the gut. That much he could understand. This wasn't possible. He screamed as the pain of a thousand fires shot up and down his arm. His stomach repulsed as he choked down the urge to vomit.

Snap!

Agony! His other wrist now shattered. *How!* He couldn't take it anymore. Dazed and defeated, he looked up into Tuuth's face. The orc's chest was heaving as he wiped the sweat from his brow. Venir didn't even realize his hands were freed. He couldn't feel them. They hung limp as his sides. He couldn't bear to look at them. Broken. Foolish. Ashamed.

"I didn't say mercy," was all Venir could manage to say.

Tuuth shook his fist, saying, "No, Stranger. I've no words for it. But you'll wish that you did." Tuuth then let out a cry of triumph to the cheers of his fellow soldiers.

Venir closed his eyes. *I can't believe it. What happened?*

The dogs howled.

The leader said, "Button it up, men."

Venir opened his eyes in time to see the small party scrambling around. Tuuth shoved him face first to the ground, held a knife to his throat, and said, "Keep silent, Stranger, if you want to live."

In all his life, Venir had never felt more helpless than when the underlings arrived.

55

D*ID JUBBLER JUST SAY THAT?*
No one else was around. Lefty removed the other nail from his ear. Jubbler picked at his beard and twitched his large nose.

"Did you say something?" Lefty asked.

"Huh."

Lefty huffed. He muttered. He cursed.

"I see you've picked up a few words in the Nest, now haven't you?" Jubbler said. The rugged dwarf's maniacal tone had turned around into something serene and wise.

He looked over at the Quartermaster, who was still down the dock.

"You did say that!" Lefty exclaimed, picking up his hammer. "Do you really know Gillem, or are you just acting crazy?"

Jubbler reached over, took Lefty's hand in his, and said, "I'm crazy because I want them to believe me to be. But I'm quite sane all the time. Now Lefty, pay attention. You don't have much time." It was Jubbler's turn to peer around. "Keep tapping. I'll start talking."

Tap. Tap. Tap. Tap. Tap ….

Lefty didn't know what to make of it, but the sound of a friendly voice energized him. Connecting with another living person elated him. All of his aches, pains and hunger subsided under a tide of hope.

Jubbler cleared his throat and spoke in a low and rich tone, his comments quick and direct.

"Master Gillem. Murdered. Let me say he was my friend and yours as well. But, he and I were doomed scoundrels from the start. Nothing but bad blood running through the both of us, most all the good parts long gone …" Jubbler drifted off and wiped his eyes.

Lefty scooted away. Was this dwarf someone he should be listening to?

"… but even the worst of us have some honor and loyalty. A code, you might say. A redeeming quality we can take to our deaths one day. Master Gillem served us all well, but he had enemies: Palos, Thorn and that dreadful Diller among them." Jubbler punched his gnarled fist on the deck. "It wasn't always this way in the guild. Palzor followed the code, but his deranged son does not. At least not anymore. It's one thing for a thief to be greedy, but Palos has taken it to another level. Our tributes and contributions are outrageous, almost triple what they'd been. And the clientele above, the additional costs for their commodities, well, they aren't so happy. Heh. Heh. Not happy at all. They ask for less for the smuggled goods, and Palos charges more."

Tap. Tap. Tap. Tap. Tap. Tap …

Lefty was enthralled. His small body filled with new energy. *I cannot believe the same person speaks.* From roughshod and rambling, Jubbler was now a polished stone, poised and in control.

"Us pick pockets are getting antsy, and with your arrival, the Royal woman and her baby, well, our bones were unsettled. Something must be done. The thin ice he's put us on is about to break." Jubbler clenched his hand and teeth. "Master Gillem was a friend, and many want him avenged." He stuck his knotty finger at Lefty's nose. "Most thieves come and go, their lives given as little consideration as their deaths. We've seen Palos snuff members out before. The man rules with an iron gauntlet. Cruel and unpredictable. But killing Gillem," Jubbler wiped his eyes and cleared the lump from his throat, "that was wrong. Wrong as a dwarf mating with an orc."

Crack!

The Quartermaster was coming back their way, eyes baring down on the both of them. Lefty picked up the pace.

Tap. Tap. Tap. Tap. Tap. Tap. Tap. Tap. Tap …

"Do some work, Jubbler, you babbling runt!"

Crack!

Jubbler squealed as the lash licked across his back and shoulder.

Lefty kept his head down and hammered away.

Crack!

"Ow!" Lefty cried out, the hammer slipping from his lashed wrist.

The orcen man growled, "Pick it up, Halfling!"

Tears streamed down Lefty's face as he reached for the hammer.

Crack!

Fingers an inch from the hammer, the lash caught him across the fingertips.

Blasted orc!

"I said, 'Pick it up!'"

Lefty snatched it like a snake strikes its prey.

Crack!

The Quartermaster missed.

"You'll pay for that, you blond-haired rodent."

Lefty balled up. Anchored down by the absidium chains, what else could he do?

Splash!

"What the!" the Quartermaster said, head and big shoulders whipping around. "You hooved fools. Clumsy as blind kobolds!"

Toward the other end of the dock, a wooden crate of goods found its way into the lake. A small craft capsized. The Quartermaster stomped down the dock, saying, "Someone's going to die for this!"

"Are you well?" Jubbler said, rubbing his shoulder.

Lefty shook his hand. Red and swollen, it hurt worse than it looked. He opened his fist in and out a few times. "I'm fine, but that hurt! What about you?"

"Heh, nothing but a sting, is all. A dwarf's hide thickens as he gets older, but it's not as flexible." Jubbler winked. "Just can't stay out in the sun too long. It can dry you up like a seed. Now, we have the get you out of here. Plans are now in motion."

"What do you mean?" Lefty said. "What plans?"

Jubbler snorted.

"You don't really think a bunch of cutthroats and smugglers accidentally dropped crates of goods into the lake, do you?"

Lefty perched his eyebrows and said, "I suppose not."

Jubbler grabbed him by the shoulder and gave it a tug.

"The Quartermaster, well, he's another Palos recruit. Not one to belong here. He'll have his hands full for now. But we have to get you going and out of here. Once it starts rolling... we can't stop it now."

Lefty had no idea what Jubbler was talking about, but he was willing to try anything to help Kam and Erin. Anything at all, he was ready. He held up the absidium chains that dangled in his fingers.

"Ah, yes." Jubbler rubbed his chin. "I never figured those out, not like Master Gillem. I was certain you would figure it out, however. Can you not do it, Boy? You have to be free if this plan's to roll."

Lefty looked at his bleeding, swollen and throbbing hand.

"How much time do I have?"

"Little! Make haste. You can figure it out. Gillem said so."

Lefty began to fidget his fingers and tug at the bonds. The chains constricted like a living thing. "Why would you and Gillem talk about these chains? Seems odd. Did he foresee my incarceration?"

"Ho-Ho. No, not at all. We had a bet, was all. He said you could, and I said you couldn't. I've never seen another trick the chains before, but Gillem was like a magician. Juggled ten coins at once, he did."

"Really?" Lefty continued wrestling the chains, twisting and turning his tiny wrists all sorts of ways. The more he twisted, the deeper they dug. It was killing him.

"I saw it for myself," Jubbler said, a smile turning to a frown, "but I never seen my coins again, either."

Lefty huffed out. "Blast! I can't do this, Jubbler."

"Hurry, Boy," Jubbler urged, motioning his finger in the air. "You have to trick it. That's what Master Gillem said, but I could never figure it out."

Sweat glistened on Lefty's face. Maybe Gillem broke them, but they'd said they were unbreakable. *Oh no, I cannot do this. I cannot!*

"Hurry, Lefty, time is short! You must save the baby before they take her."

"Take her where? Ow!"

Lefty's hands were purple and red, both wrists bleeding now.

"Palos has another deal. He's ransoming the baby girl. It seems there are people above that want her. Much money they shall pay."

"Who? Don't they want Kam?"

"No, just the baby. Hurry now, there's little time before they move her."

He had promised Kam he'd take care of Erin, first and foremost. But he couldn't leave Kam behind. How was he supposed to get out of here? What if Jubbler lied? He didn't know what to think or believe anymore. *Think! Move! Act!*

"Did you see Gillem use anything?" Lefty asked. "Maybe he had a key hidden."

"Maybe a pick? But I didn't see." Jubbler reached inside his vest and produced a small key, similar to the one Diller used to lock the chains. "Perhaps this will work."

Lefty snatched it.

"It's too big! What's that for, anyway? Drat! I'm undone. I … Am … Undone."

Jubbler tossed the key in the lake and sighed.

"I don't remember. An unfortunate thing this is, very unfortunate. Still, the plan moves forward. You must go, chains or not."

Lefty eyed the shackles on his wrists and feet. It wasn't possible. He'd be seen. But what choice did he have at this point? He at least had to try and save Erin.

"Jubbler, what do I do? How can I even get her out of here? It will be impossible to cross the lake unnoticed." He held up his chains.

"There is another way." Jubbler eyed the giant smoke stack. "It's dangerous, but if you can get the baby, you can take her up there."

Lefty looked up at the massive smoke stack, red brick marred by soot, smoke puffing from gaping holes in the brick. "You can't mean that?"

"I do. And you have to move. Your feet are forming a pool."

"Bone!" Lefty's heart was pounding in his chest. Something was wrong. He could feel it. Kam and Erin both were in grave danger.

56

"WHAT HAVE WE HERE?" DILLER said, shoving Kam to the ground.

She cried out as Thorn twisted her arm and shoved his knee into her back.

"Let go of me! Palos! Have you not treated me badly enough?"

Palos's soft eyes revealed something darker inside as Diller handed over the gems.

"She's turning into a thief, it seems," Diller said, chuckling. "Perhaps we're wearing off on the Royal wench."

Kam scraped her chin on the floor as she got a better view of Palos. The Prince of Thieves studied the gems in every detail, eyes dancing in the firelight. He kneeled down before her and spoke with a venomous tone.

"Where did you get these? I've never seen the likes before."

She held her tongue.

Thorn grabbed a handful of her hair and snapped her head back.

"Stop doing that!" Kam said.

"Answer the Prince."

"Certainly," she said, spitting blood. "I took them from your own coffers, you sot. Not that you could ever keep track of every bauble in your hoard." She laughed. "I thought you'd craft me a pair of earrings. I think I've earned them," she batted her eyes, "dear Prince."

"Diller," Palos ordered, "bring me that halfling. I'll be having words with him." Palos grabbed Kam's face with his pudgy fingers. "I've a feeling you and the boy are conspirators, Kam. And when I discover the truth, I've a feeling another halfling will be dead." He smacked her hard across the face. "Earrings, my arse. Though, they certainly have a unique twinkle to them. Perhaps they'll make a fine gift for my next Royal conquest." He snorted as he rose up. "One of your sisters, perhaps?"

Kam remained silent as Thorn picked her up and slammed her into the chair. At least Palos hadn't mentioned Erin again. But now Lefty was in danger. *What a clumsy fool I am. I should have attacked when I had the chance. Now, things are worse than ever!*

Palos sat down at the table, placed an eye piece in his head, and held up the gems.

"Fascinating. Hmmm …. The inner core sparkles like a piece of broken coal." He let out a haggard moan. "The cut is unlike most stones. Polished. Oval." He muttered and groaned, switching stones and studying every last detail.

I need those! I must get them back. She glanced at the sword. Had her father, Kamdroz, really given Palzor that? She didn't have the best relationship with her father. He was a withdrawn and mysterious man who dabbled in politics and other powers she didn't care for. And there were many things she never understood or cared about in the Castles and Towers where her family resided. People of all questionable backgrounds and character came and went in the night. Palos had revealed many things. The thieves were the main vein of supply for wizards' spell components. She had always wondered where the weird and rare items came from, and now she knew.

"Tell me more about my father, Palos, and the sword. I don't think you were finished with your story."

"Quiet!" Thorn said, pressing knife to her throat.

Don't push it. The last thing you need is a gag in your mouth. Think up a spell. Have it ready.

"It's quite alright, Thorn," Palos said, still looking at the underling eyes, a softer tone in his voice. "This is quite a find. I'm possibly grateful. Huh, yes, your father and the sword." Palos set the gems down on the table, locked his fingers on his chest, and teetered his chair on its back legs. "One doesn't reach the top without playing dirty, you naïve woman. He's had help, much help from the likes of me and my father. You might even say, to some degree, we're Royals as well."

"You can fill your mind up with all the lies you want, but it still doesn't change the lowly person you are and ever will be," Kam remarked.

"Said like a true Royal. Always justifying their position." Palos laughed. "Perhaps you'd be more tolerable if you understood your own family's history. As I recall, all in this city were beggars and thieves at one time. You'd do well to remember that." Palos coughed. "My throat is dry, and it seems my last bottle is empty. Thorn, grab two more from the rack."

Thorn twirled his knife into his belt and lumbered away. Palos picked the gems back up, juggling them in one hand, eyeing them with glee. *This is it, Kam. Do it now!*

Thorn returned, back towards her, blocking Palos's view. She whispered and muttered as Thorn refilled the goblet. A spring of mystic energy came forth. Remembering Palos's words about the sword burning skin and also the sword's promise to help, she let her suggestion out. *Thorn.*

The tall man stiffened, turning his chin her way.

She had his attention. Eyeing the great sword, creating a perfect picture in her mind, she made a powerful suggestion.

GRAB.

Thorn turned, looking at her, his burned face a mask of confusion. Kam felt another level of exhaustion seep into her bones. She was almost spent. Her consciousness drifting. She needed those gems. The underling's eyes. Thorn bent over, hand reaching for the great blade.

Palos stopped juggling, set the stones on the table, and said, "Thorn, what are you doing?" He glared at Kam. "What have you done, Witch? Thorn, don't touch that blade, I COMMAND YOU!"

Thorn wrapped his big hand around the hilt and lifted up the sword. A rush of energy filled the room, blowing the hair back from all their faces. Thorn turned, a dark look in his eyes, his mind no longer his own.

"Drop that blade, Thorn! Drop it now!" Palos jumped on the table and drew his dagger. "What have you done to him, Kam? Make him stop now!"

Swish!

The heavy blade cut where Palo's legs a moment earlier had been standing.

"I am Zorth, an Avenger, a King, a Giant Slayer." The voice was unnatural, strong, powerful. "You," Thorn's body pointed at Palos, "are a flea."

Kam had never seen fear in Palos's eyes before, but it was there, real, his forehead crinkled.

Palos lunged in, stabbed Thorn in the thigh, and jumped back.

Slice!

The blade licked out over Palos's head, clipping his ear.

"Bone!" Palos said, holding his bleeding ear. "Thorn, stop this madness!"

Kam fought to rise on her weakened knees. The spell had taken a toll on her. She needed strength. *Get the gems!*

The possessed Thorn jumped over the table and chopped.

"The time has come, Rodent Prince. Your evils shall be undone."

Kam slipped behind Thorn and grabbed the stones. *Yes!*

"No! Help! No, you witch! You cannot use magic! How did you do this?"

Thorn, great sword of Zorth in hand, chopped and sliced, but Palos was quicker than a rabbit to his oppressor's charging bull. The prince of thieves evaded all of Thorn's lethal blows, but they were getting closer.

What does he have in his hand?

Palos had a vial. He dove away from the next decapitating blow.

Kkk-rang!

The sword of Zorth chopped into the metal tub, hewing half way through the metal until it stuck. Thorn fought to free the blade.

Kam rushed over to the front door. *Where's Palos?* Scanning the room, the man had disappeared. *No!*

"You cannot escape your evils!" the possessed Thorn yelled. "There is no escape for your kind. I shall purge this city once again."

She summoned the power in the gems. *Clatch.* Palo's bedroom door locked shut. The front door was still sealed. *Where is he?* Her body turned clammy. She realized what had happened. The vial must have turned him invisible.

Wham! Wham! Wham! Someone pounded on the front door.

"Are you in there, Prince? We heard you shout!"

"Death awaits you, fools! Come and greet him!" Thorn cried.

A silence came from the other side of the door.

Kam backed towards the corner, stones clenching in her fists, glowing like fire. *Where are you, Bastard!*

"Er, Thorn, was that you? Let us in. We'll sort it out," a man said from the other side.

The great blade slipped free of the tub, and the possessed man said, "A moment in life … a moment in death … comes the cold kiss of vengeance." Thorn strode across the room to the door and shoved the sword through one side and out the other. Men wailed behind the doorway.

Kam shivered. *Oh my!* Something grabbed her from behind by the neck and squeezed. *No!* It was Palos. She knew his grip, his scent, every vital detail.

"Drop those gems, Witch! Drop them now!" he warned. One arm held her tight by the neck, the other held the dagger at her belly. "I'll not waste another moment on you. I'll gut you and let you watch your innards spill out!"

She could feel his tongue on her ear. *No!* This was her last chance. There would not be another. It had to end here, one way or the other. *I'm sorry, Erin!*

"Kill me then, you bastard!" Her hands became brilliant balls of energy as she summoned the power forth.

"So be it, you crazy whore!"

Palos choked her with all his strength and slid the dagger in her stomach. Her eyes popped open. The gem stones dangled in her grip. She clenched them one last time. *Come, Snake! Come!*

A glimmering snake of green and yellow burst from the fireplace, eyes a brilliant white fire. It came fast, slithering over the planks like living fire and coiled itself around Palos and Kam.

Palos screamed. His grip slackened, the dagger clattering on the floor. Kam fell to her knees, holding her belly, eyes watering. "No," she murmured. "I can't die."

Behind her, the snake struck and squeezed Palos, who she could now see, wailing and thrashing like an animal gone mad. *Good!*

Thorn pulled his sword free of the door, the blade streaked red in blood.

"Come! It's time we free ourselves!"

Kam was numb. Washed over with nausea. She was dying, she was certain this time. "You must take my…" she gasped, blood spitting from her mouth, "find my baby. Save her, Zorth. Save her …"

"You'll pay for that!" a man screamed from the other side of the door. "That was my brother!"

Wham! Wham! Wham!

Something heavy hit the door.

"Just pick the lock," another cried.

Straight and true, Zorth rammed the sword through the door again.

Zorth's voice was hollow, loud, direct.

"No evil shall escape. No power can stop my edge. I am Zorth."

The unseen force of Palos screamed for mercy. None came.

Kam collapsed on the floor. *Erin. I tried. I'm sorry.*

57

"A WANTED MAN, YOU SAY?" MELEGAL said, righting his slouch and facing Rayal.

Rayal smiled, her teeth white, her face as pretty as a rainbow.

"Certainly wanted. However, I've heard nothing but the highest of comments from Lorda Almen. She's very keen on you." Rayal stepped over and pulled the blanket from his shoulders and straightened his cap. "And she is far from easy to please, Life Saver."

Why must they smell so good? Gives me the weak knees of a swooning woman, it does. How do they do that?

"I only do what is expected of my service, Rayal," he said with a slight nod. *She does not know. A lift in fortune for one miniscule moment for the day. Still, persistent and nosy. Aren't they all? Scars on my knuckles. Should've stuck them in a hog waller first.*

"Odd, Detective, seeing you in the barns, and going to great lengths to steal a pail of water ... my bratty sister's at that." She took a deep breath into her chest, straining the leather cords on her riding corset, and yawned. "I'd hoped Elizabeth's enemies had the best of her. So, is this an investigation of some sort? And don't be coy. The Lorda and I share many things."

Rayal's escorts, one tall and lean, the other stocky and gruff, fingered the hilts of their long swords, eyes on Melegal. Between them, Rayal stood out like a sunflower planted between two beds of jagged rocks: hair and features dark, warm and mysterious. Was she not the one betrothed to Tonio? Such an odd situation that all their lives were intertwined. Clearly, *beauty cannot compensate for good senses.* He didn't sense the same level of cunning Lorda Almen had, either. But it was clear Rayal was sharp. *In another decade or so, she'll have it down. For now, take advantage of what she lacks.*

"I'd rather not trouble you," he said, switching the pail from one hand to the other, "but perhaps I can fill you in later."

"No. Now would be a good time. After all, trouble abounds from all corners with underlings about. They press from within and without. Many fear the great walls of Bone will come down. And I find it peculiar you are not within the walls of Castle Almen, affording protection." Her escorts bristled as she tossed her hair and folded her arms over her chest.

I don't have time for this. Brak is dying. I must act. Do something!

Melegal gave another slight bow. Added a nervous stammer and some desperation to his voice. "I-I apologize. As a commoner, I've my own troubles I'm trying to, oh how can I say it?" He grabbed his hat and wrung it, then placed it back on his head, "Rectify. I'm certain it would be frowned on by the Lorda, as it's outside of my tasks. I've much to do and little time."

Rayal's eyebrows perched.

"Perhaps I can help? I insist."

Melegal let out a slight sigh.

"A friend is injured. He lies in the stable bleeding and hot with fever."

Rayal's hand fell over her heart as she gasped. "Take me to him. I can help."

"But, Rayal, I could not impose."

With a hot look in her eye, she grabbed him by the arm and said, "Ooh, those blasted Almens only care about themselves. Just take me to this friend of yours. I'll help in spite of them."

"Eh," Melegal said as she pulled him away.

"I bet this is the barn, isn't it?" She gasped. "That's a lot of blood."

Large drops were just outside the door, but they weren't noticeable to an untrained eye.

"In here?"

Melegal nodded. *Play it through, and be ready to run.*

"Rayal," one of the soldiers said, shoving past Melegal, "let me enter first."

The other soldier stood holding his arm out between Melegal and the door.

"It's clear," the soldier yelled.

Rayal stepped inside, followed by Melegal and the last soldier.

Brak still lay in Jubilee's lap, pale as a sheet, unmoving. Haze was holding a bloody rag on his belly. The smell of death was in the air.

"Melegal," Haze said, her voice cracking, "I don't think." She sobbed.

Rayal looked at him and said, "Is this your family?"

NO!

He gestured.

"So to speak."

Rayal kneeled down alongside Brak and pulled off the chain that was around her neck. Haze glared at Melegal. He shrugged. At the end of the chain was a locket of some sort. Rayal popped it open.

"Let me see the wound," Rayal ordered in a firm but pleasant tone.

Haze revealed a gaping hole with blood seeping out.

"Mother of Bish! And yet he still breathes," Rayal dumped the contents of the locket, ground herbs of a strange pink and blue hue, on the wound. She rubbed it in and snapped the locket shut.

"What was that?" Jubilee said, wiping her eyes. "Will it help him?"

Rayal shook her head and sighed, "Not if I'm too late, Little One. I hope that I am not."

Brak's body remained still. The sweat that once beaded his face was now gone. Silence crept into the stable. Everyone took a moment to look around at one another.

Strange group. A stallion among the hounds.

Rayal broke the silence.

"Are you the Detective's sister?" she said to Haze.

Haze looked at Melegal, then back to Rayal and said, "No."

"Look," Jubilee gasped, pointing at Brak's stomach.

The bleeding stopped.

"So much blood lost, yet he mends," Rayal said, incredulous.

Brak's chest began to rise and fall again. His eyes snapped open as he rose up.

Melegal felt the sadness in his heart melt away with exhilaration. One life was saved today. *Now what am I going to do with them?*

Rayal rose to her feet and said, "It seems you owe me now, Detective." She smiled at him and looked down at Brak, who had Jubilee all over him. "What an odd looking fellow. I've never seen the likes of him. And he's got blood all over him. Some of it black. Who did you battle?"

"Underlings." *And Royals.*

Rayal made her way past him and said, "A moment outside, Detective. Ladies," she looked at Haze and Jubilee, "I'll just have him a moment."

Haze frowned while the soldiers followed him outside.

Good thing Haze is not a lycan. She'd tear Rayal's head off. Nothing like a jealous woman to tear the skin from your bones.

"I'm grateful, Rayal. My friend's loss would have been quite difficult to bear, I'm afraid. And I'm not one to mourn." He hated to say the next line, but he felt compelled to. "How can I repay you?"

Rayal leaned against the stable door and twirled her fingers in her hair. She licked her tongue over her perfect apple-red lips, thinking. Melegal quickly glanced from her toes to her head. Riding clothes couldn't be any snugger, from her long leather brown boots to the stitches in her leather breeches. He would have ridden with her anytime, anyplace, anywhere. *No need to be smart if you don't have to.*

"Tell me more about these *friends* of yours," she said, looking him dead in the eye. "The girl, in particular. She has the mannerisms of a Royal, among other things."

Oh my, she's one of those. Melegal knew the type. Rare, but honest. Rayal was proficient at discerning the truth from a lie. *Slat.* She'd caught every last detail up to this point. It wasn't likely she would miss one now. Of course, Melegal was as good a liar as any, but why risk it now? It was time to gamble. He didn't owe Jubilee anything, anyway.

"Can we have more privacy?"

"Give us some space." Rayal ordered.

The soldiers walked out of earshot.

Melegal continued in a quieter tone.

"Rayal, it may disturb you to know that my service with the Royal Almens is questionable."

He watched her eyes, but her expression remained unchanged.

"There was an incident. A battle in the Royal Arena that went wrong."

Rayal clenched her fists, "Ooh, I hate those bloody games. Cruel it is. Savage! Am I to take it that man in there is a survivor?"

"And the girl, but the woman, she is my friend."

Her brow perched over one eye.

"I see. And then who are those ..."

Melegal held his finger up.

"A moment, I've hardly finished. Underlings. They infiltrated the castle and attacked. Lord Almen fell, but his condition remains unknown. It seems no one has been accused of this infiltration but the Castle Cleric, Sefron."

Rayal's eyes drifted away from his as she looked at her guards.

Get ready to run, Melegal!

She returned her gaze back to him.

"Oh, he's a sickly one. Bulbous and perverted. I could wear ogre skin, and his bulging eyes would still strip me naked." She slapped her hand on his shoulder. "Detective, the Almens are my allies, but they are not my favorite people. The Lorda, I enjoy: how could one not? She's the most charming creature I've ever known."

The both of you, I'd say.

"But, I only owe them one thing."

"And that is?"

"My hand in marriage to her beloved Tonio. My beloved as well."

Melegal could feel the palpitations under his skin, but he kept his eyes on her. *Can my shallow grave go any deeper? This woman betrothed to a murdering abomination. This world will not be rid of him soon enough. Slat if that impudent man isn't what got us into this mess in the first place.* Melegal cleared his dry throat and said, "I've a feeling I know what you'll require of me, Rayal."

"So you can read minds, then?" She came closer. "Tell me what I ask for."

"You want to know what happened to Tonio."

Rayal combed his hair behind his ear, bringing an erotic shiver through his spine.

It's not fair. Not fair at all.

She said, "I've had many conversations with Lorda Almen. She said if anyone could find him, you could."

I wonder if she told Rayal the brute almost killed her. That I saved her? So to speak. How can this woman notice every last detail, yet be fooled by Tonio?

"Eh, did she say anything else?"

She came closer, lips so close he could feel her breath on his ear.

"She adores him as much as I do, but, I know of all the things rotten in his core, and if I am pledged to marry him, I'll be a dutiful Almen. It will strengthen my family as well as theirs." She reached over and ran a hand down his shoulder. "But if Tonio does not appear, our alliance will erode like a rotting log."

What is going on in that head of hers? She makes no sense at all.

"I need you to find him, and both you and I will be served well," she said, stepping away.

Bah, I don't need to play such games. She's more likely to marry a kobold than that butcher. I'll not find the man! Not for Lorda. Not for her. Not for a thousand gold. Well, maybe.

"So, Rayal, I'm not certain where we stand," he said, frowning.

"Check with me in a few days. You know where to find me," she said, waving to her guards, walking away.

Zip!

Melegal ducked. Something very fast flew through the barn, stirring up hay and dust. An eerie fluttering of bat-like wings came from the rafters above.

"What is that thing?" one of the soldiers said, drawing his sword and shielding Rayal.

Melegal got his first look at the creature. The muscles in the small of his back knotted as his hands fell to his swords. *Slat!* He'd taken them off to complete his disguise. The eye, a single eye bigger than his fist, was fixated on him, blinking. A hulking little creature about three feet tall hissed, clutching its black-clawed fingers in and out. Whatever it was, it was evil, menacing, dreadful, and from all appearances more than capable of ripping him into shreds.

"I've never seen such a thing!" one soldier exclaimed.

"Is that an underling?" the other added.

Something about the creature seemed both horrifying and familiar, as if Melegal had seen it somewhere before. Venir had mentioned such a thing during his battle at the great Forest of Bish. Melegal felt his bones turn cold as it licked its eye with its serpent tongue, pointed its clawed finger at him and hissed, "Time to eat!" Its red snake-like tongue whipped about as it patted its belly.

58

"WHO DARES?" VERBARD SAID, UNABLE to shake the nervousness in his belly. *What is Master Sinway up to now?* Kierway crawled out from under the Vicious, gasping and wiping the blood and mud from his face. No one else moved, not one soldier, Juegen, albino urchling, or the other creatures that creeped and crawled.

Stone-faced, Verbard dusted the debris that had fallen from his robes. A robed apparition floated his way, eyes gleaming in the darkness. The Vicious, hobbled, rose along his side. *Strange, I've not ordered the Vicious to stop. Only one underling is superior in my command.* Verbard squeezed the Orb of Imbibing, which pulsated in his hand. It wouldn't surprise him one bit if Master Sinway had shown up to execute him. Maybe killing his son wasn't such a good idea after all.

The closer the apparition came, the more solidified it was, robes black as night with intricate patterns of silver woven in, similar to his own. It floated past Kierway, who was stuffing his knives back into their sheaths.

You only have one superior, Verbard, but you also have an equal …

The underling pushed back his hood, revealing his golden eyes.

Brother.

Verbard let out an audible gasp. He'd experienced many things in his life. Shock. Amazement. Pain. Joy. Elation. Dismay. But what he felt now could not be explained. His brother, Catten, once cinder and ashes, now lived. There were no words for that. None at all.

Kierway slogged his way from the mud, arms dangling at his sides, shaking his head. At Verbard's side, the Vicious stood like a mute, studying its missing fingers.

Catten's smile stretched from one side of his head to the other as he softly landed on Verbard's throne.

"Verbard, I can see you weren't expecting my arrival, but here I am. And it would not have been so without you." Catten motioned him over.

Verbard remained where he was. Catten, yes, it was his voice, his eyes, but the body was not what it had been. The body was taller, thinner, the chin more knobby at the end. But there was no mistaking that the mind of Catten was within. It was eerie. It was his brother, yet it wasn't.

"Have you checked in with your family?" Verbard asked of his brother, smiling. "I'd be curious to know their reaction. I'd think they'd be even more overwhelmed than I."

Catten bounced his fingertips together and said, "Oh, that can wait, Verbard. I've a more important mission right now. And I don't think Master Sinway restored me for the sake of reuniting me with my family, aside from you."

"Why are you here, then?" Kierway said, stuffing a knife back inside his bandolier.

Catten spoke with a sinister look at Kierway.

"To save your life for one thing, you fool! If your brain acted as fast as your swords, you'd be more useful, Kierway. Not only are you under my brother's command, but now mine as well."

Verbard came forward.

"This is my command, Brother. Not yours. Your timely appearance garners you nothing without Master Sinway's express authority."

"It will all be clarified soon enough, Verbard. Please, Brother, I'm here to offer my thanks and assistance."

"Yet you sit on my throne," Verbard fired back. He didn't like his brother's tone. There was a lack of sincerity about it, more so than even before. "That's what almost got Kierway killed in the first place, until you interrupted."

They locked eyes. Gold glaring at silver. Silver at gold. Verbard felt Catten's gentle knocking in his mind. He opened the door.

Verbard, I cannot openly show my gratitude to you, my dearest brother. It would be construed as weakness. I am grateful. You saved me. Vanquished the Darkslayer without me. You did alone what we could not do together. I'm humbled, but still resourceful. This is your command, your charge, but I sense you need me, as I've needed you. You stand at the threshold of greatness, set to conquer the great City of Bone. You lead, I'll follow. I know to trust your instincts now.

Verbard was overwhelmed by the sincerity, but Catten was holding back. He knew it.

And as time permits, I'll explain more of what I know of Sinway. He revealed things to me I believe I was not meant to know. It might be just what we need. I need you. You need me.

Verbard liked the cunning thoughts behind that.

Now, let's join armies and release the Underland's greatest terrors on the world above!

Verbard returned his own thoughts.

I welcome you, Catten, but we still have much to talk about.

There was nothing like family to give one new strength. For months, Verbard had felt alone and wayward. Now, his brother, best friend and confidante had returned. For most of their lives, each had been the right hand to the other. Cocky. Calculating. Condescending. Cruel. They did whatever they wanted, whenever they wanted. Now, at the threshold of the most impossible mission of his life, he needed a friend he could count on. And if he could pick anyone in the world to see this through, it would be his brother, Catten.

"My Lord," Jottenhiem arrived at his side, "more barges of soldiers have arrived …" he noted Catten and grunted.

"How many soldiers did you bring, Brother?"

"Oh, enough to destroy a few castles or more." He rose to his feet. "And what lies on the outside of those walls is enough to destroy the rest."

"Even without the keys?" Verbard asked.

"Master Sinway said, 'What would be easier *with* them will still be done *without* them.'"

Catten rose in the air and put his hands on Verbard's shoulders.

"And, I've already sent a few terrors into the streets above. Consider it a gift. There's nothing like a few rain drops before the storm."

Master!

Verbard blinked his eyes. It was Eep.

I've found the human! Kill?

I need the keys, Eep! If he does not have them. Bring him to me. Alive!

Then I eats?

Verbard shook his head.

Only then! Do not fail, Eep!

"I see our little friend is still with you," Catten said, "and he bears good news, eh? I can see it in your eyes. Well done, Brother."

Verbard nodded, but having Catten around was going to take some getting used to. He needed to re-establish himself now.

"Master Kierway, prepare your soldiers for the underground assault on Castle Almen. Commander Jottenhiem, prepare yours and my brother's reinforcements for the surface attack above."

Kierway dug his sword from the mud and said in a smug tone, "So, one moment you're having me killed, and in the next, I'm taking back my command."

"Have you not learned your lesson, then?" Verbard said. The Vicious turned towards Kierway, teeth barred. "You can always pick up where you left off, but the mud will be deeper next time."

"Pah … Verbard, it bodes you well to know that I'd rather see human blood than yours." He sneered at Catten, walking away. "The same goes for you."

"I like how you handled him, Brother," Catten said. "I couldn't have done better myself."

No doubt you really think you could have; I'm certain.

59

"**W**HAT IS THAT THING?" MIKKEL yelled.
It was big, almost a story tall on its spider-like legs, a round horse-sized hairy circle with four fanged mouths above four hairy insect legs. A host of well-armed underlings now crawled out of the hole with it. It was the weirdest thing Mikkel had ever seen. There was nothing like the unknown to get your blood flowing. All his instincts told him to run. But the screams of the scattering people galvanized him to stay.

Twang!

Twang!

Two arrows sunk into the black bulk, but it charged on, unfettered, its barbed tongues, as coarse as wire, licking out over the streets. It snatched one man by the leg and sucked him screaming into its fanged maw.

"Find cover!" Billip ordered, stepping back. He sent two more shafts into an underling's chest.

Mikkel was on one side, Nikkel on the other, crossbows ready.

Clatch-Zip!

Clatch-Zip!

Both bolts hit center of the monster's mass, but it didn't slow. Its tendrils whipped out, killing one person after the other.

"This is bad, Billip! Really bad! How can we stop that thing?" Mikkel said, taking cover behind the pile of stones Nikkel had been working on before.

The monster was having its way with the people. The underlings dashed over the cobble stone road, a swath of well-organized devastation. Trinos's sanctuary was coming undone.

"Father, I'm scared!" Nikkel said, his eyes wide with horror as he struggled to reload his crossbow.

Mikkel lowered himself beside his son, grabbed him by the neck, and bumped his head. "Listen to me. Find somewhere safe."

Nikkel, trembling, was shaking his head.

"No! I'm staying with you. Like you said. I'll live a fighter; I'll die a fighter. I'm not leaving you!" Nikkel locked the string in place and loaded his bolt. "I'll do the best I can."

Mikkel never had a prouder moment when he said, "Son, it's better to fight scared than not fight at all, but if you see me running, you better run, too."

"Slat!"

Twang!

"That monster's snatching up people faster than I can load my bow," Billip cried.

The monster dashed left, right, backward, forward in short bursts of speed. Mikkel had never seen anything so big move so fast. He kneeled down along Billip's side. The tide of chaos and blood was rising. He was used to the sounds of battle, but not the sounds of slaughter. The people of District 27 didn't stand a chance. One fell right after the other, some of them being devoured.

"Run, you idiots!" Mikkel roared. "Where in Bish are they going?"

Billip punched him in the shoulder.

"Fool! Better them than us! Now listen. Go for the underlings first. There's not so many. We'll just have to figure out how to deal with the monster later." He pulled the bow string along his cheek. *Twang!* An underling attacking a woman pitched forward, an arrow in the back of its head.

Clatch-Zip!

Another underling spun and fell.

"Good shot, Nikkel!"

Clatch-Zip!

Bolt Thrower's missile cut though the neck of one underling and into the chest of another.

Nikkel looked at his father and said, "Can I use that?"

Mikkel grinned. "One day, Son. One day soon!"

Twang!

"That's the last of them," Billip said. "Now let's get after that monster."

There it was, feeding on dead bodies. Its barbed tendrils swiped back and forth as its legs dashed left, right, back and forward, destroying everything in sight. Mikkel wasn't sure what to do, so he reloaded. He'd rather fight a dozen underlings than fight it. He understood them, but this thing was bizarre.

"What are we going to do?" Nikkel said, peeking over the wall. More than a dozen people were dead already, and at the rate that thing was going they'd all be dead soon enough. He looked at Billip.

"Keep firing and hope it stops?"

"Should we shoot the legs? The mouths? That's all that thing's got!"

Billip grunted a laugh and cracked his knuckles.

"I'll take the legs. The mouths are much bigger targets."

"Ten gold to the man who drops it, then," Mikkel added.

Twang!

Twang!

The creature wobbled, two arrows sticking in one leg.

"Easy," Billip said, "I shoot five to your one. I'll have this beast down in no time."

"Don't be so sure," Mikkel said, taking aim.

Clatch-Zip!

The bolt was true, sailing through the creature's teeth and into the back of its mouth. It lurched up, all mouths squealing in a high pitched frenzy.

Clatch-Zip!

Nikkel let it have another.

It shuddered and charged their way.

Twang!

Twang!

"Get of here, Mikkel! The both of you! We can't stop this thing!" Billip yelled, reloading.

Two tendrils whipped out, one wrapped around Billip's waist, the other catching Nikkel by the leg.

Nikkel screamed, sending a jolt of lighting through Mikkel's spine as the monster began dragging the men towards its snapping maw. "Father, help!" Nikkel cried, fingers clawing at the ground.

Mikkel snatched his club from the ground and charged, all concern for safety abandoned. He had to save his son. The first blow smacked the monster dead center over its mouth, jolting his arms. "Bish!"

He swung again.

WHAM!

And again.

WHAM!

The creature slung Billip aside, skidding him hard over the road.

"Look out, Father!" Nikkel warned.

He could see his son still being dragged towards the mouth, the rows of sharp teeth snapping up and down.

Skull Basher rose and fell, driving the body of the creature down. It hissed and recoiled.

"Hang in there, Son!" he gasped out. "It's almost—*ulp!*"

A tendril coiled around his neck and squeezed. Mikkel could feel his eyes bulging from their sockets. He tried to yell for Nikkel, but could not. But he caught his eye. He could see his son being dragged to his death. *NO!* He had to stop that.

He forced a smile and winked at his boy. *I'll live a fighting man! I'll die a fighting man! But I will save my son!* He raised Skull Basher high over his head and brought it down with all his might.

WHOP!

The tendril released from Nikkel's leg.

WHOP!

Billip was pulling Nikkel kicking and screaming away, fingers grasping wildly in the air. Mikkel's club rose and fell two more times and fell no more.

60

F RIENDS OF FIRE. *WHAT IS **that supposed to mean?***
Barton's deep voice was still crying out with childlike fear. "Get them off me! Get them off!"

More than a dozen underlings had the giant pinned down, piercing weapons poised to strike. Fogle's boots slid down the bank, where he stopped and drew back his arms. There was no time to second guess himself, or Barton would be permanently blind.

You better be right, Boon!

He drew his arms out and summoned the power within. The air in the ravine rushed over him, swirling his robes. A spark ignited in front of his face, turning from a small flame into a fire, the air and his energy feeding it. Before his eyes, a ball as big as his fist grew to twice his own size. Fogle poured whatever he had left into it and let it loose. The fireball roared over the ground and slammed into the unsuspecting underlings and giant.

KRA-BOOOM!

The entire area was engulfed in flame. The small bodies were afire, scrambling and screaming. Fogle shielded his face in his robes. The fire was real now, no longer the magic power he could control. It hit. It touched. It burned.

The underlings were decimated, dying, burning in a pyre of flesh. Somewhere beneath the flames lay Barton. Either alive or dead, he did not know which. The roar of the flames grew louder, and black smoke began to roll. The stench of burning underlings had returned to greet his nostrils.

He held his nose. His eyes watered.

"Ew!"

He fanned his hands in front of his face and coughed. The wind hadn't done him any favors, and he was well aware that underlings still abounded in all directions. He couldn't decide whether to shout or be still. *Find Barton.*

Fogle had taken ten steps when he found himself face to face with a pair of underlings patting the splashes of flame from one another. Their emerald eyes sparked to life as they bared their claws and charged. Fogle ran, caught his foot on his robes, and tumbled to the ground. He screamed as a claw ripped open the back of his leg. He rolled and swatted. He needed another spell. He caught one in the nose with his heel. The other drove its fist into his face.

Smack!

It was a sickening sound. Fogle swore his jaw was broken as pain filled the space behind his eyes. His scream gave him little reassurance as the underling pinned him down and dug its claws deep into his shoulders. It was his turn to make a plea.

"Boon! Hel—"

Crack!

It felt like a rock hit him upside his head. Maybe it was, but he was too dizzy to know. As his blood dripped into his eyes and onto his robes, he fought to cry out once more, but his efforts faded, and only the sound of evil chitters remained. He thought of Cass. *I'm certain she's safer without me. I make a lousy adventurer.*

The underling was ripping up his robes when a powerful force tore the underling from atop him. Through the corner of his eye, Fogle could see a giant naked form of a man with steam rising from his body. Through the smoky haze, he hoped it was Barton because the giant slammed the two screeching underlings into each other like dolls before pitching them away. Fogle found relief from his pain, but his limbs were spent, making him unable to rise.

"Come on, you fools! They close fast!" Boon said from atop one pony and leading the other.

"I can't move!" Fogle screamed.

Two big arms reached down, picked him up, and leaned him over a shoulder like a baby.

"Wizard help Barton! Now, Barton help wizard."

Odd and humiliating, but I live.

Boon led the mounts back over the hill where they'd started, and Barton's steps shook the ground as he followed. Fogle had a better view of the vast ravine now. Underlings, dozens, were in pursuit, and even one of his apparitions remained in chase. *Slat!* It wasn't possible to outrun them on horseback. In minutes, they'd catch up and overwhelm the party.

"Boon," he shouted, turning his eyes to the front, "where are were going?"

Boon did not slow. He charged ahead, white hair whipping in the wind. That's when Fogle saw it. Another swarm of underlings had cut them off from the north and were closing in.

"Boon, are you mad?"

Less than fifty yards away, the underlings closed in like a black sea of fury, hundreds if not a thousand. In moments, it would all be over. He was certain of it. Fogle tried to form another spell on the tip of his tongue, but the jarring steps of Barton only clattered his teeth. Two dozen yards separated them all now from life and death.

"Boon! What are you doing?" he yelled.

A black shimmering hole opened up, as tall and wide as Barton. Boon and the horse rode through and disappeared. Two giant steps later, Barton charged through. Fogle's entire world and life flashed before his eyes coated in black. A brilliant glare emerged a split second later, drawing colorful spots in his eyes.

Barton grunted and lowered him down onto the ground. Fogle rubbed his eyes and blinked. It was the Outland. Same time of day, different place, no underlings. But where, exactly? And where was Cass?

"Boon?" he said, holding his head and looking around.

A raspy voice replied, "Easy now, Grandson. We're safe at the moment. And you look like death rolled over you. Save your strength while I sort things out, huh?"

Fogle looked up Boon, who had a curious look on his face, his eyes elsewhere. Barton stood, blocking the suns, scratching his naked buttocks, and looking around.

"I better see if I can find a spell to remedy that, but that one I just used..." he shook his head and grimaced, "It's gone from the book forever."

Fogle pressed his robes onto his bleeding head and said, "Well, you always told me, 'You lose it, you lose it, so you better make it count.' My breath reassures me its magic was not wasted, and I'm grateful for that." He noticed Boon's face was unchanged. The old man looked like a master who'd lost his dog.

"You almost didn't use it, did you? You contemplated full peril after all!" Fogle grabbed his head. He swore it was about to split open. *He's crazy!*

"Well, don't misunderstand me, Grandson. I'm not used to fleeing from underlings, is all. I'd rather die taking as many as I can with me. I just can't stand the thought of them living in my daylight."

If Fogle had the strength, he'd have stood up and punched Boon in the jaw. The man was obsessed with the evil brood. His actions were dangerous and irresponsible. It was time to corral his grandfather's impulsive behavior, else they might not live to see another sundown.

Through the hole in his robes, he checked the gash in his thigh. It burned and needed stitches. *That will leave a scar. I wonder if Cass will like that?* His narrow shoulders were sore and bleeding as well. He grunted.

"Yes, Fogle, you fought hand to hand with an underling and lived. That feeling will stay in your blood now. The burn will always be there."

Fogle nodded towards Barton.

"I had some help, and *no*, I'm not on some mission to wipe out the entire race of underlings." He managed to make it back to his feet. "I'm going to find Cass, that man, and that dog—and after that, I'm going back to the City of Three, with or without any of you." He dusted the dirt from his robes and grimaced. "Except Cass ... maybe."

The truth was, she was all he cared about now. It seemed the dog was all she cared about. And he wasn't so sure anyone cared about him other than himself. And what his grandfather cared about, other than killing underlings, he was the least sure about.

"Barton help you."

The giant spoke with his broad back to him, his voice somber.

"Wizard saved Barton from the tiny people who tried to poke out my eye. I help you little man with big head. Find dog, pretty woman," Barton scooped dirt into his hands and rubbed it into his wounds "and find the tricky man that hid Barton's toys."

Fogle couldn't help but feel touched.

"Well, thank you, Barton. It's good to know that someone is looking out for me, but I believe you saved me as well. I was as good as dead before you came."

"Ha. Saving people is easy. Saving a giant is hard," Barton said, resting his chin on his knees, and gazing into the dipping horizon. "I help."

"We need to find safe ground to rest," Boon said, "and, as for the dog and woman, I'm not sure as of yet how to track them down. A little more study in the spell book might be needed."

"I thought you had it memorized," Fogle said, shuffling towards one of the horses and reaching into his pack.

"Mostly," Boon said, smirking. "I'm still foggy on a few pages."

"The dog goes where the man is. And if we can find the man, we can find the dog and the druid," Fogle said, loosening the cords tied around an object in burlap. "And just because it didn't work last time, doesn't mean it won't work better this go around." He tossed Venir's long hunting knife onto the ground, reached under his robes, and dumped the totem of his bird familiar Inky beside it.

"Good thinking," Boon said, fingering the knife in the pile. "Interesting blade this is. Very interesting, indeed." He ran his finger over its keen edge. "A shame we don't have a lock of the dog's hair, or the woman's, for that matter. A shame, indeed."

Fogle snatched it away and tossed it down.

"Whether it works or not, at least we can have a scout. And who knows? Maybe they'll find us." He set some component bottles along the ground. "Otherwise, we travel south."

Fogle took a seat. He was battered and exhausted, but he was getting used to it. Underlings were everywhere, and it seemed unlikely Cass and Chongo could avoid them. *They're better prepared than me.* It wouldn't have been so bad if Mood was here, or Eethum. A few dwarf trackers would be good. Instead, it was he and his grandfather, relying on magic to do things for them their natural instincts could not. Weary and worried, he began to cast his spell, after he made a silent promise to himself. *I will see this through.*

61

E MPTY. EMPTY AS A DRY gulch. Barren as the Outlands plains. Broken like a glass window pane. Tuuth grabbed him by the hair, pulled him to his feet, and bound his broken wrists behind him. Venir didn't respond. He was listless, eyes averted from his captors. Underlings. Two had become four, and four had become eight. Everything inside him recoiled, yet he had no fight left inside him. It was disgraceful.

"Two dead," one said, gesturing to the black bodies Venir had broken earlier.

He could feel the underling's eyes looking up at him, glowering. His typical urge to slaughter and destroy was gone. Now, only a growing concern for his safety remained. He closed his eyes and tried to remain confident. *Let it play out.*

The underlings chittered back and forth, checking the wounds on the dead bodies.

"Where are his weapons?" the underling said, its common accent clear as a man's. "What did he kill with, orcen one?"

Venir felt Tuuth shift in discomfort. He knew what that was about. Tuuth wanted his weapon for himself, but that wouldn't make for much of an explanation.

"Here, I have it," the leader of the men said, stepping forward, holding a long sword. "It's a fine blade, and I'd considered keeping it for myself."

The underling snatched it from his hand and ran his clawed fingers over the blade. He made a sharp chit, and the other underling soldiers spread out and began a search of the area. The underling lifted Venir's chin up with the tip of the sword. So many underlings he'd fought and killed, but he'd never gotten as close a look at a living one as he had now. Usually, they were dead before he extended any formal pleasantries. For the first time in his life, he gave an underling a study.

Its features were a smooth granite under its thin rat-like pelt. The nose, eyes, and chin were similar to a man's, more lithe and refined, but the features tight and calculating. Something primordial and evil lurked in the depths of its eyes. Natural. Deep. Compassionless. Cold. Maniacal. They were like humans, and the other races for that matter, but lacked the empathy of men, even of orcs. No, even as Venir had killed multitudes of underlings without mercy, he'd had a reason. The only way to stop their killings was to kill them. *The underlings hunt me, not the other way around.* They enjoyed killing and torture, it seemed. Venir, he only killed because he had to, or did he?

"Human," the underlings hissed, "and such a large one at that. You are even bigger than this orc, such a strong one at that. What brings you here? Here on this hill? A spy, perhaps?"

Think. Venir had to set his emotions aside. Having a conversation with an underling was foreign to him. It began to stir his blood. He leaned forward over the underling and said, "I was hunting wild boar, but I found this orc instead."

The underling jabbed the sword tip an inch into his thigh.

Venir clenched his teeth in silence.

"I don't enjoy your chatter, Human, but I do enjoy drawing your blood," the underling said, "Now, tell me: why are you here?"

Another underling appeared with Venir's backpack in his hand, along with the signal cylinder Jans had given him earlier.

"What's in that? Dump it out."

The contents were spilled on the ground, including the sack, which the underling opened and revealed nothing. Tuuth grunted in his ear. *At least that is safe.*

The underling leader picked up the cylinder and waved it in his face.

"Tell me what this is, Human, or else I'll make your life more miserable."

Venir was certain he was going to do that anyway. *Stupid. I should have put that in the sack, too.* He clenched his teeth. *String them along. Let them think they need you.*

Venir looked away.

The underling twisted the blade in his thigh. He screamed at the top of his lungs until his throat was dry. He sank down on one knee when the underling pulled the blade from his thigh.

"Bring him along," the underling said, flipping the canister up underneath his arm. "We'll let the underling master decide his fate." The underling turned and led the way up the hill.

"Grab him," Tuuth said to the other humans. Two men came over and helped Venir limp up the hill as Tuuth drifted back.

"Borsh!" Tuuth said. He was seething. He couldn't find the axe or the armor anywhere. All that was left was the leather sack, backpack, a pair of canteens and a few other supplies. There was something about that axe and helm, something powerful he craved. He looked at his trembling fingers. The Stranger had almost broken them, should have broken them with all the pressure he felt. That man was more than a man. It had taken much of his magic to bring the man down.

"Who is that stranger?"

It bothered Tuuth.

He rubbed the leather bracers on his wrists. The rich hide texture was beginning to fade, and the leather cords that laced them were beginning to wither. How many charges were left until the magic was gone completely? It was the only thing he had to protect himself and his family. He grabbed the shirt of armor and tossed it into the backpack along with everything else, slung it over his shoulder, and hoofed it up the hill.

The southern gate of Outpost Thirty-One was big, but nothing like the City of Bone. Venir couldn't remember being so close before. He half limped and was half carried under the metal portcullis, where another set of massive doors waited to be opened.

"Blind him," the underling ordered. "The Master always likes to be the first to see their reaction and expressions. Heh, Human, consider this compassion. It will take time for your mind to adjust to what lies within."

Venir would like to think that he could handle seeing anything, for he'd seen many horrors before, but the odd smell suggested otherwise. He offered the underling one last scowl as a burlap sack was tied over his head. The big doors creaked open. Limping, blinded, wrists broken, he was led inside Outpost Thirty-One. He must have taken a hundred agonizing steps in stark silence before they stopped.

"Lock him up and leave him," the underling's voice said.

A heavy device was locked around his neck and wrists, both feet bound and chained. *A stockade?* The sound of footsteps became distant and faded. Only the throbbing in his neck, legs, wrists and knees remained to keep him company. *Bone.*

62

"T̲ake this and go," Jubbler tucked a dagger inside his belt. "And this," the old dwarf said, stuffing a vial inside his pocket. "Now go!"

"What does it do?" Lefty said.

"Just take it when you need it."

"How do I know when that is?"

"There's no time," Jubbler shoved him away, "just go!"

Lefty ran. Small feet splashing over the docks and away he went, darting from one alley to the next, blending in, and avoiding prying eyes, just as he'd been taught. The odd thing was, not so many people were to be seen. The Nest was vacant.

Erin. I have to get Erin.

It took several minutes before he came to his first stop and caught his breath. It was the apartment of Palos's nanny. He'd sniffed out her and Erin's whereabouts early, while Gillem was still alive. He crept down the alley and hid beneath the stairs that led up to the nanny's door. Two guards had been posted there before, one at the top and the other at the bottom. No one appeared to be there now.

Lefty sprang up the steps in three hops. At the top, the door was cracked open. His heart fluttered in his chest. He was too late to save Erin. He pushed the door inward and paused. Inside, he heard the nanny humming a lullaby and a rocker creaking. *Yes! She's here!* He glanced down the stairs, over his shoulders and back and forth. No one was in sight, but his keen ears picked up a commotion in the distance.

He slipped inside the room that was dimly lit by candles and had no windows. A bassinet and cupboard stood alongside the wall, and a clay bottle rested on the table. The nanny was huddled up with the baby, facing the corner. *That's odd.*

Lefty felt a pinching on his wrists. The absidium chains would make things difficult. Strange that they were so light and quiet. He wondered what their true intention was.

As the old nanny hummed and rocked, Lefty crept behind the woman. He drew the dagger from his belt. A slight blue sheen illuminated his face. It was his dagger. The one he'd been given from Melegal. How did Jubbler get it?

"Eh? Who is there," a haggard voice said. "I'm feeding the baby. Do not disturb. Do not disturb the baby."

She's insane. How do I snatch a baby from a crazy woman? He looked at his blade. *What would Melegal do?* He made up his mind: he'd stab her in the leg if he had to. He stepped around her backside, rose on his dripping tip toes, and sought Erin's face.

"No," he said, unable to hide his voice. It wasn't Erin. The nanny was nursing a baby mintaur. The vulgarity of the moment dropped his stomach into his toes. It was another moment in the nest he hoped he'd never comprehend.

Wham!

Lefty jumped as the door slammed shut.

Diller stood before it, toothpick rolling from one side of his mouth to the other.

"I've been looking for you," Diller said. "Heh-heh. I see you're looking for the baby girl, aren't you?" He stepped forward, leveling his crossbow to his chin. "Well, she's been gone for a good while now. Not likely me, you, or even Palos will ever see her again. Now, come quietly, Little Rodent. Palos wants to see you, and I won't hesitate to skewer you and haul you in like a little beast."

Lefty fidgeted. Diller had him dead to rights and cornered. His heart sunk, realizing Erin was gone and even worse, that it was all his fault. Maybe it was time to give up, already.

"Diller, you hush, Old Fool! I'm feeding the baby."

Lefty positioned himself between the old nanny and Diller.

"Cut that out, Boy. I'm not in the mood."

"There now, he's a cute little fella. I'll nurse him, too." She started to pull the rest of her blouse down.

Gads! This can't get any worse. A thought struck him. It was Jubbler saying, 'Take it when you need it.' He uncorked the vial in his pocket and sipped it down. An airy feeling washed over him. He held his fingers up to his face. They were gone.

"Ack! Where did the little fella go?" the nanny cried, jumping from her rocker. "It's a ghost, a ghost I say!" She swatted blindly in the air.

"It's not a ghost, addle headed woman. Just a boy and a magic potion." Diller pressed himself along the door. "I don't know where you got that, but if it's one of ours, it won't last but a few minutes. I can hold the door that long. Heh-heh. I bet you've never used the stuff before. Makes you sick, it does. You'll pay for it. Soon pay for it, you will."

Lefty kept his mouth shut, charged across the room, and stabbed Diller in the leg.

The man let out an awful howl as Lefty snatched the keys from his belt, backed off, and unlocked his absidium chains. He slung them, hitting Diller in the face.

"Fool!" Diller slammed the chains on the ground. "You won't get away. The magic quickly fades! In a moment, I'll have you!"

Lefty checked his fingers. He was beginning to reappear.

Diller lunged, a slice of his dagger grazing Lefty's chest.

"The ghost is back! The ghost is back!" the nanny yelled and charged to the door. "I must protect the baby." She ran into Diller, and they toppled into the door.

"Blast you, Woman! Get off of me!"

Lefty grabbed the absidium chains, swung them around Diller's neck, and yanked back.

"Urk!"

Diller stumbled from wall to wall, trying to knock Lefty free. His back was slammed into one wall after the other as Diller fought against the chains. He was choking the man, giving it everything he had, but Diller was strong. Every blow his small arms absorbed weakened them further. *Hang on for Kam! Hang on for Erin!*

The nanny opened the door and stumbled through.

Diller produced a knife and stabbed blindly back behind his head, poking at Lefty's eyes and shoulders. He ducked and dodged, crying out as the dagger poked a hole in his arm and face.

Lefty heaved back with all his might. Diller let out a rasping sound, tongue juttering from his mouth. The door started to close shut. *Move or die!* He leap-frogged over Diller's head and dashed out the door.

Whew!

There was no way Diller could catch him now. His feet were moving as if they were on air. *I have to try and save Kam.* He had no idea where Erin was, but that was another matter. On magic feet, he sped into Palos's tavern, ducking underneath the swinging doors.

Chaos.

Lefty hadn't heeded the sounds before he headed in. He only assumed it was carousing run amok. It had happened before. This time was different. The tavern was a battlefield packed with cutthroats, cut purses, and thugs. Every man and woman fended for themself. Brigand fought brigand. Hidden knives whipped out and fell. Lefty crouched behind the bar as the shouts of pain and anger reached a crescendo. It seemed Jubbler was telling the truth after all. The rebellion was on.

Get up the stairs and inside. Now was his best chance to save Kam.

One voice, odd and eerie, could be heard above the rest.

"I am Zorth! I tolerate no evil! None shall remain that cross my path!"

Thorn! What is going on?

Lefty jumped away as a body was hurled over the bar. Thorn stood atop the steps, a man possessed. He swung a massive sword that flashed like lightning over a pile of dead bodies at his feet.

"Zorth, the Slayer of all evil things!"

The great sword arced down, hewing one man in half. Down the steps Thorn came swinging: The sword judge. Jury. Executioner. Lefty was certain all in the tavern were condemned, including him.

I'm small. Maybe he won't see me. His hand trembled. He had to summon his courage. He owed it to Kam. As Zorth made it to the bottom landing on the steps, he sprang over the bar, ducked a rogue's knife chopping at another's head, climbed beams on the back of the steps, and dove inside Palo's door.

"Whew!" he wiped his forehead.

"I am Zorth, the greatest blade of all!" The sound wasn't coming towards him, but away. "*Nothing can withstand the wrath of Zorth. No giant, no dragon, and no misguided pieces of flesh!*" Thorn's odd force blended into the chaos. "*I'll be free, but for vengeance I thirst.*"

Lefty shook his head. So much had been going on. He had to get his bearings. *Kam!*

There she lay on the floor, unmoving, where a pool of blood formed.

"No! Kam!" In an instant, Lefty had her hand in his, holding it in his lap. "Kam! You can't die! Don't be dead! Please!" Tears were streaming down his cheeks. The wound in her belly was deep. He tried to stop the bleeding with her robes.

"Lefty," she said in a hoarse whisper. "Where's Erin? Did you save her?"

He shook his head, tears dripping down his cheeks onto her face. He wasn't going to lie to her again. He couldn't do that to her. Not again. Not ever.

"I went to get her, Kam," he sobbed, "but they have sold her." He shook uncontrollably. "For ransom, I'm told."

Kam's green eyes had a glossy look in them, her face expressionless as she grabbed his shirt collar and pulled him down.

"Promise me you will save her, Lefty. Promise me you will find her."

"I-I will! Oh dear, I promise that I will save Erin!"

Kam's eyes closed. Her fingers twitched, the gems twinkling inside her hand. Lefty blinked more tears from his eyes. Her chest rose and fell no more …

"Heh, heh, heh, heh …" laughed a wicked voice. It was Palos. He lay on the floor a broken man, clothes smoldering, all the hair singed from his body. He huffed a puff of smoke. He looked like a log that had been patted out.

"You'll never find the girl, Halfling. She's gone a hundred leagues by now already." Palos coughed. His body contorted in pain. "Much coin she fetched. Much, indeed! Hah-hah! Better for the girl. A favor I did. *Hack. Hack.* Seems she has no mother anymore. Tis a shame to see such a vibrant body like that go. *Hack.* But my blade was much sharper than her tongue."

Lefty's tears stopped. Rage swelled inside his chest as he pulled out his blue-bladed dagger and dove at Palos's chest.

Kam stood in a cold river, its waters black, the chill as deep as bone. Her thoughts were of Erin, her daughter's innocent face. It was all she could hold onto. Her last spring of life.

Live and serve? A voice from beyond said.

"What?" her voice echoed. She felt her strength fading. Her memories going. Only a faint red light remained.

Live and serve?

Erin. She had to find Erin.

"Yes." She felt her mind touching another's.

We are bound.

Kam lurched up, gasping for air. The gems in her hand washed the room in red light. The agonizing pain in her belly was gone. Her strength returned.

"I'll kill you! I'll kill you, Palos! You killed my friend!" Lefty was on top of Palos, the Prince of Thieves' arms holding him at bay.

Kam wrenched Lefty from Palos with a single thought, and gently set him down.

The bewildered halfling couldn't hide his shock and the elation that enhanced all the features on his face.

"How!" Palos exclaimed. "You should be dead, you red-haired witch."

But she wasn't. She lived and felt more power than she ever felt before. The potential to pull Palo's bones outside of his skin was hers. But for now she needed him alive. Her eyes turned to burning green flames.

"Where's my daughter, Palos!"

EPILOGUE

T IME STOOD STILL. MELEGAL WAS certain of it. It was as if everything in the barn no longer moved except the dreaded creature that eyed him. It sat in the rafters gnashing its teeth and slowly flapping its bat-leather wings. It said it was going to eat him. Melegal had no doubt it thought it would. If Melegal could step outside of his body, into another, anybody at all, he would. He'd reached the limit on all the running, all the fighting, all the lying he could take. He couldn't do this forever. He was ready to die.

Beside him, Rayal huddled behind her guards, who stood firm, but fearful.

Within the barn's expanse, underneath the rotting rafters and accompanied by the smell of ripening manure, Melegal realized it was as good a place to die as any. Where McKnight had, his mentor. Melegal folded his arms across his chest.

"Come and eat me then, Imp."

The horrible creature's wings buzzed to life. It dropped from the rafters and hovered before Melegal like a giant evil hummingbird.

"Keys," it said in a raspy voice. Its knotted arms reached out with four taloned fingers that looked as if they could cut through stone.

One of Rayal's guards struck the imp over the head with a two-handed chop of his sword. The blade glanced off the creature's steel hard skin. The bewildered guard looked back up just in time to catch the imp's claw in his throat. The other guard, the taller of the two, lunged at the imp.

Blink!

It disappeared.

"Sweet mother of Bish!" the man cried out, eyes blinking wildly, scanning all directions. One second the man stood in astonishment, in the next he was fighting for his life. The imp appeared on the man's back, pulling the skin from his bones. In two seconds, it was all over. Only the blood splattered imp, Melegal and Rayal remained. He wasn't about to move, and Rayal wasn't about to, either. A clever girl Rayal was. As smart as she was beautiful.

The imp hovered in front of Melegal once more, reaching out, blood dripping from its claws.

"Keys!" It demanded this time.

Perhaps all of Melegal's problems before hadn't been as bad as he'd thought. Maybe doing dirty deeds for the Almens wasn't so bad after all. Now, the feeling in his gut told him he'd become a part of something much bigger. The keys he had, the underlings wanted. They needed. They'd invaded the city for them. Oh, how valuable they must be! Oh, the power that maybe he could wield. If he had something so truly valuable in his hand, something that had helped the Almens rise to such power, then that was something maybe he should keep for himself. His shock and despair were replaced by a greater feeling. A stronger feeling. One that a thief could clearly understand: Greed. If the keys had the power the underlings wanted, that the Royals protected, then there was no way on all of Bish he was about to let them go.

"What keys?" Melegal asked, allowing a gentle bend in his knees.

"Do not play, Human. My master awaits. Give me the keys, or I shall rip them from your flesh."

Melegal could feel Rayal's eyes boring into him and the imp. Her fear and worry was heavy in the air. His own palms began to glisten with sweat.

The small door in the stable opened. It was Haze.

Not taking is eyes from the imp, Melegal said, "Get. Back. Inside."

Haze screamed as the imp eyed her.

"I just kill the women then, Skinny Man." It hissed at Haze and Rayal. "I eat them. I eat you. Alive I do."

Melegal had no doubt the creature could do it. Its mouth was as bigger than a man's. Its teeth were like dagger tips. Despite its lack of size, it reeked of raw power. He had to be careful what he did next. *But you won't get these keys.*

Melegal held up his hands.

"Easy. Easy now. I'll give you what you want." He started to reach into his vest. The imp's head jerked left and right like a little bird.

"Hurry! Eep hungers!"

Eep. The little fiend has a name.

Melegal could feel his heart in his chest now. The imp was going to kill him. Keys or no keys. He was certain of it. But the imp didn't know he had them. It was time to play a game. *How smart can an imp be, anyway?*

"I'll have to take you to the keys."

The imp hissed. *Blink.* Disappeared. Reappearing with both its claws wrapped around Haze's scrawny neck. The pressure was building in her face. Her eyes filled with terror. Melegal expected her neck to snap at any moment.

Let go! Let go! Let go!

The inside of his mind was glowing. Commanding. Splitting. Haze was about to die. He could feel it in his bones. Blood dripped from his nose.

"Eep don't like when human lies. Keys or no keys, you all die now!"

Crack!

Melegal fell to his knees as Haze's body sagged to the ground. He heard Rayal panting behind him and nothing else.

"No," he murmured, unable to hold his head up. "No …"

Call it instinct. Brak wasn't old enough to understand such things yet, but he'd heard plenty of talk about it. It was another sense, they said. Something that made your hair stand on end.

While he and Jubilee huddled behind, Haze went to check on all the commotion. Once she made it out the small door, he only saw part of her body. Her entire body stiffened, petrified with fear. Jubilee gasped at his side. His hair stood on end. Grabbing whatever he could, he was moving. That's when he saw it. A bat as big as a dog, with horns on its head, arms wrapped around Haze's neck. He hadn't even crossed the threshold when he swung.

Crack!

He hit the foul creature square in the head with the white ash cudgel that glowed with inner life. Haze crumpled to the ground like a sack of rags. The bat-like thing looked up at him now, a large red eye with a black pupil, a ragged tongue lurching from its mouth. Someone was screaming at him.

"Hit it again!"

Womp!

It was the raven-haired woman who saved him.

Womp!

Why was Melegal on his knees, head downcast, holding his heart?

Womp!

Whatever the creature was, it didn't break. It just hissed underneath the weight of every powerful blow. It was like beating a sack of cow-hide filled with sand. He went to swing one last time.

Blink.

It was gone.

"It's gone, Melegal. It's gone."

He knew the voice. It was Rayal. But that gave him little comfort or reassurance. But she smelled good. Haze was there, too. Alive and well. She didn't smell so good, but he was fond of her anyway. Inside him was an urge. An urge to hug them both and whoever else. It seemed they lived to face the next tragic moment in their lives. But he wasn't sure that it would top this one.

"Me! Me!"

Someone was screaming inside his ear. A soft familiar nicker of a pony could be heard.

Huh! Quickster and Georgio. Where did you come from?

"Me! It's me! Wake up, you sack of bones!" Georgio said. He could feel the boy shaking him, but it didn't do him any good.

"If he's dead, I get his hat," Jubilee said. "Uh … sorry Haze. But if you don't want it."

No! Not my hat! And the keys! What happens if they find my keys!

He couldn't move, though. Not one muscle. He couldn't tell if his eyes were opened or closed, but he couldn't see anything. He could barely feel his fingers or his toes. He didn't understand what had happened, either. One moment, Haze was about to die. In the next moment, his mind exploded. All he had left was his ears. All the rest of his body was damaged parts. He was certain his hat had something to do with that.

"I'll take him to the castle. I can care for him there," Rayal suggested.

"And what about us?" Haze responded, her voice heated.

"I'll see what I can do, but we need to get him to safety."

"I'm not going in any Castle," Jubilee said. "And who are you, exactly?"

"I'm Georgio. Who are you?"

Melegal was fading. His head swirling. The conversation around him becoming incomprehensible. *Maybe I'm dying.* It was his second to last thought. *Georgio better be feeding Quickster well, or I'll bust that fat arse of his.* His consciousness sunk into the darkness.

Series 1   BOOK 6

THE DARKSLAYER

Chaos at the Castle

CRAIG HALLORAN

1

B *LINK.*

Eep looked like he'd been chewed up by a dragon and spit out. He lay quivering on the cave floor. His eye was red. Swollen. The wings on his back were mangled, and many of his teeth were broken. He let out a ragged hiss.

"Masstersss …"

"I hope you have the Keys, Imp," Verbard said, his eyes glowering with silver fire.

Eep opened his palms. They were empty.

"Vicious!" Verbard snapped.

The hulking figure emerged from the shadows, snatched Eep by the neck and squeezed.

Verbard kept his rage in check as Catten chuckled at his side.

"Brother," Catten began, "we will get the Keys in due time, if need be, but let's find out what happened first before you pull the imp apart, like old times."

Verbard wanted nothing more than to destroy something or someone, but Eep was his most trustworthy servant. Master Kierway wanted his head, but Master Sinway had saved it. Jottenhiem was a loyal soldier and comrade, but even he couldn't be trusted. Now, his brother, Catten, had returned, and that only made him all the more uncomfortable. He should be relieved, but he was far from it.

"What happened, Eep?" he said, looking right into the imp's great eye.

Eep's eye bulged in the socket. He could not speak.

"Ease up!"

Eep gasped.

"Thank you, Mastersss —"

Verbard snatched his snake-like tongue and said, "It's Master."

Eep glanced at Catten, then back at Verbard and nodded.

Verbard released his tongue.

"Pardons, Master Verbard. Ah … the skinny man I found under heavy guard. I had him, but a man, a large man, smote me with white magic. Cracked bones. Eep had no choice. Return or be banished."

"Next time," Verbard said, "I'll have to keep watch on things. Can you find this man again, if you have to?"

"Certainly, Masterss … er … Master."

"You were supposed to bring the Keys or the man, Eep. You have failed," Verbard said, letting a wave of energy course through him. Eep wasn't of any use to him now. The creature was broken and would need time to heal. He couldn't tolerate failure. Not from the imp or any other. He'd make an example of the imp, and he'd do it now.

Save your energy, Brother. Catten had entered his mind. *Banish the imp. Bring him back later. The Keys can wait for now.*

Verbard wanted to smite his brother. Everybody. But, he let his magic ease.

It's time we talked about the Keys.

"Be gone, Imp!" Verbard ordered.

"But Master, I hungers," Eep hissed.

"Be gone!"

Blink.

Catten still sat on his throne, sipping port.

"Up, Brother."

Catten rose, poured another goblet and handed it to Verbard.

Verbard took his seat. Eyeing his brother, he sipped.

"Alright, Brother. Now that we are alone, tell me everything. And don't mince words. I want it all. Your resurrections. Master Sinway's plans. This ludicrous notion that the underlings once lived in this city, and what is so important about these Keys."

Catten's gold eyes brightened. His voice was almost cheerful. He said, "Certainly, Brother. Where would you have me start?"

Verbard patted the Orb of Imbibing that now rested within the folds of his robes. Its presence gave him comfort. An edge he didn't have before with his brother.

"And don't be humble, Catten. It's unlike you. It's difficult to think that you are actually you, seeing how you have changed bodies. It will take some getting used to. Now tell me about your resurrection?"

Catten held his fist to his mouth and coughed.

"Unpleasant. It was bad enough when the Darkslayer ran me through, but merging into another body was far worse than that. The pain was excruciating—"

"I don't care how much it hurt! What happened?"

Catten stiffened, a darkness falling over him as he came closer and said, "I was getting to that, Brother."

That's more like it.

"Good. Continue."

"Master Sinway was alone as he moved me from one body to another. It seemed not all underlings were fit for my powers. Some died and others remained blind in the process."

"I don't care," Verbard said, taking another sip. "What happened?"

"There is a tomb in his Castle filled with many well-preserved underlings. He merged me with one of them."

It was one thing to raise a dead underling, but quite another to raise one without a body. The eyes of the underlings held many powers, and on occasion those eyes, if powerful enough, would be collected and turned over to the master underling. Verbard always suspected he hoarded the magic in them. That they gave him power.

"He merged you with the dead?"

"Yes. The corpse with the best likeness to me. My eyes and essence filled his body." He fanned out his hands. "And now here I am." He coughed. "I lay catatonic at first while Master Sinway let me recover. He told me about your mission and that you would need help. I, like you, Brother, felt him to be insane, but the part about the underlings living above in Bone might be true. He showed me glimpses of his past. He took me across the world. I saw where we underlings finally have men on the run. They are collapsing. Darkslayer or not."

Verbard rubbed his finger under his chin. "There are many humans, Brother. The city above alone holds many more than all of us."

"But, they are not united. They squabble with one another. They fight over power and gold. 'We have corrupted them before, and we can corrupt them again,' Sinway says."

Men could be bought, that much was certain, but Verbard would rather kill them then work with them. After all, the greed of men had led to the fall of Outpost Thirty One and many others. But taking the entire city of Bone still seemed ridiculous.

"Am I to assume that we are to live among them? Make them our slaves?"

"We will use fear against them. Taking one Castle, this Castle Almen, will lead to the capture of others."

"Does this have something to do with the Keys?"

Catten smiled. "'The Keys are only one means to an end,' Master Sinway said. Having them could aid us in the battle, but they are no guarantee of victory. But, he insists that we acquire them, for they are powerful weapons in our enemy's hands."

"Or they are worthless baubles? Hah! Kierway has spent years trying to find them, and now we are being told we don't need them. Tell me more, Catten. Something is not well with Sinway. You know that. I know that. What did you find out?"

"We should not speak of such things, Brother," Catten said. He eyed the Vicious.

"What? Do you think the Vicious can send a message? It can neither write nor talk. They follow orders. They kill. Now out with it, Catten. What did Sinway reveal to you?"

I feel your suspicions are correct, Brother. He's going crazy.

Verbard sank back into his chair. Catten was lying. Or was he? Verbard hoped that he wasn't. If Master Sinway was falling to madness, that thought was comforting. It would lend a greater understanding to it all. Besides, destroying the humans and taking their city wasn't a bad idea. Just a grand one. A grander one than he'd ever imagined before, hence opening the doorway to his doubts.

"Why do you say that, Brother? Is it because of this conquest, or was it something else?"

"Brother, I'm elated with the idea of overtaking the city, if not the entire world. I'm tired of sitting beneath the world of men, and clearly Master Sinway is as well. There is something ancient that he knows, that he remembers, that has come to life and begun to burn. A vengeance hotter than the hottest of fires. An impatience that spreads like a forest fire on a gusty day. He's bringing them out, Brother."

A deep crease formed on Verbard's brow as he sat up and leaned forward.

"The legions."

Verbard nodded.

"How many?"

"All of them."

The Legions consisted of every armed force in the Underland: soldiers, mages, clerics armed with metal and magic from head to toe. They had defended the Underland in centuries long gone, and now they were coming above ground. They would be a black plague on the land. They would destroy everything in their path. If they won, they won everything. If they lost, they lost everything. The Underland would not be defended. It was an insane idea.

Catten shrugged.

Verbard smiled. He loved the idea.

"Well, Brother, let the havoc begin. Jottenhiem!"

2

"NAY, RAYAL! THEY CANNOT ENTER. Your father left the strictest of orders," the sentry said. The tall figure stood, spear at his side, in the entrance of Castle Kling.

It was a spectacular thing. Spires jutting into the moonlit sky, copper tiles twinkling like gold. It was the tallest building in all the City of Bone.

Georgio gawped at its highest point.

"Let me in, Cletus!" Rayal shouted back. "I demand it."

"You can come, and your guards, certainly Rayal, but not the others. Klings and Royal Klings only," the man returned.

The sentry stood firm in his coat of mail and helmet that bore the Royal insignia. A longsword was strapped at his waist. Georgio could see callouses on the insides of his palms as he held them out. This soldier had seen many battles, maybe even been to the Warfield. There was just something about him, but still, he was mindful of the raven-haired woman who seethed with outrage before him.

Her fists were balled up at her sides. She said, "Cletus! My father has his affairs, and I have mine. I owe these two my life." She gestured to Melegal and Haze.

Melegal was draped over Quickster's back. Georgio held him tight. The skinny woman he thought he recognized as Haze. She was one of the women who had rescued him from Tonio and McKnight. She was draped over the shoulder of a large man, called Brak. A girl, Jubilee, hung on to Brak's arm.

Cletus shook his head. "I don't care if they saved your father, you mother, and the grand ones of your family. They are not coming in, Rayal. I'm not losing my head over them, and you might just lose yours as well if you don't get inside these walls now."

"Don't you dare talk to me like that, you oaf. I'll have you quartered."

Cletus tugged at his beard. His face flushed.

"Er, Rayal, you know I am fond of you, but I cannot abandon my duty, no matter how much I'd want to." He bowed. "Forgive my directness, Rayal, but underlings!" He peered over the streets behind them. "They crawl through the city now, leading monsters and horrors that I've not even heard of. I've seen underlings, Rayal. I've seen what they do to people. I cannot bear the thought of them getting hold of you. Please, come in so we can talk about this. We'll find another remedy for those people." He looked Georgio and the rest of them over as if they were little more than urchins. "Perhaps a supply of food and water will help."

"Pig," Rayal said.

Georgio heard the girl, Jubilee, giggle. He turned. Brak's eyes locked on his. There was something there. Something familiar. Something sad in the man's eyes. Blinking, he turned towards Rayal. Everything from her hips to her lips was perfect. The young woman was angry, but poised. She was one of the most gorgeous women he'd ever seen. How the sentry, Cletus, resisted her, he did not know, but he'd dive into a barrel of fire for her if she asked. Wiping his sweaty palms on his clothes, he realized something. *I like brunettes.* He cleared his throat.

"We'll go," Georgio said.

Rayal spun on her heel. "Excuse me?"

"Uh … I said, 'We'll go.'"

She reached over and twirled Georgio's curly locks in her fingers. "What was your name again?"

He blushed. "Ah … Georgio. Uh—"

"How well do you know these people, Georgio? Are you their leader?"

"No. I'm no one's leader, but Melegal is my friend." He patted Melegal on the back. "Well, not really a friend so much. More of an acquaintance. But we've been together a long time. I used to live with him and Venir."

Georgio saw that Brak's gaze fell on him and that his eyes narrowed.

"What?" He shrugged. "It's true." He looked back at Rayal, smiling a little. "I don't know those two so well, but the woman over his shoulder saved me once. She saved me from that monster, Tonio."

"What!" Rayal stood up to her full height. Her nostrils flared.

Cletus stepped forward, reaching for her arm.

She jerked away.

"Rayal, Please! You must come inside now. We've word underlings are all over. The menace grows, Rayal!"

"Silence, Cletus." She cusped her hands under Georgio's face and calmly said, "Georgio, tell me more about this Tonio. When did this happen? What does he look like?"

She smells so good. So beautiful.

Rayal pinched his cheeks.

"Tell me!"

Georgio swallowed hard and started blurting words out. "He's a monster! A murderer! Insane. He keeps trying to kill Venir. He's dead, but lives. He tried to kill us days ago in the stables. His face is split. Venir killed him once, but he lives again. No, he killed him twice, actually."

Rayal's eyes were wide as saucers. Her delicate fingers slid from Georgio's face.

"The boy rambles, Rayal. Come in," Cletus said.

She staggered back. Lost and uncertain.

"Did you know him?"

Rayal nodded. "Does Detective Melegal know all this?"

Georgio felt chilly. It seemed he'd already said more than he should have. And this woman was a Royal. No matter how wonderful she seemed, Melegal and Venir both had warned him Royals could not be trusted. *What do I do?* He wasn't a fast talker either. Not like Melegal or Lefty. He wondered how his former halfling friend was doing. He could use his quick wits right now.

"I can't say," Georgio said. "All I think he knows leads me up to the last time I left Bone. And I was getting ready to leave Bone again when I ran across him again."

That part was most of the truth. He'd seen Melegal only once before, this time in Bone, but they hadn't said much, and there'd been no mention of Tonio. Just the Blond-Haired Butcher.

"Sentries!" Cletus said. The soldier grabbed Rayal by the wrist and held her fast.

"Let me go, Cletus!"

"Stop that!" Georgio said. He jumped off Quickster and grabbed at Cletus.

Whop!

Cletus slugged him right across the jaw.

Georgio's knees wobbled. It might have been the hardest he'd ever been hit.

Rayal fought against her bonds.

"Cletus! Unhand me, you pig-headed soldier!"

Half a dozen men in coats of chainmail and brandishing spears stormed out the door. They shoved Georgio, Brak, Haze, and Jubilee back with the tips of their spears.

"That man comes with me, Cletus!" Rayal said. She kicked, thrashed and screamed. "Bring them in the castle with me, or all of your soldiers will suffer the penalty!"

The soldiers paused.

"Get her in there!" Cletus said. "Lord Kling will show no mercy to any who don't follow his direct orders. I won't either! The guillotine is wet enough with blood already."

"Unhand me!"

Catching her eyes, Georgio started to wave. The butt of a spear caught him in the back of his head. When he looked up again, it was pouring rain. The angry wails of the beautiful woman were gone. He rubbed the knot on his head. *I hope I see her again.*

The soldier named Cletus stood at the door with his hands on his hips.

"Get out of here, you over-sized urchins! Hide before the underlings get you. If you stick around any longer, we'll be more than happy to put you out of your misery ourselves."

Wiping the rain from his eyes, Georgio took Quickster by the reins and backed away until he could see the gate of the castle no more.

Brak and Jubilee followed.

"What are we going to do now?" Jubilee asked. Her eyes were bright. Inquisitive.

Georgio didn't know who the big lout Brak and the droopy girl Jubilee were, but he could only assume they were Melegal's friends. If Melegal woke up, maybe he'd know what to do with them.

Something exploded in the air. Everyone flinched. Despite the rain, smoke and fires could be seen lighting up the city in all directions. The City of Bone always had an element of danger, but now it was taken over by something dark and eerie. He wondered if Billip and Mikkel were all right. Perhaps they needed him.

He put his hand on Melegal's back. The thief was so scrawny he could feel his bones. *He's breathing, I think?* He shook him a little, but nothing happened. He knew what a light sleeper Melegal was. A dropped feather would wake him. *I just need to get out of here! That's what Me would do.*

Scratching his head, Georgio looked at Brak. "Don't you have any ideas? You're the oldest who's awake. I just want to get out of here."

Brak leered over at him. Big faced. Unreadable. "I just want to find Venir."

"What? Why would you want to find Venir?"

Jubilee started to chime in. "Because that's his—"

Georgio felt the muscles tighten behind his neck. Something creeped and crawled over the cobblestone road nearby. He ripped out his sword.

"Underlings!"

3

"**W**HERE'S MY DAUGHTER, PALOS!"

It was Kam. Half naked. Bleeding. Green eyes blazing with mystic fury unlike anything Lefty had ever seen before. Earlier, she'd been dead; he was certain of it, but now she was alive. Alive as ever. Radiant. Powerful. But, one thing was different: the dark red gemstones glowing through her fist.

Palos chuckled. A bubble of snot formed in his nose and busted. The man's arms were tied behind his back where he sat on a high-backed chair alongside the roaring fire place. His ankles were bound to the chair legs. Sweat dripped down his paunchy face, and his hair was wet and matted on his head. Lefty had never seen the polished man so out of sorts before.

"You won't kill me, Kam." He coughed. "You wouldn't let the halfling kill me, nor would you. You are a good woman, unwilling to cross the line of evil." He eyed her cleavage and licked his lips. "But, you certainly have some very wicked ways. Mmmm. Very wicked indeed."

Kam shoved her fist under his chin. "I'll show you wicked, Palos."

"By all means—"

She slung her arm back and punched him in the nose.

Palos howled. "You broke my nose! You broke my nose, you—"

Smack!

Palos's head rocked back into the chair. He fell silent.

Kam shook her glowing fist in his face. "I'll bust every bone in your face if I have to."

Lefty flinched. Kam was already mad enough at him for getting her into this mess. He'd tried to make it up by saving her daughter, and he'd failed at that. He eased back towards the door.

Without even turning, Kam said, "Don't you move, Lefty. I'm not finished with you either."

A chair slid across the floor and scooped his feet out from under him. "Sit!"

His chin dipped down into his chest. "Y-Yesss, Kam."

Lefty had been nothing short of miserable for days, if not weeks. Palos had ruined his life. Even worse, he'd ruined Kam's.

But at that moment, Lefty felt a little sympathy for the Prince of Thieves. The man was rattled. His bloody nose dripped onto his chest, and his eyes watered in anguish. As much of a demented oddball as Palos had become, it seemed the man's glory days were at end.

Kam was going to find out what she wanted. Lefty was convinced. Even if she had to pull it out of the man one piece at a time. Something bad was going to happen. He sat still, his tiny feet dripping on the floor.

"Kam, you cannot do this to me," Palos said. "My father and your father are allies. Release me, and I'll see no harm comes to you." He shrugged. "Why, I'll even see if we can't somehow locate your daughter, or at least find one that bears a close resemblance to her." He flashed a bloody smile. "Eh?"

Palos was as disgusting a man as there ever was, but he was no fool. No, Kam knew he wouldn't give any information up that might lead to his death. Still, she could feel the fear in the man, actually feel it. And that wasn't all she could feel.

Lefty's heart pounded like a frightened rabbit's where he sat frozen in his chair. And beyond the door she had sealed, a revolution was taking place. Palos's loyalists were at odds with his usurpers. The Prince of Thieves was undone, unless reinforcement of some sort arrived.

She grabbed a log poker and stuck it in the fireplace

"What are you doing, Kam?" Palos said. He eyed her and the poker. "The fire is plenty hot from where I am sitting."

Kill him. I can find your daughter. Kill him. It's time to serve. The gems were speaking to her. The force within had saved her. And now, whatever it was, she owed it service. But at what cost?

Kam's hand drifted to her stomach where the hole that almost took her life had been. It recoiled. Her stomach was in knots. Something bad was happening to her. But the power was so strong! So fulfilling. The gems gave her strength and a confidence that she'd never felt before.

Not looking at him, she twisted the poker in the flames.

"Where is my daughter, Palos? And before you offer a foolish response, I'll remind you that I stuffed Thorn in a fireplace once and I'd have no reservations against doing the same to you."

Palos swallowed.

"Kam, I'm not privy to that information after it reaches a certain point. I merely give the order. Collect the gold. Many other hands work under my directions. Eh, it's a thief's way of avoiding attachment." He blinked the sweat from his eyes. "Ahem. For example, if I were to sell something or someone as precious as you, I wouldn't want to be privy to where you went. I might be tempted to steal you back. And that would not be good for my business."

She jammed the poker deeper into the fire, scattering the coals.

Her voice took a darker tone behind her clenched teeth. "Palos, where is my daughter?"

"Uh … er … Kam, surely even you can sense that my father will not stand for this. I am —"

"A wretch." She jammed the poker into the coals.

"A bastard." Again she did it.

"A swine," she said, pulling it out and eyeing the glow of the red-hot tip.

Kill him! I will find your daughter. Delay me further, and I will not aid. You serve.

The urgings were strong, compelling, even forceful. She tried to open her fist, to release the gems. She didn't need them now. Her fingers were locked around them like a vice. *Blast. What have I done?*

Kill him! I have waited long. It is time to go.

"Agreed, Kam," Palos said. He groaned and shifted in his chair, "I am all those things and worse. But please consider: you can make plenty more children with those lovely loins of yours. As a matter of fact, I would be a bit surprised if a new seed was not sprouting inside you now."

Kam took the red hot poker and laid it on Palos's seat between his knees and crotch. His eyes widened. His lips trembled.

"And I assure you, Palos: if you don't tell me where my daughter is, you'll have no more seeds to spill."

"I admire your obsession with my nether region, Kam. It's simply thrilling, even in my condition."

Slap!

"Where's my daughter, Palos?"

"Do you ever get tired of repeating yourself, you milk-laden whore? I'll tell you nothing!"

Kam grabbed him by the hair on top of his head.

"We'll see about that."

Twirling her fingers in the air, the leather cords that bound him groaned. His wrists and ankles turned blood red.

"Stop this, you maddened wench! I'll have your head for this!"

"Lefty, find Diller! Bring him here!" she ordered.

Lefty slid from his seat and looked around uncertainly. "But, how can I?"

"How can you not, halfling fool that lost my daughter!"

Quickly, Lefty made his way to the door, but it would not open.

"Uh, K—"

With a wave of her hand, the door flew open. "Hurry up, Halfling!"

Lefty dashed out onto the balcony, peeking inside one last time. The door slammed shut.

"As for you, Palos! Your misery has just begun if you don't tell me what I want to know." She stepped behind him and drove her fingers into his temples. She muttered. Incanted. Locked her mind with his. "Where is my daughter, Palos?"

Palos was a silver fox. Quick. Shifty. Darting through a dark forest laughing.

She tracked him down with hounds.

He evaded.

Her hunters shot at him with arrows.

He disappeared. One moment, Palos stood alone on a rocky hilltop, looking down on her, a fox with his eyes in his mouth. In the next moment he was standing behind her with a dagger at her throat.

"Clever, Kam, but like the lactating fool you are, you've done just what I wanted," he said, licking her ear.

Once a woman of power and fury, she found herself under his will. Bound by his vile thoughts. Penetrating her inner weakness. Bringing her to her knees. Once again, she was helpless. His prisoner.

"No, you shall not take me. You shall not take my baby!" she said, trying to yell back, but her voice was weak.

Palos smote her to the ground. "I take whoever and whatever I please." He grabbed her by the head and pulled her down into his suffocating darkness.

4

"FINALLY!" CASS WAS PANTING.

How long and how far the druid woman had been running after Chongo, she didn't know, but she couldn't have been more grateful that he stopped. Transforming from a large, slender white wolf, she returned back to her lithe form. She rolled from her hands and knees onto her back, still fighting for breath.

Chongo, both tongues hanging out of his big mouths, panted over her.

"I didn't think such a big dog could run so far and so fast before." She reached up and patted on of his cold wet snouts. "You really are a thing of beauty. Like a gallant stallion and mighty lion in one."

He sneezed all over her.

"Uck! Yet lacking in their grace." She giggled. Grabbed him by thick fur under his neck and pulled herself back to her feet. "Now, Chongo, what is it you finally stopped for? I was certain you wouldn't stop unless I died. Maybe not even then."

Chongo moaned a little, noses sniffing in the air, tails stiffly wagging back and forth.

The land had been barren for most of the length of the run, not that it mattered. Cass didn't have the time to stop and smell the flowers, or rather the Thorn Brush Lilies and Bone Trees. At last, the landscape was becoming more accommodating. Tall fields of wheat grass were in the distance, and small trees and shrub groves were scattered over the valley. The brisk wind stirred her long white hair as she followed Chongo up the hill, toward the horizon of the setting suns.

"Where are you taking me?" She looked back over her shoulder. "Lords of Life, how far have I chased you, anyway?"

Nature gave Cass comfort everywhere she went, but there was still much on Bish that she'd yet to see. Behind her was nothing but the hot rugged landscape that was common in the Outlands, harsh and unyielding. Though she loved the warmth, there was little comfort to be found in it. She preferred the forest or the high mountains.

"Not exactly the kind of terrain I'd care to settle in, Chongo. I need more streams, flowers and creatures to feel more comfortable." She grabbed him by one of his tails and followed the big dog up the hill. "You'll just keep on going, won't you? I can barely move my legs. Oosh! I need some rest, Chongo."

One of the giant heads swung back. Drooping eyes gazing at her, tongues hanging from his mouths. Cass swore there was a smile in his big jaws. Chongo was more than a common animal. He had a deeper intelligence in his eyes. He was part of a race of his own.

She gazed up at the hill's peak. "Whew, I see we are almost there, wherever up there is. I must admit it seems strange, you leading me up here like this. Shouldn't we be staying in the valleys?"

Chongo turned away, lion-like feet padding up the steep slope, until they stopped at the crest. He snorted, yawned, and lay down on the ground.

Cass lay on his back and draped her arms around his necks. "This better be spectacular." She gazed over the edge. A stiff wind whipped her white locks of hair into her eyes. Pushing them aside, she held her fingers under her nose. "Such a foul and unnatural odor is about, Chongo. Ugh." She spat. "What is—?"

Her pink eyes widened into circles.

Down in the plains, small black figures moved with purpose through the landscape.

Cass dug her nails into Chongo's furry mane. Underlings. She'd never seen so many before. They were a swarm of black ants moving through their fields. Tending to their macabre garden.

"Are those …" she muttered.

She cupped her hand behind her ear. What she heard made her stomach cringe.

"Shovels?"

Shovels. Spikes. Screams.

Squinting her eyes, she couldn't hide her disbelief.

The underlings were chopping into bodies. Men, women, and children of all races. The blood watered their twisted version of a garden. They threw the dead bodies head first into their holes. Buried them head first. Legs jutting from the ground. Their tombstones were bloody heads on spikes. Row after row, the field went on and on.

Cass's hands turned clammy. She clutched at her head and squeezed her eyes shut. Nothing rattled her … ever, but this did. This churned inside her core. All of her sympathies and compassion for all things living had changed. It was one thing to fight for your survival, but it was another when you were cruel. A vicious child that pulls the wings from a beautiful butterfly. She'd never dealt with the underlings. She'd always figured they had their reasons to do things, just like any other race. Until now. Maybe men weren't so bad after all.

"Chongo, we must go." She tugged the fur on the back of his neck. She'd been weary before looking down there, but now she was exhausted. "This is too dangerous. We need to go back. We need to be with Fogle."

Fogle Boon. She hadn't given him a single thought since she chased after Chongo. Suddenly, he was all she could think about. She liked him, but now she felt like she needed him. Not that she ever felt she needed anyone for anything, especially a man, but she wouldn't mind having him around now. She felt like a fool. He must be days away now.

"I hope he's looking for me."

Chongo's ears perked up. His necks growled.

The hairs on Cass's neck turned to icicles.

Down the steep slope, a hoard of underlings armed with swords and shovels scurried up the hill. Their chitters meant death.

5

T HE SUNS SET OVER THE southern horizon like two bloodshot eyes before collapsing into the mist. Fogle Boon lay flat on his back, his pillow a pile of dirt and stone.

Barton picked at his skin and complained.

"Barton wants to go find his toys now, Wizard. Why's this take so long? Hmmm. I'm ready. Ready now." He punched his fist into the dirt. "NOW! NOW!"

Fogle coughed. He fanned the dust away from his face.

"Will you stop that, Barton! *You* wouldn't have to wait if *you* hadn't *crushed* my familiar in the first place. And putting him back together is taking longer, no thanks to *you*." He dusted off his hands as he stuffed many of his bottles into his traveling sack and groaned under his breath, "Dolt."

"What did you say?" Barton poked his finger at Fogle's chest. "Dolt? What is *dolt*?"

Fogle took a hard swallow, but he didn't back away. Barton, a deformed monster-child, was one of the scariest things he'd ever seen. Barton had once held Cass in his grasp like a children's doll. Fogle had seen the man smash and eat underlings like bugs. He swallowed again. Barton used to be that scary until they fought Tundoor. That giant was from another world. How they survived that, he'd never know.

Fogle raked his finger over his sleepy eyes and replied in a complimenting manner. "A giant with a man's brain."

Barton rubbed his chin, peering up in the sky. "Hmmm … Dolt. Like a smart man, right? Like the man who took my toys, right?"

Fogle shrugged. "You could say that."

"But I'm a bigger dolt, right? Stronger dolt than him, right?"

"Oh, absolutely. There's no doubt about that. He is a pretty big dolt, but not nearly as big as you, Barton."

Barton stuck out his chin and grinned.

"Good. Barton is the biggest and strongest dolt of all."

Barton turned, thumped his chest with his fist, and walked away.

Fogle let out a sigh and took a seat by the fire. His grandfather snored on his earthen cot without a care in the world while he stewed with doubt and worry. Cass was long gone. Underlings were cropping up everywhere. He'd almost died a dozen times since he left the City of Three and wasn't so sure he'd live to tell anyone about it. *I must see this through.* He tightened his robes around his shoulders and rubbed his hands over the fire.

"Bish," he muttered, "I feel a hundred years old."

Alongside the fire, a small black figurine sizzled with mystic fire. It was his familiar, Inky, the ebony hawk he had made. Barton had crushed the bird days earlier, losing many of the key components.

"This better work." Fogle reached over and touched the object. The black bird was cold to the touch. "Ah, what am I missing?" He eyed the bird with his green eyes, scanning the ground. "Oh yes." Reaching over, he picked up Venir's hunting knife, and with a small scalpel-like dagger, he shaved off part of the carved horn from the hilt.

"Son of a Bish!" he exclaimed as the knife slipped and he gashed his thumb. The blood dripped freely to the ground. "Just a scratch, Fogle. A tiny wound of the flesh." He pulled the shaving from the hilt and pushed it into the figurine.

He checked his thumb.

"Still bleeding. Ugh. Stop bleeding."

Cass would be laughing at him if she saw the look on his face. He didn't care for the sight of his own blood running down his arm. *She'd probably laugh at me. That two-headed dog would, too. Toughen up, Fogle Boon.* He scooped a pile of dirt up in his good hand.

"I wouldn't do that if I were you," Boon said. The man blinked. Rubbed his eyes and sat up. "You aren't giant flesh, you know."

"Do what?" Fogle said. He dropped the dirt and stuffed his bloody thumb in the folds of his robes. His green robes, once garish in their own way, now looked little better than what a starving nomad would wear.

Boon stood up. His bearded silhouette was formidable against the night sky.

"You know what. You aren't made out of mud, you know." Boon reached over. "Let me take a look at it."

Fogle shifted away.

"I'll be fine, Boon."

"Well, at least wrap it up, will you? We can't have you dripping all over Bish. Underlings can smell the blood of men for miles, don't you know?"

Fogle sighed. It was pretty hard to believe that underlings could smell his blood from miles away. "It's more likely that they'd smell the odor of Barton long before my fragile wound. Besides, I wouldn't be surprised one bit if you were excited that they were right on our trail. Looks like you are plenty rested up for another battle, aren't you?"

Scratching his chest, Boon groaned. "Well… I admit that I wouldn't be against it, but I'd rather have a trap set first. There's nothing quite like seeing a look of surprise on an underling the moment before their face melts away. It tickles my teeth every time."

He's insane. I'm the spawn of a madman.

"Tell you what then, Grandfather. You stay here." Fogle pointed at the ground. "Set a nice magic booby trap while me and Barton go and search for our friends. Does that fit into your plan? Because I'm not sticking around so you can get us all killed. Sure, I realize the underlings are evil, but there is a time and place where you pick your battles."

"NO! You are wrong, Grandson. The time is anytime. The place is anywhere. Every chance you get to kill them, you take it. You don't let evil linger around. You can't let it take root. You must destroy it because if you don't!" Boon seemed as tall as a giant, but his voice was deep and cold. "It will destroy you."

Fogle tucked his chin into his chest and swallowed. He knew the truth when he heard it. Everyone did. The difference in most people was they ignored what they believed, rather than acting on it. He'd been locked inside the mind of one underling already. Even if it had only been a glimpse, an underling's mind was the darkest, most sadistic thing he'd ever seen. The underlings took pleasure in all the vile things they did.

"I understand that. We should kill them. We should kill them all. But right now," Fogle stepped nose to nose with Boon, "I need you to help me find Cass, that dog, and that man. I need your word, Boon. Will you help me find them first?"

Boon rubbed his bearded chin and made some clicking sounds with his mouth.

"Boon?"   Fogle   said.
"I … well … hmmm … well, you really are fond of that gorgeous woman, aren't you? I'd fight a thousand underlings for a woman like that."

"You'd fight a thousand underlings for pleasure."

Boon huffed a laugh.

"You take as much joy in killing them as they take in killing us, don't you?"

"Well, it's not worth doing if you don't enjoy doing it, Grandson. You wouldn't be pursuing the druid if not for her libidinous thighs. Certainly you enjoy them?" He perched his eyebrows up and down. "Hmmm? Hmmm?"

"I pursue her because it's the right thing to do, not because of anything else. Her thighs, her hair—"

"Her bosoms?"

"No—not her bosoms!" Fogle turned away. "And stop changing the subject!"

"I remember the first time I saw your grandmother. She had the most amazing bosoms, like those of three well-formed women in one. She was bathing at the Three Falls. I'd been trying to catch a peek for weeks…"

Fogle stuck his fingers inside his ears. In the process, he ripped his bloody thumb from his robes. "Ow!" *Blood maddened Wizard. He'll get us all killed. I wish Mood were here.* He kicked the dirt. "Bish! Bone! Slat!"

He looked north, where the moons were rising. How long would it take to get back home and sip some wine? *Will I ever see the City of Three again?* And how far was it, anyway? The truth was, he didn't have much of an idea where he was or where Boon had taken him. He paced towards the forest where Barton had trotted off. There was no sign of the giant, but he noticed a track. Mood would be proud. *I can track a giant.* He sniffed. *Humph. I think I can even smell him as well. Pah, why am I looking for the giant, anyway?* He headed back towards camp. For all he knew, he was on the other side of the world.

"Boon, where in Bish are we anyway?"

The old wizard pointed one finger toward the dipping suns and the other at the rising moons and spun around slowly three times. "Let me get my sense of direction. You know, in the Under-Bish, the suns and moons were quite different." He stopped and shrugged. "Well, I don't know where we are, exactly."

"So, maybe we are farther away than we started then? That would be convenient, now wouldn't it? Next time, why don't you send us straight to the Underland? You'd like that, wouldn't you?"

"Why don't you just rest, Grandson? Things will be better when you rise up tomorrow." Boon patted his stomach. "I could use some food about now. Say, where's Barton? I bet he could scare something up."

"Boon!" Fogle grabbed him by the arm and squeezed it. "Get your own food. As soon as my familiar is ready, we are moving in whatever direction it leads us toward Cass. And there's rations in the saddle. I don't think we need to be making too much noise about it. Have you forgotten that giants are still after us too? Not to mention the underlings and Bish knows what else that lies out there. Now, give me your word you will help me find her, or else!"

Boon peeled Fogle's hand off his arm. "Grandson, you have my word, but don't tussle with your elder unless you want to lose that hand."

"And don't tussle with your grandson if you want to keep yours!"

They stood eyeing each other. Unmoving. Unblinking.

Boon's eyes were as hard as diamonds: passionate, powerful and fearless.

Fogle admired them. He wished he had them.

Irritated, Boon said, "Tell me about those golden and silver-eyed underlings, Catten and Verbard. Why did you give those eyes back to them? Did you not realize what you had? Burning them would have dealt a blow to the entire Underland."

"How do you know their names?"

"Never mind that." Boon motioned him over toward the fire and patted the ground. "Just have a seat."

Fogle did so with a sigh. He'd forgotten the conversation they were having earlier when the hoard of underlings attacked. Now it was time for both of them to satisfy each other's questions. As for the golden eyes of the underling he'd given away, he was certain he'd done the right thing, but there was always doubt inside him. He remembered what Mood had said. *You cannot bargain with evil. Evil wins every time.*

With a wave of Fogle's hand, a small book floated out of his sack.

"It was the only way to get the spellbook back. A trade. The eyes for the book." He swallowed. "And the robes too."

"Pah!" Boon spat. "You cannot bargain—"

"I know! With evil! Yes, I know, but you can't sit there and honestly tell me that you wouldn't have done the same." Fogle waggled their spellbook under Boon's nose. "Huh? Wouldn't you?"

Boon took the book from his hand. "Well, I could always make another spellbook." He ran his hands over the leather binding. "And I know it wouldn't be the same, but there is only one golden-eyed underling. And he's one of the most powerful ones. He's the one known as Catten. The other is Verbard, and how did I learn their names? I discovered them when I fought some of their allies. Gold eyes. Silver eyes. The only two of their kind. They were close. So close. I felt them. They felt me. I was young, like you, decades ago." His voice trailed off. "I'd say Catten is fully restored by now."

"What do you mean?"

"Underlings can bring back their dead so long as they have the eyes. That's why people burn them. Why else would his brother, Verbard, have wanted them?"

Fogle shivered. He sprinkled mystic energy from his fingertips on his ebony hawk. It was almost ready. "He was killed once already, you know." He grabbed the knife. "He had this punched through him. Venir did that. And I say if he can be killed once, he can be killed again."

"Give me that." Boon snatched the knife away. "I knew there was something unique about that blade. I could smell it. I might even be able to track that underling down with it."

"No! You gave your world we'd find Cass! You won't be getting any help from me on that quest!" He grabbed the book and closed it. "And you won't be taking this book."

"Grandson, if we can catch them, surprise them, kill them, and burn their eyes up, then it will be the end of them. The underlings would sink back into their holes and not come out for decades."

"That's never happened, Boon. You're delusional." Fogle scoffed. "You have to quit obsessing over them."

"No." Boon's eyes glazed. Drifted. He ran his fingers over the blade. "They must be destroyed."

"You're mad."

Boon shook his head.

"You're a fool. You don't realize the peril this world is in. I've never felt so many underlings on the surface before. They have invaded. This is not some skirmish. It is full-blown war!"

"Well, if you want to kill them, then I think your best chance is to find Venir. Find The Darkslayer. And if you help me find Cass first, I think I can have a quicker way to find those underlings."

"Oh?" Boon grunted. "Tell me now."

"First, I'm going to prepare some spells for our quest, and when I'm done, you can prepare some as well," Fogle said.

Boon's forehead wrinkled. "Grandson, tell me what you know now."

Fogle tapped his head with the tip of his finger. "I'll keep it safe from you until the time comes." *I'm in control now, you crazy bastard.*

6

TWO DAYS. LONG, HOT AND miserable. Slim had bitten his nails down to the skin since Venir left. He sat alone, despite being surrounded by a few hundred of the finest horsemen that had ever been. He didn't feel safe. Not because he feared them, but because he'd have felt safer with Venir. Since the warrior left, a feeling of dread had crept into his belly, and it wouldn't go away. *Come on, Venir. Send that flare up.*

The horses nickered. The Royal Riders muttered. The foreboding sense of doom continued to grow. Early in the day a scout had returned, reporting another small army of underlings was leagues away. Bigger than the last one they'd fought. The Royal Riders were bold, brave, fearless as any, but they wouldn't be trapped and slaughtered. They'd fight until they bled their last drop, but it would be on their terms. Given the choice.

"Cleric," said a large man with a long mustache and plate armor, "we can't wait much longer. It's time we go." It was Commander Jans. A good man. A better soldier. His eyes were hard iron. He stared up into the gloom of the forest. "He was a good man, your friend, Venir. A good one."

"Still is a good man, Jans. He's not dead, you know." Slim rose up to his full height and looked down on the weathered soldier. He felt woozy. His blood still felt as thick as mud. Those spiders had taken a toll on him. "You don't know him like I do. He probably hasn't made it inside yet."

Jans stuffed a wad of tobacco into his mouth, sucked on it, then spat.

"Mmmm… now that's worth dying for right there. I should have sent some with your friend." He held his tobacco pouch out, shaking it. "Care for some? It's the best. Dwarven."

Slim held up his hand. "No, I don't think my stomach can handle it. Besides, there are other things I can do to unwind, but now is not the time."

Jans sucked and spit. "Well, so long as I have some chaw in my mouth, I think I'll die a happy man. Of course, I want my horse between my legs and my lance down an underling's throat, too." He made eyes up the hill. "Used to be you could see the flags at the top from here. Seems two lifetimes ago."

Slim nodded. "I remember. The last five years have been long."

And they had been, even for Slim, who had been around longer than most men. Over the decades, he'd seen men, dwarves, orcs and underlings go at it time and time again, but he'd never seen anything like this. It was as if the world was coming to an end. The underlings were creeping up from every corner. In the past, they'd struck terror in the night, keeping the world on edge then moving on. Now, they were getting as thick as a plague of locusts, overtaking and devouring everything in sight.

"Jans, do you think you can hold off another day? There is nowhere for you to run. Our best chance is to see if Venir comes through."

"Another day? Hah! Man, don't you realize that this might just be our last day? All of us." He pointed his mailed hand at Slim. "Now you listen to me, Slim. When the scouts come in with the next reports, if it's not good, we're leaving. And when I say we're leaving, I say we aren't just leaving this spot, but we're leaving our bones to Bish. And we're going to take as many of those dark fiends with us as we can." He patted Slim on the shoulder before he walked off. "I suggest you do the same."

Slim squatted like a vulture by the campfire and scratched his fingers through his hair. He fully expected Venir to come through in his mind, but his gut told him something else. Ever since the rangy warrior dashed up into the forest, Slim couldn't shake the feeling that he'd seen his friend for the last time. Perhaps, it wasn't Venir who wouldn't survive. Maybe it was him. Maybe his time had come to perish battling the underlings.

What was I thinking? I shouldn't have let him go alone! I should have died with him!

He nibbled at his fingernails and took another long look up the hill where Outpost Thirty One sat.

"A thousand underlings against one man," he said. Sadness fell over him. "No one could survive that."

7

"Rumph."

Venir's eyes fluttered open, but there was nothing to see. The bag on his head was still in place. His tongue was swollen with thirst, and the stinging sweat that once dripped in his eyes was gone. He groaned.

Every time he dozed off inside the stockade, a biting pain inside his wrists awoke him. The small bones in both wrists ached in a way that such small things had no business aching. His fingers were black and blue, but he could move them. Several hours had been tolerable, but now he'd lost all track of time. He couldn't tell which was worse: being in the Mist, or being shackled and wounded in a fort full of underlings.

Must escape.

Venir had been hopeful at first.

Just wait it out until my enemies reveal themselves.

But the nagging pain in his wrists kept reminding him that he couldn't do anything. He was crippled. Invalid. Diminished. And the Royal Riders who were waiting on him would be slaughtered. He had failed them. He had failed Slim. He'd failed everyone.

His stomach groaned. His tongue was as thick as wool in his mouth.

"Waterrr …" he moaned.

Venir had never begged for anything before, not even when he was a starving young boy, but his conditions were beyond miserable. He was shackled inside the darkness. Hungering. Thirsting. No chance for escape. He flexed his limbs and fought against the restraints. They didn't groan. Days ago, they would have.

Bish.

Hours ago, it had been *Son of a Bish*, but now his deteriorating thoughts couldn't even muster that. Memories of the Mist sprung forth, worsening his fears. In the Mist, at least he could move; he could walk and talk, and there was water in abundance. In the Mist, there were sounds of life. Here, there was nothing.

Here, it was black. Painful. Agitating. Eroding and sweltering. The minutes felt like hours. His great strength faded. His will was breaking. This wasn't like the dungeons in the City of Bone. This was much worse. A hundred times worse, it seemed.

Fool.

Images were coming and going inside his mind. Friends and foes, distinct and drifting. What had he done in life that had led him here? Into the belly of his very enemy? Georgio and Melegal, what had become of them? And the tiny boy, Lefty? He'd forsaken them so he could pursue his enemy. Perhaps Billip and Mikkel were still looking after them. It seemed like decades since he'd seen them.

His knees trembled. He sagged to the ground. His feet were numb from countless hours of standing. The middle of his back felt like an anvil was stuck inside it. He wanted to sit, rest, but his pinned and swollen wrists wouldn't allow it. He hung. Locked in the stockade. His suffering increasing by the minute.

No. Must fight it. Focus.

It was hard to even think, but the beautiful face of Kam found its way inside his mind. Why would any man leave such a magnificent woman? Only a bull-headed fool would do that. And he had no lust for her now. Only the desire to see her face and to know that she was alright without him.

Many other memories came to mind. The Battle in the Pit with Son of Farc. As devastating as that had been, he'd rather risk another beating than die like this. And the blonde-haired half-orc woman, Dolly, with the snaggled teeth. Why did he wonder about her?

Jarla.

Was that when all the madness started? The day of her betrayal? The day he took the armament from the sack and hewed down the gnolls, Throk and Keel? His swollen fingers twitched in the darkness. His life had been nothing but underlings after that. He'd hated them even before. They'd killed his family when he was a boy. They'd buried him alive. Yet he'd survived somehow.

Mood.

Chongo.

They had saved him before. He lurched inside the stockade. Rocked his bullish shoulders back and forth, on his toes.

"Grrrrr … *umph!*"

Nothing moved but him.

He tried again with the same result.

"Bish!" His voice was more of a croak than a sound.

He'd failed his friends and his dog. He'd failed them all, and they would all die at the hands of the underlings in the end. Now, all he could do was sit in misery and wait for his slow death to come. His thoughts drifted back and forth, between reality and some other world, hour after hour, day after day for all he knew.

His inner fire was dim, but not out. Not as long as the scent of underling skin that he knew so well was about. Hatred kept his heart beating when most men's would fail. Vengeance stoked the coals in his belly. Somehow, if he could get ahold of one more underling, he could die satisfied. If he could even just sink his teeth around one of their throats.

Dead silence. His ragged breathing. His only company until the familiar sound of a key being turned in a lock clicked in his ears. It might as well have been a trumpet blast that jostled Venir from his sleepless slumber. Stiff as a board, every joint in his body ached. He tried to move. The gash in his thigh where the underling stabbed him throbbed with its own life.

"Water," he said. It wasn't audible. The deep recesses of his mind blurted out another warning.

Be quiet, Fool! Shut up! Listen!

A steel door swung open and banged against the wall. A rush of cool air followed. Chill bumps rose along his arms, igniting each and every hair.

I'm still alive after all.

Booted feet entered. Rubbing plates of armor and weapons jangling followed. It was music to Venir's ears—until someone poked him in the ribs.

He jerked in his shackles and moaned.

Bloody bastards!

"Check the cuffs on those leg irons, and unfetter the stockade," a man said. His voice was familiar.

Venir turned his head. It was the leader of the Brigands. The ones posing as Royal soldiers he'd encountered in the gorge. Venir tried to recall how many men the leader had said they had. Less than a hundred, was it? His blood thickened in his veins.

"Tuuth," the leader said, "keep that spear on his back in case he makes any sudden moves."

The orc snorted. "He's not going to move anywhere. He won't be able to walk. Look."

Venir could feel the light from a lantern on his face. The others came closer.

"Gad! That is disgusting!" the leader said. He covered his mouth. "Give me that torch."

"No," the orc said. "The underlings like this. It's not ours to mess with."

Venir felt a lump form in his throat. What was going on? What was wrong with his legs?

"Give me the torch, Tuuth," the leader said. "The Bone with the underlings. This man's a warrior, and he doesn't deserve to die with his legs eaten off."

"It'll be your legs sticking out of the ground, not mine, Fraggon," the orc said. "You humans are so soft. Like buttered bread."

"And you orcs are rotten like basilisk eggs. Look at this!" Fraggon held the light closer. "So vile."

Venir heard another man squat down beneath him and gag.

"Blecht!" Another one spit a mouthful of bile from his mouth. "All these years, and I still can't stomach it."

Tuuth shoved one man onto his back and hunched his big frame down in the light. "Bone. That is nasty. Heh. Heh."

Venir raised his neck from the stockade and groaned. His head felt like it weighed a ton. He mumbled something incomprehensible. He was trying to say, "What's wrong with my legs?" He couldn't even feel them.

"Keep him steady while I burn these things," said the leader, Flaggon. "Hold him, men."

Tuuth clamped his arms around Venir's chest. Pinning his arms at his sides.

The others grabbed his legs.

"It's for the better, Stranger. An act of mercy I don't normally give, but you've earned that much respect from me," Tuuth said into the bag over his head.

"Mercy?" one brigand soldier started. "He'll need more than that. These grubs have eaten holes so deep in his flesh I can see the bone." Venir heard the man swallow. "Ah slat, I'm getting sick again."

"He's lucky for the leaches; that much is certain," Fraggon said. "They suck the blood and numb the pain. Gad, you don't usually see both like this." He took a dagger out and sliced one off that was bloated with blood and as big as his hand.

"How this man lives, I'll never know," the other brigand said. He spit more bile from his mouth. "He should be dead."

"Well, the grubs eat the skin, but they cauterized the holes somehow. I've seen men with tunnels of holes all over them that still live. But you're right; he should be dead, and I don't think the underlings want that yet."

Venir felt heat on his legs. His heart pounded inside his chest like a war drum. He'd seen grubs and leeches and what they did to the flesh. It horrified him.

What have they done to me!

Fraggon continued. "You've been blessed and cursed it seems, Stranger. The grubs and leeches are enjoying their meal, and a big beefy man like you can feed them for days. Well, what's left of you, anyway. But I don't think the underlings want you dead just yet; else they wouldn't have sent for you. But, I can't guarantee you'll live through this next step either. I mean, you might live, but I don't see you ever walking again. A shame too. You have him secured, Tuuth? I'd say there be some fight in him."

"Should I take the bag off and let him breathe? Let him bite down on something?"

"Are you volunteering your finger, Tuuth? My, so compassionate you've become for the stranger. No, just leave it on. It'll muffle the screams well enough. Not that the underlings would mind that one bit anyway. Stranger, may Bish be with you."

I don't have the strength to – "YEEEEEEEEAAAAAAAWWW!"

It felt like the tendons of his muscles were being pulled from his skin. Inch by inch. It was unimaginable. Excruciating. Mind numbing. His body shuddered from toe nail to chin. The top of his skull was on fire.

Flaggon pulled cord after cord from within and seared his skin with the torch.

Venir screamed. Stopped. Screamed some more.

"My, he's a gusty one," Tuuth said.

"That grub's as long my innards!"

"Keep pulling it out!" Flaggon said. "It's almost out! Get the knife ready so we can cut the head off!"

It felt like a cord of thick rope was being pulled through his body. He yelled at the top of his lungs, "GET THAT BLASTED THING OUT OF ME!"

"There's the head! Oh slat! What's in the mouth of that thing! Keep it still!"

"Kill it!"

The sound of steel cut through the air.

Slice!

"You got it! Bish! Barely! It almost got us!" Flaggon said. "How's the man, Tuuth?"

Tuuth shrugged his broad shoulders. Venir wasn't moving. "He's breathing, not that it matters. He's crippled now. A peaceful death being eaten alive would have been better."

What have the underlings done to me!

Thoughts were racing through Venir's mind despite the agony. How much suffering would they put him through?

Someone pulled the bag off his head

When he managed to look up, it was into the big pale face of the orcen man, Tuuth.

"His eyes still have some fight in them, Flaggon. Look at this?"

Flaggon stepped into view, eyed him and said with avid curiosity, "Can you stand, Stranger?"

"Can underlings die?" Venir said. He pushed against the stockade. Wobbling on his feet.

Tuuth and Flaggon looked at each other, astonished.

"Can you walk?"

Venir took his first step and collapsed face first to the stone floor.

"Help him up," Flaggon said.

"No!" Venir said.

He was free. Despite all the pain, he was going to enjoy it. Unable to use his hands because of the pain in his wrists, he rolled onto his elbows. He pushed himself over and sat himself up. He felt like he would pass out.

Bone!

He saw his legs. They were raw. Scarred. Pale as the orc. There was a hole in his thigh that led to the bone. That was the first one he saw. To the side, the grub lay dead on the floor, six feet in length. It looked like a hairy earthworm as thick as his thumb. Its head as big as his knuckles and filled with tiny teeth. His stomach churned bile up to his throat, but nothing came out.

"Well, Stranger," Flaggon said "you can't walk, but we'll let you crawl if you like. Else we can carry you."

"No," Venir said.

He was numb. Looking at his arms, the bracers on his aching wrists were loose. The bulges in his arms were gone. What had been done to him? The only thing left whole on him it seemed was his beard.

"Then get moving, Stranger. The underlings are expecting you." The brighter tone that Flaggon carried changed. "And seeing how you survived this much, I can only warn you that the worst is yet to come."

Venir swallowed hard. On elbows and knees, trembling, he crawled forward.

Tuuth rubbed the bracers on his wrists. The haggard form of Venir crawling stirred him. In the little amount of time the man had been imprisoned, he'd become a husk of the man Tuuth had battled earlier. Tuuth would never forget the shock in the man's granite face when he cracked his wrists. It should have broken the man. But it hadn't. The Stranger still had fire in his eyes. An anger. A thirst.

Watching Venir crawl up the steps, he shook his head. Tuuth unslung the man's backpack from his shoulders and pulled out the sack. He'd already been into the woods and back again, searching for the man's armament. Opening the neck of the sack for what might as well have been the hundredth time, he reached inside and found nothing. Stuffing the sack inside the backpack, he hoisted it back over his shoulders. There was something going on. There had to be. Magic had to be the answer; he'd keep the stranger's clothes.

Grabbing the cloth bag that hung on the stockade, he caught up to the stranger and stuffed it over his head.

"What'd you do that for?" Flaggon said. "It's bad enough he crawls on all fours, and now you've blinded the man too. At least let him enjoy the sights before he gets there. Heh-heh."

The torchlight flickered over Venir's haggard form that kept crawling inch by inch up the steps. Tuuth wasn't the only one that grimaced a little as Venir dragged his mangled legs over the steps.

"It'll take him hours to get there at this rate," Tuuth said. He picked Venir up and hoisted him over his shoulder. "Let's get this over with."

"Suit yourself, Tuuth. I've not the interest to carry the big lout," Flaggon said. "Come on, men. Let the friendly orc handle this. Seems he has an interest in big helpless men."

Snickering, they headed up the steps and out of sight.

Several steps up, Tuuth set Venir back down. "Where are your weapons and armor, Stranger?" Tuuth tore off the burlap bag and grabbed him by the head of hair. "Where is it? Is it magic? Can I summon it?"

Venir's eyes fluttered open. He shook his head. "Comes and goes," he said.

Tuuth wrapped his hands around Venir's thigh and squeezed.

Venir groaned and sputtered.

"Do not lie, Stranger. I will have those weapons and armor. Tell me, and maybe I can get you some water."

"Humph," Venir said. He spit out a laugh. "Like the wind, fool orc."

Tuuth squeezed again.

Venir groaned. He stared back in Tuuth's eyes. "Maybe you didn't look hard enough, Orc."

"Perhaps I should break your ankles as well," Tuuth said. He squeezed harder.

"Perhaps," Venir said, "you should take a bath, you filthy or—" Venir's eyes fluttered up into his head, and his body slumped forward.

"Borsch!" Tuuth said. He grabbed Venir by his head of hair and dragged his heavy body up the stairs.

8

Beneath the clouds above the City of Bone, the most beautiful woman on Bish stood, watching the unraveling chaos below. Trinos. Her world. Her rules. Life and death meant nothing. Meant everything.

Running her elegant fingers through her thick locks of platinum hair, she sighed.

"What to do? What to do?"

In the past, she'd been detached from the lives and deaths of all the colorful people, but now, watching them suffer and cry out, she felt something.

"I wonder where Scorch is, and what he's doing."

Scorch had meddled with her creation for his own entertainment. She sought him out, to hold him accountable. It was the most alive she'd felt since she was immortal. She was feeling all kinds of things.

She imagined Scorch was feeling the same, or was he? Shortly after their encounter at the Void, the two infinite beings had agreed that rather than suffer the endless expanse surrounding the tiny world, they would share a fate on the world of Bish. Each had buried the majority of their power in the heart of the world's center and set out on their own. They hadn't seen each other since.

Soaring the sky, the high winds billowed the robes along her perfectly figured body. She stopped. Hovered and touched a cloud.

"I imagine he isn't nearly so attached as I feel. I wonder what he will do?"

Below her, The City of Bone was in turmoil. The Royals that ruled it had made conditions unpleasant enough to begin with, but now the citizens were in deeper straights. The underlings came. A black menace of small people designed to bring nothing but restlessness and terror to the world.

"Humans win; underlings lose. Underlings win; humans lose. I've seen it so many times before. But they come up with the most interesting ways to destroy one another."

Bodies fell. Burned. They were dragged over the cobblestones and torn to bits. It was having an effect on her. The longer she stayed on Bish, the more attached she became. The world itself, a living and breathing thing. She felt it. So many people were dying, screaming, wailing, and begging for life to be over. Some fought. Most ran, and the Royals, the so called protectors, ignored their pleas. The people pounded on the walls of the castles. Their cries were not heard.

Trinos's fists clenched at her sides when a woman and her children were shot down as they tried to force their way through a gate to find safety. She wasn't sure which angered her more: the underlings or The Royals.

"The hearts of men are so unpredictable."

With little thought and a few gestures with her fingers, the Royal soldiers were lifted off their feet and dropped into the street. Two seconds later, a score of underlings appeared and tore into them. She smirked.

"Well, that was entertaining. What else can I do? Should I bring the underlings to men or the men to the underlings?" She closed her eyes. Her mind probed the thoughts of the people within the castle. "Ah, there you are, you catty little sorceress. I've got another surprise for you, Manamis."

With a wave of her hands, a score of underlings were lifted from the street and dropped into one of the courtyards of Castle Kling. Several more were vaulted onto the rooftops and others through the windows.

She heard one voice in particular shriek out. She laughed. Trinos had dropped two underlings into the bedroom of Manamis Kling, the haughty old sorceress who had challenged her at the fountain.

"Surprise!" Trinos said. She clapped her hands together and smiled. "I like it!"

Manamis shrieked. She shouted. White light burst through the window. The shingles crackled. A loud explosion followed that tore the walls down, hurling underlings through the air. Dead. Smoking. Trinos laughed again as the leathery old woman stood in the smoking hole where the wall once stood, looking around. Trinos grinned. Manamis screamed out orders and blasted the underlings with balls of blue fire.

"Bitter, but strong that one is. Crafty, too. I better keep an eye on her."

Trinos moved on from one incident to the other, observing, interfering, while trying to sort it all out in her mind. Below, she heard many of the people crying out for her in the 21st District.

She'd known the underlings were coming, but she hadn't warned the people. She wanted to see what happened and was curious how it would affect her. Corrin, Billip, and Nikkel had survived, while most of her people fell. The fountain was bloody and marred with death. The survivors had dragged the bodies of man and underling from the fountain, and the waters had cleared.

Why did I let this happen to them?

The men were valiant in their efforts, but the price was great. The big black man with a wonderful smile and cavernous voice, Mikkel, had fallen. His son was on his knees, sobbing and drenched in tears. Even Corrin's hard eyes were dampened.

Trinos felt something stir inside her. Sympathy. Worry.

Focusing, she located Georgio. She liked the young man that was full of hope. Determined to find a friend he so admired. There was something special about him, good, honest and pure. He and his friends were in a bind. The underlings had chased them down the streets and cornered them in an alley.

Georgio and another strange large man stood their ground, each of them battling with the ferocity of many warriors in one, but it would not last forever. They would all die. Even the shaggy bellied animal called Quickster.

"I can't save them all, but I can at least save the ones I like."

BLINK!

The colorful eyes of the underlings widened in the alley when the men, women and pony disappeared. Below Trinos, alongside her fountain in the 21st District, the small party re-appeared, dismayed.

"Where in all Bish did you come from?" Corrin cried out.

It was music to Trinos's ears.

9

"**M**ERCY!" JOLINE SHOUTED INTO THE kitchen, "Get out there and take some orders. We're busy, you know."

"I'm coming, Joline, just give me a moment."

The past several days had been the hardest in all Joline's life. Her best friend Kam was gone. The baby girl, Erin whom she adored, was kidnapped, and for all Joline knew they were dead. She'd taken word of the predicament to Kam's family, but they'd made their thoughts perfectly clear. Kam was on her own. Her daughter too. Of course, she hadn't spoken to Kam's mother but some other family member who was supposed to send the word out. *No wonder Kam left.*

Mercy bustled through the door. Her pretty eyes dull. Long hair tied in a knot on her head. She refused to let anyone fix up her appearance with an enhancement spell.

"Look at you, Mercy," Joline said. "You're too pretty to go around looking like that." Joline straightened the young woman's apron and wiped a smudge of batter from her face. "And pull that lip up. The customers want smiles, not pouts. You look like a frog when you make that face — so straighten up."

Mercy's eyes began to water.

"Ah, now don't you start that again, Mercy. Mother of Bish, we can't both be crying, not now. Not right now." Joline stammered. A lump formed in her throat.

There had been a lot of tears since Kam and Erin disappeared, a lifetime's worth if not more.

And everyone else fun was gone, too. Joline had grown fond of Billip in particular. The man was ornery but a protector. And Mikkel, the Big Charmer, she liked to call him, had the gutsiest laughs she'd ever heard. It seemed like she'd had a new family that she'd grown quite fond of. Tears dripped down her cheeks as she thought more about the halflings, Lefty and his wonderful friend Gillem, who brought the most beautiful flowers. What in all of Bish had happened to them? She couldn't shake the dread that overcame her when she thought of them.

"I miss Georgio," Mercy said. She didn't bother to dry her eyes.

"Are you crying again, Mercy? What are you crying for?" one of the other serving girls said, darting towards the kitchen. "We're busy, you over-grown child! Get out there and help!"

"No need to be nasty," Joline shot back, but the girl was gone.

The Magi Roost was almost at capacity and had been every day since the underlings showed up and attacked. The Royals had taken action, and soldiers had been dispatched. The City of Three was ready, and the citizens liked nothing more than to head into a tavern and talk about that.

Mercy was shuddering. "When's he coming back, Joline?"

"Oh, Girl, you are too young to fall for a man!"

"I am not too young. I'm older than him."

"Well, er..." Joline started, but she didn't know what to say. Mercy had teased the younger man from day one, but Joline had figured she was only being ornery. She remembered those days. But when Mercy found out that Georgio had left without saying goodbye, she'd been heart-broken. "Mercy, all men are the same. You'll meet someone when the time is right. Most of these men are plenty kind to you." Joline rubbed her shoulder. "You know that."

"They aren't like Georgio," Mercy whined. She blew her nose in a rag Joline handed her. "He was sweet and adorable."

True. Joline liked Georgio, and she figured if Billip and Mikkel didn't spoil him, he'd become an excellent young man. Still, she tried to think of something bad to say.

"He ate like a pig."

Mercy's eyes faded to the past. "I loved watching him eat. He really loved it. It was as if every time he ate, it was the first time."

Joline huffed a little. "Well, his hair was always a mess and dirty. And he didn't bathe much either."

"I loved all those curls, and his hair was so soft and thick."

"And his manners were horrible. Just horrible. He couldn't pass from one room to another without farting."

"That always made me giggle."

"You're hopeless," Joline said. She started fixing some drinks at the bar. "Now, wipe those tears away and drink th—"

"What is it?" Mercy said.

"Uh ..." Joline stared at the entrance of the Magi Roost. "Nothin but a-a ..."

Mercy followed her gaze to the figures at the front door. Her tears and sobbing stopped.

"I'll get him a table!"

"No, I'll ..." Joline said, reaching out.

Mercy avoided her grasp and headed over to the two people in the doorway.

One was a man, adorned in a fine looking traveler's tunic. His face was impossibly handsome, every feature perfectly formed from his chin to his teeth to the golden blond hair on his head. When his eyes met hers, he nodded at her, and she was at a loss for breath. The man was striking, mysterious, and incredible all at the same time.

He must be a Royal, maybe a member of Kam's family.

"Shall I find you a table, Sir?" Joline heard Mercy say.

"Something by the bar, little thing," a stocky woman said. She was taller than most women, garbed in outdoor leathers. Had a brassy voice. She was rugged too. A knife strapped to her wide hips and a bow and quiver slung over her shoulder. "And, do you have any pickles? My friend here really likes pickles."

"Uh … well, yes, we have some pickles. Does is like them raw or fried?" Mercy said. She hadn't taken her eyes off the man.

The man, surveying the room, didn't say a word, but the mention of the word pickles brought the slightest smile to his lips.

The outdoorswoman stuck her hand in Mercy's face and snapped her fingers. "Honey, I didn't ask what kind you had. I just asked if you had them." She looked around at the curious faces. "Now where is our table? We need a seat; my feet are aching."

"Certainly," Mercy said, looking at Joline.

Joline nodded at two stools at the end of the bar where Mikkel and Billip used to sit. Joline usually didn't let people sit there unless it was very crowded.

As the two were about to take a seat, an exhausted group of travelers pushed their way inside.

The stocky woman stormed at them and yelled at the closest one. "March your arses out of here! Wait until we come out."

"But we're hungry, Darlene," one man said. He was old. Eyes pleading. "We have some money."

Darlene grabbed the man by his jerkin and pulled him down face to face with her. "I don't care where you eat, as long as it isn't here. Scorch wants to dine alone, and I've already warned you to keep your distance. And you know what can happen if you don't."

The small group of people shook their heads, averting her gaze.

"Idiots, do I have to remind you?" Darlene held out her fist and flicked open her fingers. "Poof! Just like the underlings."

They started backing through the door, their eyes filled with horror.

"Eat somewhere else, and I'll let you know when he needs you."

Darlene walked towards Joline, spun on her heel and whistled. "Nice place you have here. Mmmm-Hmm. So what do you have that's special to drink? I tell you what, Miss. I'm so thirsty, I think I could drink a goblet of goat pee."

Taken aback, Joline said, "We don't have any of that here, but you and your companion might like this." Without thinking, she reached up and grabbed a half-moon bottle of Muckle Sap from the shelf and poured a sample into a tumbler.

What am I doing?

She glanced at the end of the bar, toward the jaw-droppingly handsome man called Scorch. He seemed to be watching everyone in the room at the same time.

They might not even have any means.

She pushed the tumbler to Darlene. "Try this, a, Darlene, is it?"

"You are pretty quick, uh—"

"Joline."

"Yes, Joline. You know, I had a cousin named Coline, but she stopped talking to me when we were children."

"Oh, why is that?"

"I kicked her in the crotch for being ornery. She said she couldn't pee straight after that, but how can you tell?"

Joline tried to hide her laugh but couldn't. The woman, for all her abrasive manners, was likeable.

Darlene took the entire glass, knocked it back, smacked her lips and smiled. "Mmmmm. That is good. Very good! Scorch, you have to try this … uh … what is it?"

"Muckle Sap."

"Muckle Sap, Scorch. It makes Jig taste like goat piss."

Joline briefly looked up, wondering if indeed the woman had ever drank goat piss.

I certainly hope not.

"Would you like the entire bottle, Darlene? That first taste is a courtesy sample, and it is our most expensive."

"Oh, well, I… Scorch, do we have any coins?" She nodded. "He says we can buy all the Muckle Sap we want."

"But he didn't say anything?" She looked over, saw his smiling face and blushed. "Did he?"

Mercy walked past the bar beaming, a large jar of pickles in one hand and a plate of fried pickles in the other. She set them before Scorch.

"Mercy, I didn't hear him ask for that?"

"I didn't either."

Another barmaid crossed Joline's path, a plate of cheese, bread and meats in her hand. She dropped it in front of Scorch, smiled from ear to ear, bowed, and giggled away.

"What in Bish is going on here? The man hasn't said a thing."

Darlene reached over and patted Joline on the shoulder. "Don't you worry about what is going on here, and everything will be fine. You see, my friend Scorch, well, he pretty much does anything he wants. And you don't want to be on the side of what he don't like."

Joline took a long look at Scorch. She couldn't tell if it was a thrill or a chill that went down her spine. But something wasn't right.

"This place is a lot better than Hohm City, isn't it Scorch?" Darlene wiped her sleeve across her mouth and burped. "Did you try this Mu-Mookle Surp? It's something. Like, really good."

It was the best Darlene had felt since she could ever remember, being here, in a wonderful tavern full of all different sorts of people. No doubt the City of Three was the place to be. She was never bothered before by the misty city she called home, but she didn't see herself going back now either. She shook her head, rubbed her red eyes and took another drink. "To the City of Trees!"

At her side, Scorch had been eating one pickle after another, washing them down with Muckle Sap, and he hadn't stopped for hours. His broad smile was all Darlene needed to see to tell that he was having a good time.

"Barmaid, tell me—Joline is it?" Scorch smiled.

Her face lit up as she nodded.

"So, you take the pickles, wrap them in cheese, and dip them in boiling…" he paused.

"Lard," she said, wiping the same spot on the bar she'd been at for over an hour.

"It's one of the most incredible things I've ever experienced in the entire universe!"

"The what?" Joline said, cocking her head.

"Universe!" Darlene blurted out, slapping the bar with her hand. "He talks about it, but I don't get it. I think it's in the Underpants—*Hic*—I mean the Underlands."

"And this Muckle Sap isn't half bad either," Scorch said. "I bet Morley would enjoy this." Scorch looked around as if he was searching for an old friend. "Oh, never mind."

"Who's Morley, Scorch?" Darlene said. "And why are you always talking about him?" Whenever she heard that name, her jealous side came to life. Scorch was her friend and her friend alone.

"Darlene," Scorch said, "I told you not to think like that."

She grabbed his sleeve, started petting it with her dirty hands and said, "I'm sorry, Scorch. *Hic*. Won't happen again. *Hic*."

Hopping off her stool, she'd started teetering away when she heard Joline say, "Is she going to be alright?"

"She'll be alright, Joline," Scorch said. He reached over and patted Joline's hand. "But please, tell me about all your worries."

"I'll be alright!" Darlene said. She knocked a bottle from one table only to excuse herself and knock a bottle from another.

The men laughed behind her back as she sauntered away, ignoring the obvious stares. The place was nice, very nice, but the people she wasn't so sure about. Many of them were impeccable in clothing, even the handful of dwarves that smoked around the tables. But their manners were lacking. *Oh!* The fire was welcoming on her back as she took a seat on the corner of the fireplace hearth.

"Woo!" she said, slapping her knees. "Sure is nice in here." She fanned herself. "Getting really hot, though."

The tavern chatter was about many things, including underlings, but there was something else going on she couldn't put her finger on. A couple of robed men's faces were masks of concentration, staring hard into one another's eyes inside a small group that gathered around and added more coins to the piles on the table.

"Ten seconds," one said, rubbing his chin.

"Twenty."

Sweat beaded on both of the robed men's foreheads.

"Thirty seconds," the man said.

The bigger of the two men locked in a stare jumped from the table, banging his knee and holding his head.

"Fodor wins!"

Darlene applauded along with the rest of the men, even though she didn't have any idea what was happening. "Say, what kind of game is this, anyway? A staring contest?"

A couple of the scholarly robed men chuckled while another man sneered and walked away. The smaller man in a bright green tunic seated at the table smiled and waved her over.

"Please, come over here and have a seat. I'd be happy to explain," he said, smiling.

"Really?" Darlene said, "My, you men sure have a different way about you. And your clothes." She grabbed the sleeves of one man's robes and rubbed them. "They look more like something a woman would wear. By Hohm, that sure is soft. What kind of fabric is this?"

The man named Fodor cleared his throat. "Ahem, Miss, what was your name?"

"Oh, Darlene. I'm from Hohm City. Home of the Mists, and that over there," she pointed, "is Scorch. My friend. He kills underlings."

Fodor made a polite nod. "I see. Well, Darlene, let me tell you about this game we play…"

"Excuse me, but are you Royals?" She grabbed another man's sleeve. "Where can I get a shirt like this? It's so pretty."

He leered at her and pushed her hand away. "This clothing is made for Wizards, not for a grubby sheep herder."

A couple men chuckled. Others gathered around.

Darlene looked them over. "I'm a hunter and a trapper, and a fine shot with a bow. I bet I could out shoot any of you. And you better watch your manners." She slipped a knife underneath the man's privates. "Or for certain you'll be wearing that fancy shirt as a woman."

The man gawped, eyes wide.

"Certainly, Darlene," Fodor said. He lay his hand on her shoulder. "Please, put the knife away. My companions don't have the best manners when it comes to travelers."

Darlene slid her knife back into the sheath and burped.

"You can say that again. So," she drummed her fingers on the table, "tell me about this game again, Fodor. Is it something I can play?"

"Certainly," he said, clasping his hands on the table. "And it's really quite simple. Even for you."

She swayed forward.

"Well, what do you mean by that?"

"I say that because it's your first time, is all. No insult about your intellect intended."

She nodded. "That's what I thought you meant."

Fodder smiled and continued.

"So, it's called a Mind Grumble. It's a game for everyone, but a mage or wizard must link it. What happens is our minds are linked together and we engage in a mental arm wrestling contest. A test of wills. Do you understand, Darlene?"

"I think I've heard of this before. I had an uncle that was a wizard, or at least my mother said he was, well said he was my uncle, but I'm not so sure why she'd be sleeping around with my uncle." She shrugged. "Maybe it was on account that my father, my uncle's brother, was no longer around. But he said he did something like this and gave a man a bloody nose for it."

Fodor shook his head. "Who said he gave a bloody nose for it?"

"My uncle."

Fodor looked at her for a long moment as if waiting for her to speak.

"Huh … I see, Darlene. Are you finished?"

She rubbed her nose. "Will this give me a bloody nose?"

"It's unlikely, but it has been known to happen before. See the floor?" He pointed with his eyes and chin.

There was a dark stain on the floor near their table.

"Is that from blood?"

"Aye, for the bloodiest nose I ever saw. Fogle Boon, one of our kind, arrogant and mysterious, locked minds with a stranger, somewhat like yourself. A rugged wilderness warrior whose name I can't recall."

"What happened?"

"To our shock and amazement, the big fellow won and Fogle Boon's nose was broken."

Darlene gulped, covering her nose.

"Darlene, that won't happen to you, I promise. That night, if anything, was an unfortunate accident. Rather unexplainable, it was. But, in the spirit of things," Fodor snapped his fingers, and a pretty waitress in a short white tunic dress strolled over, smiling, "I treat you to a bottle of wine. Are you ready?"

She eyed the men that surrounded her and the table. They had a shifty look about them, but she felt all right. "You promise it won't turn my mind to mush or anything?"

"It's already mush if you ask me," one wizard said. He had a crook in his jaw and a partially bald head. "Shouldn't hurt a thing."

Darlene's hand dropped to her knife.

"I don't like you."

He stepped away.

Fodor continued.

"Don't mind him, Darlene. He never wins. And if you find yourself feeling uncomfortable, you just need to close your eyes, or look away. It's quite simple. And for all I know, you might give more than I can handle." He smiled and chuckled. "Such things have been known to happen before."

She rapped her fist on the table. "I'll try anything once! Let's do this!" She learned forward on her elbows and stared into Fodor's eyes. "You have nice eyes." She licked her lips. "Now what?"

Fodor loosened the top button on his tunic, nodded to one of the other wizards, and then turned his focus on her. The petite man's eyes were like ice blue water, hypnotizing like a snake.

The men around the table quietly talked among themselves in a strange gibberish and gently laid coins on the table.

"Are they betting for me or against me?" she said.

The mage with the crook in his jaw muttered quickly, twirled his fingers, and then touched her forehead with one finger and Fodor's with another. "What's he doooooo …"

Darlene didn't feel anything, but the man across from her's face turned snake-like, red tongue licking out of its mouth and striking. It was her, watching herself standing in the dark woods facing off a great snake. She didn't scream, just whipped out a knife and cut off its head.

"Is that it? Is it over? Did I win?" Her voice echoed. But the scene changed. A white mist surrounded her, and the sound of rain filled her ears. "Say, where's the rain?"

In the distance, a man stood waving.

The mist turned from clouds to an Outland desert, and she was hot and thirsty. She watched the man drop a canteen. She was trotting towards it when an orc came from out of nowhere. She shot it with her bow. A gnoll popped up behind her, swinging a bastard sword. She ducked and stabbed in in the thigh. It disappeared. The suns beat down on her as she crawled hands and knees towards the canteen. She grabbed it, tipped it up to her mouth—and drank a mouthful of sand.

"Ugh! No!" she sputtered.

Nearby, Fodor stood, hands on hips, laughing.

"Have you had enough, Darlene?" he said. There was something mocking about him.

She threw the canteen at him. "No!"

He picked it up and poured water down his throat and all over himself. "Ah!"

"This game is stupid, Fodor," she said. She tried to yell, spitting sand from her mouth. "I quit." She closed her eyes and opened them. Nothing happened.

"Why am I still here?" she said, looking around.

"You half-wit!" he said. He stormed across the sand, sneering. "This game isn't over until I say it is over! And you, such audacity to speak with me and sit at my table. Oh, you shall pay for it. After this, you'll tell no more of your stupid stories to anyone again."

"What are you doing!" Darlene cried out.

"Teaching you a lesson you'll never forget, inbreed!"

Darlene grabbed her head. Her nose was bleeding! The sound of laughing voices was all around her now, jeering and making fun. Her fears overcame her, and darkness closed in.

NO! STOP THIS!

"Ha! Ha! Ha! Look, she peed herself," someone from somewhere said.

Angry and embarrassed, Darlene tried to fight back. Lashing out, her figure struck at Fodor with a knife. He rose above it, laughed, clapped his hands, and the knife was gone.

"Foolish woman, you are not clever enough to beat me!"

An invisible force squeezed her mind, suffocating her.

What is going on?

She felt a sudden loneliness that she'd never felt before. Deep down, painful despair. No one liked her. No one needed her. No one cared for her. Not even her father or mother. Her brothers and sisters even abandoned her. She had no one. She was no one.

"That's right, Darlene, no one cares about you at all. Your life doesn't even matter," Fodor laughed.

Tears were streaming down her cheeks, dripping onto the table.

I'm not so bad. I'm not so terrible.

A giant snake coiled around her and spoke through its fanged mouth.

"But you are!"
It took the breath right from her.
She deserved to die. She had no friends at all she could count on.
Or did she?
SCORCH!

Joline had just spent the last several minutes pouring her heart out to the man named Scorch. He was a wonderful listener and something to look at, too. She'd just finished telling him about what happed to Kam and the baby Erin when he turned his attention away.

"Pardon me," he said. He was looking for his friend, Darlene.

"Oh my, how did she wind up with them?" Joline said. "I'm sorry, I wasn't paying any attention."

Darlene sat in her chair, catatonic, while the men laughed because she'd peed herself.

"I'll take care of this," Joline said. She rushed from behind the bar straight for Darlene's table.

"You men cut that out! She's my guest—"

Plerf!

The first man that looked up's head exploded.

"Mother of Bish—"

Plerf!

The man next to the man whose head exploded's head exploded as well.

An arc of red sprayed across the room like a rainbow.

Plerf!

Plerf!

Plerf!

One right after the other, three more men's heads exploded. Five bodies fell. Blood was everywhere. Silence fell.

Joline was shaking. Blood was sprinkled all over her hands and apron. At the table, Darlene wiped the blood from her face, gaping at her.

"Did I do that?" Darlene said.

Joline's tongue clove to the roof of her mouth.

Darlene turned and looked at Fodor. He sat wide-eyed, blood-coated and trembling in his chair.

"Did you do that?" Darlene asked him.

He shook his head.

Plerf!

His head exploded.

"Guess not," Darlene said. She grabbed the bottle of wine, pulled the cork out of the bottle with her teeth and started drinking.

Scorch was laughing. Everyone else screamed.

10

T HE NEST WAS IN CHAOS.
Find Diller! Save Erin!

Lefty picked his way through Palos's blood bath and into the streets, where skirmishes among the thieves had broken out everywhere. Screams, shouts and cries of alarm echoed up and down the alleys and across the docks, where members of the thieves' guild sought escape from one another—and from another predator: the wrath of Zorth's blade.

Two thieves tumbled through a storefront. One collapsed in a heap, begging for his life. The other drove a dagger into his chest. Lefty darted away.

I have no idea who is on whose side. I need to find Jubbler!

Wind rushing past his ears, Lefty made his way to the docks that had become the battleground of the bloody revolt. Somewhere in the throng, a deep eerie voice rang out.

"I am Zorth! Vanquisher of all evil!"

The pleas and cries of men came to an abrupt halt.

"Get that halfling!" someone cried. "He's responsible for this!"

Glancing over his shoulder, he saw two men and one dwarf coming his way. Behind them was the orcen Quarter Master.

The big orc cracked his lash over his head. "Bring that little blond head to me!"

Lefty dashed down into the Quarters, wedged himself between the crates, and began pushing himself to the other side. Booted feet rushed over the planks.

One. Two. Three. He counted as they passed by his spot.

That was close!

"That's a dead end, rogues!" The Quarter Master yelled. His broad back blocked the narrow space between the crates. "Wait a minute. I smell something. *Sniff. Sniff.* I smell fear!" The Quarter Master turned and peeked into the space." Ah, there he is!" He reached inside the space, fingers clutching, catching hold of Lefty's shirt. "I have you now!"

No!

He pulled away, but the grip of the orc was strong.

Come on, Lefty!

He dug his little fingers into the next crate and held on for dear life.

"Hah! Hah! Hah! You aren't going anywhere, little halfling, except into the murk when I'm through torturing you!"

The orc's pimply and pitted face was pale, merciless. Lefty never imagined facing death would be so horrible. Desperate, he bit down on the orc's finger with all his might.

The orc roared, but held tight, yanking him out from between the crates with one powerful tug, skinning his face. The Quarter Master held him up by the scruff of his collar and stuck the long yellow nail of his finger in his face. He bared the canines of his teeth.

"You bit me like a yellow-headed rodent; now I'm going to bite you!"

The three other thieves gathered round.

"Take a hunk off his leg!"

"No, bite his ear off!"

The dwarf pulled out a long knife and said, "Let me cut off his toes."

Lefty kicked and flailed.

The orc laughed.

"What's the matter, rodent? Are you offended that I won't cook you first?"

"No! I'm offended by the smell of sewage in your mouth."

"Hah! Ha — *urk!*"

Lefty drove his foot into the orc's throat.

The orc hoisted him over his head and slammed him into the ground.

He saw bright spots and felt his shoulder pop out of place. His eyes watered.

The orc stood over him, rubbing his greasy neck.

"Ooo, that little fit cost you, didn't it, Halfling? Hah! The little bird cannot fly away with a busted wing. Tie him up. Once this fight is over, we'll put him on a spit!"

"Heeeee!"

"Hooooooo!"

"Huuuuuuuuuuuh!"

Three burly figures leapt from the crates over them, each landing on a different thief.

One was Jubbler. The crusty dwarf drove a short sword into the neck of the dwarf. The other men's bellies were run through with spears.

Huffing, three dwarves stood there, squaring off on the Quarter Master. The orc ripped his swords from his scabbards.

"Come on then," the orc said.

Lefty scooted back behind Jubbler. The dwarf with pig tails in his beard stepped between him and Jubbler.

"The revolt is over, Quarter Master. Palos's reign is done. Drop those blades of yours, if you want mercy! Huh!"

"Huh!" the orc said. "Fool babbler! Think you I'll surrender! Think I want mercy?" He beat his chest. "The only thing I'm going to do is skin the hide from your thick dwarven necks, you loon, Jubbler!"

The Quarter Master sunk his blade in the nearest dwarf's chest.

"Hah! I'm a warrior, not a thief!"

The other dwarf jabbed his spear at the orc's knees. The Quarter Master spun away, knocked the shaft aside, and stuck his other blade into the dwarf's skull. The orc flashed them a nasty grin. "I'm gonna carve you both into troll food. Tiny little bits that are easy to swallow."

Lefty felt like he was going to vomit. Jubbler was dragging him back, but the dock was running out of room.

"I've a confession to make. Huh. Lefty. Huh. I can't swim," Jubbler said. The dwarf eyed the lake and the orc.

"Everybody knows dwarves can't swim. Don't feel bad. I don't think I can now either," he said. He was wincing and holding his shoulder. He could maybe run if he had to. Dash right past the Quarter Master. He couldn't leave Jubbler though. But he needed to find Erin.

What to do!

The orc wrenched his dripping blade from the fallen dwarf's skull.

"I'm going to enjoy this!"

Can life get any worse in this world? I've failed at everything!

"Tis a shame, Lefty. Huh. We have this thing won! Huh. Huh. Palos's rule is over!" Jubbler said. He shuffled back another step. Only a few feet of planks left between them and the water. "Tell you what. Huh. I'll fight. Huh. You run. Huh. Tell them I need help. Huh. They'll run this pile of pig slat through. Huh."

"Bravery, the blood-letter of fools," the orc said. The Quarter Master was within striking distance.

Jubbler stopped, stood up and wrapped both hands around his sword.

"Nice knowing you, Lefty. Huh. And remember. Huh. Master Gillem would be proud. Just make sure you master those absidium chains." He raised his sword. "My hide and skull much thicker than my brother's, Orc!"

The Quarter Master banged his steel together. "We'll see about that!"

Lefty's heart sank. He didn't have many friends left. The last one he'd lost, Gillem, he wasn't close to getting over yet. Something swelled inside his chest. With his magic feet, he might be able to run right past the orc and find safety. After all, he had to find Erin. But the thought of another friend dying tore at him.

NO!

The orc swung.

Jubbler parried.

Slice.

Chop!

Bang!

Clatter!

Jubbler's sword skidded over the deck and plopped into the waters.

"Run, Lefty!" the dwarf said.

Fight or die!

On magic feet he charged. "NOOOOOOOOO!" He slammed into the Quarter Master's chest, barreling him over.

"What!" the orc cried out.

Lefty kicked. It was all he could do. His shoulder was useless.

Jubbler did the same.

Whop!

A steel pommel hit Lefty in the head. Blood oozed over his eyes.

Crack!

Jubbler fell face first onto the deck.

The Quarter Master gathered his feet under him and stood over them.

"Nice try, little people." He snorted and licked his lips. "But now it's time to die. Mmmm. I'm going to be eating good tonight." He raised his swords over his head.

Exhausted, Lefty couldn't move an inch. Beside him, Jubbler lay face first on the deck. Out cold. Lefty spit blood. He'd fought with all he had in him.

It was the right thing to do. Save a friend a little longer. It had to be. Fight or Die.

He closed his eyes.

I'm sorry, Kam and Erin.

"I am Zorth!"

Lefty's weary eyes snapped open.

Thorn's face and haggard figure quickly approached, wielding a gleaming sword as long as a man in his hands.

"Vanquisher of Giants! Dragons and Evil Doers!"

"What! Thorn!"

The Quarter Master roared and charged.

"You'll not be robbing me of my —"

SLICE!

Thorn swung through the big orc, shattering his blades with one stroke. Blood spilled from the slit in his waist.

The orc gawped. The great sword sung again, ripping the head from his shoulders. It bounced off the deck and splashed into the waters.

"I am Zorth! The end of all evil is at hand!"

Lefty leered up at the tall and rangy man. His face was charred and pink. His eyes black. The man he'd known as Thorn was gone and wouldn't be missed. But now, whoever had him possessed was a far superior threat. Lefty lost his breath when Zorth looked down on him with burning black eyes. Blood was dripping from the blade.

"I am Zorth! No evil shall remain!"

Am I evil?

Lefty watched the blade go up like it was a mile high in the air.

Or is he insane?

Blue eyes wide as saucers, he watched the blade descend.

Clatch-Zip! Clatch-Zip! Clatch-Zip! Clatch-Zip! Clatch-Zip!

Crossbow bolts ripped into the big man's body.

Thorn turned and faced his agitators. Filled with bolts in his chest, legs and neck, he stormed up the deck.

"I am Zorth! Avenger of Good. Vanquisher of Evil!"

A dozen thieves greeted him. Crossbows rocking.

Clatch-Zip! Clatch-Zip! Clatch-Zip! Clatch-Zip! Clatch-Zip! Clatch-Zip! Clatch-Zip! Clatch-Zip! Clatch-Zip! Clatch-Zip! ...

Zorth crashed into the ones at the top of the bank. A dozen bolts in his chest. The Sword of Zorth rose and fell. Bones were splintered. Cries went out. Many rogues twitched on the bloody deck. Others searched for their limbs.

"I am Zorth! Destroy—

Clatch-Zip!

A bolt went inside his one temple and stuck out the other.

The great sword clattered to the deck. The remaining rogues chopped Thorn into ribbons.

Lefty wiped the blood from his eyes.

Thank Bish!

A strong hand squeezed his bad shoulder. He flinched.

It was Jubbler. "You alright, Huh!"

"Aye!" Lefty said, swallowing.

Erin!

"Jubbler! Do you know where Erin is?"

11

T HE WORLD OF PALOS WAS dark, sadistic, perverted and dreary. Kam was choking in the man's darkness with only his laughter echoing inside her ears.

"Kam," he taunted. "I told you that you'd be my whore forever. Now I have you."

Light of a candle flared, illuminating a small wood paneled room with no doors. Tears swelled up in her eyes as she sat on her knees, now a little girl with all the insecurities in the world. Bugs the size of her fist scurried over the room. Each with a different facade of Palos for a face. One crawled up her bound arms and spoke with antennas twitching.

"Are you afraid, little girl? Do you fear the night?" He shape-shifted into a rat. "The rodents. The creatures that slither across the floor!" He turned into a burning green snake and coiled his tail around her neck. "Shall I burn your mind the same as you did my belly?" He hissed. "Hmmm... you lactating witch!"

She couldn't tear her gaze away. She was hypnotized with his power.

"What am I doing here?" she cried out. "Where am I! Where am I!"

The candle went out. Everything was gone. Only the sound of her sobs remained.

What am I doing inside the mind of Palos?

She had to find him. Find something. Find a way out of his maze.

"You never should have come here, Kam!" His voice screamed. "I'll never let you out!"

The sound of a heavy metal door banging closed. She found herself inside a room, her full adult body bound up in chains. It was freezing. She shivered without control. Her chin quivered. Her teeth clacked.

Palos appeared before her, dressed in warm white clothes, handsome and captivating. He lifted her trembling chin into his soft hands and looked her straight in the eye.

"Kam, swear yourself to me. Be my slave, and I'll end this misery," he said.

She tried to look away, but his words, his warmth, were so inviting.

But I hate you.

A tear dropped down her cheek and froze on her chin.

He kissed her forehead.

"You don't hate me, Kam. You desire me. You want me. Give in to me, and all will be well again," he said.

Why am I here?

She shook her head and looked down at the frosty chains that covered her naked frame. Her breath was frosty.

"So cold … I can't think," she said.

She was disoriented, lost and frozen. All of her memories, her passions, feeling and anger were gone. If she had an issue with Palos, she couldn't remember it. Why would she be angry with Palos? He was such a charming man.

Isn't he my friend?

"Of course I'm your friend," he said. He stroked her hair with the back of his soft hand. "I'm your only friend now. I can save you. Just swear yourself to me. I'll protect you and your daughter."

"What …" she said, fighting against her dream-like state, "daughter?"

The one you are looking for … A dark, powerful voice spoke.

"Who?" she said. She looked around.

"Who are you?" Palos demanded, jumping back from her. "Who is this, Kam? Who are you?"

There was fear in the voice of the Prince of Thieves now. It was an alarming sound. An awakening. The cold chains that bound her faded away into her green mage's gown. She shook her head.

The dark voice spoke again, more demanding this time. *Where is her daughter, Palos?*

"Erin!" Kam screamed.

A dark figure of shadows emerged between Kam and Palos. Its eyes were two burning rubies, and it had a hooked nose. Its gaze sent a chill straight through her.

Palos's face filled with horror. "Get away from me!" He drifted back into the metal door, panic in his eyes. He turned and pulled at the handle. It would not open.

"Where's my daughter, Palos!" Kam shouted. Her strength was returning.

"I'll never tell! I'll never—AYEEEEEEEE!"

The black figure's fingers stretched out like tendrils, filling Palos's nostrils and mouth, burrowing into his ears. *Where is the girl, deceitful one?*

Palos shook his head. He ground his teeth.

"No!"

Then I shall dig it out myself!

The black figure reached deeper into Palos's mind.

The Prince of Thieves screamed.

The black figure ripped out his mind.

Kam's eyes popped open. She was gasping. Lying in a pool of her own sweat by the fireplace on Palos's apartment floor. Rubbing her head, she looked up and found the Prince of Thieves still bound to his chair. His eyes were rolled up inside his head. He babbled. Drool spilled from his mouth onto his chest.

"What happened?" Struggling to her feet, she scanned the room, worried. "Where are you? Where is Erin?" She looked down at her hand. It was glowing like fire. The red gems she no longer held. They were now embedded inside her hand.

"No! What madness is this?" She tried to rake them out on the chair. On the table. She screamed. "You said you'd help me find my daughter. Tell me what you found out from Palos!"

His mind did not escape the inquiry. Time to serve, Kam!

Exhausted, Kam fell to her knees, gaping at her hand. What had she done? She'd wanted to live so desperately that she would have done anything to see her daughter again. Now she was bound with a force she couldn't have dreamed of. Only moments ago, she was going to be the slave of Palos, and now she was the slave to something else. And she still didn't have Erin.

Wiping her sweaty locks from her face, she said, "What would you have me do?"

I must return to my home.

She glanced at Palos. He was drooling like an imbecile.

Serves him right.

"And where is that?" she said. "What!" Her body was propelled to the table.

I'll tell you when we get there, but for now, I need to see through your eyes and ears. Ah … it's good to smell again, even though it's not like my home.

She grabbed a carafe of Palos's wine to her lips and drank.

The voice inside her head, eerie and dark.

This is good, a fine, exquisite taste, but I have no need for more.

Kam forced the carafe away from her lips and set it down. "Can I—or we—at least try to find my daughter on your way home? Please!"

Not likely. I've waited long enough already.

"But—"Kam said. The front door burst open. "Lefty!"

The halfling boy limped inside, holding his shoulder, face bleeding.

"We've got Diller, Kam," he said. He eyed her then looked at the ground. "But no word on Erin … I-I'm afraid to say."

A dwarf with a strange beard entered along with four other rogues who dragged a chained Diller in and slung him on the floor. Palos's reliable lieutenant Diller's eyes widened when he saw his boss.

"What happened to him?" he said.

"He didn't tell me what I wanted to hear!" Kam said. She stepped forward and stretched out her glowing hand. "And if you think you will get off any easier than him, Diller, you better think again."

Lefty, Jubbler and the rest of the men moved backward. Diller struggled in the absidium chains.

"You might break me, Princess, but you'll always be Palos's whore!"

With a wave of her hand, Kam slammed Diller into the ceiling and back down into the floor face first.

"LAST WARNING, FOOL!" she yelled. The entire room shook.

Lefty trembled.

"Huh-Huh-Huh. Mercy, never seen the likes of that—Huh—before," Jubbler whispered. The other men ducked out of the room without a glance. "You sure she's a friend of yours? Huh."

Kam whirled on the old dwarf, green eyes like blazing emeralds.

"*I tire of you tiny people*," she said. Her voice was not hers. "*Away with you!*"

Jubbler was lifted from his feet and went sailing out of the room. The door slammed shut behind him. "*Don't move, Halfling!*"

Lefty tried not to shake but couldn't help it.

"Where is my child, Diller?" Kam's words lifted him in the air, slowly spinning him around, upside down.

Nose dripping on the floor, he rolled a bloody toothpick from one side of his mouth to the other and stared at Palos's vacant, babbling face. "Promise you'll not do that to me. Your word. I was going to protect you from that monster, Kam. I swear I was."

There was some truth to his words. Kam could feel it, but he was a liar. They all were.

"That's the risk you'll have to take, Diller, but the longer you delay, the more dire your future will become." She slapped him so hard he spun in a complete circle. Two gemstone scorch marks were on his cheek. She was losing control.

I'm losing my patience, Kam.

"TELL ME NOW, DILLER!"

"She's here!" He stammered.

"Where!"

"Below. In the tunnels. I'll show you! Oh Kam, I don't want to die. I'll take you right there. I swear it! My word!" He eyeballed Palos, who was vomiting on himself. "Anything at all!"

Diller's body fell hard on the floor. Groaning, he rose to his feet.

"Do you know about these tunnels, Lefty?"

He started to move his neck.

"SPEAK!"

"No Ma'am!" he said. "Never been or heard of there."

She released her spell. Diller fell to the floor and slowly got up to his feet. He rubbed his head.

"Lead, Diller, and if you do anything stupid, you'll be eating your drool with a spoon."

"Certainly. Certainly, Kam!" he said. He headed out the door and shuffled down the steps.

"Come," she said to Lefty. "Shoulder hurt?"

"Yes."

"Good."

The once lively tavern was occupied only by Jubbler, a few other rogues, and the dead. All the living eyes were wary as Kam passed. She could feel their fear. Clutching her hand open and closed, she felt great power—and liked it.

Diller made his way into the kitchen, put his shoulder into a cupboard, and shoved it across the floor, revealing a set of stairs.

"It's Diller," he yelled. "And I'm coming down, with company." He turned towards Kam with a worried look in his eyes. "She's not alone down there, but I can't speak to her condition. Not seen her in a while."

"Go!" she said.

A torch was lit at the bottom of a tunnel that burrowed straight through the ground. Wooden rafters held it up like a mine tunnel. A series of chambers and tunnels greeted them at the bottom.

"This is where Palos keeps his hoard," Diller said. "Josh! Are you back there?"

A man in chainmail lumbered forward from the gloom with a longsword ready. He had a hard face, but was stout with a neck full of muscles.

"Where is Palos? And who are these two?"

Time to serve, Kam. I grow impatient!

"Not without my child," she said.

"Who is she talking to?" Josh said. The guard eyed her. "Is this the mother of the baby? The baby is not well."

"Shut up, you fool!" Diller said.

A charge of fire shot from Kam's hand. Josh was incinerated.

"Erin! Erin!"

Somewhere, a baby cried out.

"Erin!

She ran through the ashes and into the darkness.

"Kam, wait!" Diller shouted. "There's more men in there. This is Palos's—"

A grown man screamed. Another followed, echoing in the chambers. It was a horrifying sound. Lefty pulled out his dagger. Even though Diller's arms were chained behind his back, he was still dangerous, and it had only been minutes since they tried to kill one another. But the man didn't move. He didn't move a muscle.

Lefty looked at his sweaty feet. They'd been like that ever since he entered Kam's room. The beautiful woman he so admired was no longer herself. She was something else. Something dark and powerful had overtaken her. He thought of those gems. He'd given them to her, so her possession was his fault as well.

Can I do nothing right?

"Do you think she's going to kill me?" Diller said. His eyes were fixed on the dark tunnel.

"I think she's going to kill both of us if her Erin isn't alright."

Diller shook his head. "If I live through this, I swear to Bish I'll never do bad things anymore. That Palos, I was scared of him, but nothing like this angry mother."

Diller was spooked. Lefty was astounded. The man had been nothing but cold and cruel since the moment they met, but now there was something different about him. If Diller could change, perhaps he could change too.

Kam's eyes were glowing as she stormed up the tunnel, a baby swaddled in her arms. The baby cried and coughed, a wrenching sound. It was Erin; Lefty could feel it inside his bones. She was alive, but not well.

"Kam, anything to help, I will," Diller said. His eyes were pleading. His arms open. "I'm so sorry for all of this."

She clenched her fist and twisted.

Crack!

Diller's neck snapped. He fell to the ground.

Lefty gulped.

She's going to kill me.

She glared at him, shook her fist, and stomped up the stairs. "Don't ever lose my baby again, Lefty! Now find my father's sword! Whatever might bring Erin comfort, and meet me at those docks."

Tears dropped from Lefty's eyes. His tongue clove to the roof of his mouth. He wanted to say thank you out loud but could not.

Oh mercy! Thank you!

"And quit crying! You've shed enough tears already!"

Time to serve, Kam!

She didn't care who she served now that she had her baby. Erin nuzzled her chest as Lefty shoved the gondola off and waved good bye to Jubbler and his ilk.

"We better not wind up here again, rogues, else I'll kill you all!" Kam shouted.

"Huh! No worries, Crazy Lady. Huh! None at all!" Jubbler waved.

Irritated, Kam summoned a flaming snake onto their deck, bringing fire to everything in their paths. "Piss on them and you." She eyed Lefty. "Row, blast it!"

"My shoulder. I-I can't."

"Is it broken?"

"N-No. Just dislocated."

She held out her hand and spread her fingers.

Lefty's eyes widened like saucers. His head beaded with sweat.

"That hurt?" she said.

He shook his head.

Pop!

"Better now?"

He nodded and rubbed his shoulder.

"Don't thank me," she said. "Just be quiet. Be still."

Time to serve, Kam! I'm losing patience.

"We are leaving, fiend!"

She snapped her fingers.

The oars came to life, whisking them over the dead waters and away.

Time to serve! Time to serve! Time to serve!

12

Cass held on to Chongo for dear life. She was exhausted. The big dog was fast, but not tireless. She could feel him laboring for breath. For over an hour they'd run, chased down by underlings that rode on the backs of spiders as big as horses. It sent a chill through her.

"Run, Chongo! Run!"

Thirty minutes into the chase, she was certain she'd lost them, but that's when more spider riders appeared. Not just a couple either. An entire patrol. Their riders had weapons raised. The spiders' fangs were bared. They scurried right after them.

Sheesh! Those are sick looking things!

Animals were one thing with Cass, but bugs were another. Many druids like the bugs, but they weren't part of her nature. It was fine when the blue bees made honey, but spider webs and slimy toads grossed her out. As a girl, she was fed crunchy bugs once, and she'd never gotten over it.

Chongo dashed into a large grove, paws ripping into the ground beneath him, stirring up dust. Cass hunched down. The branches whipped over her face and legs, stinging her and drawing thin lines of blood on her pale skin.

What have I done?

Digging her nails into the thick mane on Chongo's neck, her free thoughts turned to regrets. She'd left Fogle Boon to blindly chase a two headed dog she now shared a bond with, much further than she ever imagined. Chongo, tongues hanging from his mouth, was going after his master. He'd made it clear he wouldn't stop for anything until he got there. Now she was lost.

"I hope you know where you're going!"

All she could see were glimpses of the sky as they ran under the trees. They needed to hide, outdistance themselves or do something. Behind her, she could hear the spiders crashing through the trees, getting closer.

Don't look back!

She did.

A spider and rider were so close she could see the red in all their eyes.

I've got to do something!

She couldn't think of anything.

Something!

Wind whipping through her hair, Cass struggled to hang on. Chongo raced full speed through the grove and into a ravine. His feet were trampling through a wide creek, bend after bend, when he came to an abrupt stop at the edge of a drop off. It was unlike anything Cass had ever seen before. The creek dropped over one hundred feet, waters crashing into a pool below. She gasped. The underlings and the spiders had caught up with them.

Chongo turned, lowered his heads, and growled.

There were five spiders in all, hairy legs creeping over the creek waters while the underlings chittered and hooted. Cass summoned every ounce of magic she had left.

Bish, give me strength!

Chongo's barks echoed up the ravine. The hairy black spiders hitched up on their hind legs and spewed webs, covering the ground and sticking to Chongo's legs. He let out a howl, trying to tear free.

"No, Chongo! You'll make it worse."

Cords of webbing caught her by the waist. They tugged at her.

"Never Insects!" Magic swelled inside her chest. Fire burst from her hands. She stroked the big dog and moaned. In an instant, both she and Chongo were consumed by flame. The webbing burned away. Chongo charged the nearest spider, jaws tearing off its legs and chomping the underling rider. Everything Chongo touched caught fire. The brush, the spiders, the underling soldiers. The beast tore into them with ferocious fury.

Hold on!

Her strength was already waning.

Two spiders and riders twitched and burned in the creek. Chongo pounced on the third, slinging Cass to the ground. She hit her head on a stone.

"Ugh!"

The flames left Chongo, surrounding her and her alone. She regained her feet.

Focus Cass! Focus!

Thickt!

Thickt!

Thickt!

Cords of web shot all over the big dog, sticking him to the ground. Chongo's jaws remained locked on an underling. The two heads tore the screaming underling in two parts.

Two underlings on spiders closed in on the beast. They launched black lances into his side.

"NOOOO!" Cass yelled. She dove onto one spider's legs, spreading her fire all over it.

It pitched upward, bucking its rider and sending the underling to the ground. She dove on top of it, wrapped her hands around its throat, and watched its flesh burn to the bone.

Too-wah! Too-wah! Too-wah!

Arching her back, hands out, she felt sharp things lodge deep inside her back and shoulders. Her flames went out. She couldn't move.

What's happened?

A forceful hand grabbed her by the hair and pulled her around. A pale blue-eyed underling in dark mail armor, holding a blow gun, stood over her, flashing a row of sharp teeth. He laughed and stepped away, clearing a view of Chongo.

Chongo was coated in webs so thick she could barely see him.

What have I done?

And the ravine, where they'd fled, was filled with the speckled eyes of underlings as far as she could see.

This can't be happening!

There was nothing she could do. The underling reached down, fondled her hair, and wrapped a rope around her neck. Chittering an order, another hulking albino underling, the likes of which she never imagined, grabbed the rope, jerked her stiff body to the ground and dragged her up the ravine through the creek.

She could feel everything.

13

"J UST TELL ME," BOON SAID.

They were doubled up on the horse's saddle, and Fogle had gotten tired of telling Boon no. It did feel good however to have his grandfather by the short hairs of his beard for a change. Still, he wasn't going to tell his secret about how to find the underlings.

"No!"

It felt good saying it.

Ahead, Barton led the way with great strides, swinging his heavy arms that almost dragged on the landscape. Fogle still had a difficult time wrapping his head around people being so big. It didn't seem natural or possible, yet in the City of Three, there were three giant statues in the park he remembered seeing as a boy. The stone-faced figures seemed so real at the time, but as he got older he gave them little thought.

And all this time they said the city was named after the great waterfalls. How many other lies have I been led to believe were true?

Boon hopped off the saddle, scowling. "I'm tired of riding."

"Good," Fogle said.

It was dark, overcast above, the clouds giving off a dull light from the moons.

"Tis a good way to travel, with the clouds out. The moons cast too many shadows, making it easier for things to hide," Boon remarked.

"Well, what are you up to now?"

Boon was floating along his side, arms crossed over his chest, smiling.

"Are you using magic? I thought you told me to save my power for battles. In the book it says, and you wrote it yourself, 'Not for frivolous use'." Fogle's brows were knitted.

"I didn't write that for myself, but for you. Besides, I have a great deal more power than you."

"What?" Fogle began to object.

But Boon floated high in the air, stretching his arms out exclaiming, 'Weeeeeeeeeeeeee'."

Fogle huffed.

Madman!

As he watched his grandfather swoop up and down in the sky, he couldn't help but be a little jealous. He wished he could be carefree and dangerous at the same time. He wished he had Boon's fearless edge.

How did he get like that?

Barton stopped, eyeballing the floating wizard. He pointed his log of a finger at the man, looked back at Fogle, and giggled. "Barton wants to float like birdie too, Wizard. Can you send me up there? Hee hee!"

I'd love to send you both sailing away. Nothing would delight me more.

Fogle rode his horse alongside the giant, stared into Barton's good eye, and smiled. "No."

"Aw." Barton kicked up a chunk of dirt. "I've never flown before. If I could fly, I could beat that dragon!" He punched his fist into his hand. "Hate that dragon!"

Dragon?

"Barton?"

The giant was staring into the sky, looking for Boon, who'd disappeared.

"Barton!"

"Hmmm?" Barton still eyed the sky.

"What dragon are you talking about?"

"Blackie." His fingers clutched in and out.

Whatever Blackie is, Barton really doesn't like it.

"Eh … can you tell me more about Blackie?"

Barton yawned and started walking away, watching the sky and craning his neck as he did so. "I can tell you about Blackie. Barton hate Blackie. Barton hides and Blackie always finds him. Picks him up and flies him home."

"Picks you up? All of you?"

"Blackie's big. Strong wings. Picks Barton up like a hawk and rodent. Hate Blackie. Hate him."

Oh great. Giants, underlings, and dragons are after us. And all I have is this horse to ride on. Bish! I wish Mood were here! What else is there in this world?

"Barton, tell me more about where you come from. Are there many giants and dragons?"

"Oh yes. Many of both, but more giants." He scratched his head. "I think so. Barton likes to hide in the Mist. Many things do."

"Is this dragon, Blackie, coming after you now, you think?"

"Hmmmm … well, little man with axe said he chopped Blackie's wings. Maybe, maybe not, but you'll know. 'Whump. Whump. Whump.' You'll know. Hate that sound. 'Whump. Whump. Whump.'"

All of his life, Fogle had seen many things named after dragons. Taverns. Streets. And so on. But he never knew anyone that admitted to seeing one until now.

I wonder if Mood has seen one? I wonder if it's true.

Fogle dug his heels into his horse. It lurched forward and caught back up with Barton.

"What else can you tell me about where you're from? Is it just like this, but bigger?"

"I guess so. But, I've only seen little of this place. More water though. Much more water. Splash. Splash. I like the water. I like to drown Blackie in water. Yes! Yes! Drown Blackie!"

He's demented.

"Are there people my size?"

"Yes. Many."

"Are there underlings?"

"Those little black peoples that try to kill Barton?"

"Yes."

"No."

Feeling a little foolish, Fogle realized that if he ever got the time, perhaps it would do him some good to ask his grandfather more about where he'd been and what he'd seen. And to remember that Venir had been there too.

Barton stopped.

Fogle pulled on his reins. An eerie feeling fell over him as he watched the backs of Barton's ears bend up and down with a life of their own. Thoughts of a giant black dragon dropping through the clouds raced through his mind.

"Woof. Woof."

"Blackie?" Fogle said. He crouched down, eyeing the sky.

"No. Woof. Woof. Like dog. Big one."

"Like Chongo?" Fogle said, sitting up, excited.

Barton nodded and pointed.

"That way! Uh oh." His ears wiggled.

"What!"

Barton looked back at him, scratching his shoulder, sniffing the air. "I hear many of those little black things too."

"How far?"

"Pretty far for you, not so far for me," Barton said. He turned and jogged off.

Fogle snapped the reins. Inky, his ebony hawk, swooped down from the clouds and soared above him. Focusing, his eyes and Inky's became one.

Scout ahead.

Inky darted through the air, a black streak in the night, soaring by Barton's head and out of sight.

Cass! Is she close?

"Slow down!" Boon said. He dropped from the sky. "I can only float so fast!"

Fogle wasn't listening. He was galloping.

Come on! Come on! Cass, where are you?

Inky's vision was different than a man's. Where a man saw shadows and the dark shapes in the night, Inky saw pale illuminating lines that separated one object from another. Ahead, rocks and brush, typical of what they saw, but they weren't heading south anymore. They were heading west, or so Fogle thought.

"Barton! Slow down!"

The giant kept going. One mile became two, then three.

How far can he hear, anyway?

Inky, flying ahead, didn't pick up anything extraordinary, but a series of jagged cliffs was ahead. Fogle whipped the reins. He was right on Barton's heels.

The giant labored for breath, clutched his side, and slowed. He waded into a pool of water. He pointed towards the top of some cliffs, where a small stream of water gushed like a waterfall.

Fogle's horse clomped into the water, bent its neck and began to drink.

"Hold on, Barton," he said. He closed his eyes.

Inky soared along the edge of the cliff, and Fogle could see everything.

Trees. Trees. Bushes. Creek. Is that a giant spider? "Mother of Bish—Underlings!"

Speckled eyes were like bright dots in the forest as Inky sailed by. A series of crossbow bolts assailed the bird.

Fogle lurched in his saddle and toppled into the water.

"What happened? Barton said. He helped him up.

"Slat happened! That's what! They're up there, Barton." Fogle pointed. "I can feel it."

Barton dug his hands into the ravine rock and began climbing up. "I know."

Fogle sent Inky into the fray above.

"I'll be ready this time," he said, wringing the water out of his robes.

Inky sailed above the top of the grove, dove down and landed high in the branches. He could see the pale figures of the underlings heading back up the creek, dozens of them. And clumps of black hairy flesh on the ground were burning.

What is that?

Bringing up the rear, they were dragging something, something shaped like a—

Woman! Cass!

Grabbing the vines at the base of the cliff, he climbed. Ten feet up he went. Ten feet down he came.

Splash!

Wiping the water from his face, he yelled, "Come back and get me, Barton!"

But the giant was already halfway up a hundred foot scale.

"Save Cass!" he said. "Bone! I have to get up there qui—*ulp!*"

Two strong arms hoisted him for the pool and took him upward.

"You need a lift, I see," Boon said. "Prepare a chain of energy, Fogle."

"No! That will kill Cass! This is a rescue, not a battle!"

"How many, Fogle?"

"Dozens at least." They floated alongside Barton. "And giant spiders too."

Barton laughed. "Many fun. Wizards make many fun."

"Hurry up, Boon," Fogle said.

The thought of Cass being dead rattled him. He could still see her limp form being dragged away.

"We need a plan," Boon said. "Barton, when you crest that edge, get after them. Fogle, you and I will grab the woman, but you need to focus. They'll have darts, poison, paralyzation at their disposal. We'll need thicker skin to drag her out of there. Much thicker."

Fogle knew immediately what Boon was talking about and summoned his power. He'd readied the spell in his mind earlier. His skin toughened like hide leather. Boon dipped under his added weight.

"Well done. Now, when you get her, grab her and get out of there. I'll handle the rest," Boon said. He stopped just below the crest. Barton hung on the rock at their side. "Can you make that jump if you have to, Barton?"

His big face leered down. He said, "Barton will make big splash!"

"And don't forget about the dog," Boon said. "Now listen to me, Fogle, don't come back for me. Get to safety. I'll catch up if I have to. Ah, and one more thing."

Boon led them over the edge and set Fogle down. Barton cleared the lip and rolled to his feet. Fogle could see the underlings and spiders heading back up the path less than thirty yards away.

Boon held out his hands.

"Barton, give me your finger."

Barton extended his hand.

"You going to make me fly?"

Boon wrapped his hands around the giant's finger and smiled. "No. I'm going to make you fast. Very fast! But it won't last long, so make the most of it."

Barton's face brightened like the suns.

"Go! Go! GOOOOOO!" Barton said. He smashed his fist in his palm. "This is gonna be fun!"

Fogle could see every underling stop and turn. Like black coyotes, they dashed down the ravine. Angry. Chittering. Two spiders the size of horses scurried over the waters at full charge.

Barton met them all head on. His fists drummed like giant flails. "Barton hate bugs!"

The first spider and rider were turned into piles of goo. More underlings and spiders piled on the giant. Barton was a hurricane of flesh in their midst. Snatching, stomping, tearing and rending them like bugs.

"I see the dog." Boon pointed. "Move now, Fogle. I'll try to cover you."

Without thinking, Fogle ran up the wall of the ravine. Through the ebony hawk's eyes, he could see Cass's form still being dragged along. He pushed his way through the branches and caught one in the face. *Blasted trees!* His chest was heaving when he emerged in the clearing. He cut into the underling's path.

The underling stopped. Pale blue eyes leering at him. It pulled a short jagged sword from its belt and charged.

Fogle summoned a word of power, shattering its blade.

The underling kept coming. Slammed into him full force, driving him into the ground. In an instant it wrapped its claws around Fogle's throat.

He couldn't breathe. It was strong as a man, but Fogle was stronger. The iron skin he'd summoned saw to that. He grabbed the underling by the wrists and started pulling them away.

"Must! Save! Cass!" he said. He gave it a heave, tearing its arms away.

It hissed, sinking its teeth into his shoulder.

Fogle didn't feel a thing.

It bit again. Its claws ripped at his robes.

"These are my only robes, you fiend! The Bish with you!"

Grabbing a round rock from the stream bed, he clocked it in the head.

The underling held on, determined, like a hungry badger.

Fogle muttered a word of power, ignited his rock-filled hand, and smote the underling again in the skull. *Crack!*

Its head busted open like an egg. Its jaw slackened.

Fogle shoved its dead body off him, gasping for breath.

"Cass!"

Pitching the rock, Fogle scurried alongside her. Removing the rope from around her neck, he lifted her limp form up in his arms and backtracked.

Ahead, the battle raged on. Barton's bellows echoed up the ravine like thunder, and bright bursts of energy sizzled and crackled into the underlings from all directions. Even the barks of two angry hound heads could be heard. But the woman in his arms was not moving.

"Hang on, Cass." He was shoving his way through the thicket. Inky, in the branches above, shrieked. Fogle stopped. Something else was moving their way, and moving fast. He surged through the forest.

"Boon! Boon!" he said. Finally, He emerged where he'd started.

Barton and Chongo were finishing off the underlings. Boon's hands were smoking.

"I see you got her!"

"Boon, you know that spell for the portal?"

"Yes, why?"

"We could use it now." Fogle tried to contain his panic. "Underlings are coming. I can see them. Hundreds are close and beyond them, thousands!"

"Go then! Continue your quest, Grandson! I'll slow them down. Use the spellbook!" He looked over the falls. "Make it count!"

Fogle could see Barton and Chongo's work was finished. Both were bleeding, but the underlings and spiders were pulverized.

"We'll all flee together, Boon! You gave your word."

"To save the girl and the dog, not the man!"

"But, he has all the power, you said." Still holding Cass's limp body, Fogle muttered, summoning a cushion of air along the falls. "Barton, Chongo, come!"

Obeying, they came, stepping off the drop into mid-air where they slowly lowered.

"Come on, Boon! They're close! You can't take them all!"

Boon stared back at him with a grim smile on his face. "They're so much more fun to kill in bunches!"

Drifting down past the lip, he lost sight of Boon. He shook his head until they landed at the pool in the bottom. Barton rinsed the blood from his hands. "That was fun. We do that again soon, right Wizard?"

Fogle draped Cass over the saddle and swung himself up onto the horse.

"Sure, Barton." He dug his heels into his horse.

Barton and Chongo followed.

Inky soared above the grove, showing Fogle swarm after swarm of underlings piling inside. They coated the landscape like black moss.

One moment, the grove was calm and quiet. In the next was a series of explosions and bright colorful spots.

"Enjoy, Grandfather." Fogle didn't look back. He couldn't fight the feeling he'd never see his grandfather again. *No one could survive that. Not even The Darkslayer. Come, Inky.*

14

T*OOWHIP.*
Toowhip.

Toowhip.

Venir opened the heavy lids of his eyes, squinting in the brightness. It was daytime. It was pain time. Everything from head to toe throbbed.

Toowhip.

Toowhip.

Toowhip.

Something struck his face again and again, like tiny stinging insects. His arms rattled, and his wrists ached. From the corner of his eye, he saw a long metal needle jutting from his face.

What?

There were needles in his arms, dozens of them, each leaving a red swelling mark. His head felt like it weighed a ton. He lifted his chin and locked eyes with a ruby eyed underling. One of many. His arm trembled in his bonds. *This can't be!*

It was Outpost Thirty One, but filled with a different ilk, underlings. Hundreds of them were at work within the walls of the huge fort, pushing carts over the courtyard, hammering steel by forges, and ordering motley assortments of men, orcs and kobolds about. Remnants of the Brigand Queen's army. It was a vision of Venir's world turned inside out. A nightmare.

Toowhip.

Toowhip.

Three underling soldiers, little more than five feet tall, adorned in black leather armor, had Venir surrounded. Each reloaded a small blowgun and spat a needle at him. One chittered, pointed at his face with the long nail of his finger, and spat.

Toowhip.

Struck him on the tip of his nose.

"Come closer, Underling, and I'll shove that up your arse," he said. But it was unintelligible. His tongue was thick as wool.

Ignoring the throbbing, Venir scanned his conditions. He was on a set of scaffolding two stories tall and shackled to the wooden blood-stained deck. On the corner of the deck, a bucket sat, with moisture on its lip. He thirsted. Below him, underlings were at work, some staring up with gemstone eyes to catch a look at him. They chittered and gestured. Some laughed before looking away. He'd never heard an underling laugh before. It was a disturbing sound. Shrill and creepy.

One of the underling guards made his way down a ladder, hopped to the ground, and disappeared into one of the buildings below the massive catwalks. It seemed Venir's awakening required the attention of somebody.

Dying of thirst, Venir eyed the other two underlings. He fought the urge to ask them for water. He'd never ask an underling for anything. He'd die first. Despite the ache and stiffness in his wrists, he plucked out a dart and flicked it away.

Toowhip.

Toowhip.

For every dart he picked, a half dozen more replaced it. His arms, legs and torso were covered with a hundred little stings. He kept plucking. Watching. Fighting the pain and ignoring the mocking chitters of the underlings.

Two underlings were whipping an orcen man in the stockades. Other humans pulled carts with weapons and armor, while underlings clad in black armor trained. The underlings moved about the confines of the fort like parts in a well-oiled machine, running drill after drill. Their sharp blades moved fast, glinting in the light of the two suns.

Venir's thoughts drifted to Slim and Commander Jans. Did the underlings know they were near? "Ugh!"

A dart caught him in the lid of his eye.

He reached to pluck it away.

The underling grabbed his wrist.

"Get your claws off me, Fiend." Venir said.

One underling clocked him in the head with a long stick while the other kicked him in the thigh.

Venir yelped. "Bone!" He reversed his grip, snatched the underling's wrist, and jerked it to the ground. Wrapping the underling's neck in the nook of his arm, he squeezed, ignoring all the needles being driven farther into his arm.

The other underling guard beat on his head with fury.

Whack! Whack! Whack!

Venir held on. He'd kill one more underling before the day was done. He heaved. The underling's tongue writhed out of its mouth. Claws stretched out for its last grasp of life. It shuddered and convulsed. Venir crushed its throat. The sound of steel being ripped from a sheath caught his ears. He whipped around. The underling guard's arm coiled back to strike his throat.

A commanding voice shouted out in underling.

The underling sentry stayed his hand, chest heaving. Nostrils flaring.

The platform groaned as a figure made its way up the ladder.

A burly underling warrior, the size of two in one, appeared.

Venir had never seen such an underling before. Dark plate covered its chest, and its arms and chest were as thick as an ape's. Dark ruby eyes glowered at him as it walked over and struck him in the face with its mailed gauntlet.

Venir saw spots. Tuuth's big pale frame appeared behind the underling commander, holding the canister he had carried to signal for the Royal Riders.

A moment of awful clarity. Venir realized his plan was not such a good plan after all. He'd never considered the consequences of the canister falling into underling hands.

Bish, I'm a fool!

All he could do was hope the underlings wouldn't figure out what it was there for.

The burly underling commander grabbed Venir by the hair and pounded the tiny needles deeper into his chest, one blow after the other.

The excruciating pain was blinding. He cried out.

Tuuth was wincing.

"Big human. You should have known better than to kill underlings. Now tell us, why are you here?"

Clutching his chest, he replied, "Hunting red-eyed arseholes."

The underling commander looked up at Tuuth and asked, "What is *arsehole*?"

Grimacing, Tuuth pointed at his butt.

Chittering with anger, the underling grabbed Venir's hair by both hands, dragged him over the planks and slung him off the platform.

He landed flat on his back. "Ooooph!" All the fight he'd had left in him was gone.

Above, the underlings and Tuuth peered down at him.

The underling commander snatched the canister from Tuuth and waved it in the air. "I know about your Royal army. I know what this is. We are ready. Very ready to slaughter them all." The underling ripped the top off the canister, pointed it skyward and whacked it on the bottom.

A ball of energy shot high in the air, darting over the giant logs of the fort and out of sight.

The sound of the Southern gate being opened caught his ears. The underling tossed down the canister, and it clocked him in the head.

"Get a rope, Orc!" He pointed down at Venir. "And drag this *arsehole* back up here by the neck. I want him to see the devastation we shall inflict on his people."

15

IT WAS HOT AND HUMID. Just another day on Bish. The Royal Riders had just about finished breaking down their camp when a myriad of bright spots sparkled and sizzled above them. Every Royal Rider in the area stopped and stared.

Slim was among them.

Commander Jans held his hand over his visor and exclaimed. "Ready your horses, men!"

New energy spread over the spirits of the hard-driven men.

"Seems your friend hasn't perished after all, Healer. Look!"

"I'll be. He did it," Slim said. A surge of energy coursed through him. "Jans! What do you say now?"

All eyes in the camp were on the commander as he pulled himself up into the saddle. The Royal Rider stroked his long mustache, watching above as the twinkling lights from the signal fizzled out. When he raised his sword above his head, the rustling armor of all the hardened men fell silent as Jans opened his mouth to speak. Jan's voice was like a canyon filled with thunder when he spoke.

"Today, men … We ride!"

A chorus of cheers rang out, steel gleaming in the air.

"Ride! Ride! Ride! …"

Jans's war horse reared up on its hind legs as he cried out.

"RELEASE THE HOOVES OF CHAOS!"

It was a moment. One of those moments when the will of men convinced them they could do anything.

Slim, still weary from the sand spiders that almost took his life, teetered over to Jans.

"Shields ready! Spears! Leave the lances on the bottom!" Jans ordered the nearby Lieutenant. "I want two columns going up, a tight formation. I want them ready."

The man saluted. "Yes, Commander!"

"What is it, Healer?" Jan's said. There was nothing but fire in the exhausted commander's eyes. He and his troops were as weary as men could be, but the thought of battle gave them new energy. "Are you riding? If you are, you'll need heavier armor." He smiled. "Can you poke a spear or swing steel?"

"Neither, Commander, but I've been known to play the lute on occasion. Do you think that might help?"

"Not without a lute it won't, and I don't see one." He looked around. "So what worries you, Healer?"

Slim's long frame standing was almost eye to eye with Jans on horseback. "Trap, Jans."

"Aye, Healer." Jans shoved his sword back into his sheath. "We've been trapped for days, if not weeks."

"No—and call me Slim at least once before you die."

"Certainly, Slim, but elaborate your meaning."

"Maybe it wasn't Venir who released the signal. Maybe he's fallen. Maybe the underlings fired it off."

"So?" Jans stroked his mustache, eyeing the hill.

Slim felt silly. Clearly, Commander Jans had considered everything.

"Healer… er… Slim, keep these worries between us. I don't need my men's heads filled with doubt." He spat out some brown juice and wiped his jaw. "We've got the black fiends all around us now. Our best chance of survival is within the walls of that fort. So we are going to ride up that hill and trample every fiend we can find into a spot of greasy slat." He spit again. "And I wouldn't worry yourself about healing my men. You need to be worried about killing underlings, if you can." He reached over and put his hand on Slim's shoulder. "See you at the top of the hill, Slim. And if that gate's closed, we'll try to ride through it. Hope you make it."

They're crazy!

Slim had to admit: the sense of foreboding that had overcome him was alleviated by the energy of the men. The Royal Riders had survived this long, and any fear they had before going into battle had now fled. Still, how was Venir going to open the gate without the underlings finding out? It was a bad plan, a silly plan to begin with. But, anything was possible on Bish.

If I only had more strength.

Slim wanted to shape shift, fly into the sky and scout from above, but he didn't have the strength. He'd patched up several men and sealed some bleeding wounds. He was spent.

Over the next several minutes, all the men in camp got on horseback, their energy flowing and nervousness settling in their eyes as they headed up the dark hill of the forest.

Slim felt useless as he stood in his sandals and watched them trot by.

"You, Healer!" A soldier in a full suit of chainmail was riding his way. "Get on."

Slim extended his arm, and the stout soldier pulled him up into the saddle.

"Commander Jans charged your protection with me. My, I don't see how I can protect a man so tall, but I'll do what I can."

"I'll be careful of the low branches," Slim said. He reached down and grabbed the shield on the saddle hitch. "And, can I use this?"

"It should cover your neck, but I don't know about the rest of you."

Slim chuckled. *Might be the last laugh I ever have.*

Column by column, up the hill they went, leaving nothing but thunder and hoof prints.

16

"E ASY, CORRIN," A STOUT DARK-HEADED man said, "it's Georgio."

The man, shifty and lean, whirled his blades back into his belt. "I can see that, Billip, but I've no idea about the rest of them. Where did they all come from?" He peered into the sky. "Out of nowhere. Meaning," he rubbed his chin, "maybe Trinos is afoot."

Brak didn't know any of these people, aside from the skinny man named Melegal, slumped over the saddle.

Beside him, Jubilee hugged his leg, blinking, whispering. "How did we get here, Brak?"

He shook his head and slung the dark blood from his cudgel. They'd been running through the streets, dashing from corner to corner, avoiding the underlings, when fortune ran out and they were cornered. He and Georgio had fought like wolves, stomping and hacking at every moving underling in sight, but it wasn't going to be enough. They'd been a moment from being hacked up and forgotten. His stomach groaned.

"Who are you?" the one called Billip asked. "And where do you come from?"

As Brak opened his mouth to speak, Melegal slid from the saddle and collapsed into the street.

"Slat, Georgio!" Billip grabbed Melegal and dragged him over to the fountain. "What happened to him?"

"I don't know. He was like this when I found him at the stables. He had been fighting an imp or something."

"Nikkel," Billip ordered, "Fetch that pail and fill it with water."

The young black man frowned, slumping his shoulders as he did so.

Brak heard Billip speak to Georgio under his breath. "Mikkel has fallen, Georgio. Tread Nikkel with caution."

Georgio fell onto his haunches, holding his head. Brak could see sadness in the young man.

Eyeing the streets, Brak lumbered over to the fountain and took a long drink. It was cool and refreshing.

"You're not a horse," the one name Corrin said, "get a pitcher or use your hands."

Brak kept drinking. He also soaked his blood-stained fingers in the water, only to see the blood quickly wash away.

"Did you see that, Brak?" Jubilee said. "I've never seen water do that." Pale eyed and haired like her grandfather, Jubilee scooped her hand in and drank. "This must be water from the Everwell, but they remain below. How did it get here? How did we get here? Ew!"

For the first time, Brak noticed the scores of dead bodies scattered everywhere. Men, women, children and underlings were dead. Many mutilated. But the most disturbing figure was the black hairy bulk of a long legged monster that lay in the street, some of its barbed tendrils still twitching.

"What is that thing?" Jubilee pinched her nose. "Is that what stinks?"

A sad looking young black man with pale blue eyes walked over with a pitcher of water and handed it to

Jubilee. "That's the thing that killed my father." He nodded over to the corpse of a large black man laid out on the cobblestone road. "Who killed that beast to save me. Trying to save us all."

"Doesn't look like there's many of you left," Jubilee said.

Brak nudged her in the back.

"What? We're all going to go sooner than later if we don't get out of Bone. Besides, it's not like you didn't just about die less than second ago, Brak." She took a drink from the pitcher and offered Nikkel her hand.

Nikkel pulled her up.

"I'm Jubilee, and I'm sorry about your father. It seems families don't last very long around here. My grandfather…"

Brak didn't pay her any more attention. Instead, he made his way over to the woman named Haze, who lay alone on the blood-smeared cobblestone road. She was light as a pile of rags when he lifted her up in his arms and poured a swallow of water from the pitcher down her throat.

She sputtered and flailed, eyes blinking.

"Get that thing off me!"

He held her tight.

"It's gone," he said.

Her scrawny neck whipped around, left, right, high and low.

"Where in Bone are we?"

Brak shrugged. By the looks of things, they were still in the city, but where exactly, he had no idea. He was lost again. And it bothered him. All he wanted to do was find his father. The Bone with the rest of these people.

"Can I have some more of that water, uh… what's your name again?"

He set her down. "Brak. And sure."

She took another drink.

A commotion started by the fountain.

"Where's my hat, Georgio? And where's Quickster?"

"He's right over there, Me." Georgio was pointing, and he looked angry.

Quickster lay on his back, facing the suns, legs up, knees bent downward.

"I'll kick your fat arse if he's dead, Georgio."

"I just saved your arse, Me. And you better watch what you say to me."

"Get my hat!"

"Son of a…" Georgio stormed away. "Jubilee! Get over here and bring me that hat."

"Ah, the skinny man lives," Jubilee said. "Drat! I like this hat. Makes me feel smarter." She tossed it to Georgio. "But if he dies, I've got dibs on it, got it?"

"Gladly!" Georgio threw it at Melegal.

The Rat of Bone snatched his hat from the air and scowled as he placed it on his head.

"Where's that case of mine?"

"It's on Quickster's saddle. Now will you—"

"Be quiet," said a voice as smooth as polished silver and as strong as hammered iron.

Brak felt his limbs go numb.

A magnificent woman with platinum hair had taken a seat by the fountain. The edgy man named Corrin stepped to her side, eyeing them, guarding her. No one else moved or said a word.

Trinos found the group before her both interesting and colorful, bonded together for one reason or another. Like the rest of the men and women on Bish, they were survivors, but with something in common. All had been in contact in one way or another with the equalizer, a powerful force Trinos had put in place to keep the scales of good and evil in balance. Something that she had almost forgotten about. Something that whispered in the burst of hot air called The Darkslayer.

Gracefully, she walked over to Georgio and tussled the curly hair on his head.

"You seem disappointed, young man. Don't you realize I just saved your life and the lives of your friends?" She gestured towards the rest of them. "I saved you from certain peril." She folded her hands over her chest, waiting. "Well?"

No one moved.

The skinny man who'd complained about his hat was eyeing her with suspicion.

Billip wiped drool from his mouth.

Corrin's fingers twitched over the pommels of the daggers on his belt.

Even the girl with a penchant for talking was mute.

"Oh… I see." Trinos dipped her chin and waved her hand past her face.

Corrin sighed. "I hate it when she does that."

Blinking their eyes and shaking their heads, the rest of the people took a closer study of her rich brown hair, sun browned skin, common though somewhat exquisite garb, and softer Bish-born features.

The question now was, would they still listen to her.

"As you can see, Bone, your home and my home, has been invaded by the underlings. There are now hundreds of them taking over the streets, and thousands more below and all around us…"

Melegal raised his nose at her. "And who might you be, a Royal? A do-gooder mage from the castles coming here to what, help us?"

"Shut your vile tongue!" Corrin edged between Melegal and Trinos.

"Or what, you saggy jawed bastard?"

"I'll poke a dozen holes in you!"

Billip stepped between them. "Corrin, stay yourself. Melegal's not known for his manners." He dipped his head at Trinos. "Please forgive him and continue, Trinos."

"Forgive? Forgive what, you sawed off slackard!" Melegal said.

Billip grabbed Melegal's sleeve. "That's it, Melegal. Everything was fine until you showed up. Show some respect for our friend over there, will you? She saved your life, you know."

Melegal pulled his sleeve loose. "Oh, pardon me, pretty lady with impossibly perfect teeth. Thank you for saving my life." He bowed slightly. "Without my permission, I might add."

"Fool!" A blade appeared in Corrin's hands.

Haze gathered herself alongside Melegal, a long knife in her hand.

Words and expressions the likes of which Trinos never experienced before came forth.

"Slat sucker!"

"Orcen whore!"

"Sweat from an ogre crotch!"

"Your father bites the heads off chickens!

"Vomitus Pisswiller!"

Trinos didn't know whether to be amused or offended. "Enough!" she said.

They kept arguing. As if she wasn't even there.

She put a little more power behind it. "SILENCE!"

Everyone stopped and turned to face her.

"First, I am not a Royal. Second, I do command magic, much of it. Third, you don't owe me any 'Thank you' that you don't want to give. But, as surely as my suns rise and fall, you," she pointed at Melegal, "would have perished without me."

Nikkel stepped forward. "Couldn't you have saved us from that monster? Saved my father?" The young man's eyes watered. "Where were you then, Trinos? One moment you were here, and then you left—and the underlings came!"

"Mind your tongue, Boy." Corrin said, "She doesn't owe anyone here anything."

But Nikkel was right. She could have stopped it if she wanted. She couldn't be there for everyone all the time, but in this case, she'd offered these people protection and then abandoned them, all just to see if she could let it happen. People were dying on Bish all the time. Some in the most horrible and violent of ways. Was that indeed how she wanted it? It was, wasn't it? *How cruel. I wonder how Scorch is doing.*

Melegal looked up into the bright lights of the sky.

'My suns'? What a loon! Very pretty. Even smells nice despite the decay, but I've got things to do.

As Trinos continued to enamor the crowd by the fountain, Melegal made his way into the shade behind the walls.

What in Bish is going on?

The last thing he remembered was fighting the imp. Ordering it to stop killing Haze, who now sat slack-jawed by the fountain, hanging on Trinos's every word.

She's a scrappy one. I'll give her that.

Alone with his thoughts, he slid his back down along the wall and checked his pockets.

One. Two. Three. Four. Five. Six. Seven. Excellent.

The imp wanted the Keys for the underlings. The vile little monster was by far the most terrifying thing he'd ever faced. He wiggled his fingers and toes.

All there.

He took the hat off and rubbed his head. It still ached, but wasn't anything so sore as before he blacked out. And he'd been blinded too.

Slat. I've used it too much. Can I use it again?

He placed it on his head.

We'll see.

So much had happened over the past few days, he didn't know where to start. Rayal, what happened to her? She wanted him to find Tonio. Lorda wanted him to find Tonio. Lord Almen, he didn't know if that man was still alive or dead. But what had Rayal said on the matter?

Nothing. I can only assume Lord Almen is alive.

The image of the half-naked cleric emerged inside his mind.

Kill Sefron!

He'd almost pulled it off once already in Castle Almen's arena, but the cleric still lived. He rubbed his dart launchers on his wrists.

Perhaps it's time I used poison.

Closing off the sights and sounds of the other people, Melegal closed his eyes and mediated.

Put it all together, Melegal. What to do next?

The City of Bone was his home. He had no intentions of leaving it again, underlings or not. He had no desire to fight those nasty little creatures or that imp, but they were coming for him.

Perhaps it's time I slid out of here. I'm sure the City of Three would be nice.

Rayal wanted him to find Tonio.

Slat on that.

But she might be his only protection if Castle Almen came after him.

All Royals are the same.

He fingered the Key that had taken him from the chamber below Almen's study to the place he and Haze called home.

Now that's power.

And where would all the other Keys lead? What could they do?

I must know.

He looked around the wall, watching the group still gathered around Trinos. Brak stood tallest of them all, thick arms folded over his chest. Melegal shook his head, ducking back behind the wall.

Things were so much simpler with the big lout around. All I had to do was bail him out. Of course, he's probably the reason I'm in this mess to begin with. But with all the underlings, you'd think he'd be here in the thick of it.

Melegal contemplated many things: Haze. Brak. Trinos. The Almens. Rayal. Mikkel. Quickster. Georgio. The imp and the underlings. Hours later, he concluded his thoughts. Out of all those people, only one promise came to mind.

Get on with it, Melegal. Kill Sefron. The Bone with everything else!

The detail was horrifying. Trinos, despite her elegance, didn't sugar coat what was going on in the world of Bish. Instead, she made it perfectly clear that everyone's nightmare was coming to life. The underlings were taking over.

It was the least of his worries, however. All Georgio wanted to do was find Venir.

"Georgio, where are you going?" Billip took him by the nook of the elbow.

Georgio jerked his arm away. "I'm going out. After my family. After Venir."

"Me too." Brak stood behind Georgio.

Over the past hour, everyone had come clean, thanks to Jubilee who'd blabbed to everybody about everything.

"This is Melegal's sister, Haze, *wink, wink*, and droopy face over here is Venir's son."

Georgio, startled as he was by the statement, felt a connection. Brak had disclosed how he'd come to the city to begin with and lost his mother, Vorla, in the process. The big man who turned out to be no older than him had asked Georgio questions about his father, which Georgio had been more than happy to answer.

Billip put his hands on his hips. "And where exactly do you two fools plan on going?"

"South," Brak said.

Georgio nodded.

"Did you not hear Trinos?" Billip motioned at the woman, who was busy assisting the wounded with Haze and Jubilee. "The south is covered with underlings. The west is too. You wouldn't make it from here to the Red Clay Forest. If you're smart, you'll go north to The City of Three, Georgio. At least up there, Kam will look after you."

Georgio scowled. "I don't need looking after, Billip."

"Ah, you're still mad at Lefty, aren't you? Why else would you not go there?"

"Lefty who?"

"Hah! 'Lefty who' my eyeballs. Sheesh, you haven't been the same without him." Billip thumbed through the feathered shafts in his quiver. "As for you, eh, Brak is it? Let me tell you something about your father. Venir, that is. He can take care of himself. And it might do you some good to go north and meet with your sister, or half-sister. Erin, that is. I'm sure Kam wouldn't mind the help."

"What?" Brak scrunched up his face.

Georgio hit Brak in the arm. "That's right, you've got a little sister. Congratulations. Bone, Billip. How many urchins—"

Brak walloped in in the shoulder.

Georgio's jaw dropped wide.

"Ooooooooow! I felt that!"

Brak glared at Georgio. His father's fire was in his eyes.

"I'm not an urchin."

"Er … Sorry, Brak. But how many Venirs are scattered across Bish, do you think?" Georgio rubbed his arm and looked at Billip. "Are you a father too, Billip?"

"I don't think that's something we need to concern ourselves with now, seeing how the entire city is coming down around us." Billip rolled his shoulder. "Feels great. Strong. That woman Trinos did something to me. I feel ten years younger." He grinned. "So, what will it be, boys? And make it quick, before the City Watch comes back with the Royals to recruit you."

The City Watch, henchmen of the Royals, had made their demands known. Any able bodied man was to be drafted into the ranks to battle the underlings. They'd be given weapons, possibly armor, and the great honor of defending their city.

Billip and Corrin laughed out loud.

"We'll send the Royal soldiers back to get you," one of the two Watchmen had warned. "And see to it you make it to the front of the ranks."

It wasn't a laughing matter. No one, formidable as they might be, could overcome the Royals when they came for you. 'Either fight the underlings, or fight the underlings and the Royals.' Both Corrin and Billip had seemed torn, but after many minutes of heated deliberation, they had agreed that the Royals were still the lesser evil of the two. They had even spit on it.

"North or South, Nikkel?" Georgio asked. "Or are you staying?"

He shrugged and looked over at Billip.

"He's sticking with me, I guess."

"What do you think, Brak?"

Jubilee jumped in. "He wants to go north, to the City of Three! Right, Brak?"

Slowly, he nodded his head.

"Aw, is everyone going?" Georgio whined.

Billip slung his bow over his shoulder. "Before long, no one will be going anywhere, by what Trinos says. There's enough underlings out there to surround this entire city. Georgio, get out now, while you can, else you might not ever be leaving."

Georgio rubbed his rumbling stomach. "Well, a bowl of Joline's stew sounds awful good."

Brak's stomach growled so loud that Jubilee jumped.

"Whoa, and I thought my stomach was loud." Georgio eyed Brak. "I bet you can't out eat me."

A grim smile formed on the corner of Brak's thin lips. "We'll see."

"And what about you?" Georgio asked Billip.

Tugging at his goatee, he smiled as Trinos approached, followed by Corrin.

"I'll be fighting alongside her."

"That's sweet, Billip," Trinos said, brushing her arm along his. "But I cannot guarantee your safety. The underlings are many, and they could overtake these walls any day now."

"They say no force can take this city. We have the walls. We have the Everwells. We just need to vanquish the scourge that is among us."

"Every city falls eventually, Brave Billip."

"Yes, Trinos," Corrin agreed, "but no other place in Bish is as comforting to a wretch like me. I live here; I'll die here." His blades blinked in and out of his scabbards. "Just give me all the help you can give."

As Trinos, Billip, Nikkel and Corrin stood before him, an itch to fight overcame Georgio.

"I'm staying as well."

Someone laughed.

"Who's laughing?" Georgio said.

It was Melegal, leading Quickster his way and handing him the reins.

"Get your fat arse out of here, Georgio," the thief said, sliding a slender box from the saddle.

KAAA-VOOOOSH!

A burning building collapsed in the nearest district, sending up a tower of flames and grey smoke.

"Go, find Venir," Melegal continued, "and tell him when you see him, he's doing a lousy arse job killing underlings."

As Georgio, Brak and Jubilee headed south towards the stables, Melegal felt some wetness in his eyes. *I'll probably never see Quickster again. Fat Arse better feed him.*

Haze wrapped her slender arm around his bony shoulders. "How are you?"

"I'd be better if you went with them, Haze. You too, Billip. You need to take your knuckle cracking self with them as well. That boy can't handle the Outlands on his own. You know that."

"I'm staying here, you thin-necked copper snatcher!"

"Alright fine, Billip. I'll let you win, just this once."

Go with Georgio.

"You say you want to go with Georgio, fine. But he'd be much better off with me, and you know it."

Go with Georgio.

"And don't you forget it!" Billip blinked and stared at Melegal.

Go ... with ... Georgio.

Billip grabbed his gear and trotted after Georgio.

Melegal pinched the bridge of his nose.

Bone, that hurts!

"What just happened?" Haze said.

A confused looking Nikkel was chasing after Billip, strapping on his pack.

"Interesting." Trinos touched Melegal's cheek.

A tingling revitalization raced through his body. It felt wonderful. His headache was gone.

"Are you shaking?" Haze scowled at Trinos. "What did you do to him?"

Trinos grabbed Haze's hand. The woman's lithe frame gently collapsed to the ground.

"Take her away, Corrin, and see to it she's well cared for."

Melegal stretched his limbs. He felt better than he ever remembered feeling before.

"How did you..."

Trinos put her fingers to his lips. "What is it you want, Melegal?"

He cocked an eyebrow at her.

"Besides that."

"Can you get me inside Castle Almen? I have unfinished business."

His vest clanked when she patted it.

"You already have a way in. Just find a door and go."

You smell so incredible.

"I know." She grabbed hold of his hand. "Be careful. The Keys go many places. Many people seek them. Seek you."

"Sounds dangerous. Perhaps I should destroy them."

"Perhaps."

KAAA-VOOOOSH!

Another building crumbled and fell.

A squadron of soldiers on horses could be heard galloping their way. Like a deer, Melegal took off running in long bouncing strides.

Kill Sefron!

The Royal soldiers on horseback thundered past Trinos, Corrin, and all of the other 21st District survivors, but none of them saw a living thing.

"Did you do that?" Corrin said.

"Certainly."

"So, what are we to do now, wage war on the underlings? If so, we could use more people."

Trinos took her seat on the bench by the fountain.

"No. We'll do what we have to when we have to, but I think I've done enough for now." She stretched her arms out and dipped her toes in the water. An image of the lives on Bish formed.

Corrin's narrow eyes widened. "Is this what I think it is?"

"I would not deceive you. Besides, sometimes all you can do is sit back, watch, and hope for the best. You never know what is going to happen on a world like this."

17

B ATTLE CRIES AND HOWLS OF pain filled the air. Steel punched through bone and metal. Standing on the balcony of Castle Almen's keep, Lorda Almen's eyes were transfixed downward, in awe.

"Kill them, you worthless curs! Kill them all!"

The underlings had laid siege on Castle Almen, and Sefron, standing off to her side, could barely contain his glee.

Oh, you'll be mine soon, Lorda Almen.

He licked his lips, gazing over her hips and legs.

All mine and mine alone.

Her sharp words interrupted his thoughts.

"How many of those fiends are there, Sefron? It looks like hundreds at the wall!" She pointed. "What in Bish are those things?"

"Spiders, and those pale little things, I've no idea."

"Insects!" She recoiled back into his arms.

Oh my, so vibrant, alive … Delicious!

His hands drifted down on her hips.

Smack!

"I should remove your hands, Sefron! You pervert!" She clasped the plunging neckline of her elaborate dress. "Throw him over!"

"Apologies, Lorda, I only meant to comf—*urk!*"

One Shadow Sentry seized him by the arms, the other by the legs, lifting him over the edge of the balcony.

She means it!

"Lorda, your husband, Lord Almen, needs me!"

"Hold," she said. "Hmmm … hang him over by the legs."

Sefron clung to the Shadow Sentry's arm with desperation.

The sentry whipped out a knife and jammed it in his hand.

"Ow!" Sefron let go of the sentry's arm and dangled over the edge, held by his feet. "Lorda, please, have mercy! You need me. Lord Almen needs me."

He tried to pull himself up, but he barely managed to lift his head.

Lorda Almen wasn't even looking at him. Instead, her cat-eyes were focused on the raging battle below.

Every soldier of Castle Almen was fighting along the wall, ramming their blades into the faces of every underling that tried to climb over the parapets. Spiders climbed over the walls and into the gardens, carrying small albino underlings with thick shoulders. The heavy crossbows from the towers rocked out, filling the spider and underling creatures with giant splinters.

Sefron flinched.

A dying creature's maw opened and closed stories beneath him.

The men shouted orders and screamed for help. It didn't seem possible that the underlings could take over, not with one thousand, not with ten thousand, for Castle Almen was well defended. Between the towers, turrets and massive keep, the outer wall of the Castle could be defended from every angle. Archers and bowmen manned the towers and turrets, raining down death with deadly accuracy.

Half a dozen underlings cleared the wall, only to be feathered with many shafts.

"Lorda, let me up please. I'm sorry!"

Outside the Castle walls, underlings came from all directions, filling the streets as far as the eye could see.

Surely someone is doing something, Sefron thought.

The blood rushing to his head had turned it purple. Gazing around, he noticed the bordering Castles firing into the hordes of underlings as well, but they weren't falling, not as fast as they should be.

Slat, this Castle will never fall if I don't help the underlings.

The arms of the sentry started to tremble.

"Lorda, he's going to drop me! Please," he whined. "You need all the help you can get. At least let me check Lord Almen once again!"

"Pull him up," she said, not looking. "And punish him."

Sefron felt his body lifted through the air like a baby and slammed into the ground like a stone.

"Oof," he said.

He felt a punch in the gut. In the face. Then nothing but pain. He heard his blood dripping from his nose.

"One more transgression," Lorda said, "and it's over the parapet for you. My word on that, you grotesque fiend."

Through his one good eye, he watched the sway of her hips as she departed.

Mine, all mine.

Pushing himself up, he swallowed the taste of blood in his mouth.

We'll see who begs for mercy next time.

Rubbing her neck, Lorda moved across the stone floor and took a seat by her husband's cot. The strong visage of the man she knew was gone, replaced by a paler, weaker shadow of himself. Pulling the cloth from his head, she dipped it in a bowl of water and replaced it.

"Lorda," Sefron wheezed, limping over, "I should handle those dressings. It is my honor. Please, rest yourself."

"Get this toad out of my sight," she said.

The sentries grabbed him under his arms, lifting him up, toes dangling from the floor.

It was hard to look at the flabby man, with his bulbous belly and spindly legs. But she needed him, for now.

"Sent him to the bottom of the keep. If he causes a stir, send him out."

Sefron gulped.

"And keep him away from my servants. Send a couple up."

"As you wish, Lorda," a sentry said.

The cleric wheezed and grumbled, but Lorda found relief when the door closed, leaving her alone with the sentries. She was safe. She knew it, but her thoughts were troubled.

What do these underlings want with us?

Underlings had invaded her castle before, and now they were back again, forcing their way from outside and from within. And the other Castles along the great wall, they weren't drawing near the amount of attention that Castle Almen was.

"What have you done?" she whispered to Lord Almen.

He had many secrets. He always had, and she was more privy to them than she let on. But, the biggest mystery was what had happened to Tonio. He was still out there, somewhere, deranged and mad. And Detective Melegal, he knew more as well, but she liked him for some reason. Maybe it was because Sefron clearly hated him. And because Lord Almen shared information with Melegal that he did not share with her.

"Hmmmmm," she smiled. She liked men with secrets. She liked to find out what was inside them.

She was stroking her husband's cheek when two servant girls entered the room, fell to their knees, and bowed. Their pretty faces were worried, their hair and clothing unkempt.

She sat up. "What happened to the two of you? You look like urchins."

"Apologies, Lorda. We're cut off from our means."

The younger of the two clutched at her growling stomach.

"Humph, well you better keep your little tummy quiet while you rub my feet, else I'll feed you both to the under—Aaaaaaa!"

A pair of dog sized spiders climbed over the parapet and onto the balcony.

Thwipp! Thwipp!

Spider silk shot out from beneath them and snatched the girls. They kicked and screamed.

The Shadow Sentries burst into action. One caught his blade on the web. The other charged onto the balcony. Another spider scurried through the window and scrambled toward Lorda, its mouth full of dripping fangs.

"Eeeeyaaaah!"

18

DISTRICT THREE IN THE CITY of Bone was overrun. Underlings by the hundreds filled the streets, alleys, and storefronts—slaughtering everything in sight. One building burned, another one fell, all to the bewilderment of the Royals on the other side of Castle Almen's walls. Not a single man or woman remained alive. The humans who weren't killed instantly were burned alive. Smoldering corpses lined the streets, and their heads were tossed over the walls. It should have demoralized the Royals, but it did not.

Verbard hovered alongside his brother, silver eyes glinting in frustration.

"Jottenhiem, why haven't we penetrated the wall yet!"

Jottenhiem wiped the blood from his shaven head. "It will take hours if not days at this rate. We need siege weapons. The walls are ten feet thick. And they hold superior position from the turret and towers. These castles are made to hold through all-out war."

Catten chuckled, rubbing his chin over his lip.

Verbard sneered at him.

Chuckling now are we, you stiff?

He recalled the days he might have laughed the slightest in situations like this, to Catten's irritation. Carefree he was then, unlike his brother, who'd been all too serious about all things. But now, things were different. They had changed. He eyed the nearest turret.

"If it was aid you needed, Jottenhiem, all you had to do was ask."

Taking a deep breath, he summoned energy. Tendrils of lightning lit up his robes, coiled around his arms. His hands then struck out. A bolt of energy streaked over the wall, slamming into the turret, scattering chunks of rock and flesh through the air.

The underling army howled with glee.

"Excellent, Brother! I like how you are thinking now!" Catten said. He summoned his own blast of light.

Ka-Chow!

Another Turret filled with archers was gone, leaving a smoking hole in the castle wall.

This is more like it!

Verbard's black blood was like rushing waters. He let another scintillating bolt fly, striking one of the taller towers. Bodies of screaming men plummeted toward the ground, disappearing behind the castle's wall.

"What is that, Brother?" Catten said.

Several robed men appeared at the top of the keep, shouting and pointing their fingers. Purple and green lights glowed from the towers and turrets, covering them like a mushroom with a shimmering cloud of energy.

"NO!" Verbard said. He fired another bolt at the tower.

Ka-Fizzzzz …

"And there be wizards," Catten said. "I suspected as much." He turned to Verbard. "Seems they've drawn us out, Brother. I say we take it to them. Just us. They can't be nearly as powerful as we."

Verbard looked hard into his brother's eyes.

Are you mad?

"Our shields won't hold forever, and we have plenty of magi that can take them. For now, let's try something else."

He's been put into the body of a fool! I liked you better when you were dead.

Catten flashed his teeth. "Well said, Brother. I couldn't agree more."

Catten's smile didn't seem natural. His resurrected brother had smiled more today than in the past three centuries. It unnerved him.

Who is this underling?

Verbard sent a mental signal to the underling magi.

Hold your energy! Send more spiders over the walls! Onto those towers now!

One by one, the robed underling magi's arms went up, lifting dozens of spiders with their albino urchling riders over the wall, sending them off quickly towards the towers.

Let's see if these shields can stop livin —

Verbard jerked his arm up, shielding his eyes from a brilliant light that burst forth from the top of the keep.

BAA-ROOOOM!

The force of the blast sent him drifting back, slamming him hard into a wall.

At his side, Catten was dusting the debris from his robes and Jottenhiem was knocked from his feet. A smoldering hole replaced the spot on the street where over a dozen underling soldiers stood with one mage. The burnt scent of underling flesh was overwhelming.

Verbard grabbed his brother by the collar of his robes. "Did you know they had such power, Catten!"

"Of course I did!" Catten said, trying to push him away, but Verbard held him tight. "Only a fool wouldn't suspect it, Brother! This is war, you know! And their magic, like their rations, won't last forever."

Verbard clenched his fist and socked his brother in the gut. "You are a fool!"

Catten fell to the ground, grimacing, breathless, trying to speak.

"This is only one castle of many!" Verbard said. "And they have power! They have people! If this city organizes, then they'll gallop right through us! Go! Find Kierway, and see to it he penetrates from below. If he does not, we are doomed!"

Catten floated up from his feet, eyes like golden lava. "As you wish, Brother. As you wish!"

With a clap of his hands, a black door appeared. Catten stepped through and vanished along with the door, leaving Verbard floating there, uncomfortable.

Jottenhiem stood, staring at him with an odd look in his ruby eyes.

Verbard rubbed his fist. "I've always wanted to do that."

"Me too," Jottenhiem said. He formed the closest thing he had to a smile.

"Check in with your scouts, Commander, and report back to me quickly. We can't have the Royal forces rallying the city. Keep pressing the wall. We've got to find a way to bring those towers down."

"Yes," Jottenhiem saluted, "Lord Verbard."

Eyeing the top of the keep, Verbard's stomach started to churn.

This is a suicide mission. I know it!

19

"**N**OT YET!" KAM SAID.

Lefty tied the gondola off on the dock. He'd seen Kam broken and busted up but not beaten. However, now she was something else. Her red hair frizzed all over her head. Her robes were disheveled over her body. Heading towards the stairs that led up to the city, her sultry movements were gone, replaced by the gait of a man.

"Wait up, Kam. You'll need a lantern to navigate those steps." Lefty snatched a lantern from the post and blew on the wick inside. An eerie green illumination came forth.

Kam turned, her face contorted, her features almost unrecognizable.

"Quiet, Little Halfling," she said. The voice was not hers. "Put that light out. I don't need it."

Lefty gasped, shuffling backward.

What is going on with her!

Earlier, he'd seen her kill Diller, snapping his neck with the flick of her wrist. She'd left Palos in a pile of his own drool. And as they rowed across the dark lake beneath the City of Three, he'd found no relief in his liberation, only fear at Kam's muttering and arguments with herself.

He stayed back. She strolled up the stairs, the twinkling of the red gems embedded in her hand giving off the faintest of light. He didn't know what to make of it.

Is she possessed? By what?

The step groaned. She stopped and looked back at him, her eyes glowing with green fire.

"Did you say something, Halfling?" she said.

He shook his head. "No. No, Kam, nothing at all."

Turning, she growled in her throat and headed back up the steps, clutching Baby Erin in her arm like a loaf of bread.

Lefty followed, feet splashing over the dock and up the steps. They were soaked in his sweat all the way up to the ankles.

What is going on? I should be celebrating my freedom right now. How did it get even worse for me?

He wanted to flee as soon as he got topside, but what about Erin? She had to be in danger. But in the hands of her mother?

This is madness!

Staying back a flight of steps, Lefty fell in step behind her. At the top, Kam pushed the door open. The dim light of the alley gave Lefty new life. He had doubted he'd ever see the world above again, and now he was only steps away. Kam stepped over the threshold, through the doorway.

Don't lose her, Lefty. Don't lose Erin.

Reaching the top step, the door slammed shut in his face.

"What?"

Jiggling the handle, nothing gave. It was locked.

Nooooooooooooooooo!

"Kam!" he pounded his tiny hands on the door. "Kam!"

Suddenly, the door shoved inward, the edge cracking on his head, knocking him down to the landing. He rolled up to his feet.

The silhouette of Kam stood atop the doorway. "Get the sword, Little Fool!"

The door slammed shut again.

Downcast, down the steps he went, rubbing the knot on his head.

HURRY! A voice yelled down inside his head, watering his eyes.

Lefty's heart was pounding like a tap hammer when he reached the bottom.

The great sword lay in the gondola, completely wrapped in burlap. He reached in, wrapped his hands where the hilt should have been, put his back into it, and heaved.

How can anyone wield such a long and heavy thing?

He towed the Great Sword of Zorth behind him up the stair. The door swung open at the top. Chest heaving, he stepped out into the alley that guarded the secret entrance to the Nest.

Somebody should be out here.

The alley always had eyes and ears open.

A signal would get an unrecognized thief through. Palos kept strict control on things, and someone should be there to ask questions. It was odd that there was nothing. A stiff breeze whipped down the alley, bringing the foul odors of rotting food and excrement to full splendor. There was something else as well.

Squinting, he saw three forms slumped against the wall, the faint steam from the warmth of their bodies turning thin. At the end of the alley, Kam stood, back to him, chin up, observing passersby. Swallowing, Lefty dragged the sword past the three dead thieves. Their tongues hung from their mouths, and their throats were crushed in. He quickened his pace.

Oh my! Oh my! Oh my! Kam shouldn't be killing people. What is wrong with her? I wish Billip and Mikkel were still here. And Georgio! I've been a fool.

Kam strode down the street, startling the passing folks who came too close. They murmured and whispered while they scurried away.

Behind her, Lefty struggled to keep up, lugging the sword behind him. He wanted to scream at her, "Where are you going?" but the thought of doing so only tightened his neck. So he followed her, past the storefronts, past the high towers, to the edge of the city, where she came to a stop.

"No!" she muttered angrily to herself. The red gems in her hand flared with new life.

Baby Erin began to cry.

"I'll not do this with my baby!" Her body shuddered and convulsed. "Get out of me!" Her knees wobbled beneath her.

Lefty let loose the sword and rushed to her side just in time.

Kam's eyes rolled up inside her head.

Lefty got Erin just as Kam fell. The baby girl was wailing.

Kam lay sprawled out on the ground, bleeding from the nose, her once vibrant form harrowed.

"Easy, Erin," he patted her and bounced her in his arms. "I'll get your mother help. I promise."

There were faces. Some she recognized, others she did not.

"Kam, are you in there?" one voice said. It was Lefty; she was sure of it, but he sounded like he was miles away.

You will do as you promised. You will serve!

The voice inside her was angry, hateful, controlling. But there was something else. Desperation. It needed her; she didn't need it. That much she'd figured out. So she fought. She fought for herself, for Erin, to regain her life again on this world.

"I'll not serve. I'll not fulfill your evil will." Her mind thrashed against the unseen force.

You will!

Something grabbed the inside of her chest and squeezed it.

"Kam!" Lefty wailed.

"Mother of Bish! What has happened to this woman? She is sick!"

A crowd had gathered.

"Possessed!"

"Bewitched!"

"I'm not anything of the sort!"

But none heard a thing she said. Unknown to her, they whisked her frame through the streets of the dark and dropped her on the porch of the Magi Roost.

"You're on your own, Halfling," one said.

"Don't give up, Kam. We're home!"

You will serve me! You will obey!

Kam had agreed to serve in order to save Erin. Palos had almost killed her before she rescued Erin, but she had made a deal with the force inside the gems. It had assured her the safety of her baby. And now, men were dying. She'd even almost killed Lefty, and more death was coming.

"No!"

She would not bring more death into the world. She was not a killer! Was she?

"I'll die first!"

Yes, yes you will!

Her heart pumped slower and slower and slower. A dark force squeezed it. Burned it. Suffocated her with power.

Kam stretched her arms out.

"Erin, where are you? Erin? I will hold you. See you one last time!"

You'll see nothing ever again!

"Lefty!" an excited voice cried out. "Where have you... KAM!"

"Jo—line?" she said.

The pressure on her chest eased.

What is this?

The force inside her retreated.

She lurched up, gasping for breath, clutching baby Erin in her arms.

"Get some water, Lefty!" Joline ordered. "Mercy! Prepare some clothing. Kam! Lords! My dear, where have you been?"

As the darkness that clouded her eyes lifted, Joline's sweet face took shape. The woman was as distressed as she had ever seen her before. She smelled nice, like flowers. Tears formed in Kam's eyes. She hadn't hoped to ever smell flowers again before.

"You don't want to know," she said, coughing.

"You can tell me later," Joline said. Her friend helped her to her feet and led her to a comfortable chair by the fire.

"No," Kam said, eyeing the flames. "I'd rather sit somewhere... *else*?"

Her word froze on her tongue. The Magi Roost was not what it once was. Flies buzzed in the air, and the scent of blood was strong. Four men lay on or near a table with their heads blown off. She puked.

"Oh dear! Get a bucket too, Lefty!" Joline kept her strong arm around Kam's back and led her to the bar. "You look like you could use some Muckle Sap."

A bottle slid across the bar and refilled a goblet on its own.

"Who..." Kam's voice drifted off. An incredibly handsome man, blond headed and blue-eyed, smiled from the other end of the bar. Beside him stood a rough cut woman that looked like she made a living splitting logs.

"Joline?" the man said. His voice was purposed and poetic. "Can I be of further assistance?"

Lefty returned with a pitcher of water and a bucket.

The bucket clonked off the floor, and he began to shiver.

Kam followed his stare to the headless men at the table. She'd never seen so much blood before. Not even when Fogle mind-grumbled Venir. She retched again.

"Look at that! Just look at that, Scorch!" the rough cut woman said. "I've never seen such an adorable halfling before. Can I keep him?" She waved her arm. "Get over here, Little Fella!"

"That's Darlene, and the man's name is Scorch," Joline said. "And you better drink this and drink it fast. The pair of them have almost finished off the entire stash."

Lefty crept behind the bar and disappeared.

Kam sat up, clasped the neck of her robe, pulled her shoulders back, and shot down her Muckle Sap. There was nothing normal about these people. And where were all her patrons?

"My name is Kam. And this is my tavern. And I'd like to know what in Bish you strangers have done to it!"

"Easy, Kam." Joline patted her arm. "They did that."

"Is that your baby?" The rough cut woman, Darlene, reached out towards Erin. "Can I hold her? We've heard so much about her!"

The woman reminded Kam of a feisty raccoon.

"No. But what you can do," Kam said, "is stop answering my question with a question and give me the answers I seek." She tried to summon her powers, but nothing came forth. She was empty, the force inside her silent, hiding and waiting.

"Easy now, Kam." The handsome man, Scorch, formed the words on his lips in an engrossing manner. "We had an incident. The men over there sought to make sport of my friend, so I taught them a lesson."

"I just love the way his mouth moves when he speaks," Joline said. "Isn't it fascinating?"

It was, but not enough to overcome Kam's anger. All she'd been through. She was home now! She wanted answers.

"So you blew their heads off!" She chucked the bottle at his face.

It stopped an inch from his nose and settled quietly on the bar.

Darlene hopped on the bar and ripped out her knife.

Scorch snatched her by the ankle and dragged her down.

She landed hard, her cheek bouncing off the bar.

"Settle yourself, Darlene. This is her establishment, not ours." Scorch twirled his finger. Darlene rolled over the bar onto the hardwood floor.

"Ooooch!" Darlene bounced up, rubbing her cheek and hindquarters. "I'm sorry, Kam. I'm not known for my manners." She took another seat at the nearest table, groaning as she sat down. "It won't happen again."

"Here," Joline said, "let me take baby Erin, Kam. You need to rest yourself."

"No!" Kam said. She held Erin tight to her chest. "She won't be leaving my sight for quite some time, not after all I've been through." She eyed Darlene. The woman didn't come across as dangerous. If anything, she seemed bright and friendly, but there was something that just didn't sit right. "Especially a stranger. But, her bassinet will do. Fetch it, will you?"

"Certainly, Kam, certainly," Joline said.

Darlene started whistling and clapping her hands like she was calling a puppy.

"Here, little halfling fella! Come to Darlene!"

Lefty didn't appear. He could have been anywhere.

Returning her attention to the man, Scorch, Kam caught a glimpse of herself in the mirror behind the bar. The locks of her auburn hair were matted and frayed. Her eyes were sunken, and her cheek was swollen. She rubbed her lip that was split in two places. To top it all off, her robe barely covered her cleavage—or the rest of her.

"I wish I had a figure like yours," Darlene said. "My mother always said I had part dwarf in me on account of these stocky parts. But I didn't think dwarves could breed—*hic*—with other peoples." She closed one eye looking at Kam, shaking her head. "Ain't no dwarf in you, though."

Scorch chuckled. "Forgive Darlene. It seems she's over indulged in your Muckle Sap, which I must admit, is quite delightful."

"So, was it *you* who killed all those men?"

"With a single thought," he said. His teeth were white. Perfect. "And I'm sorry for the mess. I just don't understand why Trinos picked such leaky people. But I have to admit, it does offer a more profound effect."

"You should have seen all those people—*hic*— running out of here like their arses were on fire," Darlene said. "I don't know what was funnier. That or all those heads exploding. It was like blowing up pumpkins with whicker wonkers when I was a girl, 'cept there weren't any seeds in their heads."

That's when Kam got a closer look at all the dark stains on Darlene's clothes. She was covered in them from the waist up. She turned away as Darlene started swatting at flies again and calling for Lefty. "Here little …"

"When did this happen? Haven't the City Watch come to ask questions? There will be a trial for this! And who is Trinos?"

"The City Watch?" Scorch posed in thought. "Oh, I see. The men in the black billed hats that came to conduct an investigation. Simply put, they showed up and didn't see a thing." He waved his hand over at the men at the table. "See?"

Glancing over her shoulder, the main floor of the Magi Roost was in perfect order. The tables were cleaned, the fire crackled, and there was no proof of another living thing other than themselves. A chill went through her.

Bish, he's powerful!

"And I told a convincing tale about how the cause of the rumors and speculation most likely was those dreaded little underlings people have been talking about. I even procured several wild goose chases to keep the Watch of this fine city busy. It'll be days if not weeks before they figure it out."

"Goodness," Joline said. She was coming back down the steps with Erin's bassinet in her arms. "Where did all of those horrid bodies..."

Scorch's illusion dissipated. The bodies, flies and blood returned.

"... Oh." She shook her head and set the bassinet down on the bar.

Kam held onto Erin, keeping an eye on Scorch, fear creeping over her. The man wrapped a slice of cheese around a pickle and stuffed it in his mouth. It only made her situation all the more disconcerting.

Time to serve. Leave now.

"Can I at least change my clothes?" Kam said.

"Of course you can," Joline said. "Mercy, poor thing, as terrified as she is, laid some out on your bed. And is fixing you a bath. All the others left."

Scorch had finished his pickle. His eyes narrowed. "Who are you talking to, Kam?"

Leave now!

Slowly, Kam placed Erin in the bassinet and took a step towards the door. She fought it. Sweat burst on her brow. Her knees trembled.

Scorch rose from his seat, stepping into her path.

"Who said that?" he said, looking around. "I can feel it, hear it, smell it."

"Maybe that little halfling is playing—*hic*—tricks. What's its—*Buuurrp*—name, anyway?" Darlene clapped her hands and cooed again.

Kam was exhausted, and as much as she wanted to fight, she could not hold the force back any longer. It had dug in deep. It was taking over.

"You should move, Scorch," she said. She looked back at Erin. Joline was rocking and singing gently to her. She headed for the door.

"Eh," Joline said, "Where do you think you're going, Kam? You get back here. You get back here right now!"

Tears streamed down Kam's cheek. "I can't. I must go. I must pay my debt."

Leave now!

Compelled, she stepped left.

Scorch was there.

She stepped to the right.

He was there.

"Who are you speaking with, Kam? Show me."

"Lords, help me." She tried to lift her hand, but it would not move. Her lips sealed. Her body lifted up off the floor.

Whatever was inside her had complete control over her now. Its magic melded with her mind, summoning magic and sending her over.

"What is that light from?" Darlene turned around. "Uh! Look! Her hand! It's as red as the suns!"

Kam rose higher in the air, her toes floating above Scorch's chin, her head almost touching the rafters.

He snatched her feet, pulled her back to the floor, and shoved her in a chair.

Get away from him! Get away from him now!

The jewels in her hand flared with life. Her elbow cocked back.

Whack!

Power coursed through her arm. She punched Scorch in the face with all her might. His head rocked back. His nose broke. She waited for him to fall. It should have killed him. At least knocked him out. It didn't. His nose didn't even bleed.

"Darlene!" Scorch said.

He snatched Kam's arm and pinned her glowing hand to the table.

The wilderness woman yanked her shortsword from her sheath.

Shing!

"NO! What are you doing! STOP!" Kam said in a voice that was not hers.

CHOP!

Her jewel-embedded hand was severed from her slender wrist.

Joline screamed.

Lefty screamed.

"Is all that blood...

" Kam's eyes rolled up in her head.

Mine?

20

OUTPOST 31 WAS A HIVE of activity. Underlings, more than Venir had ever seen before, scurried over the complex, preparing for a full scale assault. Some were decked head to toe in armor; others' chests were bare. They all checked weapons and buckles and stuffed small knives into their boots. All he could do was watch. Above, they readied the ballistas on the towers and pulled large vats filled with burning pitch onto the massive catwalks. The smell of battle tickled his nose, raising the hairs on his neck.

"Hurk!"

The underling commander jerked the rope around his neck.

"Arsehole," it said. "Soon your people shall die. Soon you will follow."

Face beet red, Venir's fingers fumbled at the coarse cord of rope around his neck that burned like fire.

The underling jerked it.

Venir fell to his knees. He groaned.

"Is it too tight, man with holes in his leg? Arsehole."

If he got the chance to kill one more underling, it would be him. He hated that one. He'd never heard one talk so much before. He was going to rip its beady ruby eyes from its skull. "I'm going to kill you, Bastard," he said, wiping the spit and blood from his mouth.

The underling commander jerked the rope again. "Orc, what did this man say?"

Tuuth shrugged his big shoulders. "Something about killing bastards, I think." Tuuth glanced at Venir and turned away.

"Bastard? What is a bastard? Hmmm… arsehole." The underling paced around him. "A mighty tongue this one has." It chittered, glared at Venir, shook its gauntlet in his face. It pointed to one of its bulging biceps, then the other. "Power, Arsehole. Which one has more power?"

Crack!

The underling struck him across the jaw.

"No more words from you, Arsehole." It drew back the other arm.

Crack!

Venir's nose caved in. Blood spurted down his chin and over his chest.

"So which one is it, Arsehole Bastard? The one on the left?" It flexed. "Or the one on the right? I'll point, you nod."

Venir balled up his better hand. Punched at the underling's crotch.

It knocked the sluggish blow away with ease with its boot and chittered. A form of cruel laughter. The underling gave Tuuth another order.

"Put him in the stockade. We'll whip what's left of him when it's over." It eyed Venir, a smile forming on its jagged teeth. "Arsehole Bastard. Almost funny if it wasn't coming from you." It jerked the rope hard once more, lifting Venir from his knees and sprawling him onto the deck.

He'd jammed his aching wrists again, and he was choking.

Bone!

His face felt purple. A pair of rugged hands loosened the rope on his neck, slightly, and pulled him up by the hair.

Venir moaned.

"You should be dead, Stranger. I've never seen a man survive so many wounds." Tuuth eased him into the stockade. "What is your name? It should at least be remembered if I ever make it out of this fort. Heh, never seen a man call an underling an arsehole or bastard and live to tell about it."

Venir couldn't speak. He was beaten from head to toe. The stockade Tuuth shackled him to only added to the agony. Within moments, his back stiffened and burned. The rest of his body shuddered.

How in Bish did I get into this?

Nose dripping blood, he watched through swollen eyes everything and anything going on. Bish's ultimate survivor had to find a way out of this jam, but in his bones he knew his chances were grim.

Tuuth took his spot against the rail, leaning against it, facing him, grinning.

Turning his head from Tuuth, Venir tried to find anything helpful. A familiar face. An unguarded exit. He could barely think. Everything hurt too much. His head ached, and his eyes were swollen. His hands were almost useless.

I could still strangle an underling if I got the chance.

The platform was over two stories tall. His view was as good as from anywhere but the towers, and there were dozens of those. The ballista alone would be more than enough to skewer a man to his horse.

Coughing, he noticed the South Gate beginning to rise. It was a massive mouth of wood and steel, almost three stories tall and half as wide. It almost rivaled the main gate of the City of Bone. One by one, well organized underling soldiers spilled outside, armed with spears and small crossbows, disappearing into the green foliage of the woods.

"Won't be long, Stranger. Won't be long at all. It should be a good fight for the Royal Riders, but it'll be their last one. And it won't last long after that." Tuuth pointed at the catwalks. "Once they charge in here, they're through."

Hundreds of underlings manned the catwalks, peering down, waiting. No force would be able to penetrate their superior position. But the underlings had, five years ago. Deceived by their own, the Royals had opened the gates, and the overwhelming numbers of the underlings, combined with the Brigand Army, had overtaken the fort. The battle had lasted longer than it should have, thanks to Venir, Billip and Mikkel's arrival, but in the end, it hadn't been enough. The powerful dark magic of the underlings had confused the well-trained soldiers, and they'd fallen.

Over five hundred men fell that day inside the fort, their bones ground into dust. Now, such men, a small force, only a few hundred at best, were being baited into a return. And it was his idea, not that the Royal Riders had much of a choice. They'd survived in the Outland as long as they could. It was time for one last ride into glory.

Venir shuddered a sigh. He wished he could join them, but all he could do was watch. So long as he didn't pass out.

The minutes passed like hours while the entire fort fell gradually silent.

Venir lifted his head.

Hooves. In the distance, like a machine, they pounded the ground.

The underling soldiers stirred. Every weapon was in place. Every sharp object gleamed.

"They come." Tuuth gripped his weapon, an orcen Fang. "Stranger, let your last day be a long day. At least you'll see more underlings trampled this day. But what they do to the men that survive?" He shook his head. "You won't be ready for that. But if you want mercy, ask for mercy." He held his blade's tip under Venir's chin. "Perhaps I'll cut your head off before the underlings peel your living skin from you."

Venir didn't hear a thing. Just the thunder of hooves coming his way. His heavy head wanted to sag. His fingers stretched and crackled. His heart pumped a little more blood. But his eyelids were heavy.

Stay awake, blast it! Stay awake!

21

C HITTERS AND SHORT SIGNALS ECHOED through the spreading fog that was as thick as Boon's beard. He didn't need to see the underlings to kill them, but they needed to see him. He squatted in the crooked arm of a moss-covered tree. Waiting. Biding his time to strike.

Come on, black rodents. Your date with death is at hand.

An entire battalion scoured the grove now. Fogle Boon and company had departed while Boon held the underlings off at the edge of the cliff. Clapping his hands together and screaming up a mighty force, he'd sent a shockwave through the creatures, blasting them into the foliage. Now he waited for them to come looking for him.

Below him, a giant spider crawled, unhindered by the fog. Boon could almost make out the riders on its back. They still sensed he was near. He formed an O with is bearded lips and cast forth a soft popping sound. Somewhere, far away, a commotion stirred, sending the underlings away from his direction.

That should keep them busy.

He should have gone, left, fled while he had the chance, but he wouldn't. He wanted to kill them. Kill as many as he could. Trick them. Trap them. Slaughter them. They were many, but he was one.

Blast, I wish that staff still had its extra oomph. Just get on with it, Boon!

He muttered a spell.

On cat's feet, he drifted through the woodland. Up the creek away from the wary eyes of the underlings. His robes blended in perfectly with the fog as he did so. He stopped, heart pounding in his chest, as three underling soldiers chittered past him. With further caution, up and away he went.

This should do.

He pressed his palm into a tree, scorching the bark. One by one, he did the same to many trees in a row, staying parallel to the search line of underlings, all the while maintaining the sound commotion illusion to keep them away. It was tedious work, but the results would be divine. Over a hundred trees later, he sat down, rested his back against the tree, and closed his eyes. He could hear the chitters of the underlings. The sounds repulsed him.

Ah, what is this?

A breeze started to dissipate and lift the fog. Above, a pair of robed underling magi hung in the air nearby.

As I suspected. Perfect timing.

The wind pushed the fog down through the grove, down the ravine towards the falls.

Boon summoned a word of power.

The last tree he touched burst into flame, igniting the next one, and so on. The chain reaction was quick and devastating. The underling magi's spell to rid the ravine of the fog only hastened the affect. The wind sent the flames jumping from tree to tree. In moments, the grove was a crackling bonfire of smoke, sealing off escape for the battalion of underlings.

Laughing under his breath, Boon crept out of the grove. He could picture the underlings now, burning by fire or leaping from the ledge and plunging to their deaths.

It's a good start.

Zzrcak! Zzrack!

Two red balls of energy struck him in the chest, knocking him down. He rolled to his feet. Spit dirt from his mouth. The two underling magi stood before him. Yellow gem eyes boring into him.

He grimaced, rubbed his chest, and coughed. "Is that all you have for me?"

They flung their arms forward. Balls of bright energy shot out towards him.

Boon caught one ball in one hand, one in the other, and shoved them together. "Amateurs!" He hurled the orb of energy into the nearest underling, catching it full in the chest.

Boom!

Flesh and robes scattered.

"Perfect!" Boon said.

Vines burst from the ground, entwining his legs, pulling him down.

"Don't you have anything new to offer?"

The remaining underling let out a shrill whistle.

"Calling for help won't save you from me!"

Boon shot a green dart of energy from the tip of his finger.

Zing!

It punched through its throat. The underling clutched at its neck and collapsed.

"Blasted vines!" He reached down and ripped them away. "You'd think they'd have gotten more creative by now."

The grove was an inferno. Its smoke a black tower. There was no need for the one remaining underling mage to send a signal; the blaze would attract every underling for miles.

What to do?

Ahead, the barren landscape of the Outlands awaited. If he was smart, he'd try to catch up with Fogle and his friends, but something told him he needed to stick around. See what was going on. He had plenty of spells and energy left.

One more strike, Boon. If you can take one battalion, you can take two, maybe three.

It was his way. Trap and ambush. Trick and destroy. He'd drowned underlings in riverbeds. He'd suffocated them in their sleep. He'd burned them alive in fires. With magic, illusions and a crafty mind, he baited them. Fishing for underlings he enjoyed; killing them he relished.

Boon narrowed his eyes, scanning the horizon. He had no place to hide. He was exposed, but over a mile in the distance, another large grove of trees waited. Could he get there before the underlings saw him? And how much longer could he last on his own?

"I swore if I ever got out of the Under-Bish, I'd take the fight back to the underlings again. Let's go, old man, while your bones and muscles still bend."

Running, he headed straight for the grove, sandaled feet digging into the ground. Ahead, the trees weren't tall, but they'd offer sanctuary, a place to burrow in and hide maybe. Rest. Recharge. Renew the fight on the morrow. He didn't want to use all his spells either. He didn't have the spellbook to renew them. The ones he'd memorized for a lifetime were few.

A blur of black sped his way. Faster than the fleetest deer, it stopped twenty feet away. An underling hunter, armed in leathers, clawed fingers wrapped around the jagged blades of a dagger, barred his path.

Boon sent a green missile its way. A foot from its face, it ricocheted away when two more underling magi appeared in the sky. Another underling sped into his path, followed by another, and another. The shock troops had arrived.

Face grim, jaw set, Boon ground his feet into the dirt.

"So be it then!" Boon muttered a spell.

Arcs of light shot his way. The underling hunters closed in.

Rocks exploded beneath his feet. He dove away and rolled up on one knee.

"This is more like it!"

His beard bristled in and out of a see-through suit of mystic armor, which shimmered bluely around him. A shield wavered in one hand, a black sword of energy in the other.

They came at him. Fury and murder in their eyes. Armed and armored, they were the superior force. Experienced fighters. Killers one and all.

Boon's scintillating blade sheared through one's leg at the knee, dropping it. He gutted the belly of another.

Another stabbed its dagger at his chest, skipping off his chest plate.

Boon caught it in the jaw with a back swing. He was a trained soldier, had been part of the old programs in the City of Bone, before he took to wizardry. He liked fighting, but it couldn't destroy things as fast as he could with wizardry.

Zzrcak! Zzrack! Zzrcak! Zzrack!

Bursts of energy careened off his shield, his chest, his mystic helmet, chipping fragments of energy from it all.

The underlings' weapons gouged and cut. They were useless against his magic. Angry, they slung their weapons to the ground and jumped on top of him.

Boon staggered back under the weight and crashed to the ground. His black sword was too long to stab. *I'll try this!* Concentrating, he shrunk it into the size of a dagger and jammed it into an underling's skull.

An underling jumped on his arm, pinning it to the ground, while the other wrapped its arms around his legs.

Zzrcak! Zzrack! Zzrcak! Zzrack!

He jerked his shield up. Energy exploded out of it, cracking it apart. He kicked and flailed at his underling grapplers.

"I'll try this then, roaches!"

His shield transformed into a dagger, his dagger a shield.

He sunk the mystic blade into the underling's skull and ripped it out.

"No more chittering for you!"

Reversing his grip, he slid it between the other underling's ribs, drawing forth a howl. He extended the blade, shooting out the other side of the underling, cutting its breath short, jaws locking in the air.

Vines exploded from the ground, entwining his legs.

"Not again!" He cut them away. Huffing for breath, he rose back to his feet, ready. "Who's … eh … next?"

Gem speckled eyes, on the ground and off, had him surrounded. Rows and rows of them.

He banged his mystic sword into his shield.

"So be it then!"

Bolts of lightning struck from all over, shattering his armor, pounding him into the ground. Everything tasted like metal, and his beard was smoking. Flat on his back, his eyes fluttered open just in time to see an iron net drop from the sky.

22

MILES AWAY, FOGLE BOON COULD no longer see the smoke in the distance. All signs of his grandfather were faded and gone. In front of him, Cass's limp figure was slumped against him in the saddle. His arm held her tight around the waist.

"Cass," he whispered in her ear, "can you hear me?"

She hadn't moved, but she breathed. Fogle felt a great deal of anger when he got a closer look at her face. It was scraped up, bruised and swollen. She looked awful. *They'll pay for this.*

"Where did Puppy go?" Barton said. Scratching his head, his arms were like tree trunks as he ambled forward. "I like the puppy. He has two heads. Hee. Hee."

It was a good question, but the answer was obvious.

"He's going after Venir," Fogle said. He shifted in his saddle. His back was in knots already.

Barton smashed his fist in his hand

"The man with Barton's toys! Get him, Puppy. Get him!" Barton stopped and leered back with his one good eye. "Wizard, how are we going to find the doggy again?"

Fogle pointed upward. Inky, his ebony hawk was circling in the sky.

"Oh … that's right. Good thinking."

It was good thinking, especially this time around. Taking no chances, Fogle had cut off a lock of Chongo's mane while the beast was licking Cass, then fed it to the bird. The familiar should have no problem tracking Chongo, but he wasn't so sure that the sliver of horn from Venir's long hunting knife would allow Inky to find the man.

We'll just have to wait and see what happens.

Cass pressed her back into his chest. He could hear her smacking her lips. Reaching around, he put a canteen to her mouth and felt her delicate hands wrap around his wrists. A fire went through him as she sighed, drank, gulped and sighed.

"Is that you, Fogle?" She reached back, nails gently scratching the stiff hairs on his cheek. "Did you save me?"

Despite the weariness, he felt his chest swell.

"You could say that," he said in her ear, "but I wasn't without any help."

Without looking back, she gulped down more water from the canteen.

"How did you find me?"

"Barton heard Chongo barking, I believe."

Cass straightened her shoulder and leaned forward.

"He's gone, isn't he?"

"Yes, but I'm tracking him, see?" He pointed into the sky. "We're going right after him."

"Hmmm... I'm impressed, Fogle Vir—, oh, sorry, Fogle Hero. Seems you're getting a knack for this adventuring after all..." Her voice trailed off.

"What? What is it, Cass?"

"Where's Boon?"

Good question. Dead most likely.

"He held the underlings off while we escaped."

"And you left him?" she said.

"No, he could have come, Cass. But he didn't want to, and I couldn't make him, not with a hundred men."

It was the truth. The pair of them had prepared more than enough spells to bail them out in a pinch if need be, but Boon had made it clear. He'd rather save his energy to kill underlings.

Cass turned her hips in the saddle and draped her sensuous legs over his. Her long-lashed pink eyes bore into his. "He's a crazy old man, isn't he?" She brought a smile to her battered lips.

She understands. Thank goodness for that.

He couldn't help but smile back. Despite the bumps and bruises, she was still the most beautiful thing he ever saw. A sparkle was in her eye.

"That might be a mild way of putting it." He cleared his throat. "Cass, I'm glad you're—*mmrph!*"

Cass grabbed him by his thick locks of hair and kissed him. The long, hot wet kiss was beyond words.

She gasped and sunk into his chest. "I'm glad you're well too."

Fogle wanted to jump off the horse and have her right then and there. He pulled her in for another kiss.

She pushed his chest back.

"Control yourself," she said, "We won't have time for that until the danger is over. And that won't be any time soon. So, do you have any idea where we are? I lost track leagues ago."

There had been a time when Fogle took a great deal of pride in knowing everything. He knew all about the City of Three and its histories, its people, its place, the names of all the Royals and the wizards in the towers ... But now, stranded in the Outland, he realized that he knew next to nothing. Torn, he didn't know whether to be ashamed or fulfilled. It was as if he'd been reborn over the past several weeks, and he was uncertain whether he liked it or not. But, judging by the legs that hugged his hips, he was getting used to it.

She still smells amazing.

"Fogle," she said, shaking his chin. "I asked you a question. Are you fantasizing about me?"

"No," he said, matter-of-factly.

She folded her arms under her splendid breasts, pushing them up a little.

"Oh really, so you are fantasizing about someone else?"

"Uh ... no, never!"

Cass wrapped her arms around his neck, giggled and kissed him on the cheek.

"You're always so serious, Fogle, aren't you?"

One second Cass was expressing her concerns about the danger, in the next she was teasing him. He didn't know what to think.

She might be crazy.

He squeezed her thigh.

She squeaked.

But I can get used to that.

"I'm serious about you," he said.

She ran her finger under his chin.

"Oh, I like that, Fogle. I like that a lot." She turned in the saddle. "But, I am concerned where we are headed. Do you have any idea?"

I'm not a Blood Ranger, you know.

He wanted to say it, but held back. He was in charge now, and at worst, he needed to act like he knew something.

"My familiar is in the air, and whatever it can see, I can. If there's any danger, I'll know, but at the moment, things are clear."

Clear as mud.

The terrain was virtually all the same, miles in every direction. Rocky. Sandy. Sparsely vegetated. He didn't let Inky scout too far ahead, for fear he'd lose him. Instead, he focused on the more immediate threats, particularly the underlings. In the back of his mind, something Barton had said worried him. What about the giants and the dragon?

"What can you see now, Fogle? Are there any forests or streams near? I need to rest somewhere that thrives with life." She shielded her face from the suns. "This is not good on my body. I need water. Natural water." She slumped back into him. "I tire again."

The suns above seemed to be beating down on him all of a sudden, sucking his life through his tattered robes. Above, Inky was soaring west at a gentle southern angle. Soaring above the land, he saw only bone trees and cacti scattered about, with little hope for water or natural vegetation in sight. For all Fogle knew, it might take over a week to traverse the Outlands to get where they were going. His stomach growled, and he thirsted.

She's right. I need to find better shelter. We'll never survive out here if it's too long.

"Follow the birdie," Barton began to sing, eyeing the sky. "Go where the birdie goes and find the puppy. A two headed puppy. And find the man that stole Barton's toys. And smash him."

Cass's head flopped over. Exhausted, she slept.

It worried Fogle. What would happen if he didn't find water or shelter? What would happen if the underlings caught up with them? He sent Inky back for a look.

Barton stopped and turned. "Say, where is the birdie going?"

"He's just making sure no one is following us."

Barton sat his big body on the ground and began rubbing his feet. "Tired of walking, Wizard. Barton wants to fly now."

Inky was almost a mile away when he noticed something. The landscape hadn't changed any, and none of their known pursuers were in sight, but something was coming, something dreadful. It was a swarm of some sort. Inky flew right into it. Whatever they were, they buzzed. Had tails, stingers and teeth.

Fogle turned his horse around.

"Get on your feet, Barton—it's time to run!"

"Why?" he groaned.

Fogle was already galloping away.

"Run, blast you! Run!"

A wall of insect creatures was coming after them like a heavy rain.

23

T HE SPIRE. IT HAD AS good a bird's eye view of the City of Bone as one could get, at least within the district Melegal frequented. He climbed the worn stone steps to the top, scattering the pigeons as he did so. Brushing the cobwebs away, Melegal stepped inside the room and made his way to the opening, where the remnants of a window were still intact.

It seemed like a lifetime had passed since the last time he stood here, a place he came to often, for seclusion and fantasy. He envisioned a magnificent castle and family, relatives of his long past, towering over the streets. When he was young, he'd convinced himself he was a Royal and played his own version of Royal games here. He'd commanded the street urchins from this roost for a while, but as time passed he'd grown out of it.

The wind bristled his clothes. He crawled through the frame and gripped the lip of the tower top above him. Whatever that woman, Trinos, had done, he'd never felt better in years. Fingernails digging into the terracotta tiles, he inched his way another twenty feet upward.

Bish, I haven't considered this since I was an urchin.

Tiles slipped under his boots.

Slat!

His fingers gripped the edges of the tile, holding on for dear life. Three tiles skittered off the roof and shattered on the decayed stone walls below.

There are far worse ways to go, I suppose.

The high winds tearing at his clothes, he continued his ascent at an agonizing pace. Near the top, he stretched out his skinny fingers. A long metal pole, once a place for a castle banner, jutted from the highest point of the tower.

Stretch, you skinny bastard, stretch!

His fingers licked at the metal. His boots scraped, sending more tiles careening off the tower and crashing on the ground.

Almost there, Rat. He stretched. *Almost.* His fingers slid around the pole. *Got it!*

He pulled himself up and coiled himself around the pole. The first time he'd done that, long ago, he'd told himself he could do anything at all. But all he'd learned from it was that he could make an awfully hard climb to an awfully old pole. Still, he kissed it.

I'd like to see anyone else do this.

The viewpoint was unlike any other in the City of Bone. He could see the tops of the buildings and all the way from one massive City wall to the other. None of the intact Royal Castles lined up against the Wall of Bone had as high a spire. How this one stood here so long as it had, while the old castle and everything else around it fell, he'd never know. His keen eyes scanned the chaos.

Smoke from the burning buildings rolled past and beneath him. The massive gates in the four walls of the city were crowded with throngs of thousands of people. Soldiers patrolled the streets on foot and horseback, while squads of underlings darted in and out of the alleys and attacked. The entire city groaned in horror, despair and disbelief.

This place is going to the slatter.

He turned his keen eyes to Castle Almen. His jaw dropped open. Underlings, hundreds of them, surged the main wall. Every tower was lit with mystic illumination, and spiders the size of dogs and ponies scurried over the parapets, up the walls and towers. A chill raced down Melegal's spine. How long could the Royals hold out? And why were the underlings attacking there? His hand drifted to the Keys.

Sefron wanted them. The underlings wanted them. A picture of the imp invaded his mind. *What if that thing shows up here?*

Something was not right.

Think, Melegal. Think!

He squatted down, flattened himself on his belly, and crept back down the steep tower, thinking all the way.

Sefron works for the underlings. Underlings want inside the castle. Sefron is in the castle. Kill Sefron. Stop the underlings. Ridiculous.

As much as Melegal despised the Royals and all their cruel and twisted games, he knew the underlings were a far greater threat. Venir had shown him at least that much. Catching the lip of the tower's edge like a spider, Melegal crawled headfirst back inside.

Whew!

Alone in the tower, his thoughts went to his friends. He hadn't seen Venir since that last time he was here, and despite his anger towards the man, he'd like to be with him now. If anyone knew how to deal with underlings, it was Venir.

I wonder how Lefty's doing as well.

So far as he was concerned, ever since they all left, his life had been far from normal. If anything, it had gotten worse. He smoothed his cap over his head.

"Well, I suppose if no one else is going to defend my home, I'll just have to do it my—"

A small black blur jumped through the outside window over the top of him. Melegal ducked and rolled, the sisters out and ready. A pair of pearl white eyes greeted him.

"Octopus!"

The big cat circled his ankles, lay down and rumbled. Melegal couldn't have been gladder to see his most reliable friend. He reached over and stroked the cat's back.

"And to think, I actually worried you might be underling food."

Octopus stretched out his eight claws that twinkled in the night.

"I should have known better," Melegal said, rubbing behind his ears, "because you have plenty of lives, don't you?"

After the short reunion, thoughts heavy on his task ahead, Melegal made his way down the deteriorating steps. Octopus darted away when he reached the bottom.

Must be a big juicy rat somewhere. Besides me.

Aside from all the distant shouts of alarm and screams, the streets in this quadrant were barren for the most part. Even the urchins and thugs that frequented the remains of the abandoned castle had become ghosts.

Maybe the underlings aren't so bad after all. They're keeping the stink out.

Down the street he went, tugging and knocking on doors as he did so. Reaching inside his vest, he produced a Key. It was the same one he'd used before.

Hmmm. What did the woman at the fountain say? Just find a door and go?
From building to building he went, searching for a key hole, but none were found.
Drat it.
With all the pickpockets, urchins and thieves about in Bone, using keys to secure common doors and entrances wasn't always the securest way to go. Many shop keepers barred their doors from the inside because they lived there. Melegal imagined most were holed up inside right now. Of course, whenever a door was barred from the inside, it only meant someone must be home. Most citizens of Bone never, ever left their home or store empty.
Never cared to rob the places filled with the living.
He made his way farther up the street.
There must be a keyhole somewhere.
He stopped at the next block and stood in front of an entrance to a corner store, where a big black keyhole forged with brass greeted him. Melegal bounced the ancient Key on his chin.
It's not going to fit in there, is it?
Lowering the Key towards the hole, he froze. His neck hair rose. He sniffed.
Smells like a wet dog.
Wapush!
A tail of black leather encircled his wrist and jerked the Key out of his hand.
Melegal twisted his wrist free. *Who in Bone?*
Wapush!
The tail of the whip caught him by the leg and pulled him down.
Bark! Bark! Bark!
An oversized Rottweiler was snapping at his neck.
"Bloody Watchmen!" Melegal cried out. "Back off! I'm a Royal—"
Wapush!
Another whip wrapped around his throat.
"Watchmen! Ha! Hear that, men? This one thinks we're part of the local brute squad." A tall, limber man stepped into view. He was no Watchman. He was savvy. Buckled. Clean. A different breed.
The other two were stout. Menacing. "Ha! Watchmen, and you were about to say you were a Royal! Eh, Melegal?"
He couldn't answer. The whip choked his neck.
Bark! Bark! Bark!
"Heel!"
The dog quieted, but still loomed over him, growling.
That's when Melegal saw it. The insignia on the man's hand. His blood ran cold.
Bone! The Royal Bloodhounds are after me too!
Melegal had heard plenty of stories of the most vicious bounty hunters of all.
The speaking man squatted down beside him, long fingers stroking the finely groomed auburn hair on his chin. His eyes steely flecks of brown and green. Hair brownish red. Intelligent. Cocky. A good manner about him.
"So, a Royal Detective, as I understand. Pretty crafty I'd say, to be serving Lord Almen." He pulled a long dagger from his sheath. "Roll him over, men. Unfortunately, I need to cut those thews behind his skinny knees. Can't have you running off now, can we?"
Melegal started to speak.
Whop!
The Bloodhound leader slugged him in the face.
"No talking," the man said. Almost polite. "Now get him rolled over."

24

L ORDA ALMEN COWERED BEHIND A chair, trembling.
        "All clear!"
It was a man's voice. Strong. Labored. She peeked.
A few feet away, a dog-sized spider twitched, webbing spewed from its mouth and stuck to the floor.
Glitch!
The shadow sentry rammed his sword through its brain, bringing its convulsions to a stop. The sentry wore a helmet of black mesh armor that covered his face. The rest of him was splattered in spider gore. He extended his hand.
"Are you alright, Lorda?"

She shook her head, trying to stand, too weak to speak. Sprawled out on the floor, her servant girls were dead. A Shadow Sentry sat in the corner, coated in webbing, a nasty wound on his face. It appeared the acid from the spider's fangs had burnt straight through his mesh helmet.

You are in command, Lorda. Act like it!

Reaching out, the sentry caught her under the elbow and lifted her forward. He was strong. His girth reminded her of her former high guard, Gordin. She missed him. Her son Tonio had killed him, and Melegal had saved her, so she was convinced. She shook her head.

"Remember these words, Sentry: from this day forward, Spiders are banned from the Castle." She tossed her hair over her shoulder, pulled her shoulders back, and straightened her bodice. Outside, the battle was raging. Explosions, screams and the disturbing chitters of the underlings could be heard from all around.

"Secure the openings, men. See to it nothing again ever enters this room!"

A half dozen soldiers made their way into the room, followed by two more Shadow Sentries.

Making her way to her husband, Lorda lost her shoe. It stuck to the floor. She clenched her fists by her side.

"BONE!"

One of the soldiers grabbed a torch from the wall and burned the webbing. Lorda covered her nose.

Must all evil things stink?

She picked up a small bottle of perfume that lay near a table that had been knocked over, dabbed it on, and stepped in something that splashed.

"What?"

At her feet, water from Lord Almen's bowl had spilled, and the wash cloth from his head now lay on the ground with spider guts on it. Reaching over to grab it, she withdrew her hand.

"Disgusting."

"I'll take care of that, Lorda," the Shadow Sentry said. "Shall I send for the cleric?"

She glanced at Lord Almen.

"Eeeeeek!"

His bloodshot eyes were wide open.

25

"**N**EVER SEND AN IMP TO do an underling's job," Master Kierway said, flatly.

It was dark, aside from the glow of the small underling lanterns that cast shadows through the caves.

"What is that, Kierway?" Catten rubbed his gut. His thoughts were still heavy from his brother, Verbard, punching him there. Verbard had changed, changed much. He couldn't decide whether he should admire or hate him.

I'll get him back when the time comes.

"The Keys," Kierway said. "If we had the Keys, we'd have overrun this Castle already. They can get into anything, anything at all, even that door."

Catten remained silent. Master Kierway had a small army at his disposal, filling the caves alongside the Current beneath Castle Almen as far as he could see. All he had to do was get them in there. Time was running out.

Kierway chopped the top off a stalagmite. "Well, Mage? Did you come here to help overtake this castle or to conspire against your brother?" Kierway chopped another top off. "Or both?"

Catten lifted his chin.

"What are you talking about?"

Kierway flashed the sharp grey teeth in his mouth.

"Oh come now. Do you really think I believe you're on your brother's side? You? Then you wouldn't be the Catten I know. And besides, I already know my father can't stand him. Why else would he bring you back to life?" Showing off with his sword, he split a drop of water falling from above. "To see Verbard dead, of course."

"I'm sure there is nothing you'd rather believe, now that my brother has taken over your charge. The one you've spent years on and failed. The Keys. You dare mention them? You should have secured them, but you failed. And my brother, he's not a disappointment to your father, quite the contrary. But you are." Catten's gold eyes locked on Kierway's copper. "Sinway put you at my brother's will and pleasure, and I am here on his behalf. Now, tell me, why isn't this door open?"

Kierway's eyes narrowed. He slid his swords into their sheaths on his back. The master underling had a way of squeezing out of things, but at the moment, both Verbard and Catten had the upper hand on him. It only figured that Kierway would seek an alliance so he could get out from underneath the will and pleasure of Verbard. Kierway made his way to the door. Two robed underling magi were on their knees chittering an incantation, while another made arcane markings along the door's edges.

"It was only wood before when we destroyed it," Kierway said, "but it's been replaced with iron and stone, sealed by magic. There isn't even any key hole."

"So, how would those precious Keys have worked then?"

Kierway shrugged.

"Nothing to say, eh, Kierway?" Catten floated closer to the door. Over eight feet in height, it was more of a slab than a door. "Have you even tried to crack it?"

Kierway motioned to the battering ram propped up by the stalagmites. It was a six foot metal tube with handles

"I was confident the magi could get us in, like the last time," Kierway said. He picked up the small battering ram with a groan and tossed it at Catten's feet. "Perhaps you should give it a try?"

"Perhaps I should... Fool."

With a flick of his wrist, the battering ram lifted from the ground.

"Magi, finish your spell. Kierway, ready your warriors."

"They're ready." He folded his arms over the bandoliers on his chest. "For what, I can't imagine."

Focusing, Catten grabbed the handles on the ram and filled it with energy. It glowed red and hummed with new life, hovering over the cave floor. The symbols drawn on the door flared with life. The underling magi floated backward. The slab door groaned. The light of the battering ram became brighter and brighter as Catten filled it with more power.

No mortal man is more powerful than I!

The giant missile shot forward, striking the door with mind-jarring force.

KA-CHOW!

Stone cracked. Metal groaned. Parts of the door exploded.

A human cry of alarm went up from the other side.

Catten was about to say, "Get in there, Kierway," but the man and his soldiers were already on their way. Juegen in plate mail, Badoon warriors of all sorts, and albino urchlings stormed through the black hole, led by the Son of Sinway.

"Go!" Catten ordered two magi through the opening.

Yes! He clutched his fist.

The underling force jammed at the entrance.

He blew at the wispy fibers of energy that lingered on his fingers. He never would have imagined it possible, but in moments, he was going to be taking up residence inside the walls of the City of Bone.

Perhaps Sinway isn't losing it after all.

An army of underlings with access to the Current could hold that castle forever. It was brilliant.

We'll take them one castle at a time.

Finally, he would have one victory where his brother had failed. He'd penetrated the castle, and in minutes, it would be his.

Elation had filled him, but the underlings up front cried out in disappointment.

"Impossible!" he cried out.

The door he just destroyed had returned. He and the majority of his underling army were trapped outside. Kierway and his men were trapped within.

26

Allies and enemies. Jarla the former Brigand Queen had been on both sides of the war against the underlings. Unlike the Royals who had betrayed her, defiled her, humiliated her and destroyed her trust in all men, good and bad, she wasn't heartbroken to see the City of Bone under siege. Instead, she was thirsty.

Dragging her shoulder along an alley wall, carrying an empty bottle in her hand, she was making her way back to the stables. She just needed to find Nightmare and ride out of here. But there was a problem. She was lost.

"Bastards," she moaned. She stepped over one bloodied corpse after another. "Probably had it com-*hic*-coming."

Dried out and tired, she was rubbing her short locks of braided black hair when she found herself staring at a large road known as the Royal Roadway. A team of soldiers trotted down the street, away from her. She tried to get her bearings.

I know where this is. Hic.

Sauntering along the store fronts where the Royals used to shop, her mind wandered back to her life long ago. Her mother, a seamstress, had been the mistress of a Royal. As a little girl, Jarla watched the proud women come and go, but never desired to be one. She was cut from a different cloth, always fancying the work down in the smithy shops. Down there, as she grew older, she helped in a forge, along with her father who was also a soldier.

She recalled the last day she saw him. Taller than her, eyes blue, black hair long, he'd said, "Jarla, if I don't return, be sure to help your mother." He rode off on a horse and was gone. No word ever came of what happened to him, and her unfaithful mother moved within the walls of the castles. She had never spoken to her mother since. Instead, she enlisted. She had the right through her father, and she passed. Her steel was quick, her determination unrivaled, and after years of training and field experience, she carved her way up the ranks. Then, they betrayed her. She'd been the Brigand Queen ever since.

All the doors she passed by were boarded up or locked, and few of the stores had windows. That would be too dangerous. A pair of long-faced urchins shuffled by.

"Can you help us?" one said. He was pitiful, dirty, scraped up and trembling. "Our parents are dead."

She laughed, handed the boy her bottle, patted him on the head and walked away. "And soon you will be too," she said. She crossed the nearest alley, booted feet clopping over the storefront porch, and stopped. Something rustled inside the store. She pressed her ear to the door. A pair of bottles clinked and rolled. She jerked her head back. Someone inside busted a bottle on the door. Looking up at the sign that hung above her, she licked her lips. It read: Wine Blossoms.

"Where there's glass, there's wine."

Stepping back, she noticed the windows were boarded up and the door had no handle. She cast a glance over her shoulder, noting the streets were empty but distant sounds of battle and destruction could be heard. If anything, there should be widespread looting, but it seemed the underlings had spooked even the looters. The entire city was not itself.

Why not? Someone is in there.

She knocked on the door.

The rustling stopped.

She tried to decide if it would be best to be a member of the City Watch or a person in need. *Besides, I don't think underlings would knock.* She tried again, harder this time.

Knock! Knock! Knock!

She considered speaking. Saying hello. Sounding polite and customary, but such manners weren't in her anymore. Over the years, she'd grown accustomed to taking what she wanted.

"Blasted cowards," she murmured. She pressed her ear to the door again, closed her eyes and listened. Nothing. She was thinking maybe there was another way in when she heard more chittering. Closer this time. Coming her way. Her hand fell to her blade.

Now the little fiends show up.

Jarla didn't fear the underlings as most people did. She didn't fear anything. Besides, she'd seen them bleed the same as anything else. She'd battled them by the dozens when she was a Royal Soldier and found out that their skulls split just as easily as men's. She pressed her back against the doorway. The underlings, so far as she could hear, would be upon her any moment. And by the sounds of things, there were many of them, at least a dozen. If she only had her axes and the armament, she could have handled them.

Slat! I hate running!

Thump.

She heard a heavy footstep on the other side of the door, followed by the sound of a bolt scraping over metal.

She turned just as the door swung open. She took a sharp breath.

"Welcome," a man said. "Won't you come in?"

The man that filled the doorway spoke like his throat was full of broken glass. He looked and sounded like nothing she ever noted before. A hole dotted the center of his forehead. It was unnatural. She blinked and took a step back, hand still on her sword.

Neck cracking, the man bent his ear. "Seems company is coming, huh, Little Lady."

Her eyes drifted to the jug of wine in his grip, then back to his face. His eyes were dark, almost black, and a thick scar parted the brown hair on his head and went down past his neck, stopping at the armor that covered his broad shoulders. Jarla felt something in her bones that she hadn't felt in years. Fear.

"Shall you stay or shall you go?"

She fanned her hand in front of her face. His breath was foul and unimaginable. Everything about him defied reason. Her keen eyes noted the fresh blood stains all over his armor. Swords and long knives hung from his belt and behind his shoulders. His rotting smile turned her blood cold.

He shook his jug of wine. "It's been a long time since I drank with such a lovely lady."

She pulled back her shoulders. "And it's been a long time since I drank with such a fine man." She snatched the jug from his hand and stepped inside.

He closed the door behind her and slid the bolt back in place.

Taking a seat at the bar, the first thing she noticed was what was left of the dead people on the floor. "I'm Jarla." She tipped the bottle her lips.

The man bowed. "And I'm Tonio."

She almost spit all over herself. Something about the half-dead man's name was awfully familiar.

"Bad wine?" He smirked.

Her eyes flittered towards the door. Tonio stepped in the way, a haunting glimmer in his eye.

Slat! I should have snatched the jug and ran.

Staring at the woman, Tonio felt a degree of fascination. Her scarred face gave him comfort and solace. She wasn't like the rest of the people in this world. He grabbed the jug of wine she'd snatched and drank from it.

"Jarla," he said. It had a ring to it. There was something in a portion of his mind that clicked. "Jarla."

Her eyes narrowed, and her sword inched out of its sheath.

He chuckled. Even though his thinking had begun to clear, his memories were still scattered. "You can leave that where it is, Jarla. I have no reason to harm you."

Scowling, she looked over at the people on the floor. "Is that what you told them?"

"Heh, heh, heh… no, they would have died anyway. They were weak, but you," he eyed her athletic frame up and down. It stirred something in him, "are strong."

"You have better judgment than most men I know," she said. She pulled out a dagger and stuck it in the bar. "Just don't get too close."

Tonio grabbed another bottle and poured it down his throat. It warmed his bones, made him feel alive. But in the back of his mind, the nagging continued.

Kill the Vee-Man.

The image of Venir was still as clear as a bell in his mind. The man had mocked him in the jail cell, in front of his comrades. He could still see the man splitting him in half with that axe. The whistle of the blade woke him up whenever he drifted off. Only vengeance would give him rest.

"Kill the Vee-Man," he growled.

Jarla looked at him and said, "What?"

He slammed his fist into the bar. "Kill Vee-Man!"

Jarla jumped back, ripping her sword from her sheath. "Keep silent, you three-eyed fool! There are underlings out there!"

Underlings, they meant nothing to Tonio. Or did they? A memory came forth, the memory of the underling named Oran. Violet eyed. That underling had saved him after the giant dog's chewing almost killed him. That underling had found the Vee-Man before. Maybe underling help was what he needed after all.

He headed toward the door.

"What are you doing?" Jarla jumped into his path and stuck her sword at his belly.

"The underlings will help me find the Vee-Man," he said, coldly.

"Oh no they won't!" She shoved her sword through his belly.

Tonio didn't feel a thing. He shook his finger at the wide-eyed woman. "You shouldn't have done that, Jarla."

Smack!

He back-handed her across the face, sending her sprawling to the floor. He pulled the sword from his belly and tossed it clattering by his side. Outside, he could hear the chittering of underlings gathering at the door.

Jarla dove after her sword. A second later she was ready. "I can't let you do that, you split-faced bastard!"

"I must find the Vee-Man, and you can't stop me." He pulled a blade from the sheath.

Clang!

Metal crashed into metal. He knocked her swings away, parrying one after the other. With his other hand, he reached the bolt and started to pull it free.

"No!" Jarla said. She poked at his eyes.

Tonio flinched.

"Almost got me, Beautiful."

Jarla gasped and turned away.

Angry churts erupted. Bright underling eyes, teeth bared, poured into the room, surrounding them.

"Didn't you secure the door in the back? You idiot!"

Tonio shrugged at her and turned to the underlings. "Take me to the Vee-Man."

One underling chittered a series of orders; the rest bared their teeth, raised their weapons and charged.

27

O UTPOST THIRTY ONE WAS UNDER attack. Rider after rider stormed through the gate: three horses wide, twenty horses deep. Their banners streamed in the air, bright and colorful, a symbol of hope among the despair.

His fires stoked inside. Venir fought against the stockade.

The big orc said, "Say anything, and I'll cut your tongue out," then turned his eyes on the burgeoning battle below.

At the front of the riders, Venir could see Commander Jans. His long auburn mustache whipped in the wind as he thundered in.

"Let the Havoc begin!" Jans cried.

Perched on the catwalks and in the towers, the underlings fired. Crossbow bolts, spears, lances and ballista bolts ripped into the men. Hot pitch poured down on them.

Venir wanted to scream, "Turn back!" but he didn't have the throat or the breath for it.

The Riders kept charging, thundering through the giant courtyard, looking for an enemy to strike. One barrage after the next punched into the flesh of men, while other bolts were deflected by their heavy armor.

Venir grimaced. Many men caught ballista bolts in the face. Tuuth pointed and laughed.

Ride out, Jans! Ride out!

Venir's mind was racing. More Royal Riders stormed through the gate and inside. It was just what the underlings wanted. The riders thundered straight into the next assault. Crossbow bolts, heavy and small, ripped into them, separating horse and rider. One rider caught a bolt in the neck. Another was pinned to his horse. Pitch burned horses and riders alike. A dozen horses went down in an instant, and still the riders kept pouring in.

The well-organized ranks of the riders turned to chaos. The underlings splintered the groups, sending them in all directions. Over a hundred warriors rode purposefully around the fort, looking for something to strike. Something to trample. Something to kill. Another volley cut them down.

Blast their black hides!

Venir's fists clenched beneath his broken wrists. He'd cut off his arm to get down to them. They needed help. They needed to get on those catwalks.

Men yelled. Cried out. Horses whined and buckled. The Royal Riders' organized ranks had become chaos. Some circled the courtyard, while others tried to hide. But there was nowhere to go. The underlings fired from every angle, every corner. Venir felt helpless. Miserable. Standing there watching good men get slaughtered.

Run, blast you, Run!

A dark cloud rolled overhead, blotting out the sun as the southern gate was lowered and sealed shut. The Royal Riders were trapped.

"Won't be long now, Stranger. And once they're all dead, it won't be long for you either."

Venir would have stabbed him in in the throat if he could have. But he couldn't do anything right now. He couldn't even hold a weapon. He could barely walk or keep his eyes open. Through his hazy eyes, he caught something. Massive stone towers jutted up from every corner. Smaller towers lined the inner wall every thirty yards, linking catwalk to catwalk. At the bottom of each corner tower was a huge wooden door. The underlings cried out as one of these doors exploded.

A tall lanky man appeared, waving the riders inside.

Slim!

Commander Jans and his steed disappeared inside, appearing moments later on the catwalk.

"What's this?" Tuuth's jaw dropped in astonishment.

Spears lowered, the Royal Riders galloped into the sea of underlings on the catwalk. Jans caught two on one spear with his first pass.

Venir wanted to jump for joy. *Yes, by Bish!*

Underlings were trampled and gored. Men were pulled from their saddles. Underlings were hurled off the catwalks.

Boom!

Somewhere, another door exploded. Men surged into the tower and up onto the western catwalks.

The underlings were caught off guard. Flatfooted, they scrambled for weapons, only to have their brains dashed into the wood. The Royal Riders cheered and charged, tearing into the underlings with everything they had. Somewhere someone shouted, "Take the towers!"

One by one, the underlings on the catwalks fell under the heavy steel of the Royal Riders. The underling rout was over, but the battle had only just begun. The underlings were many. The Riders were already reduced to half the force they rode in with. The underlings, despite their losses, were somehow still at full strength.

Commander Jans was at the other end of the Catwalk, beside the South Gate entrance, throwing an underling over the railing. He was shouting, but Venir couldn't make out what he said. Were there still more Riders to come? Had Royal reinforcements finally arrived?

KA-CHOW!

An arc of energy struck Jans full in the chest, blasting him into the main wall. Above, a host of underling magi had appeared. Arms spread wide, fingertips aglow, they let the Royal Riders have it.

KA-CHOW!

KA-CHOW!

KA-CHOW!

"Nooooo!" Venir's hoarse voice cried out.

Tuuth back-handed him in the face. "Quiet, Fool!"

Men were knocked from their horses. Bodies of animal and man exploded. The triumph of the Riders took a sharp turn into a dark tunnel. Venir turned just in time to catch Commander Jans rising back his feet. Blood coated his mustache. He kept shouting. Pointing at the towers.

Two ballistas swung in his direction. An underling mage hung in the sky, guiding them. Venir's heart sank. The underling pointed at Jans. The big warrior saw them and beat his chest, yelling.

Clatch-zip! Clatch-zip!

Two long bolts ripped through the sky, striking Jans square in the chest. He was pinned to the wood. He shouted once more, hand rising in the air, pointing towards Venir and died.

"Ew… that must have hurt," Tuuth said. "But there are far worse ways to go. You'll find out soon, I bet."

The Royal Riders fought long and hard, but they were no match for the underling numbers and mystic forces. A wall of fire encircled dozens of horsemen on the ground. The horses bucked and whined. Riders were tossed from their saddles into the fires. More missiles from the crossbows and ballistas came, skewering the men and scattering others. Minute after agonizing minute, Venir watched the brave men get picked off. The underling magi cleared the catwalks, and the dead underlings and men were piled up in heaps of torn flesh and metal. The hot fort air wreaked of death.

Slim!

Venir didn't see any sign of him.

An hour later, the men of the Royal Riders could swing no more. The last twelve of them surrendered.

"Not bad, Stranger. Not bad at all, for Royal soldiers. But I think a host of orcs would have fared much better." He slapped Venir on his back. "At least you'll have some company. And who knows, they might have you peel the skin from them before they peel the skin from you." He snorted a laugh. "Now wouldn't that be something?"

For the first time in his life, Venir had nothing to say.

28

Lefty dashed from behind the bar, shaking his head, tears streaming from his eyes. Everything happened so fast. *What do I do?*

Everyone was screaming at Scorch, but he paid them little mind. Instead, he pushed his broken nose back into place.

"What have you done!" Joline screamed.

Kam's jaw dropped just before her eyes rolled up inside her head.

Joline caught her on the way down.

But Scorch wasn't paying attention to that. It was the hand that held his eyes. It twitched on the table. "Fascinating." Picking it up, he resumed his seat at the bar. "I've never experienced a talking hand before."

"Lefty! Lefty!" Joline cried.

Lefty stood there next to Joline, but still was unsure what to do. There was blood everywhere.

"Scorch!" Joline shouted. "Why, Scorch? Why!" Joline's tone was delirious.

Lefty trembled.

"Oh, put a sock in it, or whatever you people say." Scorch shook his head. "I'll never understand why Trinos picked such leaky beings." He wiped Kam's blood splatter from his forehead. "I can only presume it gives the dramatic more flare."

"Is there anything I can do?" Darlene said. "I can make a fine tourniquet."

"You could've not cut her hand off, you imbecile woman!" Joline said. Tears streamed from her face as she held Kam in her arms. "What possessed you to do such a thing?"

"He told me to. I do what he tells me," Darlene said. The husky woman handed Joline a rag.

"Would you cut your own hand off if he told you?"

"Probably."

The woman defied reason. Scorch defied reason. Everything Lefty had been through seemed to defy reason. But right now, Kam's bleeding had to stop. And Joline needed to stop screaming.

Lefty leapt onto the bar and kicked Scorch in the jaw. "Fix this, you—"

Blink!

Darleen stood by the table, dumbfounded.

Kam, Joline, the Halfling, and the baby were all gone. She wiped the sweat from her brow and swallowed. "What happened to them?" she said. She started looking under the tables.

"Could you bring me your knife?" Scorch said.

Darlene wiped the blood off her trousers and asked, "Sure, what for?"

Without looking at her, he snapped his fingers, popping her ears.

She hurried over, ears ringing, and handed the blade to him, handle first.

He showed her the hand, the gems embedded in it. "Is it customary to wear gems in this manner, Darlene?"

"No." She took a closer look. "I have to say, I've never seen anything like that before." She grimaced. "Looks painful, but you know, there are bugs that'll crawl right inside you and lay eggs. It's the vilest thing. One time this fella was drinking some jig back in Hohm when these eensy weensy bugs came crawling out if his nose and earholes. Huh! He screamed, I screamed, we all screamed for lice cream!" She popped her lips. "I got my chubby arse out of there after that."

Scorch, so far as she could tell, was ignoring her. He always did, but whenever she thought he wasn't paying attention, he'd say something to her. She'd been trying to figure it out, but she'd come to the conclusion that she just wasn't smart enough. Two minds were better than one anyway, she figured.

Scorch dug the knife under the gem inside Kam's palm.

"It seems my little red friends are determined to stay put, Darlene. Any suggestions?"

She propped her elbow on the bar and chin on her fist. "Maybe we should burn it. I can stoke the fireplace up over there, but let me warn you: it'll smell something awful."

The hand twisted away from Scorch's grip. Like a spider, it scrambled away.

Darlene jumped out of her stool. "Great Guzan!" Look at that thing go!" Heart thumping, she chased after it. She knocked over tables and chairs, diving on top of it as it reached the exit door. She held it up with both hands. "I got it, Scorch! I got it!" It felt like a dry wiggling fish in her hands. "Should I throw it in the fire?"

"Hmmm…" Scorch took a bite out of a pickle. "I have a feeling it doesn't want that. Bring it back over here."

"Certainly." Her arms wiggled. The hand was strong. Unnatural to hold. "Maybe you should cut the fingers off. I've got another knife, you know." *Thunk.* She pinned the knife to the table and handed him the hand. "This is the strangest thing I ever saw, Scorch. What are you going to do with it?"

His eyes lit up like infernos. He looked straight at the gems and said, "Time is short." His other hand became a brilliant blue fire. "What will it be?"

The hand clutched and writhed.

"I grow impatient," Scorch said.

The red gemstones popped out of Kam's hand and clattered on the floor.

"Whoa!" Darlene leaned in closer. "You know what, Scorch? Those things kinda look like eyeballs."

Dangling Kam's hand by one finger, he said, "A shame to see such a functional appendage go to waste." *Plop.* He dropped it in the pickle jar.

Darlene let out a snort, watching it float down, but a sinking feeling fell upon her.

Where did those people go?

"Don't worry about that, Darlene," Scorch said. The gems floated up to his fingers.

And that's when things became odd.

Scorch talked to himself, ate pickles and cheese, and sipped Muckle Sap for the next hour. He laughed. Scoffed. Mocked. His handsome features changed from one expression to another. Grim. Scary. Bold. Enlightened. But for the most part, he giggled and used the word 'fascinating.'

Bored, she began to clean up, whistling a lullaby as she picked up the chairs and tables she'd knocked over. She stopped at the dead bodies and smashed a few flies between her hands.

"How am I going to dispose of these guys?"

She had an idea.

"Uh, Scorch?"

He sat there, eyes transfixed on the red stones he'd set back on the bar.

"Scorch, could you?"

Slowly, he turned, a dark look in his eye.

Walking over to him, she tossed a rag over the gemstones.

He blinked at her, eyes regaining their luster. "What is it?"

She jutted her thumb at the headless bodies.

"Oh," he sighed. "Just find some sand and sprinkle it on them."

"Sand?"

"Never mind," he said. He snatched the rag off the gemstones.

Puff! Puff! Puff! Puff! Puff!

"Whoa!" she said.

The dead men had turned to statues of sand. Walking over, she poked the nearest one and watched it implode over the planks on the floor.

"Whoa. Thanks, Scorch."

But he wasn't paying her any mind. Instead, he rolled the gemstones in between his fingers. "I've got to see this." He said more, but that was all she understood.

She tried to ignore the butterflies in her stomach. She'd never had those before, but Scorch had never acted this way before either.

The door to the entry way cracked open, and one of their followers peeped his gray-haired head through.

"Darlene, er … well, any needs?"

She placed her hands on her hips. "Drag in two more of you, and find me a mop and broom."

Glancing over at Scorch, she almost peed herself. Only the hand and the pickle jar remained. Scorch was gone with the red gems.

"I got a bad feeling about this."

29

"**W**HAT IN BISH ARE THOSE things?" Fogle yelled. But Cass wasn't listening. She wasn't even moving. "Cass!" Nothing.

Ahead, Barton's giant feet shook the ground. Running full stride, his arms swung like giant hammers at his sides.

Fogle whipped the reins on his horse. "Eeyah!"

Behind him, the angry buzz of the insects got louder, like a hunger. Fogle had heard about swarms before. He recalled the stories of insects that picked the flesh clean from the bone. Inky's vision of the insects, each as long as Fogle's finger, was a chilling site. Sharp rows of snapping teeth, black bug eyes, wings and a stinger like a scorpion for a tail. He glanced over his shoulder.

"They're getting closer! Eeyah!"

They'd made it over a mile when his horse began to labor for breath. Ahead, Barton began to clutch at his side. *No! Think of something, Fogle!*

No spells came to mind that could put a stop to thousands of insects, and anything from the spellbook would take too much time.

Looking over his shoulder, he screamed again. "Cass!" The insects were getting closer. His horse was slowing, and ahead, Barton's feet stumbled. "Come on, Druid! I need you! You're the one that's supposed be able to talk to things in this world."

The buzzing became louder, not so much a buzz, but more like the sound of thousands of tiny metal scissors opening and closing. Fogle fought the image of his flesh being ripped from his skin one tiny chunk at a time, a thousand times over.

Do something, Wizard! What had Mood said? *You can die doing something or nothing. It's your life. Make it count.*

Fogle flung his arm back, flinging tendrils of energy from his fingertips. The energy punched into the grey swarm, creating a hole. An eruption of tiny explosions in the sky followed. A second later, the hole closed. Fogle shook his head. He was angry. Every time he overcame one obstacle, he found himself faced with another that he was even less prepared for.

You can't be ready for everything. Boon had said. *Just be ready to act.*

"I'll be ready to act, all right. Act dead!" He whipped the reins. "Barton! Think of something. We're about to have company!"

He couldn't tell if Barton could hear him on not, but the giant slowed and turned.

"Keep moving, Giant!"

Barton just leered at him, clutching at his sides, huffing for breath.

"What are you doing?" Fogle said, riding up to him, stopping.

"No more running, Wizard. No more. Wooooo. Barton tired." His hands fell to his knees.

Fogle tried to summon his energy but couldn't think of anything to cast. It was too late. The swarm was only seconds away. He pulled Cass tight and looked up at Barton.

"I guess this is good-bye, Barton."

Barton scooped out two massive handfuls of dirt from the ground and reached for him.

"What are you doi—ingggg!"

Barton picked them both up off the horse, set them in a large divot in the ground, and huddled over them.

Fogle tried to squirm away, but an infant could have done better. "Get off—mrph!"

Everything went black. Fogle and Cass were trapped beneath the hot sweaty mass of Barton's belly flesh.

I'm going to suffocate in sweaty lard!

Barton's body groaned and twitched over top of him and Cass. He could hear the muffled cries of the deformed giant's moans of pain. All he could imagine was the insects eating Barton alive. How long would Barton hold them off until they got to him? Would he suffocate first?

"Cass." He caught a drop of Barton's sweat in his mouth. "Yecht!"

He tried to think of something. Anything that might help. He needed air. Barton needed help. He grabbed Cass's face and stroked it tenderly. He held her tight. Above him, Barton's big body shuddered. He didn't know who to feel worse for, the giant or himself. Inside him, he wanted to fight, but there was nothing he could do.

This is pathetic.

A minute passed, then two. Barton's moans and cries subsided slowly.

He's dying! The bugs will be through any moment.

Barton's body stopped shuddering. The only thing Fogle could feel or hear was his own heartbeat. He pushed up on Barton. "Let us out!" He drove his knee into his belly. What if Barton died and they were trapped? "No! Blast it, Barton, get up!"

He summoned his energy. His fist lit up and he drove it into Barton's belly.

Ssssrack!

Barton's body lurched upward and rolled over. Fogle gasped, basking in the white daylight that greeted him. He could breathe again! One last breath of sweet air before the bugs got him. He crawled out of the hole that Barton had dug and scanned the sky. It was empty aside from a few clouds. The humming of bugs was gone.

"Where did they go?" he said, spinning around.

Barton groaned. The big giant lay flat on his back with hundreds, if not thousands, of red welts all over his body. "Oooooh," he moaned. "My belly hurts."

Fogle stood over his side and patted his belly. "Uh… looks like you've had too much bug poison. I'm sure it will go away."

Barton rolled his big neck his way, staring at him with his one good eye. "You alright, Wizard? Barton helped you, right?"

"Indeed, Barton. I'd be dead without you."

"Pretty lady alright too?"

"She just needs something better to drink than your sweat, but she should be fine. Can you get up?"

Slowly, Barton rose to a sitting position.

"Belly hurts," he said, rubbing it. "Like I got whopped by a giant. Did you do that?"

Fogle turned away. "Have you seen the horse?"

Barton pointed east.

"Ah," Fogle said. Making his way over to the mount that stood basking in the haze of the hot day. "Oh." When he got close, a chill ran through him. The horse still stood with the saddle and his bags intact, but every ounce of flesh and skin had been picked clean. Only the bones remained. He glanced back at the giant. Barton's thick skin had saved them all. All but the horse, anyway. He grabbed what gear he needed, headed back, and tried to make Cass as comfortable as he could.

"How are you feeling, Barton?"

"Dizzy. Little bugs stung me and bit me, but Barton too tough. Too strong. Belly still hurts though. They didn't bite my belly. I don't understand why it hurts." Barton scratched his head. "Was something else underneath me with you? Huh, Wizard?"

Feeling guilty, Fogle was ready to confess.

"Barton, I—"

The giant's eye closed, and he fell backward.

Thoom!

"Great! Just great!" Fogle put his hand on Barton's chest. It still rose and fell. "I guess he's alive." He kicked the dirt.

Now what, Wizard? Now what?

Cass had curled up like a baby, and Barton began to snore, leaving him as alone as he ever felt before. He found a place beside Cass in Barton's ditch and took a seat. *Inky!*

Closing his eyes, he tried to summon the familiar. The last thing he remembered was the bird flying into the swarm, and he'd completely forgotten about the bird after that. He gave it a minute or two and gave up. He pulled at the locks of his hair with both hands.

What have I done? What have I done? What have I done?

Little more than an hour ago, he had things under complete control. Cass was fine, Barton cheerful and his horse reliable transportation under his legs. They were going after Venir, the Darkslayer. Following the dog Chongo. His ebony hawk would lead straight to them.

Now, all of his plans were crushed. Inky was gone. Barton and Cass were almost comatose, and his horse was dead. He could only think of one thing. Well, two things.

Go east. Or sleep—and wake up dead.

Going east should have been simple, but it wasn't. The suns and moons didn't always rise in the same places, not than anyone ever thought about using them as a compass. Mood had always complained that getting around Bish would be easier if the suns and moons rose in the same places. Instead, you had to know the terrain.

Look for the signs.

A keen eye could see for miles in any direction, and the layout of Bish was simple. All you had to know was where places were and how to get there. Just don't be too forgetful. To make matters worse, some days, especially in the Outlands, were longer than others.

Probably have our bones picked clean out here.

He noted a bird of some sort circling above.

Great. Probably man-eating condors. Let's hope I can handle them.

Fogle pulled his spellbook from his pack. It fit on his hand at first, then, opening and closing, it got bigger and bigger, until he had to set it on his lap. He thumbed through the pages.

There ought to be something in here.

Meanwhile, Barton's snoring made the ground rumble.

Page by page, Fogle scanned his book, finding nothing immediately useful. He'd need more time and rest to learn anything new, and he had other spells in mind he had to keep until he used them. He nudged Cass. Her pale pink lips were cracked and dried. He poured a little water from his canteen on her lips, bringing forth a sigh. *Poor thing.* The feisty woman seemed so vulnerable right now, leaving him uncomfortable.

He stuck his nose back inside his book and read through more of Boon's spells. A bad feeling crawled through him. Was Boon still alive or not? The old man was crazy enough to fight an entire army of underlings and willing to die for it.

Bish, don't' let me get that crazy.

Spell after spell he read, not recalling hardly any of them. He felt ashamed now at his reluctance. Boon's written pages were a treasure that never should have been ignored. He giggled at one of them. *Breast replenishment.* With a special note. *For aging wife.* Fogle shook his head. Much of the magic in the City of Three was used to upkeep images, a practice which Fogle, unlike most, found detestable. He wondered if Boon was one of those who created such a spell to begin with. Page after page he went. Transfigurations. Polymorph. Elementals. Enchantments. Transmutations. Conjurations. A dozen forms of evocations and illusions, and so on. The ones that were most effective on underlings were highlighted. But there wasn't anything he could find that would give him directions. Fogle marked a few pages and closed the book.

"Now what, Cass? Now what?"

She didn't stir.

If only Mood or Eethum were here.

He sat for a while, before he got back up. Nightfall would be coming soon.

"Don't worry, I'll take the first watch." He stretched out his arms and yawned. "No, no, you two go ahead and rest. I'll take the second one too." Instinctively, he started to gather sticks and pile them up together. "What am I doing? I can't build a fire now, can I?" He shook his head. "Am I talking out loud to myself? Am I?"

I can't be. I can't be. I can't be.

He poked one of the nasty red stings on Barton's arm with a stick. Nothing. Barton kept snoring. "Well, I won't fall asleep with you around, that's for sure. And we can't have you drawing any underlings, giants, nasty bugs or dragons straight to us either." With both hands, he tried to pinch Barton's nose shut.

Barton snorted and started to roll over.

"Not on top of me!" he said, jumping to the side.

Barton lay on his stomach now, no longer snoring.

"Sheesh!" Fogle got up and dusted his tattered robes off. "Aw, what's the point?" He snatched up the spellbook. "I need something else to keep watch in case I fall asleep," he said, yawning.

Every scrape, bump, and bruise began to settle in on him, and he wondered if the Outland was making him tougher or deteriorating him faster.

I'm no dwarf. That's for sure.

Instead, he was a man. A lost man. A lamb in the Outland waiting to be devoured by Bish.

"There's always tomorrow if we live that long," he said to Cass. Something strange howled in the wind. He eyed the sky. "I really hope you wake back up by then, because, even though you're small, I can't carry you too far."

Barton stirred and farted.

"Ah!" Fogle held his nose. "Hmmm… I think I have an idea. Did a fart inspire that?"

Stop talking to yourself!

Over the next hour, he dove into the spellbook, eyes pouring over and committing to memory what he could. He muttered a cantrip after his final yawn. A Wizard's Alarm should wake him if anything got too close. He needed rest. He had to risk it. Besides, he couldn't wake them up anyway. "Forgive me, Cass." After kissing her forehead, he closed his eyes and drifted off to sleep, oblivious to a unique sound in the distance.

Whump. Whump. Whump…

30

MELEGAL SQUIRMED. HE WAS ONLY a few seconds from being a cripple if he didn't twist away.

"My, you're a shifty one. I'll give you that," the leader said. "Like a big fish in man's clothing."

Think of something, Thief!

Melegal had been captured before, sometimes willing, sometimes not. But when being pinned down by a superior force there were a couple of ways you could play it. Fight with everything you had, or panic.

"Help!" he screamed.

Or at least act like you were panicking.

One of the Blood Hounds slugged him in the gut.

"Ooof!" Melegal groaned.

The one that hit him said, "His stomach's harder than old leather, Creed."

"Is that so?" Creed drew back and also socked him in the gut. "That ought to soften it some. Sorry, nothing personal. Just business, squirmy one." He pinched Melegal's face in his hand, grabbed his hat, and stuffed it in his mouth. "Any more of that, and your gonads will be dog food. Understand, Detective?"

Melegal blinked twice.

"Good. Now, be peaceful about this, or we'll be forced to kill you."

Melegal's eyes widened.

"That's right, but you're wanted alive rather than dead. Good thing for you."

One of the dogs snapped in his face. He resisted less and began to turn over. He forced a hardy cough, spit out his hat, and screamed.

"Blast it! Just knock the man out," Creed said. His voice was refined. Confident. Patient. "Hand me your black jack. We've enough fooling with this. Underlings might be crawling all over us if we're not more careful."

Melegal coughed again, dodging.

He felt Creed's hand rise up with the black jack.

Now or die!

Slick as a snake, Melegal twisted free of all of them and took aim.

Zing! Zing! Zing!

"Aarggh!"

The dart launchers caught one man holding him in the face and Creed in the chin.

He rolled beneath another man's fist.

Zing! Zing! Zing!

The man wailed out, clutching at his eyes.

Zing!

One dog yelped.

Zing!

Another dog fled, dart protruding from its neck.

"Yer gonna pay for that," one said, ripping a heavy sword from his scabbard.

Melegal slid out his swords, the Sisters, and faced off the goon.

"Nice trick, Detective," Creed said, plucking the dart from his beard, watching. "But hardly effective."

Melegal shrugged. "What the dart won't do, the poison will?"

Creed drew his longsword and smiled.

"Then you'll be going down with us."

Run!

It was the preferred resolution for his survival, but there was a problem. His hat and case were on the ground, and he wasn't willing to part with them yet.

'Greedy gets you killed,' they say.

Melegal shifted his footing, gently bending his knees.

Creed nodded to his man. "Let's see what the Detective is made of. Take him!"

The man took three quick steps and lunged.

Melegal sidestepped and stabbed.

Glitch!

The man's sword clattered to the ground, and he clutched at his chest. Melegal ripped his sword from the man's heart. His own heart was pounding.

I did it!

He shifted his focus to Creed. The tall man gawped while Melegal slung the blood off his sword.

"Impressive, Detective, I must admit. I didn't think you had that kind of fight in you. But I don't think you'll have the same fortune with me." Creed smiled. It wasn't an evil smile. Just a confident one. A dangerous one. A 'cat about to eat the rat' kind of one. He drew forth another blade that shone brighter than the other.

Oh slat!

Melegal could tell by Creed's stance, his posture, he was …

"I'm a swordsman. My comrade, not so much. Besides, I didn't like him anyway. Slow and stupid, but a good grappler." He sliced his blade through the air and twirled it with his wrist. "Hmmm… I'm feeling spry this day, and well, I don't think that dart was poisoned after all." He lifted his brow and smiled. "And, I think I can disarm you in six seconds. I can maim you in ten. But, it's nothing personal. Just business."

Melegal stood his ground.

Still time to run if you don't think of something.

He renewed his stance: blades up, elbows down.

"Tell you what, Detective: come along quietly, and I won't turn you into my dog's dinner. Not all of you, anyway."

Swish!

The sword flashed like a stroke of lightening.

Slat, he's good. Melegal narrowed his eyes.

He immediately recalled his battle with Teku in the alley months ago. It had taken everything he had not to die then, and Teku had been just an assassin, not a master swordsman.

"So, you're taking me to the Almens, eh…"

"Creed, Royal Bloodhound Knight."

"Oh please, you're no Royal or Knight, but a scavenger."

"Like you," he smiled.

Melegal shrugged.

"Like me, indeed then."

Creed scoffed. "I hardly think so. Sefron's message was abundantly clear. You are little more than an overachieving urchin. I, however, am of Royal blood."

Creed could pass for a Royal, in some circles, but Melegal knew better. The Bloodhounds claimed to be a Royal house, but instead they were little more than a house of mercenaries and bounty hunters of the true Royal houses. But, because of their unique position and the secrets they kept, the Royals ignored their overstated positions.

It was Melegal's turn to laugh.

"Sefron? You took a charge from Sefron? Ha! You might as well be taking charges from the urchins that scrub pots in the kitchen and clean the slat from the bird cages. Hah! Are you even sure I'm the one he really wants?"

Creed's eyes shifted, sword tips dipping a hair.

Melegal kept pressing.

"Creed, you are a fool. Have you not noticed that the underlings are storming Castle Almen? How do you suppose to get me in there? Collect your reward? It wouldn't surprise me if Sefron was dead right now. Can you imagine him fighting an underling? Have you ever fought an underling? This City's doomed, Creed. A smart man would save himself. Not carry out the charge of a fool when total destruction is about."

Creed was thinking. Melegal could see it, the hardness in his eyes weakening.

"What are you thinking, Creed?"

"I'm thinking that a Bloodhound never gives up on a charge until he gets his man."

"Is that so, then?"

Creed raised his blades, flashing a thin row of white teeth.

"So it is, and taking into account all you've said and done so far, I think it's best for me if I take you in dead."

Melegal raised his blades.

I'm dead if I don't run. Think, Melegal. What did McKnight say long ago? 'The mind is faster than the sword.' He glanced at his hat on the ground. *If I can just squirm my way to it.*

"Creed" The man Melegal had shot in the eyes stumbled along the storefronts. "I can't see, Creed, what do I do?"

"Silence, Dolt! I'll tend to you in a moment."

Melegal started left and Creed started right, both men circling.

Good.

Creed stopped, lunged and chopped.

Clang!

The sound of clashing steel echoed through the alley and down the street. Melegal held back his grimace. Creed struck again. *Clang!* Again. *Clang!* Again. *Clang! Clang! Clang!*

Creed pressed, Melegal parried. The man was a true swordsman. His moves perfect. His swing quick and powerful. Melegal's hands were numb seconds into it.

"Not much of an offense, I see," Creed said, backing away, cutting his swords through air. "But, you've an excellent defense; I'll give you that, Detective. I underestimated you. Problem is, how long can those bony arms of yours hold out?"

Not long!

"Long enough to wear you down," Melegal said.

Creed darted in, blades stabbing like striking snakes. "I don't think so."

Melegal battled one blade away, only to shift and catch another.

Creed kept stabbing at his legs, a hungry grin behind his lips.

Slice!

Creed caught Melegal in the inner thigh. He felt every bit of it.

"Hah!" Creed said, jumping away. "First blood to me. Oh, that's already staining your clothes."

Run, Melegal! It's not worth it!

Behind him, the hat and slender case lay unmolested on the ground, but he had no chance of getting them. Creed would pin him to the ground if he tried.

"My, your shoulders are already dipping," Creed said, cutting his longsword over the ground. "More of a fencer than a soldier, clearly. But, I think I've summed you up enough." Creed sheathed one sword, left the other one that gleamed like the sun out, and shrugged. "I feel the need to challenge myself." He motioned Melegal closer with his hand. "Come on, Detective. Attack."

Melegal remained wary. Creed might be cocky, but he wasn't a fool either. Even though the odds had shifted more in his favor, he knew better. Creed had something up his sleeve.

"I'll fight my way; you fight yours. Come on then, Hound. I'm curious to see what you can do with a single sword to my two."

Creed leapt and swung.

Melegal parried and struck.

Pour it on, Rat!

Clang! Clang! Clang! Clang!

Creed parried, dodged and ducked.

Clang! Clang! Clang! Clang!

Melegal stabbed, chopped and cut, but Creed anticipated everything he did. Focused. Determined. Waiting for a weakness.

Move, Melegal!

Out of nowhere, Creed's blade licked out like a rod of lightning. Melegal squatted down. Creed kicked him in the face.

Bang!

Melegal felt his sword ripped from his hand.

Bang!

The other skipped over the cobblestones. The next thing he felt was the tip of a sword under his chin.

SLAT!

"Heh, heh, heh — woot!" Creed wiped the sweat from his brow. "I can't believe you still have your head, Detective. Ah! I missed it! You are fast. I'll give you that."

Melegal started to raise his arms up.

"Ah, ah, ah, keep those wrists down. I can't have you shooting anymore holes in me. I must admit: I'm surprised you didn't try something earlier. But, eh, I figured you were out."

Melegal could feel the sword cut his neck as he swallowed.

I should have run! Idiot!

"EEEYAH!"

A block down the street, someone screamed.

"Eh?" Creed grabbed Melegal by his head of hair and pulled him up from the ground, stepping behind him and keeping the sword at his throat.

That's when Melegal saw them. *Underlings!*

"What in Bish is that thing crawling on the ground?" Creed said, unable to hide his alarm.

Both ends of the road were blocked off. Speckled eyes and spider legs were coming.

"I can get us out of here, Creed. But your word you won't kill me."

"I know better than that."

"There's no time, Creed. You can kill me and die. Or you can trust me and live. And I don't want to die. I've no issues with you."

The chitters became louder, the small bodies closer.

"Cut my throat then, Creed! I'd rather die at your hands than the underlings'!"

Creed's rapid breath was in his ear.

"My word I won't kill you. Your word you won't kill or betray me."

"My word," Melegal said.

Hurry up, Imbecile.

"Done!"

Melegal was a blur of motion, swooping over to snatch his cap and case and darting for the door he'd tried to get in earlier. "Come on, Creed!"

The underlings let out evil howls and charged.

Melegal pulled out a Key.

"What in Bone?" Creed said, looking at the lock. "That won't fit!"

Melegal jammed it inside the lock and turned.

"Sweet Mother of Bish! It wo — *urked!*"

Clatch-zip! Clatch-zip! Clatch-zip!

Creed's face contorted as he stumbled forward. The sound of the underlings was overwhelming.

Melegal shoved his shoulder into the door and pulled the man behind him through.

Bolts zipped past his head. He fought to pull the door closed.

Something slipped in past his legs.

What was that! Hmm — I'll have to live with it.

He kept pulling on the door, catching a pair of hands in the process.

The underlings were pulling it back open.

Melegal grabbed the handle and pulled on the door with all his might.

"No!"

He was sliding forward.

A flash of light ripped through the air.

Slice!

Underlings howled and hissed in fury. The tips of their fingers disappeared, shooting black-red blood everywhere.

Melegal flew backward and felt the door close with a bang.

Creed was huffing at his side, wiping black blood off his blade.

"That was close," Melegal said. "And you better hang onto your stomach."

"Why-yeeeeeeeeeee…"

Melegal remembered hearing that and something else that growled as his body and mind were turned inside out.

31

"Ashur!" Lorda Almen said. "You have awakened!"

The face was hazy, but the voice familiar as Lord Almen tried to rise.

"Ugh!" he said, clutching at his side. The area was tender, painful.

"Easy, Darling," Lorda said, gently pushing him back down. "You don't need to tear the wound." She sobbed. "Ashur, I'm so happy to see you."

She nuzzled him. Gently. Wet tears dripping on his cheeks.

"My darling," he said, "I'm quite alright."

Still, she held on, trembling.

It was a good feeling, the scent of his wife and the curves of her body against his, but despite his awakening, something was wrong. He sniffed.

"What is that smell?" Blinking, the haze from his eyes began to clear. Two Shadow Sentries stood at his bedside with gore of some sort on their armor. "And what is that sound?"

Somewhere, a battle raged. His heart ignited.

"Help me up, Sentry," he said, pushing Lorda aside.

Sitting up, his head began to spin. He collected his thoughts. The last thing he remembered was being inside the arena. The haggard face of Leezir the Slerg was there, and a big man. A very big man that went berserk, chopping up people like wood.

"Dearest, lie down, please," Lorda said.

He slid onto the floor and with assistance from the sentry stumbled towards the balcony.

"Why are there underlings at my walls?"

It was insanity. Castle Almen was under a full-scale attack. Black armored underlings and oversized spiders filled the streets and alleys.

"How long, Lorda? How long have I been down?"

"Many days, Lord Almen. Sefron saved you. It was the underlings that infiltrated and stabbed you. I thought you were to perish."

A flood of memories washed over him. Everything that happened in the arena became crystal clear up to the point where he could feel the dagger sliding between his ribs.

The scowl on his vulture-like visage returned.

"Melegal."

"Pardon, my Lord? I ordered Sefron to send the Bloodhounds for him—"

He cracked her across the face, dropping her to her knees.

"You hired those Gormandizing Bastards? And Melegal! He's not here? He lives?"

Lorda's eyes were narrow, dangerous.

She started to rise.

"What is the meaning of this that you would dare strike me, Ashur? I'm guilty of no wrong—"

He drew back again, causing her to flinch.

"It was Melegal that slid the dagger in my ribs. Not the underlings. Not any other!"

Lorda shook her head.

"No, Sefron said it was the underlings."

"Pah! Sefron! Where is he, anyway?" He grabbed a Shadow Sentry by the collar of his armor. "You, go and fetch him yourself, and do not fail me. And see to it word spreads that Lord Almen lives!"

Melegal. The man had gotten him, and he had to admit it was impressive of the man. He would have admired it if he'd not been the victim… But now his entire castle was under siege! And he knew why. The chamber room. The underlings wanted it.

"How long has this siege been going on?" he demanded.

"Several hours, Lord Almen," a sentry replied.

"And the Keep is secure?"

"Yes, Lord Almen."

"And the castle?"

"Casualties along the wall, Lord Almen. Nothing else to report."

Lord Almen folded his arms behind his back, stepped past Lorda, and began to pace. He wondered if his neighbors would come to his aid. Or would they see him perish first? After all, that's what he would do.

"Hmmm."

He reached down and lifted Lorda up. She slapped him in the face.

"I'm —"

She slapped him again.

"I'm —"

She swung, but he caught her by the wrist. "I'm going to throw you off the balcony if you do that again."

"You wouldn't dare!" She was almost smiling.

He did smile. "Oh, of course not." He lifted her chin and kissed her cheek. "I'm sorry, my dearest."

"I'm glad you're back, Ashur." She hugged him. Then she looked him in the eye. "I'm sorry. I never would have suspected Melegal. But we'll find him, and when we do, we'll throw him off this balcony together. "

"Oh, we'll do much worse than that."

Lorda took the next few minutes explaining to Lord Almen everything that had been going on, but he was confident the Castle would hold for days. At some point, the other Royals would have to arrive.

Minutes later, the sentry that left to find Sefron returned.

"Where is Sefron?" Lord Almen demanded.

The sentry bowed. "Lord Almen, I have grave news. The underlings have penetrated the bottoms of the Castle."

"What!" He wanted to strangle the man. Ignoring the pain in his side, he dashed out of the room. He had to get to his study, secure the chamber and the Keys before it was too late.

32

I N ONE OF THE BOTTOM quarters of the Keep, Sefron stared in a mirror, dressing his wounds.

"She'll be mine," he said, stitching the side of a nasty cut on his cheek, "all mine."

"What's that, Cleric?" It was one of the sentries posted outside his door.

Fool! "Eh … nothing, just trying a cheerful tune. Oh, how it soothes the wounds." Sefron crept over towards the man, letting the needle and thread hang from his face. "My, you are a fine specimen of a soldier. I bet you have a steady hand." With a shaky hand, he reached towards the man, who jerked away. "I need some assistance with this."

Another sentry appeared and shoved Sefron back.

"Keep your hands to yourself, Toad, or I'll slit your throat. We know plenty about what you do around here." His hand fell to his dagger. "And it'd be my pleasure to cut your throat."

Sefron fell back, hands up. "Easy now. You don't want rumors leading you to something foolish, do you? After all, I am Lord Almen's trusted servant."

"As trustworthy as a slimy weasel in a hen house. Now leave my men alone!" He shut Sefron inside the room.

Sefron resumed his position in front of the mirror.

"My, I'll never understand why people aren't more taken by my charm." He smiled in the mirror, noticing how his eyes bulged outside his dark sockets and folds of flabby skin dangled under his chin. He was a sickly shade of pale, and his belly jiggled over his scrawny legs.

"Never a finer specimen of a man on Bish," he said, wheezing. He licked the blood from his purple lips. Then started sewing the gash in his face again. "That should do it." He took a seat in a nearby chair, crossed his dirty feet and lounged. "Hmmmm…"

He rubbed the eye that Kierway had stuck with a dart. The underlings waged war from the outside. Perhaps they'd found Melegal. Perhaps they just needed a little help to penetrate the wall of the Castle. He could sense the power beginning to shift. He was an agent for the underlings, and now was his time to move.

And then I'll have Lorda Almen and her servants all to myself!

He sat up.

"Time to get out of this Keep."

Reaching inside a pouch that hung from a string belt, he withdrew grains of an unusual sort. Rubbing one between his fingers, he murmured to himself. Seconds later, the mystic energies he tapped from Bish filled him, rejuvenated him. *Yes!* So long it had been since he last harnessed his energies, waiting, plotting, and scheming for the right time to recall them. He had hidden them long, oh so long. His skin tightened. His muscles flexed and stretched. His haggard body replenished, his crooked spine crackled as he rose to his feet. Smoke streamed from his mouth and nostrils, slowly filling the room.

"What's that smell?" A sentry threw open the door.

Sefron blew the grains of dust into the air.

The smoke in the room poured out into the next. The sound of men choking and gagging was music to his ears.

"Not so talkative now, are we?" He crossed the threshold, upright on a solid six-foot frame. He pulled the dagger from the gagging sentry's sheath and stabbed him in the spine. "I've been meaning to do that for quite some time."

Two more sentries remained, hacking and spitting, blinded to his presence.

Sefron stabbed one in the neck and left the dagger in the other's heart. He cracked his knuckles, went back into his room, and took another look at himself.

His countenance wasn't handsome, but strong and dark, his skin no longer pale nor sagging. His stomach was tight and his legs firm. His damaged eye was still gone, but better. He felt good. He'd been saving up decades for this, and now his time had come. "Let the powers of Bish last as long as they can last."

He focused on his personal quarters in the castle, closed his eyes, and drew in more power. A portal appeared. He stepped through it, back into his room.

"Ah yes."

It felt good, being back inside his place. Very good. Incredibly good. He grabbed his robes from the wall and tied another belt with pouch around his waist. From the corner of the small disheveled room—littered with vials, jugs and old bits of food—he grabbed a crooked staff.

"It's been a long time," he said, kissing it before exiting his door.

Despite the battle raging outside, the massive hallways were quiet. Everyone in the Castle was either fighting somewhere or dead. No longer shuffling, Sefron strolled, whistling rather than wheezing, on the legs of a twenty-year-old man. Making his way through one of the living rooms, he pressed a panel on one of the decorative shelves. A hidden door popped open behind it, and inside he went.

The spaces between the walls of the rooms were a set of catacombs that Sefron had discovered years ago. Even most of the Almens had no knowledge of them. They'd been used by servants at one time, short cuts through the castle, but Sefron had seen to it over time that no servant recollected them. They were where he did his spying, and they traversed through most of the castle's main rooms, except for the keep.

He hopped his way down a narrow set of steps, a smile on his face. It had been a long time since he moved so gracefully.

If I see Melegal, I'll kill him first.

Stopping, he pushed aside a peephole door and looked through. A dining room greeted him, undisturbed, still shiny in silver and crystal. No longer would he have to watch behind the walls after this. No longer would he be a servant to Lord Almen. No, he would be the Lord of this Castle. He pictured himself and Lorda sitting side by side. "Yes, she'll be—eh?"

Somewhere not too far distant, steel banged against steel. He trotted through the narrow passageway two dozen yards, the sounds becoming more distinct and profound. He lifted another peephole door open and got an eyeful.

Underlings were in mortal combat with sentries and Royal magi. Two Royal soldiers in plate mail armor swung their broad swords into a mass of well-armed underlings. Barrages of green and red missiles of light were shooting back and forth. Men were howling; underlings were screeching.

Sefron made his way down another short level of steps to a dead end. Opening a peephole on the final battle, he saw a group of underlings being forced down the steps that led down to the Current. *Yes!* It was everything he hoped for. The underlings had invaded from below as well as above, but there seemed to be a problem. The underlings were trapped. They were losing.

33

Triumph! Master Kierway felt nothing but triumph when the door shattered and he and his brethren blasted through. Leading the way, he bounded up the stairs and greeted a pair of Royal soldiers with his whirling blades.

He drove his steel through the plate covering one man's heart and cut the mailed neck of the other out. Blood, the only shade of red that he liked, dripped from his blades.

"Inward! Inward!" he ordered his underlings. "Nothing human lives! Everything human dies!"

Juegen soldiers, coated from head to toe in black metal armor, surged past, followed by Badoon warriors with crude knives and hatchets, albino urchlings with claws that could rip metal, and underling magi whose fingertips crackled with energy. Their faces told it all. Hungry. Fearsome. Vengeful. Hate filled. One by one they went. Bright colored eyes narrowed. Soldiers of war that meant business. And Kierway had hundreds of them at his disposal.

"Yes, brethren! Go! Slaughter!"

Everything was working. Within hours, Castle Almen would be theirs.

Up the stairs the underlings went. The last one, bringing up the rear, was an albino urchling, all four nostrils flaring.

"What is this?" Kierway said to himself, bounding down the steps. He hissed. The doorway was sealed. "No!" He looked for a handle, a bar, a lock, but there was nothing. "NO! CATTEN!"

Was this a ruse? Had Catten betrayed him and all his underlings? He didn't have time to worry about that now. Trapped or not, he could still pull this off. He had enough underlings, so he thought. Dashing up the stairs, he was halfway to the top when the wind and the screeches came. Mystic power flowed everywhere. At the top, underlings were knocked head over heels by an unseen force. Fire licked over them. Burning them.

"No! This cannot be!"

A blast of hot air came. One, two, three underlings tumbled backward over the stairs, landing at his feet. At the top, an underling's head was taken from its shoulders, green eyes bouncing off the steps all the way to the bottom. Kierway hesitated. How many Royals were at the top? But there was nowhere else to go. Taking six steps at a time, he charged, confronting a big warrior. A heavy blade came down at his head. Kierway sidestepped and cut the man's wrist from his arm. The man howled long enough to catch a blast of underling energy inside his mouth.

Kierway ducked under a blast of lightning that struck an underling mage full force. He rolled alongside a wall and got a better look at things. All of his brethren underlings that made it up the steps were gone.

Where did they go?

On the far side of the dining room, two robed humans were guarded by three soldiers, and the air shimmered before them.

Hmmmm.

Several feet away, an underling Badoon and one albino urchling were in mortal combat with the Royal Soldiers. Kierway chittered at an urchling that had sunk its teeth into the neck of a dead soldier and pointed at the magi at the other end of the room. Blood dripping from its fangs, it tore itself away and charged across the room. *Blink!* The urchling was gone.

Furious, Kierway sprang into action, assisting his brethren, hewing into one Royal soldier after the other. The battle raged for another minute and then the last Royal soldier fell, leaving himself, one Juegen, one Badoon and one mage left standing. He shook the blood from his blades and faced the Royals on the other side of the room. The faces of the men showed no concern, but rather, supreme confidence.

Kierway banged his blades together, calling a Royal soldier out. None of them moved, except the magi behind them. One gyrated his hands while the other one spoke in tones. Kierway slung two knives.

Sssz!

Sssz!

They disappeared midflight

The underling mage hurled a ball of fire, lighting up the room, shaking the chandeliers. It stopped, hovered in the air, and returned. He jumped out of the way just before it exploded. Tiny fires licked over his clothing while the underling mage burst into flame, screaming.

Whatever barrier the humans had put up, he knew they could not pass. It was a mystic dimension spell of sorts, and for all he knew the underlings that passed through were on the outside of Bone. Possibly imprisoned in a wall somewhere. But the spell wouldn't last forever. It couldn't. He banged his swords together.

The Royal Magi acted. A missile of mystic energy burst from the hands of one, then another, careening towards him.

He flicked his blades up. The missile smacked into them with a shower of sparks, knocking him from his feet. One by one, he and his men backed towards the stairwell. One bright missile soared after the other. Behind the human magi, another man appeared, dark and mysterious. Reaching out, the strange man grabbed the two magi by the shoulders. They choked, mouths popping open. Their skin tightened and shriveled. Their faces sunk in and dried. The space between them buckled, images contorting before returning to normal.

The dimension spell was gone. Kierway could feel it.

"Kill them!" Kierway said.

The two remaining soldiers readied themselves.

The urchling, Badoon warrior, and Juegen sped across the room. Kierway followed close behind.

The Royal soldiers braced themselves, chins down, swords up.

The heavy sword of one Royal chopped downward, burying itself in the Badoon's shoulder, drawing a howl.

The Juegen and Badoon pounced on the man, knocking him off balance and to the floor. Focusing on the other soldier, Kierway sidestepped one swing, followed by the other, staying wary of the man who had assisted him moments earlier. The man, holding a crooked staff, was laughing.

Clang!

Kierway batted away the soldier's heavy swings, one after the other, hissing and taunting. The eyes behind the soldier's metal helmet were determined but became weary. Each swing came more sluggish than the last.

Rip!

Kierway struck the man's knee, sending flesh, blood and steel across the room. The man stumbled forward.

"Urk!"

Kierway drove his sword through the man's heart. Yanking his blade out, he turned on the man who laughed. He and the remaining underlings surrounded him.

The man kneeled and said, "Master Kierway, it is I, your servant, Sefron."

Kierway could see it now. The man's good eye bulged a little in his socket, and his disturbing expression, though more vital, remained unchanged.

"Do you have the Keys?"

"No," Sefron said, flatly.

Kierway nodded to his men.

"Kill him."

Sefron's arm shot out.

"Wait! Master Kierway, I may not have the Keys you seek, but I can open the door at the bottom of the stairwell." Sefron's eye glanced over the dripping blades of Kierway's two men. "I am your humble servant, Master Kierway, now and forever."

Kierway held out his arm. The underling drew back.

"Do it then," he said, sheathing his blades behind his back. "But make it quick if you don't want underling steel fileting your back."

Sefron rose, led them across the room and down the stairwell, and stopped at the oversized door.

"Hurry!" Kierway said.

Sefron leaned his staff against the wall, pressed his hands on the door and chanted. One syllable after the other, faster, slower, lower, higher. Sweat dripped from his bald head, and his knees buckled a little. Panting, he turned.

"It's over," he said, stepping aside. "Shall I open it?"

"Of course, you fool!"

Sefron pushed it open.

A sea of underlings greeted him.

Sefron stood aside. Several feet away, floating across the great Dining Hall, Kierway was in a heated conversation with an underling whose likes he'd never seen before. His golden eyes radiated with power, and a mere glance in his direction ran his blood cold. Even Lord Almen didn't command such authority. Still, Sefron managed to pull back his shoulders and keep his chin up.

Show no fear. No fear at all.

His knuckles were white on his staff as a squad of underling fighters dashed by. They spread like a swarm of bees through the castle and into the main courtyard. Their numbers were overwhelming. Sefron knew that within hours, minutes possibly, the Castle would be taken over. He began to have doubts as to whether this was a good alliance or not.

It was inevitable. The Lorda and this castle or another shall be mine.

Keeping his head down, Sefron kneeled. Kierway and Catten approached.

"How many are in the keep?"

"A few dozen, if that." Sefron said. He kept his head down, eyes up a little. He could feel heat from Lord Catten's eyes boring into him.

"Master Kierway," Catten said, "do we have further need of this man?"

Sefron's eyes shot over to Kierway, heart pounding in his chest. Kierway rubbed his chin.

"Masters!" Sefron fell on his face. "I've betrayed my castle for your glory! I know many of its secrets I can share. And I am still assisting with the one that has the Keys. Spare me!" He looked at Kierway. "You promised me, Master Kierway!" His voice echoed in the large chamber.

"I made promises for the Keys, which you did not deliver." Kierway said. "And we have an imp that can find the man you speak of, and the Keys, whenever we want."

"But, certainly, you won't kill all of us? Underlings and men have held many alliances before. Outpost Thirty-One and Castle Almen were united on that endeavor." He wiped the sweat from his brow with his robes. "Certainly we can be united on this endeavor as well. I killed off two Royal magi who held a pivotal location." He crawled towards the two husks on the floor and lifted one up. "I am not loyal?"

Catten snapped his fingers. The entire room shook, knocking Sefron over and turning what remained of the corpses into dust.

"Kierway," Catten said, "You say this one is a life drainer?"

"It seems he has that craft," Kierway said, checking the bandolier of knives on his chest. "What of it?"

"Give him your hand," Catten ordered.

"Give him your own hand!" Kierway fired back.

"You'll do as I say, Kierway!" Catten's voice shook the chandeliers.

Sefron came forward, his limbs stiffening. The power he got from draining people didn't last forever, but the magi he'd drained would hold him for hours. He extended his hand.

Kierway sneered at Lord Catten, who sneered back.

"You're such a fool, Kierway. Stupid and cowardly." Catten snatched Sefron's wrist with a grip of iron and said, "Drain me, Human!"

Fearful, Sefron hesitated.

"Do it, else I'll have Kierway skewer and skin you like a rodent."

Sefron summoned his power. The dust stirred on the floor, mystic powers flowing through him, giving him more enriching vitality.

"You like that, do you Human?" Catten ran his tongue along his teeth. "A taste of centuries of tempered energy, something your kind cannot comprehend." He pulled Sefron in face to face. "Well, I'll share a secret with you. I'm feeding you my power, Weakling. You are not taking it."

Catten closed his eyes, holding Sefron fast.

An urge to pull away overcame Sefron.

But Catten held him in a supernatural grip.

Something was wrong. He wasn't draining the underling. Instead, the underling was feeding him dark, exhilarating energy.

"Human," Catten said, "certainly you knew that you are only capable of draining your own kind. I, however, can do both, and what I give, I can take away."

Sefron choked. His breath was gone. All of his vibrancy was being sucked dry. He shrunk. He shriveled. He wheezed, fought to stand, and teetered to the floor. He pleaded with his eyes. Catten released him. He fell down and clutched his chest.

"You really should consort with a better class of human, Kierway. But I should expect so much."

Sefron looked down at his flabby belly, and the skin jiggled under his chin. Wheezing, he pushed himself up on his staff.

Just need another fresh body and I'll be fine, thank you.

"Now, Kierway, take your flabby ally away. Take some of your men and secure the Chamber of Keys. Certainly, someone will show up eventually. As for me, I'll see to it the demise of the Castle is completed."

Sefron's shaky legs struggled to move. He was in worse condition than before. His good eye caught Lord Catten's hard stare once more. He turned away. It wasn't likely Lord Catten would keep him around if he didn't think of something.

Kierway shoved him forward, "Lead the way, you saggy piece of meat."

34

"**D**IE, FIENDS! DIE!"

Jarla's inner fires ignited with every stroke. Underlings, one after the other, fell under the precise patterns of her blade.

Chop!

Glitch!

Zurk!

She rammed a dagger into the last one's throat. Beside her, Tonio hewed the underlings down with powerful blows. A tireless machine among the chaos. The underlings, as well prepared as they might be, couldn't have been prepared for this; two skilled fighters with an unrivaled passion for killing.

Body splattered with red-black blood and gore, Jarla churned out one death after the other.

Toowah!
Toowah!
Toowah!
The darts struck her arms and legs.
"Cowards!" she said.
Whack!
She split one amber-eyed underling's skull.
Toowah!
Toowah!
Toowah!
Tonio laughed, half a dozen darts in his face, and yelled in his garbled voice, "There is no escape from me, underlings!"

They chopped at the man, jumped on top of him, tried to drag him down, but Tonio shook them off like a dog sheds water.

Jarla stayed close. Her lungs were burning behind her heaving chest. Her sword became heavy, sluggish. Still, she hacked. She chopped. Cognizant of the pounding on the door behind her. The underlings would chop through that door at any moment.

"We're going to have company!" she rasped. "I hope you can hold them all, because I can't."

"Let them come!" Tonio said, ramming his sword through one's skull.

Claws and fangs bared, an underling charged, leaping towards her from the bar. Engaged with another one of the underlings, she caught it in the corner of her eye, but couldn't turn in time.

Slice!

Tonio cleaved through it in mid-air, sending a shower of dark blood everywhere.

Over a dozen underling bodies were piled up, some twitching on the floor, behind them another dozen or so, when they backed off.

Jarla wiped the blood from her eyes, trying to catch her breath. They needed an escape route, but the only way was to carve through them.

"Think you can cut a path to the back through them?" she asked Tonio.

"Certainly, but I haven't the same need as you. I can fight them all day and all night if I have to," he said. "But you won't last that long, will you, Woman?"

Chop! Chop! Chop!

The underlings were still hewing at the door behind them, jostling Jarla's indomitable shroud. She'd never quit a fight before, but at the moment, there wasn't much fight left in her. She was exhausted, out of shape, and disappointed.

How did I let myself get like this? Lazy over-drinking bitch!

A twinkle caught her eye. She wiped the blood from the ring on her finger. It glowed a bright green color.

"What is that?" Tonio said.

Fool! How could I have forgotten!

"A way out of here, maybe." She darted for the front door, sliding over the blood-slicked floor. "Hold them off!"

Tonio's big frame stepped between her and the underlings, beckoning the underlings forward. "Come on, rodents. My blade thirsts for your blood!"

Where's the Key! Where's the Key!

Chop!

The blade of an axe emerged through the door. A sparkling eye peeked inside.

Glitch!

She jammed a dagger in its eye, let go and grabbed the Key. She jammed it inside the lock.

Chop!

The Key popped out and fell to the ground. She fumbled for it, grabbing it in her sticky hands.

Chop!

The underlings on the other side kept hacking at the lock. Chunks of wood fell.

Clatch-zip!
Clatch-zip!
Clatch-zip!

Small bolts ripped across the room, burying themselves in the door.

Tonio groaned. "Whatever you're doing, Witch, you better hurry. Looks like the rodents are just getting started."

Thunk!

A javelin juttered in the door frame.

Jarla tried to force the Key into the deteriorating lock. It wouldn't go.

"Blast my eyes! Get! In! There!"

The Key transformed, its head matching the lock. She shoved it in and turned.

Clatch-zip!

Clatch-zip!

Clatch-zip!

Bolts and spears filled the doorway. Over her shoulder, she could see Tonio was filled with them, still standing, snarling and chopping. She shoved the door forward and found herself in a black room. She stepped inside, huffing, then pushed the door shut.

Almost.

Fingers emerged on the door's edge, pulling it open. Tonio's blood-splattered face leered at her.

"Not leaving the party without me, are you?"

"Just get your dead arse in here and shut the blasted door!"

"My pleasure." He closed it on the small fingers of the underlings, crushing them in the frame.

Jarla heard their angry screeches and howls cut short. Everything spun. She wanted to vomit. Her world twisted bloody and black.

I hate this part.

35

E VERYTHING IN HER LIFE HAD been turned upside down. And now, she was home, back inside her own room, and once more a prisoner. Kam lowered her shoulder and pounded at the door.

Wham!

"Will you stop doing that, Kam?" Joline said. She was rocking baby Erin in her arms. "Can't you just be thankful you are home, safe for the moment?"

"That troll cut my hand off, Joline!"

Wham!

"And when I get a hold of her, I'm gonna shove my foot up her—"

"KAM! Enough!" Joline said, setting Erin in her bassinette.

The bassinette started to rock itself, and soothing music came forth, keeping Erin in a peaceful slumber.

Kam rubbed her shoulder with her lone hand and fought the tears coming to her eyes. What in Bish was going on? She'd just escaped the unbearable, only to find herself at home, confronted with the inconceivable. She looked at her stump, stupefied. Less than an hour ago, she'd awoken in her bed, the wound dressed and cleaned. Joline had done that for her, saying the bleeding had stopped on its own and the flesh had mended itself.

Who in Bish is Scorch?

She gritted her teeth.

Wham!

Joline grabbed her by the arm, dragged her over to the sofa, and pulled her down. Softly, the woman said, "Dear, I don't know what you've been through, and I can't explain what we are going through now, but you are home." Joline looked around and shrugged. "And safe as far as I know. You, me and Erin." She patted her knee. "A family."

Her tears flowed like raindrops. Her body shuddered with every breath. Kam's voice was a high pitched squeak. "I don't know what's happening to me. I don't understand. I just don't understand. I was so happy to be home, and n-n-now I'm a handless prisoner. Where's my hand, Joline? Why'd that woman do that?"

Joline handed her a handkerchief and rubbed her back.

She blew her nose and wiped her tears away.

"The truth is, Kam, you look better now than when you first walked in here. You looked possessed. You weren't yourself."

Serve and live.

That voice. It would haunt her forever. It had possessed her, controlled her. Empowered her. What was it? Who was it?

Kam had made a deal.

It had saved her. The power in the stones. A being was in the stones, like one was in the sword, the great sword of Zorth, the Everblade. It was her father's sword, and she was going to return it. Her father would have to answer to her about his dealings with Palos. She shivered. The thought of that man having his way with her. Pawing at her. Humiliating her. Almost killing her. What had happened to him? She'd left him mumbling in his own drool.

I should have killed him!

Joline squeezed her hand. "What is it, Kam? What are you thinking? There's murder in those eyes! You didn't kill anyone, did you?"

The question was like a slap in the face. Diller. Indeed, she had killed a man. Snapped his neck like a twig. And there had been others. In the alley. Broken. Lifeless. Had she killed them too? She looked at the hand that was no longer there. She swore she could still see it, feel it. And the dark energy from it still lingered within her.

She shook her head, sucked in her breath, looked Joline in the eye, and said, "I did what I had to do to save Erin, Joline." She blew her nose again. "And let me tell you, those bastards down below will think a hundred times before they ever come up here again."

Joline's eyes widened.

Kam got up, scooped her baby out of her bassinette with her one good arm and held her tight. "Nobody messes with me or my baby."

"Uh," Joline stammered, "how about some hot tea?"

"Got any Muckle Sap?"

"No." Joline pulled her shoulders back. "And I wouldn't give you any if we did. You need to settle yourself, Woman. I don't know what all you've been through, and you can tell me when you like, but now's no time for drinking. Just rock your baby."

Kam strolled over to the window. The glass was clear, but she couldn't see out. A busted three legged stool lay on the ground beside it. That window, whatever it was, was hard as stone. Kam couldn't help but wonder if it was all an illusion. Was she really here or not? Joline and Erin were real. Of that much, she was certain, but of the rest she wasn't so sure.

Erin yawned and stretched, letting out a little squeak. For the first time in as long as she remembered, Kam felt herself smile on the inside and out. She had the most important thing in the world, Erin. She kissed her forehead and took a seat in a rocking chair nearby.

"That's better." Joline worked the kettle on the stove. "You've got your whole world now, Kam. Erin's all that matters."

Tight as a drum, Kam yawned. Reflecting on everything she'd been through, she realized life would never be the same. Tortured and manipulated, she'd somehow survived. She was sore. Her face was swollen, and her gut hurt from where she'd been stabbed, but she lived. Erin lived. And even though they were prisoners, at least they were together. She rocked and rocked and rocked.

Joline walked over, eyes tired, and handed her a mug of steaming coffee.

"There you go. I put some Allybass in it. It always helps me relax. Are you hungry, Kam?"

Kam nodded.

"I'll fix you something to eat, and how about I run you a tub?"

"No tubs!"

Joline jumped.

"Sorry, just, I'll wash myself off later." Kam shuddered a sigh. "Hopefully, I can still cast a cantrip for it."

"Whatever you say, Kam." Joline fixed herself a cup of coffee and took a seat on the couch, playing with her greying locks of hair. "I might need you to use a cantrip on me, too. I feel like I've been rolled in sow waller."

Kam let out a short giggle.

It was followed by a long silence.

Kam felt safe in her heart. Restless, but safe. And the loss of her hand had been a small price to pay for Erin's life and her freedom. Perhaps Scorch, at least it would seem, had done her a favor. Shown her compassion, though a bit harsh, and merciless. Still, the image of that rough-cut woman chopping off her hand disturbed her. *She's a maniac.*

"Kam, I'm sorry to ask, but was Master Gillem a part of all this?"

Kam closed her eyes. So much had happened that she hadn't had time to take in. She blew a lock of hair from her face.

"You could say that," she said. "He poisoned the well. He seduced Lefty. But, I don't think he had a choice. At least, it was either that or death."

"Oh." Joline sat back. "I, I just really liked his company and the flowers he'd bring. He said the nicest things and told the most amazing stories. One time he told me…"

Kam let her talk, but she wasn't listening. There wasn't any sense in spoiling Joline's memories. 'There's good in everyone,' her mother always said, 'but it's often harder to find in some than others.' Of course, Kam used to believe that, but not anymore. There was no good in Palos. He was rotten to the core.

"Joline?"

"… and those fragrances he made. So… oh, sorry. Did you say something?"

"What happened to Lefty?"

"Well…" Joline looked around. "I, I don't know. I just assumed he was… oh my."

"Oh my?" Kam leaned forward. "What do you mean, oh my?"

"The last I saw him, he was kicking Scorch in the nose." Joline clutched her chest. "You don't think they cut his hand off too, do you?"

"Why'd he kick him in the nose?"

"He was mad. He was telling Scorch to fix your hand I think, then poof," Joline fanned her fingers out, "here we were!"

Kam's chest tightened. What in Bish had happened to Lefty? An image of him stuffed in a pickle jar popped in her mind.

Knock. Knock. Knock.

Kam and Joline lurched up, looking at each other.

Knock. Knock. Knock.

"Uh… er… Do you want me to get that?"

Kam handed her Erin. "No, I better do that." She walked over to the door, grabbed the handle and looked back at Joline.

The older woman mouthed the words, "Answer it."

Slowly, to her surprise, it pulled open. A familiar figure stood in the doorway.

"You!"

It was Darlene.

"Look, Lady." Darlene looked down into Kam's eyes. "I'm sure you're still upset about your hand and all, but I didn't have a choice in the matter."

"Huh!" Kam was baffled.

"But what Scorch says, I does."

"You are a Maniac!"

"A what?" Darlene rubbed her sweaty neck.

"Maniac! A crazy person! Out of your mind! Do you understand that, you featherless turkey!"

Darlene put her hands up. "Easy now, Lady. I'm not a Mannyack or a Turkey. *Hic.* 'Scuse me. Must be that last bottle of Muckle Sap. Anyhow, I'm a hunter, trapper, and a proud underling slayer. And, I'll warn you once: don't cross Scorch again. He did you a favor, and you know it."

Speechless, Kam tried to measure the woman's words. Darlene still seemed amiable, though taller and formidable.

"So," Kam said, "what is it you want?"

"First, sorry about your hand," Darlene said. "I guess you'll just have to learn to wipe with the other." She winked, pushing her way inside. "Say, this is nice. Better than I imagined it."

"What do you want?"

"Well." Darlene grabbed Kam's cup of coffee from the table and took a sip. "Mmmm… that's fine coffee. Did you make that, uh…"

"Joline," Kam said.

The rocker groaned when Darleen sat down.

"Joline. Like Darlene. I like it." She slurped another mouthful. "Mmmm, that's good. Not like that Muckle Sap, but still plenty good." She kicked her legs on the table.

"What do you want, Darlene?"

She scratched her brown hair, stirring the little flakes that fell out. "Things are getting busy downstairs. I need some help."

"Help with what?"

"Serving the people."

"Customers?" Kam said.

"Yes. You see, I don't have much experience running a tavern. I've always wanted to, but I never had the money. But thanks to Scorch, I now own this one."

"This is my tavern!"

Darlene got up and looked down at Kam. "Nope. It's my tavern now. And you're going to help me ruin it … *hic.* I mean, run it."

36

B^{LINK!}

"Say!" A dwarf, black-haired and mangy, couldn't hide his surprise. "Where'd ye come from?"

Lefty tumbled onto his butt, shaking his head. "I-I don't know."

The dwarf slammed his fist on the table.

Lefty jumped.

The surrounding men and dwarves erupted in laughter.

Lefty shook his head.

What has happened? Where am I?

He was in a tavern. That much was clear by the layout, the drinking and eating that surrounded him. A fireplace sat cold at his back, and suspicious eyes drifted over him and onto the next patron. There was something else, something weird about where he was. It was misty.

Gathering his thoughts, he looked to the dwarf, who now had his nose buried in a tankard of ale. "I'm from the City of Three, I think."

The dwarf eyed him from behind his tankard, gulping it down.

Clonk!

"Bring another and one more for my out-of-the-city friend here. Say!" The dwarf rubbed his beard. "You're pretty small, even for a halfling. Humph. The City of Three, ye say. Well, that might explain your appearance. Are you one of those magi or wizards I hear about there? I didn't think halflings could take to magic with such fashion."

Lefty crawled up on the chair and sat down. He wasn't certain what to say or think at the moment. The last hours of his life had been incomprehensible enough.

"Dwarf, uh, my name is Lefty Lightfoot, and I really have no idea where I am. Can you tell me?"

The dwarf guffawed as the barmaid, heavyset but not uncomely, set down their tankards, laughing as well.

"Can't ye tell?"

Lefty scanned the room. It wasn't the City of Bone; there were no dwarves there. And it couldn't be the City of Three; the distant roar of the falls didn't catch his ears. And other than the few other places he'd been in his life, he didn't really have any idea at all. It wasn't a village or a logged outpost. He shook his head.

"Have a drink, Halfling," the dwarf said, reaching over and squeezing his shoulder. "Hmm. Hmm. Hmm."

Being polite, Lefty took a sip, glancing around as he did so.

There were women, some dressed in thick but scant clothing, and the men were of a dour but rugged sort. A pair of full orcs sat in the corner, quiet and unusual. At the next table over was a man that might have been half-gnoll with a heavy sword on his belt. Somewhere he couldn't see, someone played a flute, another strings. A sad tune, a slow tune that settled over the room.

"Are you going to make me guess … Apologies, but may I have your name?"

"No, you might just ferget it. Dwarf will do, and no, I'm not telling you where you are."

"I could ask someone else, I suppose."

The dwarf's bushy brown brows buckled, and his calloused hand reached under the table. Lefty heard a dagger or knife slip from his belt. The dwarf leaned inward.

"Ye could, but I'd consider that rude. And I don't like rude people. You aren't rude, are you?"

I might as well be. After all, I'm a thief, a liar, a disappointment, a failure, a lousy friend, and a wretched urchin. Why not be rude too?

The dwarf, who appeared as rugged as they come, reminded him a little of Jubbler, just thicker. Besides, it didn't look like Lefty had any friends in the world anymore. Maybe it was time he made a new one.

"I'm sorry, Dwarf. The truth is, I'm not rude, just really confused. I don't know how I got here. I don't know where I am. I-I—Sheesh, I guess it's for the better!"

"Ho-ho!" the Dwarf said, "Little one, yer frustration will do ye little good. Take a breath, a drink, and tell me a little about yerself, and if I'm satisfied with your tale, I'll tell ye where ye is." The dwarf winked.

Over the planks of the room, Lefty noticed a creeping fog that swirled as the men and women passed through it.

That's odd.

"Where should I start?" Lefty's feet were sweating.

"Wherever ye want, Lefty. Wherever ye want. I've got all the time in the world." The dwarf lit up a cigar, leaned back, and kicked his heels up. "And just so you know, yer a long, long way from whence you come."

A few more solemn faces joined them at the table, each one less friendly than the next. Lefty's feet were as damp as they'd ever been before.

Drip. Drip. Drip.

37

"CAN YOU HOLD A SHOVEL?"

Venir hesitated, thinking of his aching wrists, then nodded. He was disgraced. Humiliated. Defeated. He reached out with his busted wrists.

Tuuth shoved it in his chest. "Better off digging than dying, for now anyway, Stranger."

Grimacing, Venir wrapped his hands around it and shuffled away, half dragging his feet. He could barely walk. He was dizzy. Thirsty. Hours ago he'd barley had the strength to watch the masses of the Royal Riders be slaughtered, but he'd held on through the bitter end. Watching the underlings chop brave men into bits and pieces was hard. Watching them burn in a pyre was even worse. The stench of burning flesh stung his eyes. It was suffocating.

"Stranger." Tuuth blocked his way with his big body. "What does that tattoo on your back mean, 'V'?"

Venir said nothing. He wasn't even sure himself, so long it had been since he'd even thought about it. Slowly, he trudged forward, joining the surviving Royal Riders, all twelve of them. All busted and broken in one way or the other.

"Stranger, does it stand for Vanquished?"

He looked up at Tuuth through his swollen eyes and said nothing.

"Villain? Vile? Vulgar? Vain? Victorious? Ha! Ha! Ha!"

It happened long ago. Venir couldn't remember if he was drunk when he'd done it or if someone had done did it to him when he was drunk. Melegal used to say it meant Vociferous and claim that he'd done it, but in truth, even Melegal didn't know when he got it. It was almost as if it just happened.

"Start digging, Stranger."

Wuhpash!

"You three, dig as well."

Venir sank the nose of his shovel into the dirt, thinking of all the bodies that would be stuck in the ground. For all he knew, he'd be buried alive again, and suffocated. His thoughts were interrupted when the underling commander showed up.

"Arsehole Bastard can't dig, you stupid orc!" The commander extended his hand towards Tuuth.

Wuhpash!

The underling cracked Tuuth across the arms, watering the orc's eyes.

"Next time you do something so stupid, you'll be digging a hole for yourself. We don't have any need for you, Orc, or any of those men. I'm tired of looking at humans. I'm tired of you all." He held his nose. "And you stink so bad when you burn!" The underling spat on Venir's chest then slugged him in the gut, dropping him to his knees. "I don't like this one, but I like to see him suffer."

Head downcast, Venir listened to the sound of shovels digging into the ground. He hated that sound. It made him think of the day the underlings overtook his village. Groaning, he rose back to his feet.

"Strong, stupid and stubborn, this man is," the underling commander said. "Like an orc." He hissed and chittered to himself. "Let him watch these men shovel until they die. Let him watch us strip the armor from their dead bodies. Let this stubborn man watch it all while you whip him." The underling reached up, grabbed Venir's chin and looked him in the eye. "And if he passes out, wake him up and whip him some more." The underling shoved the whip in Tuuth's chest. "Maybe he'll die before your arm gets too tired, Orc."

"Yes, Commander," Tuuth said.

Venir locked eyes with Tuuth when the commander walked off.

"Men," Tuuth said to some of the brigand army soldiers, "hitch him to the lashing post." He cracked the whip. "Normally, I'd enjoy this, Stranger. But, in your case, I feel a bit sorry for you and your stupid tattoo."

Wuhpash!

38

THREEP! THREEP! THREEP! THREEP!

Fogle's eyes snapped open.

Threep! Threep! Threep! Threep!

Sluggish, he rolled onto his knees, yawning.

Threep! Threep! Thr —

With a simple thought, he shut off the Wizard's Alarm he'd set it in his mind. It was an awareness, like a familiar, a piece of him outside himself. *Careful, Fogle.* He scanned the harsh Outland. Anything could be coming, be it flesh-eating bugs, giants or underlings. Squinting his eyes, he didn't see anything, but the sore muscles between his shoulders told him something was wrong. *Never felt that before.*

Dust Devils swirled over the landscape. Nearby, covered in a thin layer of dust, Barton snored, flat on his face.

"Am I the only real adventurer left around here?" Fogle said to himself, brushing off his robes. "Ah! Why do I continue to bother with that?" He took a deep breath, scanning in every direction. "There has to be something; why else would my alarm go off?"

He nudged Cass's curled-up form. She looked innocent, at peace. He pushed her white hair back over her ear and whispered into it.

"Cass."

She stirred.

"Cass?" he said, shaking her some more. He was getting tired of being the only one awake. "Cass!"

Her eyes fluttered open. "What? Who are you yelling at? Not me, are you?"

Elated, he couldn't' help but hug her.

Feebly, she hugged him back. "Fogle, where are we?"

He helped her up to her feet.

"And is Barton dead?"

Disappointed with what he had to share, Fogle caught her up, explaining to her what little had happened since she fell asleep. Well, little aside from the swarm of flesh-eating bugs killing their horse and weakening Barton.

She made a shivering face when she saw the remains of the horse. "So, you protected me, did you?" She smiled a little and grabbed his hand. "My big-headed hero." She kissed him on the cheek. "But, if you had some water, now, that I'd be more than willing to give you a kiss for. Oh, and my lips would be so much moister."

Fogle felt his dry mouth begin to water as she turned away, hips swaying as she walked up to Barton. He could make water if he wanted to, but she'd made it clear before that his kind would not help. "I'm sure there is some nearby, but Cass, I've lost my familiar, and the truth is, I'm not the best at determining the direction in the Outlands. But, we were headed that way, east, I believe."

Cass fingered one of the red welts on Barton. "Stingers and teeth?" She continued her inspection, eyes wide with fascination. "Even I've never seen such a thing. Strange."

"How are you feeling, Cass?" He wasn't certain how long they'd slept, but it must have been a few hours at least. He felt a bit better than before, anyway.

"Mmm… not so bad, just stiff." She rolled her neck. "How are feeling, Fogle the Brave?"

"Never better now that I know you're well." He was unable to contain his grin.

"Oh, is that so?" Cass came closer, her busted lip and bruised face all smiles. "And how well am I, exactly?"

Drat! I had one good remark. I wasn't expecting to need two! "As well as a soldier in a tavern full of whores?"

"What!"

"Er … Better than a dwarf on stilts?"

She folded her arms over her chest.

"Like a cat in a room full of rats?"

She shook her head. "You need to know when to be silent, Fogle Fool. Now—"

Suddenly, Barton jerked up into a sitting position, eye alert, craning his neck.

Fogle could see the muscles tense in the giant's back. Something was amiss.

"What is it?" Cass said.

Barton's hand covered her chest and face.

"Hear that?" Barton said, his voice a low rumble.

"Only the wind in my ears," Fogle said.

Barton's head turned towards the cloudy sky. His jaw jutted out, and he grinded his teeth. "We must go," Barton said. He reached for Cass.

"What are you doing?" she said.

"We must hide," Barton said. "Can you not hear that? Can you not hear that, Wizard?"

Fogle, eyeing the sky, shook his head. "I don't hear anything." Still, he grabbed Cass and held her tight. "Barton, what is it? Giants?"

Barton took a stiff breath through his nose and shook his head. "Not giants. Blackie. Barton hate Blackie."

That's when Fogle heard it. Distant. Foreboding. Massive.

Whump. Whump. Whump.

"A net," Boon grumbled to himself. "Of all things, I fell to a net."

Mile after mile Boon was marched, barefoot on the hot land. His bleeding and blistered feet burned like fire with every step.

Surrounding him, underling soldiers marched at his side, one holding a rope around his neck, jerking it hard from time to time.

Boon glanced over at it. Its red eyes glared back like beacons of death.

"I'll kill you first, you black roach," Boon spat. He looked at another. "Then you." And another. "And you." He was certain they didn't understand a word he said, but he understood them.

They hadn't killed him, but he was fairly certain he wished they had. No, they would torture him. Mutilate him. Cut his tongue off and feed it to him maybe. Of all the races on Bish, it was the underlings that delighted abnormally in peeling the flesh from the bones. The single thought of it disgusted Boon. Everything they did, he despised. He remembered the first time he saw them kill a man, a friend of his. They took pleasure in it. It stirred Boon. It made him sick.

"Ooof!"

Underlings shoved him to the ground, chittering with diabolical laugher.

His body wanted to stay down, but he wouldn't let it. He wouldn't give them the satisfaction. "Kill me now, fiends, before it's too late," he said. Rising, his legs trembled beneath him.

Still, they laughed in their own sick way, his threats as meaningless as the ants that scurried beneath his toes. Chests out, sharp teeth bared, the soldiers marched him over the dusty ground, pushing, pulling and jerking him by the neck mile after mile, one agonizing step after the other. *Walk or die, Old Man. Walk or Die.*

Before Fogle realized what was happening, Barton had snatched him and Cass up and started running.

"We must hide! Barton must hide! I won't let Blackie take me again. I won't!"

Over Barton's shoulder, Cass was screaming in the giant's ear. "Put me down!"

Fogle wanted to scream, but couldn't find the breath. Barton had him pressed over his shoulder too tight. *The dragon might want you,* he thought, *but I don't think he wants us!* Reassuring himself, he patted the spellbook in the pocket of his robe.

Barton's feet sounded like giant mallets pounding over the landscape, clattering Fogle's teeth and jostling his senses.

A dragon.

A black one.

Watching the clouds above, Fogle tried to imagine what to expect. There was a wizard's tower in the City of Three with a great hall filled with the most wondrous and colorful pictures. Battles. Cities. Ancient people of Long Ago. Men and dwarves battled orcs, ogres, gnolls and minotaurs. Wizards fought harpies, chimera, dark sorcerers. So many monsters roamed Bish, yet so few were ever seen, but one picture came to mind. A dragon: beastly, monstrous, little bigger than a horse attacking a host of men. It was a terrifying creature, scales a deep red, but other than that, it looked to only be a big lizard.

"Barton!" he said, "you don't even know where you're going!"

"I don't hear any dragons!" Cass screamed over at him, then looked to the air.

Whump! Whump! Whump!

Their eyes locked on one another's. Cass's widened with uncertainty.

Barton picked up the pace. "NOOOOOO!"

Fogle craned his neck, searching in all directions. Above him, a massive black shadow darted through the clouds.

Whump! Whump! Whump!

A powerful gust of air sent a chill right through him

Barton's running came to a sudden stop.

WHUMP!

Ahead, the sound of something heavy hit the dirt, followed by a roar so long Fogle felt his ears splitting. He stuck his fingers in them. *This is it!* Another roar followed, louder than the last. *I'm going to die.*

Barton lowered both him and Cass to the ground, setting them behind him.

"BARTON HATE YOU, BLACKIE! YOU WON'T TAKE BARTON HOME TODAY!"

There was a loud snort and a blast of furnace-hot air.

Fogle could smell sulfur and brimstone. He opened his eyes and looked. *Oh slat!* His knees warbled. His stomach recoiled. His warm blood went cold.

Blackie wasn't only taller than a horse; he was taller than five horses, maybe ten. His scales were black as coal. Hard as iron. His citrine eyes burned with life. Intelligent. Crafty. Teeth tall as a dwarf and sharper than spears. A great tail swiping back and forth like a preying cat. His giant claws dug into the hardened ground like it was mud.

"RAAAH-OOOOOOOOOOOOOOOR!"

The sound was maddening. Without realizing it, Fogle found Cass's arms wrapped around him, eyes shut, trembling.

"Please don't roar again," she said. "Please don't roar again."

Fogle could barely hear her words. Even Barton's bellowing shouts seemed muffled compared to the dragon's terrifying sounds.

"BARTON KILL YOU, BLACKIE! BARTON KILL YOU NOW!"

Fogle was shaking his head. *You aren't going to kill that thing.*

The dragon's wings seemed impossibly long as it spread them and roared once more.

Cass was screaming, tears appearing in the corners of her eyes. They huddled on the ground like two babes in a storm. *This is happening!*

Fogle could feel the hot coals of the dragon's breath getting hotter. Then Barton said the unthinkable.

"BARTON HAVE WIZARD TO HELP HIM NOW. ATTACK HIM, WIZARD!"

The dragon's long neck moved his head from Barton down on the ground facing him.

That thing can understand Barton. Stupid giant! What can I do? Think, Fogle, think!

"HA! HA! HA! BLACKIE GOING TO GET IT NOW!"

The giants were terrifying enough, and he'd had help with them. The dragon was something entirely different. It wasn't shaped like a man. It was shaped like a monster.

The dragon snorted and sniffed. A strange cackling erupted in his long neck.

"WHAT ARE YOU WAITING FOR, WIZARD? KILL BLACKIE!"

"He doesn't want me. He wants you, Barton!" Fogle yelled.

That's when Cass looked up at him with weak eyes and said, "Do whatever you have to, Fogle. I'll fight with you."

From behind Barton's monstrous leg, he touched foreheads with Cass and said, "Fight or Die, my sweet. Fight or die!"

"WHAT?" Barton said, leering down at him with his good eye.

Do something or die, Wizard. A spell came to mind. *Huh! Am I ready this time? For a dragon?* He wrapped his arm around Barton's ankle and yelled upward. "Barton!"

"WHAT?"

"How much to you hate that dragon?"

"A LOT!"

"Get ready then! Help's coming!"

Closing his eyes, he summoned his power. Words of magic filled his head. Rolled from his tongue. Churned from his lips like hummingbird wings. Seconds later, he sagged, Cass holding him up.

"HAMMER!" he said.

A glowing hammer, with a head like an anvil, materialized at Barton's feet. It was longer than Fogle was tall, radiating with energy. Barton snatched it up and slung it at Blackie, striking him full in the chest.

KAROOM!

The dragon let out an angry screech, flapping backward and away.

Barton charged over the landscape, snatching the hammer up in his mighty arms, swinging.

WHAM! WHAM! WHAM!

Fogle felt the air shake with every blow. Blackie screeched and clawed, angry, hateful.

"BARTON KILL BLACKIE!"

WHAM!

"FEEL THAT, BLACKIE!"

WHAM!

"BARTON HATE BLACKIE!!"

The two titans fought and clawed over the ground, but Blackie was still bigger, quicker, and deadlier. Barton was a man fighting a giant-sized lizard.

Like a snake, Blackie struck, biting Barton's hammer-swinging arm.

"AARGH!"

The hammer fell from his grasp.

Barton cocked his elbow back and socked Blackie in the eye.

The pair thrashed and rolled through the dirt.

Barton was flailing and screaming.

Blackie clawing and biting.

It was an awful sight. Fogle grabbed Cass, pulling her as far away from the Chaos as he could.

"NOOO!" Barton squeezed.

Blackie pinned Barton under his weight, an adult atop a large child.

The giant's fingers clawed at the dirt, clutching for the hammer.

Blackie swatted the hammer away with his tail and hissed in Barton's face.

Fogle could see the giant's futile squirms under Blackie's power and weight. Barton, a giant, yet still a boy, couldn't overcome his adversary, his oppressor. It was a sad thing when the fire in Barton's eye went out, defeated.

"Help me, Wizard?" Barton said, exhausted, fingers feebly clutching at the dirt.

Fogle did nothing. The dragon didn't want him or Cass. It only wanted Barton. Keeping Cass behind him, he watched Blackie dig his black claws into Barton's shoulders.

"OW!" Barton cried. "Wizard, help!"

Whump! Whump! Whump!

Stirring the air like a small tornado, Blackie was up and off, with Barton in his grasp.

The betrayed look on Barton's face would haunt him forever, but he had to protect Cass.

Behind him, Cass cleared her throat.

"What?" he said, watching Blackie and Barton slowly sail away.

"Do something, Fogle Idiot! Shoot that dragon down!" Cass ordered.

The power of a dragon was one thing. The power of a beautiful angry woman was another. Without thinking, Fogle's body charged with power. Flashes of lightning shot from his fingers across the sky, striking Blackie full force.

Blackie roared, this time with pain, not pleasure.

Barton slipped from the dragon's grasp and plummeted a hundred feet to the ground with a thud.

"That's better," Cass said.

Blackie hung in the sky, hovering, flapping his great wings, struggling to stay afloat.

"Whatever you did, I don't think that dragon liked it. Do it again?"

Fogle shook his head. "I don't have enough power to kill it. I'd better protect us."

The dragon's citrine eyes leered at him like burning suns. He'd hurt it. He'd made it mad. Now it was coming for him.

It flapped over towards them, long great neck swaying back and forth.

Fogle grabbed Cass, pulled her close, and summoned a spell.

Hanging like a black cloud over them, Blackie opened his mouth and breathed.

The blast of a thousand furnaces came out.

Fogle stood tall, a mystic bubble protecting them, scattering the flames around them.

The heat was intense, like standing at the mouth of a blacksmith's forge.

The magic shield kept them away from instant incineration. Sweat poured from Fogle's face. The shield would only hold up as long as he could.

How long can this thing breathe! He felt his air begin to thin, his lungs labor, his concentration waver.

"Hold on, Fogle!" Cass encouraged him, her face as red as a beet, "Hold on!"

He couldn't. He fought with all his will, but his will was out.

"I'm sorry, Cass!" He shook his head. "I can't. Cass … I—"

The fire stopped.

Blackie reared up, screeching. Barton was on the dragon's back, holding onto its wing with one hand and pounding it in the back of the head with the hammer in the other.

Fogle took Cass by the hand and tried to run away.

SWAT!

Blackie's tail licked out, knocking them from their feet.

Fogle gathered his knees beneath him and summoned more lighting in his grasp.

In front of him, Blackie slung Barton from his back. Wary, Blackie's eyes focused on Fogle's glowing hands.

"You don't like that, do you?" Fogle rose to his feet. "Stings, doesn't it, Lizard?"

A growl rumbled in the dragon's throat. The creature was intelligent, thinking, planning.

"Leave us be, Dragon," Fogle yelled. "Else I'll unleash all of my fury!"

Twenty feet from his nose, the Dragons' red tongue licked out over its fangs. There must have been a thousand of them.

"AAAIIEEEH!" Cass screamed.

The tip of Blackie's tail encircled her waist and dragged her away.

"NO!" Fogle yelled after her.

The dragon tucked her into his chest, playing with her in the palm of his hand like a tiny doll.

Fogle could swear it smiled.

Whump! Whump! Whump!

Up it went, Cass stunned in its grasp, leaving Fogle devastated on the cracked terrain as they disappeared into the clouds.

"CAAAAASSS!!!"

39

Castle Almen, a character in its own right, had many secrets. Many lost over the centuries, others found. It was spotless; no cobwebs or dust coated the dark wood and velvety furniture. Every piece of metal was polished. Every crystal gleamed.

Lord Almen closed the drapes to a large bay window and sealed the balcony door shut. This was once the bedroom of his father. He and his best Shadow Sentry, a long limbed man, fled the Keep and traversed the castle utilizing the secret corridors, avoiding the commotion caused by the underlings.

Still weak, Lord Almen rummaged through the drawers of a black walnut desk until he placed his hand around a dagger and stuffed it into his belt. Quickly, he made his way over to the fire place and stood on the hearth.

"Come, stand with me," he ordered.

The sentry obliged, stepping onto the mosaic hearth, fingering the pommels of his swords.

"Tell no one of this," Lord Almen warned, shoving back a marble block on the fire place mantle. The colorful tiles shifted beneath their feet, then disappeared, leaving a black hole. The lanky warrior in the black ghost armor cocked his head. Rapidly, they were sinking.

"You may want to close your eyes, Virgil."

A quick rush of air followed, the feeling of one flying, the weightlessness of a feather, and an abrupt halt that bobbled his stomach. Opening his eyes, the first thing Lord Almen saw was his office beneath the kitchen, and the front door was still closed.

Beside him, Virgil's knees wobbled, his long arms stretching out for support. Lord Almen didn't bother. Instead, he searched his office. No one would have suspected a single thing was out of place, but he knew. It angered him. Whoever had been here had some idea what to look for and what they were taking. Tonio's sword was gone. The shelf that concealed the small secret door was out of place, and the door was open. A variety of footprints had disturbed the dust. *Melegal* was the first thought that came to mind. *Sefron* was the second. But, more than that, something lingered in the air. The scent of underlings.

"Virgil, see to it that door is secure," he said, opening a small case full of vials. "You be keeping post and sending warning if anything comes through there."

"I hope it's underlings," Virgil said. He cracked his neck side to side and eased his sword from the scabbard. "Or any arsehole, for that matter."

Lord Almen couldn't see the man's face behind his cloth mask, but Virgil was one of his best soldiers. A survivor of the Warfield. A friend of danger. Lord Almen favored men like that. Cold blooded killers.

Lord Almen drank down one of the vials, followed by the other. He tossed one filled with a pale red liquid to Virgil.

"Take that," Lord Almen said. He rolled his shoulders. He was feeling better and stronger already. "It will give you stamina. Improve your focus."

Virgil pulled up his mask—exposing his rugged chin, split lip and rotting teeth—before he swallowed it down.

Lord Almen took a deep breath through his nose, filling his lungs to capacity and slowly releasing.

Virgil thumbed his blade. "This sword is the finest blade I've ever owned, Lord Almen, and I'll put it to good use in your defense." He pulled his mask back down. "I feel like killing."

"So do I."

Disappointed that Tonio's sword was gone, Lord Almen grabbed another blade, a poniard with an ivory hilt, and set it on his desk table. Opening a wardrobe, he grabbed his own suit of ghost armor and slipped it on. It fit like a glove, coating him like a thick flexible skin. A smile came to the corner of his lips. *It's been too long.*

"Sir, you look dangerous, but I plan on killing them all before they make it to you."

Almen put his hand on Virgil's shoulder. "You do that, and I'll give you your own room in this castle and a personal servant girl, too."

Black masked, Virgil saluted with his sword. "My life for my Lord. Their life with my sword."

With that, Lord Almen stepped through the small door's opening and headed down the stairs on cat's feet. Stopping, he closed his eyes and slowed his breath. He heard nothing. Not a shuffle, nor a scuffle, nor a scratch. Breathing through his nose, nothing caught his potion-heightened senses. As they passed the bottom of the stairwell, the torches came to life. The large chamber cast his shadow. All six doors were closed.

Where is she?

Making his way back to the alcove where all the Keys usually hung, he noticed the empty pegs on the wall. How in all of Bish had they escaped his grasp? *Melegal.* It had to be. Or had they been taken by the underlings?

He chuckled, remembering the first time he and his father found the chamber. There'd been more doors. More pegs. More Keys. And rings. Many came, many went. He tried his best to understand it. It seemed the chamber had a will of its own. It would serve him, so he thought, so long as he fed it. A mystery. An advantage he didn't hesitate to press. No wonder the underlings wanted it. But how did they know about it? Who made it? *Seven Keys last I counted. Eight with the one I gave to Jarla. I hope she still has it.* He looked at the floor. The slightest sucking licked at his boots.

Lord Almen paced around the circle of the great chamber. His castle was under siege. The underlings had penetrated for the second time in days. He could have held out in the keep, but the Keys were what he was certain they wanted. He had no plans to part with them. They gave him power. Control. To go whenever and however he wanted to go. And until several days ago, only few knew about his secret. Now that secret had been compromised.

Standing in the center of the room facing the alcove and the ancient doors, Lord Almen stood, watching and listening. *Where is that Brigand Queen?* He twisted the finger ring that he used to summon her. She never appeared at the same duration, but always she came. Minutes, an hour maybe, but never a day. He frowned.

Perhaps she's dead.

She had a Key and a ring. Her Key would open the doors and give him access and freedom if the underlings took over. And if the underlings had the other seven Keys, the Keys that they knew about, what would they do? They could strike day or night all over Bish if they wanted to. Just like he had. He couldn't fight the smile on his lips.

The minutes passed, leaving Lord Almen alone in his thoughts, his memories.

For years Lord Almen had used the Keys, slipping into rival bedrooms and parlors, strangling or cutting their throats while they slept. Already a Master Assassin, the Keys had made his job all too easy. Castle Almen had moved up the ranks quickly on account of it. The ancient chamber was a recent discovery, come upon by accident by his father. Slowly over the years, they had abused the power of the ancient chamber, never truly understanding it. But he knew, he'd always known, someone would come after the power one day or another. And now it seemed that day had come.

He froze. Up the stairwell echoed the sound of wood exploding into splinters. He shifted his stance. Readied his sword. Chitters and the clash of steel followed. A human cry of alarm went out. Silence fell. The room went cold.

Something clopped down the stairs, rolling to a stop at the bottom. It was Virgil's head. A clean cut through the neck. Blood spilled into the mosaic. A sucking sound followed. Lord Almen sheathed his sword.

The first past the torches was an underling, copper eyed with a bandolier of knives around his chest. He was tall, over six feet, the tallest underling Lord Almen had ever seen. Blood dripped from the tip of his sword, and a fierce grin parted his lips. Behind him, others came: two, then four, then six. Some were in black plate armor that didn't clank or rattle; the others wore little more than leather or a cloak. Blades of many kinds hung loose in their grips, and their eyes were bright with color.

Lord Almen rubbed the sweat from his hands. So many adversaries were to be expected, but everyone else in the castle flooded his thoughts. It was entirely possible that his family were being wiped out one by one. *I hope they made the Keep at least.*

Still, he stood tall, a statue by comparison. "I am Royal Lord Almen, Liege of this castle, and I request a parlay."

Coming closer, the copper eyes of the first underling narrowed to slits, a sinister chuckle erupting in his throat. "Parlay," he said, slipping his sword in the sheath in a wink of an eye. "I don't see any need for a parlay, Human Lord. After all, we've seized your castle, within your city. I think there is little you can do to help us."

About then, a wheezing sound caught his ear. Sefron the Cleric was huffing down the stairs, oversized robes hanging from his body, his gnarled staff clacking on the steps. Lord Almen's usual frown expanded when they locked eyes. *Traitor!* Lord Almen didn't hide his rage as the underlings formed a tight circle around him.

"Sefron, you sickening slaggard! It was you that gave up the castle! I'll cut open that fat belly of yours!"

Sefron groaned, straightening the bend in his back with a chuckle. He rubbed his saggy chin and blinked his bulging eye. "Master Kierway, may I have this one?"

"Fool," Kierway said, "this man will prove to be a better resource than you, certainly."

Sefron came closer, trying to push past the underlings, his hand reaching out.

Lord Almen recoiled back the ever slightest. He knew Sefron's secret and what the man was capable of. It was why he recruited him in the first place.

"Don't you dare, Servant," Almen said.

"Stay back, Sefron, you disgusting fool." Kierway shook his head. "You bother me, but this man, he doesn't bother me so much, other than being a human." He scratched his cheek with his long black nails. "Tell me about this *parlay*, Lord Almen. I'm curious."

Tearing his eyes away from Sefron, Lord Almen cleared his throat. "I've a history with your kind, Master Kierway. It was I who aligned myself with you at Outpost Thirty-One."

"So you are a traitor?"

"A survivor." Lord Almen nodded. "A master planner. My family and my castle are what mean the most in life to me. I dare not guess what the underlings have in mind with my castle or this city, but I will assist you. I'm a man of many secrets. Tell me what you want, and I assure you that I can help."

Kierway moved with the ease of a cat, sauntering through the chamber, tugging on one door handle after the other. Standing in the alcove near the key posts, he said, "This architecture is strange, but similar to many chambers in the Underland. Hmmm, so, Lord Almen, tell me, where are the Keys?"

Lord Almen kept his relief concealed. He'd lost track of much while he'd been down for several days. He eyed Sefron briefly. He could tell the cleric must have had something to do with that, or had he? The wound between his ribs should have been fatal, and he vaguely remembered Sefron coming to his aid, only to betray him now.

"Stolen," Lord Almen said.

Kierway crossed his arms and leaned his shoulder over one of the doors. "So, you are waiting for the thief to return with them? Certainly that wouldn't happen in the middle of a siege. Not unless the person with the Keys would have a reason to come back, and into that question you might have more insight than I." He raised his eyebrows. "Of course, perhaps you are down here because you are expecting someone else. Seven pegs. Seven Keys. Six doors. Interesting opportunities."

One of the most frustrating things that Lord Almen had encountered about underlings was that they weren't stupid. Every one he'd dealt with had a calculating mind and cunning demeanor. He admired that about them. And something else. Unlike men, they weren't greedy, at least not in terms of material things. Instead, they thirsted for something else without distraction. Power.

"I can't readily say, and I cannot refute the possibility either."

There was a long pause. Surrounding him, standing like statues poised to strike, the breathing of the underlings was barely audible. Lord Almen glanced over at Sefron, who now sat wheezing on the stairs. He should have rid himself of the slaggard long ago, but Sefron was so resourceful when it came to digging information from his enemies. And there was another thing. Perhaps Sefron was still his ally. The man gave no sign of it.

One by one, Kierway slid three throwing knives from his bandolier. He juggled them with one hand. The blades flashing in the air, hand moving in a blur. Kierway's expression was lax and bored. "We wait, if need be, Lord Almen, but it might be a very long time. Of course, through our sources, we know where the Keys are. They are with a man, one of your own. What is his name, Sefron?"

"Melegal."

Feigning surprise, Lord Almen said to Sefron, "And how do you know this?"

Sefron sat with his legs crossed and sighed. "He's the last one we saw with them in here." He pointed at his ruined eye. "Thanks to him I have this."

Kierway snapped his wrist.

Thunk!

A knife jutted in the support beam by Sefron's head, causing him to jump.

"No." Kierway's eyes narrowed at Sefron. "Thanks to me you have that." He turned to Almen. "This man, Melegal, created the ultimate dilemma. Acts like an underling, that one. Cool and cunning." He resumed his juggling.

Inside of himself, Lord Almen was astounded. Melegal had found the Keys! But how? And why? *Hmmm… I see. The underlings recruited Sefron to find the Keys, meaning they must have known they were here. But why now? Why after all these years? It seems they have even darker secrets than I.*

"What's this?" Putting away his knives, Kierway drew a sword.

By the stairs, Sefron rose to his feet.

A faint yellow glow outlined the door where Kierway was leaning. "Chit! Chit!" he said. Underlings moved into the shadows. Some in full armor, some little, others none. "You, stay with Lord Almen!" He pointed to one then to another. "You, stay with the other one."

Lord Almen was pushed back into the alcove, where on tenterhooks, he and two of the underlings waited. *Finally*, he thought. *For what little good it will do.*

The yellow light disappeared, and the ancient door swung open.

40

"**W**HAT IS THIS PLACE?" CREED fumbled through the dark.

"Silence, Creed." Melegal held his stomach.

You'd think I'd be used to this miserable feeling by now.

Creed moaned. "Slat, I feel like I'm hung over. What just happened?"

"You'll see." Melegal searched the darkness for a handle or a knob. "Listen to me, Creed. When I open this door, we're going to be in a chamber. People might be there, and underlings for all I know, so get your guts in order, and be ready for anything."

Creed scoffed. "I'm always ready for anything; just give me a moment."

Melegal pressed his ear to the door. If anything was moving on the other side, he wouldn't know. The door was as thick and hard as stone—and magical, for all he knew. Still, he worried. He assumed the Key took him back to the chamber beneath Castle Almen, but maybe it didn't. Maybe it took him somewhere else.

"What's that?" Creed huffed. "Did you feel something? Something's in here."

Melegal, still frozen, felt a gentle brush between his legs. Looking down, he saw two pale white eyes. "Octopus," he murmured.

"What's that?"

"Don't worry about it, Creed. Now listen to me. Do you want to go in hard and fast or quick and easy?"

Truth was, Melegal had to wonder what would happen if others were in there. Could he slip back in and seal the door? He hadn't thought long enough about it; he'd had no choice. And what if the underlings were inside? He straightened his cap. *Be ready for a nose bleed.*

"I don't suppose there really is a fast and easy way, is there?"

"I don't think we've much choice. Just be ready to fight..." Melegal found the handle and started to pull.

"...or Die," Creed finished.

Quick. Quick. Quick.

Melegal pressed the latch downward and shoved the door open. He darted straight forward, rolled, and rose to his knees, swords ready.

Creed spun along the wall, blades whirling.

The massive chamber was silent, torches flickering, forcing a wavering light.

Narrowing his eyes, Melegal noted the figures lined against the walls in the shadows. Their eyes were glimmering. *Bish! It's underlings!*

Whamp. The door they came through shut.

Leaning against the wall with two swords crossed over his back was an underling as tall as him. His copper eyes glowered at him.

"Ah... you must be the one called Melegal."

The other underlings emerged from the shadows.

The tall underling continued. "I just missed you the last time, it seems. You are the one Sefron calls The Rat."

Stupid! Stupid! Stupid! I should have taken my chances in the streets! One. Two. Three... Seven underlings. No crossbows. No darts. Two torches. Where to go? Where to go?

That's when he caught the heavy stare of Royal Lord Almen. A sword was pressed into the Vulture-like man's back. Wary, Melegal turned in his spot. Sefron's eyes were on him as well.

The cleric shuffled, wheezed, and squirmed at the side of an underling that held a blade to his belly.

Melegal allowed a grin and returned his focus to the copper-eyed underling.

"I am that rat. And who might you be?"

"Master Kierway." The underling pushed himself off the wall.

"Oh, so you are the one that Sefron wanted me to get the Keys for?"

Lord Almen shot Sefron a look, but the cleric remained silent.

"Indeed, and I assume you have those Keys?"

Slowly, Melegal nodded his head. There was no reason to lie now. All they would do was kill him and take them. He searched Lord Almen's face and saw nothing of help. It seemed the Castle was at a loss. But even if the underlings didn't kill him, he was certain Lord Almen would. After all, he'd tried to kill Lord Almen and failed.

How will you squeeze out of this one, Rat?

He glanced at Creed. The man stood tall, eyes darting from one underling to another, ready to fight anything and everything.

"I do have the Keys." Melegal sheathed his swords. "And they are yours to have."

Lord Almen's face turned pale.

Melegal reached inside his pockets.

Creed harrumphed. "Let them take those Keys from your dead body. Don't make a deal with the underlings, Detective. There are only a few of them."

"Mind your tongue, Bloodhound," Lord Almen said. "It's not your back that's dancing with a sword."

"Huh," Creed said. "At least I'll die with one in my hand, not in my back."

"As much as I'd rather not admit it," Kierway said, "I agree with this man over here. I'd rather die than make deals with the enemy. That's the kind of fighter I am. But at the moment, that's not my mission. The Keys are. Let me see them!"

"Certainly." Melegal fumbled through his clothes. *No rush. Not too fast. Not too slow.* Producing the 1st Key, Amethyst, he placed it on the floor.

Every eye in the chamber widened.

"And, Master Kierway," Melegal said, "considering my inevitable death, I would like you to consider another request." He set the 2nd Key, a diamond set in a brass setting, down on the floor. Out of the corner of his eye, he saw Lord Almen fidget the slightest.

Sefron's wheezing picked up.

"Say whatever you like, Human," Kierway said, "as you are intelligent to realize that your death is inevitable."

Melegal stood up and pointed.

"Let me sink my blades into that bug-eyed bastard, Sefron. He's the reason I came back. To cut his throat. I can't imagine you have any practical use for him. He failed to get the Keys. I didn't. And now I lay them at your feet with that one tiny request."

Sefron managed a fearsome snarl.

Melegal jumped. Still, he set the 3rd Key down.

"Let's just fight them, Man!" Creed urged. "I've killed underlings before." He eyed Kierway. "Dozens."

"Perhaps you'll get your chance, Human," Kierway said, still focusing on Melegal. "But first, let me see another Key. And maybe, assuming you do have all seven, I'll grant your request."

It made sense, what Creed was suggesting. If they fought and made it to the doors, they could escape. And so far as he understood it, he could go wherever he wanted, if he used the same door. *Two-Ten City might be nice right now.* As for the other doors, where did they go and which Key fit which door?

Of all the things to forget, he hadn't noted which Key was on which peg next to which door. It had been dark when he took them. *Clumsy fool!* For now, all he could do was buy a little more time and see what happened.

He set the 4th Key down. Its gem burned like orange fire.

As for overpowering the underlings in the room, it didn't seem likely. The ones in plate armor were of the likes he'd never seen before. He ventured any of them would be a match for Creed, who was certainly a superior fighter to himself. And Master Kierway wasn't at all worried. The underling and his brood made the men look wholly inadequate. *He didn't even ask us to disarm ourselves.*

"You'd made a fine Bloodhound," Creed said, "on account of you wanting to kill that Cleric and all."

Melegal ignored him, his shoulders and back tightening as he laid the 5th Key down. So much had happened since Lord Almen had acquired his service and made him a detective. He remembered those days in the man's office, the pressure, the fear the man put into him. He could feel Lord Almen's eyes heavy upon him, but he no longer felt that fear. *I wonder what he has in mind. He must have some plan.* Reaching inside his vest, he felt the long case he had tucked away. *Might not ever get a chance to use this. A shame.*

"Here is the 6th Key, Master Kierway." He knelt and rubbed his hands on his pants. "Can I cut that cur's throat now? Before I hand over the 7th? Just let me take his life, and I'll freely give you mine."

Kierway came closer. "You've made it interesting; I'll grant you that. Perhaps, I'll make you prisoners and lock you in a cage together instead. I think we underlings would find that entertaining."

"Would you want to be put in a cage with him?" Melegal said, unable to help himself.

"Well spoken!" Creed said, shifting on his heels.

Kierway showed him his sharp teeth. "Sorry, Human Called Melegal, but I see no reason to make such a deal." He paused and gestured. "I wouldn't be what I am, giving such consideration to a human. Now," he held out his clawed hand, "the 7th Key, please."

Shing!

In a blink, Kierway had pulled out his blade and put it at Melegal's throat.

For the first time in recent memory, Melegal felt beads of sweat on his forehead.

"You worry me, Human Called Melegal."

Melegal swallowed. "And why is that?"

"It seems foolish that you keep all the Keys on you, understanding their value. If it were me, I'd keep them hidden in many places. A bargaining chip if my life depended on it. A smart man would have hidden them all, would he not?"

I can't be that stupid. Of course I should have hidden them. Am I really going to die a fool?

Melegal's memories flashed to his friends: Venir, Georgio, Lefty, Billip and Mikkel.

I can't be as stupid as them.

But he had thought briefly about hiding the Keys and concluded that so long as they thought he had even one Key, they'd hunt him—the Royals and the underlings—forever and ever. *A clean slate or a clean death is what I'm going for. Let the rest of Bish plot and scheme all they want.*

"I did think of that, Master Kierway, but why risk the torture? They say, 'A quick beheading has no sting.'" Clasping his hands around the final Key, he summoned power from the hat that rested on his head. His mind cleared. Blood and mystic energy mixed in his veins. *Faster. Quicker. One step ahead.*

Everything around him slowed: Sefron's breath. Creed's blinking. The flickering of the torches. The clutching of Kierway's fingers.

Ahead of Melegal, behind Lord Almen, the outline of the ancient door glowed with new life and started to open.

Kierway's sword arm flicked backward.

Move or die! Melegal. Move!

Kierway's arm came forward.

41

Catching her breath, Jarla fumbled for the latch on the door. In the darkness, she was alone with Tonio's ragged breathing.

"Don't do anything foolish," she said, brushing against him and pulling away.

"Where are we?" he said, heavy feet shuffling around.

At the moment, Jarla wasn't so sure whether or not it would be a good idea to tell him. It didn't really matter either way. Lord Almen would be waiting, and what other surprises he had in store she couldn't imagine, but he must have needed her.

"Just be ready, you bloodless goon, because you're going first."

She pushed the door open.

Over Tonio's shoulder, the torches were bright beacons. It took a couple of seconds for Jarla's eyes to adjust to the figures in the room. Lord Almen, a few other men, surrounded by underlings.

"Father?" Tonio's body tensed in front of her.

Lord Almen had a look on his face she'd never seen there before. Surprise.

Behind him, an underling had a blade pointed at Lord Almen's back.

It stirred Jarla, her energy renewing, her senses firing a warning.

"Father!" Tonio's garbled voice echoed in the chamber.

Jarla stepped forward.

Another underling stepped between them and Lord Almen. Two long knives were gripped in his hands, ruby eyes glinting, bare muscular chest stuck out.

Across the chamber, two more underling soldiers armed with barbed spears filed inside as well.

Other than that, no one moved.

"The odds aren't going to get any better than this!" an unfamiliar voice shouted.

Clang!

Bang!

Lord Almen moved. Fast as a cat, he spun behind his underling oppressor and drove a dagger in its throat.

The bare-chested underling closed in, cutting out a portion of Tonio's chest armor.

The big man rammed his sword through its belly, lifted it from its feet, and slung it into another wall.

"Jarla!" Lord Almen screamed.

When she turned to his voice, an underling in black plate armor stepped in her path, swords moving like striking snakes.

Clang! Clang! Clang!

Parrying with two hands, she found her back against the wall.

Fast and fluid it came. Jarla parried and countered, stabbing its chest, her sword glancing off the armor.

"What in Bish are you?" the underling yelled at Tonio.

Krang!

Tonio hit it so hard he knocked it from its feet.

A split second later, Lord Almen kneeled down and jammed his dagger under its chin, piercing its skull.

Huffing, Jarla found Lord Almen's eyes.

"Get the Keys!" He ordered.

"What Keys?" she said.

"On the floor! Don't let the underlings have them." Ducking under an underling's arm, Lord Almen ripped out a long poniard and started swinging.

"Keys!" Tonio was pounding his way through his underling assailants. "Get for Father!"

Another underling adorned in black leathers surged at her, two short swords in its hands, sharp teeth bared.

Slice!

It howled and jumped back, clutching its split and bleeding chin.

"Don't you chitter at me, you little fiend."

When Tonio emerged through the door, Melegal swore he heard his heart stop. The Yellow-Haired Butcher had arrived. Behind him, the insufferable woman, Jarla. He was uncertain whether to be glad to see either one of them. They both deserved horrifying deaths so far as he was concerned. *Perhaps they'll get them.*

Tonio's face showed an ounce of humanity as he called for his father.

Jarla's scowling face, riddled with scars, showed creases of concern.

Behind Melegal, Sefron wheezed.

Kill Sefron.

The footfalls of more underlings came down the stairs.

Creed took in a deep breath. "The odds aren't going to get any better than this!"

Kierway hissed through his teeth, glowered at Melegal, and cut at his neck.

Everything in the room moved slowly except the underling's blade.

Melegal jerked his head down and jumped away.

Swish!

He touched the thin red line dripping on his neck.

Slat, that was fast!

With a brush of his foot, Melegal scattered 6 of the Keys in all directions.

Clang!

Whew! Keep him busy, Creed. Keep him busy.

Kierway caught Creed's swords in a crossed sword parry.

"Sefron," Kierway ordered, "get those Keys while I cut this man to ribbons! Brethren, help him!"

Man and underling squared off, lightning fast strokes ringing off each other like bells.

But Melegal had his own problems to worry about. He tucked the 7th Key back inside his clothes. *Slat on the Keys! Kill Sefron! Save yourself!*

The battle was furious.

Underlings swarmed, jumping out from all directions at the human attackers.

Tonio stood in the middle, a one-man army.

Jarla's sword darted at underling throats, her eyes darting after the Keys.

Lord Almen. *Slat! Where is he?*

Melegal let his heightened awareness take over. *Ah, there he is.* The haunting form of a man hung like a shadow near the wall, striking down an unsuspecting underling that crossed his path. *Interesting!*

A dozen yards away, Sefron slowly shuffled over the floor, bending over to grab one of the Keys.

Melegal extended his dart bracers and let Sefron have it.

Clatch-zip! Clatch-zip!

Sefron whined like a dying sheep, falling over, clutching at his legs.

Melegal crossed the room—deftly avoiding the melee—and kept shooting.

Clatch-zip! Click! Click!

Melegal overpowered Sefron and straddled his belly, pressing a knife to his throat.

"Remember my friend, the servant girl? You know, the one you almost whipped to death?"

Sefron's bulging eyes were merciless. "Hard to say. There's been so many." He licked his lips. "And there'll be many more to come, I assure you, long after you're dead."

Melegal felt Sefron's clammy hand wrap around his wrist. It was cold, ice cold.

"No, slug, it's you who'll be dead. And if I had the time, I'd whip you to death myself."

Melegal pushed his dagger into Sefron's throat, but no blood came forth, just Sefron's cackle.

"Fool, do you really think I'm so weak that a rodent such as yourself could take me?"

A wave of nausea overcame Melegal. *What's happening!*

Sefron's grip became as solid as iron, squeezing his wrist to the point of breaking it.

His dagger fell from his numb wrist.

Before his eyes, Sefron changed. His hair thickened. His teeth straighten. His body firmed like a fighter's beneath him.

No! What is this!

Melegal watched his hand curl and shrivel. It horrified him.

"No!" he groaned, trying to pull his rawboned body away.

Sefron cackled and sucked his teeth.

"Ah, such succulent life from such a scrawny man. Surprising."

Creed's father had told him that the first time he picked up a blade and swung, he was three. He'd cut into a leg of mutton and saved the butcher some trouble. He'd been swinging steel ever since.

Bang! Chang! Clang! Swish. Swish. Chang!

His opponent: an underling that weaved steel with skill he'd never seen. He thought he'd seen everything. He'd thought he knew everything.

Creed parried, dodged, ducked, and jumped backward. Forward and followed up with a chop-chop-chop.

Always attacking at the same time, the copper-eyed underling batted every blow away.

Not possible! Creed backed away.

The underling's blades were of the finest craftsmanship, archaic and curved at the very end. They moved like black flashes of lightning. Quick as a blink of an eye.

Creed had trained all his life, defeated every man he faced in fence or battle. The ones that would fight him, that is. Many Royals never gave him the honor. It bothered him. And now, entering his prime, for the first time in his life, he was worried.

"I never believed an underling could be so fast," he stalled. "Quite remarkable."

Kierway showed his sharp teeth. "Remarkable is my lowest level of skill, Human. Whatever it is you've done, I've already done a hundred times a year over a hundred years. You should know: this battle is over."

Creed wiped the sweat from his forehead with the back of his hand.

"Then I suppose this is what I've been training all my life for. Ee-Yah!"

In a flash, his gleaming blade leapt at the underling's throat.

Kierway deftly shifted his body a foot out of the way and swatted into the backs of Creed's legs with the back of his sword.

"Ugh! Blast it!" Creed cried out. He could feel the blood dripping down over his thighs already.

The floor made an eerie sucking sound.

Creed's face showed horror. "What in Bish is going on?"

"Interesting," Kierway replied. "It seems the floor hungers. I think I shall feed it."

Creed banged his blades together. One blade the finest of steel, the other enchanted by a mystic forge master. Until today, he'd always felt himself invincible with them and his skill, but it seemed for the first time in his life he'd met his match. He banged his blades again and muttered angrily to himself. "Come on, Creed! Draw his blood at least!"

Use your reach. You're longer!

Steel scraped against steel. Sweat mixed with blood.

They say, 'When your final battle comes, you'll know.'

His father had told him that, years ago, hours before he died at the Warfield. He'd always wondered who killed his father. A great sword. A great hound. Now he'd never know.

He charged. One sword high, the other low, he swung.

Kierway caught both blades on the outside with a smirk.

Creed's booted toe lashed out into Kierway's chin, clattering his teeth and splitting his lip.

Shocked, the underling hissed.

Creed kept swinging hard and fast.

Bang! Clang! Chang! Chang! Bang!

Back and forth the pair went. One master. One ancient master.

The underling's arms were strong like steel, but tireless and flexible as snakes.

For seconds, Creed pressed the advantage.

Slice.

Kierway ended it with a lightning fast stroke across Creed's thigh.

Slice.

Followed by another one across his belly.

Slice.

A hunk of flesh fell to the floor. It was Creed's.

"Hear that, Human? It's the sound of your death getting closer."

Parry, Fool! Parry!

Blue sparks showered the air.

Kierway pounded at his blades. Knocked Creed's steel down, numbing his hands.

That was Creed's plan. To beat his opponent's arms down until they felt like lead. But now his own arms felt like lead. Laboring for breath, he struggled to keep up with the blinding speed of Kierway's blades. Below, something sucked at his feet on the floor.

"You tire, Human." Kierway swatted Creed's blades away like toys. "Drop your blades, and I'll give you a merciful death."

"No. I'm going to cut you just once, Black Fiend. I can't go down like this. I can't."

Bang!

Kierway ripped one of Creed's swords from his hand and paused.

Creed's lone sword arm trembled. He grabbed his wrist with the other to support it.

"You are a fine swordsman, Human. But I've faced many better. All dead now, of course. So take note that you'll die at the hand of the finest swordsman this world has ever known."

Creed labored for breath.

Kierway was barely winded, his eyes darting around, looking for something.

"So be it then, Underling." Head down, Creed took a knee and set down his sword. "Vanquish me."

"With pleasure."

Catching a glimpse of Kierway's nearest knee, Creed lunged forward with everything he had, stabbing with a dagger concealed in his bracer. The blade sank into flesh and hit bone.

Kierway howled.

"I swore I'd cut you!"

Kierway's blade came for his head.

42

C ORRIN RUBBED HIS EYES. FOR hours he'd sat watching the images in the fountain, mesmerized. Trinos had shown him the world outside the City of Bone, the home he'd never left. It was all fascinating and horrifying at the same time.

"What do you think?" Trinos said.

Corrin stretched out his stiff arms and shook his head. "It's a horrible, horrible world out there." He cleared his throat. "And just as bad in here."

Trinos lifted her brows without making a crease in her perfect forehead.

"How so?"

Corrin wasn't sure how to respond at first. After all, he was a murderer and cutthroat, even though he was pretty certain that was all behind him now. Watching all he'd seen—people dying of thirst or getting lost in the Outlands, battling for honor in a place she said was called the Warfield—it seemed as if someone was always fighting something else somewhere in this world. All his years, he'd assumed Bone was the worst the world had to offer, but it clearly wasn't. The entire world was in a struggle, and the driving force behind it all was the underlings. Or was it? He wasn't so sure.

He took an apple from a wicker basket, started peeling it with his knife, and looked into her eyes.

"I always figured there was solitude somewhere in this world. But if there is, I've never seen it. And I've never experienced it. At least not until you came around."

"Well, Corrin, you've only seen what I've shown you. Don't you find it entertaining?"

"I can't tear my eyes away from it, if that's what you mean by entertaining, but I have to ask, is all of this real?" He stuck a piece of apple in his mouth and chewed. "Or is it an illusion? Are these places you've been to?"

Trinos's smile was warm and radiant, creating a soothing vibration in his chest. He almost felt ashamed just for looking at her, and even when he tore his eyes away from her, he glanced at her perfect figure constantly. Trinos was a mystery. Powerful. Unlike anything he could imagine in this world, but real. He didn't know what to make of her, but he'd do anything she said.

"Do you want to keep watching, Corrin?"

He shrugged, staring back into the waters where a new image started to form. This time it was different. His jaw dropped. This time it was people he knew, and they were in danger. He felt his heart speed up inside his chest, eyes transfixed.

"Perhaps you'd rather see something," she stuck out her hand and the waters wavered, "more pleasant?"

"No-No!" he said, shoving his hands over the water. "I want to see how this ends."

The waters steadied, and the image cleared. Trinos leaned towards the fountain and said, "Me too."

43

MELEGAL FELT HIS STOMACH TIGHTEN into knots. The cleric's hair grew and thickened. His sagging jawline toughened. Sefron's disturbing features transformed into the countenance of a man full of strength and vitality. It was unlike anything Melegal had ever seen before. In seconds, Sefron went from a hapless weakling to a formidable foe that was about to kill him.

"Oh yes, Rat." Sefron's teeth were straight and strong. "You thought you would take me. Avenge the honor of a worthless little slut, but now, just imagine what I'll have in store for her the next time I see her. She'll think I'm handsome, will she not, you fool? She'll be having me instead of you."

Melegal wanted to scream for help, but his tongue shriveled in his mouth, and his throat was dry. The chaos surrounding him was in full force where men and underlings battled. The Keys skittered over the mosaic floor. In his mind, he could hear them, count them all. *One-Two-Three-Four-Five... Forget the Keys! Save yourself!*

"Oh, this feels so good." Saliva dripped from Sefron's mouth.

In horror, Melegal watched his own age spots and crooked fingers form. It felt like Sefron had the grip of an ogre. *Am I to die like this? A rotting old man?* His doubts overwhelmed him. His anger and surprise turned to shock and confusion. *What do I do?*

"Heh-heh-heh." Sefron gloated, licking his lips. "It's time to die, Melegal."

Die? He let out a feeble cough. The air in his lungs felt thin. For the first time in his life, he wheezed. He was confused.

"Ha! Painful, isn't it?"

Melegal shook his head. *Can't let this happen! What do I do?* His mind was drifting. The pain was growing. His focus deteriorating.

"I think I might have what's left of you for soup. Melegal stew, stirred with your own bones and sautéed with your eyeballs."

Now, Melegal's eyes looked at Sefron like a complete stranger. He tried to withdraw. Fear overwhelmed his feeble mind. *Let go! Let go! Let go!*

The hat on his head ignited.

Sefron's grip popped open, eyes blinking, shaking his head.

"Why—why did I let you go?" Sefron reached over, grabbed his staff and raised it over his head. "No matter, I'll just bash your sock ridden he—"

Glitch!

Melegal stabbed him in the heart, plunging his blade hilt-deep in the chest.

"No!" Sefron coughed up blood, groaned, and gurgled before falling over, dead.

Melegal pulled out his dagger and stabbed him once more.

Sefron's stare was glassy, and the cleric's body reverted back to normal.

Filthy Bastard.

Melegal fell flat on his back, sucking for air. Rolling onto his belly, he groaned. "Slat, I feel like I'm a hundred years old." He crawled over the floor, aching from head to toe.

Nearby, Creed was about to die.

So much for him.

He turned his attention elsewhere. *Get to one of the doors!* He had a Key; he could still feel it, but at the rate he was moving the nearest door might as well have been a mile away. Going up the stairs looked impossible. Everyone was fighting everything everywhere.

Bone, I'm not going anywhere! I might as well die right here.

Clang!

The sound of clashing steel was music to Creed's ears. He rolled away and sprang to his feet, limping. The underling, Kierway, was tangled with a big, ugly menace of a man he would not have known had he not called Lord Almen Father. Tonio had changed.

"I like these odds!"

Rejuvenated, Creed jumped into the fray, stabbing his gleaming sword.

On the other side of Kierway, the big ugly brute hammered away with fast, heavy blows.

Kierway parried, the man on one side, the monster on the other, with speed and expertise Creed never before imagined. Still, Kierway was hobbled, blood dripping from his thigh onto the blood-sucking floor. *Wear him down!*

Bang! Bang! Bang!

Creed pounded at the underling's steel. Now, Kierway's chest began to heave, and sweat dripped from his nose. *Stab!*

Kierway poked straight through the monster's belly and ripped it out.

The monster grinned.

"You're no man!" Kierway exclaimed, side stepping a heavy swing and chopping into its leg.

"Nay, underling. I'm a monster the likes you've never seen!"

It chopped high.

Creed sliced low.

Kierway howled, tumbling to the floor.

The Bloodhound swordsman felt his sword hit bone.

Kierway's sword clattered over the stones; with the other one, he still parried. In the next instant, Kierway stuck a small whistle in his mouth and blew.

Creed smacked the whistle from Kierway's lips with his blade.

Two more underlings emerged, but Tonio was already assaulting them.

"Time to finish this!"

"Hah, Human! You think you've defeated me. I still have one sword," Kierway said, rising.

"And a really bad limp." Creed huffed. He didn't have much left in him, if anything at all.

"Tell you what, Human. Let's settle this with a draw." Kierway lifted his eyes and made the motion to sheath his sword.

"You first." Creed panted, wiping the sweat from his brow.

Kierway slid his steel over his back and extended his hands. "Now you?"

Creed did the same, over his hip.

"First one out gets the first swing." A wicked smile formed on Kierway's lips.

Creed swallowed the little spit he had left. He'd never been beaten in a draw, but this underling was quick. At least it was an honorable way to go. At least he'd bought more time to live. *Come on, Creed! Think of all those years of training. All those Royals snubbing you. Fight or die.*

"On my wink, Underling."

"Perfect." Kierway casually dropped his hand over his head.

Creed took a half breath, cleared his mind and focused. *One. Two. Three.* He blinked one eye and drew.

Kierway's blade was already out.

Impossible!

44

MELEGAL INCHED HIS WAY OVER the floor towards the nearest door in sight. *Look away! Look away!* So far, his plan seemed to be working, either from his hat, or the confusion that was going on around him. *Not my kind of party. Look Away! Look away!* He had to go at least two dozen feet more, every movement in his joints stiff and painful. Still, he was aware of everything.

Jarla cut an underling down with a stroke to its throat.

Lord Almen buried a nasty-looking dagger in the spine of another.

Tonio and Creed battled the one called Kierway with flashes of lightning and the resounding sound of steel meeting steel.

No, it wasn't his kind of party at all. *Vee! I need you. Come through that door any second now.* Grumbling, he slid over the floor: one foot closer, then two.

Down the stairs the underlings kept coming: one to a man, then two.

All the while, the floor seemed to wriggle, draining the life of the fallen, turning their bodies to husks.

They'll never make it out of this.

Everything was happening so fast, but he was moving so slow. *What did that Cleric do to me?* He clutched at the Key inside his clothes and touched something else. *What is that?* Curious, he produced the black rectangular case he'd take from Lord Almen's study above. Opening it, he found a wand-shaped rod made of dark wood with ornate carvings.

Out of nowhere, Lord Almen came and snatched it from his hand. "You just gave your worthless life a few more precious moments, Detective. Enjoy them while they last." Lord Almen snapped his wrist. The rod flared with life, a glowing purple tendril of energy extending from it.

Melegal shielded his tired eyes.

WUHPAZZ!

Two underlings whirled on Lord Almen, ruby eyes wide.

"Taste this, underfiends!" Lord Almen stroked the mystic whip of energy.

WUHPAZZ!

It sheered the arm off one, shooting blood over the room.

WUHPAZZ!

It coiled around the other one's neck. Its skin sizzled. Its eyes rolled up under its head.

Lord Almen popped its head from its shoulders with a yank, and then methodically made his way around the chamber.

The underlings, even the armored ones, were cut up with the whip, like butter with a hot knife.

WUHPAZZ! WUHPAZZ! WUHPAZZ!

Melegal, keeping his eye on Almen, continued towards the door. *I'm going to steal that… again.* Less than ten feet away. *I'm going to make it out of this slat hole!* Five feet away.

WUHPAZZ! WUHPAZZ!

Good for you, Lord Arsehole! He reached inside his shirt and wrapped his hand around the Key. He was all alone. Out of the corner of his eye, he caught someone else.

A golden-eyed underling floated in. Surveying the room, it shook its head, sneered, and opened its mouth.

Melegal's hat pulsated on his head. *Move!* Mustering all the strength he had, he lunged for the door.

A single word burst forth from the golden-eyed underling, turning the chamber asunder.

A wave of energy slammed into Melegal, jarring every bone, every fiber. The Key fell from his grasp, but he didn't hear it land. All he wanted to do was cover his head. Instead, he collapsed, unable to move, hands twitching. He'd never felt anything so painful before. *Please don't do that again. Kill me first instead.*

In the center of the room, Lord Almen, Jarla, Creed and all the underlings aside from Kierway were sprawled out over the floor. Alive or dead, he did not know.

Tonio still stood, listlessly dragging a gore-dripping sword around the room.

Melegal's Key twinkled nearby.

He stretched out his fingers. *So close.*

Kierway stepped on his hand and picked up the Key.

Melegal's vision faded. The last thing he saw was Kierway's dripping blade.

Will death be as painful as life on Bish?

45

"**I**'M HUNGRY." BRAK MOANED.

"You aren't as hungry as me," Georgio shot back, pushing back his sweaty brown locks. "Nobody gets as hungry as me!"

"Am too, hungrier!"

"Please stop it! Both of you," Jubilee shouted from Quickster's saddle. "You two idiots ate all our food!"

Billip wanted to kill both the young men. They'd all departed the City of Bone in a rush, but were amply supplied, a couple of weeks' worth anyway. But three days into it, the food was almost gone, with maybe a day left, maybe two, and it was still at least another week to make the City of Three.

"I didn't eat it all; he did," Georgio said.

Brak, whose big feet shoved the dirt like a plow, chucked a rock at Georgio, smacking him hard in the back. "I'm going to cram the next one in your biscuit hole, so you'll be swallowing your teeth."

Good, Billip thought, stopping to look. *I hope they beat each other to death.*

Georgio picked up a rock as big as his hand and slung it back. "Eat this!"

Brak jerked his forearm up.

The rock skipped off his wrist and clocked him in the head, drawing blood.

Brak's eyes widened then buckled, his big face drawing up. "You're going to die for that!"

Georgio widened his arms and slapped his chest. "I'd like to see you try, you droopy face bastard!"

"You shut up, Georgio!" Jubilee shouted. "Go beat the crap out of him, Brak!"

Closing the distance in two long strides, Brak took the first swing.

Georgio raised his arms up, blocking the blow and laughing. "You're too slow for me, Goon. I'm going to pummel you — *oof!*"

Brak upper-cutted him in the belly, lifting him from his feet.

Billip winced.

Jubilee gasped.

Face reddened, Georgio scrambled to his feet and charged. Slamming into Brak, he lifted the bigger young man from his feet and drove him into the ground. Georgio's fists hammered into Brak, hitting ribs, face and gut. "You're gonna pay for that! I'm gonna beat you to death!"

Brak, the bigger and much older-looking of the two, had his hands full.

Georgio, a big young man himself, was the quicker of the two, sneaking in punches through Brak's blocking forearms.

Billip yawned. He'd seen old three legged dogs fight better.

"Get him, Brak!" Jubilee yelled, shadow boxing in the air. "Bust his jaw so he can't eat any more."

Over the dirt they tussled, kicking up dust, yelling and growling at eat other.

"I'm going to kill you!"

"I hate you!"

"You skinny ogre!"

"Potbellied urchin!"

Billip took a small sip from his canteen, which was getting light. They'd run out of water soon. The past day had worried him. Normally, hunting game of some sort, be it a pheasant or an Outland fox, wasn't much of a problem, but thanks to the mass exodus from the south, game was harder to come by. And Billip had led them on a more difficult path as well, fearing that other weary travelers would be after them or the meat of Quickster.

He shook his head.

Only days ago, he'd been dead set on staying in the City of Bone, helping Trinos to fight and battle the underlings. The next thing he knew, he was leading the young men and Jubilee north towards the City of Three. Did Melegal talk him into it, or was it something Trinos had done? *I'm going to get that thief one of these days.*

Turning his attention away from the mirages that littered the barren landscape in the distance and back to the boys, he shook his head.

Georgio had his meaty fingers around Brak's neck, and Brak had his around Georgio's.

"Stop them, Billip!" Jubilee said.

He waved her off.

Crack!

"Ow!" Brak exclaimed.

Crack!

"Ow!" Georgio moaned.

Nikkel stood over them, his father's club in his hand.

Both young men panted for breath. Brak wiped the dust and blood from his nose, and Georgio popped his dislocated finger back into place, grimacing.

Something tugged at Billip's heart as he saw Nikkel standing there with Mikkel's club in his hand. The strapping young man would be a spitting image of his father in a few more years.

Rubbing his head, Georgio said, "What did you do that for, Nikkel? I was winning."

"Were not," Brak said. "I'm so hungry."

"I'm hungrier," said Georgio.

Nikkel, who'd been glum and quiet ever since they left, showed the slightest smile.

"Well, Nikkel," Billip said, "You found something, didn't you?"

Nikkel shrugged his muscular shoulder. "I think so. Come on."

Following Nikkel and Billip, Georgio glanced over his shoulder from time to time. Jubilee sat on Quickster's back, frowning and holding her stomach. The girl looked like she hadn't eaten in days, and her hazel eyes were sagging. Beside her and Quickster, Brak walked in long slow strides, but he was able to keep up, eyes forward, chin up and casting a scowl at Georgio before looking away.

Georgio clenched his fingers in and out of a fist. Even though he healed quickly, they were still sore. Hitting Brak was like hitting rock. The man, or young man, whatever he was, was tough. Unnaturally so, but so was Georgio.

"What are you looking at?" Jubilee said. "You're fortunate, you know. Brak could have killed you. He was holding back."

Georgio turned and stopped.

"You want to walk or ride?"

"I'm a Royal, you should know," she said, folding her arms across her scrawny chest.

Georgio rolled his eyes. Jubilee had made it a point to mention that at least a dozen times since they left, and he was getting sick of it. And if she was a Royal, how'd she wind up with them? *Venir's right: all Royals are a pain in the arse.*

"Quickster is mine, little girl, and if you don't mind your mouth, I'll have him buck you from the saddle." He glared at her and put his fingers to his mouth, ready to whistle.

Jubilee looked away and mumbled something under her breath.

"What was that?"

She tightened the cloak around her body and said nothing.

He glared at Brak.

The big man stood at Jubilee's side like a watchdog.

"You three quit boogering around, else we'll leave you!" Billip said. "And don't tempt us! We'd all have been much better off if we left you to begin with!"

Georgio didn't even bother to run and catch up. He didn't have the energy, and it didn't seem that Jubilee or Brak did either. Instead, they followed the men up ahead, one ravenous step after the other under the blistering heat.

As for Brak, Georgio still hadn't sorted out all of his thoughts on him. He hadn't even seen the big man smile as of yet, and that disturbed him. Brak's face was familiar. Like Venir's but different. If it weren't for the man's blue eyes, he'd have little resemblance at all. Brak was quiet, whereas Venir was loud. It just didn't sit well. Other than that, when they weren't fighting over food, Brak was alright.

He put his canteen to his lips. Nothing came out. "Ah…"

And of all things, the two of them could only talk about food, and that's what got them in trouble to begin with. Staying on watch one night, while the others slept, they got caught up with themselves, talking about food and eating most of it the same night. When Billip woke them up the next day, he was furious. Not only had they fallen asleep, but almost all the rations were gone. It seemed one had been blaming the other ever since, and they were taking their guilt and hunger out on one another.

Ahead, Billip and Nikkel stood on top of a ridge, talking to each other and pointing downward. Georgio climbed the rocky hill and stood between them.

"What is it?" Georgio said, looking over the ridge.

A field of cacti lay below: some tall, others round, some three times bigger than a man.

Georgio held his rumbling stomach. "So, Nikkel found some cactus. I don't see how that's of much help to us. Maybe the round ones would help, but there's no way to get to them. What are we supposed to do, Nikkel? Feed on Cactus needles?"

Billip shot him a look. "There's game in those needles, Boy. All we have to do is roust it out."

"And how do you suppose we do that?" Jubilee said with a smug look on her face. "And what kind of game are we talking about?"

"Pheasant, antler rabbits, and foxes to start," Nikkel said. "Not to mention the water in the round husks."

"There's no way to get to them!" Georgio said. "It's impossible. Let's just keep moving north. All we've done now is waste time by moving east."

All of them were hungry and weary. Eyes were tired and full of grit. Their clothes and armor coated with Outland dust so thick you couldn't tell what color they were. They'd have been better off staying with the caravan, but Billip had talked them away from that. Now they stood, baking in the sun with nothing to eat or drink but sand and needles.

"Get your bows ready." Brak lowered himself over the ridge like a giant-sized sloth.

Jubilee jumped from her saddle. "Brak! What are you doing? Get back up here, Brak! Get back up here!"

"You fool, get up here!" Billip shouted. "We don't even have a plan yet! There're snakes down there, vipers and such. Step in a nest of those and you're in for! Slat, he's still going in."

Brak ambled down the incline another thirty feet before he stumbled and rolled into a wall of needles at the bottom. Groaning, he got up and started to growl.

"Hungry." He pulled Tonio's sword from its sheath. "Tired of being hungry."

Georgio looked at Jubilee and the others, swallowing. "What's wrong with him?"

There was a wild look to the man. An inferno erupting within. The man Georgio had wrestled with moments ago was gone, replaced by something else, something savage.

"Oooooh," Jubilee said. She took her place beside Billip. "I've seen this before."

In a clap of thunder, Brak turned from man to monster, hacking furiously through the impassable wall of needles.

"He's gone mad," Billip exclaimed, readying his bow.

"No, he's gone berserk!" Nikkel said.

"RAWR!"

Georgio hopped back. The maddened sound of Brak's voice rose the hair on his arms.

Brak hewed through the green cacti and needles like tall grass. A wild man.

"That fool's bound to get snake bit in there!" Billip said, drawing his bow string alongside his cheek. "Look!"

Three antlered rabbits, bigger than cats, darted across the valley of cacti.

Twang!

Clatch-Zip!

One rabbit tumbled into the dust with two holes in it.

"You got him!" Jubilee shouted.

"Nikkel, you shot mine!" Billip said. "You take the rear; I take the front." He nocked another arrow. "That's how Mikkel and I used to go."

Nikkel cranked back the line on his crossbow.

"Got it!"

A silence fell. They all watched the rustling of the towering cacti swaying back and forth, many falling down under the sub-human roars of Brak the Berserker.

"What kind of man fights cactus?" Nikkel exclaimed, eyeing Jubilee.

"A hungry one. A very hungry one."

"Georgio," Billip said, "Get down there and fetch that rabbit before a fox gets it."

"But…" He looked toward the path Brak had created. "What about—"

"Get your hungry arse down there! Run back up here if you're scared!"

A bloom of pheasant burst out of the cacti and into the air.

Clatch-zip!

"Hold your shot, Nikkel!" Billip said, "You have to wait till they clear the grove. Slat. Do I have to do it all myself?"

Twang!

Twang!

Two rock pheasants spiraled out of the sky, falling along the jagged rim.

"Get down there!" Billip ordered, nocking his bow and searching the grove.

"RAWR!"

Georgio's boots slid over the slope, over the loose rocks and dirt, until he hit bottom and fell on his back. "Blast it!" He plucked needles eight inches long from his arms.

A dozen feet away, the rabbit lay just outside the cacti, an arrow and bolt in its belly and thigh.

He glanced down the path that Brak had hewn down. Cacti lay fallen and torn, leaving an ugly path behind, but there was room, just very little. He plucked another needle from his thigh. *I must look like a porcupine by now.* He grimaced.

"Toss up the rabbit," Nikkel yelled, his black face glistening with sweat.

"I will!" Aggravated, Georgio snatched it up off the ground and slung it up the hill. "Happy now?"

Nikkel disappeared, but he could see Jubilee's eyes peeping down at him over the lip of the ridge.

"Go get Brak," she ordered.

Georgio yelled back up, "You go get him!"

"You're already down there, Stupid! Besides, you ate all the food too! So go fetch it!"

"Aw, I'm going!" He stomped off into the cacti.

She was right, but he wasn't very comfortable going after Brak, not after the last look he'd seen in the man's eyes. It wasn't human. It was something else. Something that rent flesh from bones with its teeth or bare hands. *He can't kill me. He can't kill me. Could he eat me?* He shook his head. *He would have to be hungrier than I am, to eat me.*

Tip-toeing his way down the path, he was twenty yards in before he heard Brak's mad snarling and mutterings again. It tickled his spine.

"Brak," he said, barely audible.

White-knuckled hand on hilt, he took a deep breath and forged ahead, painful needles biting into him time and time again. He could hear Billip calling out for him. *If they want me, they can come and find me themselves.*

"Blasted needles!" he cursed, wiping the sweat from his eyes. There was no avoiding them, no matter how much he tried, and they burned too.

Twenty feet deeper, he twisted and turned.

Ahead, a small clearing opened up, with Brak standing in the middle, plucking a yellow fruit from a plant Georgio had never seen before. Two at a time, Brak was stuffing them in his mouth, chomping and squirting the pulp down his chin and jaw. The man had more needles in him than Georgio could ever count. They were in his face, his arms, thighs… Tiny droplets of blood ran over his face and down his clothes. It was painful to look at. How Brak ate only fruit and no needles, he didn't know.

"Alright Brak, you win; you're hungrier than I am." Georgio sheathed his sword. "What kind of fruit is that anyway?" He got closer. "I've never seen it before. It might be poisonous, you know."

Turning, Brak snarled, raising his sword.

Georgio froze.

"Easy now! Go ahead, eat all you want. I can wait." Georgio plucked some small needles from his meaty forearms. "But save some for everyone else."

Brak kept eating, grunting and swinging his sword.

"That used to be my sword, you know. Venir gave it to me."

Brak didn't understand. His face was still sub-human, a wild animal ready to strike at any moment. Georgio didn't care. He was too hungry. Too tired. He sat down.

As ten more fruit disappeared down Brak's throat, the sword in his arm lowered, and the growling stopped. Stuffing another fruit in his mouth, Brak blinked at Georgio and held his hand out. "Hungry?"

Georgio nodded, extending his hand.

"Good," Brak said, tossing it over. A smile riddled in needles crossed his lips.

A long shadow rose up behind Brak. It was a snake. Big, thick and hooded. Eyes like emeralds and a red flicking tongue.

"Brak, look out!"

Brak turned, but too late. The snake sank its fangs into the back of the big man's shoulder.

Georgio jumped to his feet and ripped his sword out.

Two more snakes slithered from beneath the cacti, rearing up and blocking his path.

Georgio struck first, clipping one's pale yellow underbelly.

Something like a hot knife sank deep into his thigh, numbing his leg.

Instantly, the bright light of the suns swirled.

46

T HE GIANT'S FEET MADE A cloud of dust with every step.

Listless and weary, robes dragging on the ground, Fogle Boon followed Barton. His sunburnt face peered into the clouds. Cass was gone again, and the suns of Bish had already set twice since then. He was miserable. Sick.

"Hold up." He fell to his knees.

Barton stopped and turned, scratching his head. "What are you stopping for, Wizard? We're almost there."

Fogle scanned the area. There was nothing aside from the bone trees and tiny lizards that scurried across the ground. Still, he'd been following Barton, wandering aimlessly, empty, with no idea where they were going. He hadn't had any luck finding the remnants of his ebony hawk, Inky. If he ever did, he could summon it again. He wiped his cracked lips on his dusty sleeve and spat.

"Barton getting thirsty. Make water, Wizard. Make water now." Opening a mouth that was big enough to swallow Fogle whole, the giant stuck his enormous tongue out, pointing at it. "Dry. Need water. Make water, Wizard."

He could make water, but he didn't want to. Instead, he wanted to suffer. He deserved that much. *I failed, Cass. I deserve to die. Right here. I'll just wither away into the rock and stone.* He pulled his knees to his chest and dipped his head between them.

"Just go on without me, Barton."

"What?"

Shaking his head, he said it again, louder. "Just go on without me!" He could hear Barton scratching his head.

Barton took a seat beside him. "Ah. Wizard still sad that Blackie take his woman?"

He felt a big hand patting his back. It knocked the breath from him. "Will you just go away!"

"Sheesh, Wizard getting grumpy. Make water, Wizard, so we can be happy. Barton is thirsty."

He looked up at Barton. The reddened dot inside the giant's disfigured eye stared back at him, unable to blink. The good eye shifted back and forth.

"Barton, what makes you think I can make water?"

"You're a Wizard. You can do anything, right?"

"No, if I could do anything, we wouldn't be lost out here. I'd have killed that dragon too. And Cass would be with me."

"Hmmm." Barton stretched out his arms. "But you can make water, can't you?"

No sense in him suffering. I guess I can make myself not drink it. And I only hope the spell works.

"Maybe." Fogle dusted off his hands and got back up. "But, I need to know something, Barton."

"What?"

"Do you think Cass is dead or alive?"

Barton shrugged.

Fogle felt his face redden. He'd been asking questions on and off, but the giant was reluctant to help with anything. All Barton wanted to do was find Venir and get his toys. And for some odd reason, the giant seemed to know where he was going, which left Fogle feeling more lost than he already was. *I wish Boon were here. He'd know something about that dragon. Why didn't that old fool come with us? Why!*

"Tell me something, Barton. Give me some hope at least." He kicked Barton in the toe.

"Ow!" Barton grabbed his toe and hopped up and down, big eye blinking. "What did you do that for?"

Fogle limped away, clutching his head. He wanted to pull his hair out. *What am I doing? Can I not outwit a giant now?* He looked up at the clouds. "Pull it together!"

Barton got up, looked up into the sky and said, "Pull what?"

"Tell you what, Barton: I'll make barrels of water, more than we could use in a month, but you have to help me find Cass."

"Blackie took her; she's gone."

"That's not going to get you any water, Barton. You'll have to do better than that."

Barton folded his arms over his chest. "Make the water first, Wizard."

The shadow the giant cast when he looked up at him gave Fogle little comfort. It made him feel insignificant. He had once been the cockiest mage in the City of Three, and now he was a rattled mess. It made him angry. He summoned his energy, filling his lungs with power.

"ANSWER ME, GIANT! OR DRINK YOU WILL NOT!"

Barton took a step back, covering his face. Peeking through his forearms, disfigured face bunched up, he said, "Yes! Yes! I will tell! I will tell!"

That felt good!

Fogle hadn't often used the Wizards Voice before, always feeling it was more show than effect.

I'm going to have to use that more often.

"OUT WITH IT!"

Barton's lips tightened.

"BARTON…"

"Ah, Blackie will take her to the giants' castle." He lowered his voice. "Or to his lair. Many bones there. Many bones of the dead."

The way Barton said it didn't seem genuine.

"ARE YOU LYING, GIANT? I DON'T LIKE LIARS!"

Barton covered his face again. "No bones! No bones! Just the castle. Blackie takes people to the castle, and they never leave there. Impossible."

"You will take me there then." The power in his voice was gone.

"No! Barton will not go back there. You'll go yourself. Now make my water. My throat hurts."

Fogle rubbed his throat. It felt like he'd swallowed a mouthful of dirt now. "Hold out your hands and make a cup," he managed in a dry voice.

Waving his hand over his water skin, he summoned the spell. "Decanterous! Everless! Fill!" He tipped the water skin over. Clear liquid poured out like a rushing spring.

Barton sucked up a dozen handfuls, and Fogle, head riddled with guilt, thoughts only on Cass, drank until his throat no longer burned. He capped the water skin.

"Feel better now?"

"Much." Barton patted his stomach. It rumbled like a giant bullfrog. "Now make food."

Fogle laughed. "Water will have to do for now. Plenty of that. If you want food, you'll have to hunt it yourself."

"Alright." Barton wandered off.

"Barton!"

The giant didn't slow.

"Barton, where are you going?"

Barton stopped and turned. "To find the doggie and get my toys."

"What about Cass? You need to help me go and find Cass!"

"She isn't going anywhere. Barton not going back there, but you help Barton find the doggy and the toys, I'll take you there." His smile was wide and creepy. "I promise."

They walked, suns down to suns up, resting little in between.

Fogle, even with all the water, was exhausted, his legs shaking with every step. He'd given up on trying to convince Barton to go back. The little giant wouldn't listen. And Fogle didn't believe all of what Barton said about the castle and Cass being there and safe. He remembered those citrine eyes of the dragon. They had a murderous intent. *Is she dead?*

He stumbled and fell to his knees.

"Get up, Wizard."

Fogle didn't move. Instead, he lay staring into the sky, hoping to see a black dragon pass by. *I deserve to die here. Bake my flesh, Bish. I'll make a fine meal for the buzzards of this lousy world.*

Barton kept on walking.

47

P AIN. IT WAS ALL THAT remained of Venir's life. His burning skin looked like raw meat on his back, and there was little left to be seen of his tattoo. Tuuth had whipped him until the rawhide was soaked with blood. Venir had fought the first few hours, making derogatory comments about the orc and his kind.

"That's a nice lash. Did you borrow it from your mother?"

Wupash!

"What's it like being an orc? Stinking and stupid all the time?"

Wupash!

"Is your arm getting tired yet? My back's just getting warmed up!"

Wupash!

"Bone! That's feels good!

Wupash!

"Say, Tuuth, don't they think you can do anything harder than this?"

Wupash!

"If I survive this, I'm going to skin your hide and make a whip out of you!"

Wupash!

It had gone on like that, back and forth, until Venir couldn't say a word, or remember his name. Unable to wake him after the first day, they had dragged him off to his cell, only to drag him back out again and hitch him to the post. That was three days ago.

Wupash!

He remembered watching the Royal Riders stripped of their armor, mutilated, tortured, buried and burning. He saw how the underlings celebrated their handiwork. They'd strolled inside the fort, arm in arm, mugs raised high and chanting strange sounds that would make hound dogs cry. It all made Venir sick. What he could remember of it.

Still, some men survived. Chained and cuffed from the neck to ankles, they served, performing one menial task after the other. Venir caught glimpses of it here and there, but his memories faded until he worked again to suffer another tortuous day.

Now, lying face down in the slime of his cell, he stirred. It was dark, but a pool of yellow light shone through the door. He tried to sit up. Something was on his back, picking at it.

"Wha—?" he mumbled, forcing himself up.

He heard a buzz.

A sharp stabbing pain shot through his back to his chest.

He slammed his mangled back into the moldy wall.

Something crunched and squished.

A sliver of fear raced through him. His blood coursed behind his ears. Something was feeding on him. Something had chewed up his legs, now it felt like bugs were making a nest in his back.

"Nnn—"

He slammed his back into the wall again. Bright spots of light burst in his eyes, leaving him woozy. He sagged down, slumping to the floor.

"Venir."

His eyes popped open, searching.

"Venir."

Somewhere, a tiny voice was speaking to him.

"Lie still, you idiot, and stop squishing the bugs. They're healing you."

"Slim?"

"Quiet."

He felt tiny insect legs crawling over his shoulder to his ear.

"Yes, it's Slim, and I'm getting you patched up… again."

Something crawled off his shoulder and stood before him. It was an insect, like a mantis, but mostly had Slim's face, except brownish green and bug-eyed.

"Uh…"

"Just be still, you big fool!" Slim put his insect arm to his face. "This wouldn't be so bad if you weren't so stubborn. As soon as that white orc whips you, pretend to pass out. Stop running your mouth. Bish, you've got a lot of nerve calling him stupid and stubborn. You should be dead already, you fool, but I've been having the bugs patch you up. You heal fast. Very fast."

A bug the size of Venir's finger that looked like part cricket, part spider scurried up to Slim's mantis-like form. Its antenna twitched back and forth in short furious motions, then it scurried away.

"Listen, you big lout: you smash any more of them, they're leaving, so just lie there and be still. I can't keep you alive forever, you know."

"Water."

Motioning to a stone bowl that was tipped over, Slim shook his head. "You already drank it. You don't remember, do you?"

"Just get out of here, Slim. Escape, tell others. There's nothing more you can do here. If I die here, then I die here. Enough have died here already. You don't need to die too."

"That's a great idea, but the safest place right now is here, under the enemy's nose. I've been keeping a look out. More underlings have come since we rode in here, and they talk as if the City of Bone has fallen. They talk as if they've conquered the world, Venir." Slim blinked his glowing bug eyes. "I've seen it pretty bad on Bish before, but this? I've never seen it this bad, but something's got to happen. It just can't keep going like this. It can't."

Venir never figured Slim's age, but for all he knew, he was as old as Mood. As for the underlings, he'd never seen them with such an upper hand before either. Usually, he'd been able to face them with the mystic armament when things got bad, but now it was gone. Perhaps the underlings had it. *If I could wrap my paws around Brool's handle one last time! Bone!*

"Just do what you can and go, Slim. It's like you said, 'Bish Happens.'"

"I did say that, didn't I? Huh, that's a good one." He scurried over Venir's shoulder and spoke in his ear. "Now you just be still while I have the bugs stitch you up. And remember, keep your mouth closed tomorrow. You're better off dying digging holes than being whipped to death, I'd figure. Of course, I'm a lot smarter than you."

"Thanks, Slim—Yeouch!"

It felt like something crawled into his spine.

"Be still, I say! It's going to hurt, you know. Yesterday you slept right through it, leaving me wondering if you were getting better or worse."

"Worse." Venir bit his lip. Helpless, he lay there listening to Slim guiding the creatures all over his back. "Don't you have any of that blue ointment?"

"Heh, the underlings would sniff me out in a second if I used that. I've got it hidden. Besides, I'm saving the good stuff for me."

"Great…" Venir said just before dozing off.

Slim the Healer kept his astonishment to himself. Venir should have been dead. The man's back was a grotesque mat of blood and skin. The first time he saw it, he felt his own skin turn inside out. Yet somehow, Venir had prevailed.

The bugs scurried over Venir's back, attacking the puss that seeped through the pores. *If he gets the fever, he will be dead.* If he did, there was no way of helping the man, no way at all. Still, it was a mystery. What kept Venir together this long? One by one, the bugs pushed the flaps of skin back into place and sealed them up with a thick gummy spit.

"Aside from all the blood, you don't look half bad," he said, dusting his insect hands off. "I can even see the tattoo. 'V'. Hmmm, what did that drunken fool put it on there for? What was her name? Vorla? Ah, time to crawl back into my hole. Sleep well, Venir, and don't run your mouth tomorrow."

Venir snored.

"That might be a good thing."

On his six insect legs, he made his way from Venir's cell and followed the other bugs into a small hole they had bored into the interior of the fort's wall. Squeezing through the dark and narrow path, he popped into a hollowed-out room inside the massive log from the Great Forest of Bish, big enough for several men. Exhausted, he reverted back to his normal form and stretched out in the dim green light provided by the Elga Bugs from the glowing sacks on their bellies.

Resting the best he could, he couldn't help but worry—as he had on all the previous nights—that Venir would not return alive.

"How much will the underlings put up with, and how much more can he take?" Closing his eyes, he whisked his hand, and the Elga bug lights went dim.

If Venir's no longer The Darkslayer, then who is?

48

CASTLE ALMEN WAS NO LONGER under siege. It was overtaken. Lord Almen sat on the marbled tile floor, arms shackled behind his back, and sighed. A corpse of one of his prized Shadow Sentries lay dead at his side, his mesh mask melted to his face. The rest of the room, his throne room, was in good order. But now, where there had been one high-backed chair of mahogany wood trimmed in the finest metal and jewels sat two. Both were empty at the moment.

His stomach rumbled as he shifted on the floor. He'd been fed, but very little, and he was stripped down to his shirt and trousers. All of his rings and baubles were gone. Closing his eyes and leaning back, the same thought raced through his mind.

How could I let this happen?

He rolled his shoulder and cracked his neck side to side. Something scurried out of the corner of the room. A spider, big as a dog and quick as a cat, on silent legs crawled over towards him. Another nearly his size dropped from the ceiling, jaws opening and closing. They were the underlings' watch dogs. Creepy things. Hairy black creatures with white stripes and venomous teeth that he'd seen suck the marrow from his own nephew's bones two days hence. The revolting sound still rang inside his head. The sucking. The screaming. The anguish. For the most part, Lord Almen delivered quick and silent deaths, but the underlings enjoyed the torment at another level. They delighted in the suffering of others.

He remained still, beads of sweat dripping from his nose onto the floor. A minute passed, then two before the spiders backed away and curled up out of sight.

How did I let this happen?

Until now, there had never been a day when Lord Almen hadn't felt in control, but other things had led to his fall. Melegal had undone him. Sefron had betrayed him. Most men dared not look him in the eye, nor did they have the courage to attack him. But Melegal had. As for Sefron, the man's own lust and fear of the underlings clearly led to his betrayal. However, Lord Almen could not imagine why Melegal had tried to kill him. He raced through that day. What had happened before Melegal stabbed him? Had Melegal done it on his own? Certainly he'd wanted to. Or had Leezir the Slerg pulled off a suggestion? *Hmmm...*

Lord Almen thought through it until his lids became heavy and he drifted into sleep.

Clap!

His head snapped up.

"Almen," a silver-eyed underling named Verbard said, "rise up."

He nodded.

The underling sat on one of the thrones, his golden-eyed brother, Catten, at his side. Between them stood another creature, a hulking black humanoid that reminded him of a panther. The underlings' eyes pierced him as he rose up to stand tall. With a single word, he felt one or the other could destroy him. He'd dealt with underlings before, but not like this. The cleric Oran had been formidable, but the might of these two? Another scale. No, these two had made his finest magi look like carnival enchanters: leaving one in a pile of ashes, the other with a gaping hole in his chest.

"The time has come to negotiate," Verbard said.

"With?" Almen replied.

Catten tapped his fingernails on the arm rest, a callous look on his face.

Verbard took a deep draw through his nose.

"Do you smell that, Almen? The delicious scent, so pungent, so sweet? A dead child? A dead wife, perhaps?" Verbard rubbed the rat-like fur under his chin.

It wasn't what Lord Almen smelled that bothered him so much as what he didn't smell. His castle had always been filled with fresh flowers and the burning of scented candles, oils and such. Now, the beauty of his Castle—that he and Lorda took so much pride in—was gone. The gardens trampled and smeared in blood. Many of his men buried in them. As for Lorda, he had no idea if she lived or was dead, but the Keep had fallen a day later, after the rest of the castle fell. He could only presume she was dead. It was the best way to avoid manipulation.

"I smell death. Decay. What else is there?"

"More, much, much more." Verbard floated off his chair and right past him. "Come. I'll show you."

Lord Almen glanced at Catten and the Vicious. The underling filled his goblet with a bottle of wine, and the Vicious fell a half-step behind him and shoved him forward. He limped but kept up as Verbard made his way through Castle Almen as if it were his. Underlings were posted throughout the castle, their countenances evil and alert.

Grimacing, he followed Verbard into the keep, taking the stairs that led onto the roof. He was panting when he reached the top, rubbing the bandage on his leg where he'd been stabbed at the battle in the chamber.

Verbard floated still higher in the air, robes billowing, turning towards him. *Can you see it? Can you smell it?*

He heard it in his mind.

He did see it and smell it. Black smoke was rolling up over the great wall of the City of Bone, not on the inside but on the outside. Eyes watering, he covered his nose.

Play along, Almen. Play along.

Walking across the top of the keep and stepping into a small tower that led to its highest point, he got his first glimpse over the wall in years.

Underlings. Legions of them.

They were everywhere. It wasn't just underlings either, but giant spiders and strange creatures he'd never seen before, tossing one dead human onto one flaming pyre after the other. His fingertips went numb.

He looked Lord Verbard in the eye. "Would you have me negotiate the terms of surrender for the City of Bone?"

"Serve us well, Lord Almen. You and a select few of your choosing can be our liaisons."

Lord Almen had made deals with the underlings before. He'd supplied Oran with people for various poisons, potions and such. He'd even conspired with others to see the fall of Outpost Thirty-One. It had led to his rise from the 6th house in the City of Bone to the 3rd. But now, in hindsight, it seemed that move might also have led to this.

"I welcome the opportunity." He bowed. "How may I assist?"

"We just need to know which Castles need to fall first. You see, with the Keys, we can infiltrate any of them and slaughter them all. But 'Which falls first?' is the question."

Lord Almen wanted to laugh. *I can send the underlings to do my bidding for me! But to what end?*

"After that, you can negotiate with the weaker houses and on down. Once we control them, then we control everything."

"I see, Lord Verbard. And once they surrender, what are your plans for them? Slaughter? Slavery? A mass exodus into the Outland?"

"Those are excellent suggestions and most likely a great deal for them all, but you shouldn't worry about that. Not for your own sake."

Verbard pointed at Almen's chest and hissed.

"No, you should just worry about yourself."

49

THE DUNGEONS BENEATH CASTLE ALMEN hadn't changed any over the past few months, but the guards had. Now, they were underlings. Wiry with gem-speckled eyes that didn't hesitate to punish if you so much as snored.

Melegal sat with his head between his bony knees, contemplating. Contemplating his next move. He'd been doing it for days, but he didn't have a next move.

Keys. Keys. The Keys. Wretched things got me into this mess. The wretched things could get me out.

Two underling guards in dark leather armor dragged a tall man in and shackled him inside an adjacent cell. Stripped down to his trousers, the man's chest was bruised and knotted with painful lumps.

Melegal could feel the man's green eyes on him, but he kept his head down.

The underlings didn't whip the quiet ones, but Creed, he couldn't help himself. You'd think someone of his ilk would know better.

"Ooof!"

An underling kicked Creed in the gut, locked the cell and walked away.

Don't speak. Don't speak. Don't speak.

Nearby were the rest of the survivors.

Jarla lay in her cell, facing the wall in the back. The Brigand Queen hadn't acknowledged any of them since they'd been there. Instead she, despite her condition, maintained her air of superiority somehow. Melegal wouldn't be surprised if she was there as more than a prisoner, but a spy. After all, she had assisted the underlings in getting into Outpost Thirty One.

What are you going to do, Rat? What?

Stripped down to his own trousers, Melegal might as well have been naked. His hat was gone. Worry gnawed at his stomach: that an underling had discovered its powers, powers that he himself had only recently begun to unlock. It had been long ago when he acquired it, and it had become a companion of sorts. He wasn't comfortable without it. Not at all.

Get the hat, get the Keys. Get the Keys, get the hat.

Hiding his yawn, he couldn't stop his stomach from rumbling.

One of the underling guards stepped over and banged on his cage.

He kept his head down, but was unable to contain the next loud sound his stomach made.

The ruby-eyed underling, brandishing a black club, opened the door to his cage, stepped inside, and cracked him in the head, drawing bright spots in his eyes. The underling drew back again.

Slat on this!

In a single motion, Melegal swept its legs out from under it, snatched its keys, scurried out, and slammed the door shut, locking the underling guard in his cell. He tossed the keys to Creed's outstretched arm.

Slice!

The jagged teeth of the other underling's sword ripped over his head.

Melegal leapt over a torment table, snapped up a spear from the wall, and braced himself. The creature, swift as a cat, batted the weapon away and lunged inside. Melegal twisted away, the underling's blade slicing the skin on his back.

What am I doing? What am I doing!

He knew he couldn't overpower the underling. They might be small and lithe, but their bodies were hardened like animals. He'd seen them rip overconfident men to pieces a time or two. The underling came at him, hard and fast. Melegal sidestepped again, pinned its sword arm on the table, and drove a long metal torture needle through its hand.

It screeched, ruby eyes widening, and then back-handed Melegal in the jaw.

His knees swayed.

The underling pounced on him. Its clawed fingers wrapped around his neck and dug into his skin.

Melegal's eyes bulged. *At least I killed Sefron. I'd kill him again if I could.*

Glitch!

The bloody tip of a sword burst through the underling's chest.

It fell over dead.

Creed stood tall, eyes cold and dangerous.

"Now this is more like it. Just what I've been saying all along." He grabbed Melegal's arm and pulled him up like a doll. "What's the plan now?"

"Yes, what is the plan, Fool?" Jarla pressed her angry face against the bars. "To get us all killed?"

"'Die doing something, or die doing nothing.' That's how I saw it." Melegal hunched over, catching his breath. "And I don't recall making you part of any plan. Any of you, for that matter."

Creed gave him a look.

"No offense. I needed you to kill that underling, but I didn't figure it'd take you so long to operate a keyhole."

"Why you sneaky little scarecrow," Creed was smiling. "I like it. But, I took a moment to kill that other underling first." He pointed to Melegal's cell.

The other underling lay back against the wall, a large gash in his head.

"At that point, I wasn't certain I needed you either." He winked. "But you won't be going anywhere without me." He wagged the dripping sword in Melegal face. "At least not without my sword sticking through you."

"Hah, hah, hah." Jarla was still sneering. "You don't have any plan. Do you, Fool?"

Actually, I do. Just not a very good one.

Melegal had learned many secrets about Castle Almen in his stay here, many thanks to Sefron. He knew of the secret rooms and corridors, not all, but some. He figured that should be enough to save himself.

"No, no I don't, but right about now, you're in the cage, not me."

Creed grabbed his shoulder and squeezed it. "We'll need all the strong arms we have if we're to carve our way out of here."

"Let out! Let out!"

It was Tonio's voice, crying out from behind a wooden door with a closed-off portal.

Melegal hadn't forgotten about the man, but he wished he had. The deranged man rattled even the underlings, who seemed to avoid him.

"We're going to need that big fellow too, you know." Creed was making his way around the room, gathering up weapons. "I don't know what he is, but he swings a heavy piece of steel like a needle. Let the monster out." Creed gazed at Jarla up and down. "Perhaps this raven-headed princess can control him."

"You dare! You, a misfit from the Royal hounds of the sewers?"

Creed forced a laugh, shoulders dipping.

"You have the cell keys, Creed. Do what you want." Melegal made his way over to the iron door. It didn't appear to be locked. He pressed his ear against it.

"Let out!" *Wham!*

Melegal shook his head. So far as he could tell, the way past the iron door was clear, for now, but they needed to move fast.

Just lead them out, Melegal. Once they start swinging, you'll disappear and be fleeing. Heh. Heh. Crafty as a serpent, I am.

"Let the monster out then," he said, looking at Jarla, "and Tonio too."

I hope she dies first.

Sword ready, Creed unlocked Jarla's cage.

"Idiot." She made her way across the room and sorted through the weapons on the table.

Melegal kept his eyes on her.

Tall, dark and arrogant. A Queen of Brigands indeed. Other than those hips and legs of hers, I'll never understand what Venir saw in the evil hag.

"Your word: you won't be stabbing any of us in the back, Jarla."

Her smile looked as dangerous as a viper. "Unlike you? No, I'll not be giving you my word, you little ghoul of a man. As a matter of fact, I see no reason to follow you." She came closer, sword ready. "For all I know, you'll lead us into a trap."

Creed stepped between them. "The underlings are the enemy now, Jarla. Survive their invasion. We can settle our differences later. Now, I'll give my word. You give yours, Jarla, and Detective, yours as well."

Bang! "Let out! Give Word! Let out!"

"The word of a liar is as useless as the slat of pigs." Jarla stuffed a dagger in the waistband of what was left of her clothes. "All men are liars. All men are filth. But I'll give you both my word—and my word is 'Slat on you both.'"

Melegal huffed a laugh.

That's good enough for me." Creed eyed her up and down again. "And if we do indeed survive this, I'll like to share some drinks."

"Pig!" She slung a pair of shackles at Creed.

He caught them against his chest and winked. "Just lighting a fire in you, Man-hater. Now, let's get on with this." He tossed the cuffs to the ground. "You've got some ornery ideas for such a fine woman."

Jarla's face reddened. "I'll clip your—"

"That's enough!" Melegal stepped around Jarla and strapped on a sword. "Creed, get the door."

Creed unlocked Tonio's door.

The tall half-dead man stepped outside, morbid and scary, rubbing the hole in his head.

Melegal's spine tingled.

Hate that man.

Even Jarla's breath hastened.

Creed's eyes were wary. "Grab some metal, Tonio. Detective, lead the way."

Swinging the dungeon door inward, Melegal felt something crawling in his stomach.

Why haven't they killed us already? What do they need with us, anyway?

He remembered what he'd seen and what he'd been told. The underlings would mutilate some and send them out to spread fear in the world.

Shouldn't we be dead or crippled?

Up the stairs he went, followed by Jarla, Creed and Tonio's heavy steps.

He'll get us all caught.

The dungeons beneath Castle Almen weren't deep, but more or less a sublevel of the basement with a lone entrance at the top. In this case, Melegal knew where he was, but there were places in the Castle he'd never explored. A lone door awaited them at the top. He knew it led into one of the main basement corridors. It was perfect. All they needed to do was overpower any guards, and Melegal knew a few secret corridors with hiding spots down there.

Alright, Rat. They fight. You run.

Running his fingers through his salt and pepper hair, he felt naked without his hat.

Forget it. Just run, Rat. Run!

He mouthed the next words to his followers.

"Ready?"

Creed nodded.

"One."

"Two."

He grabbed the door handle.

"Threeeeeeeeeee...."

The door transformed into a black mirage and enveloped them.

Suddenly, Melegal was free falling.

Creed was yelling.

Jarla was screaming.

In the next instant, he felt himself land hard on the ground. Spitting the dirt from his mouth, he sat up only to face the heads of many spears lowered in his face.

I know this place. All too well.

They were inside Castle Almen's arena.

"What kind of bloody magic was tha—ulp!"

Creed bit his tongue thanks to the barbed spear at his throat.

"Well, finally, some new opponents come." It was Master Kierway. "And just when I was beginning to wonder whether or not you would show."

Kierway wasn't alone. He was accompanied by several underlings, warriors one and all, being served by men and women, barely clothed, and shackled at the neck. One was kneeling by his side, holding up a plate of fruit. It was Lorda.

"Ah," Kierway rose up, "these will be much better opponents for my Juegen to spar with. The others," he gestured toward the wall of the arena, "didn't last so long."

At least a dozen human heads on spikes encircled the inner wall.

So this is what they were saving us for. Games. Underling games.

Melegal's head felt heavy, and he couldn't stop his chin from dipping. His stomach rumbled. All he could think about was Brak here in the arena. His wailing. His moaning.

How in Bish did I get here?

It was pretty clear that nothing was going to save him now. Not Brak, not Venir and not himself. All those years he fought to escape the horrors of the Castle, and he still wound up here. He locked his eyes on Lorda. She was still captivating despite the scrapes and bruises on her face, and he'd never seen her voluptuous body in such revealing clothing before.

"Who's that?" Creed whispered in his ear.

An underling jabbed the butt of a spear in the back of the Bloodhound's head.

"I hope they let me fight you first," Creed said, "Black fiend!"

Whack!

Creed hit the ground.

"Secure them all, except the skinny one," Kierway ordered, copper eyes on Melegal. "We'll whittle what little is left of him down first."

Melegal raised his brows and allowed himself a smile.

Lorda showed a grim smile back.

Well, it's over. Nothing like a little flirting before you're dead.

50

"**W**ATCHA LAYIN' THERE FER?" A gruff voice said. "That ain't what I had in mind when I taught you about adventurin'."

Fogle didn't move. He couldn't. Instead, he lay in the sun, baking like a biscuit in a roasting oven. Still, he forced his eyes open, trying to blink the hallucination away from his mind, his thoughts.

"Go away, Mood. I'm done for," he said with a dry throat.

"What's the matter? Did ye lose your little druid friend? And now yer tender heart is broken, so you quit? This is Bish. You quit, you die. Now get up!"

Fogle didn't. Instead, he closed his eyes, but the scent of Mood's cigar drifted into his nose.

This is one powerful hallucination.

For hours, maybe days, he'd lain there, letting his inner self fight it out. He'd failed. He wanted to go home. Crawl under a rock and bury himself.

He'd been here before. Back when Venir beat him. Busted his mind and his nose. A broken man, he'd left the Magi Roost. It had taken him years to understand his failures. His fears.

Now, those fears returned with a vengeance. The Outlands. The sweltering heat, the chronic battle to survive, and the threat of the unknown had rattled his brilliant mind.

I can't do this anymore. I can't.

"Just leave me alone," he said, rolling over.

"Get up, Wizard!" the gruff voice prodded. "Get up, else I'll kill you myself."

He curled up, covering his face.

"Go ahead," Fogle said. "If my hallucination doesn't kill me, I'm sure something else will. Perhaps a giant will step on me, or some bugs will eat my flesh," he cackled, "or a dragon will roast me like a log." He cackled again. "Or the underlings will cut my throat. So many ways to go. Getting killed by my imagination seems more soothing than the rest. So Mood, my long gone friend, I'm prepared for the worst."

A silence fell. Even the hot winds slowed. The scent of Mood's cigar drifted to his nose again. Fogle sighed. "That's much better." He curled up and pulled his robes tighter. "Sorry, Cass. I failed you."

A minute passed, maybe two.

"GET UP, I TELL YA!"

Fogle's eyes popped open. In the next moment, water was pouring over his head. Down it came, second after second, soaking his hair, his robes.

"GET UP!"

Spluttering a mouthful from his lips, he forced himself to an upright position. Water was still being poured over his head by the figure of a large stout man. When the water finally stopped, he wiped his eyes.

Two emerald eyes under bushy red brows were staring right at him.

"Mood? Are you real?"

"As real as a mole on an ogre's fanny." Mood puffed on a cigar stuck between his two meaty fingers. "Are you finished belly aching now?"

Fogle stretched out his arms and hugged him.

"But how? You were, well, in such bad shape." He patted the rocky muscles in Mood's thick shoulders.

"True, but I was still breathing. And I'm King of the Dwarves. Soon as I fell, the lady dwarves came running. They patched me up leagues away, where Eethum caught up with me."

That's when Fogle noticed Eethum, the big black dwarf, arms crossed over his long blood red beard, standing like a mighty oak. He wasn't alone either. More Black Beards, each just under five feet tall, but stout as keg barrels, sat on the back of dwarven horses.

Fogle couldn't hold his tongue from catching Mood and Eethum up on everything that had gone on.

"A dragon, ye say? Woot! It's been a long time since I've seen one of those," Mood said, taking a knee, wincing.

"Mood, you aren't fully well, are you?"

The ancient dwarf shot him a look. "Ye need to mind what you say, Wizard." He grabbed Fogle by the forearm and squeezed. "I'm well enough to snap you in two."

Biting his lip, Fogle tried to pull away. "No need to be so cranky. I was just concerned."

Mood squeezed harder. "You were what?"

The fingers on his hand went numb. "Nothing! Nothing!"

Mood released him and blew a puff of smoke in his face.

"Mind yer manners." Mood reached into a pouch on his trousers and tossed him something in a cloth.

Fogle unfolded it and found the remnants of Inky.

"Thanks," he said, fanning the smoke. "How'd you find me?"

Mood rolled his thick neck towards Eethum, who said, "We're Blood Rangers. Once we got yer scent, we could track you anywhere, but we did lose you for a bit." He glanced at Mood.

"I hate to admit. You disappeared into thin air."

Fogle knew what he was talking about. It was the spell Boon had cast that got them out of the jam when they fled a wave of underlings.

"Still, why can't you follow Chongo?"

"He doesn't have a scent."

Fogle raised an eyebrow. "I guess not."

Mood handed him his water skin. "Yer gonna need this. We've a ways to go." He grunted as he swung his leg up on his horse. "Get on."

Mood looked like a giant atop his dwarven Clydesdale, large axes strapped across his back.

"Where are we going? What about Cass?"

"We're going after that giant," Mood said, "Find him, most likely we'll find her. Now get on. Time's a wasting, and I suggest you find ye some good spells."

"Why's that?" Fogle said, getting on.

"'Member them giants that socked it to me?"

"Yes," Fogle said, looking over his shoulder as the horse lurched forward.

"Well, they ain't done. YAH!"

As the first dusk settled, Fogle got his first glimpse of green tree tops in the distance, but it brought him little relief. When he wasn't focusing on his spells, he was thinking about Cass and those piercing eyes of the Dragon that Barton called Blackie.

I'll get you back, Cass. I swear it. Even if I have to find a way to the Under-Bish all by myself.

Eethum led the way, followed by the Black Beards, then Mood and himself. The King of the Blood Rangers had little to say, however, unlike before. He seemed grim and angry for some reason. Fogle was about to ask him if something else was wrong when Eethum brought them to a halt less than a mile from the lush branches of the jungle.

Mood rode forward.

"You want two ranks or one?" Eethum asked, bushy red brows raising up and down.

"Two. But no more than thirty yards between us. It's as thick as my beard in there."

"Well, I'm certain the giant left a noticeable trail," Fogle said, dropping from the saddle and stretching his limbs.

Mood huffed.

"Wouldn't he?" Fogle said, gulping down some water, looking around. None of the dwarves had taken a single drink, now that he noticed, and now that he'd gotten used to it, he'd been sipping every hour. He held it out to Eethum. "Drink?"

The dwarf showed his teeth and shook his head.

"Trusting the giants are ye now, Little Wizard?"

"Well, no, just following him. But he's helped me, and I've helped him. I see no harm in it." He plugged his ever-flowing water skin. "Besides, he seems to know where Venir or Chongo is. Where else would he be going?"

Mood and Eethum just looked at him.

Fogle shrugged. "What? I'm not a dwarf, you know."

"A good thing fer us you ain't, Wizard. Now hush your mouth and get back on. We've got a ways to go."

Fogle pulled at his sweat-soaked robes. Hoping for relief in the shade of the jungle, as opposed to the dry Outland heat, he instead found himself overwhelmed by the chronic dampness of the humidity.

"Like walking through water," he muttered.

"Aye," Mood agreed, "but don't worry: you'll never get used to it."

They'd traveled through night, the jungle as black as a cave, before the dawn of a new light. Fogle found little comfort in it, swatting at mosquitos as big as his hand and smashing them on Mood's back.

"Ye want something?"

"Uh…" Fogle wiped his hand on his robes. "No… But, shouldn't we have caught up with Barton by now?"

"Barton? Is that what ye call yer friend?"

"Never mind."

Mood had been plenty clear on his hatred for the giants. He'd even shared a horrible tale of another one called Horace. The insane giant had slaughtered more than a hundred dwarves. Some of Mood's sires. One of his wives. But, how Mood captured the giant, tethered and killed him was another thing. It seemed the giants had a mystic way to come and go as they pleased. Fogle was curious about that.

"Look." Mood pointed his sausage-thick finger toward an opening in the trees.

Squinting, Fogle shook his head. "What?"

"Not thata way." Mood grabbed Fogle's chin and turned his head. "Thata way."

A stark log-made structure like a giant's home sat atop a mountainous hill.

"What is that?"

"Men call it Outpost Thirty-One or somethin'."

"Are you serious?" Fogle knew the history of the fallen outpost that gave the underlings the upper hand in the southern lands. 'Nothing on Bish has been the same since the fall of Outpost Thirty One,' the travelers from the south said.

It was rumored that whoever controlled Outpost Thirty-One controlled the South and would gain a foothold on the North. Now, it sat there alone, abandoned so far as he could tell. The logs that made up its framework were five times as thick as the surrounding forest trees. That was the other odd thing. The fort, a safe-haven for men, had been built by giants, they said. It reminded him of the City of Three, where a few structures still stood that marveled the others in size.

"Mood, you're a giant dwarf. Who built that? The giants?"

"It don't matter who built it. It only matters who's in it."

"Then who's in it?"

Mood shook his bushy bearded head and snorted the air.

"Well, I'll be slat on a stick. I think Venir is in there."

"Alive?"

"Don't know, but there's only one way to find out." Mood dug his boots into his horse and lead the Black Beards towards the mountain.

"I thought the fort was run by an army of underlings."

"So?"

"Well, there's only fifteen of us. Can I assume the King of the Dwarves has a plan?"

"I'll let ye know before we get there. It's still a bit of a ride ahead."

"That's not a plan."

"It's better than whatever you got."

51

"**O**RDER UP! ORDER UP! ORDER up!" Darlene clamored. "Move your boots, ladies! There's hungry fellows out there!"

"I heard you, Darlene!" Mercy said, grabbing a tray of food from the kitchen and rushing it over to a loud and eager table.

Kam had been rubbing the black polish on the bar for over an hour, trying to ignore the rough cut woman. Now, her elbow was sore, and her cheeks burned.

I'm going to kill her!

Over the past few days, the Magi Roost had been turned upside down and inside out. No longer the quaint establishment it once was, it was now a seedy den for travelers from all over the land. It hadn't ever been this bad before, not even when Venir was here. Not by a long shot. And all of Kam's patrons, many of whom she adored, were gone, replaced by anything from an orc to a halfling. The City of Three had become a harbor for Southern refugees, and it was a problem.

"I hope you aren't planning on going through with that."

Taking the dust rag off the stump of her hand and slinging it over her back, she turned and faced Scorch. The man's comely looks were startling. He'd been sitting in the same spot at the end of the bar for days. He never left, and she couldn't get used to it. But, she'd gotten used to it enough.

Eyeing her hand in the pickle jar and blowing her red locks from her face, she said, "And if I am? Are you going to cut off my other hand?"

"Certainly not. It was Darlene who did that, not I. But Kam, I must warn you: I'm not comfortable with murderous thoughts." He refilled his goblet. "I want this to be a happy place. A place of celebration. A place of fun."

She could feel her missing fist clenching. Through gritted teeth, she said, "A place I cannot flee, because you will not permit me to. No, Scorch. If you want this place to celebrate—then leave!"

His blond brows creased a little.

She felt her breath thinning.

"Kam!" Darlene said. "We're shorthanded. Get over to that table of half-orcs. I like those guys. They tell the filthiest jokes. Here," she held a pitcher out, "they need replenished!"

Cheeks flushed, Kam shot her a dangerous look. "You do it!"

Go! Scorch's voice rattled her head.

More on his will than her own, she grabbed the pitcher of ale and started over.

"And show more cleavage," Darlene shouted after her, "they'll pay extra for that. And hide that stump of yours. I don't want the patrons uncomfortable."

52

"HOW'S HE DOING?" BILLIP ASKED.

Shaking his head, Nikkel wiped the sweat from Brak's head with his sleeve.

"He's still burning up. I could fry an egg on his big head."

Brak lay still, his big swollen face creased in a frown. His back was red and purple where the snake had bitten him, leaving the man bloated.

Georgio groaned on Quickster's saddle. He was swollen a little himself, and his stomach still hurt. He didn't remember anything after the snakes struck. Instead, he'd awoken on a stretcher of sorts, being dragged by Quickster. That was two days ago. All he could figure was his body's special gift for healing itself had saved him. But Brak, he wasn't so sure about.

"He's still chewing," Nikkel said, widening his blue eyes. "I've never seen a man who could eat in his sleep before." He shrugged. "At least he isn't dead. But it doesn't look like he's going to get up for a while."

Brak's body convulsed, and thick saliva dripped out of his mouth.

"Yech," Nikkel said, tossing Jubilee a rag. "You can wipe that up; he's your friend."

Jubilee lifted her chin up and strutted over to Brak. "I'd be happy to."

Georgio felt miserable. Part poison, part other things. Brak hadn't done anything wrong aside from being hungry, and in all truth, it had been Brak's berserker's fit that saved them, all of them. The man-boy had scared up plenty of food, and Brak's clearing in the cactus pit had revealed many round cacti filled with water. He had filled them all up, but Georgio didn't feel like eating any more.

He pulled at the locks of his curly hair. *It's not my fault.*

"This is all your fault, you know," Jubilee said at him. "If you hadn't gotten him all riled up, he wouldn't have gone berserk, Fatboy Idiot!"

"That's enough, Jubilee!" Billip intervened. "It's not anyone's fault. Things like this happen in the Outlands. You *children* just aren't used to it."

"But—"

"But!" Billip turned on Jubilee, nostrils flaring, knuckles cracking, "I'll tell you about *butt*, Little Girl. I'm going to bust yours from two halves to ten if you don't close that big mouth of yours."

She folded her arms across her chest and stuck her tongue out. "No one's ever whipped me, and no one ever will."

"Don't tempt me," Billip said, taking out an arrow and smacking it into his palm.

"You'd enjoy that, wouldn't you, Rogue?"

He smacked it into his hand with a loud whap. "I certainly would."

"Pervert."

Georgio thought Billip's face was going to crack.

But Nikkel, calm as well water, stepped between them. "Let's not kill each other. Because if we do, who'll take care of Brak?" His smile, which hadn't been seen in days, was beginning to show more.

"Quickster, I guess," Georgio said, starting to chuckle.

"Well, I hope Quickster doesn't understand what she's saying," Billip added, "else he'd kick her in the teeth."

The men started laughing.

"I wish I'd thought of that," Nikkel said, smiling. "Let's give her some rawhide to chew on. That might keep her quiet."

"Stop laughing at me!" Jubilee whined.

They ignored her.

"Stop it, I said! Stop it!"

Georgio felt a little better, and it was good to see Nikkel smile again. He looked even more like his father when he did that. He even noticed a little moisture in Billip's eye.

"How much longer, Billip?" Georgio asked. "This is taking twice as long as it did when we came down here. We aren't lost, are we?"

"No. But we've got a ways yet. I'm certain we'll make it, but I don't' know about Brak. I'm afraid if we can't get him some healing soon... Just keep feeding him bits of the green snake meat."

Everyone looked at Brak again. It was a sad sight. Somehow, he'd managed to save them, but they had no way of saving him.

Georgio fought back the tears in his eyes. He missed Venir. He missed Mikkel and even Lefty. He pinched the tear ducts in his eyes.

"You alright?" Nikkel asked, patting his shoulder.

Georgio pushed his hand away. "It's just dust in my eyes."

"Sure, Georgio, sure. I got some of that too."

53

"**K**EEP MOVING," TUUTH SAID. *Wupash!*

It was early. The suns hadn't crested the fort's high walls yet, but all Venir could think about was the long day ahead. Everything but his fingernails ached. Every step was full of lead, and his back felt like it was on fire all the time. It was misery, but knee deep in an underling slat hole, he kept shoveling muck from one pit to the other.

"Smells good, doesn't it, Stranger?"

Venir kept his head down. His mouth shut. Tuuth had been taunting him day and night, but he wouldn't take the bait. He had to hold out. He dipped his shovel in the muck and slung it over his sagging shoulders.

"You don't look well, but you haven't died." Tuuth spat a snot ball in the muck. "Even the underlings are talking about it. Funny thing, Stranger, the underlings aren't so different than men. Believe it or not, they're betting on you. How much longer you'll live." He spat again. "I'll tell you this much: I lost my wager days ago. So I don't have any motivation to see you live any longer, so die already, will you?"

Tuuth spat again and took a long drink from his flask before he continued.

"One of my comrades, Flaggon, will win if you don't make it through the night. That's a nice bit of script he'd get with the underlings, and he promised the rest of us enough wine to drink all night." He stuffed a large wad of tobacco in his mouth. "So plan on a few whippings and more digging. They won't be stopping at all today unless your heart gives."

It didn't even stir him. He dug. Busted wrists and all. His once taut muscles now sagging on his arms. The thought of men consorting with underlings had infuriated him once, but now it didn't seem to matter. Now, the only thing that mattered was digging from one day to the other.

"Huh," Tuuth said, walking away, "I think I liked you better when you talked more."

Venir kept shoveling, glancing around from time to time.

Watch. Listen. Learn.

The remnants of the Brigand Army and the renegades from other orders were fewer than one hundred, including Flaggon and Tuuth. But the underlings were a different story. Venir had never seen so many different colored eyes before. He hadn't realized there were so many underlings in the world. He'd managed to count over a thousand of them one day, but the next day when he woke there'd been almost two thousand. They weren't all coming in through the gates either. Instead, squads of them came from inside the Outpost walls, out of a building that was once the Royal Headquarters.

And Venir knew there was no way that building could hold them all. Dread filled him.

Have they taken over the entire world?

Digging, he tried to make sense of what was happening, but he could barely think.

Brool.

His war-axe entered his mind. It seemed his days of devastation were over. What a fool he'd been, to remove the armament and leave it behind. And for what? His pride!

Am I a fool?

He couldn't shake the feeling he'd seen Brool and the rest of the armament for the last time. He'd do anything to be reunited with it again.

Curse me for a buffoon.

He slung more muck over his shoulder. One shovelful. Two. Fifty. A hundred. Two hundred.

Steam rose from the muck. The big flies and mosquitos swarmed.

A tall man walked over with a jug of water. It was Flaggon.

"You seem to attract the rottenest things." He fanned the bugs away. "Here, drink."

Venir took a swallow and made an ugly face.

"What did you put in that?" Venir tried to hand it back.

"Keep drinking, Stranger, and make it quick. That's vinegar added to it. You need it."

Venir eyed him.

"I thought you'd win the bet if I died today."

"Ah." Flaggon's brows lifted. "Tuuth told you about that, did he? Well, the truth is, Tuuth doesn't know what's going on. I already have plenty of wine, and there's no such thing as money here. We barter a little with the underlings." He winked. "But Tuuth's not very good at bartering. Besides, now that you've survived this long, I hate to see you die. Ye've defied the odds, ya have." He scratched his head. "And something's to be said for that."

Venir took another drink, finishing it off, and tossed Flaggon the canteen.

"How long do you think they'll keep you around?"

Flaggon shrugged. "I don't have any choice in the matter. No more than you. But I'll tell you this: the underlings are running the show on Bish now. They aren't going to kill everyone, but they will be killing everyone who opposes them. And I figure I'm better off with 'em than against 'em."

Venir scowled. "You make me sick."

"Ha!" Walking away, Flaggon waved at him. "I see they haven't broken your spirit yet, Stranger. See you tomorrow. Dead or alive. I've a bottle of underling port to crack."

Digging and simmering, Venir filled the other hole, crawled over the ridge between the pits, and stepped in it. Rolling his shoulder, he realized no one, not man or underling, even noticed. Instead, they all went about their business. A digging corpse, he was already forgotten.

They were Chittering back and forth with one another, even smiling, some of them.

Could it be true? Had the underlings taken over? He even saw one playing an instrument, similar to a lute. But the thing that disturbed him most was—he was getting used to it. Their smell. Their gray faces and their faint fur-like pelts.

Another hour passed, then two.

"Dig, Arsehole Bastard. Dig!"

It was the underling commander.

Venir ventured a look at him.

His bulging arms were crossed over his barrel chest. A razor-edged sword hung by his side.

"On your knees, Arsehole Bastard," the underling said. "You are now a servant of the underlings."

It felt like all the eyes of the fort were on him. Those of both underling and man. Dying of thirst, tongue swollen, Venir kept shoveling.

"Orc," the commander said, "is this man deaf? I told him to bow, not to shovel. Make him bow, Orc. Make him bow!"

"On your knees, Stranger," Tuuth said.

Venir kept shoveling.

"He looks like he can't hear." The commander slid a sharp dagger from his belt. "So he doesn't need those ears." He extended it towards Tuuth.

Hesitating, Tuuth said, "You want me to cut them off?"

"No, I want you to carve him a new arsehole, Stupid Orc."

Tuuth snatched the blade. "Fine then. Stranger, get out of that puddle."

"No!" The underling pointed. "You get in the puddle, Orc. What's the difference? You always smell like dung."

The surrounding underlings chittered in agreement.

"Last chance to bow down, Stranger," Tuuth warned, an angry look growing in his eyes. "If I step in the mire, I'm going to do more than cut your ears off. I'll cut your tongue out as well."

Venir glared at them. "What are you waiting for?" He slung a shovel full of muck on the both of them.

Ruby eyes flashing, the underling let out a hiss.

Tuuth roared, jumping in, splashing muck all over.

"You couldn't keep your mouth shut, could you?"

Crack!

Venir's head rocked back, falling into the sludge.

The underlings and men let out cheers.

"That'll shut him up, Tuuth!"

"Bust him again, good!"

"Make him eat that slat he's diggin'!"

Even the underlings chittered words of encouragement.

"He'll not talk after that punch!"

His legs felt like anvils, his arms like sandbags, but Venir got up and raised his hands on his busted wrists, squeezing them into fists. Dripping in muck, he eyed Tuuth.

"Fight or die."

Tuuth walloped him in the belly.

He sagged to his knees.

"He's bowing now, ain't he!" a brigand said.

Venir rose again.

"Cut his ears off, Orc!" The underling commander said as two other underlings wiped the muck from his armor. "I want them for a necklace. I might have you add some fingers and toes as well." He spat and wiped his mouth. "I want the tongue too."

Tuuth grabbed Venir by the hair, yanked him up to his feet, and put him in a head lock.

Struggling, Venir's face was beet red, but a ten-year-old boy would have fared better. His strength, what little he had left, was not enough.

Venir grinded his teeth and tried to pulled away.

"You!" Tuuth ordered to one of the brigands. "Get in here and grab his feet."

"Slat on me," the heavyset man said, stepping in and rolling up his sleeves. "Just make it quick, will you? It smells worse than an ogre's outhouse."

"Try not to scream, Stranger," Tuuth growled in his ear.

Slice!

His ear dropped into the muck.

"Did you hear that, Arsehole Bastard?" the underling commander said.

Every eye from the underling camp was watching now. From the towers, the catwalks, sitting on the parapets. If you were within eye shot, you could see.

Fight, blast you! Fight!

Venir's struggles were in vain.

Slice!

His last ear fell in front of his eyes, floating atop the grime.

"Good, Orc, good," the underling rubbed his chin. "And I like your idea. Cut his tongue out as well. No more talk, Human. Instead, you will scream so we can't hear."

"You two, get in here," Tuuth ordered.

One man rolled his eyes; the other one groaned.

"Get in there, idiots," Flaggon said, shoving them forward.

They sloshed through the muck, one holding his nose.

"Get his arms," Tuuth said, and then looked down on Venir. "Any last words, Stranger?"

"You're all orc, Tuuth. And it smelled better before you got here."

Ptui!

A gob of spit hit Tuuth square in the eye.

Tuuth rose his dagger high.

"Just the tongue Orc! Do not kill him!"

THROOM!

Everyone in the fort flinched, eyes searching the southern gate.

THROOM!

All the men murmured.

The underlings chittered, scrambling to their stations.

The wooden portcullis cracked and buckled.

THROOM!

The alarm was sounded, high pitched.

"Move it, men," Flaggon ordered. "Tuuth, leave him. He's not going anywhere."

"Not until I have his tongue first." He rested the knife on Venir's chin. "Hold him."

54

S HACKLED TO A STAKE WITH mystic purple bands, gagged, arms behind his back, Boon sighed.

The fight is over.

All his life he'd been in control. Dominant. A powerful force. Even when the giants had custody of him, as powerful as they were, he'd had a say in his destiny. But now, his say had run out.

Surrounding him, in an underling camp in the Outland, were more of the fiends than he cared to count. Thousands, and they were still arriving. He'd never seen such a large force. He hadn't even imagined one so large.

Nearby, a brood of underling magi watched over him. Their light blue and green eyes in study.

He wondered why they kept him alive.

"Water," he said, licking his lips.

They said nothing to him, chittering to themselves from time to time and inspecting his robes. The only stitch he had left on him was a pair of cut-off trousers. Even his sandals were gone. The suns gave a nice red layer to his back.

He tried to stand, but his knees wouldn't bend.

He never thought he'd ever ask an underling for anything, but he asked again, "Water."

Nothing. But it would come. It had come yesterday and the day before. A humpback urchling had fed him some food that was horrible but digestible. And so it had been. Day in. Day out. Hour after hour.

"I always imagined I'd die battling you fiends. Never a prisoner. Now look at me. An underling's beggar." Again he sighed. "I can't even insult you."

After dozing off, for how long he didn't know, he was rustled. Two underling warriors picked him up, leading him on trembling legs through the camp. The black grey smoke burned his eyes. He closed them until they stopped. An underling chittered at him with an angry tone. He knew what it meant.

Open your eyes, Human.

He knew what to expect. He didn't mean to open them, but he did.

They led him to the edge of camp, where a graveyard of the living and the dead waited.

Trains of people—men, women and children—fell under the lash and spade. They screamed, cried and wailed. Mercy was asked, but none was given. They dug graves. And were buried in them by their own.

A tear fell onto Boon's wispy white beard.

One underling pointed. The other one laughed.

It gnawed at his gut.

"To take such pleasure in it is sick."

They led him through the graveyard until his legs failed.

How could this happen? The armament must be gone. Or the underlings must have it.

55

A S QUICK AS HE MIGHT be, Melegal was no fighter. He was a thief. A cutpurse. Shadow. Survivor. Rat. The swords in his hands were heavier than those he was accustomed to, his blades, the Sisters.

"Just get in a quick jab between the ribs, Detective," Creed said. "You have it in you."

Tonio and Jarla stood nearby, surrounded by underlings with long spears, leaving Melegal in the center of the arena, all alone.

Still, Lorda's long-lashed eyes intent upon him gave him a bit of a charge.

Master Kierway chittered to one of his men.

An underling with dark ruby eyes stepped forward, a razor sharp sword in each hand. The steel flickered around his body in a lightning quick display of skill and speed.

Great.

"That's all show! Go for the ribs," Creed said. "Like you did to my man. That was a good jab." Creed muttered to Jarla something under his breath. "He doesn't have a chance."

Melegal glared back at Creed, who shrugged.

"Let's get this started, shall we?" Kierway said, raising up his hand.

Melegal swallowed hard and squared off with the underling. *If I only had my hat.* But it was gone. Everything was gone. The Keys. The hat. His friends. *Maybe they'll survive this. But at least Sefron is dead. Was vengeance worth it?* He thought about Sefron. The man had been much more than he appeared to be. Was anything in Bish what he thought it was? He'd seen so many things the past several years.

Melegal glanced at Lorda one last time.

She blew him a subtle kiss.

I'll be.

Kierway dropped his hand.

The underling sprang, swords chopping high and low.

Melegal backpedaled and parried the snake quick strokes.

Clang. Clang. Clang. Clang. Bang.

"Keep 'em up, Detective!" Creed said.

Drained and starving, Melegal didn't have the strength to fight. *Fight or die.* It rattled in his head, but he didn't have it. He didn't have anything. *Die.* He broke it off and threw down his swords.

The underling paused and looked over at Master Kierway.

"Don't go out like that. Pick the blade up and finish like a man!" Creed said.

Skinny chest heaving, Melegal clutched at his sides and dropped to his knees.

Creed frowned. "He's got nothing left in him. Coward."

No, Melegal wouldn't die fighting. He sucked up all the air he could and fixed his gaze on Lorda. *If I go out. I'll go out doing what I want to.* He winked at her and mouthed good-bye.

She clutched her painted fingers at him, eyes watering.

"Finish him," Kierway ordered, dropping his thumb. "And get the woman ready next. Sad, but I bet there's more fight in the woman than the man. Pathetic humans, letting their women fight with them and against them. Weak."

The underling warrior raised his blade, sharp teeth showing a savage grin.

Melegal kept his chin up, eyes on Lorda.

"CEASE!"

The entire room shook.

The underling warrior froze.

Lord Verbard, silver eyes sparkling, floated down the stairs with Lord Almen and a hulking Vicious right behind him.

"How dare you?" Kierway said, jumping up from his chair. "This is no concern of yours, Verbard, you insolent underling! My father—"

"Your father agrees! You can ask him yourself," Verbard said. "He's coming soon, and no doubt he'll want to evaluate your failures."

Kierway's hard jaw slackened. His ascent up the steps stopped.

"Lord Almen, are these the humans you want?" Verbard said, pointing down into the arena at them.

"Just three of them: Lorda, Jarla, Tonio, Come!"

"Tonio!" Lorda shot Almen a look. "Our son?" She looked at her son. Total shock on her face. She didn't know him.

"Aye, now get moving, Dearest Lorda," Almen said. "I'm out of parlays."

"And that woman, the black-haired witch? Are you bringing your mangy whore along?"

"What about me, Lord Almen?" Creed said. "I'm a loyal Hound at your service! You know that."

Lord Almen shook his head. "A hound, yes. No more, no less. I've plenty of curs at my disposal." He grabbed Lorda by the wrist.

Creed scowled at Almen, muttering to himself.

Lorda twisted away and continued her ascent, giving Melegal one final glance. "If you get her, then I want him."

Lord Almen's jaw tightened. "Be grateful you live, Woman. You can stay with me, or you can stay with Master Kierway."

Lorda called him a bastard, called out for Tonio, and moved away.

CRASH!

A boulder as big as a pony burst through the glass dome, crushing two underlings into the arena stairs.

The castle shook. Shouts of alarm when up.

"We're under attack!" Lord Almen said. "It seems my neighbors have awakened." He looked for Verbard, but the underling Lord was already moving.

"Get your men ready, Kierway," Verbard said. "The next battle has begun."

A large white-yellow ball of energy floated through the broken glass and hovered over the arena.

Kierway chittered a command.

Melegal balled up, covering his ears, closing his eyes.

Ka-Chow!

Something fell on top of him. It was the underling he'd been fighting. He shoved it off.

What in Bish!

Its red eyes were blinking and its limbs were loose. Melegal, despite his weakness, could still move. He grabbed a sword and stuck the underling.

Glitch!

Creed was on the move. Snatching up a sword, he tore a stunned underling's head from its shoulders.

Escape, Fool! Run!

Chaos unfolded. The dazed underlings were gathering their wits, heading for the doors. Kierway and Verbard were moving, ordering, unfazed.

The Vicious, a hulking predator, pounced into the arena and darted towards Creed.

Clank!

Melegal and Jarla froze.

A large leather sack had landed along the arena wall in front of Master Kierway's chair.

Slat on me! Venir?

Long legs churning, Jarla dashed over and dove on the sack. With a ravenous look in her eyes, she opened the sack and reached in.

Tonio was confused. His father was there, calling for him. His mother didn't seem to know him, and then she called for him too. And the underlings were in charge. Deep in the recesses of his mind, he knew he should be able to put it all together, but he couldn't. It was frustrating.

"Mother?" he said.

A rock fell from the sky, and a brilliant white flash followed. He grunted. Clutched his head and shook it. "Mother!"

A creature with a cat-like face shoved his mother down. Down the steps it bounded. He didn't know what it was, but he was going to kill it.

"Tonio kill!"

A pair of underling warriors stepped in his path.

"I'm getting used to this underling steel!"

Stab!

Creed yanked the blade from the underling's neck. Black-red blood gurgled from the hole and seeped into the ground.

The underling, though stunned, recovered quickly.

Creed, Master Swordsman from the House of Bloodhounds, pressed his advantage.

Slice!

He disemboweled one.

Chop!

He chopped another's neck open.

"Who do I have to kill to get some food and ale around here?" Creed shook the dripping blood from his blades. "I'm so hungry I could eat one of you fiends! Where's the kitchen?"

He caught a shadow in the corner of his eye and whirled.

"What in Bone are you?" he exclaimed.

The Vicious. Wicked rows of teeth. Claws like razors.

"I see you're missing some fingers," Creed said. "Let's see if I can even you out and remove a few more."

Creed lunged.

The Vicious sprung away and hunched down like an ape.

Creed felt something crawling in his belly. He'd never seen anyone that big move that fast.

"Yer not born of this world, are you? No matter. I'm still going to gut you with my blades." He banged the swords together. "Give it a go again. I'm ready for you."

The Vicious pounced, arms sprawled out, chest bared.

Slice!

He cut it across the belly and rolled out of the way and back to his feet.

"Let's see how you fight with your guts hanging out."

The monster turned, showed its fangs, and smiled. There wasn't a mark on it.

Creed felt his skin turn pale. "I'm in for."

The Vicious lunged.

Creed chopped with all his might. The blade shattered on its forearm.

The Vicious ripped a hunk of meat from Creed's chest.

"Urk!"

The Vicious snapped him up by the neck and squeezed his neck like a fresh fruit.

Eyes bulging from the sockets, Creed flailed and kicked.

At least I took some more of them with me.

"Mine!" Jarla said, licking her lips, eyes wild.

It was her salvation. Her liberation. The sack, after all these years, was back in her grasp, and nothing would ever stop her again, ever. It would fill her. Restore her. Any kind of enemy Jarla faced, even be they Royal or underling, she would prevail.

Reaching inside, her fingertips tingled in anticipation. The shafts of her axes. The power surging through her bracers. The awesome awareness from her helmet. Down to her shoulder she reached, fingers outstretched as far as they could go.

"Where are they?" She reached deeper. "Where are they!"

Her heart emptied. Nothing was there.

"No," she sobbed.

A shadow fell over her. She looked up. It was the rawboned detective. He held a heavy club with both hands. She sneered.

"That's not yours," he said. "It's Venir's."

"What? Are you mad? I'll never let that lou—"

Whack!

Melegal clubbed her across the jaw.

She tried to speak, but no words came. Only pain. Then darkness.

"That felt good," Melegal said, gathering the sack, "and I haven't forgotten that Lorda wants you dead. But I'll let the two of you fight that out."

Explosions were still erupting all over the castle, so the concerns of Lord Almen and the underling leaders were elsewhere right now.

Hidden along the arena wall, no one had sight of him.

The stunned underlings that were coming out of the mystic blast were focused on the fighting in the middle.

Now I just have to hide until I find Venir. I knew that fool must have caused this.

It was simple. All he had to do was find a place between the walls until he figured out where Venir was. Then he could free him and let him deal with this mess. And he just might be able to get his cap and Keys back. *Just the cap. The cap would be good.*

A doorway, up the steps on the other side of the arena, was open with no one to bar his path.

Move or die.

He was darting along the arena wall, concealed for the first twenty steps, when he heard a familiar voice shout out.

"Seize him!"

It was Lord Almen pointing and shouting, his face filled with rage.

Melegal jumped up, grabbed the lip of the wall, and slung himself up.

Two underlings bolted towards the door, cutting off his path, weapons ready.

He was too late.

Bone!

Two more were closing in from behind. All he had was a club and a sack. Expecting Venir to appear any second, he shook his head.

Where is that brute?

Dropping the club, he sat down, laying the sack on his lap.

56

"MMMPH!"

Tuuth tried to pry his mouth open, but Venir wouldn't give. Teeth clenched, he fought on.

"Hold him still!" Tuuth ordered.

The brigands, stout as they might be, struggled. Each slipping into the mud from his efforts.

"Blast you, Tuuth! You hold him! I'm not swimming in slat on account of this wretch's tongue! He's done for!"

"Aye!" the other agreed, letting go and crawling out of the slime.

"You'll both be in the stockade for a week, maybe longer!"

"Pah!"

Still in a headlock, Venir's nostrils flared.

Tuuth cranked up the pressure.

"This isn't over," Tuuth said, looking around.

All the brigands and underlings had abandoned the pit, shouting orders and gathering gear, leaving the two of them all by themselves.

Tuuth shoved him down in the muck and held him under, waited several seconds, and jerked him back out.

Venir coughed and spat.

"Enough of this," Tuuth said, trolling out of the muck and slinging it from his fingers. "Let the underlings kill you themselves, like everyone else."

The ground shook.

"What?" Tuuth stopped in place, arms out.

Venir felt it too, but it was of little notice. Sitting in the muck, he was in agony. Reaching down, he plucked one of his dirty and bloody ears from the muck, tossed it aside, and grabbed his shovel. He pushed himself up with it, legs shaking. Wiping the filth from his eyes, he was watching the southern gate, which was rising, when another clamor went up.

"It's a giant!"

Tuuth tucked the underling's dagger into his belt and looked back. "Don't go anywhere!"

He wasn't. He couldn't. Even if he could, where would he go? Though tempted to at least climb up out of the muck, he remained in what little cover the pit provided, keeping his eyes transfixed on the slow rise of the southern gate. Hundreds of underling soldiers, dark armor and helms gleaming in the sun, stood ready.

A moment later, a collective gasp followed.

There he was.

Tethered by thick ropes and chains, towering more than three times the height of the underlings, a giant stood. They pulled, poked and prodded him. He was angry and confused, each footstep shaking the ground. Bolts and javelins jutted from his body like briars.

Venir's eyes widened.

It was Barton.

The young giant growled and yelled. Slung his weight against his captors to no avail. They had him chained by the neck, the arms, and the ankles. Enough chains to forge an armory.

Venir felt pity. Barton's expression was tormented. A confused child. Miserable.

Barton stomped. Rocked and reeled.

"LET BARTON GO! LET BARTON GO!"

But the underlings had him under control. They chittered. They laughed.

Sitting down on the edge of the muck pit, he watched the underlings bind the giant further. Venir recalled his time in the Mist. It had been Barton who freed him. It had been Barton he tricked, and it had been Barton who said he'd come for him—and he had.

Of all people, he remembered me.

Of course, it wasn't Venir he wanted, it was the armament. The toys. Venir wanted them too, but he was certain the armament was gone.

Barton's going to be disappointed, if he lives to find out.

Barton was bound to the exterior wall, a mere ten yards away, but under heavy guard. He yelled and whined, but after several minutes, he fell silent.

Venir resumed his shoveling. *Nothing I can do. Sorry, Barton.* Whatever happened was going to happen, and there was nothing he could do. Two more hours he dug. He was dying of thirst.

"Dwarves!" One of the brigands shouted from the catwalks. "Dwarves!"

Venir lifted his head up. Stout black-bearded men, shackled, were herded inside like cattle. Some limped. All bled. Hard looks on their grim faces.

"Who's in command of this place?" a commanding voice said.

Mood? He cupped his hand behind his missing ear, peering forward.

"Come on, rodents! Bring yer leader out!"

Venir shielded his eyes from the blazing suns with his hand. Mood, bushy and broad, stood over the rest, a green glimmer under his brows.

The underling commander strutted forward, chest out.

"Blood Ranger, you have no business here. Not on my mountain. The penalty is death."

"Ye'll release us all, Underling," Mood said. "We hunt giants, all over Bish, and where they go, we go. Underlings or no. It's our right. You best let us go, or the entire dwarven world will come for you. Not to mention more giants."

An underling cracked a spear over Mood's head.

The Blood Ranger didn't flinch. All he said was, "I'm warning you."

"Say all you want, Blood Ranger. You'll be dead soon, so it doesn't matter. Bish is ruled by the underlings now, so your threats are of no matter." The underling commander started to walk away. "Flay them. Flay them all. But save the giant for last."

"It's easier to flay a stone than a dwarf, you fool!" Mood said. "We'll dull your knives after the first cut."

Venir shook his head and resumed his shoveling.

"Stay here."

Those were the last words Mood had said to Fogle Boon before he'd departed with the Black Beards and headed towards Outpost Thirty One, leaving him alone with Eethum. That had been several hours ago, and at the bottom of the massive hill they waited. He'd been clutching at handfuls of his hair ever since.

"Eethum, what's the plan?"

Solemn as always, the black Blood Ranger replied, "I don't know."

That was the same answer he'd given five times already, and Fogle was tired of it. He had to know, and even though Fogle didn't question dwarven integrity, he had his doubts.

"So, am I to understand that we are to *stay here* forever? And you're comfortable with that?"

Eethum eyed the long branch he'd been whittling for hours.

"He's the King. I do as he says." He stuck his knife in a tree stump and admired his work. "Look at that. Straight as a dwarven bolt." He smiled at Fogle. "I can make a fine spear with it." He tossed it to Fogle. "Or a Wizard's walking stick. Ha! Ha!"

Fogle wanted to crack it over Eethum's head. He slung it to the ground.

"We can't wait here forever, Eethum."

"We won't," Eethum said, grabbing his knife along with another branch and whittling again.

Pacing around him, Fogle said, "I'm not a dwarf. I can't stand here for a hundred years and do nothing, like you."

"I'm not doing nothing; I'm carving wood. Just find yourself something to do. Study your spellbook. Always be ready for something."

It was easier said than done. Fogle didn't know what was going on. So he turned his attention back to Inky. His ebony hawk familiar stretched out its black metallic wings. It was ready.

He glanced over his shoulder at Eethum. The Blood Ranger didn't pay him any attention.

"Alright, I might have to stay here, but that doesn't mean I can't try and figure out what's happening."

Grabbing Inky, he placed Venir's hunting knife in its talons. "Give this to Venir if you see him. It will be some time before I can connect with you again." He tossed the bird in the air. Black wings flapping, it soared into the sky, disappearing into the tree line.

He turned and faced Eethum.

The Blood Ranger's arms were crossed over his chest.

"What?" Fogle shrugged. "I'm staying here."

Eethum shook his head. "There's at least a thousand underlings out there. Your little bird's done for."

"Why do you think that?"

Eethum batted an eye at him. "Wizard, have you seen a single bird since we've been here?"

Fogle tucked his chin into his neck. "No."

"There's a reason for that." Eethum put a finger to his lips, then pointed upward. "Hear that?"

Fogle cupped his ear. Something hummed in the sky. "I can always bring him back to us."

"Don't do that. You'll just lead them right to us."

"Them?"

"Stirges. Flocks of them. They destroy every flying creature in sight."

"But Inky doesn't have any blood."

"Maybe so, but they don't know that."

57

"YOU SHOULD EAT SOMETHING, CORRIN."

"What?" he said, blinking.

"Eat," Haze said, motioning to her mouth. "I heard your stomach growling from over there. You've been staring in the fountain for hours. Take a drink already. Or a bath even. Just do something other than sit there."

Corrin gaped at the skinny woman. "Don't you see them?"

She leaned over and peered in. "What? Fish? Spooks? I don't see anything except water."

He looked back in the fountain. The living images were gone.

"No!" he said, reaching in the water, shaking his hand. "Where are they?"

"You've lost your wits," she said, walking away, "but I'll still get you something to eat. Get some shade at least. The suns probably cooked your noodles."

"Aw!" he said, smacking the water. "I'm going to miss it. Trinos!" He looked everywhere. She was nowhere to be found. "Hate it when she does that!"

Trinos had told him strange things. She spoke of Bish as if it were her own child and the things that worried him would take care of themselves. There was order among the chaos, she'd said. Sanity with the madness. Good where there was evil.

But, he disagreed. There wasn't any good in the underlings. He was a hired killer. A murderer. But he took no pleasure in it. The underlings did, and he made it clear to her that despite the Royals' lust for power and control, the world would be better off without the underlings.

"No one is ever in control," she had said. "I have planted many seeds to see to that. But nothing will last forever. I tire. When it ends, it ends."

Corrin didn't understand it one bit. All he knew was people were dying and underlings were living. When it came to the battle for Bish, he wanted in. He buckled on his sword.

"First, I'm going to fill my belly with food, and then I'm going to fill gray bellies with steel."

Trinos sighed.

Her world was everything she'd imagined it to be, but worse. It drained her. The people were strong, full of life, bold—but always shadowed in darkness. Peace had come in the past. Only to go and come again.

Scorch had changed that. Now, peace was a lonely cry from the highest mountain top.

She walked, her toes drifting over the sand in the Warfield. Of all the places in Bish, it was the one most at peace right now. Hot and barren, both underlings and men had avoided it among the turmoil that had broken out everywhere else.

Shall I stay? Can I go? Is this what I want?

She knew she couldn't go. Not without Scorch. They had both buried most of their power deep in Bish when they arrived. One could not tap it without the other.

In the meantime, her own power, vast as it might be, had weakened. Bish was feeding on her. Her powers waned. What had been effortless required effort now. She filled her chest with hot air and slowly let it out. Despite the change, she felt as alive as she ever remembered. Emotions, long forgotten, went up and came down.

Does Scorch feel this as well?

Should I track him?

So she walked, toes sinking into the sand, becoming another part of the world she'd created.

Behind her, two disfigured people followed, covered head to toe in Outland robes, swords hanging from their hips, sandaled but no longer insane.

58

C REED KICKED THE VICIOUS IN the face. It was a last ditch effort.
        It head-butted him.

Crack!

He saw bright spots and stars. He was choking. Sharp claws dug into his neck. His own blood trickled down his chest. He always figured he'd die before he was gray. A match of steel against a younger, stronger opponent like himself. Where he held on with skill and cleverness to the end. But this, to fall in the brutal hands of a monster, was unbearable.

If I only had my sword again.

The brute held him by the neck, pushed him up with its long arm like a child, and shook him like a doll.

Purple-faced, he gulped for air.

Such a cowardly way to go!

He kicked at the Vicious again and again, but there was laughter in its evil eyes.

"Blast you, fiend!" Bloody saliva flew from his mouth.

Creed felt his body closing down. The light dimmed. The pain subsided.

This is it, Bish.

The Vicious released him.

Creed fell to the ground, coughing and choking.

Tonio was there. Arms latched around the creature's neck in a headlock of some sort.

Crawling through the dirt, Creed searched for a blade—a knife, anything.

"Perhaps I'll get in one last swing."

"Mother!" Tonio growled. "You hurt my mother!"

Strength versus strength. Power versus power. Two titans thrashed with one another. The Vicious, an underling abomination of magic brought to life in humanoid form. Tonio, a dead man revived, raging within like a forest fire.

He didn't know what he was or how he came to be. He knew he should be dead but he lived, stitched up by the spiderish arachna-men. Magic gave him life, and nothing could give him death. So he fought. His vengeance unfilled against the yellow-haired Vee-Man.

The Vicious twisted out of his choking grip and socked him in the face.

He staggered back.

The creature pounced on him. It punched and clawed at him, one blow as quick as the other.

His skin shredded. His bone exposed. Tonio didn't feel a thing.

The creature let out an angry howl.

Tonio punched his fist inside its mouth.

Its eyes widened. It pushed away.

Tonio shook the spit from his hand and flashed a split-faced grin. "You can't hurt me!" He pounded his chest. "Nothing can!"

The Vicious leapt. Kicked him in the chest. Knocked him to the ground.

Tonio laughed and rose to his feet. The underling was quick. He matched it blow for blow. He slammed it into the wall.

It bit off a part of his leg.

Tonio hoisted it over his head. Slammed it into the ground. Stomped on its chest. It's head.

Back and forth they went. Two monsters. Evil. Tireless. No quarter given. No hatred spared.

Underlings closed in.

Melegal's instincts took over. He reached into the sack, clutching for a weapon. Something. Anything. Bony fingertips stretching. Tingling. He felt something. Cold. Living.

What is that?

Smack!

An underling cracked him over the head with the pommel of its sword, splitting his vision from two to four.

Spine like jelly, he slumped over the benches, the sack slipping from his grasp.

The one underling grabbed him by the leg and dragged him. The other tossed the sack over the rail, into the arena.

Head bouncing off the benches, Melegal stared at the broken glass dome above. The suns gleamed on the broken glass edges.

Venir, you lout, where are you?

Creed crawled. Huffing. Bleeding. Busted inside and out. A rack of weapons awaited him against the way. And that wasn't all.

"I'll be," he said.

His sword lay on the rack. Steel glimmering under the dust. Tonio and the other monster thrashed behind him. *Move, Creed!* He gathered his feet and stumbled over.

"I bet Pearl can poke a hole in that thing."

He stretched out his fingers and grabbed the hilt.

"Bone! Ah!" The sharp stabbing pain of broken ribs bit into him. Something fell over his head, blocking his sight. *What in Bish?*

He tore it off his face and beheld a worn, stitched-up sack of leather.

Where did this come from?

His stomach rumbled. He hadn't eaten in days. A savage instinct overcame him.

Maybe there's a loaf or some cheese. I don't fight well when hungry.

Ravenous and wild-eyed, he set down his sword and reached inside.

Lorda Almen squatted along the wall at the top of the arena, hiding in a doorway, trembling. A boulder the size of a sofa had almost smashed her, and a creature as dark as night had shoved her down. Her home, her castle, had become a den of madness, and it had only just begun.

"Lorda, get out of there," Lord Almen cried out, his long arm waving her over.

Underling soldiers were whisking him away, and two more were coming for her. She shook her head.

Down on one side of the arena, her son Tonio smashed two underlings together. He attacked the hulking beast that had shoved her, and he was about to break the neck of another. On the other side, Melegal, a man she'd become fond of for some reason, was pinned in by the underlings, awaiting a certain death.

She tried to catch his eye, but a strong armed underling jerked her off the ground and hissed.

"Come with me, Woman. I can't have my pets running loose, now can I?" It was Kierway. He looked over his shoulder. "I've got more pressing matters than watching humans die."

"Unhand me!" she said.

He backhanded her.

Her legs swayed.

"Speak to me like that, and you'll never speak again."

59

COULD HE BE DEAD?

Slim the Healer crawled out of his hiding spot and scurried outside. Being king of the Elga bugs was getting old. He needed to stretch his legs. Not the six he had now, but the two he preferred to walk on as a man.

This is tiresome.

Still, he would do whatever he had to do to keep his friend alive. Something had to happen. Something always did. But this time things didn't seem right. His friend, Venir, was being whittled away, one chunk at a time.

Crawling up one of the Outpost walls, he found a good spot, away from the soldiers.

Oh my!

A man the size of three men was inside the camp, talking like a loud child and fighting against his bonds.

A giant!

A dwarf was whipping his blood red hair in the air, screaming and yelling at an underling like an angry bugbear.

Mood! And Black Beards? Captured? What in Bish is going on?

Bug eyes shifting back and forth, he glossed over a man shoveling in the muck.

Ew! But that's what Brigands should be doing.

Still searching, he couldn't find Venir, so he looked for the orc called Tuuth. The big orc was watching over the dwarves, arms crossed over his chest. Fluttering his wings, Slim found another spot and started searching faces all around.

Venir? Where is that brute?

The man was nowhere to be found. Turning back to the man in the muck pit, he took a closer look. Earlier, he'd been looking for blond hair and muscles. But the markings of a 'V' tattoo still shown through the muck. *Venir!*

A sinking feeling started inside his insect belly. Doubt flooded his mind. Over the centuries, he'd seen many things, but he'd never witnessed such a dire scene before.

The underlings singled out one dwarf and chained him to the wall. Above, in one of the fort's turrets, a pair of underlings grabbed the winch and cranked back the draw string on a ballista. Then loaded a bolt as long as a man. The black beard looked up at the underling, set his chin and raised it high.

Slim closed his eyes.

Ballista bolt sticking out of his chest, the Black Beard let out his final gasp, "For the King!" His head dipped. His helmet fell to the ground.

The underlings let out a loud raucous cheer. Venir had never witnessed underlings celebrating so. They danced and jumped. Loaded another ballista. Replaced the dead dwarf with a live one.

"Yer gonna pay for that!" Mood bellowed, fighting against his bonds.

Venir's heart dipped. Mood's rescue attempt was going to cost the lives of all his men, and then that of Mood, himself. This wasn't how the giant dwarves were supposed to end. They should have known by now that his friendship only brought death.

"King of the Dwarves," the underling commander said, flexing his arms and pumping up his soldiers, "what is it like to see your subjects die? It is customary that we kill the leader first, but I like to watch your eyes. I want to make them water. Making a dwarf cry will be a first." He pointed up at the fort tower and dropped his arm. "Fire!"

THWACK!

Another Black Beard fell. The bolt sticking out of his skull.

"That probably stung," the commander said, "but not for very long."

The crowd chittered, sharp teeth gnashing in agreement.

"Two down, many more to go."

Venir was used to people dying, but not when they weren't in battle. Not without a fight. Watching the dwarves fall ate at him. It wasn't right. It wasn't natural. Hands white-knuckled on the shovel, he thought of Brool. The white hot power surging through his hands. A hollow feeling overcame him. An old friend lost. Lost forever. He had lived this long without it, but could he live anymore? He was broken. What there anything else he could do to help this savage world?

"You?"

Barton's hanging head tilted up and looked right at him. The giant sniffed the air.

"Ah-hah, you are hiding in the stink, Venir?"

Tuuth faced the giant. "What did you say, Giant?" He pointed at Venir. "Are you talking to him? Is he *Venir*?"

"Go away, Orc! I do not like your stink!" Barton's eye rolled back over to Venir. "Give me my toys!"

"Gag that giant!" Tuuth ordered his men.

"What's going on?" the Brigand Flaggon said.

"This man, Commander, has a bounty on his head. A big one. This is Venir the Outlander, the one who destroyed the Brigand Army."

Flaggon rubbed his chin. "I thought there was something familiar about him." He kneeled alongside the pit. "Your bounty is big, and the penalty is death. Get his shovel, men. Tuuth, clean him up a little before you cut off his head. We'll want to bring it as a trophy, if we ever make it back to the Brigand City."

Throughout the fort, everyone's heads snapped up.

The sound of trees snapping like twigs echoed in the distance.

"What now?" Flaggon said.

Tuuth kept his eyes intent on Venir. "Get him out of there."

The ground shook. Not like before, but worse.

Thoom!

It shook again. More trees snapped and cracked. Branches sounded as if they were being crushed into the ground.

Thoom!

Above, Venir glimpsed several robed underlings soaring above the walls, clawed hands filling with color.

Wumpf!

An uprooted tree soared over the wall, smacking into an underling mage and crashing them both into the ground.

"Oh No!" Barton said. "They've come!"

The underling magi fired balls of energy over the wall.

The soldiers in the towers fired their ballistas.

Rocks bigger than men flew over the wall.

Men and underlings scrambled.

A rock smashed into a turret. Underlings fell to their deaths.

"They're after the dwarves!" The underling commander cried out. "Prepare for parlay! We'll hand them over!"

"Hah!" Venir heard Mood say. "If there's anything giants hate more than dwarves, it's the underlings!" Mood snapped his chains and punched the wide-eyed underling commander in the face. "But none hates more than I do, Fiend." Mood let out a gusty word. "*SHARLABOTZ!*"

The leather and metal that bound the Black Beards withered and snapped. The dwarves burst into action. In seconds, they were an armed force. Hacking and slashing into the off-guard underlings.

Venir stirred. A fire ignited within. He raised his shovel and brought it down on the back of Tuuth's head.

Snarling, the orc turned, grabbed Venir by the hair, and slung him to the ground. The orc pinned him down. Wrapped his fingers around his neck and squeezed.

Venir couldn't breathe.

"You're done for now, Venir!" Tuuth pushed him towards the muck pit. "And your grave's even ready. Your bones will be right where they belong, Outland Scum."

60

T HUMP.

Thump. Thump.

Boon's heart still beat. His nose still breathed. But that was all he could to. Beat and breathe. Barely. *Is this all I have left?* The mystic cuffs tightened with every move. Biting into his wrists and burning at the same time. Inside, his own mystic fires still burned, but he could not summon them. His mouth was bound tight as well. Eyelids heavy, heart skipping and slowing, it was his magic that kept his fiber together. Without it, he would have died long ago.

Oh, to wield the armament one last time! I'd give these fiends a show.

Sagging on the ground, he was oblivious to the commotion that stirred the camp. His mind was somewhere else, fighting to keep his body on this side of the threshold between life and death.

Fire fell from the sky.

"Eh..." He opened his eyes.

Smoke began.

The hairs on his arms and beard curled and singed.

Hot smoky air filled his nose and lungs.

A cry of Chaos went up.

A clamor spread through the underling camp. Underlings barked orders. Flames spread from tent to tent.

Someone grabbed hold of him. Pulled him to his feet. Cut his bonds and yanked the gag from his mouth.

"Eat this!" his rescuer said. A fruit of some sort was stuffed in his mouth.

He sunk his teeth right in. Juice dripped down his beard.

"Come with me!"

He followed, blinking the dark smoke from his eyes. Flames surrounded them. Underlings screamed out. They burned. They burned alive. The sound of underlings suffering was music to his ears.

Is this real? Or am I dead?

"Grab this and get on!" the voice ordered, placing his hands on a rope.

"What?" he started to say, but was cut off.

Something huge lurched beneath him, stirring up a cloud of dust and fire. Off the ground they rose. Boon fought to hold on. He slipped, but a strong arm grabbed him and held him tight.

"Am I on what I think I'm on?"

"Keep silent, and hold tight!"

61

CREED'S FINGERTIPS TOUCHED LEATHER. HE dumped out the contents of the sack. A sword belt. Different. Two pommels with a dull gray finish were shoved in short scabbards on it. Compelled, he strapped it on. *Two short blades are better than none.*

"Food! There must be something." He reached back inside.

Behind him, Tonio and the Vicious were still having it out, but it didn't matter to him if either one died, so long as it wasn't him. "Just a morsel, eh? Or maybe a skin of wine? Please?"

Instead, the sack served up soft fabric.

"What's this?" Creed held a dark, intricately woven cowl, big enough to cover his head and shoulders.

The cowl throbbed with a life of its own, telling him something.

He traced the tiny swirling rows of stitches with his fingers. "Bish, what kind of garment is this?" Creed's keen eye understood fine craftsmanship. He'd crafted his own blades with intricate designs. But what he now beheld was nothing short of marvelous in his eyes.

"Huh, a bit much for keeping the rain off," he said. He put it on. And forgot his hunger.

The Cowl filled him with great awareness.

He jumped from the ground. "Mother of Bone!"

The Vicious caught Tonio in the nose, rocking the half-dead man, flattening him. It turned on Creed, jaws snapping, claws bared.

Tonio moved, but slowly.

Creed didn't have a stitch of armor on him aside from The Cowl. He wasn't worried. He felt thick. Tough. He sized up the monster.

Its arms were long like an ape's. Its skin tough, like black steel. The claws on its fingers were ten blades to his two.

Creed's hands fell to the steel pommels at his hips. *Maybe they can cut this thing.* He jerked them out. Steel. Dark. Razor sharp.

"Great Bish!"

The blades were long! And heavy, but light in his hands.

The Vicious charged.

Quick as it was, Creed was quicker. Like a cobra he struck.

Slice!

Slice!

One monster hand fell, then the other.

The Vicious howled, fangs dripping with saliva.

Glitch!

The tip of one blade punctured its eye.

Glitch!

The other its throat.

The Vicious sagged to the ground, dead.

Creed looked at his blades. "I'll be." Spun them around. "I could get used to this."

His head throbbed. Underlings were coming. His eyes glimmered. Two underlings surged down the steps and leapt into the arena. Behind them, Detective Melegal's scrawny body was sprawled out on the benches, unmoving.

Creed smiled. He twirled one sword in his hand. Held the other behind his back.

Flanking him, one underling came in low, the other high, curved swords licking out like serpent tongues.

Creed swatted their blades away.

They pressed.

He pressed back, laughing. *If the Royals could see me now! Hah. They'd never face me.*

All his life, he'd been training to fight. We wanted to be respected. Fight the Royals in their arenas. Be their champion. But they wouldn't let him. He wasn't their blood. They claimed he wasn't worthy. Still, he continually perfected his skill and craft. Designing his own steel and other weapons. Now he wielded two as easily as sticks. He felt like he could swing forever.

"Hah!"

His steel flashed.

He clipped through the nose of one.

Zitch!

He tore the lip from the other.

Bleeding, the underling's eyes were focused. Ready.

Creed folded his swords behind his back, stuck his chin out and shook his head.

Chittering, they came at him.

Creed lunged. Stabbed both through the chest.

Their swords fell. Their bodies right after.

"If only my hounds could see this."

He slung underling blood from his swords and scanned the arena. Only one underling was left. Its eyes furrowed beneath its brow.

Creed waved him down.

"Time for a rematch, you copper-eyed roach."

Tonio pushed himself off the ground, shaking his head. The black creature was fast. It confused him. Still, he would make it pay.

Turning to face his predator, he saw something he didn't expect. The Vicious was face first in the dirt, hands missing and dead. He had a sinking feeling when he looked over and saw the next thing.

A faceless man battled the underlings. His swords were fast. Strokes of lightning.

A chill went through Tonio. He looked at the scars on his arms and ran his hand down the split in his face. Something about that man distraught him. He had to get away.

"No," he said, recoiling. The black forest came to mind, the webs. He noticed a gleaming sword near the arena wall and took it. Then, he headed to the nearest door and ripped it open. His mother, Lorda, was screaming after him, but he didn't hear her. He had to hide. He had to plan.

"Detective."

Melegal groaned.

"Detective." It was the soft voice of a woman. Her lips brushed his ear. "We must hurry."

Melegal found himself gazing up into the beautiful eyes of Lorda Almen. His heart thumped in his chest. He reached out and grasped her hand, feeling her breasts brush against his chin as she held him. He savored the moment.

"We must go," she said, lifting his chin to face her.

A moment ago, he'd been ready to let his suffering in Bish end. He'd had enough of facing one bad day followed by another. But for now, he had a new purpose. He fought the pain and discomfort and wrapped his hand around her sensuous waist. *Fight and fondle.* He was going to help the Lorda.

"How many underlings?" he said, coughing a little.

"Hundreds. They come and go. From where, I don't know. It's an army." She pushed her black hair from her eyes. "It's madness, is what it is. We have to get out of here." She pushed him. "Let's go."

Melegal started to go, then froze.

"Venir?"

In the arena, a man in a dark cowl was squared off against the underling, Kierway.

The sight sent chills through Melegal.

The man under the cowl was tall and muscular, but not savage and brawny like Venir. His face was obscured a little. The man moved like a predator, dark blades whirling at the underlings like storms at small boats out at sea.

Melegal then noticed the pants. Well-trimmed auburn hair around the mouth.

Creed?

Sadness fell over him. Despair filled his belly. If his friend was no longer The Darkslayer, then was his friend no more?

"Fool!" Lorda said, pulling him along. "You're supposed to be saving me; I'm not supposed to be saving you."

They made their way to the door Melegal had tried to approach earlier. He passed through it before her.

A corridor led around the arena toward many other exits. There was a clamor everywhere. Chandeliers fell. Vases were busted. Footsteps scrambled over the marble. Castle Almen was under attack, but the usurped were fighting back.

"C'mon," Melegal said. He took her hand. One corridor was blocked off by rubble. Another was overrun with underlings. "There should be more options in a castle so large." Jogging back down the corridor by the arena, they took another path. Melegal had spent considerable time following Sefron and learning many secrets. Others, he'd discovered on his own. He eyed the framework of the wall. "Aw, where is it?"

"What?" Lorda said.

Chitter. Chitter. Chitter.

Underling soldiers were prowling the halls, coming from both directions.

Dripping with sweat, chest heaving, Lorda's eyes locked with his.

Melegal caught her voluptuous form in his arms and kissed her on the mouth.

She dug her nails into his back. Kissing him back. Her soft lips were hungry. Passionate.

They finished, gasping.

"You know," Lorda said, "death is the penalty for that."

Underlings cut them off at both ends.

"Obviously," Melegal answered, pushing her behind him, "but it was worth it."

62

THE CASTLES IN THE CITY of Bone were all lined up against the great wall: some looking over, some not as tall. On both sides of Castle Almen, the other two attacked. Small catapults hurled heavy stones, and piles of logs and ballista bolts crisscrossed.

Standing on top of the keep, Lord Catten laughed.

"It seems the Royals have decided to engage," he said to his brother, "but it's a bit too late."

Verbard knocked debris from his shoulders. "Or, perhaps it's their way of taking down an enemy. Putting an end to the Almen house, which has betrayed so many."

Lord Almen stood tall and stone-faced. Nails digging into his palms. He would have done the same thing, but seeing it happen to himself and his people and family was a hard thing. "Spare your people, Lord Catten and Lord Verbard," Almen said. "This isn't a full assault, but rather a test of strength."

"And how long will this test go on?" Catten said.

"Several minutes at most," Almen said, giving a quick nod. "Perhaps after that I can begin a parlay with them. Certainly their eyes are on me." He gestured at one of the other castle's towers. "They'll be expecting something."

Floating inches above the roof of the Keep and staying half a head taller than Almen, the molten eyes of the underlings bore into him.

"Mind your place, Human," Verbard said. "Your suggestions are annoying."

"And your Castle is boring," Catten added.

Out of the corner of his eye, Lord Almen glimpsed a missile coming his way. He ducked. The ballista bolt splintered on an invisible shield of magic.

"Such a fool, Brother," Verbard said. "Did you pick him out?"

"Nay, Brother," Catten said. "I believe it was you who suggested we keep him around, but I see little need for a man who flinches at such a feeble attack."

Lord Almen regained his feet. Eyed the attacking castle turret next door. They were reloading. He caught the glimmer of a spy glass turned on him.

"Interesting, Brother," Verbard said. "I don't even think that attack was meant for us, but rather meant for him."

"I agree, but there is only one way to find out." Catten floated to Almen's left.

Verbard nodded and took a place on his right.

"Stay right where you are, Lord Almen. My brother and I have a wager of sorts."

It was hot. Sweat dripped off Lord Almen's brow and nose. In all truth, the underlings didn't have any need for him. They had his Castle. Key sections of the City.

It would take a unified Royal force to prevail against the underlings. *Not likely.* His only sanctuary was knowledge, but he was certain the underlings would risk losing that. They could just learn it for themselves.

Rocks and pitch-coated burning logs sailed overhead, slamming into the castle. Soldiers in the turret were winding the ballista winch back. The one with the spy glass had pointed right at him; he was certain.

"Any last words, Lord Almen?" Catten asked, arms folded over his chest.

Lord Almen took a silent draw through his nose.

"If I die, kill all those bastards."

"They'll die anyway," Catten said, "but if it makes you feel better, you can believe we did it that way."

Don't blink. Don't flinch. Don't move.

Lord Almen didn't have any idea if they kept their shield up or not, but certainly they'd protect themselves now, wouldn't they?

Twack!

The bolt sailed. Lord Almen's quick mind watched in slow motion. Closer. Closer.

Rip!

It tore straight though his leg. He spun to the ground. Three feet of wood jutted through his thigh.

"Hmmm… Brother," Verbard began, "it seems their aim isn't very good. Not good at all. I can't really say if they were aiming for him or us. It was such a bad shot."

"Agreed, Brother," Catten said, turning away, "but I can't fool around here all day. And I don't think our enemies are interested in this human's parlay. No, let us leave him up here and we'll check back and see if they spared him or not."

"Fair enough. Besides," Verbard said, "I think we need a better eye on our neighbors. I think our imp would be a much better ambassador."

"Agreed."

Lord Almen watched them walk away, a hard grimace on his face. Through the door they went, closing it behind them. Lord Almen and his Royal enemies were all alone.

The spy glass reflected in the suns.

He stood up, bit his lip, and searched for cover. *Get to the ledge.* He hopped as fast as he could. Another bolt ripped through his shoulder.

63

T UUTH APPLIED PRESSURE TO VENIR'S throat. "I'm going to enjoy this, Outlander." Saliva dripped off the orc's canine teeth. "I want a clean-cut earless trophy."

Venir's kicks glanced off the big orc's sides. He tried to speak. Tuuth squeezed harder.

"No more words from your loud mouth," Tuuth said. "Perhaps it's another challenge you want? Perhaps another insult towards my kind? If I had your ears, I'd stick them in your mouth."

Venir's eyes rolled up in his head. Sound faded.

"NOOO!"

WHAP!

An oversized hand sent Tuuth spinning away. There stood Barton. Fists clenched at his sides. Chest heaving.

"Get my toys first!"

Venir gulped for air. Gasped. "I… I don't have them."

Barton slammed his fists into the ground.

"NO!"

"Giant!" Tuuth beckoned with his finger, one hand still behind his back. "I know the toys you're looking for. Stoop down, and I'll tell you where they are."

Barton grunted, leaned downward, cocking his head.

"Where are they, Orc?"

Tuuth's gauntlets flashed.

WHAM!

He struck Barton in the jaw.

Barton quavered. His eye rolled up into his head. He collapsed.

Tuuth thumped his chest.

"I just broke a giant's jaw." He looked down on Venir. "Imagine what I'll do to you."

The ground shook.

Three giants jumped off the walls, crushing a dozen underlings.

"Can you knock them out too?" Venir said.

"I'm not worried about them." Tuuth swung.

Venir blocked the punch. His bones clattered. He fell in a heap.

"I can't die like this," he said, looking up. "Not to an orc."

Tuuth glowered at him. "You can, and you will." He kicked Venir in the gut.

Everywhere, underlings by the hundreds swarmed the giants. Cutting, Stabbing, and screaming. They crawled over them like angry black ants.

There was another explosion.

The southern gate was shattered. A giant bigger than the other three, with brown hair tied in knots, stormed inside. He swung a hammer as big as an ogre. Dozens of underlings were crushed and swept aside. Their bones powdered on impact.

Tuuth snorted and gawped.

"Where in Bish did they come from?"

Something from the sky fell at Venir's feet. It was a long knife in a scabbard.

"Huh?" Tuuth said.

Venir dove for it.

Tuuth kicked it away.

"Nice try, Venir!"

The orc grabbed him by the hair and pounded his face and chest. Ribs cracked.

Venir lost his breath and collapsed.

Tuuth readied the underling's knife and thumbed its edge.

"This is it for you."

Venir groaned, struggling to rise. He couldn't even open his eyes.

Tuuth pushed him down with his boot.

"No, you won't die on your feet. You'll die in the muck."

Something growled.

Venir's eye popped open.

Tuuth turned.

There stood a giant a two-headed dog. Fangs bared. Hair raised on its necks.

"What the…"

Chongo pounced. Sank one head's teeth into Tuuth's arm.

Tuuth punched the giant dog's other face.

Chongo held on. Growling. Snarling. Shaking his heads.

"Let go of me!" Tuuth screamed, still punching, his gauntlets charged with energy.

Venir crawled over to his knife. A new fire in his belly. He closed his fingers around it.

Chongo's massive jaws crunched the bone in Tuuth's arm.

Still, the orc kept swinging.

Pow!

One head yelped. The other let go. Shaking, Chongo backed away. Sluggish, Growling. Teetering.

Arm limp on one side, Tuuth shook his glowing fist.

"I'm going to kill you, dog."

Venir stepped between them, knife behind his back, swaying.

"You have to kill me first," he said, "and you haven't done that yet, orc."

"I'm going to rip your head from your shoulders, Venir." Tuuth came at him.

Venir braced his feet.

Quick. Quick. Quick.

Tuuth drew back. Gauntlet glowing. Everything was in his swing. The big fist came.

Like a panther, Venir leapt up out of the muck pit and struck. Venir cut through armor. Muscle. Bone.

"Urk!"

The orc's yellow eyes widened. Blood filled his mouth. Tuuth punched.

Venir held on. Driving the knife deeper, he drove Tuuth to the ground. Twisting the blade one last time.

"I hate you, Out—"

Tuuth died.

Shaking, Chongo came by his side and lay down. Both heads licked the muck off of him.

Venir grabbed his mane. "You're too good to me, Boy."

A black bearded dwarf sailed high overhead, slamming into one of the ballista on the towers.

"No time to rest now," Slim said.

"What?"

Slim appeared from behind a wall of cornmeal barrels. "This party just started. They'll need your help. Ew, Chongo! Oh well. Now grab some weapons and gear, Venir. You've got underlings to slay."

"I've got a knife, Slim. I can barely lift it. The armament is gone, Slim. It's gone."

Snap!

With two underlings on his back, Mood continued to pummel the underling commander into submission.

Crack!

"Ye little underlings think yer a match for a Blood Ranger? Their king at that? I'll make a greasy smear of all of you."

Face broken, the underling commander jammed a dagger in Mood's side.

"Ho! Poking me with a tooth pick, now that's just insulting, stabbing me with anything smaller than a sword."

He brought his ham-sized fist down like a mallet into the underling commander's face, knocking it out cold. He tore the other two underlings off his shoulders and threw them to the ground.

Black Beards hacked them down.

Mood yanked the dagger from his shoulder and sunk it in the underling commander's heart.

A Black Beard, grisly from beard to toe, handed him his axes.

"By the bearded goats," he said, assessing the chaos, "we've got work to do!"

Underlings swarmed from all directions, their focus on the giants—the dwarves an afterthought. All the Black Beards huddled in a battle circle, striking with planning and precision, but they weren't here to roust the underlings. They were here to save Venir. The giants were just a distraction. A good one. But Mood had led them here.

They might be big, but they ain't so smart. They'll be after us soon enough.

One giant, with black hair down to his back, was scooping up underlings and throwing them over the wall. Another, heavyset as an ogre, stuffed the black fiends in his mouth like roaches, crunching bone and metal like canes of sugar.

"Get along the walls! Away from the giants!" Mood commanded. He swung, splitting an underling's face in half.

It was a battle. It was war.

I should've brought more dwarves.

A giant swinging an axe stepped into the fort through the southern gate. He was chopping up the catwalks like kindling when a blast of magic caught him in the face, sending him reeling into a store house. The giant's twin followed, helping his brother up before jumping up and destroying a fort tower with a lethal strike.

Underlings were dying. By dozens now. It was a great thing.

"Black Beards! Find my friend!" Mood said. "We need to get our wrinkled hides out of here!"

Days earlier, Mood and the Black Beards had tracked down a lone giant and killed it. That was what they did. Now, the giants were not only after their kin, Barton, but they had vengeance on their minds as well. Mood would deal with them when he had to. He never imagined Barton would lead them to Outpost Thirty One. They'd let themselves be captured. It couldn't have worked out better. The giants caught right up with them. He couldn't have asked for a bigger distraction.

"Hurry, Dwarves!"

A shadow fell over them. A giant with a gore-splatted club in his hand attacked. The first swing crushed two dwarves.

Fogle sat on the back of Eethum's horse, grinding his teeth.

The jungle erupted. Trees snapped, and footsteps shook the ground.

"Giants?" he asked.

Eethum shook his head yes.

"Aye, let's just hope they're not too late. Come."

"Late?"

"Hold tight, Wizard, and have your craft ready. Ee-Yah!"

Less than a mile away, they galloped up the mountainous slope. Fogle readied a pair of spells on his lips, squeezed his eyes shut, and summoned his powers. He was used to fighting underlings now. For a change, he'd be prepared.

"What are we supposed to do when we get there?" he shouted in Eethum's ear.

The big dwarf was silent, long red beard whipping in the wind.

Bloody dwarves are nothing but secrets.

Something big crashed into the branches above them and fell to the ground. Two underlings lay dead, one with a broken branch stuck in his eye. Fogle smiled.

Good. But what in Bish did that?

The horse burst through the trees and onto the road, hooves thundering over the path.

"Yah!" Eethum whipped the reins. A giant wearing a one horned helmet stepped in their path.

Fogle's neck stretched upward.

The giant was as tall as the oaks. Three underlings floated in the sky, surrounding it, shooting lighting from their hands.

Zzzraam!

Zzzraam!

Zzzraam!

The giant roared, swinging blindly, covering its eyes with its arms.

The underling magi pressed their attack, shooting out the lightning that coiled up and down their arms.

"I'll show them," Fogle said.

He pointed and shot a bright green missile from the tip of his finger.

Zing!

It pierced one underling skull and entered another before blowing out the other side and into the third one's mouth. It gagged, hissed and swallowed a moment before it exploded. All three forms fell from the sky and thudded to the ground. The giant stomped each and every one of them, grinding them into the ground before moving onward.

Eethum stopped the horse, turned and eyed him.

"Don't do that again."

"What, kill underlings?"

"We're not here to kill underlings. We're here to save your friend—and my king, if need be. Protect yourself and your friend. When the time comes, you'll know."

"Killing underlings does protect us," Fogle said. "Killing giants does too, for that matter. And since when do you dwarves decide when killing is and isn't allowed? I say we go in there, kill them all, and sort it out later."

Eethum flashed his teeth and harrumphed.

"Aw, I like the way you think, Wizard Warrior," the Blood Ranger said.

Did I just say what I thought I said? I must be going mad.

Fogle thought of the image of his grandfather's blazing eyes and wispy white beard. The man enjoyed killing underlings more than anything else. *I'm not like that.* He glanced back at the giant footprints of underling goo and laughed. *Well, maybe I am a little.* He jumped off the horse.

"What are you doing?" Eethum growled, grabbing him by the cloak.

Fogle twisted away.

"Why wait to kill the evil bastards later when you can kill them now? I'm going in."

Eethum jumped off his horse and slapped it on the rear. Whipping out his axes, he said, "Mood was right, as always."

"About what?"

"The best wizards are the crazy ones."

64

M ASTER KIERWAY ENTERED THE ARENA, head high. The underling's eyes were more curious than they were fearful. Creed's confidence dipped.

The Cowl on his head urged him forward.

Blood charging through him like a rushing river, Creed faced Kierway for the second time. Chill bumps ran down his arms.

"Fool, no man nor underling can best me, no matter the steel he swings." Kierway eased his swords from the sheaths on his back. "Your death was only delayed by circumstance." He shifted his stance. Circling.

The underling grandmaster of the sword was the fastest he'd ever seen. When they battled in the chamber, it had taken all of Creed's skill just to parry. *I'm faster now. Better now. Aren't I?*

The Cowl assured him he was. The swords in his hands said they were parts of him now. Like a snake's head and tail.

"I beg to differ," Creed said, "It was your death that was delayed."

Creed lunged.

Kierway spun out of reach.

Stabbing a fly would have been just as easy.

"Blast!"

"So, you grumble already, Human. Good."

Eyes flashing, Kierway attacked.

Ching! Ching! Ching!

Creed was on the defensive. Parrying the lightning fast blows. He'd never seen anyone move so fast before. It was astounding.

Rolling his wrists like a human windmill, he batted the attacks away.

The underling's blades were unrelenting.

Rip!

Kierway clipped him under the ribs.

Rip!

Across the thigh.

"Bone! You can't be so fast," Creed said, jumping away.

Kierway twirled his blades and laughed.

"Maybe you should stop talking and start fighting. You've swung once to my twenty," Kierway said. "Still, it's entertaining." He pressed forward.

Creed backed away. It was embarrassing. He'd been taught everything there was to know about the sword. Offense. Defense. Counters and strokes. But in seconds, the underling had negated all of it with superior speed and power.

'Loosen up, Bloodhound,' his mentor once said. 'Being too stiff will kill you. All the skill in the world won't save you when your instincts fail. Trust in them.'

Creed always had good instincts. He could size up an opponent quickly. A dipped shoulder. A slouched posture. Too much weight on one leg. Short arms. Long arms. Everyone had a weakness to exploit. Not this one.

Holding one sword behind his back, Kierway swung.

Clang!

"There. I'm making it easy for you. Swing back."

He wanted to swing.

The Cowl on his head wanted him to swing.

But one mistake would be fatal. He almost died the last time. He didn't want to die today.

Clang! Clang!

Kierway swung.

Creed parried. Backward he went. Stepping around dead bodies.

"Are you going to bleed to death?" Kierway said, eyeing his wounds. "I thought you wanted to fight. Give me a challenge, Human. Give me a fight of some sort before you die like the coward you are."

"Coward?" Creed said, his voice a little less mortal. It made him mad. His mind surged. "You—whose kind strikes at women and children in the darkness—are calling me a coward?"

"Yes, a soft one. A coward and a shoddy swordsman."

Torn between caution and rage, Creed had to choose. *Sometimes you have to trust your instincts and let loose.* He lowered his chin. *Swish. Swish.* "Let's finish this."

He attacked.

The Cowl rejoiced.

But Kierway was already spinning away. He'd seen the move before it happened.

Slice!

Creed clipped Kierway's shoulder. Red-black blood was spilled.

Kierway snarled and cut at his belly.

Creed sprung backward ten feet.

"Did you feel that, Underling?"

Kierway's eyes were molten.

Creed noticed something. An awareness. A second sight. *Go with it, Creed. Go with it!*

Steel crashed against steel like an armory caught in a tornado. Back and forth they went. Blood was let. Sweat dripped. Attack. React. Anticipate.

Creed's mind, body, and blades were one. His skill and instincts melded together. He turned. He changed. From a swordsman into a fearless fighting machine.

Slice!

Kierway ducked and countered.

Chop! Slice!

The underling's blade ripped into Creed's shoulder.

He drove his pommel into the underling's chin.

Kierway stuffed his knee in Creed's gut.

Steel flashed again. A pair of tireless storms trying to wipe out one another.

Duck!

Jump!

Parry!

Strike! Strike! Strike!

Creed didn't know if it was him commanding his body or The Cowl, but he was doing things he'd never done before. The underling's strikes came, precise and fatal, but they missed their mark, time and again. He bled. He fought. He learned.

"Such improvement, Human." Kierway said, "Unexpected. Impressive."

Master Kierway's hardened face lathered. His thin coat of fur showed a sheen.

Creed's own chest was heaving. He'd never fought so long. So hard. Pressed. Possessed. He fought on. *Kill the underling!*

Seconds passed that felt like minutes. Sparks of hot metal flew in the air.

Clip!

He caught Kierway below the knee cap.

Clip!

And under his left sword arm. His blades cut armor like bread.

"What manner of man are you that fights like many?" Kierway said, breaking off his attack, wiping the blood from his lips. The underling lowered his blade and stuck one in the ground. "A parlay, perhaps?"

Creed opened his mouth to speak.

Whish! Whish! Whish!

The underling's knives flicked through the air.

Creed battled one away, then two, catching the third in his chest.

"Now that's just dirty! Who's the coward now, Underling?" Creed plucked it out and slung it back.

Kierway ducked under it and laughed.

"Such words have no meaning to our kind. Your time to die has come, Human."

Chest burning, Creed shrugged is broad shoulders and stood tall in the face of his enemy. He might not have much time left to live, but he still felt like fighting. *Make the most of it!*

Kierway's swords came at his neck and thigh.

But Creed had seen them coming two steps ago. Lunging forward, he punched his right sword through Kierway's side.

Bang!

He head butted Kierway in the face, breaking his nose.

Kierway hissed, tearing himself away and clutching at his bloody side, copper eyes wide as saucers.

"Impossible!" he said, eyeing Creed as if he were someone else.

"Nothing's impossible!"

Creed charged. Inspired. He spun. He swung.

Kierway's swords were ready.

Creed shattered both of the underling's blades with his first blow.

Slice!

Kierway's head popped from his shoulders with the second blow. Blood sprayed. The underling fell.

Creed clutched at his chest and fell to his knees, sucking for breath and spitting blood.

"Now that was some glorious fighting. If I can only live to tell the ladies about it."

65

I T WAS STRANGE, STANDING ALONGSIDE one of the most powerful women in the City of Bone, having her huddle in his arms.

If we had a soft bed and a secure room, I bet I could teach her a thing or two.

In little more than a stitch of clothing and without even a weapon in hand, Melegal prepared for his last stand.

"They won't kill you, Lorda," he said, pushing her between the wall and his back. "But I don't think they'll spare me."

"True," she said, her nails wrapped around his belly "but I may be able to convince them otherwise."

The idea had promise, but sooner or later, the odds of surviving were bound to catch up with him. *Cats have many lives, but perhaps rats have more.*

"I appreciate that," he said, "but you don't need to risk yourself. No one lives forever. Save yourself."

"How noble, Detective. You have a charming tongue. I wish we had more time."

Melegal's ears perked up, and Lorda Almen gasped.

Two underling soldiers came closer, black hair braided and old gold hoops in one's ears. One scraped his hand-axe along the wall, and the other let out an unfriendly chitter.

Melegal's grip tightened over Lorda's hand as the other pair closed in. Dark faced and armored in leather, there was something evil about them. Something sinister. Melegal never meddled in the affairs of underlings; he let Venir The Darkslayer handle that. The stories he heard and the things he had seen were more than enough to keep him away from the twisted breed.

Lorda pressed her soft lips into his back. "Sorry, Detective." She stepped into the clear.

The underlings stopped.

She pointed at Melegal. "I am the Lorda of this castle, and this man is my servant. No harm should come to me or him, Underlings." She had a convincing way of speaking. "Seize him if you must, but don't you dare lay a hand on me."

The nearest underling, red eyes glimmering, lowered his weapon, walked over and back handed her in the face. "Silence, Human."

Lorda fell to the ground, gaping, rubbing her reddened cheek.

Another underling lowered a spear at Melegal's belly.

Melegal crept back into the wall, the spear tip nicking his exposed belly.

"This man will die, a painful death," the underling said, "but you, Woman, your death will look like an accident."

"You wouldn't dare," she said, shocked. "My husband is in good standing with your Lords. They'll punish you for this."

"No," the underling said. He pinched her face in his hand. "Human life has no meaning to us. No use to us. They'll be rid of you soon enough."

"You overstep your bounds, Black Swine. You've no order to kill or harm me, just him," her eyes flicked to Melegal, "… maybe?"

The longer they talk, the longer I live. His stomach groaned. A shadow darted between the walls. *What was that?*

"Put a hole in the noisy one's stomach."

Chop!

An underling's skull was split open.

Slice!

The head of another underling leapt from its shoulders, freeing Lorda.

Melegal twisted. The spear tip jabbed at his center.

Slice!

The underling spear-wielder lost both hands from forearm to finger.

Melegal turned.

Taller than him the battle-splattered warrior stood, eyes glowing a pale green through a dark cowl. Melegal blinked, thinking of Venir, but his man was different. Agile and swift. Quick and merciless. The face was obscured somehow. But he was certain it was Creed.

The last underling charged Lorda Almen, cutting at her throat.

Melegal dove for her, but he was too far away.

In one long stride, Creed cut the underling off and ripped his sword across its belly, spilling its bowels.

Creed sheathed his swords and clutched his chest. Reaching down, he lifted Lorda back to her feet.

"Who are you?" she said. Her fingers grazed his broad chest. "You're wounded."

"Aye, but it's already getting better." He bowed a little. "I'm Creed the Bloodhound, Lorda."

"No," Melegal said, getting back up, "that's not what you are, not right now." He craned his neck. "And more soldiers are coming." Melegal grabbed her arm. "Anything left in the arena?"

"Just the dead."

"Good," Melegal said. "That'll be our way to sanctuary then. Come on."

Through the entrance, down the steps and over the wall they'd gone when Melegal's keen eye caught something in the rack of weapons.

"I'll be," he said. He rummaged through the rack, strapping his swords, the Sisters, around his waist and finding something else. "Yes!" He grabbed his dart launchers and snapped them on. "Where is it?"

"Where is what?" Lorda said, trying to help.

"My cap."

"I'll buy you all the caps you want," she said, running her finger over his ear.

"No," he said, looking at her. "Have you seen it? Do you remember—"

"Yes, I remember. Last I saw it, well," she picked at her lip and shrugged. "It was in my husband's throne room, under heavy guard."

That bothered Melegal. Had they discovered the secret of his cap? Why else would they guard it? *Must get it back.*

"And the Keys?" he said.

"Same place."

"How many did you see?"

"Five, I think. But Kierway had one."

Finishing the last buckle on his dart-launchers, he searched the headless body of Kierway. Nothing. "Are you sure he had a Key on him?"

"I'm certain."

His neck snapped to the last spot he'd seen Jarla. She was gone.

"Slat! The witch has it!"

"What's so special about those Keys?" Lorda asked, brushing her hair out of her eyes.

The question struck him. There was little reason to believe that Lorda knew anything about the Keys. Lord Almen was a man of many secrets. As for the Keys, the easy way out of this was gone. He had no idea which Key went where, or what they all did. Did they need a door from the chamber or could they be used elsewhere instead?

"Did you notice the gemstone in it?"

Lorda's perfectly plucked eyebrows scrunched down.

"Sapphire, I believe," she said. "I only caught a single glimpse of it."

I didn't matter. It wasn't the one Melegal had used anyway.

Swish. Swish. Swish.

Creed was whirling his blades around his body in a marvelous fashion.

"Astounding," he said, "I cannot tell if it's the blades or me." He extended the keen edges outward, eyeing them. "I don't prefer hand guards." *Swish!* "But these are so flexible."

"And how about that… cowl… on your head?" Melegal started.

Creed slipped his blades into their sheaths. He didn't move. Instead, he stood still, cocking his head back and forth.

"Are you coming?" Melegal said. "Or are you waiting for more underlings to arrive?"

"There are so many," Creed said. "I can feel them running through the halls. Their hearts beat in my ears." He cast a dark foreboding glance at Melegal, and his voice changed a little. "I can kill them." His body tensed. "I can kill them all."

"No," Melegal said, "if you could do that, they'd be dead already."

"What makes you say that?"

"I know. Now…" He tossed Creed the sack. "You'll need that." He jammed two fingers down his throat.

"Ew, Detective, what are you doing?" Lorda asked. "Are you ill?"

Melegal spit a metal gob into his palm and rubbed the spit off. He flashed the light of his coin in their eyes and grinned.

"Follow me."

"You're resourceful, Detective. I'll give you that," Creed said. The man was chewing on jerky and flipping his coin of light. "This is the best jerky I've ever tasted."

"You don't have to call me detective, Creed. Melegal will do." He was sifting through a trunk in what used to be one of Sefron's hidden rooms. "Or not."

If Castle Almen didn't have so many secrets, we'd be dead already.

Of that much, Melegal was certain. And as for Sefron, his pasty nemesis, the cleric had been storing up for something. This room barely held the three of them, but it was filled with provisions, and it was only one room within a sprawling network. *I could spend a year exploring this castle, maybe more. I wonder how many secrets are in this world.* He looked at Creed and crunched into some fruit.

The man had finally pulled his cowl down off his head so it rested on his shoulders, and Melegal could make out his face. *Good.* For the time being, Creed was himself again. An overachieving thug in the ranks of Royals.

At least he doesn't have his loud and smelly dogs with him.

"Melegal," Lorda said, chin down, rubbing her arms. "Do you think all my family are dead?" She sobbed. "I saw them gut my niece and butcher one of my uncles before my eyes. They're monsters, aren't they?"

Just a little more so than your husband.

"There's no time to mourn, Lorda. Just escape."

"But?"

He put one hand on her shoulder, lifted her chin and looked into her eyes. "Be strong."

A tear fell down her cheek. Lorda had family, and they meant something. He was certain they were wiped out. Most all of them anyway. If he understood anything about underlings, he knew they didn't need people for anything, other than amusement. They were like cats that played with mice.

He fondled a small ring he'd found in one of Sefron's chests earlier. It was a flat metal with odd symbols, dust coated, and set with a variety of smooth gemstones. There were other baubles, but he had no pockets to stick them in.

"You're gorgeous," Creed said, staring hard at Lorda.

"What?"

Creed game closer, adjusting the bracers he'd pulled out of the sack and put on his arms earlier.

"You're more gorgeous," he repeated, "than the morning light in the gardens. Captivating."

Lorda pulled tighter around her form a gown Melegal had scrounged up for her.

"Mind yourself, Bloodhound," she warned. "I'm not some tavern trollop who'll swoon at your clever phrase of words. The finest troubadours in the land haven't swayed me, so how could a smelly hound like you?"

"Pardon, Lorda." He bowed with a grin. "It's a sincere compliment. But I'd be lying if I didn't admit that I'd cut my own arm off just for a—"

"Don't you dare, Heathen!"

"Shhhh! The both of you," Melegal said. "There's a hundred underlings out there looking for us."

"A taste of those sweet lips," Creed said, "was all I was going to say. What did you think I was going to say, anyway? I'm a Royal too, you know."

Lorda scooted farther away.

The last thing Melegal needed was a conflict with Creed. The man wasn't a brute, but he was all fighter. They needed him. They might have to carve their way out to escape.

Creed resumed his seat and tore back into his jerky. "What's the plan, Melegal?"

Melegal envisioned the last thing he'd seen from his spire before he came in here. Underlings were everywhere. The only safe way out was the same way he'd come in. With a Key.

Slat! And to think: I had seven of them, along with my freedom, and I came right back into this infernal Castle. What a vengeful fool I am!

"We need a Key, Creed. I think one Key is all it will take to get us free and clear. It's either that, or we're going to have to lay low in here, and it won't be long before the food runs out or they find us."

Eyeing Creed, Lorda said, "I'm ready to get out of here. I don't think this man can be trusted with me in these close quarters."

Creed perched his eyebrows. "My intentions are nothing but honorable. You'll need protection, Lorda. You can't expect me to believe you'd prefer the company of underlings to me?" He shrugged and looked at Melegal. "Then again, maybe you prefer the small gruesome kind. No offense."

"None taken."

Creed slipped The Cowl back over his head. "Let's be about our business." He held a finger up. "Wait, something comes."

Melegal stepped in front of Lorda, pushing her behind him. He hadn't heard a thing when a dark shadow slipped into the room.

Creed drew his sword.

"Wait," Melegal said.

"What is that?" Lorda said.

"It's my cat. Octopus."

Lorda let out a sigh.

Creed flipped him his coin. "That's the ugliest cat I ever saw. And those eyes. What is it, blind as a bat?"

"Blind as a bat and meaner than ten of your dogs."

"Huh."

Octopus rumbled, the hairs raising on his back.

Creed froze. "They're close."

"How close?"

Dust and debris fell from the ceiling above.

Wham!

Something pounded the floor above.

"Is that close enough for you?"

Bone! They're onto us.

66

S LIM DANGLED THE PINK FLESH of Venir's missing ear in his face. "Hold still. This is going to sting. I can put it back on, but, I'm sorry, I couldn't find the other one."

"That's alright," Venir said. "I never listened much anyway. I don't think putting my ear on is going to do me much good eith—*urk!*"

Grabbing both sides of his head with extra-long fingers, Slim's hands glowed.

"Argh!"

Venir's bones crackled. His skin felt like it was on fire. It wasn't pain, not like all the other torments he'd faced the past few days, but it was uncomfortable. Disturbing. Unnatural.

"Bone! What are you doing, Slim?"

A storm raged between his temples. His bones moved. His skin crawled. His arms and legs thickened.

Slim's long, youthful face changed. His hair thinned. His eyes sunk back in their sockets.

Venir blinked hard.

Slim's red lips turned gray, and the skin on his body became mummified and dry.

"No, Slim! No!"

He tried to push his friend away, but Slim's lanky arms didn't budge.

Finally, Slim let out a ragged sigh, released him, stepped back, and fell to the ground. His long frame little more than a husk of skin and bone.

"Slim! Slim!" Venir said.

The cleric's teeth were cracked when he smiled.

"Don't worry about me, Vee. I'll be fine. Go get you some underlings."

One of Chongo's big heads licked the man.

Then Slim's eyes rolled up in his head.

Venir's head dipped to his chest, and his hand was white-knuckled on his knife. He was whole. So far as he could tell, he was as whole as he'd ever been. He'd been living in such pain.

Grabbing Chongo by the mane on his neck, he swung himself into the saddle. "Let's find me an axe and shatter some bones!"

Chongo surged forward.

Outpost Thirty One was in total disarray. A hundred underlings or more dragged one giant to the ground. A dozen underlings at a time were being stomped, leaving black smears in the dust. A wagon cart was tossed into one of the towers, and a giant bigger than all the rest beat his chest and roared, slamming his weapon across the ground, sweeping underlings away like bugs.

"Now that's an axe!" Venir yelled.

Chongo barreled through the sea of underlings, biting some and trampling others. Venir's eyes locked on the battle axe of a fallen brigand who'd been smashed into a bloody mud hole. Riding by, he snatched it off the ground. A second later, he gored an underling's head.

"It's sharp! It's metal! It ain't Brool. Yah! But it'll do!"

He brought the heavy axe down, busting armor and splitting through a clavicle. He was free. Unfettered by his helm, he had clarity. Sweeping the battle axe from one side to the other. In seconds, gore coated his arms and chest.

The distracted underlings didn't see him and Chongo coming.

Crush!

Crumble!

Chomp!

"Over there, Chongo!"

Venir had spied an ailing Black Beard surrounded by a thicket of underlings. Chongo pounced on them. Venir dove into the ones he missed. Swinging left and right with all his might, opening chests and crushing in skulls. *Who needs the armament!*

Two strokes later, his corded arms turned to lead. His lungs caught fire. Out of the corner of his eye, he saw another pack of underlings closing in on him.

"Seems fear of the giants has rerouted their attack," he said, raising his axe over his head. "Come on, get them!"

Eethum led. Fogle followed. The Blood Ranger's axes sang to the underlings. A tune of death and destruction. Fogle tasted their oily blood in his mouth and spit it out. Above, the towering giants had failed to take over. Scores of underlings kept coming. Overwhelming the giants with sheer numbers. They crawled all over.

Fogle was torn. *Whose side should I be fighting for?* Even if they defeated the underlings, wouldn't the giants turn on him and the dwarves?

Thump!

Thump!

The entire fort shook. One of the giants, eyes close together, was slamming himself into one of the corner towers. Underlings spilled out, screeching on their way to the ground.

"Help the dwarves, Fogle!" Eethum said. "Keep your eyes out for Venir!"

Find Venir! And get out of here!

Wading through underlings and dodging oversized feet and weapons, Eethum led them up the stair onto the catwalks.

"See anything?" Fogle said.

"No!" Eethum said. The Blood Ranger was holding them off.

"There!" Fogle pointed.

Two Black Beards were fighting for their lives in the corner. Fogle unleashed his power. A bolt of lightning leapt from his fingers.

Sssram!

The chain of lightning ripped through one underling, then another. Piles of ash were scattered in the air.

A giant, bald and cock-eyed, leered down at him, raised his axe and swung. Eethum shoved Fogle out of the way. The catwalk shattered. They tumbled hard to the ground.

Breathless, Fogle got back to his feet just as the giant reached down for him.

Wham!

The ugly giant roared.

Somebody swung a club the size of a tree into its knee. It was Barton.

"Leave my Wizard friend alone, Haddad!"

Whack!

Haddad struck Barton across the face, knocking him from his feet, and turned back to Fogle.

"I'LL EAT YOU, WIZARD!" He patted his belly. "YOUR MAGIC MAKE HADDAD STRONG!"

Eethum burst into action, chopping into the bone below the giant's knee.

"ARGH! BLOOD RANGER! YOU SHALL PAY!" The giant was quick. It snatched Eethum off the ground and squeezed him.

Fogle drew his arms back, summoned his words, and started to cast.

Clonk!

A sling stone ricocheted off his head. Blood trickled in his eyes. The next thing he saw was Eethum flying through the air and the giant reaching for him.

I don't want to fly like that.

Fighting to lift his arms to swing, Venir's knees buckled when an underling's shield clipped the back of his chin. Trying to shake it off, he was too late. The underlings piled on top of him, clawing and tearing at his throat.

"Heeyah!" a familiar voice rang out, scattering the underlings like bloody moths.

Mood's arms pumped those axes into one underling after another, rekindling Venir's fire.

Venir caught his breath and burst into motion.

"Ain't so savvy without that helmet on, are ye?"

Venir, arms high, sunk his axe down into an underling's chest, shooting black and red blood up everywhere. "No!"

Two more black beards joined in, the five of them forming a circle, keeping the underlings at bay.

"Where in Bish are all these roaches pouring out from, anyway!" Mood shouted, deflecting a chop at his neck on the blade of his axe.

"Northside War Room! There must be a tunnel in there!"

Hundreds of underlings lay dead, but where one fell, two more were coming. So far as Venir knew, the underlings never had a tunnel to the Outpost, but they could have dug one over the past few years. Chopping away, he watched another giant fall, leaving only three.

"What was your plan, Mood?"

"Carve a way in and rescue you! Carve a way out to freedom!"

That wasn't going to happen. The underlings covered the gates, and many were watching the giants fall. Ropes, grappling hooks, and magic cords wrapped the giants' legs and pinned their arms. Another giant pitched and stumbled, his head slamming into the wall. He roared while the underlings cut and stabbed at his back.

Thwack!

One of the Black Beards caught another ballista bolt in his back.

"Bone!"

"Tis a shame," Mood said, still swinging.

"What!"

"We could have made it, if not for all the extra underlings."

Fogle's plan had unraveled. He'd had on his lips the same spell he'd used to fight Tundoor and his breed. It was lost. Now, mind addled, he tried to recall another spell before he was crushed, then eaten.

One foot from his nose, the giant's fingers stopped. An enormous black shadow fell from the sky, shaking the ground.

WHUMP! WHUMP! SNORT!

Fogle's heart skipped. Two citrine eyes bore into him.

Blackie!

A tide of flames ripped through the underlings.

Ka-Chow!

Ka-Chow!

Ka-Chow!

Bolts of lightning fell from the sky, blasting underlings off the ground. Every portion of the battlefield was either lit up in a spectacular array of fireworks or consumed by flame.

Venir's attackers paused. Their hesitation was fatal.

Chop! Hack!

Two underlings fell.

"Head for the North Gate," Venir said. "The south is on fire!"

In front of them, the giants waded through the flames like they were water, stomping and chopping at every underling in sight. The black bodies were burning and dying by the dozens now, the others trying to flee.

Venir led Mood and the remaining Black Beards north under the catwalks, picking their way through the dead.

"We can take the drainage tunnel, if we can get to it."

"MOOD!"

The loud voice shook his bones. The biggest giant of all, hefting a battle axe over its shoulder, was coming after them.

"I'VE GOT YOU NOW!"

The Black Dragon was the last thing Fogle expected to see, until he saw Cass, sitting on its back.

"Cass!" he yelled, but nothing cut through the chaos.

Inspired, Fogle launched a magic missile into the hesitating giant's eye.

"ARGH!" it roared, stumbling backward.

He sent another one past Cass's face.

She jerked back, pink eyes hot with anger before she caught his gaze.

He waved and ran toward her at full speed.

Blackie whipped his serpentine neck in front of him, opening his mouth that was full of flames.

"No, Blackie!" Cass cried. "He's on my side."

One spell. One spell. One spell.

Boon soared off Blackie's back and floated into the sky.

Above Outpost Thirty One, five underling magi hovered, attacking the giants. He let them have it.

Ka-Chow! Ka-Chow! Ka-Chow! Ka-Chow! Ka-Chow!

Lightening ripped out of the clouds and through their robes, sending them twirling and smoking to the ground. Below him, Blackie, flames shooting from his mouth, landed on the ground.

"Burn them! Burn them all, Blackie!"

The smoke was black and thick, and the smell of burning flesh foul, but Venir and Mood waded through it, trying to avoid the giant.

"I CAN SMELL YOU, MOOD!"

CRASH!

The giant was destroying everything in its path, trying to get at them.

"GIANTS! SECURE... THE... GATES! THE... KING OF THE DWARVES... IS HERE! KILL HIM... AND... HIS KIN!"

Ka-Chow!

The giant's face was lit up by a lightning strike.

Venir stopped and took a look.

"Are ye mad?" Mood said. "Keep moving."

Venir gazed up at the man floating in the air. It was the old wizard, Boon, scraggly hairs whipping in the wind, eyes filled with power.

Where'd he come from?

"PARLEY!" Boon said in a voice that was loud like thunder.

The giant, Haddad, rubbed his temples. "WHAT, WIZARD? HAH, YOU... CANNOT... PARLEY... WITH US. WE... HAVE... YOU. ALL... OF...YOU."

Venir tugged at Mood's shoulder. "Let's move."

Mood rose his hand up. "Nay, let them parley, Venir. It buys us time, if nothing else."

Behind Haddad the giant, another one had Barton slung over his shoulders. The deformed giant was kicking and screaming.

"TOYS! VENIR, GIVE ME MY TOYS! BARTON WON'T GO BACK WITH YOU, HADDAD! BARTON HATES YOU ALL! AND BLACKIE, TOO!"

"THE TOYS ARE GONE, BARTON!" Boon said.

"LYING WIZARD TRICK BARTON JUST LIKE VENIR DID BEFORE! BARTON WILL SMASH VENIR. CRUNCH HIS BONES. HE IS A LIAR!"

Haddad the giant reached back and walloped Barton in the head.

"NO MORE... TROUBLE FROM YOU... TEASER OF DRAGONS!"

Barton's hand went to his eye. He started to cry.

"HE STARTED IT!"

"SIIIIILENCE!" Haddad said, shaking everything on the ground. "WIZARD, I OFFER THIS! I TAKE PRISONER THE BLOOD RANGER KING, MOOD. BLACKIE THE DRAGON AND THE TINY GIANT," He pointed at Barton, "MUST COME HOME." He spat a giant gob onto the ground. "THE REST CAN LEAVE."

Another giant stepped forward, squeezing a black beard between his fingers.

Venir swore the black-faced dwarf was purple.

Giants are liars. But are they good liars?

Remaining still, Fogle's eyes were transfixed on his grandfather, who was negotiating with the giants. Out of nowhere, a pair of warm pale arms wrapped around his waist.

"Miss me?" Cass said. She kissed him on the cheek.

He struggled to choke out the words. "I thought I'd lost you, Cass. I'm so—"

She put her finger to his lips.

"Shush, Fogle, I'm alright." She gave him a reassuring embrace. "And Blackie, believe it or not, has been quite good to me."

He glanced over at the dragon. There was jealousy in those yellow eyes.

"But, how?"

"I'm a druid, remember. I can communicate with all living things. And Blackie and I," she said, nodding at the dragon with great admiration in her pink eyes, "we understand one another."

Fogle chewed on his lip. He'd seen that look in the eyes of women before. Her arms around his waist had already slackened. *No. This can't be happening.* What had Venir told him on the trail before? *'Bish is full of surprises. And women even more. Get used to it.'*

"You're going with the dragon, aren't you? Over me—A man!"

She caressed his face, looked up into his eyes, and said, "Oh Fogle, you knew it could never last, me and you."

It tugged at his chest, but he knew she was right. The two of them couldn't be any more different, but what they had shared had been wonderful. He didn't want to let that go.

"I never really thought about it. I was too worried whether you were alive or dead." He stepped away from her a little. "And now," he glared at Blackie, "you choose a beast over me?"

"Don't be that way, Fogle."

"What way? Sane?"

"No," she said. Her cheeks reddened. "A grown man acting like spoiled child who lost his favorite toy. Shame on you, Fogle. I'm not yours to claim. I never was."

"I risked my life for you! I fought that dragon! And this is the thanks I get? Come on, Cass!"

"Oh Fogle, don't be so dramatic," she said, walking away and onto Blackie's back. "It's not manly. An adventurer should know that." She sighed. "At least you'll know what to do with the next pretty woman you meet."

Fogle turned away.

Of all the ridiculous things.

"Here," Mood said to Venir, handing over his axes.

"For what?" Venir said, feeling a little foolish for some reason.

"'Cause you'll be needin' them, I'm certain. I'll not where I'm going."

"You can't be serious, Mood?" Venir said. He looked at the giant that talked with Boon. He couldn't understand it. He turned back to Mood. "You're the King of the Dwarves. You can't leave your people."

"It's better to be a live King than a dead one." He winked. "And don't worry; they can't hold me forever. I'll outlive them first."

Venir took the axes. Mood walked out to the giant. "Alright, Haddad! I'll come with you, but all my dwarves and people stay!"

Chongo stammered his paws on the ground. Black tails flicked back and forth like whips. His big jaws snapped.

Venir got in between both heads and hugged Chongo's necks. The dog would do anything for him. He'd do anything for the dog. But things had changed. He could feel it in his bones. Without the armament, the underlings would catch up with him sooner or later. They would catch Chongo too, if he stayed with Venir.

He couldn't protect his dog. The dog couldn't protect him.

"I've got to let you go, Boy." He rubbed his forehead on Chongo's big chest. "Go with Mood." He pointed at the dwarf.

Mood stood, shoulders stooped, holding his side a little.

"Mood needs you, Boy. He's getting old."

Both of Chongo's heads licked Venir one last time.

Venir rubbed his dog behind all four ears. "Take care of him, Chongo. If anyone can lead the old curmudgeon out of there, you can." He hugged the muscular necks once more.

Chongo, with one head looking backward, walked away. Venir wiped the blood from the corner of his eye.

"Dog come with Barton? Good. Barton like that." Barton sighed in the clutches of two other giants, like the child he was. He struggled in vain. His chin dipped. They were bigger and stronger than him.

The other giant set Eethum down, and one by one the giants faded into mist, along with Chongo, Barton, and Mood, whose thick arms crossed his bearded chest.

Whump! Whump! Whump!

Cass and the dragon lifted off the ground and into the sky. Fogle's head was down, but Boon waved goodbye to Cass, a big smile on his face. Only three men, a handful of dwarves, smoke, fire and carnage remained.

"Now what?" Fogle said. "Is it over?"

"Or has it just begun?" Boon cried out, pointing.

The underlings that had fled earlier were coming back now. There were well over a hundred.

Venir readied his axes and dug into the ground.

"So be it, men!" He yelled out at the top of his lungs, "RELEASE THE HOUNDS OF CHAOS AND CRY BISH!"

"Wait, Venir. There has to be another way to get out of here," Fogle suggested.

"To the last, Grandson! The time for a final stand has come!" Boon said, lightning racing up his arms.

Eethum the Blood Ranger shouted over all of them.

"Over there! Look!"

One of the Black Beards was waving them over from the entrance to the War Room.

Venir growled. "That's where the underlings came from earlier."

"Well, they're not coming from there now!" Fogle started running.

"Slat! Let's go then!"

Dashing across the courtyard, the small party barreled through the doors, stepping over dead underlings, ignoring the ones that still burned.

The Black Beard led them through a panel in the wall that Venir had never noticed before and down a wide set of carved out steps. At the bottom, a long corridor ten feet tall and just as wide led to another door, which was open.

"Fool! What does this do, lead to the Underland? I'm not going in." Fogle turned away.

Behind them, the underlings were coming. Chittering and screeching as they entered the War Room.

"We either fight them out here, or in there, but having that big door between us will buy us some time to prepare, at least," Boon said. "I say we go in."

"Well, time's a wasting," Venir said, watching the underlings tear up the corridor. "It's now or never, Wizard."

"Fine!" Fogle said, being the first to enter.

Boon was next, followed by the Black Beards, Eethum and Venir, who pulled on the door handle, trying to close it.

"See any underlings yet?" Venir said between clenched teeth.

No one said anything.

Venir and Eethum kept pulling, but the underlings fought them on the other side.

"Heave!" he yelled.

Eethum grunted.

Venir pulled with all his might, pinching underling fingers around the edges.

"Hurk!"

The door sealed shut. Eethum slammed the bolt in place.

"Whew!"

Suddenly, Venir's instincts caught fire. He knew he'd made a big mistake. In the distance, something evil chittered and twisted.

67

"**D**OGS," CREED SAID. "HAS TO be."

Melegal could hear nails scratching at the ceiling above them.

"It's your cat that led them to us, Melegal," Creed said, "but I can handle them if they catch up. Just lead us."

With Lorda hanging onto his hand, Melegal led the way through the winding secret passage until the clawing above them came to a stop.

"See? They're stuck in one room, and we're beneath another, so it's not my cat." Shining a tiny beam of light forward, he realized Octopus was no longer around. *Good.* He wasn't going to admit it, but Creed was probably right.

"They're still going to catch up with us," Creed said, eyes glowing in the dark through The Cowl.

Melegal shook his head. Something about the man disturbed him. Creed was eerie. Unpredictable. And to make matters worse, he was a Bloodhound. Part of a notorious bunch of chaotic goons. *Keep your back in the front and front in the back.* There was no telling what the man would do, and he had the armament now. Melegal remembered Jarla, who had it before. She was the most evil woman Venir ever knew.

"Just keep your swords ready, Creed. We've still got a shot at getting out of here yet."

"Are we going to the Throne Room?"

"Aye. We're going to steal a Key." *Or as many as I can get my hands on.*

Melegal's eyes glared through a peep hole.

The Throne Room was empty. No guards. No underlings. No Keys. No hat.

Where in Bone could they be?

"What is it, Melegal?" Lorda clung to him. "What do you see?"

"Nothing," he said, "see for yourself. It seems they've moved the bloody things."

"If I were a Key, where would I be?" Creed said, oddly.

On the one hand, Melegal was relieved he didn't have to face the underlings. On the other hand, he'd have to start all over again, with the underlings already looking for them.

"Perhaps I can find out, Melegal," Lorda suggested. "Lords Catten and Verbard are working with my husband. If I can get to them…"

"No! They tried to kill you once already. Besides, I can only assume they are either in the Keep or the Chamber."

"Perhaps the Chamber is where we should go. The Keys will be there at some point, won't they?" she said, pressing up against him. "We could hide and wait them out."

"I've already thought of that," he said, rubbing his aching neck. He brushed up against Lorda who brushed back. *So amazing. Even in perilous times.* "But they probably have more guards there than anywhere."

"Then I'll have to kill them all," Creed said.

The madness never ends.

All Melegal wanted was his hat, at least one of the Keys, and his own castle. He was pretty sure his own castle was the most attainable of the three.

"Move or die, Detective," Creed said. "Move or die."

"I'll be," Lord Verbard said. "He's butchered."

Lord Catten was holding up Master Kierway's head, unable to hide the shock in his golden eyes.

"Do you think Master Sinway will be angered or pleased?" Catten said, handing the head to one of his Juegen.

Verbard gawped at the mutilated Vicious on the ground. "Probably more angered about the Vicious than his son." He shook his head. "What do you make of this, Jottenhiem?"

"A swordsman," the red-eyed commander said. "An outstanding one at that. Master Kierway was one of the finest swordsmen in the Underland, after me and a few others, of course."

"You boast, Commander," Catten said. "Much as I hate to admit it, Kierway's skill was without rival."

Jottenhiem glowered at him. "If you say so, Lord Catten."

"Stay close, Commander," Verbard said. "Whoever did this… well…"

"Might be The Darkslayer, Brother? Is that what you're thinking?"

It was exactly what Verbard was thinking. It worried him. It more than worried him.

"Eep!"

The bat-winged imp buzzed up to him out of nowhere, rubbing its taloned fingers together.

"Yess, Lordsss. Is it time to kill?"

"It's always time to kill," Verbard said, "but the hunt must go on first. Find who did this, imp, and report back to me, immediately."

"As you wish, Lordsss Verbard," Eep hissed and looked at his brother, "and Catten."

Blink.

With Eep gone, Verbard and Jottenhiem were continuing their brief investigation when he discovered something else.

"We've another problem," Verbard said.

"Oh, and what is that?" Catten replied.

"Master Kierway's Key is gone."

"Well, Master Sinway won't be happy about that either, but he said we only needed one Key. We still have seven. Kierway's Key didn't do much of anything."

"It did enough to help anyone escape."

Catten twirled a dark gray cap on his fingertip. "Are you suggesting The Darkslayer fled?"

"We don't know that it was The Darkslayer." Verbard's nails dug into his palms. "And what is that on your finger?"

"A mystical item."

"What does it do?" Verbard's hand slid inside his pocket over his Orb of Imbibing.

"I don't know yet, but I will soon."

"It's ugly."

"It's charming."

"Well, I wouldn't be wearing it when Master Sinway arrives."

Catten slid it into his pocket. "I suppose the time has come to greet him." He pulled a Key from his pocket. "Shall I let him enter, or shall you? I could lead him to your Throne Room, if you like."

"Or I could lead him to yours, Brother. But we'd better be rid of this scourge first."

Verbard tossed Lord Almen's whip to Jottenhiem.

"Soon you might get your chance to prove who is better: Kierway or you, Commander."

68

Venir felt like one side of his body was going out the other.

"Bish! What is happeningggg?"

He felt the wind whoosh through his hair. A split second later he stopped.

"Fight, Man! Fight!"

It was the old wizard, Boon, yelling. Yellow strands of light licked from his fingertips, striking at the hive of underlings surrounding them.

Choking down the queasiness, Venir lashed out.

Slash!

An underling warrior fell dead with its neck open.

"You fight well, Warrior." Eethum banged one attack away and countered another. "But can you fight long?"

Glitch!

The Blood Ranger gored the underling's chest.

Venir, brow buckled, did what he did best. He swung and swung, giving no thought to where he was or what he did.

"Fight and die!" he cried

Fogle's first question wasn't 'Where am I?' but 'How much longer am I going to live?'

He blasted the first underling he saw in the face, knocking a hole in it and barreling two more over. In the dim light, he caught glimpses of a large chamber that was rows deep in underlings.

I can't be in the Underland! I can't be!

He summoned a mystical shield and glanced over his shoulder. The door they'd come in was sealed.

There must be another away out of here.

Two underlings converged on him, mouths wide, curved swords low. The first struck hard, its edge glancing off his shield, cracking it. The other slammed into him with its full weight, pushing him backward. They kept swinging, chipping away shards of magic one piece at a time. Something ignited in Fogle.

No!

The underlings. They'd caused so much anguish. So much pain. He'd lost Cass because of them!

NO!

He shoved his arms forward. His attackers were flung backward, clearing a hole at the bottom of a wide torch-lit stairwell that was otherwise filled with more underlings coming down.

"Hahahaha," he heard his grandfather laughing, "Brilliant, Fogle! Brilliant!"

Boon flung a ball of smoke up the stairwell. It exploded in a puff of air, leaving behind it a wall of stone. Those underlings were sealed outside the chamber.

"Have at them, warriors!" Boon cried, eyeing the hoard of underlings that still surrounded the party. "Let's route these fiends once and for all! Hahahaha!"

Like two Juggernauts, Venir and Eethum gored every black thing breathing.

"Bish!" Fogle lifted his feet from the suction of the floor. The fallen were being sucked dry. Dry husks in an instant. A nasty chill went through him. "What is this place?"

"Eight!"

Chop!

"Nine!"

Slice!

Arms heavy, chest filled with fire, Venir kept swinging. Mood's well-crafted axes could cut metal, but they weren't as light and balanced as Brool's keen edge that he'd grown so accustomed to over the years.

Gashed from chin to toe, he fought on and on, mindless of anything else. He'd gotten his wish. He'd sent more underlings to the grave. He could die complete. Happy. He buried one axe in the next underling's chest.

Large drops of dark blood showered the odd mosaic floor, which sucked every bit up.

"Venir!"

Eyes blazing, he whirled.

"They're all dead," Boon said. "Look around."

Twenty underlings, maybe thirty, were being sucked dry by the floor, their flesh withering.

"Aw." Eethum knelt down at the armored shell of a Black Beard. The dwarf was one of only three that now remained.

Venir's wounds dripped like sweat, feeding the yearning floor. His skin crawled. "We need out of this cursed place." He walked over and tugged on the handles of many doors. "Hurk! Get over here, Eethum, and help me!"

The dwarves remained kneeled, holding hands, heads bowed over their fallen comrade.

Venir tried the next. Then another after that.

"You need a Key, Venir," Boon said, with Fogle standing by his side, panting.

"I've got my own Key." Venir swung Mood's axe into the wood, juttering his arms. "Son of a Bish! It's harder than stone."

"It's magic," Boon said, taking a stroll around the room. "Hmmm… six doors." He peeked into the alcove, where seven lonely pegs remained. "I'll be. Strange. Tricky."

"What?" Fogle's face was drawn up as he shook underling guts from his robes.

"This room," Boon said, his voice filled with wonder, "I believe is an ancient device I've read about before. It's a Chamber of Transportation. As I understand, it can take you anywhere in the world. Very mysterious magic this is. Ancient. Dark. Dangerous." He ran his hand over one of the doors. "If the underlings have the Keys… my… well, that would explain a lot of things."

"Any idea where we are now?" Fogle asked.

"If you still have a map in that spellbook, we can certainly find out."

"And what of that barrier you created, Boon?" Fogle said. "How long will that hold?"

"Hours, unless they bust through it or have a mage to dispel it, and I don't think they do."

Venir made his way around the room, testing the doors anyway while he gathered his thoughts. Fogle had changed a great deal. The lines on his face were hardened, and his skin was darkened and tough. The wizard even had a ragged beard covering his face, giving him a dwarfish look.

Fogle caught him staring. "I'm glad we found you, Venir. And I'm sorry about your dog—and Mood. I spent a great deal of time with the both of them, looking for you."

Venir nodded and turned away. So much had happened. He didn't know what to think. His friends, the best ones he'd ever known, were all gone on account of him. The armament was gone as well. He felt naked without it. Still he lived. And Slim, what had happened to him? Had that man given Venir his very life?

"Aw, give me that book, Fogle," Boon grumbled, taking it away. "You're got mintuar hooves for fingers. It's a wonder you managed to write down anything."

"At least I don't waste what I've written."

"Pah, here it is," Boon said, fingering the book. "Just give me a few minutes."

Leaning against one of the doors, Venir squatted down, took a deep breath, and closed his eyes. He was tired, and his bones were aching.

Boon and Fogle stretched out a mystic map on the mosaic floor and gawped. Then one said to the other, "We're in Bone!"

"What?"

"Venir," Boon said, waving him over. "Look at this."

Venir raised his big frame off the floor and sauntered over. Boon's aged and crooked finger was pointing down on a map that shrunk and grew with a wave of his hand. Venir could see everything. He pointed at a red dot that was located on a drawing of a castle.

"I can see the entire city," Venir said, wiping his brow with his forearm. "I can even see the alleys. Huh, that's Castle Almen."

"Are you certain?" Boon asked, perching one eyebrow.

Venir glared at him. "I'm certain."

Boon rose to his feet and tugged at his white beard. "Hmmm… They've taken over a Castle. Possibly many of them."

"Or the entire city," Fogle said.

"Then that means they'll be coming right back for us," Boon said, eyeing the stone wall that protected them.

"Any minute now. We're at the very heart of the battle now. Hah! We may have just squandered their plans after all. But I sense something. Someone familiar."

"I sense something too, Grandfather," Fogle said. "Are you thinking what I'm thinking?"

Venir didn't know nor care what either one of them was thinking. He just watched. They clasped hands.

But knowing that they were back in Bone? A place he thought he'd never see again? That sent a charge right through him! He was ready now. Ready to tear the wall down and carve a bloody path back to the Drunken Octopus. He warmed his hands on the glow of one of the torches.

Boon and Fogle cried out. The pair, fingers locked, were shaking. Eyes rolled up in their heads.

Venir tried to separate them, but Eethum stayed his hand.

"No," he said in a stern voice, "there's nothing we can do now. They're in a battle they must fight on their own."

Crack.

Boon's wall of stone cracked and began to crumble.

Eethum and the two other dwarves surrounded the interlocked wizards. "We'll protect them as long as we can."

Venir took his place at the bottom of the steps. "I'll kill underlings as long as I can."

69

"**L**EAD THE WAY, DETECTIVE," CREED stepped aside.

Still holding Lorda's hand, he brushed past Creed's chest.

"Beg Pardon," the man said. "But that's worth risking your life for."

"You incorrigible, Piiii—"

Two clawed hands burst through the wall. Lorda was yanked through the wood and plaster, leaving a gaping hole.

"What in Bish was that thing?" Creed said.

Melegal darted through the hole and found himself facing his worst nightmare. It was Eep the imp, hovering in the air, holding Lorda Almen by the neck in his clawed fingers.

"We meetsss again, Skinny One," the imp said. Its long tongue licked up and down Lorda's dangling body, which kicked and flailed.

Melegal only had one dart in his launcher. He took aim.

Better make it count.

"Drop the woman!" Creed said, stepping into the clear, swords ready. "Slat, you're an ugly thing. What in Bish are you?" He looked at Melegal.

"An imp."

Creed shrugged. "Drop her, Imp, or taste my steel."

Eep laughed, rose twenty feet high into the throne room, and dropped her.

I've found them, Mastersss.

Found who? Verbard replied.

The Skinny Man who had the Keys, a woman, and the murdering swordsman you seek.

Where?

In the Throne Room.

"That was fast," Catten said. "Even for an imp."

Suddenly, Verbard's and Catten's eyes locked.

It cannot be, Brother, Verbard thought.

"But it is," Catten hissed through curled lips.

Someone was searching for them. An old enemy. A great foe. An enemy they'd fought decades ago.

"Boon! And his grandson, Fogle!"

"How did they get here? Where did they come from?"

"They must be in the chamber."

Verbard fingered the Keys in his pocket, as did Catten. They were all there except the one Kierway had lost, the one that led to Outpost Thirty-One.

"So they were the source of all the commotion? They're here? How did they make it through an entire army?" Catten was outraged. The surrounding castles were still attacking, and he'd sent all their reserves to Outpost Thirty One for reinforcements. How many giants had arrived down there?

"What do you want to do, Brother?" Verbard said.

Catten slipped the cap on his head. "Boon is not what he was; I can sense it. And his grandson is still green." Catten rubbed at his side where Fogle had zinged him months before. "I think I can hold them."

"Then I'm after that swordsman, whoever he is," Verbard said. "Jottenhiem, come with me and bring every soldier you can spare. We'll wipe this out quickly."

70

FOGLE'S KNEES KNOCKED. HIS CHIN rattled. His mind rocked and reeled. The image of the golden eyed underling Catten snickered in his head. He and Grandfather were somewhere else. A battlefield in the inner mind, inescapable and chaotic.

"Grandfather! Grandfather!" he sputtered out, fingers knotted around Boon's.

The old man's body withered and sagged to the ground, making a feeble gasping sound.

Fogle remembered the last time he'd locked minds with Catten. It had almost killed him, and now, the underling was prepared. Enlightened. More powerful.

"You will die, Human. You and the old man both."

Biting into his lip, Fogle felt his mind collapsing on itself, turning dark and filling with despair.

Hold on, Fogle. Hold on.

The voice was weak and distant.

The underling was slowly ripping Fogle's mind from his grandfather's. A great gaping maw filled with razor sharp teeth was ready to devour them. Swallow them into an abyss forever. A long yellow knotty tongue lashed out around his grandfather's waist and reeled the old man in. Boon's face was sagging and withered, his grip, once strong as iron, struggled to hang on.

I won't let him go! Fogle's feet anchored themselves to the warbling floor. *I beat you once! I can beat you again!*

Catten chuckled and spiked a shard of power in his head.

"Aargh!"

The pain stabbed between his eyes. Excruciating. His entire body felt like it was melting into a gooey drop, ready to be swallowed whole.

Think, Fogle! Think!

His fingers slipped from his grandfather's.

On the other side of things, Catten was laughing and dusting his long nails on his robes.

"This cap is amazing," he said to himself, making his way out of the arena. He thought of his brother and Master Sinway. "It gives me that edge I've been seeking."

The stone wall crumbled. The first underling rushed through. Its head was splattered all over the walls.

"Ten!" Venir roared.

But the stairwell was three beasts wide, and the ranks of underlings deeper than a well.

Hack! A clawed hand was lost.

"Elven!"

Crunch! A chest caved in.

"Twelve!" Blood spurted from an underling's neck.

Glitch!

Venir took a punch to the shoulder, lost his footing and stumbled backward.

"Blast yer hides!" he screamed, swinging wildly, keeping them at bay.

"Get over there, Black Beards!" Eethum yelled and ran at the same time.

Three dwarves in heavy armor rushed forward, plugging the stairwell. Steel clashed on steel. Axes splintered bone. Long knives sifted through weak points on armor. Slowly, the dwarves, busted and bleeding, were being pushed backward.

Venir took a quick glance over his shoulder. The wizards had collapsed on the floor. Like their bones were missing. They twitched. He growled. The underlings had taken his friends, and now they had taken his city. He was tired of losing. A raging storm ignited inside him.

"Rrrrrah!"

Charging, he leapt over the dwarves into the underlings.

Yes, Fogle. Yes! Boon said to him, his withering voice stronger than before. *Do it! Do it quick!*

Fogle hung on. Struggling for his sanity, bearing every cruel twist and turn, searching for a weakness in the underling's probing mind. He summoned The Darkslayer. The underling laughed. One door slammed closed. *Find another.* Fogle found something. *Yes.* The green amulet that he'd given to Venir to track him. *Yes.* He'd put it in Catten's robes when he exchanged them for his spellbook. It was a little something he'd planned on sharing with Boon when the time was right.

The time is right now! Boon said. The old wizard's eyes were opened wide. He grappled with the tongue that held him. Grabbing the lip of the beast that tried to swallow him, his arm now held a pick-axe, which he sunk into its lip and held on. *I can hold on! Let me go and strike!*

"NO!" Fogle said, "I can't risk it!"

You've no choice now. The iron in Boon's eyes had returned. *Do something. Quick! Before he finds out!*

"I can't get out of here." Fogle said.

Do it!

Boon, geared up in his mystic armor and sword, dove into the belly of the beast and disappeared.

"Nooooooooooo!"

71

Melegal and Creed arrived at the same time, catching Lorda, who'd fainted.

"Nice catch," Creed said, looking upward.

Eep's wings buzzed. He was laughing. *Blink!*

"Watch out!" Melegal said.

Eep popped up behind Creed. *Slash! Slash!* Tore into his back.

Blink!

"Argh!" Creed said. "Bish!"

Melegal's head swiveled on his shoulders. He'd seen the imp tear men into dog food in seconds. *Run! Get Lorda and get out of here!*

Creed turned his back to him and said, "How bad is it?"

Two bloody gashes formed a nasty X beneath his shoulders.

Eyes intent, Melegal took a quick glance.

"Just a scratch."

He moved away. *Where is that thing?* His eyes drifted towards the only exit. "No," he said, shoulders sagging.

"What?" Creed said, looking around.

Several underlings entered the room.

Eep buzzed alongside a floating underling with bright silver eyes. Accompanying him was a burly underling soldier with a shaven head and dark ruby eyes. Lord Almen's whip glowed in his grip. Four other underlings in dark chain armor escorted them. The floating underling hesitated in midair a moment, pointing at Creed as it spoke.

"Jottenhiem, Eep, kill him. Leave the skinny one to me."

Creed could feel them. Sense them. They were going to kill him.

"Let's give it a go then. Shall we?"

One by one, the four underlings, brandishing a variety of sharp blades, surrounded him. He glanced at Eep, his keen ears keeping track of the buzzing. *Not going to let that happen again.*

The bald underling with the whip chittered out a command. The well-trained team of underlings struck in unison.

Creed was already moving. He stepped into one underling. *Stab!* Piercing its heart in a lightning fast strike. *Swish!* He ducked under the next cutting blade.

Clang! Slit!

He ripped the sword out of one's hand and took its throat.

Gulch!

Gored the face of another.

Slice!

Tore the innards from the third.

Chop! Chop! Chop! Chop!

And butchered the fourth's head like a melon.

He took a bow.

"Next."

The imp and the whip-wielding underling circled him.

Blink!

The imp was gone.

The bald underling uncoiled the mystic whip and grinned.

Wupash!

"Oh, Great."

He backed towards the thrones. He had no sense of where the imp was. He needed a barrier on his backside. *You won't be getting to my back again.*

Blink!

Eep re-appeared right in front of his face and latched onto his chest.

"NOOOO!" Creed yelled. He dropped his swords. Grabbed the imp by the throat. The creature was solid. Muscle. Hard knotty skin and bone. He was no wrestler. "Get off me!"

Eep was merciless. Talons dug deep into his flesh. Its oversized jaws bit hard into his shoulder.

Creed punched the imp. It was like hitting a rock. He'd been in hundreds of fights, but he'd never faced anything supernatural like this. He punched and punched.

Wupash!

Eep blinked away, reappearing alongside Jottenhiem.

Creed sagged to his knees, fingers searching for his swords.

Wupash!

The whip coiled around his neck and jerked him to the ground.

Creed's head was burning hot. He clutched at the air.

Melegal's feet were lifted from the ground. He sailed right into Lord Verbard's powerful grasp. The underling squeezed his neck.

"Interesting for a human, you are. A survivor. I might have a use for you yet."

The words registered, but the meaning was lost. *I'm choking to death.* He twitched and recoiled from the depth of evil in those silver eyes.

A long shiver went through him when Verbard said, "Of course, it all depends on how long your breath can last. Can it last longer than my grip, Little Rat?"

72

"EH…" CATTEN MUMBLED, HIS GOLDEN eyes flaring.

Boon, a forgotten nemesis, had become a great fish hooked and struggling on his line.

"So be it, Enemy! I'll kill you first and take your grandson next."

He released his grip on Fogle Boon's mind, blasted every stitch of armor from Boon's body with a single thought, and started shoving Boon's broken form into a deep, dark, grave.

Fogle gasped. Breathing again, recollecting his senses, he crawled over to his spellbook and thumbed through the pages. Blinking hard and trying to block out the sounds of battle that echoed in the chamber, he found the page he needed.

He pressed his finger on the first word.

"I never thought I'd do this." He touched his grandfather's unmoving form. Boon was ashen and cold. Knowing it would erase the spell, Fogle read straight from the book.

The first word was soft, like a drink of sweet wine. The next syllable exploded in his mind, taking it yonder and back in a split second. His face lit up. His back straightened when the last syllable fell. "Eethum, get ready!" The page of the spellbook faded into smoke.

The air sizzled, shimmered and crackled.

Underling Lord Catten materialized before them, his wizened face gaping.

"What!" he said, outraged. Bewildered. "You shall pay for—"

Slice!

Eethum's stroke took his head from his shoulders. Its bright golden eyes rolled over the ground.

"I did it," he said, looking at Eethum. "He's dead. He's really de—"

Clang! Bang! Crunch!

Fogle whipped his aching head around. *Venir!* Buried in underlings, the big man was in for.

The underlings. Their hatred was deep. Venir's was deeper.

Chop!

Rage. They ignited it. He hated them. The smell of them. The sight of them. The oily stink of them. And he was going to kill them. Kill them all.

Hack!

He was a hurricane. Dwarven steel gone wild.

He launched a fatal blow into a bright blue-eyed underling's chest.

Sixteen!

Venir was no longer a man, but now a savage animal. Hungry. Starving. Battling for survival. For supremacy!

He brought both axe-blades down hard on a helmeted underling's head, splitting its skull to the teeth. Wrenched his blades free.

Two underlings jumped on top of him, pinning down his arms.

Slice!

A curved blade lashed out across his leg.

Down he went with five underlings on top of him. He fought like a tiger. He fought like a beast. He lost his blades. Something hard, heavy, struck his head. He could not feel. His vision blurred. He swallowed blood. He spit blood. He saw blood.

Small blades rose and fell.

He was going to die. He was certain. He booted one in the nose.

"Remember," he said. "I killed a thousand of you, and you only killed one of me!"

Crack! Stab Slash!

Venir didn't feel a thing. *Fight and die.* Everything faded. Fuzzy. Black.

Chop! Chop! Chop!

What was that?

Something was stuffed in his mouth. He tried to spit it out.

"Chew!" the Blood Ranger ordered. The Black Beards, the two that were left, kneeled along his side, beards dripping wet.

It hurt to swallow, but he did. Then he glanced at his burning belly. It was open, in more places than one.

"Got any Elga bugs?" Venir looked over a Black Beard's shoulder. "Say, what happened to that underling?"

The stone wall was back. A breathing underling was stuck inside it.

Eethum tore a piece of string off his sleeve with his teeth, threaded a fine needle, and started sewing Venir's belly up.

"Hold on," Venir said to Eethum.

Rising to his feet and holding his innards in, Venir limped over, grimacing, and jammed his axe in the trapped underling's head. Sat and lay down again.

"Here," Fogle said, holding a canteen to his lips. "Drink."

Venir pushed it away. "I'm not an infant, and I'll have no part of a bearded nanny."

Boon forced himself up into sitting position and put his throbbing head between his knees.

"Did you get him?" Boon said, holding his stomach.

"One of them," Fogle said, holding Catten's head up by the hair.

Boon blanched.

"You cut his head off! With a sword!"

Fogle smiled. "Eathum did. With an axe as big as my head."

"Well, that's a big axe alright, but," Boon paused, "the other one, Silver Eye?"

"Haven't gotten him yet."

Boon sighed. "How much have you got left?"

"About as much as you, I'd guess."

Boon rubbed his forehead and held his trembling hand out. The fire was back in his eyes. "Give me that spellbook."

73

JOTTENHIEM YANKED ON THE WHIP, jerking Creed from his feet and slinging him across the room into the hard wall behind a tapestry.

Creed felt every bit of it.

Wupash!

The dark purple light of the mystic whip ripped the skin from his arm.

Wupash!

It coiled around his other arm, burning like fire. Jottenhiem pulled him across the floor.

Creed screamed. The pain was maddening. It shocked every inch of his body.

"Let me eatss him!" The imp said, wringing its taloned hands and gnashing its over-sized jaws. They opened so wide, Creed could see his entire body fitting inside the imp's mouth.

He grabbed at the whip and cried out.

Jottenhiem slung him into another wall.

Wupash!

He cracked the whip into Creed's blood-seared back again and again.

Wupash!

The whip coiled around his neck with only The Cowl protecting him.

"Go ahead, Imp," Jottenhiem said, flashing his sharp teeth, "I'll hold him still. You eat."

Eep smacked his thin lips and slowly buzzed over.

Creed tried to scream, but he couldn't. All he could do was scream in his mind.

NOOOOO!

Rage mixed with helplessness. The urgings from his cowl now shrouded by the pain. Creed outstretched his arms and flexed his fingers.

I'm not going to die like this!

The imp was fifteen feet away. Ten. Five.

No! Not like this! Where are my swords?

Two sharp objects shot across the room into his hands.

My blades!

Eep paused and blinked.

Creed sunk one blade through its eye before the lid could open.

Slice!

He cut the whip away. The imp twitched and howled, sporadically flying all around.

Slice! Slice!

He clipped one buzzing wing, then the other.

Blink! The imp vanished.

Creed took a deep breath. *That was close.* His arms were shredded. He dripped blood. He hobbled when he moved. He wanted to rest. Heal.

The Cowl wouldn't allow it.

Suck it up, Creed.

Jottenhiem tossed the broken whip away and came running with his swords. They collided at the center of the room, sword hilts locked together. Shoving back and forth, Jottenhiem held his ground. The underling, though smaller, was far stronger than he looked.

Jottenhiem cracked Creed in the jaw with his head, bringing painful spots and slicing right at him.

Clang!

He deflected a blow.

Clang!

Then another.

Jottenhiem sneered, reversed his grips, and came after him slicing, stabbing and spinning. The bald underling was almost as fast as Kierway, but a different skill of fighter. Hours ago, Jottenhiem would have been far better, but that was hours ago. Much had changed in the past few hours.

Creed whipped his blades under Jottenhiem's nose in a flurry.

"Smell that, Underling?"

Jottenhiem's lips twisted.

"Smells of death, doesn't it?"

The underling tore into him. Blades clashed. Showers of sparks went everywhere. Creed felt his hatred growing. His skill increasing. The battle led out of the Throne Room and into another.

Clip! Slit! Clip!

Jottenhiem bled from three separate wounds.

Slit! Clip! Slit!

One ear dangled, and an X on Jottenhiem's forehead dripped blood into his eyes. He broke off.

"Thinking about running, aren't you, Underling?" Creed shrugged, gasping. "But there's no honor in being a coward, is there? Come on, then." He waved him over. "At least you don't have a whip around your throat."

Something propelled him forward, attacking the underling with unrelenting fury.

Bang! Bang! Bang!

Jottenhiem's corded arms started to give, snapping back up slower and slower. It was fatal.

"Enough of this!"

Creed ripped at Jottenhiem with all his might, tearing one sword from his hand.

Jottenhiem gasped.

Flash!

Creed tore the other one out.

Jottenhiem's ruby red eyes were full of hatred. Anguish.

He shook his head, took a knee and bowed.

Creed's next stroke was lights out.

"No!" Verbard moaned. "No!" His silver eyes darted around. Looking for a ghost.

Clutching Melegal with both hands now, the underling's silver eyes filled with anger and dismay. Whatever happened had been bad for the underling. Whenever bad things happen to underlings, worse things happen to people.

Melegal clutched at the underling's wrists and tried to kick at its guts.

Let go!

The ring from Sefron's chamber glimmered on Melegal's finger, and a charge of energy coursed through him.

Zzzzt!

Verbard's brows lifted. His face contorted. His jaw dropped open. "Argh!" The underling yelled, releasing Melegal and clutching his head.

Coughing, Melegal hit the floor, legs moving towards Lorda. The woman had sat up and was rubbing her head, blinking. "Get up, Lorda. Head for that door!" He glanced back.

Verbard spun in the air, shaking his head, arms coiling with mystic energy.

Here it comes!

Zzzzram!

Tendrils of lightning leapt from Verbard's finger, striking Melegal full in the back.

He skittered across the floor, reeling in pain, mouth tasting like metal and stone. Teeth screaming. He couldn't move, but he twitched, fingers curled, stomach knotting, his nose filling with the stench of his seared skin and hair.

Verbard floated over, gloating, and raised his arms.

This is it, Melegal. He found Lorda's eyes once more and mouthed the words, *So long.*

She reached for him.

Melegal crossed is arms over his face.

Zzzzram!

Boom!

Creed didn't stop with Jottenhiem. He didn't stop with the imp. He kept going. Limping. Hunting. Sliding from one room to another like a shadow, he slaughtered every underling he honed in on.

I know where you are.

Most of them didn't see him coming. For those who did, it was too late. One dead underling became two. Two became four. Four became eight. It was a glorious thing.

Melegal's shaking slender fingers patted over his body. *I'm still intact!* He wasn't alone either.

Two robed men stood in front of him, coated with transparent swords and shields. One's hair was long white and wispy, the other looked like he'd just crawled out of the woods. They were accompanied by a blood-bearded giant dwarf and two smaller black beards.

Melegal didn't stick around to thank them. Instead, he scooped Lorda up and headed for the door.

"Heh…" he breathed, stretching his aching fingers into his clothes and grabbing one of three Keys he'd pilfered from the underling Verbard's robes. He shoved the Key in the nearest door and turned. The door opened. "Let's get out of here. Shall we?" He'd hesitated, starting to turn back, when the room shook in its entirety. Shards of marble careened through the air.

A powerful figure shoved him inside and closed the door behind them. His mind and body started to spin. *Creed!*

74

"**Y**OU FIRST," BOON SAID AFTER opening up a black dimension door.

Fogle gave him a look.

"I cast the spell, and I'm your elder. If it makes you feel any better, take the dwarves with you."

Fogle summoned his power, coating his body in a transparent layer of blue energy and a shield. Armor, mystical or not, wasn't something he was at all accustomed to. As a matter of fact, he'd never worn so much as a bracer before.

"Let's go," he said to Eethum.

Holding his stomach, Venir said, "I'll go too."

"No, we'll need you to pull us out if things go wrong," Boon said, handing him the end of a rope tied to his waist. "If you hear us scream, tug it."

"Let the dwarf tug it," Venir growled. "I'm going in… oof!" Clutching his stomach he took a knee.

"Go, Fogle," Boon said, "I'll be right behind."

Stepping through, they found themselves in the Throne Room facing the back of a robed underling that hovered over a man and woman he did not recognize.

Fogle flicked a green missile into its back. *Zip!*

The underling's arms sprawled out.

Zzzzram!

Boom!

The underling's energy, meant for the man and woman, shot up into the ceiling.

Eethum and the Black Beards charged.

The underling, Verbard, whirled around, silver eyes flashing. With a wave of his hand, he knocked the dwarves around the room, slamming them into the wall.

"Let him have it, Grandson!" Boon yelled, energy erupting from his hands.

A bolt of power slammed into the underling's chest and dissipated. Fogle fired his own charge, which careened towards the underling and disappeared into the underling's robes.

The underling reached into his robes and pulled out a glowing orb of power.

Fogle started to fire again, but Boon stayed his hand.

"This is not good for us."

Verbard laughed.

A burst of energy blinded them.

Fogle heard his grandfather scream.

Facing the black doorway, Venir tugged at the rope. Nothing happened.

"I better get in there," he said, staggering towards the black door.

Srrit!

It disappeared.

"Slat!" He rubbed the back of his head. "Stupid mages! I knew I should have gone with them."

He could see it now, the two of them fighting the underling mage with the silver eyes. He knew it was him. They had said so. Now, he was trapped inside the blood hungry chamber with nowhere to go.

Fogle's wall of stone cracked again.

Venir picked up Mood's axes.

"It's just you and me, underlings."

Creak…

Behind him, one of the six doors opened.

Venir's jaw dropped.

Out came Melegal, whose eyes were as wide as his.

"Vee?"

"Me?"

"I knew you were behind all this!" Melegal said.

"Uh!"

A beautiful black-haired woman was shoved to the floor behind Melegal. The skinny thief jumped away and whirled.

"Creed, what are you doing?" Melegal said, backing away.

A tall rangy form stepped from beyond the threshold. He pointed a gleaming sword at Melegal's scrawny chest with one hand and held a jug of wine with the other.

Venir wiped the sweat and red grime from his eyes with his forearm and locked eyes with the man he'd all but forgotten about months ago.

"Tonio!"

"Vee-Man!"

Nullified.

That's what happened to the plan.

Boon had planned on overwhelming Verbard with his grandson, spell after spell, while the dwarves wove in and out, attacking. It might have worked if it weren't for something Boon hadn't foreseen. The Orb of Imbibing.

"Defend yourself, Fogle!"

Zzzram!

Zzzram!

Verbard launched one blast into them after the other, shattering their mystic armor and skipping them across the floor.

Boon tried to summon the dimension door again, but could not.

Verbard pressed the assault. Not letting him get a word out. The underling hovered over them now, draining their powers.

"Which one of you killed my brother?"

"I did," Boon lied, "and it was quite satisfying. Like a tender piece of veal cooked just right." Boon licked his lips. "The death of underlings is an excellent dessert."

One Black Beard had been crushed inside his armor. The other was out cold. Eethum lay on the floor bound up by yellow magic cords. Fogle's grandfather was a horrible negotiator.

Be silent, Fogle wanted to say, but his tongue was made of wool. Fogle had thought he was ready for anything by now, but he wasn't ready to not be able to use magic.

He gazed at the orb that pulsated in Verbard's hand like a beating heart. *Bish is just one excruciating surprise after another.* He tried to lock minds with Verbard.

"You dare!" the underling Lord hissed, squeezing his telekinetic fingers around his neck. Fogle was choking. Beside him, Boon clutched at the invisible fingers wrapped around his own neck, face turning purple. Verbard was getting stronger as he got weaker. There was nothing, nothing at all he could do. Was there? Searching the deepest recesses of his mind, he had to find the answer. He had to find the key. He heard his neck crack. Or was it Boon's?

"Finally," Tonio said, shattering his wine jug against the wall, "I'll have your head."

Shoulders lowered, axes bared, Venir charged in. "No! I'll have yours!"

Krang!

Tonio's gleaming sword tore Venir's axe from his wrist. The half-dead man was powerful and fast.

Venir ducked under a decapitating cut and tore a gash across Tonio's belly.

Tonio laughed. "You already killed me, Vee-man! You can't kill me again. Sorry yet?"

Whack!

Venir cut across his leg, but Tonio countered, punching Venir's bullish form in the face, cracking his nose open. Spitting blood from his mouth, Venir squared off again, shoulders dipping, belly aching. Whatever Tonio was, it wasn't mortal.

"I've been searching for you a long time, Vee-Man." He ran his fingers down his gash. "I'm going to split you in half as well. Show you how bad it feels. You ruined my life. You ruined everything!"

Venir forced a laugh at him. "Especially your face!"

Tonio grunted and stuck his sword into the stone. "Come on then," he said, walking over, "see what you can do with that little axe of yours."

"I'll be glad to show you, Tonio!"

Slic—

Tonio caught his arms and wrenched the axe free from Venir's hands.

Venir dug in, punching at the monster's ribs with his hardened fists.

Tonio didn't feel a thing.

Whop! Whop!

Venir's head snapped back. His knees buckled.

Melegal had seen Venir brawl with anything from underlings to half-ogres, but he'd never seen him fight something that couldn't be hurt or broken.

Tonio's speed and strength were Venir's match. Toe to toe, blow for blow, they fought and wrestled over the mosaic floor.

Come on, Vee!

Venir hammered away, an angry juggernaut, but his strength was fading.

A lightning fast strike caught Venir in the chin, wobbling him.

"Your head is mine, Vee-Man!"

Tonio wrapped his arms around Venir's head and squeezed. It turned red, then purple, his blazing blue eyes rolling up.

Move, Melegal!

Fogle thought of Cass. Dying, he still found himself angry with her for abandoning him—for a dragon of all things— and now, leagues from his home that smelled of flowers and sweet wine, he was going to die.

Verbard's fading face was gloating from above, sneering at him and his grandfather.

"I'm disappointed. I thought the pair of you would have more power that I could store in my orb. But the power I have should be enough to bring my brother back, once more, if I must."

Glitch!

A dark bloody sword burst into Verbard's chest and disappeared.

Glitch!

Another blade followed. In and out.

"No," Verbard said, incredulous, turning on his captor. "Where did you come from?

The man in the cowl with the glowing eyes stood tall, swords held in his thick wrists.

"Are you The Darkslayer?" Verbard said, splitting up blood and sagging to the floor.

Creed swung both swords at once.

Slice!

Verbard's head slid from his shoulders.

"I guess I am, Underling."

Fogle clutched at his chest, gasping.

Boon was doing the same. The old man, coughing, reached over and grabbed the Orb of Imbibing.

"Grab my hand, Fogle, so I can restore you. Quickly!"

Melegal whipped out the Sisters and struck Tonio in the back of the knee, tearing out tendon and flesh.

"What? You skinny flea!" Tonio teetered, losing his balance.

Venir bull rushed the man onto the floor and started to 'ground and pound' him, one blow after the other.

Tonio swatted the blows off and clutched at Venir's throat.

Stab!

Melegal pinned one of his swords through Tonio's shoulder.

Tonio caught him by the ankle and jerked him down.

Melegal tried to twist away from Tonio's grasp.

Snap.

His ankle cracked.

"You break like a twig!"

Venir was drunk with battle. He punched, kicked and clawed, almost oblivious to his opponent, but the arrogant tone in Tonio's voice kept him going.

"Ahhh!"

Melegal, his best friend and confident, cried out.

Tonio had the man's leg and still hung onto Venir's throat, holding them both in his vise-like grip.

Venir's instincts took over. He fumbled for a weapon. Found his long knife strapped to his leg. With both hands, he raised it over his head and drove it straight into Tonio's heart.

Crunch!

"That won't work, Vee-Man!" Tonio said. His grip was getting stronger. "I have no heart!"

Venir twisted the knife inside Tonio's chest.

Tonio's eyes widened. "Urk!"

Tonio's body shuddered.

"Grab an axe, Melegal!" Venir said, wrapping his arms around the monster, holding him to the ground.

Melegal hopped over towards the axe. "And do what?"

"Chop his head off!"

Melegal caught something in the corner of his eye.

I have a better idea.

Tonio slung Venir off and ripped the knife from his chest. "You already killed me! I'll make you sorry!"

Venir, huffing for breath, was too slow.

Tonio closed in, stabbing at him.

Melegal! What are you doing!

The thief was fooling with the underling on the blood-sucking floor.

Venir tried to dodge. Tried to block.

Glitch!

His own hunting knife caught him in the leg.

Twisting away, Tonio ripped a hunk out of Venir's back.

Slash!

Getting cut to pieces but still standing on his feet, Venir watched Tonio's final blow start down.

The monster's split face had a cruel smile on it. "Time to die, Vee-Man."

Tonio stopped, not moving a muscle, the bloody blade no longer coming down, a surprised look on his face.

"Venir," Melegal yelled, "catch!" The thief tossed him Mood's axe. "Be quick about it!"

Venir snatched it out of the air and whirled full force into Tonio's neck.

Slice!

Tonio's head bounced off the floor and rolled. His big body collapsed on the ground.

Venir collapsed as well. He snorted for air. Tried to shake the spots from his eyes. He reached over and pulled his knife from Tonio's grip.

"I knew I should have killed that Royal brat in the first place."

Pinching his nose, Melegal adjusted the dark cap on his head with the other hand, admiring Tonio's' corpse. He wiped the blood that dripped from his nose. *That was close.*

On the floor, Venir looked as bad as he'd ever seen him. It tugged at his heart a little. *Big lout.*

He helped Venir back to his feet.

"You know, you should have listened to me—"

"Don't start, Me."

75

"So we all agree then," Boon said, standing in the alcove, eyeing the Keys on the pegs.

They were all there except one, which Melegal believed Jarla had.

Fogle didn't care much either way. The only thing that mattered was that the underlings didn't have the Keys. He looked back over at the Stone Wall he'd produced. It was still holding. Behind it were—he had no idea how many underlings.

The party all knew now that despite their victory today, the underlings were penetrating the City. The battle for Bone had just begun.

"Shouldn't we destroy the Keys and the chamber?" Fogle suggested.

Boon rubbed his brow. "That's up to you, Fogle. Take a Key and do with it what you like, but remember, it always leads back here. And as I understand it, the room is here now, but it might be elsewhere later."

"You mean it moves?" Melegal said, leaning against the wall, arms folded across his chest.

"That's how I understand it. But, I could be wrong. It might just stay here forever."

"And the big Key," Melegal said, eyeing the Key on the center peg, "who gets that? Does it work all the doors? Or just one?"

"I don't think we have time for that now," Boon said, twisting his beard. "The goal is to get the Keys out of the chamber and away from the underlings. Once we are free of this, you can do what you wish. Keep them or destroy them."

"Will you destroy yours?" Melegal said.

"Well, er," Boon added, "that's my concern. I think it might come in handy if I get stuck back in the Under-Bish." He looked at Venir. "It could increase our chance of freeing Mood from down there."

Melegal had already told them what his Key did. It would take him wherever he wanted to go, but it always led back to the chamber, where he would have to start all over again. Certainly the underlings would soon have a heavy guard on the chamber. He looked at Venir.

"What do you think?"

"Let's take them to the furnace and destroy them." Venir nodded over at the bodies of Tonio, Catten and Verbard. The underlings were eyeless now. "Or," he said, eyeing the sack that hung over Creed's shoulder, "we can drop them in there?"

"Hmmm…" Boon rubbed his chin. "I have another idea. Creed, would you oblige me and open the sack?"

Creed, cowl down, tossed the sack over to Boon. "Open it yourself."

Boon's eyes widened.

So did Venir's.

"Fogle, let me have the staff."

Taking it out of his backpack, Fogle tossed the staff to Boon, who dropped it into the sack.

"What did you do that for?" Creed said.

Boon stuck his arm inside, down to the elbow, and withdrew nothing.

"Care to try?" Boon held the sack out to Venir.

He took a breath and a step forward. He longed to have the armament back, but he longed for his own freedom too. "I'll pass."

Boon handed the sack back to Creed. "Try not to get too used to it, whoever you are."

Creed couldn't keep his gaze off Venir. The big man looked like he'd been chewed up by a dragon and spit out, but was used to it. Still, the dark circles under the man's bright eyes concerned him. He had the look of a man who'd faced every horror and form of death hundreds of times. He was elemental. Forged in iron.

"So, you used to have this?" Creed said as the others squabbled over the Keys.

"Aye, but it was different, as different as you and me."

"You like women?" Creed said, his voice deep and rugged.

Venir eyed him.

"You like wine?"

"Grog."

"You like fighting?"

"You just described every soldier in Bish."

"We're not so different, you and I."

Venir turned and faced him. Looked him up and down.

"I don't think so."

Creed, bigger than most men, felt small in that moment.

"Maybe one day we'll share our tales together," Creed said, smiling at Lorda. "Chat with some ladies. Share some wine … er … grog."

"No doubt you'll be hearing tales about me," Venir looked down at him, patting his shoulder. "That much is certain." Venir coughed a laugh. "And you'll need more than a goblet of wine to deal with that mantle."

Creed nodded, extending his hand. Venir took it in his. Hard as a rock. Like a vice. Creed grimaced a little.

"We've come to a decision," Boon said, snagging the Keys from the pegs. Keeping the big one for himself, he handed Keys to Eethum, Melegal, Fogle, Venir, Creed and Lorda. "Just give us a few minutes."

Fogle sat down and started reading from the spellbook while Boon held the glowing Orb of Imbibing in his hand. It pulsated with mystic life.

Minutes later, Boon said, "We're ready."

Fogle said, "Melegal, lead the way."

"Where are we going, Me?" Venir said.

"The furnace."

Venir walked over and pulled Tonio's shriveled head up off the sucking floor. "Good idea. We better burn this."

Melegal opened the door with the Key he was accustomed to.

"Everybody inside," Boon said.

One by one they entered, leaving the throbbing orb behind.

"And what is that for?" Eethum asked, pulling the door closed.

"It should destroy the chamber," Fogle answered.

"And possibly the castle," Boon added.

Lorda gasped as the door closed.

The stone wall Fogle Bone had created finally evaporated, to the glee of a stairwell full of underlings. Each of them watched the orb spinning in the room, getting bigger and bigger and bigger. Spinning faster, it started to whine and crackle. The underlings' gem-speckled eyes flittered back and forth at one another, gaping in confusion.

Finally, one said in underling, "Flee!"

Lord Almen was tattooed with long bolts sticking out of his legs and chest by the dozen. He kissed his mystic ring. The assault on him had stopped, and he crawled over to the door on top of the keep. Shaking and bleeding, he pulled it open.

I'll live! I'll avenge!

KA-BOOM!

The entire keep shook and then collapsed. Lord Almen fell through the roof that opened up, landing at the bottom in time to watch the rest of the keep collapse on top of him.

One by one, they tossed their Keys into the furnaces that fired beneath the busy streets of Bone. Hot and fiery flames reflected all over their shadow-cast and oily faces.

Boon pitched two pair of underling eyes in as well. One pair silver, the other pair gold.

Venir took one last look at Tonio's face, his mind eating at him. Had one isolated incident been the start of it all? What would have happened if he never fought Tonio to begin with?

"You aren't thinking, are you?" Melegal said.

Tonio's grey eyes popped open.

"Vee-Man!"

Lorda jumped, but the others remained still. "Tonio," she said, extending her hand and touching her son's face. An odd silence fell.

"Mother," Tonio said, black eyes returning to normal.

"Good-bye, Son," she sobbed, turning to walk away.

"But Mother," he said. His eyes turned black. Brows buckled. Lips curled. "You can't kill me, Vee-Man."

Venir held Tonio's head out over the vat of fire. "Maybe you can't be killed, but I bet you'll burn, Brat." He pitched him over the rim.

"Noooooooooo!"

"The city holds for now," Corrin said, taking a good look at the present company. "The Royals finally got off their arses and stirred a fight. I think the collapse of Castle Almen lit a fire under them."

Lorda Almen was crying on the bench by the fountain.

Melegal caressed her head. The woman had lost her home. Her entire family. He felt bad.

"Where to now, Melegal?" Venir said, drinking from the fountain. "You want to stay and fight, or do you want to go? You should have left for the City of Three last time, you know."

"Just a moment," Melegal said in Lorda's ear, releasing her petal-soft hands.

He limped his way over to Venir.

"Itching to see your family are you, Vee?" he said, smiling.

Venir stopped drinking and said, "What family?"

Splash! Splash! Splash! "Help!" Lorda Almen sounded like she was drowning. "Detective!" *Splash!* "Help!"

Turning, he saw Haze had Lorda's head stuffed down in the water. He hobbled over. Pulled her away.

Haze ripped a long blade across Melegal's chest.

"Are you mad?" he exclaimed, twisting the dagger from her hand.

She slapped his face. "I'm a one-man woman, and you're a one-woman man. Got that?"

He snickered. "Absolutely, my Lorda."

"Good," Haze said, "and I want to go to the City of Three. You promised me."

"No, I did—"

She glared at him.

"I suppose I did."

Corrin then said, "You aren't going anywhere. The city's under siege out there."

"You ever been out of the city before, Corrin?"

"No."

"You want to leave?"

"No, I'm going to stay and fight."

Creed stepped alongside Corrin. "This is where I'll be, as well."

"This is where you're supposed to be," Venir said.

"And what about me?" Lorda said, slinging her dripping wet hair over her shoulder.

Creed put his arm around her. "You're coming with me. The Bloodhounds can always use another queen."

The wizards approached.

"Get all the gear you can handle, men," Boon said. And then he noticed Haze's glare, "and woman. The underlings aren't going to let us congregate here forever. I can teleport you miles from the city, but you're on your own after that."

"I said I would never leave Bone again," Melegal said, shaking his head. "And I'm still certain you're the root cause of all this, Venir."

Limping towards the black dimension doors, Venir said, "Well, at least you have someone to blame. And what family are you talking about?"

Somewhere far away, the Elga bugs came. Slim's body went.

Master Sinway waited on his throne. Catten, Verbard and Kierway never arrived. He petted one of the Cave Dogs at his side and said, "This isn't over. It's just begun."

EPILOGUE

BRAK'S OVERSIZED BODY HELD TIGHT on the reins of Quickster as they rode into the City of Three. The poison had passed. He lived, but was far from back to himself again yet.

"Don't worry, Brak. We're almost there. We can get you a bed, healing and a comfortable room. And the stew you'll eat! As soon as you smell it, your mouth will water," Georgio said.

Georgio had been nicer to him since he almost died. But that probably had more to do with the City of Three than actual concern.

He wiped from his face the mist that blew in from the massive waterfalls he could see in the distance.

"Isn't that beautiful, Brak!" Jubilee said. "I've never even imagined anything like it. Billip, can we go there?"

"Yes," Nikkel said, "can we go there?"

"Soon enough. But I'm getting a gullet full at the Magi Roost first!" Billip said, smiling underneath the grit and sand that covered his face.

"I'm filling both my gullets!" Georgio said.

"You don't even know what a gullet is," Nikkel said, laughing.

"I do too."

"What is it, then?" Jubilee said.

"Uh… it's your belly."

Jubilee and Nikkel looked at each other and laughed.

"Isn't it?"

Everyone's mood lightened when they saw the city. Even Brak, who still felt as feeble as a kitten, felt better for it. He looked once up and down at the tall towers whose spires seemed to reach the clouds, but he wasn't impressed. He just wanted to rest. He was wondering about his father, Venir. He hadn't had any dreams about him lately. *Maybe he's dead.*

"This is it," Billip said, stopping in front of a building where a sign hung that read in bright letters, **THE MAGI ROOST.** Billip started dusting himself off. "Joline will kill me for going in there like this."

Georgio took off his boots, poured the rocks out and banged them together. He took a deep draw through his nose. "I can taste the stew already." He sniffed again and made a funny face. "And something else."

One at a time, Billip leading the way, they entered.

"Welcome, Travelers," a tall husky woman said. "Have a seat, and I'll get you some help."

Brak saw Billip and Georgio's hands fall to their sword belts.

"Just who in Bish are you?" Billip said, "And what have you done to this tavern?"

The Magi Roost was darker and filled with a seedier sort of characters. All the long robes and noses were gone. The smell of cheap wine and ale was in the air.

"And how did such an unattractive woman get in here? Where's Kam?" Billip demanded.

"Oh," the woman leaned over Billip with her hands on her hips. "You're one of her friends, are you?"

"Billip!"

It was Joline. She ran up and threw her arms around him, tears streaming down her face. "You're alive. I'm so glad you're alive." She kissed his cheek, then whispered in his ear. "But you need to get out of here."

"Joline!" a man sitting the bar said in a warning tone.

Billip gawped at him. He'd never seen such presence in a man before. Handsome, refined, distinguished, with eyes as blue as water.

"Don't dally with Darlene's patrons. She's likes to welcome them."

"I'm hungry, Joline," Georgio said, patting Joline on the back.

She shook her head. "You've changed so much, Georgio. You're a full grown man."

"Ah, I haven't been gone that long. Where's Kam?"

"Just grab a table," Joline said, "I'll get her."

"Mercy!" Darlene bellowed, "Get these folks a table!"

Mercy scampered over, chin down, and led them to their table.

"How have you been, Mercy?" Georgio said, hitching his arm over his chair and smiling.

"Georgio?" She seemed to wake up from a daze. "Georgio!" She sat down on his lap and hugged him. "I thought you'd never come back!" She whispered in his ear. "Just stay away from them." Her eyes flittered towards the woman Darlene and the man at the bar.

"Who is that?" he said. "I can handle him."

"No, no," she said, grabbing him by the collar. "Just leave them be, and they'll leave you be." She hopped off his lap. "I'll get you stew, to start." She eyed all of them. "And a big bowl for you, Georgio." She saw Brak. "And one for your friend, too." She patted Billip on the head. "I'm so glad you're back. So glad!"

"There's something spooky going on here," Billip said. "I don't recognize any of these people."

"Seems alright to me," Jubilee said, looking around. "Say, who's the beautiful lady with only one hand up there? That's kinda sad."

"What? There's no one in here with one hand," Georgio said, looking around. "Kam!"

She stood on the balcony in a long green dress, sunken eyed and waving her one-handed arm.

"Do you know her?" Jubilee said.

Billip said in disbelief, "What in Bish is going on here?"

FROM THE AUTHOR

U NFORTUNATELY, THE ENDING IS NEVER as much fun as the journey.

As for this first series, there is more, I decided to wrap it up with this 6th book. It was time. I think readers wanted some resolution. That's what made it so difficult. I had a bunch of characters spread out all over Bish. That said, I didn't want to end it. Originally, I wanted this to be an ongoing saga, but I spread myself too thin and my writing was suffering for it. This first segment of Venir's life ends. But it feels good for me, finishing a full-length fantasy series.

Fear not, Darkslayer fans, the adventures of The Darkslayer will continue in the *Bish and Bone* series. Venir and Melegal's escapades are not over, if anything, it's just beginning, so hang in there. But I'm not spoiling things.

Next. THANK YOU! It has been my pleasure writing for you! Your support is a dream come true to me. My goal is to improve and write even better stories for you, but don't hold me to that. That way you won't be disappointed. ;)

So, will Venir and Brool be reunited? What do you think? But there is only one way to know for sure. Check out the next series, *Bish and Bone.*

Again, check in with me at The Darkslayer Report by Craig on Facebook. I want to hear what you thought of this series. And if you have time, I'd appreciate a sincere review.

Fight or Die,
Craig Halloran

ABOUT THE AUTHOR

Craig Halloran resides with his family outside of his hometown of Charleston, West Virginia. When he isn't entertaining mankind, he is seeking adventure, working out, or watching sports. To learn more about him, go to: www.thedarkslayer.com

OTHER WORKS BY CRAIG HALLORAN

The Darkslayer Series 1
Wrath of the royals (Book 1)
Blades in the Night (Book 2)
Underling Revenge (Book 3)
Danger and the Druid (Book 4)
Outrage in the Outlands (Book 5)
Chaos at the Castle (Book 6)

The Darkslayer Series 2
Bish and Bone (Book 1)
Black Blood (Book 2)
Red Death (Book 3)

The Chronicles of Dragon Series
The Hero, The Sword and The Dragons (Book 1)
Dragon Bones and Tombstones (Book 2)
Terror at the Temple (Book 3)
Clutch of the Cleric (Book 4)
Hunt for the Hero (Book 5)
Siege at the Settlements (Book 6)
Strife in the Sky (Book 7)
Fight and the Fury (Book 8)
War in the Winds (Book 9)
Finale (Book 10)

Zombie Impact Series
Zombie Day Care: Book 1
Zombie Rehab: Book 2
Zombie Warfare: Book 3

The Supernatural Bounty Hunter Files
(Coming 2015)
Smoke Rising
I Smell Smoke
Where's there's Smoke
Smoke and Mirrors
Smoke on the Water

CONNECT WITH HIM AT

Facebook: The Darkslayer Report by Craig
Twitter: Craig Halloran